May 14, 1972

marvelous
mother of our kids.

MW

"Immortality means being loved
by many anonymous people."

Sigmund Freud

Also by Irving Stone

BIOGRAPHICAL NOVELS

LUST FOR LIFE
(Vincent Van Gogh)

THE PRESIDENT'S LADY
(Rachel Jackson)

IMMORTAL WIFE
(Jessie Benton Fremont)

LOVE IS ETERNAL
(Mary Todd Lincoln)

ADVERSARY IN THE HOUSE
(Eugene V. Debs)

THE AGONY AND THE ECSTASY
(Michelangelo)

THE PASSIONATE JOURNEY
(John Noble)

THOSE WHO LOVE
(Abigail Adams)

BIOGRAPHIES

SAILOR ON HORSEBACK
(Jack London)

CLARENCE DARROW FOR THE
DEFENSE

THEY ALSO RAN
(Defeated Presidential Candidates)

EARL WARREN

HISTORY

MEN TO MATCH MY MOUNTAINS

NOVELS

PAGEANT OF YOUTH

FALSE WITNESS

BELLES-LETTRES

WE SPEAK FOR OURSELVES
(A Self-Portrait of America)

THE STORY OF MICHELANGELO'S
PIETÀ

WITH JEAN STONE

DEAR THEO
(Vincent Van Gogh)

I, MICHELANGELO, SCULPTOR
(Autobiographies through
letters)

COLLECTED

THE IRVING STONE READER

EDITOR

THERE WAS LIGHT
Autobiography of a University
Berkeley: 1888–1968

LINCOLN: A CONTEMPORARY
PORTRAIT
(with Allan Nevins)

BOOKS FOR YOUNG READERS

THE GREAT ADVENTURE OF MICHELANGELO

THE PASSIONS OF THE MIND

The Passions
of the Mind

A NOVEL OF SIGMUND FREUD

by Irving Stone

DOUBLEDAY & COMPANY, INC., GARDEN CITY, NEW YORK, 1971

Grateful acknowledgment is made for permission to include excerpts from the following copyrighted works:

Psychoanalytic Pioneers edited by Franz Alexander, Samuel Eisenstein, and Martin Grotjahn, © 1966 by Basic Books, Inc., Publishers.

The Freud Journal of Lou Andreas-Salome, translated and edited by Stanley A. Leavy, © 1964 by Basic Books, Inc., Publishers.

A Psycho-analytic Dialogue: The Letters of Sigmund Freud and Karl Abraham 1907–1926, edited by Hilda C. Abraham and Ernst L. Freud, translated by Bernard Marsh and Hilda C. Abraham, © 1965 by Hilda C. Abraham and Ernst L. Freud, Basic Books, Inc., Publishers.

The Origins of Psycho-analysis: Letters to Wilhelm Fliess, Drafts and Notes: 1887–1902 by Sigmund Freud, edited by Marie Bonaparte, Anna Freud, Ernst Kris, translated by Eric Mosbacher and James Strachey, © 1954, Basic Books, Inc., Publishers.

Free Associations: Memories of a Psycho-analyst, by Ernest Jones, © 1959 by Basic Books, Inc., Publishers.

Volume I of *The Life and Work of Sigmund Freud* by Ernest Jones, M.D., © 1953 by Ernest Jones, Basic Books, Inc., Publishers.

Volume II of *The Life and Work of Sigmund Freud* by Ernest Jones, M.D., © 1955 by Ernest Jones, Basic Books, Inc., Publishers.

Psychoanalysis and Faith: The Letters of Sigmund Freud and Oskar Pfister, translated by Eric Mosbacher, © 1963 by Sigmund Freud Copyrights, Ltd., Basic Books, Inc., Publishers.

Volumes I, II, III, IV, and V of *The Collected Papers of Sigmund Freud,* edited by Ernest Jones, M.D., Basic Books, Inc., Publishers.

Studies on Hysteria by Josef Breuer and Sigmund Freud, translated from the German and edited by James Strachey in collaboration with Anna Freud, assisted by Alix Strachey and Alan Tyson, Basic Books, Inc., Publishers.

The Letters of Sigmund Freud, selected and edited by Ernest L. Freud, translated by James and Tania Stern, © 1960 by Sigmund Freud Copyrights, Ltd., London, Basic Books, Inc., Publishers.

Three Essays on the Theory of Sexuality by Sigmund Freud, translated and newly edited by James Strachey, © 1962 by Sigmund Freud Copyrights, Ltd., Basic Books, Inc., Publishers.

All used by permission of Basic Books, Inc., Publishers, New York, and The Hogarth Press, Ltd., London.

The Interpretation of Dreams by Sigmund Freud, translated and edited by James Strachey, Basic Books, Inc., Publishers, and Allen & Unwin, Ltd.

To my wife
JEAN STONE
who has been
EDITOR IN RESIDENCE
through twenty-five
published books
and in her spare time
runs a beautiful home
manages our business affairs
reared two children
maintains an exciting social life
helps in the causes of her community
keeps a difficult husband happy

With gratitude and love

THE BOOKS

BOOK ONE

FOOLS' TOWER

Fools' Tower

THEY moved up the trail vigorously, their slim young figures in rhythmic cadence. In a nearby meadow yellow flowers grew in the short grass. Though the pasqueflowers with their silky petals had been dead since Easter, there were spring heather, primroses and dog rose to weave a colorful carpet under the beeches.

He was not a tall man, barely achieving five feet seven inches when holding himself erect. Yet he felt himself exactly the right height for the girl moving so gracefully at his side. He stole a shy sideward glance at Martha Bernays' profile with the strong chin, nose and brow. He found it difficult to believe what had happened. Here he was, only twenty-six, deeply involved in his physiology research in Professor Brücke's Institute, a gaping five years away from the possibility of love and a full ten years away from marriage. He had been a mediocre student in chemistry but should he not have learned that love and calendars wouldn't mix? He said, "It's impossible. It can't have happened!"

The girl turned to him in surprise. The light in the woods was shaded and mellow, for the elephant-gray birches had been stripped of their lower branches and the high green umbrella of leaves shielded the sun's rays. Perhaps it was the soft shadows of these woods above Mödling that made Martha's face seem the loveliest he had known. She made no pretense of being a beautiful woman but he found her wonderfully attractive: large gray-green eyes, sensitive, gentle, with a penetrating quality and resolutely independent. Her thick brown hair was parted in the center, making a precise white line, and then combed behind ears molded flat to the head. She had a good nose, slightly retroussé, and a marvelous mouth, or so he judged, with red, full-bodied lips. Her chin was perhaps disconcertingly strong for so slender a face.

"What is impossible? What can't have happened?"

They had come to an angle in the trail where the green roof was leaking sunshine.

"Did I speak aloud? It must be the quality of silence in these woods. I'll have to be careful if you can hear me so clearly."

Now they were at a midway plateau where they could step onto a flat rock formation and see Mödling below them. Faint strains of music drifted upward from the band playing in the Kurpark. Mödling was a charming rural town an hour from Vienna by train. It had become a fashionable holiday resort for the Viennese: a small Red Sea of tiled roofs gleamed in the warm June sunlight; and beyond, the vineyards climbed the slopes pregnant with swelling bunches of grapes whose "new" wine the Viennese would be drinking the following spring in the *Heurigen Stüberln* of Grinzing.

Martha Bernays was visiting with family friends who had a house on the Grillparzergasse in Mödling. Sigmund had taken the Südbahn, Southern Railway, from Vienna that morning. They had walked through the Kaiser Franz Josephs-Platz with its ornate, gold filigreed Pestsäule, the column commemorating the conquering of a past plague, continued up the Hauptstrasse to the Old City Hall with its clock and onion-on-onion spire, then followed the Pfarrgasse past the fountain to St. Othmar Kirche towering above the town. Opposite the church was a circular stone tower.

"It looks like an Italian baptistery," Martha observed, "but Mödlingers insist it's an old bone tower. As a medical doctor could you tell me how they throw bones in there without the rest of the person?"

"As a fledgling doctor with neither practice nor experience I haven't the faintest idea. Why don't you write a research paper about it and I will submit it to the Medical Faculty and apply for your degree? Would you like to be a doctor?"

"No, I would like to be a housewife and mother, with half a dozen children."

"These are not extraordinary ambitions. You should have no trouble fulfilling them."

Her eyes had a way of turning emerald when she was deep in the woods.

"It's after fulfilling them that I don't want the trouble. You see, I'm a romantic. I would like to love my husband and live in peace with him for half a century."

"You are ambitious, Martha! You remember the lines from Heine:

> " 'I should have remained unmarried,'
> Many times poor Pluto sighed,
> 'Since I carried home my bride,
> I have learned: without a wife
> Hell was not yet Hell nor harried.
> Bachelor life was joy and glamor!
> Since I Proserpina wed,
> I wish daily I were dead!' "

Her eyebrows arched upward. "You don't really believe that?"

"I? Certainly not! Marriage was invented for simple folk like me. Once the ceremony is performed I shall become an addict."

"Was it Goethe who said that hyperbole is used by people who want to conceal their true feelings?"

"No, my dear Miss Bernays, it was you who just invented that quotation."

He had known her too little time to have enumerated to himself all of her endearing qualities but he was enchanted by her voice. Martha was twenty-one. She came from Hamburg, the proudest of all the Hanseatic League cities. She spoke High German, pure, precise, so unlike the swift, comradely, easygoing *Schlamperei* of the Viennese tongue. She had told him why she had preserved this purity of diction even though her young girl classmates at school had badgered her as being arrogant, superior, prideful: charges most Viennese made against the powerful, prosperous, fiercely free and rigidly bourgeois Hamburgians. Martha's father, Berman Bernays, had served for ten years as the invaluable assistant to the famous economist Lorenz von Stein of Vienna University, until Bernays' sudden death two and a half years before, in 1879.

"When I first started school in Vienna," Martha told Sigmund, "I was only eight. Naturally I picked up the pronunciation of my classmates. For the word *Stadt* I said *Sch-tadt*. For *Stein* I said *Sch-tein*. My father took me into his study and said, 'Little one, what you are speaking is not German, it is a corruption. We do not say *Sscch-tadt* or *Sscch-tein*. We say *S-tadt* and *S-tein*. That is pure German.' The next day I told my parents I had had a new kind of cake called *Schtrudel*. My father said, 'I don't know what a *Schtrudel* is. But whatever it may be, we will call it a *S-trudel*.' My classmates finally decided it was an affliction for which I should be pitied, like stuttering."

They continued their walk up one of the branching trails each of which had a different-colored stripe of paint on its bordering trees so that hikers would not become lost in the magnificently dense woods which extended southward from Vienna. The path underfoot was covered with pine needles which made it slippery and little more than proper that Sigmund should grip Martha's elbow so that she did not fall. The sun was hot now, the umbrella pines did not quite meet across the trail, but the scents were delicious from the bed of pine needles and the resin.

From high above there was an echoing:

"Hallo! Hallo! Come along, you laggards."

They thought that Eli, Martha's brother, a year and a half older than she, was being discreet in moving so swiftly up the trail ahead of them.

In truth, Eli had a passion for side trails and had to move twice as fast as anyone else to cover the same amount of ground.

It was another quarter hour to the crest. Here they had a staggering view: the Kahlenberg, called Vienna's domestic mountain, silhouetted to the north some ten miles away, stood sentinel over Vienna.

There was a small cafe nestled under the towering trees. The Saturday family groups sat on benches at rustic tables having coffee or beer. Sigmund found a small stone-topped table surrounded by wicker chairs and ordered three bottles of raspberry-flavored *Kracherl*. When the bottles arrived, Martha, Sigmund and Eli raised a thumb and with a simultaneous movement pressed sharply on the glass marble closing the neck. The marbles submerged behind a loud "Pop!", after which they drank the cool sweet soda. Eli downed his in two extended drafts and bounded off like a buck to find other trails. Over his shoulder he threw an admonition:

"Don't wander away. I'll be back to fetch you."

2.

They sat with their faces turned up to the benign sun, its warmth so eagerly anticipated through the raw Vienna winter. Tuscany had ceased to be influenced by the Austro-Hungarian Empire twenty-two years before but the sky was the robin's-egg blue that blesses Florence in the spring.

He stretched out an arm, put his hand palm up on the center of the table. She laid her hand in his, lightly. It was cool to his touch, quiet, waiting, her skin fresh and moist in his grasp. Martha looked at him closely, head on, for the first time. Though the families had known each other, she and Sigmund had met less than two months before. He had a strong, rather bony nose jutting imperiously out from the declivity between his eyes; thick, lustrous black hair which he combed at an angle across his forehead toward his right ear; a narrow chin beard and mustache; a high forehead and, dominating the attractive face, large luminous dark eyes, a little brooding perhaps.

"Tell me about your work. I don't mean to intrude but all I know is that you are a Demonstrator in Professor Brücke's physiology laboratory."

"Yes, I prepare the slides for Professor Brücke's lectures."

He hitched his chair closer, scraping its legs over the gravel bed. "Shall I start at the beginning or at the end?"

"The beginning, where everything should start."

"The first four years of my medical studies were not exciting except that when I was twenty my zoology professor, Herr Carl Claus, sent me twice to Trieste where they had founded a zoological experimentation station. I worked on the gonadic structure of eels."

"What does 'gonadic' mean?"

Eli came flying by, crying, "Time to start back," and disappeared into the shadow of the woods. Martha and Sigmund followed reluctantly, taking the green trail. After a few moments they came to a huge tree that had fallen across the path. He had to help her over the rounded trunk; and it was beyond his powers of physical resistance not to notice that the girl had a pair of handsomely trim ankles. The road then swerved sharply and ahead they saw a clearing with sunlight pouring into a ravine. Woodchoppers were stacking their logs into four-foot rows with mathematical precision.

"Wouldn't it be nice," he murmured, "if we could arrange the days and the results of our lives as neatly as those woodcutters pile their wood?"

"Can't we?"

"Can't one? Isn't it possible? I think so, Martha. At least I hope so. It's in my nature to love order and flee chaos."

They walked along in silence for a moment, the earlier question hanging above them. If he refused to answer she would not raise the question again, but unless he did make a reply as he would to an equal, Martha would know that he had judged her and found her wanting. He spoke in the quiet academic tone he used with younger medical students who came to him for tutoring.

"The dictionary defines 'gonadic' as 'an undifferentiated germ gland, serving as both ovary and spermacy.' My task was to locate the testes of the eel. Only one man, Dr. Syrski, had found even a faint clue. I was to substantiate or disprove his findings."

Martha had almost missed a downward step when he mentioned the word "testes." But not quite. She turned to him and asked:

"What is important about locating the testes of an eel? And why weren't they discovered a thousand years ago?"

"Good question." He linked an arm lightly through hers. "Except in mating season there is no way to recognize the male organ. Before they mate the eels put out to sea. No one has ever caught them at it. No one has ever found a mature male eel. Then again, perhaps no one has been interested."

"You found what you were after?"

"I believe so. Dr. Syrski was right and I helped document his theory. Professor Claus read my paper at a meeting of the Academy of Sciences and it was published in the Academy's *Bulletin*. That was five years ago. No one has yet disputed my findings."

There was a ringing pride in his voice, as though the best thing in the world a man could do was conscientious work. The approval in her eyes encouraged him to go on. He found himself pouring out his inner convictions in a way he had never communicated to a woman, young or old.

"The whole problem is much larger than the practical application of Professor Claus's theory about hermaphroditism in animals, though the eel looks as if it might fit into this category. Research science must operate outside any realm of conventional morality. In science all ignorance is bad and all knowledge good. We were born into this world a long time ago, millions of years, Charles Darwin suggests. In the beginning we knew nothing of the forces surrounding us. But for all these millions of years the human brain has been chipping away at that ignorance, storing up hard-earned wisdom. This is the greatest adventure of mankind: to find something that was never known before, or understood. Each new piece of knowledge does not need to have a specific or functional use, at least not at the moment. It is a sufficient triumph that we have learned something and proved it by documentation, that had formerly been part of the darkness."

It was her turn to reach out and grasp his hand: warm, bony-knuckled, trembling with excitement over the vision he had tried to capture for his new-found friend.

"Thank you. No one has ever spoken to me that way before. It makes me feel like a . . . a person. No, like an adult. You could not have given me a finer gift if you had shopped for it on the Kärntner Strasse."

They returned to the house in the Grillparzergasse in time for the *Jause*, afternoon coffee. Sigmund and Martha preferred theirs in the garden. Eli remained indoors with their hosts. The walled back garden of the house was small but the lime trees were in bloom, filling the air with heavy perfume. Martha brought out to the arbor a plateful of white blossoms of the elderberry bushes; they had been dipped in batter and fried. She sat beside him on the rustic bench. He watched her arms and shoulders move gracefully under the brown zephyr dress with its wide white collar as she held the two pots aloft, the streams of coffee and milk intermingling in the big cups. They picked nuts out of a silver bowl.

"Look," she exclaimed, "a *Vielliebchen*, a double almond. Now we have to exchange presents."

"I love omens, particularly when they come down on my side. Sit closer and that will be better than any gift you could buy me in the Graben."

She sat so close that by leaning almost imperceptibly he could touch shoulders. His eyes danced with joy. He loved this girl, though he had only once before had an intimation of what love meant. His parents had sent him to Freiberg for a vacation when he was sixteen, and he had stayed with friends from an earlier day, the Fluss family. Sigmund had developed a crush on their fifteen-year-old daughter Gisela, walking through the romantic woods with her, and fantasying about the beautiful married life they would have together. But he never told Gisela; and the pretty young girl vanished from his mind when he returned to Vienna, entered into the excitement of his next to last year at the Sperlgymnasium; he and a companion taught themselves Spanish so that they could read Cervantes' *Don Quixote* in the original.

He dared not tell Martha of his love for her; it was too soon, she might think him frivolous, for they had been acquainted only seven weeks. Besides she had given him no reliable clue. He murmured to her, " 'My cup runneth over.' "

"That's from the Psalms."

"My father read them to me when I was a child. 'Thou preparest a table before me in the presence of mine enemies; thou anointest my head with oil . . .' "

"Do you have enemies?"

"Only myself."

Her delighted laughter rang in his head like the bells of St. Stephan's. He was no longer able to contain his rush of emotion.

"I will tell you of a real omen. Do you remember that first evening I saw you, when I came home with a library of books under my arm, eager to get to my room for a four-hour bout of study? There you were, sitting at our dining-room table with my sisters, talking cleverly while peeling an apple with those delicate fingers. I was so disconcerted that I stopped short in my flight and sat down to join you."

"It was the apple. Ever since the Garden of Eden."

"You didn't know that that was the first time I had done more than nod to one of my sisters' friends. I said to myself that roses and pearls fell from your lips as with the princess in the fairy tale, and that one was left wondering whether it was goodness or intelligence which had the upper hand with you."

He was unprepared for her reaction to what other girls might have considered a romantic flight of fancy. Color flooded upward on her cheeks, then quite as suddenly she paled and tears glistened in her eyes. She turned her head away. When she turned back her eyes were serious.

"How long have you been at the university?"

"Almost nine years."

"You recall the day we strolled in the Prater with my mother? When we returned home I asked my sister Minna, 'Why did Herr Dr. Freud ask so many questions of me?' Now it is my turn. You are a doctor of medicine yet you do not practice. Why is that?"

He rose abruptly, took a quick swing around the garden. It was important to him that Martha Bernays understand his reasoning and approve his choice. She sat quietly, hands folded in her lap, looking up at him with an expression serious and receptive.

"It's true I have my medical degree. Though in fact I was dilatory about it, taking three years longer than I needed, and only then because my circle of acquaintances at the university began to accuse me of being lazy or scattered."

"You seem a most concentrated person."

"Only in what I like. I studied for five years in the Medical School because that was the best way to get a thorough scientific training; we probably have the greatest Medical Faculty in Europe. For the past few years I have been working full time in Professor Brücke's Institute of Physiology. Brücke is one of the founders, along with Helmholtz, Du Bois and Ludwig, of modern physiology. Under his guidance I have already completed four pieces of original research and published papers on them: in 1877, before I was twenty-one, I did a paper on the origin of the posterior nerve roots in the spinal cord of the ammocoetes; the next year I published my findings on the spinal ganglia and spinal cord of the petromyzon; and the year after that the *Centralblatt für die medizinische Wissenschaften* printed my notes on a method for anatomical preparation of the nervous system."

Martha smiled at the combination of youthful exuberance and precise technical phraseology.

"I also completed a study of the structure of the nerve fibers and nerve cells of the fresh-water crayfish. This is the kind of work I'm best at. For me it is the most rewarding job the world has to offer, full of excitement and gratification: every day we learn something new about living organisms. It was never my intention to care for patients. I know how praiseworthy it is to alleviate individual suffering, but through research in the laboratories and increasing knowledge of what makes the human body function, or not function, we can find ways of eradicating entire diseases."

"Could you give me an example?"

"Yes. Professor Robert Koch at the School of Medicine in Berlin only this year has offered evidence of having discovered the bacillus which causes tuberculosis. Then there is Professor Louis Pasteur, working at the Sorbonne in Paris, who two years ago isolated the germ that causes chicken cholera. He has also been inoculating sheep against anthrax, a deadly disease. Working on this formula of inoculation, we should be able to wipe out cholera in human beings. Then there was the Hungarian, Dr. Ignaz Semmelweis, who graduated from our Medical School in 1844. Singlehanded, Semmelweis found the cause of puerperal fever, the childbed fever that was killing a high percentage of our hospital's maternity patients. The doctors at our General Hospital connected with the Medical College crucified him for his monomaniacal

quest; yet all over the world thousands of mothers will live because Ignaz
Semmelweis proved to be an indestructible researcher and medical scientist."

His voice rang out over the garden, his face was shining, the dark
eyes crackled with excitement. She spoke softly.

"I am beginning to understand. You hope through your work in the
laboratory to wipe out still other diseases."

"There are many illnesses not caused by germs or viruses that we recognize; the doctor can offer the patient little more than attention and
sympathy. But please don't mistake me, I have no idea that I am a Koch,
Pasteur or Semmelweis. My ambitions are much more modest. Most
cures are based on the work of hundreds of researchers, all of whom
make minute contributions. Without their findings, bits of knowledge
piled on bits of knowledge, the ultimate discoverer could probably not
find his way to the cure. I want to spend my life as one of those researchers."

Eli put his head out the back door of the house and called, "The sun
is setting. Time to gather ourselves together, say good-by and walk to
the train."

They collected their belongings. By the stoop, Martha reached up to
break off a sprig of the lime to take home. They were standing very
close, with Martha's arms in the air. Sigmund glanced toward the door
to make sure they were alone. He thought, "Now is the time. But carefully, carefully. If she is not ready, if she has not begun to love me, I
may offend her."

Though only a few inches separated them it seemed to him an interminable time before he covered the distance of all the world, of all
his life. Martha had already plucked the small branch but she had not
yet lowered her arms. Her eyes were still enormous from the import of
what he had revealed; she was breathing deeply, her lips slightly parted.
Would she welcome him? He could not be sure. But she seemed so
vital, so lovely and warm and happy.

Slowly, so that he could stop at any instant without embarrassment
or revelation of his intent, he put out his arms, placed them about her
slender waist, drew her to him. With his lips only a breath away she
lowered her arms as gently about his neck as the falling lime blossoms;
and his lips met hers, alive and palpitant with the sweetness of life.

3.

He left his parents' apartment in Vienna's Second District a little
after seven on Monday morning; in his exuberance he closed the door
with the number 3 on it none too gently behind him. The *Hausmeister*
had not yet turned out the gas light over the stair well, a good thing for

his safety since he was taking the steps three at a time without bothering to hold onto the wrought-iron balustrade. A sharp turn took him
through the decorated entrance hall with its stucco filigrees and arabesques into the brightness of the just-awakening street. Most of the
houses in this Second District where the Freuds had lived since arriving
from Freiberg, Moravia, in 1860 when Sigmund was four, twenty-two
years ago, were a story and a half, of modest wood frame. This fourth
of the houses through which the Freuds had struggled laboriously upward since Jakob Freud lost his respectable fortune in Moravia was the
most solid and handsome on the block, near the corner of the Taborstrasse, on the wide tree-lined Kaiser Josefs-Strasse, connecting the
French garden of the Augarten with the promenades and rolling
lawns of the Prater, a favorite route of the royal court. Sigmund had
frequently seen the Emperor Franz Josef and his resplendently accoutered attendants riding horseback or making the short journey in
elaborate cream and gold French carriages.

He stepped out vigorously on his favorite hour-long walk, inhaling
the light fragrant spring air as though it were an elixir. After he had
passed the Zum Hl. Josef pharmacy, with ornate chemical jars in its
windows, he turned left into the Taborstrasse, passing the fine shops,
coffeehouses and restaurants that had been built for the Vienna World's
Fair of 1873 and continued to prosper. At the corner of the Obere
Augartenstrasse he could see through the trees to the French pavilion-
like buildings in the park. At the corner of the Grosse Pfarrgasse was a
four-story house, its top floor held up on either side by plaster torsos of
two Amazons with heroic breasts and the classical headdress of the
ancient Greek women.

Sigmund bowed formally without breaking his stride, murmured:
"Küss' die Hand!"

He chuckled as he thought of his friend Dr. Adam Politzer's apartment building on the Gonzagagasse with its two pillars of lightly
swathed, big-hipped and big-bosomed Viennese women coiffured to
look like the women of Caesar's court. There was a joke among the students at the university:

"We learn more about anatomy from Viennese architecture than we
do from the medical books."

He quickened his pace to the Haidgasse where he gazed upward at
his favorite building in the district, topped by a bulbous red spire that
seemed to him Oriental. His next landmark was the Leopoldstädter
Children's Hospital, after which he turned west on the Tandelmarkt-
gasse with its workshops and storehouses, keeping ahead of the early
morning flow of horse-drawn cars and *Einspänner*, inexpensive one-
horse carriages; street cleaners with country-made straw brooms brushing the refuse to the curb with the help of water hosed out of a

cylindrical white barrel drawn by white horses; *Dienstmänner,* young-ish, clean-shaven men wearing a uniform of peaked hat, coat with epaulet and large badge, pushing carts loaded with merchandise for the shops. These errand men, licensed by the city, stationed themselves at the corners of the main thoroughfares and delivered anything from a letter to a handcart full of boxes for four kreutzer a kilometer, their average charge being ten kreutzer, four cents, for any message or errand within the city. He made his way past the stream of men walking to their day's work, and to the center of the ancient plank bridge with its customs shed guarding each entrance. This was his resting spot, half-way between his home and the Physiology Institute. These were the few contemplative moments available to him, his thinking helped by gazing down into the swiftly moving waters of the Danube, or *Donau* Kanal, its banks lined with poplars and willows.

This morning's conference with Professor Ernst Wilhelm Ritter von Brücke would be a crucial one. He asked himself, "Why have I put it off so long?" But he knew the answer. He had long since made his decision: to remain here and to work his way up the academic ladder of the University, the Medical Faculty and the Allegmeine Kranken-haus, the General Hospital: to a first assistantship under Brücke, on to his *Dozentur* and the right to lecture to classes; then to *Extraordinarius,* assistant professor; and finally to *Herr Hofrat, Ordinarius,* full profes-sor; and head of an institute as had Brücke in physiology, and the renowned Theodor Meynert, head of the Second Clinic in psychiatry. Both professors had encouraged him, even as his parents had continued to support him, supplementing the small fees he earned as a Demon-strator and tutor.

He had been happy in the laboratory; his two former teachers, Sig-mund Exner von Erwarten and Ernst Fleischl von Marxow, though only ten years older than he, were the most brilliant associates any man could hope to work with.

Whistling a bright Viennese ballad a full sixteenth off key, for he cheerfully admitted that he was tone deaf, he continued on to the other end of the bridge, enjoying the view of the Ruprechtskirche, the oldest church in Vienna, with its stand of tall poplars, and to the left the towers of St. Stephan's narrowing upward to a point of infinity in the powder-blue sky. He had read that Paris was the mother of all cities and the most beautiful but he believed that for walking Vienna could have no equal; every few steps, such as this very moment when he came onto the Schottenring, the eye was greeted with such breathtaking beauty that one gasped with delight.

The Physiology Institute, a part of the University of Vienna Medical College, was housed in a former gunworks on the corner of the Währ-inger Strasse, just a block from the sprawling complex of the General

Hospital and catercorner from the Votivkirche and the university itself. The two-story Institute had the same gray-colored walls as the guns
it had manufactured. The other half of the block-long building was the
dissection laboratory where Sigmund had worked on cadavers for the
first two years of his medical studies. He skittered around the corner of
the Schwarzspanierstrasse, made his way under the arch and through a
short dark tunnel toward the inner court. On his right was the auditorium where Professor Brücke lectured every morning from eleven
o'clock until noon. In each of the nichelike cubicles around its walls
was a desk or laboratory table loaded with specimens, electric batteries,
books, notes, mechanical equipment and students bent over their microscopes. When the professor came in to lecture the students had to go
elsewhere for the hour, despite the fact that there was nowhere in the
totally inadequate building to work. Sigmund himself had occupied
practically every one of these auditorium niches during his three undergraduate years of training with Professor Brücke.

He took the stairs up to the second floor with the same gait that he
had come down the two flights from his apartment. It was a few minutes before eight but the laboratories were humming with activity. As
he walked along the corridor facing the court he passed the room
which he shared with a chemist and two visiting physiologists from
Germany. The next room was a small laboratory shared by his two
associates, Ernst Fleischl and Sigmund Exner, both from titled Austrian
families. At the corner of the building was the brain and nerve center
of the Institute, Professor Brücke's combined office, study, laboratory
and library.

All doors were kept open. When he stuck his head into Exner's and
Fleischl's room his nostrils were assailed by the aromatic odor of the
oxidation of electrical batteries and the chemicals used for anatomical
preparations which, until two days ago in the garden in Mödling when
he had buried his face in Martha's hair, he had thought the most desirable scents in a man's world. The room was neatly divided in half,
each man's workbench occupying one full wall. Exner, though only
thirty-six, was growing bald and his untrimmed beard verged on the
scraggly. That was about all Exner was missing, except a sense of
humor. In the university it was said that every male Exner must become
a university professor, which a wag had reversed to: "Every university
professor must be an Exner."

The room itself was dominated by two complex machines, the one,
a "neuroamoebimeter" improvised by Exner, consisting of a metal
strip which vibrated one hundred times a second and was used for
measuring psychic reaction time of the human brain; the other invented by Fleischl for his pioneering work in brain localization.

Sigmund watched the two men affectionately as they went about their concentrated chores. Exner had been his professor in medical physiology and the physiology of the sense organs, while Fleischl had taught him physiology and higher mathematics. The two men could not have been more completely opposite in temperament. Exner, who came from a wealthy family that had long been entrenched in the court life of the Austro-Hungarian Empire, was an accomplished technician and administrator who was determined to become, at Professor Brücke's retirement, Professor *Ordinarius* and Director of the Physiology Institute. Sigmund considered him an attractive man, with absorbed gray eyes overhung with heavy brows and heavy lids.

Ernst Fleischl's family was as old and wealthy as Exner's but its long-time entrenchment was in the art, musical and theatrical world of Vienna, probably the most stimulating in Europe with its robust Hofoper and Kärntnertor, its Philharmonic and symphony orchestras, and rich national repertory theaters. Vienna abounded with composers and playwrights; its concert halls and theaters were always full. Fleischl was a handsome man with a stand of thick black hair, a fastidiously trimmed narrow beard, a high rounded forehead, nose of sculptured precision, a sensitive, always-in-action mouth which could quote and pun in six languages; and certainly he was the best-dressed man to parade past the Opera of a Sunday morning. His mercurial mind had neither liking nor talent for administration and so he was no rival of Exner for the directorship. He had an irreverent wit which he used against the pomposities of the Hapsburg court and the unique character of the Viennese. He had asked Sigmund:

"You know the story of the three girls? The first one was in Berlin, on a bridge over the Spree. A policeman asked her what she was doing. She replied, 'I am going to jump into the river and drown myself.' The policeman hesitated, then said, 'All right, but are you sure you paid all your taxes?' The second girl, in Prague, jumped off a bridge into the Moldau but after she hit the water started crying out in German, 'Save me! Save me!' A policeman came to the edge of the bridge, looked down at her and said, 'Better you should have learned to swim instead of learning to speak German.' The third girl, in Vienna, was about to jump into the Donau Kanal. The policeman said, 'Look, that water down there is very cold. If you jump in I must jump in after you, it's my duty. That means we will both catch cold and have to go to bed. So why don't you just go home and hang yourself?'"

Fleischl had suffered an outrageous stroke of bad luck ten years before; while working on a cadaver his right thumb had become so badly infected that part of it had had to be amputated. Granulated tissue known as "proud flesh" formed, the skin had trouble filling in from the sides, the thin layer kept breaking open, causing ulceration. Professor Billroth operated at least twice a year; the further cutting of the nerves only added to Fleischl's misery. His nights were racked with pain but no one could tell this during the working hours of the day when he experimented with his dozen wax models of human brains injured in accidents, attempting to relate the areas of damage to impaired functioning: aphasia, blindness, paralysis of facial muscles.

Fleischl was the first to see Sigmund standing in the doorway. His face lit up with an engulfing smile. The younger man was one of his two or three closest friends; Sigmund spent many a night trying to entertain and engross Fleischl so that he might forget the excruciating pain in his thumb.

"Herr Freud, what do you mean by coming to work in the middle of the morning?"

Exner looked up, amused. He said:

"Fleischl was depressed this morning because not one injured brain came into the hospital from all those Sunday mountain climbers."

Fleischl said to Sigmund with mock seriousness:

"How am I going to determine which tiny area of Professor Exner's brain creates those bad jokes if I never get a brain-injury case of a flatulent humorist?"

"Be consoled, Ernst," Sigmund replied. "I'm about to ask Professor Brücke to make a momentous decision in my life. If I fail, I shall throw myself off the Leopoldsberg head first . . . with your name and address in my pocket."

4.

He knocked on the jamb of the wooden door and walked into the room.

"Grüss Gott."

"Grüss Gott. Herr Professor Brücke, could I speak to you alone for a few minutes?"

"But certainly, Herr Kollege."

A tremor of joy went through Sigmund: Brücke had called him a colleague. This had happened only once before, when the professor had been impressed by Sigmund's work on laying bare the central nervous system of the higher vertebrate. It was the finest compliment a head of an institute could pay a lowly Demonstrator earning but a few kreutzer a day.

The two students who were working at opposite ends of Brücke's crowded workbench gathered their papers. Josef Paneth, who had a small desk under the window from which one could look down the hill of the Berggasse, a desk at which Sigmund himself had worked for a year, tipped him a comradely wink and left the room. Paneth, a year younger than Sigmund, twenty-five, had taken his M.D. two years earlier. He sought out Sigmund's company because Sigmund was the only one of their circle who did not seem to know about the considerable portion of his family's fortune that Paneth had already inherited, and which so embarrassed him among the impoverished students whose company he enjoyed that he wore shabbier clothes than anyone else, and when the group went to a coffeehouse for talk and the raillery so dear to students' hearts, ordered the cheapest *Kleinen Braunen* and plain cake.

Paneth closed the door behind him. The room was permeated with the familiar smells of alcohol and formaldehyde. Sigmund gazed at the man he admired most in the world. Ernst Wilhelm Ritter von Brücke, now sixty-three, had been born in Prussia of a family of academically trained painters. Brücke's father had encouraged young Ernst to follow in the family tradition; he had studied painting techniques, traveled in Italy, collected a Mantegna, a Bassano, a Luca Giordano, a Ribera, as well as Dutch landscapes and German Gothic canvases. Some of the paintings had hung on these laboratory walls for years, mingling with the professor's collection of anatomical slides and histological specimens prepared for the microscope. Brücke's decision to become a medical scientist had not been based on a lack of artistic talent; in the drawing room of the professor's big apartment on the Mariannengasse Sigmund had seen a self-portrait done when Brücke was twenty-six, the drawing incisive, the coloring of the red hair and fair skin adroitly applied, the modeling of the head set forth with the fist of a penetrating realist. Nor had Brücke actually abandoned art; he had published books on *The Theory of Pictorial Art, The Physiology of Colors in Applied Art, Representation of Motion in Art,* which established him as an authority.

When Ernst Brücke had been brought from Königsberg to the University of Vienna in 1849, at the incredibly high salary of two thousand gulden a year, eight hundred dollars, because all of Europe sought him, he had been given a spacious suite of offices in the palatial Joséphinum with a fine view of the city. But Professor Brücke had not come to Vienna to be comfortable or to admire the scenery. He gave up the luxurious quarters, moved to the old gunworks on the corner and, without running water or gas—one handyman brought in buckets of water from the outside tap and took care of the animals being used for experimentation—by sheer brains and dedication gradually turned the dilapidated old building into the most important Physiological Institute in Central Europe. It had been only three years before Sigmund took his first course here that water had been piped in and gas for the Bunsen burners.

Professor Brücke sat behind his bench watching Sigmund with the blue eyes that were known as the coldest in the university; disgruntled students claimed that one glance could freeze any catch of Danube fish. On the professor's head was an omnipresent dark silk beret; wrapped around his knees was a Scotch plaid blanket; and in the corner of the room stood his enormous Prussian umbrella which he carried even on the clearest summer day while making his early morning tour around the Ring to watch progress on the newly building Parliament, Greek, after Athens; the Rathaus, Flemish, after the City Hall in Brussels; the two Museums of Art and Science, facing each other, after the Italian Renaissance. Professor Brücke was reputed to be a most courageous and daring scientist; he feared only the diphtheria which had killed off his mother and young son; the rheumatism which had crippled his wife; and the tuberculosis which ran in his family.

Sigmund had never found Ernst Brücke to be cold. He had been reproved only twice over the years; once when he had come into the laboratory at one minute past eight, to have Brücke comment:

"To be a little late to work is to be too late for your work."

Young Sigmund had felt incinerated.

Another time he had put aside a discovery he had made in the staining of nerve tissue in order to let the idea lie fallow.

"Lie fallow!" exclaimed Professor Brücke. "That is a euphemism for evasion."

These reprimands were as nothing compared to the one Sigmund's neighbor in an auditorium niche had received. The student had written in a report, "Superficial observation reveals . . ." Brücke had scrawled angrily across the paper, "One is not to observe superficially!"

Sigmund knew that he would have to begin this difficult conversation himself; Professor Brücke had lost his fund of small talk when a young man and had never again been able to raise even a modest stand.

"Herr Hofrat, a change has come over my life. Only last Saturday the young woman I love gave me an intimation . . . It happened suddenly; I was taken by surprise. Of course we are not yet engaged . . . marriage is years off . . . but this is the woman with whom I am convinced my future happiness lies."

"My congratulations, Herr Doktor."

"Herr Hofrat, I know that you will not consider me guilty of flattery if I say that I have found full satisfaction in your laboratory, and men whom I can respect: yourself, Herr Professor, and Drs. Fleischl and Exner . . ."

Brücke tipped his beret a trifle lower on his forehead, a gesture he used when no reply presented itself. Sigmund took a deep breath and plunged in once again.

"In order to become engaged and look forward seriously to marriage I must have a position and the possibility of advancement at the university as my work warrants it. Would you recommend me to the Medical Faculty for the position of your Assistant? I know I must start modestly but here I will have a chance of making a contribution worthy of your teaching and confidence in me."

Brücke was silent. Sigmund could feel fragments of sentences forming and being discarded. He studied Brücke's nearly clean-shaven face, the high-ridged cheekbones, the full-lipped mouth, the rounded chin, the eyes still beautiful at sixty-three. Sigmund had sometimes felt about Brücke that he was a passionate man who waged a constant battle to keep his feelings in check.

"First things first, Herr Doktor. Would I want you for my Assistant? Assuredly. Can I engage you as my Assistant? I cannot."

Something inside Sigmund's chest plummeted. The thought flashed across his mind, "As a physiologist I ought to know what it was within me that just dropped. But I don't." Aloud he said, "Why can you not recommend me, Herr Professor?"

"The regulations of the Medical Faculty do not permit me to. The Institutes are allowed only two Assistants. To get the Ministry of Education to add a third would take years of struggle . . ."

Sigmund felt sick to his stomach. Had he known this limitation all along and deceived himself?

"Then there is no place for me here?"

"Neither Fleischl nor Exner will ever leave the Institute. Until I die and one of them can take my place, they must continue here as my Assistants . . . at one hundred dollars a month."

"But they could be called to head a department at the University of Heidelberg or Berlin or Bonn . . . ?"

Brücke came around his workbench and stood before his favorite pupil. His voice was gentle.

"My dear friend, isn't the problem considerably deeper than whether you can get an assistantship here? Under our present structure pure science is for the rich. The Exner and Fleischl families have had wealth for generations. They do not need a salary. You've told me of your father's struggle to support you through these university years. Have things improved at home?"

"No. They are more difficult. My father is growing old. I must start to help my parents and sisters."

"Then doesn't it follow, Herr Doktor, that you must find another route? If I were successful in bringing pressure upon the Ministry you would have to work for the first five years for forty or fifty dollars a month. At middle age you would be earning little more, unless Exner

and Fleischl were both dead, and the Medical Faculty appointed you
director instead of going outside for a famous name."

A darkness flooded Sigmund's eyes as though a squid had squirted
his inky fluid into them. Professor Brücke had been at the University of
Vienna for thirty-three years, long enough to recognize this particular
form of bitterness. He read it, shrewdly.

"No, Herr Kollege! It is not anti-Semitism. Several on our Medical
Faculty are Jews. Among the student drinking clubs, yes; but no first-
rate medical school could be built on the sewage of religious prejudice.
Professor Billroth's unfortunate attack, which I heartily regret, was an
exception."

Sigmund's mind went back to Billroth's *The Medical Sciences in the
German Universities* and the chapter which attacked the quality of the
Jewish medical student, even as Professor Brücke, more heatedly and
more wordily than his usual self, was saying, ". . . I was three things
Catholic Austria hates most, a Protestant, a German and a Prussian.
But after a year I was elected to the Academy of Letters. For the first
time in their history a German was made dean of the Medical Faculty
and then rector of the university. You are too good a man to seek refuge
in the thought of anti-Semitism."

"Thank you, Herr Hofrat. But if I cannot earn a living here, what
am I to do? There is no other department where I could . . ."

Brücke shook his head, took off his beret and wiped the perspiration
from his brow. Only then did Sigmund realize that his mentor too
had been laboring under heavy emotion. Brücke went to the window
and stared out for a moment, his chunky back turned to the younger
man while he gazed at the corner of the Berggasse where the wide street
flowed downhill to the Kai and the Kanal. The half-song of a country
woman, her hair covered by a head shawl, came through the window:
"I have lavender. Who wants my lavender?" When Brücke turned, an
expression of serenity was back in the fine eyes.

"You will have to do what all young doctors do if they have no
private income. Practice medicine. Take care of patients."

"I don't want to practice private medicine. I never intended to. I
went into medicine only to become a scientist. One should have the
talent, the feeling for the sick . . ."

Brücke returned to his chair and adjusted the plaid rug over his lap
though the room seemed stiflingly hot.

"Herr Doktor, is there really another way? If you wish to marry? The
young woman has no dowry?"

"I believe not."

"You will have to return to the Krankenhaus for fuller training in
all the disciplines. So that you can become an able as well as a successful

practitioner. You are young, you will adjust. It should not take more than four years of hospital experience before you have your *Dozentur* and can put out your sign. Vienna needs good doctors."

Sigmund mumbled, "Thank you, Herr Hofrat. *Grüss Gott.*"

"*Servus.*"

5.

He struck out blindly, up the Währinger Strasse, past a side entrance to the hospital grounds which was used by students, doctors and attendants. Beyond the arched gate loomed the five-story circular stone Fools' Tower.

"That's where I belong," he muttered, "in one of those cells, chained to the wall. Lunatics should not be allowed abroad."

Walking in Vienna was no longer exhilarating; every inlaid stone and cobble lacerated the soles of his feet even as his chaotic thoughts and recriminations bruised the central nervous system which he had been so successful in laying bare in the animals of the laboratory. He thought:

"We know that sight is controlled by the occipital lobe and sound by the temporal lobe. Surely I'm the right man to discover which lobe of the forebrain controls stupidity!"

He plunged dazedly onward toward the Hirschengasse and Grinzinger Allee, making for the Wienerwald where generations of Viennese had exalted their joys and vented their sorrows while hiking through the thickness of its forest. The village of Grinzing, bustling with *Hausfrauen* carrying baskets on their arms, ran uphill toward the lower vineyards which were also planted with peach and apricot trees. The *Heurigen Stüberln* had evergreen wreaths above their entrances to indicate that in these little wine houses the vintner's new wine was available in the garden under chestnut trees, from vines that had grown in the lee of the Wienerwald for two thousand years, long before the Roman legionnaires seized the settlement then called Vindobona. He did not stop.

The winding path upward was overhung with shade, but Sigmund Freud broiled in the heat of his mortal agony. Paroxysms of emotion swept over him: shame, fury, defeat, confusion, fear, frustration, anxiety, each state of distress quite separate, leaving a different residue of gall in the mouth.

He left the path used by the villagers and plunged upward through the deep woods surrounded by silver birch and pine that went back a century to their beginning roots. There was an engulfing stillness here, and quietude; only the occasional note of a bird or a distant woodchopper's ax broke the silence. The chlorophyll of a forest of leaves is the best absorbent; it can assume any amount of man's grief without withering the branches. But today not even the magnificent trees could bring him absolution. The lush spring foliage, the sense of having returned to a beneficent green womb where all were protected and the hostile world shut out, which had refreshed his soul over the years, failed him now as he oscillated from anguish to rage and back again.

He reached the peak and the garden restaurant of the Kahlenberg. People were eating their picnic lunches out of rucksacks and drinking steins of *Gösser Bier* brought by waiters with oversized trays. He was parched and tired now, having trudged for eight miles, but he took off immediately on the crestline trail to Leopoldsberg and its ruined castle. Below him lay Vienna, held between the Wienerwald and the Danube. To the south rose the alpine peaks leading to Italy, to the east the lowlands rolling toward Hungary, along which the invaders from Asia as well as Huns, Avars, Magyars and Turks had besieged and sometimes overrun the Imperial City. He could see nothing but the misery inside his own head: for he had fallen into a Sargasso Sea of self-pity.

How could he ask Martha to become engaged to him now, when his future was so clouded? How was he going to explain to her this unforeseen setback and defeat of his plan to be a scientist? How was he going to support himself, let alone help his family, in the next years? How was he going to endure four years of hospital training in surgery, at which he was inept; in dermatology, which he had found dull; internal medicine, for which he had little diagnostic gift; nervous diseases, about which he knew only what his friend Dr. Josef Breuer had taught him? Psychiatry, which meant brain anatomy, under Professor Meynert would be interesting; he had already studied clinical psychiatry under Meynert, who favored him and could teach him all there was to know about "localization." But since the patients who would eventually come to his office would not want the tops of their skulls taken off so that he could study their fissures, what good would such training do him?

Halfway back to the Kahlenberg he dropped down a narrow, rutted ox trail to Klosterneuburg. At the foot of the mountain, every muscle of his body aching, he turned his back on the road to the Cloisters and began walking homeward along the bank of the Donau Strom, pausing occasionally to splash water over his feverish face. He had another several hours to walk but he knew by now that he had to put an end to the flagellation and despair, not to mention the excoriation of the University, the Medical Faculty, the Allgemeine Krankenhaus and the Ministry of Education, in which he had been indulging. Men took their punishment even when it was applied to the bare back with knotted whips; they gritted their teeth and refused to cry out in pain. They went on to the next day of their lives. What choice was there?

It was late afternoon before he made his way, emotionally spent, to the home of Dr. Josef Breuer, his confidant and closest friend. Known in Vienna as "Breuer of the Golden Touch," Josef was personal physician to the larger part of the university's Medical Faculty, an accolade that made him one of the most sought-after doctors in the Austro-Hungarian Empire. His fame rested on his diagnostic skill. Breuer often achieved cures where others failed. At the Medical School it was said that he "divined" the causes of hidden ailments. The townspeople translated the word literally to mean that Dr. Breuer's knowledge came from a divine source. The Viennese were puzzled as to why their Catholic God should reveal the nature of their illnesses to a Jew, but they did not allow theology to get in the way of Dr. Breuer's cures.

Josef Breuer was a genuinely modest man. When people praised him as being prescient he replied:

"Nonsense! Everything I know I learned from my chief, Professor Oppolzer, in internal medicine."

He had indeed learned a great deal from Oppolzer, who had taken him into his Clinic while Josef was still a student, only twenty years old. Five years later Oppolzer appointed him Clinical Assistant, and was grooming the young man to take his place as chief. But Oppolzer died in 1871. Breuer was only twenty-nine. The Medical Board had gone outside the faculty to choose an older and better-known man, Professor Bamberger of Prague and Würzburg, to succeed to the directorship. What happened next Breuer had never revealed; he had either resigned in disappointment or been released by Professor Bamberger, who wanted a Clinical Assistant of his own choosing. Breuer had entered private practice while continuing to research in Professor Brücke's laboratory on the fluid in the semicircular canals which he found decisive for the control of movements of the head. Here, working unofficially, he had made important discoveries on the otolitic apparatus as the organ for the feeling of gravity. Here too he had become fast friends with Fleischl and Exner, and here he had met young Sigmund Freud, fourteen years his junior and not yet an M.D. Breuer began taking Sigmund home with him for midday dinner. His wife, Mathilde, and their children adopted Sigmund into the family to replace Josef's younger brother, Adolf, who had died some years before.

The Breuers lived at Brandstätte 8, in the Central City, two short blocks from Stephansplatz and the fashionable shops of the Kärntner

Strasse and the Rotenturmstrasse. From their apartment the Breuers could see the noble spire at the rear of St. Stephan's Cathedral, the two Romanesque towers at the front, the sharply slanting mosaic slate roof, the giant bell, *Pummerin*, the Boomer, which summoned the city to fires as well as worship. First started in 1144, when it stood outside the original medieval walls, the cathedral was, like the capital it served, a fascinating potpourri of seven centuries of architecture. Its interior was majestic, its exterior far more pragmatic, for there was the open-air pulpit from which the clergy had exhorted the besieged Viennese to drive off the infidel Turks, a Christ on the Cross with such lines of pain in his face that the passing, irreverent faithful crossed themselves while calling him the "Christ of the Toothache"; a praying bench for those in a hurry to join their *Stammtisch* in the nearby cafe; and, the most important economic guideposts in the Empire, a circle carved into a stone block so that the Viennese shopper could measure the freshly bought "round" of bread, a horizontal, deeply etched meter on which to check the purchase of cloth to make sure there had been no cheating by the width of so much as a fingernail paring.

The *Portier* of the apartment house slid back a tiny glass window in his ground-floor apartment and waved Sigmund in. He climbed the flight of steps and rang the bell just above Dr. Josef Breuer's handsome bronze plaque. A *Dienstmädchen* admitted him. To his surprise he found portmanteaus and a trunk standing in the spacious foyer. When Mathilde Breuer heard his voice she came quickly to greet him. She was thirty-six, with a bright open expression, light complexion, smoke-gray eyes and copious braids of chestnut hair wound on top of her head. Though her fifth child had been born three months before, Mathilde had already recovered her slim figure.

But not her merry, infectious spirits. Even before the child had been born, Sigmund had noticed that Mathilde was silent and a little morose; the atmosphere in the house had become restrained. He attributed it to some kind of physical illness resulting from this fifth carrying and thought he should not drop in so often. He was rebuked by both Josef and Mathilde, and been given to understand that he was not to abandon them in their hour of trial.

Now all that seemed changed. Mathilde's eyes were sparkling as she greeted him with her old-time cheerfulness and energy.

"Sigi, we are going to Venice. Josef is taking me for a month's vacation. Isn't that delightful?"

"I'm so happy for you. When do you leave?"

"In a few days . . ." She stopped abruptly. "What happened to you? Your clothes are dirty and your face is caked with sweat. You look as if you are parched."

"I'm fasting. It's my Day of Atonement."

"What was your sin?"

"Self-deception."

"The first thing Josef would do is chase you into the bathtub. That's the best place to wash away your guilt. We have plenty of hot water on the stove."

The stubby tub stood off the floor on four cat's paws. The serving girl brought in wide, squat bottles of hot water, arranging them on the floor beneath the petroleum pump. When she left, Sigmund attached the pump to the first bottle and, while the water was piped up the back of the tub, undressed and put his soiled linens on a chair outside the door. They would be replaced by a set of Josef's linens. When he had transferred the pump to the last bottle he jumped into the tub and lay flat on his back so that the water from the pipe would pour over his head. Then he scrubbed himself.

The hot water drained not only the stiffness from his legs and body but the tensions from his mind. He wondered if a good part of the world's problems might not be solved in a hot bath. The Freud family had never had a bathtub. When Sigmund, his five sisters and brother Alexander were young, every other Friday afternoon a large wooden tub with jars of hot and cold water would be brought by two husky carriers from the nearby bathing establishment and put down on the stone flags of the kitchen. His mother soaped each of her young standing up, then dunked them in the tub. The next day the two men would return for their pay and take away the tub. In warm weather Sigmund bathed with his friends in the Danube; in the winter he went to the newly built *Tröpferlbad*, trickle bath, where for five kreutzer, two cents, he could take a shower while his mother rented a cabin at an adjoining bathhouse, with a tub and roaring fire in the corner stove. The sisters brought along apples which they left on top of the stove to roast while they lathered themselves.

There was a knock on the door. Breuer's voice called:

"Come out, Sig. Mathilde is setting supper for us upstairs in my office. She says we may eat in our shirt sleeves."

6.

He dried himself and dressed, smelling of the lavender which Mathilde kept in small porous sacks in Josef's bureau, then went upstairs to Breuer's office.

Breuer wore an oblong, precisely trimmed black beard, one of the most capacious in Vienna, perhaps to make up for the fact that he was prematurely bald.

"Mathilde told me you came in looking crushed. 'Pulverized' was her exact word. What hit you? I'm all ears."

Sigmund smiled for the first time that day. Josef was indeed all ears; they stood out at right angles to his head like the handles of a water pitcher. No one had ever called Josef handsome, but his eyes had a rare combination of strength and tenderness.

The upstairs office was small, with a desk for Josef to write at, just off his laboratory. The maid had put a crisp white cloth over a board table and laid out a platter of cold chicken left over from the midday dinner, some cold vegetables, a bottle of cooled *Giesshübler*, mineral water, and half a *Guglhupf* dusted with icing sugar. When Sigmund had dispatched two slices of breast and a second joint, he leaned back in his chair to gaze at Josef's craggy nose and eyebrows. He knew every shade of Josef's expression from the hundreds of hours of riding in a *Fiaker* with him through Vienna and the countryside while Dr. Breuer called on his patients.

"Josef, it's good to see Mathilde happy again."

"We're going to Venice for a month's honeymoon."

"That's the cure. What was the disturbance? Or is it indelicate to ask?

"I can tell you, now that it's over. It was Bertha Pappenheim. That's her real name, the one I've been calling Anna O. I've been treating her for two years now. Most amazing case I've ever handled, in the field of neurology at least."

"That's the case you described as 'the talking cure'?"

"Yes. Or, as Miss Pappenheim labeled it, 'the chimney sweeping.' During the past few months Mathilde has felt that I was spending too much time with Fräulein Bertha. I wasn't, of course; she needed me. But apparently I talked about her too much. I couldn't help it, you see, because I was getting such fantastic results from hypnotizing the girl and wiping out the symptoms of her paralysis. But that's over now. I pronounced her cured this morning, and came straight back home to tell Mathilde to set out our valises. —Now, I want to hear your story."

Sigmund told it quietly; how he had received an "intimation" from Martha Bernays that she loved him; how he had made his decision to ask Professor Brücke for an assistantship; how the professor had told him that there could be no future for him in academic life, that he must enter the Allgemeine Krankenhaus for deeper study and his years of internship, then set up a private practice.

"Martha Bernays, from Hamburg? The daughter of Berman Bernays, who was Professor von Stein's private secretary?" asked Josef.

"Yes. He died two years ago."

"I know. I studied the history of economics under Von Stein at the university."

"Josef, I can confess to you that this has been the most agonized day of my life. I just don't see any way out for myself."

Breuer appeared singularly undisturbed.

"There isn't. There is only a way *in*. You've told me that you prefer to eradicate generic illnesses rather than individual pain. I have always felt there was a touch of the messianic in that wish."

"What's wrong with the messianic, if it serves as a spur to accomplishment?"

"Nothing. But it should come as a result, not a beginning. You know, Sigismund, a long time ago I discovered under the surface of your timidity an extremely daring and fearless human being."

Sigmund stared at his friend, openmouthed.

"I have thought so too, Josef, but how does that help me in my present predicament? I have always looked forward to the university as a way of life, with full time for research and teaching. I feel at home amidst a constant stimulus of ideas. I never wanted to struggle for my existence on a competitive basis."

"You prefer the cloister."

"Yes, except that the university is a cloister where men are seeking the knowledge of the future rather than the buried forms of the past. And frankly, I don't like money."

"You don't like money, or you don't like to think about earning money?"

Sigmund had the good grace to blush: for Breuer frequently came to his rescue when he was desperate for funds, insisting that, since his own income was large and Sigmund's had not yet commenced, he should have the right to make life more bearable for him. Sigmund kept a meticulous account of the money he owed the Breuers, several hundreds of gulden by now; but it would be years before he could begin paying it back.

"Sig, you have made a good case for the academic life but you wouldn't be happy there for long. You would lack freedom. You would have to conform. You would be allowed to be radical only along strictly conventional lines. You would have someone over you, directing you to shift your focus, hurry publication on something they approved, or destroy that which made them uncomfortable."

He left the table and paced the room.

"Sig, this will make you stand on your own feet. The first part of medical science is seeing patients, taking care of them. From this basic work, which every doctor should perform, you can make greater discoveries than peering through a microscope. Come into the laboratory."

Years before, Breuer had removed the wall between two connecting rooms, just under the roof. There was a long workbench under windows overlooking a back garden, and on the adjoining wall cages for the pigeons and doves, rabbits and white mice with which he was working, also glass bowls of fish. Scattered about the room were electric batteries and machines for electrotherapy; jars of chemicals, boxes of slides, microscopes and, spread over the workbench, pages of Breuer's scientific writings.

"Josef, you *have* been working."

"Indeed. This laboratory is a three-way station. What I earn in fees I pour into machines and experiments. What I learn from my experiments I use to help my patients. I've now got twenty years of research on the semicircular canals of pigeons alone. But this is the important part for you, my young friend: I have total freedom to work and experiment and discover. I must tend my patients but the rest of my life is my own."

There was a sharp knock on the door. It was Mathilde. She had a sealed message in her hand.

"One of the servants from the Pappenheim house just brought it."

Breuer ripped open the envelope, turned pale.

"It's Fräulein Bertha. She has been seized with violent abdominal pains. I must go at once."

"Josef, you promised me you were finished with that case."

"Not while I am still in the city."

Tears came to Mathilde's eyes. She went slowly down the stairs. Breuer checked his black bag, said:

"Sig, please wait for me. Try to explain to Mathilde . . ."

Mathilde had locked herself in her bedroom. Sigmund went into the library, sat in Josef's high-backed chair reading the titles of the reference volumes that stood against the brass-rod railing at the end of the desk. It was a charming room with a high, decorated ceiling, a sharply curved black walnut piano and an eighteenth-century peasant chest ornamented in bright colors and holding silver candelabra. Spotted about on the bookshelves were archaeological findings from new digs.

Sigmund knew that it would do no good to talk to Mathilde now. She was too distressed. Yet, given Josef's background, it would have been impossible for him to do less than his duty. The Breuer grandfather had been a surgeon near Wiener Neustadt, serving the village and countryside until he died at a rather young age. Josef's father had had to educate himself; at thirteen he had walked the fifty miles to Pressburg to study at the theological seminary, and at sixteen had walked nearly two hundred miles to Prague to complete his course. He had become an outstanding educator in Prague, Budapest and Vienna, teaching the Hebrew language, history and culture. Breuer had proudly told Sigmund about his father who, he claimed, had helped replace "Jewish jargon by literate German, and the slovenliness of the ghetto by the cultured custom of the Western world." Josef's father had raised him on the teachings of the Talmud; Josef would never be able to escape being a moral man.

Sigmund's thinking turned to Anna O., now identified for him as Fräulein Pappenheim. She had been a school friend of Martha's. Her people had come from Frankfurt. It was indeed a strange and fascinating case as Josef Breuer had chronicled it for him over the past two years. Fräulein Bertha was a slender, twenty-three-year-old beauty, bubbling with intellectual vitality, daughter of a prosperous but rigidly puritanical family which had denied her further education when she finished the lyceum at sixteen, and allowed her no books or theater for fear her maidenly innocence might be corrupted. Bertha, of a kindly nature, revolted from the arid monotony of her life by creating her "private theater," daydreaming fairy tales based on the pictures in Hans Christian Andersen's stories.

In July of 1880 Bertha's father had fallen ill. Bertha devoted her energies to nursing him, allowing herself so little rest or sleep that no one was surprised when her own health failed. The first signs were weakness, anemia, distaste for food. She took to her bed. Breuer, the family doctor, had been called to treat her severe cough but had found a more serious illness: Fräulein Bertha was suffering from "absences"; her mind went away. At the same time she had hallucinations, seeing death's-heads and skeletons in the room; her hair ribbons appeared to her as snakes. She alternated between high spirits and deep anxiety, complained of profound darkness in her head, feared she was going deaf and blind. Severe headaches were succeeded by paresis of one side of the face and then one arm and leg. Her speech became disorganized, she lost words, then syntax and grammar, became unintelligible. Finally she lost her power of speech completely.

After a year of illness her father died. Fräulein Bertha could no longer recognize people, sank into deep melancholy, destructively tore the buttons off her nightclothes, would take almost no nourishment. Dr. Breuer was beside himself with frustration and self-condemnation: his golden touch had turned to brass, for he could find nothing physically wrong with Bertha, and here this witty, poetic and lovely girl was dying under his impotent care.

That is, until he stumbled across his first clue. Bertha began to live not in this June or July of 1881, but in the events of the year before, when she had been nursing her father. Breuer saw that she achieved this by autohypnosis. He was able to verify her memory-reversion by consulting a diary that had been kept by Frau Pappenheim. At this point Breuer came to several conclusions: that Bertha was suffering from a hysterical illness; that if she could hypnotize herself he could hypnotize her; and that if he could get her to relate the beginnings of her symptoms he could discuss them with her and suggest cures.

The method had worked, though curiously, for Fräulein Bertha answered Breuer only in English. Under hypnosis, she was able to remember the progress of her problems. Breuer discussed them with her and "suggested" that she could and should eat; that her eyesight and hearing were sound; that her paralysis would disappear when she willed it to; that, although her father had died, all parents die, and she could live her life without melancholy or crying out "Tormenting! Tormenting!" in the few hours she slept.

One by one Dr. Breuer had removed the symptoms. After a time he no longer needed hypnosis, Bertha preferring to "talk out" without it. She got out of bed, took exercise, returned to speaking and reading German. Although there had been regressions, by the end of the second year Breuer had been satisfied that his patient could maintain a normal existence.

Several times while Breuer was talking about this strange case of "Anna O.," Sigmund had asked:

"Josef, after you learned of the hysterical base of the symptoms, what could you perceive of the causes of the hysterias?"

Josef shook his head in resignation.

"You mean beyond grief at her father's illness, and perhaps self-castigation because she was not a perfect nurse? How can anyone tell? These are the closed areas of the human mind. No one can get into them. Nor do we need to so long as we eradicate the symptoms and restore the patient to health."

Breuer was back in far less time than Sigmund could have believed possible. His face was ashen, the fingers of his left hand clenched as though to hold down a body tremor. Sigmund was shocked.

"Josef, the girl can't be dead?"

Breuer poured himself half a glass of port wine, drank quickly. He then slumped into his high-backed chair, picked a cigar out of his box of Havanas, motioned to Sigmund to light one also. When he had taken a few quieting puffs he leaned across the desk.

"When I reached the house I found Bertha doubled over with pain. She did not recognize me. When I asked her what had started the pains she replied, 'Dr. Breuer's child is coming.'"

"What!"

Breuer took a folded handkerchief from his pocket, wiped beads of perspiration from his brow. His collar was soaked with sweat. Sigmund stared at his friend in incredulity.

Josef blurted: "She's a virgin. She doesn't even know what makes a woman with child."

"A hysterical pregnancy! Did her family hear?"

"No, mercifully. I hypnotized her and left her in a sound sleep. She won't remember the scene when she wakes in the morning."

A shiver went through Breuer.

"God Almighty, Sig, how could this have happened? I know the inside of that girl's mind like a book and there has never been one iota of sexuality in the case . . ."

Mathilde came into the library. Her face was puffy. Josef sprang up and took her in his arms.

"My dear, how would you like to leave for Venice tomorrow morning?"

Color rushed to Mathilde's cheeks.

"Josef, are you serious? But of course you are, I can tell. It's an early train but I will have everything ready."

Sigmund let himself out the street door, locked it behind him and dropped Josef's key into the slot lettered *Hausbesorger*. His own problems had been driven out of his mind. He found himself wondering about Bertha Pappenheim. Obviously, Fräulein Pappenheim was a long way from cured. If it were true, as Breuer had said, that there was not the slightest sexual element in the illness, then why did Bertha choose, of all the hallucinatory symptoms available to her, the idea that she was about to give birth to her physican's baby? And how was it that she did not recognize Dr. Breuer? Could it be because she could not then have said, as though to a stranger, "Dr. Breuer's baby is coming"? What could give rise to such a fantasy when the abdomen she was clutching was as flat as unleavened bread?

Making his way up the Kaiser Josefs-Strasse toward his house, a chuckle escaped him. As he went through the inner court of his apartment house, having paid the *Hausmeister* ten kreutzer for admitting him, since it was long past ten o'clock, he murmured:

"Apparently there are more hazards to private practice than Josef has indicated."

7.

The following noon he poured hot water from a pitcher into the bowl on a stand in his bedroom, washed his face with as much spluttering as soap and, with a towel tucked into his pants, scrubbed his chest, shoulders and arms. He rubbed himself with a bath towel until his skin tingled, took a shirt from the tiny wardrobe that contained his other suit and slipped into its crisp starched whiteness with a nod of gratitude for the laundering done by the *Wäschermädel* in the neighborhood laundry. He fitted his one good necktie, a black cravat, under the white collar which came to a low V exposing his strong, trunklike neck, then turned to the mirror over the washstand to see with what he was confronted now that he had made the most of his assets.

The mirror was only wide enough to show his face, shirt and tie. If he wanted to see how the dark-lapeled coat was sitting on his left shoulder, he had to move the right half of his head out of view. But what he saw looked good even in the one-eyed vision; for the barber had cut his hair and it was combed back with a dark glow from his forehead, and trimmed sharply around the ears. The beard was but a faint shadow down the line of his cheekbone. His mustache had been shaped to tilt saucily upward. What astonished him was how healthy he looked despite these last days of dislocation.

He went about straightening his room, where he hoped to bring Martha after the group of young friends who were invited in had had dinner, to show her his books and where he worked. It was a longish narrow *Kabinett,* a half room in the extreme corner of the apartment, pasted up alongside the next building, but with a window overlooking the Kaiser Josefs-Strasse. Though the room appeared to be an appendage left over when the rest of the apartment had been designed, he thought it the perfect spot for him because it gave him privacy from his growing sisters and, when his schoolmates came in for an evening of exuberant discussion, prevented them from keeping the family awake. In one corner he had put the equipment and books he had brought home from Brücke's Institute.

The six years the Freuds had lived here had been good ones for him. He had slowly added to his reference library of medical scientific treatises and filled the shelves above his desk with literary works in six languages, not including the Latin and Greek texts left over from the Leopoldstädter Kommunalgymnasium: Goethe, Shakespeare, Schiller, Balzac, Dickens, Heine, Mark Twain, Byron, Scott, Zola, Calderón, Ranke, Grillparzer, Fielding, Disraeli, Nestroy, George Eliot, Fritz Reuter. In a special place of honor, held by two silver bookends, was the prize of his library: the German edition of John Stuart Mill's *Essays,* the translation rights to one volume of which had been secured for him by Professor Brentano under whom Sigmund had studied philosophy. He had done the translation when he was twenty-three and stationed at the Garrison Hospital across the street from the Allgemeine Krankenhaus during his year of military service.

He made his way to the kitchen, located at the rear of the apartment overlooking the court. Amalie Freud stood at her coal stove alternately basting the goose that was roasting in the side oven and wiping down the gravy stains which fell onto the white tile with which the stove was faced. She was swathed in a white apron covering her party dress. Next to her was her oldest daughter, Anna, past twenty-three, tending the asparagus cooking on its iron plate. At a sideboard was her daughter Rosa, twenty-two, cutting up fresh fruits for dessert.

Amalie saw her son standing in the doorway, hung up her ladling spoon on the brass rail surrounding the stove and came to him with an affectionate smile. This was her favorite child, her favorite human being. When he had been born with a caul, an old country woman had announced to Amalie:

"With your first-born you have brought a great man into the world."

Amalie had not the slightest doubt of this. Though he had dark hair and dark eyes, she dotingly named him "my golden Sigi."

She fussed over his cravat, straightened the wide lapels by moving them slightly around on his shoulders. Neither piece of grooming had been necessary. Sigmund loved his mother deeply though not blindly. She was from East Galicia, a part of the Austro-Hungarian Empire with a reputation for having bred a peculiar people, different from every other race in Europe, filled with tempestuous emotions and liable to passionate outbursts over irrelevant causes. They were also known as a people of tremendous courage; in fact, a kind of indestructibility.

"Sigi, you look uncommonly handsome. For which of the girls are you wearing your best shirt and tie?"

Much as she adored him, there was no jealousy in Amalie's nature. She referred to the "day when Sigi can be married and give me beautiful grandchildren." She had five robust daughters, all of them doubtless as fertile as their mother, but the idea of their having children had not yet come into her head.

"For you, Mother."

Pleased that the ritual had followed its prescribed course, Amalie leaned up to peck her son on the cheek. His sisters gazed at the scene with amusement. It was no secret that their mother was foolish about her older son, just as it was no secret that sixty-six-year-old Jakob Freud was still excessively in love with his wife. In a family of nine there was more than enough affection to go around.

Amalie turned to a cutting table where she had made a long roll of dough. Now she began pulling off bits, rolled them between her hands and dropped the dumplings into a pot. Then she opened the oven to look at her goose. Sigmund, Anna and Rosa exchanged an indulgent smile as they watched their mother pour hot water from the kettle into the big pan in which the goose was roasting. Sigmund thought, "She has bequeathed all seven of us her insatiable appetite for life."

During the more prosperous Freiberg days the Freuds had been able to afford a nursemaid for their two little ones, but since coming to

Vienna there had been long dry spells when Jakob Freud could bring
little money into the house. Amalie had had to care for her growing
brood of seven children herself, content to have an occasional cleaning
woman, and to send the personal linens to the neighborhood laundress.
Amalie had spent prodigiously of her own substance to make up the
deficit. If there was no flour for the *challah*, she kneaded herself into
the loaf; if there was no cambric for the girls' dresses, she sewed
herself into the fabric.

He went into the *Wohnzimmer*, the room he cared for least, for
the parlor was nearly always kept dark: heavy black mahogany chairs
and sofa, double coverings for the windows with brown velours draperies gathered at each side, a worn Persian rug that had been left
from Jakob's first marriage. Yet there were a few things in the room
he liked: the coffee table with the old Hebrew Bible that had come
from his father's side of the family; the bookcase in the corner with
its bamboo facing; and the pull-down writing desk against the back
wall holding Amalie's most valuable possessions: three family photographs covering a period of eighteen years, each taken in a sudden
spurt of prosperity when the Freuds could buy new clothing and engage a good studio.

The first had been taken of the two men of the family—Alexander
would not be born for another two years—when Sigmund was eight and
being tutored by his father in preparation for entering the Sperlgymnasium. Sigmund was dressed in a handsome jacket, the coat buttoned
high, just under the soft shirt collar; and wore long trousers with a raised
seam at each side. Jakob wore a long dark coat, wide uncreased pants,
and a blue polka dot cravat. He was holding a book in his hands with
affection and confidence.

"Father, you were a mighty good-looking man," Sigmund said aloud,
and then laughed at his vanity: for even in this old picture the son
was a startling reproduction of the father.

The second picture was taken eight years later, when Sigmund was
sixteen and had been at the head of his class at the *Gymnasium* for
five consecutive years. He wore a vest now, with a gold watchchain
slung maturely across it, and a modest mustache. He was leaning
against an elaborately carved desk, his foot reaching out to touch his
mother's black taffeta hoopskirt. She too was holding a book, but away
from her, sliding downhill on her lap as though to admit quite honestly
that she did not hold a book too often or too naturally.

His mother, ten years younger then, was fastidiously groomed, her
face slender, sensitive. He liked the handsome gold earrings hanging
on delicate threads, the gold chain around her neck, the locket hanging below the white lace collar-inset of the black gown, and Amalie's
crowning glory, the gleaming black hair braided and coiled on the

back of her head. In Vienna it was said that the women from Galicia "were not ladies of exquisite manners"; but gazing intently at his mother now, he saw before him a woman of grace.

The third photograph was the largest and latest, taken only six years before, with six of the Freud children and Amalie's young brother, Oberleutnant Simon Nathansohn, as short in leg and torso as he was long in mustache, but looking every inch Austro-Hungarian Empire in his smartly tailored uniform with the light-colored buttons down the front of his jacket, the sword at his side dwarfing him. Sigmund saw himself standing at the center of the group, twenty now, deep in his medical studies, and wearing his first thin line of beard. His mother was sitting just in front of him, leaning on the arm he had placed on the back of her chair. On the floor was ten-year-old Alexander, the baby of the family. On Sigmund's right was Anna, a big strong girl with her mother's head of black hair, copious bosom and slim waistline.

Next to Anna stood Pauli, the youngest daughter, only twelve in this picture, tall and well developed for so young a child, plainer than the rest of the girls, with a buttonlike nose and round face. Her brother had found her easy to tutor but impossible to impose upon. On the other side of him stood Marie, called Mitzi, fifteen in the photograph, one braid worn forward over her left shoulder, irresolutely gazing out at the world beyond the camera. In the front row, next to their mother, was Dolfi, fourteen, on the other side of Amalie, Jakob, leaning forward to meet the camera head on, as though to impress his imprimatur on the portrait as master of the family.

Jakob Freud chose that moment to walk into the room. He was taller than his son, broad across the shoulders; his hair and beard were turning white but his mustache was a youthful black. His son thought him to look more and more like an Old Testament prophet. Jakob had an accumulated fund of stories to lighten any situation.

"Well, Sig," his father said, "you are nattily gotten up for our little festivity."

"I'm celebrating my entry into the medical profession."

Jakob blinked a few times while he absorbed this bit of intelligence. The entire Freud family had forgathered in the Aula of the university the previous year, on March 31, 1881, to watch Sigmund receive his diploma and become Dr. Freud. Jakob also knew that his son did not mean to practice medicine.

"I'm serious, Father. In a few weeks I'll be back in the Allgemeine Krankenhaus preparing myself for private practice."

"That's good news, son."

"Only in part. It will be several years before I can begin earning. I know that will be hard on you."

"We'll manage."

That had always been the key to the Freud household. They had coped. Jakob had managed to have ready the fees needed for the eight years of the *Gymnasium* and the six years of classes at the Medical School. But in recent times, as father and son both knew as they faced each other in the dark living room, the fare had been thin gruel.

Jakob showed signs of aging and did not always feel well. Although he had been married when only seventeen, to Saly Kanner in Tysmenitz, he had gone into the wool and fabric business for himself and prospered. He was the local agent for merchants in Prague and Vienna. In one year alone he had sold thirteen hundred bales of raw wool, involving large sums of capital and profit to match. When he and Saly moved to Freiberg, Jakob had taken out a license, paid substantial taxes and been a respected man in the community. Though he had had only a few years of formal education, mostly in religious school, he trained himself in the German classics. Saly had apparently been equally bright, for when Jakob was away on his frequent trips through Moravia, Galicia and Austria, buying and selling sheep and oxen, beef and hides, tallow, hemp and honey, Saly raised her two sons, took care of Jakob's account books, managed his storehouse in the neighboring village of Klogsdorf.

Saly had died when she was thirty-five. Sigmund had not heard the cause mentioned; in fact he could never remember hearing his father's first wife's name mentioned in Amalie's house. During his trips to Vienna Jakob had done business with the Nathansohn family, immigrants from Galicia, but now well entrenched in the Austrian wool business. He had watched Amalie grow up and had been fond of the child. Five years after the death of Saly he married Amalie, who was twenty at her marriage, and took her to Freiberg. She was an attractive girl with a good dowry; she had not had to marry a forty-year-old widower with two sons if she had not wanted to. But Jakob Freud was a strong, attractive man, successful, gentle of nature and well mannered. Sigmund believed that it had been a love match and not a marriage of convenience arranged by two business associates.

Jakob's and Saly's older son, Emanuel, was already married when Jakob brought Amalie back to Freiberg. Saly's other son, Philipp, who was nineteen, lived with the Freuds and became an older brother first to Sigmund, then to Amalie's second son, Julius, who died at the age of six months, and finally to Anna, who was born eight months later. Up to the age of three, Sigmund had had difficulty in determining his relationship to Philipp, who was almost the same age as Amalie; there were moments when he thought that Philipp was his father and Jakob his grandfather. Even more baffling at that time had been his relationship to Emanuel's son John, who was a full year older than he, and to Emanuel's daughter, Pauline, who was his own age. These difficulties vanished when Amalie and Jakob moved Sigmund and his sister Anna for an unsuccessful year to Leipzig and then to Vienna. Emanuel took his family, and his brother Philipp, to Manchester, where they set up in the textile business. Sigmund did not see his half brothers, nephew or niece again until he was nineteen and Jakob was able to give him a promised summer in England for having passed his *Matura* and qualified for the University of Vienna.

With his second marriage Jakob Freud's fortunes began to decline. The new Northern Railway from Vienna bypassed Freiberg; the inflation and then depression of the 1850s caught him and many others unprepared. He was unable to meet the debts arising out of his considerable commitments. When he lost his business and arrived in Vienna with his four-year-old son and year-and-a-half-old daughter, he came up against established firms with entrenched capital. Without funds he could not compete. On the records of Sigmund's Sperlgymnasium Jakob Freud had filled out "Wool trader" for his profession; but the sad truth was that Jakob never again became a merchant in wool. He had never taken out a license or paid taxes but had been employed in a variety of jobs in the wool and textile trade. When Jakob had a good job they bought a piano for Anna, one of the new petroleum lamps which could be raised and lowered on chains for over the dining-room table; they bought clothing for the family, had their picture taken, raised Sigmund's allowance at Deuticke's bookstore. When the job was a poor one, or Jakob was laid off, as was becoming increasingly frequent, the Freuds lived in a moneyless world heeding Amalie's stricture: "There is nothing to spend."

Yet until recently the Jakob Freuds had managed to cling tenaciously to the *Mittelstand*, the social class of teachers, officers at the Ministry, musicians who earned from three hundred to five hundred gulden a month, a hundred and twenty to two hundred dollars, a middle income, not good but sufficient.

There was one factor Sigmund alone knew from his summer with Emanuel and Philipp, who were prospering in the wool business in Manchester. In Emanuel's house, Sigmund had heard his half brothers speak of Saly as an astute businesswoman. Though they sometimes had to send money to Vienna when things got too bad in the Freud household, they had no criticism of Amalie. It was just that if Saly had been alive she would not have permitted Jakob to plunge so heavily in his commitments.

"But then," mused Sigmund as he smiled at his father, "if Saly had been alive in 1855 my father would not have married my mother. I, Dr. Sigmund Freud, such as I am, would not be here on the Kaiser Josefs-Strasse, on a warm June evening, waiting for the girl I love."

8.

The bronze hand of the clapper on the outside door fell with three rings against its metal plate. Sigmund rushed from the living room to greet Martha, but Anna and Rosa got there first to greet their young men: Anna was secretly engaged to Eli Bernays, and Rosa was keeping company with one of Sigmund's schoolmates, whom everyone called Brust. Behind Brust came Minna, Martha's younger sister, with Ignaz Schönberg, to whom she was secretly engaged. Minna was a big girl, tall, broad across the shoulders and hips, but flat-chested, as though nature had decided that it had to economize somewhere. Ignaz was Sigmund's university friend, a fleshless string bean of a fellow who had long suffered from the tuberculosis which beset so many of Vienna's young people. He was acknowledged at the university as the brightest Sanskrit scholar to emerge in a generation, and was already translating and editing a volume of Sanskrit fables, *Hitopadesa*, for publication in German. Bringing up the rear was Eli Bernays, with his sister Martha.

Eli was a commanding young man of twenty-two, heavy-set, with an aquiline nose, omnivorous eyes, who dressed in fashionable suits and wore high black kid shoes. When Eli was nineteen and about to enter the university under Professor von Stein's patronage, his father had died. Without a faltering step he had taken his father's job as secretary to the professor and begun supporting the Bernays family. Along with ferreting out side paths in the woods, his one idiosyncrasy was that he fastened his socks to his underwear with safety pins. Each night before he went to bed he set out the six pins on the identical spot on the rug; each morning he put on his underwear and fastened three of the pins into each sock.

"By the same token, no other portion of Eli's life plan can conceivably fall down," Sigmund commented.

Now at last he could greet Martha. Had she held back purposely? As he took her hand she flashed him a smile that left him standing on one foot, feeling weak. Greetings were exchanged between the young couples, then Amalie and Jakob Freud were greeted:

"*Grüss Gott! Grüss Gott! Guten Abend, Gnädige* Frau, *Guten Abend,* Herr Freud."

Eli and Ignaz had brought little bunches of flowers.

The dinner table had been extended by a board at each end and was covered with a white Danish cloth and napkins rolled in silver holders, still an intact dozen from Amalie's dowry. At each place was set a large plate for the main course, and on it a soup plate. Across the top of the setting lay the dessert spoon; each place had its glass for the *Giesshübler*. The youngest daughter brought in the large round loaf of *Hausbrot*, sliced through in triangular pieces, which made the circuit of the table; then Anna brought in the soup tureen, from which Frau Freud filled the plates as they were passed to her. Next, Rosa brought in the goose on a platter, Mitzi carrying the platter of asparagus and Dolfi the red cabbage. Now came the most delicate moment of the evening; the carving of the goose was a stratagem which Frau Freud would not trust to her husband, since it had to be divided into thirteen parts, which meant a judicious halving of each leg, second joint and each side of the breast.

Anna had arranged the oblong Meissen place-card holders, putting all the secretly engaged couples next to each other; secretly engaged meaning that everyone knew they were in love but were too young and poor to think about marriage. Anna had placed Martha's card next to Sigmund's, for which he blessed his sister; but it was soon apparent that Rosa's Brust was none too happy about his own intimate arrangement. He sat on the edge of his chair as though poised for flight. Rosa was the beauty of the family, her friends comparing her to Eleonora Duse: wide-spaced eyes, the features and coloring of the Delphic Sibyl on the Sistine vault, a young woman of charm and grace who held her head cocked just a trifle to one side with a bemused interest in life. Brust could not stay away from Rosa but he was also frightened. Sigmund wondered of what.

The petroleum lamp had been pulled low and cast a warm glow of light over the table. On the wall over the buffet with its gleaming array of trays and silver service were framed photographs of the "bourgeois Ministry," Herbst, Giskra, Unger, Berger and others from the university's graduates: it had been one of the triumphs of the uprising and street fighting in Vienna in 1848 that the merchant middle class had at last been allowed to hold important government posts, among them several Jews. Sigmund had been so impressed, sitting opposite these imposing portraits each day at dinner, that toward the end of his preparatory training he had thought perhaps he might like to study jurisprudence. Reading Goethe's *Fragment Upon Nature* had changed all that:

> "Nature! We are surrounded by her, embraced by her—impossible to release ourselves from her and impossible to enter more deeply into her. . . . She creates ever new forms; what exists has never existed before; what has existed returns not again, everything is new and yet always old. We live in her midst and yet we are strangers to her. She speaks constantly with us but betrays not her secret to us. We are continually at work upon her, yet have no power over her. . . . She is forever building, forever demolishing, and her workshop is not to be found. . . . She is the sole artist. . . ."

Eli was holding forth.

"The post of editor of an economics journal is opening up; Professor von Stein says he is going to recommend me for it at the end of the year. I've had some conversations with the Austrian Minister of Commerce; one of their officials is retiring and they're considering me for the job. On the other hand, I know of an opening in a private travel bureau. There's a lot of money to be made in travel. Which of the three jobs should I take?"

Anna replied mischievously, "All three. You know you have enough energy to fill them."

"Then perhaps I ought to go to America? They like people who can do three jobs simultaneously."

A discussion broke out as to which was the best country in which to live. Sigmund, who was the only one who had been to a foreign land, said:

"England. I'll tell you why: in England everything is allowed except what is specifically forbidden. In Germany everything is forbidden except what is specifically allowed."

"What about Vienna?" asked Ignaz.

Jakob replied quickly, "In Vienna everything that is forbidden is allowed." He added, "I heard one at my *Stammtisch* today." His eyes lighted with warmth. Jakob loved the Viennese custom of the round table of friends who met every day at the same hour, in the same coffeehouse, at the same table. It was here in the brown leather booths behind etched-glass doors, the walls lined with racks of newspapers, that Vienna visited.

"A mother gave her son two neckties for his birthday. The next day, to show his appreciation, the son wore one of the ties. His mother cried, 'What's the matter, don't you like the other one?'"

Everyone laughed except Amalie, who never could find any humor in jokes told at her expense. Jakob blew her a kiss across the table.

Sigmund had suddenly lost his appetite and laid down his fork. This was the first time since the Saturday walk in Mödling, and their kiss, that he had seen Martha. On Sunday, because of the twin almonds they had found, he had sent her a copy of *David Copperfield* and she had sent him a cake she had baked herself, the secret gifts passing from the Bernays and the Freud houses through the kindness of Eli. Martha did not know about his disappointment at the hands of Professor Brücke. He could not fool her, for he had made too ringing a statement about his love for research. Yet neither could he divulge that he had made his decision because he would sacrifice anything to become engaged to Martha before she returned to Hamburg for the summer, the following Sunday. Suppose she asked, "Why have you suddenly changed your mind? Are you not a stayer?"

He said in a voice that came out a little larger than he had intended, "Eli, you are not the only one who is changing jobs. . . . I'm returning to the Krankenhaus when the new courses start in August. Within a few years I should be able to cure you of every known ailment except acute alcoholism."

Martha turned full face to search for his meaning. He felt her mind probing his.

"Then you *are* going to become a doctor!"

"Of course he's going to become a doctor," said Amalie. "Why else would he take his medical degree?"

Martha groped for his hand under the table. His confidence returned. When all eyes were on Ignaz, who was telling about the Sanskrit fable he had translated that day, Sigmund leaned over and appropriated Martha's place card. He whispered:

"Among primitive tribes there is a superstition that, if you possess something that belongs to another person, that person is in your power. It's magic. You will them to do something and they cannot resist."

"Now that you have me in your power, what is it that you are going to will me to do."

"If I revealed it you might break the spell."

"So easily?" She was beautiful when she smiled as she did now, teasingly, but with affection. "When you worked in those alchemist laboratories, didn't you find an even stronger magic that put one person in the power of another?"

"That wasn't an apple you were peeling the first time I saw you. It was me. Round and round in those long, delicate fingers, cutting away my cover in one continuous ribbon, right down to the core."

9.

Two days later Eli dropped by. When he was leaving, Sigmund said, "I'll walk you home."

Not unexpectedly, Eli invited him in for a cup of coffee. Mrs. Emmeline Bernays received him politely. She and Amalie Freud had been friends, but that did not reconcile Mrs. Bernays to the fact that her son Eli had fallen in love with Anna Freud. Mrs. Bernays liked Anna but she thought it an act of lunacy for a bright and promising young man like Eli, whom the matchmakers were pursuing with offers of up to fifty thousand dollars, to marry a girl with no dowry whatever. Had she thought that Minna was serious about Ignaz Schönberg or Martha interested in Sigmund Freud, two penniless *Yeshivabucher*, perennial students, the hair under her *Scheitel* would have turned white.

Mrs. Bernays' family, the Philipps, had come from Sweden. Her husband's family were solid Hamburg merchants and professors. Berman's father, Isaac, had been chief rabbi of the German-Jewish community. His brother Jacob moved on to the University of Bonn as professor and chief librarian. His other brother, Michael, was brought to the University of Munich by King Ludwig II of Bavaria, who created a special chair for him. The Philipp family had been equally prosperous and respected.

Though Emmeline Bernays, at fifty-two, was an old woman by general standards, she had refused, symbolically, to practice the Hindu custom of suttee after her husband's death, maintaining that she was too young and vigorous to go up in flames. She insisted that she was now head of the Bernays family, which brought her into conflict with her son, who maintained that since he was the man of the family and supporting them he was entitled to be the master of the household. As Martha served the coffee and *Kipfeln*, Mrs. Bernays got off on her favorite subject of returning with her family to live in Hamburg and the charming suburb of Wandsbek, about which she had been quarreling with Eli. She was a bright, educated and disciplined woman. Her outstanding passion was a detestation of Vienna.

"Ever since the Congress of Vienna in 1815 people have believed this city to be a place of wild, fun-loving 'live today, we die tomorrow' gaiety," she exclaimed. "It's a contorted myth. Actually most Viennese live in despair; the music, the songs, the eternal waltzing, the forced, senseless laughter, are a tattered cloak they wear to hide their nakedness from the world. It is true 'In Berlin things are serious but not hopeless; in Vienna things are hopeless but not serious.' In Hamburg we do not pretend to be gay when we are sad or troubled. We don't end each sentence with a foolish trilling as they do, though they may be announcing the death of their mother. If we don't like a person we don't treat him in our most ingratiating manner, then stick a gossip-knife through the ribs of his reputation. I do not care to spend the rest of my life turning realities into appearances. I am a Swede and North German, and I refuse to laugh the rest of my days out of existence. We should never have left Hamburg." Abruptly, she turned to her son. "Eli, you are remaining home? Then I will go for a visit with Frau Popp."

Eli made desultory talk for a few moments and then, his duty done, said, "Excuse me, I have to write some notes for Professor von Stein."

Martha was sitting in her favorite brown chair. Sigmund moved to the hassock at her feet. The Bernays apartment, on the Matthäusgasse in the Third District, close to the Wien Fluss and Stadtpark, was a comfortable one, somewhat overstuffed with all the solid furniture the Bernayses had brought from Hamburg. On the walls were paintings of forest scenes and seascapes from an early Hamburg school of painters.

"Why are you going to Wandsbek?" he asked.

She turned a little pale.

"It was planned . . . some time ago. . . . It's a way to visit the family and have a summer in the country. There are lovely groves to walk in. You would like them almost as much as the Vienna Woods."

"Could that properly be considered an invitation?"

She opened her eyes wide, one corner of her mouth twitching in a mischievous smile. Every fiber of his being yearned to embrace her, to use in his own interests the few moments Eli was affording them. Yet his background conquered him. Inside his head a thought ricocheted:

"It would be a violation of hospitality."

Eli returned. "How about a stroll in the Prater?"

It was a clear mid-June dusk, the sun flooding the western sky with rose-lavenders as it made a spectacular setting. Eli bounded about, never in their sight but actually not out of it. They entered at the Praterstern, then walked arm in arm along a side path of the Hauptallee. Double rows of chestnut trees lined the center road busy with handsome carriages, the women gowned in double-skirted dresses and big hats, the men in dark suits and top hats, the drivers smartly turned out in short light brown coats with hats of matching brown.

They turned into a path which led them across the Kaisergarten with its carefully tended lawns, clipped trees and bushes, and found themselves in the Volks Prater, the amusement area, crowded with visitors from every part of the Empire: men from Croatia selling wooden spoons and baskets, women from Czechoslovakia in misshapen country boots with rough straw trays strapped around their necks, hawking carved animals and toys; the country people from Bohemia and Moravia looking as though they had walked every mile; the Poles selling slices of black blood sausage; the boys from Silesia and Bosnia selling glassware and porcelain cups; the cooks from Bohemia on the arms of their newly found soldier friends, headed for the pavilion. On their left a women's band was playing at the expensive restaurant, the Eisvogel. On their right small children were swinging in a rocking boat. Ahead was the famous Fürststheater with a poster reading: "*Die Harbe Poldi.*" Martha asked:

"In what way is Poldi not very friendly?"

"It's a euphemism for 'not very obliging.'"

Martha studied the price list. "Who would want to pay eight gulden, three dollars and twenty cents, to watch a girl who is not going to be obliging?"

Sigmund missed his step completely.

"Why, Dr. Sigmund Freud, I do believe I shocked you."

He put an arm about her waist and hugged her.

They had reached the Rondeau where a crowd was assembled in

front of Calafati, the giant revolving Chinese statue which delighted
the children. They were now in the center of the fun area with its
merry-go-rounds, mini-giant wheels, shooting galleries where soldiers shot
clay pigeons to win roses for their girls, exhibitions of the Siamese Twins,
the Thick Girl, the Hairy Woman, and all around them beer gardens
and restaurants.

They turned back to the Grosse Zufahrtsstrasse and, as Eli suddenly
materialized, stopped at the Liesinger Bier Depot and listened to the
music from the two famous restaurants opposite, Zum Weissen Rössl
and Schweizerhaus. In the street between them thronged the young
girls in their brightly colored dirndls, the Bavarian women in *Dirndlkleid*,
wide blue skirts, aprons and scarves; and, crying out their wares in
a familiar cacophony, the woman carp baker, the coffee *Sieder*, the
Limonehandler, the *Schokoladenmacher*, the fruit sellers and vendors of
salads and radishes, the water pourer. Sigmund bought them each a
portion of baked carp with a *Mohnkipfel*, a poppy seed roll, while
Eli ordered mugs of beer. They murmured, *"Prosit!"*

Sigmund gazed across the table at Martha, at the almost fragile oval
and the warm eyes so serious and honest. His feelings went out to her
in a rush of joy and compassion. He felt a need to protect her. Yet
he had not even been given permission to call her *du*. She was leaving
on Sunday for the summer. That gave him only two more days. He
was chilled with fear that she would get away without his being able
to make a declaration of his love; that he might lose her to someone else before he could see her again. Martha broke the silence.

"Sigmund, can you be happy giving up the work you like best,
going into a private practice you had not planned on?"

He knew that his answer would be important to her.

"Yes. 'Love is the flame; work is the fuel.'"

She passed this sentiment by, knitting her brows as she leaned toward
him. Was it the eau de cologne that tightened his insides, or the natural
scent of her hair in which he had buried his face for that one marvelous
instant in Mödling?

"Then this is something you must do? It had to come, sooner or
later?"

"Without doubt I must find a way, as quickly as possible, of helping
my parents and the girls. Alexander too, because he has two more
years at the *Gymnasium*."

She studied his face thoughtfully before speaking again.

"You don't sound . . . unhappy . . . chagrined. I don't know why
you changed so suddenly but apparently you are reconciled."

"Yes and no. I will practice as best I can, after I am equipped.
Probably in nervous diseases, since this is Josef Breuer's field and he
will be there to help me. But at the same time I do not intend to

abandon research. I will always want part of my life for exploring the science of medicine. I have the energy, the strength, the determination . . ."

She put a hand on his, fondly, as a loyal friend might. And he knew that soon, though not at this moment when they were surrounded by eating, drinking, laughing crowds; but very soon now, he would have to make his declaration, the one that would determine his happiness.

When he returned home he sat down at the desk in the tiny *Kabinett*. He had found the German language strong and precise for expressing thoughts in science. Now he found it tender and evocative when speaking of love.

> *Dear Martha, how you have changed my life. It was so wonderful today in your home, near to you. . . . I could have wished that the evening and the stroll had had no end. I dare not write what moved me. I could not believe that I should not see your dear features for months, nor can I believe I am running no danger when fresh impressions affect Martha. So much of hope, doubt, happiness and privation have been condensed into the narrow space of two weeks. But there is no longer mistrust on my side; had I doubted ever so little I should never have revealed my feelings in these days. . . .*
>
> *It won't come. I cannot say here to Martha what I still have to say. I lack the confidence to finish the sentence, the line that the girl's glance and gesture forbids or allows. I will only allow myself to say one thing: the last time that we see each other I should like to address the loved one, the adored one, as 'Du,' and be assured of a relationship which perhaps will have for long to be veiled in secrecy.*

10.

Eli said he would smuggle the letter past Mrs. Bernays. Sigmund had all day Friday to worry about the rashness of his message. Suppose she did not feel about him the way he did about her? She would leave on Sunday without answering and he would be left dangling for the entire summer. Nor could he invent another pretext for visiting the Bernays home so soon. Mrs. Bernays would descend on him from her "arrogant Hamburgian heights" and put an end to the affair.

Saturday was like a river of minutes; he swallowed each drop deliberately as it went past him. He wandered through his house, through the streets, through his own mind. He could not achieve two consecutive thoughts. At five, when he was pacing in the two-foot stream of space between the desk and the bookshelves on one side of his room, the cot and bureau on the other, trying not to knock his knees on either bank, he heard voices in the hallway and rushed out to find Ignaz, Minna, Eli and Anna just back from a walk and bringing Martha with them.

Five o'clock coffee is the most pleasant time of the day for the Viennese. Midday dinner is serious, eaten for the purpose of nourishment; supper is light, the leftovers of the day's food and happenings. Coffee is the truly social hour, lively, good-natured talk pouring out at the same flow and consistency as coffee from the pot's spigot: the deep-burnt aroma, the relaxed stimulus of friends as *Gemütlichkeit* reigns: the feeling that each has a place in the world, no matter how simple; that there are things to say and to hear, not important but never abrasive; the comradery of being accepted, of laughing for laughter's sake; the confidence of there being one hour in the day that no man could confiscate and no man corrupt.

Alexander told the story of the Nestroy play he had seen at the Volkstheater a short time before. Anna reached for the Sacher Torte so rarely purchased by the Freuds these days and handed out the thin slices of chocolate cake in stiff layers covered with raspberry jam and then a dark chocolate icing, hard and shiny of surface. A gleaming white mound of *Schlagobers* passed from hand to hand, the thick whipped cream to be piled on the cake. The Sacher Torte was at the very heart of the Viennese civilization.

Covertly, Sigmund stole glances at Martha at the other end of the table. He realized that he had been sitting in his chair like a dummy for a considerable time now, and would soon be conspicuous by his silence.

"I am reminded of the argument between Sachers and Demels about who invented the original Sacher Torte," he said loudly enough to capture everyone's attention. "Matters got so acrimonious it was decided to submit the dispute to Emperor Franz Josef. One Sunday all of Vienna jammed into the gardens behind Schönbrunn while inside the royal palace the Emperor and his Cabinet sampled first the one Torte, then the other. At the end of the day they appeared on the balcony. The Emperor raised both arms and announced:

"'After due tasting and comparison, the Empire has come to its decision. *They are both the original!*'"

Sigmund thought he saw Martha raise one eyebrow quizzically. He rose and made his way down the hall to the parlor. The draperies had been opened but the room was cool, shaded from the sun of the Kaiser Josefs-Strasse by Amalie's white lace curtains. He waited in the center of the room. Martha followed. Here they would have as much privacy as though they were in the Prater meadows searching for the first violets of spring.

"Martha, did you receive my letter?"

"Yes, Sigi, but not until this morning."

It was the first time she had used the diminutive of his name. A tremor ran through him. He was angry with himself at his shyness and lack of courage. But had he not declared himself in his letter? It was up to Martha now.

"I thought of you while I was in Baden yesterday," she said in her low, quiet voice. "I brought back this sprig of lime blossoms for you."

He took the branch, buried his nose in its tart fragrance . . . came up against something hard. Blinking, he stretched the branch out in front of him. There was a golden glint among the white blossoms. Fumbling along its length, he drew forth a gold ring enclosing a pearl.

"Martha, I don't understand. . . . It's a ring . . ."

"The one my father wore. I want you to have it."

He slipped the ring onto his little finger, the only one it would fit, put the lime blossoms down and took Martha in his arms.

"What a wonderful way to answer my letter! Oh, Martha, I love you so dearly."

"I love you too, Sigi."

He held her so resolutely that it was obvious he could never let her go. She put her arms about his neck, locking her fingers. He kissed her on the mouth. Her lips were not as cool as they had been in the garden, but warm, slightly open, as though to all of love and life.

They sat on the sofa, holding each other. He had never been so happy. When at length he could bear to take his lips from hers, he said:

"I have no gift for you, Martha. But I will have this ring copied so that you can wear it. Then your mother need not know. Our engagement will have to be secret, and a long one."

"How long is long?"

"Our early ancestors decreed seven years."

"I'll wait."

She walked to the coffee table and picked up a small package she had placed there, brought out a teakwood box. "Do you remember what you said at dinner when you took my place card? About the primitive belief in possession? I've brought you a better token."

It was a photograph, taken a short time before. He held it straight out ahead of him at arm's length. The pictured Martha gazed back at him, the wide-spaced eyes a little too large for the slenderness of her face, the lips a little too full, the nose and chin too firm in their fragile setting. "But altogether," he decided, "the loveliest lady I've gazed upon."

He had difficulty turning away from the reproduction and returning to the original. Martha had been watching his face, bemused by the emotion that swept unguardedly across it.

"Sigi, when Eve tempted Adam, do you suppose she stopped to peel the apple?"

"I doubt it. They were in too much of a hurry to get out of the Garden of Eden and into the sinful world."

"Is it sinful?"

"I'm almost as innocent about that as you are. I locked myself in a laboratory until I experienced Martha's magic."

"You do believe in magic?" she asked.

"In love? Incontestably. Martha, my darling girl, we have to become conspirators. How am I to get mail to you? A flood of letters in a man's handwriting would appear strange in your uncle's house. Could you address a number of envelopes in your own hand?"

"Yes, I could do that."

"You are a very sweet girl. Perhaps that is what I love most about you: your sweetness."

She released herself from his arms abruptly.

"Sigi, don't confuse sweetness with weakness. Beware of genuinely sweet people: they have a will of iron."

He was more amused than alarmed.

"I know you are strong; but in the right ways. I don't feel any hidden or concealed traits in your nature. I believe you to be what you purport to be. I am the complex and confused character in this relationship. My friends have always called me a cynic. As a trained scientist I never thought of myself as a sentimentalist. I have enjoyed and been enriched by the classic love stories, but I never thought about myself as a lover. Oh, one day love would come, slowly, cautiously. . . . But that it should spring on me like a panther from a tree in the forest! Incredible! How could I be so defenseless? After all, I am twenty-six. I have dissected the world's love poetry as thoroughly as the cadavers in the laboratory. If I can watch this mystery unfold before my very eyes, what right have I to reject so categorically the mysteries of the Burning Bush which an angel of the Lord set on fire before Moses? Or for that matter, Christ's feeding the multitude with loaves and fishes?"

She leaned her back against his chest, turned her cheek gently to his.

"Do you know what I would like as an engagement gift? Some of the love poetry you've been speaking about."

"Heine or Shakespeare?"

"Both."

"First Heine:

> *"Just once more I'd like to see you*
> *And sink upon my knee*
> *And speak to you while dying:*
> *'Madame, ich liebe Sie.'"*

"Much too sad. Nobody's dying. Is Shakespeare more cheerful?"

"He has the Clown speak the lines in *Twelfth Night*:

> " '*What is love? 'Tis not hereafter;*
> *Present mirth hath present laughter;*
> *What's to come is still unsure:*
> *In delay there lies no plenty;*
> *Then come kiss me, sweet and twenty,*
> *Youth's a stuff will not endure.'* "

She turned a serious gaze on him. "It's not going to be easy, is it, my dear?"

"No, Marty, there will be hardships we can't even guess at. But we will rewrite the Clown's last line. 'Love's a stuff that will endure.' "

BOOK TWO

THE LONGING SOUL

BOOK TWO

The Longing Soul

THE ALLGEMEINE KRANKENHAUS, where Sigmund Freud would spend the next three to four years, had been slow in growing. A Poorhouse had first been built on the site in 1693, a hundred and ninety years before, its First Court being called Der Grosse Hof. By 1726 a building was completed around the Second and adjoining Court, The Marriage and Widows' Court. During the next half century half a dozen other buildings were constructed and occupied: the Sick Courtyard, the Housekeeping Courtyard, the Artisans' Courtyard, the Students' Courtyard. . . . Then Emperor Josef II, an idealist and visionary, traveled through Europe incognito and, in 1783, decreed that the Grossarmenhaus, Large Poorhouse, be converted into a Main Hospital, and patterned on the Hôtel de Dieu in Paris. It was to incorporate all the latest conveniences and discoveries. The courtyards were rebuilt and modernized, sewers and cesspools installed, chimneys moved from the center of the room, kitchens installed, windows enlarged, the space allocated to each bed increased to five feet. All refuse from the hospital was to be burned on a special lot across the street from the hospital; it was forbidden to throw dead animals into the Alser Creek which ran close by. Nurses would serve quarantined cases food and supplies through the windows only.

The University of Vienna Medical School was moved in and the Allgemeine Krankenhaus began its spectacular rise to eminence among the world's great hospitals and research centers. Its professors were among the most respected men in the Austro-Hungarian Empire, while the hospital developed an awesome reputation for the brilliant research coming out of its laboratories.

The General Hospital became a community unto itself. A dozen large quadrangular buildings housed its twenty departments and fourteen institutes and clinics, each enclosing a large, beautifully landscaped court connected by means of long tunnel-arches the width of the building above, the entire two hundred and fifty acres securely enclosed against the outside world by stone walls. The water was brought in from Semmering, high on the mountains, in special pipes; there was running water on each floor; the food although contracted to outsiders was cooked in the hospital's kitchens. There was a reading room for the doctors, and a lending library for the twenty-five thousand patients who occupied the two thousand beds over the course of a year. The courts were lighted by gas lamps, new inventions such as electricity and the telephone being used only experimentally. *Füllöfen*, coke stoves, heated the wards in winter; in summer the upper part of the windows could be swiveled to let in fresh air. There was a Catholic chapel and, in the Sixth Court, an octagonally shaped synagogue for the Jewish patients and doctors. There was a bath-house in the Fourth Court with private rooms for tub and steam baths. All wards had adjoining tea kitchens and, at a distance safe enough to keep away odors, water closets with flush toilets. The unhygienic straw mattresses of earlier years had been replaced by three sections of horsehair which could be changed about to keep them flat and firm. The mortality rate was low, only fourteen percent; the fees ran from four gulden a day, a dollar and sixty cents, for first-class patients, to seven cents a day for indigent Viennese, to free medication for paupers. The well-populated maternity wards, which trained midwives as well as doctors, charged their patients thirty-six cents a day for room, board and delivery.

2.

An air of excitement hung over Dr. Theodor Billroth's operating room on the second floor of the Surgery Clinic overlooking the First Court, with its tall Greek frieze separating the operating table from the steep amphitheater. Sigmund had stopped at the central office to register for the course and found the tiers of the amphitheater jammed. The surgeons of Vienna had turned out to watch Professor Billroth perform the second test of his newly discovered "resection." It had long been known that a man could have an arm or leg cut off and still live; war had proved that. But it had not been known that a part of a man's viscera containing a tumor or obstruction could be cut out and the severed ends of the intestines or stomach sewed together.

Sigmund joined a group of some twenty doctors sitting on the window ledge and standing on the steps beyond the frieze. During his thirty hours of courses in clinical surgery under Billroth he had learned a good deal about pathology but little about surgery. Part of the fault had been his: he had never intended to operate on patients. Part had been Billroth's, who announced: "To give special courses in operating for students is futile. The typical operations are discussed and demonstrated to the students on the cadaver; they also see them in the Clinic."

Billroth had been a brilliant lecturer, the halls had been crowded with admirers, yet Sigmund had never been given the opportunity to meet the Herr Professor, or to exchange the simplest greeting with him. Now that he was preparing for general practice it was imperative that he learn how to perform surgery. In an emergency a patient's life might depend on his skill with a knife or scalpel. There was no help for it if he was going to become a good doctor, and he had no intention of becoming a bad or mediocre one.

Professor Theodor Billroth had helped to transform surgery from a crude handicraft practiced by the town's barbers into a precise and documented art. He was also the first with the courage to publish reports on his operations; since surgeons lost more cases than they saved, the reports were macabre reading. But Billroth insisted, "Failures must be acknowledged, at once and publicly, without glossing over our mistakes. An unsuccessful case is more important to know about than a dozen successful operations."

The book he had published six years earlier, in 1876, was a slashing attack on the medieval methods still used in medical schools, with a plan for reorganization. A gratuitous five pages of it had constituted a disastrous blow to the hard-won harmony enjoyed at the Medical School. Under the heading "Student Types, The Jews at Vienna," Billroth had written:

> It has been rightly said that at Vienna there are more poor students than anywhere else, and that they ought to be assisted because living at Vienna is so expensive. Yes, if the question were one of poverty alone! . . . Young men, mostly Jews, come to Vienna from Galicia and Hungary, who have absolutely nothing, and who have conceived the insane idea that they can earn money in Vienna by teaching, through small jobs at the stock exchange, by peddling matches, or by taking employment as post office or telegraph clerks . . . and at the same time study medicine. . . . A Jewish merchant in Galicia or Hungary . . . earning just enough to keep himself and his family from starving, has a very moderately gifted son. The vanity of the mother demands a scholar, a Talmudist, in the family. In the face of countless difficulties he is sent to school and passes his final examination with great effort. Then he comes to Vienna with his clothes and nothing else. . . . Such people are in no way fitted for a scientific career. . . .

It was this pronouncement that Professor Brücke had been so sensitive about. Up to this time whatever latent anti-Semitism may have existed had been kept underground. Jew and Gentile had mixed freely on all intellectual, artistic and scientific levels, if not social ones. Billroth's public attack, the first to come from an official source since Emperor Leopold I forced the Jews out of the Old City in 1669–70 and across the Donau Kanal to settle in what had become the Second District, had once again made prejudice respectable.

Theodor Billroth had wanted to become a musician but his parents had persuaded him to go into medicine. His closest friend was Johannes

Brahms; many of Brahms's scores were first played by Brahms himself in Billroth's home. In his love for music Billroth was very much like Professor Brücke: half scientist, half artist.

Now his seven Assistants and Professors Extraordinarius were standing in a circle about the patient awaiting the arrival of their chief. The windows were closed against the stifling August heat, there was an air of reverential quiet, with all eyes fastened on the door. Sigmund had grown inured to the hospital odors during his student days.

In strode Dr. Billroth, a handsome man of fifty-three with a short gray-white beard and rimless spectacles low on his nose. His Assistants stood at attention, the students and visiting surgeons simply stood. Billroth, who was called upon to operate on emperors, kings and potentates from Turkey, Russia and the Orient, was expensively clothed. Sigmund had heard that he earned a hundred thousand dollars a year. The hospital, the surgical rooms and equipment, his Assistants and young professors were all at his disposal without cost. He also had his own private hospital. Billroth's Assistants at the Krankenhaus earned thirty-six dollars a month, the *Extraordinarii*, a hundred and sixty, despite the fact that several of the latter were already middle-aged men with families to support. Nor were they permitted to practice privately without Billroth's consent. He allowed each of them an occasional private operation for a fee, enough, Sigmund judged, to keep them from desperation.

Dr. Billroth pushed back the sleeves of his English wool suit. He did not allow white aprons in his operating room because he felt they would make the surgeons look like barbers. No one wore gloves. Nurses were not permitted in the room. He nodded to the head of his staff, Dr. Anton Wölfler, who raised the report he had been holding and read aloud in a flat voice:

"The patient is Josef Mirbeth. Age forty-three. Appears to have drunk some nitric acid from a vodka glass, mistaking it for lemonade. Symptoms: can only drink liquids. Vomits everything he swallows. Strong pressure on the stomach and pains in the back. Diagnosis: tumor of the stomach."

One of the Assistants covered the patient's face with six layers of gauze. Chloroform was dropped onto the gauze. Billroth made his incision neatly parallel to the ribs, a cut twelve inches long and two centimeters under the navel. He cut the blood vessels between the stomach and the large intestine. This freed the stomach, making it mobile. The Assistants put clamps on the blood vessels and metal retractors to hold the wound open. Others sponged up the blood, though Sigmund was surprised to see how little there was. Billroth made detailed observations as he moved along which an Assistant wrote into the patient's record book, beneath a precise drawing of the incision.

By putting his hand under the floating stomach and duodenum Billroth was able to cut into them easily with his scalpel. He saw at once a white, fanlike spreading cord on the outside of the pylorus. He stopped abruptly, lifted his head and said to the room:

"We were in error. This is not a tumor, or a withering from the acid scars. The duodenum has been thickened to such an extent that only a pin could be put through. We will have to excise ten centimeters of duodenum and stomach."

While an Assistant continued to sift drops of chloroform onto the gauze, Billroth proceeded to cut out the obstruction. Because the duodenal opening was only half as wide as the stomach opening, he first sewed up half of the stomach with sutures before he matched the two openings for size. He then sewed them together, making sure the connection was totally sealed, that there could be no leakage of food or liquid. This done, he closed the incision with silk ligatures.

The operation was completed. It had taken an hour and a quarter. The sections that had been cut out were put in a jar for the pathology laboratory. Billroth washed his hands in a solution of bichloride. His youngest Assistant handed him a towel. He dried his hands, rolled down the unsoiled sleeves of his street coat, bowed formally to his staff and audience and went majestically out the door.

There was a buzz of admiring talk among the doctors and students who filed out, leaving only Billroth's staff and a group of some ten surgery students, including Sigmund, standing in a tight circle around the operating table. Billroth's Chief Assistant, Wölfler, prepared to operate on the next patient, who had abscesses on his head, pain in one hip and the inability to move one of his legs.

Dr. Wölfler said, "I don't know whether there is any connection between the head abscesses and the immobile leg. We'll puncture this bad kneecap and draw off the pus."

They drew off the yellow fluid, then cauterized the wound and bandaged the knee. Sigmund walked home to the Kaiser Josefs-Strasse for midday dinner, regretting that he would see nothing more of Billroth's wizardry for a couple of months, as the professor was leaving for a vacation in Italy to join his friend Brahms.

As an Aspirant in surgery, Dr. Sigmund Freud would work in the wards from eight to ten in the morning, from four to six in the afternoon, and read from ten until midnight. The bedside reports of the patients had to be kept up meticulously. In the hours between his ward duties he had to read the literature on surgery, the articles being printed in the medical journals, and attend all operations. The operating room would become his headquarters: a big, pleasant whitewashed room flooded with summer sun from the high window overlooking the First Court, where the convalescents in their blue-striped nightgowns could wander in the shade of the linden trees.

Returning to the ward for his afternoon service, he found that Billroth's patient, Josef Mirbeth, was feeling nauseous but insisted that the pain in his stomach was gone. Sigmund was amazed at the speed of the recovery and the fact that there was little fever.

The next patient was fifty-year-old Maria Gehring, who underwent a breast operation for cystosarcoma; then seven-year-old Lenasse Anton, whose leg had become foreshortened from a previous operation and who now had to have it broken again and cleaned out; next Jakob Kipflinger, forty-five, with a swollen and infected arm. Mixed in between were the patients who were found to be inoperable and were sent home to await death.

Sigmund was not allowed to handle a knife but he assisted with other chores: draining wounds, applying clamps, bandaging. With Billroth gone the staff relaxed, brought each Aspirant close to the patient to see how the surgical instruments were used. There was a good deal of comradery, particularly among the young unmarried men who established their own little *Stammtisch* at a nearby coffeehouse for late supper.

The patients under Sigmund's care did well. One by one they were sent home, all except Mirbeth, who began to develop complications four days after his operation. His recovery had been important to the entire department. Sigmund had given him special care, but on the sixth day Mirbeth became semi-conscious. He had been coughing for several days but this had not seemed serious. Now his fever was high and his pulse rapid. Sigmund checked his book; every detail was faithfully recorded, including the fact that Mirbeth had also begun to suffer from sharp pains in the stomach.

When midnight came, he could not tear himself away. Two of Billroth's Assistants also stood by. They tried simple remedies, cold packs, but Mirbeth was sinking rapidly. He died at three in the morning. Sigmund felt a sense of personal loss.

He was back before eight the next morning to speak with Dr. Wölfler, a man of thirty-two with a finely trimmed mustache and beard. He was a gifted surgeon, as Sigmund had cause to learn from watching him repair the harelip of an infant, remove a man's cancerous eye from its socket, perform a gynecological operation that seemed to cut out half the woman's abdomen. He asked:

"Herr Dr. Wölfler, will there be an inquest on Josef Mirbeth?"

"None is indicated, Herr Kollege. The body will go over to Dissection but we are not asking for a report."

"Then how will we know whether he died of peritonitis, pneumonia, reblockage of the stomach . . . ?"

"Dr. Freud, death is not looked on with favor here. It presents too many intangibles. But, as you saw, Herr Mirbeth would have been dead by now of starvation. Count it as a gain that the operation gave us further experience with working inside the stomach and duodenum. We will probably lose the first hundred cases. But by then the technique will be perfected and surgeons all over the world will be able to perform the operation successfully."

Sigmund bowed his head slightly.

"I wish to thank you, Herr Doktor, for your patience with me." But as he moved down the ward, saw Mirbeth's empty bed, he thought:

"How is Billroth going to publish the results of this case 'without glossing over the failure,' to use his own words, if we don't try to find out what went wrong? What have we left from Mirbeth to instruct with? We have detailed diagrams of the operation and ward records; but what actually caused his death?"

3.

For a man who has never been in love, the landscape of jealousy is as obscure as the dark side of the moon. He was distressed, having already gone through several bouts of possessiveness of which he would not have believed himself capable. The first incident had taken place two days before his visit to Mödling. Calling at the Bernays home, he had found Martha working on a musical portfolio for Max Mayer, a fond and older cousin. As he watched her bending happily over the sheets he had been flooded with jealousy: "It's too late. She loves Max. There is no chance for me. I'm going to lose her. . . ." He had stopped dead in his tracks. "Whoa! Whoa! She is only preparing a scrapbook to take to Hamburg to a cousin. She doesn't love anybody yet. It will be you; but slowly, slowly. Don't let her see you acting like a fool."

The second episode had broken into the open. The engagement of Martha and Sigmund, as far as their young friends were concerned, remained about as secret as a July sun. Fritz Wahle, a painter and long-time friend of Sigmund's, had brought Martha several books on the history of art to read and discuss with him. Though Fritz was engaged to Martha's cousin Elise, Sigmund became uneasy:

"Fritz, artists and scientists are natural opponents. Your art somehow provides you with a key to open feminine hearts, while we stand helpless in front of the citadel."

He then avoided Fritz and stopped speaking to him. Ignaz Schönberg brought them together for a coffee at the Cafe Kurzweil. Wahle stirred his *Grossen Braunen* as though it were a thick beef and barley soup. At length he looked up, his underlip protruding.

"Sig, if you don't make Martha happy, I will shoot you and then myself."

Embarrassed, Sigmund laughed, a few artificial notes, but enough to outrage Wahle.

"You laugh, do you? If I write to Martha and instruct her to drop you, she will do as I ask."

"Now, Fritz, you are no longer Martha's teacher and you can't instruct her in anything."

"We'll see about that! Herr Ober, bring me paper and pen."

Fritz dashed off a note in white heat. Sigmund pulled the sheet from Fritz's hand and saw that Fritz had been writing the same kind of passionate lines that he himself had been sending to Martha. Fritz was in love with Martha and not her cousin Elise! He tore the letter to shreds.

Fritz stormed out of the cafe. Sigmund slept little that night. Had Martha encouraged Fritz? He wrote to her:

"I am made of harder stuff than he is, and when we match each other he will find he is not my equal." He was engaged to Elise, but "only in logic are contradictions unable to coexist; in feelings they quite happily continue alongside each other. . . . Least of all must one deny the possibility of such contradictions in feeling with artists, people who have no occasion to submit their inner life to the strict control of reason. . . ."

Exercising his own "strict control of reason," he told her that she would have to break off her relationship with Fritz. Any other solution was unacceptable to him. Martha refused. She replied that her friendship with Fritz had been a good one and it would be cruel to destroy it. She had a right to innocent friendships, and she was writing to Fritz to assure him that nothing had changed.

Sigmund had known that Martha Bernays was an independent spirit. She herself had warned him that sweet people can have a will of iron. He had welcomed the idea; but now, seeing her will set in opposition to his own, he went through torments of self-doubt, rage. How could Martha really love him if she would not observe his wishes in so fundamental a matter?

He thrashed his way through the streets trying to wear down his emotions against the cobblestones. The fierceness of the midsummer sun, even at this late afternoon hour, had turned the city into a caldron and emptied the thoroughfares. Perspiration streamed down his face as, returning home, he poured out a letter of stormy protest, sparing himself and his fiancée nothing of the tempest racking his inexperienced heart. Should he hide his feelings from Martha? But how could they achieve a permanent relationship that way? They had agreed to be totally honest with each other and to reveal as friends, rather than sweethearts, everything they were thinking and feeling. To himself Sigmund observed:

"I am the one who insisted on this. I can live no other way. But when I made the stipulation did I have any idea of the agonies involved?"

To Martha he confessed unashamedly, "I lose all control of myself. . . . Had I the power to destroy the whole world, ourselves included, to let it start all over again—even at the risk that it might not create Martha and myself—I would do so without hesitation."

What unsettled him was that it took four days for letters to be exchanged. By the time he had gotten over his seizure, Martha would be reading his most tortured outpourings. He forgave himself for these transgressions only because he acknowledged to himself though not yet to Martha that he and his sister Rosa had "a nicely developed tendency toward neurasthenia."

He returned to surgery to watch the daily succession of ailing, crushed, deformed bodies brought to the operating table. Some cases were simple, such as reshaping eighteen-year-old Johann Smejkal's legs in plaster-of-Paris casts. Others were long and intricate, taking four or five hours: the excision of Rupert Hipfel's abscesses in the anal area; removing Walburga Gorig's goiter, taking a section out of Johann Denk's jaw.

Sigmund cared for the several wards of patients during his two shifts of duty. "Though in truth," he mused, his eyes dark with concern, "there is little I am called upon to do: keep the wounds dry, watch for fever, order changes in bandages or drugs, write down the developments in the record books." Resourceful surgeons were instructing him, but the closer he watched the more he became convinced that he had no talent for the art of surgery. It might be a full two years, including the performing of these operations on the cadavers stretched out in the dissection laboratory, before he would even be permitted to operate on patients. In all truth would he not be better advised, once he was out in general practice, to rush any patient in need to a qualified surgeon? It was the conviction he had arrived at six years before.

There was no prescribed course for the Aspirant, unpaid candidate for a post, at the Allgemeine Krankenhaus. The young doctor could apply to any department in which he wished training, and remain as long or short a time as he thought he needed. No one told him which discipline to move into next. It was expected, in a general sort of way, that he would take training in every department so that he would be equipped to do everything from delivering a baby to wiping out a plague. But nobody checked or cared. The doctor was his own man.

He decided to serve out the full two months; any less would be an admission of defeat as well as an affront to Professor Billroth and his staff. Having made the decision, he did not feel badly about it, any more than he had when he found during his undergraduate years that he had no gift for chemistry. A man had to face his limitations and move on to fields in which he could be master of his materials.

Nevertheless he was confused.

He became depressed, wrote to Martha how black the future looked, with formless years of work, much of it useless to him, stretching bleakly ahead without her. It seemed impossible to go anywhere in this frozen structure where one man alone could rise to the head of a clinic, institute or department and the others were doomed to remain obsequious workhorses. The only way to break out of this academic and administrative prison was to abandon it to others and start afresh somewhere else. He wondered if Martha would consent to move to England with him when they were married. English medicine, the hospitals and the schools had seemed to him during his summer stay with his half brothers to be less stratified; "ossified" was the word he had used at the time. He had been impressed by the way Philipp and Emanuel lived: as English gentlemen, in big comfortable Tudor-style homes, having acquired the manners and hospitality of the English gentleman. He wondered why he could not become an English gentleman, wearing well-cut suits instead of this shapeless gray jacket and these wrinkled breeches. Young doctors and scientists were welcomed by the British medical profession providing they were well trained; and England, like Europe, stood in awe of the accomplishments of the Vienna Medical School.

"We could be independent. England knows about independence. It practically created it for individual man; or at least re-created it from the Greeks."

Martha was growing used to his moodiness, the soaring flights of hope in one letter, the dejection in the next. She answered with consolation and affection, managing to keep herself on an even keel despite the half dozen pages of tumultuous handwriting which arrived nearly every day signed "Your faithful Sigmund." He had long ago exhausted the supply of envelopes she had addressed.

Toward the end of August he developed a sore throat. When he could barely speak or swallow food he asked a Billroth Assistant to look at it.

"But of course you have pain. It comes from a case of Ludwig's angina. The infection is beginning to form an abscess near your tonsils. Better let me lance it before it spreads to the floor of your mouth."

He accompanied his friend into the surgical room where a knife was cauterized, then stuck with a deft movement into his throat. The pain was so intense that, unable to cry out, he banged his hand hard on the wooden table at which he was sitting. The pearl broke loose from Martha's ring and went skittering to an opposite corner, under a cabinet. More stricken than by the surgeon's knife, he jumped up, sank to his knees before the cabinet and fished out the pearl. The surgeon said:

"I see I have removed two baubles with one lance!"

Sigmund grinned woefully, spat up the infectious material, clutched the pearl in his left hand. He made his way home and went to bed with fever and general misery.

He was up in a few days but found himself preoccupied. Something was still sticking in his throat. It was the pearl. He wrote to Martha, "Answer me on your honor and conscience whether at eleven o'clock last Thursday you happened to be less fond of me, or more than usually annoyed with me, or perhaps even 'untrue' to me, as the song has it. Why this tasteless ceremonious conjuration? Because I have a good opportunity to put an end to a superstition."

It was also an opportunity to tell her how he felt about her absence.

". . . a frightful yearning, frightful is hardly the right word, better would be uncanny, monstrous, ghastly, gigantic; in short, an indescribable longing for you."

4.

Martha returned early in September, after nearly three months. If the summer had not matured her, Sigmund's tempestuous letters had. What had seemed to be a pure love idyll at the time of their engagement had begun to show fissures. He was the first to concede that the leverage needed to pry them apart had been provided by him. When he had spent the last of his gulden to send her a gift she took him to task in her return letter, telling him that he must not be extravagant. He wrote back like an outraged husband:

"Martha must give up saying so categorically, 'You mustn't do that!' " and then went on to inform her, with all the possessiveness of his nature, that she was no longer a daughter or older sister but rather a young sweetheart.

"When you do return you are coming back to me, you understand, no matter how your filial feelings may rebel against it. . . . For has it not been laid down since time immemorial that the woman shall leave father and mother and follow the man she has chosen? You must not take it too hard, Marty . . . no one else's love compares with mine."

He had tipped his hand now: he was going to be the master and she was to become a docile *Hausfrau*. But he had not yet taken a proper gauge on his sweetheart. She wrote a tart reply which he had the good grace to acknowledge he had earned.

That the tiffs had not hurt their love he learned the afternoon after her return when they walked hand in hand to see the developments in the magnificently burgeoning Ringstrasse. Chaperoned by Eli, Minna and Ignaz, they made their way along the Verbindungs Eisenbahn, entered the Stadtpark with its high elms and ash trees, then followed a path running through thick shrubbery and found an open green area where the Viennese drank coffee and listened to the band on Sundays. They came out on the Parkring.

What was now the Ringstrasse had for hundreds of years been the high fortification walls enclosing the Central City with its surrounding moats and, beyond, the broad glacis or drill grounds for the army. As long as these bastions remained in place Vienna was imprisoned; the Innere Stadt remained a medieval walled city. These walls were important, the Austrian army said, to protect the prosperous, upper classes within the city from the working people who lived in the suburbs.

Emperor Franz Josef rejected the reasoning. In December of 1857 he ordered the abolishment of "the circumvallation and fortifications of the Inner City as well as the surrounding ditches." The process was a long one, taking some five years to tear down the walls, fill the ditches, integrate the glacis. But the polygon Ringstrasse that emerged in its place by 1865, with its horseshoe opening facing the Donau Kanal lined with palatial apartment houses; its splendiferous Opera; broad, tree-lined boulevard with its white Acropolis-like Parliament, neo-Gothic City Hall, new University and open gardens with lime trees fragrant in June and roses blooming through late summer and fall, made Vienna one of the most modern and beautiful of cities. To the Viennese the Ringstrasse was as magnificent as the Champs Élysées in Paris. It became the symbol of the Austro-Hungarian Empire, which would always rule an important portion of the Western world.

Twilight had settled in. The *Laternenanzünder* were lighting the high gas lamps with long extendible poles, first opening the glass door with a hook, then turning on the gas jet, next applying a flame from the hissing end of the pole before adjusting the burner, closing the glass door and moving on to the next lamp.

"Do you know, Sigi," Martha exclaimed, "after spending a couple of months in my own city, I found that I missed Vienna."

"Could I be part of the reason?"

He kissed her affectionately.

"I have the feeling that I am going to mix a few metaphors but it is true that a relationship is the more seaworthy if it has weathered a few storms. All hands now know that the ship isn't going to founder in the first squall."

Martha lodged herself firmly against a chestnut tree.

"I get seasick in rough weather. Couldn't we confine our battles to the enemy? It seems so wasteful to fight the people one loves. Why don't you stay on the bridge and navigate this ship you have introduced, and let me be the engineer? Both officers are equal on board but they have separate powers."

He was amused by her adroitness, but sombered. "I don't even know which harbor I'm looking for."

She nestled her shoulder against his.

"Why have you been so dissatisfied with your efforts this summer?"

"Because I don't think I've progressed enough to justify the expenditure of two months' time, vis-à-vis our marriage, I mean."

"Then you're letting the idea of our marriage become a burden to you. You should think only of completing your studies."

"Probably what I'm upset about is which department I should go into next. Dermatology is important for general practice but not a very appetizing field. The course I enjoyed most was under Professor Meynert in clinical psychiatry, brain anatomy. Meynert favored my work when I was a student and I have a deep veneration for him. He says I can start my training with him right now. At the same time there is a rumor that Professor Hermann Nothnagel is being invited to come from the University of Jena to take over our Clinic of Internal Medicine. If that is true, he will need Assistants. . . ."

Eli signaled them to turn back. Martha murmured, "I told Mother I was bringing you home to supper."

"Does she know?"

"She suspects."

"How is she reacting?"

"She says, 'Why do all three of my children choose penniless partners? What is the virtue in being poor?' "

When Sigmund heard that Nothnagel had been officially invited to come to Vienna he sent a message to the Breuers asking if he might join them for the *Jause* and bring Martha with him. They decided to tell Mrs. Bernays where they were going, since they would need no chaperon. Martha wore a blue silk dress with crocheted collar and cuffs. She knew that Sigmund had chosen the Breuer home as a model for his own. She also felt that she would be on trial.

Mathilde Breuer had no such idea. She ushered Martha and Sigmund into the dining room where the table had been covered with a fresh white cloth. On it she set the platters of *Guglhupf*, chocolate cakes and, as Josef came down from his laboratory, the platter of linked pairs of sausages. "A pair" was immutable and sacred in Viennese custom; it was as unthinkable to serve one sausage or three as it would be for one person alone or three together to attempt marriage. As Mathilde put a roll on each plate she cut the link binding the pair; the snipping indicated that the afternoon repast could begin.

Mathilde was in fine fettle. The month in Venice had healed all the wounds. Martha barely touched her food. She sat quietly listening to the spirited byplay of the three old friends. Mathilde knew how difficult it must be for a newcomer, particularly a young girl, to break into a long-established friendship. She paid Martha a good deal of attention.

When Sigmund told Josef of Nothnagel's appointment and of his hopes for an assistantship, Josef cocked his head to one side with a bemused smile.

"For a young man who has reconciled himself to the rigors of private practice, I must say you are decamping mighty fast."

"Only at the first opportunity!"

They all laughed, the tension snapped.

Then Josef said, "But you're right to move in this direction. Let's see, Nothnagel's two most famous books, besides his original *Handbook of Pharmacology*, are *Topical Diagnosis of the Illnesses of the Brain* and *Experimental Investigations of the Functions of the Brain.* The man he'll admire most in Vienna is Theodor Meynert. You must secure a card of recommendation from Meynert at once."

Professor Hermann Nothnagel had barely moved into his apartment when Sigmund arrived, carrying a card from Professor Theodor Meynert recommending him for his "valuable histological work" and expressing gratitude if Professor Nothnagel would give Dr. Freud a hearing. Though the new flat still smelled of varnish, the waiting room in which the maid asked him to wait was handsomely furnished in the best Thuringian style. Professor Nothnagel, like Professor Billroth, was fortunate: as director of a university medical clinic instead of an institute such as Professor Brücke's, he could practice private medicine at the same time. It was said that he rarely returned home without finding ten patients at ten gulden a head waiting for him.

On the walls were pictures of Nothnagel's four children and on an easel stood a portrait of Frau Professor Nothnagel, who had died two years before. Under it was a vase of fresh flowers. After his wife's death Professor Nothnagel had said: "When one's love is lost nothing remains but work." Having been trained in the poetry of Schiller to adore and worship women, he felt that they should be protected from the world, kept delicate and sensitive. He was an adamant opponent of any woman being allowed to study medicine at the universities where he taught.

Hermann Nothnagel was an idealist. He told his students, "Only a good man can be a good physician." On the bookshelves Sigmund was now scanning there were the German classics, Greek and Latin plays, English novels and an extraordinary set of Bibles in Aramaic and Greek. Evidently Nothnagel's interest in literature was as great as Professor Brücke's devotion to painting, Billroth's fascination with music. Sigmund wondered:

"Do these men have a deep involvement in the arts because they have universal minds? Or has the same faculty which empowers them with the imagination and bold flights of intellect to make startling discoveries in the sciences also enable them to grasp an art?"

A door opened at the far end of the room. Professor Nothnagel entered, dressed in a heavy black suit with a silk vest, silver buttons and a black silk tie covering much of his shirt front. His head and face were covered with a sandy blond hair, the same shade as his skin. His eyes were quiet. There were two large warts, one high on his right cheek, the other on the bridge of his nose. Yet for all its plainness it was a good face, the kind men liked in their associates.

"Professor Nothnagel, I have been asked to bring you greetings from Professor Meynert. With your permission I should like to hand you this card."

Nothnagel motioned Sigmund to a leather bench.

"I set great store by a recommendation from my colleague, Meynert. What can I do for you, Herr Doktor?"

"It is known that you are about to engage an Assistant, Herr Professor. I understand that you value scientific research. I myself have done some scientific research but at the moment I have no opportunity to continue. For this reason I am presenting myself to you as an applicant."

"Have you some reprints of your papers with you, Herr Dr. Freud?"

Sigmund took the monographs out of his coat pocket. Nothnagel read the titles and first paragraph of each. Sigmund continued, "At first I studied zoology, then I changed to physiology and, as Professor Meynert indicates, I have researched in histology. When Professor Brücke told me there was no assistantship open and advised me, a poor man, not to stay with him, I left."

Nothnagel turned his dark eyes upon his young visitor.

"I won't conceal from you that several people have applied for this job. As a result I can't raise any hopes. I will put your name down in case another job turns up. *Qui vivra verra*. I will hold onto your publications, if I may."

Sigmund swallowed hard.

"I am now serving as an Aspirant in the General Hospital. If you can't offer me the prospect of an Assistant's job, I would serve with you as an Aspirant."

"What exactly is an Aspirant?"

Sigmund explained that in the Allgemeine Krankenhaus structure an Aspirant was a young man who already had his M.D. and aspired to complete his technical training. When Nothnagel asked further questions Sigmund attempted to outline briefly the organization of the sixteen clinics and ten institutes as part of the University of Vienna, used primarily for teaching and research; the Medical Faculty composed of the professors, all paid by the Imperial Government and the Ministry of Education. The twenty departments were "the hospital"; each had at its head a *Primarius* who could not be connected with a clinic and was under the jurisdiction and budget of the District of Lower Austria. A career under the control of the Imperial Government was separate and distinct from one in the departments. There was no crossing back and forth.

Dr. Nothnagel raised his eyebrows in astonishment. Sigmund smiled. "The Allgemeine Krankenhaus has grown by accretion over a period of a century. It follows no logical plan except that of trying to keep the professors happy, each in his special domain."

"How very odd all this is. Dr. Freud, I advise you to go on working in the scientific field. But first you've got to live. Well, I'll keep you in mind. *Qui vivra verra.*"

" 'Who lives will see,' as Herr Professor Nothnagel is so fond of saying," groused Sigmund as he closed the door behind him. "I intend to do both. But surely a slightly improved view of the future couldn't do me any irreparable harm?"

5.

The internal medicine wards were on the second floor overlooking another of the nine hospital courts. Each held twenty beds, ten to a side, in large pleasant rooms with whitewashed walls and high windows, three on each side and up to the ceiling, allowing all the light and sun that were available in Vienna.

Sigmund arrived before eight on the first morning of Nothnagel's clinical demonstration to his Aspirants and undergraduates. He was no stranger to these wards, having taken thirty hours of courses under Professor Bamberger. He made his way up the winding staircase, so narrow that the attendants carrying the emergency cases had to bend the stretcher and patient around the curves. Next to Nothnagel's office were several small rooms for first-class paying patients whom Nothnagel could bring here at his discretion. The rooms would also be available to Nothnagel's Assistants for private patients when Nothnagel gave his consent; though the fees which the Assistants could charge were prescribed.

Professor Nothnagel was already in his office, surrounded by his newly chosen staff.

"*Grüss Gott*, Professor Nothnagel."

"*Grüss Gott*, Herr Doktor Freud."

Sigmund looked with envy at the thirty-six-dollar-a-month Assistants, several of whom he had known from his work in the laboratories. When Professor Nothnagel rose to make his way to the first ward, his entourage followed. There was a rigid caste system. As the professor stood at the bed of the patient to be diagnosed, only two of the older doctors or visiting colleagues could be at his side. In the second row would come his Assistants, in the third row the Aspirants and then, grouped as far back as necessary, the dozen or so students from the Medical School, the last of whom could see little of the patient.

Two nurses were at work in the ward. They were broad-bosomed country women who arrived in Vienna, generally at the age of fifteen, knowing only the robust art of scrubbing; the Krankenhaus was one of the best-scrubbed hospitals in the world. Many of them had come to Vienna seeking not only work but husbands. Few found them. The girls put in years of training, mostly in menial tasks, before they were permitted to handle patients. They piled their hair on top of their heads, wore short-sleeved plaid blouses, skirts down to the middle of their shoes, and white aprons, narrow over the bosom and wrapped around at the waist. They were allowed out only twice a month on a Sunday afternoon. It was a hard life.

Professor Nothnagel took one look at the nurses' short-sleeved blouses and banished them from the wards.

"No woman will be allowed to show any flesh in my department," he cried. "You will return with sleeves that come down to your hands!"

Sigmund was dumfounded at the outburst.

Nothnagel turned to the assemblage, said in a low, stern voice: "Let me make something clear to all of you. When examining patients, either male or female, only that part of the body being studied may be exposed."

He approached the woman in the first bed. She was eighteen. There was a greenish tinge to her complexion. Her chart declared the case to be one of chlorosis and anemia. She had been a finicky eater, having "a depraved appetite." She craved clay, slate and other indigestible articles. This condition had been thought to be mental; Nothnagel assured the group that it was dietary. He turned from the bedside toward his followers. This was a different Nothnagel. There was a glow on his face and his eyes were warm and sparkling, the dedicated teacher.

"My first warning is that you must exercise extreme care in making your diagnoses. It is no longer sufficient to examine only the organ the patient complains about. A conscientious physician examines the patient from head to toe, and only after a thorough observation does he unite the various elements into a unified diagnosis. Always remember that a human body is a complex living organism, every last element of which can influence every other element. A pain in the head can be caused by something that has gone wrong at the base of the spine. The only unforgivable sin in internal medicine is a lack of that sense of duty which demands that the patient have every conceivable attention and all of your powers of observation." Turning back to the patient, "We believe that chlorosis may be connected with the evolution of the sexual system, but we are not certain just how. She must be given malt liquor, muscular exercise . . ."

Sigmund reflected on Nothnagel's declaration. This was the approach known as "Nothnagel's revolution"; it was the first time he had heard these principles enunciated for internal medicine.

When they moved on to the next bed they found a middle-aged

woman with typhoid fever. It was she who was responsible for the sickening odor of feces in the ward, for she had been defecating in her bed. Sigmund recalled the saying, "Every case of typhoid represents a short circuit from one person's anus to another person's mouth."

Nothnagel pointed out that the patient had a fever of 104 degrees, with a slow pulse. She had pink spots over her trunk. He cautiously exposed a few of these spots.

"There would seem to be intestinal bleeding. This can lead to death through ulceration. The patient can also die from pneumonia or peritonitis; but we can bring her fever down with cold cloths, a good deal of liquid to drink, plenty of rest. This disease is caused by a parasite, but we don't know which one."

The next bed held a thirty-four-year-old woman with chronic nephritis, Bright's disease. He analyzed the symptoms. "The treatment for Bright's disease, gentlemen: limit the salt in her diet, give her no meat but make sure she gets small doses of bichloride of mercury. We will hope that this will improve her kidney condition. She should never be allowed to become pregnant again. Her condition can go on anywhere from a month to ten years."

They moved to the next bed, a woman of twenty-eight with toxic goiter. She complained to Nothnagel how hot it was in the ward. Nothnagel replied, "The temperature is low." The patient kicked off her covers, exposing herself. Nothnagel set his lips in a quick gesture and replaced them. He asked her to stick out her tongue, pointed out that it had a "fine tremor." He then took a measurement on the goiter, declared it not a large one:

"This kind of toxic goiter is rarely fatal but it debilitates the heart. Her heart is already overloaded by going 120 to 140 a minute. This is almost double the normal. We don't know yet why goiter has this effect on the heart. We must take away from her all coffee, tea and mental excitement. Give her tincture of aconite; it is a poison but not dangerous in small doses. We can only hope that the disease will subside before her heart breaks down."

"And how does one keep the doctor's heart from breaking down?" Sigmund asked himself quietly. There was no question about the thoroughness of Professor Nothnagel's diagnoses. Neither could there be any question that, although the specialist in internal medicine could make an accurate diagnosis of the symptoms, there was no corresponding body of knowledge of the cure.

As if he had heard Sigmund's thoughts, Nothnagel stopped in front of the bed of a thirty-four-year-old woman who was suffering from thrombosis and embolism.

"The greatest medicine is nature. Nature has all the secrets of its own cures. Our task, colleagues, is to ferret out these secrets. Once we ferret out the secrets we can implement her work. But if we go against nature's laws, we can only injure the patient. For example, the operation that I have heard was performed here recently, when a surgeon removed part of the stomach and duodenum. I believe this to be against nature. We must cure without cutting into the body of the patient."

Sigmund Freud soon found out what Nothnagel meant when he said, "When a man's love is lost, nothing remains but work." As far as Nothnagel was concerned there was nothing but work whether a man had love or not. "Whoever needs more than five hours of sleep should not study medicine," he announced. Each morning Sigmund followed Nothnagel through the wards for from two to four hours, learning something every hour in the art of diagnosis from the "bedside demonstrations." Nothnagel expressed his delight at the "richness of the source material": the twenty-four-year-old male with a rheumatic heart; the man of sixty-two dying from dehydration caused by cancer of the stomach; the sailor who had returned with malaria from an African port; a case of an old gonorrheal stricture which had developed multiple opening fistulas between the anus and genitalia, and a "watering pot" perineum because the urine flowed out through his skin; the diabetic; the aphasia case, with the man losing all ability to talk; the unending stream of new patients, all minutely examined and diagnosed before Sigmund's eyes, of pellagra and scurvy; pleurisy, anemias, gout, leukemia, hepatitis, angina pectoris, tumors, paroxysms . . . all the ills the flesh is heir to, and nearly every sickness that would present itself in Dr. Sigmund Freud's consultation room. He was fascinated by the poetic imagery and breadth of vocabulary which Nothnagel had taken from the world's literature and brought to bear on such subjects as gallstones or valvular lesions.

Nothnagel spent his free hours in his laboratory where he was continuing his work on the physiology and pathology of the intestinal canal, using live animals for his experimentation. As an Aspirant, Sigmund was not permitted to carry on research. However he faithfully attended the demonstrations, read himself blear-eyed until one or two in the morning.

The months passed. No appointment as an Assistant was indicated. By late October another fact became clear: he had no intuitive resources for diagnosis of the kind demonstrated by Professor Nothnagel. Nor would he be able to "divine" the nature and causes of illness. He would be able to recognize symptoms based on his training but internal medicine could never be the focus of his life.

Martha was puzzled.

"Then why have you worked so hard, Sigi, if it is not to be your field? We have seen each other only one evening a week."

He grinned sheepishly. "In medicine there is no way of knowing whether there is a career for you unless you accumulate training; you can't learn that a book is useless until you've read it. I am inching forward with the sideways movement of the crab. Without research possibilities, without publishing or lecturing . . ."

His voice trailed off. They had just crossed the Josefs-Platz with its large equestrian statue of Josef II and majestic Hof-Library. Sigmund had secured written permission, through the office of the Medical Faculty, to enter Die Burg. This Hofburg was a city within a city, the very heart of Imperial Vienna. Each succeeding emperor had added new stone wings, squares, façades, chapels, fountains. They came opposite the gold-encrusted Swiss Gate, inside which they could see the first quadrangle built about 1220 and cornered with bristling defense towers. True to the city itself, the Hofburg was a mélange of architecture and decoration, classical Greek, Gothic, Italian Renaissance, Baroque . . . The Burgkapelle of the mid-fifteenth century differing sharply in style from the Amalienhof of the sixteenth, which bore little relationship to Emperor Leopold I's apartments of the seventeenth and even less to the Neue Burg which had been started by Emperor Franz Josef only two years before. Yet the palace had its historical continuity, and it was a poor day for a Viennese when he could not find an excuse to cut through the series of monumental squares from the business district of Michaelerplatz at one end to the stately Burgring with its long view of the gardens between the twin museums on the other.

Resting on a bench in the Stadtpark for a moment, the pale April sunlight brittle on their faces, Martha reverted to Sigmund's serious comment before they had entered the palace grounds . . . that he was moving forward with the sideways movement of the crab. Sigmund waved an arm encompassing the overpowering Hofburg surrounding them.

"Ah well, I never was one who could not bear the thought of being carried off by death without having his name carved on a rock."

She answered quietly, "Sig, the fact that you could evoke such an image proves it is in your mind. You deprecate yourself when all avenues of progress appear blocked."

6.

The financial situation was growing increasingly difficult in the Freud household. Jakob was getting only an occasional bit of work in the textile district. Sigmund could not determine whether his father had more illness because he worked less, or he worked less because he was often irritable. The five Freud daughters, all now over eighteen, bright, educated, hearty girls, could not help because no one would employ females except as a *bonne*, nursemaid or companion to elderly women.

Anna was planning to be married soon, but Brust had disappeared from Rosa's life. The four unattached girls offered to take jobs and contribute to the finances but Jakob and Amalie were in agreement that such jobs were for lower-class girls from the workingmen's district, or those newly arrived from the country. The Freud girls would seriously injure their marriage possibilities; it would be an announcement to the world that the family was *in extremis*. Better to suffer the privation.

The immediate ray of hope was Alexander. Though he had not been an enthusiastic student, caring little for theory or abstract thought, he passed his *Matura*. After the graduation exercises Alexander walked home with his older brother.

"Sig, you know I'm practical by nature. I like business. I'm sure I'll be good at it. I want to get a job right away where I can learn. I also want to start bringing wages into the house."

Graduation and maturity had arrived hand in hand. Alexander was still several inches shorter than Sigmund, clean-shaven, with his hair cut short; otherwise they looked quite astonishingly alike, as though their parents had come back to an original formula after a lapse of ten years and five quite different-looking daughters. Alexander had been named by Sigmund, at Jakob's invitation, after Alexander the Great, known as a protector of the Jews. He was subject to ups and downs of emotion and labored under the illusion that this was not true of his older brother, whom he idolized, for Sigmund concealed his recurrent depressions from his family as a burden they should not have to share. Alexander had Sigmund's high forehead, wide-spaced eyes, attractively shaped nose and chin; his expression was plain, forthright. However a basic difference in their temperaments had begun to emerge. Sigmund's philosophy was, "Anything that can possibly go right will go right." Alexander maintained, "Anything that can possibly go wrong will go wrong." He had long been the one in the family who repaired whatever broke, from the rung of a chair that needed regluing to the stuffed-up water tank that had to be removed and cleaned out.

"What kind of work would you like, Alex?"

"I love trains. Remember, Sig, when you used to take me to the Nordbahnhof to watch the trains come in? Then we went into the yards to watch the giant green- and mustard-colored locomotives get ready for long hauls across Europe. I wouldn't want to be an engineer. But I'd like the business of keeping them loaded with freight and passengers. Do you know anyone who can get me any kind of job?"

Sigmund pondered on this. "After all these years in medicine, I don't have any friends in business. The only approach we have is Eli."

Eli Bernays persuaded Professor von Stein to give Alex a job in the office where his economic research was carried on and his journal published. There was only one catch. Alex had to begin as an apprentice, without salary. "But as soon as I can prove to the professor that he is useful," said Eli, "we can get him a wage."

Alexander groaned. "How long might that take, Eli?"

"Not too long. A few months. Trust me."

Alex went to work the following Monday, his black coat buttoned up to cover half the white shirt, only the knot of his tie showing, and in the center of the knot Alex's one bit of finery: a large pearl stickpin. He was happy, excited, but not nervous.

It was not the kind of job Alex could do well; there was too much theory involved. When after three months Sigmund told Alex he should demand a salary, Alex, honest with himself, asked:

"What do I do if they refuse? I haven't really been able to make myself useful."

Eli could not get a salary for Alex. "Give me until the first of the year," he demanded.

Alexander located a small company that specialized in railroad transportation, freight rates, routes. It was owned by an elderly, childless man by the name of Moritz Muenz who had been looking for a bright young lad. Alex walked in with his shining face and love for railroads. Muenz offered a good wage for a sixteen-year-old, six gulden a week. Alexander, when he brought his first pay home and placed it in his mother's hand, was the proudest young man in Vienna.

The snows began early in November, the first flakes, as Sigmund watched them from his window, small, hardly larger than raindrops, just a white tinge sifting down at an angle, thickening into a heavy white blanket as though pressure-driven from above, melting before they reached the pavement, leaving the ground as wet as though rain had fallen. He noted the small coveys of sparrows, never more than ten, wheeling in the cold gray skies as though they did not know which way was south. The next fall of snow was considerably heavier; walking to the Allgemeine Krankenhaus, he saw the buildings as though through white satin. But the big flakes melted when they hit the remaining leaves of the trees or the slate roofs. The pillows and bedding that had been put on the window sills in the early mornings to air were gone now; the people emerging from the houses wore heavy overcoats, put up their umbrellas, holding them tightly toward the top so that they would not pop upward with the first strong gust of wind.

The walnut trees were the reluctant givers. They clung to their leaves and the leaves to their greenness through the snows and early cold; but by the end of the second week in November the high winds tore them loose and raced them at rooftop level through the streets like flocks of green birds.

Sigmund knew the fierce, capricious winds of Vienna; knew them too well from his long years of trudging to school. They had the sense of direction of a compass: at any given hour they blew only through the east and west streets. Another day it would be north and south. He would be walking in comparative warmth, take a right-angle turn and instantly be met by a blast of icy wind that almost blew him from the sidewalk. Like sailors, the Viennese wet a finger and put it into the wind to see if they could walk home in a direct line.

Being with Martha was his only delight during these hard-pressed months. His embraces became so ardent that she developed dark circles under her eyes. He blamed himself. They loved each other and after days of separation when they came together he could not stop kissing and holding her close.

"Marty, let's tell your mama we are engaged. Then the whole world can know and we'll feel better. At least I will. What is common knowledge has to be true."

Martha saw how thwarted he had become; she yielded.

"Eli says he is going to tell Mother about his engagement to Anna on Christmas Day. Why don't we join them?"

Instantly his dejection was gone.

"Wonderful. We'll buy her a gift. What do you think? A book? It will be a good day for us, a way station."

The three couples, Minna and Ignaz, Eli and Anna, Sigmund and Martha, brought gifts to Mrs. Bernays, Sigmund having chosen a copy of Schiller's *Glocke*. Mrs. Bernays did not receive the news of the engagements very well. She sniffed slightly, as though someone had burned the roast. But it was her son Eli who bore the brunt of the storm. After a week Eli showed up at the Freud house red-faced and ashamed, to announce that he could not see Anna any more. Anna took the news quietly. Sigmund was outraged. When Eli had left, he cried:

"What kind of a man is he to allow his mother to force him to commit a dishonorable act? He knows he loves you and that you are the right girl for him."

"Give him time," replied Anna stolidly.

He had even less success in quarreling with Martha over the break.

"I can't take sides against my family," she insisted. "A woman who would denounce her own mother and brother would, given time and provocation, take sides against her husband as well."

Only a few weeks later Eli apologized, took Anna in his arms, kissed her warmly . . . and set their wedding date for the following October. Still Sigmund would not forgive him. Mrs. Bernays withdrew from the contest. Outraged with Eli, she moved in with the Freuds, assuring Anna that she had only wanted to delay the marriage, not prevent it. She then announced that she was going to move permanently to Hamburg and Wandsbek and that Martha and Minna would live with her there. If the two young couples wanted to be engaged, they could do so at a distance of five hundred miles.

Sigmund commented, "I'm not going to worry now about something your mother is threatening to do next June."

Martha slipped a cool hand into his, murmured, "That's the Herr Dr. Freud I love."

"It will be a poor marriage if you are only going to love me when I'm wise."

Ignaz Schönberg was not in sufficiently good health to take any reverse calmly. When Mrs. Bernays, whom Ignaz had showered with affection, announced that she would take Minna to Wandsbek, he hemorrhaged and became prostrate with grief. Sigmund stopped by the dispensary to pick up a bottle of tonic for him and went to sit by his bedside. He found Ignaz pale and listless, the freezing February weather aggravating his cough.

Ignaz had two brothers who were doing well in business and helped maintain their mother's house but would give Ignaz nothing. They said, "You have to support yourself. Who ever heard of making a living out of Sanskrit?"

Mrs. Bernays too had been hounding Ignaz. Not because of the Sanskrit. Her husband had imbued in her a respect for university life and its revered titles. But because she felt that he was malingering; that he should graduate at once so that he could get a teaching job.

Ignaz cried: "I need more years of study. It's a vast field. I should master it before I take my degree."

"I thought a scholar worked all his life to become an expert," retorted Mrs. Bernays. "Why must you finish the job before you start?"

Sigmund had aroused the same accusation before he forced himself to take the exams for his M.D. He could sympathize with Ignaz. He gave him a double dose of the tonic.

It was not until early April, when the fountains were turned on again in the Stadtpark, that the big opportunity arrived for Sigmund. Dr. Bela Harmath, an acquaintance, declared his desire to resign from Primarius Theodor Meynert's Psychiatric Department in the hospital. Harmath had been a *Sekundararzt*, roughly the equivalent of an Assistant, but connected with the General Hospital rather than the university. He did no teaching or lecturing, lived in the hospital, and took care of patients in the wards. He was a resident physician. Since the District of Lower Austria supported the hospital, Sigmund knew that he would have to apply to the Lower Austrian Municipal Government for the job.

Though the regulations expressly forbade a man to be both *Primarius* of a hospital department and *Hofrat* of a university clinic, drawing funds from the Imperial Government and the district government at the same time, Professor Theodor Meynert was allowed to break the rules so that he could carry on his brain research for the university clinic and care for mental patients in his hospital wards. Sigmund's opportunity had arisen in these wards, *but how far from the wards could the research laboratory be?*

He went at once to see his old teacher and friend in his office on the ground floor of the Third Court, with large windows overlooking the chestnut trees, and a series of small windows so deeply recessed in the beamed ceiling as to give the room the appearance of a chapel. These quarters and the work going on there were indeed holy to Theodor Meynert.

He was a stumpy, sturdy, barrel-chested man with an unruly mane of hair flying on top of an enormous head; nature was trying to make up in cranium what it had neglected in shin and thighbone. He was a fighter, an individualist, eccentric and crammed with intelligence. Meynert was born in Dresden, son of a dramatic critic and a singer at the Hofoper. He was a poet, balladeer, historian, drama critic, master of half a dozen languages, none of which he could speak worth a kreutzer. His neuroanatomic work had earned him the title of "father of the architecture of the brain."

He did not claim to have invented anatomical brain investigations; he gave credit for this to a long line of antecedents: Arnold, Stilling, Koelliker, Foville and in particular to his teacher, mentor and supporter in his fiercest battles: Professor Carl Rokitansky, chief of pathological anatomy. What he did claim was that he was the "chief cultivator of anatomical localization." Starting with the mole and bat, he had worked his way through a hundred species to determine which area of the brain controlled which parts of the body, calling attention to the cortex of the brain as "the part of the brain where the personality-building functions are stationed." He taught psychiatry, a term coined some forty years before, but rejected the term, insisting:

"All emotional disturbances and mental confusions are caused by physical illnesses, nothing else."

His career had been a stormy one. During the years that he had worked at the Lower Austrian Insane Asylum, he had spent his time on the microscopic methods of brain and spinal cord research, considering psychopathological patients as good material for exact scientific investigation . . . the cortex of the brain, the ganglion cells, the posterior central part of the brain as sensory, the anterior central part as motor. His critics, who were many and bitter, said:

"To Meynert the only good lunatic is a dead lunatic. He can't wait until they die to get their brains for dissection."

It was here that he came in conflict with the German psychiatric-humanitarian movement, the medical doctors who conceived it their job to study the mentally ill, classify their symptoms, set down their family histories since all insanity was hereditary, and attempt to alleviate their sufferings. Theodor Meynert's superior at the asylum, Dr. Ludwig

Schlager, had worked for ten years to improve the lot of lunatics and the protection of their property and human rights, casting off the chains with which they were bound, releasing them from dungeons and prison cells, giving them care, food, living conditions and humane study that was accorded to other ills, to be defeated, so he insisted, by Meynert's proclamations that only the laboratory work being done in his own Psychiatric Clinic had any value. Meynert was neither a cruel nor a callous man, but he maintained that he never saw a lunatic cured. The only cures would come from the brain anatomist who, when he knew everything about how the brain worked and what caused its malfunction, would eliminate mental illness by getting rid of the causative disease.

The battle at the asylum became so bitter that Meynert was fired. He worked alone, in his private laboratory, continuing his anatomical dissections, abandoned as well by the university Medical School as having caught the dread disease of craziness from the asylum. Only two people stood by him: his wife, who thought him a genius, and his proctor, Rokitansky, who knew he was a genius. Rokitansky prevailed and, in 1875, just two years before Sigmund became his pupil, a Second Psychiatric Clinic had been founded at the Allgemeine Krankenhaus and Meynert placed in charge. All cures for the ills of the mind would now be found in the brain anatomy laboratory.

As a follower of Theodor Meynert, Sigmund knew that his teacher was entirely right. His ambition now was to get back into his laboratory.

"Professor Meynert, I just heard that Bela Harmath is resigning and I've run all the way here. If I don't appear out of breath it's only due to my powers of dissembling."

Meynert laughed. He had always liked this eager, gifted young man. They were well acquainted with each other's temperament, though Sigmund had not actually worked under Meynert's direction since he had taken an intensive course in clinical psychiatry some four years before. Like many another scientist-artist at the University of Vienna, Theodor Meynert had created a salon of writers, musicians, painters and actors as well as their patrons in high Austrian society. As a favored student, Sigmund had occasionally been invited to these soirees. He had seen that the artistic world was as much a part of Meynert's life as his laboratory; though of course the guests suspected that Meynert's eyes were forever piercing their skulls to determine which local area of the forebrain made one man a dramatist and another a sculptor.

"So you want to become my *Sekundararzt*, do you, and get back into psychiatry? Can't say I blame you."

"Herr Professor, I've got a research idea you will like."

"Tempting me, are you? Very well, what's the brilliant concept?"

"To begin an anatomical study of the brain of newborn infants and fetuses as early as we can get them. There could be some developmental studies that would give a comparison with the brain of adults."

Meynert smiled to himself.

"You know, Herr Kollege, that the *Primarius* of a department such as mine has no power to appoint his *Sekundararzt?*"

"Indeed, Herr Professor, I've long known that story."

"And you realize that you must apply to the Lower Austrian Municipal Government for the post?"

"I have already written out the application."

"And even if they are willing to appoint you, you must be named by the Directory of the Allgemeine Krankenhaus for any department that needs a *Sekundararzt?*"

"I understand that you cannot intercede on my behalf."

"Unheard of. Prepare to commence work on May first."

He rose, stretched out his hand with a paternal grin.

"I will be happy to have you working with me, Herr Doktor. You have a natural aptitude for brain anatomy. But not a word, you hear. We must handle this matter delicately."

7.

On May first Sigmund moved out of his parental home. It was a happy event for the family because it meant that he was taking his next step in the long journey. The break would not have been a severe one in any case, for Amalie had already moved the family to a smaller, less expensive apartment four blocks down the Kaiser Josefs-Strasse, at number 33.

Young women were not allowed in the doctors' rooms at the hospital but Sigmund got permission from the Directory to bring Martha there on his moving-in day to help him get settled. He supervised the *Dienstmann* he had hired on the corner, who loaded into his cart the portmanteau of linens and personal belongings as well as boxes of medical books. He and Martha walked arm in arm to the hospital.

The sky was a clear blue. It was an intensely exhilarating spring day, when the air of Vienna, straight down from the vineyards and forests of the Wienerwald, was intoxicatingly buoyant. Simply to breathe was an act of joy. It was the rebirth of the city after its cold wet winter. The townspeople were on the streets on their way to the shops, the coffee-houses, to transact long-delayed business; and with them were the throng of colorful characters who plied the sidewalks as they plied their trades: groups of wandering musicians playing guitar, clarinet and violin; decorated two-wheeled ice cream stands; street vendors selling oranges; a pot salesman carrying his merchandise in a wide wisket on top of his head;

women from Croatia in high boots selling toys; the handsome, mustached man selling cheese from a leather saddle hung over one shoulder, salami from the other; the bread man with his wooden tub of bread strapped to his back; the "pots and pans" repairman; the organ grinder, bootblack; the pretty young *Wäschermädel* with flowered dress, puffed sleeves, black ribbon about her neck, delivering laundry to the nearby barracks; butcher boys in aprons down to their shoes delivering packages of meat; the *Wurstelmann* serving hot sausages and rolls from a stand on the street corner to handsomely garbed gallants and sweaty workmen, eating side by side. Young girls in straw hats with aprons over their dresses were coming home from school carrying bookbags; chimney sweeps, black with soot from the winter's fires, in black leather cap and jacket and long black pants, had coils of wire strung over their backs and their hands filled with black brushes. There were knife grinders with emery wheels; a Croatian selling handmade wooden baskets and spoons, the winter's accumulation of merchandise sticking out in front of him like a woman nine months pregnant. Men on stepladders pasted posters of the new plays, operas, symphonies on the circular kiosks. And everywhere the buxom country women with their baskets of *Lavendl* called in their insistent music, "I have lavender. Who wants my lavender?"

"What a day to be alive in Vienna," murmured Sigmund.

Martha breathed deeply.

"What a day to be alive anywhere."

They entered the hospital and made their way to the Sixth Court. Though, as *Sekundararzt*, he would have no official time off, for the *Hausordnung* said that he had always to be within reach, the young doctors living in the hospital traded hours and filled in for each other. He would be able to get home for dinner once or twice a week.

His room on the second floor was twice the size of his *Kabinett*, twelve by twenty; the walls were of whitewashed plaster; there was an eleven-foot ceiling and, at the far end, facing south, an arched window that rose to the ceiling and occupied two thirds of the wall, with a deep window seat. The room got a great deal of sunlight; the scrubbed plank floor and throw rugs were warm underfoot.

"How pleasant!" Martha exclaimed. "Oh, Sigi, I think you can be happy here."

"I had better be. It's going to be my combined medical office, study, bedroom and dining room for the next several years."

She studied the room as it had been left by Dr. Bela Harmath. In the middle of the right wall, behind flush doors, was the wash cabinet with a pitcher and porcelain bowl on a thin marble shelf. Above the bowl was a mirror with towel racks on either side; hooks to hang his white gown. Next to the wash cabinet was the stove, a supply of wood on one side, on the other a bucket of coal and a shovel.

"Wouldn't you like to move your bed to the far end of the room, by the side of the window?" she asked. "With this piece of tapestry on the wall above it, you'll see how gay it becomes. Then if you put that round table in the center of the room you could keep your bowl of fruit and nuts on it and there will be plenty of space for books and magazines. Your mother sent a white cloth, and I've brought some flowers. Sometime later I think you will want your study desk on the other side of the window. It will give you the most light and privacy, especially if your door has to remain open any part of the time. Then you can move those bookshelves to the wall next to your desk."

"Let's do it now," he said enthusiastically.

Together they rearranged the room, put his medical books on the shelves, then opened the package she had brought with her: five colored cushions for his bachelor bed. She set them against the wall, fluffed them. He stood with his back to the window, amused.

"I'll ask your mother to send you a more cheerful bedspread." She stepped back. "Above your desk we will hang the pictures of Goethe and Alexander the Great from your study at home, and now I put my picture in the center. *Fertig!* Done! Now it seems more like your own room."

He took her gently in his arms.

"You are going to make a good housekeeper."

"I'm already a good housekeeper. It's just that I don't have a house to keep."

The waiter arrived from a neighboring cafe bringing pots of coffee, boiled milk and trays of little cakes. Behind him came the young doctors he had invited to meet Martha: Nathan Weiss, *Sekundararzt* First Class, in the Fourth Medical Department specializing in nervous diseases, the coming neurologist of Vienna and by universal agreement the world's most complete monomaniac; Alexander Holländer, Professor Meynert's Assistant and the hospital's Beau Brummell; Josef Pollak, an ophthalmologist also in Professor Scholz's nervous diseases; Karl Koller, an intern in ophthalmology and an old friend; his friend Josef Paneth from Brücke's physiology laboratory.

Martha poured coffee and milk. Sigmund could not take his eyes off her. He engaged in his favorite fantasy: they were married, this was their charming home, friends had come in for supper and lively talk . . .

"Fräulein Bernays, you don't have to worry about Herr Dr. Freud," Weiss teased; "we'll scan all the female patients to see that he gets the ugly ones."

"And we'll make sure that only the old crones are allowed to clean his room," Holländer added.

Martha blushed.

"Gentlemen, you are kind."

The coffee was passed again and the cakes all eaten. Sigmund's comrades bade them *Auf Wiedersehen.* It was six o'clock, time for Martha to leave also. They found it difficult to tear themselves apart.

"Please sit in this big chair, Marty. So. Then each time I come into the room I will see you there." He knelt before her, whispered:

"The love-inflamed poet says, 'We are cast in flesh but must live as iron.'"

Tears sparkled in her eyes. Sigmund put his arms about her and held her to him.

He enjoyed the rigorous routine of the hospital: up at six, down to the basement for a hot shower or tub, back to his room where the charwoman had left him a basin of hot water for shaving the center of his cheeks; putting on his long white ward coat. Then a checkup of the wards to see what emergencies the night had provided; again to his room for a breakfast of milk-coffee concocted of barley chicory with a few drops of real coffee in it, rolls, butter, marmalade; then to the *Beobachtungszimmer,* the B.Z., Observation or Examining Room, to which patients had been sent from the "Journal," the hospital's Central Admitting Office, to take the case histories of the newly arriving patients. Midday dinner was brought in from a neighboring restaurant; each doctor ate alone at the round table in his room. The leftovers were kept for supper. The pay was thirty gulden a month, twelve dollars; his food cost forty-five cents a day, adding up to thirteen dollars. But now that he was working in the hospital, students were referred to him for tutoring, for which he earned three gulden an hour. As a *Sekundararzt,* even though Second Class, he was allowed to practice medicine on the side, during those hours when he could be free from his duties. He could even go out to visit a patient, providing he arranged with another doctor to cover his rounds. Sigmund had no private patients, but Dr. Josef Breuer promised to share a few of his long-standing cases.

There were many changes for him in his new assignment. Working under Billroth and Nothnagel, he had been an Aspirant; under Meynert he was a doctor, spending seven to ten hours of his working day, which he felt was "barely enough," treating and prescribing for patients who were not primarily demonstration models for classes or Aspirants. Meynert's Assistants taught and lectured, the rest of their time they had for laboratory research. *Sekundarärzte* were not permitted in the laboratories but Meynert had little love for regulations. By the second week of his service Sigmund was putting in two solid hours a day in the laboratory and, every evening after seven when the patients were retired for the night, working by lamplight amidst the jars of human brains preserved in formaldehyde.

He slipped quietly into his role, relieving the tensions of the emotionally disturbed and mentally ill, a full panoply of whom was represented in the male and female wards through which fourteen to sixteen hundred patients passed each year. Though Professor Meynert described his Psychiatric Department to Sekundararzt Freud as "the only State Insane Asylum of Austria," this was untrue. There was the large asylum on the Lazarettgasse, where Meynert had originally worked. Nor were these wards an asylum in the strictest sense: an asylum kept patients until their death. Meynert's Clinic was a classifying, diagnosing and teaching center from which patients were sent home or to other institutions, sometimes being walked over to the Lower Austrian Insane Asylum a block or two down the Spitalgasse, then inside an admission gate and up a little hill planted with lawns, flower beds and trees.

All that Sigmund Freud knew about mental illness he had learned early on from Meynert when the professor had lectured at each of these beds in wards, classifying the patients by the title of their disturbance, relating the family background to show from which antecedent the patient had inherited his insanity, putting the confused or deranged ones through their recurrent attacks so that the student could see the manifestations and be able to recognize them.

"This man has dementia praecox, that one amentia, or confusedness. This woman is catatonic. That young man has alcoholic delusional insanity; this case is cretinism, the other one dementia paralytica; this is a manic depressive, this is senile dementia, this one has paranoia, that one a traumatic neurosis."

Complete records were kept on every case. Progress was being made: young Emil Kraepelin, working at the University of Leipzig, had just published an exhaustive categorizing book, *Clinical Psychiatry*. Krafft-Ebing, professor at the University of Graz and administrator of the Feldhof Insane Asylum, was expanding his *Psychiatry* by adding dozens of minutely observed cases to each new edition.

No one knew the cause of these disturbances. The doomed, according to Meynert, Krafft-Ebing, Kraepelin, simply inherited them from their parents or grandparents much as they did the color of their eyes or the way they walked. Nor were there any cures; what was inherited obviously could not be hung back on the family line to bleach. Happily there were some few methods of alleviating the symptoms: electric massage, warm or cold baths, the quieting bromide drugs. Beyond that, one could only wait for nature to return the minds to normal.

The first time Sigmund went into Meynert's office he saw a manuscript titled Psychiatry on the desk. Meynert was still researching his last chapters, Weights of Brain Divisions and Influence of Cortex upon Vaso-Motor Center. Sigmund looked at the new drawings of the midbrain and *nervus facialis*.

"Your book is practically complete, Professor Meynert!" he exclaimed with pride.

"It has taken seven years," responded Meynert. "Now I have proved once and for all that the forebrain can never give rise to hallucinatory phenomena; nor are its so-called memories possessed of the slightest sensory qualities."

"No soul there, Herr Professor?"

Meynert grinned, though weakly. Sigmund was teasing him, for Meynert was the chief opponent of the existence of the human soul, maintaining that all the work of psychologists searching for the seat of the soul, attempting to erect a science of ethics in human conduct, was not only wasteful and futile but also confused; the true work on the human brain was being done in the laboratories.

8.

Professor Meynert assigned Sekundararzt Freud to the male wards. Sigmund was of several minds when he started his work with these hospital patients. He had no prejudice against them, as many doctors had. They were sick people and it was his job to train himself to take care of the ill, whether it was an infection in the foot or a delusion in the head. But neither had he any special interest in their illnesses. He made a circuit of the first ward to get his bearings. Some of the cases were simpler than others. The chronic alcoholics were drying out; once they were over their delirium tremens they could be sent home until the next crisis. The accident cases were of a different category, so were the manic depressives, the persecution manias, the hallucinatory cases, the surprising number of patients who heard "voices." Here was a carpenter who had fallen off a third-story scaffold and landed on his head. His vision was impaired so that he saw everything double, his speech was too slurred to know whether he was thinking sequentially.

Then there were the paralytic cases, with facial tremors, tics and paresis reflecting damage to the brain or nervous system caused by tumor, inflammation, abscess, tubercular meningitis, syphilis. Though the disease itself was beyond the reach of the physician, and could be understood only after death when an autopsy of the brain and spinal cord had been completed, treatment might clear up their mental confusion. Many of these cases should never have been sent to Psychiatry, but to Primarius Scholz in Department Four, specializing in nervous diseases. However the young Sekundarärzte working in the Central Admitting Office nights and Sundays, as Sigmund would also have to serve one day a week, could not always judge what was wrong with a patient whose speech or hearing or behavior was affected.

It was fifty-year-old Theodor Meynert's ambition to record thirty thousand brain examinations. As Sigmund moved about the ward, seeing every manifestation of physical ailment combined with mental confusion and irrationality, he wondered how Meynert decided, once he broke down the fissures of any one brain, just what malfunction had caused the combined physical and psychic illness.

"Relatively easy," Meynert assured him. "Take that case in the center bed. He's dying now. When I get his brain I'll find a tumor as big as a ripe tomato!"

In the corner bed Sigmund found an old Benedictine monk whose diagnosis read *Confusion*. When admitted to the clinic he had thought he was in a military bunker in the midst of a war. He could not find his bed once he had left it, nor could he recognize any of the doctors or attendants. When Sigmund asked him how he was feeling he recited his history quite accurately, through the elementary school, *Gymnasium* and stays at various monasteries; but for the past eight years he had been in a state of amnesia. He drank water constantly, a sip between each sentence, asked for a new bottle every few minutes:

"I was at Hütteldorf, I was not able to get out of there as well as here. At Hütteldorf I have—I don't know it, Lord, I don't know it! I am the greatest liar, if I knew that. What did they do at Hütteldorf? Lord, I don't know it! Since I suffered from typhoid dysentery I have not been able to remember anything. Maybe I am in an insane asylum. What are you doing here? Lord, I don't know it! I am too confused. Which month do we have now? . . ."

Sigmund left the man's bedside; surely this was a case of advanced senility? In the next bed was a young son of a farmer, whose diagnosis read *Mania*. At home he had become uncommunicative, had not listened to what the family said, refused to answer questions. At night he took off his clothes and ran around the courtyard naked, then returned to cut to shreds his trousers, jacket and boots. He had been declared unfit for military service but his one ambition was to enter the army. He would not talk to Dr. Freud until Sigmund had found the right clue:

"Wilhelm, what do you intend to do in the army?"

This unleashed a storm of exposition. "I want my clothes back. I came to Vienna with the mayor of my village to enter the army. The mayor promised to meet me here again. I do not feel sick. I've always been healthy except for a fever when I was young. I must go home. There is so much work on the farm. If you don't give me my clothes I'll bring an ax against everybody at the Provincial Court. I have been stabbed and shot several times. What are you writing down? You don't need the name of my father, my father does not concern me. I was arrested for poaching. They beat me over the head with a gun. I was indicted by the court for larceny. That made me sad. I did not like to talk to people any more. I want to be in the army."

In the next bed was a fifty-two-year-old bachelor shoemaker. He was a small man with a pale bloated face and flabby muscles.

"I'm not a fool. I don't need to be locked in the Fools' Tower. I am being persecuted by several persons. I'll name them for you. Also by a Sunday child who wanted to thrash me and stab me. My brothers and sisters tortured me because I satisfied myself with a goat. I know I must atone for this crime. My elder brother is feeble-minded."

"Do you know why you came here, Franz?"

"Because they made a fool of me at home. I hear scolding voices at the window in the night. They shout, 'Drunkard. We will beat you.' That's why I locked myself in. The Sunday child saved me from my persecution. Five years ago I satisfied myself with a goat and also with little children. I should be in prison. For two years I have been drinking. My father was a potator too. He died from alcoholism."

An attendant came to say that a patient in one of the isolation rooms was asking to see the doctor. It was a married grape grower who had fallen into a rage the night before. Sigmund went into the room, closing the iron door behind him. The chart said that the man suffered from confusion, delirium tremens, anxieties, excitements, hallucinations of eyes and ears and feeble-mindedness. Less than a month before he had suddenly become frenzied and run away, then after he returned, prayed on his knees for as long as five hours at a time. He maintained that he had come to the hospital in order to be cured of an ailment of his throat.

"How is your throat now?"

"I've always been healthy. Only for two years I've been suffering from a cough. The neighbors locked me in because they thought I barked. I was only clearing my throat. I smashed the window and ran away."

"You didn't eat anything yesterday, Karl."

"Because all the food is poisoned. I am not going to let you kill me. I bought a house in Haugsdorf for six hundred gulden. You can't keep a rich man locked up."

Professor Meynert asked Sekundararzt Freud to take the morning stint in the B.Z. Sigmund had by now read several hundred "Admitting Reports" and knew precisely what was required of him as the first examining doctor. Each morning the cases flooded in, brought by the police, by families, by doctors and by the patients themselves. Some were incoherent, mumbled meaningless sounds and broken words. Others talked a streak in disconnected phrases and sentences. His first case was a twenty-five-year-old Roman Catholic graduate law student. "Medium height, moderately nourished, pale complexion," Sigmund wrote in the record book, "brown hair, reddish beard, blue eyes; the left corner of his mouth is

lower, which may be due to scabious scar. Chest and heart normal."
Heinrich related his story to Dr. Freud:

He had been a weak child with a speech defect, measles, scarlet fever,
diphtheria. Since his sixth year he had been frequently punished for
petty thefts, which he denied having committed. He had flung a chair at
his brother when he was ten. He had to leave the Schottengymnasium
after the seventh grade and was sent to Krems to relatives. He spent
large sums buying fashionable clothing in order to show off. He passed the
Matura with average success and entered the School for Law in Vienna.
He had social intercourse with the high aristocracy, took only a *Fiaker*
as a means of transportation, had mistresses, defrauded the students'
fund when he was twenty-one. He passed the first law examinations but
failed the third and last. He had the feeling of being tubercular, sometimes consulted doctors five times a day. He had spent one year at the
Provincial Court studying but had been forced to give up his job because
of debts. He decided to go to America with his family, but escaped from
them, sold his ticket for half price and wandered about Europe living by
theft and fraud.

Sigmund jotted down very carefully: *Megalomania, Insane and Feeble-
minded behavior, cure improbable.*

"How am I going to go on with my career, Herr Doctor, if I am locked
up here? It is my brother who wants to ruin my career. I have never done
anything wrong. Everybody is against me. I can't work too steadily because I have syphilis and tuberculosis."

"Heinrich, I seriously doubt that you have either syphilis or tuberculosis."

"I have piercing pain in my left lung. If I keep all the records for the
ward will they let me out of here?"

Sigmund assigned him to a bed, prescribed potassium iodide.

He was called to check on a young married man admitted during the
night. The diagnosis read *Disturbance of the Mind.* He had refused to
eat or drink.

"You know why I won't eat or drink, Doctor, it's because I've got so
much mucus, and because of this I have to die. I'm parched but I can't
drink any water because I've got so much mucus in my throat."

Sigmund checked the man's chart. The patient had never been physically ill. His first symptom of mental abnormality was that of poisoning
mania: he refused to eat at home because he thought his wife wanted
to poison him. He went instead to a public house. He had become
hyperexcited, unable to sleep, in the morning he refused to dress or go
out to work because "I've got too much mucus."

Sigmund studied the patient. He was physically emaciated, had recurrent shivers, motor restlessness. Now he was shouting:

"I am the spitting master of the world. At home I lay on the sofa for three weeks and was spitting all the time. My wife is a whore."

"Albert, do you know where you are? And when you came here?"

"No, I only know that I am going to die."

Sigmund watched the man's face. The reaction of both pupils was slow, his skin was cold, he was physically very weak. He probably was going to die because something had gone wrong in his brain, some disease had taken over. But what kind of disease made a man spit for hour after hour because he had too much mucus?

It was ten o'clock at night when a joiner, a day or two away from being discharged, asked to consult the doctor. He had requested to be committed to the hospital because of acute pains in the limbs but en route had gotten drunk and on arrival at the Krankenhaus had been sent to Psychiatry. He was a married man with three children, healthy. After sobering up he was convinced that other patients pursued him about the ward and threatened to put his eyes out.

"Do you realize that that is a hallucination, Karney?" Sigmund asked.

"Yes, I suppose so. I want to go home and back to work. But I suffer from sleeplessness so much, and from anxiety. And then I begin to drink . . ."

Sigmund stood staring out the window; only the dimmest lanterns lighted the darkness of the court.

"Why his eyes? What sickness does this arise from? The only thing I can think of is the line from Matthew, 'If thy right eye offend thee, pluck it out, and cast it from thee.'"

9.

Martha's departure for Wandsbek in mid-June was more painful than either of them had anticipated. Eli intimated that he would be willing to keep his two sisters with him but there were years of waiting ahead for both of them. Sigmund felt that the separation was dangerous for both couples; at the same time he acknowledged that if their love could not endure a separation it could not last at all.

He put his arms about her. Kissed her.

"Once your mother started this action there was nothing either of us could do to prevent it. We have no choice. We must have faith in my work. That is the only thing that can bring us together again."

The next day they met for a moment on the corner of the Alser Strasse. They were so dry of lip that neither could utter the word "Good-by." Too upset to return to the hospital, he went instead to visit Ernst Fleischl. Josef Breuer and Sigmund alternated as Fleischl's physician, in between Billroth's several operations a year, though there was little either of them could do except rebandage the thumb and provide morphine against the pain.

Fleischl lived in a handsome apartment house built by his grandfather and decorated on the outside with enormous male and female nudes, Greek columns, porticoes, arabesques, plaster cherubs. The elder Fleischls occupied the entire second floor but Ernst had arranged an independent apartment by breaking through the landing with a new door to give himself a large corner bedroom, behind that a smaller dining room, and on the opposite corner a combined library, study, office and sitting room where he spent his tortured, sleepless nights.

Fleischl's manservant admitted Sigmund. One wall of the study was solidly faced with books. On the other walls hung the Italian paintings his grandfather had gathered on his carriage journeys from Milan to Naples. Numerous stands, desks and tables held fragments of marble sculpture from Asia Minor, female torsos, heads of Roman generals, friezes, an Etruscan Bacchus off the Temple at Veii.

"Sigmund, what a pleasure to see you. I had just told the cook I wouldn't be eating any supper, but with you for company we'll have a fine spread."

He picked up a tube from behind a velvet curtain and blew into it. When the manservant appeared he ordered a generous meal. Sigmund took off the bandage to check Fleischl's thumb. Billroth had amputated again only two months before. He cleaned the wound and redressed it while they chatted animatedly. Fleischl had just taken up Sanskrit so that he could read the Veda in the original. Sigmund suggested some coaching by Ignaz Schönberg.

Supper was brought in; Fleischl's good-sized dining table was filled with archaeological artifacts brought back by his grandfather from his journeys in Egypt and the Holy Land. There was barely room to set down the two soup plates. Fleischl explained:

"When I eat alone I feast my eyes on these lovely pieces. It's as though I were absorbing them instead of the liver dumplings. When I die I'm planning to take these treasures with me."

Sigmund did not like to hear thirty-seven-year-old Fleischl talk about dying, even in a joke; but the harsh truth had to be faced. This thumb of Fleischl's was never going to cure, and every time Billroth had to operate he took more years off Fleischl's life. The pain of the wound was intense; morphine had become the only solution. To Sigmund it seemed a travesty of justice; Ernst Fleischl had everything to live for. His soaring intellect took him into realms that the rest of medical Vienna could not follow.

"You know, Ernst, if I didn't love you I could be mighty envious," Sigmund quipped. "The last man who knew everything knowable was

Leibnitz, back in 1716. If you don't start rationing yourself you're going to displace him."

An involuntary spasm of pain shot across Fleischl's handsome face. Sigmund gave him an injection of morphine. During the day Fleischl was engrossed in his work in Brücke's laboratory; but the nights were long. Sigmund stayed until one in the morning, playing Japanese Go. He was uneasy: somewhere along about four in the morning, unable to endure the pain any longer, Fleischl would give himself another injection. He was addicted by now; both Breuer and Sigmund knew this, though they were the only ones who did. Walking back to the Krankenhaus through the deserted streets, he thought:

"We've got to get Ernst off morphine. That will kill him quicker than his thumb." No one could endure that kind of pain without a means of relief, but surely there must be something less lethal?

The hospital, Sigmund learned, was run by the *Sekundarärzte*, of whom there were ten of the First Class and thirty of the Second Class, as he was. The *Primarii* were middle-aged men of wealth and outside practice who spent only a couple of hours of the day in their hospital offices and the wards. That left forty men to supervise and care for the twenty departments. Though the specialties were confined to their specific courts there were several places where the *Sekundarärzte* could meet and become friends: the Journal, the central reading room, around the gas stoves in protected recesses where the young men gathered for a cup of coffee and "*bassena* talk": named from the gossip of women who gathered about the single water spout on the outside balconies of lower-class apartment houses. Their shared omnipresent problem was money. Because it was a common plight they developed a Freemasonry that made a common pot of their scarce gulden and kreutzer. One of the men in Dermatology had an embroidered sampler above his desk from John 12:8, " 'The poor always ye have with you.' That's US!" The First Class *Sekundarärzte* earned more, thirty-two dollars a month, and had accumulated a few more patients, but they were also older and had greater obligations. Everyone scrambled for extra gulden: by tutoring, reviewing medical texts, seeking patients. They were all in debt to their families, friends, booksellers, stationers, tailors, coffeehouses.

One morning Sigmund needed five gulden for Amalie. He tried two friends; they sifted their fingers through empty pockets. After the midday meal Josef Paneth came hurriedly down the hall. He was poorly dressed as usual, his thin blue eyes reflecting not only his shy, sensitive soul but the tuberculosis which in Vienna struck those from rich backgrounds as well as those from the poor. Paneth, always uneasy lest his comrades exclude him because he did not share their poverty, made it a point to give the parties. Any excuse served: birthday, promotion, publication. He went to the restaurant early, ordered the dinner, tipped the waiters and paid the bill, then sat happily by.

"Sig, I just heard you need a few gulden."

"I can't borrow money from you. It's an unwritten law."

"Why am I excluded?" It was a wail.

"Because it isn't proper to borrow from a man who doesn't need to be paid back. It smacks of begging."

"You're a pack of snobs! Why should poor people be allowed to lend and rich ones be frozen out?"

"Very well, Josef. When we want money for prodigal living and sin, we'll borrow exclusively from you."

Paneth walked to Sigmund's desk, picked up Martha's picture. "How are you enduring the separation?"

Sigmund grimaced. " 'Enduring' is the exact right word for it. And how is Fräulein Sophie Schwab? You know you love that girl and ought to marry her. You've been searching for a poor girl long enough."

"I agree. We're planning the marriage this summer."

Sigmund enjoyed particularly the companionship of his associates. Robert Steiner Freiherr von Pfungen had recently been awarded his *Dozentur* in neuropathology; he did most of the bedside teaching for the courses under Meynert. Sigmund had to be present at these lectures and demonstrations since he was responsible for caring for the patients being used as teaching models. Von Pfungen had had excellent training under the great professors at Vienna: Brücke, Wedl, Stricker, Redtenbacher, Schneider and Barth, from which he emerged with a solid background in medicine, chemistry, the physiology of the kidneys and the mechanics of the cortical disorder of speech. He was particularly well liked because he never questioned anyone's request for materials or supplies. He was also possessed, in an amiable way, of therapeutic monomania.

"Sig, we're looking for clues on what makes patients' minds go through alternating periods of clarity and confusion. I've found the answer: in the peristaltic cycle: the movement by means of which the contents of the alimentary canal are propelled along it."

"Would you mind clarifying that, Herr Doktor?"

"What I would like you to do, Herr Kollege, is to keep a record of the patients' bowel movements, with precise timing from the beginning of the movement through the act of evacuation. Then collate this schedule with the times that their minds are clear or in confusion. I think you'll find an inverse relationship: while the peristalsis is working the patient's mind will be confused. Once the evacuation is over, the mental faculties become clear and will remain so until the next movement has its inception. What do you say to all this?"

Only one word floated tubularly to the surface of Sigmund's mind: *Scheisse!* But Von Pfungen was much too fine a fellow to offend. He promised to watch his patients as he had requested.

A few weeks later Von Pfungen developed a new theory. This one concerned the cause of bronchial catarrh.

"It has to do with the washing of the back of the patient," he explained while they made their rounds of the wards. "I have enough evidence now to conclude that the right side of the bronchia is less often affected because the left, or weaker and lazier hand, does not wash the right side of the back as strongly as the right hand washes the left side. An interesting approach, don't you think, Herr Doktor . . . ?"

But the man Sigmund saw most often, and not always willingly, was Dr. Nathan Weiss, who at the age of thirty-two had already been living in the hospital for fourteen years, the last four of them as Senior *Dozent* in Department Four. Weiss was known as Herr Allgemeines Krankenhaus. Josef Breuer, when he learned that Weiss was making Sigmund his new confidant, said:

"Nathan reminds me of the story of the man who asked, 'My son, what do you want to be?' The son replied, 'Vitriol, the stuff that eats its way through everything.'"

Nathan's gigantic self-importance was matched only by his appetite for work, his ability to burrow into things and hold on by his fingernails. He was forever in motion, delivered brilliant monologues, knew a little bit about everything; but by concentrating on nervous diseases had become an authority in the field. He had fallen in love once, as a student, been rejected, and been frightened of love ever since. Instead he ran the Fourth Department.

Dr. Nathan Weiss began dropping in for a companionable chat, sometimes inviting Sigmund out for coffee or supper. At first Sigmund thought he was just a new ear for Weiss's extraordinary vocal cords but he learned that this was unfair. Nathan liked him and respected his judgment.

"Freud, when you've finished your training with Meynert, why not come over to me? I'll be *Primarius* by then. I'll make you my Senior *Sekundararzt.* I'll turn you into the second best neurologist in Vienna."

"How close do you think I can get behind you, Nathan?"

"There will always be an unbridgeable gap between me and the next greatest neurologist. When you finish in Nervous Diseases you will bear the mark of Nathan Weiss upon you."

"'And the Lord set a mark upon Cain. . . . And Cain went out from the presence of the Lord, and dwelt in the land of Nod.'"

"I know. Genesis 4:15-16. My father tattooed the Old Testament line for line on my epidermis." He went to the door, turned and said wistfully:

"Sig, you have some sisters at home. Could I meet them? I'd like to marry a doctor's sister. As soon as I'm *Primarius* I want to set up my own home. It's time for me to be married now . . . past time . . ."

10.

All of the research laboratories were the same size, ten by twelve feet. Professor Meynert occupied one by himself with space set aside for his young Assistants to make demonstrations when they had progress to report. Von Pfungen shared the next laboratory with a Russian, Darkschewitsch, whose ambition it was to take modern neuropathology to Moscow; Sigmund had the next laboratory with Dr. Alexander Holländer; and in the last room was the first American he had ever worked with, Bernard Sachs, a twenty-four-year-old who had taken his A.B. at Harvard University, his M.D. at the University of Strassburg the year before, and was now doing his postgraduate work in brain anatomy under Meynert. Sigmund found him amiable and intelligent and enjoyed speaking English with him. Dr. Sachs had a position waiting for him as instructor in diseases of the mind and nervous system at the New York Polyclinic. The only argument Sigmund had with Sachs was over the use of the word "mind." Sachs kept talking about "diseases of the mind." Sigmund said:

"Barney, that specimen you are looking at through your microscope is not a thin slice of a human mind. It's a slice of brain."

"How can you separate the mind and the brain?" Sachs insisted.

"The brain is a vessel, a physical structure built to contain. The mind is the content: words, ideas, images, beliefs. . . ."

"Indistinguishable, my dear friend."

Sigmund entered his own laboratory by a door in the corner. A workbench had been built around the room against the wall except for an area near the door where there was a sink and under it a big wastebasket for the rejects: pieces of brain, broken slides. On high shelves were the jars containing the brains sent over from the dissection room, floating in formaldehyde and wrapped in muslin sacks supported by string so that they would not settle to the bottom of the bottle and flatten out.

Sigmund removed his coat, hung it on a hook behind the door, took one of the brains out of a jar and released it from its muslin sack. He held the brain in his two hands; it was soft, intriguing, disturbing. Always with adult brains he had the feeling that there had been life here only a few hours or a few days before.

The brain was oozing in his hands. For Sigmund it had a slight feel of jelly: pale, cream-gray-white in color. He washed off the particles of blood and set it on the board next to the sink. He picked up an eight-inch-long kitchen knife, not too sharp, and sliced the brain as though it were sausage, in cuts of a half to a full centimeter in thickness. He found a certain resistance. The room now stank with the odors of formaldehyde, alcohol and cut brain; a peculiar death odor, musty, pungent and disagreeable.

He moved the slices of brain to his workbench where he had to push aside earlier slices in slotted boxes piled one on top of the other with handwritten notes between. He used his microtome for the very thin specimens he needed. In a row at the back of the workbench were the bottles containing his solutions, in front of them his staining bottles arranged in the sequence in which he had to dip his slides. He took each slab of brain with his forceps, and with a small scissors cut out the section that was most pertinent and typical of the pathology.

A messenger from the dissection laboratory brought a package containing the brain of an infant that had been stillborn the night before. It had not yet been put into formaldehyde. As Sigmund held it he found that it too was soft, slippery, but with more ooze to it. The emotional impact was difficult to take. As he sliced the brain and put the specimens under the microscope he saw why this infant could not have lived: it had developed a congenital abnormality, hydrocephalus, water on the brain.

"If we can discover why the water ventricles contained too much fluid, what plugged up the openings so there could be no outflow," he said to himself, "then we're on the road to preventing it."

His immediate task was to discover a method of staining the slices so that certain areas of the nerves, nerve roots and cells, which had never been seen clearly because there was no way of making them stand out sharply from the surrounding gray matter, could be discerned. This was proper work for a histologist. But all of his attempts spoiled the cross section. He was amazed to find how many hours could go by, working by himself in the laboratory until midnight, while each new combination of chemicals either caused it to be too brittle, or to shrink, overhardened the tissue or threw it into folds.

Dr. Alexander Holländer, who had been in the clinic for seven years, followed his work closely. Holländer was the son of a Hungarian physician, well educated in languages, philosophy and literature, a brilliant diagnostician and brain anatomist who often lectured to the students in Meynert's absence. His thesis *On the Theory of Moral Insanity* was much admired. A charming man from a solid family, he dressed elegantly, smoked expensive cigars and did his work with the courtly manner of a grand seigneur. Meynert claimed that no one had a greater capacity than Holländer to learn what other investigators turned up. Though the technical work of dissecting and mounting specimen tissue bored him, he never tired of watching Sigmund put together improbables in the hope of finding the right mixture.

"I say, you are stouthearted in the face of failure. I wish I had your endurance."

"I wish I had your knowledge. Besides, you're only a failure up to the thousandth try; if you succeed on the thousand and first, you're a genius."

"Then you must be mighty close to genius."

"Why not come in with me, Holländer? I think I'm getting close to something for handling the embryo and newborn brains. We could complete the experiments and write the paper together for the *Centralblatt für die medizinische Wissenschaften*."

"Say, I haven't published in some time now. When shall we start?"

"We've started. Take off that handsome English coat and put out the cigar. Here, watch what happens when I harden pieces of the organ in bichromate of potash . . . or here, in Erliche's fluid. . . .'"

Holländer was a splendid teacher. Sigmund had only to turn to him with a simple question and he would receive a recondite lecture on brain fissure. He was also an amusing man, with droll tales of the current theater, opera and Vienna society. His one limitation was that he left the laboratory early in the afternoon to prepare for his evening of pleasure, occasionally dropping back about midnight to see how Sigmund was getting on. When urged to help, he replied:

"The light is too bad. Besides the technique is difficult. . . ."

"It is, thank God. Otherwise anyone could do it. Holländer, why don't you try hard work sometime?"

Holländer laughed good-naturedly.

"You'll never believe it, Freud, but while I was in Medical School I was the hardest worker in my class. I was absolutely determined to master brain anatomy, which I did."

"No one disputes that."

"Well, my dear chap, since I have acquired my expertise, why labor further? My war is over. Before long I am going to open my own sanatorium and be independent. You'd be surprised how many rich families have one crazy member locked in a rear bedroom somewhere. Peering down those microscopes is for fanatics, like you."

When he had gone Sigmund sat idly on a high stool for a moment, his head down, thought:

"You mean *poor* men like me, who need discoveries and publications and *Dozenturen* and patients and earnings and a wife and a home. . . ."

He was transferred to the women's wards to round out his training. The mornings were spent in the B.Z. examining the newly admitted patients. The first-of-July heat was suffocating. Not the tiniest breath of air came in through the open windows. In the outside court the foliage drooped despondently in the fierce white glare of the summer sun. Sigmund did not own a lighter-weight suit; his body burned under the heavy winter clothing.

The first woman brought in was a thirty-five-year-old from Galicia who insisted on speaking in Polish. She had been arrested at the Schönbrunn castle for tacking pictures of saints onto the walls and trees. God had ordered her to do so, and her reward was that she would be the only one permitted in heaven. She refused to allow Sigmund to make a physical examination; when he unlocked the corridor to the female wards she picked up a chair and attacked another patient with it. Sigmund immediately ordered her put in the isolation ward. When she hit the attendants who attempted to clean her cell, she was transferred to the asylum at Gugging.

His next case was an oldish wife of a landowner from Weissenbach, a small meager woman with gray eyes and no teeth except her incisors. He found that she suffered from erysipelas which covered her bottom, genitals and the inner part of her thighs almost to the knees, for which he prescribed dressing with carbolic acid, ice and quinidine. She told him that she had been beaten by her husband on the head, once until she lost consciousness; another time he tore part of her hair out and threw her into the yard where she lay for an hour in the snow. Her husband had exclaimed when she came back into the house: "The beast is not yet dead!"

The woman bared her breasts. Sigmund called for a female attendant. The patient got very excited, lifted her skirt, behaved indecently, then soiled herself. Sigmund turned her over to the attending nurse.

Waiting for him was a middle-aged unmarried household maid with a thick nose. She was in deep depression. She had gone to the police herself, complaining about her sad condition, and asked to be sent to the hospital.

"Why are you melancholy, Fräulein?"

"I did household work for a high civil servant for eight years. I was dismissed with an excellent certificate. But this certificate destroyed me. When I go for a job everybody thinks I'm not suitable for a modest job. I haven't had work for two and a half years. Three months ago I tried to commit suicide by drinking vitriol but the hospital cured me. I'm afraid of going back into the world because there are many people but no human beings. In the street people look at me strangely. When I show people my actual certificate they tell me there was a punishable relationship between me and my employer. That's why I want to die. Doctor, if I stay here, will you help me get some poison?"

He examined the young wife of a grape grower from Lanzendorf. She was small and delicately built. She paced back and forth in the room with her head on her chest, gave her name correctly but would not answer any other questions. When he asked her whether she was married, she replied, "I don't know. Sometimes I can't remember anything. Even earlier I was forgetful."

"Would you like to stay here with us for a while, Frau Granz?"

"No, I must not live in a beautiful building like this. I have too many sins."

"Would you tell me what the sins are?"

"I don't deserve any meals. I've been bad and am becoming worse. I should be thrown out or killed. My parents should not have been so stupid as to marry. Then I would not have been in this distorted world. After their births, my parents should have been thrown into a well. I married a farmer I did not like in order to get out of my home. At home everything is distorted. Here everything is in order."

A nurse summoned him to come into the ward to care for a young unmarried tie sewer from Hungary. She had been admitted by Dr. Meynert, who had marked her diagnosis *Madness* because of hallucinations and hyperexcitement during which she spent hours on the window ledge trying to find a way to jump. Her records showed that she had been complaining about pains in the back of the head; that she was being persecuted by men; that she was compelled to approach them because voices demanded her to do so. During her first night she had had to be restrained in a rope crèche.

Sigmund ordered the netlike covering of her bed opened. The woman jumped up and tried to embrace him. She wept, complained about the bad treatment. Sigmund quieted her, asked when the pains had begun.

"Ten months ago. From an ailment in the stomach. I had always kept away from men and now I got the idea that I can only be healed by a man. I began to run at every man and to kiss and hug them. My family locked me in a room at home. I tried to escape by jumping out the window. That's when they had me brought here."

"What is that blood on your arm, Fräulein?"

"I bit myself. There is a man in my bed who wants to burn me."

She jumped out of bed, tore a piece of her dress, wrapped it around her throat and tried to strangle herself. Sigmund ordered two grams of chloral hydrate to be administered. She was soon asleep.

And so it went, this parade of pathetic souls: the thirty-seven-year-old spinster daughter of a farmer who had had a stillborn child as a young unmarried girl and was trying to convince everyone that she had not killed it, committed for running naked through the woods and telling the townspeople that every night someone was murdered in her parents' home and their bodies hung in the attic; the attractive married Viennese woman who saw ghosts and the Devil each day, saw the ceiling of the ward opening and people sticking their tongues out at her; the fifty-seven-year-old single-needle worker who heard voices and shooting, and saw her daughter lying full of blood in her own bed after being chopped by her husband; the woman in her late thirties who could not sleep nights because the body of her lover, Alexander, walked around with the head of her husband stuck on him, and who asked that a sofa be brought into the ward because the Holy Ghost would come and make love to her; the elderly spinster who heard the voices of police and the barking of dogs, and who saw city people staring at her and accusing her of taking dogs into her house to have intercourse through the mouth; the forty-year-old wife of a bank cashier, educated and well mannered, who believed that the whole city hated and avoided her because she had had illegitimate sexual intercourse, had acquired a venereal disease (she had none), and had infected her husband, who left her because of it. . . .

There were even more difficult patients to be served: the incoherent, disjointed, unfocused, living back ten, twenty, forty years, unable to recognize that they were in a hospital or that they were ill. He spent hours each day reading the cases being reported from Graz and Zurich, from Prague and Paris, Milan and Moscow, London and New York. Intense studies were being made of the hallucinations and delusions, the fantasies, anxieties, fears, the persecutions divided into minute categories so that the doctors could tell, as indeed Sigmund had determined from the monographs and books lying open on the desk before him, that these sicknesses did not arise in any one time or place or special set of circumstances. They were universal. The hospitals, the sanatoriums, the nursing homes, the asylums of the Western world were crowded with hundreds of thousands of these people.

Their ailments were diagnosed: craziness, madness, dementia praecox. The treatment was simple. Quiet them with chlorides and other drugs, give them rest, try to make them see the difference between reality and illusion, give them warm baths on this day and cold ones the next, electrical therapy and other massage; but very little of this, as far as he could fathom, had any appreciable effect. Sometimes, if the patients were at the beginning of a sickness, they could be reassured and returned home. However the records were discouraging; most of these unfortunates had recurrent attacks, were returned to the hospital or to prison or died by their own hands.

During these months Sigmund committed three patients to the Lower Austrian Insane Asylum, walking them over to the building on the knoll of the hill. Von Pfungen committed the same number, but Holländer's number was larger, with seven incurables, and Professor Meynert, who was called upon to judge the most difficult cases, was highest with thirteen.

The time in the "disturbed" wards had both an emotional and physical affect on him. He ate little, slept poorly, lost a number of pounds which his lean frame could not spare. The combination of heat, crowded wards and the continuing outbursts of violence and mania had caused his eyes to sink in their sockets and put a thin crease down each cheek. As an intern, or custodial physician, he was not supposed to become any more involved in the miseries of those suffering in the mind than those suffering in the body. Yet there was a subtle difference. For the patient with a goiter or gallstones a doctor felt sympathy; with the patient suffering from mania the doctor experienced fear. It was an instinctive reaction. Since he had never intended to work with the mentally deranged, he had not thought that he would get so deeply immersed. Now he began to sense, albeit dimly, that these unfortunate creatures had come too late to the fair.

For the pathologist it was an enormously rich field; there was so much about the human brain that still had to be understood in terms of structure and function. But for the attending physician who could give so little help? And for the patients, most of whom seemed to be beyond help? Looking back over the months and the hundreds of males and females he had treated, Sigmund thought dispiritedly:

"It is unfruitful, this psychiatry."

BOOK THREE

WALK A FINE LINE

BOOK THREE

Walk a Fine Line

IGNAZ SCHÖNBERG walked over twice a week from the university for a
visit, sharing Sigmund's light supper. The two friends read and studied
together under the light of the oil lamp on Sigmund's table. Ignaz,
who wanted to marry Minna as soon as possible, had undertaken a
heavy schedule. One evening he looked pale and listless. Sigmund put
his stethoscope to Ignaz's back and chest, tapped a finger laid over his
ribs.

"Ignaz, you need a rest."

"Some other year, Sig," Ignaz replied wearily.

"No, this year."

Sigmund decided to call on Ignaz's brothers. Alois was away but
Geza invited him to supper. Sigmund had seen a good deal of the
brothers because of his years of friendship with Ignaz. Geza was
heavy-featured and heavy-set, a hard worker who, early in life, had
declared that books were the natural enemy of man. Sigmund considered
him stupid and conceited and lost no time on the amenities.

"Geza, Ignaz's T.B. is getting worse."

"What do you want from me?"

"Money. Enough to give him a few weeks in the mountains."

"Why am I supposed to pay for him? I break my back for the gulden
I earn."

Sigmund softened his tone. "We all have to look out for ourselves.
But Ignaz is very precious."

"Why is he so precious? Because he reads poetry in Sanskrit? You
can't feed a hungry mouth with Sanskrit."

"If I can persuade Alois to contribute, will you give something too?
I'll take him myself. I don't want him traveling alone."

"All right," grumbled Geza. "I give. Don't I always?"

Sigmund took Ignaz to Stein-am-Anger in Hungary, leaving him with
stern instructions about taking care of himself. He had been home
a short while when Josef Breuer sent word to meet him at Fleischl's
apartment. The thin layer of skin over Fleischl's latest amputation had
broken open again. Fleischl was in misery. Breuer, who had brought
the morphine, gave him a shot of it. They were walking back across

the town in the steaming mid-July evening with the very stones of the sidewalks and buildings exuding heat, when a man came up to speak to Breuer. Sigmund dropped a few steps behind. Later Josef waited for Sigmund to catch up.

"That was the husband of one of my women patients. His wife had been behaving so peculiarly when she was out in society that he brought her in for treatment as a nervous case. There is little help I can give. These cases are always *secrets d'alcôve*."

"Whatever do you mean?" Sigmund asked in astonishment.

"The alcove containing the marriage bed, where neurotic cases begin and end."

Sigmund thought about this for a moment, then exclaimed, "Josef, I think you fail to realize how extraordinary the *matter* of your statement appears to me."

Breuer was silent. Sigmund walked by his side, puzzled. He had had no experience with "secrets of the alcove"; he sensed a potential danger here for a man who still had several years to wait for his own alcove. He could not readily grasp the idea that married couples did not always do well in their marriage beds. Certainly he and Martha would.

And yet . . . and yet . . . he had grown up in Vienna, a city which had earned the reputation of enjoying the greatest sexual freedom in Europe. He knew about the attractive young prostitutes in special houses, and the demimondes (call girls) who were always available. The more prosperous and less serious of his fellow students entering the university had quickly found themselves *Süsse Mädeln* from the country or the outlying workers' districts, keeping them as mistresses until graduation, at which time their "sweet girl" shed a few tears and dried them in time to see clearly which of the entering freshmen would be the next lover. Married women were approachable for assignations; he had observed a raised eyebrow by a fashionably dressed woman having five o'clock cakes at Demel's, a whispered word by a man to a lady alone at a coffeehouse; and there followed, he knew, the adventure and carnal excitement of a rendezvous. If one were caught there was always the danger of a challenge by an outraged husband; but the duels rarely proved fatal.

Sigmund Freud and his group of friends had known about this charming sexual *Schlamperei* since their Sperlgymnasium days but they had neither purse nor passion for it. They had been raised in the rigid moral code of the Old Testament; they believed in romantic love; spare and sparse gulden were wanted for the dozens of books they desperately coveted. But most important for these intellectual bookworms was the time and concentration that they guarded for their studies, discussions, clashes of ideas and philosophies. Dr. Sigmund Freud, who had dissected a dozen dead females, had grown up in sensual innocence of the live women about him.

Once home Sigmund and Josef Breuer sat in Breuer's upstairs office. Mathilde sent up a plate of refreshing *Kraut mit Rahm,* finely shredded cabbage cooked with sour cream and sprinkled with caraway seeds.

Josef commented, "If some of my cases didn't come from wealthy families they would be in your wards instead of my consulting room. There is a wandering group of neurotics in every city, running to each new doctor in the hopes of miracle cures for non-existent illnesses. The wandering band with wandering pain! Today it is in the head, tomorrow the chest, the next week the kneecap. It does no good to exorcise the pain from the shoulder or bowel; it is a monster that grows as fast as a doctor can cut it off. All doctors have witnessed this; it is part of their burden. But why? What causes it? Thousands of bright, healthy men and women who need an illness, need a pain. A new patient came to me yesterday, a middle-aged man important in the Viennese financial world who, when he walks the streets, sees himself surrounded by monsters, gnomes, bats. They brush past him and fly around his head. When he goes into a meeting, instead of seeing the faces of his associates he sees devils and creatures from horrible nether worlds. His business is prosperous, his wife and children are in good health. Yet he is living in a world of terror. I can see *what* he is suffering; but what is he suffering *from?*"

Josef shook his head in puzzlement and frustration.

"Tell me, Sigi, what are you getting these days in the wards?"

"I'm getting Johann, for instance, thirty-nine, a bachelor, former clerk of the Franco-Austrian Bank. For some weeks before he was admitted there had been increasing absent-mindedness, indecency at home as well as in public places, panic restlessness involving rising at four in the morning to rush about the city. He bought things without purpose, stole senselessly. Today he smashed several windows in the ward; when I asked him why, he replied:

"'My brother is a glazier and he should have some work. My father was a glazier, he died when he was seventy-one; my mother is alive and well. She runs through the city for eighteen hours a day. I only came here to see the pictures. There are no insane people here, only nice people. The food and service are excellent. I am going to write an article about it for the press. I speak five languages; I am enormously rich. I am going to hang myself if I am not taken out of here soon. I am going to give you a million gulden. Go to the *Börsenmakler* and buy securities from the lists.'"

"The classical symptoms. Madness moving toward idiocy," observed Josef.

"Then there is the patient whom I questioned in the B.Z. yesterday. He was quiet while I examined him but once made ready for bed he climbed on a window sill and threatened to jump through the glass. I had to put him in isolation. He told me, 'I don't know why I am here, I'm perfectly well. For eight nights I couldn't sleep. I always dream of the

Madonna. I have seen her in my bed. Parts of the world have perished, monkeys have become men and will reign over them. Look up, do you feel the sun dragging out your brains? It's pulling out my brains, sucking them out. . . .'"

Breuer mused over Sigmund's cases for a moment.

"The Psychiatric Clinic has always been a transmission belt for the asylum. Even so, you don't get the worst cases. The really bad ones are tried by the police and sent to the prisons. The ones that come under the heading of 'Moral Insanity.'"

"The kind Krafft-Ebing has been trying to defend in the courts of Germany?"

"Yes. The sadists who stab women in the streets, usually in the upper arm or in the rectum, and have an ejaculation at the same time. The fetishers who slash women's clothes or steal their handkerchiefs to masturbate into; the men who dig up dead bodies to have intercourse with; the pederasts who attack young boys; homosexuals caught committing obscene acts on each other in public lavatories; the male perverts who dress like women and solicit men; the exhibitionists who display their genitals in parks and theaters; the flagellants who whip each other; the female perverts who practice cunnilinction and are turned in by the girls they seduce . . .

"You're lucky, Sig, that you don't have to handle these moral insanity cases."

Sigmund shook his head morosely:

"Warm baths, quieting drugs, rest at a spa. We give them a few days or weeks of absolution. But we can't operate on the skull the way Billroth does on an intestine, cut out a diseased area and stitch the ends together. We have no quinine for this fever. We cannot take them off sugar the way we do diabetics, prop up their milk legs until the inflammation subsides. Brain anatomy has not yet provided us with a single cure."

Josef got up and paced the room.

"Sig, I had a purpose in asking you about your cases in the psychiatric wards. You cannot make a living from brain anatomy, much as you enjoy working in the laboratory. You cannot make a living from the insane unless you want to join your friend Holländer in opening a private sanatorium. You simply must get over to the Fourth Department under Scholz, and into nervous diseases."

2.

The best hour of the day generally came late, when the hospital was quiet and the chores finished. He sat relaxed, happy in the vivid presence evoked by Martha's picture on his desk, seeing her wave to him as she came up the path of the Belvedere garden to meet him, or walked by his side along the Beethovengang in Grinzing, embarrassedly turning to the side of the road to straighten a faltering stocking. As he read and reread her letters which reached him nearly every day he could hear her voice speaking the written lines, the low cultivated tone, the purity of diction, her gentle laughter.

He wrote her long, intimate letters, withholding nothing of importance: his work in the wards and the laboratory; how much he enjoyed the company of the other *Sekundarärzte*; his suggestion to Fleischl that he use the gold staining device for examination of the retina of the eye and Fleischl's acceptance. "To my joy because to teach an old teacher something is a pure, unmitigated satisfaction." How Breuer had suggested that he move on to nervous diseases. How he roared with delight while reading *Don Quixote*; and longed for her when he read Byron.

He loved to write, came alive with a pen in his hand. He wrote as he breathed, naturally, for writing resolved his ideas and refreshed him. He had considered himself a stylist ever since he had been given an *Excellent* on his German paper for the *Matura*. His professor had told him, "You possess what Johann von Herder, the German poet and philosopher, so nicely calls 'an idiotic style: at once correct and characteristic.'" Seventeen-year-old Sigmund Freud had taken the comment as a compliment, writing a friend, "I advise you to preserve my letters, have them bound, take good care of them—one never knows."

Martha's presence in his room did not fade; her scent overcame the smells of the laboratory that he brought back with him no matter how much he scrubbed with the hard brown soap. Her picture was the first thing his eyes rested on when he re-entered the room. Yet when he suffered an attack of sciatica or became exhausted, discouraged, depressed, he quarreled with her via the post. He could not reconcile himself to Mrs. Bernays having taken her daughters away from Vienna. Martha's first loyalty was to him! He accused her of weakness and cowardice in choosing easy paths instead of facing painful situations. Martha answered these pugilistic letters with:

"I love you and I love my family. I will give up neither and be disloyal to neither. I will not allow any relationship to be destroyed."

The upward turn came quickly, within a day or two, after some rest, a long walk in the woods, a bit of encouragement in his work. He realized that he was using these letters as a catharsis, working off his impatience and frustration at his slow progress and the bleak years ahead. He also realized that Martha was bravely facing a difficult situation: her fiancé! Then he would sit before her picture, grateful that it was not judging him, and write from two to ten pages of repentance, apology and protestations of his love. Since he always managed to get these letters to her by the seventeenth of the month, the anniversary of their engagement, he sensed dimly that his moods swung round the sun on their own cycle over which he was exercising no control. He was secure with Martha; he could not destroy her love. Was that why he indulged himself?

Toward the end of July the Breuers joined the exodus out of Vienna for their summer house in the mountains of the Salzkammergut. "I would like you to take care of a patient of mine, Herr Krell, who lives in Pötzleinsdorf," said Josef. "Ride out with me and I'll introduce you."

"What is Herr Krell suffering from?"

"Amyotrophic lateral sclerosis. He is a little past fifty. About a year ago he began to feel some clumsiness in his walk. Six months ago this was accompanied by a slow shrinking of the calves. During the past two months he has had increasing difficulty in drinking; he gags and chokes on liquids and some comes out of his nose."

"What is the cause?"

"We don't know."

"And the prognosis?"

"We can alleviate the symptoms, not the disease. Under the best of conditions, two to three years. Otherwise a year, no more."

"How do you help him?"

"You will see."

It was a comfortable middle-class home with well-tended gardens, furnished in the best Biedermeier, curved lines in the chairs and sofa backs, rails and supports, and straight lines richly decorated on the cabinets and chests.

Breuer introduced Herr Dr. Freud as his associate. Mrs. Krell offered coffee. The patient's ataxia had apparently increased since the last visit. Sigmund recognized the seriousness of his irregular stumbling gait. Breuer examined the patient's calves, then called for a glass of water and mixed into it a bromide powder.

"August should be a fine month for you, Herr Krell. Spend the days in your garden. Walk about as much as you like. And, Frau Krell, don't worry. Herr Dr. Freud can be reached at the Krankenhaus day or night and will come at once if you need him."

Back in his room he found Nathan Weiss waiting for him, excited and flushed. "Sig, I've made up my mind. Remember that mother and two daughters I told you about? I've decided to marry the older one. She won't be an easy conquest, I can tell you that. I am going to need help from an old boulevardier like you."

The courtship went badly. The girl was twenty-six, had already turned down a number of eligible suitors and quite honestly told Weiss that she did not feel any need for love. She criticized his manners, his loquaciousness, his statement of "I am the center of my universe." She insisted that he would have to change his entire personality. He brought Sigmund two letters she had written, asking for an opinion of her character as shown by what she wrote.

"From the letters, I would say she is sound, sober and respectable," responded Sigmund. "But I see little feminine refinement in her handwriting or expression."

"What are you talking about? She's extremely feminine. All I have to do is set her on fire with my love."

"But if she told you she feels no need for love?"

"How can she know if she needs love until she's felt love? The whole thing is an abstract theory until the right man comes along."

Sigmund asked quietly, "Nathan, are you sure you are the right man for this particular Brünnehilde? She seems reserved, demanding and not very yielding."

Not long after, Nathan declared:

"I'm depressed. She's grown melancholy, weeps for no reason, and takes no pleasure in my company. I set an early wedding date, her family is enthusiastic . . ."

"Nathan, the girl is conscientious. Don't press her too hard."

Taking advice was not one of Weiss's virtues. He spent a thousand gulden on presents for his fiancée, invested the balance of his savings to furnish their bridal apartment. Then he ran to Sigmund heartbroken.

"Sigmund, when I took her to see our magnificent home she said, 'Nathan, why don't you marry my sister instead?' "

"I implore you to accept the idea that she does not love you," urged Sigmund. "Take a long trip. You'll come back detached . . ."

"I don't want to be detached. I want to be attached. I can't bear the fact that this girl could refuse me. Granted, she's cool and prudish; after marriage I can force her to love me the way I've forced my way to success in everything else."

The marriage took place. Nathan, about to leave on his honeymoon, embraced Sigmund warmly.

"I'll see you in two weeks. I have a marvelous trip planned."

Dr. Freud turned his attention to Breuer's patient. The first few times he was summoned to Pötzleinsdorf it was for comfort and assurance. There had been no deterioration. A depressing heat clamped down on the narrow streets. There was not a breath of air. The patients in the enclosed courts of the Krankenhaus sopped up perspiration by rubbing their striped pajama tops across their chests. The only street activity was the occasional *Dienstmann* with cart, moving yet another family to a foothill village in the Wienerwald. Vienna seemed deserted. Then came a call on a beastly day. Sigmund was limp and dispirited. He did not feel that the long trip—Josef had warned him to take a *Fiaker*, no doctor could travel in an *Einspänner*, the one-horse carriage, or his patient would suffer a relapse of mortification—would serve any purpose. The instant he entered the Krell house he knew he had been wrong. Herr Krell's ataxia had taken a decided turn. That morning when he stood up and closed his eyes he had lost his balance and fallen to the floor.

And for the first time Dr. Sigmund Freud knew what it meant to be needed in a family home, as a physician. His listlessness fell away. He gave Herr Krell chloral hydrate to quiet him. When the man gagged on the liquid, he put him to bed, applied cool packs to his calves, massaged him. When Herr Krell dropped off to sleep, Sigmund calmed the anxious wife.

"It's just the summer heat. He'll be much quieter for the next day or two."

"We thank you, Herr Doktor, for coming all the way out here in this miserable weather."

Riding back to the city, enclosed in its ovenlike stone walls, he could not ignore the personal gratification he had experienced in being needed. He had entered a home filled with dread and left it with the family reassured.

He thought: "Poor man, he'll be dead this time next year. I didn't do anything to help him, except for the next few hours. Then why do I feel so exhilarated, as though I've been of some value in this world?"

Now he knew why so many doctors loved their practice and felt so strongly about their patients.

He was summoned twelve times to the Krell home before Josef Breuer returned. Herr Krell sent him sixty gulden, two dollars a visit plus his *Fiaker* fare. It was the largest sum of money he had earned. He gave forty gulden to his mother, paid something on account to Deuticke, the bookseller, settled half a dozen small debts around the hospital, and still had enough left to send Martha the dictionary she had been wanting, meager consolation for the nights when his loins ached so sorely for her that he had to jump out of bed, don his clothes and tramp blindly through the streets in an effort to exhaust himself by dawn.

The Sundays he spent in the Journal gave him a chance to read and write quietly; not many people chose or were obliged to be admitted to the hospital on the Lord's Day. The younger Aspirants came to him for counsel. When a disagreement arose between the *Sekundarärzte* and the Administration, Sigmund was selected to present their grievances. He logically laid out the points that needed correcting. The director agreed that the rules could be loosened in several directions.

Nathan Weiss returned to work but failed to visit him. The first time Sigmund encountered him at a meeting, he asked:

"How is marriage?"

Nathan looked away. "I've known better things."

A week later they met again. Nathan's only comment was, "I've been a wretched failure."

Early one morning Dr. Sigmund Lustgarten broke into Sigmund's room, green of face. Sigmund was still in bed.

"Have you heard?" cried Lustgarten. "It's Nathan Weiss. He hanged himself! In a public bath in the Landstrasse!"

It was a shattering blow. The entire hospital was struck dumb. This was the last man to commit suicide! Many reasons were propounded: he had been done out of a promised dowry; he had spent his savings for a domestic disaster; his rage had been caused by rejected passion. . . . Sigmund credited none of these theories. He found himself unable to talk about Nathan with his associates. Instead he sat at his desk and spent hours writing Martha a letter relating the story. He then went to call on Josef Breuer. The two men discussed the suicide.

"It is the most mysterious sickness of all," Josef said, "almost impossible to diagnose."

"Nathan seemed to have an egomaniacal passion for life . . ."

"Apparently not, or he couldn't have left it at the first adverse turn of fortune."

"Josef, I have the strange feeling that Nathan knew he was driving himself to defeat; that in pursuing that unfortunate girl he was providing himself with a reason to be dead."

3.

He made his discovery of a viable brain dye, though it took him several more months of lonely work deep into the night. He stayed with the original concept he had enunciated to Holländer, a mixture of bichromate of potash, copper and water. He evolved the further steps in the hardening process by placing the brain specimen in alcohol. The thin sections were washed in distilled water, then put into an aqueous solution of chloride of gold. With the aid of a wooden rod each specimen was removed from the solution some four hours later, washed and placed in a concentrated solution of caustic soda, which rendered it transparent and slippery. After two or three minutes he used a toothpick to take the preparations out of the soda, allowed the superfluous liquid to drain off. He then put the sections into a ten percent solution of iodide of potash, where they almost immediately became a tender rose color, changing into darker hues of red during the next five to fifteen minutes.

He transferred the preparation from an adult brain into alcohol and mounted it in the usual way. For the specimen from the brain or spinal cord of a newborn or embryo, he evolved a method of delicately bringing the preparation onto a glass slide by means of a camel's-hair brush, drying it without pressure and covering it with a piece of filter paper. It was an involved, tedious process, yet it enabled him to preserve the most sensitive slices.

By his new method the fibers showed pink, deep purple, black or even blue and were brought distinctly into view, scattered everywhere through the white and gray substance. In the embryo, the nerve fibers were strikingly clear. Those bundles which were already possessed of a medullary sheath were distinguished by darker coloring from the others. Examined under the highest possible microscope, the single axis-cylinders were so well defined as to enable him to count their number. It proved of great service in his tests on the nerve tracts of the central nervous system of the newborn child.

He called in a group of friends to show them the process. Meynert and Von Pfungen were as surprised as they were pleased. Lustgarten asked to use it on some skin tests, Horowitz on his bladder experiments and Ehrmann on his studies of the adrenal glands. That night, exhilarated by their enthusiasm, he began writing A New Method for the Study of the Course of Nerve Fibers in the Central Nervous System, which was later published in the Centralblatt für die medizinische Wissenschaften, as he had predicted to Holländer.

He wrote triumphantly of his success to Martha; every success and forward movement, no matter how small, brought them closer to their wedding day.

Two more weeks of experimentation brought him the fixative he wanted; now the slides could be stored in the reference filing cabinet and be used for future studies. He was elated. He took the preparations to the physiology laboratory to show to Fleischl and Exner. Professor Brücke appeared.

"Anything to be seen, Herr Doktor?" he asked.

"Yes, Herr Professor, brain gildings."

"Ah, that's very interesting, especially since gold has the reputation of not being much use for this."

"But this is a new method, Herr Hofrat."

Brücke concentrated on the microscope, murmured, "I see." When the series was completed he straightened up, his fierce blue eyes pleased and proud.

"Your methods alone will make you famous yet."

Now that his system was perfected he wrote an expanded version for the Archiv für Anatomie und Physiologie; and later wrote in English a similar account for the British Brain: A Journal of Neurology. Barney Sachs corrected it for him to make sure his English was perfect; Sachs was a favorite in the laboratory, for he was also translating Professor Meynert's now completed Psychiatry for publication in London and New York. Darkschewitsch asked if he could translate the article into Russian for his native neurological journals. That night he wrote to Martha:

"Apart from its practical importance, this discovery has an emotional significance for me as well. I have succeeded in doing something I have been trying to do over and over again for many years. . . . I realize that my life has progressed. I have longed so often for a sweet girl who might be everything to me and now I have her. The same men whom I have admired from afar as inaccessible, I now meet on equal terms and they show me their friendship. I have remained in good health and done nothing dishonorable; even though I have remained poor. . . . I feel safe from the worst fate, that of loneliness. Thus if I work I may hope to acquire some of the things that are still missing and to have my Marty, now so far away and lonely as her letter shows, close by me, have her all to myself, and in her tender embrace look forward to the further development of our life.

"You have shared my sadness; now today share with me my joy, beloved."

When he had sealed the envelope he wrote on the back of it, in English: "Hope and Joy."

Despite Nathan Weiss's death, Professor Franz Scholz informed him that there would be no opening in the Fourth Department until after the New Year. Sigmund promptly got himself admitted to Dermatology, the department of syphilis and contagious diseases, continuing to be a *Sekundararzt*. He started on October first, to be greeted by young Dr. Maximilian von Zeissl, whose father had been chief of the department until the year before.

Von Zeissl was Sigmund's age, a blond with a small downy beard and agate-blue eyes. His father, Professor von Zeissl, had brought the boy into the wards when he was six. The syphilis wards contained some of the most horrible sights to be seen in any hospital, decayed noses, gangrenous eyes, green ulcerated cheeks, chancre upon chancre eating out ears, a mouth, half a chin . . . Instead of being repulsed, the boy had been fascinated. Once he had finished at the university and had his M.D. he had gone straight as an arrow for Dermatology. He had only recently become a *Sekundararzt*, but it was his intent to succeed his father as chief of the division.

He welcomed Sigmund into his office; the world's literature on syphilis was neatly stacked on the shelves.

"Let me take you under my wing," he said. "I love to teach and it will be the first time I've had an opportunity to work with a man who has had your background in histology and pathology."

"Just assume that I am an undergraduate, Herr Doktor, I am completely untrained in this area."

"I will remedy that situation. First and foremost, our bible in these wards is mercury. When we pray we thank God for its therapeutic power. Did you know that the Arabs used it as much as five hundred years ago? Despite this there are many hospitals and doctors in Europe who refuse to use mercury. I am well aware of the abuses; I know that not all cases of syphilis are cured with quicksilver; I know that the treatment is not suitable to all the different periods of the malady. But I have also seen how much help we have given, even to those who are going into mental deterioration. . . ." He laughed. "As you can see, I am a fanatic on this subject. You have no objections to fanatics, Herr Doktor?"

Sigmund laughed.

"If you mean single-mindedness, what other kind of man can make a great discovery?"

"I've heard of some that have been made by sheer accident! Come, let us go into the wards. We have our patients divided into Fournier's categories and we work through four methods. First there is the dermic method, putting the unction on the part of the skin where the sweat glands are most numerous, in the armpit, the groin, the soles of the feet." He indicated a case of very early outbreak. "We simply touch these sores with tincture of iodine or Van Swieten's solution. In the secondary period we use mercury. After some two months of treatment we send the patient home for two months to overcome the effects of the medication. Then we bring him back in for a tertiary period in which we treat with iodide of potassium only."

Next he demonstrated the hypodermic method, beginning with the subcutaneous injection of chloroform:

". . . in the hip, right at this spot. It is painful to men and nearly always unendurable for the women."

A disagreeable odor of bisulphite of carbon hung over the wards. During the next weeks Sigmund listened intensively to Von Zeissl. He was never going to become a dermatologist but needed to learn how to handle the cases that might come into his office.

"We plan to treat our serious cases for three to four years," said Von Zeissl. "The patient will be getting mercury only ten months out of the first twenty-four months. At the end of the second year, along with the mercury, we administer iodide of potassium. In the third and fourth years we drop the mercury and go with iodide of potassium alone. Sometimes we've been brought in too late, sometimes we cannot check the disease and the patient dies. However, we manage to arrest a good deal of the syphilitic spread. The physiological action of mercury is obscure. I am working on that; also an attempt to isolate the virus syphiliticus."

Sigmund learned how much mercury to mix in the baths; the respiratory, or dermopulmonary method, in which he stood the patient in a box, closed the door and burned medicinal tablets of cinnabar or corrosive sublimate to rout the virus out of the lungs. Using the alimentary-canal method, he fed the patient metallic mercury, blue pills of bichloride of mercury, or iodide of potassium in a syrup of orange peel; learned when to start the cathartic milk diet. He watched Von Zeissl prepare solutions of gold, silver and even copper, hoping to find quicker ways of arresting the disease.

Partly because he could not get the smell of bisulphite of carbon out of his nostrils or his clothes, he buried himself in the hospital for the first weeks of his training, even refusing to attend the wedding of his sister Anna to Eli Bernays, with whom he was still feuding. He made his rounds, served his turns in the Journal as admitting physician, continued to work in Meynert's laboratory between his rounds of the wards, and spent the evenings reading the periodicals.

Syphilis was a venereal disease and as such was a dirty name. There was no way one could acquire the illness with honor or respectability, like tuberculosis or angina pectoris, though there were plenty of wives in the female wards who had contracted it innocently from husbands who had not so innocently contracted it from the prostitutes of Vienna. Soldiers, who had the highest incidence of syphilis in the country, were sent to the military hospital but all others who wanted care were brought to the Allgemeine Krankenhaus, since few, if any, of the other hospitals would take in anyone with a communicable disease. As with the mentally ill who did not get to Meynert's Clinic, there were many syphilitics hidden away by families who could not bear to face the disgrace. Like the psychiatric patient, these people were pariahs. Sigmund found himself caught up in an emotion compounded of revulsion and pity.

4.

The IV Medizinische Abteilung was a catch-all for the baffling illnesses, particularly the nervous disorders which the Central Admitting Office of the Allgemeine Krankenhaus did not know how to dispose of. It was supported by the District of Lower Austria and the municipality of Vienna and had to accept any patient from Vienna or the surrounding villages who needed hospital treatment. Primarius Dr. Franz Scholz had found ingenious ways of getting around that stipulation, as Sigmund found on New Year's Day, 1884, when he was escorted through the five wards of the Fourth Department. There were one hundred and thirteen beds to accommodate the huge numbers of sick. Scholz conceived it his duty to remove every patient from his clinic as fast as he could; sometimes before the diagnosis was complete or control of the illness anywhere in sight.

"Wards 87 through 90 are a clearinghouse," Dr. Scholz told his new Junior *Sekundararzt*. "They are not a rest home. Examine, record and move the patients out."

Dr. Scholz, sixty-four years old, had become famous in medical circles twenty-two years before for developing and perfecting the technique of subcutaneous injection, using a hypodermic syringe. He had started as a philosophy student at the University of Prague and come to Vienna for his medical education. For some sixteen years he had been in a position of power at the General Hospital, first as chief surgeon, then in charge of medical research. Sigmund knew his reputation. In his young years Scholz had been a brilliant innovator; he had published in the Vienna medical journals, had made important contributions to the contamination statistics of syphilis, done a study on *Mental Diseases of Prisoners in Solitary Confinement*. In his early forties, after the medical world put into general use his technique of subcutaneous shots and honored him for his pioneering work, the flair for original investigation died out. He had settled back comfortably into the role of administrator.

He was a heavy-set man, wearing thick coats and vests, with one of the most effulgent stands of mustache and beard favored by the hirsute of Vienna. To compensate for the baldness on top of his head, he wore his back hair several inches thick and down to his coat collar; a formidable-looking man, it was conceded, with his huge bony Roman nose and sharp eyes. To Sigmund it seemed tragic that he no longer searched out scientific problems but was content to keep down the costs of his department and considered balancing the budget an act of faith. The *Sekundarärzte* were denied expensive medicines or new drugs, electric machines or other equipment which they thought might help the patient. Sigmund was immediately told of Scholz's passionate insistence that the beds in the wards be the regulation distance apart.

"But you will find that this is a good department in which to learn," said Senior *Sekundararzt* Josef Pollak, six years older than Sigmund. "As long as your methods don't require money, Scholz will let you strictly alone. If you have to cadge extra days for the really sick ones, that will serve to develop your ingenuity."

Sigmund was glad to be in Nervous Diseases at last, the department in which Josef Breuer thought he would have his greatest opportunity. Yet it was a sharp turn in the road; not only was there no teaching, lecturing or demonstrations, there were no research laboratories attached. Josef Pollak was working with Exner in Brücke's laboratory on otological machinery. He said *sotto voce*:

"I want to specialize in disturbances of the ear. I've had enough of nervous diseases! I feel as though I'm about to catch a few of the more revolting ones myself. By the way, all young doctors working under Scholz have to remain staunch friends; it's the only way we can put down the *Primarius*."

Sigmund asked Professor Meynert's permission to continue in the brain anatomy laboratory.

He found his charges in the Fourth Court a mixed group, result, in good part, of the "eyesight" judgment of the *Journaldienst* who admitted them off the street. The process kept Primarius Scholz furious: his beds were filled with patients who patently belonged in other departments! He transferred them fast. The other *Primarii* were not offended; every department was interested in nervous diseases, for the nervous system affected the health of every part of the body.

By getting up early Sigmund could finish his round of the wards by nine-thirty and be in Meynert's laboratory by ten. He made a second round of the wards after midday dinner, finishing by five. He then read and studied through supper and returned to Meynert's laboratory to work until midnight. So many cases of facial paralysis were coming into both Meynert's and Scholz's wards that he decided to do a study of these pareses, and facial tics as well.

Early in his first week an impoverished tailor's apprentice was admitted to the ward. He had had a bad attack of scurvy. Sigmund found his body to be covered with the black and blue blotches caused by hemorrhages below the skin. The young man proved apathetic under examination; there were no other symptoms. The next morning the chap was unconscious. The evidence suggested a cerebral hemorrhage. Sigmund returned to the bed after he had toured the ward and remained most of the morning and afternoon, annotating the development of the illness. There was nothing he could do but it was important to learn what was wrong. At seven o'clock that evening a symmetrical paralysis developed. An hour later the man was dead. That night and the next morning Sigmund wrote an eighteen-page paper on his observations and his diagnosis of which part of the brain had been affected. When the autopsy proved him right, he sent the paper off to the *Medical Weekly*. It earned him ten gulden he badly needed, and established him among his associates in the Fourth Department.

The department also had its *Beobachtungszimmer*. The B.Z. was under the command of Dr. Josef Pollak, who enlarged Sigmund's diagnostic techniques. Sigmund's first case was a forty-two-year-old woman suffering from acromegaly. Over the past five years she had noted that her shoe size had gotten considerably bigger, that her hands were growing larger. Her husband had been aware that her facial features were becoming gross. She was not ill, though she had a general sense of weakness. Sigmund diagnosed it as a tumor of the pituitary gland.

"What begins it, and what's the treatment?" he asked Pollak.

The Senior *Sekundararzt* shrugged.

"Nobody knows, Sig. And there is no treatment. The grossness occurs where there is bony structure. The prognosis? She can live for fifty years. The grossness will increase up to a plateau, then level off."

"How long do we keep her here if there is no treatment?"

"Just long enough to study her."

The next patient it was his duty to examine was a twenty-five-year-old man who had developed sudden and excruciating head pains during intercourse. He described them as mainly from the back of the head, "a feeling of hot water" going down his neck. Neither Dr. Freud nor Dr. Pollak had any notion what could be bothering him. They sent him home. Ten days later, while having a bowel movement, he had another severe pain in the head and collapsed. By the time they brought him into the hospital he was in a coma. Primarius Scholz was called. He declared it apoplexy. Pollak looked at the man's fundus with the ophthalmoscope and saw a hemorrhage in the eye. He said in an aside to Sigmund:

"It's an aneurysm. There is a balloon on the wall of the artery which gets bigger and makes the wall thinner, until it bursts. It's a congenital anomaly; he was born with it."

The man died that night. Under autopsy they found the loose, ruptured aneurysm. The attacks had been caused by straining: at intercourse and to get a bowel movement. The strain had raised the blood pressure and exploded the balloon. Josef Pollak had redeemed himself.

The next morning he said to Sigmund, "Come with me into ward 89; I'm going to try an experiment. It's that thirty-year-old attractive woman who has been in the hospital for months and hasn't been able to move her legs. She also suffers numbness to the waist. Yet there is not one objective evidence of disease. Her reflexes are normal."

They went into the ward. Pollak said gravely:

"Fräulein, last night we completed tests on a new drug. It can produce a movement of your legs within sixty seconds. However it is extremely dangerous; it can cause death. If it were my legs I would take the gamble. What do you say, Fräulein? I have a dose of the medicine in this hypodermic syringe."

The patient shuddered. She whispered, "It can kill me, Herr Doktor? How soon?"

"Within a week. But you could also be cured of the paralysis within sixty seconds. Wouldn't you rather be dead than be paralyzed for the rest of your life?"

The woman closed her eyes for a moment, shocked at Pollak's bluntness, then opened them wide.

"Inject the medicine."

Josef Pollak made the injection high on the arm. Sigmund knew there was no such new drug and was terrified that the patient might react to Pollak's suggestion and expire before their eyes. Before half a minute had passed he saw her legs begin to tremble under her gown and at the end of a minute she had moved one of them up into the air. She cried, "I can move. I can move my legs! I am not paralyzed any more!"

Pollak patted her shoulder, wiped the perspiration off her forehead. "You are a brave woman. You have saved your own life. Now you can return to normal."

As they walked away Sigmund asked quietly:

"What was that miraculous new drug, H_2O?"

"Precisely. This was a case of hysteria. I doubt that it was malingering."

"Why did you frighten the poor woman so?"

"Because the element of danger must be there. Sometimes the resolution to face death gives the courage to face life."

Sigmund shook his head, bemused. "Herr Doktor, you ought to be acting for the Karlstheater. That was one of the most convincing performances I've ever seen."

Pollak threw him a shrewd look. "What makes you think a doctor doesn't have to be an actor? We act all the time. To the man with a fatal disease we turn a reassuring smile and tell him that he is suffering from nothing that cannot be cured by a strong physic. When a neurotic woman tells us that no doctor has been able to help her, we put on our serious face, inform her that she has a rare disease and give her a bottle of sugar pills. This cures her . . . for at least thirty days. If we are completely baffled by a patient's symptoms we put on our most intelligent expression and murmur, 'Yes, yes, we have our diagnosis now and should start getting results very quickly.'"

Sigmund thought with some longing of the comparative honesty of the laboratory. What could be proved to be true under a microscope was true, and what was false was false.

5.

There were times when it appeared that the stars must be conjoining against him. His thirty-six-dollar salary as *Sekundararzt* was all he had. Even the tiniest additional income ceased. There were no patients, no students requiring tutoring, no medical publications to review for the journals. His clothes were growing threadbare and he could no longer afford to go to the barber to have his hair or beard trimmed. He went for days without a gulden in his pocket, cut off from his *Stammtisch* in the coffeehouse and his occasional companionable supper with the other interns. He became too embarrassed even to browse among the new publications at the bookstore. Though he had had scant money to spare for the theater, he had been able occasionally to join a group of his companions at the university at six in the morning to wait in line for the tickets which would allow them to stand in line again at five in the afternoon at the Hofoper or Theater an der Wien to buy a standing-room ticket, then race up the stairs to get a front position where one had a protective railing to lean against. He had stood from five in the afternoon until midnight to hear Mozart's *The Magic Flute, Figaro* or *Don Giovanni*.

Since the middle years of the Sperlgymnasium he had saved his pocket money, sometimes for weeks, to see the finest plays of German literature done by the repertory actors of the National Theater near the Hof: Goethe's *Faust*, Schiller's *Wilhelm Tell*, Grillparzer's *Die Ahnfrau*. The greatest treat of all was when his parents or a friend took him on his birthday to see Shakespeare's *Hamlet* or *Macbeth* or *Twelfth Night*, whole passages of which he knew by heart. In the summer months he was amused by the light comedies and bawdy farces in such outdoor theaters as the Fürst in the Prater, or the Thalia. The theaters of Vienna were the most effective matrimonial agencies; the young people promenaded during the several very long entr'actes, catching an eye, wangling an introduction, starting the flirtatious "salon chatter" that led to invitations, friendships, marriage. Sigmund and his friends had been too poor and had too far to go in their professions to be caught in the marriage mart, but elaborately gowned and groomed young folk from all over the Empire had come to the capital city to make a handsome and convenient alliance. The spectacle was often as interesting as anything being acted on the stage.

The Philharmonic played in the Musikvereinsgebäude, and one o'clock of a Sunday in the Musikvereinsgebäude was *the* place of the week in Vienna. Sigmund had been able to get in only once or twice because a subscription to the concerts was frequently a family's most valuable possession, handed down from father to son. The *Abonnenten*, those who had the same seats every season, would have incurred more social obloquy for selling their subscription than their virtue. Genuine music lovers who could not get in complained that half of the orchestra seats were occupied by the legendary "Frauen" Xanthippes who, all Austria insisted, slept nine times through Beethoven's Ninth Symphony.

The deprivation of the Philharmonic concert was not far-reaching. Vienna resounded with music. Military bands blared away; Viennese popular marches echoed from the Ronacher Theater by the famous Deutschmeister regimental band; in the Kursalon of the Stadtpark an orchestra played romantic melodies; in the Volksgarten one could hear Mozart and Beethoven; in the Gartenbau Restaurant, enchanting Viennese waltzes. In the evenings folk singers entertained in the beer and wine gardens, under bowers surrounded by trees.

"Why should we not love music?" the Viennese asked. "Did we not invent it? Most of the world's great music was written right here, or

in the villages surrounding us, by Mozart, Beethoven, Schubert, Haydn.
. . . What other city could match such an array?"

Vienna loved her music. "And why not?" asked her detractors. "Can
you imagine a better way to keep from thinking?"

Sigmund finally reached the point where he had no kreutzer with
which to buy the stamps for his letters to Martha. He went home only
rarely, for he did not want his parents to see how seedy he looked.
The family was in dire straits as well, the cupboard bare. Amalie awoke
each morning to pray that manna would fall through the kitchen ceiling. Guilt weighed heavily on him; here he was, nearly twenty-eight,
a highly trained professional, but he could contribute nothing to the
family, which was barely subsisting on Alexander's wage of six gulden
a week. Mitzi had been promised a job as a *bonne* in Paris, but not
until summer. Dolfi and Pauli were also looking for jobs. Jakob had
been persuaded by a Rumanian cousin to make a trip to Odessa where
a good business opportunity was presenting itself. He had returned
empty-handed, and crushed.

Sigmund bumped into his father accidentally one chilly April afternoon on the Franzenring between the Rathaus Park and the gleaming
white Burgtheater, ten years in the building and still several years
from completion. Jakob was half a block away, his thin chin buried
in the collar of his heavy overcoat, scuffling a little. Sigmund loved
his father deeply; he had had nothing but warm affection and support
from him from the moment of his birth. He put a bright smile on
his face, stood still on the sidewalk and let Jakob walk into his arms.
He kissed his father on both cheeks, then conjured up the biggest
lie he could think of.

"Papa, how wonderful to meet you. I was coming home for the
Jause to tell you the news. I have some money coming, a respectable
sum."

A small humorous smile came into Jakob's eyes. "Sigmund, your
little toe is cleverer than my head; but you should stick to medical
science. You have no talent for fairy stories."

"Is there something on the horizon for you, Papa?"

"Of course. I have good projects and high hopes."

Sigmund raced through the park, past the university and up the
Währinger Strasse to the Krankenhaus. Once in his office, he wrote a
letter to his half brothers in Manchester asking that they send Jakob
enough money each month to preserve their father's health and dignity.
As soon as he could complete his training he would support Jakob,
meanwhile they owed it to their father . . . Philipp and Emanuel sent
a generous sum.

A few evenings later in response to a summons, he went to visit
his old friend, Professor Hammerschlag, who lived with his wife and

children in the Brandstätte. Hammerschlag had been Sigmund's teacher at the Sperlgymnasium. He was retired now, after fifty years of service, on a modest but adequate pension. Hammerschlag had a paternal attitude toward Sigmund; he had loaned him small sums during his university days. At first Sigmund had been ashamed to accept money from a man in such modest circumstances. Hammerschlag told him:

"I suffered great poverty in my own youth. I can see nothing wrong in accepting help from those who can afford it."

Josef Breuer, also helping Sigmund, agreed. Sigmund said, "Very well, I guess I can be indebted to good men and those of our faith without a feeling of guilt."

Fleischl, when he heard this sentiment as he too was trying to lend Sigmund a few gulden, nearly took his head off.

"Now what kind of parochialism is that? You are willing to be indebted to 'good men of your own faith.' Does money have a religion? Is there a difference between Jewish debts and Catholic debts? When you are a prosperous doctor are you going to refuse to lend money to a Christian medical student who needs help? You are not! Sig, you have fewer ghetto remnants than any Jew, and I've worked with the best of them. Prejudices are chains. You refuse to conform to any of the externals of your religion, yet somewhere in the back of your mind you're still making invidious distinctions. You simply must batter down the residue of those walls."

"You're right, Ernst. I will try," Sigmund had answered thoughtfully. "And thank you for the loan."

Hammerschlag combed his scant white hair forward over his forehead, leaving only his gentle Talmudic eyes and short nose visible between the white mustache and beard.

"Sigmund, my son Albert needs help at the Medical School. He's having problems in one or two areas. Can you do anything for him?"

"Of course. Have him come to my apartment between five and six. I'll brush him up in his weak subjects."

"I knew you'd say that. But that was not my reason for asking you to drop in. A rich acquaintance has given me fifty gulden for a worthy young man in need. I mentioned your name, and he agreed it should be you."

Sigmund walked to the other end of the room, gazed sightlessly at the Hammerschlags' worn furniture. How could word of his desperate straits have reached Professor Hammerschlag? And how could the man afford to give up fifty gulden of his small monthly pension? It was an incredible act of kindness.

"Professor Hammerschlag, I won't conceal the fact that I need the money. But I simply cannot take it."

Hammerschlag pressed the notes into Sigmund's hand. "Use it. Lighten your burdens."

Sigmund gulped. "You know, Professor, I must give it to my family."

"No! I am against such a move. You are working hard and cannot afford at this moment to support other people." Then Hammerschlag relented. "Very well, give half the money at home."

These were times when Sigmund thought, in the privacy of his own brainpan, that the astrologists might have a point: at certain periods the planets became obstructionist and everything went badly; then, for no reason one could discern, everything started to go right. A medical pupil was sent to him for a complete course in brain anatomy, for which the student would pay handsomely if Dr. Freud would cram it into a four-week period. A friend sent him a patient, the fruit seller from the Three Ravens, where one turned off the Seitenstettengasse. She suffered from a continual buzzing in the ears. Sigmund had her ears examined by Dr. Pollak to make certain there was nothing organically wrong, then treated her with electricity. The noise of the machine must have drowned out the buzzing, for she went home cured. The next morning she returned with a basket of fruit for the Herr Doktor. Josef Paneth sent word from the Physiology Institute that he would like to visit with Sophie, whom he had married six months before, and would drop in for the *Jause* the following afternoon, bringing little sandwiches and cakes. Would Sigmund please prepare the coffee? The Paneth wedding had been beautiful; after the religious service there had been dinner for nearly a hundred at the Riedhof Restaurant; a band played waltzes, an afternoon of entertainment had been provided by the finest singers, dancers and acrobats Josef could find. He did not need to play the poor boy. He had a *gemütliches* wife who kept open house so that his friends could enjoy good food and drink and cigars at least one day a week. Frau Paneth had begun to dress Josef in the best woolens, shirts and boots available. His days of living like an anchorite had been dissolved.

Sigmund commented on how well he looked.

"I have found to my delight that my bride has more brains than I have," exclaimed Josef. "See this marvelous idea she came up with. Sophie, show Sig the bankbook. *The Sigmund Freud Foundation.* We have deposited fifteen hundred gulden into an account in your name. The interest each year amounts to eighty-four gulden, which will enable you to visit Martha."

Sigmund stared at his friend, uncomprehending.

"Josef, Sophie, what are you saying? . . . Fifteen hundred gulden in the bank for me? So that I can use the interest to go to Wandsbek? . . ."

Josef chuckled. "Oh, nothing so restricted. The fifteen hundred gulden are yours to use for any purpose. If you want to marry right away, the money is yours. If you want to set up your medical practice here in Vienna, or flee to America, the money is yours."

"Josef, it is a story out of Hans Christian Andersen." His hand trembled; he spilled some of the coffee from the pot onto the cloth. Sophie took the pot from him. He murmured, "I have received acts of friendship; perhaps I've been able to do a few modest ones in return. But this is magnificence! My children will bless you unto the seventh generation."

When the Paneths had left, Sigmund took the bankbook, the first he had ever owned, and set it on the desk next to Martha's picture. He determined that the money was not to be frittered away on momentary needs, no matter how pressing. The interest he would withdraw as often as the bank allowed and turn it over to his parents. However the master sum would have to be saved for a very urgent purpose; either marriage as Sophie favored, or, as Josef had said, the opening of his private practice.

The planets did indeed seem to be orbiting properly. Ignaz Schönberg also received good news. Professor Monier Williams invited him to Oxford University to work with him in editing a new Sanskrit dictionary. He offered a salary of £150, and Ignaz's name on the title page as collaborator. It would be most important in getting his university professorship. The Bernays sisters would receive letters of good cheer.

The sick continued to pour into Scholz's Nervous Diseases even as they had into Billroth's Surgery, Nothnagel's Internal Medicine, Meynert's Psychiatry and Von Zeissl's Dermatology. A woman of thirty had fallen off a ladder and hit the back of her head on a rock. She had been brought into the hospital unconscious. Sigmund got her two hours later; blood was coming out of her left ear. He recognized a brain concussion with a basal fracture of the skull, the fracture going through the petrous bone, with a tear in the eardrum. The proper procedure was to let her alone. She would probably wake up by that evening. They had only to guard against a meningitis infection of the brain covering. He would be able to send her home in four days. This he did, though she still had a headache and deafness on the left side.

For the following patient he needed Dr. Karl Koller in Ophthalmology: a bookkeeper complained of headaches and could not see the numbers on the right side of his ledgers. He also had haziness on the left side of his vision when he looked straight ahead. Koller put his hands on the side and to the rear of the man's head. Slowly he brought them forward. First the doctor's right hand entered the patient's field of vision, and then, when it was close to him, the left. Now Sigmund knew from his brain dissections where the tumor would be: in the pituitary area, pressing up between the optic nerves. The man would be blind in one to five years. There was no help for him; no use to keep him except to complete the record. He was advised to find work at something where his eyes were not so important.

Day after day they came; hundreds of them, all ages, sizes, shapes, with all degrees of illness. There were the patients with amyotrophic lateral sclerosis, suffering clumsiness in their walk and ataxia; there was cerebral thrombosis with one side or the other paralyzed; there was locomotor ataxia; progressive muscular atrophies with the slow wasting away of the muscles; cases of multiple sclerosis accompanied by convulsions; strokes; lead poisoning; brain tumors; meningitis; patients who jerked, trembled and fell; patients with sciatica, hernia, aberrations of the senses.

The most difficult task of the doctor in Nervous Diseases was the alleviation of pain. There were bromides in a solution of water, chloroform, opium. He gave himself a course in the *Materia Medica,* learning the natural history of drugs, their physiological properties, dosage and remedial application.

And then there were the hysterics, all of them women, since the word "hysteria" came from the Greek word *hyster,* meaning uterus. Men did not have a uterus and therefore could not become hysterical. Early medical books stated that if the uterus moved around in a woman it caused various kinds of outbreaks; the treatment was to get it back into its proper place. Sigmund recalled the case of the woman to whom Dr. Pollak had given an injection of water. Yet he found that it was also easy to be fooled. He judged one case to be hysteria, and when the patient died a few days later the autopsy proved there had been a cancer. The hysteria had existed side by side with the fatal malady. He reasoned:

"Let that be a warning to me that I must never oversimplify! Behind illnesses there are other illnesses, and behind those perhaps even a third complicated row of disturbances."

Here was an area of investigation that could be as important and exciting as the research in Meynert's laboratory.

6.

He came upon the subject by accident, while reading the December issue of the *Deutsche medizinische Wochenschrift,* an article by Dr. Theodor Aschenbrandt about experiments performed on Bavarian soldiers during the fall maneuvers. The article was called The Physiological Effect and Importance of Cocaine. Certain phrases jumped out of the page at him: ". . . suppression of hunger . . . increase of the capacity to endure strain . . . increase of all mental powers." Dr. Aschenbrandt reported on six cases. Sigmund found himself reading with intense interest:

"On the second day of the march, it was a very hot day, the soldier T. collapsed from exhaustion. I gave him a tablespoonful of water containing twenty drops of cocaine *muriaticum* (o,5:10). About five minutes later T. got up by himself, continued the march for several kilometers to the point of destination; in spite of a heavy pack and the summer heat, he was fresh and in good shape on arrival."

He read through the next five cases, asking the key questions and searching for answers. Did this renewed energy on the part of the soldiers come out of their own reservoir of strength? Or had the twenty drops of cocaine created a totally new strength? What were the properties in cocaine that created the endurance?

There flashed into his mind an article he had read in the *Detroit Therapeutic Gazette* a month or so before on the same subject. He went down to the reading room, found the *Gazette* in an elongated row of magazines and took it to his room for study. He then glanced at his watch on the desk before him and saw that there was still time to get over to the library of the Surgeon General's office. In the Index Catalogue he found an article, *Erythroxylum coca*, which contained a bibliography of the literature on the drug. He made his way back to the physiology laboratory. Ernst Fleischl gave him an introduction to the Society of Medicine, which had a good medical library, and wrote a note assuming responsibility for any books Dr. Freud might use.

The evidence, when put together from a dozen sources, was staggering. "In fact," Sigmund thought, "it strains one's credulity." In a series of articles from Lima, Peru, stories were told of how the Indians used coca as a stimulant from early youth and continued to use it throughout their lives without harmful effect; they employed it when they were facing a difficult journey; when they were taking a woman. When their strength was going to be called on for great and continued exertion they increased their customary dosage. Valdez y Palacios maintained that "by using coca the Indians are able to travel on foot for hundreds of hours and run faster than horses without showing signs of fatigue." Tschudi's articles cited a case in which a half-breed had been able to work at the hard manual labor of excavation for five days and nights without sleeping for more than two hours a night, consuming nothing but the coca. Humboldt wrote that when he went to equatorial countries this was a generally known fact. There were reports that if taken in excessive amounts cocaine could lead to digestive complaints, or emaciation, depravity and apathy; in fact many of the symptoms were similar to alcoholism and morphine addiction. However no such case was reported where the drug had been taken in moderation.

What fascinated Sigmund even more were the reports, as early as 1787, of the beneficent effects of coca on psychiatric patients. Antonio Julian, a Jesuit, reported on a learned missionary who had been freed from severe hypochondria; Mantegazza claimed that coca was universally effective in helping the functional disorders of neurasthenia; Fliessburg wrote that cases of nervous prostration could be considerably improved by the use of coca; and Caldwell, in the *Detroit Therapeutic Gazette*, attested to its effectiveness as a tonic for hysteria. The Italians Morselli and Buccola had tested the drug with a group of melancholics under their care, using subcutaneous injection, and reported "improvement in . . . their patients, who became happier, took nourishment. . . ."

He began to wonder if coca could not help fill the gap in the Allgemeine Krankenhaus' psychiatric medicine chest. While he had cared for the patients under Meynert, he had had a good supply of drugs for reducing the excitation of nerve centers but neither he nor anyone else had had any drug which could improve the reduced functioning of the nerve centers. As he sat in the library of the Gesellschaft der Ärzte reading the articles he added up the evidence that coca had been effective not only in hysteria and melancholia but for hypochondria, inhibition, stupor, anxiety, fear.

And if all this were true, surely there must be other valuable uses for the drug which no one had touched on? How was he to verify this material? Would Professor Meynert allow him to test it on the patients in the psychiatric ward or Professor Scholz allow him to give it to the patients suffering from nervous diseases? The drug, as he learned by walking over to Haubner's Engelapotheke am Hof, was very expensive.

Professor Meynert would not allow him to test it on his patients; Professor Scholz would not buy one kreutzer's worth. Obviously if he were going to test it he would have to be his own patient, test tube and treasurer. He wrote to Merck's in Darmstadt, who had provided Aschenbrandt with the coca for his experiments, ordering samples. His tutoring fees from two students just covered the cost. When it arrived in the mail he let it sit on his table until he was suffering a slight depression brought on by fatigue.

He mixed 0.05 gram of the *cocainum muriaticum* in a one percent water solution and drank it down. He then stretched out on the bed fully clothed to see what would happen. After a few moments he experienced an exhilaration and feeling of ease, of lightness. He got up, went to his desk. There was a certain furriness of his lips and palate followed by a feeling of warmth. He tried a glass of cold water which was warm on his lips yet cold in his throat. He jotted down the line:

"The mood induced by coca in such doses is due not so much to direct stimulation as to the disappearance of elements in one's general state of well-being which cause depression."

During the hours that passed he was stimulated to such an extent that it would have been impossible for him to sleep. He felt neither hunger nor fatigue but a desire for an intense intellectual effort. He picked up some of his more technical books and began to analyze the abstruse material. He worked for a number of hours with clarity and spirit; then slowly the drug wore off. He glanced at his watch, saw that it was two o'clock in the morning. He undressed, washed his hands and face, went to bed and fell asleep. He awoke promptly at seven feeling no sense of fatigue, got up and went to the desk to look at the volume of hand-written pages and the amount of text he had absorbed.

"Is this the effect of the coca?" he asked himself. "Or could I have accomplished as much without it?" But since he was feeling depressed, could he have forced himself to sit down and work in the first place?

During the following weeks he tried the same dosage of cocaine a number of times. Not once did it fail him. He wrote that through the coca he achieved "exhilaration and lasting euphoria, which does not differ in any way from the normal euphoria of a healthy person." He could perceive an increase of self-control, vitality and capacity for work; it was difficult for him to believe that he was under the influence of a drug. He performed intensive mental labors without fatigue; ate well but had the clear impression that the meal was not required. He had no craving for further use of cocaine; rather he felt a certain unmotivated aversion to it.

After a dozen experiments he decided to take the result to Josef Breuer. Breuer was working in his upstairs laboratory. On learning what Sigmund had been doing, he set his work aside. When Sigmund finished reporting he asked Breuer quietly:

"Josef, do you think we might try this on Fleischl? I've brought accounts from a number of cases where people have been broken of morphine by the use of coca."

"What have you told Fleischl about this?"

"Nothing. He knows about my reading because he gave me a letter of introduction to the Gesellschaft der Ärzte. I have not told him about my experiments."

Josef squinted his eyes as though to see through to a truth, then shook his head a little apprehensively.

"What about cocaine addiction?"

"The Peruvian Indians use it all their lives. That's addiction but it doesn't appear to have done them any harm. Ernst is constantly increasing his morphine dosage. Isn't it worth a try?"

They found Fleischl in total torment, his eyes bloodshot, his arm twitching with pain. Sigmund recounted the coca experience. Fleischl was enthusiastic. Sigmund put 0.05 gram into a glass of water. Fleischl drank it. They sat quietly in the study. After a few moments Fleischl experienced a considerable lessening of pain. His eyes cleared, he raised his head, began striding around the room.

"Sig, Sig, I think you've found it. I think it's going to work. I know I'm taking too much morphine but I can't control myself when this thing festers."

Josef Breuer said, "We know what you're suffering, Ernst. But the coca has only been partially tested. We must use great discretion."

"I'll do what you tell me, Josef. Sig, can you get it for me?"

"Yes, I've already talked to the manager at Haubner's. It's only a little more expensive than sending to Merck."

Once a day Sigmund, Breuer or another friend of Fleischl's, Dr. Heinrich Obersteiner, manager of a mental sanatorium in Oberdöbling, gave Ernst his portion of coca, in every instance holding it to the 0.05 level. When they were afraid to give him any after dark because it kept him sleepless most of the night, Fleischl cried:

"What does it matter? This way I feel well, I can read and work on my experiments and do some writing. The other way I am in misery and don't sleep anyway."

It took only one week for the roof to cave in. Sigmund climbed the flight of stairs and knocked on the door of Fleischl's apartment late of an afternoon but got no answer. He kept knocking. There was a sound inside the apartment which he could not identify. He ran to the physiology laboratory for help. Exner came back with him. Josef Breuer and Obersteiner were both summoned. When they managed to break into the room they found Fleischl lying on the floor semiconscious. They undressed him and put him into a warm bath. He came to slowly. Both he and his friends were shattered by the experience. Sigmund would not leave before he had secured a master key to the apartment. He gave it to Obersteiner, who agreed that he would come in at this same time every afternoon when he finished his special work at the Krankenhaus.

Sigmund and Breuer walked home at dawn. They bought a hot sausage and a roll from the *Wurstelmann* behind his stand and ate hungrily, suddenly remembering they had had no supper. Ahead of them the lamplighter in his hat with the long peak and *Zundstongen*, extendible pole, was opening the glass doors of the lamps and turning off the gas. The Am Hof market was already going full force, the early shoppers commandeering the best produce while the country women drank hot tea to keep warm. A man with a box carriage on small wheels, a ladder and bucket of paint hanging behind him, passed on his way to paint posters on a wall. The crew of street cleaners, their horse-drawn water barrels tilted downward, were sprinkling the streets from the opened plugs. Groups of elegantly dressed men in high silk hats and capes came out of the brilliantly lighted cafes to yawn their cheery good nights.

"I'm uneasy," persisted Breuer. "He shouldn't have been in that condition from pain. . . . Has he been getting any extra coca? I mean from Haubner's?"

"I'll be there when they open to ask."

The news was bad. Fleischl had been buying a large quantity of coca and taking it surreptitiously. Was coca then as safe as the literature made it sound? What constituted an overdose? Obviously there were dangers.

He made no attempt to keep his experiment secret. He revealed his findings to his colleagues, some of whom tried the drug and brought him corroborative reports that it was the equivalent of an ample meal, that it dispelled extreme fatigue or roused sufficient strength to take a long walk. Josef Pollak reported the successful use of the drug on the control of the mucus membrane and muscular system of the stomach.

After his scare, Fleischl cut down on the coca. Sigmund himself continued to take the prescribed dosage whenever he felt he needed it, gave some to his sister Rosa and sent some to Martha, who found that it helped her during periods of stress. Breuer was still cautious but Sigmund's faith in the cocaine was renewed. He found reason to believe that it could help control vomiting, gastric catarrh, as well as deaden the pain of trachoma and cutaneous infections. He gave some to his friends Karl Koller and Dr. Leopold Königstein, suggesting that they use coca to lessen the pain of non-operable eye ailments.

When he had all his materials assembled he wrote a twenty-six-page paper On Coca which was published in the *Centralblatt für die gesammte Therapie* in which he collated the published materials he had found in five languages, quoted his authorities and then set forth with enthusiasm the case for the value of the drug in digestive disorders, dyspepsia, anemia, febrile diseases, syphilis, the control of morphine and alcohol addiction, impotence . . . If even half of this amazing potential should be realized, his name and fame would be made. He wrote to Martha:

"We need no more than one stroke of luck of this kind to consider setting up house."

Ignaz Schönberg's mother developed a complicated heart ailment. Sigmund gave up his spare hours at the hospital to care for her. He brought her back to health. Ignaz left for England but failed to say good-by because of embarrassment over the fact that his brothers had not paid Dr. Freud's token charges. When at length the money arrived, sixty gulden, Sigmund bought an electric massage machine he would need for his private patients, then arranged to send ten gulden to Martha so that she could buy herself a jersey jacket she had been wanting.

7.

The summer heat of 1884 clamped down on Vienna and the streets emptied of Viennese as the carts and wagons moved the families to the country. Sigmund went to the barber, had his hair cut quite short, the dark beard trimmed to a thin line, and even ordered a lightweight suit to be made by Tischer, the tailor who served most of the young doctors at the Krankenhaus. It was over a year since Mrs. Bernays had taken her two daughters back to Germany.

Breuer offered Sigmund a patient suffering from a severe neurosis who would pay the Herr Doktor one thousand gulden if he would spend the summer traveling with him. His colleagues urged him to accept. Sigmund refused; he was not going to serve as a male nurse to a lunatic. Besides, he needed the months to complete his work in Meynert's laboratory and his investigation of coca.

It was Primarius Scholz who went on vacation. He left Dr. Josef Pollak and Dr. Moriz Ullmann, who had been assigned to the Fourth Department shortly after Sigmund arrived there, in charge. When a serious outbreak of cholera occurred in Montenegro, the news spread through the Krankenhaus that doctors were sorely needed. Pollak and Ullmann heard of it instantly, volunteered, then went together to Sigmund's room. They caught him writing furiously about his experiments in measuring muscle reactions under the influence of coca. Pollak, hard-working and serious in the wards, liked to create fun when he could close the doors behind him. He stood before Sigmund, clicked his heels together ceremoniously, bowed low, exclaimed:

"Herr Doktor Primarius Professor Freud, we have come to congratulate you. You have just been promoted by the Minister of Education to become superintendent of the Fourth Medical Department."

Sigmund looked up with his mouth slightly open. He was accustomed to Pollak's pranks but could make no sense of this one.

"When did this great honor befall me, gentlemen?"

Ullmann broke in with a grin. "It happened to you ten minutes ago. And we are the ones who brought this distinguished honor upon you."

"Come on, you two clowns, what is this all about?"

"It's no joke, Sig," said Pollak. "Ullmann and I have volunteered to go to Montenegro. There is a cholera epidemic there. They need every doctor Vienna can spare."

"Good, I'll join you."

"You can't, Herr Hofrat," cried Pollak. "You have to mind the store. There is absolutely no one to take your place. We'll bring you back some souvenirs."

As acting chief of the Fourth Medical Department he grew up fast. Prior to this time he had had patients to take care of but the final responsibility rested with either Scholz or Pollak. Now the responsibility was his, not only for the admitting of patients, their diagnosis and treatment, but for the uses of the money available for supplies, drugs and equipment. Excitedly walking the wards as the *Primarius*, he mused:

"This is the first time I've really known what it means to be a hospital doctor."

There were life-and-death decisions to be made every few minutes. To admit this patient and reject that one. To send a third patient home because there was still another more in need of hospitalization. He commanded one hundred and thirteen beds, but there were times when five hundred patients were trying to get into them . . . with variations of trauma, seizures, tumors, as well as motor and spinal paralysis. The beds were no longer the exact distance from each other that the regulations and Herr Dr. Scholz demanded.

Sometimes he did not get to bed until three in the morning. As a lowly Junior *Sekundararzt* he had been allowed to sleep until seven o'clock. As *Primarius* he was up at six. Yet even in his exhaustion the thought flashed through his mind:

"Josef Breuer and Nathan Weiss were right. Herr Dr. Freud, you are at long last becoming a neurologist."

Primarius Scholz returned at the end of August, freeing Sigmund for a vacation, a long-hoped-for visit with Martha. She met him at the railroad station in Hamburg, waving to him as she ran down the platform against the flow of disembarking passengers. He set down his valise, waited until she was in his arms, then whispered against her ear:

"I wrote you not to meet me at the station unless you were prepared to be kissed in public."

"I couldn't let you come into Hamburg and not be welcomed."

"Martha, Martha, how good to hear your voice again!"

She had engaged a carriage to take them to Wandsbek, some five miles from Hamburg; the driver watched for them to emerge from the station. They sat locked in each other's arms against the leather button-studded back of the seat. Fourteen months was such a long time out of a man's life, and out of a young woman's. He held her away from him, studying her face. It was a little slimmer than he remembered; her eyes were radiant with the joy of being with him again. She still parted her hair in the center and had obeyed his instructions to take a long walk every day. She was wearing a silk summer dress. His old gray suit and white shirt were rumpled from the journey and the black soot of the giant engine.

"Was it a good trip? I've been counting every hour since you left Vienna."

"You know how crazy I am about trains, just like Alexander. Did you find me a room?"

"Yes, but not the attic you asked for. Some friends on the Kedenburgstrasse had a front room to spare. You'll like it, it overlooks the Eichtalpark. The month's rent is not high."

"You're a bright girl."

Hamburg's suburb of Wandsbek seemed charming. The room he was taken to was hung with cream-colored wallpaper with a pattern of yellow daisies. Martha waited in the parlor while he washed, changed his shirt and put on his new suit, then they walked the short block to the house Mrs. Bernays had rented on the Steinpilzweg. It was a modest cottage set in a garden, on a quiet street, and furnished with furniture Sigmund remembered from the apartment in Vienna, including the comfortable brown chair and hassock in which he and Martha had spent happy hours.

Sigmund had not looked forward with any pleasure to meeting Mrs. Bernays again. But when he entered the house he saw that she was thin and haggard from a long illness. All antipathy fled; in its place came remorse and sympathy. He stepped forward, said, "*Grüss Gott*. It's good to see you again, Mother," bent over and kissed her hand. He asked how she felt, then said solicitously:

"You must let me prescribe a special tonic and watch over you while I'm here. I believe I am beginning to be a reasonably good doctor."

Mrs. Bernays too had been braced for a chilly meeting, perhaps even a contest. Sigmund's interest in her well-being vanquished her opposition.

"That I never doubted," she replied, with more tenderness than he had ever heard in her voice. "My only worry was how long it would take you. I know that your friend Dr. Ernst Fleischl has been engaged to the same poor girl for ten years, or is it twelve? But I also know now how deeply Martha loves you. Let us be allies, Sigi."

When she left the room, Martha leaned forward and kissed him on the forehead. "Thank you. You see now how right I was to keep the family peace? An argument not waged is a war won."

"Agreed, Fräulein Aristotle. Your logic is impeccable."

Minna came in, her broad face wreathed in a smile as she engulfed the smaller Sigmund in a bear hug.

"I'm so happy to see you. You look wonderful. Now quickly tell me

about my Ignaz. Have you had letters from Oxford? He never tells me
how he feels. Is he thriving on the work . . . ?"

"Whoa, whoa, little sister, you mustn't drive me like an *Einspänner*.
You will have the news of our Ignaz. He is working well on the dictionary.
Before long he should be earning the three thousand gulden a year needed
for you to marry."

Minna waltzed around the parlor and ended by taking both Martha and
Sigmund in her capacious arms and kissing them lustily on the cheek.

In the early mornings they walked in the woods surrounding Wandsbek,
with the dew still fresh on the grass, the September sunshine warm as it
filtered through the network of trees. Martha wore a loose-fitting brown
walking dress and a big hat. Sigmund declared, "These greens here are
so all-pervading your eyes look like emeralds. The Prater is a paradise but
there were never less than a hundred people trudging the path in front
and behind us. This Wandsbek grove is more beautiful because we are
alone, like Adam and Eve. . . ."

They chatted quietly about their future. At eleven o'clock they would
stop for the *Frühstück* at a small inn, the tables out under the trees.
While this was no Viennese "fork breakfast" of goulash, a waitress brought
them fresh-baked bread, sweet butter, cakes and milk. Then they walked
home, stopping to pick the last of the wild flowers, to midday dinner
cooked by Mrs. Bernays and Minna, who had decreed that Martha was
to do no housework for the month of September "as long as Sigi is
here." Of a late afternoon they rode the horse-drawn streetcar into Hamburg to buy the shirts that Jakob had said were better than the Vienna
shirts; or to gaze, doe-eyed, into the window of the furniture stores with
their displays of mahogany dining-room sets, armchairs and sofas for the
parlor, bedroom suites with high headboards and carved footboards. The
Hamburg furniture was more stolid than the Viennese.

"It looks as though it is built to last several generations," he remarked.

"Oh, it is," she replied emphatically. "Hamburg families buy one house,
then furnish it to last a century."

"When I went to the Electrical Exhibition in Vienna last year there
was a series of rooms, lighted by electricity of course, but furnished
charmingly by Jaray's furniture store. I was in ecstasy thinking how much
you would have enjoyed seeing those beautiful things. Then I realized
that we could be unhappy on a Jaray's lovely sofa, and happy in any
well-used armchair. The wife should always be the most beautiful orna-
ment in the house."

She gazed at his reflection in the store window. "Sigi, you think you
are a scientist of the breed that believes only what it can measure. Not
so, my dear. You are a poet."

Toward the middle of the month there were two days of rain. They sat cozily in the Bernays parlor reading aloud to each other from Heine, and novels, *Nathan the Wise* or *Vanity Fair*. Sigmund rested after the hard-working year in the wards and laboratories of the Krankenhaus. He enjoyed every moment with Martha and the Bernays family. They spent a full day walking the busy docks and canals of Hamburg. He told her of the offer he had received to accompany Breuer's sick patient abroad.

"A thousand-gulden fee is a big one. You could have used the money in a dozen directions," she exclaimed.

"Yes, but it would have held up my work for three months, and held back our marriage for the same length of time."

"I am hindering you," she said.

He took her by the shoulders and shook her.

"My beloved girl, you must utterly banish from your mind such gloomy thoughts. You know the key to my life: I can work only when spurred on by great hopes for things uppermost in my mind. Before I met you I didn't know the joy of living and now that 'in principle' you are mine, to have you completely is the one condition I make to life, which I otherwise don't set any great store by. I am very stubborn and very reckless and need great challenges. I have done a number of things which any sensible person would be bound to consider very rash. For example, to take up science as a poverty-stricken man, then as a poverty-stricken man to capture a poor girl; but this must continue to be my way of life: risking a lot, hoping a lot, working a lot. To average bourgeois common sense I was lost long ago."

There were tears in her eyes as she linked her arm through his.

Eventually he came around to telling her of the travel grant given by the Medical Faculty. The fund had been started by the rector and Consistorium of the university in 1866. "It's for six hundred gulden, two hundred and forty dollars," he explained, "and it goes to the *Sekundararzt* at the Krankenhaus whom the Medical Faculty considers can benefit most from it. It means the chance to travel to another country, study under a master in your field. The winning of the grant is like an honorary degree."

"Oh, Sigi, do you think there is a chance for you?"

"It's only a matter of rumor. If I win I want to go to Paris and study at the Salpêtrière under Professor Charcot. He practically invented modern neurology singlehanded." He looked at her apprehensively. "It would mean that I must spend one more year of training at the Krankenhaus, then I could come here to visit with you for a vacation, and after that go to Paris."

Martha closed her eyes, rested her chin on her folded hands as though she were praying.

"What a beautiful dream. May it come true."

8.

The first person Sigmund saw when he came through the court of the Fourth Department on his return from Wandsbek was Dr. Karl Koller. Koller, twenty-seven, was practically the only clean-shaven man in the hospital; his hair was cut short, on either side of the center part he wore a little curl combed forward. His only nod to convention was a long, thin mustache whose ends turned up in straggly fashion. He had an open good-natured face with well-proportioned features but there was a difference between Koller's genial face and his personality, which was abrasive. He was irritable, blunt, fault-finding.

"Karl, what are you doing up here policing my area? Have we suddenly taken over Ophthalmology?"

Koller cried, "No, Ophthalmology has taken over you."

Sigmund took off his coat and shoes, put on a pair of slippers. Koller circled the furniture.

"Sig, I owe it all to you. You remember how you demonstrated the effects of cocaine to us and gave us each a little. You commented on the numbness it caused in the mouth. Well, I was in Professor Stricker's lab and I had a small flask with a trace of white powder in my pocket. I showed it to the professor and his Assistant, Dr. Gärtner, and told them, 'I hope, indeed I expect, that this powder will anesthetize the eye.' Stricker asked, 'When?' I replied, 'Any time that I want to start the experiment.' Gärtner said, 'What's the matter with right now?' He got me a big lively frog and held him immobile while I dissolved the coca in water and trickled drops of the solution into one of the protruding eyes. We tested the reflex of the cornea with a needle. Sig, I swear to you it was only an instant before the great moment came: the frog permitted the cornea to be touched and even injured without a trace of reflex action or attempt to protect himself. You can imagine how excited we were. We promptly got a rabbit and a dog and trickled cocaine into one eye. We were able to do anything to it with a needle and a knife without causing the animal pain."

Sigmund sat staring at his friend.

"My God, yes, of course, Karl. If cocaine will numb the tongue it will numb the eye."

"Our next problem was the human being. We didn't dare test it on any patient in the wards, so we trickled a solution under the lid of each other's eye. Then we put a mirror in front of us, touched our cornea with a pin. Almost simultaneously we cried out, 'I can't feel a thing!' Sig, would you believe it, we could make a dent in the cornea without the slightest awareness of the touch? Do you realize what this means? We can now operate for glaucoma and cataracts without inflicting pain on the patient, and at the same time keep him quiet until our task is completed!"

Sigmund jumped up and embraced Koller.

"You've made a breakthrough. You must set down your findings and lecture to the Society of Medicine, then publish the paper."

"I have already had a friend present a preliminary report at an oph-thalmological meeting in Heidelberg. I wanted to do it myself but I couldn't scrape up the funds." Tears came to Koller's eyes. "It means that I will be able to move up, the first step to building a private practice. I'll open a little hospital on the outside and before long even take over one of the departments here. That has been my dream."

"We all have the identical dream, Karl." A smile settled on one corner of his mouth. "Just as soldiers have the identical dream of picking up a pretty girl in the Prater and taking her into the woods."

The next morning Leopold Königstein, also an ophthalmologist, came to see Sigmund. Though he was a man who rarely showed emotion, there was a pounding excitement behind his voice.

"Sigi, I'm so glad you're back. You remember the discussions we had about your cocaine, and its numbing effects on various parts of the body? You suggested that I try it on the eye. I have. Sig, I think we've got the anesthetic we've been searching for all these years."

Sigmund groaned. "Leopold, have you talked to Karl Koller about this?"

Königstein stood in silence for an instance, not happy about the question.

"Why do you ask?"

"The two of you have made the same discovery."

Königstein went pale. "How do you know this?"

"I found Koller pacing the hall when I got home last night. He had tested the cocaine on several animals as well as himself. He hasn't operated on human eyes yet."

"I haven't operated on human eyes either, but certainly I will do so."

Sigmund was troubled.

"Leopold, I'm very happy for you. I know how important this is. But if you and Koller have made the discovery simultaneously, you must present your papers to the Society of Medicine simultaneously. You and Karl will have to share credit."

Both men were bitterly disappointed. Sigmund worked on them. When he thought he was not making sufficient progress he asked for help from the burly, physically powerful Dr. Wagner-Jauregg, who was working across the street at the Lower Austrian Insane Asylum, because Wagner-Jauregg had been in and out of the Stricker laboratory and had watched some of the experiments. They convinced Koller and Königstein to give their reports on successive evenings and to acknowledge that the work had been done simultaneously.

Later when his father came to the hospital complaining of a pain in his eyes, Sigmund took him to see Koller. Koller diagnosed Jakob's problem as glaucoma. He advised an immediate operation. Königstein made the same judgment. A few days later, in the operating room of the Ophthalmological Department, Sigmund helped Koller administer the cocaine anesthetic while Königstein performed the operation. When it was over Koller said with a shy smile:

"It's a happy moment. Here we are, the three men who made such operations as these possible, all working together."

Koller's new-found fame was seriously jostled; the ripples extended to all those who had so happily celebrated his achievement. An accident befell him, one of the first to happen in the Krankenhaus in such flagrant form in many years. Sigmund had just finished his rounds in the wards when he was summoned to Koller's room. He found half a dozen of his friends crowded there, all of them bitterly angry.

Koller looked up from the chair into which he had sunk.

"I was on duty in the Journal with Dr. Zinner, one of Billroth's interns. A man with a seriously injured finger was brought in. Upon examining it I saw that the rubber bandage was constricting the flow of blood; if I didn't remove it there was danger of gangrene. Dr. Zinner said the patient should be sent immediately to Professor Billroth's Clinic. I agreed, and made a note of his request in the book, then started to loosen the bandage. Zinner objected, saying that I should touch nothing but send the patient to Billroth's at once. I was afraid to take the chance, so I quickly cut the bandage from the finger."

He hoisted himself out of the seat. "Zinner screamed, 'Impudent Jew! You Jewish swine!' I was blinded with fury. I swung with all my might and caught him on the ear with my fist. Zinner cried, 'My seconds will call on you and arrange the duel!' "

Sigmund was deeply shocked. The hospital administration fought to protect the reputation of its Medical Faculty and Allgemeine Krankenhaus. Anti-Semitism had been subtle, rarely overt, a bouquet of which Sigmund and his friends, sensitive as they were to such matters, occasionally caught a whiff. Dr. Billroth's tract had been duly condemned, yet an unmarked line existed in the Krankenhaus. Christian and Jew did not associate outside the hospital or mix socially. It was a cliquishness practiced by both groups. "Cliquism for comfort!" Julius Wagner-Jauregg had called it, his green eyes serious. Son of a civil servant in Upper Austria, Catholic, Wagner-Jauregg had retained what the Austrians called a "countrylike" appearance: clean-shaven except for a sand-colored mustache and a thick stand of sand-colored hair cut short in military fashion; a chin as granitelike as his forehead; the powerful arms and torso of the woodcutter whose clothes he liked to wear while mountain climbing. Wagner-Jauregg did not presume on his strength to intimidate others; it was simply there as a naked force. He had worked with Koller and Königstein to develop a method of using cocaine to anesthetize the skin.

"Freud, I like the Jewish doctors in the A.K.," he had exclaimed. "They are sometimes brilliant, honest. I have learned much from them. I could work at their side in the clinics and laboratories from six in the morning until six at night and never remember that we belong to different religions; such matters are extraneous to science. But when night falls and I leave to join my friends I want to be with my own kind. Not that they are better, but simply that we have grown up together and know each other well. In all fair-mindedness, you would not call that anti-Semitism?"

All knew that it was more difficult for a Jewish doctor to rise in the Medical Faculty hierarchy, it took more time and talent. Yet no Jew was kept out of the Medical School if he had the qualifications, and there had always been a goodly number of Jewish doctors on the staff.

Someone murmured, "Karl, when did you last handle a saber?"

"I picked one up several times when I served my year of military service."

"Zinner can kill you. He's been a duelist from his student days."

Koller sighed heavily. "That possibility has occurred to me. But if I refuse to accept his challenge I dishonor us all."

Dr. Zinner's seconds arrived to issue the formal challenge. The duel was to take place at the cavalry barracks at Josefstadt. They were to use espadons, honed foils with very thin, light blades. There were to be no bandages; the seconds were not to interfere, neither were they to be permitted to fence off certain thrusts. The fight must continue until one party or the other was totally unable to defend himself.

To everyone's amazement it was Koller who inflicted the cuts on Zinner, wounding him on the head and upper right arm.

"Sig, I honestly don't know how I managed to nick him. He took three passes at me, I was just waving that sword around trying to defend myself."

Drs. Koller and Zinner were summoned to the office of the *Staatsanwalt*, the Public Prosecutor. Koller refused to repeat the insult that had been hurled at him. Zinner told the story quite freely, maintaining that he had had to issue the challenge or he would have forfeited his officer's rank as *Oberarzt* of the Army Reserve. He offered neither justification for his outburst nor an attempt to defend himself against the now public opinion that Dr. Koller had been right to remove the constricting bandage. An article in the *Neue Wiener Abendblatt* praised Dr. Koller for insisting upon doing his proper duty to the injured man; it castigated Dr. Zinner for "hurling insults."

Koller's victory was simply not acceptable in the Krankenhaus. By

winning he had somehow committed a crime of the same proportion as
Dr. Zinner's insult. He came to Sigmund's apartment sleepless, gaunt,
sorely troubled.

"Sig, I need counsel."

"Make yourself a cup of coffee, Karl. I'm not sleeping either."

Koller boiled the coffee, poured them each a cup.

"I think I'm being frozen out. They don't want me around here any
more."

"Is your work being obstructed?"

"No. That could never be charged against the Krankenhaus. But there
are a hundred signs."

"Couldn't you pull into your shell and let the thing die out?"

"I've told myself that, and I try. But I find myself worrying more
about what the other doctors are thinking, and how I can reprimand
them, than I am about the work I should be doing."

"That's the worst thing you've told me."

"Am I imagining this, Sig?"

"I've sensed it."

"It looks as though I'm going to have to move away. Apply to Berlin,
or Zurich, or even try to find a place in America. I've been thinking
about America a lot lately."

Sigmund smiled. "The promised land? You know why it's a promised
land, don't you? When any of us get discouraged we decide we'll just
pack up and go to America. We don't go but the fact that it is always
there helps us in our darkest moments. I suppose I have considered moving
to America at least a dozen times in the past two years."

"Sig, if they want me out of here, I can't stay. Yet the university and
hospital are my life. I want to spend my years here, teaching, researching,
practicing, operating."

"Then I would recommend a leave of absence. Not immediately. That's
too much like fleeing. When spring comes go to Salzburg or some other
beautiful place for several months and compose yourself. After all, you're
now known over the world. You've made a fine contribution. Vienna needs
you. Perhaps a period of being away will convince them of this."

9.

It was easy to give advice to a friend, not so simple to see clearly for
oneself. He had returned from his month with Martha refreshed. Now
he pushed himself as hard as he had before but the spontaneity had
vanished.

It helped when a group of American doctors, the Messrs. Campbell,
Darling, Giles, Green, Leslie and Montgomery, asked him to give them

a course in clinical neurology . . . in English. Dr. Leslie collected the
fees and kept the records in return for his tuition. Sigmund lectured for
one hour a day for five weeks. Although his spoken English had limitations, the Americans were delighted to understand a complete lecture or
demonstration instead of the occasional phrases and sentences with which
they had had to be content in the long, somewhat discursive lectures in
German.

He received the regulation fee of twenty gulden from each doctor,
and put the considerable sum of forty dollars in the antique box Martha
had bought for him in the old section of Hamburg. From it he made a
substantial contribution to his family and sent a few gulden to Wandsbek:
"From now on Marty and Minna are going to drink port"; then indulged
himself in a sorely needed pair of winter trousers.

The course was a success. He was asked to repeat it. This time he
had eleven subscribers, quite good for a young man not yet a *Dozent*,
university lecturer. Although the Americans may not have been good
linguists, they were well-trained neurologists who occasionally caught
"teacher" in a diagnostic *gaffe*, such as the time he described a persistent
headache case as "chronic localized meningitis" when the patient had
no serious illness but a neurosis in full blossom! It was a baptism by
fire he thoroughly enjoyed.

He continued his rounds in Scholz's wards, was interested in two new
cases, a baker on whom he had made the admitting diagnosis of endo-
carditis with pneumonia, together with acute spinal and cerebral involvement. No one in the department knew what to do to help the patient.
Sigmund kept close records on the case. The baker died in the middle
of December and the autopsy proved that he had been right in his
diagnosis. Again he published his detailed account; a reviewer for the
Neurologisches Centralblatt wrote, "This is a very valuable contribution
to our knowledge of acute polyneuritis."

The second case was that of a weaver. Sigmund diagnosed syringomyelia,
an uncommon disease of the spinal cord; the man had lost sensation of
pain and temperature in both hands, although he felt pain in his legs.
Sigmund gave him special care for six weeks. The patient did not respond
and was sent home. This case he reported to the *Wiener medizinische
Wochenschrift*. A few months later it was reproduced in the *Neurologisches Centralblatt*.

Yet even this good work could not dispel the gnawing feeling that he
had come to an impasse. He was dissatisfied with himself. The reason
became clear on a Sunday morning when he was enjoying an eleven
o'clock *Gabelfrühstück* of *Kleines Gulasch* with Josef and Mathilde
Breuer. He told Josef of his growing sense of discontent, his feeling that
he did not belong in the Krankenhaus any longer.

"I know I'm not trained to deliver a baby, and certainly there are diseases of the bone and the blood that are beyond anything I have studied. But I think I've completed my apprenticeship. I am frustrated."

Josef smiled. Sigmund persisted.

"I'm getting too old to be a Junior *Sekundararzt*. I know that between the application and certification for the *Dozentur* it can take up to a year. I'm beginning to feel naked without it. Once I am a *Dozent* I can hang out my sign anywhere."

The title of *Privatdozent*, without which no man could build a first-class practice in Austria, carried with it the privilege of giving lecture courses at the university, though not on any subject included in the regular curriculum. The *Dozentur* brought no pay, nor were the *Dozenten* permitted to attend faculty meetings. Yet this official approval of the Medical Faculty gave the general public confidence. The Viennese never said, "I am going to see the doctor"; they said, "I am going to see the professor."

"You're on the shoals called 'administration backwaters,'" said Josef. "You must convince the Medical Faculty that you're ready for promotion and should also receive the travel grant."

Mathilde leaned over the table. "I already have the design for Sigi's street plaque: glass with black background and gold letters. The one for the inside door will be porcelain."

Sigmund tendered his application for the *Dozentur*, dated January 21, 1885:

"If the Honorable College of Professors will grant me the lectureship on Diseases of the Nerves, then it is my intention to promote in two ways the instruction in this branch of human pathology. . . ."

A committee was appointed by the Medical Faculty to investigate Dr. Freud's application and qualifications for the *Dozentur* in neuropathology. It was composed of Professors Brücke, Nothnagel and Meynert. Fleischl was amused:

"Herr Dr. Freud, you have stacked the deck!"

Professor Brücke volunteered to review Sigmund's work and write the report which would nominate him. He had to analyze such of Sigmund Freud's histology papers as *The Posterior Roots in Petromyzon* and *The Nerve Cells in Crayfish*, which Brücke labeled "very important," and shorter, appreciative abstracts of his methods. Brücke wrote:

"The microscopic anatomical papers by Dr. Freud were accepted with general recognition of his results. . . . [He] is a man with a good general education, of quiet and serious character, an excellent worker in the field of neuroanatomy, of fine dexterity, clear vision, comprehensive knowledge of the literature and a cautious method of deduction, with the gift for well-organized written expression. . . ."

Professors Nothnagel and Meynert enthusiastically signed Professor Brücke's recommendation.

The contest for the travel grant narrowed down to Dr. Sigmund Freud, Dr. Friedrich Dimmer, a *Privatdozent* and Assistant in the Second Oculist Clinic; and Dr. Julius Hochenegg, from the Surgery Clinic.

It was surprising how the weeks could speed by while he did little but plead his cause with the members of the Medical Faculty. The professors he had worked with received him warmly; they wrote letters to their colleagues and arranged with friends or friends of friends to intercede for him. Sigmund maneuvered for further appointments, kept a chart of how the votes were distributed, abandoned hope when after an exposition a professor murmured *"Servus"* with no word of encouragement.

His little group of friends plotted his campaign with what they called "military strategy." Josef Breuer undertook the persuading of Professor Billroth's vote, and secured a commitment. Dr. Sigmund Lustgarten undertook the appeal to Professor Ludwig. Young Dr. Heinrich Obersteiner's father owned a psychiatric sanatorium with Professor Leidesdorf in Oberdöbling. Obersteiner through Leidesdorf promised to bring in the vote of Professor Politzer.

By the end of April Sigmund and his friends believed they could count on eight votes. He labored under the disadvantage that some votes would be cast against him because he was a Jew. However if the other two candidates, both Catholics, were to divide the balance of the vote Sigmund would emerge with the largest number. Then Dr. Hochenegg withdrew on the grounds that he was too young. This left the contest squarely up to the supporters of Dr. Freud and the supporters of Dr. Dimmer. He wrote to Martha:

"This has been a bad, barren month. . . . I do nothing all day."

He thereupon went down with a mild case of smallpox. The professor in charge decided that the case was too light to isolate him in the Infectious Diseases Department, but his friends were told to stay out of his apartment for a number of days. He was well cared for by the nurses, who brought him food and fresh linens.

When he had recovered he walked home to reassure his parents. As he neared the front door of their apartment building he saw Eli enter. Turning quickly, Sigmund made his way to his sister Anna's house to congratulate her and visit with his infant niece. Anna was too happy to be angry at her brother's neglect. It was becoming increasingly difficult for Sigmund to remember why he was quarreling with Eli.

On May thirtieth the Medical Faculty met to decide the winner of the travel grant. The meeting ended in a stalemate.

Sigmund was low in his mind when young Dr. Obersteiner asked if he would like to go out to Oberdöbling for a few weeks of work in the sanatorium to replace a doctor who was going on vacation.

He was delighted at the opportunity to get out of the Krankenhaus, as well as to earn the extra money. He secured a "sick leave" and packed.

The sanatorium in Oberdöbling, an hour out of Vienna, stood in a park toward the end of the Hirschengasse, on the road to Grinzing. It was a big house of two stories, built on a hill and surrounded by smaller houses. Across the road there was a nursing home for the serious cases. The suburb was still sparsely settled. As Sigmund walked up the Hirschengasse, jauntily swinging his walking stick, he felt as though he were going to spend a few weeks in the country.

Co-owner of the sanatorium, Professor Leidesdorf, was the teacher of Meynert; as superintendent of the Lower Austrian Insane Asylum, he now held the title of associate professor of psychiatry. He walked stiffly from a severe case of gout, wore a wig and was, Sigmund soon discovered, a shrewd observer of mental illness. Professor Leidesdorf's daughter had married young Obersteiner, a former pupil of Brücke, skinny, undistinguished-looking but a decent man. Obersteiner took Sigmund on a tour of the sanatorium. The rooms were large, filled with sunshine and good views, and were cheerfully furnished. There were sixty patients on the grounds, manifesting every symptom from slight feeble-mindedness to serious withdrawals, dementia praecox. The inmates came from wealthy families. Sigmund was amazed to learn how many of them carried titles; nearly everyone was a baron or a count. There were two princes, one of whom was the son of Marie Louise, the wife of Napoleon. These members of the nobility, Sigmund thought, looked seedy and dilapidated; not in their dress, which was frequently colorful, but in their expression and manner. With some of them he never was able to determine the ratio of eccentricity to psychic disturbance. It was not part of his job! He had simply to keep them comfortable and tend any physical ailment they might claim.

He was surprised at how amiable life could be in the sanatorium. The food was excellent; he was served a robust second breakfast at eleven-thirty and then a very good dinner at three o'clock. Young Obersteiner lent him his own library to work in, a lovely cool room with a view of the hills and Vienna. There was Obersteiner's microscope and a superb literature on the nervous system which had been accumulating now for two generations.

He made his rounds of the rooms from eight-thirty until ten in the morning, then went to his office where he had to be available until about three in the afternoon. He got along well with the patients; recognized their symptoms from his months of work in Meynert's psychiatric wards. Wealth and nobility changed the outward form of the eccentricity but there was little that he had not already observed and treated. The inmates were apparently satisfied with their surroundings, they ate well and slept well, though one occasionally called for a sedative or a purgative or electric massage. From three to seven he made his rounds of the rooms again.

Life was even more pleasant after he finished his first rounds with Dr. Obersteiner, Sr., and made several astute diagnoses. From that moment he was trusted and given additional time to read and study. Professor Leidesdorf said, "Herr Doktor, may I tender a bit of advice? Let me recommend that you become a specialist in nervous diseases among children. All too little is known about it."

"Ah, Professor Leidesdorf, if only one could get an official call for this! There is great work to be done in that area, I know, and I would like to try my hand at it."

He thought, "I must write Martha. One could live an idyll here, with a wife and children. If I don't get my *Dozentur*, and I fail to receive the travel grant, I must ask if she would like to live in such a place."

The Medical Faculty was to meet again on June twentieth to decide not only the winner of the travel grant but whether he would become Privatdozent Sigmund Freud. The week before dragged. He tried to "kill time," which died reluctantly. The minutes were wet sponges underfoot; the more he tried to crush them out of existence the more they oozed up on either side of his feet.

The simple anxiety was enhanced when he learned that Ignaz Schönberg had left his position in Oxford and arrived in Wandsbek gaunt, hollow-cheeked and feverish. Mrs. Bernays and Minna put him to bed; Martha went for the family doctor. The prognosis was bad: one lung was destroyed, the other probably riddled with disease. Nowhere, except conceivably on the Sahara Desert, could he live with what was left of one collapsing lung. Ignaz had apparently abandoned hope. He got out of bed, despite the high fever, packed his suitcase, informed Minna that their engagement was broken and that he was returning to Vienna. Sigmund determined that as soon as Ignaz reached home he would have him examined by Dr. Müller, an experienced chest man. Sitting in his room waiting for word from the Medical Faculty that would determine so much of his own future, he thought back over the years of friendship he and Ignaz had enjoyed since they attended the Sperlgymnasium. He reflected:

"We cannot turn the man who has to work into one who can simply afford to enjoy life and take care of his health. It's not the disease that is incurable, it is a man's social standing and his obligations that become an incurable disease."

A messenger from the university brought the good news in the late afternoon. Herr Dr. Freud had been granted his *Dozentur* by a vote of nineteen to three. He had also been awarded the travel grant by a vote of thirteen to nine.

It was a moment of intense joy.

After being warmly congratulated by Professor Leidesdorf and the two Obersteiners, he went to his office to write to Martha, then hired a carriage to take him into Vienna, first to the post office to mail his letter, then home to tell his family. Then to the Breuers to thank them for their wonderful help and finally to spend the evening in celebration with Ernst Fleischl. Fleischl opened a bottle of champagne.

"Sig, I've heard most of what went on. For your *Dozentur* there really was no contest. Why three voted against you is beyond me. But the fight for the grant was heated. Professor von Stellwag made a first-rate presentation for Dimmer. What won for you was Professor Brücke's passionate intercession on your behalf. He described you as the finest young scientist to come out of the university in years. He caused a general sensation. No one had seen Herr Dr. Brücke so worked up, so convinced that he was right, that the Faculty must sponsor you with this grant because of the important results that would come out of your work with Charcot in Paris."

Sigmund was silent for a long time. He took a sip of the champagne. Dr. Brücke's clear, hard, blue eyes confronted him in the crystal glass.

"How does one thank a man for doing a thing like that?" he murmured plaintively.

"One works," said Fleischl. "One achieves the results Professor Brücke predicted for you. Your trial lecture comes at twelve-thirty on June twenty-seventh in Brücke's auditorium. . . . You'll need a top hat."

Suddenly complete realization struck him.

"Ernst, I just can't believe it. Now I can go to Paris and become a great scholar and come back to Vienna with an enormous halo, and then Martha and I can get married, and I will cure all the incurable nervous diseases."

"*Prosit!*" cried Fleischl, lifting his glass.

BOOK FOUR

A PROVINCIAL IN PARIS

BOOK FOUR

A Provincial in Paris

E ARRIVED in Paris in the first week of October 1885, and found a
pleasant room on the second floor of the Hôtel de la Paix, his front
window overlooking the Impasse Royer-Collard and the gardens of
the apartment house at the dead end. It was a quiet street close to
the Luxembourg Gardens and a half-hour walk to the Salpêtrière. The
hotel was only three windows wide, held snugly in place by more
pretentious private dwellings on either side. There was a throw rug
beside the bed to warm the random plank flooring, a wardrobe embar-
rassingly large for his scanty clothing, a cheerful wallpaper of red roses
against a gold background, and on the wall opposite his bed a pine
table on which he put his books and Martha's picture.

Martha's picture . . . He continued to gaze at it after he had turned
down the lamp, opening the window to admit the cool autumnal air
and the faint sounds coming from the Boulevard St. Michel. What a
wonderful month they had enjoyed together in Wandsbek. He felt
calm, rested, secure, happy in his love. He fell asleep, the curtain blowing
a little from the breeze.

He was up early and walked to a cafe opposite the entrance to the
Luxembourg. The tables were already crowded with men on their way
to work and students who had only a block to walk to the Sorbonne. When the white-aproned garçon approached with the matching
coffee and milk pots Sigmund let him pour, then said in the precise
French he had learned from a tutor at one gulden a lesson before
leaving Vienna:

"Du pain, s'il vous plaît."

The garçon shook his head, demanding, "Comment?"

Sigmund was annoyed at himself. He thought, "Is it possible that I
have read French since the Sperlgymnasium and still do not know how
to ask for bread? Am I going to be reduced to the ignominy of pointing
at that basket on the next table, as though I were illiterate?" Then he
remembered what the crescent-shaped Kipfel was called. When he
triumphantly uttered the word the garçon sighed with relief and brought
him a basket of croissants.

As he drank his coffee he turned his ear to the surrounding tables. He could not grasp one sentence, or for that matter a single word. He groaned:

"How am I going to understand, let alone utter these wretched sounds? What happened to all those vowels I used to pronounce so distinctly when I read aloud from Molière and Victor Hugo? These Frenchmen swallow them faster than their delicious hot coffee."

He went into the crisp October air, setting forth to conquer Paris with the only weapon at his command: his feet. He thought, "He who walks a city vanquishes it, takes possession, as intimately as a man does a woman. I want to absorb Paris the way I do a new book, devouring every street, shop, crowd of people as though it were a city under siege, and I the invader."

He made his way to the Seine, walked along the riverbank, browsed in the open bookstalls, admired the architecture of the Ministries facing the Quai d'Orsay, crossed the river on the Pont Alexandre III and found himself in the broad tree-lined Champs Élysées, the boulevard filled with sunlight, the leaves turning from purple to gold to brittle brown.

He had known that Paris was two to three times larger than Vienna but he was amazed at how the streets went on for miles, as though one had a clear view to infinity. After reaching the Étoile, the high knoll of the Champs Élysées, he descended to the Bois de Boulogne. The women riding by in their carriages were exquisitely gowned. In the park, on his way to visit the zoo in the Jardin d'Acclimatation, he passed wet nurses feeding infants, older children riding in goat-drawn carts and watching marionette shows, starched-white nursemaids quieting children's quarrels.

It was late afternoon before he made his way back to the Boulevard St. Michel, delighting in the flood of amber light in which the city was bathed. Everything in Paris was new, different, startling and somehow . . . whole. Unlike Vienna, this was not a composite city, attempting to simulate every culture and civilization. Paris, he grasped, was fiercely itself, French. He understood now why the Viennese referred to it as being "in Europe" in the sense that Vienna was not. The Austro-Hungarian Empire was an area, dynasty and culture unto itself, unique, incomparable. Yet Paris was "the mother of cities." He was tired now but triumphant, for every block he had walked was his, every building he had studied, architecturally within his grasp; the Seine, the bridges, the park, an ineradicable part of himself.

He reached the crossing of the Rue de Médicis with the Boulevard St. Michel, opposite the entrance to the Luxembourg. Here there were a dozen outdoor cafes, their tables close together and filling with wives meeting husbands for an apéritif, young men with their sweethearts, students finished for the day at the university, painters out of their studios in berets and velvet coats, chic young girls walking home in groups or with their young men friends, talking and gesticulating animatedly, in love with Paris, with life, with each other. To his astonishment he saw boys and girls break into a series of dance steps, as though it were a spring day and they were not in the midst of passing crowds but alone in Elysian Fields. He thought:

"No such sight is conceivable in Vienna. How wonderful to dance in the streets because one is young and in Paris."

Then it hit him, as though someone had swung a club into his viscera: he was suddenly and totally alone, a foreigner in a strange land, knowing not a soul, unable to communicate, desperately lonely for Martha of the clear eyes, the tender smile and loving lips. How was he to get through these next five days before he could go to the Salpêtrière and present his letter of introduction to Professor Charcot?

He returned to his hotel room, closed the shutters, pulled the draperies over the curtains, flung off his coat, threw himself on the bed, aching in every joint and fissure of his brain: homesick, lovesick, despairing of accomplishing anything. Why should Professor Charcot receive him or help him? Why should the staff at the Salpêtrière put themselves out for a stranger from a foreign land? Why had he come?

The travel grant was an honor no poor man could afford! He went over the figures in his head, as he had a hundred times before. The Medical Faculty had given him only half of his prize, three hundred gulden, a hundred and twenty dollars, to come away with; the second half would be paid when he returned to Vienna and submitted his report. Before he could leave home he had had to pay his debts: a hundred gulden to the tailor; seventy-five to the bookseller; thirty gulden for a trunk and packer with which to travel; eight gulden to his charwoman at the hospital; seven to a shoemaker, five to his French teacher, three at the police station for the forms when he filled out the questionnaire for his *Dozentur*. He had put twenty gulden in gold pieces into Amalie's coffee mug in the kitchen cabinet, bought his railroad ticket to Hamburg for thirty gulden, set aside the two hundred gulden he would need for his visit in Wandsbek, then another thirty-five for train fare from Hamburg to Paris . . . He was in debt before he reached Salpêtrière!

He groaned, "I should have become a bookkeeper instead of a doctor."

The physicians at the Allgemeine Krankenhaus who had studied in Paris assured him that he would need at least sixty dollars a month to live on, or a minimum of three hundred dollars. He had to have another sixty dollars for a month of study at Berlin's hospitals on the way home, and still another sixty-five gulden for his train fare from Paris to Hamburg to Berlin to Vienna.

He had realized that he was caught in an impossible situation; only the fifteen hundred gulden given to him by the Paneths could save him. The fund was intact except for the interest which he had used to help out at home and for last year's trip to visit Martha. He spent a weekend with

Sophie and Josef Paneth, who had rented a villa in the cool white birch forests of the mountains of Semmering. Sophie and Josef agreed that the money would possibly best be spent for training under Professor Charcot.

He jumped up from the bed, took his wallet from his inside coat pocket, laid the money on the pine table. No matter how often he counted it, it came only to a thousand francs, all that was left of the Paneth "Foundation" money. He opened a writing pad and began figuring. This two hundred dollars would allow him three months abroad, half the time he needed. In order to make the most of the journey he would require another three hundred gulden. But how was he to earn it? He needed every precious hour for study with Charcot.

He threw himself back onto the bed, frustrated and unhappy. With the shutters closed, no sound of Paris intruded. At length he fell into a dream-laden sleep.

The next morning he felt better, annoyed with himself for giving way to despair. Yet in the days that followed he found himself acerbic about Paris and the French. He walked through the Tuileries to the Louvre, going first to the Greek and Roman sculpture rooms. He saw women standing in front of male nudes whose private parts were blatantly exposed. He was shocked.

"Don't they know the meaning of shame?"

He returned to the Place de la Concorde with its obelisk from Luxor, studied its superb carving of birds and men and hieroglyphs, but also gazed at the voluble Frenchmen who were speaking and gesticulating with a sense of abandon. He muttered to himself:

"The obelisk is three thousand years older than this vulgar crowd around it."

There was a by-election taking place in Paris, the Republicans trying to oust the Monarchists. He bought two papers a day, reading them over coffee in the cafes, grateful that he was able to follow the written developments if not the spoken word; but the shouts and cries of the newspaper vendors hawking four and five editions a day he found not only deafening but unseemly.

The following night, going to the theater with John Philipp, a young artist cousin of Martha's, to see the great Coquelins play Molière, he paid one franc fifty only to find himself up in the *quatrième loge de côté* from which he could see a sidewise slice of the audience but nothing of the stage. He declared it "a disgraceful pigeonhole box," was struck by the lack of elegance in the women's formal gowns and put off because there was no orchestra as in the theaters of Vienna. He was also struck by the primitive three hammer blows behind the curtain which announced the beginning of the play.

"Why in the world can't they simply lower the lights?"

When *Tartuffe* was played, and then *Le Mariage forcé* and *Les Précieuses ridicules*, all three of which he had read in French as well as German, he found that by leaning perilously forward he could not only watch the Coquelins act but catch phrases and sentences. He was furious at the women actors, of whose dialogue he could understand nothing, and developed a migraine headache. "I don't think I'll come to the theater very often."

He was unnerved by the high cost of everything. The restaurants were expensive. When he went into a pharmacy to buy some talcum, mouthwash and tar he was charged three francs fifty, which staggered him.

He fell into a strange confusion, identifying the French whom he was seeing in the streets with the historical French who had gone through so many bloody revolutions. Standing in the Place de la République in front of the huge statue which represented a bas-relief history of the last hundred years of civil war and revolution, he decided:

"The French are given to psychical epidemics, to historical mass convulsions. And Paris is a vast overdressed Sphinx that consumes every traveler unable to solve her riddles."

Late that afternoon, the last before he was to present himself to Professor Charcot, he was walking to his hotel along the Boulevard du Montparnasse when he chanced to catch a full picture of himself in the glass of a store window, every detail of face and clothing, posture and stance. He exclaimed aloud, to the astonishment of a passer-by:

"My heart is German provincial, and it hasn't accompanied me here!"

He studied himself objectively for the first time since he had come through the Gare du Nord, saw his heavy, almost funereal Austrian suit, the Homburg hat, the Vienna beard, the black silk tie tucked spinsterishly under the rigid white collar, the stern, sober, academic expression in his eyes and around his mouth . . . He confessed:

"I'm the one who has been at fault. I am the foreigner here, not only my clothes and beard and accent but my rigid set of German values and judgments. When I admitted that my heart wasn't here, it meant I didn't want to come. I am holding my loneliness, my not belonging—and how should I belong to Paris after four days of wandering her streets, unable to speak to a soul, uncertain of my future?—against the city and her people."

He turned away from the window, a little smile on his face.

"Forgive me, Paris, it was I who was the barbarian."

2.

The Salpêtrière hospital was located in the southeast end of Paris, just off the Gare d'Austerlitz, a vigorous walk from his hotel. He had studied a map of Paris and seen that there was no direct route. Promising himself more exploratory paths later, when he had come to know the neighborhood, he made his way to a corner of the Luxembourg Gardens, then took the wide Rue Lhomond to a joggle of streets where, with a few sharp turns left and right, he found himself on the teeming Boulevard St. Marcel which led directly to the front entrance of the hospital.

He felt at home at once in the Salpêtrière, for like Professor Brücke's Physiology Institute it had originally been built to store the city's gunpowder. Later a royal edict converted the barnlike structure into a Hospice Général for unwanted women and the infirm. The Salpêtrière was then filled with the prostitutes of Paris; later the beggars of the city were confined within the walls. Finally called an "asylum," its doors were opened to the indigent. One whole section had become an old people's home; then buildings were added for cripples and incurables, for children suffering from mysterious maladies, for insane women. In the infirmaries the idiots, paralytics and those suffering from cancer were all mixed together, and sleeping three and four in a bed. In the eighteenth century a maternity ward was established for unwed mothers, who were obliged to breast-feed the numerous foundlings picked up by the Bureau of the Poor.

During the sixteenth and seventeenth centuries little or no medicine was practiced in the Salpêtrière; it simply gave asylum, food and shelter to the afflicted. In the eighteenth century a physician and a surgeon from the medical services of the Hôpital Général visited the Salpêtrière twice a week to confer with the two resident surgeons. It was not until Dr. Jean Martin Charcot became chief of the Medical Service in 1862 that the Salpêtrière became a full-blown and functioning hospital.

The moment Sigmund walked down the broad cobblestoned approach, lined on both sides with trees, and entered the middle of the three arches with its high-turreted windows, octagonal cupola and white-faced deck, he was back in his own familiar surroundings of quadrangular buildings, landscaped courts, nurses and doctors walking briskly by.

The Salpêtrière, like the Allgemeine Krankenhaus, was a world unto itself, occupying seventy-four acres of land, all enclosed by a high brick wall, with forty-five separate blocks of buildings. It now had a permanent population of six thousand patients; an unoccupied bed could not be remembered by the oldest nurse in attendance. Between the buildings were spacious yards with gravel walks and old shade trees. Some of the buildings had projecting roofs, like Swiss chalets. Unlike the Allgemeine Krankenhaus, the Salpêtrière was bisected by a number of streets, roads and paths, making it unnecessary to go through a series of courts to get from one department to another as in Vienna.

Upon reaching Charcot's office he was informed by a nurse that the staff had gone to the weekly *consultation externe* and that he should report there. He found the rooms quickly, a detached suite for the outpatients, people who were coming for the first time to be examined. He made his way into a small room where a dozen doctors were crowded together in a semicircle before an examining table. Behind this table was Charcot's *Chef de Clinique*, Dr. Pierre Marie, youngish, clean-shaven. Sigmund presented his card. Dr. Marie said politely:

"Won't you join our group, Dr. Freud? Professor Charcot will be here in a few moments to begin his consultation."

He made his way to the last empty chair, was nodded down by a doctor on either side. It was to be a morning of considerable surprises. On the stroke of ten Professor Jean Martin Charcot strode in. He was a man approaching sixty, tall, with a sturdy figure and square-cut shoulders. He wore a double-breasted black coat that came down to his knees, and a top hat. He too was clean-shaven, his black hair was tinged with gray at the temples and brushed back severely from one of the broadest and most powerful foreheads Sigmund had ever seen. The entire head seemed sculptured; strong, overhanging brows, a big bony nose that was in proportion only because it was set in a broad face; ears set flat and considerably back from the plane of the other features; full protruding lips, a stone-carved chin; dark eyes. Sigmund felt the enormous strength of the face, yet it was without any touch of superiority or arrogance.

"Rather," he thought, "like a worldly priest from whom one expects a ready wit and an appreciation of good living."

The Assistants and visiting doctors had risen when Charcot entered. He waved them down with a smile and a rolling gesture of his right hand.

For Sigmund Freud there now began the most exhilarating medical experience of his young life. Charcot, once the patients had been sufficiently undressed to reveal the extent of their illness, began to make neurological diagnoses as though he were alone in his private office, a kind of improvisation that the Viennese professor would never risk. The patients were not suffering from obvious, run-of-the-mill maladies; they had been screened by Drs. Marie and Babinski to make sure their cases were both interesting and complex. Charcot questioned the patients closely to lay bare the background of the illness, broke down the symptoms into neurological categories, proffered a diagnosis and suggested treatment. Sigmund, who had imagined himself reasonably well trained in neurology, was awed to hear Charcot as he reasoned out loud, bringing into his analyses similar cases, proposing original theories about the cause and nature of the maladies before him. When Charcot decided he had made a mistake in judgment he quickly admitted his error, and went forward to a corrected version.

The first patient was a middle-aged woman suffering from exophthalmic goiter, an illness which Charcot had been the first to make known in

France. He demonstrated the symptoms: accelerated pulse, protrudent eyes, heart palpitations, muscular tremor, and the goiter which had swelled out of the woman's neck. Then came a young workman suffering from multiple sclerosis, with its accompanying spastic paraplegia, tremors, disturbances of speech. Charcot illuminated the sharp distinctions between this disease and Parkinson's disease. Further to point up the differences he summoned an older woman with paralysis agitans to indicate the deformity of the hands, the stiffness and slowness of body movement, and the frozen expression of the face.

Dr. Marie next presented a young girl suffering from aphasia, the inability to bring forth words, their place being taken by unintelligible sounds. Then came cases of mutism, cardiac disturbances and cases of urine incontinence.

Toward the end Dr. Marie introduced a woman of fifty, stricken with progressive muscular atrophy, visibly wasting away. Sigmund recognized the symptoms from patients he had tended in Scholz's Fourth Court. After Charcot had made his analysis, on which he and Marie had recently published a definitive treatise, Charcot turned to the semicircle of doctors.

"This is one of the most unfortunate of diseases: hereditary and familial. There is no hope of recovery and never was, from the moment of her birth." He turned away for a moment, then brought his soft dark eyes to meet those of his disciples, speaking in a low-timbred tone:

"What have we done, Oh Zeus! to deserve this destiny?
Our fathers were wanting, but we, what have we done?"

A fascinating part of the experience for Sigmund, as the patients succeeded each other, was that the Assistants and visiting doctors were expected to interrupt and question, contradict Charcot or express conflicting views. This was unheard of in German-speaking countries, where the professor was a god never to be questioned on the tiniest detail of his diagnosis. At one point a visiting doctor from Berlin broke in:

"But, Monsieur Charcot, what you say contradicts the Young-Helmholtz theory."

Charcot replied gently, "*La théorie, c'est bon, mais ça n'empêche pas d'exister.* Theory is good, but it does not put a stop to facts."

A few moments later an Assistant made an observation that appeared sound, though at variance with Charcot's judgment. Charcot replied:

"Yes, but that is more clever than correct." He then pointed out obscure elements of the case before him, caustically but affectionately urging his Assistant to probe deeper. A Belgian doctor asked:

"Monsieur Charcot, if we cannot recognize a patient's symptoms, how are we to perceive exactly what damage has occurred in the nerve structure?"

Charcot came from behind his examining table, stood in the well of the semicircle, so close to Sigmund that he could have touched him by putting out a hand, and reflected:

"The greatest satisfaction a man can have is by seeing something new. That is, to recognize it as new. We must be see-ers. We must look and look and look until ultimately we see the truth. I am not ashamed to confess to you, my confreres, that today I can see things in patients that I overlooked for thirty years in my hospital wards. Why is it that doctors see only what they have learned to see? That is the way to freeze medical science. We must look, we must see, we must think and meditate. We must permit our minds to go in any direction that the symptoms take us."

At the end of the session Dr. Marie gave Sigmund's card to Professor Charcot. Charcot fingered it for a moment, then asked:

"Where is Monsieur Freud?"

Sigmund went forward, handed Charcot a letter of introduction from Dr. Benedikt, a neurologist in Vienna who had worked with Charcot in earlier years. Charcot smiled with pleasure as he saw Benedikt's name; he stepped aside to read the letter, then returned to Sigmund and said with a friendly expression:

"Charmé de vous voir! Would you like to accompany me to my office?"

Sigmund was surprised at how few formalities there were in the French medical world and how readily he understood its language. Though he had been nervous about meeting Charcot—in fact he had come to the Salpêtrière the morning before, only to realize that he had unaccountably left Dr. Benedikt's letter of introduction at his hotel—he felt immediately at ease.

Charcot took Sigmund into his office, a modest-sized room whose walls and furnishings were painted black, with a single window admitting light. There were engravings by Raphael and Rubens as well as a signed portrait of the pioneering English neurologist, Dr. John Hughlings Jackson. The room was sparsely furnished, with a wardrobe for Charcot's coats, a small table and a chair, and several chairs for the interns when he called them to a meeting. Sigmund had already learned that in this small dark room Charcot had made many of the discoveries which had turned neurology into a systematized medical science.

Charcot showed him the laboratory behind his office. There was space only for a couple of tables and a minimum amount of equipment. Ophthalmological experiments were also conducted here, and one corner could be closed off as a darkroom. Charcot murmured:

"Yes, yes, I know the quarters seem small and cramped. But for me they have always been commodious because when I started my first laboratory experiments thirty years ago the only space available was a section of a narrow hallway. Let us go up to the next floor. I will show you through our wards."

Jean Martin Charcot had been born in Paris, son of a carriage builder of modest circumstances. He was trained by the Faculty of Medicine at the Sorbonne, became an intern at the age of twenty-three, at which time he opened his first office in a modest apartment in the Rue Laffitte, combining private practice with a slow climb up the ladder of both the Medical Faculty and the Parisian hospitals. His important awakening took place when he first walked through the wilderness of the Salpêtrière clinics, its thousands of patients writhing out their agonies with no apparent help. Seeing these hopeless creatures huddled together in their unnamed tortures, Charcot said:

"*Faudrait y retourner et y rester.* It is necessary to return here and remain."

Charcot had been thirty when this vision came to him. The road back was long and tortuous but he had fought his way, and by the time he was thirty-seven had managed to get himself named *Médecin de l'Hospice de la Salpêtrière.* Nobody gave him money or help. He assembled his own crude equipment, set up a laboratory in the dark corridor he had mentioned to Sigmund. Yet he had made urgent discoveries in the pathological anatomy of diseases of the liver, kidneys, lungs, spinal cord, brain. When he started training courses in neurology, the Medical Faculty could find no space for his lectures except a vacated kitchen or abandoned pharmacy. Nor were the medical students any more interested. The first year one intern attended the lectures.

None of this had bothered Jean Martin Charcot, who was engaged in the quiet revolution of converting the Salpêtrière from a custodial asylum into a remedial hospital, a scientific center for research, the training of young doctors and the throwing of light into the nature of neurological illness, most of it a dark secret since the beginning of time. He brought the patients to his office for a meticulous clinical study, classifying, categorizing, minutely analyzing the differences between the thousand ills, separating the patients into specialized wards, writing up hundreds and then thousands of cases over the years, publishing papers and books which documented shaking palsy, progressive rheumatism; arterial spasm; lesions of the joints; vertebral cancer; the effect of uric acid on arthritis; muscular atrophies subsequently named after him. Sigmund Freud had heard it said of Charcot: "He explores the human body the way Galileo explored the skies, Columbus the seas, Darwin the flora and fauna of the earth."

Moving now at Charcot's side through the large, well-lighted wards, seeing Charcot stop at each bedside for a moment of conversation, watching the expression of idolatry on the faces of the stricken, he realized that these patients, many of whom had been here for years, were Charcot's children, and he the father responsible for them all. Although some of the cases were incurable, Charcot's studies had brought many of them at least a partial arresting of the disease. Between the beds Charcot stated in a low voice what ill each patient was suffering: a variety of hemiplegia, cerebral hemorrhage, aneurysm, locomotor ataxia . . . not unlike the wards at the Allgemeine Krankenhaus. Most frequent was the wide variety of paralyses of one part of the body or another.

On the way back to his office Charcot turned full face to Sigmund and said earnestly:

"You have heard this before, Monsieur Freud, but you cannot escape my introductory lecture: from your stay in the Salpêtrière you must return to Vienna a 'visuel.' "

"Forgive my spoken French, Monsieur Charcot, it is wretched; but I know the structure of your language fairly well. If the word 'to see' is voir, is the word for see-er not voyant, prophet?"

Charcot replied with eyes snapping:

"A see-er as a prophet is one to whom divine revelations are made. How could I have had divine guidance if for years I looked at this multitude of cases and did not, could not, understand them? I watched the progress of a disease over decades, painfully putting together fragments of comprehension, and finally had them add up to the truth, and often not until after the autopsy. Does that signify a vision? Or is it rather a devoted craftsman learning his trade?"

"You are considered an artist in neurology."

Charcot thoughtfully gathered strands of loose hair and tucked them, housekeeping-fashion, behind his ear.

"They're referring to my alleged sixth sense? I'll define the sixth sense for you, Monsieur Freud: a high degree of honest perception, working against rigidly disciplined years of observation and exploration, seeking answers to questions not asked before!"

When they returned to Charcot's office, he said, "I would advise you to make your working arrangements with the Chef de Clinique."

"Monsieur Charcot, you have been kind to a newcomer and a stranger."

"We must not be strangers in neurology; we must be confreres. The work demands it."

Sigmund paid three francs to a clerk from Administration, was given the key to a locker in the laboratory and a tablier, an apron. Walking out through the main gate, he took the receipt from his pocket and saw that it had been made out to M. Freud, élève de médecin. He exulted:

"Ah, this marvelous French language. All I have to do is to put an accent over the third e instead of the second, and I change from a medical student to a doctor, heroic, eminent, lofty!"

With which, pangs of hunger overcame him and he dashed unceremoniously across the Boulevard de l'Hôpital to the nearest restaurant.

Early the next morning he showed Charcot some of his Vienna slides. Charcot was impressed.

"How can I best further your work here, Monsieur Freud?"

"I need some children's brains; and some materials on secondary deterioration."

"I will write a note to the professor in charge of autopsies."

Sigmund opened his locker, took off his coat, put on his apron and went to the long bench along the rear wall of the laboratory where he had been assigned a microscope. Half a dozen interns and foreign doctors were already at work. Dr. Marie brought him tissue specimens. Sigmund climbed onto his stool; there was hardly room to lift an elbow without lodging it in a companion's ribs. He adjusted the microscope, peered into it and saw . . . Vienna . . . Meynert's laboratory, himself on a stool peering into a microscope. . . .

He straightened up, muttered:

"I've come a long way only to find myself back home. I came here to study neurology! The brains of Parisian children are no different from those of Viennese."

3.

The most important day of the week was Tuesday, when Charcot delivered his weekly lecture in the auditorium-amphitheater with its deep stage, seats rising in steep tiers and, on the back walls of the stage, an oil painting of Pinel striking the chains from the insane at the Salpêtrière in the year 1795. These were now the most popular lectures in Paris, attracting a large number of medical students, doctors and laymen seriously interested in science.

Sigmund came early to acquire a front-row view. The professor who entered the door was not the man with whom he had become acquainted, who had vivacity and a joke to lighten a serious moment; but a man solemn and somber under his velvet cap. He had aged ten years.

On both sides of the stage, and packed behind him, were the medical students. Charcot nodded formally to them, then to the jammed amphitheater, then began reading, half from memory, the formal, tightly knit lecture which he had rehearsed before his staff and corrected after an analytical discussion of the medical implications. His voice was subdued, his diction impeccable; what he said was couched in a rhythmic French prose. His own findings he buttressed with citations from German, English, Italian and American medical journals. Remembering the formlessness of the lectures he had heard in Vienna, Sigmund was impressed not only by Charcot's obvious desire to avoid platitudes and banalities, but by his daring concept that a medical lecture could and must be literature.

As he had already discovered, his surprises here had only begun. When Professor Charcot reached a point in his lecture where he considered even his lucid words insufficient he gave a signal and his Assistants brought onto the stage a group of waiting patients, men and women, all suffering from the same malady. Charcot put down his manuscript, went from one patient to the next and illustrated that they had similar deformities of hip, leg or foot, that when they walked their crippled gaits were identical. He had them take off their gowns to show the corresponding deformities; made them bend, kneel, sit, go through a series of gestures until the pattern of the clinical manifestations was apparent to all.

When these patients had been replaced by a new selection, Charcot grouped together those with differing types of tremors and different forms of paralyses to show the important ways in which they differed. An accomplished pantomimist, and once again his younger self, Charcot threw his features into a series of facial tics and paralyses, acted out the muscular rigidity of those suffering from Parkinson's disease, demonstrated with his own hand what happened in the case of radial nerve paralysis, giving shattering reproductions of the half-animal sounds emerging from the throats of aphasia victims.

When the last of the patients were returned to their beds, Charcot's Assistants set up a large blackboard, brought in statuettes and plaster casts of the cases Charcot had analyzed during the week, as well as charts, graphs and diagrams which were now tacked to the side walls of the stage. With colored crayons, Professor Charcot drew on the blackboard the intricate regions of the nervous system where the maladies originated; then, with the room darkened, showed photographs taken of his patients particularizing every manifestation of the deforming and crippling caused by the diseases he was lecturing about.

The demonstrations ended, the curtains were pulled back to admit the light, the stage cleared of blackboard, casts, graphs. Professor Charcot sat down, composed and dignified, in his chair in the center of the stage, adjusted his velvet cap, became a decade older again and quietly read the concluding pages of his lecture. When he had finished, the audience and students rose in respectful silence, not moving so much as a toe or eyelid until Charcot was out the door, and the near hypnotic spell broken.

Sigmund left the Salpêtrière half stumbling, half walking on air past the Gare d'Austerlitz, crossed the Seine at the Pont d'Austerlitz and finally found himself at the Bastille. It was deep into the noon hour and the streets were largely deserted. He was dominated by a sense of exultation. Charcot had given him a new concept of perfection.

Yet the most extraordinary development came on the following Tuesday when Charcot entered the lecture room and announced that he would address himself to the subject of "male hysteria." To Dozent Dr. Sigmund Freud of Vienna this was an incomprehensible suggestion. During the years of his medical training he had been taught that hysteria was found only in females.

A twenty-five-year-old cabdriver who had been in the wards since April was brought on stage. He had had an accident, falling from his horse-drawn cab onto his right shoulder and arm. The fall had been painful but there had been no bruising. Six days later, after a sleepless night, Porcz awakened to find that his right arm hung motionless, incapable of all movement except for the fingers of the hand. The arm dropped heavily after being raised by an Assistant. Charcot demonstrated that it was insensible to pain, heat, cold.

"To epitomize," he announced to the class, "we have absolute motor paralysis of the shoulder and arm, complete loss of the sensibility of the skin. But it behooves us to notice that there is only minimal atrophy because of lack of use, and the reflexes are normal. These considerations lead us to reject the idea of a cortical lesion, a spinal lesion or a lesion of the peripheral nerves. With what then have we to deal?"

Sigmund leaned forward in his chair, spellbound. Charcot concluded:

"We have here, unquestionably, one of those undestructive, non-organic lesions which escape our present means of anatomical investigation, and which, for want of a better term, we designate *functional.*"

While Porcz was being led out and the next patient brought in, Sigmund took charge of his whirling reactions. What Charcot was proving was that there was no physical damage to the shoulder or arm and hence authentic paralysis was untenable. The accident caused the driver a shock; the paralysis was a result of that shock, that trauma, and not of injury to the arm. Since Porcz had not hit his head, had not lost consciousness, there could be no physical brain damage. This was "male hysteria." Sigmund thought back to the woman in Scholz's ward whom Pollak had cured with psychology and a minute injection of water. Yet hundreds of men met with minor accidents, bruised a shoulder or knee, felt pain for a few days, then forgot the incident. Why, with Porcz, did a paralysis result?

The next patient was a twenty-two-year-old mason. His mother and two of his sisters had been judged hysterics. Three years before his first attack he had taken pomegranate bark to rid himself of a tapeworm. The sight of the tapeworm in his excretion had so unnerved him that he had suffered temporary colic and trembling of the limbs. Two years later a stone was hurled at him in a quarrel. Although it missed him, he was again seized with trembling of the limbs and nightmarish visions of his voided tapeworm. After fifteen days he suffered his first convulsive attack, repeated at regular intervals. The day after he entered the Salpêtrière he had five successive attacks. Examination showed loss of sensation and diminution of the field of vision, and what Charcot described as "an almost perfect imitation of the symptoms of partial epilepsy." In order to demonstrate, he exerted moderate pressure on one of Lyons's two spasmogenic points, just below the false rib on the right side.

Before Sigmund's eyes Lyons complained of epigastric constrictions, then of the feeling of a ball in his throat. His tongue stiffened, was retracted. He lost consciousness. Attendants laid him on a cot. His arms were extended but his legs remained flaccid. Colonic convulsions began, then his arms and legs were shaken by vibrations. He became tormented by visions, crying out:

"Scoundrel! Prussian! . . . struck with a stone. He is trying to kill me!"

He sat up, still unconscious, tried to disengage a tapeworm that was circling his leg. He was moving on to the next epileptoidal stage when Charcot put pressure on the same hysterogenic point of the floating rib and Lyons awakened. He appeared dazed but swore he could remember nothing of what had happened. The attendants returned him to his ward. Charcot concluded his lecture on "hystero-epilepsy," promising to demonstrate a dozen more such cases.

After everyone had gone Sigmund sat alone, the amphitheater and stage wrapping a protective cloak about him. He was shaken to his very fibers. How had Charcot gained this fantastic piece of knowledge when the excellent doctors of Austria and Germany were completely unaware of its presence? Only a few hundred miles separated Paris and Vienna, yet in respect to male hysteria Vienna could have been located in the mountain highlands of Afghanistan.

His mind returned to his fourteen months in Primarius Scholz's Nervous Diseases. All the paralytic cases there, the patients with odd fits, those suffering from loss of pain sense, known to the neurologists as "anesthesia," all had been diagnosed and treated as somatic disturbances, organic illnesses of the body. As he brought the cases back before his eyes he recalled disquieting facts: the man whose legs were paralyzed but who could wiggle his toes; a case of mutism to whom speech was suddenly restored, without any known reason; the patient whose head and arms appeared to be paralyzed but who could breathe well, anatomically impossible because the diaphragm would be paralyzed if the head were paralyzed.

He rose from his chair feeling drained. As he made his way to the door he remembered what Charcot himself had said when he walked through the swampy wilderness of the Salpêtrière's wards thirty years before:

"It is necessary to return here, and to remain."

4.

His quarters at the Hôtel de la Paix were comfortable in the austere manner of quiet bachelor rooms around the world. He ate his meals alone in the restaurants favored by the Sorbonne students, where the food was plain but ample. When he was not at the hospital he spent his time at the Louvre and in Notre Dame on the Cité, where he frequently

climbed to the platform near the top of the tower for a breath-taking view
of the Seine as it made its sweeping curve past the Invalides to the Bois
de Boulogne in the southwest corner of the city. If he had no friends outside the hospital, his love affair with Paris made up for the sometimes
lonely hours. His greatest satisfaction came when he crossed a corner by
the Church of St. Germain des Prés thinking in German and discovered
when he got to the opposite side of the boulevard that he was thinking in
French.

Now this was to change. He had been at the Salpêtrière two weeks when
he was caught on his early morning walk by a sudden beginning-of-
November rain squall. The doctors in Professor Charcot's laboratory
loaned him dry clothes and a pair of slippers. He arrived at the *consultation externe* a little late and had to take a seat behind the semicircle of
doctors. He saw before him a narrow pale skull covered with thin, fair hair.
The owner turned, nodded with a warm smile. Sigmund recognized
Darkschewitsch, of Moscow, with whom he had worked in Meynert's
laboratory, and who had translated into Russian his article on the gold
staining method. After the consultation the tall, lean, melancholy Slav
invited Sigmund to his room for bread, cheese and excellent Russian
tea. They had never grown close in Vienna but here they met as old
friends, particularly after Sigmund learned that Darkschewitsch too had
been engaged for years to a girl he loved devotedly but would not be able
to marry until he completed his training, wrote a textbook on the subject
and received a promised professorship at the University of Moscow.

Darkschewitsch introduced him to another Russian studying under
Charcot. Klikowicz, Assistant to the Czar's physician, had learned enough
about Paris to teach Sigmund how to shop in a *crémerie* where he bought
for thirty centimes what would cost sixty in a restaurant; and initiated him
into a number of small family-run restaurants where the food was inexpensive and excellent. Klikowicz was young, vivacious, shrewd and amiable; they spoke an atrocious French together and one night went to see
Sarah Bernhardt at the Porte St. Martin in Sardou's *Theodora*. Sigmund
thought the four-and-a-half-hour play pompous and interminable. To
Klikowicz he said during intermission while they were standing in the
street enjoying the night and eating oranges:

"How this Sarah can act! After the first words uttered in that ultimate,
endearing voice, I felt I had known her all my life. I've never seen a
funnier figure than hers, but every inch is alive and bewitching. As for
her caressing and pleading and embracing, the way she wraps herself
around a man, the way she acts with every limb and every joint, it's
incredible. . . ."

Klikowicz laughed. "You make her sound like an anatomy lesson. We
all fall in love with Sarah, regardless of how poor the play is."

Then an older couple adopted him, a Viennese-trained neurologist of Italian descent by the name of Richetti, and his German-born wife from Frankfurt. The Richettis had moved from Vienna to Venice where, the doctor told Sigmund, he had been so successful as to accumulate a fortune of a quarter of a million francs. His wife, concededly a homely woman, had brought to her marriage an enormous dowry. Childless and alone in Paris, they insisted on taking Sigmund to midday dinner each day at Duval's. He enjoyed their clucking over him. They went together to Notre Dame for mass on Sunday. The next morning Sigmund bought a copy of Victor Hugo's *Notre Dame de Paris*, which he had already read in Vienna but which now opened up an understanding of Paris and the French he had not been able to grasp before.

In the laboratory he found the anatomical research hard going, even though the famous histologist Dr. Louis Ranvier welcomed him and spoke well of his work. He was getting nowhere with his children's slides, perhaps because his imagination had been captured by Charcot, who was not only giving him a priceless training in neurology and male hysteria but was kind enough to correct his French and allow him to start clinical studies of interesting cases in the wards. He had hours of depression, of feeling a stranger, of loneliness for Martha; and he was constantly worried over what he called "this confounded money." He committed what he considered a supreme act of folly: going into a bookstore on the Boulevard St. Michel to buy a *Mémoire* by Charcot which was listed at five francs, and finding it out of print, he permitted the owner to sell him the set of Professor Charcot's published volumes for sixty francs, "a bargain." It cost him another twenty francs for an annual subscription to the *Archives*.

When he had made his way into the Impasse Royer-Collard and up the narrow steps to his second-floor room, he kicked himself from the bed to the desk to the wardrobe and back again. He had been putting away a franc or two a day in order to take Christmas presents to Martha and the members of her family who had been kind to him; and here he had just spent seventy-five francs more than he had intended . . . though the Charcot *Archives* would be indispensable for his work.

His money began to run out sooner than he had figured. He knew he had only himself to blame, for he had not lived as cheaply as possible. How could he be in Paris and not see the Opéra Comique so that he could report to Alexander, whose passion, after trains, was light opera? How could he not go to the Comédie Française and hear the purest French spoken anywhere in the world? How could he not make the trip to Versailles . . . ? These were opportunities that might never come again in his lifetime.

He sighed, "Ah well, what can't be afforded must be lorded."

Charcot's demonstrations with male hysterics became the most fascinating part of his Salpêtrière experience. There was Marcel, sixteen, who had been in the wards for a year. He was intelligent, of a joyous disposition but subject to paroxysms of anger in which he broke everything he could lay his hands on. Two years before he had been attacked in the street by two men, had fallen and lost consciousness. There had been no discernible wound yet he had developed nightmares and bouts of hysteria. Hard as they searched, no doctor at the hospital could find evidence of injury or deterioration of any part of Marcel's body.

Then there was the thirty-two-year-old patient Guilbert, a metal gilder, also admitted the year before. He had been suffering four or five convulsive attacks a month. Though Dr. Charcot could not find any serious impairment, Guilbert lost all tactile sensibility on one side of his body. He committed suicide by swallowing an enormous dose of chloral. The autopsy proved the diagnosis of hysterical epilepsy to be accurate, for no injury to brain or nervous system was found.

The weather during the first week of December turned foul: slate-gray skies swirling downward in charcoal cones of rain; then cold so intense that it froze the wet sidewalks and made the simple act of walking a precarious feat. Cold in a strange city seemed more piercing than at home.

At the first Monday *consultation externe* in December, and the day after the soul-searching Sunday in which he realized that this would have to be his last month in Paris, that he could visit Wandsbek for Christmas, have only a few days in Berlin, and then must return home, Charcot mentioned in passing that he had not heard from the German translator of his lectures for a long time. Sigmund recalled the incident in the Psychiatric Clinic when Professor Meynert had just completed his book on psychiatry and the young American doctor, Bernard Sachs, had offered to do the English translation. For the next few months none of the other doctors could get near Meynert because he was giving all of his attention to Dr. Sachs. Could this be a way to get closer to Charcot? And wouldn't the translation fee afford him the extra months he needed?

At dinner he said to Dr. and Mrs. Richetti:

"An idea has occurred to me. Today Monsieur Charcot mentioned that his German translator has disappeared. Do you think I might ask him for permission to translate the third volume of his *Leçons?* I can explain that I suffer only from motor aphasia in French; I wouldn't like him to think I read the language as miserably as I speak it."

Mrs. Richetti answered with maternal enthusiasm. "Assuredly you should try."

They spent an hour composing the letter, speaking of the service Sigmund would be rendering to his compatriots in the German language.

A few days later Charcot took Sigmund aside.

"I consent most happily to your translating my Volume Three into German; not only the first half, which has already been published in

French, but also the second half, of which you have been hearing some of the lectures, and which I have not yet released to the printer."

That afternoon Sigmund wrote to Deuticke offering him the German rights. The contract arrived in Paris by return post. Sigmund took it to Professor Charcot's office; together they went over each clause in detail. Charcot seemed pleased that the publishers were immediately interested.

"But I do not see anything in the contract for your translation fees, Monsieur Freud," he declared. "That must be stipulated, must it not?"

"Yes indeed, Monsieur Charcot, I shall ask for four hundred florins, a hundred and sixty dollars. That will support me for several more months." He looked up from the papers, his eyes serious. "And give me the very great pleasure of returning to your tutelage after Christmas."

"*Bon.* I shall want to help you with your translation. I know how hard it is for German-speaking doctors to accept my thesis of male hysteria. It will give you an opportunity to see a good many more cases of this strange phenomena. Then perhaps you will be able to convince your confreres at the University of Vienna."

5.

Winter closed in as Christmas approached. He bought a box of *Chocolat Marquis* for Minna, a French scarf for Frau Gehrke, the Bernayses' charwoman; since the train stopped in Cologne, he would buy Mrs. Bernays a bottle of *eau de cologne* there. He had promised Martha a golden snake bangle "because all *Dozents'* wives wear them, to distinguish them from other doctors' wives." But he had not accumulated enough money to buy the gold bracelet. In Hamburg he found a silver snake that slipped onto the wrist without a clasp. He bought it at once; it would be a promise partially fulfilled.

Five days before Christmas, mercifully dry and pleasant, he moved out of the Hôtel de la Paix, storing his box and trunk with the Richettis, who loaned him a traveling bag and a rug to keep him warm on the train. For his return stay he had found a more pleasant front room in the Hôtel de Brésil, a block away from the Impasse Royer-Collard, and a few steps from the busy colorful Boulevard St. Michel.

He looked forward to talking with Martha and Minna. Since he had arrived in Paris he had spoken to no woman except Madame Richetti, and the wife of the Freuds' early doctor in Vienna, Frau Dr. Kreisler, who had brought her son Fritz to Paris in the hopes of developing him into a concert violinist. There were plenty of girls on the streets but Sigmund did not think them as pretty as the strolling Viennese girls in the Kärntner Strasse. It seemed a rather shaky platform for chauvinism and he restrained himself from sending the piece of intelligence home.

Mrs. Bernays had invited him to stay with the family. He occupied the spare room down the hall from Martha, was up early every morning and startled Martha out of sleep with kisses. As soon as she heard their voices, Minna came in from the kitchen with a silver pitcher of coffee and boiled milk and a tray of *Kipfeln* with fresh butter and jam. After Martha had washed and brushed her long brown hair, they propped her on pillows against the headboard, then sat cross-legged at her feet, telling stories. It was all highly irregular and would have been condemned out of hand by the Hamburg bourgeoisie. Mrs. Bernays closed her eyes to the irregularities, which she termed "Vienna-Paris moral *Schlamperei.*"

They walked in the leafless woods in the cold late December air, bundled up to their ears in greatcoats; when it rained they read aloud before a wood fire in the living room. On sunny days they rode into Hamburg to mingle with the holiday crowds.

The day before Christmas when she served him the five o'clock *Jause* of coffee and *Guglhupf*, a cone-shaped, ten-inch-high yeast cake made with raisins, blanched almonds and lots of butter, she asked quietly, "How long now, Sigi? What are your plans?"

He stretched out his legs before the fire, contentedly relaxed after their run to outdistance a thunder and lightning storm, and studied Martha's face as she poured the steaming hot coffee. Martha was now twenty-four and a half; it was three and a half years since she had agreed to wait for him. During this time she had matured from an eager girl, poised expectantly on the brink of life, to a young woman. Her eyes seemed larger and more communicative, the oval of her face had slimmed, her hair was combed a little more rigorously from the central part. He reached over, kissed her long on the lips. She wound her graceful arms about his neck and ardently returned his embrace.

"How soon, Marty? Let me lay out my plans. I will spend two more months with Charcot; I'd like to work with the hysteria cases as much as possible, in the meanwhile completing my translation of the *Leçons*. After that I will spend a month in Berlin at the Charité to study their treatment of hysterical paralysis, and at the Kaiser Friedrich Hospital to observe their treatment of children's neurological cases. Then I will go back to Vienna to give my travel report, which is expected at that point, open my first office, and accept Dr. Kassowitz's offer to start a children's Neurological Division at the Erste Öffentliche Kinder-Kranken-Institut. . . . The Institute doesn't pay anything but it will afford me materials for research and publishing. Another advantage lies in the reputation one can acquire in this way as a specialist. I'll try to build up my income as quickly as possible to the hundred dollars a month needed to support a home and office."

"How long might that take, Sigi?"

"Probably until the end of next year. The following spring at the latest. In the long run a doctor's practice depends on his skill; in the beginning it rests on luck. It's as big a gamble as *Tarock* or the trotting races in the Prater."

Martha sat on the floor to one side, an arm resting lightly on his knees. When she looked up she wore a thoughtful expression.

"I come under Milton's category of 'they also serve who only stand and wait.' Sigi, you once said that the time to be foolhardy is when one is young; that middle-aged folly is an act of desperation rather than faith. I'm not afraid to gamble. I think you'll earn that twelve hundred dollars a year faster if married than single and alone."

He twirled the silver snake around her wrist but remained silent.

On Christmas morning big, rawboned, broad-faced Minna asked Sigmund to take a short walk with her. They went to the little park across the street from the Bernays house, on the Steinpitzweg, its *Kirche* filled with worshipers but the rest of the park abandoned to leafless trees and its paths covered with snow.

"Sig, I've heard no word from Ignaz since you saw him last summer. It breaks my heart not to have seen him all this time, when he needs me. . . ."

"Minna, Ignaz's illness has destroyed his mind and his will before his body. That's why he broke his engagement with you, he is too exhausted to think of love."

"But how can he be so ill when he went to the theater with you in Baden, smoked a cigar and was happy?"

"It is the nature of the disease. Whenever a T.B. patient in the hospital tells us that he wants to go home tomorrow because he feels fine, we know he will be dead by that time the next day."

"Then Ignaz must die?"

"I wasn't satisfied with my own examination. I took Dr. Müller out to Baden with me a couple of days later. You simply must prepare yourself, Minna; the word of Ignaz's death will reach us any day now."

Minna turned away so that he might not see her tears. He put an arm about her shoulder to console her.

"Minna, you are young, only twenty. Fate has dealt you and Ignaz a cruel blow. It would have been easier on you had you been able to be together to the end; then you would have had only his death to mourn." He turned her about to him, kissed the tears sideways out of each eye. "My dear sister, you have a long life ahead of you. There will be another love. When Martha and I are married you must come to Vienna and join our little circle."

She rested in his arms for a moment, towering over him, her head on his shoulder. Then she trembled and raised her head resolutely.

"Come, Martha said she would have hot red wine with cinnamon waiting for us. It will warm the outer regions of our souls."

6.

The Hôtel de Brésil was a good deal more luxurious than the Hôtel de la Paix. His room overlooked the Rue de Goff. It was no larger than his former one, but the ceiling was higher and the bed and table against one wall, the secretary opposite, were of better quality. It had carpeting on the floor, red velvet draperies over the windows, a bidet and washstand in a corner, hidden behind a screen. The one decoration, a mirror opposite his bed, proved to be of dubious value, for when he awoke the first morning, bolting upright to figure out where he was, he saw himself stark alone again, a man in a furnished room, with no fiancée down the hall whom he could awaken with a kiss.

"I'm a hopeless Philistine," he thought, gazing at his dark eyes, hair mussed from sleeping; "with all the exotic and romantic adventures that are open to free and courageous young men, I want only Martha, marriage, a home, children and a living from my work."

He spent New Year's Day translating Charcot. It was a pleasant occupation, for as he read Charcot's lines he could hear the professor's voice speaking the words in his lecture auditorium. Later that night he wrote to his parents and friends in Vienna wishing them a Happy New Year for 1886: the Breuers, the Paneths, Fleischl, Koller, ending with, "I shall drink to your health." The only trouble was, he had nothing to drink but water from the pitcher; it seemed rather forlorn to raise his water glass to the molded ceiling in a salute.

He returned to the Salpêtrière the following day to begin work on a group of neuroses resulting from trauma known as "railway spine" or "railway brain," a group term, as Mr. Page of England had recently named it. As a result of the extensive train travel in England, Europe and America accidents were fairly frequent, and a new nervous illness had developed. Five French doctors had written theses on the subject; Putnam and Walton in America as well as Page in England had documented the fact that frequently cases of "railway spine" were simply manifestations of hysteria.

There were nine cases of the trauma in the Salpêtrière which Sigmund had the opportunity to study. From their symptoms he realized that several of the cases he had treated in the Allgemeine Krankenhaus' nervous diseases wards had been this same kind of illness. He followed the recuperation of the patients after the legal trials and the payment to them of damages. Charcot emphatically declared to the group of doctors:

"These serious and obstinate nervous states which present themselves after collisions, and which render their victims incapable of working, are very often hysteria, nothing but hysteria. But take heed, only occasionally are they cases of malingering or fraud."

Sigmund moved about the wards studying the other forms of hysteria. An eighteen-year-old mason by the name of Pinand, who had fallen from a six-foot scaffold but was only slightly hurt, had three weeks later suffered complete paralysis of the left arm. Now, ten months later, he was brought into the Salpêtrière. Examination showed a violent arterial pulsing in the neck, with complete cutaneous anesthesia, making the arm and shoulder impervious to cold, pricking, intense electric therapy. His arm hung flaccid and inert; but with no evidence of atrophy. There was also no evidence of spinal lesion, nor did the motor paralysis of the arm involve at any time the corresponding side of the face. Hysterogenic zones were found under the left breast and on the right testicle. When these were pressed Pinand lost consciousness and went into an attack of hystero-epilepsy of a violent nature. He bit his left arm, became abusive, incited imaginary people to murder: "Hold! Take your knife! Quick . . . strike!"

Several attacks took place during the following days, in one of which the patient's left arm suddenly became agitated. When he awoke he was able to move the arm and shoulder, of which he had had no use for ten months. To all intent and purpose he was cured.

"Of what, gentlemen?" Charcot demanded. "Was Pinand malingering? He was not? Then how could his arm and shoulder muscles be almost normal after ten months of alleged paralysis? Was he exercising in the dark when no one could see him? Possibly. These are riddles we still have to resolve. But of the fact that this is a case not of brachial monoplegia but of hysteria, you have now seen the proof."

At about this time the patient Porcz, who had fallen from the seat of his cab and ended with a paralyzed right arm, had a violent argument with another patient over a game of dominoes. His anger and emotion were so great that he sprang up and physically threatened his opponent. Full movement came back to his hitherto paralyzed limb. Within a few hours he had packed his bag and left the hospital. Sigmund was in Charcot's office, along with Marie and Babinski, when Charcot dismissed Porcz.

"You were right, Monsieur Charcot," Sigmund murmured, "the patient was never paralyzed at all."

"Ah, but he was!" replied Charcot, bemused. "Perhaps through some minor lesion of the nervous system. Induced by the trauma of the fall. He cured that lesion by another trauma, the shock of anger so strong that he needed to wave both arms threateningly at his opponent."

"Monsieur Charcot," Sigmund asked, troubled, "aren't we now in the realm of psychology rather than physical illness? Wasn't Porcz's illness ideational?"

"No, no," retorted Charcot sharply. "Psychology is not part of medical science. Porcz's hysterical paralysis was somatic, arising from a cortical cerebral lesion, principally localized in the motor zone of the arm, but not in the nature of a gross material alteration. We hypothetically suppose its existence in order to explain the development and persistence of the different symptoms of hysteria."

"We hypothetically suppose! Monsieur Charcot, isn't that another way of saying we don't know?"

Charcot replied blandly, "Quite true, Monsieur Freud, but don't let the news get outside the medical profession."

When Charcot had gone Sigmund turned to the *Chef de Clinique*.

"Monsieur Marie, have you ever performed an autopsy on a hysterical paralytic who died of other causes, one you 'hypothetically supposed' had lesions?"

"Several."

"Did you find the lesions?"

"No."

"Why not?"

"They disappear at the moment of death."

Sigmund threw his arms in the air, frustrated.

"And what causes some men, after relatively unimportant accidents, to become hysterical paralytics, while others pass them off?"

Dr. Marie stood staring at him in silence, then murmured: "Hereditary weakness of the nervous system."

He learned that Professor Charcot was going to give one of his now infrequent demonstrations of *la grande hystérie*. Although he had heard that these hypnotism demonstrations were popular in Paris, he was unprepared for the throng that came through the door and filled the rising tiers of the amphitheater: fashionably gowned women from the *haut monde*; former court society; boulevardiers in their high gray hats and walking sticks; actors from the Comédie Française; journalists, painters and sculptors with sketching pads; all chatting and with the air of suppressed excitement Sigmund had witnessed in the French theaters before the three hammer blows announced that the play was to begin.

Just as Charcot had made male hysteria worthy of serious study as a disturbance of the nervous system rather than a practice of malingerers, so too in his earlier years he had practiced hypnotism, describing it as "an artificially induced neurosis which can be induced only in hysterics," and set down his clinical findings. In Vienna, Dr. Anton Mesmer, who had graduated from the Vienna Medical School more than a century before Sigmund entered, had gained wealth, fame and power from his hypnotic "animal magnetism" séances before being forced by the Austrian authorities to stop his practice, and later run out of medical circles in Paris as a charlatan. Jean Martin Charcot had once again made the subject respectable, though here in the Salpêtrière he had only categorized and illustrated the nature of hypnosis; he had not, as had Josef Breuer with Bertha Pappenheim, utilized the possibility of hypnotic suggestion for therapy.

Four attractive young female patients from the wards were waiting in an adjoining room. Charcot's Assistants under the direction of Dr. Babinski took turns hypnotizing them as they were brought in, seating them in the center of the stage and having them fasten their eyes on a metallic object or glass ball. Each of the girls in turn quickly succumbed. The Assistants conducted the introductory experiments; Charcot would come later to the three stages of his "grand hysteria."

The first patient was told that a glove, which an Assistant threw at her feet, was a snake. She shrieked in terror, lifted her skirt to her knees and tried to back away. The glove was retrieved, the patient told she was happy again. She broke into a broad smile, then giggled. The second patient was given a bottle of ammonia and told it was aromatic rose water. She smelled it with intense pleasure. The bottle was taken away, she was informed that she was in church and should pray. She slipped to her knees and, with her hands clasped together, recited a prayer. The third patient was given long thin pieces of charcoal and told they were chocolates. She nibbled on the sticks, savoring the bites. The fourth young woman was told that she was a dog; she got down on her hands and knees and began to bark. Ordered to rise, and told that she was now a pigeon, she flapped her arms vigorously and tried to fly.

The first part of the demonstration was over. Sigmund turned in his chair as an appreciative murmur arose behind him. He straightened out in time to see Charcot rise from his armchair at the side of the stage. Today he was young-looking, clean-shaven, his hair trimmed on the sides and back in the current short style. He was dressed in a fastidiously cut black frock coat, with a fashionable shirt and cravat, his feet shod in shining black boots.

A patient was brought in, a comely brunette with her hair gathered at the nape of her neck, wearing a light bodice which slipped easily over her shoulders and down along the cleft between her breasts. She was accompanied by two nurses.

Silence descended over the amphitheater as Charcot reiterated that hypnotism was an artificially induced neurosis which could be brought about only in hypersensitive people and those not well balanced; that he had been the first to study it as a neurologist, to chart its path and to evolve a scientific theory which described its manifold stages. Around Charcot stood his trusted aides, Babinski and Richet. Dr. Marie was missing. An Assistant put the girl into the first stage, somnolence.

Charcot spoke about the relationship of somnolence to genuine sleep and suggested the differences. Then, by use of a bright light shone into the patient's eyes, he put her into the second stage: catalepsy. There was great rigidity of the limbs, they were insensible to stimuli, even the pain of pin pricking; the skin turned pale and the respiration slowed down. Charcot concentrated on the physical conduct of the body, demonstrating what was known as the "iconography of the Salpêtrière." He could make the girl go into every kind of paralytic stance, with arms, legs, back, neck, hands, rigidly contracted and, in the great "culminating arc" of his theory, with eyes closed, lean so far over backward that anyone in a waking state would have fallen.

Charcot then brought his patient out of catalepsy and put her into the third stage, a relaxed sleep. When he awakened her there was evidence of lethargy with no sign of the paralytic stances remaining. She answered questions fluently. Around the edges of his thinking Sigmund was aware that in his demonstration Charcot had made no attempt to interpret the phenomenon. What caused it? Were the actions committed under hypnosis solely physical? Was the body its own master as it moved into the grotesque and crippled postures? Or was there another force Charcot was tapping in these hysterical patients?

Charcot received a thunderous ovation from his audience. He bowed formally, to the left, then to the right, put on his top hat and disappeared through the door.

Sigmund found himself walking beside a young Scandinavian doctor whom he had seen at several of the Tuesday lectures. He had not heard the name clearly and was too embarrassed to ask the tall blond, blue-eyed man to spell it out. He saw that the face of the doctor towering above him was a mottled red, his eyes blazing. He turned to Sigmund and said with a knife-cutting sharpness:

"It's a fraud! A theatrical performance! These girls have been through these acts so often they can do them in their sleep. Go up to the ward at any time and give them one lead-in word and you will see the entire demonstration acted out before you."

Sigmund was stunned.

". . . but . . . are you suggesting . . . it can't be that you're accusing Professor Charcot of a swindle . . . ?"

The doctor said harshly, "Certainly not. It's his Assistants. They have trained these girls the way they do the ballet dancers at the Opéra. The girls know what is expected of them; they love an audience; they are favored and petted patients because they deliver exactly what Charcot wants. This is not hypnotism. Nor are these girls hysterics to begin with. They are being used. I've just come back from several weeks of study under Liébeault and Bernheim at Nancy. They are authentic hypnotists! With thousands of case records behind them. I've seen a hundred cases helped through suggestion, the symptoms alleviated, the illness brought under control. Charcot has refused to use hypnotic suggestion to help his patients; he thinks of hypnotism as a subdivision of neurology to be demonstrated as *la grande hystérie* instead of being used as a therapeutic tool. Drs. Bernheim and Liébeault are honest men. It's a thing you should see one day, then you would know how dangerous this kind of demonstration is to the medical profession and to Charcot's reputation."

Sigmund said in a low voice so that none of the people now making their way toward the Boulevard de l'Hôpital could hear:

"But Charcot is the creator of modern neurology!"

The doctor calmed down, said more quietly:

"He has taught the world more about the function of the various organs of the body, as well as its central nervous system, than anyone since Hippocrates. This is his one terrible mistake."

"Have you spoken to Charcot of this?"

"I mentioned Dr. Bernheim to Charcot once. He flew into an absolute rage and forbade me ever to mention that name again in the Salpêtrière. But take my word for it, the Nancy school is right in this matter of hypnotism, and the Salpêtrière school terribly wrong."

A few days later Sigmund learned that the young dissenting doctor was in trouble. He had stumbled upon an attractive country girl who had come to Paris, gone to work in the kitchen of the Salpêtrière, and then been found to be an excellent subject for hypnotism. She was now living in one of the wards. The man had hypnotized the girl and ordered her to slip out of the hospital and come to his home—"anyone can guess for what purpose!" Dr. Babinski told Sigmund. The girl had been caught in a confused state as she was leaving the ward and had informed the authorities of what the Scandinavian had told her to do. Charcot had summoned him to his office, charged that his was a dastardly crime against an innocent victim, and ordered him out of the hospital. Only because he did not want to hurt the reputation of the Salpêtrière had he not turned him over to the police!

Sigmund felt sorry for the man, then puzzled. Why would he risk his career by such a ridiculous act as bringing a pretty young girl to his home under hypnosis when there were a thousand equally pretty young girls roaming the streets of Paris looking for just such a rendezvous?

7.

One Saturday morning he was chatting with Dr. Richetti outside the Neurological Clinic. Dr. Charcot came up to them to invite them to his regular Tuesday soiree, famous for the celebrities who thronged the house. Charcot's staff was often included but visiting doctors rarely. Charcot turned to Sigmund and added, "And will you also come on Sunday at one-thirty? We will discuss your translation."

On Sunday he set out from the Rue de Goff as the chimes rang out from St. Germain des Prés. It was one of the rare January days in Paris when the sun was scattering islands of warmth on the cold stones of the city. He made his way to the wide, prosperous Boulevard St. Germain, stopping in front of number 217, looking up at what he surmised must be one of the most beautiful homes in Paris. The original had been built in 1704 for Madame de Varengeville but the mansion and grounds had been so extensive that a hundred and fifty years later, during the Second Empire, when the Boulevard St. Germain was built across the Left Bank, the street cut diagonally across Madame de Varengeville's courtyard. Charcot had married the daughter of a wealthy Parisian tailor, and his private practice had grown to include the royal families of Europe. He had been able to buy this magnificent home a few years before, then add two modern wings, one of which was the library-study into which Sigmund was ushered by a butler.

It seemed as large as any apartment he and Martha would ever move into, two stories high, the far half modeled after the Medici Library in Florence, with dark wood bookcases up to the ceiling, a flight of stairs leading to a narrow balcony and several thousand richly bound volumes. It was more like the library at a small university. Short projecting walls divided the room; one end was devoted to Charcot's scientific books, the other half in which Sigmund stood transfixed was filled with deep comfortable chairs, a long refectory table covered with periodicals and, in front of the windows overlooking the parklike garden, inset with fragments of stained glass, Charcot's elaborately carved oak writing table with its formidable array of inkpots, manuscripts, annotated medical books. Behind it stood a high imperial leather chair. On the walls were Gobelin tapestries, Renaissance Italian paintings; before the fireplace at the far end of the room there were tables and museum cases containing Chinese and Indian antiques.

Charcot came into the room, shook his hand warmly, invited him to sit down at the worktable, handed him ten sheets of the unpublished lectures.

"Now, Monsieur Freud," he said, "show me your beginning pages. I speak German badly but I read it well."

Sigmund explained that he had not striven for a literal translation but had attempted to get the neurology absolutely clear and faithful to Monsieur Charcot's scientific thinking.

"Bien, bien, let me read," Charcot responded. "You will not mind if I mark your pages?"

They worked for an hour. When Charcot made suggestions and corrections they were proffered as between collaborators. The work finished, he said, "Shall we take a turn about the garden? Let me tell you a little of the history of this Hôtel Varengeville. These paths we walk have felt the feet of every important royal personage, diplomat, scientist, author, artist of these two centuries. . . ."

For the Tuesday salon Madame Richetti obliged her husband to buy a new pair of trousers and a hat but Richetti decided that his redingote would be sufficiently formal. Sigmund wore the black tailcoat made for him by Tischer. He bought a new white shirt and white gloves and had his hair cut and beard trimmed in the French mode. When he looked at himself in his bedroom mirror, he exclaimed:

"The German provincial is gone. I must say I look very fine in my new black Hamburg tie. In fact, I think I make a favorable impression on myself."

He laughed gaily, went down the narrow winding steps and onto the Rue de Goff as the Richetti carriage drove up. Richetti was trembling with nervousness. Mrs. Richetti said in mock despair, "Sigi, wouldn't you think he was an impoverished student coming tonight to beg Charcot's help in getting admitted to Medical School?"

They entered the main salon with its crystal chandeliers, thick carpets, tapestries and wealth of art works. Monsieur Charcot introduced them to Madame Charcot, to his son and daughter, to the son of the famous author Alphonse Daudet, to Louis Pasteur's Assistant, Monsieur Strauss, known for his work on cholera; and assorted French doctors, Italian painters.

Mrs. Charcot was a pleasant-looking woman, short, plump, vivacious. She confessed that she spoke nearly all languages, then asked:

"And you, Monsieur Freud?"

"German, English, a little Spanish, French . . . badly."

Dr. Charcot intervened. "Not at all. Monsieur Freud is too modest, he lacks only the practice of the ear."

Sigmund drank beer and smoked several of Charcot's excellent cigars. Circulating among the guests, he met Paul Camille Brouardel, professor of forensic medicine, who invited him to attend his lectures in the morgue; Professor Lépine, a shriveled, sickly man, one of France's most famous clinicians, who suggested that he come to Lyons and work with him there in neurology. Toward the end of the evening he was joined by Mademoiselle Charcot. She was twenty, with a handsome figure, full-bosomed, and looked amazingly like her father. She had her mother's natural way with visitors. As he listened to her speak the slow precise French she knew would be a help to such newcomers as Sigmund Freud, he thought:

"How tempting it would be to court this charming young woman! She looks so much like the great man I admire. . . . Mon Dieu, I shall have to confess this aberration to Martha when I write her about the reception."

The weeks were enlivened by Charcot's *jours fixes* though they were not uniformly stimulating. There were always crushes of forty to fifty guests and plenty of food and drink in the dining room. Sometimes he took nothing but a cup of chocolate and vowed not to return; but of course he did.

The week before he was to leave Charcot said:

"I am expecting you *chez moi* this evening, but for dinner this time."

There were only the four Charcots, Dr. and Mrs. Charles Richet, Charcot's Senior Assistant, a Monsieur Mendelssohn from Warsaw, who had also been Charcot's Assistant, Emanuel Arène, an art historian whose articles Sigmund had enjoyed in the daily press, and Toffano, the Italian painter. The after-dinner guests this Tuesday were particularly interesting: Louis Ranvier, the famous histologist of the Salpêtrière; Marie Alfred Cornu, professor of physics, known for his experiments with the speed of light, a Monsieur Peyron, director of the Assistance Publique.

Sigmund was standing with Professor Brouardel listening to Charcot tell about some patients with whom he had been in consultation that day, a young married couple who had made the journey to Paris to consult him. The wife suffered from a variety of severe neuroses; the husband was either impotent or so awkward it amounted to impotence. Professor Brouardel asked in astonishment:

"Are you suggesting, Monsieur Charcot, that the wife's illness could have been caused by the husband's condition?"

Charcot cried with great vitality:

"*Mais, dans des cas pareils c'est toujours la chose génitale, toujours . . . toujours . . . toujours.* But in this kind of case it's always a question of the genitals . . . always . . . always . . . always."

Sigmund was equally astonished. He watched Charcot wrap his arms around his stomach and jump up and down with insistence. Sigmund immediately thought of Josef Breuer the night they had walked home from Fleischl's and Breuer had been interrupted in the street by the husband of a patient. Breuer had exclaimed about the wife's strange behavior, "These cases are always secrets of the alcove, the marriage bed."

The incident had happened three years before. Breuer had never mentioned it again. Yet here was Charcot saying the same thing and they were two of the most knowledgeable neurologists.

"But what," he pondered, studying Charcot's face, "can they mean? This is no part of any medical science I have found in my reading or seen in a ward. On what evidence do they base their conclusions if it is lodged so lightly in their minds that it bursts out like a desert spring and then vanishes again beneath the sand?"

The evening having thrown Dr. Josef Breuer and Dr. Jean Martin Charcot together in his mind, he lay awake, his hands under his head on the pillow, recalling Josef Breuer's "Anna O." Had Josef Breuer come upon a new healing device which Bertha Pappenheim called "chimney sweeping," the "talking cure"? He decided to tell Charcot about it. The next morning he was in Charcot's office early. Sigmund asked if the professor had some moments to spare to hear of a strange case that had been helped considerably by hypnosis. Charcot settled back in his chair, his eyes noncommittal.

Sigmund quickly gave Charcot the background of the Pappenheim family, the nature of the oppression of Fräulein Bertha by a puritanical moral code, the illness of the father, her months of nursing him and the beginning of her attacks, ending with some thirty separate physical manifestations of illness: paresis of the neck, severe headache, muscle rigidity as well as hallucinations, the inability to recognize people . . . He described how Dr. Breuer, by leading the young woman back in her memory while under hypnosis, had enabled her to get to the origins of some of her obsessions and talk about them freely. How the open talk had relieved many of the symptoms, though there had been setbacks, and the partial cure had taken two years. Finished with his story, he hesitated a moment, then asked:

"Monsieur Charcot, what do you think? Did Josef Breuer open an important avenue of study? Is it something we should follow? Can hypnosis serve as a therapeutic tool, particularly when we are frustrated?"

Charcot flung out the fingers of his left hand in a dismissing gesture. "No, no, there is nothing of interest there."

Sigmund dismissed Bertha Pappenheim from his mind.

8.

Charcot was so pleased with the translation of each day's *Leçons* that he kept Sigmund by his side during his hours at the hospital, correcting his French and neurology simultaneously. Darkschewitsch, for his part, discerned some startling material on Sigmund's gold staining slides. He and Sigmund spent hours examining the slides under the microscope in Darkschewitsch's room, and when they were certain of their findings wrote a paper, On the Relationship of the Restiform Body to the Posterior Column and Its Nucleus. Sigmund said with a grin: "It will never rival *Notre Dame de Paris* as a popular title."

The *Neurologisches Centralblatt* of Vienna accepted the paper for March publication. Encouraged, Sigmund set to work on a project he had been annotating for several weeks: a short book to be called Introduction to Neuropathology which would attempt to be in German what

Darkschewitsch was now completing in Russian: a textbook for doctors and medical students. He finished his first section in three days of concentrated writing, then returned to his translations.

In Paris all was going well. The news from Vienna was not good. His sister Rosa wrote that Ignaz Schönberg had died. Though Sigmund thought he had been reconciled to the inevitability, he found himself brushing tears from his eyes as he stood disconsolately at the window staring out at the Rue de Goff, thinking bitterly:

"How meaningless! A great scholar, a first-rate brain, buried in a cemetery before he could even begin his work. And what were the causes, really, that gave the tuberculosis bacillus such a fruitful breeding ground? Bad living conditions? Overwork? The poverty that kept him from retreating to a warm dry climate for a cure? How long will it take before medical science eradicates the hateful disease?"

He returned to his desk, poured out a long letter of sympathy and love to Minna.

Next, the publishers of his Charcot lectures, having agreed to pay him four hundred gulden for his work, sent on a contract in which they had knocked his fee down to three hundred gulden. It was a small loss, but he had figured his remaining expenses in Paris to the last franc, and his month in the Berlin hospitals to the last mark. Now he would not be able to afford it. He was humiliated to have to borrow from Josef Breuer still once more, angry at the publishers for having taken advantage of him, and depressed because he would have to confess his lack of business sense to Martha. Moneyless as he was, he went out and bought a dynamometer to study his nervous condition so that he would be better able to prescribe for himself.

In this state his letter to Martha was inordinately long, analyzing once again his nature and character with a piercing and sometimes mordant wit. . . . His depression and tiredness were caused by all the work and worry of the past years. He had made criticisms of her and picked her to pieces but now he realized that he wanted her precisely as she was, and as a change he would pick himself to pieces instead! He had known for a long time that he had no spark of genius, and in fact could not comprehend why he wanted to be burdened with talent; the only reason he was able to work in such a disciplined fashion was that he had no intellectual weaknesses; he had thought that under perfect conditions he could achieve as much as Nothnagel or even Charcot but, conditions being bad, he would have to settle for a middle accomplishment. While at the Sperlgymnasium he had always led the boldest opposition and never hesitated to defend an extreme stand, even when he had to pay a price for such eccentricity. . . . Miraculously his neurasthenia vanished when he was with her; he had to try immediately to earn the three thousand gulden a year which would entitle him to marry. . . .

It was the last week in February, and his last week in Paris, when he came up with a culminating idea which could bring his work at the Salpêtrière into focus. He would write a monograph on A Comparison Between Hysterical and Organic Symptomatology. In setting down his notes he defined "organic" as "physical damage to the spinal structure or brain." For "hysterical" he gave himself the definition: "representational paralysis," one representing an idea rather than somatic damage or the ravages of disease. His aim was to determine whether the two different origins of paralysis, one physical, the other mental, produced differences in the nature of the paralyses themselves.

He hoped to make three points clear: that a hysterical paralysis could be isolated in one part of the body, such as an arm, without other parts being affected, whereas an organic paralysis due to brain disease was usually extensive; that in hysterical paralysis it was the sensory changes that were more pronounced, while in cerebral paralysis the motor changes were more pronounced; that the distribution of motor changes in cerebral paralysis could be explained and understood in terms of anatomy. *In its paralysis and other manifestations, hysteria behaved as though anatomy did not exist!* It derived its changes from ideas, observations and imagination. What he wanted to establish was that under hysteria the paralysis was set according to the *patient's* concept of its limits.

He wrote a letter to Charcot outlining his idea, gratified at how much his French had improved. Yet he hesitated to hand it to him. To Martha he wrote, "I know that in sending such a letter I am risking a good deal, since Charcot does not like people intervening with clever ideas."

Where he had departed from Dr. Jean Martin Charcot, though he had not said so in his letter, was that Charcot believed hysterical paralysis resulted from a lesion, a wound, in the nervous system, if only a slight one; and that recoveries took place, as in the cases of Porcz and Lyons, when an arising emotion was so strong that it overcame or cured the lesion. Sigmund Freud had come to doubt this, since no one had ever found a cerebral lesion in a hysterical paralytic alive or dead. *The lesion was in the ideas of the mind.*

"But how can an idea, which has no physical contour, be wounded?" Darkschewitsch demanded, when Sigmund discussed it with him.

"I don't know. It's like that night I got back to my room at the Hôtel de Brésil very late and had no matches to light the lamp. I undressed by the light of the moon . . . without a sliver of moonlight! But I just can't grant Charcot the right to 'hypothetically' assume a lesion. If medicine is to remain an exact science we can't settle for a hypothecation. We have to learn how a human mind can so thoroughly anesthetize a mass of its own flesh that a needle can be driven into a shoulder, or a lighted candle held against a leg until it blisters, and the patient feel no pain. If I'm right in thinking that it is the human brain which accomplishes this incredible feat, then the human brain is the most powerful and resourceful *mechanismus* on the face of this earth."

Darkschewitsch's eyes had retreated deep into his head, following his thoughts.

"But, Sig, there's no way of seeing ideas. It's clear from our work here that the patient never knows. How are we going to find out?"

Bertha Pappenheim flitted across his mind, and how Breuer had been able to get inside her memory, had helped her wash out her neuroses by a cascading torrent of words. But Charcot had said there was nothing to be learned from this case.

"I guess we're going to have to make an exact science out of psychology, Dark, if such a thing is possible. What do you say, does the idea have enough merit to warrant my showing the letter to Charcot?"

A mop of hair fell over Darkschewitsch's eyes.

"It's a valid area of research."

Sigmund placed his letter on Charcot's desk the following afternoon. Charcot summoned him. He waved Sigmund to a seat, picked up the letter, which he apparently had read several times.

"Monsieur Freud, the ideas contained in this letter are not bad ones. I myself cannot accept either your reasoning or your conclusion; but neither will I contradict them. I think it might be worth while to work them out."

"Your approval gives me great pleasure, Monsieur Charcot."

"No, no, not approval! Consent. When your material is ready send the paper here to me. I will publish it in my *Archives de Neurologie*."

A few days later Darkschewitsch came to his room in the Hôtel de Brésil to help him pack. He was already packed. He had only one phobia of which he was conscious, and this one, oddly enough, was attached to one of the greatest joys of his life: train travel. Whenever he thought of himself as actually boarding a train, he broke out in a profuse sweat. For twenty-four hours preceding any departure he was in a state of nervous excitation. A sound sleeper at all other times, the night before his departure he thrashed about in bed, torn between joy and apprehension. He went to the station days before to recheck schedules and try to buy his compartment seat in advance. On the morning of his journey he was ready to leave hours before the train was made up, and had to exercise the utmost restraint to keep himself from dashing out the front door, valise in hand, to make a wild scramble for the station. At the same time he was possessed by a feeling of dread so strong that he became slightly nauseous, and yearned to unpack the valise. On every journey he had to overcome this anxiousness.

While it was true that there were frequent train accidents on the Continent, Sigmund was convinced that his anxiety was not caused by a fear of physical injury. Then how could he explain this amorphous trembling in his soft viscera?

He had never lost his excitement over the colorful drama of the trains themselves: climbing mountains, penetrating tunnels, trestling rivers and gorges, hurtling through vast fields of wheat and barley . . . Then why the omnipresent reluctance to board a train for the ardently desired journey? Why did he pace the platform after throwing his suitcase onto the rack above a window seat, unable to force himself to board until the shrill whistle and peremptory "All aboard" of the conductor?

Sigmund had been so caught up in the excitement over Charcot's promise of publication that he never returned to his manuscript of The Introduction to Neuropathology. Darkschewitsch had virtually completed his own text on brain anatomy. In a year he would be back in Moscow, send his book to press, prepare his lectures for the winter classes at the university, and marry his sweetheart. Drs. Freud and Darkschewitsch were on almost the same timetable; the long months and years of training were over, they were about to take their places in the professional and scientific world. And yet, riding in a carriage through the streets of Paris to the Gare du Nord, Sigmund felt a little sad.

"Or is it just nostalgia, Dark? I've come to love Paris, the Salpêtrière, Charcot . . . even you, you melancholy Slav."

Darkschewitsch blinked his eyes hard. "Thank you for those parting words, Sig. I haven't had a close friend since I left Russia. Do you imagine we will meet again?"

"I'm sure we will, Dark. Think of all the Neurological Congresses in the capitals of the world where you and I will be reading competitive papers."

They both laughed in enjoyment of the prospect; but as he sat at the window of the third-class compartment, gazing out at the backs of two-story stone houses, Sigmund realized that in the difficult moment of parting he had been consoling Darkschewitsch and himself as well. The past was gone; he would probably never see Darkschewitsch again, or the Salpêtrière or Charcot, for that matter. It was time now to set his face resolutely to the future. In two months he would be thirty, surely time to stop being a student.

Then, suddenly, the train left the suburbs and began puffing through the green fields of France. Joy washed over him like a sweet summer shower. He had done well in Paris, worked hard, won the friendship of the staff at the hospital and finished more than half of the Charcot translation. He had written some good papers and secured Charcot's approval—no, *consent*, to do an original study that might have pioneering value. Equally important, he was now as well trained as any young neurologist in Central Europe.

In the reflection of the train window he saw his own face smiling back at him. His hair had thinned at the part, where he brushed the left side sharply down toward his ear. He noted that there was a faint tinge of gray in his short chin beard. To his surprise he saw that his face had filled out in Paris. He quite frankly liked the clean-shaven appearance of his cheeks with only the faintest beard line. But best of all he saw that his eyes were clear, wide open, bright and eager for all the goodness of life and love and work that lay ahead. There would be the usual irritations that young doctors faced when first entering practice; but he could perceive no serious obstacles. He had come through the marshy lowlands and reached a point of elevation where he could see his life in perspective. He felt his strength surge within him.

Man's Estate, at last!

BOOK FIVE

A DOCTOR'S PRESCRIPTION

A Doctor's Prescription

B ACK in Vienna in early April he found a practical setup for a bachelor physician: two furnished rooms and foyer offered by a childless couple who occupied the *Parterre* apartment, up a few steps from the entrance hall, at the foot of a broad staircase. The rent of thirty-two dollars a month included the services of a young Austrian *Zimmermädchen* who would answer the door between the hours of twelve and three to admit patients. One door of the foyer led to Sigmund's waiting and consultation rooms, the one on the side permitted the maid to answer the door from the main part of the apartment.

His suite was located in a massive six-story apartment house at Rathausstrasse 7, facing a small park at the rear of the Gothic City Hall, a block from Rathauspark, the Franzenring and the nearly completed Burgtheater, the best possible location in Vienna for a beginning doctor. The baroque entrance hall had rust-colored marble insets as wall panels, fluted marble columns and a plenitude of gold-leaf decoration in the ceiling. In his foyer there was a three-section wardrobe with a mirror in the center, a place to hang hats and coats, racks at the bottom for walking sticks, umbrellas and rainboots. The waiting room had a three-cushioned sofa, a coffee table and enough chairs for a fledgling practice.

His main room was large, with draped windows looking out to a court, wallpaper which simulated cut velvet, hard and soft chairs, a tall Dresden clock and a Dutch tile stove of dark green. At the back of the room a curtain concealed a narrow cot, nightstand and oil lamp. In one corner of this bed-space was a cabinet-closet in which he put his ophthalmological equipment; in the opposite corner a door led to the communal bathroom, with locks on either end. He brought in his own desk and bookcases from the Allgemeine Krankenhaus, shelving the medical reference books within reach of his desk chair.

Mathilde Breuer fulfilled her promise to design Dr. Freud's two medical plaques. Late on Saturday afternoon, the day before Easter, the three of them took a *Fiaker* from the Breuer apartment, each man with a plaque under an arm and Mathilde holding a shopping basket with cakes from Demel's. Sigmund borrowed a screwdriver from the *Hausmeister*. He and

Mathilde held the glass plate with the gold letters on the black background: *Privatdozent Dr. Sigmund Freud,* while Josef twisted the screws into the deep-pitted stone block of the building next to the street door.

They went to the rear of the entrance hall where Mathilde brought forth the porcelain plaque to be attached to the door. While Josef took a tour of the suite and Mathilde put some lilies in water, Sigmund rang for the maid to bring in coffee. Mathilde cut the *Guglhupf* on the plates Amalie Freud had provided, set out cups and saucers, cream and sugar. They sat around the coffee table in the waiting room in *gemütlicher* fashion.

Breuer's hair was retreating in a precise oblong from the deep wrinkle in his forehead; he now trimmed his beard in an oblong of precisely the same dimension.

"Sig, I remember how discouraged you were that day Brücke refused you an assistantship, four years ago it is."

Mathilde exclaimed, "You've become positively handsome, in a rakish French sort of way." She was forty, a handsome matron who had abjured the luscious sweets of the Viennese *Konditorei* and retained her slim figure. Her braids of chestnut-colored hair were wound meticulously on top of her head, her smoke-gray eyes seemed brighter than ever. "Seriously, Sigi, you went to Paris as a promising young student and have come back a mature physician. You can't know how good it is to see pools of wisdom in those warm brown eyes instead of a hutch of impatience."

Sigmund leaned across the coffee table and planted a kiss in the air about three inches from her cheek. He thought, "Mathilde has more confidence in me than Josef." When he had told them that he intended to marry Martha before the end of the year, Mathilde had approved. "The sooner the better. You have burned for years and I don't think that's good for any young man." Josef had cried out:

"For God's sake, Mathilde, don't egg him on. Sig, my advice to you is to wait. For at least two years. By then you will have built up a solid practice, your wife and family will be secure . . ."

"Why, Josef? All I need is three thousand gulden a year. Surely I should be earning that much by the end of 1886? My translation of Charcot's book will have been published; the editor of the *Wiener medizinische Wochenschrift* has agreed to print two of the lectures. I have sent out two hundred cards to the doctors of Vienna, many of whom I have worked with. Surely they will be sending me some patients . . ."

Mathilde, aware that Sigmund had become uneasy, interrupted.

"Sigi dear, when will you put your announcement in the newspapers?"

"Tomorrow, Mathilde. In the *Neue Freie Presse.* Let me show you what I inserted. It cost me eight dollars, by the way; no wonder newspapers make so much money." He went to his desk, rescued a paper from under a batch of notes and read aloud, "*Dr. Sigmund Freud, Dozent in*

Neuropathology in the University of Vienna, has returned from spending six months in Paris and now resides at Rathausstrasse 7."

Mathilde declared, "Very good, but shouldn't you have added, '. . . *six months in Paris at the Salpêtrière working under Professor Charcot*'? People might think you spent the six months at the Moulin Rouge with a series of cancan girls."

Josef was amused at his wife's sally. He stroked his oblong beard, said "That wouldn't be *comme il faut*. Vienna might think he was bragging, in particular those two hundred doctors who haven't had a chance to study at the Salpêtrière. But, Sig, why in heaven's name did you place the announcement for Easter Sunday? That's unheard of."

Sigmund grinned. "I thought of that. But people have more leisure to read on a holiday; they'll be startled to find my announcement in the issue and will remember the name more easily."

After coffee, Mathilde sat back in the deep chair while Sigmund discussed the developments in male hysteria which Charcot had set forth. Breuer was thoughtful. He said tentatively:

"I would caution you to go slowly, Sig; be discreet. Don't fly in the face of Vienna's ridicule of male hysteria. You can do yourself nothing but injury."

Sigmund paced his waiting room nervously.

"But, Josef, surely you're not asking me to abandon what I've learned?"

"Use your insight and training on your patients. Build up a portfolio of proof."

"Once my translation of Charcot appears in German the conclusive material will be on hand for everyone to read. I will be committed."

Breuer shook his head, demurring. "They will read Charcot's neurology with vast respect; when they come to his material on male hysteria they'll dismiss it as a passing peccadillo of an otherwise great scientist. As for your part in the book, you are translating, not advocating."

"Josef, I was planning to write on the subject for my lecture at the Medical Society . . ."

"Then don't! It's too dangerous. Skeptics can only be convinced at their own rate of speed, not that of the proselytizer's."

That evening he sat at his desk writing to Martha. The family was coming the next day to visit his new quarters. Amalie and the girls had promised to bring the robust Sunday *Jause*. A host of emotions chased themselves across those mysterious areas of the brain which his anatomical studies had not yet localized: fear that no patients would show up, contesting with a blind faith that a workman was worthy of his hire; ambivalence over having ended in private practice after all, and reassurance over Dr. Meynert's enthusiastic welcome in the psychiatry laboratory to complete his study on the brain structure of infants, and Dr. Kassowitz's urgent invitation to open the Neurological Department of the Children's Institute immediately.

Coupled with these swirling thoughts and feelings were his ambiguous sentiments about being back in Vienna. During his seven months away from the city he had reassessed its hold on him. He had not been born here, perhaps that made a difference; and yet he could remember little of Freiberg in Moravia. As an intellectual who had spent his adult years in Professor Brücke's physiology laboratory and the Allgemeine Krankenhaus, he had known only the serious, scientific Vienna, an altogether different world from the Vienna of the mass of its people, the Vienna dominated by the composer geniuses, Mozart, Beethoven, Shubert, the Strausses, in whose melodic music the Viennese floated through life.

There was no doubt in his mind that, reluctant lover though he had been, he had become enamored of Paris; the sunlight on Notre Dame, the Seine winding through the city on a dark night, the tranquillity of its indigenous architecture, wide boulevards and open areas, the numerous sidewalk cafes where one listened to the newsboys hawking extras in the streets, watching pert young people singing their way along the Boulevard St. Michel; the quick-moving, light-stepping tone of the people in general, the modern feeling of its republicanism. There was something in the air of France, a bouquet, the look, feel and smell of free men. He had sensed it only once before, when he had visited his half brothers in Manchester.

From Berlin he had written to Martha that he would not worry about anything until he saw with his own eyes the "detestable tower of St. Stephan's." And yet in all fairness he knew that the tall tower was a thrilling thrust into infinity of the architect's art; he was holding against it the fact that in its shadow he must make his stand. He mused, "No man loves his battlefield; not until he has conquered there." From Berlin, where he had spent his month studying with Dr. Adolf Baginsky, professor of pediatrics and director of the Kaiser Friedrich Hospital, and with Drs. Robert Thomsen and Hermann Oppenheim in the Nervous and Mental Diseases Department of the Charité Hospital, he had written a line to Martha from Schiller: "How different it was in France!" and then added, "If I had had to travel from Paris to Vienna, I think I would have died en route."

Alone, the lamp wick turned low, he pondered on the meaning of Vienna in his life. Of much of it he knew only what he saw in holiday parades: Emperor Franz Josef, the Empress and their children; the nobility, the brilliantly attired military officers who were the gods of the city; the landed gentry who ruled the countryside; the ministers by whom the Empire was administered. He knew about these things from what he read in the *Neue Freie Presse* and the *Fremdenblatt*. The Hapsburgs had been ruling here for hundreds of years, controlling the largest, richest empire since the Romans. Paris also had its nobility, reduced by the three revolutionary bloodlettings; yet it elected its officers, its laws were made and enforced by representatives. Would he have felt differently if he had entered a Paris ruled by Louis XV?

And yet, the Austrians did not miss their freedom; they adored and worshiped Emperor Franz Josef, who in turn gave them solid, honest, responsible bourgeois government in which they participated in some small measure since their uprising in 1848. But there were differences in attitude; the Austrians who identified with their beloved Emperor turned themselves into subjects by that very act. The French were their own political masters. Sometimes wasteful, inattentive, stupid, they wore their freedom like a loose cape, sloppily fitted and looking a bit incongruous on some, but still, as free men.

As Parisian architecture was its own, so was the French character. Little borrowed, and nothing begged. Vienna's was powerfully polyglot, Austrian, Bohemian, Hungarian, Croatian, Slovakian, Polish, Moravian, Italian. . . . As the Imperial City it wished to represent every segment as "the recapitulation of all world civilization; opulent, baroque."

Yet he was happy to be home; eager to commence his work. He had ample reason to revere Vienna's university, Medical Faculty, scientific institutes, Allgemeine Krankenhaus. The city had given him, a poor boy from an immigrant family, a superb education and professional training that could not be surpassed in Berlin, Paris, London or New York. He could be accused of knowing little more than the university-medical-scientific world of Vienna. Need he know more? Was not every city a honeycomb of compartments, each occupied by a portion of the population? To the military man Vienna was the army; to high society, it was the Emperor; to the actor it was the Karlstheater; to the musician, the Opera, the Beethoven and Mozart Halls; to the businessman, the banks, shops, textile district, Börse.

Each man knew his city. Certainly the one in which he worked and lived attracted the finest minds and spirits not only of the Empire but of the entire German-speaking world. He, Sigmund Freud, had gone to school to them. They had been kind, helpful, generous. They constituted a great Vienna. He did not desire to live in any other Vienna!

Nor for that matter did he desire to live in any other city, Paris included. His roots were here, burrowing deep into the cobblestones. True, he was a Jew inside a Catholic enclave, which was not always comfortable; but the Jew had been a wanderer since the Temple was destroyed, and had had to live in the midst of someone else's religion. As far as he had read history it did not seem to matter which was the host culture. Emperor Franz Josef had been consistent in his protection of the rights of the Jews within the Empire.

He rose, paced the room for a moment, then went to the window overlooking the little park behind the Rathaus. Through the curtain he saw a few couples walking slowly on the paths under the flour-white gas lamps. He turned back to his desk.

Vienna must allow him to earn a living, support a wife, afford him the opportunity to study, research, discover, write in his chosen field. . . . Here he and Martha could work, prosper, propagate.

2.

An hour before noon the Monday following Easter he sat at his desk, manuscripts stacked neatly on either side of him: the travel report to be given before the *Gesellschaft der Ärzte;* the chapters of the Charcot book already translated, notes for his Introduction; beginning pages for a paper on hypnotism which he would present to the Physiology Club and then to the Psychiatric Society; abstracts of neurological literature in Vienna for Mendel's *Neurologisches Centralblatt* and of children's neurological literature for Baginsky's *Archiv für Kinderheilkunde* which he had promised both doctors in Berlin.

His total assets at this moment of commencement were four hundred gulden. The three hundred gulden he had had to borrow to see him through his latter months in Paris and Berlin he would be able to repay in July when he received his fee for the Charcot translation. The second installment of his travel grant, which he would have in hand when he submitted his written report, was also owed. He had borrowed small sums from Fleischl over the years, frequently at Fleischl's insistence. When Sigmund told Ernst that he should be able to repay him within a year or two, Fleischl said:

"Forget it, Sig, I have had a hundred times that much in medical service from you. Not to mention those long nights when you sat up with me arguing and playing Go to help me forget my pain."

"That was friendship."

"Do small sums of money lie outside the realm of friendship? Were your time and medical attention worth nothing?"

"Just about! I'll find other ways of paying you back."

Fleischl gritted his teeth. "Invent a way of grafting a new thumb onto this bloody hand of mine."

His biggest debt was owed to Josef and Mathilde Breuer. It amounted to a full two thousand dollars. He had suggested that he begin paying them small sums each month. Breuer waved this aside with a vigorous gesture.

"That's no good, Sig. We don't need the money now. Take a ten-year reprieve. At the end of that time you will be earning substantially."

There was little likelihood of his earning the necessary hundred dollars over the first months of his practice. Some of his associates at the All-gemeine Krankenhaus had considered him foolhardy to start out with so little reserve. Dr. Politzer, the otologist who had called him in for consultation when he was back in Vienna only a day or two, and earned him fifteen gulden, said, when he heard that Sigmund was planning to be married in the fall:

"I'm shocked. I know from our meeting only a few days ago that he has absolutely no means. Why does he insist on marrying a penniless girl when he can get a dowry of a hundred thousand gulden?"

His reverie was interrupted a minute past twelve by a heavy knocking at the front door. The *Zimmermädchen*, a little flustered by her new role, admitted two officers from the police building on the Donau Kanal. They had both been sent by Josef Breuer.

He attended the older man first, the one with the barrel chest and protruding egg-shaped stomach. He had scuffled with a thief when arresting him, and had neck pains radiating down his left arm, associated with tingling pins and needles which involved the thumb and index finger. Dr. Freud judged that the officer was suffering from a brachial neuritis. He prescribed traction. The officer returned several times and soon Sigmund was able to pronounce him cured.

The younger of the two officers, totally bald and with his head set deep in his shoulders, told Dr. Freud that he had difficulty in knowing where his legs were when he placed them ahead of him during his night shift, and was conscious of a marked sense of insecurity unless he was able to visualize where he was placing his feet. He described flashes of pain girdling from his back around his abdominal wall, increasing in intensity over a number of months. Dr. Freud brought the man back for a variety of tests; however the end diagnosis was what he had suspected from the beginning: syphilis, with evidence of locomotor ataxia.

Professor Meyers of the University, learning that Sigmund had opened his office, sent his wife in to see if he could furnish her some relief from her sciatica. He suspected a rupture of an intervertebral disc which produced severe pain at the bottom of her back and down her left leg. He prescribed bed rest, posturing exercises and a support placed in the low area of her back. The thin fibrous plate that lay between the bodies of her vertebrae and acted as a rubber cushion slowly moved back into place.

Breuer's "roving band of neurotics" found his office. The first to reach him was Frau Heintzner, plump, attractive, fortyish. She appeared with a skin rash which Dermatologist Freud cleared up with salves. A few days later she was back with a stiff neck which kept her head twisted to one side. Electrical Therapist Freud loosened her neck muscles with faradization. At her next appointment she was suffering from sharp abdominal pains. Internist Freud massaged her stomach and soft viscera, which relieved the cramps.

"Dr. Freud, you are a marvelous physician. You can cure absolutely anything I get."

He replied somewhat hollowly, "Our motto at the Medical School, Frau Heintzner, is: 'Anything the patient can contract, the doctor can subtract.'" But while Frau Heintzner laughed, straightening her dress and adjusting her hat on her piled-up tawny hair, he thought, "What does one do with a person who can get attention only by conjuring up new symptoms? My meager medical experience can never keep up with her imagination."

The life of a beginning physician, he found, was busy, fraught with uncertainties and perils, filled with gratifications and disappointments. Professor Nothnagel sent him the Portuguese Ambassador, whom he relieved of a minor ailment; but Professor Nothnagel's next two recommendations to patients that they see Dr. Freud were ignored, the people preferring older doctors. Next he was summoned to treat an acquaintance from his *Gymnasium* days, bedridden and penniless. He had gone without supper for three days to save his gulden; now he walked an hour each way to save the *Fiaker* fare. That night he had an urgent message that the man was dying. The rented cab took the savings from his three supperless nights, but he did manage to keep his old schoolmate alive.

It was Breuer who sent him Frau Dr. Kleinholtz, who was seeking help for her husband. Dr. Kleinholtz had been going through personality changes, alterations in his habit patterns. Formerly scrupulous in his grooming, he now went about unkempt, developed an inability to concentrate, and had been making faulty judgments in his business affairs. He also complained of headaches.

The patient seemed confused. When Dr. Freud could find no organic evidence of illness or disturbance of function, he thought that he might have an authentic neurosis on hand. However he had sternly warned himself not to be prejudiced in favor of neuroses and hysterias, but to keep an open mind and examine every patient objectively. During the two weeks of tests Dr. Kleinholtz developed a weakness in the right hand, with increasing headaches. Sigmund recognized these symptoms. Dr. Kleinholtz was suffering from a tumor in the left frontal lobe.

One particularly cool morning a young Assistant from the Allgemeine Krankenhaus sent him an American doctor who had come to the hospital for a refresher course. He was thirty-five, with a clump of red hair and dressed in a double-breasted blue jacket.

"How can I help you, Dr. Adamson?"

Adamson sprawled in the big chair across the desk, then tried to push the stand of red hair back off his brow.

"I'm embarrassed, Dr. Freud. My wife and I saved enough money for this stay in Vienna, but I have little left for medical expenses."

"Suppose you tell me what is wrong? If I am qualified to help I will be happy to extend professional courtesy."

"Thank you. I am suffering increasingly severe headaches. They fall into a pattern: a bandlike sensation around my head with a sense of pressure on the very top, combined with blackout spells which are not truly blackout spells but episodes during which I am aware of everything that is going on."

"You are a trained physician, Dr. Adamson. Have you identified any organic disturbance?"

Dr. Adamson gazed at the shelves of medical books, then turned back with a troubled face.

"I am apprehensive because I feel that jealousy regarding my wife has been causing me to become somewhat mentally unbalanced. She is young and beautiful. We have been happily married for several years. I must confess that I don't know what has happened to her. When we go to parties she behaves in a forward fashion with the men about her. Nothing like this has ever occurred before. But my real problem is her increased sexual appetite. It is draining my energies. What's more, our act of coitus has changed its character. She becomes more and more . . . aggressive, almost obsessively carnal. She is emotionally upset part of the time, and now she has me mentally upset as well."

"I will give you a thorough examination. After that we will discuss your wife. Could you bring her in?"

The next afternoon Dr. Adamson was accompanied by his wife. He had not underestimated her charms: she was an ash-blonde with luminous blue eyes and a figure which she clothed in a dress one size too small, outlining her breasts, flat abdomen and legs.

Dr. Adamson returned to the waiting room. The moment he left, Mrs. Adamson shook the tresses of her blonde hair coquettishly and gave Dr. Freud a bold smile. He came around the desk to talk to her. As he did so the picture of Martha, which had been sitting comfortably toward the back of the desk, fell to the floor. This startled him; he did not believe he had brushed the picture or shaken the desk sufficiently for it to fall off.

He got little from Mrs. Adamson except talk about how gay she found Vienna. However after insistent questioning she did inform him that six years earlier she had had a prolonged episode of double vision; when that had cleared she had noted some numbness in the left arm and in her face. At the end of a half hour, since her husband was waiting, he asked her to return the following day.

As Sigmund came forward to greet her, Martha's picture again fell off the desk. He stood staring at it on the floor, dumfounded. How could this have happened twice? True, Mrs. Adamson had walked into the office swinging her hips, holding her head back so that her breasts were pointing at him. "But surely," he thought, "not enough to knock Martha off the desk!" Mrs. Adamson said with a coy smile:

"Your fiancée, Dr. Freud? It looks as though she is about to fall out of your life."

Sigmund picked up Martha's picture, dusted it against his coat and set it in the geometric center of the desk. He plunged at once into the question of Mrs. Adamson's hypersexuality, trying to find when the change had taken place. Mrs. Adamson denied that her sexual demands were excessive.

"It's just that I feel I am growing younger and more alive every day, Doctor; and my husband, poor man, working as hard as he does, grows older."

Sigmund was perplexed. Was this an emotional problem? Or was there some organic disturbance? He felt certain that Dr. Adamson was telling the truth and that his wife was not.

He thought, "The first and indicated course is to examine her gynecologically; but I know so little about the field. I wouldn't know what I was looking for. Besides, considering the expression on Mrs. Adamson's face, that might be a dangerous procedure. I think I'll go talk to Rudolf Chrobak instead."

Late that afternoon he dropped in at Dr. Chrobak's apartment. The gynecologist, though only forty-three, had been appointed professor of gynecology at the University of Vienna. Sigmund had done no work under him at the hospital, but they had liked each other and become good acquaintances. He told Dr. Chrobak about the Adamsons; he stroked his formal Vandyke beard in rhythm with his thoughts, but could give no help.

A few weeks later the case took a sudden turn. Dr. Adamson brought his wife in; but it was a different Mrs. Adamson. There was nothing flirtatious about her; she was holding her head to one side as though in pain. She spoke slowly, her lips stumbling around the words:

"The symptoms I had . . . six years ago. . . . They're back. But different. My left eyebrow . . . is numb. And I have trouble moving my right foot. . . ."

He escorted the woman behind the screen, then examined her painstakingly. There was no numbness in any other part of the body, no anesthesia in her legs or back, abdomen or chest. His first light came when he recalled that in multiple sclerosis there was often an increased sexual appetite.

When he had conducted additional tests he was certain: this was multiple sclerosis. He did not inform the patient, but the beautiful young woman would suffer increasing tremors, disturbances of speech, and finally paralysis. There was nothing in medical science that could arrest the disease. Its severity would depend upon the seat of the lesion in the brain or spinal cord. Dr. Adamson would soon be cured of his ailments; but the marriage would face another and more traumatic shock.

3.

His thirtieth birthday, May 6, 1886, fell on a Thursday. He had collected few gulden during the past weeks and there had been no one in his waiting room for several days. He groused, "That descriptive term is misused: it's the beginning doctor who waits, not the patient."

The postman knocked early in the morning with an evergreen plant from Martha. Behind him came his sister Rosa, bringing a blotter for his desk, framed on either end with red leather stamped with Florentine gold. Since the frightened, apprehensive young Brust had disappeared Rosa had not had another beau. Sigmund wondered why, she was such an attractive girl, with a stimulating mind. She seemed happy, high-spirited, with a bemused attitude toward life, though she also suffered Sigmund's wide range of emotional reaction. She fingered a button of his coat which was hanging loose on its threads.

"Sigi, you're being neglected. Do you have needle and thread? And look at your shoes! They need repairing. You have another pair; I'll take these with me when I leave."

He chuckled, put an arm lightly about her shoulder.

Pauli and Dolfi arrived carrying a Makart bouquet of dried palm branches, bamboo, reeds and a peacock feather. Behind them came Mitzi and her newly acquired husband, Moritz Freud, a distant relative. She brought a framed wedding picture of herself. His parents arrived, Amalie with a *Wiener Torte* she had baked that morning, and Jakob with a copy of a book by the Englishman Disraeli whom Sigmund admired. Both parents took him in their arms and kissed him precisely as they had on his tenth and twentieth birthdays. The last to arrive was Alexander, who had gotten up at five that morning to stand in line in front of the box office of the Theater an der Wien to buy two tickets for Johann Strauss's *Gypsy Baron*. One night a week Alexander went to hear light opera, *Die Fledermaus, Tales of Hoffman*; the week before he had deprived himself of this one splurge in order to have enough money to take his brother with him on this thirtieth birthday.

Dolfi made coffee on the grill in the ophthalmology closet, Amalie set the cake on Sigmund's desk, Alex brought in the chairs from the waiting room. The family gathered close together in a *Kaffeeklatsch*. Anna arrived, out of breath, six months pregnant, a basket of flowers from the Naschmarkt under one arm, her fourteen-month-old daughter under the other, wished Sigmund "thirty more, thirty better," and deposited little Judith in his lap. Sigmund, feuding with Eli Bernays this time because Eli was tardy in returning some dowry money Martha had put in his care, managed enough birthday good will to inquire after his brother-in-law's health.

Jakob had been working of late and bringing home a wage. Sigmund knew his father was happy because he was telling jokes again.

"Sig, there was an impecunious Jew who stowed himself away without a ticket on the fast train to Karlsbad. Again and again he was caught, pummeled and put off. At one of the stations he was met by an acquaintance who asked him where he was going. 'To Karlsbad,' he replied, 'if my constitution can stand it.'"

It was late when the operetta let out. Sigmund thanked his brother, then walked home alone. He entered his little apartment feeling depressed. He, too, was traveling without a ticket, toward marriage, a home, a practice . . . if his constitution could stand it.

He had had to buy a couch on which to examine his patients and it had taken practically the last of his cash. He was learning what he had always known, that there was a sharp difference between practicing medicine and earning money. If Dr. Politzer had not called him to a second consultation the day before, he would have passed the entire week working like a demon and not earning a kreutzer. He sat down at his desk, adjusted the light from the lamp so it would cover only the sheet of paper and his hand, and wrote to Martha, "I would like to think that the next birthday will be as you describe it, that you will be waking me up with a kiss and I won't be waiting for a letter from you. I really no longer care where this will be. . . . I can put up with any amount of worry and hard work, but no longer alone. And between ourselves, I have very little hope of being able to make my way in Vienna."

The next morning, after he had posted the letter and was on his way to Meynert's laboratory, he thought, "I'm like Rosa. My emotions are as fluid as the tides of the sea."

It was said that, while the earth turns on its axis, patients turn on their pains. During the next days half a dozen paying patients settled themselves in his waiting room, and during the afternoon he was called to the Krankenhaus Wieden by an associate to look at a newborn infant who had, at the lower part of its back just above the buttock crease, a soft growth about the size of a lemon. Dr. Freud examined the stretched skin and the hair growing from it, then checked the rest of the infant's body.

"A congenital variation, nothing more," he assured his associate. "I've seen several such growths in adults. The baby will grow up without difficulty."

"Would you please tell that to the mother?" the doctor asked.

The following morning he was summoned to the home of a former nervous patient of Obersteiner's at Oberdöbling, whose baby had been born paralyzed from the waist down and was desperately ill. When Dr. Freud touched the sphincter of the rectum, the gate of the anus, he found the muscle completely loose. The paralysis also involved the bladder and bowels. It was a case of myelomeningocele. The child would be paralyzed for life. However if he could keep the fever down, hold off convulsions, watch for bladder infection . . .

He spent all day Saturday and Sunday with the infant, sleeping overnight on a couch. His major problem was that there was little drainage; the bladder filled and acted as a culture for germs inside the urine. He had reason to believe that the baby would die from a kidney infection; it might take two years or it might take only two months. Yet he had been trained to fight for life as long as there was the tiniest discernible spark. Fight he did, keeping the baby alive until the family's doctor was able to take over.

He had set himself a rigidly disciplined schedule: up at six for his bath, dressed, he admitted the maid who brought hot rolls from the neighboring baker, and a cup of his own coffee which she had ground in the kitchen. By seven the girl took the breakfast dishes and cloth from a corner of his desk and he started work on the translation of Charcot's last chapters or his travel report. By ten he was in Meynert's psychiatry laboratory working on the origin of the auditory nerve in the human fetus. At eleven he walked across the street to a restaurant for the *Gabelfrühstück* consisting of a double *Kleines Gulasch*, each small enamel pot containing two or three pieces of meat with potatoes and gravy, since his consultation hours left him no time for the big midday meal.

He returned to the laboratory for another half hour with his slides and by twelve sharp was behind the desk in his consultation room. The waiting room now was frequently filled, for word had spread that the new young doctor handled his charity cases with the same care as his paying patients. He had not earned his expenses for the first month but he was glad to have the "free patients"; Vienna said that if a beginning doctor got no charity patients, no one else would want him either. And, like the goulash, spaced among the frequent potatoes was the occasional bite of beef or veal: those who, unlike the Portuguese Ambassador who never did pay his bill, dug into their purses or wallets to pay their medical fees as they went along.

The following month when the new quarters were ready, he would leave at three on Tuesdays, Thursdays and Saturdays for the Erste Öffentliche Kinder-Kranken-Institut in Wien, where he would set up a Children's Neurological Department. For the other days he extended his office hours until four, asking those patients who sought free diagnosis or electrical massage to come at this later hour so that he would not have to keep his paying patients waiting. In the late afternoon he met a doctor friend at a coffeehouse, Paneth, Obersteiner, Königstein, who also served at the Children's Institute, Widder, Lustgarten; they discussed their common medical problems and, if he were not in the usual bachelor fashion suppering at the Breuers', Paneths', Fleischl's, ate a light supper and returned to his desk for concentrated reading and writing until midnight. He fell asleep instantly his head touched the pillow. On Sundays he had midday dinner with his family; each Sunday he dropped a few gulden into the coffee mug with the broken handle which Amalie kept in a kitchen cupboard. Neither mother nor son mentioned this modest, ritualistic act, but it gave them considerable pleasure, particularly toward the end of the second month when his practice increased and he saw he was going to take in half again as much as he needed to pay his expenses and could leave ten or fifteen gulden in the cache.

In spite of the crowded eighteen-hour workday he found time, always late at night, to miss Martha. He wrote to her nearly every day, describing his patients and cases, happy when the consultation-room chairs were filled, despondent when he sat from twelve until three and no one came but the *Schnorrer* and *Schatchen*, beggars and matchmakers who found Vienna's young doctors their natural prey.

And as exciting to Sigmund as the beginning of his private practice was his work in creating the Children's Neurology Department at what was now being called the Kassowitz Institute after its director, Dr. Max Kassowitz, considered to be Vienna's outstanding specialist in children's diseases. Because he had tried to cover the entire area of childhood ailments Kassowitz had at one time thought smallpox, chicken pox and measles to be the same disease; earlier he had imagined that rickets were caused by an inflammation. Yet he was the first in Vienna to put the study of children's diseases on a scientific base. When he learned that phosphorus was important in the treatment of rickets and other weaknesses of the child's body, Kassowitz searched for an emulsion which would hold the chemical together and enable the child to take it. He finally fixed on cod-liver oil, considered useless medically. The phosphorus accomplished miracles for children suffering from rickets, tuberculosis and anemia.

Only a few months before Sigmund's return to Vienna, Kassowitz, who had completed his training at the Allgemeine Krankenhaus seventeen years before, had moved himself and his family out of a spacious eight-room apartment on the first floor of Tuchlauben 9, above A. Moll Apotheke, one of the oldest drugstores in town, to other rooms in the same building, and converted his former apartment to an expanded children's day clinic for outpatients. The Institute was a free clinic. The children came from the poorer classes who could not afford to pay. All of the doctors were volunteers, receiving no fees or salary of any kind. The former Kinder-Kranken-Institut was supported by private contributions, laying out only a thousand florins a year for indispensable medical supplies.

Sigmund made his way down the Tuchlauben, past the drugstore on its triangle of land, thronged at all hours of the day with those, including mothers suckling their young, who wanted to buy Kassowitz's preparation. The pharmacy had three people doing nothing but make the mixture. He then swung into the Kleeblattgasse. Here on the sidewalk were mothers and children waiting in line to climb the outside flight of stairs to the Institute.

Dr. Max Kassowitz greeted him. He was an intently serious man, looking a quite old forty-four. He was bald, but with such a beautifully shaped head that the lack of hair was not unattractive; nor did he attempt to compensate by growing a hirsute beard, contenting himself with a pepper-and-salt patch on his chin. The eyebrows were black as a raven's, a solid inch in width, forming dramatic semicircles over the deep-sunk, compassionate eyes. He dressed well, as was *de rigueur* for a doctor in Vienna, with a wide-lapeled pearl-gray vest under the precisely tailored dark coat.

He showed Sigmund the operating hall, the lecture room, the laboratory, the department for internal medicine, the rooms that had been reserved for skin, ear, nose and throat ailments, infectious diseases. Sigmund saw some of the young scientists with whom he had gone to the university, and whom he had known at the Allegemeine Krankenhaus: Emil Redlich, Moritz Schustler, Karl Hochsinger, who was Kassowitz's Chief Assistant. Sigmund had time to note as he went from room to room that all of the doctors were Jewish. He wondered why, since it was obvious that only a small portion of the children being treated were Jews. Had Kassowitz not invited Catholic doctors to serve? Or had the Catholic doctors not been interested, since the Institute was going to be directed by a Jew?

When they came to the end of the long hallway, Kassowitz showed Sigmund into a room in which mothers and children were either standing or sitting on the few available chairs. He said:

"Herr Dr. Freud, this is your area of operation. We hope that one day you will create an Institute for Children's Neurology. However, until you can become an Institute, I herewith bestow upon you the title of *Abteilungsleiter*, department head. That's not quite as important as being a department head at the Allegemeine Krankenhaus, but it is as good a place as any to start."

During his stay in Berlin Sigmund had had ample opportunity to examine children suffering from nervous diseases. That experience was of incalculable value to him now.

The children had been immaculately bathed and dressed, the little girls' hair tied in ribbons. For the most part the older children were not in pain, and uttered few complaints: the diseases that had ravaged them had already done their destructive work. The ones in pain were the parents as they brought a child forward to explain under the doctor's gentle prodding the background of each case. The parents held themselves guilty for what had happened, even though nature had sometimes run amok while the child was in the mother's womb.

His first patient was a six-year-old boy suffering from meningitis: an infection of the coverings of the brain, of the fluid surrounding the brain and the brain itself. The child had been perfectly normal, suddenly became cranky, developed high fever and a stiff neck. This was now two days later; he was sleepy and lethargic; his face showed a marked flushing. When Dr. Freud took his temperature it registered 106 degrees. He looked at the boy's hand, on the fingernails he saw tiny red dots, hemorrhages of the capillaries of the skin.

There was nothing he could do except cool down the fever. The boy would develop convulsions, generalized jerking, clonic actions of the arms and legs, and die. . . . And three days ago he had been a healthy, happy boy. Meningitis was caused by bacteria. It was found in the air. He could have gotten it just by breathing it in.

He examined a seven-year-old girl who, while she was talking, would stop for perhaps three seconds, turn her head slightly to one side, stare, and then continue as if nothing had happened. This had been happening four or five times a day, the mother explained, and had begun about a month before.

Dr. Freud watched the child, recognized the "absences" as *petit mal*, even though epilepsy as a general term was a relatively poor one for describing such seizures. He could find no evidence of abnormal blood formation, scarring from an earlier injury or brain tumor. He reassured the mother, explaining that certain changes took place at puberty—Fleischl had documented these changes in brain-wave patterns—and that the disturbance would vanish.

Gradually the room emptied . . . except for a nine-year-old and a mother who had been shrinking into a corner. The child looked normal, though the mother said that he had been complaining of headaches and nausea. The woman flushed, blinked her eyes rapidly, looked down. Sigmund urged her to reveal why she had brought the boy in.

". . . Doctor, I'm embarrassed . . . shy . . . it's why I haven't brought him sooner. . . ."

"Please go on."

". . . my son has a . . . a . . . large penis . . . lots of hair around the area, as though he were fourteen or fifteen. Am I foolish . . . Doctor . . . to be concerned?"

Sigmund's tests, coupled with his years of experience in brain anatomy, indicated that the boy had a tumor in the central portion of his brain, a cancer, in effect, involving the floor of the brain, which altered the impulses going from the hypothalamic area to the pituitary and changed the sex characteristics, accounting for the abnormally large sexual organ. There was no medication and no treatment. He did not tell the mother so, but the boy would develop more headaches, more vomiting, become lethargic, go into a coma, and be dead within the year.

He remained at his desk until dark, deeply moved, wrote up his notes on the cases he had seen. Then he walked home through the Am Hof, not bothering to look up at the exquisitely decorated six-story house that he considered the loveliest in Vienna. In the Freyung he stood before the fountain, letting the cool mist bathe his face as the faces of the young patients he had seen that afternoon flashed on a screen before his eyes.

4.

His work and his practice settled into a steady stride. His written travel report was accepted by the Medical Faculty. He read a paper on hypnosis before the Physiological Club. Two chapters from his Charcot translations were published in the *Wiener medizinische Wochenschrift*. He was invited by the Psychiatric Society to repeat his lecture on hypnosis; encouraged, he tried hypnosis on an Italian woman who suffered a seizure amounting to convulsion every time she heard the word *Apfel* or *poma*. He felt awkward and self-conscious at this first serious attempt but the patient was either unobservant or indifferent. When he finally got her into a light half-sleep, he suggested that since an apple was not a live creature which could attack or injure her, when she heard the word "apple" she was to visualize a tray of fresh apple strudel in a bakery window. He thought this a rather clever suggestion, but since he never saw the patient again he could not tell whether it had helped. When he described the case to Breuer, Josef exclaimed:

"What do you suppose 'possessed' her?"

"It has to be worms, Josef. She must have bitten into a wormy apple. We had a male hysteric at the Salpêtrière, a young mason named Lyons, who saw a tapeworm in his excreta; the sight of it gave him colic and trembling of the limbs. Years later the tapeworm image came back when someone hurled a rock at him, and he ended up with epileptiform attacks."

Breuer shook his head in bemused despair.

"Our bodies are incredibly intricate machines that could only have been produced by the hand of a genius. The greatest work of art on earth, as Michelangelo has proven. And what do we do with them? We pour sand in the locomotive until the wheels grind to a halt."

"By sand, Josef, you mean . . . ideas, images, illusions, figments of the imagination . . . ?"

"If I knew what 'sand' meant, my dear Sig, I would be a psychologist instead of a specialist on the semicircular canals of pigeons. Birds don't shrink in horror from worms, they eat them."

His second month of practice had earned him the gratifying sum of a hundred and fifty-five dollars. He needed to hypnotize himself only slightly to believe that marriage was now a supportable idea. Martha agreed with the suggestion; they set the date for the end of summer.

The bad news arrived the last week in June in the form of an official government letter: First Lieutenant Dr. Sigmund Freud, Reservist, was summoned into the army for a full month's service, to start on August tenth. The Austrian War Office was concerned lest last year's war between Serbia and Bulgaria break out again. Lieutenant Freud would be in charge of the health of the troops during the military maneuvers at Olmütz.

It was seven years since he had put in his year of army service in the Military Hospital across the Van Swieten-Gasse from the Allgemeine Krankenhaus, where he had translated the John Stuart Mill book during his leisure hours. He was not given to profanity, but now he stormed through his consultation and waiting rooms, fortunately empty at this hour of the morning, using every disapprobatory term he could bring to mind to indict wars, the military, call-ups, maneuvers . . . and his own bad luck in particular. At any time during the three years that he had been in the Krankenhaus it would have been simple for him to have gone off. By the following year he would have been exempt.

"Why now?" he demanded. "When I am just getting started! When I have patients coming in, when I'm beginning to earn my keep. How can I vanish now, break off my practice? I'll have to begin all over again. I can't pay another quarter's rent when I won't be here. What am I going to do about my marriage? I must have time to find a proper home to bring Martha to. *Verdammt!*"

He jammed a hat on his head, crossed the Rathauspark and did an agitated swing around the Ring, pounding out his frustration and sense of outrage against the pavements.

By the time he got home his brain was as bruised as his feet, but he was not too tired to write Martha a long letter about the misfortune that had befallen them. She wrote back an undisturbed note advising him not to march too long in the hot August sun!

Wryly amused at the casual manner in which his fiancée had deflated him, he went to his parents' apartment and asked Amalie to dig out his old uniform from the moth balls in her storage trunk. Though it was musty and wrinkled, it still fit him. The light-colored ceremonial coat buttoned straight down from the right shoulder with eight silver buttons; the collar dark, high under the chin, the wide cuffs dark to match. The trousers were as black as the boots. The hat was tall, round and dark, peaked in front, with a medical insignia in the center. Jakob, who had paid for the tailored uniform when Sigmund was twenty-three, commented:

"My Sig is smart. He knows enough to get called up in times of peace."

"But not smart enough to miss out altogether," Sigmund retorted.

"You can use a month in the country," said Amalie. "Look how pale you are from all that hospital air."

There was no quarreling with the War Office. However he did have to be practical. The best month of the year for doctors in Vienna was October, when the Viennese returned from their summer vacations in the mountains, settled into their homes and decided that the illnesses which had been bothering them in the spring, but which they had been too relaxed and happy to think about in the magnificent summer mountain air, had better be tended to. He would have to plan to be married a day or two after his discharge from the army. They could then take a two-week honeymoon and be back in Vienna by October first. He simply must have an apartment so he could recommence his practice at once.

He spent the next few days scouring Vienna's vacancies. It had to have the proper arrangement for a medical office. Viennese couples, particularly professional men, remained in one apartment all of their lives. It had to be a convenient location for his patients to come to. It had to be in a reasonably prosperous district so that they might not think Dozent Dr. Sigmund Freud was a failure. Rosa inspected a dozen apartments or more; Amalie and Jakob trudged the streets looking for signs and notices. The apartments were either too large or too small, too inconvenient or too expensive.

It was not until the middle of July that he stumbled onto a discovery that made sense. Emperor Franz Josef had just completed an elaborate apartment house in the best neighborhood, off the Ringstrasse. The architect was the same Schmidt who had designed Vienna's imposing City Hall. The rents were modest, the rooms large, the building constructed with a handsome inner court, stairways and filigrees of ornamentation to delight the ornate heart of the Viennese. Yet twelve attractive apartments stood empty! This *Sühnhaus*, House of Atonement, had been built on the very site of the Ringtheater which had been swept by a great fire on December 8, 1881, burning almost four hundred Viennese to death. The association proved so morbid and melancholy that the people were refusing to move into what was now the most modern and handsome apartment house in Vienna.

It satisfied Sigmund's requirement: an advantageous location, only a block from the university, the Votivkirche with its park, and another block or two from the Allegemeine Krankenhaus. When the *Hausbesorger* showed him through an apartment on the first floor in the corner overlooking the Maria Theresienstrasse, a wide, tree-lined shopping boulevard, he found it ideally laid out. The rent was a little more than he could afford at the moment, but then, "Anything is more than I can afford at the moment!" he mused. The apartment was worth double that amount in the Viennese real estate market. Sigmund himself felt no compunction about moving in; it seemed an opportunity not to be missed.

He wrote to Martha, however, telling her the story, leaving out none of the gruesome details of the fire. He asked if she would mind moving into such a house since it would be a splendid place for them to begin their married life and practice. Martha promptly telegraphed him to accept. She also agreed that he and Rosa should furnish the apartment, basing their judgment on those suites which they had looked at in Hamburg. Thanks to gifts from her aunts and uncles, Martha had a two-thousand-dollar dowry with which to furnish the apartment. They were to buy substantial, long-lasting furnishings for the parlor, dining room and bedroom, as much as her money would allow. Rosa was to send her samples of the carpets and draperies. She would send the money as required to pay the bills. They were not to buy any dishware, silverware, glassware or linens; there would be many gifts from the Bernays family and Philipps, the Freuds and Sigmund's friends.

Sigmund blessed his fiancée for her calm good sense; not so his impending mother-in-law. He received a letter from Mrs. Bernays, who had just been informed of the fact that Sigmund intended marrying Martha in the middle of September instead of the end of the year despite the fact that he would be out of practice over six weeks. The letter was the worst dressing down he had ever received. Mrs. Bernays accused him of "recklessness," of marrying out of despair, declared him impractical as well as irrational, irresponsible and downright stupid!

5.

At first sight he judged the army camp at Olmütz a filthy hole. However he got little chance to brood about it, for he had to be up at half past three in the morning and march with the troops across stony fields until noon under simulated attack upon the black and yellow Austrian flag. There were sieges of a fortress during which Dr. Freud treated the soldiers who had been designated to receive wounds from the blank cartridges. The soldiers were also reservists and apparently did not meet the approval of the General Staff. As they lay out in the field while cannon shot was being fired over their heads, a general rode past and cried hoarsely, "Soldiers, do you think you would still be breathing if we were using real ammunition? You would all be dead!"

In the afternoon Sigmund lectured on field hygiene. The course was well attended by the soldiers. He suspected the attendance might be compulsory, but in point of fact the lectures were so well regarded that the officer in charge ordered them translated into Czech, and promoted Sigmund to *Regimentsarzt*, Captain. He had thought he was going to hate the month bitterly; to his amazement, by the end of the first week his worries, problems and anxieties about the future had vanished in the hot sun. He developed a tan, ate heartily in the officers' mess, enjoyed the sleep of physical exhaustion. He behaved with exemplary courtesy to his senior officers and took care of the hospitalized, mostly cases of dysentery, sunstroke or fractured ankles. A crisis arose when one of the soldiers developed what looked like paralysis agitans. Dr. Freud handled the soldier with great caution, starting him with arsenic injections. By the end of a week the symptoms had vanished. Sigmund did not say so in his written report but in his opinion it had been a case of hysteria. At the end of his month's service the reviewing board gave him excellent marks, not only for his medical service but for his attitude toward the maneuvers and the Austro-Hungarian army in general.

He returned to Vienna, changed into civilian clothes and caught the first train to Hamburg. In his suitcase he had his frock coat, ruffled white shirt and black tie for the ceremony at the City Hall. He had had no time to spare and was already settled into a corner seat of a second-class compartment before he missed his usual apprehension. He had gone to Olmütz hating the idea. Now he was glad he had had the month. He had never been in better physical health.

"Every man should have a month of rigorous army training before he goes on his honeymoon," he exclaimed happily.

Martha and Minna kissed him warmly when he reached Wandsbek. Mrs. Bernays had apparently forgiven him for ignoring her dire strictures and raised her cheek for his welcoming embrace.

Martha had a mischievous gleam in her eye.

"All right, Marty, out with it. You're hatching something at my expense."

"Not really, Sigi. Suppose we take a turn in the garden."

It was not a request but a command. He linked his arm through hers and they began circling the gravel paths beside the Bernays house.

"Very well. What is on your lovely chest?"

She blushed, but that did not delay her statement, which she apparently had been preparing for weeks.

"Sig, I know this is going to come as a blow to you, but if the ceremony is performed at the City Hall our marriage will not be legal in Austria."

"What *are* you talking about? That's absolute nonsense!"

"Yes, dear, I knew you'd think so. That's why I had the law copied out. One of my cousins found it. Here, read this: it says that no marriage can be considered legal in the Austro-Hungarian Empire unless there is a religious ceremony."

"Now, Martha, you know we don't have time to be converted to Catholicism." His eyes twinkled.

"I'm being converted to marriage, and that's quite enough adventure for the moment. We can be married in a ceremony at the City Hall. But after that we will have to come back here and go through a religious ritual. Until a rabbi signs our papers we are still only affianced."

He saw she was not to be put off and stormed through the garden, flinging phrases of protestation over his shoulder. Though Jakob Freud had belonged to a synagogue in Freiberg, where he had had his two sons by Saly Kanner *Bar Mitzvah*, he had not obliged either Sigmund or Alexander to go through the ritual which took place at the age of thirteen and admitted the young boy to manhood. There had been no formal religion practiced in the Freud household since Jakob moved to Vienna, when he became a freethinker. The only observance with which Sigmund had grown up was the Passover Seder, the dinner and services commemorating the Exodus of the Jews from Egypt, and the crossing of the Red Sea. Sigmund had enjoyed the traditional ceremony because Jakob knew the service by heart and, seated at the head of Amalie's sparkling white table, passed the three matzoths under the folds of a large napkin, the roasted shank bone, the bitter herbs, the *charoses*, finely chopped nuts, apple and cinnamon; the parsley cut into small pieces; the salt water and the cup of wine for Elijah. He recited the ancient story of Israel's redemption from bondage in beautifully articulated Hebrew.

Sigmund came back to Martha.

"I don't believe in religious ritual. It's senseless to go through empty forms. Marriage is a civil contract. The City Hall is the only place where we should be obliged to take our oaths. I've told you for four solid years that I will not go through a religious ceremony. You can't make me."

"It's not me, Sigi dear," she answered sweetly. "It's your beloved Emperor Franz Josef and his Ministry. You must not blame the Austro-Hungarian Empire on me."

She sat down in a white wrought-iron chair, her hands clasped in her lap, her attitude one of bemused sympathy. Finally, worn out by his emotionalism, he slipped to his knees and put his arms across her legs, grasping her two hands.

"Martha, you know that I am not attempting to flee our heritage. The forms I am protesting against brought the old Jews happiness because they afforded them shelter. We just don't need that shelter. But even if we don't seek shelter, something of the core and the essence of this meaningful and life-affirming Judaism will be present in our home."

"Does that mean that you consent?"

"I capitulate. Marty, please don't think that I've been pretentious about this. I know that empty protest against forms can be as foolish as the forms being protested. Now, what do I have to do?"

"First of all, you have to memorize your *Brokhe*. My Uncle Elias Philipp will teach the prayers to you."

"Why do I have to memorize them? Why can't I just read them?"

"Sigi, even illiterates are able to memorize that set of prayers. You have two full days, Privatdozent Freud. Hamburg thinks little enough of the University of Vienna as it is. You wouldn't want to deal your Alma Mater a lethal blow?"

"What else must I do?"

"You stand under the *huppah* with me so that we will be married, symbolically, inside the walls of the First Temple. I have persuaded the rabbi that we'll be content with the ceremonial prayers, and that you won't be in need of the sermon about the responsibilities of married life. When the ceremony is over you will stamp on a wineglass to break it. And that will bring us good luck in our marriage. The family will toast the bride and groom with wine and your ordeal will be over."

During the next three days the house was a hubbub of activity; flowers, candy, gifts arrived continually. Finally the wood lattice of the *huppah* was trimmed with green leaves. Sometimes Sigmund watched, leaning across the open doorway; sometimes he felt so much in the way that he spent his hours tramping along the dock identifying the ships arriving from foreign ports.

Returning late one afternoon, he put his hands lovingly on either side of Martha's face, kissed her.

"I wouldn't go through this for anyone else in the world."

She returned his kiss, gratefully.

"I wouldn't attempt to persuade you for anyone else!"

They spent their two weeks radiantly happy at Travemünde, a resort town on the Baltic north of Hamburg; sleeping lazily in the mornings, awakening to resume the embraces that had put them blissfully to sleep the night before; eating a late breakfast on their secluded balcony overlooking the sea: pots of steaming hot chocolate, hot rolls wrapped in white napkins, fresh sweet butter; bathing in the gentle swells of their cove, napping after lunch, walking the white sands of the near deserted beach. Theirs was a complete rapport: to a couple who have loved each other faithfully and waited through four years of hardship, struggle, privation and sometime differences, marriage comes not only as the end of a long siege in which they have been embattled, but as the end of a war. Now was the time to enjoy the fruits of victory. They had persevered and prevailed, conquering a seemingly hostile world.

"We were ambitious. Only modest aspirations are fulfilled quickly," he murmured as they lay in bed and watched the filling moon throw light on the sea.

6.

They arrived in Vienna on an afternoon in late September. His parents and sisters were at the Kaiser Ferdinand Nordbahn to welcome them, Dolfi and Pauli carrying flowers for Martha.

A *Dienstmann* put their suitcases in his cart to trundle through the streets to the *Sühnhaus*. Rosa got into the *Fiaker* with them in order to show Martha how well she had carried out her written instructions. The rest of the Freuds walked home, but only after the newlyweds had promised to come to the parental home at seven for the *Nachtmahl*.

Sigmund asked the driver to pass by the front of the *Sühnhaus* on the Schottenring. Martha exclaimed with pleasure when she saw the cathedral-like façade with its impressive two-story Gothic-arched entrance, inset circular stained-glass window above the arch, elaborately framed Italian Renaissance windows and balconies, at the roof level cupolas, cornices, turrets, towers, spires and, along the front, heroic sculptured figures, male and female. Emperor Franz Josef had hoped through the ornate richness of design to heal the wounds of the catastrophe.

The Freuds' entrance was around the corner on the Maria Theresien-strasse; it had a touch less *pasticcio* in the decoration but a handsome bent-elbow wrought-iron banister leading past the mezzanine to their first-floor apartment. The *Hausmeister* escorted them to their front door, unlocked it and ceremoniously handed over the keys. Sigmund gave the man a four-gulden gold coin for having brought up Martha's heavy boxes and crates from Wandsbek containing the fruit of her four years' labor hand-making her trousseau.

Martha ran her fingers over Mathilde Breuer's porcelain plaque. Sigmund opened the door. She walked into the anteroom, which was large enough to seat a dozen waiting patients, then took a quick look at each room before she turned to her right and went to the bedroom, standing at the open door with her face wreathed in a smile. Though letters had streamed back and forth between Rosa and Martha containing swatches of materials of varying textures and colors, and even rough sketches of the furniture "suites," Martha had nonetheless taken a gamble in letting Rosa and Sigmund furnish her home and this most personal of rooms; for hard as Rosa had pleaded at Jaray's and Portois und Fix, the best she could do was an agreement that Frau Dr. Freud could return one set, and only then by paying haulage costs both ways. Martha hugged her with a bright flash of pleasure. Rosa sighed deeply with relief.

"*Gott sei Dank!* I had so hoped you would be pleased. *Auf Wiedersehen.* Until seven."

It was not hygienic to have an entire bedroom covered with carpet, so Rosa had placed on each side of the bed a brightly patterned copy of the Oriental rugs now being reproduced in Vienna. A valance box had been built over the two windows which looked out on the large enclosed court of the *Sühnhaus,* and from it were hanging wine-colored draperies, gathered low at each side of the closely set windows with tie-cords and tassels. The bedspread was also burgundy velvet. The bed was of elaborately carved wood, the headboard as tall as Martha, hand-grooved with flowers, circles, squares, diamonds, rolling curved edges and arabesques by the finest Austrian woodcarvers.

Sigmund put his arms about his wife's waist, standing behind her and holding her to him.

"Does it look sturdy enough? Can we found a dynasty there?"

She turned, kissed him lightly: "Yes, but not right this moment."

She ran a hand affectionately over the tall, inlaid mosaic wardrobe for their clothing, the stand in the corner with two bowls and pitchers on a thin marble slab, and below them matching cabinets for storage. In the opposite corner was the fourth piece of the set, a linen cupboard with four deep drawers.

"What do we need the pitchers and bowls for," he grumbled, "when we have a bathroom just beyond that door, with a completely modern tub, sink and hot water heater!"

"They come with the set. We wouldn't have saved a gulden by leaving them behind in the furniture store."

Returning down the hall, she nodded with approval that the kitchen door was immediately opposite the front door. "The *Zimmermädchen* will be able to admit your patients quickly," then stepped into the kitchen, exclaiming, "Ah, what a nice size. Even bigger than the one we had when Father was alive. With a blue clock and blue curtains. Look, even the rolling pin and bottles of vinegar and oil are in place."

The floor and wainscot were of stone tile; under the shelves there were hooks for stirring spoons, dippers, kitchen cloths. The dishware cupboards were of pine; on top of her spice cabinets were china canisters labeled Salt, Coffee, Tea, Sugar, Flour, Semolina. On the bottom of the icebox was a block of ice, while in the food compartment above Amalie had put butter, cheese, sausage, Hungarian salami from the Naschmarkt. There was bread in the metal breadbox, fruit in a bowl, and on the worktable a philodendron. On the wall above the worktable was a *Nudelwalze,* a "noodlewalker," and a doily embroidered by Amalie:

"*Eigener Herd ist Goldes wert.* A stove of your own is worth gold."

Martha murmured, "True. In Hamburg they say a good oven is more important to a marriage than a good bed."

There were three rooms on the side of the foyer opposite their bedroom. The farthest of the three was to be Dr. Freud's consultation room, already furnished with his desk and chair, bookshelves and black couch. The middle room, the smallest of the three, but wood-paneled, was occupied by a huge mahogany dining table with a thick slab top, carved flower arabesques, its legs sculptured square columns with vaselike figures, joined by carved rails which met in the center to make a platform. The eight chairs were upholstered in leather, as Martha had requested, with seats broad enough to hold the posterior of any middleaged Viennese who had eaten his fill of liver dumpling soup and *Tafelspitz.* There was a carpet under the entire length of the table as etiquette required, and dominating what was left of the wall space an enormous *Kredenz* combining a buffet, drawers for the silverware and glass-door cabinets above for the best china and goblets, every millimeter carved into an urchin, cherub, cornicle, fruit or flower arrangement.

Sigmund commented, "It's true that the Austrians abhor a vacuum. Every inch of undecorated surface is considered naked and hence raw."

The combined effect was one of solidity, its owners stable and prosperous.

The living room was so spacious that Rosa had been able to fulfill Martha's sketch by placing on either side of the wide window a large glass-doored bookcase sitting atop a cabinet. In the bay there was a three-inch-high platform, covered by a Turkish rug, with a love seat on one side, a mandolin on the wall above it, and a cushioned bench on the other, above it, a Makart arrangement on a tiny half-moon shelf. Against one large wall was a divan covered in brown velours with a circular roll at each end and tassels cascading nearly to the floor. On the opposite wall were upholstered chairs on either side of an inlaid table. Next to the door there was a tall glass curio cabinet for Martha's Dresden figures and bric-a-brac. In one corner was a brown ceramic tile heating stove, in the other a tall clock from Hamburg which Rosa had found in the Viennese Doroteum, where furniture from the provinces and other countries of Europe left behind by their owners was auctioned off. Martha was touched.

"What a nice thing for Rosa to do. Nostalgia for the bride." She put her arms about her husband, kissed him warmly. "Nothing has to go back!" She smiled whimsically; there was also nothing left to buy. It was as complete as any apartment could be, its furniture as beautiful as any Viennese burgher's. It would last a lifetime.

"But what I like best about our home," she announced, "is that it is all brand new. No one has been here before us."

"*Virgo intacta*," he murmured, "like us innocent children."

The next morning he splashed around in the luxury of his first privately owned bathtub, remembering the Breuer bathroom into which the hot water had to be pumped from jars on the floor as he let in hot water from the heater above the toilet. He dressed, hung away his nightclothes and was seated at one corner of the dining table reading the front page of the *Neue Freie Presse* when Martha returned from the bakery with fresh-baked bread. When she came out of the kitchen with her pots of coffee and hot milk, he stared at her in astonishment. The part in the center of her hair, which he had known from the first instant he had seen her, was gone. She had brushed her hair straight back off her face and bound it in a *Knödel*, the dumpling, neatly fixed with a hairnet. She had frequently served him breakfast in Wandsbek, but that had been her mother's house. There was an entirely different expression on her face now as she helped him to sweet butter and marmalade: she was mistress of all she surveyed, a competent body who had already taken over the management and control of her empire. He leaned over to stroke her cheek.

"That's quite a transition, Frau Dr. Freud! If I had stumbled upon you in the dark I might not have recognized you."

"Ah, I think you would. Is my coffee as good as the coffee you drank in the French restaurants? If you will ask the *Hausmeister* to open my boxes and crates I'll be off to the Labor Exchange to find a young Bohemian girl; they are the best cooks and all-around houseworkers."

"Would you also make sure she is bright? She has to admit my patients, boil my instruments and help sterilize the injection needles on that stove of yours."

He was not certain they would be able to afford even the beginning wage of four dollars a month earned by a young *Dienstmädchen*, but they were obliged to have a maid at once; it was absolutely *verboten* for a doctor or his wife to open the door for patients.

He was at his desk arranging his papers in their proper folios when there was an agitated rapping of the front door knocker. A man who identified himself as a "bystander" asked Dr. Freud to come quickly to the Schottenring side of the *Sühnhaus* where a young boy had been knocked down by a carriage. Sigmund half ran across the enclosed court; a few feet away on the sidewalk of the Ring he found a tow-headed lad of about fourteen lying in the center of an angry crowd which was threatening the driver of the carriage. The boy was being racked by a series of body tremors.

Sigmund had to make a quick decision: if there were serious injury he would have to get him to the Allgemeine Krankenhaus at once. He ascertained that the boy had not struck his head in falling, no bones were broken; the carriage wheels had not passed over any part of his body. He asked two men to carry the trembling lad to his office. He gave him a sedative and searched for bruise marks. By the time the frightened parents arrived, he was able to reassure them.

Martha returned with a plump, rosy-cheeked girl, off a subsistence farm in southern Bohemia about fifty miles away, and in Vienna only since the evening before. She was dressed in a spotless dirndl. Martha introduced her to Professor Freud as Marie, then took the girl with her little bundle to the *Kabinett* off the kitchen, a room the size of the one Sigmund had occupied in his parents' home, and returned to Sigmund's office to learn with pleasure of his first case.

"How useful those plaques are by the street door," she commented; "better than an announcement in the *Neue Freie Presse*."

"Not really," he replied; "it's just that one is not permitted to announce twice in such a short time. Besides, at the moment we can't afford the eight dollars. You seem pleased with your Marie."

"Have you ever been in those Labor Exchanges? There were at least twenty girls sitting around three walls on benches, with several spurious 'Frau Tanten' sprinkled among them. These are older women who eavesdrop the interview and can be sent for if the newly hired maid finds the home or job unattractive. The first girl the Bureau asked me to interview was Hungarian. She asked, 'Do I get a key to the apartment so I can come and go?' The second was from Galicia; she wanted the nights off after washing the supper dishes because 'I have a lover.' The third one, from Rumania, wanted to know if we gave frequent parties so that she would have a good chance for tips. Then came Marie. When I asked her what she wanted most from her job she replied shyly, 'To be part of a family, and be treated well.' I asked her if she had a *Frau Tante* there. She said, 'No, *Gnädige Frau*, I do not approve of this fakery. If something is wrong I will tell the *Gnädige* myself.' I think we're in luck."

The *Portier* finished opening Martha's boxes. Sigmund could not believe his eyes: hand towels and bath towels by the dozen, all monogrammed; high piles of sheets and pillowcases; supplies of washcloths, dishcloths, dustcloths; blankets, feather beds, pillows, bedspreads, doilies, crocheted throws for upholstered chairs and sofas; damask tablecloths and napkins for parties; colored sets of linens for everyday use, household linen to last a solid twenty years. Then came Martha's underclothing and "bed lingerie" also in quantities of dozens, the nightgowns not trimmed with lace, which was too expensive to clean, but with decorative hems and sailor collars; shirts, handkerchiefs decorated with thread-work, peignoirs made of soft, colored cottons and wools; jerseys for walking in the mountains; and lastly milady's underdrawers, complete with pink and blue ribbons that tied in bows just below the knee.

He became convulsed with laughter at the seemingly inexhaustible supply.

"You certainly haven't been idle during these four years, have you? You have enough merchandise here to stock a shop."

"You would not have wanted me to come into marriage naked, would you?"

He took her in his arms.

"You are going to create a charming home. You will always be the mistress, and I will be your well-behaved guest."

7.

The young boy who had been knocked to the pavement was back to normal after several faradic treatments. When the father came in to pay the bill, and Dr. Freud attributed the cure to the electric massage, he replied:

"Perhaps so, Herr Doktor, but that's not what my Johann thinks. He told his mother and me that it was your kindness and your wonderful eyes that helped him."

" 'Perhaps so, Herr Doktor,' " Sigmund groused to himself a few days later, "but my wonderful eyes have not gazed upon a new patient in days. I paid a full month's rent for September just so we would be ready to accommodate the hordes that would beat on our door in October. We hired our *Dienstmädchen* to open it properly, and even the charity patients haven't returned to me. . . ." After the initial expenses of moving in, Martha's purchases of the few things she needed, a pot for soup, skillets, and the payment of the balance of the first quarter's rent, four hundred gulden, they began their domestic life strapped. The first thing to go was Sigmund's gold watch, which he pawned, holding onto the gold chain still strung across his vest to save face. Previously this would have sent him into a spin of depression; now he was too wonderfully happy to worry: with Martha, their love, their companionship, this charming home to which their friends continued to send welcoming flowers and plants. Each day a messenger arrived from Papke with a silver coffee set, a gift of the Breuers, from Foerster with a stunning silver platter sent by Fleischl, a set of silver fruit bowls from the Paneths, Meissen china, cut-glass vases, small Oriental rugs, lovely Dresden figurines for the coffee table and Martha's curio cabinet, all sent by well-wishers.

When he saw that he would not earn even fifty dollars during the month of October, and had to tell Martha that her watch would soon be on its way to the pawnbroker to sit ticketed on the shelf next to his, Martha said plainly:

"Why don't we borrow from Minna instead? She would be happy to help. She has her trousseau money and won't be wanting it for a while."

"You know, Marty, walking home from the pawnshop the other day, I entertained myself by rewriting Genesis. *Money* was really the apple in the Garden of Eden. Eve got fed up with her unenterprising mate and told him, 'Why should we stay in this tucked-away nook, where we have nothing we can call our own? You work all day, Adam, tending the orchards and what do you have to show for your labors? Not even a pair of pants to cover your nakedness. At any moment we can be put out! Empty-handed, as naked as the day we entered. And what kind of a Boss are you working for? All he ever does is give orders. 'Do this! Don't do that!' It isn't fair. We should be feathering our nest, accumulating wealth against our old age. Adam, think of what we could do outside this Garden of Eden. Own millions of acres of land, sell the fruit of the trees and the grain of the fields. We can be rich! Monarchs of all we survey. We will rent land to everyone who comes after us, a few thousand acres at a time, build ourselves a castle, with servants and trained troops to protect us, clowns and acrobats to entertain us . . . Time to grow up, Adam, to face reality. Let's get out now before we're too settled in our ways. There's a world to conquer.' Adam says, 'It sounds right, Eve, but how could we get out? The Boss won't let us go. He means to keep us here forever.' Eve replies, 'I'll think of something.'"

The last week of October was the most difficult because he had no *Haushaltsgeld* to give Martha. But in November Dr. Rudolf Chrobak turned their luck around. He sent a note to Sigmund asking him if he would take care of one of his patients. Since he had been appointed professor of gynecology at the Medical School he no longer had time to attend this particular woman. She lived close by, on the Schottenring; would Herr Freud be there at five so that he, Dr. Chrobak, would make the transition a comfortable one?

He found Frau Lisa Pufendorf in an ornately furnished sitting room, just off her bedroom, stretched out on a rose-colored satin divan. She rose when he was announced by the maid, pale, wringing her hands as she paced the room. Though under forty her face was ravaged, with deep circles under her eyes. Sigmund asked:

"Frau Pufendorf, Herr Dr. Chrobak informed you that I was coming?"

Her eyes darted about the room as though she were looking for an escape.

"Yes, yes, but he isn't here. He isn't here. Where can he be?"

"He will come within a few moments. Please calm yourself. It might be helpful if you tell me what is wrong."

She feverishly rearranged the bunches of dried flowers, grasses, thistles and peacock feathers in the Makart which stood on her crowded mantelpiece. Sigmund watched her.

"We must find out where Dr. Chrobak is," she insisted. "I have to know." She whirled from the fireplace, her eyes deep pools of fear. "I have to know where he is every minute. That is my only security, so that I can reach him immediately if anything happens to me. I must know if he is in his office or at the university. I must locate him!"

Dr. Freud spoke soothing sounds. The woman quieted a little. Dr. Chrobak came in. Frau Pufendorf collapsed onto the divan. Chrobak patted her paternally on the shoulder, said:

"Excuse us for one moment, my dear Frau Pufendorf. I wish a consultation with my colleague."

Chrobak took Sigmund into a formal drawing room. Here they sat on two fragile gold chairs. Chrobak was a gentle man who had fallen into the habit of speaking to his confreres in much the same comforting manner he did to his patients.

"My dear Freud, you saw the state Frau Pufendorf is in. There is absolutely nothing wrong with her physically. Except that, although she has been married for eighteen years, she is still *virgo intacta*. Her husband is and always has been impotent. There's nothing a doctor can do for such an unfortunate woman except to extend his friendship to the marriage, comfort the wife, and keep their problem from the public. I must warn you, my dear *Kollege*, that I am not giving you the best possible case. When her friends learn that Frau Pufendorf has a new doctor they will be hopeful and expect you to achieve great results. When you don't, people will talk against you, saying, 'If he's any kind of a doctor, why can't he cure Frau Lisa?'"

Sigmund was baffled by Chrobak's attitude. "Aside from the bromides and other quieting drugs she can assimilate, is there no other advice you can give me for her treatment?"

Chrobak shook his head with a sad smile. "Her husband doesn't need medical care. His impotence does not seem to derange him. As for your patient, there is only one prescription for such a malady. It will be one you recognize, but there is no way that we can effectively prescribe it. It would read: *Rx: Penis normalis dosim repetatur*."

Sigmund was taken totally by surprise. He gazed at his friend in some bewilderment, shaking his head over Chrobak's cynicism. He thought, "*Rx: a normal penis, dose to be repeated*. What kind of medical advice is that?"

Josef Breuer's voice echoed in his ears. "These cases are always matters of the marriage bed." Charcot's exclaimed, "In this sort of case it's always a question of the genitals . . . always, always, always!"

"Come, Herr Kollege," Chrobak said quietly, "let us return to our patient. One thing you must understand if you are to undertake this case: Frau Pufendorf must know where you are every minute of the day and night."

"That won't be too difficult," Sigmund answered quietly. "I keep to a rigorous schedule. But if there is nothing physically wrong with Madame Pufendorf, why does she have to know our whereabouts at all times?"

Chrobak polished his rimless spectacles with a handkerchief, as though he might see the small print of the answer more clearly when the lenses were clean.

"I've puzzled over that for years. Perhaps you can solve the riddle."

Before he left the apartment, Sigmund sketched out his daily schedule so that Frau Pufendorf could get a message to him in a matter of minutes.

He walked home, slowly, sunk in thought. What was the meaning of these judgment-outbursts on the part of Drs. Breuer, Charcot and now Chrobak? Where was such a sentiment expressed in a lecture or clinical demonstration? What scientific book or monograph had taken the stand that a person's sexual activity, male or female, affected the physical health or mental and nervous stability?

Could there be any medical truth in so radical and unseemly an idea? If so, how was one to find out? Where was the laboratory where one could dissect the phenomena of sexual intercourse even as one studied, under a microscope, stained slides of brains?

The entire concept was impossible. Breuer, Charcot and Chrobak had simply not intended their extracurricular remarks to be taken seriously. The act of coitus was normal and natural. There were accidents, yes. Abstinence, yes. Had he himself not gone without intercourse until the age of thirty while living in the most licentiously sexual city in the world? But problems?

No, there was nothing there. He was a scientist. One believed only what could be measured.

BOOK SIX

THE BONDAGE OF WINTER
IS BROKEN

The Bondage of Winter Is Broken

H E WAS invited to give his paper On Male Hysteria at the Society
of Medicine's first meeting of the season, always well attended
by the Austrian and German press, University Medical Faculty
and doctors in private practice as well as from smaller Vienna hospitals.
He ate some *Selzstangerl* at five, long salty sticks with a sprinkling of
kümmel seeds, but declined supper. Martha had had his best suit pressed,
his white shirt prepared. Marie polished his boots. His hair had been cut
and his beard trimmed. Martha surveyed him proudly.

The meetings of the Society of Medicine were held in the Konsis-
torialsaal of the old university, now dwarfed in the shadow of the new
university which had been completed two years before. The meeting
room held up to a hundred and forty listeners. He saw Professor Brücke,
flanked by Exner and Fleischl, Breuer sitting next to Meynert, Nothnagel
with his group of young internists; his associates from the Kassowitz
Institute. The meeting was opened by retired Professor Heinrich von
Bamberger, under whom Sigmund had studied years before. The hall
was filled, the air heavy with cigar smoke. He moved restlessly in his
chair while Professor Grossmann, the laryngologist, reported a case of
lupus of the gums. Then it was his turn.

The group was friendly at the outset, until he plunged into a
portrayal of male hysteria as Charcot had established the type and
"proved the existence of a clearly defined order in hysterical symptoms,"
destroying the prejudice that classed hysterics as malingerers. Professor
Meynert squirmed and then, while Dr. Freud outlined the cases he
himself had studied at the Salpêtrière, gazed at the ceiling. By the end
of twenty minutes Sigmund had lost the attention of most of the
audience, many of whom were whispering to each other.

Chairman Bamberger commented that there was nothing new in Dr.
Freud's paper; male hysteria was known but it did not cause seizures
or paralyses of the kind which Dr. Freud had reported. Meynert rose,
his long gray hair falling forward over the corner of his eyes, a smile
on his heavy-featured face which Sigmund mistook for indulgence. The
tone of voice quickly dispelled any such illusion.

"Gentlemen, this French import which Herr Dr. Freud has brought through the Austrian customs may have appeared a solid substance in the rarefied neurological atmosphere of Paris, but it was converted to gas when it came across our borders and emerged into the clear scientific sunlight of Vienna. In my thirty years as a pathologist and psychiatrist I have seen and located many diseases of the forebrain. I have traced the activity of the cerebral mechanism under morbid conditions of the mind. Nowhere in my studies of the cortical and ganglionic fibers or the connection of these fibers with the pyramids of the brain have I found any indication of male hysteria, or the possibility of such disturbances causing paralysis, aphasia or anesthesia, all of which depend on predisposition as a form of disease."

He paused, bowed benignly down at Sigmund. "However I would not want it said that I lack the broadening qualities of travel or the resilience of some of my younger and more daring colleagues. I therefore want to confirm my interest in Dr. Freud's startling theories, and invite him to bring 'male hysteria' cases to this Society so that he can prove the validity of his assertions."

Sigmund was so stunned by the hostile reception that he could not hear a single word of the excellent report which Dr. Latschenberger, the physiological chemist, gave On the Presence of Bile and Fluids During Grave Illnesses of Animals. By the time he bestirred himself and struggled to his feet, he found the room empty. Outside the Aula several of his younger associates had waited to murmur a word of praise. Breuer had disappeared with Meynert as had Fleischl with Brücke.

He walked home alone through the sharp mid-October night, each step producing a dull ache. Meynert had offered up his former *Sekundararzt* to ridicule before the greater part of the Viennese medical profession.

Martha greeted him in the foyer, a long blue wool peignoir covering her sailor-collared nightgown. One look at his face and her eyes darkened.

"Sigi, what happened?"

He took off his tie, unbuttoned the shirt, ran his hand consolingly over his chafed neck. His spirit was equally chafed and sore.

"I met with a bad reception."

They sat together in the alcove of the parlor while he sipped a cup of chocolate. "I hope I am not being oversensitive, but it was as though I had behaved like a naughty student before the masters and been drummed out of school."

He took a nervous turn through the assorted coffee tables. She had never seen him as emotionally upset, his closed lips moving sideways over his teeth. He returned to loom above her on the raised platform of the alcove.

"It has always been said among the younger members of the Society that the older men want us present only as an audience. They have never wanted to listen. I've watched Bamberger and Meynert be rude before to young researchers, but never have I heard them phrase their objections on such hasty non-scientific judgments. I suppose I should have begun by assuring the Viennese Medical Faculty that the Parisian Faculty had nothing to teach them. To suggest that more advanced neurological techniques are being used in Paris makes me an ingrate. Worse, an apostate! Meynert's invitation was not only facetious but scornful."

"But Meynert is devoted to you."

"We had a collision. In a dark tunnel. Two trains. Head on. I have emerged with 'railway spine.'"

He put an arm about her, said quietly, "This is an unexpected advantage of marriage: a sympathetic shoulder on which to prove that I am right and the world is wrong."

Late the next afternoon, when he joined Breuer and Fleischl in the Landtmann Coffeehouse, with its tranquil brown walls and booths, its brown-streaked marble tables, men sitting about after their day's work chatting or reading newspapers in half a dozen languages, he learned that he had been wrong as well as right. Breuer and Fleischl excoriated Bamberger and Meynert for their rudeness, then told their protégé where he had made his mistakes. Josef said:

"Sig, you should have reported Charcot's work on male trauma without touting his theories on hypnotism. His *grande hystérie* is suspect anyway. Ever since our fellow alumnus Anton Mesmer scandalized Vienna a hundred years ago with his 'animal magnetism,' hypnotism has been the harshest word of opprobrium in the Austrian medical lexicon."

Fleischl nodded his head in agreement. It was not easy for them to chastise their friend, but they sensed that he had involved himself in something more serious than a passing flair of jealousy or bad manners. Breuer continued:

"Then too, you could have left out the material on 'railway spine.' It is tangential and beyond your major thesis that there are no symptomatic differences between male and female hysterics. We have been trained to treat all paralyses as resulting from palpable physical damage to the central nervous system. If you tell us that these disturbances of muscular function and sensory disorders can derive from neurasthenia, you put the older practitioners out of business."

"But what am I to do? Retract? I have watched hysterical cases recover in an instant, after months of seemingly physical paralysis. You know Charcot is right and Meynert wrong."

Fleischl signaled the waiter, who brought them another round of tea and rum and a tray of *Schinkensemmel*, sliced ham on fluffy salty buns. Fleischl resumed the argument.

"It's not Charcot who needs defense in Vienna, it is you. Meynert is hurt. Mollify him. You still believe he's the greatest brain anatomist in the world. Then tell him so. Every day for a month."

"Am I to ignore his challenge as well?"

"No!" Josef broke in firmly. "You must demonstrate a case. But don't do it combatively, to prove yourself right and Meynert wrong. You have to go along with Meynert or he can do you incalculable harm."

The logical place to find his demonstration case was in Primarius Scholz's Department Four, Nervous Diseases. But Scholz had become angry on several occasions when his young *Sekundararzt* implied that it was more important to bring in the proper medicines for the patients than to keep their beds precisely apart. Now Scholz refused to allow him any examination or use of his patients. Word spread through the Allgemeine Krankenhaus with the speed of a fourteenth-century bubonic plague: Dr. Sigmund Freud was *persona non grata* in the nine major courts.

With everyone, that is, except Professor Meynert. Meynert accepted his stumbling pleasantries with good grace, his smile of acquiescence a hairline out of focus as he said:

"But of course, Herr Kollege, you can search my male wards for a demonstration case. You know I am the last man in the world to stand in the way of medical research."

He went into the wards where he had served his apprenticeship in psychiatry three years before. In the first bed was a former innkeeper with a limited paralysis of one arm, described by his chart as "suffering from disturbances of the mind." He had been sad since his wife's death. Dr. Freud watched the patient go through an epileptic fit, then cry out that he would overthrow the Ministry. He became abusive, ran about beating other patients until restrained in a rope crèche.

Sigmund turned away: this poor fellow had half a dozen illnesses all mixed together.

The next morning he tried another patient, a waiter with a disturbance of speech and facial paresis. His chart read *Madness with Paralysis*. He welcomed Dr. Freud's attention, confided to him that God appeared to him at least a hundred times each day . . .

". . . so why am I being kept in a police station? The attendants here torture me. They bruise my scrotum."

When Dr. Freud got him out of bed he proved to have a staggering gait, tremor of his fingers and a shivering tongue. These were possible evidences of hysteria but there was so much megalomania and mental disturbance he reasoned nothing could be proved by the case. In the next bed was a thirty-three-year-old coachman who drove an *Einspänner*. He suffered from delirium tremens and manic excitement but it was apparent that the disturbances arose from alcohol. The Viennese coachmen drank heavily, even in the early mornings, in an attempt to keep warm.

In the Second Ward he found an actual trauma case: a tile setter who fifteen years before had fallen from a roof. He now had delirium tremens and hallucinations. His last act before being brought to the hospital had been to beat up his daughter when she tried to take him home from a *Weinstube*. Since the original fall he had been drinking so steadily that he was continually falling. Did the man drink and was he partly paralyzed because he fell off the roof? Or had he fallen off the roof while drinking?

"It's hopeless," he thought as he walked home for his eleven o'clock consultation hour; "where alcoholism is a constant factor it would be too difficult to prove what causes trauma. I wonder if anyone ever tried to find out what causes alcoholism?"

His anteroom was nearly filled with half a dozen patients, all ceremoniously received and seated by Marie. For now, in the chill, rain-swept end of October, his practice had bloomed. The charity patients were back, though the marriage brokers were taking their offers elsewhere. Breuer, Nothnagel, Obersteiner sent him their overflow. Professor Brücke, who had heard Meynert's rebuff of their jointly sponsored protégé, but who had said no word about the lecture, now spoke his piece in his usual quiet fashion by sending him a visiting German pathologist in need of neurological care. As his work progressed at the Kassowitz Institute his colleagues there, as well as family doctors faced with neurological problems, summoned him to homes and hospitals. Sometimes he could do nothing, as with two newborn infants, the first with a small mass falling out of the back of the skull like a pigtail; the second, a case of hydrocephalus, the head growing bigger by the day because of excess fluids collecting within the ventricle system of the brain. He kept the child alive for several weeks until it succumbed with pneumonia.

He confided to Martha, "I went into this field knowing that most of the diseases in children's neurology are incurable."

"Why did you, Sigi, if it is so disheartening?"

"For the same reason that other neurologists go in: for the purposes of research, study of the pathological entity of the diseases: describing, classifying, creating diversity from other forms. . . . We have to know, before we can start on our long stumbling journey toward a cure. A hundred years from now, perhaps only fifty, doctors will have learned how to save those two infants I just lost."

A deep sigh rocked his chest.

Yet he did help and sometimes saved the youngsters brought under his care. There was the seventeen-year-old boy who suddenly went into a *grand mal* seizure, foaming at the mouth, biting his tongue until the blood came. By careful questioning Sigmund learned that the boy had been hit on the head with a rock when he was eight and had suffered a depressed skull fracture. The wound and infection had cleared in a month, but a scar had formed on the right side of the brain causing irritation, and now a burst of electrical impulses had triggered the attack. Dr. Freud could not remove the scar tissue or end the seizures; but he did outline a rigidly disciplined routine. He was brought a pituitary dwarf, bright and perfectly proportioned except that everything was in miniature. He put the apprehensive parents on bromides, the boy on a forced diet and inquired among his medical friends for a chemical to feed the pituitary gland.

He repaid the debt to Minna, redeemed his gold watch, resumed his placing of gulden in Amalie's coffee mug.

2.

He was indeed a guest in his own home. All that Martha demanded of him was that he stop work and be in his seat at the table, napkin across his lap, at least one full second before Marie came in from the kitchen with the tureen of hot soup. That Martha was a well-organized and capable housewife came as no surprise; but that she took her household duties as seriously as he did his medical ones he learned only slowly. Yet she was no martinet who cleaned up behind him with broom and dustpan before he and his cigar were out of the room.

A couple of mornings a week, when the weather was clement, she woke him early. On Friday mornings she took him down to the Franz Josefs-Kai on the canal where the boats brought in their catch of fish. Martha liked first choice. Their carp or perch in the family basket, they continued along the Donau to the Schanzelmarkt for her fresh fruits, brought in from the countryside in the deep of night by peasants in lanterned farm wagons. On Saturday mornings she led him on a fifteen-minute walk from the Ring down the Wipplingerstrasse to the Hoher Markt and then on to the Tuchlauben and the Wildbretmarkt, the week's best poultry market with its clacking, foot-tied live chickens, geese, ducks, turkeys, pheasants, the country women in their caps, shoe-length skirts and capacious aprons crying out the excellence of their wares, the husbands killing and dressing the *Hausfrau's* choice before her wary eyes. They were back for Marie's breakfast by seven.

The high spot of the early morning junkets came on Wednesdays when they left the house at five, the dawn still an unverified suspicion of gray paint on the eastern horizon, for the most colorful spot in Vienna, the Naschmarkt, with its hundreds of covered stalls containing the finest and most exciting foods to be found, known as "the golden streets for *Naschen*": for nibbling sweets, dainties, delicacies, exotic flavors to inflame the mind and seduce the body. It would not be fair to say the Viennese loved his Naschmarkt more than his opera or concert hall but there was something in the commingled riotous smells, colors and shapes that made him feel that he was eating his way around the world. Sigmund was enchanted by the cacophony of the Naschmarkt. He said to Martha:

"The Viennese will remain happy and carefree because they love so dearly to eat. Besides their five meals a day they manage always to be nibbling at something. There's the ultimate secret of life, *meine Frau*, keep your gastric juices flowing."

First came the flower stands, fifty stalls in a row on either side of two long blocks, each one small but stocked with riotous autumnal-colored blooms and plants. Next were the fruit stands with their oranges, peaches, grapes from Albania and France, Bulgaria and Rumania, honey-dew melons from Spain, bananas from Ecuador, nuts and raisins from Czechoslovakia. They stopped at stalls selling only eggs, followed by numerous bakeshops selling a round *Linzer Torte* with three holes showing jelly through them, *Nustrudel* and *Honigkuchen*, a honey cake, and an original Tyrol bread with ridges on top and the sides filled with white powder as though the loaves had been plowed instead of baked.

They ate stuffed heart of veal to keep warm as they made their way through stalls with jars of cauliflower, cabbage, cucumbers and sauerkraut, fresh paprikas, *gemischter Salat*, white peppers, herring salad, beets. Then came the vegetable stands: eggplants, oblong tomatoes, curly leaf cabbage and *Kohl*. Next the stands of sausages: liver, pork, beef, *Lungenbraten*, big black blood sausage from Cracow, Hungarian salami, *Heurigen* salami of which the Viennese said, "There once was a man who loved his wife so much he even ate *Heurigen salami!*", salamis tied longways and roundways with string, smoked pork and ham, black in color. Then came the fresh meat stalls with *Gulasch* meat, *Rindfleisch*, beef, trays of oxtails, brains, pigs' feet, lung; a Bavarian stall with *Geflügel*, the back wall decorated with deer horns. There were stalls for candies and biscuits, one for ground paprika, sage and *Kuttelkraut*; one concentrating on spices, curry and sassafras; grocery stands with rows of white sacks bursting with rice, lentils, navy beans, barley, yellow peas, limas; barrels of pickles, bundles of mixed soup greens; lemons from Italy, onions from Spain, cranberries from Sweden, cheese stands selling Bulgarian goat cheese; wild mushrooms called *Schwammerl*.

Sigmund joked as he carried home the basket of specialty foods which would last the week. "Every country represented in our basket is either now under the Hapsburgs or was at one time."

She liked to pick up his jocular tone in these carefree hours. "Then we are entitled to say that the sun never sets on Hapsburg foods."

He received a note from Dozent Dr. von Beregszászy, a laryngologist who had attended the abortive lecture at the Society of Medicine. Could Dr. Freud meet with him at the Cafe Central, the favorite coffeehouse for Vienna's intellectuals, novelists, playwrights, poets, journalists, bright young lawyers and doctors? It was important. The cafe was jammed with crowded tables and humming conversation now that cold weather had closed the three-sided sidewalk section. Dr. von Beregszászy waved to him from a small marble-topped table at the side of the coffeehouse, away from the clicking of the billiard balls, the movement of waiters, the buzz of amused and exhilarated conversation that had been going on at the same tables by the same participants for a lifetime.

Over coffee and *Semmel* Dr. Julius von Beregszászy, who was nine years older than Sigmund, a Hungarian Catholic trained in medicine in Budapest as well as Vienna, said, "I may have the case you're looking for: an intelligent, twenty-nine-year-old engraver, a victim of cerebral hemi-anesthesia and loss of tactile sensibility on the left side of his body. I have been treating him for three years. He was an unending source of puzzlement to me until I heard your paper. Unless you find something physically wrong with him that I have been unable to locate, August is a prime case of hysteria arising out of trauma. Let me give you some background."

Sigmund felt the pulse in his temples begin to throb, a subdued tension grip him. It was a chance to repatriate himself with the Allgemeine Krankenhaus.

"Please do."

"The father was a violent man, a heavy imbiber of alcohol who died at forty-eight; the mother suffered from headaches and died of T.B. at forty-six. Among August's five brothers, two died at an early age, another died from a syphilitic cerebral infection, one suffers convulsions, another deserted from the army and has disappeared. At the age of eight August was run over in the street, suffering a ruptured right eardrum. The accident brought on several months of intermittent fits. Three years ago he had a quarrel with his brother, who owed him money; the brother refused to pay and stabbed at him with a knife. Although he had not been cut, August went into shock and fell unconscious at his own front door. For weeks he suffered feebleness, violent headaches and intracranial pressures on the left side. He told me that the feeling in the left half of his body had altered; that his eyes were tired; but he continued to work. Then a woman connected with the engraving business accused August of being a thief. He developed violent palpitations of the heart, became depressed, threatened suicide . . . and began the first of a series of tremors in his left arm and leg, along with intense pain in the left knee and left sole when he walks. He came to see me because he felt as though his tongue was 'nailed' to his throat.

"August has never been guilty of malingering. He has worked at his engraving straight through. He doesn't like being ill, as some patients do; he desperately wants to be cured. Shall I send him to you?"

"By all means." He laid a hand over the older man's. "I want to express my appreciation for your confidence in me."

The next day August came to Sigmund's consulting room. Sigmund asked a number of searching questions, then made a physical examination. There was no atrophy of the muscles. Except for a dull heart palpitation he could find nothing wrong. However he noted in both eyes what he jotted down as "the peculiar polyopia monocularis of hysterical patients and disturbances of color sense." He also found that August had lost the use of his sense organs on the left side. However his hearing in the left ear was intact. . . . Could August be retaining the hearing in the left ear because if he did not he would be stone deaf?

He took the man to Dr. Königstein to be examined. The eyes were still the best open doorway to the brain. Königstein reported August to be physically normal. Sigmund then determined precisely the areas of the anesthesia which affected the left arm, the left side of his trunk and left leg. He was able to stick a pin into August's left side without evoking reaction or pain.

Yet certain aspects of the patient's behavior convinced him that the anesthesia was not valid, that the disturbances of August's mobility in moving his arm or leg depended largely on external conditions. When he took him for a walk along the Danube and told him to watch his process of walking, August had great difficulty in putting his left foot out in front of him. However when they strolled about the Ring and Sigmund described the glories of Vienna's neo-baroque architecture, August set the left leg down as securely as he did the right.

On the man's fourth visit Sigmund told him one of Jakob's Peter Simpleton stories and, while August was laughing, ordered him to undress. He did so, using his left and right hands with equal facility. With August's attention diverted, he asked his patient to close his left nostril with the fingers of his left hand. August automatically did what was directed. However when Dr. Freud stood before him as the concerned physician and instructed him to make a series of movements with his left arm or hand, and to think about them carefully, in every instance August failed: he was unable to lower his arm, tremors arose in his fingers, the left leg went through a shivering process.

The evening of November 26, 1886, was just another weekly meeting for the Society of Medicine, and few who gathered were concerned about Dr. Freud or his patient. Sigmund was certain that he could convince his colleagues. He acknowledged his indebtedness to Dr. von Beregszászy, asked Leopold Königstein to give his report on the ophthalmological examination, which was negative; then made the report of his month's findings, putting August through the full spectrum of experiments.

He concluded his demonstration, "The hemianesthesia in our patient exhibits very clearly the characteristic of instability. . . . The extent of the painful zones on the trunk and the disturbances of the sense of vision oscillate in their intensity. It is on this instability of the disturbance of sensitivity that I found my hope of being able to restore the patient to normal sensitivity."

There was polite applause. No questions were asked or comments made. The meeting adjourned; those whom Sigmund thought of as the "higher-ups" formed little groups and walked out of the building together. He felt flat-footed. Dr. von Beregszászy congratulated him on the clarity of his presentation, then a number of friends came up to shake his hand: Kassowitz, Lustgarten, Paneth. While Sigmund knew that he had not proved a total case of male hysteria, he thought that his demonstration had indicated that many kinds of anesthesia and malfunction arose out of hysteria. However he could tell from the attitude of the older doctors that they had not thought the experiment important.

Professor Meynert failed to mention the demonstration. It was as though he had forgotten about it or, as Sigmund suspected from an edge of coolness in Meynert's manner, that the demonstration had been meaningless.

Nobody ever brought it up again. Sigmund became the more determined. He gave August a half hour every day for vigorous hand massage, electrical treatment with his faradization machine, insisted that area after area was clearing up, that sensitivity would return to the skin, the tremor vanish from the hand.

The results were slow in coming but they were definite and marked. Within another three weeks August was back at work in the engraving shop full time, although he never recovered total use of his sense organs on the left side. Sigmund was tempted to give a third report to the Society of Medicine but decided that it would be useless; the older men would no more believe August cured than they had believed his symptoms to be hysterical.

3.

His practice continued to grow, slowly: a referral here, a recommendation by a patient there. Since Martha would not permit him to go without his midday dinner as he had when he was a bachelor, he was in his consultation room from noon until one, had dinner, and returned to his office at two. At the Institute for Children's Diseases the number of neurological cases put under his care increased. He analyzed his patients' symptoms, wrote exhaustive notes and attempted to establish order by dividing the nervous diseases into some thirteen distinct categories. He told Martha:

"I lost a rabies case today; the family doctor did not recognize what it was until the child began foaming at the mouth. But I will be able to keep alive one of my new children, a cerebral palsy. We may yet train him to move about, hold a restricted job."

When he sensed that the atmosphere at the Allgemeine Krankenhaus was beginning to lighten he made a bold move. One of the privileges of having earned his *Dozentur* was that he was entitled to give lecture courses at the University Medical School. To project such a series and have the university announce it, he had to have Meynert's permission. Meynert was sick in bed. There were stories around the academic and medical circles that his chronic heart ailment had increased his robust appetite for alcohol. Sigmund paid no attention to these rumors: one of the by-products of a coffeehouse civilization in which men spend countless hours talking over cups of thick sweet Turkish coffee is that, when there are insufficient true stories to go around, collateral stories are invented or improvised. Sigmund splurged; he bought a box of the Havana cigars that Professor Meynert doted on, and paid him a visit.

"Herr Hofrat, I'm sorry to see you indisposed. But knowing it was not a respiratory ailment, I've ventured to bring you a box of your favorite cigars."

Meynert was touched. He had a temper, he was jealous of his position, but most of what Charcot knew about brain anatomy he had learned from Meynert's writings. Sigmund Freud had been one of his best students and *Sekundarärzte*; he had held high hopes for him. He had been hurt as a father is hurt when he hears his son lauding someone else's father as great, or greater.

"Thank you, Kollege. It was thoughtful of you; and must have put a dent in your wife's *Haushaltsgeld*."

Sigmund blushed.

"Herr Hofrat, do you recall last spring when I returned from Paris, you suggested I take over your lecture course in brain anatomy?"

"Of course I remember. You were the best to handle the lectures . . . if only we hadn't sent you gallivanting into the fictional fields of Paris."

"No hysteria, Herr Hofrat, and no hypnosis." Then smiling crookedly, "Not even 'railway spine.' Just solid authentic brain anatomy, as taught to me by Professor Meynert."

Meynert opened the box of cigars, slowly selected one, rolled it between his fingers, smelled it, squeezed the end, reached for his knife, then lit it. An expression of benign calm came over his face.

"It's a good cigar, Herr Kollege. Keep your lectures equally mellow. Collect the fees yourself, rather than have them go through the university."

This was an unusual request: the bursar always collected the fees and paid them over in a lump sum to the lecturer. Was this Meynert's way of chastising him? If so, it seemed a small enough price to pay. He readily agreed, thanked the Herr Hofrat and departed in high spirits.

The announcement for his first official university course read:

> Anatomy of the Spinal Cord and the Medulla Oblongata. An Introduction. Twice weekly. By Privatdozenten Herrn Dr. Sigmund Freud. In the Auditorium of Herrn Hofrat Professor Meynert.

It was a Wednesday afternoon in late October, the days darkening early, when Sigmund entered the auditorium for the first of his lectures. He found a fair group of medical students, young Assistants and Sekundärärzte from the Allgemeine Krankenhaus who felt they needed more knowledge in this highly specialized field of the nervous system. As he stood before the class he felt a warm glow come over him. This was his organization, his political party, his religion, his club, his world; he had no other and wanted no other, not since he had passed through the childhood games of planning to be a warrior in the tradition of Alexander the Great, or an advocate serving on the Vienna City Council. A lot of water had flowed under the bridges of the Donau Kanal in the two years since he had lectured to six American doctors: he was a Dozent now, a Medical Faculty lecturer, trained by Charcot, a department head at the Children's Institute, a happily married man with enough patients in his waiting room to enable him to support his home.

On the luminous screen behind his eyes he saw a picture of himself as he had stood before the mirror of the wardrobe in his bedroom: the handsome dark gray suit that had just been tailored for him, the white shirt and black bow tie he had worn in Paris at Charcot's salon and for his wedding; at thirty, a touch heavier, his beard and mustache close-cropped, with a sprinkling of gray which had not yet appeared in his thick black hair, neatly combed to the top of his ear on either side, his eyes reflecting his excitement and happiness. Maturity agreed with him. He knew he had never looked better. Professor Brücke had been right four years before to force him out. Had he remained a pure scientist in the Physiology Institute his knowledge of medicine would always have been inadequate. He would have become a laboratory mole. Now he combined the best of two worlds: one half of his life for private practice, which would earn him his independence; the other for teaching, researching, discovering, publishing.

He acknowledged to himself that frequently he had been impatient, in a hurry to find, reveal, achieve position and fame. This feverishness had abated. He was home again in the ambience in which he had always been comfortable: a classroom, a group of men come together to think, to learn, to reason, to advance the magnificent science of medicine. Though he admitted to himself that once again he was starting on the bottom rung of the ladder, he was content with the long stretch of years ahead during which he could eventually rise to be an *Ordinarius*, full professor at the university, and in charge of one of the nine courts of the Allgemeine Krankenhaus. He wanted to become the kind of professor that Ernst Brücke was, Theodor Meynert, Hermann Nothnagel; and the breed of men who long before his time had made the University of Vienna Medical School a beacon to the world: Skoda, Gall, Hildenbrand, Prochaska, Hebra, Rokitansky, Semmelweis, Kaposi, pioneers who had created modern medical science.

With a start he saw that the class was still standing, awaiting his signal to be seated. His eyes smiling, he rolled the fingers of his left hand outward. The men sat down. He opened the notebook on the podium, glanced at the structural outline he had organized, began speaking in a quiet, contained voice. Immediately he and the students were plunged into the intricate and infinitely marvelous anatomy of the spinal cord.

He saw Lisa Pufendorf every day, stopping at her home on his way to the Kassowitz Institute or to a patient at a private hospital. She received him in her sitting room, crumpled handkerchief wrung in perspiring hands. If his work obliged him to stop off later than he expected, he would find her in tears, having taken to her bed. He gave her sedatives but sparingly, hoping that his calming words could take their place. Messages reached him everywhere; Frau Pufendorf was having a crisis of nerves, could he come immediately? He did, as often as possible. He was encouraged to learn that she was still running her home responsibly; he urged her to have a woman friend in for coffee and a chat each afternoon. At the end of the month when he added up the more than fifty visits he had made to her apartment he saw that he was going to have to submit a substantial bill for his services. Herr Pufendorf thanked him and paid him at once.

As he cared for Frau Pufendorf over the winter months of snow and rain, he found that Dr. Chrobak's prediction did not materialize: the members of her family did not criticize him for failing to cure his patient. They had come to accept that Lisa was a highly nervous woman who would never change. Once or twice he imagined he caught a glint in the eye of a male uncle or cousin which indicated that Herr Pufendorf's sad deficiency was known. The other half of Dr. Chrobak's *obiter dicta*, what Frau Lisa needed to cure her, he slowly and reluctantly concluded was the truth. According to the family, she had been healthy and happy up to her marriage, and for a year or two beyond. Only then had the nervousness come on. Frau Pufendorf's disturbance obviously arose not from the past but from an inescapable fact of the present. If like the considerable number of morally easygoing Viennese wives she could flirt with strange men in coffeehouses and engage in a series of clandestine love affairs, all would be well. But this kind of conduct was not in her character. Until her husband was cured there could be no relief for Frau Lisa Pufendorf. He speculated over the use of hypnosis on the distracted woman but decided against taking the risk.

After a time he came up the loser in a bout of conscience. The Pufendorfs could well afford his medical fees; the money was more than welcome in the Freud family. Yet after the hundredth visit he had to ask himself what, as a physician, he was really doing for Frau Lisa. As a doctor he was not supposed to indulge in emotional reactions to his patients, but this patient put him through the wringer of frustration, wrath and even boredom when he had to repeat the same tranquilizing formulas. He went to see Professor Chrobak in his overheated office at the Medical Faculty.

"Herr Doktor, I think I must retire from the case."

Chrobak leaned forward in his leather chair, replied' in a stern tone, quite unusual for him.

"Saving life is the doctor's first task. Frau Lisa cannot exist without an attending physician. If she is no better than when I called you in, she is certainly no worse. You are keeping her hysteria under control. This is as important as keeping an infection under control."

Sigmund squirmed uneasily, trying to loosen his collar in the sealed-in heat of Chrobak's office.

"But it's awkward knowing that all I can do is give her a dose of verbal bromides."

"My young friend," said Chrobak, "you have told me many times that neuroses and hysteria can be as fatal as blood poisoning." He walked over to Sigmund. "If you abandon her she will find another doctor and then another; if the poor creature runs out of doctors she will end up in one of those rope crèches you used in Meynert's Clinic to restrain the violent."

One late March afternoon he came home from the Kassowitz Institute tired, wet from a sudden rain, and out of sorts. Martha had returned to the house just before him; she was bubbling with news which quickly put an end to his crankiness.

"Sigi, you'll never guess where I have come from. I visited my old friend Bertha Pappenheim. We met in the bakery and she invited me home for coffee."

Sigmund took a fast breath. Josef Breuer had kept him up to date on the girl of the "talking cure." She had had two relapses since Josef ended the relationship when she cried, "Dr. Breuer's baby is coming!" She had been in a sanatorium in Gross Enzersdorf but fled because a young physician there had fallen in love with her. Breuer had despaired for her life.

But that had been five years before. After Martha had made him get out of his wet coat and put on dry socks and slippers, she continued:

"During the day Bertha is well, goes out, sees a few old friends, attends concerts. Mostly she reads and studies, quite seriously, she tells me, in German periodicals about the new 'Women's Rights' movement. She and her mother are moving back to Frankfurt where Bertha intends to work with the organization. She claims she will never marry, that she wants a career and a life of service. She feels it is the only thing that will save her."

"From what, Marty?"

"The dark. She looked so beautiful today. All the symptoms of her illness are gone. But at night she feels a darkness in her head. In Frankfurt she intends to work nights as well as days and not return home until she is utterly exhausted. She has promised to tell me more about women's emancipation."

"I happen to like you the way you are. Don't listen too hard."

"I'm not likely to . . . at the moment." She sat down in the chair beside him, settled her back comfortably against his chest, spoke softly without looking at him. "I paid a visit today to your friend Dr. Lott up the street."

"Dr. Lott. He's an obstet . . ."

"Yes, dear, I know." She turned, put her cheek on his. "You are going to become a father along about October . . . so Dr. Lott assures me. I knew, but I wanted to be certain before I told you."

A flash of joy surged through him; it was the ultimate fulfillment of their love. He took her face tenderly in his hands, kissed her on each cheek, then chastely on the lips.

"I couldn't be happier. For you. For me. I've always wanted us to be a family."

She wrapped both his arms about her from behind, holding his hands securely within her own.

"That is the best word a pregnant wife can hear."

4.

The weeks of spring, 1887, sped by. Fulfilled love and a congenial home of his own brought him such personal happiness that he even made up with Eli Bernays, realizing faintly that he had nurtured these quarrels with his admirable brother-in-law without tenable reason. Marriage and his acceptance in the medical community had removed his nervousness and self-deprecation as well as the thrashing about for the quick and easy solution, what he had termed "spontaneous combustion of fame out of a Bunsen burner and a microscope." His body and mind were working together in a glow of health, resilience and energy. In the years that he had been engaged to Martha he had ached in all the places where a penniless romantic young man can ache; and they were legion. Now there was no more talk about moving to Manchester, New York, Australia. He revised his timetable; since he could not make a master contribution by thirty, having already achieved that august age, he would make it at forty. If he were still in process at forty, he would bring his work into focus at the age of fifty. In spite of his earlier denial to Martha he still wanted to carve his name on a rock; but he had become reconciled to the fact that it could not be etched with one's fingernails.

As the warm weather came on they began spending Sundays and holidays in the Vienna Woods, picnicking among the late spring flowers in the "new wine" sparkle of the clear air and the view from the heights of the Leopoldsberg: the tan-gray roofs of Vienna with its green church domes rising above the sea of slate and chimneys that surrounded them; the winding valley of the Danube with the river gleaming in the sun, the mountains to the south still snow-covered where the Alps peak into Italy.

Martha had an irrepressible enthusiasm. She climbed to neighboring knolls for a special view, served the lunch from her wicker basket, popped the *Kracherl* and drank the sweet raspberry soda from the bottle: high color in her cheeks, her eyes filled with joy, at one with nature and the universe as the infant grew in her womb. During the long work evenings she sat with Sigmund in his office reading a recent novel while he wrote his medical book reviews for the *Wiener medizinische Wochenschrift*. At the breakfast table he fell into the habit of interpreting aloud to her from the *Neue Freie Presse*.

"The whole front page is a dispatch from England reporting the crisis in the Cabinet since Lord Churchill resigned. On page two there's a story from Prague about a German Club being formed there; our government is suspicious of its motives. Here's a discussion from the Landstag about the parliamentary law passed last year making education mandatory from ages six to fourteen; in the provinces the parents don't want to keep their children in school that long. A man got killed in the Zoological Gardens in Berlin by a rhinoceros. Another man committed suicide in a cemetery, on the grounds that it would be more convenient for everyone. . . ."

Dr. Sigmund Freud's most gratifying success came from his skillful use of his electric machine. He devoted an increasing number of hours to treating patients with it. He kept his fees modest, and since the patients went away feeling better, word of his skill spread. Dr. Wilhelm Erb's definitive *Handbook of Electro-Therapeutics* was always at his elbow; he reread Erb's prescriptions for "galvanic" or "faradic" current, slowly achieving mastery over the complicated apparatus, the most beneficial tool at his command as a neurologist; learning to measure what Erb called "the absolute strength of the current," the use of rheostats, electrodes, the application of Ohm's law, using the equipment to best advantage on the nerves of the skin and muscles, on the brain and spinal cord, for hypochondriasis and diseases of the sexual organs.

He was able to put away some money against the birth of the baby and contribute enough to the running of his parents' home so that Jakob no longer had to worry about his spasmodic jobs of work. That is, until summer set in with its warmth, its cauterizing bright sunlight, fascinating cloud puffs drifting through a Tiepolo sky. The Viennese sat for hours at the outdoor cafes, separated by green potted plants from passers-by in the street, reading the newspapers and periodicals served with the coffee ("Coffee is food for the body, newspapers food for the mind"), calling forth a succession of small glasses of water, a teaspoon balanced on top to indicate that the customer was welcome even though he was not ordering anything more. The townspeople brought their children or grandchildren to run in the flower gardens of the Stadtpark and listen to the band play romantic waltzes for tea; or sunned themselves in the lower Belvedere. Colds dried up, coughs disappeared, neuralgias vanished, neuroses went underground. The Viennese evacuated their city for vacations in Salzburg, Berchtesgaden, the Königssee and the Thumsee. Even the Pufendorf family departed for their mountain home in Bavaria, where the high altitude had a pacifying effect on Frau Lisa.

Martha commented on their plight, "Professor von Stein liked to tell my father: 'You're neither rich nor poor by what you earn in a week or a month; add it all up at the end of the year and you'll know whether you're solvent or bankrupt.'"

"Good for the economists; they know a lot of truths we doctors might never suspect."

She patted his shoulder comfortingly.

"I'm trained to be frugal when it's necessary. You won't even suspect I'm spending less."

In the fall, knowing that Martha would soon be confined to the house, the Breuers asked the Freuds if they would care to see the production of Sophocles' *Oedipus Rex* which was to be performed in the old Hofburgtheater in the Michaelerplatz the following Monday evening.

"Oh, Sig, could we go?" Martha pleaded.

"Yes, I'd like very much to see the play. Look here at the cast announced in the *Wiener Extrablatt*: Mr. Robert is playing Oedipus, Charlotte Röckel Queen Jocasta and Mr. Hallenstein Creon. They are excellent. Marty, I haven't read *Oedipus* since my fifth year of Greek at the Sperlgymnasium, but I remember it as a harrowing play. Are you sure it won't bother you, in your condition?"

"What's wrong with my condition?" A flush spread over her cheeks, which had filled out with the rest of her body.

The following Monday they walked to the Breuers' for a light supper. The Breuers lived near the theater. Before seven Sigmund had checked the women's wraps at the *Garderobe*. Mathilde had been able to secure four seats in the first row. When they were settled Sigmund turned to gaze upward, remembering how often he had sat in the fourth gallery because the seats cost only one gulden apiece. He took out the slim volume of *Oedipus Rex* in the original Greek which he had slipped into his coat pocket before he left home, and read a few lines as the curtain rose to show a Priest of Thebes, with a crowd of children gathered before an altar in front of the palace of Oedipus. King Oedipus emerged to ask the Priest why he and the children were sitting there as suppliants. The Priest related the terrible curse that had fallen on Thebes: the crops were dying in the fields; there was a blight on the cattle; the mothers were barren; children who were born died in the streets. Oedipus replied that he had sent Queen Jocasta's brother Creon to Apollo in his Pythian temple to learn how the city could be saved.

Creon returned at that moment to report that Apollo had announced that there was a pollution upon their land: a murder-guilt.

The tragic story now unfolded. At Oedipus' birth the oracles had decreed that he would murder his father and marry his mother. His parents, fearing the prediction, gave the infant to a shepherd to be put out on a hillside to die. But the shepherd had instead given the infant to a shepherd from distant Corinth. Here the child had been adopted by the King and Queen of Corinth and raised as their son. At manhood, learning the forecast of his life, Oedipus had fled his supposed parents and Corinth in terror. En route he was roughly handled by a party of travelers and beaten over the head by an old man. In retaliation, Oedipus had killed him. Coming a short time later to Thebes, he found the city under a curse, its guardian Sibyl having propounded a riddle which must be solved. Oedipus solved the riddle, saved the city and in gratitude was made King of Thebes. He married Queen Jocasta, widow of the mysteriously slain King Laius; and had children by her.

The one servant of Laius' party who had escaped and returned to Thebes was now brought to the palace. Oedipus learned that the old traveler he had killed was King Laius. Still believing himself the son of the King and Queen of Corinth, he rejoiced when a messenger arrived from Corinth to inform him that his father Polybus had died of old age; half the oracle's curse seemed to have vanished. Yet he was still frightened and demanded of Jocasta:

"But surely I must fear my mother's bed?"

Jocasta replied:

"As to your mother's marriage bed,—don't fear it.
Before this, in dreams too, as well as oracles,
many a man has lain with his own mother.
But he to whom such things are nothing bears
his life most easily."

The messenger from Corinth later confessed that he was the shepherd who took the infant Oedipus to Corinth. Oedipus was determined to find the first shepherd. Jocasta cried out:

"I beg you—do not hunt this out—I beg you,
if you have any care for your own life.
What I am suffering is enough."

When Oedipus insisted and sent for the original shepherd of the household, Jocasta cried:

"O Oedipus, God help you!
God keep you from the knowledge of who you are! . . .
O Oedipus, unhappy Oedipus!
that is all I can call you, and the last thing
that I shall ever call you."

She rushed into the palace, grief-stricken. The old shepherd was brought in, revealed the truth: Oedipus was the child of Laius and Jocasta. Oedipus cursed the man who saved him from death:

"Then I would not have come
to kill my father and marry my mother infamously.
Now I am godless and child of impurity,
begetter in the same seed that created my wretched self. . . .
O marriage, marriage!
you bred me and again when you had bred
bred children of your child and showed to men
brides, wives and mothers and the foulest deeds
that can be in this world of ours."

Jocasta had hanged herself. Oedipus cut down her body and, tearing off the two gold brooches that held her gown, struck them against his eyeballs, destroying them. His two daughters, Antigone and Ismene, led him away, blind, penniless, to wander the world in search of penitence.

When the curtain fell the party of four friends sat breathing hard, deeply shaken. Josef suggested the Cafe Central for a snack. It was a mild fall evening. They walked the one long block and one short one down the Herrengasse. Since the Breuers were *Stammgäste* their *Marqueur* knew what they ate and drank after theater. Josef explained to Martha why the Central was such a favorite of the Viennese men: it was expert at "tuft-making," granting more titles than Emperor Franz Josef. Anyone wearing glasses was called Doctor, authentic doctors were called Professor, genuine professors were elevated to the nobility, with a "von" in front of their names.

Sigmund pulled out his copy of *Oedipus Rex* and began leafing through it, half audibly translating from Greek to German.

"Josef, something is perplexing me," he confessed; "did you gather from the performance that Jocasta knew all along she was married to her own son?"

"No . . . oo. But she realized the truth before Oedipus did. That's why she killed herself."

"But early in the play Oedipus tells Jocasta of his meeting with Phoebus, who

"'foretold other and desperate horrors to befall me,
   that I was fated to lie with my mother . . .
   to be murderer of the father that begot me.'"

"Yes," interrupted Josef, "but Jocasta could not have assumed from the similarity of the evil oracles that Oedipus was her son. She believed he had died in infancy on the hillside."

Sigmund skimmed the text while Josef bit into his *Powidle*, purée of prunes encased in a light pastry shell.

"But when the messenger arrives to tell Oedipus that his father Polybus is dead, and Oedipus is still afraid of the other half of the prophecy, Jocasta says:

"'Best to live lightly, as one can, unthinkingly.
   As to your mother's marriage bed,—don't fear it.
   Before this, in dreams too, as well as oracles,
   many a man has lain with his own mother.'

It appears to me that she is putting a good face on an evil situation."

"That doesn't prove, Sig, that she knows."

"Then consider this," he insisted. "Jocasta is not present when the herdsman identifies Oedipus as her son. She has already hanged herself!"

Martha interposed, "I see what Sigi is driving at: even if Jocasta is just learning the truth, she does everything she can to prevent their relationship from being revealed."

Josef shook his beard almost independently of his head.

"I agree that she did not appear to be taken totally by surprise. Could it be that Jocasta had known, but not consciously?"

"I think so, Josef; she has to have been living with this knowledge for a long time in order to accept its dreadful import and fight to preserve her marriage."

Mathilde asked quietly, "Gentlemen, isn't this a rather involved analysis of an ancient Greek drama?"

"No, Mathilde," said Sigmund. "It is contemporary as well."

"But how? We have no gods on Mount Olympus, no sons who are 'fated to lie with my mother . . . to be murderer of the father that begot me.' That's long ago and far away, like Jason's voyage to find the Golden Fleece."

"All great literature is universal; if it is not, it perishes; that means that *Oedipus Rex* is contemporary. Heinrich Schliemann discovered Troy just fifteen years ago and excavated through nine cities, each built on the other. Until then only Homer had believed there was a Troy."

"Then you think there are nine cities buried in *Oedipus Rex?*" Joseph asked.

"I don't know what I think. But listen to these three lines that the blind prophet spoke to Oedipus:

> " 'I say that with those you love best
> you live in foulest shame unconsciously
> and do not see where you are in calamity.' "

"Ouch!" exclaimed Martha.

Sigmund looked at her in alarm.

"The baby just kicked me. I think the kick was directed at its father."

They all laughed; Sigmund a little shamefacedly.

Martha was most cooperative; she decided to have the baby on a Sunday when her husband would be free of patients and hospital work. She awoke at three in the morning with her first labor pains. Sigmund asked if he should go for Dr. Lott and the midwife. She said:

"Let's wait."

At five he could contain himself no longer. After a short examination Dr. Lott said, "Things are moving very slowly; it could last all day and night."

Martha was calm. She had decided to avoid anesthetics. When the pains increased in intensity in the late afternoon she could not suppress her screams, but each time she apologized for her conduct. By seven-thirty in the evening Dr. Lott said:

"The child isn't advancing. I think I ought to use the forceps."

Sigmund looked at his wife. There was danger here, more to the child than the mother.

The birth took a quarter of an hour. Though the room was cool, Sigmund could feel the sweat running down his face. Martha made jokes during the ordeal, which Dr. Lott and the midwife seemed to find amusing. Then the baby came along nicely, Martha declared that she felt fine, ate a plate of soup, took a good look at her daughter to make sure she was normal and unmarked, and fell into a fast sleep.

Sigmund, happy and exhausted, held his daughter, whom they called Mathilde, after Mathilde Breuer, weighed her at seven pounds, decided that she had a beautiful voice when she cried, and put her to sleep in her crib, commenting:

"You don't seem upset by your great adventure."

At midnight he sat down in his office to write the news to Mrs. Bernays and Minna, ending by saying:

"I have now lived with Martha for thirteen months and I have never . . . seen her so magnificent in her simplicity and goodness as on this critical occasion, which after all doesn't permit any pretenses."

Babies bring their own luck. The next morning his anteroom was filled with patients.

5.

Professor Theodor Meynert was at long last given the Department of Neurology he had been seeking. In the years when Sigmund had been close to Meynert he had had the right to hope that he would be chosen as Meynert's Chief Assistant. Now it was too late. Yet it was a source of pride to be lecturing in Meynert's auditorium; and he was grateful to the older man for his bigness of mind in not allowing continuing disagreements to deprive Herr Dr. Freud of the official blessing of the Psychiatric Clinic.

For his second series of lectures, coming a year after the first, he tacked onto the wall behind his desk drawings of the cerebellum and forebrain. Only five applicants turned up for the course. They sat strung out along the second row of seats like swallows on a picket fence. The errant thought went through his mind, "All I will be earning for the five-week course is twenty-five gulden." But he was not going to allow the little group to see that his pride was hurt.

"Gentlemen, won't you gather here in front of the desk?"

Reluctantly, because they felt they were rattling in space, the three medical students and two doctors moved to the spot in front of him. It took him only a few moments to forget the size of the class and plunge into the exciting materials. Afterwards he walked quickly through the chill dark streets, with the students in their long white coats rushing home after the day's classes.

Three days later, when he entered the auditorium to give his second lecture, he found standing by his desk a newcomer in a handsomely tailored wool suit with a faint gray stripe and a butterfly bow tie with gray flowers against a dark background. But it was the newcomer's face which fascinated Sigmund; he had never seen a countenance so vividly alive; large, widely spaced, dark eyes whose vibrancy seemed to illuminate the entire auditorium, in crepuscule so late in the afternoon; wavy black hair fitted close to a perfectly shaped head; a virile, assertive, half-wild beard and mustache of the intensest black, a wide mouth with glistening lips standing out like a streak of red paint in the dark forest surrounding them; cheeks and forehead with the healthy glow of a young boy.

Feeling Sigmund's eyes upon him, the stranger looked up. Sigmund felt himself engulfed in one of the most endearing smiles he had ever seen on a man. The stranger put out his hand.

"You're Dr. Sigmund Freud. Dr. Josef Breuer recommended that I take your course; in fact, he insisted upon it. Said it would make my stay in Vienna memorable. I'm Dr. Wilhelm Fliess, a nose and throat specialist from Berlin, come to spend a month here with family friends and medical associates. You will accept me? I'm sure the month of lectures will be of permanent value to me."

Sigmund shook hands with Fliess. Even in this, so simple a gesture, Fliess was galvanic, holding Sigmund's hand firmly in an avowal of pleasure.

"Dr. Fliess, it is good to welcome you. The class will be enriched by your presence."

So it was. Fliess sat off to one side, as he felt a newcomer should, but his power of concentration was so great that after a time Sigmund felt he was lecturing directly to the Berliner. Dr. Fliess was one of those rare students who can take legible notes without removing his eyes from the lecturer; the intensity of the gaze, the apparent rate of absorption was a new experience for Sigmund. At the end of the hour, after the group had left, Fliess came to the desk.

"A dynamic experience, Dr. Freud. Your approach to brain anatomy opens new concepts to me. But then, I am trained as a biologist; I could envy you your physiology under Professors Brücke and Meynert. Could we stop at one of your delightful Viennese coffeehouses for a beer?"

"Yes, let us walk, and talk. Tell me about Berlin. I spent a month there, working with Drs. Robert Thomsen and Hermann Oppenheim at the

Charité, and Dr. Adolf Baginsky at the Kaiser Friedrich Hospital. You practice medicine rather differently than we do in Vienna."

"Yes, different, but not better," Fliess replied as they crossed the Lazarettgasse and made their way to the Alser Strasse. "We have a little more freedom to try new approaches. Our practice has no seasonal drop-offs. Here, this looks like a pleasant cafe, the Universität. I have an engagement for the evening, but I am not expected until eight-thirty. It is a soiree at the Wertheimsteins'. You know the family of course?"

"I know little of them," replied Sigmund frankly as they entered the warmth and bustle of the cafe; "though my first important assignment came out of that very salon. One of Theodor Gomperz's translators of John Stuart Mill died inadvertently; he mentioned this at a party there, and my professor of philosophy, Franz Brentano, recommended me for the job."

"Ah, how important these great salons are! So many of our young artists find a voice there, and patrons to promote their work. But let me tell you something about myself."

Wilhelm Fliess was twenty-nine, two years younger than Sigmund. He had been born into a prosperous Jewish middle-class merchant family and, being precocious, had pushed through his medical studies so that he already had established a widespread practice and was regarded as one of the top otolaryngologists in Germany.

His voice was vibrant, coming like an opera singer's from deep in his chest. He kept it low so that Sigmund alone could hear him, yet the people at the surrounding tables could not take their eyes off him.

"My dear Dr. Freud, I have been an admirer of yours for a long time, since I read your papers on cocaine. I tried it experimentally, and now I can report that I am able to ameliorate specific symptoms by administering cocaine to the nasal mucous membrane."

Sigmund hitched closer to Fliess in the tan leather booth, confiding:

"You can't know how much that means to me, for my work on cocaine has been seriously attacked."

"For heaven's sake, why? Your discoveries have enabled the eye surgeon to perform hitherto impossible operations. In my own field, cocaine has enabled me to discover reflex neuroses proceeding from the nose."

"Reflex neuroses . . . from the nose? What precisely do you mean?"

Fliess's eyes snapped with excitement at the prospect of proselytizing. His words and phrases stumbled and fell against each other like puppies playing on a downhill lawn.

"Ah, my dear Doctor, the human nose is the most neglected organ of the human body, and at the same time the most significant: a veritable bellwether of all the ills that besiege the *soma* and *psyche* of life. There it sits like an erect penis, night and day, for all to see, measure, diagnose. I have made discoveries that enable me to tell by scientific tests on the nose what has gone wrong in other areas of the patient's body. Did you know that within a few years I'll be able to prove there is a connection between the nose and the female sexual organs?"

Sigmund was staggered. He had never suspected that any such work was going on, let alone in the process of documentation. He gazed at the younger man beside him, who was quivering with emotion, asked:

"Dr. Fliess, what first got you so interested in the human nose? Certainly not any difficulty with your own: it's the most beautiful Greco-Roman nose I've seen in years."

Fliess laughed delightedly.

"Yes. I've always been proud of my nose. Had it been twisted or bumpy or at broken angles I could never have become an otologist.—But I must not keep you from home any longer. You know, Dr. Freud, I'm completely enchanted with your young Viennese girls: they are so much softer, more feminine, desirous of pleasing than our Berlin girls. . . ."

After an hour Sigmund staggered his way home, forgetting to buy a bag of roasted chestnuts from the elderly vendors who plucked them hot and charcoal-blackened from the braziers. He had not been so exhilarated since he emerged from Charcot's first lecture in Paris. He apologized to Martha for being late; but when he tried to picture Fliess for her he found that he could not compress the pyrotechnical personality and mind into a few descriptive words.

The following week, after the lecture, Fliess suggested they walk to his favorite *Literaturcafe*, the famous Cafe Griensteidl, for a *Kaffetscherl*, one of Vienna's loving expressions for a "little coffee." Settled at a table overlooking the street many Viennese used, some walking as rapidly as though they were on a mission, others strolling arm in arm involved in conversation, Wilhelm Fliess provided Sigmund with still another surprise: he refused to talk about himself.

"Ah no, my dear colleague, last time I was greedy, I was so stimulated by your lecture that I was unable to constrain myself. Today I want to know about you, from the beginning of your researches in histology. In particular I would like you tell me about Charcot's work in male hysteria. Josef Breuer tells me you got into hot water for lecturing on the subject to your superiors."

Fliess's alert, serious eyes were glued to Sigmund's, drinking in every word. Sigmund found himself talking uninterruptedly for well over an hour. He was embarrassed.

"Heavens, that's the second lecture of mine you've had to listen to this afternoon. It's your own fault, you know; you have a way of making people feel that everything they say is important."

"Everything you said to me was indeed important," Fliess replied quietly. "You know, Dr. Freud, we're very much alike in that we've never allowed ourselves to be frozen into academic or professional attitudes. We believe with Heraclitus, 'All is flux.' Every day we must learn something new in our science, or we have not lived that twenty-four hours. Like you, I come out of the Helmholtz school: everything has to be tested according to the laws of physics, chemistry, mathematics. On this solid base we carry on our practice, I in otolaryngology, you in neurology. But in truth we both have divided our lives into two parts: one half in which we practice the best of accepted medicine, the other half for exploration into the hypothetical realm of ideals and concepts, bold approaches to the human condition."

Sigmund turned away from Fliess and watched the passers-by huddle into their winter coats as a cold wind began sweeping them down the street.

"Yes. Life for me would be dull without speculation. Every medical doctor, to be worth his salt, has to project his science at least one jot into the future."

"Precisely. The present dies unless it multiplies for the future. How good it is to meet a kindred soul."

Puzzled, Sigmund asked, "But surely you must have many such associates in Berlin?"

Fliess hooded his eyes for a moment.

"My dear colleague, in my medical practice I have many friends and admirers. You will hear nothing but praise for my work in the hospital and medical meetings. But my speculative work I must keep to myself."

Fliess remained in Vienna three weeks. Sigmund saw a good deal of him: at an evening at the Breuers', where he was accompanied by two lovely young women: at the Breying und Sohn Restaurant to which Fliess invited the Freuds; and finally at home, where Sigmund invited him for Sunday dinner. After each lecture they stopped for a companionable beer and talk. Sigmund felt that he had never lectured better; he was constantly amused, stimulated, enlightened by Fliess's flow of perception, his insistence that "medical science is like an embryo in the mother's womb, changing, growing, becoming more viable every day." He was sorry to see him go.

Before he left, Fliess turned over to Sigmund a patient by the name of Frau Andrassy, explaining that he was her family doctor in Berlin but had been unable to help her.

Frau Andrassy came to see him the day after Fliess left. She was twenty-seven, a short sandy-haired woman with sand-colored eyelashes, plain in an honest poised fashion. She was the mother of two young children. Since the birth of her second child she had lost considerable weight, become anemic and developed a recurrent foot spasm, accompained by a heaviness in her legs that made it difficult to walk. Fliess had

had her examined by Josef Breuer; both men thought the evidence indicated neurasthenia without physical causation.

Frau Andrassy had been in his consulting room only a few moments when a foot clonus came on, a rapid contraction of the muscles. He had her take off her shoes but nothing more: Viennese women had to be examined through their clothing. He massaged her foot until the spasm passed, then used the faradization machine on her legs and back. He examined her muscular system for symptoms of drawing or pressing, areas of burning, pricking, numbness. He could find none. After she had returned to his desk, he asked:

"These foot spasms apparently do not depress you?"

"No, Herr Doktor, I would not compound my difficulties by letting my spirits fall as well."

"Then your condition does not cause you anxiety?"

"Not anxiety. I do not have the worrying disposition. Though naturally we are concerned, my husband and I, that it grow no worse. After all I have two small children to raise."

"Dr. Fliess left this diet for you. It is urgent that you put on the weight you have lost since the birth of your child. I recommend several hours of rest in the afternoon. Come to see me Thursday."

After she left he sat motionless at his desk reflecting on the case. Fliess and Breuer had agreed that the illness was a neurosis. He could find no trace of what to him were the most significant symptoms of neurasthenia: anxiety, a profusion of new maladies, hypochondria. In neurasthenia these were never absent. She was thinking about her children rather than herself; she was happily married, enjoying a full relationship with her husband. These were not symptoms of hysteria. All the evidence pointed toward an organic disturbance. He must find it.

Frau Andrassy put on weight, regained her strength. After a couple of weeks of massage and faradization the foot spasms stopped and the heaviness began to lessen in her legs, but he knew he must get to the original cause of the difficulties.

"Frau Andrassy, the giddiness you describe of a few years ago sounds like nothing more than a temporary fainting spell. Did you never have trouble with your legs before?"

"When I was a child I had diphtheria. When I got out of bed my legs were paralyzed."

"But, my dear Frau Andrassy, why have you not told me?"

"It was seventeen years ago. I was completely cured. . . ."

Dr. Freud turned to his medical bookcase on the wall behind him, took down one of Charcot's volumes. But it was Dr. Marie's voice he heard, saying to the group at the Salpêtrière, "We can attribute disseminated sclerosis to acute infections incurred in the past." Nothing happened until the patient became undernourished and physically depleted; under such conditions the weakest point in the spinal cord would revolt; which was exactly what had happened to Frau Andrassy.

"How have you been feeling these past days?"

"Better than at any time since the beginning of my illness."

"Splendid. We now know how to keep you feeling that way."

He was elated over the results. He had not only helped Frau Andrassy, he had reassured himself.

"Now I know I can treat each patient objectively and not ride the neurosis hobbyhorse!"

6.

Spurred by his reassurance in the Frau Andrassy case, he turned his mind to the perplexing cases in which he had been unable to help the patient. Three of them had previously consulted other doctors, whose efforts also had been fruitless. His colleagues were convinced that the illnesses were somatic. Sigmund was beginning to have serious doubts. He sent to the bookseller in Paris, who had sold him the Charcot *Archives*, for a copy of *Hypnosis and Suggestion*, published five years before by Professor Hippolyte Bernheim of the University Medical School of Nancy. Bernheim maintained that hypnotism was "the induction of a psychical condition which increased the susceptibility to suggestion." Though he did not agree with all of Bernheim's theses, particularly when Bernheim differed with Charcot, he was fascinated by the dozens of case histories Bernheim had set down with fastidious detail in which the use of hypnotism and suggestion had been a therapeutic tool. Several of his own patients, he believed, were suffering from neuroses similar to those involved in the hysteria cases he had studied at the Salpêtrière and now found before him in the pages of Bernheim's book. By the time he finished a second reading he had decided that he would write to Professor Bernheim in Nancy and ask if he would like to have his book translated into German.

It was not a doctor's job to find out what idea had made his patient ill; no one knew the answer to that riddle in any event, not even the sick person. But was it not his task to ameliorate the symptoms? And since it was patently impossible to extirpate an idea which neither patient nor doctor could formulate, why should he not proceed to implant in the patient's mind a counterforce that could rout the enemy and allow a new concept, that his symptoms had been overcome and he could be well again, to take command? It was a suggestion that could be made to the patient a thousand times while he was awake and be rejected; but somnolent, under hypnosis, when he could not fight the suggestion . . . ?

He went to see Josef Breuer, for this was extremely dangerous ground in Vienna; hypnotists were told to confine their performances to the theater. The most vociferous enemy was Professor Theodor Meynert, who had thundered for thirty years that hypnosis was a whore who should not be allowed admission to respectable medical circles.

Sigmund knocked lightly with an index knuckle on Josef's library door and entered his favorite room in Vienna. Breuer was in his high-backed chair, writing at his desk. Sigmund told him he wanted to attempt hypnotic suggestion, and described the cases. Josef was slow in responding.

"Sig, have you hypnotized any patients other than that Italian woman who saw worms every time she heard the word 'apple'?"

"Two or three, in the wards in the Salpêtrière, just to see if I could bring it off. But those women had been hypnotized so often by Charcot's Assistants they fell asleep before I could say, 'Close your eyes.'"

"Then you don't know whether you're good at it?"

"I doubt I have any exceptional talent. By the way, you haven't mentioned using hypnosis since the Bertha Pappenheim case. Have you abandoned the practice?"

Josef flushed. He looked away, muttered, "No, I . . ." stopped, walked over to a wall of bookshelves and patted a few books that were already precisely in line. When he turned around he had regained his composure.

"Sigmund, why don't we try it right now? I'm meeting Dr. Lott at a patient's house in a few minutes. Frau Dorff. I'm worried about her and nothing Dr. Lott or I can do has helped at all. I'll recommend to the family that you try hypnotic suggestion."

It was a penetratingly cold day but the skies were clear. The mountains and woods stood out as sharply as though they were a block away. Josef murmured, "In Vienna we walk in beauty. These mountains are as much a part of our daily lives as the food we eat and the patients we examine. Those green hills, with the cloud puffs hanging over them almost caressingly, how many times have they brought me back to the goodness of life and nature when I was walking the streets harassed, perplexed."

Josef was standing still in the piercing cold, gazing at the hills with adoration. Sigmund linked his arm through the older man's, said, "Come along before your teeth start to chatter. And tell me about Frau Dorff. What must I suggest she do?"

"Breast-feed her baby."

Frau Dorff had had her first child three years before, though already in her early thirties. She had wanted to breast-feed the infant and was perfectly well, but her supply of milk was poor. Any tugging brought sharp pain. She had been so disturbed that she could not sleep. After two unhappy weeks a wet nurse had been called in, whereafter both the mother and child flourished. Now, three years later, Frau Dorff was having more serious trouble with her second child: as feeding time approached she threw up her food and, when the infant was brought in, became so agitated at her failure to nurse the baby that she wept.

"Dr. Lott and I agreed this morning that we couldn't risk endangering the mother or child any longer; we decided that we would instruct the family that they had to find a wet nurse immediately."

"Josef, she's your patient. You're a skilled practitioner. Why don't you hypnotize her?"

Breuer said flatly, "For a departure in treatment I think a new doctor is indicated."

They found Frau Dorff in bed, red with rage that she had been unable to do what she called "every mother's duty." She had eaten nothing the entire day; her epigastrium was distended and her abdomen tender to the touch. Sigmund drew a chair up to the bed, began speaking in a slow heavy voice.

"You are going to sleep. . . . You are tired. You want to sleep. Your eyelids are growing heavy. . . . Sleep is coming. You will sleep. Your eyelids are closing. You are going to sleep. . . . You are going to rest. Your eyes are closed now. You're drifting off to sleep. . . ."

It had not taken long but, thought Sigmund, "considering the patient's state of exhaustion, it should have taken half the time." He hitched his chair closer to the bed, began talking in a voice filled with confidence and assurance.

"Have no fear! You will nurse your baby excellently. The baby will thrive. You're a healthy normal young woman. You love your baby. You want to feed him. It will bring you joy. Your stomach is perfectly quiet. Your appetite is good. You are looking forward to your next meal. You will eat and digest your food in comfort. When the baby is brought in you will feed him. Your milk is good. Your baby will thrive. . . ."

He kept up the flow of suggestion for five minutes, then awakened Frau Dorff. She remembered nothing of what had taken place. Herr Dorff came in glowering, told the doctor in a voice loud enough for his wife to hear:

"I don't approve these goings on. A woman's nervous system could be destroyed by hypnosis."

Dr. Freud replied quietly, "Not true, Herr Dorff. Hypnosis has never hurt anyone. It is merely sleep, very similar to ordinary sleep. Your wife already looks rested. Should we not base our decision on the results? I will look in again tomorrow."

Herr Dorff was not mollified.

When he returned the following afternoon he learned that he had had a partial success: the patient had eaten a good supper and slept comfortably all night. That morning she had breast-fed the baby quite satisfactorily. However, sitting at the dining table at midday, she again began to be troubled and, when the platters of food were brought in, vomited.

In the afternoon she had been unable to nurse the child. She was depressed.

"There is no need to be," Sigmund assured her; "since your disorders disappeared for half a day, the battle is half won. We now know that we can banish your symptoms. Come, let us try again."

This time he kept her somnolent for some fifteen minutes, going over the same ground a dozen times, allaying her fears, assuring her that all would be well, that she would feed the baby that evening. At the last moment, on an impulse, he suggested that five minutes after he left the house Frau Dorff would be cross with her family, demand to know where her dinner was and how they expected her to feed her baby if she had nothing to eat herself. He then woke her. When he returned the following evening he found that Frau Dorff had eaten all her meals and had breast-fed her baby with no problem. She declared herself entirely well and declined another treatment.

Herr Dorff walked him to the door, telling him of the odd thing his wife had done after Dr. Freud left the house: she had spoken crossly to her mother and demanded to know why she was not being given her food. Dr. Freud kept his own counsel. In saying good-by, Herr Dorff made it quite clear that nature and time had cured his wife; that Privatdozent Dr. Sigmund Freud had done nothing at all . . . though of course he would be paid for the three visits.

He was jubilant. He had posited a cure! He would have to keep in touch to make sure there was no regression, but from her attitude it was indicated that she was well. The force of his own suggestion that she could feed her child had driven out her self-imposed suggestion that she could not. Professor Bernheim was right: there were certain specific forms of illness which were ideational, arising originally in the mind and acting as cruel masters over the defenseless body. This was a new instrument in the leanly packed kit of therapeutic tools! Charcot was wrong to ignore it.

Martha quickly responded to his exhilaration. When deep in thought she raised a wrinkle between her eyebrows and then stroked it abstractedly with a forefinger.

"Sigi, am I right, you planted an idea in Frau Dorff's mind which dissolved another idea which was making her ill?"

"Yes. I didn't dissolve it as I would a lump of sugar in a cup of coffee; but the effect was the same."

"And where did her idea come from?"

"There you have me, Marty. That's in the speculative realm of psychology. If doctors started speculating on the origin of these malady ideas, we'd leave the scientific world altogether."

"Is hypnosis scientific? Can you take a cut of it with a microtome and put it on a slide?"

"In effect, yes. That's what Bernheim is doing at Nancy. I'll have to go there one day and study his methods. Particularly if I get permission to translate his book. The key is Bernheim's line, 'Hypnosis is a state of heightened suggestibility.' Why can't the same thing be accomplished when the patient is in normal sleep? Answer, I don't know. Question: Then there is an essential difference between regular sleep and hypnosis? Answer: Yes! Question: What is that difference? Answer: I don't know."

A few days later he tried again. Dr. Königstein sent him a young man with an eye tic, explaining that there was nothing organically wrong with the eye. The young man was suspicious, hostile. He categorically refused to succumb to hypnosis. Sigmund's efforts were to no avail. Late that afternoon a fifty-year-old patient was brought in who could no longer walk or even stand up unassisted. The referring doctor informed Dr. Freud that neither he nor his associates could find a physical impairment.

Sigmund made his own examination. There was no shrinkage or atrophy of Franz Vogel's leg or hip muscles. He then set down the development of the symptoms: first the heaviness in the right leg, then in the left arm, a few days later inability to move his legs or bend his toes. Franz Vogel's illness had developed in stages over a period of ten days. Would it not be wise to take him on the road to health at the same pace?

He put Vogel to sleep without difficulty, then suggested that when he awoke he would be able to bend and wiggle his toes. When Vogel awoke he followed the suggestion, considerably to his amazement. The next day Dr. Freud suggested that when he awoke, though he would not be able to walk, he would be able to raise his right leg up and down while lying on the couch. Again Vogel followed orders. At the third session Sigmund suggested that Vogel would be able to stand unassisted. Vogel did so. The following Monday Sigmund suggested that Vogel would be able to walk to the end of the room and back. He complied. At the end of ten days Vogel was back at work in his business office. There remained only some slight heaviness in his right leg where the difficulty had originated. Several more sessions of hypnosis failed to remove the trace. The following Sunday morning when Sigmund and Josef were taking a fast walk around the Ring under the cold ash-gray sky, he asked Josef:

"Does the heaviness remain because there might be some slight physical disturbance, quite independent of the psychological one? Or have I failed to root out the original germ of the possessive idea?"

Josef was swaddled up to his ears in a greatcoat; his voice sounded as though it were coming through a bolt of wool.

"Or was the last germ of Vogel's idea protecting itself? If you could bring him back to absolute normal in ten days, might not people think he had never been ill at all? Herr Doktor, don't quarrel with your cure."

Sigmund's words came out into the freezing air accompanied by puffs of frosted breath.

"How much we know about the brain's physical structure, and how little about what causes ideas to ricochet through that mass of gray matter. . . . Yes, Josef, I know: ideas belong to the psyche, brain anatomy to the soma. But sometimes I feel frustrated not knowing *why* a man thinks *what* he thinks."

Before the year ended he had two more occasions to test hypnotic suggestion. His friend Dr. Obersteiner sent him a twenty-five-year-old *bonne* who had been with a good Viennese family for seven years. For a number of weeks Tessa had suffered a nervous attack every evening between eight and nine, when she had to leave the family and retire to her room. Convulsions followed, after which the girl fell into a trancelike sleep. When she awakened she ran out of the house and into the street only partly dressed. She was a big-boned girl and had lost thirty pounds in the past month. She had not swallowed a bite of food for days. After trying several doctors, her mistress had decided that she had better put Tessa into a mental hospital. Dr. Obersteiner suggested that she be taken to see Dr. Freud first.

He found Tessa bright, willing to talk and totally unable to understand what had happened to her. He diagnosed it as a case of hysteria. He put his fingertips lightly on the girl's eyelids, spoke reassuringly. She fell asleep. He then suggested that she was basically a strong and healthy girl; that she was going to be cured; that she no longer needed to fear retiring to her room; that her appetite would return; that she would sleep peacefully the entire night. He awoke her after ten minutes. Tessa opened startled eyes, cried:

"Herr Doktor, I can't believe it. I'm hungry. I shall buy a sweet roll and eat it on the way home."

The next day Tessa returned. She had eaten well but had awakened during the night and had to restrain herself from running out of the house. He hypnotized her again, this time stressing that she would feel safe while she slept; that there was no reason to run out of the house, that she was happy in the house and respected by the family.

The third day Tessa reported that she had awakened at three in the morning, restless and disturbed, but with no desire to run. After one more session Tessa was back to normal. A week later her mistress dropped in to pay the bill.

"Herr Doktor, how does it happen that several of the best professors in Vienna could do nothing for Tessa? That I was so desperate I had decided to put her into a sanatorium? Then within a few days you have her back to her healthy lovely self?"

Sigmund lightly stroked his beard to gain time. Was it wise to tell that he had been using hypnosis, and then perhaps have to justify it in a city that had only contempt for the method?

"It sometimes happens this way," he said quietly. "You brought Tessa to me at the moment a cure was possible."

The woman took some gold coins from her handbag, placed them on the desk. When she left she was still shaking her head in puzzlement. Sigmund said to himself:

"You are not the only one puzzled. Why after seven years did Tessa develop an acute aversion to going to her room at night? What caused the convulsions? What drove her into the street, half dressed? And why was she incapable of eating?"

Into his mind flashed the trio of answers afforded in passing by Breuer, Charcot and Chrobak. "These things are always *secrets d'alcôve!*" "In this sort of case it's always a question of the genitals—always, always, always." "*Rx: Penis normalis dosim repetatur!*" But those patients had been married women. Tessa was only twenty-five, single and, he was certain, virginal. This kind of thinking could not apply to Tessa.

Then to Sigmund Freud came the case that, for him, answered monumental questions and opened the massive doors to the future. It also changed his life.

7.

A *Dienstmann* brought him a note asking him to come to Josef's apartment when the last of his patients had departed. Before he could leave, a maid brought a second note, from a Frau Emmy von Neustadt, who was staying at one of Vienna's most expensive pensions. Dr. Breuer had mentioned his name. Could he please call that afternoon; it was urgent.

It was the first of May, a pleasantly warm day in Vienna, with the country women in the streets singing, "I have lavender. Who wants my lavender?" At the street corners fiddlers in baggy pants were elbowing off-tune waltzes. Sigmund walked with his face turned up to the sun, welcoming its brightness and warmth. He found Josef in his laboratory, in shirt sleeves, working with his pigeons. The attic window was thrown open to the weightless spring afternoon air. The two friends stood by the open window, overlooking the back garden.

"Sig, I'd like you to take over a difficult case for me. Frau Emmy von Neustadt. I've been handling her for six weeks, since she came from Abbazia with partial paralysis of the legs. I've done everything I could, massage, electric treatment, quieting drugs, but she has become dissatisfied. Yesterday when she thought I wouldn't notice she even started to make fun of me. At that moment I casually dropped your name into the conversation. She thinks I did it by accident. You probably heard from her today."

"Yes. She asked me to call this afternoon. Thank you for dropping my name into the pot. Is it really urgent?"

Josef rang for cold drinks. They sat on hard wooden chairs across the workbench on which Josef kept his microscope, slides and the diary of his experiments.

"Yes, Sig, it is. Let me tell you what I know about Frau Emmy von Neustadt."

Frau Emmy, as Josef now began calling her, came from the landed gentry of northern Germany, with a town house as well as a country estate near the Baltic. When she was twenty-three, a well-educated woman, she married a widower in his early fifties who had several children by a first wife. Von Neustadt was a man of high talent and intelligence, who had built a large industrial empire. Frau Emmy bore him two daughters during their three years of marriage, which was a happy one and gave every indication of being a love match. She also established a salon where there congregated writers, artists, theater people, scientists, university professors. Then Von Neustadt died of a stroke. Frau Emmy's second daughter was only a few weeks old. After her husband's sudden death she became ill for a considerable time, as did the infant. Later she played an important part in the management of her husband's industrial complex. She continued her salon, traveled, had many lively interests. But in the fourteen years since her husband's death she had suffered a variety of unaccountable illnesses.

Sigmund arrived at the fashionable pension in which Frau von Neustadt had installed herself with her two daughters, a governess and a maid, and took the lift to the top floor. The maid admitted him to the living room. Here he saw a still young-looking woman lying on a sofa, her head resting on a leather cushion, a throw over her feet. He observed that it was a face full of character, with finely cut features and sea-green eyes which, although freighted with pain, looked most intelligent. Her silken-textured blonde hair was combed meticulously on top of her head. She was dressed in a flowered silk morning dress.

He stood just inside the doorway studying his patient for a moment before crossing to her. There was a tense, strained look on her face; the cords in her neck muscles stood out like columns; and there was a ticlike slide of a muscle under the skin of the left side of her face; a movement up and down in smooth clocklike motion. She was clasping and unclasping her fingers agitatedly.

"Frau von Neustadt, I am Dr. Sigmund Freud. How are you feeling today?"

Frau von Neustadt replied in a low cultivated voice.

"I am not at all well today, Herr Doktor. I have sensations of cold and pain in my left leg which seem to originate from my back . . ." She stopped abruptly, horror spread over her face. She threw her right hand toward him with the fingers extended, and cried in a voice choked with anxiety, "Keep still! Don't say anything! Don't touch me!" She then dropped her hand, the fingers relaxed. She continued in the same low tone as before, "I also have considerable gastric disturbance. I have been unable to eat or drink anything for two days now. Every bite or drop makes me ill . . ." She stopped, closed her eyes; suddenly from her lips came a clacking sound, a "tick—tick—tick!" uttered with her tongue against her teeth, then a pop of the lips followed by a hiss. The pain vanished from her face. She propped herself up more comfortably on the pillow.

"My parents had fourteen children, of which I was born the thirteenth. Alas, only four of us survive. I was given a good rearing, though under intensely strict discipline by my mother, who loved us but was severe . . ." Again she thrust out her right arm, cried, "Keep still! Don't say anything! Don't touch me!" then resumed in a low voice, "Because of the sudden death of my husband, whom I adored, and the difficulty of bringing up my two daughters who are now fourteen and sixteen, and who have been ailing all of their lives from nervous troubles, I have become ill . . ." Again the "tick—tick—tick—pop, hisss. . . ."

Sigmund by-passed the woman's verbal peculiarities.

"Over the years, Frau von Neustadt, you have found doctors and treatments which have helped you?"

"Not often. Four years ago I was helped with a combination of massage and electric baths. For several months I have been suffering from depression and insomnia. I have been in Vienna for six weeks now looking for medical help but have found none." The arm jerked: "Keep still! Don't say anything! Don't touch me!" She relaxed. "It was something Dr. Josef Breuer said while treating me yesterday that made me believe that you could be of assistance."

"I hope I can, Frau von Neustadt. However my suggestion is that you leave your two daughters here in charge of your governess and maid, and that you enter an excellent nursing home that I will recommend. There we can make a complete study of your symptoms, and I will have the best chance of bringing you back to health."

Frau von Neustadt's green eyes studied him for a moment.

"Thank you, Herr Doktor. If you will leave the name and address of the nursing home I shall move there in the morning."

He emerged oblivious into a shell-pink dusk, the hard edges of the city's building stones commingled in soft contours. His brown eyes were opaque; he walked in a manner unusual for him, in a broken gait, while he tried to sort out the astonishing sights and sounds of Frau

Emmy von Neustadt. Obviously she was suffering from a major hysteria: rational and intelligent for minutes and then suddenly seized by horrifying hallucinations, apparently without knowing. Did she put out her hands as though to ward off evil when she cried, "Keep still! Don't say anything! Don't touch me"? Once this incantation had been pronounced, did the demon vanish? And what of the weird clacking sound, the tick-pop-hiss? These mental tics appeared to come from a portion of her mind which had no contact with the part of the brain which was speaking and thinking logically.

His walk brought him to the square alongside St. Stephan's Cathedral, where lines of *Einspänner* and *Fiaker* were waiting for customers, their drivers exchanging *bassena* talk in the late afternoon sun. Thoughts were whirling through his head at an uncontrollable speed; yet his emotions were lumped like heavy dough at the pit of his stomach. When he tried to sort them out he could recognize only apprehension commingled with awe. He sensed that he stood on the edge of a great chasm: the duality of human nature. After *Oedipus Rex*, Josef Breuer had said that Queen Jocasta had not known in her *conscious* mind that she was married to her own son. Sigmund had failed to make the next and connecting step, toward which the full force of his intelligence had been driving him: Jocasta had known of Oedipus' identity in an *unconscious* mind. Teiresias, the blind prophet, had actually said so:

> "I say that with those you love best
> you live in foulest shame unconsciously
> and do not see where you are in calamity."

It was to this unconscious mind that hypnotism served as a key! The patients he had helped through hypnotism had been made ill by an idea lodged in their *unconscious* minds: the mother who could not breast-feed her child; the businessman who could not walk; the *bonne* who could not remain in her room at night; and now Frau Emmy, whose unconscious mind was filled with demons which were strong enough to break through her conscious mind and assert themselves even as she talked.

He stared up at the Gothic tower of St. Stephan, sightless, his breath coming fast, as frightened and elated as he had ever been in his life. It was as though he had been standing on top of the highest mountain of Semmering, closed in by an impenetrable fog, and now the mists had lifted, showing the plains below: the contour of the human mind. It was a view the poets, novelists and dramatists had always sensed, the Unconscious. Psychology had talked about the soul, about moral faculties, and been despised as a failure. But today he had seen the unconscious mind perform. Like everyone else, he had watched it countless times before and had not perceived the meaning of what he was seeing.

Could it be? Were there two human minds functioning separately from each other? The concept was shattering. He shivered in the warm evening air, even as he imagined Vasco de Balboa had, standing on a promontory, gaining his first view of the Pacific Ocean; unknown, unheard of, unmapped, so staggering in breadth as to overwhelm puny man. What dangers lay in this bottomless deep? What monsters could emerge? What forces were at play that could lash and splinter man's tiny boat in hurricane gales? Were there great holes into which the ship would drop, its crew never to reappear? Were there no limits, no end to this sea stretching to infinity? Would they sail on and on without sustenance because there was no solid land at the other end? Would they go down to a watery grave?

What he now grasped sent his thoughts running wildly in fright, confusion, fear, disbelief of his own evidence, the sights of his own eyes and the sounds of his own ears. This was a land where no man had ventured before. Had no man dared? Over the years he had read a good deal about the conflict between the Lord and Lucifer, particularly in Goethe's *Faust*. Except as a literary or religious concept, symbolic in nature, he had never understood this contest between God and the Devil. Now for the first time he understood it. God was the conscious, logical, responsible mind, the great force that had brought man out of the sea, the jungle, the bush and turned him into a reasoning, creative creature. The Devil was the unconscious. The Evil One enthroned in a nether region fit only for monsters, gargoyles, reptiles, the habitat of the ugly, the evil, nefarious and demoniac, malevolent, noxious, pernicious, virulent, base, accursed, fiendish, the offal and excreta of the universe; its servile minions ready at the slightest opportunity to wither, corrupt, contaminate, paralyze, destroy. There could be no God, no science, no discipline, no reason, no civilization in so damned a spot; no area where a man could put his foot or his mind and not sink at once into the pestilential muck. Once so hopelessly befouled, could one ever return to reason or society?

Sigmund Freud admired brave men: Alexander the Great, Galileo, Columbus, Luther, Semmelweis, Darwin. He had always hoped to be a brave man himself, unflinching before the perils that could challenge a human. But who would not quail before this chamber of horrors, worse than anything Torquemada had devised for breaking men's bodies, their will?

Josef Breuer had stumbled into its caldron. Was the price too high to pay? Did one emerge befouled? Had he become too horrified to pursue it, even though at the bottom of the pit there might rest diamonds, pearls and emeralds of the purest wisdom and beauty? Had he purposefully turned the adventure over to his younger protégé?

Doré's illustrations for Dante's *Inferno* came to his mind. He remembered the opening of Canto 1:

> *Midway upon the journey of our life*
> *I found that I was in a dusky wood;*
> *For the right path, whence I had strayed, was lost.*
> *Ah me! How hard a thing it is to tell*
> *The Wildness of that rough and savage place,*
> *The very thought of which brings back my fear!*
> *So bitter was it, death is little more so:*
> *But that the good I found there may be told,*
> *I will describe the other things I saw.*

8.

He took several turns through the sanatorium garden before he went into Frau Emmy's room, located with a view of blue Vienna skies. She had eaten nothing and had not slept the night before. Each time the door opened unexpectedly she cringed, half jumped up in bed as though to protect herself. He ordered that no one, nurse or doctor, was to enter the room without knocking softly.

"Frau von Neustadt, in the first week I propose to build up your strength. I shall massage your body twice a day. I have ordered that you be given warm baths. I am going to hypnotize you now and put you to sleep, after which I will make certain suggestions. Have you ever been hypnotized?"

"No."

She proved to be a splendid patient for hypnotism. He held a finger in front of her eyes and ordered her to go to sleep. Within minutes she had relaxed back onto the stacked pillows, looking somewhat dazed but not at all anxious. He said quietly, "Frau von Neustadt, I suggest that your symptoms are going to disappear, that you will begin to eat with fine appetite, and sleep peaceably through the night."

It took him six days of consecutive hypnotic suggestion, along with the baths and massage, to bring Frau Emmy to the point where she was rested; her facial tics, both physical and mental, were subdued. Sigmund knew they were not gone but merely lying in wait. They would take a deeper treatment.

When he entered on a fine Tuesday morning, with the sun streaming into her room, he was at once assailed.

"I read in the Frankfurter *Zeitung* early this morning a horrible story, how an apprentice tied up a boy and put a white mouse in his mouth.

The poor boy died of fright. One of my doctors told me he had sent a whole case of white rats to Tiflis." An expression of revulsion came over her face as she hugged her arms over her breasts. "Keep still!—Don't say anything!—Don't touch me! Herr Doktor, suppose one of those rats was in my bed!"

He put Emmy to sleep, picked up the copy of the *Zeitung* which was lying on the side table and read the story about the young boy who had been mistreated. There was no mention whatever of mice or rats. Something, an idea, a hallucination, a fear, had come out of Frau Emmy's mind, interwoven the mice and rat material with what she was reading in the newspaper.

It would only be by learning what set off these bouts of terror in Frau Emmy that he could attempt to dissipate them. He had perceived by now the strong parallels between her case and that of Bertha Pappenheim's. He had tried to equate the similarities with Josef Breuer, evaluate the possibility of a "chimney sweeping" or "talking cure"; but Josef had refused to be drawn into a discussion.

He spoke to Frau Emmy for a considerable time while she lay somnolent, suggesting in a dozen different ways that fear of such animals as mice, rats, snakes, reptiles was normal, but that they would not enter her life. He suggested she stop being concerned about them, dismiss them as errant thoughts, as something common to mankind and of minor importance. He suggested, "Frau Emmy, you have the ability to make this choice."

The next time he put her under hypnosis he asked her why she was so frequently frightened. She replied:

"It has to do with memories of my earliest youth."

"When?"

"First when I was five years old and my brothers and sisters often threw dead animals at me. That was when I had my first fainting fit and spasms. But my aunt said it was disgraceful and that I ought not to have attacks like that, and so they stopped. Then I was frightened again when I was seven and I unexpectedly saw my sister in her coffin; and again when I was eight my brother terrified me so often by dressing up in sheets like a ghost; and again when I was nine I saw my aunt in her coffin and her jaw suddenly dropped."

After each of the recountings she shivered, her face and body twitching. She now lay back on the pillow, exhausted, panting for breath. He poured some water into a basin, dampened a towel and wiped the perspiration off her face, gently massaged her shoulders. He then walked to the window and stood staring out into the garden, trying to understand the apparently excruciating experience Frau Emmy had just put herself through. Each incident was separated from the other by at least a year; they would be imbedded in varying layers of her memory;

yet at a simple question she had instantly pulled all of the elements together and knit them into a connected narrative. When he asked her now how she had been able to do this, Emmy replied:

"Because I think of those dreadful scenes so often. I see everything so vividly, all of the shapes and forms and colors, as though I were living through it again, this very moment."

He stroked her eyes gently to put her into a deeper sleep, then took up the component parts of her story, handling each one separately. Could she really remember so vividly scenes from when she was only five years old? And did her sisters actually throw dead animals at her? It all seemed highly unlikely. Did she suffer from fits and spasms in her childhood? She had not mentioned this before in speaking of her early symptoms. She appeared to have been a fairly healthy girl.

"In any event, whether the incidents took place or not, I suggest that you wipe away these images. Our eyes see literally millions of pictures during our lifetime and we are not obliged to remember them all. Here again, Frau Emmy, we have freedom of choice. I suggest that you choose not to remember these scenes any more, and I think you are perfectly able to expunge them from your mind. You are strong enough and intelligent enough to do so. Let us drop a veil over them so that they grow indistinct and finally vanish altogether."

The following day, finding that she was suffering from nothing more than gastric pains, he decided to try to get at the origin of the tics. He asked:

"Frau Emmy, how long have you had the tic in which you make that peculiar clacking sound?"

Frau Emmy answered easily and with full knowledge not only of the affliction but of its point of origin.

"I have had the tic for the last five years, ever since a time when I was sitting by the bedside of my sleeping daughter who was very ill, and had wanted to keep absolutely quiet."

He said sympathetically, "This memory should not have any importance for you, Frau Emmy; nothing happened to your daughter."

"I know that. But the tic comes on me when I am worried or frightened or apprehensive."

At that moment Dr. Josef Breuer entered the room with the house physician. Instantly Frau Emmy put up her hand, cried, "Keep still! —Don't say anything!—Don't touch me!" after which Breuer and the house doctor retreated unceremoniously.

The next time Sigmund put her under hypnosis he urged her to tell him any additional experiences which had frightened her. She replied:

"I have another series of scenes and I can see them now. One was how I saw a female cousin taken off to an insane asylum when

I was fifteen. I tried to call for help but was unable to, and lost my power of speech until the evening of the same day."

He interrupted, "At what other times were you so concerned with insanity?"

"My mother herself had been in an asylum for some time. We once had a maidservant who used to tell me horrifying stories of how the patients were tied to chairs and beaten and made to turn round and round and round until they were unconscious."

During all this time she was clenching and unclenching her fingers anxiously, her mouth drawn tight in terror. He told her that she was too bright to believe the stories of a servant girl; that he himself had worked in asylums and seen the care that was given to the patients. He suggested that there was no need to be victimized by these tales, that they could not affect her.

On another day, when her body relaxed in the bed and her facial expression became more cheerful, he asked, "Please tell me the meaning of your phrase, 'Keep still!—Don't say anything!—Don't touch me!'"

Emmy replied calmly, "To keep still relates to the fact that the animal shapes which appear to me when I am in a bad state start moving and begin to attack me if anyone makes a movement. 'Don't touch me!' comes from an experience with my brother, who was so ill from taking a lot of morphine, I was nineteen at the time that he seized hold of me. When I was twenty-eight and my daughter was very ill the child grabbed me so forcibly in her delirium that I was almost choked."

Again Sigmund tackled each of the stories with a series of suggestions, all directed to expunging the memories. At their next session, after Frau Emmy was deep in sleep, he asked the origin of her stammering. Going through violent agitation and impediment of speech, she told him how the horses bolted once with the children in the carriage; and how another time she was driving through the forest with the children in a thunderstorm and a tree just in front of the horses was struck by lightning and the horses shied. She had thought, "You must keep quite still now, or your screaming will frighten the horses even more and the coachman won't be able to hold them in at all." The stammer had come on from that moment.

He went over and over every suggestion he could think of to expunge this new set of "plastic" memories. When he had finished, he said, "Frau Emmy, will you relate all of those episodes to me once more." Frau Emmy did not respond to his command. He wakened her. She did not remember what had taken place under the hypnosis. The stammer appeared to be gone. He felt a sharp sense of elation.

Frau Emmy von Neustadt became the focal center of his practice. He spent two hours each day with her, one in the morning after breakfast and another in the early evening. But fascinated as he was with the developments, he had little time to think of them between visits, for his clinic at the Kassowitz Children's Institute had become so busy that he spent three full afternoons a week there. His personal practice had also expanded, and he frequently spent four hours a day caring for the patients who came to his consultation room. He was functioning as a neurologist, seeking and oftentimes finding the somatic cause of his patients' illnesses. Ironically, now that he was developing a fresh approach to neuroticism, not one patient suffering from hysteria showed up. Though he became a little thin and drawn by the volume of work, he spent the hour before midnight, with the apartment quiet about him, Martha asleep, sitting at his desk meticulously writing down every word that had been said that day with Frau Emmy. It was an effort designed to come out with a topographical map of the weird wilderness of the woman's unconscious.

By the end of Sigmund Freud's third week of attendance on Frau von Neustadt he learned that she was a veritable laboratory of ideational illnesses. There had been a six-year interval between Josef Breuer's termination of the Pappenheim case and his own taking over of Frau Emmy; to the best of his knowledge no such therapeutic method, no "talking cure," had been attempted anywhere during these years. It was exciting for him to be translating the Bernheim book on *Hypnosis and Suggestion* at the same time that he was using the therapy. He knew also that his suggestions under hypnosis were getting only half the job done; the other half was being accomplished by Frau Emmy herself through the "talking cure." It was apparent that none of the stories which she was now pouring out had ever passed her lips before; it was equally doubtful that any of them had previously been able to make their way forward from the back of her mind into consciousness. Josef Breuer had known the power of his therapeutic method yet he had refused to use it again. Why? Certainly he had been able to diagnose Frau Emmy's illness and could have employed the same catharsis he had used on Bertha Pappenheim. Why had he been unwilling to seek a cure for the woman at his own hands?

Sitting at his desk each night, he wondered too what proportion of the patients who came into doctors' consultation rooms and into the hospitals had been made ill by ideational rather than infectious bodies. Not all, certainly; and not even most; he had worked too long in hospitals and seen too many people die of physical diseases not to know that the majority of them suffered from the malfunction of an organ, diseases of the lungs or heart, blood, from cancerous growths. Yet he could not escape the intuition, as he continued to treat Frau Emmy each day and translate more chapters of Bernheim each night, that the ill ones were all too frequently doing themselves in. It was a slow and subtle form of suicide, unbeknownst to patient, family, friends or doctor!

9.

Through suggestion he was able to remove Frau Emmy's embarrassments and fears over the things that happened around the nursing home; she came out of hypnosis feeling cheerful, talked about her salon and her wonderful friends among the writers and artists. Yet when he returned the next morning, she would cry out:

"Herr Doktor, I'm so glad you've come. I'm so afraid. I know I'm going to die."

Under hypnosis she told him about her dreadful dream. "The legs and arms of the chairs all turned into snakes. A monster with a vulture's beak was tearing and eating at me. Then other wild animals leapt upon me. When I was young I went to pick up a ball of wool and it was a mouse that ran away; when I moved a rock there was a big toad there and I was so frightened I couldn't talk for a day."

These were further animal images, ones he had not expunged. Was she making them up out of her hallucinations? Could she continue to conjure them up as fast as he could take the earlier crop from her? Or did they come from authentic frights of her childhood? He asked, while she was relating an episode from her past:

"Frau Emmy, why do you so frequently say that you have storms in your head?"

She stiffened, said crossly:

"You should not keep asking me where this comes from and that comes from; you should let me say what I have to say, without interrupting me."

Later that night while setting down his notes he thought, "Frau Emmy is right. As long as the patient's material is flowing I must remain in the background and let it formulate as it can and must. That is the best way to get a self-portrait. I must intrude only if the source has dried up."

The following day she unraveled an astonishing tale: one of her older brothers, an officer in the army, had syphilis, and because the family was concealing the illness, she had had to eat at the same table with him while deathly afraid she might pick up his knife and fork and catch the disease. Still another brother had had consumption and used to spit across the table into an open spittoon next to her chair in the dining room. When she was very young and refused to eat her food, her mother would force her to remain at table even if it were for several hours, until she finished her meat, "quite cold by then and the fat set so hard." She was swept by a wave of revulsion. "Every time I sit down to eat I see that cold layer of fat and I cannot swallow a bite."

Gently he asked, "Frau Emmy, did any of these memories come back to you during the three years of your marriage? Did they disturb you then?"

"Oh no, even though I was carrying my two daughters for eighteen of the thirty-six months. But then you see I was so terribly busy. We entertained all the time, both in town and on our country estate. My husband initiated me into the intricacies of his affairs. When he went away on business to other countries he took me with him."

Her face became animated; she looked young. He kept her under hypnosis.

"What was the event in your life that produced the most lasting effect on you?"

There was no hesitation on her part; nor was there any horror, fear or revulsion, only a sadness that settled over her fine features and made her cheeks slightly pale.

"My husband's death." Her voice deepened with emotion but there was no stammering, no clack. "We had been out on our favorite spot on the Riviera. While we were crossing a bridge my husband suddenly sank to the ground and lay there lifeless for a few minutes; then he got up and seemed quite well. A short time afterwards, as I was lying in bed after my second confinement, my husband, who had been sitting at a small table beside me reading a newspaper, got up all at once, looked at me strangely, took a few paces forward and then fell dead. The doctors made efforts to revive him but in vain. Then the baby, who was only a few weeks old, was seized with a serious illness that lasted for six months during which I myself was in bed with a high fever." Her expression changed; one of anger and bitterness came across her face. "You cannot imagine what troubles that child caused me. She was queer, she screamed night and day, she did not sleep, she developed a paralysis of the left leg which seemed to be incurable, she was late to learn to walk and talk, for a time we believed she would be an imbecile. According to the doctors she had encephalitis and inflammation of the spinal cord and I don't know what else besides!"

He pointed out that this daughter today was perfectly healthy. "Frau Emmy, I am going to remove the entire recollection of that period as though it had never been present in your mind. You have an expectation of misfortune. That's what makes you so fearful. But there is no reason for you to torment yourself. Neither is there any reason for the recurrent pains in your arms or legs, the cramp in your neck, the anesthesias of parts of your body. . . . Since I can wipe out these memories from your mind, I can also wipe out these recurrent pains."

But she remained depressed. He asked why she was so often sunk in melancholy. She replied, "It's because I have been persecuted by my husband's family. They disapproved of me. After his death they sent shady journalists who spread evil stories about me in the neighborhood and wrote stories for the newspapers that maligned me."

He had heard similar laments too often in Meynert's Clinic not to recognize them as a form of persecution mania. Yet, mania or no, he had to remove the ideas from her mind.

He met Josef Breuer at his house at six o'clock, when he knew Josef would have finished work. They walked to the Cafe Kurzweil which they had both used as their *Stammlokal* during their student days because of the blackboard on which they could chalk messages for their friends. Its *Marqueurs* were called on to score points in the billiard matches; the waiters were the most skilled players in the Empire and were frequently asked to finish a match when a patron had to dash off to keep an appointment. As always there was a beautiful girl "residing" on a rostrum, with her cash desk overlooking the room. Sigmund led Josef to a table at the far end of the *Schanigarten*, where they could combine a breath of air and the quiet to talk.

"Josef, I have been working with Frau Emmy now for six weeks. I haven't taken even a Sunday off. I've made progress in many directions, only to come back a day or a week later to find that there are new images and new memories which have replaced the ones I have expunged. There are times when I fear that her will to be ill is going to be stronger than my will to cure her."

Breuer shook his head soberly, caressing his beard with the palm of his hand.

"I know, Sig, she's a reluctant dragon. But six weeks is a short time in which to cure a woman who has been ill for fourteen years."

Sigmund thought about this for a moment.

"Josef, if Frau Emmy's husband had lived, would she be suffering these symptoms? All the evidence indicated that she was well and happy. If she had not seen him drop dead at her feet, would she have raised her two daughters normally? It was she, in her shock and grief, who made the girls nervously ill instead of the other way around. Isn't that true, Josef?"

"Yes, Sig. I am afraid it is. Why has Frau Emmy never remarried?"

"She claims her reason for remaining a widow was one of duty: she felt that another marriage might lead to the dissipation of her daughters' estate, and she was afraid to take the chance."

Breuer whistled softly, stirring the sugar in the bottom few drops of his thick black coffee.

"That's a higher price for money than the usurer's rate, wouldn't you say? She has preserved the girls' fortunes and has suffered fourteen years of intermittent illness and, when I turned her over to you, her symptoms were so bad that she might very well have died of them."

"Josef, you once told me that Bertha Pappenheim said that she had two selves, a 'bad or secondary self,' which was leading her into a series of psychotic illnesses; and a first or normal self, 'a calm and clear-sighted observer who sat,' as she put it, 'in a corner of her brain and looked on at all the mad business.' It's apparent to me that Frau Emmy has two separate and distinct states of consciousness, one revealed and one concealed. For six weeks I have watched this process in full bloom; and now I have a portrait of that 'second force' at work. I have had a glimpse of an unknown, unexplored continent, an area for scientific investigation of crucial importance. Josef, how many of the poor unfortunates chained to the circular walls of the Fools' Tower were there because their 'bad selves,' their diseased second minds, had taken over the forebrain? How many of the patients in Professor Meynert's Clinic had been made mentally ill, and how many in the Lower Austrian Insane Asylum have become emotionally disturbed and finally irrational because they had not one mind but two, functioning independently of each other, the sick one slowly eradicating the control of the normal functioning one? I know Frau Emmy is undoubtedly a person with severe neuropathic heredity; but on the other hand, Josef, we know that disposition and heredity alone cannot create this hysteria. There have to be external reasons, such as the sudden death of her husband, or the hereditary taint may never be set in motion."

Josef Breuer shook his head in bemused despair.

"Sig, as Frau Emmy's doctor, you cannot experimentally give her a new husband. Therefore you must eradicate the material with which she makes herself ill. My advice to you is not to release her from the nursing home until she expresses a strong desire to take up her normal life."

Frau Emmy made progress. Dr. Freud, the hypnotist, continued to suggest that she was too strong a woman to be dominated by a collection of old photographs. He asked her bluntly to tear them up, to scatter the fragments to the winds.

One morning he came in to find her sitting in the chair by the side of her bed, fully dressed, her hair neatly combed and a smile on her face.

"Herr Doktor, I feel entirely well. This is a beautiful time of the year at our country home. I want to go back and take my daughters with me. I am eager to rejoin my friends and take care of the family business. I am deeply grateful for all you have done."

That night as he lay sleepless, with Martha breathing rhythmically beside him, and only the baby's head showing out of the covers of the crib, he fell into a soliloquy. It was the quiet time when men engage in much of their best thinking.

"Just what did I do for Frau Emmy?" he demanded of himself. For the moment at least he had put an end to her physical pains, routed the idea that she was subject to paralysis of her limbs, or that she was going to die. He had fed her, massaged her, given her electrical treatments and warm baths, expunged from her mind endless repulsive images. But what had he actually done about getting to the root of her problem? It was the ultimate question every doctor had to ask himself. He was ready now to ask the cause of the *ideas* that got into people's minds and devastated them. Where did they come from? What determined their strength? By what process did they become master of the house and the afflicted one the servant? It was not enough to say that Frau Emmy's mental and physical ills came from the sudden death of her husband. Thousands of young women were widowed; they remarried or remained single, worked the rest of their lives, raised their children.

The baby stirred. He rose, felt her bottom to make sure she was dry, adjusted the fine-spun blanket over her shoulders, returned to bed.

Weren't these the same questions that had been asked about every other illness? For a thousand years people had died of tuberculosis before Professor Koch asked, "Where does this disease originate? What causes it?" He found the answer: the bacillus; and now doctors were working on a drug to eradicate it. For centuries people had died of stones in the gall bladder, until surgeons learned to remove them. For generations child-bearing women died of puerperal fever. Semmelweis asked, "Why? Where does the fever come from?" He found the answer and stopped its ravages.

There was no longer any question in his mind but that neurosis was a major illness. That it could blind a man, make him deaf or dumb, paralyze his arms or legs, spin him into convulsions, make him unable to eat or drink, kill him as dead as blood poisoning, the black plague, collapsed lungs, closed arteries to the heart. Patients died as a result of their neuroses, how many he could not conceivably guess. Most doctors were well trained, conscientious; they urgently wanted to help their patients, to save them. But what of the cases that were misjudged, sent to the wrong department of the hospital or clinic, there to be given the wrong treatment, incarcerated or sent home for the wrong reasons, to die in the wrong season of their lives?

BOOK SEVEN

LOST ISLAND OF ATLANTIS

Lost Island of Atlantis

THEY took the 7:30 A.M. express to Semmering, the mountain area known as the alpine paradise of the Viennese, late in June to look for a villa in which the family might enjoy their summer refresher. Their second-class compartment was handsomely upholstered with brown leather, the head linen across the top proudly carrying the letters K.K., *Kaiserlich Königlich* (Imperial Royal), the equivalent of Imperial Rome's S.P.Q.R., which the Viennese saw a dozen times a day as they passed official buildings or the tiny shops selling tobacco and stamps. As they went through the first pitch-black tunnel, known as the Kissing Tunnel because it was too early in the two-and-a-half-hour trip to have the gas lamp in the ceiling turned on, Sigmund put his arm about Martha and bussed her soundly on the mouth. She whispered in his ear:

"Did you know, Sig, that if a husband does not embrace his wife in the Kissing Tunnel that means he is keeping another woman?"

They were rolling now through the foothill vineyards with their rows of stakes to hold the growing vines. As the train stopped in the Pfaffstätten they saw the wineshops with their garlands of green leaves tacked over the doors to indicate that they were serving fresh wine. Sigmund, whose practice seemed to have vanished the way the street cleaners' water steamed up and disappeared in the early morning sun, muttered sardonically:

"Maybe I should put a *Büschel* over our front door to indicate that I am purveying a fresh medical philosophy, just as raw as the *Heurige* and equally intoxicating."

The haycocks at the base of the House Mountains, so named because they were close to Vienna's households, were shaped like brown cupcakes. They began their climb up to The Humpback World, the Austrians' nickname for the foothills between Schneeberg and the Rax, six-thousand-foot twin snowcapped peaks. Long ago his brother Alexander had told Sigmund the story of how this line to Semmering, the first true mountain railway in the world, had been built by the visionary Karl Ghega under the sponsorship of Emperor Franz Josef. Sigmund recounted the story to Martha of the near impossible feat that had been accomplished in conquering the Semmering Pass, more than three thousand feet high, with a series of sixteen viaducts over the gorges and fifteen tunnels dug through the rock of the mountains. During his youth Sigmund had come as often as possible for a weekend of hiking.

At Gloggnitz Station three officials inspected the train, then a special engine was put at the front to help pull the cars up the mountains, while a second was added at the rear to push. At Klamm the gas lights were turned on. Sigmund observed, as they came out of the blackness of a series of tunnels into the blinding light of the viaducts, from which they could see the huge paper mills of Schlögel, and then the church Maria Schutz:

"This journey is the best symbol I know for the difference between Dante's *Inferno* and *Paradiso*. Did you know, Martha, that there are people in the world who prefer death to life?"

"It is hard to believe, Sigi. Do you know why?"

"My patients are teaching me."

It was close to ten o'clock in the morning when they finally stepped through the large doors of the Semmering Station and began their walk through the village. They breathed deeply to quaff great gulps of the heady pine and snow scents. Though they were in an upland valley ever higher ranges tumbled backwards, thrusting icily into the azure sky. Below them were open green pastures with grazing cattle; and along the narrow dirt roads that curved through the mountains like ribbon interlaced at the hem of a lady's gown, scattered villages of red tile roofs and gray slate barns.

Many of the villas had already been rented but shortly after noon they found a pleasant house known as the *Sommerwohnung*, buried in a plateau of white birch. It was large, like the houses in Baden, but Tyrolese in character, the ground floor built of stone, the second of wood, with window shutters painted green, a small wooden turret for the bell, and decorated with the horns of a stag. The owner lived downstairs. With the spacious upper floor the Freuds would have a wood-covered terrace. They sat out on the rustic chairs where they would take their coffee after meals. When the owner's wife brought them a fresh white wine as a welcoming gesture, Sigmund and Martha clinked glasses, exchanged a quiet "I love you," and decided they would name their retreat the Pufendorf villa because the Pufendorf fees were paying the rent.

"Pufendorf Palace" proved a great success. Martha and nine-month-old Mathilde thrived in the pine-scented warmth of the days while the nights were cool enough for a blanket. Marie managed her summer kitchen very well on the thin ration of utensils. She had packed two boxes of dishware, pots, silver and linen, which had traveled in the luggage van behind the train in which she and the three Freuds occupied one full seat, their *Handkoffer*, hand trunks, on the racks above them. Sigmund took the express each Friday evening at eight-fifteen, and a little after eleven was walking along the narrow country road. By midnight he was lying beside Martha in the sweet warmth of their bed.

It was many years since Amalie and Jakob had been able to afford a summer house; Sigmund invited them to visit. Alexander, who had a railroad pass, rode up on Sundays. "Not to visit us," teased Martha, "but to ride over those sixteen viaducts."

Alexander replied, a beatific smile on his face, "Even with my eyes closed I can tell you the name and number of each one: Busserltunnel, Payerbach, Schlögelmühle . . ."

Alexander at twenty-two was a couple of inches shorter than Sigmund, most of it missing from the neck; otherwise the brothers continued to look startlingly alike. Sigmund believed his brother to be a complex personality, temperamental in his relationships, impatient with people, yet levelheaded and steady in his work. He stayed at his desk until midnight. His only complaint was that the sheets of freight rates were printed in such microscopic type that he already wore glasses with a narrow metal band over his broad-bridged nose while Sigmund, ten years older, was absorbing medical print without them.

"When I become Minister of Transportation, my first official act will be to enlarge all railroad type by four times. For that one act alone I should be knighted by Emperor Franz Josef."

Alexander's firm distributed the *Allgemeine Tarif-Anzeiger*. When he had begun work the Tariff Schedule was confined to a couple of rough sheets. Now, after five years, he had turned it into a respectable journal.

"Alex, be careful," Sigmund warned, "or you'll become the Austrian expert on freight trains."

"I already am."

Sigmund found it strange to be living alone with the parlor and dining-room furniture sheeted over, the windows locked, the draperies taken down for the summer, the rugs rolled in camphor and newspapers. Since he had only an occasional patient, he spent his afternoons at the Kassowitz Institute where there was an influx of afflicted children from all over Austria. Mornings he studied and wrote articles on aphasia, brain anatomy and paralyses in children for an *Encyclopedic Handbook of Medicine*, and an introduction for the just completed translation of the Bernheim book in which he suggested that the achievement of Dr. Bernheim consisted of "stripping the manifestations of hypnotism of their strangeness by linking them up with the familiar phenomena of normal psychological life and of sleep . . . 'suggestion' is established as the nucleus of hypnotism and the key to its understanding." He claimed the book to be stimulating and well calculated to destroy the belief that hypnosis was still surrounded, as Professor Meynert asserted, by a "halo of absurdity."

The evenings he spent with his friends. Ernst Fleischl urged him to come for supper as often as possible, for he was lonely and ill, often too feverish to continue his researches in Professor Brücke's laboratory. Josef Paneth had taken over his work, doing a brilliant job with Exner on visual disturbances following operations on the hindbrain. Fleischl, whose formerly handsome face was now little more than ridges of bone, fretted over Sigmund's paucity of patients.

"Sig, why don't you go into general practice? At least until you can afford the luxury of being a neurologist?"

Sigmund laid down his fork.

"It is excruciating to sit in that consultation room morning after morning listening for patients to ring the bell. But I don't know enough medicine to be a general practitioner. Besides, there are only a handful of us specialists in neurology."

Fleischl sighed. "You're right to be stubborn, of course."

Josef Breuer transcribed the word "stubborn" to "recalcitrant." He picked up a copy of the *Medizinische Wochenschrift* and read aloud from Sigmund's preface to the Bernheim book.

"Why did you have to attack Meynert by name? You have belled the cat." He lowered his head and gazed at Sigmund from the tops of his eye sockets. "This is the lion of the jungle. He's sure to strike back, Sig. I just don't think you have the weapons yet to fight him in the open arena."

The happiest evenings were spent with Sophie and Josef Paneth in their cool top-floor apartment on the Parkring, overlooking the Stadtpark. Josef invited several other young doctors, and they played *Tarock* in front of the open living-room windows. Sigmund enjoyed the game, forgetting all about medicine, Meynert and the missing patients as he cried, "*Stich oder Schmier.* Take the trick or sweeten it!" or "*Ultimo!*" without needing to look at the two sets of hole cards; and being mildly disappointed if the opponent said, "*Kontra,*" and beat him for the sixteen points.

One evening Sophie drew him aside.

"Sigi, Josef is coughing a good deal. In the middle of the night. Once I found bloodstains that he tried to conceal. Would you find an excuse to examine his chest?"

"Sophie dear, I know the best lung man in Austria."

"Would you also ask the doctor to banish us to the mountains for the rest of the summer? Josef is so excited about his work with Dr. Exner that he's overextending himself."

Amalie was the most pleased about Sigmund's summer bachelorhood, for she got a chance to cook her son's favorite foods for midday dinner. Now fifty-three, her hair was tinged with gray but her face was still full, her energies inexhaustible. The household was too small an empire for her to administer, particularly since Sigmund insisted that she hire a maid to do the heavy work; but it was sometimes an emotional one, for the three daughters still at home were obliged to sleep in one room. Though the sisters got along well there was an occasional uproar due to the cramped quarters. Jakob fled the house at the first discordant note. Amalie refused to take sides, merely admonishing the girls to keep the peace in *her* house. Alex, the practical, would solve the immediate problem by finding space for still another clothes pole in the closet, another shelf over a bed.

Now that he himself was a father, Sigmund found his feelings for Jakob changed. He had always loved his father for his combination of wisdom and humor; Jakob had kept a light touch with his children. Yet between Sigmund and his father there had been a difference not merely of one generation but two. That difference no longer seemed important; he had joined Jakob's fraternity and recognized in his own feelings for little Mathilde the gentle affection that Jakob had showered on him. His father had been his first tutor and, after Amalie, his first admirer.

Sigmund saved an hour nearly every day for the walks that his father loved in the coolness of the Prater woods, harking back to Sigmund's childhood when they had walked together one day a week. Here, arm in arm, the two men talked about the news of the world. Sigmund had seen a notice in the *Neue Freie Presse* which advertised a good position for a doctor in a factory in Moravia; the doctor did not have to have any qualifications except that he be a Christian. This kind of anti-Semitism had not only been growing in the past few years but was becoming overt. A newspaper, *Deutsches Volksblatt*, had been founded for the purpose of fomenting and financing anti-Semitism. The United Christian Party had been formed to promote an entente with Germany, weakening relations with countries lying to the east; inherent in this movement was an anti-Semitism organized for political ends.

In a discussion of the Karl Koller duel, it was Josef who figured out that Dr. Zinner had had to lose in order not to be dismissed from the Allgemeine Krankenhaus. Having been wounded, the authorities would feel satisfied that Zinner had paid for his bad conduct. "Had Koller been smart enough to let himself be cut, he would still be there," reasoned Jakob.

The weekends were carefree. Martha and Sigmund set out early on Saturday morning, Sigmund wearing *Lederhosen*, short leather pants above his knees, heavy Bavarian suspenders to hold them up, hiking boots, thick green socks to match his shirt and a mountain walking stick. He carried a rucksack stuffed with a picnic lunch, a blanket rolled along its top. Martha wore a wide skirt and a floppy hat to protect her face from the sun. Once they left "Pufendorf Palace," they wandered the mountain trails divorced from the realm of time. Sigmund's favorite flower was the *Kohlröserl,* a small dark purple sprig with a peculiarly pungent sweet perfume. When they reached the Schneeberg, he climbed the steep grassy slope to collect the blossoms for Martha. The task was arduous and dangerous, which made the bouquet the more precious. They had a beer and ate their lunch on the terrace of a mountain inn with a magnificent view over the valley, and returned home at dusk gloriously tired, to retire early with the cool sharp scent of night pine in their nostrils. This "summer refreshing" made the city tolerable to the Viennese during the winter of rain, sleet and snow.

2.

Martha whipped up an autumnal storm by opening, airing and scrubbing the apartment. As a natural consequence, she announced triumphantly, Sigmund's practice immediately picked up. Though he was grateful to be sought out by the neurological cases, that the chairs in his waiting room were amply filled with men suffering from the aftermath of syphilis, paresis of the face or locomotor ataxia, and women with multiple sclerosis, one in the beginning stage; aphasia cases, since he was gaining a certain reputation with this problem and was collecting histories for a monograph; victims of Parkinson's disease; of chorea characterized by spasmodic twitchings; and building slowly over the winter an increasing number of young children, infants too, whose parents could afford private physicians and chose him because they heard of his work at the Kassowitz Clinic; still, he was disappointed that there was not one patient suffering from a neurosis. These cases of hysteria were his only source material for further study of the disease. Aside from the psychiatric textbooks by Kraepelin and Krafft-Ebing, there was little material in the medical or scientific monographs beyond Charcot's *Archives,* the work of the American neurologist, Silas Weir Mitchell, originator of the famous "rest cure for neurasthenia," the Englishman James Braid's *Neurypnology.* Doctors in the German-speaking world still defined neurosis as "opprobrium madness, the despair of physicians."

Meynert believed that neuroses were either inherited or caused by physical damage to the brain. Sigmund's personal mine of knowledge emerged from Frau Emmy von Neustadt, whose case had given him the clearest picture of how the unconscious mind functioned, how through hypnosis and the "talking cure" it could be voided of painful memories which were causing hallucinations. He had sent her home to northern Germany in near normal health, even as he had enabled Frau Dorff to nurse her child, Herr Vogel to walk again on legs which had appeared to be paralyzed, Tessa, the *bonne,* to sleep through the night instead of running into the street. He kept copious notes on these cases, adding fresh thoughts and speculations. Yet only from new patients could he seek out corollaries, search for and establish patterns of behavior.

An eleven-year-old girl was brought to him. She had been suffering for five years from intermittent but violent convulsions so serious that a long string of qualified doctors had decided she was an epileptic. All of the physical examinations had been made, nothing neurologically wrong had been found. Sigmund chatted with the girl for a few moments to establish confidence, then hypnotised her. She had no sooner fallen asleep than she had an attack. As Drs. Bernheim and Liébeault had advanced beyond Charcot by suggesting to the hypnotized patient that he would awaken from sleep and be without his ailment, so Sigmund went beyond the Nancy hypnotists. Instead of suggesting to the girl that the convulsion would disappear, he asked:

"My dear, what are you seeing in your mind?"

"The dog! The dog's coming!"

"Which dog? One that belongs to you?"

"No, no, a strange dog . . . savage . . . wild eyes . . . mouth foaming . . . he wanted to bite off my leg . . . !"

Sigmund examined the child's two legs. There were no scars.

"But he didn't bite you. You got away. The dog is long since gone. You've never seen him again, have you? You never will. You are completely safe. You no longer need to fear the dog. I suggest, child, that you forget the episode. It has never happened again. The picture of the dog will fade from your mind. You'll forget him."

He woke the girl, summoned the father from the waiting room and asked if the child's first attack had occurred just after she had been chased by a dog. The father remembered that they had happened at about the same time.

"Has no one ever attempted to tie these two elements together: the fright over the dog and the beginning of the convulsions?"

The father stood wide-eyed, twisting his stiff bowler hat in his hands.

"How could there be a connection? The dog never bit her. How could she catch epilepsy from him?"

"What she caught was *terror*. That is what has been causing these convulsions. This child no more has epilepsy than you or I do. My job is to suggest away the terror that is so firmly planted in your daughter's second mind. I think I've made a good start."

Sigmund saw the girl every day for a week, exorcising her terror-memory. It vanished. She did not suffer another spasm. When Sigmund handed the father the modest account, he glanced at it, took a sealed envelope from his pocket, put it on the desk and thanked Herrn Doktor Freud with great emotion for saving his daughter's life. Later Sigmund opened the envelope and gasped; the manufacturer had endowed the Freud family for their next summer vacation in the mountains.

Josef Breuer, who had been called to see a twelve-year-old boy, was having less success. The boy had returned from school one day with a sick headache and difficulty in swallowing. The family physician diagnosed sore throat. For a period of five weeks the child went downhill, declining food, vomiting if it were forced on him. He spent all his time in bed. To Dr. Breuer the boy explained that he had become ill because his father had punished him. Josef was convinced that the illness was of a psychical origin. He asked Sigmund to come in for consultation. Sigmund reported after a visit with the boy:

"I'm sure you're right, Josef, the illness is emotional at base. I sense the same terror that possessed my little girl after the dog incident. But with a difference. I have the feeling this boy knows what's making him ill. I believe it's trembling on the edge of his lips."

"His mother is a clever woman. He'll talk to her quicker than he will to me."

The stratagem worked. The following night on their fast hour walk around the Ring, Josef reported the details: on the way home from school the boy had gone into a public urinal. Here a strange man had held out an erect penis toward the boy's face and asked him to take it into his mouth. The boy had fled, shattered by this first crudely perverted thrust of sexuality into his life. Overcome by disgust, he had become unable to take food into his mouth or hold it down.

When his mother talked it over with him and assured him that the incident was not his fault and should be forgotten, he was able to eat a good meal. "He's all right now."

"We are learning, Josef, about anorexia, want of appetite without a loathing of food, and chronic vomiting: they have to do with images and ideas about the mouth, about eating. Every time Frau Emmy tried to eat, her memory went back thirty years to the cold meat her mother had forced on her. You know, Josef, it's becoming increasingly clear: *hysterics suffer mainly from reminiscences.*"

One morning at the end of January he was summoned to the home of a patient who lived in the Eschenbachgasse. He followed the Herrengasse to the Michaelerplatz and, hearing the regimental band playing in the inner court of the Hofburg, entered under the great arch and dome with its baroque male and female figures. It was a cold day, dry underfoot. A crowd was watching the changing of the guard, a colorful sight and one that Sigmund had loved since he was a child and Jakob had brought him to see the guard march in with drums beating. The band had just begun Meyerbeer's Overture to *The Huguenots* when Emperor Franz Josef's aide-de-camp rushed out of the main wing of the Emperor's quarters and summarily commanded the bandmaster to stop. The musicians flatted to an uneven ending. The crowd of onlookers was stunned; never had a regimental band been stopped during the fifty-minute concert.

Uneasy, Sigmund went on to treat his patient. It was not until he had finished his afternoon's work at the Kassowitz Institute and came into the Tuchlauben that he saw the newsboys distributing a special edition of the *Wiener Zeitung*, announcing that "His Imperial and Royal Highness, Crown Prince Archduke Rudolf, had died suddenly of heart failure" at his hunting lodge, Mayerling, in the woods beyond Baden.

Sigmund made his way directly to the Cafe Central, confident that he would find a number of his friends there; in Vienna, state tragedies were mourned in the coffeehouses. Every inch of the cafe was occupied and buzzing. Josef Breuer moved over, flicking a finger at the *Marqueur* to fit in still another chair. Josef Paneth was there with Exner, and Obersteiner had brought Fleischl, whom he had been treating when the *Zeitung* appeared with the news.

The death of the Crown Prince was a shocking misfortune. Emperor Franz Josef was viewed not only with awe but with love amounting to adulation. He was the Great Father of the Empire, faithful, hard-working, kind, dispensing imperial justice and solidity with every breath. He was not so happy in his private life. His beautiful Empress and cousin, Elizabeth of Bavaria, spent most of her time away from Vienna and the royal couch. His oldest son, Crown Prince Rudolf, had been assiduous in preparing himself to take over the Empire, until his father had refused him any part in the government. It was also said that the Emperor had forced his son into a loveless marriage with Stephanie of Belgium, and then thwarted Rudolf's plea to the Pope to have the marriage annulled. All eyes at the table were turned on Josef Breuer who, although he did not treat the royal family itself, was consulted by members of the court.

"The Crown Prince has had no history of heart disease that I ever heard of . . ." Josef reported. He looked about him cautiously, for although stories about the court were among Vienna's chief sources of entertainment, the Emperor and his immediate family had been too sacred to be touched by gossip. ". . . Though we know that he's been drinking to excess, and taking drugs."

"But surely not enough to bring on a fatal heart attack?" Exner asked, almost in a whisper. "He was only thirty . . ."

Sigmund walked home forlornly. He had never met or been in the presence of the Crown Prince, nor had there been any possibility that he ever would have; yet like all Austrians he felt so strong a sense of loyalty to the Hapsburgs that it was as though the tragedy were his own.

By the next day the nation's grief took an unhappy turn; the intelligence swept Vienna that Rudolf had not died of heart failure but in a double suicide with the seventeen-year-old Baroness Marie Vetsera. The newspapers were not allowed to print anything of this; cablegrams and mail going out of the foreign embassies was censored and delayed. But the truth could not be concealed: the Crown Prince and the Baroness had shot themselves, or each other, to death in the royal bed at Mayerling. The Baroness's body was removed and buried without ceremony in the monastery of Heiligenkreuz. Rudolf's body was brought back to Vienna and placed in the Crown Prince's apartment.

Until February fifth, when Rudolf's coffin was placed in the crypt of the Capuchin Church, Vienna lived like a city under siege. The Viennese were literally sick with grief, their minds in turmoil. All activity stopped except the hushed, unbelieving yet unending talk about how such a thing could have happened: for the Baroness was not Rudolf's first love, or even the only one at the time.

Until the new rumors started. Then, and only then, did the city return to normal. Wherever Sigmund went, to a hospital or the Children's Institute or the home of a friend, a new story had preceded him. First, it had been a lovers' double suicide because Rudolf and Marie were not free to marry. Next, Marie had found herself with child and murdered Rudolf because he would not help her. Rudolf had been killed by being hit over the head with a champagne bottle by Johann Orth, an Austrian pretender to the throne of Bulgaria. The Crown Prince had been caught *in flagrante* with the wife of a forester's assistant, who had promptly shot him. However this story was short-lived, for the witty Austrian Prime Minister remarked:

"An Austrian forester's assistant who surprises the Emperor's son with his wife does not shoot, he starts to sing 'God Save the Emperor.'"

A special kind of coffeehouse story took over: the Baroness Marie, learning that she was pregnant, had castrated Rudolf while he slept, and when he awoke he killed them both.

Vienna finally went back to its work and pleasures, content with the last rumor to emerge, that the Crown Prince had been conspiring behind the Emperor's back to lead a revolt of Hungary to take it out of the Empire, and had shot himself when the plot was about to be revealed.

For Sigmund the suicide had an immense emotional impact. That a Hapsburg, the Crown Prince of the Austro-Hungarian Empire, the highest and most exalted position in Europe, should kill himself under such ignominious circumstances was inconceivable. He remembered the last line from *Oedipus Rex*:

"Count no mortal happy till he has passed the final limit of his life secure from pain."

The factor that bothered him most was that Prince Rudolf did not leave a note for the Emperor. For his mother, yes, but not for his father. It was a deliberate omission. "We know that he was a liberal, that he felt the monarchy needed to be reformed from within, its powers curtailed," he explained to Martha. "Perhaps that is why the Emperor refused to allow him to participate in any business of state."

"Are you saying that Rudolf killed himself out of frustration?"

"What I'm suggesting is that Rudolf turned to drink and drugs and excessive numbers of women because the Emperor would not give him any serious mission. Toward the end I think he came to hate his father, and the suicide was an act of revenge."

"Now that's a rumor I have not heard circulating."

"Nor will you, Marty. And please don't quote me. I might have a difficult time documenting my thesis."

3.

Neurologists are accustomed to having their patients suffer setbacks, yet Sigmund found it severely disappointing when Josef Breuer told him that Frau Emmy von Neustadt had suffered a relapse and, on advice from a doctor in her city, had gone into a sanatorium in North Germany. It was galling to lose what he had hoped was a cure, for Frau Emmy's case was the keystone of his proof that the talking cure under hypnosis was the most important therapeutic tool in treating neuroses. He counted on his fingers, then said to Josef:

"She returned home in June feeling well, that's seven months ago, and from what you tell me she was all right until the Christmas and New Year's holidays. How bad is she now? And why did we lose our cure?"

"One of her tics has returned, and several other symptoms including partial paralysis of one leg. Perhaps some of those buried memories had been there too long, had sent down roots too strong to be exorcised by one series of treatments. Would you send her physician an account of the hypnotic theory, and on what symptoms you found it effective?"

"I'll write tonight. Well, if I have had a setback you have enjoyed a triumph. Bertha Pappenheim had dinner with us on Sunday, and left for Frankfurt on Monday. She is going into the women's rights movement in Germany. She intends to devote the rest of her life to this cause. I must say she seemed both strong and happy."

"For which of the women's rights does she intend to work?" Josef asked, his voice hoarse; "the vote, justice in the courts, control of inherited moneys . . . ?"

"The right to enter the universities and the professions, better working conditions in the factories . . ."

Josef made no further comment.

"Thank you for writing the letter, Sig; if Frau Emmy doesn't improve

I will recommend that she return to Vienna and put herself under your care again. We've seen from other cases that suggestive therapy has to be repeated until the product of the secondary state can be worn away."

Glumly, Sigmund replied, "I hope we're not talking about drops of water on a rock. If the unconscious is a rock, and not a sponge, we're going to have to find ways of turning waterfalls onto it."

The following evening at a meeting of the Vienna Society of Medicine he heard Meynert issue a scathing attack on the hypothesis of male hysteria, as originated by Charcot in Paris. "A subject," Sigmund thought, "he just can't leave alone." Though he did not mention Sigmund by name, everyone in the audience knew who was responsible for originally introducing the concept of male hysteria into Vienna. Sigmund waited until the meeting was adjourned, then went up to Meynert and said:

"Herr Hofrat, may I have the pleasure of walking you home?"

Meynert's beard and eyebrows were turning gray, his hair as it rolled down in thick clusters to cover his ears had considerable white in it. The lightened color gave his authoritative head an almost benign look.

"No, my young friend, you may not walk me home. You are the dasher type. You like to walk for the same reason Pegasus liked to fly: the exhilarating sense of motion as you tear around the Ring faster than a *Hofwagen*. However I would be happy to have you walk home with me. I am the stroller type, I like to enjoy the tactile impact every time I put one foot in front of the other."

Sigmund laughed. When Meynert was in good form he was a delightful character.

"Besides, I know you want to argue, and I don't intend to run alongside of you with my mind as well as my legs."

"Not argue, Herr Hofrat, just discuss. With respect, might I suggest that an element of confusion crept into your description of the three stages of Charcot's hypnosis . . . ?"

Meynert patiently let Sigmund explain, right up to the front door of his house. He rang the outside bell for the *Hausmeister*, clapped Sigmund on one shoulder and said:

"Thank you for the illuminating walk."

The matter might have ended there, had Professor Meynert not published his lecture in one of the medical journals. Sigmund felt that he was obliged to keep the record straight, so he also reported on what he called Meynert's "confusion" in the *Wiener medizinische Blätter*. This roiled Meynert's professional feathers. He returned to the attack with a series of three articles in the *Wochenschrift*, in which he roundly condemned Charcot's theory of autosuggestion as the underlying cause of hysterical paralyses, asserting that such paralyses were of physical origin. Meynert's *coup de grâce* was the line:

"I find Herr Dr. Freud's defense of his suggestive therapy all the more remarkable inasmuch as he left Vienna a physician with an exact training in physiology."

The row was out in the open. Josef Breuer gave Sigmund a thorough dressing down. Sigmund insisted that he had to fight back when attacked.

"Josef, Meynert wrote about me that I am 'working in this place as a trained practitioner of hypnosis.' This can create a false impression that I do nothing but hypnotize. I 'work in this place' as a nerve specialist, and I make use of all the therapeutic methods at the disposal of the neurologist. Meynert called hypnosis 'a piece of absurdity.' You and I know better than that; we've helped sick people, you first, and I following you."

Josef Breuer turned hurt eyes on his friend; he was a man of peace.

"Agreed, Meynert goes too far. But let him be the one who has to make the long journey back from misstatement. You should not get involved in a quarrel with older men in your field."

Sigmund was unable to follow the logic of this thought because he was too hurt at the fact that Josef had used the formal *sie* for you, instead of the familiar *du*. But he did not heed the advice. The next day he wrote a review of a short book, *Hypnosis*, by the eminent Swiss neurologist August Forel. He praised Forel's book, did a *précis* of its content, wrote, "The movement which seeks to introduce suggestive treatment into the therapeutic storehouse of medicine has already triumphed in other places and will eventually reach its goal in Germany and Vienna too"; then focused on Meynert, who had given Forel short shrift before a scientific audience, calling him "Forel the Southerner," contrasting him with a "more Northern opponent of hypnosis," a model of cooler thinking. Sigmund informed the readers that Forel had been born on Lake Geneva, which Meynert had apparently confused with the Mediterranean. Tired of being accused of "Disingenuous motives and unscientific modes of thought" in using hypnosis, he let fly at the professor:

"When among these opponents men are to be found like Hofrat Meynert, men who by their writings have acquired great authority . . . some damage to the cause of hypnotism is no doubt unavoidable. It is difficult for most people to suppose that a scientist who has had great experience in certain regions of neuropathology, and has given proof of much acumen, should have no qualification for being quoted as an authority on other problems."

Sigmund had decided that the time had come to learn at first hand the methods used by Drs. Bernheim and Liébeault.

"While you're in Nancy," Martha asked with a rueful smile, "would you like me to look for a lecture hall for you?"

"Meynert's not like that, Marty. He'll let me use his auditorium again for the winter term. What really embarrasses me is that I won't be here when the review appears. I wouldn't want anyone to think I ran away."

"Never fear! I gather that the Viennese scientific world thinks you're the kind of man who runs *to* a fight. I wonder if your son will inherit your temperament."

". . . my son?"

"Yes. Don't I remember hearing you say that you wanted a son?"

He caught her inflection, swept her into his arms.

"We're going to have a lovely family. And, I would say, a populous one! Shall we rent the same villa in Semmering for the summer? I will be in Nancy most of July; my sister Pauli will keep you company."

4.

He dropped off the afternoon train at the station at Nancy, near the northeast border of France, walked across the Place de la Gare to the commercial hotel and was given a rear, third-floor room, comfortably large but with walls painted a disagreeable mustard color. Out the window he had a view of the mountain range from which Nancy mined its iron ore for the industry of France.

He washed, then set out for a stationery store on the upper rise of the Place where he could buy a guidebook to the city. He still had a few hours for exploration before the early July sun would sink. He would not be able to eat his supper that night or fall asleep until he had had the city under his feet.

The guidebook informed him that Nancy had been the historic capital of Lorraine since the twelfth century. Turning the street map sideways, he oriented himself, then struck out for the cathedral in the Rue St. Georges. It had an ornate façade and two domed towers, but he found it disappointingly dull after the churches of Paris and Vienna. He then checked his map for the pride of Nancy, the Place Stanislas, built by the ex-King of Poland, Stanislas Leszczynski, when he had been made the Duke of Lorraine.

He entered the Place and exclaimed aloud with delight. It was not simply a square but a section of the city bordered by public buildings of uniform architecture, an abundance of black wrought-iron ornamentation and gold leaf. There was a Triumphal Arch in the center, lines of statuary on the long cornices; the exquisite baroque Hôtel de Ville, the Palais de Justice, the theater, the tree-planted Place de la Carrière, were held together with the enthralling harmony of a Mozart symphony. The fatigues of the long journey vanished.

The next morning he rose at six. Though the sun was up, the narrow street under his window was still dark. Workmen were hurrying along the sidewalk against a background of unlighted shops on their way to the mines and mills. He took a spongebath at the basin in front of his shav-

ing mirror, donned his Vienna medical garb of dark gray suit, white shirt
and tie tucked under the stiff collar, and sat at the freshly hosed terrace of
an open-air cafe on the Place de la Gare reading a Nancy paper over
his coffee and croissant.

It was good to be walking in a French town again, the buildings on the
main thoroughfares solid, prosperous, bourgeois and somewhat dull. He
found the hospital and Medical School on the outskirts. They were well
built, with a series of courts similar to the Allgemeine Krankenhaus and
the Salpêtrière. The buildings were immaculately scrubbed; the interior
courts had overhangs under which flower beds and blooming plants lent
an air of gay color.

As Professor Hippolyte Bernheim bade Sigmund welcome and thanked
him for the German translation of his book, Sigmund had a chance to
study the man. Bernheim was of stocky build; clean-shaven except for a
modest graying mustache; his hair, cut short, was turning gray. His eyes
were heavy-lidded, cavernous, at once compassionate and withdrawn; but
his outstanding features were his high, prominent cheekbones and jaw.
To Sigmund he looked more German than French. Now forty-nine, he
had been born in Alsace and had secured his medical education at
Strassburg. He moved to nearby Nancy early in his career, practiced
neurology for twenty-five years in a rapidly growing private practice in
his own office, and at the Hôpital Civil where he had been in charge of
clinics, taught as a rising member of the Medical Faculty and, like Meynert
in Vienna, had in his earlier years worked at the asylum attached to the
university.

Sigmund knew that Bernheim had stumbled into the field of hypnosis
six years before by way of a stubborn case of sciatica which he had been
unable to cure. He had quietly taken his patient to the outdoor garden of
a country doctor by the name of Ambroise Auguste Liébeault, part genius,
part mystic and, so said certain elements at the Nancy Medical Faculty,
part quack. Dr. Liébeault had cured the patient by means of suggestions
made during three hypnotic sessions. Still covertly, Dr. Bernheim had
taken several other patients to Liébeault, cases in which he had not been
able to find a physical ailment or alleviate the severity of the illness. In
each instance Liébeault brought considerable relief, and sometimes cures.

In the process he had converted Dr. Hippolyte Bernheim to the practice
of hypnosis.

"Monsieur Freud, I have alerted the department heads that you would
begin your work here today. I wish you to meet each one of them so that
you may observe our procedure. *No patient is allowed into our Hypnosis
Clinic until every department head in the hospital has made a thorough
examination and been convinced there is no physical illness, no sickness
of somatic origin.*" His deep-sunk eyes twinkled mischievously. "I might
also add, Monsieur Freud, that, unlike the Salpêtrière, no patient in my

clinic is seen, instructed or coached by anyone on my staff. Charcot's
three phases of hypnotism was never anything but a cultist's type of
hypnotism."

Sigmund squirmed. He did not want to get into an argument over the
competing claims of the Salpêtrière and Nancy schools. Dr. Bernheim
took him into the hypnosis wards, leading him from bed to bed, explaining the symptoms of each case and, having walked beyond earshot, suggesting to Sigmund his diagnosis.

"Here, as you will see, we have only those cases I mentioned earlier:
hysteria, neurosis, autosuggestion. We pride ourselves that our Nancy
school is thorough and scientific. There are literally thousands of cases
in our files available for your inspection. We have accumulated a large
amount of empirical material: hour-by-hour and day-by-day data on the
patient and the treatment. You will find no theorizing, no supposition.
We record the facts, and use them to help the next similarly suffering
patient. Our task is to cure. That is what a hospital is for, no?"

Sigmund said softly, "You are a lot more than a healer, Monsieur
Bernheim, you are also a scientist. That is what I constantly aspire to be."

The department heads received him cordially. They knew about his
translation of Bernheim's book and took it kindly, since they were aware
that Sigmund had also translated Charcot. They felt that they were
practicing as fine medicine as the Salpêtrière was capable of, but would
live out their lives in the shadow of the famous Parisian hospital. Sigmund
found them to be men of the highest caliber. This was one of the reasons
he enjoyed medical science: it attracted the finest brains and character of
each country.

Returning to his own quarters, Dr. Bernheim said, "I have two cases for
this morning. I think they will interest you. Then Madame Bernheim is
expecting us home for dinner."

Bernheim worked in a bare room off his office, one in which he
lectured to his students. There was a straight-backed chair for the patient.
He had the nurse bring in a married woman of twenty-seven suffering
from dysentery and bloody stools. Dr. Bernheim handed Sigmund her
chart. She was weak and nervous, had catarrhal jaundice and hysterical
paroxysm. She was also having difficulties with her husband.

Dr. Bernheim put her into somnolence. Watching him, Sigmund
realized how limited was his own gift with hypnosis. Bernheim had a
natural talent; it was not only the sleep-producing effect of his drowsy
voice but the expression in his eyes, the cast of his body, the way he held
up his reassuring hands, as though the patient would fall peacefully into
them. Dr. Bernheim explained to the woman in a quiet persuasive tone
that her troubles arose from her depressed state; that once she was in
good spirits again her pains and aches would disappear one by one. He

suggested that when she awoke she would be in good spirits. When he woke her some minutes later and asked, "How do you feel?" she replied in astonishment, "Really, quite well!" "Good," said Bernheim, "tomorrow we will give you a treatment that will stop your dysentery. Then you will feel stronger."

Sigmund asked, "How many treatments do you think it will take?"

Bernheim checked off the patient's symptoms. "I would say a week. Because I prefer that in each 'operation,' as James Braid called his hypnosis—by the way, did you know he invented the word to get away from the ill repute of 'mesmerism'?—to remove only one symptom. This singling out of each symptom gives the suggestion greater unity and strength, makes the cure more permanent."

"Yes, I too have found that," Sigmund exclaimed excitedly. "I tried it with a fifty-year-old man with paralysis of the leg, foot and toes. I let him recover at the same rate he had fallen ill."

The nurse brought in a twenty-year-old male who had been wounded in the hand. He had not been able to stretch his fingers or shut his hand since. Dr. Bernheim put him to sleep, suggested that he could open and shut his hand and extend his fingers without difficulty. For ten minutes he massaged the man's hands and fingers. Before he woke the patient he murmured, "You see, Monsieur Freud, this was not really suggestion, it was countersuggestion. This young man had already suggested to himself that his hand was crippled. All I had to do was get rid of the autosuggestion."

The man awoke, found that he could manipulate his hand and fingers without difficulty.

"I have seen injury-trauma cases like that in the Salpêtrière," Sigmund proffered. "There they merely demonstrate the ability of the patient to do under hypnosis what he cannot do when fully conscious; they do not attempt a cure. In the Allgemeine Krankenhaus there are also such cases, I'm sure, except that we don't recognize them as such. But I must ask: why this particular young man, and not the hundreds of men all over the world who hurt their hands, some quite severely, and go back to work the next day, bandages and all?"

Dr. Bernheim shook his head emphatically.

"That, Monsieur Freud, would call for a supposition. In order to keep my Hypnotism Clinic scientifically respectable I deal in fact alone. My obligation is to cure the illness. From my body of documented fact we will develop hypnosis into a scientific medical practice."

They walked home in the hot noon air. The Bernheim house was located in the center of the city, at 14 Rue Stanislas, close to the Municipal Library in the ancient university. The house was surrounded by a cool, well-tended garden. Madame Sarah Bernheim, in her early forties, was an imposing woman of enormous vitality whom an unkind fate had not blessed with children. She hovered over her husband, mothering him as though he were a brood of six little ones. Bernheim, Sigmund saw immediately, loved every moment of the spoiling. Although the Bernheims were prosperous, with two servants present to admit the doctor and his guest, usher Sigmund to a spare bedroom where he might refresh himself, and then serve a glass of white wine in the parlor before dinner, Mrs. Bernheim allowed no one else to "prepare Monsieur le Docteur's food. Only I know the flavors he likes. . . ."

Fortunately the two-story house was cool, for Mrs. Bernheim made no culinary concession to Nancy's summer sun. Sigmund, who had grown up with the traditional three-course Viennese dinner, found himself helped by a maid in a black uniform to a thick onion soup, an *entrecôte* surrounded by tiny whole carrots, peas, small clumps of cauliflower, potato chips just taken out of their cooking basket, a tomato stuffed with bread crumbs and chopped herbs, all of it enhanced by a bottle of Lorraine wine; then a green salad with oil and vinegar and an orange soufflé. It was the best dinner he had eaten in France. He did not hesitate to tell Madame Bernheim this. She glowed with pleasure.

"My husband works so hard," she said, "that I find it my first duty to keep his strength up."

Bernheim laughed as he patted his full belly.

"What you are doing, my dear, is keeping my waistline up." Turning to Sigmund, he asked, "Do you remember, Monsieur Freud, the young Swedish doctor who worked with you at the Salpêtrière and was discharged from the hospital for allegedly trying to seduce a young 'patient' of the hospital?"

"I do. He spoke highly of you."

"Then you must let me clear his name. He met the parents of the girl in the garden of the Salpêtrière. They had come up from the country to visit their daughter, who they thought was working in the kitchen of the hospital. When the doctor investigated he found that Charcot's Assistants had found her a good subject for hypnosis, given her clothes, cosmetics, and converted her into a 'hypnosis actress.' She enjoyed the attention, but the young man was convinced her sanity was at stake. He bought her a railroad ticket to return to her parents' farm, then hypnotized her to come to his home so that he could put her on the train."

Sigmund pondered this a moment.

"I remember thinking at the time that the affair made no sense."

"There are several 'affairs' at the Salpêtrière that make little sense. In the meanwhile Monsieur Liébeault will be starting his afternoon session in a few moments. I will introduce you, and then go on to my private office. Like you, I still earn the better part of my living as a neurologist."

5.

On the walk to Liébeault's house, which was located in a modest part
of town, Dr. Bernheim said, "Let me tell you about Ambroise Auguste
Liébeault. His parents, solid farmers, put him into Petit Séminaire so that
he would become a priest. By the time he was fifteen he had convinced
himself as well as his instructors that he had no talent for theology.
When he reached twenty-one he entered the Medical School at Strassburg—he was fourteen years ahead of me—and graduated in 1850 with
a thesis on the dislocation of the femorotibial. One of his professors
interested him in hypnosis by proving that nosebleeds could be artificially
induced by giving the command to do so while the patient was asleep.
After graduation Liébeault settled in a small farming village a few miles
from here, where he was kept busy delivering babies and setting broken
bones. The only time he wanted to try hypnosis, on a young girl suffering
from convulsions, her father would not permit it on the grounds that it
would be declared witchcraft and sacrilegious. Yet Liébeault could not put
down his fascination. After a few years of country practice he attended a
series of lectures in Nancy on Braid's *Neurypnology*, bought a house in
town and opened a general practice. His patients were mostly farmers
and families of working people. He offered his patients free medical
treatment if they would allow him to use hypnosis; otherwise they would
have to pay the regular fees, as well as the expense of medicine, hospital,
the like. No peasant in France could turn down an offer like that! And
few laborers, for that matter. For the past twenty-five years he has supported himself and his family, modestly, on the normal run of physical
illnesses. But his heart is in hypnosis. His first book, *Sleep and Its Analogous States*, sold one copy! Think of it. His second book did little better.
But here we are."

Ambroise Auguste Liébeault had bought himself a corner house, two
and a half stories high, without grace but looking as though it had been
built for the centuries. On their left was a small garden with a lawn and
pebble path leading to a back building spanned by an umbrella-like
shade tree. There were a dozen patients sitting on rough benches outside
the door, country people dressed in their Sunday best, workmen with a
wife or child. The line moved along the bench toward the doctor's door
as each patient came out.

Dr. Liébeault stepped into the doorway of his garden office for a breath
of air. Sigmund got a good look at the grizzled sixty-five-year-old, thin
patches of white hair on his head, a short white beard and mustache,
his brow creased by horizontal wrinkles, his complexion the ruddy red of
the country man. His face embodied a series of contradictions: a child's

gaiety mixed with the authority of the priest; the expression simple yet serious, gentle but commanding. His concepts of "verbal suggestion" and "provoked sleep" were known and respected in many parts of Europe, yet he was excluded from important segments of the life of Nancy. Patients with position or money did not dare go to Dr. Liébeault; it was not considered proper. Nor had he been invited to teach at the Medical Faculty or the University, no matter how highly Dr. Bernheim respected his work and praised him.

Le bon père Liébeault, as he was known to his patients, looked up, saw Dr. Bernheim and Sigmund, welcomed them with a paternal smile. Liébeault bade Sigmund enter the garden house. There was a small foyer in which patients waited during the cold or rainy winter days; beyond that a large room scantily furnished: shelves containing very old books, a wooden armchair for the doctor, a few rickety chairs for the patients. Sigmund looked for a filing cabinet or box where Liébeault might keep his reports; but there was none. Liébeault kept no records, made no extensive physical examination. That was why the Medical Faculty called him "unscientific."

Sigmund watched the doctor work on half a dozen patients in succession. His methods were even more simple and open than Bernheim's. His eyes were bright, concerned, his voice deep, swift, his manner assured. He held the thumbs of the patients in big, awkward, loving hands, told them to think of nothing but sleep and healing, suggested that their eyelids were becoming heavy, their bodies were slumping into heaviness, that they would soon be in a state of somnambulism. When their eyelids began to blink Liébeault said in his sonorous tone, "You will sleep," and they did.

The first patient was an eleven-year-old boy who was still wetting his bed at night. Liébeault suggested that from now on, if the boy had to urinate during the night, the pressure would wake him and he would get out of bed and relieve himself. Sigmund learned the following week that only this one séance had been necessary to dispose of the problem. The next was a fourteen-year-old girl with weakness in her legs, pain in the thighs and difficulty in walking. Liébeault described these as growing pains and suggested that another session or two would banish them. Then came a sixty-year-old carpenter with left hemiplegia, paralysis on one side. He had been coming for three weeks. Liébeault said in an aside to Sigmund:

"I have him cured and walking, though with some heaviness in one leg. He's working, but refuses to climb the ladders."

The patriarch was now facing a twenty-year-old divorced woman who worked as a cigar maker. She had suffered, Liébeault explained, "fits of passion, alcoholism, incomplete paralysis of the legs."

"I have cured up everything except her addiction to wine," he mused to

Sigmund. "While she is asleep I can get her to express distaste for wine. But awake, she still drinks it. It is most strange. But we have her back at work."

There were still patients on the garden bench but Sigmund thanked Dr. Liébeault and asked to be excused. Once again he walked the streets of Nancy, ending in the serene beauty of the Place Stanislas where he found a seat on a bench in the Place de la Carrière, the former tournament grounds of the Dukes of Lorraine. Here, under the trees that absorbed the angular rays of the late afternoon sun, he tried to work out his impressions. There was no question in his mind but that he had witnessed the performance of the two greatest hypnotists practicing the beleaguered art. Compared to Liébeault and Bernheim, he was a journeyman.

However this was not what was bothering him. What set his thoughts to swirling was the sense that something urgent was missing: speculation, a theory of causation. *Why* had the twenty-seven-year-old married woman developed dysentery? Was it because she was fighting with her husband and, in the phrase of the peasants, was "sicking out" of her marital duties? *Why* was an eleven-year-old boy still wetting his bed? Was it merely laziness? *Why* had the sixty-year-old carpenter developed a hysterical paralysis? Was it his fear of the ladders? *Why* had he become afraid of ladders after climbing them for forty years?

"The most useful word in any language: *why*," he exclaimed aloud. "If we keep building whys upon whys the way the Italian masons lay stone upon stone, eventually we will have built an edifice that will shelter us from storms."

The next morning he sat in Dr. Bernheim's office in the hospital overlooking an inner court. It was so quiet on this mid-July morning that they could hear the flies buzzing against the window screens. A nurse brought in a child who had pains like muscular rheumatism in his arm, which he could not lift. Dr. Bernheim seated the boy before him, touched the boy's eyelids. "Shut your eyes, my child, and go to sleep. You will remain asleep until I wake you. You are sleeping very well, as safely and comfortably as though you were home in your own bed." He raised the boy's arm in the air, touched the sore spot and said, "The pain has gone away. You have no more pain. When you wake up the pain will not come back. You feel that your arm is warm, the warmth increases, it takes the place of the pain."

When he awoke, the boy could raise his arm without difficulty. "Do you have any pain, my child?" "None, Monsieur le Docteur, but my arm feels warm where the pain used to be."

"The heat will subside. You may return home now."

When the boy left Sigmund said quietly, "Where did that pain in his arm come from?"

Dr. Bernheim permitted himself one of his occasional smiles.

"It was a hallucination. In truth we are all potentially hallucinating people during the greater part of our lives."

"Agreed. But where do the hallucinations come from, and *why* that particular hallucination?"

Dr. Bernheim clasped his fingers tightly across his chest, then threw open his hands and arms as though to infinity.

"How could we possibly know? Better to cure the child than plunge him and ourselves into the Stygian depths of where hallucinations come from. Even the psychologists stay away from that *bête noir.*"

Sigmund spent his mornings at the hospital studying Bernheim's techniques and records, his afternoons with Liébeault. He noted that with each new case Bernheim began by telling the sick person the benefit to be derived from suggestive therapy; that if hypnotism could not cure his symptoms it could certainly relieve them. He inspired confidence in the nervous ones by assuring them that there was nothing strange or harmful about the process, that it could be induced in everyone. If the patient was still afraid, he probed for the source of the fear, alleviated it. He said, "Look at me and think of nothing but sleep. Your eyelids begin to feel heavy, your eyes tired. They are beginning to blink, they are getting moist, you cannot see distinctly . . . your eyes are closed." If his voice alone could not accomplish the task, Bernheim held up two fingers of his hand or passed both hands several times close to the patient's eyes, then gently closed the lids, at the same time lowering his voice. With stubborn cases he would put his hands on the patient's forehead, three fingertips on each temple; if this did not work he would clench his left fist and lay the four knuckles lightly but authoritatively in the center of the patient's brow. He did not like to rely on external objects, but if after a second or third try he could not induce even a light sleep, he took a series of objects from his desk: a round glass ball, a thin shiny slab of metal on which the light danced; and now even the most fearful fell into a trance.

Dr. Liébeault believed with Mesmer that a magnetic energy passed from physician to patient, and always used the "laying on of hands." With children, Sigmund observed, he lightly stroked their hair back from their forehead, repeating, "All is well. You will sleep peacefully. You will feel better when you waken." With young adults he took the face between his big, warm hands; with older people he stroked an arm gently or pattingly soothed a shoulder, murmuring, "Restful sleep is on the way. I will close your tired eyelids now, and sleep will come. . . ."

He remained three weeks, watching Liébeault and Bernheim treat scores of cases, different in nature, requiring every device in the arsenal of the two talented men: paresis of the hand, an accountant's writer's cramp, paralysis of the legs after a pneumonia, epigastric pains, sciatica along the left thigh and calf, facial tics, bizarre seizures, impaired vision, vomiting and insomnia, loss of appetite and melancholia.

He made copious notes on the cases he had seen, documenting the progress of the patients over the weeks, the prognosis for a permanent or eventual cure, adding his own comments on how and why the results had been achieved. On quiet days he had dinner with the young interns of the hospital, talking shop: Vienna versus Paris versus Nancy for excellence of training and practice. At night he wrote to Martha, receiving letters from Semmering every day or two. But always at the back of his mind was the disturbing question:

"What is going on in the second mind, the unconscious mind that is creating these ills, and how are we ever going to understand human conduct if we don't get into that forbidden continent and map its contents?"

When he continued to press Bernheim for clues, the doctor replied, patiently, "Let us say that the human mind is a vast bowling green with thousands of balls scattered on the grass. I throw a ball down the green, in the form of a suggestion or command. It is aimed at a ball blocking access to the wicket. I careen it aside. The original blocking ball is no longer in contention. My suggestion is now in a commanding position. I have replaced my patient's hallucinatory idea with a command that the pain, contracture, vomiting, depression will vanish. For you see, Monsieur Freud, ideas are physical objects, as tangible as bowling balls. We physicians need the proper skill to knock these hallucinatory balls out of action. We fail sometimes, but we have also had remarkable results."

Sigmund rose, took a turn to the door and back, easing a finger between his tight, starched collar and chafed neck. He made an effort to keep down the excitement in his voice.

"There is work going on that you and Dr. Liébeault should know about. A new therapeutic tool, first used by Dr. Josef Breuer of Vienna, and confirmed by me last year. Could I take the two of you to supper tomorrow night?"

The Restaurant Stanislas, on one of the main business streets of Nancy, was decorated with checkered tablecloths, each lamplighted table separated from the other by high wood-paneled partitions. The two doctors sitting opposite him ate heartily; Sigmund hardly touched his food in his desire to present the "talking cure" under hypnosis; explain the dialogue between doctor and patient. Neither Dr. Bernheim nor Dr. Liébeault showed any interest. At a certain point, when Sigmund was analyzing Breuer's astute handling of Fräulein Bertha's formerly submerged but now outpouring memories, he felt that both men had made a decision, had closed their minds.

Bernheim said gently, "My dear Monsieur Freud, that would not serve any purpose for us. As I have made clear, we address ourselves to a hysterical illness and rout it with countersuggestion. We need to know only the manifestation. We are effective! That is the sole task and duty of the physician. My friend Dr. Liébeault refused when very young to become a priest; I am sure that even now he has no taste for confession."

Sigmund was crestfallen. The doctors thanked him for the fine supper and went their separate ways. Walking up the steep street past the dark imposing government buildings, Sigmund thought:

"That was precisely Charcot's reaction. He said, 'No, there is nothing of interest there.' But there is! I am convinced of it. Why do pioneers like Charcot, Liébeault and Bernheim refuse to peer through the open door of another man's vision? Why do they stop when they come to the end of their own revolution?"

6.

One of his problems when he returned from Nancy was that no one had wanted him to go, not even Breuer.

"But, Josef, why didn't you tell me this before I went, instead of after?"

"Would it have stopped you?"

"No."

"Precisely."

As far as Meynert and the Medical Faculty were concerned, his experience in Nancy had simply sunk him deeper into iniquity. His colleagues at the Kassowitz Institute did not openly disapprove, though they thought he had trapped himself in a blind unscientific alley. As a result he had no one with whom to discuss this phase of his work. He wrote to his friend Wilhelm Fliess in Berlin that he was beginning to feel isolated, that there was no one in Vienna who could teach him anything.

He began writing steadily to Fliess as a friend and confidant to whom he could reveal his innermost medical speculations. Fliess was receptive, writing encouraging and enthusiastic letters in return. Sigmund confided to Fliess that he would like to settle down exclusively to the treatment of the neuroses; but no single case of neurosis was at present in his consultation room. He was working exclusively as a neurologist treating somatic ills, as well as a family doctor for his neighborhood, stopping up leaky noses and loose bowels. His newly learned hypnotic skills had to be stored away. He had had a fine vacation with Martha in Semmering after the first separation of their married life; she was carrying well; his daughter was growing into an enchanting child. He was completely happy in his family life; yet in being denied what Professor Nothnagel had described as "the rich source material of medicine" he felt that his creative work had come to a standstill.

This was the first time since his zoology professor Carl Claus had sent him to Trieste to work on the testes of the eel that he felt he had no exploratory and potentially valuable experiment going forward. He recalled his first passionate declaration to Martha in the woods above Mödling:

"Pure science is the most rewarding job the world has to offer, full of gratification because every day we learn something new about living organisms."

Yet here he was only seven years later blocked in an effort to test, experiment, discover. He had become a simple practitioner. As he sat at his desk in his consultation room at the *Sühnhaus*, a wall of medical books behind him, the photographs of the famous men he admired hanging above the black examining couch, he thought with a cutting edge of bitterness, "Like any country doctor." The difficulty with trying to study the unconscious mind was that unless one was attached to a major hospital, the Allgemeine Krankenhaus, a Salpêtrière, or Nancy Medical Faculty, the explorer was left for long periods without unknown seas to navigate, Tibetan ranges to conquer, Sahara deserts to survive.

He vowed that he would not allow Martha to smell the dank odor of bitterness oozing through his pores. The fault was his, not hers. He had failed to find a creative niche for himself. Was Josef Breuer also growing away from him because his high hopes for his young protégé had been dashed? Josef was finding frequent excuses not to take their evening walk around the Ringstrasse.

"Martha, do you think I'm being oversensitive? Perhaps it's just that Josef is preoccupied?"

"There has been no change in Mathilde, she speaks lovingly of you when we are together. You talk of the life cycle of all organisms, how it ebbs and flows. Friendship is a living organism too. Now you are married, have a child and a practice. Josef's love for you wasn't deeper or better before; it was different."

He thanked her for her good sense and, reassured, fell into a troubled, dream-laden sleep, every detail of which he remembered vividly in the morning.

He did not succumb to despair; instead he took the opposite tack, beginning the research and writing of two long monographs, the first On Aphasia, which he felt needed doing because of the diverse and conflicting theories surrounding it; the second, A Clinical Study of the Unilateral Palsies of Children with his young friend Dr. Oskar Rie, a children's physician.

A series of events sharply demonstrated how far he had strayed from his original purpose of becoming a professor of the Medical Faculty. Two years before, Professor Leidesdorf, head of the First Psychiatric Clinic located in the Lower Austrian Insane Asylum, had suffered a heart attack during a lecture and had asked his young Assistant, Julius Wagner-Jauregg, to complete the course for him. The Ministry of Education had named Wagner-Jauregg for one term at a time. The following year Leidesdorf retired, and now in the summer of 1889 the University Medical Faculty tapped Richard von Krafft-Ebing, Professor *Extraordinarius* at the University of Graz, to take Leidesdorf's place. After Meynert, Krafft-Ebing was the most accomplished and renowned psychiatrist in the German-speaking world. The contest began to see who would succed Krafft-Ebing at Graz; to everyone's astonishment, thirty-two-year-old Wagner-Jauregg was selected.

Professor Krafft-Ebing arrived in Vienna after the summer holidays to prepare for his opening lecture. Sigmund paid a courtesy visit, bringing with him as a calling card his translations of Charcot and Bernheim. Krafft-Ebing had just moved into a freshly painted and varnished flat, the smell of which reminded Sigmund of his visit to Professor Nothnagel's seven years before, when he had sought the position of Assistant to Nothnagel in Internal Medicine.

The professor rose from behind his desk, extended his hand in a cordial welcome. Sigmund's immediate reaction was, "What an attractive man!" Krafft-Ebing had a head of heroic proportion: a massive brow from which he combed his thinning gray hair back in a gentle wave; a nose sufficiently Roman to provide a family of smaller noses; a gray and black thin beard and mustache; enormous eyes set in a commanding structure of overhanging brows, dramatic circles underneath, much too dark for a man not quite fifty; the projection of the face radiating a powerful intelligence yet at the same time a sympathetic view toward the world's grief and ugliness, of which he had witnessed more than his share.

Richard Freiherr von Krafft-Ebing had been born in Mannheim, of a high civil servant father and a cultured, kindly mother from a family of distinguished lawyers and intellectuals. When he was ready for the university his family moved to Heidelberg, where he came under the wing of his maternal grandfather, known as the German "attorney for the damned," protecting the legal rights of those culprits charged with heinous crimes, in particular sexual perversions. Krafft-Ebing studied medicine at the University of Heidelberg; his specialty was determined when he was sent to Zurich to recuperate from typhus and heard Griesinger give a series of lectures in psychiatry.

Fascinated, Krafft-Ebing wrote his doctoral thesis on "Mental Delirium," took a position as resident physician in an insane asylum, and in 1873 was called to the Medical Faculty at the University of Graz in Austria, also becoming director of the newly opened Feldhof Asylum. He immediately took up his grandfather's cause, defending in court both men and women accused of "sexual outrages" and "crimes against nature," by presenting to the court the complete medical history of the accused in an attempt to gain understanding and mercy for the deviates who aroused so much loathing in puritanical society that their civil rights were ignored. From this work came his *Textbook of Court Psychopathology*; and from his years of work in the asylum, his three-volume *Textbook on Psychiatry* which had been widely translated and, with Kraepelin's similarly titled textbook, was respected as a definitive work on clinical psychiatry; behavior patterns and motivations for human conduct, as differentiated from Meynert's brain anatomy psychiatry. Krafft-Ebing was a man of infinite patience with the inmates of asylums; his unfailing kindness had helped many patients of lesser illness to recover. He was now under a cloud for the publication of his *Psychopathia Sexualis*, which gave detailed medical reports of the hundreds of cases of sexual inversion and perversion which he had defended in court. Materials of this nature had never been published before; they were the subterranean scandals of society, not to be spoken about. Though Krafft-Ebing wrote much of his material in Latin so that it could be understood by doctors but not a prurient public, he had been severely condemned in England for "unleashing these filthy and disgusting materials on an innocent and unsuspecting world." Krafft-Ebing was a pioneer. Sigmund Freud had studied his books with care, even though they dealt with the heredity of the patient only, his physical attributes and environment.

"I take it most kindly that you bring me these two books, Herr Doktor," said Krafft-Ebing. "I hear that you are the chief advocate of hypnotic suggestion here in Vienna. And that you got your knuckles rapped by my colleague Hofrat Meynert. Never mind, within a few years we shall make hypnotic suggestion respectable."

Sigmund felt as though a sack of potatoes had been lifted from his shoulders. The words that had been dammed up since his return to Vienna poured out as he gave Krafft-Ebing a vivid reconstruction of what he had observed in Nancy. When he could bring himself to stop, Krafft-Ebing exclaimed:

"A truly remarkable pair. I thank you for sharing your experience with me. Young Wagner-Jauregg was here just before you. A strong and determined man; he will do well in Graz."

Sigmund made his way to the Lower Austrian Insane Asylum, across from the Allgemeine Krankenhaus, where sandy-haired, handsome Wagner-Jauregg had lived for the past six years as Professor Leidesdorf's Assistant, starting four months before Sigmund became *Sekundararzt* to Professor Meynert.

On the walk to the asylum he thought back to his own student and graduate days with Wagner-Jauregg, who had been born only a few months after Sigmund, took his M.D. a few months before, and received the *Dozentur* in neuropathology when Sigmund received his. Wagner-Jauregg's career duplicated his own to a remarkable degree; he too had been trained in physiology by Professor Brücke; he too had researched independently as an undergraduate and published his papers; he too had sought an assistantship from Professor Nothnagel and been refused; he too had gone into psychiatry. . . .

His reminiscences brought him to the crest of the knoll and to the front of the asylum, which had been built in monumental style, with a foyer and broad staircase fit for a ducal palace. But as he climbed the steep steps Sigmund thought, "The analogy of our lives ends right here, in this building. When Wagner-Jauregg moved in he received not only twice as much salary as I did when I moved into the A.K. to work with Meynert, but he was also fed from the asylum kitchen. He never wanted to become a psychiatrist; he told me himself he was no good at it. Yet he trained himself and stuck it out. Now he's offered the psychiatry chair at Graz, the best university in Austria after Vienna; that puts him just one rung below the top of psychiatry's ladder."

And here was he, Sigmund Freud, the same age, eking out a living as a private practitioner, lost to the university world, the only world he had ever wanted. How did it happen?

He stopped before Wagner-Jauregg's door, hand on the knob, head down. "I know how it happened. I fell in love with Martha. Wagner-Jauregg is determined to rise to the top of his profession before thinking about marriage." His jaw thrust itself forward. "Let him have his appointment at Graz; I will make my own way."

He knocked, entered the office to congratulate Wagner-Jauregg and wish him *Alles Gute.*

BOOK EIGHT

DARK CAVERN OF THE MIND

Dark Cavern of the Mind

T HEIR son was born in early December. They named him Jean Martin, after Charcot. Martha was triumphant at having produced a boy. While she slept, Sigmund made a tour of family and friends, his face beaming with joy, to spread the good word. When she awakened he propped her up in bed. He had never seen her look more beautiful, her eyes sparkled with happiness and accomplishment. He held her hands clasped firmly in his.

"Marty, darling girl, the advent of a son is one of the most precious moments in a man's life. Now I have someone to carry on the family name. The Jews are offended if they are described as Orientals, but in this one respect, the deep-seated need of a son, the description may be accurate."

"Uh-huh," agreed Martha, "and equally accurate of the Occidentals. Next time you see a christening party, follow it into the Votivkirche and watch the father with his first-born son. Mightn't Charles Darwin say that this is one reason the human species is still being perpetuated? Perhaps the mastodons and dinosaurs didn't care that much about having sons to carry on the family name?"

Sigmund chuckled.

Within twenty-four hours of the birth of his son, there walked into his consultation room the first patient with a neurosis since he had returned from Nancy; by the end of a week he had four fascinating cases on hand.

Winter fell upon them. The winds came straight down from Siberia. Martha's pillows, made to fit snugly between the double windows, absorbed some of the chill, but there was no way to shut off the icy blasts except by pulling the velours draperies over the curtains, turning the room into a dark cavern, and stoking the ceramic stove to throw off its maximum heat. Nothing could lessen the force of the storm-driven rain and hail which knocked tiles off roofs and sent them clattering to the sidewalk below. The winds blew over a number of carriages so that one had the choice of being stoned from above by tiles or tipped onto the stones of the street.

The next afternoon, after a cloudburst, the sun would suddenly appear, and with it a very large and beautiful rainbow, it's variegated colors doming a narrow ribbon over the city.

"That's Vienna," Sigmund observed. "First it freezes you, then it drowns you, then it fishes you out of the Danube, wraps you in a rainbow and murmurs, 'Forgive me, my child, forgive me for having driven you half out of your mind with my innocent excesses! I still love you. Let us have music in the park, let us waltz, let us wander in the Naschmarkt eating blood sausages from Cracow and *Königskuchen.*'"

Fräulein Mathilde Hebbel, nineteen years old, had come to Sigmund the day before Christmas. She was severely depressed and irritable. No matter how many times Sigmund gave her suggestions which she was to carry out when she awoke, he was rewarded with gales of tears. Then, during one session, the young woman became talkative. The cause of her melancholia was the breaking off of her engagement to her fiancé, which had happened eleven months before. After the engagement both she and her mother had found certain qualities in the fiancé they had not liked; yet both had been unwilling to terminate it because the young man was wealthy and well placed. Finally the mother had made the decision. The girl spent sleepless nights wondering whether she had done the right thing. This was the point at which she had become depressed.

Sigmund was confident that he could help her through suggestion to stand firm behind the belief that the marriage would have been wrong. However he could not get Mathilde Hebbel to say one more word about her problem. Then she stopped coming. A week later one of his confreres at Kassowitz Institute said:

"Congratulations, Sig, you achieved a splendid cure with Fräulein Hebbel. I was with the family last night; the girl seems fine and is getting along again with her mother."

Sigmund swallowed a couple of times, decided against confessing that he did not know how he had helped Mathilde, but dropped into the Hebbels' apartment. He said to the girl:

"I am glad to see you well and happy. Do you know how it came about?"

Mathilde exclaimed gaily, "Yes, I do. On the morning of the first anniversary of the breaking of our engagement, I woke up and suddenly said to myself, 'Very well, a whole year is passed. Enough of this nonsense!'"

It had started to rain. Sigmund found a *Fiaker* in front of the Church of the Capuchins, rode home sunk deep in the leather corner of the carriage and in thought:

"Mathilde didn't wake up on the first anniversary of the breaking of the engagement and 'suddenly' think that the 'nonsense' had gone on long enough. Somewhere in her unconscious she had decided to preserve what was left of her love until the first anniversary of the broken engagement

. . . a kind of mourning period. I didn't help her because she had no need of me. Yet Mathilde has given me my first clue that the unconscious mind has as good a timetable as an ancient calendar stone."

If he received too much credit for curing the young lady grieving over her fiancé, with the next patient he got too little. Just before New Year's Day of 1890 he took on the case of a young man who was unable to walk. The evidence pointed to hysteria. Sigmund began his hypnosis and treatment to remove a number of the surface manifestations: inability to eat, incontinence of urine, fear of walking downhill. One by one he succeeded in removing these symptoms only to find that when he had eradicated the hysteria he had before him an organic case of multiple sclerosis. The psychical symptoms had been so strong and numerous they had concealed the somatic sclerosis.

He had many fewer male hysterics than female but only because, he surmised, the men were preoccupied with earning a living and did not come to him until they fell into emotional trouble which jeopardized their livelihood. One of his simpler cases was that of an intelligent man who had stood by in the hospital while his brother had an ankylosed hip joint extended. There was such a resounding crack when the hip joint gave way that the brother had been seized by a violent pain in his own hip joint, still present after a year had passed. There was absolutely nothing wrong with the man's hip. Sigmund learned that, in his second mind, the healthy brother had become convinced that the disease was congenital.

Of a more crippling nature was the employee who fell into a frenzy of rage after being maltreated by his employer. Under hypnosis, Sigmund led the patient into a repetition of the attack, during which the man relived the triggering episode in which his employer had abused him and hit him with a stick. Sigmund tried to drain off the emotion; but a few days later the patient went down with an equally violent seizure. This time, under hypnosis, Sigmund learned that the employee had taken his superior into court and sued him for maltreatment. He had lost his case. It was the embittering frustration of this defeat that was causing him to fly into uncontrollable rages and then to collapse. Sigmund could not cure the man; he was too old, the sense of injustice too deep-seated; he had to be content with lessening the intensity of the frenzies.

The little group of doctor friends had now become a Saturday night *Tarock* club: Sigmund, Josef Paneth, Oskar Rie, Leopold Königstein, Obersteiner, sometimes Josef Breuer, Fleischl. They would play as late as one o'clock in the morning, particularly when at the Paneths' because Josef could not bear to part with his friends. Fleischl was not well enough to go out often but asked the group to come to him when it was his turn. In Sigmund's apartment the men played at the dining table, the room with its heavy wooden and leather furniture ceilinged by a low cloud of cigar smoke. At midnight Martha and the other wives brought in hot linked frankfurters, served with mustard or horseradish, and Viennese rolls. There was an hour of comradery, the exchange of the news and the humor of the week, reports of books, plays, music. One May night, when they left the Paneth home, Martha asked:

"Sig, is it wise for Josef to be up so late?"

"Yes, as long as he is as gay as you saw him tonight. The doctor says he has a couple of bad spots but they don't seem to be growing any worse."

The winter turned piercingly cold. Sigmund urged his friend to go to a warm country for two or three months. Josef replied in his gentle voice:

"Sig, I can't bear to leave Exner and the physiology lab. How can I just sit somewhere? Isn't that a form of dying too?"

"No, it's a form of hibernation. Once we get your lungs dried out you can work for thirteen months a year."

Then Josef got caught in a sleet storm, developed a chill, and by the following afternoon, with five doctor friends standing helpless around his bed, died of double pneumonia. Perhaps because he had been delicate, perhaps because of his sweetness and generosity, Josef had been the pet of the little group. For Sigmund it was a poignant loss; Josef Paneth had been a companion through all the years of Medical School. Without Josef's and Sophie's "Freud Foundation" of fifteen hundred gulden, he could not have afforded to accept the university travel grant.

It was a charcoal-gray day compounded of mist and drizzle when they buried Josef in the Central Cemetery, his friends joining in the graveside prayers. Professor Brücke, himself ailing, came to the cemetery, escorted by Exner and a haggard Fleischl. Then they returned to the Paneth home to sit *shivah* with the widow, speaking affectionately of Josef while the maid passed *Kaffeekuchen*. As they rode home in the early cold darkness Sigmund and Martha huddled together forlornly.

He was brought a young happily married woman who during childhood had been found frequently in the morning in a stuporous condition, her limbs rigid, mouth open, tongue protruding. These attacks had now begun to return. When the young woman did not respond to hypnosis, Sigmund suggested she tell him stories surrounding her childhood. She talked about her room, her grandmother who had lived with them, and one of the governesses of whom she had been fond. Sigmund could make nothing of the material. An older physician who had attended the family at the time came to his aid. The physician had discerned a far too close attachment between the governess and the young girl, and had asked the grandmother to keep an eye on them. She reported back that the governess was in the habit of visiting the child in bed after the rest of the family had gone to sleep, spending the night there. She had, from all evidence, corrupted the girl. The governess was promptly fired. When Sigmund thanked the older man for this clue, the doctor asked, puzzled:

"How will you proceed now?"

"I think there is no way but to tell her the truth. This episode, of which she apparently understood nothing as a child, is buried deep in her unconscious; she will never be able to bring it forth by a spontaneous effort. The attacks could continue for years. If I explain why this memory has been suppressed, and that memories of this nature continue to send out poisons later in life, I think she will understand that she has been victimized. If such an attack should begin again she would at least know its point of origin and have an opportunity to grapple with it."

The young woman received the information without emotional disturbance. The family doctor reported several months later that she appeared in good health. The case substantiated Sigmund's growing certainty that events which take place in childhood, though they are beyond the comprehension of the young at the time, cut ridges and gullies into the unconscious mind. The scar could suppurate at any time in the years ahead to strike down an otherwise healthy person. He believed this invaluable for a physician to learn. He also asked himself why the attacks had struck again at this particular time.

A most miraculous success was with a man in his mid-thirties for whom he could do nothing in his consultation room, and consequently sent to a sanatorium. To Sigmund's astonishment, after one week in the sanatorium the man began to recover, the facial tics and stuttering vanished, he ate well and slept well, he was no longer tendentious and was able to concentrate on the subject at hand, the lack of which had cost him his responsible position in a Viennese bank. Sigmund visited him once a week, and after three months suggested that he go home. The patient categorically refused to leave the sanatorium, became almost violent over the advice. Since there was no lack of money in the family, the man remained. At the end of six months he turned up in Sigmund's office. When he arrived Sigmund said:

"You are the greatest walking testimonial any doctor in this town ever had. What did you do for yourself to effect such a complete cure?"

The man replied with a wink, "The cure lay right next door: a very attractive woman patient. By the end of the first week we were having intercourse every night. It's been the most glorious period of my life. She left only two days ago. I have often thought that the woman was a patient of yours who was also in trouble, and that you had placed us side by side purposely."

Each case of neurosis was different and stimulating. Along with the successes were numerous failures, especially among young men, those on the delicate side. They suffered from every nervous and emotional affliction he had seen in his female patients, and a good many others he had never seen or read about; yet he could not come to grips with the basic cause of the disturbance, not even with the ones he suspected of homosexuality. What emerged from their unconscious was to him a weird and meaningless hodgepodge. When in resignation he tried the Lié-beault-Bernheim method of attacking the symptom without attempting to understand the ideational cause, most of the patients either refused to accept his therapeutic suggestions or found themselves unable to carry them out. He was impatient with these failures; the sufferings originated in a locked area of the unconscious to which he had failed to find a key.

The unconscious mind had become the passion and lodestar of his life. Interspersed with his meticulous records on each case was his own thinking, conjecturing, exploring. He felt the way he imagined Anton van Leeuwenhoek had when he peered into his improved microscope and became the first human being to see swarming protozoa and bacteria. He thought:

"The unconscious is going to become my field of refraction. It will lead to discerning and describing scientifically the causes and cures of human conduct. I'm going to be a midwife; no, I am so swollen with excitement and palpitant life that I shall undoubtedly become a mother." He threw his arms up toward the ceiling in mock horror. "I only hope the baby doesn't have two heads!"

2.

Word began to spread that Dr. Sigmund Freud was a good man to consult about what was euphemistically described as "women's troubles." Wives in their late twenties and early thirties began appearing in his consultation room, hesitatingly trying to describe a series of fluctuating illnesses which their family doctors had been unable to diagnose. He gave each a thorough physical examination, sending them to specialists when he did not have sufficient training to trust his own judgment. In most cases there was nothing organically wrong; after a sufficient time of quiet questioning it became clear that their troubles arose out of what Josef Breuer had described as "secrets of the marriage bed." Only occasionally could he get a recognizable clue, or make a prescient guess about what had gone wrong; for these women, raised in restraint amounting to strangulation at the suggestion of sexual love, were unable to speak about such unspeakable matters even to their physician. Yet sometimes, accompanied by blushes, stammerings, face hidings, the truth emerged: the husband was clumsy, hasty, inconsiderate, did not time himself so that his aroused wife could participate, "pounced on and rolled off like an animal."

Yet when Sigmund learned these facts and knew why his patient was nervously disturbed, there was little he could do to remedy the situation.

A Viennese husband would be outraged if he were summoned by his wife's physician and informed that his wife was ill because he performed the act of coitus badly. This was a subject which students, soldiers, boulevardiers, clubmen, businessmen in their *Stammlokal* discussed among themselves *ad nauseam,* down to the most intimate of physiological detail; but all such discussion was banned in the home and in the marriage as immoral and degrading. The amount of unhappiness caused by this dichotomy became increasingly evident as his case records piled up; yet neither he nor any other neurologist had learned how to help these afflicted patients out of the hand-wringing, handkerchief-tearing situation. Some of his "wife patients" were going to be ill all of their lives.

From each neurosis he learned some new, ingenious working of the unconscious. Twenty-three-year-old Fräulein Ilsa was a lively and gifted girl who was brought to him by her father, an elderly physician who insisted on remaining in the room. For eighteen months Ilsa had suffered such severe pains in her legs that she had found it difficult to walk. The first doctor had diagnosed it as multiple sclerosis but a young Assistant in the Department of Nervous Diseases thought he recognized symptoms of hysteria, and recommended the girl be sent to Dr. Freud. For five months Ilsa came three times a week. Sigmund gave her intensive hand massage, increased voltage on the electrical machine; under hypnosis he made all manner of suggestions to alleviate her pain. Nothing helped, despite the fact that Ilsa proved a willing subject. One day she stumbled into his office, held up on one side by her father and on the other by the umbrella she used as a walking stick. Sigmund lost patience with the girl. When she was under hypnotism he shouted:

"This has gone on too long! Tomorrow morning that umbrella of yours will break in your hands and you'll have to walk without it."

He awakened Ilsa, outraged at himself for having lost his temper. The next morning her father came to the apartment without an appointment.

"What do you think Ilsa did yesterday? We were walking along the Ringstrasse when she suddenly began singing '*Ein freies Leben führen wir*' from the chorus in Schiller's *Die Räuber*. She beat time on the pavement with her umbrella and broke it! She is now moving around without an umbrella for the first time in months."

Sigmund gave a deep sigh of relief.

"Your daughter has wittily transformed a nonsensical suggestion on my part into a brilliant one." He knew Bernheim or Liébeault would be satisfied with the cure. He hesitated, then plunged forward. "But the breaking of the umbrella is not enough to cure Ilsa. We must learn what in her mind suggested to her that she was unable to walk."

The next day he put Ilsa to sleep and immediately demanded to know what had upset her emotionally just before her leg pains began. Ilsa replied quietly that it was the death of an attractive young relative to whom she had considered herself engaged. Sigmund encouraged her to express her feelings about the man, her grief at his death. Ilsa's replies were so matter-of-fact that he doubted he was on the right track. Two days later Ilsa came into his office, having found herself another umbrella to lean on. Sigmund put her to sleep, then said in a stern voice:

"Ilsa, I do not believe that your cousin's death had anything to do with your state of illness. I think something else has happened to you, as a matter of grave importance to your emotional and physical life. Until you tell me what it is I cannot help you."

Ilsa remained silent for a few seconds, then under her breath muttered a long sentence in which he discerned the words "park . . . stranger . . . rape . . . abortion." Her father began to sob bitterly. Sigmund brought the girl out of sleep. Father and daughter helped each other out of the room. Sigmund never saw the patient again, nor was any word of explanation sent. If the affliction was not arrested she would soon be bedridden. Then she would be safe, withdrawn from the world. He believed that if he could have Ilsa back for another few sessions, alone perhaps, he could show her the connection between her oncoming paralysis and the earlier misfortune; that he would have a chance to reconcile her to the fact that she could walk through life despite the tragedy that had befallen her.

Fräulein Rosalia Hatwig, whose case he handled at the same time as Ilsa's, was a young musician with an excellent voice, in training for the operatic and concert stage. Everyone believed she had a promising future. Then suddenly she developed an imperfection in her middle register. The flattings were present only when Rosalia was agitated; her voice became so impeded that she could not carry on. Sigmund put her into deep sleep, encouraged her to talk. She had grown up in a family with a number of younger children and a brutal father who maltreated his wife and children not only physically but psychologically in demonstrating his sexual preference for the servants in the household. When Rosalia's mother died, Rosalia took over the defense of the younger children. While willing to battle to protect the little ones, she did everything in her power to suppress her own hatred and contempt, swallowing the lines of violent reproach she wished to throw at her father. Each time she forced back a heated reply she felt a severe constriction and scratching in her throat.

Sigmund urged her to say under hypnosis everything she had wanted to tell her father over the years, in the harshest terms she had wanted to use. Rosalia did this in magnificently irate terms. The flattings stopped but Rosalia's troubles with an aunt brought the treatments to a premature end.

Knowledge is a slow-flowing river; sometimes it backs up, laden with debris, sometimes it runs dry. Now for Sigmund it became a torrent. The next discovery, which had been trying to push itself through the crustacean wall of non-knowledge and into his consciousness, was that in another phase of his practice he had been not only an idiot but a fraud. Wilhelm Erb's prescriptions from the *Handbook of Electro-Therapeutics* which he had been using freely on patients these first five years of his practice were a gigantic hoax!

Not that Professor Erb meant it as such: he had evolved a system of ohms, currents, electrodes of brass, nickel plated, covered with sponge, flannel and linen, and worked out "the essence of electro-therapeutics" in a series of complicated mathematical formulas which Sigmund, to his present chagrin, had memorized, using them as though they were Scripture. He cringed when he remembered how many patients he had deluded by believing the lines from Erb's book, "I am not guilty of exaggeration when I say that the curative effects not infrequently astonish even the experienced physician by their magical rapidity and completeness."

"No exaggeration!" Sigmund engaged in one of his rare swear words. "Those electrodes have the same value as a sugar tit. I shudder at the fees I have taken for a few hours of relaxation that never got within an ohm of the patient's disturbances. Fortunately my charges were mild, money as well as electricity. Yet every neurologist in Europe, England and America, even the great Hughlings Jackson, has been using Erb's faradization for years. How can we be so blind for so long? Erb got international fame, and the patient got a science as spurious as phrenology."

Josef Breuer was amused at Sigmund's vehemence. They were visiting in Josef's library.

"Now, Sig, you're exaggerating. Faradization is at least as helpful as warm and cool baths, Jackson's rest cures or bromides."

"Which is . . . exactly nothing! Of course rest, sea voyages, good food create a better physical aura. But you and I know that they can penetrate the jungle of the unconscious and propitiate the demons there about as well as a stein of beer can put out a forest fire."

Josef palmed his beard, a gesture he used automatically now when he was distressed.

"Then what do we have left, Sig, if we admit publicly that we no longer have any tools to work with?"

Sigmund's eyes flashed.

"We have our new approach, Josef, the one you introduced with Bertha Pappenheim and I have been carrying forward. That is a real therapeutic tool."

Josef gazed over Sigmund's head at the wall of books. A few evenings later he dropped into Sigmund's study to discuss the case of a young woman he found medically puzzling. When he had repeated the symptoms, Sigmund said:

"Josef, it sounds to me like a case of false pregnancy."

Josef stared at him for a moment, his eyes agitated, then jumped up and left without saying good night. Martha, who had seen him hurrying through the foyer and out the front door, came into the study to ask, "What's wrong with Josef?"

Sigmund scratched his beard against the grain to symbolize his perplexity.

"I can't imagine. He asked for my diagnosis, and when I ventured a guess he ran like a deer in the woods."

3.

It was the birth of their second son, Oliver, in February 1891 that made it clear they would have to move. There was no proper children's room in the apartment. The change would be difficult; it admitted publicly that the first choice had been an indiscretion. The fact that they were moving suggested instability. "In point of fact the Viennese are more faithful to their vow of fidelity to their apartments than they are to their spouses," commented Fleischl.

Their lease in the *Sühnhaus* ran through July. Over the months they looked at dozens of apartments when there were To Let signs at the street entrance. Nothing appeared that would take care of their needs. Then one pleasant July afternoon when Martha and the children were in a villa in Reichenau near Semmering, Sigmund set out on his favorite stroll along the Danube Canal, walking in the shade of the weeping willows and enjoying the view of the bridges as the canal curved against its frame of the deep green Wienerwald. On the opposite bank there were flowering shrubs, roses and geraniums in bloom, marigolds and flowering lupine. The water moved with decisive swiftness between its dry-rock walls, a greenish brown. Young mothers were wheeling their babies in high-slung carriages. On the benches and along the low brownstone walls the townspeople were sitting with their faces turned up to the sun, eyes closed, absorbing the light and heat with the luxuriousness of lizards.

After passing the Tandelmarkt, the ancient and colorful Flea Market of Vienna, he crossed a *Platz* with five streets flowing into it, and started up the Berggasse, the Mountain Street, because it was one of the steepest in Vienna. He had frequently climbed it on the way to Professor Brücke's laboratory, which stood at the top, walking the three blocks at robust speed. Now at number 19 he stopped abruptly. Hanging from a hook on the street door was a printed paper sign ZU VERMIETEN: TO LET. He took a swift appraising look up and down the street, judging it for the first time: spaciously wide, lined on both sides with five-story apartment buildings, a few shops on the ground floor, on the opposite side the Export Academy. It was a middle-class, respectable bourgeois street, the house façades decorated but not overpopulated with Herculean sculptures. The sidewalks were paved with the usual three-inch stones, laid in semicircles.

The door was unlocked. He entered, went through the hall to summon the *Hausmeister*. While waiting he stood in the open door of the courtyard with its four shade trees, well-kept lawn, flowering shrubs, and at the rear a classic-columned alcove with a fountain and carved stone figure of a young girl. The scene gave him a feeling of well-being.

The *Hausmeister* took him up a steep flight of stairs, past the same kind of *Parterre* apartment he had occupied as a bachelor, to the first-floor apartment that was available. From the moment he stepped through the door he had a sense of expanded space; the ceilings were fifteen feet high, giving him breathing room. The foyer was a viable entity seventeen feet by twelve as he paced the floor. On his left he saw a set of double glass doors, the bottom half opaque. Opening one of these, he found himself in a large room with a parquet floor. Despite the fact that there were no windows overlooking the street, the room was awash with afternoon sunlight from a glassed-in porch at its far end.

He walked into a large bedroom with its windows looking out on the garden court and, at the far corner, set off at an oblique angle, another good-sized bedroom which would hold several children. Off the first of the bedrooms was a comfortable bath with a hot water heater over the long enameled tub and toilet on a raised platform. Conveniently off the bathroom was a walk-in closet large enough to hold the family's clothing, as well as built-in drawers and shelves for linens, pillows and blankets. The bath and closet had windows admitting to a light shaft. All the rooms had been modestly cleaned. He thought, "My meticulous Martha will work her *Hausfrau* wonders on them."

With a start he realized that in his mind he had already rented the apartment.

He crossed the foyer, opening the doors that led to the street quarters. On his right was the most luxurious room in the house, with three sets of double windows overlooking the Berggasse, and a chandelier in the center. From here he could look into the other two rooms, for there were two sets of handsomely carved sliding wood doors which stood open to his view. The parquet floor, a series of flower arrangements laid in squares, extended continuously through the three rooms. All had handsome moldings with a double curved baffle as the wall rounded into the ceiling: quiet, pleasing, highly decorative.

He entered the center of the three rooms, the smallest, which his mind envisaged as a consultation room or study; and then into the corner room, perfect for a dining room, with the kitchen just a double door behind. He was about to go away without looking at the kitchen, but realized he had better inspect it carefully so that he could take Martha an accurate report. It was twice as large as their kitchen at the *Sühnhaus*, with cupboards on either side of the wall straight up to the ceiling, a floor of checkerboard red and white stone, a six-burner coal stove, a food-preparing table under the window leading to the light shaft. As he followed the superintendent through the empty rooms he had a feeling of *déjà vu*, as though he had been through all this before.

When he asked the annual rent, it proved to be somewhat less than the *Sühnhaus* apartment. Admittedly, the area was not as elegant as their present site on the Schottenring; some people might say that its proximity to the Tandelmarkt lowered the neighborhood in the Vienna hierarchy.

"But," Sigmund calculated, "there are several streetcars feeding into the *Platz* below, still another line that runs on the Währinger Strasse just up at the corner. It's easily accessible for *Fiaker* as well, so my patients will have no difficulty getting here. There are markets in each of the five corners of the *Platz*, several parks between here and the Donau Kanal in which the children can play. We must have it; it's perfect for us."

He was torn by a need to lease the apartment on the spot but he said nothing as he walked with the *Hausmeister* down the elbow-angled stairs and stood in front of the *Parterre*, ten steps above the foyer floor.

"Who lives in here?"

"An old watchmaker. Bachelor. Name of Plohjar. Has a hole-in-the-wall shop in Central City. Spends all day there, all night at the coffeehouse on the corner with his *Zunftgenossen*, guild comrades. Don't know what he needs the apartment for; keeps threatening to move out each quarter when he grumbles out his rent."

Sigmund's heart skipped a beat.

"Could I see it? Just for a moment? It may be that I'll want this *Parterre* to go with the apartment upstairs, once your watchmaker declines to grumble out his rent."

He handed the man some kreutzer. The door was opened for him. It was a gem of five rooms, modeled after the one upstairs, in miniature, and without the string of rooms overlooking the street. There was a foyer and sitting room for his patients; two adjoining bedrooms at the rear which he could convert into a consultation room and study for himself; and a cabinetlike kitchen, useless for a family but perfect for boiling his instruments.

"How much is the rent on this *Parterre?*"

When the *Hausmeister* told him, Sigmund had difficulty suppressing a groan of delight; the rents of the two apartments together came to very little more than they had been paying these five years. Unable to contain his excitement, he took a bill out of his wallet and pressed it into the soft hand.

"This is an evidence of earnest. I must tell my wife about it, bring her here . . ."

"I understand, Herr Doktor. I will hold the upstairs apartment for you in the same hand with his money."

Martha, when he brought her in from Reichenau, managed to contain her enthusiasm. She was not happy about giving up her newer kitchen and bathroom for these older ones; yet as she moved through the big airy rooms with their high decorated ceilings and handsome parquet floors, twice the space they now had, her expression slowly began to lighten. She linked her arm into her husband's and flashed him a warm smile.

"This will be a family house," she said softly. "It's large enough to contain the future."

Mid-July's intense heat had driven the Viennese to the mountains. He sat at his desk in the *Sühnhaus* for days without a patient ringing the doorbell. With all income cut off he felt obliged to change from his imported Havana cigars, of which he gave himself the delight of smoking a dozen a day, to Trabuccos, a small mild cigar he bought at the neighborhood Tabak Trafik as the best one produced by the Austrian tobacco monopoly. Only the publication of *On Aphasia* relieved his tedium. Receiving a note from the publisher that the copies were off the press, he walked to the bookstore. There, on a flat table holding other medical titles, was a pile of ten copies of his book. As he picked up the top copy, scanned the title page, table of contents, textual material, he felt a surge of joy sweep through him. This was his first book, his formal entrance into the realm of creative medical publishing. His name had been inside three other books as translator; but this volume was wholly and uniquely his own. If not for him, it would never have come into existence. He held the copy in his hands as tenderly as he ever had Mathilde, Martin or Oliver, this living, breathing, speaking creature which had come out of the loins of his intellect.

He tucked one copy for himself under his arm, then asked a clerk to wrap and send a second copy to Dr. Josef Breuer. He did not take it himself because he wanted his friend to be totally surprised by the line which he had kept secret: *Dedicated to Dr. Josef Breuer in friendship and respect.* He did not expect Josef to finish the whole book, it ran well over a hundred pages, that day or even that night. Probably he would drop by the following afternoon for coffee, or have supper with him.

But there was no word from Josef the next day or the next. Sigmund could not understand it. By the third afternoon he could bear the suspense no longer, rushing impulsively through Stephansplatz to the Breuer apartment. Mathilde greeted him warmly; he knew at once that she had not yet heard about the book.

"Josef is in the library, Sig. Go straight along and I'll send in refreshments."

Josef was writing at his desk. He looked up, saw Sigmund enter, blinked a couple of times. Sigmund thought, "He's not pleased to see me! In fact he seems embarrassed. What in the world has gone wrong?" Aloud he said, "Josef, did you receive the copy of the book?"

"Yes, I got it."

"You've been too busy to read it?"

"I've read it." Flatly.

"You didn't like it!"

Josef made a derogatory dip of a shoulder, said, "It's not altogether bad."

Sigmund felt as though he had been struck across the face.

"You can't recollect any of its good points?"

". . . yes, it's well written."

"Thank you, Josef, I always aspired to be a great stylist." With asperity. "What about the scientific material? The new psychiatric approach?"

"I don't think you put the halves together, the somatic and psychiatric. They tend to fly apart, like antagonists. And really, your habit of attacking authorities in every field, the most respected men in medical science . . . No one will thank you for that new heresy that psychic factors have as much to do with aphasia as the physical disturbances do, certainly not Wernicke or Hitzig or Lichtheim."

"I wasn't looking for thanks, Josef, only for an objective analysis of my evidence."

Josef did not answer but instead rang for the maid. When she entered, he asked, "Has Dr. Rechburg arrived yet?"

"No, sir."

"Bring him here the moment he comes."

Sigmund felt drowned in disappointment. After the maid left he said hoarsely:

"Josef, you haven't mentioned the dedication. I wanted to honor you. I hoped you would be pleased."

". . . yes. Well, thank you."

The maid ushered in Dr. Rechburg. When he saw Sigmund he seemed to shrink back. Sigmund reasoned, "He and Josef have already discussed the book. They disapprove. That accounts for his embarrassment." He went quickly to the door, muttered an "*Auf Wiedersehen*" without looking at either man, and descended to the pavement. As he trudged wearily homeward to his empty apartment words formed themselves slowly in his mind. He fitted his feet into the thin-sliced granite cobblestones:

"My differences with Josef are growing deeper. Why? He agrees with me step by step, and then throws out my conclusions. My affectionate dedication has only embarrassed him further, as though the medical world might hold him responsible for the content. Yet he knows as well as I do that there are ideational causes behind speech impediments; and that the unconscious can be the villain behind aphasia. Why is he so hesitant to admit these things?"

The heat gave way to a rain that did not stop. The humidity and lack of patients made him cranky. It was pouring even harder when he reached the mountains on Friday evening. He climbed the Rax anyway, thinking the exercise might dispel his gloom, and picked some edelweiss which he brought home to Martha. She pressed all of the flowers. He missed the bright smiling face of Marie, who had left to be married; in her place Martha had hired an old Nanny, recommended by friends who no longer needed her. Moping around the villa the following day, he decided that the old nurse was bad for the children. He complained to Martha:

"Martin is a fine boy, affectionate, good-natured, intelligent. Did you notice that he speaks a fair number of words now? But that ancient crone is ruining our little woman! Mathilde has grown naughty, she refuses to obey, on principle, I believe, and she says 'No' to absolutely every suggestion I make. Besides, Nanny has no right to criticize the children so harshly. I don't see why you don't rebuke her. I hope you don't intend to keep her when we move to the Berggasse? I'll add something to her pension fund if necessary."

Martha replied sweetly but firmly:

"Dear, why don't you go climb the Schneeberg? The air will do you good. And please don't worry about Mathilde; it's a passing phase. By tomorrow or next week she'll again be the little girl you love."

The Schneeberg took the crankiness out of him, and the unhappiness over Josef's rejection. He came back tired, to soak in a tub of hot water; and to make it up to Martha by taking her for supper to a beer *Stube* where they sang popular songs.

4.

A former patient led him into an exciting adventure and a reconciliation with Josef Breuer: the forty-five-year-old Frau Cäcilie Mattias, a tall woman with flaxen hair, strong eyebrows, nose and mouth militarily disciplined on the oval parade ground of her face; an intelligent, sensitive person who wrote poetry which Sigmund found to contain a highly developed sense of form. Dr. Breuer had summoned him to Frau Mattias' house late one night a year before, where he had found her suffering from an excruciating neuralgia which centered on her teeth. He learned that these attacks had come on two or three times a year for some fifteen years. Once, when the neuralgia had raged for months, the family had called in a dentist who diagnosed the trouble as diseased root cavities, and had extracted seven of what Sigmund suspected, after examining the rest of her mouth, had been perfectly sound teeth. Other dentists had wanted to extract still other supposedly errant teeth, but Cäcilie had evolved a technique to defeat them: the night before her appointment to have more "criminals" yanked out, the facial neuralgia would disappear. Other doctors, called in over the years, had used the faradic brush, purges, "drinking of the waters" to get rid of a slight trace of uric acid. Nothing had helped; the scourge went through its pattern of five to ten days and then disappeared as mysteriously as it had begun. The consensus of the Viennese medical professors was "gouty neuralgia."

There was little Sigmund could offer beyond a sympathetic manner and a bromide to put her to sleep. She had come into his consultation room the next morning dressed in a checked wool suit she had designed herself. Standing tall and bright-eyed before him, she said in a clear but impersonal tone:

"Herr Doktor, do you think you might give me a hypnotic treatment? I hear that you help people who have had the same illness for years."

"Has Dr. Breuer used hypnosis on you?"

"No. The subject did not come up. But the pain in my face is intolerable now, and will continue for at least a week. If you believe that hypnosis has a chance to help me, I beg you to try."

Sigmund uttered an unworded prayer to an unnamed deity.

"Very well. Relax in this chair. Close your eyes. Rest. Think of sleep. Pleasantly. That's good. You're going to fall asleep now, quietly, easily, happily . . . sleep . . . sleep . . . sleep."

His voice was gentle, calm, soothing. But once she was asleep he changed his tone and tactics, became quite stern, told her in positive terms that she did not have to suffer from facial neuralgia, that she had the power to banish the pain; that the irritation of the second and third branches of one trigeminal was not sufficient to cause neuralgia, and that it could be made to disappear once she wanted it gone; that her intelligence and hence her capability of coping with physical disturbance was greater than the minor illness to which she had been succumbing. He had said to himself, "I must lay a very energetic prohibition on her pains, the strongest I have used yet. Since she demanded the treatment she will be able to tolerate a suggestion that is in reality more of a command."

When he woke her he had asked, the drill-sergeant manner gone, "How do you feel now, Frau Cäcilie?"

". . . better, I think." She ran her fingertips tentatively along the neuralgia paths of her cheek. "There is still pain, but considerably less. It's dull now, rather than raging."

"Good. I could come this evening and give you another treatment, if you wish. Let us see if we cannot rout this pain before it would normally fade."

He had hypnotized her three times, suggesting that, although she had not invented the original slight neuralgia pain, she had in fact used this legitimate starting point as a locomotive, such as the ones attached at the Gloggnitz Station to haul the train up the mountains to Semmering, to initiate what she herself called a "raging neuralgia" of the teeth. He had suggested that the next time she felt a twinge in the fifth cranial nerve she was to dismiss it as incapable of causing any severe pain in her jaw or teeth.

The treatment had worked. Cäcilie's neuralgia vanished. She passed the period when the neuralgia was scheduled to reappear. Nothing happened. Sigmund asked:

"Josef, don't we now have to doubt the genuineness of her fifteen years of neuralgia?"

"You're convinced it was a form of hysteria?"

"What other explanation is there? I can't cure somatic illnesses by suggestion. Nobody can."

Josef had turned a skeptical but approving eye on his younger confrere.

"Don't congratulate yourself too soon. Cäcilie is a resourceful woman. She has half a dozen other maladies which have baffled Viennese medicine since the day of her marriage."

Now, a year later, he was again summoned to the Mattias house. He arrived to find Cäcilie at the crisis of a nervous attack, again centering around her teeth. He concluded that he could not eradicate the hysterical neuralgia until he got at its cause. He put Cäcilie to sleep.

"Frau Cäcilie, I suggest that you go back to the traumatic scene which first caused your neuralgia. You will remember it because it has been carefully protected in your unconscious mind all these years."

Cäcilie fumbled with incoherent syllables, then burst into tears, her body swaying back and forth. The words began pouring forth: a quarrel with her husband shortly after their marriage, during her first pregnancy. She came to the climactic moment, when her husband had flung a cruel insult at her. Cäcilie put her hand to her cheek and cried aloud:

"It was like a slap in the face!"

"Yes," Sigmund agreed, "it was a slap in the face, but only *symbolically*. You converted that symbol into a physical reality. Since you probably had a slight toothache at the time, you focalized the insult on that existing pain, and developed it into a 'raging agony' which lasted for days. Why did you need to do this? So that you could speak to your family and the doctors about the pain you suffered over your husband's insulting remarks? In your conscious mind you did not know you were making the substitution; it was your unconscious that evolved the plot."

Cäcilie awoke. They discussed the logic of his deduction. She gazed wide-eyed at her doctor, murmured:

"You are an alchemist. You have taken the dross of my illness and turned it into the gold of truth."

Within a few days he suffered the fate of all alchemists: the plating wore off. His patient fell ill again, this time with fits of shaking and an inability to swallow food; she was frightened by witches at night and could not sleep. She came to Sigmund's consultation room utterly depressed, greeting him with the sentence, "My life feels as though it is chopped to pieces. Am I not a worthless person?" going into a long impassioned speech about what a wretched creature she was. When Sigmund tried to get at the cause of her melancholy, she described a series of unfortunate situations that had arisen within the family during the past few days. But upon investigation he learned that nothing unpleasant or distressing had actually happened. By treating and watching her carefully he learned another phenomenon of the unconscious: in its early stages of an attack it sends out feeler signals which in Frau Cäcilie's case had caused anxiety, terror, self-loathing, indicating in advance that another "memory debt" would have to be paid by its victim.

By now Sigmund had guessed the generic cause of Cäcilie's illnesses: a stern grandmother, wishing to consolidate the family wealth and social position, had affianced her to a stranger and forced a marriage of convenience. The husband had never liked Cäcilie; her intelligence and artistic talents frightened him. After the birth of their second child, years before, he had stopped having intercourse with his wife. Cäcilie had lived a continent life, while her husband's affairs became the talk of Vienna.

Sigmund's mind went to Frau Pufendorf, whose husband was impotent; Frau Emmy von Neustadt, who had been without love since the death of her husband. These women had one thing in common: they had lived for years without sexual intercourse, in situations where intercourse should have been normal and natural. There was a universal truth here, if only he could measure it, document it in a laboratory.

In the meanwhile he had a sick patient on his hands; Cäcilie had been unable to swallow food for so long she was suffering from anorexia. Under hypnosis he unblocked the passage between her conscious and unconscious. There tumbled out story after story of her husband's abrasive, cutting comments, against which Cäcilie had no defense. She had cried:

"I shall have to swallow this! Oh, God, I shall have to swallow this."

Sigmund explained. "Whenever your unconscious thrusts forward this memory, your throat locks in a hysterical aura. A voice at the back of your mind is saying, 'I refuse to swallow anything more!' Don't you see, Frau Cäcilie, it's the same symbolization as the neuralgia in your teeth."

Cäcilie awoke, accepted the reasoning, began to eat again. Josef Breuer praised his work both to Sigmund and to the Mattias family. Then Cäcilie came down with a severe heart attack. Sigmund was summoned after midnight. He listened to her heartbeat; it sounded normal. It was some time before he could elicit the germinal story of how her husband had accused her of a deceitful act. He knew by now that she was a textbook of symbolizations; he persevered until she related that, when her husband accused her of misbehavior, his charge had:

". . . stabbed me to the the the heart!"

"Frau Cäcilie, these are psychiatric disturbances, not somatic. You can put an end to them by going back in your memory and setting exact dates for the happening which precipitated the trauma."

Cäcilie tried to help herself, but the ingenuity of her unconscious kept bringing up new crises; at the height of each new attack Sigmund was summoned by a servant or frantic member of the family. The next phenomenon was an excruciating pain in the right foot. "When I was in a sanatorium years ago the doctor told me I had to go to the dining room and meet my fellow patients. The fear flashed through my mind, 'What if I don't get off on the right foot with all these strangers?' "

The most serious of the illnesses was a piercing stab between the eyes; the attack kept Cäcilie half blind. It took a long time for him to work through her partial amnesia; then in his consultation room, in deep sleep, she confessed:

"One evening, while I was lying in bed, my grandmother came in and gave me such a piercing look that it went right between my eyes and into my brain."

When they discussed it later, he asked:

"Why should she have given you such a piercing look?"

"I don't know. Perhaps she was suspicious."

"How long ago was that?"

"Thirty years."

"Would you like to tell me what it was you were feeling guilty about, so that you thought your grandmother suspected you of something?"

Cäcilie was silent, then murmured, "It's not important any more."

"But it is, since after three decades the memory of the scene is still lodging a piercing barb between your eyes."

"Stupid of me, isn't it, Herr Doktor, to still be suffering over something done so long ago?"

"Not stupid, defenseless. That piece of guilt got lodged in your mind, and you have had no way of getting rid of it, until now."

"You know the nature of my youthful sin, don't you, Doctor?"

"Yes, I think I do."

"Don't you agree that it's too embarrassing to talk about?"

"No, since masturbation is quite common. There's no evil attached to it. It's an instinctive act which lies outside the realm of morality."

"Since my marriage has been a disaster, could I have been blaming myself for its failure—way back in that second mind you speak about, on the grounds that my early sins warranted this punishment?"

"My dear Frau Cäcilie, I now see hope for your recovery. And it will have been you who established the last link in the etiology of your neurosis."

He worked at his desk all through the night setting down the full facts of the case. Frau Cäcilie had helped him pry open another battered-down hatch of the unconscious: *symbolization*. He stood at the window as the summer sun rose, burnt orange as hot as though fired out of a cannon, rubbing his eyes sleepily.

"How many more divisions and compartments are there in that spectral land?" Slowly, slowly, he was stalking the terrain. "How many years will have to pass before I can map the surface and have the right to call myself a cartographer? Where will this shrouded road lead before I shall have reached its end?"

5.

They ordered a *Möbelwagen* for August first, a Saturday; it was pulled by two dray horses, its high seat occupied by a pair of burly movers who packed the dishes in barrels, the glassware in sawdust, then disassembled whichever pieces of furniture came apart, emptied the bureaus of their drawers, carried the furniture down the iron-balustraded steps to the court, out to the Maria Theresienstrasse and then into the covered, oblong gray van.

"I'm feeling a little choked up as the external surroundings of our five years are dismantled and hauled off," Martha exclaimed, standing in her empty bedroom.

"Only a few blocks, and to another building. Nothing alters inside us."

"Now I understand why the Viennese don't like to change homes: to move is to die a little, to leave behind the years."

"We don't lose them," Sigmund said, his fingers gently stroking her smooth cheek. "The memories are all wrapped in old newspapers and packed in barrels to be taken out safely in the new apartment. The most precious ones we will swaddle in your dowry linen, or pack in soft suitcases, the way you did the porcelains."

Martha wanted to remain in town for a couple of days to sort out her possessions, bring in an upholsterer to recut the draperies to fit the new windows, and arrange her furniture against the freshly painted off-white walls. She urged Sigmund to take the early morning train to the country since he had not seen his children for a week. He rested the balance of the day and set out the following morning to climb one of the highest mountains in the surrounding range. He had his dinner in a recommended "refuge," served to him by a buxom but morose eighteen-year-old whom the landlady called Katharina. Later, after a hard climb to the peak, when he had thrown himself down in the grass to rest and marvel at the view of the three lush valleys below, Katharina came to him, said she knew he was a doctor from his name in the Visitors' Book, and could she please speak to him? Her nerves were bad. Sometimes she got so out of breath she thought she would suffocate; there was a buzzing in her head, a weight on her chest. Could Herr Doktor Freud help her?

Herr Doktor Freud would have preferred to gaze at the view; "surrounded by this grandeur, how could anyone have nerves?" flashed through his mind; but obviously this robust mountain girl was suffering emotional distress. She was eager to tell the doctor everything. Her troubles had begun two years before when she accidentally looked in a window and saw her father lying on top of her young cousin Franziska. That was when she could not catch her breath. She had gone to bed for three days, sick and vomiting. Sigmund recalled a discussion with Josef Breuer in which they had come to the conclusion that the symptomatology of hysteria could be compared with a pictographic script: in that alphabet, being sick meant disgust.

He studied the broad peasant face. Katharina had not been brought up with the puritanical restraints imposed on Viennese women. Why was her hysteria so evident, over a sight witnessed two years before? Particularly, as she informed him, since her mother had divorced her father when Franziska became pregnant by him. The experience was very likely screening another more serious maladventure of years before. He told her so. Katharina then blurted out the truth: when she was fourteen, and had gone into the valley to spend a night at an inn, her father came upstairs drunk, had climbed into bed with her and made sexual advances. She had felt a particular part of her father's body held against her, before she had sprung up. *That* was when the "spells" had begun. But she had not thought of all that for a long time!

Sigmund suggested that now she understood the original cause, she could dismiss it from her mind, breathe deeply again. Yes, she would try; she felt better already. . . .

That night, after tucking the children into bed, he sat under the light of an oil lamp, relating the day's experience to his other cases. Again and again he was finding that "an earlier traumatic moment may require a later auxiliary experience to make it flare in the unconscious. Put in other terms, *the cure to any existing trauma has to be sought in the originating trauma which probably took place many years before.*"

He left his writing table and went out to the terrace overlooking the somnolent valleys and mountains molten in the night fog. He remembered the hunters he had passed during the day, guns over their shoulders, looking for game. He ruminated, "The unconscious does not fire like a rifle; it allows its lead poisoning to trickle through to the foremind until enough has gathered to cause emotional and nervous cesspools of disturbance." Of one thing he had become absolutely certain: "*the manifestation is today; the cause lies in yesteryear.*"

The family's move into the Berggasse apartment was a happy one. They gave a series of weekly dinner parties to introduce their relatives and friends to their new home. Mathilde and Josef Breuer approved of the apartment because of its rambling spaciousness. Sigmund's parents and sisters were intensely proud. The Saturday night club declared it excellent for playing *Tarock*. His associates at the Kassowitz Institute were more formal, but they arrived carrying flowers and candy with which to bless the new abode. Ernst Fleischl, almost too weak to climb the flight of stairs, had a servant with him, carrying for Sigmund's combination study and consultation room a finely carved head of a Roman senator from the time of Emperor Augustus. Sigmund was deeply touched; he knew how attached to that particular marble Fleischl was.

Sigmund used part of the large foyer for a waiting room, the two boys had a bedroom to themselves, four-year-old Mathilde was content to have the small *Kabinett* for her own. A new Bohemian girl replaced the ancient governess, who had decided she was ready to retire to one of the pleasant homes maintained by the government for domestic servants who never married. With the move into the larger apartment Martha and Sigmund both wrote to Mrs. Bernays, inviting her to come for a visit with her grandchildren. But she had apparently had more than enough of Vienna; she replied that Hamburg suited her just fine. It was Minna who replied favorably to their invitation, saying that she frequently was nostalgic for the Ring, that "stone menu card."

Sigmund's judgment about the location of the Berggasse was sound. From the first day of October the section of the foyer he used as a waiting room was filled. He knew that his practice was flourishing partly because Austria had gone back on gold currency and was recovering the prosperity that had been wiped out in the depression of the seventies. In good times patients not only visited their doctors but as the members of the Medical Faculty were wont to say:

"They can even pay their bills without getting ill all over again."

He was able to put enough money in the bank to start earning interest. Martha, who had nothing to do with the finances of the family, preferring to have Sigmund give her the weekly *Haushaltsgeld* each Monday morning, observed when Sigmund showed her the bankbook:

"How nice that this has finally happened to us. Just think, it's money earning money, instead of you making it by the sweat of your medical brow."

It took him only three weeks to learn that Ernst Fleischl had brought him not so much a housewarming as a parting gift. He was summoned to Fleischl's apartment late one afternoon by an urgent message from Dr. Obersteiner; when he reached there and found himself preceded by Professor Brücke, Exner, about to become head of the Physiology Institute, and Josef Breuer, he knew that Fleischl was dying. He went into the library where his friend was lying on a cot but he could not find any words with which to greet him. Instead he put a hand on the cover where Fleischl's shoulder had become a ridge of bone.

Ernst Fleischl von Marxow was the least sad one in the room.

"Here I am surrounded by the best medical minds in Vienna. And what do you do for me? You hold my hand . . . the good one! Don't feel sorry for me, my friends. I've been rehearsing this scene for ten years. I even have my exit lines memorized. One of them is, Please each of you take some books off these shelves, the ones that are of special interest to you."

Brücke replied with a wan smile, "Thank you, no, dear Kollege, my failing eyesight won't let me read while crossing the river Styx. But since you're planning to go ahead of me, there are several favors I might ask. Buy me a silk beret, a plaid blanket and the largest umbrella you can find. I won't enjoy my walks in the next world without a thickly rolled umbrella as a walking stick."

"It will be waiting for you, Professor."

Fleischl asked Breuer, who was standing next to the bell cord, to pull it. His servant brought in a ceremonial supper: caviar, bottles of champagne in ice buckets, the gourmet delights from the Naschmarkt, their aromatic scents filling the room. He insisted that everyone eat and drink. The servant thumbed open the cork of a bottle and filled half a dozen glasses including one for his master. With an almost Herculean effort Fleischl pulled himself upright, raised his glass, said:

"One more drink all around! Yes, I planned my own farewell party. Why not? All roads lead to the Central Cemetery. People give parties when we are born, when we are baptized, when we are engaged, when we marry, have children, anniversaries. Why shouldn't I give myself a dying party? I knew that none of you could be persuaded to give it for me, much as you have loved me and cared for me over the years. Wouldn't it be gratifying if a man could take to the next world whatever his eyes last saw on this earth? The miser who would be counting his money would take with him a fortune in gold coins; another man, caressing a beautiful woman, would have her with him unto eternity. Another, reading Goethe's *Faust*, would have that one literary feast until doomsday; while still another, walking in the Vienna Woods, would take with him a small green forest. I'd like to take this room, precisely as it is, so that I would have exciting living quarters in purgatory, or wherever I'm going."

"To heaven," Sigmund murmured half under his breath "you've had your inferno on earth."

Fleischl heard him. "So do a lot of people, my dear Sig, in their minds, instead of their bodies. You ought to know about that from your patients. That's where the expression 'hell on earth' comes from. I've suffered pain, more than one human's allotment, but I've never been in hell in this room; not with all these books and art works. They are a better anodyne, Sig, than the coca you imported from Peru.

Obersteiner, open another bottle of champagne. It will give me great pleasure to wake up in the Elysian Fields tomorrow, blissfully healthy, and know that you all have hangovers in my honor. I'll feel I'm missed."

Obersteiner popped the cork, which hit the ceiling, and refilled the glasses. "Fleischl, you have a macabre sense of humor; I drink to it!"

They ate, they drank, they sang nostalgically the songs of their university days and romantic tunes from the light operas of Vienna. Then, when the last bottle had been drained, the trays of delicacies emptied, Ernst Fleischl turned his head sideways on his pillow, closed his eyes. Josef Breuer went to his side, searched for a pulse. He could find none. He started to put the sheet over Fleischl's head. Sigmund said softly:

"Is it necessary, Josef? He looks beautiful, even in death."

Eli Bernays invited Sigmund and Martha to an eight o'clock supper; he wanted to tell them something important. Eli and Anna now had three children, the latest, Edward, being only a few weeks old. The family lived well, for Eli set high standards for himself. He had given up his government post to develop his travel bureau, but despite his sharp business acumen and inexhaustible energies, his affairs were not moving forward as fast as he would like. At thirty-one he was still the heavy-set commanding figure Sigmund had known a decade before, immaculately dressed in suits made by one of the best tailors in town, black kid shoes also made to order and, Sigmund was certain, each sock was still meticulously fastened to his underwear with three safety pins.

"Sig, Martha, I've decided to go to America. I simply cannot bear to spend the rest of my life at the slow pace of the Austrian Empire. There's so little opportunity here for an ambitious man. Everyone I meet, everything I read, tells me that the United States is the land of opportunity. A man can build and develop there at a hand-over-heels rate, and that's exactly what I'm starved for."

Sigmund chuckled. "I'm surprised it took you so long. How can we help?"

Eli threw an arm about Anna affectionately.

"Since this can only be an experimental trip, I'll have to leave Anna and the children behind. Anna has consented. I already have my steamship ticket. I gauge I'll be gone three or four months. Will the two of you look after my family?"

"For as long as you need to be away," Martha reassured him. "Anna, wouldn't you like one of your sisters to move in?"

"Yes, I think I'll ask Rosa. She's so capable."

"What about money, Eli?" Sigmund asked. "We have some savings . . ."

"Thank you, Sig. I'm selling my travel bureau for a fair price, but I could use some help to see us through."

"Well then, leave your family to us. You just think about how you are going to bring back all that gold the streets are paved with."

6.

When Professor Ernst Brücke died in early January, the entire medical and scholarly world mourned his passing; but none more so than Sigmund and Josef Breuer, to whom he had been the greatest of scientists and teachers. They talked about Brücke until midnight, their reminiscences going back almost twenty years, when Josef had gone to work for the professor in the Physiology Institute. Josef observed:

"Sig, this has been our own special funeral service for Professor Ernst Brücke. It is right that as his students we keep him alive, with all his idiosyncrasies and all his scientific genius."

"It wasn't a Protestant service, but I think it might have been as spiritual. Josef, if love is what religion is about, then we have preached an eloquent sermon over our good and great friend. As the priests say, 'Requiescat in pace.' "

Births and deaths alternated in staggered rhythm. In April their third son, whom they named Ernst, was born. Martha commented happily:

"Now you really can consider yourself the head of a numerous clan. 'Your seed shall be dispersed by the winds of the earth.' "

"My darling Marty, don't let's lose the formula for girls, the way my parents lost the prescription for boys. I'm sure Mathilde would like a baby sister to play with."

It was a few weeks later that he heard that Professor Theodor Meynert was on his deathbed, a victim at fifty-nine of congenital heart disease. He wanted very much to go to Meynert's house and pay his respects; for in spite of their professional differences and public brawling, Sigmund loved and admired the man second only to Brücke. Along with Brücke, Meynert had favored him and fought for him as a student and a young intern. Yet he did not feel that he could intrude. The professor apparently was seeing no one in his last difficult hours.

Sigmund was all the more surprised, then, to find Meynert's servant in the foyer with a message. Would Herr Dr. Freud come to the Meynert home at once? Professor Meynert wished to see him. When Sigmund was ushered into the bedroom he found that his old teacher had not wasted away but was looking rather plumper than usual, with his long gray-black locks falling forward over his brows. If he was frightened of dying, Sigmund could see no sign of it. Meynert waved him to the head of the bed, said in a hoarse voice:

"I'm glad you didn't bring a box of Havana cigars this time, Herr Doktor; I should hate leaving some of them unsmoked."

"Your sense of humor has not deserted you, Herr Hofrat."

"No, but practically everything else has." He tried to hitch himself up in the bed. "You are perhaps wondering why I summoned you at this late moment?"

"You have always been the master of the unexpected, Herr Professor, particularly in your work."

"No. In my life. Half of my personal acts have come as a surprise to me. Shall I tell you why?"

"I think you want to, Herr Hofrat."

"How discerning of you. Prop these pillows behind my back, please. Thank you. For five or six years now you have had me under siege with your Charcot nonsense about male hysteria. Do you still believe that absurdity? The truth now; it is not proper to lie to a dying man."

"In all honesty, and despite your considerable efforts, I have not changed my mind."

"Then I too will be honest with you." A thin smile fluttered across Meynert's face. "My dear Kollege, there *is* such a thing as male hysteria. Do you know how I know?"

"No." Humbly.

"Because I was always one of the clearest cases of male hysteria. That's what got me addicted to sniffing chloroform when I was young, and addicted to alcohol when I grew older. Why do you think I have fought you so bitterly during these years?"

". . . you were . . . committed to an anatomical base . . ."

"Nonsense! You should not have been deceived. I made your theories seem ridiculous so that I would not be found out."

"Why are you telling me this now, Herr Hofrat?"

"Because it doesn't matter any more. My time is up. I feel I still have something to teach you. Sigmund, the adversary who fights you the hardest is the one who is the most convinced you are right. I won't be the last man to trap you into battle, to try to decapitate your beliefs. You're much too adventuresome not to get yourself into a lifetime of battles. You were one of my best students. You've earned the truth."

It was the first time in over thirteen years that he had worked under Professor Meynert, since his first course in the winter of 1878 in clinical psychiatry, that the professor had called him by his first name. He was so taken aback, so touched that he barely heard the last sentence. Like

Fleischl's marble Roman head, he sensed that it was a farewell gift. Meynert whispered:

"*Auf Wiedersehen!*"

"*Auf Wiedersehen*, Herr Hofrat."

Sigmund turned away with tears in his eyes.

They rented the same pleasant villa in Reichenau for the summer, the high point of which was a two-week vacation in August that Martha and Sigmund took in "the green province," spending one week in Hallstatt and the other in Bad Aussee, in Styria in southern Austria. They had been married for six years now; they had four robust children; a permanent home and, it appeared, a practice in neurology, the somatic disturbance of the central nervous system, which provided the basic support for the family, as well as a practice in the neuroses, the psychic disturbance of the nervous system, which kept him intrigued and excited as a medical researcher.

In both hotels they found rooms with comfortable balconies overlooking the rich valleys, the deepest green in Europe. They climbed the mountains, swam in the cold green lakes of Bad Aussee, drank the white Styrian wines, ate roast saddle of venison, partridge and *Palatschinken* filled with jams and raisins. Late afternoons they stretched out on their porch to glory in the riotous sunsets and to read until dark.

The years rolled away; all thoughts of children, home, patients, vanished while they reveled in the tranquil beauty of the Styrian Alps, went to bed early to love and sleep under the feather-light but wonderfully warm comforters, to awaken happy to be alive, with a viable life of their own and a place in the sun, no matter how modest.

The outstanding social event of the year was Wilhelm Fliess's marriage. Wilhelm had confided to Sigmund earlier: "I want to marry a Viennese girl; that's why I come here so often." He had found what he wanted in Fräulein Ida Bondy, twenty-three, warm, outgoing, not beautiful but pleasant to gaze upon. Though she was the daughter and heir to Philip Bondy's considerable mercantile fortune, and the Bondys were one of the best-known families in Vienna, Ida had retained her natural sweetness, without the souring note of arrogance or pretension. The Bondy family were patients of Josef Breuer; Sigmund and Martha had accompanied the Breuers to several parties at the spacious Bondy apartment on the Johannesgasse.

"As you know, I approve of marriage but dislike weddings," Sigmund observed to Martha. "But we simply must attend Wilhelm's and Ida's services."

She went into Vienna with him the following Monday to start working with her dressmaker, who would need at least three weeks for the moiré gown Martha wanted. Her eyes went dreamy. "It will have chiffon ruching along the shoulder seams and a high stand-up collar of ruching; also the fashionable V insert of smocked chiffon starting at my shoulders and ending in a narrow point at my waist. I'll have a thin belt . . ."

"Now, now, Marty, this is Ida's wedding."

The affair took place early in September at the Bondy summer home in Mödling. The ceremony was held in the Bondy garden, surrounded by towering shade trees. Sigmund need not have worried about Martha outshining Ida, though his wife looked beautiful. Ida was radiant in a tight-sleeved white satin and lace gown, with a full white satin train. After the noon ceremony the party went into the house for a wedding dinner of *Fogosch*, Tallern duck, young Gumpoldskirchner wine, and a wedding cake with Rhine wine for the many toasts. In the cool of the afternoon they returned to the garden where a dance floor had been installed. An orchestra played waltzes until sundown. Sigmund and Martha danced only a couple of times a year. The dozen toasts had made everyone slightly hilarious. The waltzing was more abandoned than usual.

Wilhelm drew Sigmund aside.

"Sig, my marriage must not make any difference between us. I will always have urgent need of you. Your analysis and criticism of my ideas helps me to hatch my ugly ducklings and make graceful swans out of them . . . or is that figure of speech slightly tipsy?"

Sigmund laughed. "We're all slightly tipsy. And why not, at such a lovely wedding? Wilhelm, I also need you. We must continue to write several times a week, everything we're thinking, send each other drafts of our papers . . . to be blue-penciled. . . ."

"We must also continue to meet a couple of times a year, congresses anywhere you say: Vienna, Berlin, Salzburg, Dresden, Munich . . ."

Sigmund patted Wilhelm lightly on the forearm. "As we say in Vienna, 'A useful knife must have two cutting edges.' . . . Have a happy honeymoon. There will be several letters waiting on your desk when you return to Berlin."

The Freud family returned to the city at the end of September. The weather remained pleasantly warm. Martha kept Sigmund company while he finished his work.

"I'll read that Arthur Schnitzler book you brought home last week, *Anatol*. Is it really as interesting as you say?"

"Yes. It's a new kind of book. Schnitzler is a doctor, you know. He was a few years behind me, working in Meynert's Psychiatric Clinic as I did. He speaks more honestly and realistically about man's sexual nature than anyone writing today."

The room was lighted by two reading lamps. They passed a few words back and forth when a thought occurred but there was no urgency to talk.

At eleven o'clock Martha brought in a pitcher of cool raspberry juice and soda water, and they prepared for bed. Sigmund was asleep within a matter of seconds; nor did the sleep seem much longer than that when he was jolted half out of the bed by an explosion, followed by a blinding flash of light in the darkness outside. Martha cried:

"Get the boys! I'll take care of Mathilde."

Sigmund passed the window just in time to see the watchmaker jump out of his ground-floor window into the court. He hurried into his large white bathrobe and went to the doorway of the boys' bedroom. Martin took one look, screamed, "It's a Bedouin, a live Bedouin!" and dove under the covers. The maid appeared with the baby.

But the light and glare had vanished. "I doubt it's a fire," said Sigmund. "I'll find the *Hausmeister*."

He returned in a few moments to reassure the family; it had merely been an explosion of the gas supply in the watchmaker's apartment. He sat on his three-year-old's bed, asked, "Now, Martin, just how did I become a Bedouin?"

"Your big white robe, Papa, like the Bedouins in the picture book you gave me. Papa, you look nice with your hair standing straight up."

The next morning the watchmaker moved out of the *Parterre*, muttering that he could recognize an omen of nature when he encountered one. By noon the *Hausmeister* was at the Freud door.

"Herr Doktor, the apartment is yours if you still want it. We'll need some days to paint where the gas blackened the walls . . ."

By the end of the week the gas equipment had been repaired, the apartment repainted an off-white. At Sigmund's orders a foyer was glassed off from what was still an ample waiting room in which he placed the chairs, sofa and hat-umbrella rack from his earlier waiting rooms. A door led into his consultation room, with a window admitting to the court, the one out of which the watchmaker had jumped. Here Sigmund installed his desk, bookshelves, the black couch he had bought for his first bachelor office-apartment, a glass cabinet to hold his equipment, and on the walls framed pictures of the great physicians who had taught and practiced at the University of Vienna: Skoda, Gall, Semmelweis, Brücke. He had gotten rid of his electric massage machine. It was an austerely professional room, one which he hoped would inspire confidence in his patients.

No such austerity was wanted or needed for his study, the angled room behind the office, which closed with rolling doors. On the wall above his writing table he hung a reproduction of a Giottoesque Florentine painting and on either side of it, strung downward in a row, the shards of pottery, medallions and inscribed plaques from archaeological diggings in Asia Minor which had been given to him as gifts by Fleischl and Josef Breuer for his birthday or Christmas, and to which he had added a few small pieces he had found in an antique shop in the Old City.

This was to be his private world to which he could retreat for hours on end when there were no patients, where he could continue his reading and research, keep his notes in proper files, write his manuscripts and maintain his correspondence—the most exciting part of which was with Wilhelm Fliess in Berlin—spread on a worktable and oversized desk, surrounded by racks of the books in which he continued to work: on aphasia, psychology, the brain. Here he could study, speculate, write, theorize. In his consultation room he was the physician handling a variety of neurological cases; in his study he was the scientist, the scholar, the medical philosopher, working his way through the labyrinths of his newly discovered nether world of the mind. The study was small, ten feet by fifteen, which he made even smaller with two side walls of bookshelves. Yet he liked its sense of compactness, of being shut off from the outside. The only sounds that came to him were the salutary ones of the gardener cutting the grass or raking leaves.

He had broken with tradition with this move; Viennese doctors had their offices in their family apartments. Yet he found that his patients appreciated the new sense of privacy: of opening an unlatched door, sitting down unseen in a waiting room without a maid to intervene. Then too there was a lavatory just beyond the foyer which they could use without anyone knowing they had to, or invading the privacy of the family; with many of his patients this was a distinct benefit. Martha scheduled the maid to go down while the family was having breakfast and scrub the tiny kitchen where Sigmund boiled his own instruments, and to give the rooms a vigorous cleaning before the first patient arrived.

The day before he settled in, Martha bought a three-foot marble replica of Michelangelo's *The Dying Captive* which had moved him so deeply when he saw it in the Louvre. She had the statue delivered while he was working at the Kassowitz Institute, setting it on a low storage chest. He was taken completely by surprise when he returned to find Martha in his study, and the marble figure installed as though it had always been there. Tears sprang to his eyes.

"My beloved Marty, how did you know?" He ran a hand caressingly over the exquisite sculpture. "See how young this Dying Captive is, how magnificently proportioned his body; look at the flawlessly carved Greek face, the divine spirit hovering over his pain-laden eyes and lips. The torment in this face symbolizes for me the agony of all captive mankind, destroyed by an unseen enemy and a ruthless fate. He must be saved! Mankind is too wonderful a creation to be lost.

"How can this Dying Captive be freed from his bonds, brought back to vigorous health? That is the question to which I want to address the whole of my life."

7.

A doctor friend asked Sigmund if he would take the case of Fräulein Elisabeth von Reichardt, whom he had been treating unsuccessfully for two years for recurring pains in the legs and a sometime inability to walk. The referring doctor had come to the belated conclusion that Fräulein Elisabeth was suffering from hysteria. Perhaps Sigmund could help?

Elisabeth von Reichardt was twenty-four, with dark brown hair and eyes, a mouth and chin set in a disproportionately wide facial structure. She seemed emotionally normal, bearing her misfortunes with a stoic cheerfulness. His physical examination showed the anterior surface of the right thigh as the point of origin of the pain, and sensitivity of the skin of both thighs, which constituted a hysterogenic zone, for Elisabeth exclaimed with pleasure rather than pain when Dr. Freud exerted pressures on the muscles of her legs. He found only one somatic disturbance, a number of hard fibers in the muscular substance. He speculated:

"Could a neurosis have attached itself to this area of mild distress, as Frau Cäcilie's neurosis had attached itself to the slight neuralgia in her jaw and teeth?"

He saw the woman twice a week for four weeks of what he described to his colleague as "pretense treatment," principally hand massage, while the Von Reichardts' long-time family doctor slowly unfolded for Elisabeth the new therapy which Dr. Freud had evolved, that of talking about her problems to get an idea of why she was ill. When Elisabeth was ready, Sigmund put an end to the massages.

"Fräulein Elisabeth, I am not going to hypnotize you. I think we can accomplish much without it. However I must reserve the right to resort to it later in case materials arise to which your waking memory is unequal. Agreed?"

"Agreed, Herr Doktor."

"This procedure is one of clearing away the pathogenic material layer by layer. We liken it to the technique of excavating a buried city. Start by telling me everything you can remember about your illness."

Elisabeth reminisced freely. The youngest of three daughters of a prosperous Hungarian landowner, she had, because of the illness of her mother, become her father's companion and confidante. The father boasted that Elisabeth took the place of a son; the relationship had decided Elisabeth against marriage except to a man of extraordinary talents. The father felt there would be greater opportunities for his daughters in cultivated Vienna and moved his family there. Elisabeth lived a full, bright life, until her father suffered a massive heart attack. She became his nurse, sleeping in his room.

After eighteen months her father died. Her mother underwent an operation for cataracts of the eyes. Once again Elisabeth became the nurse. A ray of happiness entered when her younger sister married a man who was extremely considerate and kind. The family's happiness was short-lived; the younger sister died in childbirth; the heartbroken husband moved back to his own family, taking the infant with him.

It was a sad story. Elisabeth admitted that she was lonely, embittered at cruel fate, hungry for love. But why had it resulted in a hysteria which took the form of an inability to walk? No vestige of Elisabeth's unconscious mind had peeped through her grave recital. Sigmund decided to utilize hypnosis. But try as he might he could not get Elisabeth into a somnolent state. Instead she grinned at him triumphantly as though to say:

"I'm not asleep, you know. I can't be hypnotized."

Sigmund was not amused. He was growing tired of saying to patients, "You are going to sleep . . . sleep!" and have the patient reply, "But, Doctor, I am not asleep." Yet it was imperative that the patients have access to memories and be *able to recognize connections which appeared not to be present in their normal state of consciousness.* He was after "determining causes," he needed those pathogenic origins which were absent from the patient's waking memory.

A picture flashed into his mind of Professor Bernheim using the pressure of his hand on a patient's forehead. He placed his own hands firmly on Elisabeth's forehead and said:

"I want you to tell me everything that passes before your inner eye, or through your memory, at the moment of this pressure."

Elisabeth remained silent. Dr. Freud insisted that she had seen images and remembered conversations after he applied his fingers to her forehead. A long soughing breath came out of her as she slumped in her chair, then whispered:

". . . yes, I thought of a wonderful evening . . . a young man I liked saw me home from a party . . . our conversation was deeply gratifying to me, as between admiring equals . . ."

Sigmund seconded Elisabeth's sigh of relief. He thought, "The cork is out of the bottle."

When Elisabeth reached home from the party, which her family had insisted she attend, she had found that her father had taken a turn for the worse. He died soon after. Elisabeth could not forgive herself. She never saw the young man again. . . .

The dikes were open. Sigmund noted that the patient's pain in the left leg increased when she talked of her dead sister and brother-in-law. By insistent probing he evoked a scene in which Elisabeth described a long walk taken with her brother-in-law at a mountain resort while her sister was feeling unwell. When Elisabeth returned she suffered violent pains in the legs. This was ascribed by the family to a too long walk of the day before, and to the hot mineral bath where she had caught cold. . . .

Dr. Freud did not think so. He led her, again through pressure on her forehead, to her next memory: of climbing a hill alone to a spot where she had often sat on a stone bench with her brother-in-law, admiring the view. When Elisabeth returned to the hotel she had found herself semi-paralyzed in the left leg.

"What were your thoughts when you returned, Elisabeth?"

"I was lonely. I had a passionate wish that I could bask in love and happiness such as my sister enjoyed."

Sigmund believed he was on the right track, but he had an unpredictable patient. At times the material gushed forth in chronological order "as though she were turning the pages of a lengthy book of pictures." On other days she became recalcitrant, her conscious mind remained firmly in control, unwilling or unable to bring forth rejected knowledge or memories. He fought these suppressions and concealments. "Something must have occurred to you! Perhaps you are not being sufficiently attentive? Maybe you think the idea that comes to you is not the right one. That is not for you to decide. You must say whatever comes into your head whether you think it appropriate or not!"

Sometimes days would go by before Elisabeth would yield to her second mind and the truth reveal itself: she had thought herself strong enough to live without love, without the help of a man; but she had begun to realize her weakness as a woman alone. "My frozen nature had begun to melt," when she saw the wonderful care her brother-in-law lavished on her sister; he was like her father, the kind of man with whom one could discuss the most intimate subjects. . . .

The causation became clear but it took an external incident to prove his thesis. One afternoon she had felt too ill to come to the office. Sigmund was treating her in her home when they heard a man's footsteps and an agreeable voice in the next room with Elisabeth's mother. Elisabeth sprang up, exclaiming:

"May we break off? That's my brother-in-law. I heard him inquire about me."

Sigmund spaced his revelations over several consultations.

"You have been sparing yourself the painful conviction that you love your sister's husband by inducing physical torments instead. It is in the moments that this conviction forces itself upon you that your pains come, thanks to a successful conversion. If you can face this truth, your illness can be brought under control."

Elisabeth stormed. She wept. She denied. She denounced.

"It's not true! You talked me into it. It could not be true. I am incapable of such wickedness. I could never forgive myself."

"My dear Fräulein Elisabeth, we are not responsible for our feelings. The fact that you have fallen ill in these circumstances is sufficient evidence of your moral character."

Elisabeth was not to be consoled; not for several weeks. Then slowly the full truth emerged. It was an arranged marriage; the first time the brother-in-law had come to the Von Reichardt house he had mistaken Elisabeth for the girl he was to marry. One evening some time later, the two of them had been having such a stimulating conversation that the younger sister had said, "The truth is, you two would have suited each other splendidly." And then, the most painful admission of all: when Elisabeth had stood at the bedside of her dead sister the involuntary thought had flashed through her mind:

"Now he is free again and I can be his wife!"

Sigmund taught Elisabeth to accept this truth of her love and live with it; also to accept the fact that she would never marry the brother-in-law. It was not easy, there were relapses, but one night he and Martha went to a ball which Elisabeth also attended. He watched her dance by, flushed by the music and the waltzing. Next he learned that she had married, happily and well.

There were many reasons for him to be pleased: he had brought to an end an illness of considerably over two years' duration, one that the other doctors had been unable to treat. He had demonstrated again, just as he had demonstrated a brain section in Meynert's laboratory, that if there are no discernible or serious anatomical disturbances in the body, crippling can be caused by the involuntary suppression in the unconscious mind of ideas repugnant to the conscious mind. No hysteria could be implanted like a foreign body until an idea was intentionally repressed from consciousness. In his notebooks he observed, "*The basis for repression itself can only be a feeling of unpleasure, the incompatibility between the single idea that is to be repressed and the dominant mass of ideas constituting the ego.* The repressed idea takes its revenge, however, by becoming pathogenic." That, once extracted from the unconscious, brought into the fierce light of the conscious, the ideational material can be reduced as effectively as any other virus or infection of the flesh or bloodstream.

Equally important, he had taken another step forward. He had often confessed to Martha, "I'm not truly good at hypnosis. Liébeault and Bernheim have a native gift. I'm simply forcing hypnosis on my patients and myself."

No longer need he fail patients because he was not an expert hypnotist. He could now send people into the far reaches of their memory while awake as effectively as he had ever done through somnolism. The light pressure he had used on Elisabeth von Reichardt had been maintained for only a few moments. Once she had been induced to concentrate he had no longer needed any other tool. The "business of enlarging a restricted consciousness was laborious," the forgetting of memories often intentional and desired. He must try the method again; he must document it. He trembled with excitement.

8.

Eli Bernays had made two exploratory trips to New York. He now felt ready to sever his ties with Vienna; Americans didn't throw out new ideas as gauche or radical. The streets weren't paved with gold but the air was! "With your talents, Sig, you'd own your own Allgemeine Kranken-haus within a year."

He had one more favor to ask. He was taking Anna and the baby with him, but until he was permanently established he would be grateful if Martha and Sigmund would keep six-year-old Lucy with them, and Amalie and Jakob would keep eight-year-old Judith. For perhaps half a year . . . if it was no imposition . . . ?

Martha assured him that it was not.

Sigmund divided his patients into two categories. The neurological cases could come at any time during his consultation hours, sit in the waiting room and take their turn being admitted to the office. The neurosis patient had a specific appointment which he had to keep to the minute. The previous patient was dismissed sufficiently early so that there was no chance of a meeting with the next patient.

Supportive material for the method he had used with Elisabeth von Reichardt was not long in coming. A specialist asked Sigmund if he would take the case of a thirty-year-old English governess he had been treating for two years for an inflammation of the mucous membrane of the nose. New symptoms had arisen: Miss Lucy Reynolds alternately lost her sense of smell or was harassed by hallucinatory odors, as a result of which she was suffering from loss of appetite, a heavy feeling in the head, accompanied by fatigue and depression.

"Sig, none of these disturbances would be the result of an inflamed membrane. There may be other things bothering Miss Reynolds. Would you try your approach and see if you can get at the cause? I can't do anything more for her."

Lucy Reynolds turned out to be a tall, pale woman, delicate, but who had been in good health, with a consistently cheerful nature, until the onset of her present disturbance. Sitting opposite him at the desk, she gave her history as a governess in the comfortable home of a factory director on the outskirts of Vienna; his wife had died several years before and Lucy, a distant relative of the wife's, had promised her that she would move into the house and care for the two young daughters. The father had not remarried, but Lucy had made the home a happy one for the little girls . . . until her illness. Sigmund started with the hypothesis that the hallucinations of smell were hysterical in origin.

"Miss Reynolds, what is the one smell that troubles you more than the others?"

"A smell of burnt pudding."

Her pale blue eyes watered. Sigmund was silent: "I must assume that a smell of burnt pudding was actually present during the experience which is now operating as a trauma," he speculated to himself. "The patient was suffering from suppurative rhinitis and consequently her attention would be focused on her nasal sensations. The smell of burnt pudding should be the starting point of the analysis."

He suggested that Lucy lie down on his black couch, close her eyes and keep both her features and body quite motionless. He placed his hand on her forehead and suggested that through concentration the pressure would enable her to see, hear and remember the episodes in her memory for which they were searching, and that she would be able to communicate them.

"Miss Reynolds, can you remember when you first experienced the smell of burnt pudding?"

"Yes, it was a couple of days before my birthday, two months ago. I was with the girls in the schoolroom, playing at cooking with them. The postman brought a letter from my mother in Glasgow. The children snatched it from me, crying, 'Please save the reading for a birthday gift.' While I was trying to get the letter from them, the pudding burnt. The room was filled with the strong smell. It's in my nostrils all the time now, day and night, and grows stronger when I become agitated."

Sigmund pulled up a chair and sat beside her.

"What was the emotional content of the scene that makes it so unforgettable?"

"I was preparing to return to Glasgow; the thought of leaving the children . . ."

"Was your mother ill? Did she need you?"

"No. . . . I just couldn't stand living in that home any longer. The servants accuse me of thinking I am better than they. They repeat malicious gossip to the girls' grandfather. Neither he nor the children's father backs me when I complain. I told the father I would have to leave. He urged me to think it over for a couple of weeks. It was during this period of uncertainty that the pudding burned. . . . I had promised the girls' mother on her deathbed that I would never leave them. . . ."

Sigmund thought he saw a faint dot of light at the end of a tunnel; but Lucy had to leave for the long journey to the outskirts. She could come into town only when she found someone trustworthy to stay with the girls. So much time elapsed between visits that Sigmund had almost always to start at the beginning. Lucy was using the burnt-pudding smell as an olfactory symbol, since she was having trouble with her nose. Here was corroboration of his theory that a hysteria finds its Achilles' heel. After half a dozen sessions he became convinced that Lucy was leaving one element out of her portrait. He decided to make a frontal attack.

"Lucy Reynolds, I think you have fallen in love with your employer, and you believe you have a genuine chance to take the mother's place in the home as the director's wife. Your imagined attacks by the servants arose from your fear that they were reading your mind and ridiculing you."

Lucy replied matter-of-factly, "I believe that's true."

"Then why didn't you tell me?"

"I wasn't sure . . . I didn't want to know . . . better to knock it out of my head and be sensible . . ."

The smell of burnt pudding vanished. To be replaced by an obsessive smell of cigar smoke. She did not know why, since cigars had always been smoked in the home. Sigmund gathered he had a second half of the analysis to complete. He put Lucy back on the black couch, but now she kept her eyes open quite normally. She told him the first picture that came into her mind under the pressure of his hand. It was the dining-room table, at luncheon, when the father and grandfather had returned from the factory. Sigmund insisted that she keep looking at the image. Lucy finally saw a guest there, the chief accountant from the plant, who was devoted to the children. Under prodding, Lucy at last recalled the germane scene: the old accountant had tried to kiss the two children good-by. The father had shouted, "Don't do that!"

"I felt a stab at my heart. Since the men were all smoking cigars, that smell stuck in my nostrils."

"Which of the two scenes came first, this one or the burning of the pudding?"

"This one was earlier by two months."

"If that is so," thought Sigmund, "then the burnt-pudding memory was a substitute. We're not at the bottom yet." To Lucy he said, "Go back to an earlier scene; it lies deeper than this first one with the accountant. You can remember it; no one ever forgets a scene that's stamped on the mind."

". . . yes . . . a few months before . . . a woman acquaintance of my employer's came visiting. When she left she kissed the little girls on the mouth. I got the full burst of their father's fury: I had failed to do my duty! If it ever happened again, I would be dismissed. This was during the period when I thought he loved me; he had spoken to me so kindly and confidentially about the proper raising of the girls. . . . That moment crushed all my hopes. I knew that if he could make such a terrible threat in a matter over which I had no control, he could not love me. The smell of cigar smoke hung heavy in the room . . ."

When she returned two days later, Lucy was in a gay mood. Sigmund imagined for an instant that her employer had proposed marriage. He asked what had happened.

"Herr Doktor, you have only seen me discouraged and ill. When I awoke yesterday morning it was as though a heavy weight had been lifted from my mind. I felt perfectly well and cheerful, as I always had been."

"What do you think of your prospects of marriage to your employer?"

"Non-existent. But that fact no longer has the power to make me ill."

"Do you still love the children's father?"

"Yes, assuredly. But what difference? My thoughts and feelings are my own."

Sigmund examined Lucy's nose. The swelling was gone. There was a slight sensitiveness; future colds would settle there and give her trouble. *But her unconscious would not!*

The resolution of the problem had taken nine weeks. Sigmund had thought the sessions slow, repetitive, unrewarding. Yet here was Miss Reynolds sitting before him with a confident smile on her lips, acceptance in her eyes. Months later she was still in excellent spirits.

He now felt released from subservience to hypnosis . . . five years after he had hypnotized his first patient. He hoped he would soon be free of the need of hand pressure as well. It would be his skill, his knowledge pitted against the unknown. Each patient, each case would enable him to bring another shaft of light into the dark cavern of the human mind.

His thoughts went back to the early Monday morning after his understanding with Martha, when he had entered Professor Brücke's office in the Physiology Institute, been assailed by the odors of alcohol and formaldehyde, saw his beloved teacher sitting behind his desk in his beret, agate eyes studying the face of his young demonstrator. He had asked for an assistantship and a permanent place on the University Medical Faculty and Professor Brücke had been obliged to turn him down, advising him to return to the Allgemeine Krankenhaus, earn his *Dozentur*, and go into private practice.

He had thought that that was the end of the world for him. Instead it had been, as the perceptive Professor Brücke had known, a beginning. Here he was, only ten years later, facing what he believed to be the profoundest medical discovery of his age. He was on fire to publish his cases, to present to the world this therapy he found so miraculous in helping people in deep mental and emotional stress; saving them from incapacitating illness, and perhaps even commitment to an institution, or death.

Did he dare to proceed with such a publication? To expose his findings and theories to the entire medical world? He knew that he could not go it alone: he simply did not have the position or stature in Viennese medical circles to earn him acceptance for so revolutionary a concept. There were half a dozen doctors in the city who had referred patients to him and knew that he sometimes got results. But for the rest he was unacknowledged by either the Medical Faculty or the university's scientific institutes, never asked to join their ranks. Despite the fact that his discoveries about cocaine had enabled surgeons to perform eye operations almost inconceivable before, and had forwarded Wagner-Jauregg's work on anesthetizing areas of the skin, he was still being attacked in at least one respected journal for advocating cocaine as a medicine without realizing that it could become an addictive drug; and somewhere, deep in the recesses of his aftermind, he knew this charge to be partly true.

The same accusations of hastiness, gullibility, irresponsibility were being charged against him because of his work with hypnosis. It would do him no good to pass on to his fellow practitioners what he had learned by reading Mesmer's works: that Dr. Anton Mesmer had been at least half right in everything he had originated, particularly the power of suggestion to influence both the physical and mental health of an afflicted one. It was this "suggestion" and not the "magnetic fluid" which had helped people, and upon which the later work of Braid, Charcot, Liébeault, Bernheim, Josef Breuer and now himself was based. The only thing wrong with Mesmer was that he had been a showman who had attracted high society to his group séances in both Vienna and Paris, and had turned them into Oriental bazaars.

There had been a third and more serious apostasy: his concept of male hysteria, brought back with his own modifications and extensions from Charcot in Paris seven years before. Josef Breuer and Heinrich Obersteiner at the sanatorium in Oberdöbling had known he was right, but Professor Meynert had turned the entire Austrian medical world against him by ridicule in the lectures at the Society of Medicine and the *Wiener klinische Wochenschrift*.

His first published book *On Aphasia* had, as Josef Breuer feared, been considered still one more indiscretion and hence been ignored not only in the medical press but by all scientific circles in Vienna. His friends and medical associates never commented on its content. Although published in an inexpensive monograph by Deuticke, who had outlets in every German-speaking city, it had sold only 142 copies during its first year. The sale had now virtually stopped; none of the new studies in the field mentioned his title or contribution. As far as he could perceive, it was worse than having a book fall to the bottom of the sea. It was as though by challenging the thesis set forth by mid-European research that aphasia must be traced to anatomical localization in the brain or to subcortical lesions, and by suggesting that important areas of aphasia were caused by psychological factors, he had once again, in Meynert's phrase, "left Vienna a physician with an exact training in physiology," to return as a "trained practitioner in hypnosis." He had disgraced himself in the bargain by criticizing such great authorities as Meynert, Wernicke and Lichtheim. Although he had admitted in a letter to Wilhelm Fliess just before publication that he had been rather "cheeky" in crossing swords with the famous physiologists and brain anatomists, he was smarting from the wounds of silence inflicted by his opponents' sheathed swords.

"I'm not a masochist," he thought. "I don't enjoy getting pummeled. I crave admiration and respect as much as any scientist. But how am I to move forward to publication of my most important discovery? Those who would not laugh would jeer. They would whisper to each other behind their hands, 'There goes that irresponsible Freud again, trying to set the world on fire with an unlit Bunsen burner!'"

BOOK NINE

"COUNT NO MORTAL HAPPY"

"Count No Mortal Happy"

THE RAIN slashed down the Berggasse at a forty-five-degree angle, November having betrayed the Viennese by a premature storm. Inside the Freud dining room the four friends were comfortable in the warmth emanating from the coal burning in the tall, broad-bosomed green ceramic stove. Martha's mahogany dining table now had more space around it than in the *Sühnhaus*; the eight leather-upholstered chairs with their broad bottoms no longer sat in each other's laps. She had added to the buffet and cabinet for the china and goblets an Italian Renaissance chest, inlaid with ivory and mother of pearl, above which she had hung a reproduction of Albrecht Dürer's etching of St. Hieronymus.

Another "Marie," also from Bohemia, had prepared the Breuers' favorite dinner for a drenched winter day, starting with a hot beef soup. Josef had become bald except for gray-black tufts at the back of his head, yet unlike the Viennese, who let their beards grow longer as the hair on the top of their heads receded, he had cut his shorter and rounded the oblong.

"On my fiftieth birthday," he announced, "I decided that life and its values were not as rigorously square-cut as I had imagined."

Despite Sigmund's on-and-off relationship with Josef since the *On Aphasia* dedication, Mathilde and Martha had remained fast friends. To thwart the wind-swept autumnal rain beating against the outside of her double windows, Martha had donned a gay blue cheviot wool. Though she had passed thirty, and was pregnant with her fifth child, she seemed to Sigmund no older than the flush-cheeked girl he had married in Wandsbek six years before.

After dinner Sigmund murmured, "I have some new materials to show Josef. Perhaps the ladies will excuse us for a while?"

They descended the broad staircase to Sigmund's office. The previous June, Josef had agreed to collaborate on a Preliminary Communication in which they would set forth their "theory of hysterical attacks," based on their findings in the cases they had already treated with significant results: Breuer's Bertha Pappenheim, Sigmund's Emmy von Neustadt, Cäcilie Mattias, Franz Vogel, Elisabeth von Reichardt and the dozens of others who had passed through his office in the past five years. It had not been easy to convince Breuer. Sigmund had pleaded:

"Josef, we have opened the door to a new medical field: psychopathology. We have made some tentative steps with a problem that has never previously been stated. I honestly believe that we have accumulated enough material to formulate an instrument for the scientific investigation of the human mind."

Josef had sprung up abruptly, gone to his cages of pigeons as he always did when he was troubled, and sprinkled corn in the feeding troughs.

"No, Sig, not yet. We don't have enough material. And there's no way to test it in a scientific laboratory. All we have are surmises, hypotheses . . ."

Sigmund had paced the short walkway between the cages.

"We have discovered universal truths about the unconscious mind and how it discharges hysteria. Are not fifty cases, thoroughly pursued, as revelatory as fifty pathology slides studied under a microscope?"

Breuer had shaken his head. "No. We have no vocabulary with which to describe what we are finding. We have no charts, no apparatus . . ."

". . . because the old apparatus is irrelevant. Professor Erb and his electrical massage machine is a fake. Hand massage relaxes for an hour or two. Weir Mitchell's rest cure adds little but body tone and weight. The hydrotherapy sanatoriums soak the skin but not the mind. Our few drugs, bromide and chloral, pacify the patients but never get near the ideational disturbance. Put Meynert's brain anatomy in a separate category and the field of psychiatry is non-existent except for textbooks describing the forms and manifestations of mental disease. My God, Josef, we are trembling on the brink of one of the most important discoveries in the history of medicine."

Breuer had put his hands on the younger man's shoulders, moved by the plea.

"All right, my friend, have a try at it."

During the next few days Sigmund had written feverishly, then torn up the pages. No one had yet posited a theory of hysterical attacks; Charcot alone had given even a description of them. To explain hysterical phenomena it was necessary to assume "the presence of a dissociation—a splitting of the content of consciousness." A recurrent hysterical attack was caused by the return of a memory. The repressed memory could not be a random one; it had to be a mnemic return of the buried event which had caused the original psychical trauma. He wrote, "If a hysterical subject seeks intentionally to forget an experience or forcibly repudiates, inhibits and suppresses an intention or an idea, these psychical acts, as a consequence, enter the second state of consciousness; from there they produce their permanent effects and the memory of them returns as a hysterical attack."

But what determined when and why such a person would suffer such an attack after being moderately well for weeks, months, perhaps years? He realized he could not go very far in his working hypothesis until he could offer a substantive for the precipitation of an attack. He recalled earlier discussions with Josef about their work under Brücke in the Physiology Institute. One of the first things they had learned had come out of a Helmholtz-Brücke school founded in Berlin many years before: the "Theory of Constancy": "The nervous system endeavors to keep constant something in its functional relations that we may describe as the 'sum of excitation.' It puts this pre-condition of health into effect by disposing associatively of every sensible accretion of excitation or by discharging it by an appropriate motor reaction. . . . *Psychical experiences forming the content of hysterical attacks . . . are . . . impressions which have failed to find adequate discharge.*"

He and Josef had discussed this in simpler terms: the nervous system, including the brain, was a reservoir for the storing of energy. When the level of energy fell too low, the psyche got sluggish, depressed. When the energy got too high the nervous system opened some of its sluices so that the excess energy could pour out. This was when and why an attack happened: the nervous system could no longer tolerate the superfluity of energy engendered by a memory-trauma in the unconscious, and got rid of it by causing an attack. The attack was simply the form by means of which the Principle of Constancy asserted itself. Nervous energy was like electrical power stored up in a battery; each container had a limit to the amount it could hold. So did each nervous system. When there had been an overcharge there had to be a release. The release might be subtle, taking the form of hallucinations; or it might be violent, resulting in spasm, convulsion, attacks of epilepsy. The actual discharge was somatic, traveling out through the far ends of the nervous system; but its content and causation were psychic.

He had set his thoughts down on paper and sent the notes over to Breuer. The next morning he wrote to Josef:

"Honored friend: The satisfaction with which I innocently handed you over those few pages of mine has given way to the uneasiness which is so apt to go along with the unremitting pains of thinking." He added his conviction that a historical review would serve no useful purpose, suggesting: "We should start by dogmatically stating the theories we have devised as an explanation."

Josef had apparently been thrown off by the word "dogmatic."

"Sig, if we are going to publish at all, we have to be tentative.

Dogma and science are antithetical words. We must freely and openly admit everything we don't know and cannot yet deduce before we set forth our puny hypotheses as medical knowledge."

"Josef, what I meant by *dogmatic* was a series of simple statements of belief: what we have learned as observable fact about hysteria and its unconscious controls. Surely our patients have led us to a few basic truths?"

Breuer had been adamant.

"We need to know more about the processes of excitation in the mind. While I agree that the Constancy Principle applies here, it will remain little more than speculation until we can demonstrate in terms of physiology how the nervous system serves as a conduit to discharge its superfluity of energy."

Sigmund gave up. He said quietly, "I'll do the paper over again and will include only those materials upon which we have mutually agreed. I will end by confessing that we have done no more than touch on the etiology of the neuroses."

The third draft had been more acceptable, Josef allowed; but was again followed by dozens of hours of animated debate and frequent heated exchanges over what could properly be deduced from the evidence at hand. At moments Sigmund was irked at himself for pushing Josef so hard; half the time Josef was frightened by the nature of the materials with which they were grappling, and longed for the security of the landlocked harbor of his laboratory work on the inner ear. At other times he became exhilarated by the startling postulates which his discussions with Sigmund brought into focus. It was the same dichotomy, Sigmund realized, which now characterized their entire relationship; when they were together for social purposes, having a coffee at the Cafe Griensteidl, or briskly walking around the polygonal Ringstrasse, Josef was as affectionate as in the most loving days of their friendship. But once they had started writing, Josef behaved as though Sigmund Freud were simply a medical associate who was trying to get him involved in a non-science which he, Breuer, had begun, but which he would now give anything to forget!

Sigmund unlocked the door of the *Parterre* offices and led Josef to his study. The continuing downpour allowed little light from the window to the garden court. Sigmund brought up the wick of the oil lamp so that it threw a bright glow, then offered Josef the lone overstuffed chair and a good cigar.

"You certainly can have quiet down here," Josef commented, gazing at the side walls filled with medical books. "It's too lonely for me, I would miss my pigeons."

Sigmund took what he hoped would be the last and acceptable

draft of the Preliminary Communication out of his desk drawer. He handed it to Josef, then settled back in his office chair to await Josef's decision, lighting his own cigar. He had put Josef's name first in the authors' credit line, and had hewed to all of his mentor's strictures. Watching Josef's face as the older man read the near twenty-page manuscript, Sigmund could tell at precisely which point Josef stopped to inspect the use of a new or transliterated word which they had used in their discussions but would rarely have been seen in print before: *abreaction:* the bringing to consciousness and to expression material which had been repressed in the unconscious; *affect:* the feeling tone accompaniment of an idea or mental representation; *catharsis:* a form of psychotherapy which brought repressed traumatic materials into the conscious mind; *libido:* the energy with which instincts are endowed.

Josef looked up, a pleased expression in his eyes.

"Yes, Sig, you have stated the case in as close to scientific terms as we can come at this stage. It is true, what you have claimed here: 'Certain memories of etiological importance which dated back from fifteen to twenty-five years were found to be astonishingly intact and to possess remarkable sensory force, and when they returned they acted with all the affective strength of new experiences.'"

He thumped Sigmund's manuscript with an affirmative gesture. "Hysterics, as you say, suffer mainly from reminiscences. You have documented, without claiming too much, how and why our psychotherapeutic procedure has a curative effect." He riffled through the manuscript pages, read in a strong voice, "'It brings to an end the operative force of the idea which was not abreacted in the first instance by allowing its strangulated affect to find a way out through speech.' I approve that statement." He rose, paced the room just outside the lamp's glow. "However I cannot go along with your theory on the Constancy Principle until you can prove precisely how, by pressing a button, one can trigger a somatic release of energy. Every neurologist in Europe would demand our proofs."

Sigmund was disappointed; he determined not to let Josef know it. He reached for his manuscript, said noncommittally, "Very well, Josef, I'll omit those paragraphs."

Breuer returned to his chair.

"Excellent! Now we can publish."

"The *Neurologisches Centralblatt* of Berlin said they could use it in the January first and fifteenth issues. I've also talked to the editor of the *Wiener medizinische Blätter;* they don't mind publishing after Berlin. They suggested the end of January."

"Very good. And while you're at it, why not present our material in a lecture before the Vienna Medical Club?"

Sigmund went to Breuer and hugged him.

"My dear friend, this is one of the happiest moments of my short but phrenetic medical career. Thank you."

2.

At the New Year he looked back over the past twelve months to judge his accomplishments; alas, the fingers of one hand proved to be a sufficient abacus. But 1893 ushered in a welter of work. As Josef Breuer had suggested, he prepared a version of the Preliminary Communication for the January eleventh lecture at the Vienna Medical Club, then completed his translation of Charcot's revised *Leçons du Mardi*, which was first published serially in important German medical journals; completed a final version of the article Some Points in a Comparative Study of Organic and Hysterical Paralyses which he had agreed to write for Charcot's *Archives de Neurologie* while still in Paris; and wrote a study for Dr. Kassowitz's series, An Account of the Cerebral Diplegias of Childhood.

The publication of the *Preliminary Communication* in Berlin and Vienna drew neither critical assessment nor casual comment. His lecture at the Medical Club was well attended more because Breuer's name was on the paper than because he was lecturing; but not one physician bothered to comment. The only affirmative action was that of a reporter for the *Wiener medizinische Presse* who, seeing that Privatdozent Freud was speaking from notes, took down the lecture in shorthand, which the newspaper then published.

He was surprised to find that he was not disturbed that the paper had failed to arouse interest; he was confident of its germinal power. It was Breuer's attitude which puzzled him; Josef seemed mildly relieved that no one was going to hold it against him or challenge his postulates. Sigmund reproved him for this, albeit gently.

"Josef, it just isn't like you to take a negative attitude toward work well done. Besides . . ." He paused, then plunged ahead: "I have my heart set on our doing a book about our cases; it's only by presenting the full evidence that we can substantiate our thesis."

Josef shot him a swift look of disapproval, came around the highly polished library table and stood with his back pressing into the row of bronze rods which held the reference books in place.

"No. No. That would be violating medical ethics. Patients who have exposed themselves to us have to be protected."

"So they will be, my dear Josef. We'll change the names and exterior circumstances. What we will present will be solely the medical evidence. I will write up one or two of the cases for you, perhaps

Frau Emmy and Miss Lucy Reynolds; then you will see how completely the *materia medica* can be set forth without revealing a glimpse of who the patient might be."

Josef remained unconvinced. Sigmund discreetly avoided mentioning the book again, though he already had a title for it: Studies on Hysteria. He confided to Martha:

"I'll wait for an opportune moment, perhaps when the first favorable review of our paper comes in."

The fascinating aspect of his work became the symptom most universally present in his patients, what he named the *anxiety neurosis*, based on the sexual origin of their neuroses. Neither his character nor his temperament made it easy for him to accept this. During his early cases the connection had not struck him, despite the intimations of Breuer, Charcot and Chrobak. If it had he would have dismissed it summarily. When the evidence began piling up, from ten and then twenty and then thirty patients, it became increasingly difficult not to acknowledge the sexual etiology buried deep in the unconscious. He had first been surprised, then amazed, and finally *erschüttert*, shocked; at one point of revelation, unnerved: he was not by nature the sexually possessed male who thought that life began and ended at the erogenous zones. In full truth, he had resisted the predominantly sexual nature of man and its direct influence on his emotional, nervous and mental health. Yet after a time he had had to admit that the material had been pursuing him. He would have been a poor physician had he failed to evaluate the symptoms as they emerged.

In an old and tightly knit city where interlocking circles of people know each other intimately, word quickly gets around that a certain doctor has a fresh insight or attitude which is helping patients from whom other physicians are turning away in fatigue and defeat. Most of the cases that came, frightened and almost surreptitiously, to his office ranged from the sad to the pitiful to the tragic; lingering neuroses that rendered the patients incapable of living an acceptable adult life because of traumatic happenings in their childhood: the sexual noxa having fallen upon the soil of an inherited tendency toward neurasthenia.

The men came first, some young, some middle-aged, suffering from depression, debility, migraine headaches, trembling of the hands, inability to concentrate on their work: the long-time masturbators; the impotent; those practicing *coitus interruptus*. Then the women, the married ones whose husbands gave them little sexual life; the frigid who could not endure the sexual act. He wrote in his notes:

"No neurasthenia or analogous neurosis can exist without a disturbance of the sexual function."

It was rough terrain. An attractive thirty-year-old lawyer with a flamboyant blond mustache admitted himself gingerly into the consultation room, then quickly related how his loss of appetite had cost him twenty pounds in weight; he also suffered from melancholia and what Sigmund diagnosed as psychogenic headache. Could the doctor help him? He had had one child; his wife had been ill since the birth of the baby; the disturbances had begun not long after.

"Does your wife's illness preclude your having intercourse with her?" The lawyer toed the design in the rug under his feet.

"No."

"Normal intercourse?"

"Yes . . . well, almost. I withdraw before . . . My wife can't have another child until she is well again." Then defensively, "Is there something wrong with that?"

Sigmund replied in his soberest professional voice, "Physically, yes. It is the cause of your illness."

The lawyer stared at him in disbelief. "How can that be?"

"Nature meant the male sperm to be deposited in the vagina. That is the normal and healthy completion of the normal and healthy act. When you withdraw from your wife before your ejaculation you cause a severe shock to the nervous system. It is an unnatural act. It creates what we call *sexual noxae*. Did you suffer any of your present symptoms before practicing *coitus interruptus*?"

"None. I was healthy and vigorous."

"Do you have a religious problem? Have you tried condoms?"

"Those clumsy heavy rubbers depress me for days."

"Does your wife know about douching?"

"She says it's too uncertain."

"Then our problem is to cure your wife; therein lies your own cure."

He had a dozen cases with similar symptoms. With some of the husbands it took insistent digging to get to the basic cause, since the men did not think it proper to reveal their sexual relations with their wives, even to a physician from whom they were seeking help. But Privatdozent Dr. Sigmund Freud had been evolving discreet and sensitive methods of persuading reluctant patients to reveal the truth. As the cases accumulated he saw what an enormous amount of *onanismus conjugalis* was being practiced because of rigid religious strictures and the fear of conception. It began to appear that the only men not suffering debilitation from *coitus interruptus* in marriage were those who kept a mistress or used the Vienna whores.

Nor were the wives much better off. A young mother came to him with complaints of unnamed fears and pain in her breast. She loved her husband. When he was away she was perfectly well; when he was home he practiced *coitus interruptus* because they did not want any more children. She suffered constant fear that the withdrawal might not come soon enough.

"Frau Backer, does your husband bring you to a climax before he withdraws?"

She stared at him, pale with embarrassment. "Herr Doktor, is that a proper medical question?"

"Yes, because it relates to your nervous health. Let me explain: considerate husbands will time themselves so that the wife is also satisfied. For you see, Frau Backer, a wife who is brought to a climax and then has it broken off suffers almost as serious a nervous shock as does the husband. If your husband will make sure of your satisfaction, then you will no longer suffer from the pains that are racking you."

Frau Backer shot him a fierce, penetrating look.

"But if my husband goes to that length, the danger of his not withdrawing in time increases?"

"It might."

"The cure you describe could be worse than the malady."

"Then let me give you this medical assurance: there is nothing wrong with you physically. The amorphous fears, the flashes of pain in your breast are neurotic pains, a manifestation of your anxiety. Once you resume normal sexual relations with your husband, your symptoms will disappear . . ."

" . . . to be replaced by morning nausea." She smiled thinly, thanked the doctor, and left.

There came too, the young unmarried men, some of them under twenty, and slightly older unmarried women, with a variety of neuroses, many caused by masturbation. At first Sigmund found this information even more difficult to get at, for it had been beaten into the children that masturbation was the most venial of all sins, leading to blindness and idiocy. As far as the doctor could gather, the actual act of masturbation, unless it was so excessive as to lead to exhaustion, did not do as much damage as did the accompanying feelings of guilt, with their subsequent quota of hypochondria, self-loathing, obsessive brooding. As a piece of collateral knowledge he observed that boys and young men who were seduced by older women did not develop neuroses.

It took weeks and months of probing, sometimes using pressure on the forehead before he could lead the patient back to precipitating causes: with one young woman who had suffered from a tormenting hypochondria since puberty, he traced the disturbance to a sexual assault when she was eight years old; in the instance of a hysterically suicidal young man, to an indoctrination in masturbation by a schoolmate. Unlike his treatment of earlier patients, he was no longer content to banish memories by suggestion. Since he was now probing deeper, and working from an enlarged point of view, he found this kind of therapy fragmentary; it was treating only the surface effects. As a physician he had undergone steady growth and change in his professional attitude toward his patients, and was making ever greater demands upon himself. Now he was determined to get at the underlying cause of an illness and to find the universal law that governed the disturbance. Until he could achieve greater comprehension, he would, of course, have to concentrate on prophylaxis, try to protect the patient against further onsets by bringing the repressed material forward from the unconscious to the conscious, explaining by every method available to him that the patient need feel no guilt, fear or anxiety because he had done nothing wrong; the wrong had been committed against him a long time before. It was unplowed soil, the kind of neurasthenic sexual phenomenon he was now trying to treat. Unlike the hysteria cases where he sometimes got good and tangible results, "only seldom and indirectly," he observed in his going manuscript, could he "influence the mental consequences of an anxiety neurosis." The cases that baffled him completely were those of the men who disliked all women and had never been able to overcome their physical distaste at the thought of having intercourse with one of them. What could be the ideational cause of homosexuality?

The most tragic cases were those brought to him too late, when the patient already showed signs of paranoia. There was the young unmarried woman who lived with her brother and older sister in comfortable circumstances. She had developed a persecution mania, "heard voices," imagined that the neighbors were talking about her behind her back, saying that she had been jilted by an acquaintance of the family to whom they had previously rented a room. For weeks at a time she thought she saw and heard the people on the street saying that she lived only for the day when the roomer would return; and that she was a "bad woman." Then her mind would clear, she would realize that none of her suspicions were true, and she would be in normal health . . . until the next seizure.

Josef Breuer had heard about her from a colleague and recommended that she be sent to Dr. Freud. Sigmund tried to make an incision into the story with the deftness of Billroth lancing a carbuncle. The young man had lived with the family for a year. He had then left on a journey, returned after half a year for a short stay and then departed permanently. Both sisters spoke of how pleasant it had been to have him in the house.

What had gone wrong? Sigmund was reasonably certain that the illness had a sexual base. Then he learned the truth, not from the patient, but from her older sister: one morning the younger girl was making up the young man's room while he was still in bed. He had called her to him, and suspecting nothing, she had gone. The man had then taken her hand, thrown off the blanket, and placed his erect penis in her palm. The girl had remained motionless for a moment, then fled. Shortly after the man had disappeared for good. Somewhat later the girl told her older sister about the incident, describing it as "his attempt to get me into trouble." When she fell ill and the older sister tried to discuss with her the "seduction scene," the younger girl categorically denied any knowledge of the event, or of ever having related it to her sister.

Now that he had before him the *sexual noxa* that had caused the illness, Sigmund reasoned that he had a chance to help; for what emerged from her hallucinations of being called a "bad woman" by her neighbors was the probability that she had been excited by the feel of the man's organ in her hand, and the sight of it, and consequently had been overtaken by a sense of guilt ending in self-reproaches which, since they were unbearable, she had shifted to outside sources: the neighbors. Though she had been unable to reject her own sense of guilt she could repudiate it when leveled against her by others.

What had to be exorcised was not so much the actual incident itself, since he doubted that he could totally erase the traumatic memory; but the burden of guilt which had lodged in her unconscious mind. If he could take her back to the original happening and show her that her reaction had been normal and inescapable, he might rid her of her self-reproaches. Once these were gone the need of the persecution by the neighbors would vanish, along with the voices and accusations. She would have a chance for a normal life and hopefully for marriage.

He failed, utterly. Several times he put her into a state halfway between hypnosis and free recollection, urging her to talk about the young roomer. She spoke openly of all the good things she remembered, but when he tried through searching questions to lead her to the traumatic scene, she cried out:

"No! Nothing embarrassing ever happened! There's nothing to tell. He was a good young man, always sociable with our family . . ."

After the second such outburst she sent Dr. Freud a letter dismissing him because his questions upset her too much. Sigmund sat in his office in the late afternoon, the letter before him, his arms spread out envelopingly on the desk. He was sad; for the patient had built so strong a defense against being reminded of the happening that it would literally be the death of her. It was too late for him to penetrate to the repressed material and cauterize it.

He sighed, heavily, then shook his head, turned up the oil lamp so that the room was bathed in its warm light and picked up the latest draft of his manuscript on The Anxiety Neurosis. . . .

3.

As he looked over his case records for the intensive work period since October he was gratified to find that he had helped considerably more patients than he had failed. As his knowledge increased and he sharpened his therapeutic tools, there was reason to hope that he might be able to alleviate more and more the symptoms which baffled him. Now in the spring patients were plentiful; each case brought him a jot more evidence that the major manifestation of a neurosis, no matter how artfully concealed, was anxiety; and that the anxiety neurosis arose from a repression. Since he thought even more clearly with a pen in his hand than he did while walking the streets of Vienna, he printed at the top of a page in Latin letters: PROBLEMS.

Equally as important as solving problems was the formulation of problems. "Don't wait for a problem to come to you," he observed; "it may arrive at an inconvenient or disagreeable time. Make the search yourself so that you are the aggressor; work through the puzzling, recalcitrant materials on your own terms."

Nor could there be room for timidity. Wilhelm Fliess wrote to him from Berlin, "Dare to improvise! Dare to think beyond the boundaries of what is already known or guessed at!" Sigmund decided, "Wilhelm is right; we cannot do without men with the courage to think new thoughts before they can prove them."

Was there such a thing as an innate, inherited sexual weakness or disturbance? Or was it acquired in the early years through external circumstance? Was not heredity simply a multiplying factor? What was the etiology of recurrent depression? Did it have a demonstrable sexual base?

Under THESES he listed a group of postulates which would serve as his foundation. Phobias, hallucinations, anxiety depression were at least partly the consequence of the disruption of normal sexual life and growth. Hysteria arose after suppression of the anxiety. Neurasthenia, nervous disability in men, often resulted in impotence which in turn brought about neuroses in their women. Sexually cold women developed neuroses in their husbands.

He set out for himself several collateral tasks; to read the literature from other countries "in which particular sexual abnormalities are endemic"; to build up a formidable file on the affects arising from the inhibition of the normal recognized sexual outlets; and the most difficult and important of all leads, sexual traumas incurred before the age of understanding. The exciting part of any search was for basic causes; this was what kept medical scientists enthralled with their experiments. And it was precisely what Sigmund was pursuing now. He sent expanded drafts of The Etiology of the Neuroses to Fliess asking for criticism. In a revision, when he was becoming more explicit about sexual materials, his puritanical nature overcame him. He began his letter with:

"You will of course keep the draft away from your young wife."

It was not until several days later that he realized he had been guilty of the same prudery that was practiced by so many of his rigidly raised women patients, like the one he had just dismissed who suffered anxiety attacks which ended in fainting spells the morning after intercourse with her husband, a timetable he had had to excavate with a shovel rather than a scalpel. Since their love-making was highly fulfilling to both of them, Sigmund realized that the originating cause lay archaeological layers deep in her unconscious. It took many sessions utilizing a process he had named *free association* before the patient could lead herself back to the originating trauma.

"I'll tell you now how I came by my attacks of anxiety when I was a girl. At that time I used to sleep in a room next to my parents; the door was left open and a night light used to burn on the table. So more than once I saw my father get into bed with my mother and heard sounds that greatly excited me. It was then that my attacks came on."

Sigmund had painstakingly been building up a file of one hundred anxiety neuroses. He said quietly, "Your reaction is entirely understandable; most young girls face their first exposure to sexuality with something akin to terror. Let me read to you from my records similar cases going back to an even earlier age than yours. Your major problem now is to understand that your anxiety has nothing to do with your marital relationship. It is hysteria coming from reminiscences: repressed memories. The well-being of your marriage depends on your rejecting these anxieties as belonging to a distant past, arising from as normal and salutary a relationship between your parents as there now is between you and your husband."

When the patient left he stretched back hard in his office chair, a hand massaging each side of his neck as he thought about his newest technique, which was replacing the putting of pressure on the patient's forehead. He conceived of free association as a key to the exploration of the deep-lying unconscious strata of the mind. It was a forward leap in method. "That apparently disconnected remarks should from the mere fact of their contiguity prove to be bound together by often invisible (i.e., unconscious) links was . . . a most impressive extension of scientific law." What sounded like chaos to the patient turned out to be a pattern discernible to the trained physician. It would be difficult to bilk, manipulate or deceive the unconscious. For free association was not really free; each "by chance" thought, idea, picture, memory was bound to the ones that came before and after as were links in a chain. It was the process rather than the content that was free, when uninterfered with by an act of will on the patient's part to choose selectively from among the incoming thoughts, and without the prompting, suggestion or influence of the physician.

"By this process," Sigmund concluded, "we can get a real rather than a fantasied self-portrait. Every following of a thought, after a previous one, is an act of orderly progression, even when it's a backward movement, in the unconscious. It is never an accident, cannot be irrelevant or meaningless. The process gives expression to the submerged mind." Even the most wildly incongruous and seemingly contradictory thoughts would, if followed in succession, reveal the inner structure of the psyche.

Immediately free association began to work, Sigmund encountered the strangest phenomenon, and the one he found the most difficult to understand: *the patients reacted to him as though he were someone out of their past!* They projected their thoughts, emotions, wishes onto the physician because, once their repressed unconscious material was being revived, they were taken backward in time to the infantile years and *relived that period,* sometimes positively in love and submissiveness, sometimes in hate and rebellion. Their sense of the present was wiped out, they staged the same scenes, sought the same gratification they had had when they were small children, most often in the parental home. This had not happened when he used hypnosis, or when he applied pressure on the patient's forehead. Now he learned that this *transference,* as he named the astonishing development, was inevitable in every fundamental analysis. He found that it took the patient a long time to grasp the irrationality of his conduct; and many of the transferences were as painful for the doctor to endure, when he did not recognize them, as they were for the patient to project. Some modest alleviation of the symptoms was possible without this transference of loves, hates, fears, anxieties, aggressions from the past to the living present, but certainly never a cure! Once the patient grasped and understood transference, he was on his way to understanding both the content and method of his own unconscious. From this peak of Mount Everest he could achieve self-knowledge; and Dr. Sigmund Freud then had the chance and opportunity to work toward a cure.

He had not been greatly interested in the morning mail; occasionally there was a letter from Mrs. Bernays or Minna from Wandsbek, a note from one of his half brothers in England; mostly it consisted of medical journals, announcements of meetings, bills. But since he had created his International Bank of "ideas in the offing" with Wilhelm Fliess, who was contributing a startling concept of the periodicity in human life, he waited eagerly for the postman's knock, fingering swiftly through the stack for a sight of the desired Berlin stamp. Fliess wrote often and voluminously, his letters virtually amounting to first drafts of his medical monographs: provocative, sometimes pugilistic or jejune, but never dull.

Sigmund liked to write to Wilhelm every day, usually around midnight, a recapitulation of the day's cases, new and revelatory materials, fresh hypotheses, past errors to be corrected, reformulated; the triumphs of the mind over obscure research materials, as well as his failures: to learn, to understand, to systematize his growing body of knowledge. When he could not write he missed this period of *Gemütlichkeit* and communication as sorely as other Viennese would their hour at the coffeehouses; for Wilhelm Fliess had become his *Stamm*, his familial group of friends and peers with whom one meets for a convivial hour every day of one's life. It had replaced the hours he had sometimes spent in a favorite coffeehouse.

On April twelfth Martha gave birth to her fifth child, a girl, whom they named Sophie. She had carried well, and as Sigmund commented, "Sophie came into this naughty world without a trace of a struggle." Martha was tired and pale and fell into a long untroubled sleep. The young nursemaid who had been engaged to take care of the four children during the last weeks took over the infant with authority.

Martha was up and around at the end of two weeks, assuming command over her domain, though urged by Sigmund's mother and sisters not to overexert herself. When Sigmund saw that she was feeling strong and content with her new offspring, he asked if he might take a few days to visit Wilhelm Fliess in Berlin.

"Of course, Sigi, go now while I am surrounded by your doting family. You would think I had invented the bearing of children. You've been most attentive; and I did enjoy the Mark Twain you've been reading to me."

4.

He came into the Anhalter Bahnhof in the late afternoon. Wilhelm Fliess was waiting for him with the *Droschke* which he used for his professional calls and journeys to the hospital. In the privacy of the hansom the two men clasped hands warmly; they had not seen each other since the wedding. Sigmund gazed with pleasure at his friend: the enormous dark eyes burning with the intensity of live coals; the intensely black mustache failing to cover lips as red as the bands of red paint on the trail trees of the Wienerwald; his cheeks glowing with the vitality of youth, "even though," thought Sigmund, "he's only two and a half years younger than I, thirty-four."

"This will be our first real congress," Sigmund exclaimed.

Wilhelm broke into a broad grin, "There are only two of us but we'll unloose a covey of ideas that will fly in swarms over Berlin."

The late April afternoon was still warm. Fliess asked the driver to push back the leather top of the *Droschke:* "I remember that you like Berlin, Sig."

They were headed west toward Charlottenburg, one of the many suburbs from which the city of Berlin had been made up. Sigmund gazed at the people in the streets as they moved along the Tauenzienstrasse; they had serious, almost somber expressions, even those who were walking in pairs and talking. He observed:

"The Viennese are gigglers; the Berliners are frowners. How has Ida oriented herself to becoming a *Berlinerin?*"

"For an eight-month bride I think she has accomplished miracles: she has nothing but German friends, German furniture, even a German cook who would consider it unpatriotic to make a *Wienerschnitzel.* Her only concession to Viennese loyalty is that in our living room there are no pictures of the Kaiser or the Crown Prince or of battle scenes in which the German army is gloriously victorious. She has also formed a little social group, six young married women who meet each afternoon at four in each other's houses for coffee, cake and the latest news of the day: *bassena* talk, she says you call it in Vienna."

The Fliesses had a spacious apartment on the top floor of 4a Wichmannstrasse with a fine view of the Zoological Gardens. When Sigmund stepped into the living room Ida Fliess invited him to sit down on the sofa, the place of honor in every Berlin home. Looking at the Fliesses' heavy somber mahogany furniture, his mind went back to the times he and Martha used to wander the streets of Hamburg, their noses pressed against the windows of the furniture stores, wondering if they would ever be lucky enough to have a home and such solid indestructible *Möbel.*

Ida Fliess had invited the half dozen couples of her *Kaffeeklatsch* for an eight-thirty dinner. The dining-room table was handsomely set with a heavily embroidered cloth. Sigmund noticed with some astonishment that piled in front of each place were five plates of different sizes and, except in front of his own and Wilhelm's places, an opened bottle of wine. Wilhelm explained in an aside that he had two operations early in the morning and that he thought he ought to be sober enough to perform them and that Sigmund ought to be sober enough to watch.

A variety of preserved fruits and sweet pickles was placed in the smallest uppermost of the five plates; a plate disappeared with each course; the butter was molded in the form of sheep, each with a red ribbon around its neck. As the wine level receded in the individual bottles, the noise level rose.

The next morning Wilhelm and Sigmund stood on opposite sides of a small oilcloth-covered table in the corner of the dining room which held freshly baked wheat rolls and a coffeepot on top of its heater, then made the long drive into the center of town, down Unter den Linden, past the university, to the hospital. At the stand-up breakfast and during the ride to the hospital, Wilhelm chatted animatedly, his eyes brilliant with the excitement of the ideas he was discussing, his body quivering with animation under the well-cut gray suit. When the *Droschke* reached the hospital, a different man and a different personality emerged, the eyes hooded, the lips resolutely set, the carriage as stiff as that of the military officers walking in the Königstrasse in their uniforms of dark blue and scarlet. As he entered the hospital and was greeted by the attendants, nurses, by his colleagues and then by his Assistants, his manner was stern, cool. He spoke only those words needed for the preparation of his patients. The magnificent human warmth of Dr. Wilhelm Fliess was frozen inside his skin.

Sigmund watched with admiration the sure, delicate touch of the puncturing instrument as Fliess operated on his first patient, cutting into the bone in the natural opening of the sinus to allow better drainage; and with a second patient, the submucus resection of a septum, the stripping up of the mucosa and cutting away of the cartilage.

After the two operations Wilhelm scrubbed, donned his pearl-gray coat, nodded to his Assistants and nurses in the operating room, and made his way, ramrod-stiff, down the hallways bowing formally to his fellow physicians and administrators. Sigmund did not feel that it would be proper to penetrate this formidable shield even for so pleasant a purpose as complimenting Wilhelm on the artistic beauty of the surgery.

They emerged from the hospital at eleven o'clock. Once in the carriage Wilhelm threw his arm roughly around Sigmund's shoulder and, with eyes wide and laughing, cried, "Now we are free! We can begin our congress. We'll have the driver drop us at the Stadtbahn, it's the fastest way to get out to the Grunewald . . . that's Berlin's equivalent of the Wienerwald, twelve thousand acres with rivers and lakes and a magnificent royal forest. I know every trail and tree. The restaurant where I will take you for dinner, the Belitzhof, is a lovely one on the Wannsee. Attend closely now, it's a six-mile walk if we go as our boots lie, but ten miles by the maze of trails that I've laid out for myself when I need a full day of walking and thinking. What do you say? Can you wait ten miles for your dinner? I have some startling things to tell you."

Sigmund thought, "He's two men; the face he shows one world he never allows the other to see. As Josef Pollak said years ago when he gave that patient a shot of H_2O to cure her paralysis of the legs, 'We are all actors.' "

Fliess waited until they had plunged into the womblike privacy of the dark green forest, the trail comfortably soft underfoot, before he launched into the exposition he had been holding back with considerable difficulty from the moment he met Sigmund at the Anhalter Bahnhof. Hat in hand, his sonorous voice filled the air.

"Sig, you just can't know what it means for me to have you here. My colleagues think of me only as a nose specialist." He gripped Sigmund's left arm. "Do you know what I'm onto through my periodicity figures? A solution for the problem of coitus without contraceptives!"

Sigmund gazed at his friend, puzzled. "Do you mean without conception, as well?"

"Yes, yes, precisely what I mean! I've been working out mathematical formulas based on the menstrual cycle of twenty-eight days. Do you know what I've found? *That women are not equally fertile throughout their monthly cycle.* My statistics, based on the nine months of carrying, vis-à-vis the actual birth date of the child, are now showing some staggering results." He turned in the path, said in a low, passionate tone, "Listen carefully, my friend: there are certain ascertainable periods when women do not secrete the ovum which is fertilized by the male sperm. Once I can establish these definite limits—the number of days immediately preceding and following menstruation—married couples will have a time in which they can engage in intercourse without fear of pregnancy. Think of it, Sig, an end to the *coitus interruptus* which you have found to be the cause of so many neuroses; an end to those cumbersome and unreliable condoms; an end to continence through which happily married couples deny themselves the act of love for months on end; and most important of all, no more unwanted children in this world. Is this not a revolution, if I can bring it off? Would it not be one of the most beneficent medical discoveries of all times?"

Sigmund's thoughts were winging back and forth like hummingbirds who can reverse their line of flight without first stopping their forward movement.

". . . Wilhelm . . . you've staggered me. But can you be sure? Pregnancies vary so much in actual length; so few women hit the precise two-hundred-and-seventy-day carrying period. I see what you're trying to achieve—it's fantastic! You mean to count backward from delivery date to conception date, gathering data which will tell us exactly when, in the monthly cycle, women conceive; and roughly when they cannot, or at least do not . . ."

". . . precisely. Every family will keep its own calendar. According to my present figures—oh, there are years of work ahead perfecting the mathematical formulas—married couples will enjoy about twelve days of freedom every month."

"But what will the Church say? Have you considered that? They do not approve of any form of birth control."

Fliess's eyelids flared with excitement. He had been walking so fast that they now reached the peninsula of Schildhorn, with its monument commemorating the escape of Prince Jaczo from Albert the Bear. He was too involved in his thoughts to point it out. Instead he changed the westerly direction of his interlocking trails and began to swing north, murmuring something about a lovely bay and island where they would have a cup of coffee.

"There's where the miracle gets compounded. I have talked with some of my Catholic colleagues, oh, ever so casually. They agree that this would not constitute birth control in the sense that the use of condoms or douches or the herbs taken by more primitive people definitely is. They do not feel that there would be any sin involved in simply observing a schedule. What do you say, my friend?"

Sigmund shook his head in incredulity.

"Wilhelm, if you can prove this thesis mathematically, there will be a statue erected to you in every town in the Western world."

"Sig, the greatest of all sciences is mathematics; it can prove or disprove anything. With it I can demonstrate the periodicity of every tiny phase of human life. Did you ever suspect that men too go through a continuing cycle? The figures that keep coming in indicate that the male rhythmic cycle is twenty-three days long. There could even be a menstruation involved in this male cycle; not of blood, but of what you have described in your Constancy Principle as surplus energy, or nervous electrical current, so that after a day or two of discharge a whole new cycle commences for the male in which he slowly builds up again from the low point through the twenty-three days to its climax. I have been searching out the diaries, notebooks and journals of great writers and artists. There's no doubt in my mind; the human brain as a creative force does not always work on the same level, either of energy or accomplishment. It works cyclically. Keep a close diary on yourself and you will soon see the outlines of your own cycle emerge."

Sigmund ruminated on this for a time as they sat on the terrace of the Pichelswerder drinking coffee and gazing over the bay with its connecting bridge to the island.

"I haven't seen your evidence, but I have a manic depressive patient who, at the top of her cycle, is lovely, carries herself with pride, her mind penetrating and full of self-confidence. Then slowly from this crest, as the days move on, she falls downhill; her confidence wanes, she shrinks inward, her thoughts lose their clarity, become confused, then scattered. Anxiety sets in, insomnia, loss of appetite, physical pain. . . . At the bottom of the cycle she is a desperately unhappy and unnerved human being with strong suicidal tendencies, given to storms of weeping, self-accusation, violent words and actions against those whom she loved and trusted only a few weeks before. Her face turns ugly, contorted, awkward. . . . Then the long pull up the opposite side of the cycle starts: her energy begins to return, the hallucinations vanish, her mind clears, the anxiety lessens, she resumes her work and social relations. Halfway up the curve she becomes reliable, functioning. From this point on, the last quarter to the top of the cycle, she abounds with love and confidence. At the top there are a few days of exultation . . . then the slow agonizing descent. . . ."

Fliess had been listening with intense concentration.

"Good, good," he cried, "the perfect pathological manifestation of periodicity. Sig, what was the length of the cycle?"

"Damme, I was trying so desperately to get at the cause that I failed to record the time. I would say about eight to ten weeks."

They made their way to the Havel River, then followed its bank to the Kaiser Wilhelm Turm, climbing to the peak for the panoramic view of Potsdam and Berlin. When they reached the Belitzhof Restaurant, overlooking the Wannsee, Sigmund was tired and hungry. Wilhelm ordered their dinner: a *pâté, Bouillon mit Ei*, a baked fish from the Baltic cooked in yellow sugar and served with Algerian potatoes. Sigmund ate his way resoundingly through each course; Fliess barely touched his food, sipping instead slowly from a bottle of Rhine wine.

After dinner they sat on a bench overlooking the Wannsee, the sun warm on their faces. When Sigmund indicated that he was ready, Fliess sprang up, refreshed and rejuvenated.

"A long route back to the station, or the short? I'll need time to present another thesis. I have the first half in manuscript but the second sorely needs thinking out. Follow me closely, friend, for I shall be treading on marshy soil."

Sigmund laughed. "'Lay on, Macduff, and damn'd be him that first cries, 'Hold, enough!' I will mark with blue pencil the parts that should go to the barber's."

Fliess smiled impatiently; he was an ardent listener as well as talker, but he could not mix the two antithetical ingredients.

"Sig, I'm invading your field; under the heading of Nasal Reflex Neurosis. You told me of a teen-age girl whose form of hysteria was menstruating from the nose. That is entirely understandable because there is a definite relationship between the mucous membrane of the nose and of the uterus. Did you know that the nose contains erectile tissue? I've measured it in my own patients. The nasal mucous membrane swells with genital excitement during intercourse, and during menstruation. What's more, the monthly cycle of the male as well as the female is connected with the mucous lining of the nose. More important from your point of view, almost all nasal irritations are a reflection of neurotic symptoms, in particular sexual repressions or irregularities. Every nose has a genital spot in its interior. I have been able to lessen the pain of menstruation by treating the nose; miscarriage can also be brought about by anesthetizing the nose with cocaine, whose propensities you discovered. Sig, the nose is the center of the human face and hence the human universe. You look puzzled; very well, I will prove that the rhythmic change in the mucus of the nose corresponds to the mucus of the vaginal tract. . . ."

5.

The next morning after standing at the oilcloth-covered table to have their rolls and coffee they left for a walk in the Tiergarten quarter, three blocks from the Fliess apartment, the most fashionable residential neighborhood in Berlin, with its rare, self-contained houses standing in gardens of their own. This, explained Fliess, was where he would like to live and raise his family. It was eight o'clock and the chimes of a dozen churches summoned the Sunday worshipers. They would have six hours before the family *Droschke* brought Ida, at two o'clock, to the most popular weekend restaurant in Berlin, Kroll's in the Königsplatz, opposite the not quite completed Reichstag. It was Sigmund's turn to address the congress.

"Start talking, Sig; I will surround you with a hundred ears."

Sigmund chuckled. Wilhelm's enthusiasm was infectious.

"My dear Wilhelm, you have already read drafts A and B of my Anxiety Neurosis, and so I cannot startle you the way you did me yesterday, but I have made tremendous progress in my thinking since I wrote you last. . . ."

"Make your case. No one makes my thoughts fly as fast. . . ."

"What is an anxiety neurosis? It is a clinical entity characterized by general irritability, worried expectation, fright without any associated idea, passing physical attacks such as palpitations, inability to breathe, vertigo, night sweats, tremor and shivering, diarrhea . . ."

He had learned from his practice that anxiety originated in some physical factor in sexual life. He had found it in virgin girls who received sexual information inadvertently or under inauspicious circumstances, and in virginal boys when they began having erections about which they understood nothing. It arose in people deliberately abstemious; in those who regarded anything sexual as an abomination, who translated their anxiety into respectable phobias such as excessive love of cleanliness. He had found it in women who were neglected by their husbands; in men suffering from *ejaculatio praecox*, who were unable to hold back an orgasm until its fulfilling moment. It was present in men married to women who disgusted them; who were in fact offended by the female genital organ and the need to penetrate it. He had found it in those people who thought or had been told that they had no need for coitus but only for love in its spiritual form.

They strode along at a good pace, one that fitted the rhythm of Sigmund's thought; not nearly at Fliess's breakneck speed of the day before. Nor did Sigmund's voice ring out in the clear air as had Wilhelm's. He spoke in a professional tone, affixing his arguments one to the other with logic as though they were tiles being set in the cement of a mural mosaic.

"Going back to the Constancy Principle, Wilhelm, each individual has his own threshold. In normal circumstances the physical sexual tension leads to aroused psychical libido, which leads to copulation. However where intercourse is not available or is psychically rejected, a transformation takes place, there is a deficiency in sexual libido: we have an accumulation of physical sexual tension and an anxiety neurosis. My male patients confide that since becoming anxious they have no sexual desires. Instead they develop shortness of breath, intracranial pressures, spinal irritation, constipation, flatulence. Women suffer the kind of anxious expectation which converts a child's or a husband's cold into pneumonia; they hear the hearse going by. The symptoms abound in every doctor's office in every city: vomiting, giddiness, inability to walk; fainting fits, the constant need to urinate, ravenous hunger. Then there are the phobias and obsessions: fear of snakes, of thunderstorms, of the dark, of vermin; *folie de doute* which paralyzes the confidence in one's train of thought.

"I've handled a goodly number of patients now, and I've read case histories in five languages. Certainly there are purely somatic causes for a variety of physical illnesses; the hospitals are full of them. Yet I would be obliged now to say that a large part of such illness is psychically induced. If we can find ways to cure the endemic frustrations involved in man's sexual nature we can reduce mental and emotional illness and help in areas of physical affliction as well."

They had come to the Neuer See. Wilhelm explained that he and Ida ice-skated here in the winter.

"Sig, how are you planning to curb the sexual ills of this world?"

"A cure is always after the fact; valuable, God knows, to the patient who is enabled to live a reasonably normal life. But it is modern society that creates the illness in the first place: by its deceits and hypocrisies, its concept that there is something evil and dirty about one of the most natural and basic acts the human being can perform. Among people where sexual activity is natural and omnipresent, there are none of these neurotic ills."

"True, Sig," Fliess insisted. "But until you can reform contemporary society and release the sexual act from its chains in the Fools' Tower, how do you propose to proceed?"

They crossed a broad riding path lined with tall trees whose boughs met overhead. Berlin's brilliantly accoutered cavaliers, sitting their mounts with ramrod precision, were cantering stylishly.

"By finding the normal in the abnormal. By learning everything about the unconscious mind, how it works and how it controls the individual; and then by establishing understanding and scientific measurements by means of which a person can know in his conscious mind what the censor is refusing to make manifest in the unconscious, thereby freeing himself from a cruel master. How do we prevent sexual noxae from taking hold? The ideal alternative would be free intercourse between young males and respectable girls, which could only be resorted to if there were innocuous preventive methods. Your method, Wilhelm, would serve as a releasing agent. In the absence of a healthy attitude toward sexuality, our society seems doomed to fall a victim to ever increasing neuroses which reduce the enjoyment of life, destroy male and female relationships and bring hereditary ruin on the coming generation."

Walking along the banks of the Spree, they came to the ocher-yellow Bellevue Palace, with a row of statues ornamenting the central façade. In the wooded park in the rear the benches were occupied by guardsmen and nursemaids embracing ardently.

"I tell you, my dear Wilhelm, the physician is faced by a problem whose solution deserves all his effort."

He returned to Vienna stimulated and refreshed, to find that Martha and his infant daughter were doing so well that he celebrated by taking Martha to see a ballet of *Around the World in Eighty Days* in a Volkstheater in the Prater, and then to supper in the Restaurant Eisvogel. Sigmund told her about the Fliesses and how they lived in Berlin but nothing of Wilhelm's theories. He did describe Fliess's "split personality." Martha exclaimed, "He is at the head of his profession, why need he pretend when he is with his colleagues?"

"It isn't pretense, my dear, it is simply another of the masks that humans wear. Bernheim said, 'We are all hallucinating creatures.' Speaking of split lives, shall we rent the same villa in Reichenau for the summer? I won't need to be in Vienna more than three days a week. I'll work in the mornings; in the afternoons we can go for long walks in the woods, hunt mushrooms . . ."

Martha glanced about her quickly to see that no one would notice, then kissed him on the cheek. "Oh, Sigi, I would like that, let's go early, in June, and come back late, not until October. It's good for the children to have you with them."

Try as he might, he was unable to see anything of Josef Breuer. Josef's practice was at its zenith. He was continually being summoned to the capitals of Europe on urgent cases. He simply had no time to talk to Sigmund about their proposed book on the hysterias; and so Sigmund could do no work on it. In July he picked up a copy of a French medical journal and found that Dr. Pierre Janet, who occupied an important position at the Salpêtrière, had praised *Preliminary Communication* in the highest terms . . . as confirming his own research and deductions.

He camped in Josef's library until he caught him. To his astonishment, Josef was as delighted as a child over Janet's praise.

"This is excellent, Sig. Pierre Janet is on his way to becoming the best neurologist in France. His support can be critical when it comes to controversial theses such as ours."

Sigmund smiled at his friend's use of the word "ours." Twice since the paper had been published, Josef had referred to the work as "your."

"Josef, now that we have confirmation that we're on the right track, why could we not go forward with the book itself? The only way we can convince the medical fraternity is by setting forth our case records; they demonstrate the truth of our theories."

"Yes, Sig, I think the time has arrived. Why not write up your major cases and let me see how they come out? Remember, discretion above all; we must protect our patients. I could never permit anyone to suspect that my Anna O. is in reality Bertha Pappenheim. . . ."

In August, Professor Jean Martin Charcot died suddenly. Sigmund wrote a glowing tribute which was published in the *Wiener medizinische Wochenschrift* and earned him praise in both German and French medical circles.

The woods around Reichenau were green and cool. Sigmund taught his children the lore of mushrooms and how to find them in their clever hiding places. There was a prize for the one who gathered the best haul. After an early supper he read to them from Hans Christian Andersen or Grimm's fairy tales, played "tongue twisters": *Wiener washerwomen wash white washing.* Each night he said the good-night prayer with them, even fifteen-month-old Ernst struggling valiantly with the words.

> I am tired, I lie down,
> I close my eyes.
> Father, let Your eyes guard my bed.
> All those that are near to me,
> Let them rest in Your care.
> All the people big and small
> I commend to You.

The number of days he spent in the city depended on how crowded his Neurological Department was at the Kassowitz Institute, since no new cases of neurosis came to his consultation room during the caldronlike months. Sigmund greeted the customary hiatus with an ironic smile. "The mountains, forests and cool green lakes do more for them than I can in this scorching heat." But there were always afflicted children and mothers with pain-laden eyes. Many came to his consultation room, referred by other doctors, by the departments in the Allgemeine Krankenhaus, some, whose children had suffered relapses or alarming progressions, from the Institute itself. He was proud to be a good children's neurologist, and continually heartbroken that there was so little in the range of his medical science that could be of any appreciable help.

6.

They returned during the first cool days of October. Sigmund found a lively practice awaiting him: a near frigid young husband suffering from colitis; a young wife so frightened at having a baby that she developed hysterical anxieties as night fell; a woman of thirty-five who was deathly afraid of going into a store unless accompanied. A few months earlier she had entered a shop where two salesmen appeared to laugh at her because of her clothing; the humiliation was the greater because one of the salesmen had seemed attractive to her. She had run out of the shop with an affect of fright. Under Sigmund's probing, the fact emerged that the patient had been not only well dressed but in rigorous good taste. The fantasy had to be screening another more serious memory. He was able to lead the patient back to the time she was eight, when she had gone into a candy store alone. The proprietor had fingered her genitals through her clothing. She had run away, frightened; only to return a week later. The proprietor, taking her presence as a signal of assent, had stroked her genitals for a considerable time. The repressed memory had now reemerged in an acute anxiety. Was it the assault itself that had caused the noxa? . . . no, she admitted after several sessions, it was that she had returned a second time and felt guilty of wanting to be assaulted. That was why she was now afraid to go into shops alone: not because the salesmen would laugh at her clothing but because she might want a desirable one to stroke her. Guilt plus fear created anxiety.

A medical student was sent to him from the university; he had violated his sister, murdered his cousin, set fire to the family home. It took only a cursory check for Sigmund to learn that the cousin was alive and well, the house untouched, the sister unharmed. He searched for the actual situation that was causing the overpowering sense of guilt; and found it in the medical student's compulsive masturbation. Why was the young man so mentally stricken by this lesser sin that he was willing to substitute publicly the confession of incest and murder? The doctor frankly could not tell; but he thought he knew a cure:

"Find yourself a woman with whom you can have normal intercourse, even if you have to use the money you're now spending for food. You can afford to lose twenty to thirty pounds in weight, they are recoverable; but not your sanity."

He wrote to Fliess, "The patients go away impressed and convinced, after exclaiming: 'No one has ever asked me that before!'"

Most doctors had known or suspected that they had patients whose ills were caused by sexual problems. Yet the subject had been *verboten*: Privatdozent Dr. Sigmund Freud was the first to throw a beam of light into the dark chamber. His success was helped by the absolute privacy of the *Parterre*, with no maid, family or other patient present. The scholarly, almost monklike austerity of the consultation room freed the afflicted ones to dig deeper into their unknown memories. Dr. Sigmund Freud had precisely the right temperament for this delicate confessional: grave, sober, studious, concerned, impersonal, a quiet family man, bourgeois, proper, moral to his fingertips, discreet, handling the most indelicate revelations in the cool manner of the scientist. He sat across from the patient in his formal physician's uniform: black coat and heavy vest with the gold watch chain strung across it, white shirt and collar with the black tie tucked under it, slightly graying hair and beard, impersonal dark eyes, creating an ambience of credence and trust in his methods and motives.

A long letter arrived from Eli Bernays in New York. He was entrenched in the Produce Exchange, had a growing income and was enclosing a draft for Sigmund's sister Pauli to bring his two daughters to New York. Eli's bank draft was sufficiently ample to buy new outfits for the girls and Pauli as well, also to buy a trunk and valises. Pauli came to supper bringing eight-year-old Judith Bernays. Pauli asked if she might talk to her brother. He took her into the study.

"Sigi, I didn't want to tell Mama and Papa before I had your consent. I'd like to stay in New York and not come back."

Sigmund studied his sister's face. She was not pretty but she had good features and was pleasant to look at, just as the girl herself was an amiable companion. Yet she was approaching thirty and was still unmarried.

"You're not unhappy, Pauli?"

"No, not unhappy." Her expression was calm. "Just . . . unfulfilled. I should be married by now and have a couple of children. But there just haven't been any chances. It's all right for Rosa, she has admirers, she can marry any time she wants. But Vienna seems to have passed me by."

"The more stupid they!"

Pauli shrugged. "I don't want to be a spinster. Eli writes that men arrive in New York alone from all over the world and are soon looking for wives. I'd like to try my fortune."

Sigmund put his arm around his sister's shoulder. "Then you must stay on as long as you like. I will send you pocket money each month so that you can feel independent."

Pauli kissed him. "And will you tell Mama and Papa, please?"

"I'll tell them. But not all at once. Each month that you stay on, I'll cut off another piece of the dog's tail. In that way you'll be free to come back if you wish; and if you should marry, then it will be obvious that you will remain there."

Soon he had his one hundred cases of anxiety neuroses assembled and documented. Not all were clear-cut; sometimes a patient came for help who had half a dozen maladies with no discernible sexual problem. He recorded these in good faith, even when they weakened his hypothesis. A case that stumped him was that of a forty-two-year-old man with children of seventeen, sixteen and thirteen. He had tolerated *coitus interruptus* for ten years without ill effects but six years before, at the death of his father, he had come down with an attack of anxiety so violent that he was convinced he had cancer of the tongue, heart disease, agoraphobia and dyspepsia. The patient kept repeating:

"With my father dead I suddenly realized that it was my turn next. Now I am the father; I am no longer a son; soon my sons will be mourning me. I never thought of death before my father went, and now I think about it all the time."

"Every man owes nature a death," Sigmund observed; "from the beginning of time it has been man's deepest concern. Even in our sophisticated society the fear of death is an omnipresent emotion. So you see, you are only being normal in your dread. But what is not normal is your fear of cancer and heart failure; here are the reports from the specialists I sent you to. Your tongue and your heart are in excellent condition. From your physical examination I would say that you have many years to live. Do you know what hypochondria is . . . ?"

He could not tell whether special kinds of cases came to him in cycles or simply that he had a new insight which enabled him to diagnose more deeply and learn things about his patients that he had not been able to perceive before, ideas which a few months earlier might have seemed outlandish conjectures. As with each succeeding layer of the buried cities of Troy, he was becoming able to document the remains of an earlier civilization. He was fulfilling Professor Charcot's injunction that he become a see-er. He was treating as many as eight neurosis patients a day. Since each patient was given almost the total hour, saving only enough time to get out unseen and the next patient to arrive undetected, he got Dr. Oskar Rie and Rie's brother-in-law, Dr. Ludwig Rosenstein, to take over some of his hours at the Kassowitz Institute.

The new revelation he named the *neuropsychosis of defense*. He marked this down as an acquired hysteria. From the cases at hand he saw that this "defense" arose when something took place in the ideational life of the patient which was incompatible with the rest of the ego. What he now called an act of defense consisted in the banishment of the unwelcome and insufferable idea, the ego in its defensive attitude labeling it non-existent, and the effort of the patient to turn a powerfully disturbing thought into a weak one which could not disturb him, attempting in fact to deplete the noxious notion of its affect, the sum of excitation or energy with which it was loaded. In the light of the Constancy Principle this nervous energy, this psychical excitation which had been taken away from the unwelcome idea, had to be put to use somewhere, discharged through another concept and another channel.

Hysterics utilized a process which he now named *conversion;* they transformed their excitation into a somatic seizure. With these patients, men and women alike, the repressed ideas had not been "pushed away" as his women patients told him they had done, but had taken on a different form: the rejected idea was replaced by one which was not in itself incompatible to their ego. This was how obsessions and phobias arose. It was a form of defense, unconscious in the making, which enabled the patient to pay off his debt, sometimes at usurious rates of interest. In no case did the patient understand that the obsession or phobia was a substitution for the original unacceptable idea, which had retreated into the unconscious, *or that it would stay alive as long as the originating noxious material was not dissolved or dispelled!*

And here too he found, as with his anxiety cases, the originating idea which had been repressed and reconverted into an obsession or phobia had in almost every case had a sexual origin. The cases immediately at hand made the conclusion inescapable.

A woman of twenty was suffering from a peculiar disturbance: whatever crime she read about in the *Neue Freie Presse* in the morning, she transliterated during the passing hours into her own act of guilt. If a murder had been committed in the Prater, it was she who had stabbed the victim; if there had been a robbery in a store, she was the one who had stolen the jewels; if someone had set a house on fire, she was the arsonist. She felt morally obliged to confess the crime. When it was pointed out that she could not have committed these deeds, since half a dozen people knew that she was at home at the time of the robbery or murder or arson, she acknowledged that this was true but by the next morning was again obsessed with self-reproach.

Sigmund gently touched the young woman's forehead, asked her to concentrate on the event or person that came into her mind. Cooperation was difficult to secure, but the family was persistent. Sigmund stayed with his task until weeks later the girl blurted out the fact that a somewhat older woman had led her into joint masturbating. This relationship and practice had grown with the passage of time until one night, coming home with the older woman from a formal ball, the younger partner had engaged in such intense masturbation that she became disturbed. Because of her sense of immorality and sin, she had been unable to confess her wrongdoing to anyone. As a defense, the guilt was supplanted by substitute self-reproaches; it was now possible to confess that she was doing wrong every day . . . and to allow the psychic energy to pour off in discharges of false recrimination.

A simultaneous case was that of a young woman who had been raised in a rigorously prudish fashion. She had been made to believe that everything concerned with sex was dirty and "bad," and had determined never to marry. Her phobia took the form of a psychical dread that she would be overtaken by the need to urinate and wet herself; it had become so strong that in the past year she had been unable to leave her home to go shopping, to the theater or to any kind of social gathering. She felt secure only when she was in her own home, a few steps from a water closet. She faced the prospect of becoming a total recluse.

Sigmund sent her to a urologist. He could find nothing wrong with the woman's bladder, kidneys, urinary tract or uterus. Her fear, Sigmund decided, was a defense which had supplanted another idea or experience which was less acceptable to her.

But how to find it? Weeks of daily free association provided no clue. His own mind produced no trenchant idea. Light pressure on the young woman's forehead failed to bring forth any significant data. Her attitude was that she would kill herself before discussing anything connected with the dread sexuality.

Patience paid off. Eventually there stuttered from the woman's unwilling lips the truth. She had gone to a concert at the Musikvereinsgebäude and had seen, sitting a few seats away, a man whom she liked and who, against her will, excited her. She fell into the fantasy that she was his wife, sitting beside him at the concert. Suddenly she experienced a strong sexual sensation and felt an immediate and irresistible need to urinate full force. She had had to stumble over people sitting beside her and run jerkily up the aisle to the ladies' room, where she discovered some wetting of her underpants. In the days that followed a sense of guilt verging on revulsion overcame her; she determined never to think of the man again. Yet she fell into exotic reveries centered around him, and sometimes other men who pleased her, always with the resultant imperative to urinate.

As a physician Sigmund had three tasks to perform; first, to identify the psychical need to "urinate"; second, to connect it with her healthy sexual nature; third, to convince the young woman that those who had poisoned her mind against the sexuality of love had been wrong; that sexual intercourse between people who desired each other, particularly within the security and emotional well-being of marriage, was a creative act of meaning and lasting satisfaction.

It proved to be a laborious process, drops of water trickling down through layers of incrustation to be dissolved by the oft-repeated word, phrase, sentence, bit of logic. Sigmund combined monumental patience with the grave face and manner of the schoolmaster in order to convince her that his philosophy was right, proper and livable. Then the patient met a young man whom both she and her family admired; plans for marriage were drawn . . . the patient radiantly announced herself cured.

Another case was that of a woman married for five years, with one child; "happily married, Herr Doktor. Everyone agrees," who for the past eighteen months had been obsessed with the wish to throw herself out of a window or off the balcony of her apartment. The impulse had become so pronounced that she had been forced to lock the balcony door and to put chairs in front of the windows. Each time she went into the kitchen and saw a sharp knife she became obsessed with the idea that she would stab her baby with it. She was distraught at the idea that she might commit suicide and leave her child motherless; or that she might murder the baby.

"Herr Doktor, what has happened to me?"

"Frau Oehler, the answer must lie in your unhappiness. No young, happy person has the idea of throwing herself out of a window or of stabbing her child."

"But what have I to be unhappy about?"

"My professional guess, Frau Oehler, is that you are unhappy with your marriage. Now let us talk honestly as physician and patient: what is wrong with your marriage, so wrong that you want to destroy both yourself and the fruit of that union? Lie down here on this couch, if you will. Please tell me exactly what comes into your mind. Make no attempt to censor your visions or thoughts."

There was a long silence; then Frau Oehler whispered, "The sensation of some . . . object . . . being forced . . . under my skirt."

"You know what that object is, of course?"

". . . yes."

"Then please tell me about your marriage."

The young woman burst into tears. She cried, "I almost never have intercourse with my husband. He does not want me that way. The few times that he tries, he can never bring it off. This has been going on for three years now, ever since the baby was born. But why should that bring ideas of suicide to my mind, since I am not a sensual person and I do not miss marital intercourse?"

"You never have erotic fantasies when you see or are with other men, those of whom you think highly?"

". . . yes . . . erotic ideas . . . that's when I feel something . . . forcing itself under my skirt. That makes me so ashamed of myself and I think I ought to be punished, that I ought to die. . . ."

"Frau Oehler, I would not be a proper physician if I did not admit that you have a serious problem. I realize that divorce is not possible for people of your faith. You must somehow find a way to bring your husband to the sexual act more frequently and more successfully. In this I cannot help you. However I can and must help you get rid of your obsession about suicide and the killing of your child. Your mind has set up this obsession in place of what you think is the more reprehensible sin of having erotic feelings toward strange men. You must no longer delude yourself that you do not miss marital intercourse. If you will face the idea that you have vigorous sexual needs which are going unsatisfied, and that it is not a sin for which you can be blamed or cast out of decent society, then you will get rid of this other obsession which is challenging your sanity."

"I think I understand . . . at least a little. What you are saying is that when I do have erotic desires toward other men I need not regard myself as depraved . . . or think I should be punished, so that I want to throw myself out of a window or stab my child. All I do need to know is that I have this erotic feeling because it's normal to have erotic feelings, and I must find a way to help my husband love me."

"Yes, Frau Oehler, that is precisely what I am saying. It is up to you to keep these thoughts straight in your conscious mind. . . ."

With another patient he failed completely. It was a young girl who was in love with a man who, she thought, returned her affection. The truth was that he had come to her home for other purposes. When the girl learned this, she became disappointed, depressed, and then ill. On the day of a big family reunion she convinced herself that the young man would attend and that he was coming to see her. She told her family so. She waited throughout the day and by nightfall had fallen into what Sigmund described as a "state of hallucinatory confusion": she believed the man had arrived, she heard him come singing through the garden, she rushed down in her nightgown to welcome him . . . During the following months she believed he was at her side, that he had declared his love, that they were going to be married. She was happy in this unreality. Any attempt to disrupt the fantasy on the part of her family or Dr. Freud returned her to her earlier depression. She had apparently gone too far to be brought back to normal.

Sigmund tried to explain the phenomenon to her heartbroken parents: the intolerable idea of having been rejected had taken control; it was so bitterly unacceptable that her unconscious mind in an act of defense had created a more acceptable world for her to live in. Through her obsession that the young man loved her and was near her, she was able to discharge the nervous energies that she had been unwilling or unable to discharge in the repressed idea of being unwanted.

In his notes he wrote: "So long as the patients are aware of the sexual origin of their obsessions, they often keep them secret . . . they usually express their astonishment that they should be subject to the affect in question, that they should feel anxiety or have certain impulses. . . . No insane asylum is without what must be regarded as analogous examples: the mother who has fallen ill from the loss of her baby and now rocks a piece of wood unceasingly in her arms; or the jilted bride who, arrayed in her wedding dress, has for years been waiting for her bridegroom."

7.

A middle-aged, heavy-set, almost square-headed undersecretary of the Austrian government came to him. He was being persecuted. When Sigmund asked by whom, he replied:

"By everyone. By all of the people in my office. By strangers who sit near me in the cafes. By passers-by on the street. By my family and friends. They accuse me of the most horrible crimes."

"How do you know they are talking about you?"

"Because I hear their voices. I have developed this uncanny knack. I can hear them talking even though they are in the next room or across the street. They accuse me of stealing documents from my office and selling them to the enemy. Of ordering shoddy clothing to be sent to the army and buying poisoned food for the troops."

"But you are not guilty of any of these things, Herr Müller. You are well respected in the Ministry."

"Then why is the world conspiring against me?"

"Herr Müller, no one is conspiring against you. The voices you hear are your own."

The man stared at the doctor with his mouth open.

"What are you saying? I don't talk to myself. I'm not insane. I recognize the voices."

"The voices are coming from the back of your mind."

"Why would I talk to myself? Why would I make these accusations when I know I am innocent of crime?"

"You have become obsessed with the idea of guilt. My treatment will consist of trying to find out what you genuinely feel guilty about."

Considerable time passed before Sigmund learned that Herr Müller, who was a married man with a family, had picked up a young prostitute in the Prater and come down with a case of gonorrhea. Unwilling to confess this to his family doctor, he had infected his wife. What all those voices were trying to say, Sigmund deduced, was not that he was a traitor or embezzler, but an immoral man who had brought havoc upon himself and his family. Sigmund persuaded him that he had to confess to his wife and take them both to a urologist. Herr and Frau Müller were cured of the gonorrhea, but the accusatory voices continued to pursue Herr Müller!

Sigmund was chagrined and crestfallen; he was certain his theory was right, though its application had failed. Apparently the gonorrhea was too recent a "crime" to have induced the voices. He delved deeper into Müller's past, but all he could come up with were certain underlying fears of the father, combined with nameless anxieties and hostilities toward the elder Herr Müller. It was almost as though the patient was carrying on his back a bundle of formidable guilts about his father, yet careful inquiry proved that he had been a good and generous son. Sigmund was unable to solve the problem.

Failures follow seasons of their own: a well-educated, soft-spoken man of thirty brought him a different obsession. Since the death of his father, he had had to keep off the streets of Vienna because he had an overpowering desire to kill every man he passed. For fear of giving in to his murderous impulses he locked himself into his apartment for days on end, practically terminating his career. On those occasions when he was obliged to pass through a street, he felt it imperative to know where every person had disappeared to so that he could be certain he had not disposed of the body. As with the young woman who had imagined she had created every crime reported in the *Neue Freie Presse*, he thought himself the "hunted murderer" written about in the newpapers.

Sigmund could find no solution, though whenever the analysis led back to the young man's childhood there emerged the giant figure of the father: harsh in nature, severe in discipline. The son had not loved his father, in fact had been antagonistic for much of his life; how then, Sigmund asked himself, could the death of the man so obsess the son that he wanted to kill every stranger he passed in the street? Intuitively he knew there had to be a connection between this case and that of Herr Müller and his voices, with the father the common denominator. At the moment he could not fathom what it was. It was an area to be researched!

One morning he received a patient sent by an associate at the Kassowitz Institute. An otherwise intelligent girl, she so hated the servants in her mother's household that she quarreled with them until they either quit or were fired. The situation created almost intolerable household difficulties. She was brought in by her mother.

"Could you tell me your reason for the feeling of hatred you have for these servants?" he asked after he had made her comfortable. "And you must give me the honest reason; one does not deceive one's physician."

"It's the coarseness of these girls!" she spat out. "They have spoiled my entire idea of love. I know what they do when they have their day off. They have sexual intercourse with any soldier or workman they pick up. How can one think beautifully of love-making when one knows it is being so vulgarly engaged in?"

Sigmund had to think about the answer for some time. It was, he knew, honest insofar as the young woman had any answer to give in her conscious mind. However he believed the idea was a defensive one, screening another which was unacceptable and intolerable to remember, giving her the avenue for discharging psychical energies which had become overloaded and overheated.

"Please lie down here on the couch. I will sit behind you. And do not look at the books or the art works on the wall. Look back into your own life. Into the past, where I believe the problem lies. Tell me the one most vivid episode of your childhood."

The young woman said little and what came out was censored and unusable. Sigmund became frustrated, tried false starts, asked irrelevant questions, pushed the patient too hard, which increased her sense of hostility and belligerence. This had happened before; where the failure to establish communication had been his fault rather than the patient's, because he had begun with preconceived notions about the case or had failed to recognize clues until it was too late to implement them. He would grow exasperated with himself, bemoan his lack of skill . . . until he remembered the line from the Italian: "The most beautiful word in any language is 'Yes.' The most useful word is 'Patience.'" Not for a full month could he get her to face the scene that possessed her.

". . . I see my mother . . . another man . . . not my father . . . in bed . . . making love . . . naked, both of them . . . I can see all the sights, hear all the animal sounds . . . so coarse and vulgar . . . they made me ill."

Sigmund replied in a dull voice, "So it might have anyone. It was an unfortunate circumstance that you had to encounter this. Did it turn you against your mother?"

". . . no. I loved her tenderly. At first I thought I would have to move out, go to my grandmother. I could not bear to look at her. But I could not leave my mother. She was the dearest person in the world to me."

"But don't you see the kind of transposition you have made? You're not really angry with the maids. You don't believe that they coarsen or vulgarize love. Someone had defiled love for you, but it was someone of whom you could not force yourself to remember the defiling. As a defense you obliterated this image and replaced it with the image of servant girls and their soldiers. Surely by now you can find it in your heart to forgive your mother; or at least to understand her? It could have been a period in her life when she was unhappy. You could not have understood then, you were too young. You are a grown woman and should be able to have compassion for her. Once you can achieve this you can face the repressed image and dismiss it. With that the obsession about the maids should vanish."

It did; but not until Dr. Freud had explained and rephrased his strictures every day for a second month. The mother returned to pay the bill, saying, "I don't know how you accomplished this, Herr Doktor, but it is a godsend to our entire family."

That afternoon he acquired a new patient, a woman who washed her hands thirty, forty times a day, and who would touch nothing in her house unless she had gloves on. It was an aggravated case of fear of dirt but by no means the first one that had walked into his office. He asked, "Frau Planck, how long has it been since you either saw *Macbeth* or read about Lady Macbeth?"

"Herr Doktor, I don't get the connection."

"Do you recall that when Lady Macbeth conspired to murder the king she forever after tried to wash the blood off? 'All the perfumes of Arabia will not sweeten this little hand.'"

"Are you suggesting that I have murdered someone?"

"Oh no. Shakespeare meant that symbolically. Do you wash any other part of your body as often as you do your hands?"

The woman's cheeks flushed a burnt scarlet. She replied insolently: "What conceivable business can it be of yours how often I wash other parts of my body?"

He refused to take offense.

"Frau Planck, you have just answered my question."

"Very well," she flared. "I wash my genitals every half hour. What relation has that to my nervous condition?"

"It's a symptom. Surely you must know that you are not trying to wash away dirt?"

"What then am I trying to wash away?" Belligerently.

"Guilt."

Frau Planck stared at him wide-eyed for a long moment, then burst into tears. But she would not talk; not until many sessions later.

"How could you possibly know?"

"Because I have had other cases of mysophobia, fear of dirt, and all of them resulted from some kind of moral transgression which a patient is unable to face and is working to rid from his conscious memory."

She replied in a hoarse voice: "I was unfaithful to my husband. I met a man who, for a short period, had a kind of horrible fascination for me. For about two months, in the afternoons, I met him in his room."

"And it's this infidelity which you have been trying to banish from your mind?"

"I felt nothing but remorse. But one cannot live with remorse night and day, not if one has a home and a husband and children and parents to care for. I was determined to push the episode far back in my mind."

"I had a patient here earlier today who said to me, 'Something very disagreeable happened to me once and I tried very hard to put it away from me and not think about it any more. I succeeded at last; but then I got this other disturbance which I have not been able to get rid of.' Your obsession with dirt represents a substitute or surrogate for the incompatible memory. But you are suffering more from your obsession than you would from the guilt. Has the time not arrived to face up squarely to what you have done, to forgive yourself and set yourself free for service to your husband and children? If you allow this obsession to grow it will literally devour your sanity. If you feel that you cannot forgive yourself and put down your sense of guilt, perhaps you ought to confess the episode to your husband. It will be painful, but most men and women who love each other manage to resolve the problem. This too could free you."

And so they came, the old and the young, the well to do and the poor, male and female, the afflicted ones who had never before been able to talk to a doctor. The young man who could not defecate, though his bowels and anus were normal; and who Sigmund finally learned had from some kind of childhood confusion developed the phobia that defecation was analogous to ejaculation from the male organ, an act which was repugnant to him. The woman who was suffering from arithmomania; who felt obliged to count every step as she mounted it, every board in the floor she crossed, even to count as she urinated to see if she could get up to the number one hundred. It emerged that this too was a defense act, one designed to keep her thoughts constantly busy so she would not think tempting sexual thoughts which had begun to possess her as the years passed and no love or marriage was proffered. There was the young man who had been seduced anally by an older male cousin and who in his guilt had taken a clumsy but similar revenge on his younger sister. He was now obsessed with the idea that the police knew about his crime, were watching him day and night through peepholes. He saw police officers everywhere he turned; was compelled to walk to the station four and five times a day to confess, only to flee at the last moment in terror.

Then there was the woman who was obsessed with snakes; she saw them come alive in the legs of chairs and tables, even as had Bertha Pappenheim and Frau Emmy von Neustadt; her hair ribbons were converted into snakes, as were pieces of string, belts . . . Sigmund and Josef Breuer had independently reached the concept that the snake was the primary sexual symbol, a surrogate for the extended penis. Women who felt guilty at conjuring up such fantasies and desires converted the image of the phallus into a snake. Sigmund had also concluded from the evidence of his patients and a reading of literature that the box was the universal sexual symbol for the womb.

8.

He was living at the top of his bent. Sometimes the penetrating concepts came with such lightninglike speed and clarity that it seemed as though his mind would explode. At times he became uneasy and even frightened at his unorthodoxy, the heretical concepts which, he sensed, would bring the wrath of society down upon his head once he published the materials. Then he would develop a migraine headache, or the mucous membranes of his nose would swell and he would be unable to breathe. When the pain grew too intense he dropped a little cocaine into the nasal cavity, as Fliess had advised, and in fact as Fliess himself did when his nose gave him trouble. Fliess had had a nose operation performed by Dr. Gersuny on his last visit to Vienna; and on one of Sigmund's visits to Berlin had persuaded Sigmund to let him perform a curetting operation which had given him considerable relief. He thought how strange it was that he and Wilhelm Fliess, so alike in their creative temperaments, shared the same physical ailments. Could there be a connection?

He could not discover enough hours in the day for all the work that had to be done, staying up until two in the morning to complete his manuscript on The Psychoneuroses of Defense; and to begin another called Obsessions and Phobias, all of them resulting from his cases of the past years. Martha did not mind, she saw what a creative ferment he was in; how fulfilled he was with his progress. They had already rented a villa in the mountains for the "summer refresher" and she would have him largely to herself. The only thing she asked was that he not work downstairs in the Parterre at night, but bring his papers upstairs and work in the parlor or on the outside porch if it were warm enough, so that she would feel the comfort of his presence.

A number of doctors were referring cases to him when other neurologists had failed. He now had twelve patients a day, starting at eight in the morning and going through until nine at night except for those afternoons when he worked at the Kassowitz Institute. Since he allowed only five minutes between patients, he did not even bother to have a cup of coffee brought to him. After supper he returned to his desk for several hours to write down the content of each patient's revelations and its meaning in the over-all picture of the neurosis.

As a physician he was not supposed to become emotionally involved with his patients, any more than he had in the Allgemeine Krankenhaus wards. It was necessary for him, as doctor as well as scientist, to remain detached so that he could best handle the chaotic materials, yet he underwent severe mental and emotional strain and was hard pressed not to feel what Aristotle had declared to be the basis of authentic tragedy: pity and terror.

How could he not feel for these unfortunate creatures? Particularly when they moved into a *transference* in which Dr. Freud became the mother or father, the uncle or aunt, sister or brother of ten to forty years before, overwhelmed with tears, entreaties, accusatory diatribes, of having denied them love, caused them anguish by real or fancied brutality or neglect . . . the storm-swept re-enactment of the crucial scenes of infancy and childhood, the traumas which were being relived this very hour, draining him as though he were a flannel washrag being hand-wound through the two-roller wringer by the *Wäschermädel*. The transference was a necessary part of the patient's cure, but sometimes he became so emotionally exhausted he had difficulty making his way up the one flight of stairs to his apartment.

When he became irritable through sheer fatigue, his detachable white cuffs kept crawling up his shirt sleeves. He demanded of Martha, when he had had to "shoot his cuffs":

"Are my arms growing longer or are these sleeves getting shorter?"

"'Warm air and men's cuffs rise upward.' Are you suggesting that the *Wäschermädeln* are shrinking your shirts? You know they're the prettiest girls in the Ninth District."

"I also know that's a non sequitur," he replied grumpily.

Then he encountered the first serious illness of his life. He had had minor ailments in addition to his occasional headache and nasal disturbance: an abscessed throat which had been lanced by one of Billroth's Assistants when he was in the Surgery Clinic; an attack of sciatica when he was twenty-eight, a mild case of smallpox the following year; an attack of influenza when he was thirty-three which had left him briefly with a condition of cardiac arrhythmia, a variation of his normal heartbeat. He recognized that the considerable pain on the left side of his chest and shooting pains down his left arm indicated the possibility of a heart attack.

After supper he asked Martha if she would like to walk down the Wipplingerstrasse, through the Hoher Markt to the Breuer house. He did not tell her why. It was a mild spring evening, "the best kind," said Martha, "for a slow walk."

He signaled Josef covertly, nudged him along to his library. There he explained his difficulty in breathing and the burning sensation in the region of the heart. Josef made no comment. He locked the library door, had Sigmund strip to the waist, put the plugs of the stethoscope in his ears and applied the bell to Sigmund's chest, listening and tapping, collating the beat of the heart with the pulse at the wrist. When he turned to put his stethoscope away his face was expressionless.

"Josef, you must tell me the truth: how did I come out in the test?"

Josef snapped the little black box shut and replied noncommittally, "Not too bad. There is some irregularity of pulse, but you have had that on and off for a while. Are you getting enough sleep?"

"Five hours. I wake up refreshed and excited about getting to work."

"Any money worries?"

"I have more paying patients than any time in my life."

"How much are you smoking?"

"About twenty cigars a day. Josef, it is painful for a medical man who spends all the hours of the day struggling to gain an understanding of the neuroses not to know whether he is himself suffering from a reasonable or a hypochondriacal depression. What do you think?"

"I don't think you need to stop smoking, Sig."

Wilhelm disagreed with Josef Breuer; he suspected that Sigmund was suffering from nicotine poisoning and forbade him to smoke any more cigars. Sigmund realized that he had been smoking to excess, but it was such a comfort to him, a constant source of pleasure while he was involved in medical problems and the long hours of writing. To be cut from twenty cigars a day to absolutely none was genuine torture. He found himself reaching into his vest pocket where he generally kept an array of three or four cigars; when there was none to be found there, he went fumbling into the now empty cigar boxes which he kept on every desk and table in his *Parterre* and the apartment upstairs.

He had no problem of self-discipline; he lit nothing; nor would he indulge in the substitute of chewing on an unlighted cigar. Yet the period of withdrawal he described to Martha as a "misery of abstinence," considerably greater than he could have conceived. There were times during the day when he did not know what to do with his hands. When he came up to a moment of perplexity he longed for the cigar that would remove the pressure. At some moments he felt lost, as though a part of him were not there; in starker moments he wondered how he could ever conceive of life and work without cigars. Days would go by without writing a word. Yet at the end of three weeks the automatic reaching for the cigar had stopped. He was able to watch other men smoke without feeling a sense of envy.

The abstinence exhausted his store of self-discipline; he was able to curtail neither the volume of his work nor his worry about his heart condition. He began to suspect that both Josef Breuer and Wilhelm Fliess were concealing things from him. The most painful part of the hours of idleness had been a fear that he could never again count on being able to do any scientific work. He wrote to Fliess, "I have no exaggerated opinion either of my responsibilities or my indispensability, and I should endure with dignity the uncertainty and the shortened expectation of life to be inferred from a diagnosis of myocarditis; indeed, I might perhaps

draw benefit from it in arranging the remainder of my life, and enjoy
to the full what is left to me."

His monograph on *The Psychoneuroses of Defense* was published in
Berlin in the *Neurologisches Centralblatt* in May and early June. He
considered it his most important paper to date; sound scientifically since
it was based on Helmholtz's Constancy Principle and the somatic discharge
of stored-up energies. He had high hopes for it, feeling that it would
arouse considerable discussion. It was totally ignored. He should have
taken a clue from the fact that none of the medical journals in Vienna
would accept it.

An Account of the Cerebral Diplegias of Childhood, on the other hand,
received the highest praise, was translated into French and lauded by
the top neurologists at the Salpêtrière. He could see no justice in this.
He had not wanted to write the cerebral diplegias paper, had felt that
he had nothing new to add to the existing body of knowledge; and in his
own words had knocked it together "almost casually." Professor Raymond,
who was Charcot's successor at the Salpêtrière, quoted whole passages
from the work in a chapter of his new book, with many flowery acknowl-
edgments. What frustrated Sigmund was the knowledge that his other
papers dealing with the neuroses, now in preparation, would also be
ignored.

Josef Breuer said with a faint edge, "Sig, I can't understand why you're
amazed at this. Aren't you being naïve? You remind me of the joke:
'Rebecca, you can take off your wedding gown, you're not a bride any
longer.' You're respected throughout Europe as a neurologist, particularly
in children's diseases. Everything you write on that subject is scientifically
sound, based on your fully documented records both in your own office
and in the Kassowitz Institute. The rest . . . the unconscious mind, the
sexual etiology of hysteria and neuroses, the psychoneurosis of defense,
the long list of obsessions and phobias . . . Nobody wants them because
nobody is prepared for them. You're talking about ideas as independent
entities, about the 'quantity of excitation'; the psychiatrists and neurologists
want to talk about the 'excitation of the cortex' since that's all they think
an idea is."

"Josef, not to change the subject, have you written the story of Bertha
Pappenheim yet, and have you started your last chapter on theory?"

Josef hesitated, ". . . no. But I've read your case histories."

"Are they clear? Do they follow logically step by step?"

Josef smiled, a touch wistfully.

"Of course, to the convinced. It's like any other religion. The faithful
don't need proof. To the infidel no proof is possible."

"But you will write this material in the coming months? It's a year and
a half since we decided we would publish the book. I think it will put a
solid base under us."

Breuer looked annoyed.

"Sig, I wish you wouldn't use that word 'us' so constantly. I am not a psychiatrist, I have no ambition to treat neuroses. You've known that for a long time now. I am an internist and a diagnostician. I am also an authority on the inner ear of pigeons, for whatever that may be worth."

June was a violent month, rare and unexpected for Vienna. One morning Sigmund was awakened at six o'clock by a hailstorm which broke out a window in his study. A few days later President Carnot of France was stabbed to death by an anarchist while visiting the Exposition in Lyons. At the same time one of the physicians at the Allgemeine Krankenhaus, Dr. Vragassy, celebrating the death of Dr. Billroth, resurrected Billroth's published charges against Jewish medical students at the University of Vienna and started a wave of virulent anti-Semitism. Professor Nothnagel was so outraged that he opened his next lecture on internal medicine by decrying and condemning anti-Semitism. He was hissed off the platform, an act unknown in a German-speaking university. Nothnagel prevailed; the Medical Faculty appointed him to head a committee to investigate the anti-Semitism and to deal with the culprits. He found Dr. Vragassy guilty, again denounced the attacks in the lecture room, and this time was applauded.

Sigmund called on Hermann Nothnagel, taking him a small bouquet of flowers.

9.

The moon grew full, the earth revolved on its axis; his heart trouble stopped. When the family moved up into the mountains several men patients followed him there for intensive treatment. The angle of disturbance again seemed to vary; he was getting more cases of hypochondria, several of severe depression and one of a manic depressive; and an increasing number of what he now clearly recognized as latent or overt homosexuality.

Dr. Zenter, thirty-four years old, had married four months before, only to find that he could not consummate the marriage. He was now suffering from intense flashing pain in the eyes, migraine headaches and scotoma, blind spots. His troubles rendered him incapable of carrying on his medical practice. . . . Twenty-eight-year-old Albrecht was suffering from pressures like steel bands around his head, lassitude, shaky knees, impaired potency; he also thought he was coming into a period of perversion in that he was attracted to girls in puberty, rather than to mature women. Theobald, a deeply depressed twenty-seven-year-old, son of a neurotic family, awakened with night terrors and palpitation of the heart, dogged by unnamed and formless anxieties which gave him a sensation of congestion in his chest and a feeling that something dreadful was about to happen to him. He was one of the rare patients who knew that his troubles had a sexual origin. A year before he had fallen in love with a young girl who was noted for her flirtatious manner. She had excited him sexually from the beginning, though he had had no physical contact with her. When he learned that she was engaged to someone else, he went into a state of shock.

Male homosexuality thwarted Privatdozent Dr. Freud. Those who were in no way disturbed or perplexed by their condition, who were participating in homosexual relationships without reluctance or stress, neither sought nor needed a physician. Those who came to him were unhappy, emotionally disturbed, urgently needing help. They were, he perceived, sincere in their desire to live normal lives. It had been a great wrench to lay bare their eccentricity, one which had terrorized them from the onset; and which they wanted desperately to understand and control. They talked freely, answered the doctor's questions, gave him the background of their cases, their attraction to other men both younger and older; their struggles to love a woman, to enter into intimate relationships with them, and their failure.

Yet when it came to finding a cause for the disturbance, he found himself bewildered. He used every technique he had evolved for the bringing forth of images, memories stamped into the earlier and deeper bowels of the unconscious. He spent many hours through the late summer afternoons urging the patients to yield to free association. What emerged were long involved stories of family complications; of mothers and fathers, rivalries, shifting alliances, dislikes amounting to hatreds within the intimate group, dislocations of emotions and loyalties; nothing that shed a consistent light.

He realized and acknowledged to these benighted patients that the failure was his: he was unable to unravel the skein of cause and consequence. He needed more knowledge, more insight. But the patients had no time to wait; free as Vienna was in terms of heterosexuality, gay and charming and innocent as they made seduction and adultery appear, there was little tolerance for homosexuality. It did not lend itself to the operetta form. The most Sigmund could do was suggest that they were not monsters unique in the history of the world; that some degree of homosexuality had been favored in Greece and in the Renaissance of Italy. It was poor solace but it was all he had to offer. He brooded about his failure. He knew, too, that the neurosis had to have its female counterpart, but no lesbian had yet come to him, even in the privacy of the *Parterre* apartment.

The summer was a glorious one. The mountains around Reichenau were green and cool and fragrant. He was up with the sun, before six, had a light breakfast and worked straight through until one o'clock dinner. It was rarely possible to enjoy six or seven hours of uninterrupted writing in Vienna. He ate the substantial meal, then he, Martha and the children set out for the adventure of the day: a walk through the woods, the gathering of mushrooms, seeking newly opened trails. He saw his patients late in the afternoon, at the coffee hour.

His stack of manuscript for his book with Josef Breuer grew tall as his excitement mounted over what would be his first truly creative book, in which he would break ground for a wholly new approach to neuropathology, one so revolutionary in its diagnosis and treatment, both of which he could authenticate with his own case documentation, that his discoveries would be accepted by neurologists all over the world. He began at the beginning, set down meticulously the case of Frau Emmy von Neustadt, her phobias and obsessions about animals and insanity. It was now his judgment that her brothers and sisters had never thrown dead animals at her when she was five years old; that she had not had fainting fits and spasms as a child, or seen her sister in her coffin, or older brothers who had syphilis or consumption, or that she had ever been persecuted by her husband's family.

He outlined the case of Miss Lucy Reynolds, the English governess, and her hallucinatory odors, what he now recognized as "defense mechanisms" to conceal from herself that she had fallen in love with her employer. He wrote about Frau Cäcilie Mattias, who had contributed so importantly to his understanding of how the symbol screened out the indigestible idea, and the neurosis found its Achilles' heel; the raging neuralgia of the teeth because of her husband's "slap in the face"; the severe heart attack when his accusation "stabbed me to the heart"; the piercing pain between the eyes as a result of her grandmother's glance when she caught her granddaughter masturbating.

He wrote the case of Elisabeth von Reichardt, who had developed a paralysis of the leg to screen out the fact that she had loved her sister's husband and had been pleased when her sister died. He wrote about eighteen-year-old robust Katharina, who had great difficulty in breathing since the day she had seen her father lying on top of her young cousin Franziska, but had actually been using the experience to screen an older memory of when her father had attempted to attack herself.

. . . All of the cases which had so startlingly convinced him of the sexual etiology of the neuroses; the large number of sufferers from anxiety . . .

In September he took Martha and the five children to Lovrano on the sun-drenched Adriatic, for two weeks. It was their first trip into Italy. He had always longed to visit Rome. He had read widely in its history and thought it the most fascinating city in the world. But Rome was an unhealthy city in summer, and that was the only season he could take a vacation.

Mathilde was now old enough to watch over Sophie; Martin led the two-year-old Ernst in search of seashells. Martha protected herself from the hot sun with a floppy straw hat, but Sigmund sopped up its burning rays, acquiring a fine tan and using the time of idleness to read a volume of Kipling's short stories. The balcony of their hotel overlooked the sea; after supper they sat out to watch the fishing boats and talked of their developing family in America. Her brother Eli was doing well in New York, entrenched as a grain exporter on the Exchange, the family living in their own comfortable home on 139th Street. Anna, who had had her first American-born child, Hella, at the beginning of the previous year, had just given birth to their fifth child, Martha. Sigmund's thirty-year-old sister Pauli, who had taken the Bernays children to join their parents, had found that the legend was true: the streets of America were paved with husbands; or at least with the only one she wanted and needed: thirty-seven-year-old Valentin Winternitz, a German-speaking Czech who had come to New York to make his fortune and was doing well as a representative of technical firms. Sigmund's sister Marie and her husband Moritz Freud were also preparing to leave Vienna with their three daughters. They were going to Berlin, where Moritz was expanding his import business.

Martha and Sigmund returned to the Berggasse with idyllic memories of the Italian sun and sea, pasta and veal Parmigiano.

The autumn of the year, like its June, again brought grievous disappointments and depression; what Sigmund described as "a season of anarchy." It was not merely that two bombs were thrown by an anarchist in Barcelona in an attempt to kill the Spanish Premier and the Minister of War; and that a couple of months later another anarchist dropped a bomb into the Chambre des Députés in Paris, being guillotined for his efforts. It had also to do with the nature of his practice. Nearly every issue of the daily paper carried a suicide story, many of them about young people: a twenty-two-year-old maid who took poison; the seventeen-year-old son of a tavernkeeper who shot himself. All the articles finished with an identical phrase: *Motive Unknown.*

"Of course the motive is unknown," Sigmund cried; "because no one cares to investigate. These young ones have nowhere to go when they need help. We have techniques now to get at their disturbances; we can tell what causes a death wish, and how to defend against it. But there is no way to use this knowledge to help these people."

The level of his bank balance receded the way water does in a summer pond. He grew morose. To Martha he groused, "Everything is *Kraut und Rüben,* topsy-turvy. Things are so bad in Vienna that everywhere I turn I find soup kitchens with long lines. A dozen sleeping asylums have been opened for the unemployed but they don't have nearly enough beds. In the Tenth District the workmen's clubs have opened their own hotel dormitories and claim to be sleeping two thousand indigents a night. Frozen bodies are found in the streets each dawn. The City Council has appropriated enough money to hire unemployed masons, carpenters and laborers to pull down the balance of the Gürtel. Only now, because the weather has turned wet and cold, has each district set up a collection center for used clothes, particularly shoes for poor children who are walking the streets barefooted. 'Life is like an infant's shirt, short and soiled.' The Austrians are right when they say that a hungry pig dreams of acorns."

This was one time Martha was not able to cheer him. She murmured with a slightly woebegone expression:

"What do geese dream of? Of maize. That's how I felt last Monday morning when you failed to give me my week's *Haushaltsgeld*. However, as they say in the coffeehouses, 'The situation is hopeless but not serious.' "

The severity of the depression increased. The Empress opened her own *Volksküchenverein* to feed the hungry. A quarter of a million lunches were served to school children who had no other food all day. The iron-workers of the Tenth District went out on strike; the government declared it illegal. Other workers paraded without a permit, were beaten by the police and then arrested. Socialist pamphlets were clandestinely printed and distributed. The police made frequent arrests for "subversive activities." Two thousand undesirables, including one American, were deported.

One of his new patients was a young law student about to take his third-year examinations. He came with a wild look in his eyes, protesting that he was going insane, that he would never be able to take the examinations or face life again unless Dr. Freud could help him. Soothingly, Sigmund told the young man that no one ever really went insane from masturbation. The law student, his lips twitching, said:

"Dr. Freud, I can rely on your discretion? Everything said between the patient and the doctor is privileged?"

Sigmund smiled at the legal language and reassured the man.

"Doctor, you surely must know that no man masturbates into a vacuum. What I mean to say is, we don't ejaculate without pouring our semen into a woman."

Sigmund nodded his head; this confirmed a thesis that had been forming in his own mind. The student rushed on:

"When I was in the Schottengymnasium my fantasies revolved around the beautiful actresses at the Volkstheater. When I was masturbating, the current star would be lying under me. When I moved on to the university I had fantasies about the women I saw in the expensive restaurants and in the theaters, with their low-cut gowns; they would become the objects of my fornication each night. I have even committed fantasy incest with attractive young aunts and cousins. Yet none of this seemed to bother me . . . until . . . now."

He jumped to his feet and then collapsed into the chair and broke into sobs. Sigmund sat back in silence, waiting. He wondered to what bizarre length the patient had gone to have reduced himself to this state. The man looked up.

"You will know I am going insane. The object of my fantasies now . . . the woman with whom I copulate . . . who lies beneath me . . . is my own mother. —Am I not a doomed man?"

"A fantasy is a 'dusk dream' lying halfway between a daydream and a nightdream," Sigmund replied quietly. "Once we have removed this vision from your imagination we will get down to what causes you, a young man of twenty-five, to be masturbating instead of pouring your energies into your legal studies and into love itself."

The patient never returned. Sigmund received a letter enclosing a bank check. And that was the end of his practice for the rest of the year, insofar as "neuroses" were concerned. His only steady patient was a very old woman whose son engaged him to travel to the family home each morning and late afternoon to give his mother her injections. He kept the old woman alive; her affluent son kept the Freud larder stocked.

The cycles made no sense to him, not even after rereading Wilhelm Fliess's papers on human periodicity. In the spring he had been flooded with patients and now there was no one . . . except the man who broke his leg in front of their apartment house. Sigmund helped move him to the Allgemeine Krankenhaus to get the bone set. He spent a good deal of time at the Kassowitz Institute to make up for his neglect of the previous spring. Some of the parents had means; they were not attempting to get free medical service, only to find the best. When they learned that Privatdozent Dr. Freud was available at his private offices, they brought their afflicted and crippled children to the Berggasse.

During the late winter and early spring to further confound his confusion, his neurological practice returned in full tide, with a sufficiency of patients and an overabundance of notes to be made, a condition which he found pleasing. He finished the rewrite on his case histories for the forthcoming book, Studies on Hysteria, and began his concluding chapter. At long last Josef Breuer was setting down on paper the full record of Bertha Pappenheim. In their resumed walks about Vienna he discussed with Sigmund what would go into his own final chapter on theory, what was tenable in their conclusions and what had yet to be proved. Writing firmly and rapidly in his notes, Sigmund completed his essay in French on Obsessions and Phobias for the Revue Neurologique in Paris; did a rewrite on The Anxiety Neurosis, which was being published in the

Neurologisches Centralblatt in Berlin. Deuticke, who had published his translations of Charcot and Bernheim and his book *On Aphasia,* agreed to publish Studies on Hysteria.

When he had begun to write about anxiety neurosis he prided himself on having made an original discovery. The passage of the months and a heavy bout of reading disabused him. He confided to Martha, "Every human being and every idea has a mama and a papa; their genesis, as has been proved by Darwin, goes back to the beginning of time." A Dr. Kaan had published a paper on anxiety as a symptom of neurasthenia only the year before; then Sigmund found a recent publication by a Dr. E. Hecker. In his own manuscript he wrote, "I found the same interpretation expounded with all the clarity and completeness that could be desired." However Hecker had not separated anxiety attacks from neurasthenia, actual nervous instability. Professor Möbius of Leipzig had also published materials on the psychological origin of hysterical symptoms; but he believed that nothing in psychology could serve as a curative. In a letter to Fliess, Sigmund described Möbius as "the best mind among the neurologists; fortunately he is not on the track of sexuality."

10.

Early in 1895 there appeared in his consultation room a red-cheeked young widow of twenty-eight by the name of Emma Benn who was to take him to the brink of tragedy. Emma's family, prosperous merchants, were friends of the Josef Breuers and Oskar Rie. Through them the Freuds had also grown close to the Benn family; Emma often dropped in to the Berggasse apartment for a visit. She was a straw blonde, heavy about the hips in the manner of so many young Viennese girls, with a bumpy nose and asymmetrical face which was nevertheless attractive because there was an alert and frequently combative light in her eyes. She had been suffering severe stomach and intestinal tract disorders. Josef Breuer had been the Benn family doctor for years. He had come to the conclusion that the attacks were hysterical in origin. He asked Sigmund to see her. Sigmund suggested that his kind of therapy might not work with friends. Josef overruled his qualms.

Emma was a militant feminist who resented her subsidiary position in an all-male society; she was particularly incensed over the Germanic concept of *Kinder, Kirche, Küche,* children, church, kitchen, as being the only activities proper or permissible to women, to which the more flexible Austrian husbands had added a fourth K: *Kaffeeklatsch.* Emma conjured up for Sigmund scenes and stories that were truly inventive: she saw the Devil sticking a pin into her finger and then placing a piece of candy on each drop of blood.

As a child she had suffered from nosebleeds; during the years of puberty she had had severe headaches. Her parents thought that she was malingering. Emma was unhappy that her parents did not believe her; when she started excessive menstrual bleeding she greeted this as a proof of the genuineness of her illness. She related a memory of having been circumcised; and having been sexually molested by her father. At fifteen she fell in love with a handsome young physician, suddenly developing nosebleeds again so that the family would send for him.

Emma's illnesses and fantasyings had ended with marriage. Though her husband was much older and not in especially good health, Emma had found in the five years of her marriage the love she needed. There had been no children. After her husband's death and a protracted period of grief, Emma came down with the present ills, centering around her digestive system. Because she had eaten badly for months, and her nervous system had had a profound shock, it was believed that something in the nature of an ulcer might have developed. When Breuer recommended that Emma be put into Herr Dr. Sigmund Freud's care, her parents objected. They liked Sigmund as a friend but had no faith in his methods. Breuer convinced the family that Emma should be given every chance of curing the illnesses which were making her despondent and unwilling to take part in the life about her.

Emma was both willing and able to talk. There were a number of hostilities in her; she had a poor opinion of men in general which she made little effort to conceal. Yet there was an overriding need for a man's love. Many of her stories revolved around her father, about whom she had contradictory feelings: there appeared to be deep-seated scars over his sexual molestation, and at the same time a tremendous need to be loved by him.

Then, during a session in which he urged Emma not to censor or reject her thoughts, but to let them flow freely without interposing her own judgment about their worth or relevancy, Emma became a little girl again, began acting out her memories. Privatdozent Dr. Sigmund Freud became her father. She called him Papa. She was back in her home, playing games with him, singing to him, telling him how much she loved him, relating how she had rushed home from school so she could join him for the afternoon *Jause*. Then her mood changed and she burst into tears, protesting that she had not been naughty, that she had not told an untruth, that he must not fail to believe her. Next she flared into anger, refusing to carry out the instructions he had given her, claiming she would run away from home, that she didn't love him any more . . . all the while going through a series of facial grimaces that ranged from little-girl coquettishness to hand wringing and tears that were obviously re-creations from her girlhood.

Other patients had made a transference, forgetting where they were, going through intense memory-emotion, frequently weeping, even cursing. Before he had understood the nature of transference he had had the uneasy feeling that the shouts and the curses as well as some of the more affectionate gestures were directed toward him; he had been responsible for inducing the memories. With Emma he had transference in full flower: she passed the better part of each hour reliving scenes of emotional intensity with the conviction that she was going through them with her blood father.

Sigmund was reluctant to let Emma go at the end of the hour, even though he had another patient coming. But she appeared to make the transition back to the present without the slightest memory of what had gone before. Josef Breuer considered the scenes another aspect of her hysteria. Her visceral pains grew worse, at the same time she suffered from a blocked sinus, with an accompanying variety of congestions and inflammations of the nose. He studied Fliess's article on the *Nasal Reflex Neurosis*, wondering whether Emma's intestinal pains might be caused by her inability to breathe freely. Fortunately Wilhelm was coming to Vienna for a visit. Sigmund asked Emma if he could bring Dr. Fliess into the consultation. She consented.

Wilhelm Fliess came to Sigmund's consultation room to see Emma the morning after he reached Vienna, and made a number of tests.

"There's no question, Sig, this young woman's troubles originate in her nasal passage," he announced. "Her turbinate bones need a resecting so that the air currents can get through. This condition could not only cause her gastric pains but unquestionably has an upsetting effect on her sexual organs."

"Then, Wilhem, you think she should be operated on?"

"Undoubtedly. It is a harmless operation. I have performed hundreds of them. She'll only need to be in hospital for a couple of days."

"But you won't be here to take care of her."

"No postoperative treatment is really needed. You yourself can take the packing out after a few days. She'll be back to normal activities in a week or two. Schedule the operation for tomorrow."

"We'll have it done at Loew Sanatorium; it is a well-equipped private hospital. And thank you, Wilhelm."

The operation went off successfully. Fliess returned to Berlin. Emma was taken home. The next day when Sigmund entered her bedroom he detected a bad odor. He examined her nose and saw that the mucous membrane was visibly palpitating. She had not slept the night before and was in intense pain. He gave her a sedative. The following day a bone chip broke loose, followed by a massive hemorrhage. The next day he found it hard to irrigate the nasal passage. He now realized that Emma was in trouble. He called Dr. Gersuny, who came at once. The nose specialist judged that the access to the cavity had contracted, leaving the patient insufficient room for drainage. He inserted a rubber tube with difficulty, telling Sigmund that he would have to rebreak the bone if the tube did not stay in. A fetid odor lay heavy in the room.

Early the next morning Sigmund was wakened with a message that Emma was bleeding profusely. Dr. Gersuny could not come until evening. Sigmund asked Dr. Röckel, an ear, nose and throat specialist, to meet him at Emma's apartment. By the time Dr. Röckel arrived Emma was bleeding not only from the nose but from the mouth. The odor was almost intolerable. Dr. Röckel cleaned out the nose, removing some of the blood clots and packing, then gazed intently at something, turned to Sigmund and asked:

"What is this?"

Sigmund looked, replied, "I don't know. What does it appear to be?"

"A thread. I'd better see what's going on." He took the end of the thread and pulled. He kept pulling . . . and pulling . . . and pulling . . . until he had extracted half a meter of gauze from Emma's nasal cavity that had been left there by Dr. Fliess after the operation. A veritable flood of blood poured out of Emma; she turned yellow, then white, her eyes bulging. Sigmund took her pulse; it was hardly palpable. Emma was in danger of dying. Dr. Röckel moved swiftly, packed the cavity with fresh iodoform gauze. This stopped the hemorrhage.

Sigmund fled to the next room, sick and faint. He drank a glass of water. He was in mortal agony. Had the gauze remained undetected for another few days, Emma would have died of poisoning. A new wave of nausea accompanied the growing realization that he should never have allowed the operation. Not only should it have been performed by either Dr. Gersuny or Dr. Röckel, who would have been there for postoperative attention; but, like ice water thrown in his face, came the blinding truth that Emma's troubles, either psychical or somatic, had nothing whatever to do with her nose. The operation had been a gross mistake. In this revelation he perceived that there had never been anything wrong with Fliess's nose, or his own either!

Someone handed him a glass of cognac. He downed it in a gulp, then summoned the courage to go into the next room where he made arrangements for Emma to be returned to Loew Sanatorium. Here Dr. Röckel and Dr. Gersuny repeated the operation, broke the turbinate and curetted the wound. When the doctors had left, Sigmund stood by Emma's bedside, both of them knowing full well how close she had come to bleeding to death. Emma greeted him with combatively wide eyes. She said, tapping her fingers against her chest:

"This is the strong sex."

He dreaded writing a report of the case to Fliess. He knew how disturbed Wilhelm would be. He did not blame Fliess. Fliess had performed the operation, but if Emma had died the responsibility would have been his own. Emma was his patient. He had been directly responsible for the death of only one patient during his years of internship and practice, a woman at the Allgemeine Krankenhaus to whom he had given prescribed doses of sulphonal, regarded as a harmless drug, but who had been unable to assimilate it.

He did all he could in his letter to ease Fliess's burden, told him how distressed he was that "this mishap should have happened to you"; laid the blame on defective gauze . . . "the tearing off of the iodoform gauze was one of those accidents that happen to the most fortunate and cautious of surgeons . . . Gersuny mentioned that he had had a similar experience, and that he therefore used iodoform wicks instead of gauze . . ."; scolded Dr. Röckel for pulling out the gauze without waiting to move Emma to a hospital; ended by reassuring Fliess that ". . . no one blames you in any way, nor do I know why they should. . . . Rest assured that I felt no need to restore my trust in you."

Emma took several months to recover. As strength returned so did her intestinal disorders. The nose operation had cured nothing. She came back to the Berggasse to resume her treatments. Her behavior was unchanged. There was now no doubt in Sigmund's mind that her illness was based on the fact that her love life had been cut off. He explained the sexual etiology of her neurosis, outlined the methods of suppression and defense that were so brilliantly utilized by the unconscious mind; the obsessions and phobias that arose out of the inability of the psychical energy to discharge itself properly.

Not a word of which Emma would believe or accept. When he suggested that she come out of the seclusion in which she had maintained herself since the death of her husband; that she go to parties and dances; that she invite people into her home and meet all the young men she could in order that she might fall in love and marry again as soon as possible, she grew angry.

"There's no truth in what you say. Of course I sorely miss my husband, his tenderness, his affection; yes, our marital acts as well. But they were only a small part of the over-all picture of our love for each other. That cannot be the reason that I am ill, that I have had these racking pains since my husband's death. There has to be something wrong physically."

"Yes, Emma, that is possible, even though Dr. Breuer says he can find nothing. Many of our neurosis cases are complex in that they are combinations of physical and psychiatric disturbances. But even if you do have something physically wrong, it is not the sole symptom. Emma, your mental, nervous and emotional health depends upon your making every effort to find another love and another husband. This you must do deliberately, with an organized plan. There is nothing else in your life that matters or that can bring you any semblance of good health."

Emma sprang up agitatedly. "What an undignified thing to demand of me: to rush through the streets of Vienna crying, 'I need a husband! Would anybody like to marry me?' Summer vacation is starting now. Why don't we just discontinue these treatments for a time?"

Sigmund agreed.

The manuscript of Studies on Hysteria was completed and ready to be sent to Deuticke. Breuer wrote a significant closing chapter. He did not believe that psychology or the study of the neuroses could become a laboratory science following in the footsteps of the eminent physiologists Helmholtz and Brücke, but saw it as a new realm that would have to coin its own language and owe no debt to any part of physical science. Sigmund was unwilling to accept this; he was also unable to. He had had a reputation as a scientist until he lost it through his concentration on hypnotism, male hysteria, amnesia and now the sexual etiology of the neuroses. He was in desperate need of finding consistencies and measurements within which to fit his concepts. He did not believe it to be a futile pursuit; one day the psychology of the mind would be as exact a science as the pathology of the body.

He believed that the book marked the beginning of a new era in medicine, turning human psychology from a phantasmagoria into an inductive system which would not only provide an effective therapeutic tool but also open the door to a hitherto untapped body of knowledge. Sitting with the bulk of the manuscript within the palms of his hands, his hopes once again soared so high that he caught himself in an act of euphoria: the book would earn him lasting fame, wealth and complete independence.

11.

Martha was four months' pregnant. She had not been carrying well. After five healthy pregnancies, something about this sixth one had been wrong almost from the beginning. She felt poorly, her face appeared pale and bloated; she was having trouble with her teeth. She and Sigmund decided it would be better not to go as far away as the mountains around Semmering; instead they rented a villa at Bellevue, under the Kahlenberg. The lilac and laburnum were still in bloom, soon to be replaced by the scent of acacia and syringa. Overnight the wild roses burst into flower.

The villa had originally been designed as a place for eating and dancing; its two reception rooms had hall-like lofty ceilings. The Hotel Kahlenberg advertised a "dust-free Alpine Climate." Martha claimed that this was equally true a mile or so lower down at Bellevue; and immediately felt so much better that she planned a party for her thirty-fourth birthday, inviting Emma Benn, Dr. Oskar Rie, who was vacationing with Emma's parents at their country home, the Josef Breuers and many of their friends. The reception hall would lend itself to a celebration with music and dancing.

Three days before the party Dr. Rie came to Bellevue to check on one of the children who had a sore throat. He brought Martha a bottle of *Ananas* liqueur in anticipation of her coming birthday. Sigmund quipped:

"Oskar, you have a habit of making presents on every possible occasion. When are you going to find a wife to cure you of that habit?"

After dinner, when they opened the bottle, it gave off a strong odor of fusel oil. Oskar, embarrassed, cried, "Now do you see why I don't rush into marriage? If I had given that present to my wife it would have caused a marital row!"

While the two men were climbing up to Leopoldsberg, Sigmund asked:

"How have you found Emma?"

"She's better, Sig, but not quite well."

Sigmund was distressed. There was no reproof in what Oskar had said, yet Sigmund imagined that Oskar's tone of voice suggested that Dr. Freud had promised his patient more than he had delivered. For that matter, Oskar, who loved Sigmund in the same selfless way that Josef Paneth had, cared little for Sigmund's method of treating the neuroses. He wanted Sigmund, his superior at the Kassowitz Institute, to remain a specialist in children's neurology. Some months before, hungry to find a sympathetic soul in Vienna, Sigmund had shown Oskar an early draft of his paper on the sexual etiology of the neuroses. Oskar had scanned only a page or two, shaken his head in dissent and returned the pages to Sigmund, using the identical words Charcot had uttered when Sigmund finished telling him the story of Josef Breuer's "talking cure":

"No, there's nothing in that."

Sigmund's ophthalmologist friend Leopold Königstein had also shown honest doubt, asking at a Saturday night *Tarock* game:

"Sig, can this cathartic treatment of yours really achieve an abatement of symptoms?"

Sigmund replied: "Yes, I think we can transform hysterical misery into common unhappiness."

After Martha and the children had gone to sleep, he lit the lamp in the room he was using as his study and wrote a letter to Josef Breuer explaining in detail everything in his prognosis and treatment of Emma Benn. He wrote steadily until midnight, hoping to justify himself in Breuer's eyes as an answer to Oskar Rie's implication that he had not done a good job. It took him awhile to fall asleep; toward morning he fell into a dream:

"A large hall—numerous guests, whom we were receiving. Among them was Emma. I at once took her on one side, as though to answer her letter and to reproach her for not having accepted my 'solution' yet. I said to her: 'If you still get pains, it's really only your fault.' She replied: 'If you only knew what pains I've got now in my throat and stomach and abdomen—it's choking me.' I was alarmed and looked at her. She looked pale and puffy. I thought to myself that after all I must be missing some organic trouble. I took her to the window and looked down her throat, and she showed signs of recalcitrance, like women with artificial dentures. I thought to myself that there was really no need for her to do that. She then opened her mouth properly and on the right I found a big white patch; at another place I saw extensive whitish gray scabs upon some remarkable curly structures which were evidently modeled on the turbinal bones of the nose. I at once called in Dr. Breuer, and he repeated the examination and confirmed it. . . . Dr. Breuer looked quite different from usual; he was very pale, he walked with a limp and his chin was clean-shaven. . . . My friend Oskar was now standing beside her as well, and my friend Leopold was percussing her through her bodice and saying: 'She has a dull area low down on the left.' He also indicated that a portion of the skin on the left shoulder was infiltrated. (I noticed this, just as he did, in spite of her dress.) Breuer said: "There's no doubt it's an infection, but no matter; dysentery will supervene and the toxin will be eliminated.' We were directly aware, too, of the origin of the infection. Not long before, when she was feeling unwell, my friend Oskar had given her an injection of a preparation of propyl, propyls . . . propionic acid . . . trimethylamin (and I saw before me the formula for this printed in heavy type). Injections of that sort ought not to be made so thoughtlessly. . . . And probably the syringe had not been clean."

At breakfast the dream hung heavy in his mind; it possessed him in a way that no dream had previously, and made it impossible for him to think about anything else. He surveyed its content over and over. Unlike his earlier conviction that dreams were a form of sleeping-insanity, he had perceived in his own dreams an occasional reference to something that had happened to him the day before or several days before which seemed to make a modicum of sense; some of his patients had been frightened or upset by their dreams and insisted upon relating them during their hour of consultation. In those dreams too he had occasionally been able to pick out a line or an image that seemed to reflect and, in a small way, illuminate an aspect of the patient's illness. However he had not been able to analyze these moments of clarity or relate them to each other, no matter how many dreams a patient had reported. Apparently dreams had a memory, much as the unconscious mind had; and when the individual was asleep these memory shards, after being beaten in a bowl the way a cook beats up eggs for an omelet, found a way of floating to the surface.

He glanced across the breakfast table at Martha; he had given her nothing more than a grumpy good morning.

He rose from his seat, walked around to her, put his arm about her shoulder and kissed her on the cheek.

"Forgive me for being uncommunicative this morning, but I had the weirdest dream before I woke up. It is haunting me. I simply must sit down and see if I can't make some sense out of it. I have a feeling that it may be important; and may even possibly be decipherable . . . though at the moment it looks like sheer chaos."

He closed the door to his study, filled the inkwell, stacked a pile of paper in front of him and sat down with his back squarely to the glorious view of green woods and mountains. He said to himself, "I must take this dream apart, bit by bit, the way a Swiss watchmaker dismantles a clock."

He reasoned that he would have to take each image, each piece of action and each line of dialogue quite separately and let his mind roam in the kind of free association which he urged on his patients. If what he thought seemed to make no sense or to have little relevance, he must force himself to carry out his stricture even as he obliged his patients to do. He would let his thoughts dwell on each person in the dream, then, when he had down on paper everything that came forth spontaneously, he would try to link them up to each other and to himself.

The time and place were obvious: Martha's birthday and the main hall of Bellevue where he and Martha were receiving their guests. Emma was of course the central character.

He placed the fingers of his left hand lightly on his forehead: the thought came to him, "It was uppermost in my mind to reproach Emma for not having accepted my solution to her illness. In the dream I said, 'If you still get pains, it's your own fault.' It's my belief that my services and obligations to a patient are fulfilled once I have brought forth the hidden and secret meaning of their symptoms. The cure lies in that very act. It is really not my responsibility whether she accepts my diagnosis, though of course there can be no cure unless she does. Consequently it is urgent for me that she believe in my solution and work faithfully on my suggestion. If the pains are Emma's fault they obviously cannot be mine; ergo, she has failed to cure herself and I am not responsible for any part of the failure.

"Could this be what the dream is about?

"Emma complained of pains in her throat and stomach and abdomen. Obviously I am still concerned that a major portion of her illness may be physical. As a scientist I must not miss an organic illness. To prove that I am not a monomaniac, I took Emma to the window to look down her throat and on the right side I found a big white patch as well as extensive whitish gray scabs on some curly structures modeled on the turbinal bones of the nose. Yet Emma had never had anything wrong with her throat."

Then he remembered that Emma had a close friend, also a widow, whom he, Sigmund, had come to know and had thought labored under certain hysterical patterns. One day when Sigmund walked into her apartment he had seen Josef Breuer there, examining her by the window and looking down her throat, suggesting that she had a diphtheritic membrane.

"What happened here?" he asked himself. "I have had Emma's woman friend replace Emma in the dream. Further, I noted that Emma looked pale and bloated. But Emma has always had a high complexion. It is Martha who is pale and bloated. Somehow I have made an amalgam of Emma, her woman friend and Martha. Why?"

Still letting his associations run freely, his mind went to Oskar Rie who, if Emma was the heroine of the piece, had somehow become the villain. Sigmund saw that he had made two quite serious accusations against Oskar in his dream, the first of having been thoughtless in handling chemical substances, and also of using a dirty syringe. Since he, Sigmund, had been giving injections of morphia to his eighty-two-year-old patient and never once had caused an infection by a dirty needle, he perceived he was taking pride in his own work and at the same time denigrating Oskar. By some mysterious connection his next thought was that this made Oskar Rie responsible for the fact that Emma still suffered a series of pains. Emma was ill because of the injection Oskar had given her! "Therefore if Oskar Rie is responsible, obviously I cannot be! I have exonerated myself once again."

The interjection into the dream of the drugs propyl, propyls, propionic acid . . . trimethylamin was a reminder of the fusel oil smell that came out of the bad bottle of liqueur Oskar had brought Martha as a birthday present, and was a further reproach to Oskar in the dream itself.

Now his mind moved to Josef Breuer. Their book had been released by Deuticke but there had been no reaction to it as yet. In the dream Sigmund had called in Josef to take a look at Emma's throat and the turbinal bones of her nose. Josef had confirmed his diagnosis; but why did Josef look so pale, walk with a limp, and with his beard shaved entirely off? And why had Josef said, after examining her, "There's no doubt it's an infection, but no matter; dysentery will supervene and the toxin will be eliminated." This was a nonsensical statement; the concept that morbid matter could be eliminated through the bowels was not believed by any well trained doctor.

"Here again," he thought, "in my dream I am grooming myself to be a superior diagnostician to Josef Breuer."

He wrote freely, ideas pouring forth for a number of hours. There were inferences to patients in the past whom he, Oskar Rie, Josef Breuer and Fliess had treated; a number of self-reproaches, such as the case of the woman to whom he had prescribed continuing doses of sulphonal; and the fact that he had allowed his friend Fleischl to become addicted to cocaine. There were also associations which he set forth, and then walked away from, such as the fact that Emma had been transposed into her widow friend and then into Martha Freud; that Emma spoke of pains in her abdomen when actually it was pregnant Martha who had the pains in her abdomen; again there was the syringe and the injection, which he believed to be a symbolization of the sexual act. He recalled that neither he nor Martha had wanted another child at that time. Therefore the "dirty syringe" stood as a symbol for the loaded or fertile injection which had made Martha pregnant again, and which had by now led her to considerable discomfort.

That afternoon he took a long walk in the woods, demanding of himself, "How do I connect up all these seemingly irrelevant and disorganized strains? What is the common denominator? What is it that the dream was trying to say? Or that I was trying to say through the dream? Because I don't know yet whether the dreamer is the dramatist or merely the actor whose lines have been written for him." The one thing that stood out sharpest in his mind was that the dream was self-serving. He thought, "Its basic content is the fulfillment of a wish and its motive is a wish."

Memories of earlier dreams flooded over him, as well as bits and pieces of his patients' dreams; suddenly he came to a dead stop. His body became taut. He felt his skin rise in goose pimples. He exclaimed to a thick stand of trees:

"That's the purpose of dreams! To release from the unconscious mind what the individual is really wanting. Not the masks, not the disguises, not the hidden feelings or thwarted desires; but what the individual somewhere in the core of his brain wishes to have happen or have happened! What an astounding mechanism! What an astounding accomplishment! But how could we not have known this through all of the centuries? How could everyone, including myself, have thought that dreams were the stuff of madness? That they had no pattern, served no purpose, were uncontrolled by any force in heaven or hell? All the time they could have been analyzed on a disciplined base and an enormous amount learned about the nature of the individual."

In dreams, he saw, nothing is forgotten, no matter how long ago it happened; the inventiveness of the dream, its cleverness in assuming altered forms, was a tremendous ploy of the imagination. And if, as he now had begun to suspect, dreams were an open door to the unconscious, laying bare the true wishes of the patient, he would have still another way of understanding what was making his patients mentally, nervously, emotionally ill; he would truly have the illness under a microscope. What better delineated what a man would like to have, to be, to achieve, than his wishes? And by reflex those wishes also demonstrated what he would like to have changed, altered, improved, ameliorated, made right. In his dreams a man edited and rewrote the manuscript of his past life!

He wheeled about on the trail to return home, exultant. This was one of the greatest discoveries he had yet made. The implication of where it could lead him was staggering.

12.

Studies on Hysteria was badly received. One of the best-known German neurologists, Strümpell, gave it a condescending and dismissing review. After that no one bothered to review it in any of the German-language medical journals.

Sigmund complained to Martha, "Everything that Strümpell says may be true, but he's not talking about our book. He built up a nonsense case out of his imagination which he then brilliantly demolished."

In Vienna no one discussed the book even critically, nor did any of his friends bring it up. However he assumed that it was being read because Deuticke reported that several hundred copies of the eight hundred printed had already been sold. It was more than *On Aphasia* had sold in a couple of years.

The following weeks brought a few compensations. Dr. Eugen Bleuler, head of the Burghölzli, the university Psychiatric Clinic in Zurich, who had favorably reviewed *On Aphasia* and with whom he had exchanged a number of letters, did an evaluation for the *Münchener medizinische Wochenschrift* in which he took some exception to the material but stated that "the factual account the book gives opens a quite new vista into the mechanism of the mind and makes one of the most important contributions of the past years to the field of normal or pathological psychology." There was a message that Dr. Mitchell Clarke in England had read the book and was planning a critique for the magazine *Brain*.

Sigmund opined ruefully, "Now I can once again resign myself to daily cases and economies."

Martha gave him a wisp of a smile. "Isn't that what life is made up of? Don't let your hopes fly so high, my golden Sigi, and you won't drop with such a terrible thud."

The neglect apparently discouraged and hurt Josef Breuer so much that Sigmund saw nothing of him. At the same time he noticed that his brother Alexander was growing increasingly nervous and irritable. He knew he was overworked, editing the ever expanding *Tarif-Anzeiger*, running the freight company almost singlehandedly, teaching at the Export Academy. He still lived at home, helped support his parents and two sisters; and was investing part of his salary each month toward the purchase of the business. His schedule allowed him no time for the comradery of young friends. He had not taken a vacation in thirteen years.

Martha decided the week in Venice she and Sigmund had been discussing would be a good thing for the brothers.

"It would do you both a world of good. It will be your twenty-ninth birthday present from us, Alex. I'm much too uncomfortable to traipse around Italy in the heat of summer."

Sigmund's train phobia caught him by the throat; for a full day before their departure he could think of little else. There was an element of dread mixed into the joy. He had trouble making himself pack and then arrived at the station more than an hour too early to board. Once the train headed south, he relaxed.

Venice had no peer for the sheer delight of a first visit. They took a gondola down the Grand Canal to the Royal Danieli Hotel, then plunged at once into the Piazza San Marco with its four noble horses. They climbed to the top of the Campanile, which Goethe had climbed before them, for a view of the red tile roofs of Venice surrounded by the sea from which she had sprung fifteen centuries before; made a tour of the magnificent Doge's Palace, climaxed by a reverential awe as they stood beneath Veronese's oval ceiling painting of the *Deification of Venice*. They had their supper on the outside terrace of Florian's with a string orchestra playing arias from Verdi.

Sigmund was a fanatical sightseer. They walked the ancient streets to see the leaning campaniles, visited the slowly sinking palaces built when Venice was as rich in carnival sin as silver; crossed the Rialto and Accademia bridges; swam in the warm sea of the Lido, went by boat to the islands of Torcello and Murano. Venice had been built onto the mud flats in the way other Italian villages were carved out of the sides of mountains. Best of all, Sigmund knew the story of its art: Giorgione, Titian, Carpaccio. Since much of the art of Venice was in its churches, they started with the Byzantine Basilica of San Marco, with its breathtaking marbles and mosaics, paintings and sculptures, went on to Santi Giovanni e Paolo, St. Zaccaria, the Salute.

Alexander was like a child. He walked about without a hat, letting the sun tan his face. The lines of fatigue vanished, he ate heartily of the abundant Venetian seafoods. He enjoyed riding the gondolas. But mostly he enjoyed seeing Sigmund's mind reach out to embrace the color-laden beauty of the Venetian architecture, the great ducal palaces, the Bovolo staircase and Sansovino's Loggetta. To cap off the trip Sigmund stumbled across an antique shop on one of the smaller canals where he bought, at a ridiculously small price, a bronze head of the two-faced Janus, the Roman god of "beginnings."

At the station in Vienna, when they parted, Alexander said, "Thank you for the glorious vacation. Do you know what I enjoyed most? Looking at you looking at art. I've heard you say a number of times that you are not religious by nature. Non è vero, as the Italians say; art is your religion. There is ecstasy in your eyes as you worship in front of a Giorgione or a Titian. I can see your lips moving in prayer."

Sigmund was amused. "Professor Brücke loved paintings as much as he did physiology; Billroth loved music as much as surgery; Nothnagel loves literature as much as internal medicine. If my love for a first-century marble torso makes me a religieux, so be it."

He was no sooner back than he left for Berlin. He was eager to have another congress with Wilhelm Fliess. Ever since he had delivered the completed manuscript of Studies on Hysteria there had been burgeoning in his mind a concept for another book, perhaps a hundred pages in length, to be called Project for a Scientific Psychology.

Fliess took time off from his practice; the two men spent the warm end-of-August days in the woods, discussing the project at fever pitch. Sigmund was so stimulated that the moment his train pulled out of the Anhalter Bahnhof he opened a notebook, took a pencil from his pocket, jotted down "Part I," and wrote almost the whole way into Vienna. He used a cryptic shorthand which Fleiss alone would understand, evolving a system of Greek symbols:

$$Q = \text{Quantity, the order of magnitude in the external world.}$$
$$Q\acute{n} = \text{Quantity of the intercellular order of magnitude.}$$
$$\emptyset = \text{system of permeable neurones}$$
$$\gamma = \text{system of impermeable neurones}$$
$$w = \text{system of perceptual neurones}$$
$$W = \text{perception (Wahrnehmung)}$$
$$V = \text{idea (Vorstellung)}$$
$$M = \text{motor image}$$

"The intention," he wrote, "is to furnish a psychology that shall be a natural science: that is, to represent psychical processes as quantitatively determinate states of specifiable material particles." He then moved into a neurone theory, evolved from recent findings in histology, attempting to explain how a current passes through the cells' paths of conduction, distinguishing between neurones which had contact barriers and others which allowed $Q\acute{n}$ to pass through without resistance . . . in an attempt to explain memory, pain, satisfaction, wishful states, cognition, thought, the content of consciousness. . . .

He wrote thirty pages; a few days later he began Part II, Psychopathology, in which he traced his findings in hysterical compulsion, pathological defense, symbol formation, disturbance of thought by affect; and how, through cathexis, pain and unpleasure were discharged along physical passageways. Ten days later he began Part III, Attempt to Represent Normal Processes.

He had never known so powerful a preoccupation. He confessed that he was "positively devoured" by the job of proving his theories on the basis of histology, physiology, the anatomy of the brain and the central nervous system; how the unconscious mind functioned physically through this nervous system. He invented vocabulary, evolved mathematical formulas to measure the quantity and direction of flow of memory images, drew diagrams of such important cases as the young woman who could not remain in a shop because she thought the clerks were laughing at her clothes:

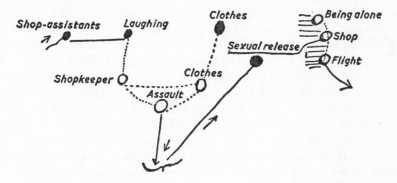

He was happy and expansive. He was being a scientist again.

Martha was fascinated by the sketches strewn over his desk. She asked him to explain them. "As a draftsman I'll never be a Daumier," he quipped, "but let me see if I can make myself intelligible. Here is a portrait of the ego as a network of cathected neurones."

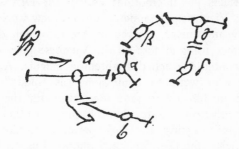

It was too technical for Martha's comprehension, particularly such concepts as "a quantity of $Q\acute{n}$ entering neurone a from $\varnothing$, the outside." "I can't grasp what your symbols stand for, Sig. That's laboratory language, isn't it?"

"Hopefully so, my dear Marty. The antagonist here, as in all laboratories, is the unknown, which has always served as a challenge to man and has frequently been his conqueror. It's simple enough to participate in exterior physical action and conflict: the men racing in the early Olympic games in Greece; the clash and clangor of opposing armies on the battlefield. Yet an adventure of the mind can be as daring and just as dangerous. I know how easy it is to romanticize oneself; but the flash of a universal truth in a human intellect can exist on the same level of excitement and accomplishment as the feat of Columbus sighting the New World from the bridge of the *Santa Maria*."

"You convinced me of that the first day we climbed the hills above Mödling; it's a part of why I fell in love with you."

"Do you remember one night last week, when you woke after two o'clock and found me still at my desk? I was writing to Fliess. I told him I was in some pain, that my mind seems to work best with physical discomfort as my antagonist, when suddenly all the barriers to my understanding fell away and I was able to perceive the innate nature of neurosis to the very detail of how consciousness is conditioned. Every part of the machine fell into place, the wheels and pulleys and cogs began to mesh. It looked as though I had evolved a self-running mechanism, including my three classes of neurones, their bound as well as free state, the track on which the nervous system runs, how, biologically, attention and defense are achieved, what creates reality as well as quality of thought, how the sexual factors operate in repression and, as a climax, the elements which control consciousness, what I define as a *perceptual function*. I tell you, Martha, the whole design holds together so logically that I can barely contain my sense of joy."

"Sigi, I'm sure you have just carved your name on a rock," she laughed gently, "but repeat after me, 'Rome was not built in a day . . . or a night. . . .'"

There were far less joyful emotions abroad for Dr. Sigmund Freud and his family. As Vienna's economic conditions grew worse the intensity of the anti-Semitic movement, spurred by the campaign of Karl Lueger for Mayor of Vienna, using attacks on the Viennese Jews as a coalescing force for the discontents, reached frightening heights. A student from the *Gymnasium* who went to confession was told, "As repentance for your sins you are obliged to pray for victory for the anti-Semites." Clergymen visited private and state schools to preach to the students, "The victory of Christianity against the dark power is coming." Crowds of young men gathered at the beer *Stuben* to shout, "Lueger! Lueger! Down with the Jews!" smashing their beer glasses and attacking any passer-by who happened to be dark-complected. The climax was reached when a Father Pfarrer Deckert concluded a Sunday sermon by advising his congregation:

"Let there be funeral pyres; burn the Jews in honor of God."

This proved too much for the Jewish community, which constituted about eight percent of Vienna's million and a half residents; and for the solid Catholic community as well. The Catholics waited upon Cardinal Dr. Gruscha, who banished Father Deckert; the Jewish committee went as a deputation to Emperor Franz Josef. He forbade the kiosks, where the Viennese were accustomed to looking for announcements of what was playing at the Opera, the Burgtheater, the Volkstheater, to be papered with the anti-Semitic posters now adorning them. Sigmund attended a staff meeting at the Kassowitz Institute. The mood was dark. One of the doctors cried:

"Today it is only a parish priest, Father Deckert; but what about tomorrow, if the one crying for funeral pyres is a chancellor?"

Sigmund was not political by nature. Now he decidedly went out to vote against Lueger and his party. To the dismay of a large part of Vienna, Lueger won a majority of the votes. Franz Josef refused to allow him to be inducted into office, stating that he was harmful to the well-being of the Empire. The city heaved an enormous sigh of relief.

13.

At last Deuticke's publication of *Studies on Hysteria* brought an affirmative result: Sigmund was invited to give three lectures before the *Doktorenkollegium*. This was not the equivalent of an invitation to speak to the Society of Medicine, which was the most important medical body in the Austrian Empire, where Sigmund had lectured earlier. The *Doktorenkollegium*, though it had at one time included in its membership all of the doctors of the university, had in the past years become less and less important. But he accepted the invitation with warm thanks. He had no false pride; if he could not be invited into the *Ärztegesellschaft* to set forth his ideas, he was happy to speak at the secondary society.

A week or two later when it became known that he was to give his lectures, he encountered another surprise. Josef Breuer turned up at the Berggasse apartment and congratulated him on the invitation.

"Sig, would you like me to speak that evening? I do want to participate, and I think my best role would be that of introducing you and in that sense sponsoring you."

Sigmund murmured his thanks without knowing just what words he used.

On the evening of the first lecture, Josef waited for him shortly before seven inside the front door of the lecture hall of the Akademie der Wissenschaften in the Universitätsplatz 2. In a few moments the chairman rapped for attention. Josef got up in front of the lectern, before the modest audience, and gave a brief sketch of Sigmund's scientific writings, starting with his work on eels and crayfish and concluding with The Anxiety Neurosis, and then the book which the two of them had done together, and of which Josef now made plain he was proud to be co-author. In his concluding lines he said:

"For a long time I did not want to believe Freud's theories were right; but now I am convinced by the abundance of facts. I agree with Freud when he maintains that the root of hysteria is to be found in the sexual sphere of the individual. This does not mean however that every single symptom of hysteria necessarily goes back to the sexual sphere. If his theory does not satisfy in every respect, his presentation makes clear that progress has been achieved."

Sigmund rose. He spoke from notes tightly integrated. He took his tone from Josef Breuer's suggestion that the experiments were tentative, that not every symptom of hysteria had to have a sexual etiology. He admitted his failures as well as his oversimplifications; he confessed to errors of judgment after which he had had to reverse his field of thinking. He conceded that he was at the beginning of his work, that there were decades of research and testing ahead; and wound up his preliminary remarks by saying that official academic medicine *had* known about the sexual factors of illness but had acted as if it knew nothing, perhaps because of a reluctance to look squarely at sexual materials. Then he went into the body of his lecture and very simply set forth the truths he had been able to find, how they had evolved and why he considered them valid.

At the end of the lecture there were a few questions asked: a mild discussion lasted for ten or fifteen minutes. The hall emptied. Sigmund linked his arm through Breuer's and walked out into the street with him, pleased with the modicum of warmth displayed by the audience. He knew he owed a good part of this to Josef Breuer's endorsement; but he also knew that he had organized his materials well and led the group of doctors from step to step with a good show of scientific precision. The crisp coolness of the October evening felt good on his warm brow. He turned to Josef and said affectionately:

"Josef, I can't tell you how much your introduction heartened me, and what it means for my future work. That's the reason the audience listened so respectfully, and gave me some applause: because you endorsed our theory of the sexual etiology of the neuroses."

Josef Breuer drew up to his full height, squared his shoulders, put his head in the air and with his lids pulled back wide above his eyes, said coldly and hostilely:

"All the same I don't believe it!"

With which he turned on his heels and walked away in the direction of St. Stephan's and his home. With a swift, almost fleeing gait, he moved out of Sigmund's sight.

Sigmund stood dumfounded. An hour before Josef had given their work a glowing endorsement. Now he not only renounced that work but by his attitude was rejecting Sigmund Freud as well! The expression on his face, the tone of his voice, his manner in rushing off would seem to indicate that Josef Breuer was terminating the loving relationship of an older and younger brother which had extended over a period of twenty years.

Sigmund shivered. He felt frozen to the spot. He could not make a move toward home. He was heartsick. What had possessed Josef to cause him to repudiate him in this fashion? What had he said to make Josef act as though he was through with Herr Dr. Sigmund Freud and his wild theories?

He forced himself to begin to walk. Slowly he covered the streets, his legs heavy beneath him. And slowly his mind began to rest on Professor Meynert, who had also repudiated his protégé . . . until he had confessed, "Always remember, Sigmund, the adversary who fights you the hardest is the one who is the most convinced you are right."

He held his breath as a conviction swept his brain. Now he understood!

Josef Breuer had told him that there was no element of sexuality in the Bertha Pappenheim case. Josef had believed this from the beginning; he believed it to this instant. Yet Bertha Pappenheim had lived through the fantasy of having had sexual intercourse with Dr. Josef Breuer; she had imagined herself pregnant by him; and the very night Josef had declared her well enough to turn over to another doctor because he and Mathilde were going to Venice, Bertha Pappenheim had felt the sharp labor pains of the woman about to give birth. When Josef reached her she had exclaimed, "Dr. Breuer's baby is coming."

Sigmund had known from his own case histories that there had to be considerable sexuality in the Bertha Pappenheim case. He had long ago suspected that the woman had fallen in love with her doctor, that she was still in love with him, that the reason she would never marry was that she intended to carry this love all her life. What he now saw clearly, and only Mathilde Breuer had known before, was that Herr Dr. Josef Breuer had also fallen in love with his patient! That was what had upset Mathilde so badly, had disturbed the peace and happiness of the marriage. For months when Sigmund came into the house he had found Mathilde red-eyed, pale. Mathilde would never have reacted so to a patient's having fallen in love with her famous and attractive husband; it had happened a dozen times before. But

Mathilde had felt endangered. Perhaps Josef Breuer did not know, and still did not acknowledge, that the depth of the love that had sprung up was shared equally by the patient and the doctor. Herein lay the threat to the family well-being.

Now for the first time Sigmund grasped why Josef Breuer had been so erratic in his attention to the Pappenheim case: he had somehow been frightened about his own emotional involvement. The kindest and gentlest of men, he would not have hurt his wife, and would have done anything to prevent it. He had apparently not had the power to remain out of love with the brainy, beautiful and utterly delightful Bertha Pappenheim; nor could he accept the fact. He had suppressed the knowledge, pushed it far back into a crevice of his mind. This could be the only explanation of his on-and-off relationship with Sigmund, his acceptance and non-acceptance of the work on hysteria and the sexual etiology of the neuroses, the year and a half it took him to write up the case . . . and now, after his most public acceptance, this utter rejection.

The evidence flooded over him, flushing his face in the cold night air. This was why Josef had stopped treating neurosis patients; why he would not use hypnotism again but sent the patients into Sigmund's care. It was why a dozen times in the past several years he had walked away from Sigmund and their researches into mental and emotional illness. And it was why tonight he had rejected his friend in such untoward and climactic fashion.

In the next few days there would appear in the *Wiener medizinische Wochenschrift* a transcript—Sigmund had seen a reporter taking notes —in which Josef would proclaim to the medical world that he backed Sigmund Freud in the sexual etiology of the neuroses.

This would be intolerable! A mortal agony to Josef Breuer! Had it been building up during the lecture and the discussion? The knowledge that he had fallen in love with his patient and would never forget her any more than she would forget him? Had Josef been all this while one of Dr. Sigmund Freud's fledgling case histories?

If Josef Breuer never saw Sigmund Freud again, if he never worked with him again, if he never had to be responsible for any of his hypotheses or explorations, could he then live at peace with himself, his medical practice, his research, his lovely wife, his solid home and solid reputation?

The clock on a nearby church struck ten times, its sound echoing over all of Vienna. Sigmund could not believe the hour. He took out his own watch to verify it. Then, bundling his overcoat up around his throat, while trembling inside its warmth, he crossed the Maximilian Platz behind the Votivkirche and strode the three blocks down the Berggasse. He felt as though it were the end of a world; that he had lost his oldest and dearest friend; as though Josef Breuer had been taken in death as had the other men he had loved: Ignaz Schönberg, Ernst Fleischl, Josef Paneth.

There was not another soul left in all Vienna with whom he could discuss his work. Now he would be alone.

BOOK TEN

PARIAH

Pariah

J AKOB FREUD died in the fall of 1896, at eighty-one. He had been in so
shaky a condition the previous June, with a series of heart attacks and
bladder weaknesses, that Sigmund decided he could not survive the
oppressive Vienna summer. He had rented a small villa in Baden for his
parents and Dolfi, the only sister still at home since Rosa had married
the month before. Jakob responded to the cool, fragrant air of the countryside, moving about and spending pleasant hours on the front porch
overlooking the verdant valley.

"Go to Aussee with Martha and the children," he had urged Sigmund.
"You need a vacation too. You have my word that I will not indulge myself in one sick hour until your return."

Jakob had kept his word. But now, late in October, with all the
Freuds back in Vienna, Jakob suffered from a paralysis of the intestines as well as a meningeal hemorrhage.

Sigmund and Alexander remained with him during his last night.
Jakob died before midnight. He had a post-mortem rise in temperature
which gave his cheeks such a ruddy glow that Sigmund exclaimed:
"See how much Father looks like Garibaldi!"

At that moment the grip on Jakob's intestines was released. The
bed was soiled. Alexander changed the linen while Sigmund washed
his father down. He then went into the next room where Amalie was
waiting. He took his mother in his arms, kissed her and said gently:
"Father had an easy death. He bore himself bravely, like the remarkable man he was."

He arranged for a simple funeral service, buying a plot in the Israelite
section of the Central Cemetery, about a fifteen-minute walk from the
entrance gate, along a path on which were large tombstones etched
with copies of Jewish temples. The nearby barber, to whom he
went every day, unexpectedly kept him waiting so that he arrived a
little late for the ritual. Alexander and Dolfi gave him unhappy looks.
That night he dreamt that he was in a shop in which a printed sign
had been nailed up:

> You are requested
> to close the eyes.

The next morning the dream came back to him. He recognized the shop as his barber's; the printed sign must mean: "One should do one's duty towards the dead. I had not done my duty and my conduct needed overlooking. The dream was thus an outlet for the feeling of self-reproach which a death generally leaves among the survivors. . . ."

His father's death had a strong impact upon him. He wrote to Wilhelm Fliess, "By one of the obscure routes behind the official consciousness the old man's death affected me deeply. I valued him highly and understood him very well indeed, and with his peculiar mixture of deep wisdom and imaginative lightheartedness he meant a great deal in my life. By the time he died his life had long been over, but at a death the whole past stirs within one."

It was an already subdued Sigmund Freud who had approached his father's death, a peaceable act compared to the subtler form of violence which had taken place months before, in which he had been both the instigator and the victim. His ostracism had been caused by a lecture, The Etiology of Hysteria, which he had given for the Society of Psychiatry and Neurology in late April. He had told Martha, "The donkeys gave it an icy reception." The disapproval of the paper and its content was total; the university medical and scientific circles would accept not one jot of its evidence or its conclusions. President Krafft-Ebing, who had been presiding in his own lecture hall at the time, declared, "It sounds like a scientific fairy tale."

Yet the real troubles did not begin until Sigmund let it be known that he was going to publish the lecture in the *Wiener klinische Rundschau,* a clinical review, in five installments during May and June. His colleagues were sternly opposed. The objectionable, inadmissible points were his findings about infantile sexuality and the sexual molestation of children. He himself had been so repulsed by the evidence that he had rejected it from the first dozen cases. How could there be so many fathers who molested their daughters, or afforded them excessive sexual stimulation? Except in such brutalized cases as that of the mountain girl Katharina, it was utterly unbelievable. When his women patients had associated back to these childhood memories, Dr. Sigmund Freud had tried to lead them into other, more credible materials. But what was he to do when he had assembled a full hundred cases, documenting the staggering fact that molestation, or sexual stimulus of some sort, was common between father and daughter as well as between mother and son?

An orderly from Professor Krafft-Ebing's Psychiatric Clinic brought Sigmund a note: could Herr Dr. Freud spare an hour sometime late in the day? Sigmund checked his appointment book and sent a reply that he would be happy to call at six o'clock. It seemed odd to be going back through what had formerly been Professor Meynert's wards where thirteen years before he had been a *Sekundararzt* and taken care of hundreds of just such patients as were now lying in these two rows of beds, ten on each side, with an occasional one contained in a rope crèche, never suspecting what might be wrong with any one of the unfortunate souls whom Professor Meynert had given up as hopeless. *How could he have been so blind? How could they all still be so blind today?* It was unnecessary to wait until these patients died, to cut the brain with the microtome and put it under a microscope to see what had failed to function. There would be nothing visible to the eye! Only in life was it possible to reach into these brains, to locate in the farthest depths of the unconscious precisely what had broken down, what in the past was causing the neuroses that ended up in these clinic beds as mental and emotional disturbances that could maim and kill as predictably as any physical disease.

Krafft-Ebing had changed Meynert's office very little; it still looked like a chapel, with its series of small high windows deeply recessed in the beamed ceiling. There were different books on the shelves, a Florentine desk set richly embossed with the Medici fleur-de-lis. Krafft-Ebing had also moved in a comfortable lounge chair covered in red Viennese damask, with a writing board across the two arms for the continuing manuscripts which poured from his indefatigable pen. He had occupied this office for four years now, since shortly after Meynert's death.

Professor Krafft-Ebing clipped his freshly scrawled pages to the writing board, rose and greeted Sigmund with a friendly smile. He had aged rather fast during these past four years; his wavy hair had thinned, receded and turned gray; there were flashes of silver in the bold, black and virile beard. But it was still one of the most powerful Roman-senator heads Sigmund had seen: deep-set eyes brooding under craggy brows, a jutting bony nose. It housed a superb brain. He was as gentle and helpful as any master of the scientific world.

There was someone reading in a corner of the room whom Sigmund had not noticed. Professor Wagner-Jauregg turned and shook Sigmund's hand warmly, almost crushing it. Wagner-Jauregg had retained his "countrylike" appearance: the powerful arms and torso of the wood-cutter. Sigmund's heart sank as he realized that he had been summoned to as influential a Psychiatric Congress as could be assembled in the German-speaking world; for Wagner-Jauregg, true to his own prediction, had been summoned back from the University of Graz to take over one of the University of Vienna's two Psychiatric Clinics. He did not appear to have aged a day since Sigmund had gone to his office to wish him good luck at Graz: the sea-green eyes, the short-cropped sandy hair, the clean-shaven, oblong blond face with its circumspect sandy mustache.

Krafft-Ebing said in his kind voice, "Thank you for coming, Herr Kollege. Ah, here is the coffee and cake. Do sit down and be comfortable."

Sigmund murmured his thanks, thought, "Comfortable, I won't be. But the coffee will help." Krafft-Ebing was not a man who smiled because something amused him but because he wanted to put somebody—usually in trouble—at his ease.

"Freud, your lecture has not done you irreparable harm; there was no reporter present, and the Society has been scrupulous in not allowing one word to be given to the press. After all, the Society is a forum open to all qualified physicians. Surely you yourself have heard many weird medical hypotheses expounded there, which never survived their maiden voyage."

"Then, Herr Professor, you think my ideas ridiculous?"

"That is perhaps too strong a word between colleagues . . ."

"I use the word without prejudice. I made myself a little ridiculous when I returned from Paris and gave my first lecture on male hysteria. That was only ten years ago, but the concept is accepted in Viennese neurological circles today. Later I made myself a little ridiculous by practicing hypnotism in Mesmer's home city . . . your arrival and faith in hypnotism as a therapeutic method heartened me. . . ."

There was a heavy silence in the room. Wagner-Jauregg paced for a moment, then said in his woodchopper's tone, every word falling like an ax on white birch:

"Freud, we went through the Medical School together, we worked side by side in the laboratories for years. I have had admiration for your work in children's paralysis. That is why I ask you: do not publish your lecture. That *will* cause you irreparable harm. You will lose the respect you now enjoy. Both Krafft-Ebing and I feel that you are moving too fast and taking too many chances. You should work for more years, accumulating additional evidence, testing your hypotheses, eradicating the possibility of error."

Sigmund felt sick at heart. He studied the faces of the two successful men before him.

Krafft-Ebing added quietly, "We have taken your lecture apart, bit by bit, and we are convinced that you are committing a fundamental error in your 'infantile sexuality' concept. It is utterly repugnant to human nature. I urge you, my dear Freud, not to let your belief run ahead of the evidential force of the observations you have made so far, as you agreed to do in your lecture. Do not abandon the ways of precise science to which you have dedicated your life. Premature publication will hurt more than your reputation."

Startled, Sigmund asked, "Whom else do I hurt?"

"The Medical School. *Rundschau* is widely read. You could do a great disservice to your university."

Sigmund groaned inwardly. He asked hoarsely, "Herr Professor, I have read some of the abuse heaped on you for your valuable book *Psychopathia Sexualis*. Surely there must have been some people who warned you against publishing such revolutionary material, most of it repugnant to human nature?"

Krafft-Ebing stood in silence, his high dark face creased in pain. Wagner-Jauregg stepped between them.

"Freud, I have a nagging feeling that there is a fundamental error built into your conclusion about the sexual molestation of children, one which you yourself will certainly catch in time, with deeper probing. That's why I urge you not to publish just yet. You know what our Austrian peasants say when they catch someone in a whopping mistake? *Du hast dein Hosentürl offen.* Your fly is undone!"

2.

Oskar Rie had asked Sigmund to join him and his brother-in-law, Ludwig Rosenstein, the following morning at a restaurant down the street from the Tuchlauben. Director Max Kassowitz was also there, a rare honor. Although the greetings were as affectionate as ever, a pervading sadness at the table kept them from eating their little pieces of veal and potato in its pink paprika sauce.

The staff of the Kassowitz Institute had been at Sigmund's lecture, backing him with their physical presence; but not one of them had been able to accept a word he said. Professor Kassowitz, now fifty-four, and deeply respected throughout European medical circles, felt that Sigmund was at a moment of crisis: that if he published his lecture there would be no turning back. Rosenstein said that Sigmund was in the middle of the ocean with nothing to hold him up but a goose feather. Oskar Rie showed him a new publication by Professors Freund and Sachs, neurologists of Breslau, in which the authors had lifted Sigmund's main ideas from his *Organic and Hysterical Motor Paralyses* without mentioning Dr. Freud's name. Oskar said with a wistful, homely grin:

"If imitation is the sincerest form of flattery, Sig, then plagiarism is admiration run wild! You're the best children's neurologist we have; almost everything that Ludwig and I know we've learned from you. Stay with us, where you can enjoy a solid, stable, respected career. Your present endeavors will keep you on the . . . fringe . . . of medical science as well as respectability. Why make such a meaningless sacrifice?"

He had walked home slowly through the late April warmth, eyes on the cobblestones, feeling as though the original bastion walls, which Emperor Franz Josef had ordered razed some years before to make the Ring, had been set up again to close him in. He was a prisoner. Two guards watched: his own inner nature, which would not allow him to retreat where he believed himself to be right; and the medical profession of Vienna, which would no longer accept him as a physician. He reported the scene to Martha word for word, as he had the meeting the afternoon before with Krafft-Ebing and Wagner-Jauregg. Her life would be affected; she had a right to know what was going on.

"Marty, these are men of good will; they want the best for me. But just as Krafft-Ebing and Wagner-Jauregg were protecting the reputation of the University Medical School, so Kassowitz and Oskar, deep in their minds, are desirous of having no untoward incident touch the Children's Hospital."

Martha was going on thirty-five. It was five months since the birth of Anna, in December of 1895, their sixth and, they were determined, last child. She had felt poorly during the end months of carrying; the delivery had been a difficult one. However the child was flourishing. Only now were Martha's health and good spirits beginning to return. Her hair, glossy black, was still pulled back tightly behind her ears; her eyes had not lost their gray-green pools of tenderness. Despite her six children, she was aging far less perceptibly than Sigmund who, at forty, was showing flecks of gray in his beard, and an embattled air.

She put her hand out to take his. During her months of slow recovery, much of it spent in bed, he had read to her for an hour each morning and evening from their favorite contemporary novelist, the Swiss, C. F. Meyer. He had kept the bedroom filled with her favorite cyclamens.

"Sigi, you are going to publish the paper?"

"Yes, I'll do a final revision after dinner and drop it off at *Rundschau* late this afternoon."

"And that, according to your colleagues, is going to be the end?"

"No, it will be the beginning . . . of a void which will close about me . . ."

Martha smiled as an indulgent mother might, murmured, "'In the beginning God created the heaven and the earth. And the earth was without form, and void. . . . And God said, Let there be light. . . .'"

Sigmund kissed her cheek as he thought, "No marriage is really fulfilled until the wife becomes maternal toward her husband." Martha continued, "You have sometimes spoken of moving to a new city. I don't think I could stand the idea of London or New York, since I have no facility with languages. But if you want to move to Berlin . . . ?"

He crouched before her chair, clasped her two hands in his.

"Thank you, darling girl, for that gift of sacrifice. But it won't be necessary. I am reminded of the Jewish story about the peddlers who roam the countryside on foot, packs on their backs, selling to farm and village. In the evenings they gather at the local inns for food and sleep, leaving their packs out in the yard. Each peddler outdoes the other in woeful lament: his pack is the heaviest, the most clumsy to carry, the most exhausting any man ever strapped on his back. Then one night the inn catches on fire. Every peddler rushes out into the yard . . . and grabs for his own pack. Vienna is my pack. Vienna is my prison. I must remain and conquer the bastion from within. My writings will be as Joshua's trumpet: enough blasts and the walls will come tumbling down."

The maid brought them a freshly brewed pot of tea. "Strong enough," Sigmund commented, "to walk upon; the best unguent for a bruised and battered ego." He sipped slowly, letting the warmth burn its way down his pipes.

"Marty, I must resign from the Kassowitz Institute. It is ten years since the day I walked into that flat above the drugstore and was assigned a room in which to begin a Children's Neurological Department. I have put in thousands of hours, treated thousands of children; I have written good and useful materials for their publications. I have wanted to resign before. This is precisely the right moment."

A frown creased Martha's brow.

"Might they not think you are resigning out of pique over their rejection of your lecture?"

"Perhaps; but they will also be a touch relieved. I'll date my resignation May sixth, my fortieth birthday. I'll become my own man, working solely in the neuroses and the unconscious. When a man has completed four decades of this arduous and uncertain life, he should have earned his freedom." He smiled wryly. ". . . 'if,' as Jakob's traveler to Karlsbad without a ticket said, after being beaten at still another station, 'my constitution can stand it.'"

The lectures were published by *Rundschau*. Doctors whom he had known for years at the Allgemeine Krankenhaus crossed the street to avoid greeting him. When he attended meetings at the Society of Medicine no one nodded or addressed him.

In Vienna a servant's luggage was referred to contemptuously as "seven plums": the ritualistic line for firing a servant was, "Pack up your seven plums and out you go!" At the Medical School the doctors were saying, when the subject of Dr. Freud arose, "He has packed up his seven plums and out he has gone." A *Sekundararzt* in what had formerly been Primarius Scholz's Department of Nervous Diseases commented about Privatdozent Freud's theories, using a common German phrase:

"*Nicht auf meinem eigenen Mist gewachsen*: Not grown on my own manure. It's not my baby."

He felt shunned and despised . . . a pariah. Time and again the cry started in his mind, though it got no farther than his locked teeth: "I am isolated! I am lonely!"

His referral practice vanished almost as completely as though he had been black-listed. There were no patients from the Allgemeine Krankenhaus, the Kassowitz Institute or the doctors who had turned to him in the past.

He continued his extracurricular lectures on Hysteria and the Great Neuroses at the university, but he drew only four registrations. He was still welcome at the Saturday night *Tarock* game, but he went rarely, feeling that his friends were pitying him. Martha tried to reassure him that Oskar Rie and Leopold Königstein were incapable of such nonsense. He wondered whether a persecution mania might be contagious. Had he caught it from that psychotic army officer he was treating?

Because there was little chance that he would be invited to speak again before any medical society, and the publication of his lecture had, in his own terms, "led to the severance of the greater part of my human contacts," he asked a former business acquaintance of his father's about a group with whom he might discuss his discoveries.

"Where can I find a circle of chosen men of high character who will receive me in a friendly spirit in spite of my temerity?"

The older man replied, "The B'nai B'rith is a place where such men are to be found. But for the purpose of the meeting you refer to, I would recommend the young people in the Jewish Academic Reading Circle."

About thirty young men assembled in the clubroom in the Ringstrassen Haus on a Saturday evening. They knew nothing of what Sigmund described as "first glimpses into the depths of the instinctual life of man," nor had they ever heard of the architectural structure of the unconscious mind. They listened in fascinated respect, then asked questions which indicated that, although they understood only the beginnings of what Dr. Sigmund Freud had to say, they were eager to know more. When he walked into the apartment on the Berggasse, and Martha saw the glint in his eye, she said:

"*Gott sei Dank.* It went well."

Fortunately the family news was good. Their relations in New York and Vienna were doing well. Pauli's first child, Rose, was born. Rosa Freud, at thirty-six, had fallen in love with Heinrich Graf, forty-four, a doctor of jurisprudence and member, after seven years of extra training, of the Institute of the Advocates, a cultivated man with a first-rate intellect and a rapidly growing law practice; an authority on trade marks and railway freight law. He was also publishing in the legal journals. Rosa had not been serious about any man since young Brust fled the Freud dining table ten years before. She had not been pining for Brust, nor had she given up the concept of marriage as had Minna when Ignaz Schönberg died; rather Rosa was a romantic who believed that somewhere in the world there was precisely the right man for her.

Sigmund had acted as best man, signed the necessary legal papers after the bride and groom had kissed under the *huppah* in the Sanctuary of the Temple of the Müllnergasse. Martha gave the wedding dinner. The apartment was filled with fragrant lilies of the valley; French champagne was served. At three they sat down for dinner, some thirty Freuds with all the children at a special table. Martha served a soup, beef with new potatoes and parsley, and then the masterpiece of Viennese desserts, a Malakoff chocolate torte with whipped cream, covered by ladyfingers. By five the bridal couple had slipped away for their honeymoon.

That left only Dolfi. Since she was a couple of years younger than Rosa, no one had worried about her being single until Rosa married. Then Sigmund and Alexander admitted to each other that there were essential differences: rather plain Dolfi had not had a man seriously interested in her.

Sigmund withstood with inner calm the attacks that were launched against *Heredity and the Etiology of the Neuroses* which he had written for the *Revue Neurologique*. Most of the commentators took their tone from Dr. Adolf Strümpell, the German neurologist who, when reviewing *Studies on Hysteria*, had given it what Sigmund described to Martha as a "disgraceful notice," casting serious doubt on Sigmund's therapeutic procedure and writing, "I do not know whether such fathoming of the most intimate private affairs can in all circumstances be considered legitimate, even on the part of the most high-principled physician."

With the *Rundschau* publication he stepped into a hurricane. He was called, quite separately, "filthy-minded," "prurient," "a sexual maniac," "a dealer in salaciousness and pornography," "a defiler of the spiritual qualities of man," "indecent, shameless, lecherous, bestial," "a disgrace to his profession," and ultimately, "the anti-Christ." His critics were, like the doctors, most sorely upset by his materials on sexuality in children, the material he had garnered when patient after patient led himself back through layers of screening to their earliest childhood and their hitherto suppressed memories of sexuality. He had learned about the various erotogenic zones which children found and on which they concentrated. After years of intensive work he had documented oral sexuality; for as he observed:

"Love and hunger meet at a woman's breast."

He was also beginning to understand some of the meanings of anal sexuality, when and how it began, and into which stage of growth it continued; some of his homosexual patients had driven back in their minds to the beginnings of their anal sexuality. What a staggering number of youngsters thought that babies were expelled through the anus . . . !

In Vienna children, and particularly infants, were considered totally innocent, divine cherubs who had no knowledge or feeling about the sometime brutish business of sex until they reached maturity. Dr. Sigmund Freud now defiled not only motherhood and fatherhood but was polluting the mainstream of child life where all was pure, carefree. . . .

"Is it better to be ill, to have one's life destroyed, than to speak of man's instinctual sexual nature?" he asked Martha, as she and her sister Minna sat having the afternoon *Jause* with him. Minna was now thirty-one. She was still the warmhearted Minna Sigmund had known at seventeen; the fact that she no longer sought personal love or a family of her own had in no way diminished her spontaneous enjoyment of life. She was a godsend to Martha, and a ray of sunshine in the Freud house during the times of discouragement. When Mrs. Bernays came from Wandsbek for one of her occasional visits, Sigmund and Martha asked if she would permit Minna to remain with them in Vienna. Minna accepted, but only after trying the plan for a few months. The children loved their *Tante*. Martha was pleased to have her sister as confidante, particularly since she had lost Mathilde Breuer.

Tante Minna found the charges against Sigmund funny.

"They couldn't have picked a more improbable candidate for their accusations," she cried. "Oh, Sigi, if only they knew what a conventional man you are! Even Queen Victoria would call you a prude. Why can't they understand that you are explaining and describing, not advocating? After all, you didn't write the plot of human nature. Doesn't Darwin say that we are descended from millions of years and thousands of species?"

"Yes," replied Sigmund, "and it would please me if one particular specie, *Homo medicalis*, walked right back into the primeval ooze it came from."

Martha looked up from her crocheting and said placatingly, "Now, dear, leave the bitterness to your adversaries."

3.

The death of his father deepened everything beyond his conceiving or understanding. His isolation, which had been bearable up to this point, became intolerable. When he confessed to Wilhelm Fliess, "I feel now as if I had been torn up by the roots," he knew that he had undergone an emotional shock of such intensity as to make him uncertain, for the first time in his life, of who or what he was. He could feel an internecine war starting inside his skull: a remembering of Jakob to keep his father alive, to keep him from being interred in the cemetery of the forgotten, and at the same time a struggling upward from the depths of his unconscious of anxieties, fears, amorphous flutterings that washed against an implacable censor with the feeling-sound of birds' wings in the dark of night; to leave him confused, inward-driven, his tumultuous half-formed feelings ricocheting between his brainpan and stomach.

He recalled the case of the forty-two-year-old man who, at the death of his father, had come down with an attack of anxiety so violent he convinced himself he had cancer of the tongue, heart disease, agoraphobia. The patient had said, "With my father dead I suddenly realized that it was my turn next. I never thought of death before my father went, and now I think about it all the time."

Sigmund had attempted to comfort him by paraphrasing a line from Goethe: "Every man owes nature a death," but this wisest of all aphorisms had failed to resolve the man's neurosis. Sigmund's efforts through analysis to reach the source of his patient's disturbance had also failed.

Now, caught in the beginnings of a neurosis of his own, Sigmund thought, "It is not our own death that frightens us; it is our father's death. Why?" Both his patient's father and his own had lived into the eighties. Both he and his patient had been good sons. Why then were his insides so tied up; why was he so depressed? "I loved Jakob, I gave him respect, I helped to support him these past ten years. I cared for him tenderly during his illness. . . . Why am I pursued by this gnawing sense of guilt?"

The Jewish religion declared it one's duty to go to Temple every day for a year to offer a prayer for one's deceased. Sigmund did not observe the ritualistic forms of religion. But symbolically in his concentration on Jakob he was doing just that: mourning work.

The immediate result of his churnings over the loss of his father was to make him dread the years ahead in which he would perforce remain an outlander in his profession and city. He could no longer tolerate the feeling that he was shunned. He needed an organization, an institution, something to which he belonged and which, in a familial sense, belonged to him.

He knew what he must do. He must get back to the University of Vienna Medical Faculty where he had always wanted to spend his life, and which he had given up fourteen years before when Professor Brücke had advised him that, as a poor young man who wished to marry, he would have to go into private practice. He wanted an academic career: offices and a laboratory at the Allgemeine Krankenhaus, continuing courses to the medical students; promotion along the way to full professor; his own department; a voice and a vote on the *Professoren-kollegium* for the running of the Medical School; the modest but steady salary. This would still leave him adequate time for his private practice and writing.

He was past forty. The depth and variety of his work in neuropathology

entitled him to an *Extraordinarius*, assistant professorship. The years had
gone by without his thinking about it, but appointment now would
solve many of his problems; it would make him a functioning part of one
of the greatest medical schools in the world, gain him automatic respect:
a professorship in Vienna was a rank which turned its holder into a demi-
god. . . . It would put an end to the cyclical nature of his practice.
Since June, when the fifth of his articles was published, through November, he had not earned enough to feed a flock of six sparrows, let alone
ravenous youngsters, though now in December he was working ten hours
a day.

But this was the worst possible time to apply!

Martha asked, "Sigi, how are you going to accomplish this miracle?
You couldn't be farther out of favor with the Medical Faculty if you
had been locked in the Fools' Tower."

"I know," he replied, "the only one left who is friendly is Professor
Nothnagel, and that's because he was impressed with my monograph for
his *Encyclopedia*."

"Perhaps you could enlist his help?"

"One is permitted to do that in his youth, seeking a travel grant or
his *Dozentur*. No, two *Ordinarii* must nominate me, the regulation
Committee of Six must investigate my work, and then the *Professoren-
kollegium* must vote for me as a body and recommend my appointment
to the Minister of Education. It is the only respectable way."

"And you are an eminently respectable man." It was Minna, teasing
him.

The members of the *Tarock* group did not show any surprise when he
showed up for the game that Saturday night for the first time in months.
Nor did Leopold Königstein, the only one in the group giving courses at
the University Medical School, raise an eyebrow when Sigmund suggested
in passing that he wished his name could be placed in consideration for
the year's appointments to the faculty. Königstein himself had been
passed over for the assistant professorship for several years.

In January, just after the turn of the year, Sigmund heard the rumor
that the recommendation for the post of assistant professor in neuropathology was going to be given to a six-year-younger colleague, Lothar
von Frankl-Hochwart. Sigmund respected Hochwart, whose monograph
on tetanus had been the first scientific description of that illness, but he
felt that his own greater age and body of research entitled him to the
position. He wrote to Fliess:

"I am left cold by the news that the Board of Professors have proposed
my younger colleague in my specialty for the title of professor, thus
passing me over, if the news is true."

During the first week of February he received the bound page proofs
of *Infantile Cerebral Palsies*, the monograph he had written for Noth-

nagel's *Encyclopedia.* He inscribed it for Professor Nothnagel and took it to his office. Nothnagel was dressed in his usual heavy black suit with silk vest, silver buttons and black silk tie. His head and face were still covered with a sandy blond hair, the two warts on his right cheek and the bridge of his nose bulbous. As the editor of the *Encyclopedia,* Nothnagel would have received these pages in any event, but Sigmund knew that the recommendations were being written for each of the departments, and that if he were to have any chance at all it would have to be right now.

Nothnagel accepted the book with his left hand and then, without looking at the inscription, thrust out his right hand to shake Sigmund's.

"Herr Kollege, this must be kept secret for a time, but Professor Krafft-Ebing and I have proposed you for a professorship, along with Frankl-Hochwart." He went to his desk and took out a sheet filled with writing. "We have the recommendation already drawn up. Here are Krafft-Ebing's signature and mine. The document is ready to go to the Board. If the Board declines to accept our recommendation, we shall send it into the *Professorenkollegium* on our own."

Sigmund felt faint. Bits of thoughts tumbled about in his head like the first fall of autumnal snow caught by a surprise windstorm. By some kind of amazing coincidence he, Sigmund Freud, Professors Nothnagel and Krafft-Ebing had thought of Privatdozent Freud as a professor at almost the identical moment. Strange, since not one of the three had made an effort in that direction in the past several years. It was not unnatural for it to have occurred to Nothnagel, for Sigmund had just enriched his *Encyclopedia* with a first-rate contribution. But Krafft-Ebing! The man who had warned him that he would be doing himself irreparable damage, and the university as well, by publishing his lecture.

"We are sensible men together," Nothnagel went on in his assured voice. "You know the difficulties. All of this may do no more than put you on the *tapis.* But it is a good beginning, and you may be sure that we will guide your nomination step by step. In the meanwhile Professor Krafft-Ebing has said he would like to see you."

When Sigmund walked into his office, Krafft-Ebing rose and wrapped both arms around his own huge barrel chest, as though embracing himself for having done a good deed. When Sigmund stumblingly expressed his thanks, Krafft-Ebing waved a hand in his face in protest, saying, "No, no gratitude. It is a thing that should have been done. What you must do now is to assemble your bibliography, all of the work you have completed, all of the research projects and all of the publications."

Sigmund thought, "What decent men they are! They are both attempting to reinstate me in Vienna's medical society. I know my chances are slight. I know how difficult it will be to get approval from the Ministry; but now I can think warmly and well of them."

Krafft-Ebing said, "Sit down, let us talk. I know what you are thinking:

that it is almost a year since I called your *Etiology of Hysteria* a scientific fairy tale and urged you not to publish the material. Yet here I am today recommending you for an assistant professorship. Why the change in heart? Well, for one thing, as you pointed out to me, I took more than sufficient abuse from my own published materials. I decided it was not a tradition I cared to perpetuate. If I don't agree with your theories about where mental illness originates, and I cannot, it is not because I don't think of you as a serious man. You are! Nor do I any longer believe you to be telling fairy stories to catch attention. That was a phrase I should never have used. I apologize for it . . ."

"You have nothing to apologize for, Herr Professor. I have been one of your greatest admirers . . ."

"Don't mistake me, Freud," Krafft-Ebing continued, his voice originating deep in the great canyon of his chest, "you are running down a blind alley. At least it looks blind to me because all of my professional life I have been trained to see the blocking wall at its end: *heredity*. I admire you for your courage and character. I shall not mention my doubts about your new theories to the Minister of Education; I shall only praise you for your good and plentiful work . . ."; he paused, "and between us, Herr Kollege, if that blind alley should happen to be in my head rather than yours, I would just as soon not have it written down in the official record."

Krafft-Ebing wrote an enthusiastic report.

Sigmund set down an abstract of his publications, which would have to be printed for the Medical Faculty Committee of Six which had been appointed to judge his qualifications.

4.

It was May. He rarely had fewer than ten neurosis patients in a day. His ability to understand his patients' illnesses and to grapple with their symptoms was enhanced by his evolving analytical technique of dream interpretation. A woman patient constantly dreamed of falling, particularly when she was shopping in the Graben, a favorite beat for the streetwalkers. Did she wish to be a fallen woman? There was the man who could not be toilet trained as a child, who had now replaced this trait with avariciousness. He dreamed of money as filth, excreta, and constantly reproached himself for desiring dirt. When he was forced to touch money, he immediately washed his hands "to remove the stink." There was the woman who was harassed in her dreams by the image of going to market with her cook carrying the basket, and being rejected by every butcher with the words, "That's not attainable any more." After a number of sessions Sigmund traced this line to a phrase which was generally similar to Wagner-Jauregg's peasant saying, *"Die Fleischbank war schon geschlossen;* the meat shop was closed." He learned from his patient that her husband no longer cared for her and had long since closed his *Fleischbank.*

He had a male patient with an intense case of anxiety, a twenty-seven-year-old who had been reduced to such a state that he could neither work nor maintain relationships. He dreamed of being pursued by a man with a hatchet, of trying to run but feeling frozen to the spot. When the patient delved into his childhood days, he confessed that he had abused his younger brother, kicking him in the head until he drew blood. One day his mother had told his father, "I'm afraid he'll be the death of him." That night his parents had come home late and the boy, who slept in the same room, pretended to be asleep. Soon he heard sounds of panting, saw his father on top of his mother in the bed. He told himself that there was violence and struggling going on. The next morning he found signs of blood in his parents' bed. Now he knew that one day his father "would be the death of his mother." Anxiety had taken root at that moment, an anxiety so severe that it took Sigmund over a year to lessen the force of his symptoms.

There was the husband who insisted that his wife take a hundred-gulden fee from him before intercourse so that he would "be sure to get his money's worth"; and who now, with his business in financial difficulties, had for five months refused to make love to his wife because he could not afford her services. Sigmund had already treated several husbands who could not persuade themselves to have sexual intercourse with respectable women and could bring it off only with those who hired out their bodies for pay.

A young girl came to him who was afraid to pick a flower or even a mushroom in the woods because it was against the will of God. "He forbids the destruction of any germs of life." The chief manifestation of her neurosis was that she could not accept anything that was handed to her unless it was wrapped up. Sigmund ascertained that her feelings about the destruction of germs arose from memories of religious talks with her mother, who inveighed against taking precautions during intercourse. The symptomatic manifestation he identified as a "condom complex," which he had come upon earlier. The young girl's illness was an unconscious revolt against her mother's teachings, a symbolic flight from authority into independence.

He was called by an internist into consultation at the home of a seventeen-year-old girl. The internist stayed in the room, as did the girl's mother. Sigmund found her intelligent but surprisingly dressed. Viennese women were meticulous about their clothing but this girl, from a prosperous family, was wearing one of her stockings hanging down; two of the buttons on her white blouse were undone. When Sigmund asked her how she was feeling she said, "I have pains in my leg," and rolled her stocking down to expose her calf. Sigmund did not examine the girl's calf, as she obviously wanted him to do; instead he asked what her principal complaint was. She replied:

"I have a feeling in my body as though there was something stuck into it which is moving backwards and forwards and it is shaking me through and through. Sometimes it makes my whole body feel stiff."

Sigmund and the internist exchanged glances. This was too graphic a description for anyone to mistake; yet when Sigmund looked over at the mother he saw that her daughter's disturbance, and her description of it, meant absolutely nothing to the older woman. He decided that the internist, who had long been the family doctor, was the one who should reveal the facts of life to the young girl.

A forty-year-old woman came to the *Parterre* with classical complaints: she had a fear of walking alone in the street; would not go out unless attended by a member of her family. She also had a fear of sitting near windows. Sigmund diagnosed the symptoms as the "prostitution wish," a vision of walking the street alone and looking for a man; as well as the custom of the prostitute in Europe of sitting in the window so that the men passing by would know she was available.

A man came to him who was well respected in the professional world of Vienna, complaining that he was afflicted by fantasies about every female he saw, including the most casual view of one on the street. The serious part of the disturbance, and the reason he had come to Dr. Freud, was that his fantasying became almost violent in nature; he went through all of the varieties and aberrations of sexual intercourse, in particular what had become his favorite form, mounting, as he had first seen it practiced by dogs in the street.

A young girl who loathed herself insisted that she was evil, ugly, worthless, should die and get out of other people's way. Before long it turned out to be a form of purposeful self-abasement; the girl had caught her father, whom she adored, having intercourse with a servant girl while her mother was ill in the hospital. She could not reproach her father, so she had made a substitution and reproached herself. Dr. Freud was able to help her understand this.

A woman patient suffered from hysterical vomiting. She had been examined by other doctors, all of whom were convinced that there was nothing wrong with her physically. After much delving, Sigmund's analysis showed the vomiting to be the fulfillment of an unconscious fantasy dating from puberty; a wish that she might be continuously pregnant and have innumerable children. Another wish, added later, was that she might have these children by as many men as possible. After puberty a defensive impulse began to operate against this unbridled wish. The vomiting was a desire to punish herself, cause her to lose her figure and looks, and thereupon make her unattractive to men.

In spite of the source material pouring through his office, and his fascination with some of the strange cases that came to him from as far away as Breslau, his emotions remained in a state of turmoil. He wrote to Fliess that inside of him there was a seething ferment, coupled to an obscure feeling that very soon something important would be added to his therapeutic technique.

The passing weeks and months had not reconciled him to the death of Jakob. He found himself unable to keep flashing images and memories of his father from intruding on his mind, even when he had disturbed patients in his office who needed all of his concentration and skill. In his small amount of leisure time, on the walks he forced himself to take along the Donau Kanal, with the woods and mountains clear in the distance, he was unable to control his reveries, his backward looks. On the surface they were pleasant memories: Jakob taking him for Sunday walks in the Prater; to hear the noon concerts in the Hof at the changing of the guard; Jakob reading to him, telling a new Peter Simpleton joke, Jakob presiding over the Passover dinner and saying the entire Hebrew service by heart; Jakob bringing him home a book on payday . . .

These memories came from an available conscious level; they were obviously not the ones causing his emotional upheaval. The only direct memory that distressed him was the scene Jakob had described one day in the Prater. "When I was a young man," Jakob had said, "I went for a walk one Saturday in the streets of your birthplace; I was well dressed and had a new fur cap on my head. A Christian came up to me and with a single blow knocked off my cap into the mud and shouted: 'Jew! Get off the pavement!'"

"And what did you do?" Sigmund had asked.

"I went into the roadway and picked up my cap."

Ten-year-old Sigmund had become bitterly unhappy, had lost respect for his father. He contrasted the situation with another which he admired in history: the scene in which Hamilcar made his son Hannibal swear before the household gods to wreak vengeance on the Romans.

The memories, good and bad, did nothing to still the inner agitation. Time, which he had thought would assuage his emotions and permit him to allow Jakob to rest in peace, was making his disturbance more intense, as though he had been seized by an invasive streptococcus which multiplied itself.

"Why can't I just let the old man go?" he asked himself. "He has been dead for half a year now; he had exhausted living by the time he died. Why has this neurosis flowered, leaving me as anxious and depressed as some of my patients?" It was no longer possible to deny it, he had become disturbed to the point of being ill.

The comparison in his mind to his own patients brought him up short. He was shopping in the colorful Hoher Markt square with its early Roman ruins, after his lecture at the university, to which only three of the four registrants had come. His patients' illnesses did not arise out of their conscious minds but from their unconscious: from early, suppressed memories that went back to their first years of life. *Hysterics suffer mainly from reminiscences!* Why then had he never applied this to himself?

He stopped dead still, his feet metaphorically caught in the cracks between the paving blocks. Cold in the windswept streets, he felt himself break out in a sweat which made him shiver. A voice in the back of his head enunciated in granite-hard words:

"My recovery can only come about through work in the unconscious. I cannot manage with conscious efforts alone!"

He walked to the nearest coffeehouse, ordered a *Grosser Brauner*, warmed his fingers by wrapping them around the steaming hot cup, then sipped the fluid in an effort to quiet his trembling. The phrase, "Physician, heal thyself," flashed before his eyes; but how could a physician uncover layer by layer the fertile earth of his own unconscious? Schliemann had deduced the precise location of the allegedly mythical Troy by an assiduous reading of Homer. Where was his Homer? He was alone in the universe. No other man practiced his craft. Fliess loved him enough to try, but Wilhelm had no part of the requisite training needed for the technique which he, the inventor and sole practitioner, had only a year before decided to call psychoanalysis: a draftsman's method for setting forth the structure of the human psyche. Had Jakob's death taken place a number of years ago, Josef Breuer might have helped through hypnosis. Certainly not now.

His body was hot inside his heavy clothing. The coffeehouse, whose warmth and smoke-filled intimacy he had welcomed only a few minutes before, became oppressive. He ran his fingertips over his perspiring forehead. If his disturbance lay in his unconscious, and there was no one who could help him to peel away the years, to get down to the bone of the matter, how was he to find his way back from hysteria to the common unhappiness that was the lot of everyman? He knew he was in serious trouble. He forced out of himself the confession that in the past months, aside from those hours when he had glued his attention to his patients' needs, he had suffered an intellectual paralysis such as he had never imagined could happen to him, a neuropathologist who understood the workings of the human psyche.

"My conscious mind cannot understand my own strange state. What am I to do?"

5.

He plunged into the external life around him. He took Martha to watch the ceremony in which the first woman was graduated by the Vienna Medical Faculty; read the numerous newspaper accounts of the parliamentary elections of 1897 in which there was a strong increase in the anti-Semitic platform; went to hear Mr. Stanley lecture on how he had found Dr. Livingstone in Africa; took the older children to watch the annual military parade and the magnificently bedecked Austrian and German Emperors. Late one afternoon he felt sufficiently refreshed to set down an idea: he had been in error to divide the human mind into two rigid categories, the conscious and the unconscious. In between there lay a much less determined area, the *preconscious,* into which parts of submerged or repressed materials which had drifted past the censor remained in a fluid, unattached form until a specific occasion and effort of will summoned them into the consciousness.

The Committee of Six processing his assistant professorship nomination did a thorough job of investigating his researches and publications. Their report to the Medical Faculty was laudatory, recommending that his name be sent to the Minister of Education. There had been some opposition at first, and the vote was delayed, but Sigmund was gratified to learn that his old companions had fought for him and voted for him: not only Nothnagel and Krafft-Ebing, but Wagner-Jauregg and Exner, now head of the Physiology Institute.

He went climbing in the mountains around Semmering with Alexander; took Martha to Aussee for Whitsun; collected Jewish jokes which, through ethnic humor, imparted both the philosophy and the survival pattern of the people. His sister Rosa, a number of months pregnant, moved into the recently vacated apartment across the hall from the Freuds. It was smaller than the Freud apartment, but well laid out, with six rooms and a spacious foyer. The kitchen, dining room and living room overlooked the back garden with its lawn and trees, and the fountain statuette in its niche at the rear.

In June the Medical Faculty voted twenty-two to ten to recommend to the Minister of Education that Privatdozent Dr. Sigmund Freud be made an *Extraordinarius.* There was nothing left now except for the Minister of Education to draw up the appointment and present it to Emperor Franz Josef for his signature. Yet Sigmund knew that few men were appointed the first time they were recommended by the Medical Faculty. There was another disadvantage. Several able men of his own religion had been denied their appointments. Königstein had gone once

to see the Minister of Education and asked point-blank whether his
religion had been holding up his appointment. The Minister had answered honestly, "Yes, in view of the present state of feeling, with all the
anti-Semitism abroad, it would not be particularly wise or politic. . . ."

One aspect of his work fascinated him, and that seemed to be going
forward on its own volition: the diagnosis and organizing of materials of
the unconscious mind which were revealed to him through his interpretation of dreams. The earliest dream he could remember, one that had
flashed back at intervals, took place when he was seven or eight: "I saw
my beloved mother, with a peculiarly peaceful, sleeping expression on her
features, being carried into the room by two (or three) people with
birds' beaks and laid upon the bed."

He awoke crying in fear and ran into his parents' bedroom. It was not
until he saw his mother's face, and was reassured that she was not dead,
that he grew calm. In more than thirty years he had never attempted to
analyze the dream because he had not known how. Now he tackled the
obvious lead, the unusually tall and strangely garbed people with birds'
beaks, who had been carrying his mother on a litter. Where did they
come from? He went to a table in the parlor where he kept the copy of
the illustrated Old Testament which his father had given him for his
thirty-fifth birthday, and in which Jakob had written in Hebrew:

"It was in the seventh year of your life that the Spirit of God began
to stir you and spake to you [thus]: 'Go thou and pore over the book
which I wrote, and there will burst open for thee springs of understanding,
knowledge and reason.'"

Die Israelitische Bibel was in Hebrew and German; it had a commentary by Reform Rabbi Philippson of Prussia, and was illustrated with
vivid woodcuts from all religions and cultures. This was the book from
which Jakob had taught Sigmund to read. Leafing through now, he came
upon several illustrations in Deuteronomy which showed Egyptian gods
wearing birds' heads. In Samuel he found one called "Bier. From a Bas
Relief in Thebes," in which a body of a man or woman with a "peaceful
expression" was being carried on a bier guarded by tall, strangely dressed
people, with birds hovering over the bier.

Nostalgia swept over him as he remembered himself as a young boy
turning the leaves of the text and illustrations; a grin twitched one
corner of his lips as he recalled that he had explored the Bible not only
for its religious text but for sexual information which other young boys
were looking for in dictionaries. He had been fascinated by the story of
King David and his son Absalom: how David had fled Jerusalem when
Absalom conspired to become king, and had left his concubines behind to
guard his property. Then, said the Bible, "Absalom went in unto his

father's concubines in the sight of all Israel." He remembered wishing he could have been present.

Now that he had identified the manifest content of the dream, what was its latent meaning? The huge birds' beaks were patently phallic symbols; in German the vulgar term for sexual intercourse was *vögeln*, from *Vogel*, bird. This brought him an image of the son of a concierge with whom he used to play on the grass in front of their house; it was from this boy that he had first learned the word *vögeln*; before that he had known only the Latin derivative *to copulate*.

His thoughts turned now to his mother. Was this the real cause of his anxiety, a dream that Amalie had died? Probably not. The anxiety was there first, from another cause; his unconscious had switched it to a more respectable or presentable form. He had been anxious in his dream. Why?

He recalled an amusing dream related to him years before by Josef Breuer's nephew, who was also a doctor. The young man, who liked to sleep late, had the charwoman awaken him. One morning she had had to knock several times, and finally called out, "Herr Rudi!" At that moment he had a vision of a chart board on a bed of the hospital in which he worked, with his name, Rudolf Kaufmann, written on it. In his dream he told himself:

"Well, Rudolf Kaufmann's at the hospital in any case, so there's no need for me to go."

A new patient by the name of Ehrlich taunted Sigmund by exclaiming, "I suppose you'll say that this is a wishful dream. I dreamt that just as I was bringing a lady home with me I was arrested by a policeman who ordered me to get into a carriage. I asked to be given time to put my affairs in order. . . . I had the dream in the morning after I had spent the night with this lady."

"Do you know what you were accused of?"

"Yes. Of having killed a child."

"Was this connected with anything real?"

"I was once responsible for the abortion of a child as a result of a liaison."

"Did nothing happen during the morning before you had the dream?"

"Yes. I woke up and had intercourse."

"You took precautions?"

"Yes. By withdrawing."

"Then you were afraid you might have begotten a child; and the dream showed the fulfillment of your wish that . . . you had nipped the child in the bud. You then made use of the anxiety that arises after this kind of intercourse as material for your dream."

He remembered his own dream of a few weeks before, when he was miffed at Fliess for going to Venice without providing him with a mailing address. He dreamed that he had received a telegram from Fliess, giving his address:

$$(\text{Venice})\begin{cases}\text{Via} \\ \\ \text{Villa}\end{cases} \quad \textit{Casa Secerno}$$

His immediate response was annoyance because Wilhelm had not gone to the pension which Sigmund had recommended, the Casa Kirsch. But what was the dream motivation? The regret he had felt at having no news of Fliess? Or disappointment because he had wanted to write Fliess about the outcome of some recent cases and was deprived of his audience because he could not send letters off into the blue? The address was a wish fulfillment; that was the manifest or surface aspect of the dream. Was there a latent content? How did these particular words get into the dream telegram? The Via came from his day's reading about Pompeii's streets, after the recent excavations. The Villa came from Böcklin's painting, *Roman Villa*, which he had seen the previous day. Secerno sounded Neapolitan, Sicilian, a manufactured word. He had already discovered that dreams could construct anything out of bits and pieces; words, buildings, cities, people; but the work was always done for a purpose, was never accidental or meaningless. So Secerno had to be a fulfillment of Fliess's promise that very soon they would have a congress farther south in Italy than Venice: Rome? The Eternal City, the eternal goal of all Sigmund's travel, adventure, fulfillment, desires. How he had longed to spend that Easter in Rome!

. . . Rome. He had four short dreams, separated by days. In the first dream he was looking out of a railway carriage window at the Tiber and the Ponte Sant'Angelo. The train began to move, and it occurred to him that he had not so much as set foot in the city. In his second dream someone led him to the top of a hill and showed him Rome half shrouded in mist. The city was so far away that he was surprised that his view of it was clear. The theme of "the promised land seen from afar" seemed obvious. In the third dream of Rome he was standing by a narrow stream of dark water, with black cliffs on one side and on the other meadows with big white flowers. He noticed a Herr Zucker, whom he knew slightly, and decided to ask him the way to the city. The final dream was the shortest, only one scene flashing by: a street corner in Rome; he was surprised to see so many posters in German stuck up on the kiosks.

He determined to treat the dreams as a series, to break them down to their component parts as he had in his dream about Emma Benn; he was convinced that there was a rational explanation for even the obscure visual images and bits of dialogue in a dream. He observed,

"Every element in a dream is traceable; every act, word and sight has meaning if one will be objective and spend the required time to think through the latent content. The manifest content of a dream is analogous to the exterior appearance of an individual; the latent content corresponds to his character."

He recognized the scene from the railroad window of the Tiber as an engraving he had seen the day before in the sitting room of a patient; the city seen in a half-shrouded mist was Lübeck, where he and Martha had begun their honeymoon. When he broke up the landscape of the third part of the dream, since he was attempting to visualize a city he had never seen in reality, he recognized the white flowers of the meadow as the water lilies he and Alexander had seen in the black marshes around Ravenna on their vacation the year before. The dark cliff at the edge of the water reminded him vividly of the valley of the Tepl near Karlsbad. He thought, "How resourceful is our dreaming; we make amalgams of places and scenes separated by time and space!"

Why Karlsbad? Karlsbad was the town to which the impecunious Jew was trying to get without a ticket . . . if his constitution could stand the beatings. Zucker? He was a man Sigmund hardly knew. It took time before the connection broke through: *Zucker* meant sugar, and Dr. Freud had sent several patients to Karlsbad who were suffering from *Zuckerkrankheit*, diabetes. In the last dream he had seen German posters in Rome. His mind went to the letter he had written Wilhelm Fliess in which he answered Fliess's suggestion that they meet for a congress in Prague. Sigmund had replied that Prague would be an unpleasant place at the moment since the government was forcing the German language upon the Czechs. In his dream he had fulfilled the wish of transferring the meeting to Rome; but posters in German had showed up on the kiosks!

"Very well, now I recognize the sights that have been manifested," he exclaimed. "What is the dream trying to accomplish? All four are connected with the fulfillment of a single wish: to get to Rome. Yet analysis has shown me that the actual wish which instigated the dream is derived from childhood. The child and the child's impulses are still living in the dreams. There must be a connecting link between the present and the past. These dreams must lead me into my unconscious. I have a phobia about Rome, both to get there and to stay away . . . in a sense, similar to my train phobia."

Moving back tortuously in time, he came upon the cache: in his latter years at the Sperlgymnasium there had been a growth of anti-Semitism. Some of the older boys had made him feel that he belonged to an alien race. In this challenge he had needed to find his identity, to "take up a definite position" as he told himself. His most admired historical figure, the Semitic general Hannibal, had vowed eternal hatred for the Romans and pledged his father that he would conquer Rome. He had crossed the Alps in 218 B.C., defeated the Roman forces at Lake Trasimeno, ravaged the Adriatic coast to the heel of Italy, then swung back to take Naples, and brought his army within three miles of Rome, ready to make the final assault. . . .

But he never did. Hannibal remained in Italy fifteen years, then withdrew his Carthaginian army. In the young Sigmund's mind Hannibal and Rome symbolized the conflict between the tenacity of Jewry and the all-pervasive Catholic Church. Dimly he perceived that Rome had become the surrogate for his own ambitions as well as his need to avenge his father for having had his fur hat knocked in the mud. It also symbolized Hannibal's failure to avenge Hamilcar, his father. On an earlier vacation Sigmund had made his own way to Lake Trasimeno, only fifty miles from Rome. But he, Sigmund Freud, could not bring himself to travel those fifty miles any more than had Hannibal. Would he always stop short of his life ambition?

With practice he became better able to analyze his patients' dreams and to use their latent content in his therapy. A homosexual patient reported a dream that when he was ill in bed he had accidentally uncovered himself. A visiting friend sitting by the bedside had uncovered himself as well, then seized hold of the patient's penis. The patient had been astonished and indignant; the other chap, embarrassed, had let go and covered himself.

"Several things come to mind about that dream, Gottfried," said Dr. Freud. "First, that your uncovering of yourself may not have been accidental; second, that you wanted your penis held by your friend; third, that you also wanted strongly to feel revulsion over the act. That has been your dichotomy. Yet I doubt that this dream can be altogether contemporary. Let's move backwards and see if we can't find the starting point in your childhood. It will be repressed."

Gottfried clasped and unclasped his fingers. He was blinking back tears.

". . . not totally repressed. Parts of it float into my mind like a bloated corpse twisting and turning down a river. . . . When I was twelve . . . I went to visit a sick friend . . . he uncovered himself . . . I caught hold of his penis . . . he rejected me . . ."

Sigmund said quietly, "In your dream you turned the story around. That was a fulfillment of a wish: that you could have been the passive boy rather than the aggressor. Your dream shows that you want to rearrange the past, that is, to be forgiven. It is an important step forward in your treatment."

He began writing on the feeling of inhibition in dreams, of being

glued to the spot, of being unable to accomplish something, which occurred so often in dreams and was so closely akin to the feeling of
anxiety. After supper he returned to his *Parterre* office to work. It was
an airless night; in the course of writing he took off his detachable
collar and cuffs. At midnight, going up to bed, he took the steps
three at a time, a sensation he enjoyed as being one of flying; it
was also proof that he had nothing congenitally wrong with his heart,
though in depressed moments he recalled Fliess's theory that he, Sigmund
Freud, would die during his fifty-first year because that was an inescapable
combination of his two controlling cycles of twenty-three and twenty-
eight years.

Halfway up to the apartment he suddenly thought how shocked anyone would be to find him returning to his living quarters in this
state of dishabille. He and Martha had a cool drink together, looked
in on the children to be sure they were not too heavily covered. During
the night he dreamed:

"I was very incompletely dressed and was going upstairs from a flat
on the ground floor to a higher story. I was going up three steps at a
time and was delighted at my agility. Suddenly I saw a maidservant
coming down the stairs—coming towards me, that is. I felt ashamed
and tried to hurry, and at this point the feeling of being inhibited
set in: I was glued to the steps. . . ."

The major difference between reality and the dream was that he had
more than his collar and cuffs off; he could not see himself plastically
but had the feeling that he had very little clothes on at all. In addition this was not the staircase leading from the *Parterre* to his living
quarters; nor was it one of Martha's maidservants coming down to
summon him or bring him a message. Rather, it was the staircase of
the old woman to whom he had been giving injections twice a day
for some five years now. The associations came rather quickly: sometimes when he went up the staircase after having been smoking heavily,
he cleared his throat and, since there was no spittoon in the building,
he expectorated in the corner of the stairs. He had been caught at
this several times by a female concierge, who grumbled her disapproval. Only two days before a new maidservant had been introduced
into the old woman's apartment, as old as was the female concierge, who
had admonished him on that very day:

"You might have wiped your boots, Herr Doktor, before you came
into the room today. You've made the red carpet all dirty again with
your feet."

This was the manifest dream, and these were the materials from
which it had been cut. What was its latent meaning? He had discovered that most exhibitionism goes back to early childhood; that is
the only time when one can be naked yet surrounded by strangers

or family without feeling ashamed. Nakedness in his dream was probably the fulfillment of a wish for exhibitionism. He knew what caused inhibitions in waking life; the motive was undoubtedly similar in dreams: a *conflict of will*, a strong act of volition coming from one's instinctual nature, opposed by a strong "No!" which arises out of background or training. He made the observation, "The deepest and eternal nature of man . . . lies in those impulses of the mind which have their roots in a childhood that has since become prehistoric."

He set down his dreams in full detail, making deductions on the basic character of dream work and its power to use an occurrence, usually of the day before, a sight or incident, as a key to open the unconscious and reveal, sometimes in cryptic form, often condensed, its stored-up content.

He wrote to Fliess, who had returned to Berlin, "I have felt impelled to start writing about dreams, with which I feel on firm ground. . . . I have been looking into the literature on the subject, and feel like the Celtic imp: 'How glad I am that no man's eyes/have pierced the veil of Puck's disguise.' No one has the slightest suspicion that dreams are not nonsense but wish fulfillment."

He had several books on dreams on his shelves: Hartmann in German, Delboeuf in French, Galton in English. Since a major part of life and the efforts of the human brain had to do with the formulating of wishes and the attempts to achieve them, dreams could help him understand not only the structure of his patients' hysterias but the normal workings of the healthy mind as well. Thus the interpretation of dreams could be a royal road not only to psychoanalysis but to the long-awaited science of normal psychology.

There was only one way to accomplish this feat: by collecting and analyzing all of his own dream material for the next year or two, as well as that of his patients and family, and write a book to be called The Interpretation of Dreams.

In early summer Minna volunteered to take the children for a fortnight to Obertressen where the Freuds had rented a villa in the middle of a woods full of fern and mushrooms, and where Mrs. Bernays could visit and have a chance to be with her six grandchildren. Tante Minna would also have the opportunity of switching from the role of aunt to that of mother.

The Freuds enjoyed their weeks of being alone together as Martha described it, though "sometimes the apartment does seem enormous and eerily quiet. Even the cook is subdued; she says she doesn't know how to cook for two when she has been preparing for a dozen." Alexander took them to hear *Die Fledermaus*. They gave the cook a week's vacation to visit her family; and ate in the outlying restaurants where they listened to the *Heurigenmusik* and drank the new wine.

When they reached Obertressen they found that the heavens had opened; it continued to rain for days, the countryside was flooded, wings of houses were demolished and washed away. Mrs. Bernays fled to friends in Reichenhall; Sigmund took Martha to Venice. Tante Minna remained with the children. In Venice, Martha contented herself with mornings of sightseeing, reading on the balcony of the Casa Kirsch during the afternoons, while Sigmund moved from church to palace to gallery to see the paintings of Giorgione, Titian, Carpaccio. When they returned to Obertressen, Tante Minna wanted a short walking tour. Martha suggested that Sigmund take her for a few days to Untersberg and Heilbrunn, ending up with a visit to Mrs. Bernays. After dropping off Minna, Sigmund returned to Vienna to arrange for his father's tombstone. While choosing the design he mused:

"Parents refuse to stay dead. They live with us to our dying day. I wonder if that is why someone conceived the idea of heavy tombstones: to keep Mother and Father down?"

Vienna's medical season opened in October, but this time without any new patients for Dr. Sigmund Freud. He was perplexed. He took two free cases, remarking to Martha, "If I include myself, that makes three non-paying patients."

He also knew that he had been prodigal over the summer. He observed, "I must not provoke gods and men by too much traveling. Besides, I should know as a psychoanalyst that a good deal of my travel compulsion is brought on by my neurosis. As soon as I solve some of my problems I'll settle into work and I won't want to go any further than the Chinese Calafati in the Prater."

6.

He had brought back from the summer vacation a piece of intellectual equipment which had not been part of his baggage when he left. While his feet had been treading the soft woodland paths of Untersberg, or the hand-made ceramic tiles of Venice's churches; while his eyes had been resting on the hundreds of variations of green in the dense forest, or the luscious colors of the Italian painters, a back area of his mind was becoming increasingly uneasy about the blame laid by his women patients on perverse acts by their fathers, evidence that had always astonished him, and which he had accepted reluctantly. He asked himself why, in those cases, he had failed to bring his analysis to a good conclusion. Why had some of his most responsive patients fled at a certain point, though some of their symptoms had abated? His findings re-soundingly demonstrated that the unconscious mind had no "indication of reality" and was unable to distinguish truth from "emotionally charged fiction." In his lecture before the Society of Psychiatry and Neurology and the *Rundschau* publication, he had taken a wrong turn somewhere, he knew that now, both as a theoretician and as a clinician.

The first indication of a breakthrough came from a female patient, a forty-two-year-old married woman, who was suffering from an insomnia that was wrecking her emotional health. The patient could give no clue as to why she was unable to fall asleep. She went to bed very tired at the end of a long day. However the moment she put her head on the pillow she began to go backwards in time, remembering fragments of scenes from her childhood, which left her unsettled, then anxious and then filled with fears that made her thrash about in her bed most of the night. Sigmund had already noted in a number of insomnia cases that the inability to go to sleep followed certain es-tablished patterns; that it originated not from undesire in the conscious mind to sleep but from the fact that closing one's eyes and getting into the posture of sleep somehow elbowed aside the censor, allowing material from the unconscious to seep into the mind like water from underground caverns, albeit frequently in transposed forms.

With this patient, as with many in the past, the fears were con-nected with muted yet erotic desires centering about her father. It took hours of intensive free association, leading her into the earliest stages of her childhood, before she began to stage the scenes of sexual attraction and molestation which had aroused the ire and repudiation of the Viennese medical world.

He had listened to these stories for almost eight years. But this patient was different: slogging backwards along the trail of her life, she would move into a description of a neurotic scene about her father, then suddenly veer off, crying: "No, no, that wasn't the way it was! It was more like this!" She would go halfway through another description of the intimacy only to falter, conjure half a dozen neurotic situations, then deny them all and break off the session . . . only to return the following day to begin from an entirely new angle a different group of fragmentary scenes of her intimate relationship with her father. . . .

Sigmund let out a groan so audible that the patient was shocked out of her state of near somnambulism. She opened her eyes, blinked hard, demanded, "What is it, Herr Doktor? Is something wrong? What have I said? What have I done?"

Sigmund replied quietly, "Nothing, nothing at all. You are doing fine. Please continue." When the woman began speaking again he took a deep breath; he felt sick at heart and sick to his stomach. With an inward groan which bruised his rib cage he exclaimed to himself:

"I have been misled! We are not dealing here with child molestation! We are dealing with *fantasy!* With what, in their earliest childhood, these patients *wished for.*" The fantasies had taken root; they had survived over all the years as scenes of reality. Covered over, carefully screened, kept from sight and view and knowledge of the adult, but there, as a living force, causing what the poor woman was suffering now as she writhed on his couch trying to wring out, almost from the time of her infancy, her wish fulfillments in relation to her father. Why had he never seen this? Why in these cases had he taken these disturbed and emotionally ill people at their word? It all appeared true; they were not lying or cheating or attempting to deceive. They were telling the truth as they saw it, overwhelming evidence of case after case of a truth that he had not wanted to accept. Yet all the time he had been unable to distinguish between the reality and the fantasy.

He had been right about infantile sexuality; it was there beyond question, earlier than anyone in the world had ever suspected or been willing to admit; but not as he had projected it. He was wrong for the right reasons. Krafft-Ebing and Wagner-Jauregg had been right for the wrong reasons! It was with a profound sense of relief that he understood at last that ninety-nine percent of the relationships had never taken place; and yet his patients thought they had, and made themselves ill just as surely as though the sexual intimacy had occurred.

He was so shaken that he asked the next and last patient of the day if he might be excused. The patient appeared relieved. After he had gone, Sigmund locked the outer door of the *Parterre*, went to his files and took out the cases of patients who had come up with infantile sexual residues. He read the material now, his heart beating so violently that he thought it would blow up the *Parterre* as had the gas main when the watchmaker lived there before him. The same evidence of fantasying was present in every record! He recalled Dr. Bernheim's statement in Nancy, "We are all hallucinating creatures"; but how could he, Sigmund Freud, have known that this hallucinatory power extended back into the earliest reaches of childhood and could exert its influence into adulthood? The signs were there, for any man with his eyes wide open: the incongruous elements, the contradictions, the improbabilities of sequence. Why had he not recognized the true nature of these grotesqueries?

He paced the room. Well, there were reasons: he had been so staggered by the discovery of infantile sexuality that he had been unable to discard any part of the evidence. There had to be a background of truth to such universal relating of father-child phenomena. He had searched the literature in the field; there was no mention anywhere of the fact that the infant was born with a full set of sexual instincts, that there were sexual feelings, gropings, instinctual strivings buried within the genes which began to manifest themselves almost at the moment of birth. But enough of this hindsight . . . granting now the revolutionary theory of infantile sexuality, why had it been inverted by the patients? Why were not the manifestations faithfully and honestly recorded in the unconscious? Did neither the unconscious nor the censor have any equipment with which to distinguish between reality and fantasy? Why was the patient and then the physician misled about what had actually happened? There was another factor with which he had yet to come to grips. These fantasies were not pointless, they were not without a purpose; they were used by the psyche for a reason. What could it be? And what lay behind infantile sexuality that was so unacceptable, so apparently heinous to the human mind that it caused inversion and denial?

He had stumbled into the labyrinth by watching where he put his feet. Observing carefully every step, he had made his way halfway through the maze. Here he stood now, exhausted. Wagner-Jauregg, in his countryman fashion, had said it right:

"Do you know what the Austrian peasant says when he catches somebody in a whopping mistake? *Du hast dein Hosentürl offen.*"

He excused himself from supper, telling Martha that he had to make an emergency call. He was looking distraught but assured her that there was nothing wrong. The expression on her face told him that his tone carried no conviction. She said simply:

"We'll keep your supper warm. Try not to be too late."

He walked for two hours, making his way through small business districts and residential sections, then through open fields and suburbs on his way to Grinzing. It was the same route he had taken some fifteen years before, when he left Professor Brücke's office after being told that there was no place for him in the scientific world. He ached in almost every part of his mind and body, even as he had then. Yet above the recrimination and self-reproach, the agony of having exposed himself with half-baked conclusions, there kept floating to the brim of his mind a scene which had recurred to him over the years since he was seven, which had frequently been in his conscious reveries, and equally often in varying forms in his dreams. He had never attempted to discern what the scene meant. One night when he was seven years old, he had gone into his parents' bedroom after they were apparently asleep; the door had been firmly closed, though not locked. As he stepped into the darkness of the room there had been a series of movements in his parents' bed, dimly seen and heard, and not understood, which upset him terribly. His father, sensing that someone was in the room, had turned his head over his shoulder to look back, seen the boy standing there and subsided in whatever he was doing. The next scene was hazy in Sigmund's mind: sometimes he saw himself urinating on the floor just inside the door, at other times he had a blurred impression of having run to the bed, thrown himself into his mother's arms and micturated there. His father was so disgusted that he had said:

"The boy will come to nothing."

He had been taken to his own bed and put to sleep by his mother with comforting words. Yet the sentence had never left his mind. Was that why the scene returned to him so often? Perhaps so; but underneath lay another element with which he had never before grappled. Why had he urinated in his parents' bedroom? Up to the age of two he had occasionally wet his bed, and when he was reprimanded for this by his father he had said consolingly, "Never mind, Papa, I promise to buy you a nice new red bed in Neutitschein." But he had never wet his bed after the age of two, or micturated in any place except where it was proper to do so. Why had he committed this outrageous act at the age of seven, without any apparent need to relieve himself, and only because he was upset by what he found going on in his parents' bed?

The answer came out of the night the way meteors flash across a dark sky. He had been jealous of his father! *He had wanted to interrupt and put a stop to what was going on!* He had chosen the most dramatic method in his power of doing so. He had wanted to oust his father from his mother's attentions and take his place in her affections. By micturating, was he simulating the very act, in the only way that a seven-year-old boy can, which his father was about to perform? Taking over from his father, and completing the love act which he had surprised in process?

But this was outlandish! He had loved his mother and his father both. He had never had any desire to come between them. Neither had he shown any preference. His father had been the greatest man in the world to him. Then why had this memory haunted him for over thirty years, concealing its meaning but never losing its poignancy?

He was glad that Vienna did not yet know about the scientific error he had committed in confusing the reality of infant sexuality with its fantasy. He was determined not to expose himself further until he could establish the motivating cause. He had not the faintest notion of what it was; yet he summoned the moral courage to put an end to his self-chastisement over assuming he had reached the end of a road when he had merely reached a halfway house. He thought:

"If I had not made my way as far as this mistake, there would be neither a need nor an opportunity to go beyond it and complete the whole of the journey."

7.

Painful as was the revelation of the scene in his parents' bedroom, his thoughts turned more and more to Amalie. By hours of free association before, after and, regretfully, sometimes during his consultations, he traveled backward to an incident that had happened before the end of his third year. It had come into his consciousness on and off ever since he was a boy but he had dismissed it as a random memory-trace. He saw himself standing in front of a large piece of furniture which he sometimes thought of as a cupboard and at other times as a wardrobe. He was screaming his demand for something, he could not remember what, while his half brother Philipp, who was twenty years older than he, held the tall door of the cupboard open. At that moment his mother, Amalie, seeming to him to be slim and beautiful, came into the room as though she had been returning from a visit. He had sometimes asked himself, "Why was I crying? Was my brother trying to open or shut the cupboard? What had the entrance of my mother to do with the scene?" He remembered thinking once that perhaps his half brother was teasing him and that his mother had come in to put an end to it.

Now, with the experiences of the past weeks upon him, he knew better. There was a central psychiatric point to the memory; that was why it had been preserved intact for thirty-eight years. He had to find that core.

Had he missed his mother? Did he fear that she was shut up in that wardrobe or cupboard? Was it for this reason that he was demanding that his brother open it? Why, then, when it was opened, and he saw that his mother was not inside, had he suddenly begun to scream? It was in the midst of this scream that his memory stuck.

That night he had a dream in which an old nurse who had taken care of him in Freiberg moved into the picture and quickly out of it; but not before he perceived some reference to the nurse being locked in a wardrobe or cupboard.

The next day after dinner he walked over to Amalie's apartment. His mother had suffered far less from the death of Jakob than had Sigmund. In fact, she seemed to have grown fifteen years younger. There was good color in her cheeks and a laugh on her lips. More than ever she earned the title her children had bestowed upon her, "Frau Tornado," moving the furniture every few weeks in order to do a thorough cleaning; driving Dolfi half out of her mind by her need for activity. It was not the first time Sigmund had noticed that widows who had loved their husbands, and whose husbands had lived a full life, grew younger in widowhood and carried around with them the air of having been let out of jail. He kissed Amalie on each cheek while she hugged him for a moment, then asked, "Mother, you remember in Freiberg when I was not quite three years old, I had a nurse. . . ."

"Yes, she was a relative of the landlord, the locksmith. Her name was Monica Zajic." Amalie laughed: "The old girl had deft fingers. While I was confined with Anna she stole everything movable that she thought I wouldn't look for. When I got out of bed again, your brother Philipp caught her and took her to court."

"Now I remember," Sigmund cried. "That was the very same time I asked Philipp what had happened to Monica, and he replied in that clever way of his, 'She's boxed up!'"

Later that night while Martha slept quietly by his side and he lay with his hands behind his head on the pillow, sleepless, he began to put many factors together. On the apparent side he remembered the scenes because of a fear of his mother having been boxed up in a cupboard; she had evidently disappeared for a few hours, even as the nurse had disappeared the day before. He was afraid that Philipp had locked his mother up. Unraveling the threads, he also began to perceive why he was aware that his mother was slim and beautiful. She had been big with child for many months just prior to this, and when Anna was born Sigmund had been jealous of the infant and the attention paid to it by his parents. In one context he did not want his mother "boxed up" as the nurse had been; but in a more profound sense he passionately did not want anything more in his mother's box. He did not want her to have any more children. Was that why he had stopped screaming and been so relieved when she came into the room thin and without child?

He rose, put on his robe, wandered through the hallway and into his study overlooking the Berggasse, aware of the dim gas lights in the deserted street and the darkened windows of the Export Academy opposite. Another and far more serious implication had come to him. About a year before the birth of Anna, Amalie had had a son whom they named Julius. Sigmund had been filled with hatred of his brother from the moment he was born, racked by infantile jealousy. The death of Julius at the age of six months had stowed the germ of guilt in Sigmund's mind. *Is not the wish the father of the act?* If he had never wished that Julius were dead, the little boy would still be alive. He had killed him! And was terror-stricken that his parents might discover that he had been responsible for the death of the infant. The days were dark; a cloud had settled over his mind.

Had he ever really come free of this guilt? He knew now that the incident had never disappeared from his unconscious. It had been repressed and allowed to leak through only in terms of screen memories. Surely this indestructible sense of having sinned could have caused him to be mildly neurotic throughout his childhood and youth. And if this sense of guilt over having killed his younger brother had lain buried and dormant, yet so vitally alive that he could recall the pain and terror of it even at this moment, what other semi-fantasies remained in his unconscious, and in the unconscious of all humanity, that drove people to incapacity and death without their ever guessing what devils or demons were pursuing them?

It was with a profound sense of shock that he realized he was already in self-analysis; for he had come to understand that he would have to be analyzed, even as he analyzed his patients. Yet the idea was unthinkable. No man could analyze himself, even though some authors had tried to come to an understanding of their earliest and deepest motivations. It was an extremely emotional moment for him, not unlike a trauma. He knew the dangers involved: there was no one to lead him or guide him; there was no one to help him back from the edge of any number of psychological abysses into which he could stumble; he had seen what had come out of the dark caverns of other people's minds; how could he force himself down through the nine layers of Dante's *Inferno* until he reached the central city of Dis, if what Dante meant by the central city of Dis was the ultimate, perhaps all-destroying truth about a man? He was not incapacitated as were the patients who came to the *Parterre* hoping for relief; nevertheless he was undergoing a withering debilitation. Was it not likely to get worse as he moved deeper into the subterranean caves?

No one had ever attempted this kind of journey alone. The trail was infested with fire-spewing dragons. He knew what an elaborate network of defenses every psyche threw up; his own materials would be as rigidly repressed as those of his patients. He would suffer the same agonies he had seen them endure as he led them on the backwards trail through time and space. He had watched in his own office while patients reverted to their earliest childhood, re-created the scenes which were at the seat of the disturbance, laughing and crying, cajoling, raging, reliving the upset as it had taken place twenty, thirty, forty years before. They had turned against him, the physician, in an act of transference, as though he were the offending mother or father against whom the accusations, reproaches and hate-laden emotions were pouring out. To whom could he make the necessary transference when there would be no one else in the room? Might he not go into shock?

For three days he was overcome by fright. It was as though two giant hands were crushing his head so that all of his thoughts were as jangled and disconnected as any group of electric wires jerked forcibly out of their connection. He ate and slept poorly, could neither read nor write, work nor laze; there seemed no way to escape his predicament. He recognized the feeling of inner binding about which his patients complained.

Caught in a threnody for his father and trapped halfway up the mountain of self-analysis, which he could neither ascend nor descend, he grew irritable, suffered abdominal disturbances, pushed his patients too hard, led them into paths where free association would not rightly have taken them, lost interest in them. He became depressed, introverted, hopeless about his own life and that of the world, invaded by the fear of his own death. He suffered pains all over his body which left as mysteriously as they had come, only to be replaced by aching muscles or sore bones. Self-reproach boiled within him; he was inhibited in all of his activities . . . even lost the capacity to make love.

With a resolute act of will he disciplined himself with his patients, managing to re-establish his technique of quiet persuasion. However he had no such success in serving as physician to himself; he could not rid himself of the gnawing anxieties, unnamed dreads, unformed infirmities hovering over him like shapeless clouds; the inner shrinkings. His feelings toward his father continued to suffer a series of traumas which caused his image of Jakob to alter radically. He remembered Jakob's Peter Simpleton story: a peasant died and his son wanted to have a picture of him. He found a painter and described to the artist exactly what his father had looked like: hair, color of the eyes, shape of the face. When the boy saw the portrait a few weeks later, he burst into sobs, crying: "Poor Father, how much you have changed in such a short time."

The portrait of Jakob was changing day by day, not merely because of his conscious remembering, but because another figure was emerging, scrap by scrap, from his unconscious. It was not so much a different and changed Jakob Freud as it was a vastly different and changed father-and-son relationship. After a year he now believed that a father's death was the most important event, the most poignant loss, of a man's life. Yet what continued to baffle and distress him was the fact that, as he reviewed the cases of a number of his male patients, there frequently emerged a death wish on the part of the child against the father. This death wish did not come down consciously to adult life. He had never entertained a death wish against Jakob! Then could what he had learned from his patients also be true of himself: that the almost universal death wish from early childhood remains fresh and festering in the unconscious? That although rigidly repressed by the stern defenses of the psyche, its emotive force breaks through when a current crisis pushes the censor aside? That there seeps out guilt, torturing self-doubts and ultimately the inability to cope with the contemporary world?

Why would any son want to have a death wish against his father? There were violent men who beat their small sons, who forced them into slavish menial labor, who deserved to be hated. Under these conditions a son might well wish his father dead; in fact he would dream of it, in some form or other, with each passing night. But most fathers were not like this, they loved their sons, treated them well, gave them as good a home as was possible. Why then did so many of his male patients, whose analysis revealed no valid reason to hate their fathers, end up with this wish for them to die?

It was a puzzle of staggering proportions.

He was rescued by his dreams.

The more he thought about his father, the more his dream material centered around his own earliest years. The realization came to him that even a three-year-old child has some kind of prehistoric, instinctive knowledge of the procreative act. One night he had a dream about enormous fires burning with almost jetlike intensity in the dark night. He stood before them for only a few moments before rushing past. Yet it was not he who was rushing past; he was being carried past, forcibly. When he awakened he had an uneasy feeling in his stomach: anxiety was there, also dread, but inexplicably mixed in, a rush of excitement, of almost sensual joy. He went at once to his study, picked up his pen and began separating the elements of the dream. At first he associated the flaring, hissing fires with Dante's *Inferno,* but this yielded no result. Then he turned to the dream element in which he was being carried . . . by what? A person, a carriage, a train . . . ?

A train! He could feel the wheels begin to move under him. It was night; he was in his sleeping clothes. There was noise of steel or iron and hissing steam as the train ground to a stop. He rose from his sleep, gazed out the window. There he saw the flaming gas jets of the station, the first he had ever seen. They had reminded him of souls burning in hell, as ardently Catholic Monica Zajic had described them to him, throwing all the passion of her religious conviction into the harrowing tales of the damned being reburned every day, so that little Sigi would never be a bad boy and go to hell when he died.

That would account for the anxiety and fear awakened by the dream. But what about the joy and excitement that were still making his insides tremble? Who could have caused that? For that matter, who else was on the train in that little room where they were sleeping above the wheels? Not his father; Jakob was not along. Monica had been left behind. Then who else was there who could have . . .

He broke out in a profuse sweat. It was his mother! He saw her standing in the small space, nude. Having put her two children to sleep, she had taken off the last of the voluminous clothing, petticoats, corset, stockings, and was just reaching down to her berth to pick up her nightgown and slip it over her head.

He rose, was swept by dizziness, sat down again. Now at last he understood his train phobia: his planning of the trip, of packing days in advance, getting to the station an hour before train time, being the first to put his bags on a rack . . . then, rushing off the train, standing on the platform, reluctant, holding himself back until the conductor's boarding whistle, flinging himself up the steps, half in dread, half in exaltation . . .

His day had been thrown into chaos. He could not think two consecutive thoughts. Was it not disrespect to remember his mother without clothing? He was forty-one, Amalie sixty-two! Why was this material surfacing about his mother now, when it was his father's death that had so severely upset him? What had happened to this memory for the past thirty-eight years, that it had never once emerged? For that matter, why did this have to be a true memory? Why could it not be a fantasy, of the kind that little girls wove into their desire to be loved by their fathers? Actually he knew nothing of such a journey, such a train, such a compartment. . . . He would simply have to find out.

That Sunday when Amalie and Dolfi came for midday dinner, Sigmund took his mother aside.

"When we left Freiberg," he asked, "did we take a train that went past flaming gas jets?"

Amalie raised her eyelids.

"How extraordinary that you should remember! Yes, when we passed through the station at Breslau, on our way to Leipzig. We lived there for a year. I was just preparing for sleep. But I saw those gas flames too. Then I saw you leaning up on your elbow. Your eyes were as big as full silver moons."

That night his dreaming returned to Freiberg; and to Monica Zajic. She was bathing him in a basin in which she had already bathed. The water was tinged red. Then he saw her rushing him in his toilet training; she had always been overly severe. "You must do your duty. You must be punctual. You must be regular." Then she was dressing him, petting his private parts and assuring him that he was the finest boy in the world, that he would be rich and powerful when he grew to be a man. . . . Then they were in church, listening to the choir and the mass; only it was Monica who was burning in the fires of hell, not he. . . .

He awakened with shards of memory flying about in his head like blind bats. The red-tinged water was obvious: Monica had been menstruating. Then why was he not now repulsed at her bathing him in it? Because as his nurse, even though she had seemed old and ugly, she had served as a surrogate for his mother.

He pursued the dream trace of the church. Monica had taken him to mass every Sunday morning. Though he had not thought of it all these years, he could smell the incense as the priest swung the censer, hear the choir boys in their white surplices; see the bleeding Christ on the Cross behind the altar, the mural of the Assumption of the Virgin Mary. He had been well trained, by osmosis, in Catholic ritual and panoply so different from the stern, unadorned Synagogue.

His mind soared: now he understood why he loved religious painting, particularly the rich, colorful Italian art; it also explained in part why he had turned away from the ritual of his own religion; and by the same token had been reasonably comfortable with the omnipresent Catholicism which surrounded him.

But why in his dreams had he consigned Monica to the fires of hell? That took hours of struggling recall, driving himself backward relentlessly until at length he reached his own prehistory, that time in a child's life before his conscious mind begins recording events and memories. In his dream Monica had encouraged him to steal ten-kreutzer pieces to give to her. He had judged the culprit guilty and condemned her.

A few nights later he dreamed again of Freiberg. It was in their home above the locksmith's shop. His mother was crying, Jakob was grim of visage. There was a tiny coffin in the room. Jakob was pointing to it, accusing Sigmund . . .

He awoke with a start, trembling. What had come to him through free association was now returning in the form of a nightmare. He poured cold water into a basin, used a washrag to cool his face, running it over his hair and the back of his head. Jakob had been right to accuse him of the crime. With Julius buried and vanished forever, Sigmund now had all of Amalie's love. He had always known he was guilty: it had not taken Jakob's accusation to bring him to justice. Perhaps now that guilt would be extirpated; exorcised by his nightmare.

He thought, "Penetrating oneself is good exercise; but excruciatingly painful."

He sensed how incomplete his analysis was; he had years of intense searching ahead. Yet he became enchanted by the intellectual beauty of the work. The euphoria was followed by days in which he moped about because he could neither understand nor decipher any part of a previous night's dream or a daytime fantasy. Self-analysis was impossible without objectively acquired knowledge, yet he would go for stretches when his will was paralyzed, as well as his power to set down words and communicate his ideas. Some of his patients wandered off, discouraged when he could not give them significant help. His weekly lectures at the university were ineffective because he did not know where his thinking was taking him. Sometimes only one or two listeners showed up. He discontinued speaking at the B'nai B'rith; even an audience of friendly faces could not resolve his perplexities.

He had a dream centered about a pile of ten-gulden notes which he gave to Martha for her housekeeping money each week. Through a chain of associations he came back to the dream of the ten-kreutzer coins which Monica Zajic had urged him to steal from his parents.

"Just as the old nurse stole my ten-kreutzer pieces and toys, so do I now get money for the bad treatment of my patients!" he exclaimed.

It was both exhilarating and chastising to see what a close watch his unconscious was keeping on his day-by-day analysis, and how sternly it was judging him. Occasionally a concept came through with the clarity of a printed truism, such as the one derived from a wealthy male patient who was miserable and hated life.

"How can that be, Herr Doktor, when I have everything I could conceivably want?"

"Happiness is the deferred fulfillment of a prehistoric wish. That is why wealth brings so little happiness; money is not an infantile wish."

As he had expected, he was experiencing the emotional turmoil which he had witnessed in his patients. The nature of the problem still appeared dark; at the same time he had the feeling that he only had to put his hand out to be able to grasp what he needed to know. The turbulence hid the reality from him. Then his mind would clear and the "inner work" get hold of him, hauling him through the past in a rapid succession of scenes like the landscape seen from a train. The words of Goethe came to him:

"*And the shades of loved ones appear, and with them, like an old, half-forgotten myth, first love and friendship.*"

To Martha's inquiries he replied brusquely:

"Don't disturb me with personal questions." Then guiltily he would explain something of the process he was undergoing. He had long ago introduced her to the unconscious mind, explaining that, "The great writers have always known that man has two minds, and that frequently he is driven by uncontrollable forces which he neither understands nor even knows are present in his nature. You'll find this implication in Sophocles, Dante, Shakespeare, Goethe . . . above all, Dostoevsky, who knew most about the unconscious, though he would not have called it by that name."

She asked, "Do you believe you can achieve total analysis of self?"

"It's the only way I know to resolve my own neuroses and to live peaceably with myself. When I accomplish it, it will help me to get to the bottom of my patients' unconscious and neuroses as well."

"Have you not, all these years?"

"Reasonably well. But since Jakob's death something has happened, and I must come to an understanding of it."

"My father said that no man should know everything about himself, that it could be shattering."

He smiled ruefully.

"It is. But no matter. I am not a dish that can be dropped and broken on the kitchen floor. What I can take apart of my own character I can put together again, as a good mechanic reassembles a machine."

8.

The revelation had been trembling on the threshold of his preconscious for weeks now, perhaps months. The series of revelatory dreams had afforded him interlocking fragments of the puzzle; as far as he could determine, the solution lay in a dream in which he relived the family's departure for Leipzig, and then Vienna, with his half brothers Philipp and Emanuel separating from them to live in England. It was at this moment that Sigmund had learned that the older man, Jakob, was his father, not Philipp, who was his mother's age. It was also at this point that he had moved into active competition with his father. It was not enough that there should be no further children growing in Amalie's stomach! Jealous, fearful that he would lose his mother's love, he had wished his father's death!

His mind reverted to the production of *Oedipus Rex* at the Hofburgtheater to which the Breuers had taken the Freuds ten years before. The answer had been there all the time; and yet he, Sigmund Freud, searching for years for the cause of neuroses which he could not unravel, had been too obtuse to recognize it. He saw Oedipus, having blinded himself, about to depart for Thebes as a mendicant; heard him cry out to his two unfortunate daughters:

> What curse is not there? Your father killed his father
> and sowed the seed where he had sprung himself
> and begot you out of the womb that held him.

But the words he heard most clearly now were:

> Then I would not have come
> to kill my father and marry my mother infamously. . . .
> If there is any ill worse than ill,
> that is the lot of Oedipus.

He had come to grips with the ultimate truth: his neurosis at the death of Jakob had been caused by the fact that his unconscious was holding him guilty of having wanted to kill his father and lie with his mother!

He wrote to Fliess:

"I have found love of the mother and jealousy of the father in my own case too, and now believe it to be a general phenomenon of early childhood. . . . If that is the case, the gripping power of *Oedipus Rex* . . . becomes intelligible. . . . The Greek myth seizes on a compulsion which everyone recognizes because he has felt traces of it in himself. Every member of the audience was once a budding Oedipus in fantasy. . . ."

It was universal then for a boy to desire his mother and a girl her father. It was also normal for these materials to be fantasied and then repressed, as he had learned at dire cost. How could any adolescent live with such knowledge in his conscious mind? Murder and incest were the oldest crimes in history, most rigidly punished. . . .

. . . punished? Yes, just as he had been tormented these last months. The father's death had suddenly made the son accountable for his sin against the older man. The shovels digging the father's grave had dug a six-foot trench from the son's unconscious to his conscious. While the censor was occupied burying Jakob, the repressed memories of childhood flooded the gate and anguished the culprit. That was what so many of his patients were suffering from.

His patients! How many he had failed, bringing them little help because he had not understood . . . good sons, who on the death of their fathers had developed omnipresent fears and murderous impulses; Herr Müller who had heard voices in the present . . . from a past Sigmund had not been able to identify; the young law student who had thought he was going insane and asked, "Am I not a doomed man?" because while masturbating he had fantasied his mother beneath him. . . . And the women . . .

But how could he have cured them when he had not known what was wrong?

He took his English copy of *Hamlet* off the shelf, plunged into the reading of the play whose lines were so familiar to him. When he had finished he put on his heavy coat and hat and went for a walk in the blinding snowstorm. He returned home exhausted in body but with his mind passionately eager to set down his revelation. He pushed aside a large stack of notes from the front of his desk, opened his notebook:

"The same thing may lie at the root of *Hamlet*. I am not thinking of Shakespeare's conscious intentions, but supposing rather that he was impelled to write it by a real event because his own unconscious understood that of his hero. How can one explain the hysteric Hamlet's phrase 'So conscience doth make cowards of us all,' and his hesitation to avenge his father by killing his uncle, when he so casually sends his courtiers to their death and dispatches his friend Laertes so quickly? How better than by the torment roused in him by the obscure memory that he himself had meditated the same deed against his father because of passion for his mother—'use every man after his desert, and who should 'scape whipping?' His conscience is his unconscious feeling of guilt."

He realized why it had taken him so many years to understand the Oedipal situation: *resistance.* Because of the strength of his own Oedipal ties he had resisted perceiving the truth about the play, his disturbed patients, and finally himself. It was only when he had seen himself going into a severe neurosis that he had forced himself, using his own method of analysis, to shatter his repression and probe to the germinal cause. Because he had analyzed himself, played on himself all the tricks of repression, regression, defense, concealment, suffered self-revealment, been "tied up" in depression, unable to work or communicate, but in the process had achieved self-analysis, he would be able to proceed step by step with his patients. He would be the more skillful in serving them.

He had a deeply emotional reaction to his discovery. If he were right about the Oedipal theme, and the evidence from his male patients told him that he was, then he had now penetrated to a focal core of the human situation.

BOOK ELEVEN

"WHENCE COMETH MY HELP?"

"Whence Cometh My Help?"

THE FIRST days of 1898 seemed to serve notice that the New Year had scant hopes for itself. With the old year having run its course without an appointment from the Minister of Education, Sigmund had to accept the fact that he had been passed over for the position of associate professor. No one had been appointed in neuropathology.

He received a note from Josef Breuer, the first in two years. Would Dr. Freud treat a relative of his, Fräulein Cessie, whom the other neurologists of Vienna had been unable to help? Cessie, whose father was dead, worked all day, earned a modest wage, and could see the doctor only at night. Sigmund summoned the young woman to his consultation room and told her that he would charge her half of his regular fee. The next morning he went to the post office to buy a money order for three hundred and fifty gulden to send to Josef, his first payment on a long-overdue debt. He asked Martha to write an accompanying note.

Josef Breuer returned the money by the first *Dienstmann* he could find in the Stephansplatz. Sigmund could tell how furious Josef was by the construction of his sentences. He had never considered the help he had given to Dr. Freud as a loan; it had been a helping hand from an older friend to a younger. He neither wanted nor expected the debt to be paid. Since Dr. Freud was treating Fräulein Cessie at half his regular fee, this three hundred and fifty guldens should be used to compensate for Dr. Freud's generosity. . . . Sigmund wrote a long letter to "Dear Dr. Breuer" insisting that money borrowed always had to be repaid.

Fräulein Cessie's illness had started at sixteen; she suffered a form of schizophrenia, blank areas where she could face neither people nor life situations. Apparently her mother was also a latent schizophrenic and had built a mutually parasitic relationship with her daughter. Sigmund likened this relationship to the lichen which is made up of two parts, one a fungus and the other an alga, which feed off each other and depend upon each other for life. Cessie's troubles had begun when she first became aware of sexual maturing, had her first contacts with young men . . . and discovered that she had no base in reality. Her mother had become ill, Cessie was terrorized at the thought of losing her source of sustenance; at the same time there had come a budding love affair with a young man. Since she had no coping mechanism for either event, regression set in, Cessie returned to an infantile state, looking for youthful solutions to adult problems. She relied more and more on fantasy, lapsed into long periods of withdrawal or depression. Though she was able to retain the routine clerical job Josef Breuer had secured for her, and nurse her sick mother, in all other aspects of life Cessie had sunk so deep into the empty spaces in her psyche that she had disappeared, particularly from her own view. Sigmund worked hard with her, but none of the techniques which had been effective with withdrawn or "absent" egos brought any results. Her resistance made her incapable of free association; in the course of each hour she fell into one of her emptinesses and disappeared as effectually as though she had fallen through a trap door in the office floor.

At the same time he was having his first serious differences with Wilhelm Fliess in their ten years of comradeship. They had had three short meetings the year before. In Nuremberg, Wilhelm had come up with a staggering conception: *bisexuality*. There was no such thing, suggested Fliess, as a "pure, one hundred percent male" or "pure, one hundred percent female." Every human being had within him the element of both sexes, both physically and psychically. Wilhelm had not yet completed his mathematical tables which would suggest the ratio of male to female in he had established to his own satisfaction that the norm would be somewhere between seventy to eighty percent of the male in the male and female in the female. Any sharp rise above this level would be abnormal and dangerous; it would create too much male or too much female, the monsters of the earth who have such a need to demonstrate their maleness that they strut, fight, plunder, destroy; or their femaleness in that they must preen, cajole, deceive, seduce. Any deviation below the seventy percent could be harmful for the opposite reasons: the male lost his "manhood," began slipping into feminine forms, of appearance, of speech, of mannerism; became soft, indirect, even simpering. The female moving down the equation scale became hard, rough-voiced, harsh of feature and body, masculine in her walk, tastes, attitudes, pleasures. What did Sigmund think?

"Wilhelm, it's just too staggering a departure for me to assimilate at the first telling. There are a few hermaphrodites of course; I had one in my office last month pleading for help. Mollusks and worms have both sex organs, and have survived for eons; but no one has ever had the temerity to suggest that all human beings are psychically hermaphrodites, two thirds male and one third female, or vice versa."

"Yet it's true, Sig." Wilhelm's face was radiant. "You'll see that I am right."

It took Sigmund only a few days after returning to Vienna to decide that the theory provided a logical answer for two of the most baffling yet any individual man, or the ratio of female to male in any one woman, but powerful elements in the psyche: repression and resistance. He noted, "It would seem obvious that the repression and the formation of the neuroses must have originated out of the conflict between masculine and feminine tendencies."

He went back to his records of earlier cases and recalled the plaintive cry of one of his homosexual patients: "I have a female brain in a male body." Alongside each of the records he made an observation:

"There is a touch of homosexuality in every person. Normally it does not reveal itself in waking hours; but it will come through in a dream fragment. . . .

"The tendency of dreams to employ the sexual symbols bisexually reveals an archaic trait, for in childhood the difference in the genitals is not known, and the same genitals are attributed to both sexes. . . . In no normally formed male or female are traces of the apparatus of the other sex lacking."

In women the clitoris, or analogue of the penis, was part of the external genitalia. Much female masturbation centered around the clitoris, which little girls regarded as a beginning penis. The male had breasts and nipples. He remembered a young woman patient who was hounded by the concept of witches soaring through the air. In her fantasies she was forever flying with a broomstick between her legs. Sigmund speculated, "Could it be that the broomstick of witchcraft is the great Lord Penis?"

The problem with Fliess arose during their holiday in Breslau after a day and a half of walking about the capital of Lower Silesia, with the bridges across the Oder River dividing the old and the new towns, exchanging their "ideas in progress." Sigmund had become indisposed and taken to bed after the midday meal, thinking to sleep for an hour; but Wilhelm drew up a chair and, combing his fingers agitatedly through his hair, cried:

"Sig, since I saw you in Nuremberg I've been able to put a biological base under bisexuality. I call the new approach *bilateralism*. Now listen closely, and your stomach ache will vanish."

Sigmund had rarely seen Fliess so excited; his black eyes were flashing, he was making wide encircling gestures with his hands and arms.

Each of the two halves of the human body contained both kinds of sex organs! The uniting of the male and female became complete in each half of the body by itself. There was femininity in the left half of a man, even if this side included a testicle and the lesser male sexual organs. Every human being contained within his body both the male cycle of twenty-three days and the female cycle of twenty-eight days, running concurrently, causing disturbances in the psyche. Since the two halves of the human body lived independent and separate existences, on certain days of the cycle the left side dominated, on other days the right. That was why people sometimes had pain on the left side of the head, at other times on the right. By plotting his own tables each person could tell in advance which side of his body would dominate, or rebel, on each particular day of his cycle.

Further, Fliess continued, his voice resounding off the walls of Sigmund's modest hotel room, he now had a valid explanation for left-handedness: left-handed men were yielding to their female cycle and were dominated by female sex organs on the left-hand side of their bodies.

He was so absorbed in reading from his charts that he did not see the look of incredulity on Sigmund's face. In one thing, however, Wilhelm was right. Sigmund's stomach ache had vanished, to be replaced by a dull pain straight down the middle of his skull. He rose on one elbow, studied Wilhelm's features to see if his friend were entertaining him with a fantastic hoax. But there was no doubt about the man's seriousness.

And Sigmund Freud was frightened . . . for the first time in his relationship with Wilhelm Fliess. Why did Wilhelm always need to run his ideas into the ground? No doctor could seriously posit such a proposition. But he couldn't tell him . . . or even question him; something was sure to get into his tone of voice. It was better to leave it alone. Wilhelm knew he did not feel well, that would be a good excuse for silence. Besides, he would have the perfect answer: "Sig, you disputed my bisexuality theory in Nuremberg, but within a week you were writing to tell me it was the greatest discovery I had ever made, that it would become one of the foundation stones of your psychoanalysis." Could this conceivably happen again with bilateralism? But no, the whole concept was crazy!

He groaned aloud, rubbing his stomach circularly on top of the blanket. Fliess took the hint, said, "Sleep it away, Sig. I'll wait for you in the lobby."

Upon reaching home, Sigmund wrote to Wilhelm, "What I want now is plenty of material for a mercilessly severe test of the left-handedness theory. I have got the needle and thread ready. Incidentally, the question that is bound up with it is the first for a long time on which our ideas and inclinations have not gone the same way."

Fliess took the defection badly, pouring out a tumultuous letter in which he made it clear that he not only took Sigmund's criticism amiss but was outraged at the rejection. In the letter was also the implication that Sigmund was rejecting the left-handed theory because he, Dr. Sigmund Freud, was left-handed without knowing it!

Sigmund's reply was gentle; he took no offense at Fliess's innuendo about his probable left-handedness; he simply suggested several reasons why Fliess's concept could have no biological base. Wilhelm would not allow a single one of his postulates to be questioned, even though he knew that Sigmund had been trained by Brücke, Fleischl and Exner, three of the world's most talented physiologists. Sigmund realized that the fault was his own; for ten years he had praised Wilhelm to the skies, declaring him to be the boldest, most inventive medical scientist in Europe. Now the pupil was repudiating the master!

Though Sigmund had urged Wilhelm to poke holes through the fabric of his own reasoning, and Wilhelm had responded to the invitation with enthusiasm, Sigmund Freud was the one man in the world from whom Wilhelm Fliess could not take criticism. But then had he, Sigmund, not known for three years now, ever since Emma Benn's nose operation, that Wilhelm was a *génie manqué*, that he made near fatal errors of judgment? By performing an operation that was unnecessary, then leaving gauze in Emma's nose to fester and nearly kill her through hemorrhaging? Looking at the naked facts with the benefit of his self-analysis, he understood that when he had written Fliess, after the unfortunate operation, "Of course no one blames you in any way, nor do I know why they should," he had been protecting his relationship with a friend who could not accept criticism, a friend he did not want to lose, a man he adored and needed. His unconscious had properly blamed Fliess. Had he now become free to risk that dearest friendship?

2.

Leopold Königstein dashed into his office late one afternoon in February.

"Sig, congratulations: I just heard the news. You're on the Minister of Education's new list for the associate professorship! It will be given to you by Emperor Franz Josef himself on December second, the day of his Golden Jubilee."

"Are you sure, Leopold?"

"Yes. I can't divulge my source, but someone saw your name on the Medical Faculty appointments."

Sigmund controlled his joy, remembering that Leopold had been rejected for six consecutive years. "And what about you, Leopold?"

Königstein looked away, regained control of himself.

"Maybe on Franz Josef's hundredth anniversary of becoming Emperor, in 1948. Remember, you're going to need a cutaway coat, morning trousers for your appearance at court . . ."

A few days later student demonstrations closed down the university because of the edict that declared that the German language had to be written and spoken throughout the entire Austro-Hungarian Empire. It had caused an uproar the year before. Sigmund's eleven men in the Great Neuroses course were a bright group and learning fast; he hated to give up his twice-a-week lectures. Then he hit upon a simple expedient; he invited the students to come at the designated hour, Wednesday and Saturday at seven, to his *Parterre*.

The idea worked well. Sigmund sat behind his desk, the students in a semicircle before him. There was a feeling of intimacy, enhanced by mugs of beer and cigars which Privatdozent Freud handed around. At the university all lectures had to be formal; nor were the students permitted to ask questions or react to the professor's presentation. Here in his private quarters Sigmund was able to speak in a conversational tone, address himself to each of the eleven men, pause in the middle of a point if he saw that someone was troubled.

"It's more like a seminar than a lecture," he explained to Martha when he went upstairs. "I enjoyed it thoroughly. There were some good exchanges, too. Someday I would like to have a permanent group like this, young people who come in of an evening for solid talk, everyone free to take the conversation where he wishes so long as he can defend his case. There's a human warmth about it that I find lacking at the university."

He had cured himself of the neurosis caused by his father's death by penetrating to the core of his own Oedipal condition, enabling him to treat his patients with added wisdom and authority. Many of the cases that had looked as though they were breaking down were back on the rails. His own analysis was by no means complete; it would perhaps take years to bring to the surface the last revenants of his unconscious. But he was confident that his mental and emotional health would never again be seriously challenged.

His noon patient was a broker who had been under Sigmund's care for almost a year and had made sufficient progress in staving off his hallucinations to be able to go back to his job in the Börse. Sigmund had not been able to cure him because he had not known the fundamental cause of the hallucinations; now it was clear because of his resolution of the Oedipal theme. However when he led the banker back to his childhood, to his obsessive love for his mother and hatred for his father, the man terminated his analysis.

Other patients rebelled at his use of this Oedipal tool. Those who started their treatment being civilized and well mannered became vulgar, untruthful or defiant; they malingered . . . until with infinite persistence he enabled them to lay bare the source of their illness so that the meaning was inescapable. Some of the patients improved, resumed their responsibilities to their families and their jobs. Others who had abandoned their treatment in despair returned a little later and made slow progress.

"There is a science of analysis," he exulted. "The analysis of the psyche. But God help me! What will Vienna do when I announce the Oedipal situation?" He was already in the stocks for besmirching innocent children. Now he would be compounding the felony by claiming that the origin of that sexuality was incestuous!

Very well, he would keep his thoughts to himself . . . for a very long time. Wasn't it Virgil who had said that no man should publish his writings until nine years had passed? Even the doughtiest warrior had a right to let the wounds of one battle heal before he entered another. He lighted a cigar and puffed away at it.

His stomach pains disappeared, his heart felt fine, his immersion in the well-being of his patients returned. So did his capacity for making love, for reading and writing and intellectual exploration. The journey into his own prehistory had banished his most persistent guilts and anxieties. He dropped his self-analysis in favor of the dream book, searching for material from ancient civilizations on the Oedipus legend; writing in a happy surge of energy such early chapters as The Function of Dreams, The Method of Interpreting Dreams, and Analysis of a Specimen Dream. He took Martha to hear Mark Twain, translating the colorful American's broad humor for her. He played "A Hundred Journeys Through Europe" with the children, read to them from Nansen's *Farthest North*. He tried to teach Martin how to write poems that scanned as well as rhymed. The family followed the trials of Dreyfus and then Zola in Paris. He read Arthur Schnitzler's new novel, marveling at how much a fiction writer could reveal about the sexual motivation of man.

He began to perceive that he had formulated too narrow a concept of the unconscious; and that he had made a mistake in passing moral judgment upon its content. Because he had derived his materials from distressed patients and from the self-analysis of his own disturbed state, he had thought of the unconscious only as a dark, evil force, lying in wait to ambush and strip bare the defenseless passer-by.

He had said from the outset that he meant to make his way from abnormal to normal psychology, from the sick and psychically disabled to the well human being who was functioning normally. It was this pursuit which led him to see the margin of his error; he had failed to take into account the other portion of the unconscious, perhaps the other half, which contained life-giving and life-sustaining instincts, creativity. It was from this part of the unconscious that most great and illuminating art was derived. He wrote:

"Creative writers are valuable allies and their evidence is to be prized highly, for they are apt to know a whole host of things between heaven and earth of which our philosophy has not yet let us dream. In their knowledge of the mind they are far in advance of us everyday people, they draw upon sources which we have not yet opened up for science. . . ."

His own dream material was gratifyingly rich, enabling him to document his manuscript. One night he dreamed that he had written a monograph on a certain plant. The book lay before him and he was "at the moment turning over a folded colored plate. Bound up in each copy there was a dried specimen of the plant, as though it had been taken from a herbarium."

He proceeded chronologically, bringing up associations in the order in which the elements occurred in the dream itself. The morning before he had paused in front of a bookstore window to look at a newly published monograph, *The Genus Cyclamen.* Cyclamens, he reflected, were Martha's favorite flower. He reproached himself. "It's a shame I don't bring Martha her favorite flowers as often as I used to."

He turned to the word *Monograph.* Despite the fact that he had displayed no talent for botany at the Sperl, he had years later published a monograph on a plant: *On Coca.* He had called Karl Koller's attention to its anesthetizing effect on the tongue, which enabled Karl, now practicing successfully in New York, to try it on the eye, and perform hitherto impossible eye operations. Koller and Königstein had then performed the glaucoma operation on Jakob.

. . . *cocaine* . . . that had to be a connecting link . . . yes, a few days earlier he had seen a copy of a *Festschrift* gotten up by Dr. Stricker's students to celebrate the twenty-fifth anniversary of his nomination as a full professor. The book had mentioned that Karl Koller had discovered the anesthetic qualities of cocaine in Stricker's laboratory, with no mention of Sigmund Freud's contribution. He had been hurt, and then angry at himself for not having stayed with the work for another few weeks and made the breakthrough to which he had led Koller and Königstein. But he had been too much in love; it was a year since he had seen Martha; he had rushed off to Wandsbek to his beloved.

Königstein . . . On the evening before the dream Königstein had walked him home from a lecture. Königstein was upset:

"Sig, you've made sexuality your favorite hobby; you are too much concerned with it. A doctor should take care of a diseased eye or lung or bone . . ."

"Leopold, try to think of the unconscious as analogous to cocaine. With psychoanalysis we will be able to perform operations on the mind that were impossible before, just as you have been performing operations on the eyes."

"*Monograph* . . . I am trying to finish my monograph on The Interpretation of Dreams" The day before he had received a letter from Fliess saying, "I am very much occupied with your dream book. I see it lying finished before me and I see myself turning the pages." So sharp was Sigmund's desire to complete the monograph that he envied Wilhelm his gift as a seer, saying to himself, "If only I could see it lying finished before me!"

The last element in the dream was the folded colored plate. It took a considerable time to scramble over the slag heaps of memory; at length the whirling picture stopped when he was five and his sister Anna three.

They were playing on the floor of one of the early Freud apartments; their father had given them a book recounting a trip through Persia. Jakob had encouraged them to pull out the colored plates leaf by leaf as though it were an artichoke. Jakob had been amused at the deflowering of the book.

What was being suppressed? Were certain elements of his interpretation screening other memories?

He persisted. Eventually the childhood memories came through, but they were of such an intimate and personal nature that he could not bring himself to write the materials into the proper chapter. He had enough troubles in Vienna as it was; how could he walk past the Opera of a Sunday afternoon, with all of the city promenading in its most stylish regalia and he, Sigmund Freud, stark naked? He used a subterfuge: he would write the materials for an article to be called Screen Memories, inventing a patient five years younger than himself. He would enter into a dialogue with the "patient," letting his other self reveal these autobiographical materials.

The first scene that emerged was a steeply sloping piece of meadow, thickly green, with a large number of yellow dandelions. Chatting at the front door of a cottage at the upper end of the meadow was a peasant woman in a kerchief and a children's nurse. He, Sigmund, then three, was playing with his half brother Emanuel's son John, a year older, and Emanuel's daughter, Pauline, Sigmund's age. They were picking the yellow dandelions when he and John agreed that Pauline had the best bunch, fell upon her and took away her flowers. She ran crying to the peasant woman, who gave her a piece of black bread to eat. The boys, envious, threw their dandelions away and ran to the peasant woman, who cut them each a slice of the bread. The bread was delicious, the scene broke off . . .

Why was this magic lantern show now available to him? What were the elements that had left it in his memory? The intense yellow of the flowers? The deliciousness of the black bread? The fact that they had treated little Pauline badly? The yellow dandelions took him back to a visit he had made to Freiberg when he was sixteen, when he had fallen in love with Gisela, the fifteen-year-old daughter of the old friends with whom he had stayed for the holidays. They had wandered the woods together during her school vacation, the girl in a dandelion-colored dress. He had not spoken of his love; when she had returned to school he walked the same woods fantasying that Jakob had not become bankrupt in Freiberg; they had not had to live in Vienna; Sigmund had grown up in his father's trade, prospered; he had married Gisela Fluss, they had been happy in these woods together.

His niece Pauline . . . When he visited her home in Manchester he had sensed that his half brother Emanuel had thought that he would fall in love with Pauline. But he had not; he had been a slave to his books and had had no emotion left over for the girl. Why not? Well, to take flowers away from a girl was to deflower her, and he had already done that! He had not realized this at the age of three; but in later years he had implanted the knowledge backwards.

Why did he remember with so much pleasure the tearing out of the colored plates from the book about Persia? Because "pulling out" refers to masturbation. Was that why he enjoyed artichokes so heartily? And why now he was remembering his first feeling for masturbation when he saw himself playing on the floor with his attractive sister Anna?

Was he visualizing Jakob chuckling with glee as they "pulled out" the colored plates because later he, Sigmund, had feared discovery as all boys do, and wished for Jakob's approval instead?

3.

Since he had some ten patients who needed daily sessions he remained in Vienna during July, while Martha and the children went to Aussee. He had midday dinner at his mother's apartment with Amalie, Dolfi and Alexander. When an unbearable heat settled down into the city, he sent his mother and sister to Ischl for the rest of the summer.

His patients, except for Fräulein Cessie, with whom he had admitted defeat, made such substantial progress that when he prepared to join Martha he was in high spirits. That evening he took Alexander to supper, good-naturedly chaffing their waiter and cab driver. He mildly resented Alexander's getting out of the carriage sooner than necessary and taking the Stadtbahn (Suburban Railway) home instead of going with him to the West Station and riding with him to its first stop. It was raining lightly when he reached the station and was too early to get on his overnight train. He arranged with a guard to be admitted to the platform so that he could get a preferred compartment. As he stood there he saw Count Franz Anton Thun, Prime Minister, drive up in an open carriage. The guard demanded Count Thun's ticket, but the Count waved him aside with an imperious gesture and ended with the best compartment in the train going to Ischl, the Emperor's summer residence.

Sigmund decided he would claim equal rights with Count Thun when his own train came in; in the meanwhile he hummed to himself an aria from Mozart's *The Marriage of Figaro*. Thinking of counts, he remembered Beaumarchais's phrase about the gentleman who had been kind enough to take the trouble to be born; and about the *droit du seigneur*, wedding night privileges, which Count Almaviva in *Figaro* was trying to demand of his lovely young servant, Susanna. He thought too of the journalists who disliked Count Thun and had nicknamed him "Count

Nichtsthun, Count Do-nothing." At that moment a man passed him on the platform whom he recognized as the government inspector for medical examinations; he had been dubbed by the Viennese the "government bedfellow." The inspector demanded that he be put in a first-class compartment and be left there alone. Sigmund had a first-class ticket and he felt that he too should have a compartment to himself. When he boarded the train the conductor put him in a corridor coach where there was no lavatory available during the night. Sigmund's complaints were without avail. Half jokingly he said to the conductor:

"The least you can do is bore a hole in the floor of the compartment to meet the possible needs of the passengers."

That night he had a dream: there was a meeting of students whom Count Thun was addressing. Someone in the crowd challenged him to make a comment about the Germans. Count Thun answered derisively, saying that the Germans' favorite flower was the coltsfoot, after which he inserted the crumpled remains of a leaf in his buttonhole. Sigmund found himself upset about this but also surprised that he cared. The scene now shifted to the Aula, the assembly hall of the university. Since all the entrances were closed, he escaped through a series of exquisitely furnished rooms. The only one he met with was a stout elderly matron who offered to accompany him with a lamp. He instructed her instead to remain on the staircase. "I felt I was being very cunning in thus avoiding inspection at the exit. I got downstairs and found a narrow and steep ascending path, along which I went."

The next problem was to escape from the city; but the stations were also closed off. After debating where to go, he decided upon Graz. Once in the compartment he noticed that he was wearing a plaited, long leaf object in his buttonhole. Again the scene changed: to the front of the station, where he was in the company of an elderly man who was blind in one eye. Since he was apparently along as a sick-nurse, he handed the man a male glass urinal. Here the man's attitude and his micturating penis appeared in plastic form.

At this point Sigmund awoke, took the gold watch out of his upper vest pocket and saw that it was a quarter to three in the morning. He was almost never awakened during the night with any physical need. He asked himself:

"Did my physical need provoke the dream, or was the desire to micturate called up by the dream thoughts?"

He deduced that his dream had been set in motion by Count Thun's aristocratic behavior on the platform. That was why he, Sigmund, without realizing the connection, had sung the aria from *The Marriage of Figaro*, an opera which had been banned by Louis XVI because it mocked royalty.

He ruminated on the dream for the rest of the night; then for the next several days wrote down his associations in an attempt to get beyond what had been manifest, to understand its latent implications. The aristocratic Count Thun led him to a scene when he had been fifteen years old; he and his fellow students had hatched a conspiracy against the unpopular German-language master. The only young aristocrat in the school, whom the boys had nicknamed the "Giraffe," was being abused by his master but nevertheless managed to put his favorite flower into his buttonhole. This flower represented the beginning of the War of the Red and White Roses. This led him to the red and white carnations worn in Vienna, the red ones by the Social Democrats, the white ones by the anti-Semitic party. Politics took him to Viktor Adler, who had formerly lived in the Freud apartment. The thought of Adler returned him to the Berggasse; from there his thoughts went directly to his mother's house. In his dream he had been in the Aula and had made his way through a series of beautifully furnished rooms. He had long surmised that rooms meant women, *Frauenzimmer*, frequently public women; he also knew that if one dreamt of the various ways one went in and out of these rooms, the interpretation was no longer open to doubt. What had he been doing symbolically in his dream: taking a series of women?

Whom did the elderly stout woman represent? The woman thought he had the right to pass; he felt he was being "very cunning in thus avoiding inspection at the exit."

Why had he finally decided to go to Graz? He had been boasting, which is a common form of fulfilling a wish; in Vienna the slang phrase, "What's the price of Graz?" expressed the vanity of a man who feels prosperous enough to buy anything.

He turned his attention to the last incident, the elderly gentleman with one eye to whom he handed a male glass urinal. Since a prince is the father of his country, Sigmund's reflections went from Count Thun to Emperor Franz Josef and then directly to Jakob, his own father. He thought again of the two early urinating episodes, the first when he was a bedwetter and had been reproved by Jakob; the second when he had entered his parents' bedroom and discovered his father's sexual activity.

In his dream he had taken pleasure in ridiculing Count Thun, then in ridiculing the "government bedfellow," authority figures standing as surrogates for his own father. He wrote in his notes: "A dream is made absurd . . . if any one of the dreamer's unconscious trains of thought has criticism or ridicule as its motive."

He was astonished at the intensity of aggressive feelings against his father which still existed in his unconscious. Jakob had had glaucoma, been nearly blind in one eye, and now the son was revenging himself on the father by being the one who stood by as the authority figure while the old man micturated into a male urinal. He had not been obliged to cut a hole in the floor for his father to relieve himself, since he was a medical man and hence knew how to buy a glass urinal. This reminded him of the story of the illiterate peasant at the optician's who tried glass after eyeglass and still was not able to read.

He felt a sense of guilt about the aggression until he remembered a play, *The Love Council* by Oskar Panizza, in which God was portrayed as a paralytic old man, who nonetheless was about to punish human beings for their sexual practices. The added point about *The Marriage of Figaro* was that Count Almaviva was a father figure who was duped, and had his sexual desires exposed, for which he was obliged to apologize.

He wrote in his notebook, "The whole rebellious content of the dream, with its *lèse majesté* and its derision of the higher authorities, went back to rebellion against my father . . . the father is the oldest, first, and for children the only authority, and from his autocratic power the other social authorities have developed in the course of the history of human civilization."

The important part of his dream, he realized, was that even after apparently resolving his Oedipal situation, his infantile feelings of jealousy, competition and aggression against his father could still emerge when given the proper stimulus. He had cured himself in his waking life but not in his dreams! Then he remembered again his oldest dream, the one that went back to his seventh or eighth year, when he had seen his mother with a peaceful expression on her face, being carried into the room by people with birds' beaks. When he had analyzed the dream earlier he had been unable to understand why he had felt so much anxiety over it. Now he knew. He had been dreaming libidinously of his mother, an act which always brings unconscious fear to a boy, in addition to terror that his father would find out. From recent male patients he had learned that what he called the *castration terror* was common, arising in a boy during his early phallic stage when most of his energy and interest centered on his genitals. Incest is the cardinal sin, for which there is only one proper punishment; that the offending member be cut off . . . and necessarily by the father, who is the transcendent authority figure.

4.

Despite the fact that there was a growing rift between them, Wilhelm Fliess was still Sigmund's sole audience and critic. He had already sent Fliess an early chapter of the dream book, which included an analysis of his first dream about Emma Benn. Now he sent him the next chapter, titled Dreams as Wish Fulfillments. Without waiting for Fliess's comments he began work on the first drafts of chapters on Distortion in

Dreams and The Psychical Processes of Dreaming. Martha and Minna knew the nature of the book he was writing, but they were the only ones in Vienna who did.

Over the summer he took various members of the family on short trips; no one would stay out with him very long because of the cyclonic tempo of his touring, what Minna labeled his "ideal of sleeping in a different place every night." Each time he returned with a small statuette or ancient artifact, the prize of his journey. He could not afford these travels, but he was living by a venerable Viennese proverb: "The way to get rich is to sell your last shirt." In September Minna and her mother took over the care of the children so that Sigmund could take Martha to Ragusa (Dubrovnik) on the Dalmatian coast. Martha loved the walled city so much that she declined Sigmund's invitation to take side trips. One morning he rented a carriage with a pleasant stranger who liked the idea of visiting a town in nearby Herzegovina. While traveling they chatted about the Turks in Bosnia. Sigmund told the man stories that had been related to him by a colleague who had practiced in Bosnia.

"They treat doctors with special respect and they show, in marked contrast to our own people, an attitude of resignation towards the dispensations of fate. If the doctor has to inform the father of a family that one of his relatives is about to die, his reply is, 'Herr, what is there to be said? If he could be saved, I know you would help him.'"

He then remembered something else his colleague had told him about the Turks in Bosnia: the overriding importance they attached to sexual enjoyment. One of his colleague's patients had said to him, "Herr, you must know that if *that* comes to an end, then life is of no value." However he decided he did not know the other man well enough to confide such a story. Instead he let the conversation turn to Italy and pictures. He recommended that the man visit Orvieto to see the fresco of *The Last Judgment* in the cathedral. This particular chapel had been decorated by a great artist by the name of . . .

. . . of? His memory failed him. He could see vividly the figures of the frescoes. But the only two artists who came to mind were Botticelli and Boltraffio.

For several days this lapse of memory tormented him, until he fell in with a knowledgeable Italian who provided the name at once: Signorelli. Sigmund cried, "Of course, Luca Signorelli. But why did I forget it? Nothing is forgotten by accident. There is always a reason, one that can be traced through logical steps."

He began jotting down his notes: the name Signorelli had been inaccessible to him, repressed, because he had just repressed the story about the Bosnian worship of sexual enjoyment. But what was the connection? Both stories about patients had begun with a *Herr* which is the German equivalent of *Signor*. Therefore the *Signor* half of Signorelli had been suppressed. Since they were discussing Bosnia, it was natural for Bo—tticelli and Bo—ltraffio to come to his mind. But why Boltraffio, not nearly as well known a name as either Botticelli or Signorelli? Because a few weeks before he had learned that one of his homosexual patients had committed suicide, the news reaching him in the Tyrolean village of Trafoi which provided the second half of the name Boltraffio. He drew for himself a schematic diagram of what he termed a *parapraxis:*

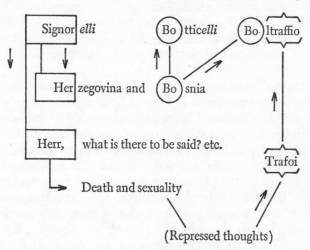

He wrote an article based on the incident, calling it The Psychical Mechanism of Forgetfulness.

When he returned to Vienna Sigmund found a paper from Fliess on a physiological discovery. Sigmund considered it too emotionally written. He also felt that Fliess had overestimated the importance of his finding. That night he dreamed a sentence:

"It's written in a positively norekdal style."

The word that was not a word puzzled him. He separated its components. Recently he had read an attack on Henrik Ibsen. Nora was the name of the heroine of *A Doll's House.* Ekdal came from *The Wild Duck.*

"The interpretation of dreams is like a window through which we can get a glimpse of the interior of the mental apparatus. . . . Dreams frequently seem to have more than one meaning. Not only may they include several wish fulfillments one alongside the other; but a succession of meanings or wish fulfillments may be superimposed on one another, the bottom one being the fulfillment of a wish dating from earliest childhood."

The common denominator of both Ibsen plays, in addition to their other plot elements, was conflict between father and son. Norekdal had been formulated in his dream because the article he had read about

Ibsen had contained a criticism suggesting that his scenes were too emotional, that he overestimated the value of the relationship he wrote about: precisely the criticism he had made of Fliess's paper! He jotted down the material as an illustration of what he called *condensation in dreams*.

He could reject Fliess's human cycles of twenty-three and twenty-eight days for male and female, which Fliess was now extending to cover the cosmos; but there was no way to reject the cyclical nature of life: the change of seasons, crops in the field, the animals dropping their young, the historical movements of industry, politics, science, nations, civilizations.

He had returned from his travels to find Vienna in a pall: the Empress Elisabeth had been assassinated in Geneva by a vagrant Italian workman, Luigi Luccheni, who described himself as an anarchist. Asked why he had killed the Empress, he replied, "As part of the war on the rich and the great." Vienna had seen little of Empress Elisabeth in the years since she became bored with Austria and left Emperor Franz Josef to wander around Europe, while the plodding, gray, mundane Franz Josef consoled himself with Katherina Schratt, an actress from the Burgtheater. Yet the Viennese were beginning to feel that a cruel fate overhung the Hapsburgs, with Crown Prince Rudolf a suicide at Mayerling, the Empress assassinated, and no one to take the aging Emperor's place except the Archduke Ferdinand, an unknown and untried nephew.

Sigmund had been back only a few days—the family was not returning until the end of September—when he became depressed with the bad mood of the Viennese surroundings. He groused, "It is a misery to live here, and it is no atmosphere in which the hope of completing anything difficult can survive." Yet soon Vienna went back to its carefree mood: the concert halls, Opera and Hoftheater were crowded, the restaurants and coffeehouses filled with excited voices, arguments, the lifetime *Stammtisch*.

In the first days of October he was overwhelmed by an "avalanche of patients" and was obliged to return to his twelve-hour office schedule, with just enough time for meals. At night he wrote exploratory pages for the dream book, exhilarated by the creative periods. Then the fount turned off, the well of his mind ran dry; ideas he had cherished proved to be erroneous; he came down with an influenza infection.

He relied heavily on being repatriated by Emperor Franz Josef when he was personally handed his scroll at the Golden Jubilee, appointing him *Extraordinarius* at the university. But when the official list was made public, Dr. Sigmund Freud's name did not appear. Dr. Frankl-Hochwart had been given the appointment. Sigmund vowed morosely that he would never again have anything to do with the Medical Faculty. He canceled his announced *Dozentur* lectures on The Psychology of Dreams. Then came self-recrimination; he had only himself to blame because, he groused to Martha, he had "kept the domain of the psychological floating in the air without any organic foundation." Why could he not explain in terms of stored-up energies and discharge just where instincts, emotions, feelings, ideas, memories, phobias, hysterias, neuroses, garnered the nervous strength with which to dispatch physiologically their content? He did his best to hide from her his disappointment and chagrin.

There were times when he was supremely optimistic about his ever deeper studies of the unconscious, followed by periods of doubt and confusion. He wrote to Fliess:

"Fate . . . has quite forgotten your friend in his lonely corner. . . . I have to deal in dark matters with people I am ten to fifteen years in advance of, who will never catch me up."

At moments he enjoyed his "splendid isolation" as he wistfully called it, because it gave him all of his hours for work. But after a few weeks of this isolation he felt as though his psyche were being crushed by a stamp mill. He brooded about the fact that the medical world of Vienna had yet to accept a single one of the precepts published by Breuer and himself five years before; that he was being shunned by his colleagues as though he were a leper who had to be kept in solitary confinement so that he would not infect the community.

When he yearned for an audience for his Interpretation of Dreams he lectured to a group at the B'nai B'rith on the subject. But he was still stumbling around in the intricacies of the dream book, attempting to canalize the work of condensation, distortion, the relation of dreams to mental diseases, detailing hundreds of dreams, his own and his patients', to show neurologists how valuable for curative purposes their interpretation could be. He would divulge none of this half-finished material for fear of hearing what Wagner-Jauregg had said about him earlier:

"You are moving too fast and taking too many chances."

With a dozen patients on hand, half of them men, he had a wide variety of neuroses with which to cope, some of them with what he had now established as classical symptoms: the persecution mania, the hearing of voices, the compulsive anxiety, the pseudoparalysis which enabled the patient to lock himself away from life . . . He enjoyed a profound satisfaction when he was able to alleviate symptoms and occasionally effect a cure; followed by a sense of personal defeat when the patient refused to penetrate the substrata of his own unconscious, or fled in terror at being faced with the psychological nature of his illness. The medical profession was trained not to take personally any errant illness which would not lend itself to a cure.

"But in my case," thought Sigmund, "it is my method that is at stake. My principles and findings are on the firing line every time I agree to take a patient." That was why he had to take Fräulein Cessie back when Josef Breuer urged him to, though a year of analysis had not brought the slightest improvement. He could not help those unfortunate ones who were too far gone to communicate with him, but when his therapy failed where he felt relief should be achieved, he deemed his new medical science to have shown itself to be inadequate. He must continue to learn, to find the truth about how the human mind worked. He must believe that in psychoanalysis the failure was the doctor's and not the patient's.

With his self-analysis there were also days when he glimpsed truths about human nature and its incredibly structured complexities that persuaded him he would one day know himself and be completely free; followed by failure to interpret either his fantasies or dreams, leaving him frightened and tied up.

As the year 1898 had begun, so had it ended.

5.

In January of 1899 Sigmund learned that the English psychologist and physician Havelock Ellis gave his work on the connection between hysteria and sexual life high praise in the *Alienist and Neurologist*. He was elated, thinking once again that perhaps he should move his family and practice to a more hospitable England. He did not know how brutally Havelock Ellis was being treated in England for his attempts to bring about education on the sexual nature of man.

His most gruesome task now was reading through the volumes on dreams in German, French and English, Spanish and Italian as they accumulated on his study shelves. He had not realized how many there were. Some were sheer nonsense, the Egyptian symbol books which taught the reader how to predict the future, even life after death. But there were others, by astute psychologists Gruppe, Hildebrandt, Strümpell, Delboeuf, who had observed accurately the effect of physical needs on dreams: heat, thirst, the need to evacuate, the relation of happenings of the previous day to the dream images; the place of anxiety in dreams. Yet for all their honest intent his predecessors had been stumbling without lanterns through unexplored caves, bumping their heads against stalactites because not one of them had suspected that there was an unconscious mind which controlled both the meaning and mechanism of the dream; and that there was a latent content going back to childhood which gave a deeper significance to the surface or manifest dream.

The annotating of this "beggar's hash" was an affliction. The interminable reading drained from his mind everything of his own that was new, yet the disembodying of the shelf of dream literature stretched ahead endlessly. When Martha saw how irritable the reading of the books

made him—he had by now compiled a bibliography of eighty volumes—
she asked:

"Why must you read every word of these books?"

"Because I cannot risk the charge of having neglected any of this work,
fragmentary as it may be."

Martha sighed.

"Won't that material have the same dulling effect on the reader that it
has had on you?"

"Unfortunately, it may."

"Well, I daresay no serious reader will be put off by an introduction of
ten or fifteen historical pages."

Sigmund rose, went to the humidor on a side table, lighted a cigar and
took a first few puffs.

"Not ten or fifteen pages, Marty. Closer to a hundred, to do the review
material justice."

Martha gazed at him in disbelief.

"A hundred pages! That's a full book in itself. Why would you want to
put that unbreachable Wall of China before your readers?"

Minna laughed. "Now, Martha, you know that the most consistent
ambition of Sigi's life is to be a martyr." She turned to her brother-in-law.
"Aren't you beating dead horses? Why quote from half a hundred authors
only to prove that they led themselves down the garden path?"

"It is the scientific way: summarize everything that has already been
written on the subject, and analyze its value."

"But what happens to the reader if he gets lost in this thicket?"

Sigmund smiled ruefully. "He will never get to see the Sleeping Beauty
within. It's a kind of ritualistic ground clearing, the way farmers burn off
last year's stubble before spring plowing."

The interpretation of dreams was the royal road to knowledge of the
unconscious activities of the mind. Into each chapter he integrated the
result of the dream work which best illuminated the method under
study. Of one thing he was certain, that the censor was a lone guard, attacked by an army of anxieties and omnipresent wishes diabolically clever
in getting themselves fulfilled. One night he dreamt that a man he knew
on the staff of the university said to him, "My son, the Myops." There
followed a dialogue made up of short remarks and rejoinders. The third
portion was the main dream. "On account of certain events which had
occurred in the city of Rome, it had become necessary to remove the children to safety, and this was done. The scene was then in front of a gate-
way, double doors in the ancient style (the Porta Romana at Siena,
as I was aware during the dream itself). I was sitting on the edge of a
fountain and was greatly depressed and almost in tears. A female figure,
an attendant or nun, brought two boys out and handed them over to

their father, who was not myself. The elder of the two was clearly my eldest son; I did not see the other one's face. The woman who brought out the boy asked him to kiss her good-by. She was noticeable for having a red nose. The boy refused to kiss her but, holding out his hand in farewell, said, 'Auf Geseres.' . . ."

Sigmund's first impression as he began jotting down his reactions was that the university staffer and his son were a screen for himself and Martin; that the dream had been caused by a succession of thoughts and emotions engendered by the play he had seen recently, Theodor Herzl's *The New Ghetto*. It concerned the Jewish problem, which was growing serious in Vienna, with prejudices now being shown more openly. Sigmund, as had Theodor Herzl in the play, felt himself concerned for his six children. According to Herzl's play, they would never have a home of their own, there would be difficulty in educating them so that they could move across both geographical and intellectual boundaries.

Rome continued to show up in Sigmund's dreams; it was still the highest ambition of his life to visit there. However, since he had never been inside the walls of the city, he had substituted a city where he had been. In this case Siena, also famous for its fountains. Siena was a particularly good substitute; near its Porta Romana Sigmund had seen a brightly lighted building which he learned was the insane asylum. He had been informed that the director, a Jew, a highly qualified man who had spent his life working up to the directorship, had been obliged to resign because of his religion. When he remembered that he had been depressed and almost weeping as he sat on the edge of the fountain the line came to his mind, "By the waters of Babylon we sat down and wept," in which Swinburne was writing about the destruction of Jerusalem and ancient Italy.

This reflected accurately his feelings about Vienna and its people. On the surface all was gaiety and charming melodies about the Danube and the eating of rich chocolate cakes at the *Jause*, yet so rife with prejudice, so bound in by the four walls of stagnation, superficiality and specious joy. But what, he asked himself, was the meaning of his need to remove his children to safety from the city of Rome? Many years before his half brothers had removed themselves and their children to the freedom of England; at the same moment Jakob and Amalie had removed themselves and Sigmund and Anna from Freiberg to what they thought would be the freedom of Leipzig, and then Vienna. Amalie had taken them on the train through Breslau.

Who was the female figure, the attendant or nun who wanted the child to kiss her good-by, the one with the ugly red nose? It could be none other than his nursemaid, Monica Zajic, who had wanted to kiss Sigmund and Anna good-by when the Freud family left Freiberg. But why had the boy, himself, he knew, said "*Auf Geseres*" when he should have said

"*Auf Wiedersehen*"? The Hebrew word *Geseres* meant suffering or weeping.

A few nights later he dreamed about a place that was a mixture of a private sanatorium and several other institutions. He set down in his notes, "A manservant appeared to summon me to an examination. I knew in the dream that something had been missed and that the examination was due to a suspicion that I had appropriated the missing article. Conscious of my innocence and of the fact that I held the position of a consultant in the establishment, I accompanied the servant quietly. At the door we were met by another servant, who said, pointing to me, 'Why have you brought him? He's a respectable person.' I then went, unattended, into a large hall, with machines standing in it, which reminded me of an Inferno with its hellish instruments of punishment. Stretched out on one apparatus I saw one of my colleagues, who had every reason to take some notice of me, but he paid no attention. I was then told I could go. But I could not find my hat and could not go after all."

He felt that this kind of dream was an example of inhibited movement, and wrote for his manuscript, "The wish fulfillment of the dream evidently lay in my being recognized as an honest man and told I could go. There must therefore have been all kinds of material in the dream-thoughts containing a contradiction of this. That I could go was a sign of my absolution. If therefore something happened at the end of the dream which prevented my going, it seems plausible to suppose that the suppressed material containing the contradiction was making itself felt at that point. My not being able to find my hat meant accordingly: 'After all you're not an honest man.' Thus the 'not being able to do something' in this dream was a way of expressing a contradiction, a 'no.' . . ."

An absurd dream puzzled him. He wrote:

"I received a communication from the town council of my birthplace concerning the fees due for someone's maintenance in the hospital in the year 1851, which had been necessitated by an attack he had had in my house. I was amused by this, since in the first place I was not yet alive in 1851, and in the second place my father, to whom it might have related, was now dead. I went to him in the next room where he was lying on his bed and told him about it. To my surprise, he recollected that in 1851 he had once got drunk and had had to be locked up or detained. It was at a time at which he had been working for the firm of T———. 'So you used to drink as well?' I asked; 'did you get married soon after that?' I calculated that, of course, I was born in 1856, which seemed to be the year which immediately followed the year in question."

Jakob did not drink, and never had. Was the dream then attempting to say that Jakob had behaved as foolishly as a drunken man might? But what had he done? There had been a hospital bill for 1851. But for whom?

Like a tiny dark cat barely peeking around the edge of a building came a wisp of a remembrance: a dropped hint here, a subtle intimation there, from his half brothers Emanuel and Philipp, that his father did indeed "get married soon after that"; to a woman by the name of Rebecca. Had the hospital bill been for Rebecca? If there had been an interim marriage, and a Rebecca Freud, what had happened to her? Had she died in the hospital? This second marriage could not have lasted long, for Jakob had been unattached for a year or two before marrying Amalie in 1855. Only Emanuel and Philipp would know. He was awed at the ingenuity with which his unconscious had kept this revenant repressed; and how his dream had subtly revealed the fragment that had lay buried in deep soil all these years.

6.

One afternoon a woman patient arrived at his office in tears. She exclaimed, "I don't want ever to see my relations again; they must think me horrible."

Before Sigmund could ask her why, she related a dream she remembered which she could not understand. When she was four years old "a lynx or fox was walking on the roof; then something had fallen down or she had fallen down; and then her mother was carried out of the house dead." The patient wept. "Now I remember something more," she exclaimed; "when I was a small child I was humiliated by being called 'lynx-eye' by a street urchin. It was the worst term he could think of to insult me. . . . Also, when I was three years old a tile fell off the roof and fell on my mother's head and made it bleed violently."

"Now you see how the elements in your dream merge and take form," Sigmund said. "The lynx shows up as lynx-eyed. He's walking on a roof from which a tile falls; and then you saw your mother being carried out of the house dead. The purpose of the dream is to fulfill a wish. You can see how you have brought your childhood materials forth from your unconscious. But there is no reason for you to be distressed. It is universal that girls fall in love with their fathers and wish to replace their mothers, and hence at some time or other wish them dead. But that happened a long time ago; and it has nothing to do with you as an adult. Your relations do not think you horrible, they went through the same Oedipal complication when they were small children."

The interpretation helped her.

A corroborating case came into Berggasse 19 within a matter of weeks, a young woman in a state of confusional excitement based on a violent aversion to her mother whom she would hit and abuse orally whenever the mother came near. When the physicians could not help her she was brought to Dr. Freud, who based his analysis squarely on the young woman's dreams: she dreamt she was attending her mother's funeral; she was sitting with her older sister at a table dressed in mourning. Accompanying these dreams were obsessional phobias in which, after she had been out of her house for only an hour, she would be tormented by a fear that something dreadful had happened to her mother and would have to rush home to confirm the fact that the older woman was all right. He was able to explain this phobia as a "hysterical counterreaction and defensive phenomenon" against her unconscious hostility to the mother. He wrote in his notes:

"In view of this it is no longer hard to understand why hysterical girls are so often attached to their mothers with such exaggerated affection."

A case similar to one he had handled several years before was that of a young man with a high moral education who at the age of seven had wanted to push his severe father "over a precipice from the top of a mountain. When I get home I spend the rest of the day preparing an alibi in case I should be accused of one of the murders committed in the city. If I had the impulse to push my father over a precipice, can I genuinely be trusted with my own wife and children?"

Sigmund learned that the young man, who was thirty-one, had recently lost his father after a painful illness. It was at this point that he remembered, for the first time in twenty-four years, his early desire to kill the older man. Sigmund led him back in his mind to a much earlier age than seven, when this death impulse toward the father had first been awakened. It took several months of analysis, plus the reading of materials from similar cases in his own files, but the patient made steady progress, his obsessional neurosis waned. He thanked Dr. Freud for releasing him from "the prison cell of my room, where I have locked myself of late so that I would commit no murder, either on a stranger or a member of my family."

A baffling case was one sent to him by Professor Nothnagel. The man appeared to be suffering from a degeneration of the spinal cord. Sigmund wondered, "Why did Professor Nothnagel send him to me? He knows that I am treating only neuroses."

The patient did not yield to psychoanalytical treatment. He denied vehemently that there could be any sexual etiology of his disturbance, or that there had been any sexual problems, confusions or activities during his early years. He declined the process of free association, of letting the first idea that came into his mind lead to the next one and from there on to the next hundred ideas or pictures or images which would bring latent materials to the surface, all on the grounds that there was nothing anywhere in the background of his mind that related in any way to his illness.

Sigmund was embarrassed by his failure. He went to Professor Nothnagel, to whose authority and medical wisdom he bowed, reported his failure and gave his opinion that the patient was actually suffering a degeneration of the spinal cord.

"Please keep the man under observation," Nothnagel replied mildly. "In my opinion it must be a neurosis."

Sigmund shook his head wryly. "That is an odd diagnosis coming from you, Herr Professor, since I am the one who knows best that you do not share my views on the etiology of neuroses."

Nothnagel changed the subject.

"How many children have you got now?"

"Six."

Nothnagel nodded his head admiringly, and then asked, "Girls or boys?"

"Three and three: they are my pride and my treasure."

"Well, now, be on your guard! Girls are safe enough, but bringing up boys leads to difficulties later on."

"Oh no, Herr Professor, my boys are very well behaved. The only alarming trait any one of them has is that he thinks he is going to become a poet. Don't laugh, Professor, you know how much our poets have suffered from poverty and neglect."

Sigmund kept the patient under observation for a few more days. Then he saw that he was wasting his time and the patient's money. He said to him:

"Herr Mannsfeld, I am sorry, but I can do nothing for you. My recommendation is that you seek other advice."

Mannsfeld turned pale, gripped the arm of his chair. He shook his head "No!" abruptly several times as though trying to knock some foolishness out of it.

"Herr Doktor, I want to apologize. I have been lying to you. I was too ashamed to tell you of the sexual matters that had gone on early in my life. I am prepared to tell you the truth now. I want to be cured."

The next time Sigmund saw Nothnagel he said to him, "You were right. Herr Mannsfeld did have a neurosis. We have made progress. There are no more signs of any degeneration of the spinal cord."

Nothnagel's wise old face wrinkled into a delighted grin.

"Yes, I know, Mannsfeld was in to see me. Stay with your treatments." Then with a rather sly expression he said, "But, Herr Doktor, don't make any false assumptions about my conversion. I still don't believe in your sexual etiology of the neuroses. Neither do I believe in your new science of psychoanalysis."

Sigmund was staggered. Was Professor Nothnagel playing a game with him?

"My esteemed Professor, you really should not confound me with such contradictions. You recognized that this patient had a neurosis and that there was nothing wrong with his spine. You sent him to me knowing that I believe all neuroses are based on sexual causes. When I tried to give up the patient because I was convinced that he had no neurosis, you instructed me to persevere. Now that I have got him half cured, you congratulate me on my fine work, and then tell me that it is what Krafft-Ebing described as a 'scientific fairy tale.'"

Nothnagel used his index finger to rub with considerable affection the wart on his nose.

"My dear Doctor, to be confounded is the common lot of medical men. Did you not once tell me that Professor Charcot confessed to having looked at certain neurological diseases for thirty solid years without recognizing them? Give me another thirty years of watching you work, and I too may become a see-er. What you have accomplished is like the feats of legerdemain that I've watched magicians perform at country fairs. And how is that poet son of yours coming along?"

7.

For the summer of 1899 they decided for the first time to leave Austria and rent a villa in Bavaria. They found a lovely one called Riemerlehen reached only by a side road from Berchtesgaden: a couple of miles up a hill, then a narrow rock and dirt road through a short stretch of pine forest to a cleared farm. It was a large villa, three stories high, capped by a cupola; an all-wood structure with gaily painted balconies held up by shaved tree trunks, a series of four piled one on top of the other. There were many windows overlooking the farm, the valley, the river and Berchtesgaden beyond.

Sigmund commandeered as his workshop a quiet ground-floor room which had a view of the mountains and got the morning sun on one side and afternoon sun on the other. He moved his lightweight writing table about so that he could bake like a lizard all day when the sun was out. He used Janus and a few Egyptian figurines, which he found in Berchtesgaden and on occasional trips to Salzburg, as paperweights so they would always be on his desk, close to him, part of his daily life. He told the children:

"Those things cheer me and remind me of distant times and countries."

He hiked for an hour, very early in the morning, and again at dusk, singing out:

"All aboard for the walking tour!"

The Bavarian countryside was a lush brilliant green.

"No wonder," Sigmund commented, "it must rain at least once every hour." Sometimes it was a gentle drizzle, at others a furious downpour of huge drops that seemed to fall from all directions. Then, when Sigmund had concluded they were in for an all-day storm, the charcoal clouds dissolved and the sun came out. Because of the just vanished wetness the sun struck their faces almost like fire. Now that the Freuds thought they could enjoy a glorious day, with the sun shining on the green fields and the cattle cropping on the sides of the mountains, just as suddenly the sun was gone and the overcast had taken its place, putting out the fire with a splash of rain.

Within the first week Sigmund and his clan learned to live like the Bavarians, who paid no attention to the rain, for it was the source of their prosperity and the fertility of their earth. When they took their late afternoon walk they passed the women from the neighboring farms dressed in their lightweight *Dirndln*, holding umbrellas over their heads and chatting merrily. When the rain stopped they closed their umbrellas without losing a syllable of the conversation.

Occasionally, when he had an involved problem to work out, the meaning of symbols in dreams, or speech, the intellectual activity in dreams, he walked alone. The Bavarian countryside fascinated him: the infinite variety of greens which the rains produced; the primeval growth which he thought must go back to the moment the earth cooled sufficiently to allow things to sprout; the trees with their slender trunks so close together that he could hardly walk between them; the mountains that went up to incredible heights, vertical crags of rock still snow-covered in July and August; the green shrubs tenaciously crawling up the stone slabs, clawing the tiny crevices to pull themselves still farther up the shinbone of alpine stone.

He particularly liked walking the one-wagon-wide dirt roads that led to farms as neat and orderly as the interiors of the homes. The haycocks were set in as precise a line as disciplined Prussian soldiers. Because of the constant rain the hay had to hang out like sheets on a line to dry. Every farm used a different haycock sculpture; the ones that Sigmund enjoyed the most were the size of a woman standing up, with a top layer of hay like a cowl over her head; they stood like a row of widows in a church pew praying for their dead. Others had a small wooden crossbar with an opening in the middle, so that he could gaze straight through a line of fifty haystacks looking like children about to play a game of leapfrog.

He came back from these walks refreshed, seeing the flower boxes on the balconies of the farmhouses and outside every window a profusion of brilliant red geraniums, bluebells and yellow blossoms making a splash of color in the deep green countryside.

His first chapter for The Interpretation of Dreams, the Method of Interpreting Dreams, had been sent to press at Deuticke's at the end of June, before he left Vienna. Here at Riemerlehen, pushing ahead vigorously on the book, he was able to send another chapter to press every couple of weeks. Deuticke would promptly return the printed galley sheets for correction. He was happy to be back in the role he loved best: scientist, psychologist, writer, creating a science of the mind based on pragmatic evidence. By summer's end the days spent thinking through and writing the final chapters of the book, including the hundred-page introduction, Scientific Literature on Dreams, filled as they were with the quiet-passing Bavarian showers and quick-passing sunshine, had been an enormous learning experience. It was now four full years since he had analyzed the Emma Benn dream and evolved the technique for getting at the hitherto suppressed materials of the latent dream. During these years he had written hundreds of cases of interpretation as supporting evidence, even as he had mounted on slides hundreds of microtome sections of the human brain, and studied them under the microscope.

There were mushrooms in the woods. The children competed with their father to find them in their hiding places. Between walks the young ones played in the fields with the farmers' children. For Martha's birthday Sigmund took his brood into Berchtesgaden so that each one of the six could buy their mother a special present. They ended up in front of a store with its windows filled with women's narrow-brimmed felt hats, the style of which had been unchanged for hundreds of years. They came in every shade of green of the fields and forests, each sporting its own saucy feather. A goodly portion of the town's womenfolk were gathered in front of the display, laughing and talking and pointing with delight: the Bavarian woman's hat was her crown of glory.

Mathilde, who was almost twelve, said:

"Papa, you know Mama won't wear this kind of hat in Vienna."

"Ah, but she will wear it on our all-day picnic tomorrow to Bartholomäe for her birthday. Won't she be lovely in it!"

To celebrate the completion of the work he took the family into Berchtesgaden for a full day's outing and dinner on a veranda high on the hill overlooking the river, the verdant valley, and their own Riemerlehen. Sigmund murmured:

"I shall always love this spot. Now I'm glad I did not take an umbrella on my walks: Rains make Brains!"

The children laughed at the rhyme, but eight-year-old Oliver quickly added, "It's been the best summer for us too. Because you were happy." Martin, who had built himself a treehouse in the woods in which to write his poetry, said, "We saw less of you this summer than other summers, Father, but we knew between the morning walk and the evening one that your work was going well."

"Thank you, Martin. How is your writing, now that you have a private studio?"

Martin thought for a moment, then replied, "Actually, I don't believe my so-called poems are really good."

That evening when the children were asleep he and Martha sat on the veranda of their bedroom, each wrapped in a coat against the coolness of the late September air. He asked if she would like to read the now completed Interpretation of Dreams:

"Everything is available to you, though I have wanted you to wait until I had a corrected manuscript so that you can see precisely what I am trying to say. But by the same token you must not feel obliged to read what I write; I won't take offense. Do skip the introduction! If there are times when you find the material disagreeable, then you must not impose the task on yourself."

"I am not going to find anything you write disagreeable, Sigi, because I am not going to make judgments. I am only going to try to understand it. If you lose your friends and colleagues, if you cannot get any of them to support you, it would be stupid on my part not to know what it is about. There is no virtue in ignorance. And what good is my sympathy if I don't know what I am sympathizing about? If we are going to live in the path of the tornado, I ought to know what puts me there. I assume that some of these materials will be distressing to me, but I am not a flower that withers at the first breath of a desert wind."

With the last chapter of the book returned to the press he was able to get a perspective on the year's work and was pleased with it. He felt drained and exhausted, yet as he packed his books and helped the family get ready to return to Vienna, he felt a high sense of accomplishment. He knew the book's worth as a pioneering effort. He told Martha proudly:

"Insight such as this falls to one's lot but once in a lifetime."

Riding home on the train through the dark green valleys, the idea popped into his head that he would die between the ages of sixty-one and sixty-two. He was startled by the explicitness of the time, though by no means upset. He thought, "I'm only forty-three, so that leaves me a decent period of grace."

He had high hopes for the book because he knew it to be his best. Besides, it was the first one on psychoanalysis that he had written by himself. In the four years since the publication of *Studies on Hysteria* he had published papers in the neurological and psychiatric journals which should have helped to prepare the ground for his new point of departure.

"I genuinely believe that Vienna has used me as their whipping boy long enough. They should be tired of the sport. I think the book will be accepted, and bring us the independence and position we have been seeking so ardently."

Martha joined her fingertips in an attitude of prayer, murmuring, "From your lips into God's ears."

Deuticke had planned to publish *The Interpretation of Dreams* in January of 1900. He printed the date 1900 on the title page, but since the volume was ready early he sent copies to the newspapers and put it on sale throughout Austria, Germany and Zurich on November 4, 1899. He printed six hundred copies, confiding to Sigmund that he had every hope they would be cleared out of the bookstores by Christmas, and he could go back for a second printing at the New Year.

The results were catastrophic. By the New Year only a hundred and twenty-three copies had been sold, Fliess having bought a dozen in Berlin to distribute to his friends. Deuticke dropped by Sigmund's office, unable to conceal his disappointment. He had not recovered his cost and had faint hopes of doing so.

"I just can't understand it, Herr Doktor! There is an established market for dream books. I've been publishing them successfully for years. People come into my shop regularly looking for just such volumes, so they can forecast their future, and know how to place their bets. But hungry as they are, even these devotees don't want your book; they thumb through it, put it back on the pile and walk away."

Sigmund felt sick at his stomach as he realized that Deuticke had not read a word of the manuscript.

As though to confirm the publisher's worst fears, the first review that appeared, on January 6, 1900, in the Vienna *Zeit*, written by a former director of the Burgtheater, heaped scorn and ridicule on the book. In March came short, negative notices in *Umschau* and the *Wiener Fremden-blatt*. An assistant at the university psychiatric clinic by the name of Raimann wrote a monograph attacking the book, though he admitted that he had not bothered to read it. Raimann then gave a lecture on hysteria to an overflow audience of some four hundred medical students in which he announced:

"You see that these sick people have the inclination to unburden their minds. A colleague in this town has used this circumstance to construct a theory about this simple fact, so that he can fill his pockets adequately."

The lecture proved to be the death knell for the book. From then on it sold only two copies a week in the entire German-speaking world. Not another word was printed about it for six months, when the *Berliner Tageblatt* published a few favorable paragraphs.

Sigmund was devastated.

"The public enthusiasm is immense," he quipped bitterly, quoting a line from the irreverent Viennese critics when an audience sits on its hands after the first playing of a new opera or symphony. "As the Austrians say when a suitor has been rebuffed: 'I have been given a basket!' "

8.

One afternoon toward the end of 1899 he found Frau Hofrat Gomperz in his consultation room. She had sent no word that she wanted to see him. Frau Gomperz was a white-haired woman who maintained a *gemütlich* if not chic salon for her husband's associates and graduate students whom he trained in philology, the science of language. It was Hofrat Gomperz who had entrusted the translation of the volume of John Stuart Mill to Sigmund when he was only twenty-three years old. During that time Sigmund had been invited to the Gomperz rambling book-lined apartment not only to go over Sigmund's German translation but for the weekly open house, where one met people from the university and professional world. Sigmund had not been in the Gomperz home for a number of years.

"Frau Hofrat Gomperz, what a pleasure to see you. How is Hofrat Gomperz? Well, I trust?"

"Yes, thank you, Herr Doktor. I am the one who is having difficulty. My family does not know."

"I am always at your service."

Frau Hofrat Gomperz's favorite hobby was knitting and crocheting. She was distressed because she could no longer do this work. She had developed a tingling numbness of the index finger of her right hand; there was pain in the wrist, which was also sensitive to the touch. She had a feeling of electric shock when she flexed her wrist. On examination Sigmund also found a numbness of the thumb side of her hand. He diagnosed her trouble as an irritation of the median nerve, put her right wrist in a splint, forbidding all activity for this hand for a few weeks.

"It's nothing serious, just the compression of a nerve. We'll have you back to normal in a month."

The woman permitted herself a sigh of relief.

"I thought I was losing the use of my fingers and wrist . . . perhaps a beginning paralysis."

"Nothing of the sort; it's the equivalent of a severe sprain. Come back in a week and let me rebandage it."

He had her out of the splint in three weeks. When she asked for a bill he declined, saying, "I will always be in the debt of the Gomperz family. It was my privilege to help you."

Hofrat Gomperz was pleased at Sigmund's treatment of his wife; along with a note of thanks came an invitation to Sunday night supper at the apartment in the Reisnerstrasse. When Martha and Sigmund were escorted into the library, crowded with a lifetime accumulation of art, rare books and manuscripts, one volume sat in the place of honor on the Gomperz coffee table before the four-seater sofa: *The Interpretation of Dreams*. Hofrat Gomperz had made a special trip to Deuticke's to ask for "Dr. Sigmund Freud's newest book," a compliment from a scholar who had been famous for thirty-five years for his volumes on classical subjects.

The most disturbing of his patients was Breuer's relative, Fräulein Cessie, who had already been with him several years. He could bring her no relief from her fear of being locked into airless places, as well as the opposite fear of open spaces; from the sweaty palms, the sense of impending disaster, of being about to collapse, to scream; the inability to speak when desiring to. Neither could she relate to Dr. Freud, though she claimed she wanted to. She still could not free-associate. Sigmund's efforts to lead her back to the Oedipal experience, to her genital and anal stages, failed. He dismissed her several times; but always she returned with a message from Breuer: "Please continue."

Since Fräulein Cessie had been unable to pay her fee for over a year, he felt obliged to take her back.

By March he was conducting his maximum of twelve hours of analytical sessions a day plus the one in the evening with Fräulein Cessie. He was earning five hundred gulden a week, was able to build up his vanished bank savings and forget about the job in a sanatorium for the following summer, which he had thought he would be obliged to take after the ignominious failure of *The Interpretation of Dreams* and the falling off of the winter patients. He went frequently to the Saturday evening *Tarock* game, resumed his lectures on dreams at the B'nai B'rith, and his *Dozentur* course at the university. For the first time in months he began to set down materials for a projected Psychopathology of Everyday Life. His wounds healed, though he told Minna that any praise *The Interpretation of Dreams* had received had been as meager as charity. He consoled himself that he was being treated badly because he was ahead of his time; but he also recognized the dangers of this form of megalomania.

What remained of the hurt was the virulence of the attack upon his personal character; for a hailstorm of slander had pelted down on his head. The man who had written on the sexual etiology of the neuroses, the sexuality of children, and now the Oedipal discovery, was called "vile," "filthy," "an evil defamer of motherhood," "a corrupter of innocent childhood," "a pervert suffering from putrescence of mind." The story making the rounds of the medical circles, reported to him by Oskar Rie, was: "It's all right to keep a garbage pail on the back porch. But Freud has attempted to set it down, with all its stinking contents, in the center of the living room. Worse, he has now put it under the blankets in everybody's bed, and allowed its stench to penetrate the nursery."

He understood that a good many of the violent rejections of his work came out of repression and fear, the inability to face the Oedipal situation, to open the doors to the unconscious, to realize what had happened to individual character because of childhood experiences, tensions and traumas; how much of seemingly rational life was controlled by the unconscious. For most people it was a demon too fierce to be confronted. It took courage to face this new knowledge of what the human mind and human nature were all about. He would not defend himself in public, for he did not conceive of science as a wrestling match. He did comment to Martha:

"They think that I am attacking them! Each one, individually. It's as though I am accusing them of heinous crimes when I am talking about universalities in human nature. It's not only that they don't want to admit these qualities in themselves; neither do they want to admit them about mankind. They prefer to keep these truths covered over with any material they can lay their hands on: all the way from dung to cast iron. Most of the forces in society are working night and day either to romanticize our instincts or to keep them locked away from man's knowledge: religion, the educational system, mores and myths, the philosophy of the ruling classes, agencies of government, such as in the time of Metternich in Austria when he acted as censor of everything that could be published in a book, magazine or newspaper, produced on a stage or expressed in a meeting of more than three people. Only the most ignorant are unaware of what goes on in the unconscious mind; everyone else has some intimation and some memory which tells them that there is a second mind at work and a second nature that is suppressed. In this sense they know that I am right, and the stronger the suspicion that I am right, the more violent the attack against me. It isn't that I lie, but rather that I am a truthteller; that is what makes me dangerous. It is Professor Meynert all over again:

" 'I am the greatest male hysteric of them all.' "

Not one word of scientific comment about his work was published in a medical journal. He felt impoverished inwardly. Outwardly, he went to his barber every day, had his tailor make him two new suits, took Martha to *Don Giovanni*, and to hear Georg Brandes, the Danish critic, lecture on Shakespeare. Martha enjoyed Brandes so much that she persuaded Sigmund to send a copy of *The Interpretation of Dreams* to his hotel. Sigmund delivered it himself, but he never heard from Brandes. He resumed his practice of taking all six of the children, his mother and sister Dolfi to the Prater amusement park for a Sunday afternoon of fun and eating fluffs of cotton candy. His near four years of self-analysis had not enabled him to take the beating over *The Interpretation of Dreams* with nonchalance, but it had enabled him to retain sound emotional health, so that he could be a good son to his mother, a good husband to his wife, a good father to his children and a good physician to his patients.

He achieved a spectacular though left-handed cure with a homosexual in so intense a state of hysteria that the word "suicide" escaped his lips every few minutes. The young man had been fired from a responsible position for erratic conduct and had cut himself off from the world, refusing to go to the concerts and plays which had been the joy of his life. He was suffering from palpitations of the heart, attacks of paralysis of the hips. . . . Instead of loving his mother, and then a surrogate in the form of a wife, this young man wanted to *be* his mother. He was an anal personality, still cherishing the childhood fantasy that that was where children came from. He wanted to be penetrated anally, and fertilized as his mother had been. He played the part of the female in the homosexual relationship. He practiced fellatio, for he had long conceived of the mouth as a sexual organ; something his mother had swallowed had made her pregnant. In the act of fellatio he made the transition in fantasy from being mother to being his mother's infant, sucking at her full breast and erect nipple, drawing forth the milk of life.

Over a period of months Sigmund quieted the hysteria by leading the patient through the Oedipal situation; he had not wanted to replace his father, he had instead wanted to punish him for being weak and dominated by the strong, aggressive mother; back through the genital stage in which he had not functioned normally, with an all-engrossing interest in his male genitals as they related to the female genitals; and finally to the anal stage, somewhere between the ages of three and four, where he had become encapsulated.

The patient worked through the anality, his physical illness abated, he found and held a new job. When he left Sigmund's office for the last time he said quietly:

"I thank you, Herr Doktor, for the help you have given me. I shall now be able to enjoy life. I shall also find a permanent husband. For you see, now that I understand how and why I became a homosexual, that does not make it wrong for me. I could never love a woman, for basically I am a woman; and I would only be exchanging homosexualism for lesbianism. But thanks to you I can now be a responsible citizen, support myself again and enjoy the better things of life. You have cured me; though I'm not certain it was the kind of cure you wanted."

Sigmund was not certain either; if his therapy could relieve the illness arising from homosexualism, why could he not eradicate the deviation itself? In his own mind he felt that he had half succeeded. But that was not the opinion of the boy's uncle, who arrived at Sigmund's the following afternoon, purple with rage.

"What have you done to my nephew? You have given him a justification for his vile acts. He was on the verge of suicide when he came to you; better he should be dead than bring disgrace on his family."

Sigmund replied in his dryest tone:

"I think not. I had a homosexual patient two years ago who did take his life. It was a bitter dose for his family and friends. Your nephew is still a deviate but no longer physically or emotionally ill. I feel certain that he will be discreet. I don't think he was born to die at his own hands; death comes soon enough to all of us. Try to accept his situation, and let him live out his life without bitterness. It would be an act of kindness on your part."

The uncle rose, pale, distraught.

"Herr Doktor, I apologize. You just can't know what a bitter pill it is to swallow: our family is an old one in the Austro-Hungarian Empire. But you are right, suicide is also a disgrace. I will try to placate my brother, who is almost out of his mind with grief. His only son . . . to end up as . . . a . . . a . . ."

9.

By Easter the brunt of his practice fell off, but in the manner he liked: several of his patients were well enough to take their leave. Of the two patients who were psychologically impotent, the pathogenic material revealed in the first one an incestuous fixation on a sister which had been repressed. The second had developed a deep fear of castration, the cutting off of his penis and testicles by the father, who he feared had learned of his Oedipal attachment to the mother. This fear had forced him into a passive role sexually, so that he was unable to achieve an erection.

After years of despair over Fräulein Cessie, he finally established a working relationship with the young woman and found that the keys he had been using in other cases now opened the lock to her neurosis. At the session during which Sigmund came upon the clue, Fräulein Cessie had been talking about her mother, and her mother, and her mother. Sigmund finally said to her:

"Look, what you are saying has nothing to do with the situation we've been talking about all these years. We've been talking about the fact that you want to be loved, you want to be cured so you can marry, have a normal sex life with your husband, so that you can have a home and children. Now all of this looks irrelevant! What you really want to do is to be a baby, a one-and-a-half- or two-year-old, and have the breast-feeding relationship with your mother that you had then, to go back to the oral period in which you got caught and in which you've been living this past twenty-two years."

A transformation came over Cessie's face. She felt an overwhelming sense of enlightenment. She did not have to hide anything any more. They had found this truth together, in a flash. The discovery was the beginning of her growth. He was able to persuade her that she could pass the oral and enter the normal genital stage; that she could fulfill some of her oral needs through the vagina, which he explained as a displacement downward. She had been virginally withdrawn; she was now desirous of sexual gratification to round out her life.

By April he felt that he had deeply and vitally altered her condition; and at last he understood that he had not wasted the four years of work on her. She had been feeding off him the entire time, using his sustenance to fill the voids, keeping herself functioning in her job and her care of her dying mother; waiting for a moment when she could rise to a higher analytical plane and be helped to create a functioning psyche. Gone were the claustrophobia, the agoraphobia, the aphoria, the fear of exposing herself to persons, places or conditions which had become anxiety situations in her unconscious: the symptoms abated and then vanished. In the middle of May she said:

"You've done wonders for me."

The next day she reported to Sigmund that she had gone directly to Josef Breuer and told him that she now felt well; and that the cure had ultimately emerged from Dr. Freud's convincing her that she had repressed the knowledge that she had a sexual organ, that it could be used to bring her pleasure, and to achieve both physical and spiritual fulfillment. When she finished telling Dr. Breuer all this, he had "clapped his hands and exclaimed again and again:

" 'So he is right after all!' "

At the same time a German editor by the name of Löwenfeld, who was publishing in serial form a big volume to be called Frontier Problems of Nervous and Spiritual Existence, asked him to do a condensed version of The Interpretation of Dreams, to be called On Dreams, perhaps thirty-five pages long. Sigmund was gratified; it was the first acknowledgment from the medical world that he had published a book on dreams.

The medical year finished well enough for him to rent once again the villa at Bellevue where five years before he had first analyzed the Emma Benn dream which had begun his work on interpretation. The rent was not excessive, and he would be spared traveling costs; for Bellevue, in the Wienerwald just below the Kahlenberg, was only an hour from the Berggasse. It was cool, there were miles of lovely woods in every direction. In a sense it was like coming home. Sigmund wrote to Fliess playfully:

"Do you suppose that someday a marble tablet will be placed on the house, inscribed with these words:

"In this house on July 24th, 1895,
the Secret of Dreams was revealed to
Dr. Sigmund Freud"?

There was an unwritten custom at the university centering around the phrase *Tres faciunt collegium,* three make a college. The year before, in the spring of 1899, Sigmund had announced a course on The Psychology of Dreams, but only one student had registered, with the possibility of a second. Sigmund had still had considerable material for *The Interpretation of Dreams* to write. "How can I afford to give a four-month course to one student?" he had asked himself.

Now in the summer of 1900, six months after *The Interpretation of Dreams* had been published, four applicants sent in their cards for the course, two of them practicing physicians. Drs. Max Kahane and Rudolf Reitler had entered the University of Vienna Medical School in 1883, had been awarded their M.D.s together in 1889, and had remained friends ever since. Neither had had any desire to enter academic life; neither had wanted a *Dozentur.* Both had gone into private practice, Kahane as an electrotherapist in a sanatorium, though he was planning to open, in partnership with an eccentric radiologist, an Institute for Physical Therapy which for the first time would use X rays and high-frequency electric shock. Reitler was a general practitioner, in which he got a good start because his father, as the vice-director of the K.K. (Imperial) Northwestern Railway, had a circle of influential friends. He too was planning to open an Institute for Therapy, in the Dorotheergasse, using hot and dry air on patients. Kahane, a Jew, had graduated from the same *Gymnasium* as Sigmund, in the Leopoldstadt. Reitler, a Catholic, had graduated from the prestigious K.K. Akademisches Gymnasium.

The two doctors had agreed to take the course together. Sigmund was delighted; it was the first time he had had practicing physicians in his course since he had become a pariah. Reitler and Kahane knew of his ostracism but were neither concerned nor intimidated. Reitler had never even bothered to join the Physicians Society. Sigmund's work intrigued him. It was a new approach, a fresh start which might prove exciting and valuable. Sigmund had never met Reitler, but he knew Kahane from the Kassowitz Institute, where Kahane had served as a volunteer in children's diseases, publishing monographs on the subject of pneumonia.

The two undergraduates were mildly interested. They reacted visibly only when he gave them object lessons in what he called "syllabic chemistry." He told them of a young male patient who had a dream that "a man had been working till late in the evening to put his house telephone in order. After he had gone, it kept on ringing, not continuously, but with detached rings. His servant fetched the man back, and the latter remarked: 'It's a funny thing that even people who are *tutelrein* as a rule are quite unable to deal with a thing like this.' "

The dream proved meaningless until the patient connected it with an earlier experience. As a boy, living with his father, he had spilled a glass of water over the floor while falling asleep. The flexible wire of the telephone had become soaked, causing an intermittent ringing which kept his father awake. The word *tutelrein* represented three different directions of the dream thoughts: *Tutel*, from whence came tutelage, meant guardianship (the father was present); *Tütte* was also a vulgar expression meaning a woman's breast (the mother was absent); *rein* meant clean; cojoined to the first syllable of *Zimmertelegraph*, house telephone, the result is *Zimmerrein*, house-trained, which the son had not been when he made the floor wet and disturbed his father's sleep.

After the lecture one of the students stopped at the podium and asked:

"Dozent Dr. Freud, is it permitted to ask a question?"

"But certainly."

"Why is it that the dreamer seems so often to be ingenious and amusing?"

"It's not unlike the use of syllables in jokes. Take the one, for example: What is the cheapest way of obtaining silver? You walk down an avenue of silver poplars (*Pappeln* can be interpreted as poplars or babbling) and demand silence. The babbling will stop and the silver will be available to you."

The student smiled, admitting that he had not heard this play on words before. Sigmund continued:

"Dreams become ingenious and amusing because the direct and easiest pathway to the expression of their thoughts is barred; they are forced into being so. In my waking life I am not a wit; yet if you will read *Interpretation of Dreams* you will find some of my dreams quite droll. That is not because a suppressed talent is released in my sleep, but because of the peculiar psychological conditions under which dreams are constructed. That is one of the things this course of lectures is about: to show how often puns and jokes are used by the unconscious to get past the censor. He's a powerful creature, but a dull dog who can be fooled by humor."

Max Kahane, who had appeared to be the brighter of the two physicians, was less open to Sigmund's psychology of the unconscious than was Reitler, who went to Deuticke's bookstore to buy *Studies on Hysteria* and *The Interpretation of Dreams*, and read them avidly. Late one afternoon Sigmund invited Kahane home for coffee; Martha had met him during the Kassowitz days. Walking through the warm spring rain, shoulders touching under Kahane's umbrella, they fell to talking about the recent advances in neurology, which were disenchantingly scant on the physical side. Sigmund could not resist a few sentences of proselytizing with the ten-year-younger man.

"Max, am I correct in saying that you still have some reservations about the psychology of the unconscious?"

"It isn't that I disagree; I find much truth in what you say, and I am absorbing new insights."

"But nothing I've said has weaned you from electricity as a therapeutic tool?"

"No."

"Your machine serves no useful purpose, aside from suggestion, because electric current cannot reach the unconscious, and there is no other way to effect cures."

"Sig, I don't think your approach has to preclude mine. I know I can help patients with physical therapy; I see them improve in my sanatorium. We help them get over their depression and minor anxieties; we improve their appetites so they put on weight. We recharge their interest in life. I just can't walk away from such results."

Sigmund studied Kahane's face, with its deep horizontal wrinkles in the forehead and corresponding vertical wrinkles down the cheeks.

"Nor should you. But what do you do when you get genuinely disturbed patients?"

"Even in some of those cases my physical therapy serves as a tonic."

"A tonic is defined as a medicine that invigorates. Once the effect of the tonic wears off, the patient is back where he started. Psychoanalysis addresses itself toward a possible cure." Sigmund shook his head in self-reproach as he braked down the steep hill to Berggasse 19. "Forgive me, I beat one of your ears off during an hour lecture, and then I deafen the other on a sociable walk home."

By the end of the second month of lectures Rudolf Reitler, lean, blond of skin and hair, a man of considerable reserve, had given himself wholeheartedly to Sigmund's cause. After Sigmund had lectured for a full hour on symbolism in psychoanalysis, Reitler waited until the others had gone, then said:

"Herr Doktor, I am fascinated by this subject of symbolism. Looking back on several of my patients whom I could not help, I realize that some of their complaints were built around the kind of symbol to which you referred in the Frau Cäcilie case. Only last night I read your material on her in *Studies on Hysteria*. Today's lecture made everything clear for me. With your permission I would like to study further in this field."

"But assuredly, Herr Doktor. Would you be free to walk home with me now? Frau Doktor Freud will give us a cool drink, and then we can analyze the materials."

10.

The summer was hot and lonely. The *Dienstmänner* had carried away the trunks and barrels of the Viennese to the cool mountains and lakes of summer resorts all over Austria. The heat bounced through the empty streets; the air, this beginning of August, was particularly oppressive. Sigmund arranged to meet Wilhelm Fliess at Achensee, a warm-water lake in the Tyrol, for a three-day congress.

On the first morning after their arrival the men set out on a hike along trails which rose several thousand feet around the lake. They were a contrasting pair: Sigmund wore high laced boots, wool knit stockings coming up under the knee, short knee pants, a vest and coat over a shirt with a striped collar, an Alpine hat with a gray band, and a stout walking stick. Wilhelm, meticulous in Berlin, went to the opposite extreme while on his summer vacation: a pair of scuffed mountain boots, an ancient pair of tan *Lederhosen* held up by battered green *Hosenträger*, a heavy faded green shirt to match his knee-length coarse-knit green stockings. For all the bravado of the well-worn mountaineer outfit, Wilhelm did not look well. He had suffered illnesses in the past two years and had undergone major surgery.

They walked through the fragrant pine forests, warmed by a south wind. Below they saw the maize stocks still standing in the fields, but the ruddy brown cobs had already been piled under the eaves of the peasants' houses, splashes of bright color against the blue lake. Above them were the towering ranges of the Karwendel and Sonnwend, rising from the dark green six-mile-long lake, in some places over four hundred feet deep.

Suddenly Wilhelm stopped in the trail, narrowed his eyes almost to slits, a feat for so big-eyed a man, and said in a harsh voice:

"You know, Sig, you're fooling yourself about those so-called cures."

Sigmund froze on the trail. What he had thought to be the silence of the woods only a moment before now burst into a dozen sounds: a wood-chopper in the distance, birds calling from the trees, cattle bawling in the valley, the tooting of the whistle of the tiny steamer on the lake. He had never seen Wilhelm look like this, the vivid personality shut down; nor had he ever heard him use such a tone. He did his best to keep his own voice emotionless.

"Precisely what do you mean, Wilhelm?"

"The thought reader perceives nothing in others; but merely projects his own thoughts into them."

Sigmund was stunned.

"Then you must regard my technique as worthless! Yet you know precisely how psychoanalysis achieves its ends. You have had hundreds of letters in which I outlined the discovery of the disturbance and gave step-by-step passage out of the illness . . ."

"I am suggesting that your method simply was not the curative factor."

"Then what was?" He was angry now. His voice had a sharp edge.

"I attribute unlimited importance to the cyclical nature of the psyche. Your patients are no more free from their own twenty-three- and twenty-eight-day cycles than any other humans. Your techniques are merely 'mothers' helpers.' Neither relapses nor improvements should be laid at the door of psychoanalysis. They are only the result of periodicity in the great changes in energy, in the ability to face tasks or the need to flee from them. You have seen my tables . . ."

Sigmund was outraged; he clenched his right fist in an attempt to control his sense of betrayal.

"After agreeing with practically every conclusion I've come to, encouraging me to carry on my research, congratulating me on my successes, are you now in the process of throwing over everything you've led me to believe for the last ten years?"

Fliess arched his left eyebrow as if in astonishment, demanding:

"Do I notice some personal animosity arising from you?"

"You could describe it that way, Wilhelm. Have you no notion of what you have just done? You have thrown overboard my entire etiology of the neuroses, and psychoanalysis as a neurological technique in dealing with mental and emotional disturbance. In short, you have just dropped my life work to the four-hundred-foot bottom of the Achensee. How do you expect me to take this?"

"As a scientist, facing an unpleasant but inescapable truth. I suggest that you examine your motives for being so distressed. Do you recall saying to me on an earlier occasion in Vienna, 'It is a good thing that we are friends. I would die of envy if I had heard that anyone else in Berlin was making such discoveries'?"

"Yes, I remember that; and many of your discoveries are remarkable. But what in the world has envy to do with this discussion?"

"Because I am, as you described me, the Kepler of biology." He put his hand inside his shirt pocket and brought out a batch of papers with columns of scrawled figures on them. "I now have my proof. If you had not behaved so badly I could have shown it to you. All mental and emotional illness is tied up in these formulas. I have only just finished tabulating them. What you describe as anxiety, repression, the Oedipal experience, the struggle between the unconscious and conscious mind, all of these are determined not by a sexual etiology but by a mathematical one. When a person's psyche is disturbed it is because his cycle is disturbed: the various sexual organs on either side of his body are battling each other . . ."

Sigmund broke into a sweat under the heavy shirt, vest and coat; then shivered as the perspiration cooled in the dense sunless woods. His back teeth had locked, and he could not utter a word in defense. Wilhelm paid no mind; he was warming to his subject now, his eyes feverishly aglow.

"Why is one man or woman more sexual than another? Periodicity! Why do some rush out to meet sexuality, spend most of their lives thirsting for it, while others shrink back in dread? Periodicity! Sig, as a practicing physician you are going to have to start working with my new tables. Go where the mathematics lead you! When they instruct you to posit a cure, you can lead an individual out of his depression, but when the tables are running against you . . ."

"I think," Sigmund said sadly, turning his head sideways and looking at Fliess but not seeing him for the thunderstorm going on inside his own head, "it is best that we return to the hotel. Nothing I can say would be of any value. I am afraid that I will only aggravate the situation. What has happened to you I cannot fathom . . ."

Fliess broke in roughly, "There is nothing more to be said."

They returned in silence. Fliess packed his bag and left. The congress was over.

In pharmacology he had read that for every poison there was an antidote. Wilhelm Fliess's rejection of his work had been the poison; the case of Dora Giesl, waiting for him upon his return to Vienna, was the antidote. Sigmund had treated Dora's father six years before. The successful manufacturer now brought his unwilling daughter to the Berggasse.

Dora Giesl was eighteen, intelligent. Her father had contracted a venereal infection before marriage which had had permanent effects: a detached retina, partial paralysis. Sigmund, after a stiff series of antiluetic treatments, had achieved a near cure. But when she was ten Dora had overheard a conversation in her parents' bedroom from which she learned that her father had had a venereal disease. The revelation had come as a shock to the child, resulting in intense anxiety over her own health. By twelve she had developed migraine headaches; later she was afflicted by a nervous cough which, by the time she reached the Berggasse, had resulted in the loss of her voice.

Dora was a tall, well-developed girl with masses of chestnut hair braided around her head, and brown eyes shot with purple specks of cynicism. Having been through the hands of a dozen doctors, she had come to ridicule them all for their failure to cure her illness. Her derisive laughter did not help buoy her spirits; she began quarreling with her parents, left a suicide note on her desk, made a feeble effort to cut her wrist, and when her father reproached her, fell into a dead faint at his feet.

The material at the forefront of Dora's mind was her family's relationship with a Herr and Frau Krauss. For a long time Dora, who despised her mother as a "house-cleaning fanatic," had adored Frau Krauss, apparently a charming woman; or at least Dora's father thought so, for he had been carrying on a liaison with Frau Krauss for a number of years. They frequently went away together on trips, or met in strange cities when Dora's father had to travel on business. Dora had learned about this love affair several years before; so had Herr Krauss, who had not gone to the trouble of breaking up the relationship.

Dora had also been fond of Herr Krauss, who apparently reciprocated: when she was fourteen Herr Krauss invited his wife and Dora to come to his office where they could have a good view of a church festival. Dora went to the office only to learn that Frau Krauss had stayed at home and that all of the clerks had been dismissed for the day so they could participate in the festivities. Krauss asked Dora to wait for him at the door leading to the upper story, then joined her, clasped the girl to him and pressed a passionate kiss on her lips. Dora swore to Dr. Freud that she had felt only disgust as she tore herself away and ran out into the street.

Recently, while Dora and her father were staying with the Krausses at their country home, she had gone for a walk with Krauss, during which he had made an overt sexual proposal to her. Dora told her mother of this incident, demanding that her father break off all contact with the Krauss family. When Dora's father faced Krauss with the incident, he denied any wrongdoing and suggested that Dora was fascinated by sexual matters, that she had read Mantegazza's *Physiology of Love* and every other book about physical love she could find in the Krauss home. Krauss described his alleged sexual advance as a fantasy. Dora's health declined.

Sigmund knew that traumas cannot become effective unless they are linked to an experience in the patient's childhood. Dora's protest now was that she could not free herself from the feeling the upper part of her body received from Herr Krauss's earlier embrace.

"Dora, could it be possible that you have repressed the exact memory that either distressed or frightened you, and have made a displacement from the lower part of your body to the upper about which you feel more free to speak?"

"Precisely what are you suggesting, Herr Doktor?"

"That while Herr Krauss was embracing you so passionately you not only felt his lips on yours but also the pressure of his erect member against your body."

"That is revolting."

"The word 'revolting' conveys a moral judgment. What we are seeking here is a truth, the truth about all of the elements which, put together over a period of years, have caused you, a bright and attractive young woman, to become melancholy, to shun society, to quarrel with your parents and attempt suicide. Shouldn't we wonder whether you may be running away from a recurrence of what you felt when you were embraced by Herr Krauss?"

"I neither agree nor disagree."

The context of Dora's obsessions for the next week or two was a long string of reproaches: against her father for lying and being insincere in carrying on a love affair with Frau Krauss; against Frau Krauss, who spent most of her time in bed as an invalid when her husband was home, but bounced around Europe to meet her father at every opportunity; against Herr Krauss for his two attempts to seduce her; against her brother, who took the mother's part in the family arguments; and against the mother, whose sole interest in Dora's health was getting her to keep their home scrubbed.

In Sigmund's experience a series of reproaches levied by a patient against other people meant that the patient was filled with self-reproach. When Dora reproached her father for not taking seriously Herr Krauss's immoral proposition to her, Sigmund concluded that this was a repressed self-reproach because for several years Dora had been a willing accomplice to her father's liaison and had been unwilling to look at it too closely for fear it might break the friendship between the two families.

Early Monday morning when Dora began a new week's sessions, Sigmund said, "You have told me that your coughing spells last from three to six weeks. When Herr Krauss had to go away on business, how long was his usual trip?"

Dora blushed. "Three to six weeks."

"Then don't you see, Dora, by your illness you were giving a proof of your love for Herr Krauss even as, when Herr Krauss returned to his wife, she took to bed so that she would not have to fulfill her conjugal duties? Your present illness is just as much motivated; there is something you hope to gain by it."

"What could that be? Do you take me for a fool?"

"No, Dora, you are a perceptive young girl. But even the best of us have trouble understanding our motivations. What you are also trying to achieve is to break up the affair between your father and Frau Krauss. You have been trying for a considerable time now. If you can persuade your father to give up Frau Krauss because of your ill health you will be victorious. Since you yourself testified that your mother and father have had no intimate relations for years, why do you call your father's relations with Frau Krauss a 'common love affair'?"

"She only loves my father because he is a man of means."

"You mean that he gives her money, gifts?"

"Yes. She lives much better and buys more expensive things than her husband can afford."

"Are you sure you don't really want to say the exact opposite? That your father is a man without means: that is, impotent?"

Dora was untroubled at this revelation. She replied, "Yes, I have long wanted my father to be impotent so there could be no sexual relations between them. However I also know that there is more than one way of obtaining sexual satisfaction."

"You are referring to oral gratification? You told me not long ago that you had been a thumb-sucker up to your fourth or fifth year. What is the source of this piece of knowledge, Dora? Would it be from Mantegazza's *Physiology of Love?*"

"I honestly don't know, Herr Doktor."

"In thinking of other means of sexual gratification, might you be referring to those parts of your body which are so frequently irritated, your throat and oral cavity? Is your cough perhaps a means of expressing yourself sexually; of your unconscious mind centering the stimulation there rather than in your genitals?"

Dora's cough disappeared. A few days later she commented, "At first I was alarmed and offended at your use of the words to describe the parts of the human body; and yet you spoke about them in a manner so clinical . . ."

"You mean, removed from the prurience with which these subjects are spoken of in good society?"

"Yes. I am sure a lot of people would be scandalized if they could hear some of our conversations, but your treatment is far more respectable than some of the conversations I have heard among my father's men friends, and Herr Krauss's men friends."

Dora's most insistent emotion at this point was her oft-repeated, "I can't forgive my father for this love affair. Neither can I forgive Frau Krauss."

"You're acting like a jealous wife, you know. You are putting yourself in your mother's place. And in your fantasy you are putting yourself in Frau Krauss's place as well. This means that you have become two women, the one your father originally loved and the one he loves now. All of which means that you are also in love with your father and that that is the cause of your inner turbulence."

"I would not care to admit that."

Weeks later Dora reported a recurrent dream: "A house was on fire. My father was standing beside my bed and woke me up. I dressed quickly. Mother wanted to stop and save her jewel case; but Father said: 'I refuse to let myself and my two children be burnt for the sake of your jewel case.' We hurried downstairs, and as soon as I was outside I woke up."

"Dora, in *The Interpretation of Dreams* I made the statement that 'every dream is a wish which is represented as fulfilled, that the representation acts as a disguise if the wish is a repressed one, belonging to the unconscious, and only an unconscious wish has the force necessary for the formation of a dream.' Now let us get on to the jewelry. How do you understand the matter of the jewel case that your mother wanted to save?"

"I had received an expensive jewel case from Herr Krauss as a gift."

"Do you not know that 'jewel case' is a common expression for the female genitals?"

"I knew you would say that."

"You mean you knew that it was true. What your dream was attempting to say was 'My jewel case is in danger. If I lose it, it will be Father's fault.' That's the reason you turn things around in your dream and present it as the opposite: your father's saving you from the fire, rather than your mother's jewel case. You asked why your mother was present in your dream when she had not been present at the Krausses on the lake during this incident . . ."

"My mother cannot play a part in this dream."

"Ah, but she does, because the incident must tie back to your childhood. In relation to a bracelet your mother refused you made it clear that you would have loved to accept what your mother did not want. Now let's turn this to the opposite and use the word 'give' instead of 'accept.' It was your wish to be able to give your father what your mother was withholding from him. As a parallel thought, Herr Krauss takes your father's place in the dream; he gave you a jewel case, so you would now like to give him your jewel case. Your mother is now replaced by Frau Krauss, who is in the house; according to the dream, you are prepared to give to Herr Krauss what his wife withholds from him. These are the feelings you have been repressing so dynamically, and which have made it necessary for the censor to turn every one of the elements of your dream upside down. The dream also proves that you were calling on the Oedipal love for your father to keep you safe from the love for Herr Krauss. Dora, look deep into your feelings; you are not afraid of Herr Krauss, are you? It is yourself that you are afraid of, of the fact that you may yield to temptation. No mortal can keep a secret."

A tremendous sigh came from Dora.

"I want no more secrets, Herr Doktor. I'm glad they are out in the open. Of all the doctors who have treated me, only you have caught me out. I despised the others because they failed to learn my secrets. Perhaps you really have set me free."

"Perhaps . . ." But he doubted it. The three-month period had been much too short.

However, Dora never returned.

Sigmund had kept complete notes on his sessions with Dora, which had taken place six days a week, until the New Year of 1901. Each night after supper he had written out the content of the day's work. Now he set down the case, with its full psychoanalytical implications, thinking to publish it as a documentary refutation to those who were attacking *The Interpretation of Dreams.* The Giesls were from the country and largely unknown in Vienna; by changing a few of the external surroundings there would be no danger of Dora being exposed.

He completed the manuscript, a hefty hundred pages, by the end of January. In June he sent it to the *Monatsschrift für Psychiatrie und Neurologie.* When the editor accepted the case history for publication, Sigmund had a sudden change of heart. He withdrew the manuscript, burying it deep in a desk drawer.

"Let it cool for a few years," he decided; "and let the public warm."

11.

He started a paper called The Psychopathology of Everyday Life. For the first time he was writing for a general public rather than a medical one; he would be able to stay away from sexual materials and not grind the moral toes of the community under his boots. The material would emerge from everyday experience: slips of the tongue, forgettings, bungled actions, misplacings of names or dates, incorrect substitutions of words, misreading . . . since he believed that it was possible to discover the psychical determinants of every smallest detail of the mind. For his title page he used the quotation from *Faust:*

> Now fills the air so many a haunting shape,
> That no one knows how best he may escape.

For the core word of his study he used parapraxis, or symptomatic acts, because they, as well as dreams made it possible for him to bring over to normal psychology much of what he had learned about the neuroses and the unconscious. If it were true that nothing was ever forgotten or misplaced by accident, but only by design, here was an opportunity to show the complex double nature of the human mind under the simplest conditions, and for healthy, normal people.

He told the story of the President of the Lower House of the Austrian Parliament who opened the sitting with: "Gentlemen: I take notice that a full quorum of members is present and herewith declare the sitting *closed!*" The roar of laughter made it clear that everyone knew how much he did not want this session of the Parliament. There was the young man who greatly admired his teacher, a well-known historian, but was humiliated by that teacher in public when he announced he was going to write a biography of a famous personage. The historian announced, "We really don't need any more books!" A few days later when they met, the young man cried, "That was a strange thing for you to say, you who have written more *hysterical* books than anyone in our field." The older teacher smiled, said, "Hysterical or historical? You have quite properly chastised me for my improper treatment of you the other night."

When Sigmund asked one of his women patients how her uncle was, she replied, "I don't know, nowadays I only see him *in flagrante.*' The next day she said, "I am ashamed of having confused *in flagrante* with *en passant,* which was what I meant to say." The day's analytical material revealed that what she very much had on her mind was somebody close to her who had been caught *in flagrante.*

There were the frequent cases of people forgetting appointments they had not wanted to make in the first place; of letters being mailed without the check that was supposed to be enclosed. One of his men patients, who was leaving the city and owed Dr. Freud a large sum of money, returned home to get his bankbook from his desk, but in a flash hid the keys so cleverly that the desk could not be opened. There was a woman patient whom Sigmund suspected of being ashamed of her family. She replied, "It is most unlikely. One thing must be granted them: they are certainly unusual people, they all possess *Geiz,* greed—I meant to say *Geist,* cleverness." Another young woman patient could not remember, in mixed company, the title of Lew Wallace's novel because in German the words *bin Hure,* I am a whore, sounded so like *Ben Hur.*

He wrote:

"There is far less freedom and arbitrariness in mental life than we are inclined to assume—there may even be none at all. What we call chance in the world outside can, as is well known, be resolved into laws. So, too, what we call arbitrariness in the mind rests upon laws which we are only dimly beginning to suspect."

He used an anecdote about himself to illustrate his theory that numbers rarely come out of the mind by accident or haphazardly, but are governed inexorably by the unconscious:

He had gone to a bookseller to buy a series of medical books and asked for his usual ten percent discount. The next day he took an armful of medical books which he no longer needed to another dealer, asking a fair price for them. The dealer wanted to pay less, ten percent less, Sigmund thought. From there he went to his bank to draw out 380 kronen (the new unit of Austrian money, worth half a gulden and just introduced) from his savings account of 4380 kronen; but when he wrote his check he saw that he had made it out for 438 kronen instead, ten percent of his savings!

Not wanting to offend the general public, he included only a few examples with a sexual base: the woman patient who was trying to re-create a forgotten memory of childhood in which a man had seized a certain part of her body with a lascivious hand. The woman was unable to remember which part of her body had been touched. A few moments later when Sigmund asked where her summer cottage was located, she replied:

"On the *Berglende*, hill-thigh . . . I mean *Berglehne*, hillside."

He met on holiday an acquaintance from his early university days. The man made an impassioned speech about the dubious future of their race in Austria, attempting to end with a line from Virgil: "Let someone arise from my bones as an avenger!" But he stumbled over the Latin, forgot a key word, then changed their order: "*Exoriar(e) ex nostris ossibus ultor.*" Embarrassed, he exclaimed, "Sig, I missed something in that line. Help me; how does it go?"

"I'll help you with pleasure: '*Exoriar(e)* ALIQUIS *nostris ex ossibus ultor.*'"

"How stupid to forget a word like that! By the way, you claim that one never forgets a thing without some reason. I should be very curious to learn how I came to forget the indefinite pronoun *aliquis*, someone, in this case."

"That should not take us long. I must only ask you to tell me, candidly and uncritically, whatever comes into your mind if you direct your attention to the forgotten word without any definite aim."

"Good. There springs to my mind, then, the ridiculous notion of dividing up the word like this: *a* and *liquis.*"

"And what occurs to you next?"

"What comes next is *Reliquien*, relics, liquefying, fluidity, fluid. Have you discovered anything so far?"

"Not by any means yet. But go on."

"I am thinking," he went on with a scornful laugh, "of Simon of Trent, whose relics I saw two years ago in a church at Trent. I am thinking of the accusation of ritual blood sacrifice which is being brought against the Jews again just now; and of Kleinpaul's book in which he regards all these supposed victims as incarnations, one might say new editions, of the Savior."

"The notion is not entirely unrelated to the subject we were discussing before the Latin word slipped your memory."

"True. My next thoughts are about an article that I read lately in an Italian newspaper. Its title, I think, was 'What St. Augustine Says about Women.' What do you make of that?"

"I am waiting."

"And now comes something that is quite clearly unconnected with our subject."

"Please refrain from any criticism and . . ."

"Yes, I understand. I am thinking of a fine old gentleman I met on my travels last week. He was a real original, with all the appearance of a huge bird of prey. His name was Benedict."

"Here are a row of saints and Fathers of the Church: St. Simon, St. Augustine, St. Benedict," said Sigmund.

"Now it's St. Januarius and the miracle of his blood that comes into my mind," continued the man. "My thoughts seem to me to be running on mechanically."

"Just a moment: St. Januarius and St. Augustine have to do with the calendar. But won't you remind me about the miracle of his blood?"

"Surely you must have heard of that? They keep the blood of St. Januarius in a phial inside a church at Naples, and on a particular holy day it miraculously liquefies. The people attach great importance to this miracle and get very excited if it's delayed . . ."

"Why do you pause?"

"Well, something *has* come into my mind . . . but it's too intimate to pass on. . . . Besides, I don't see any connection . . . I've suddenly thought of a lady from whom I might easily hear a piece of news that would be very awkward for both of us."

"That her periods have stopped?"

"How could you guess that?"

"That's not difficult any longer; you've prepared the way sufficiently. Think of *the calendar saints, the blood that starts to flow on a particular day, the disturbance when the event fails to take place* . . . In fact you've made use of the miracle of St. Januarius to manufacture a brilliant allusion to women's periods."

"And you really mean to say that it was this anxious expectation that made me unable to produce an unimportant word like *aliquis?*"

"It seems to me undeniable. You need only recall the division you made into *a-liquis*, and your associations: relics, liquefying, fluid."

"I will confess to you that the lady is Italian and that I went to Naples with her. But mayn't all this just be a matter of chance?"

"I must leave it to your own judgment to decide whether you can explain all these connections by the assumption that they are matters of chance. I can however tell you that every case like this that you care to analyze will lead you to 'matters of chance' that are just as striking."

When he later published the story, many of his readers agreed with him.

On January 22, 1901, Queen Victoria of England died in the sixty-fourth year of her reign. Sigmund had read enough English history to know that an age had ended, one which, by the very nature of the monarch, had opposed every tenet of Dr. Sigmund Freud's sexual nature of man. In this, the first month of the second year of the twentieth century, Sigmund permitted himself the hope that the new age would be more open-minded, less prudish, less bigoted and frightened about the normal sexual attributes of man; that it might even admit that women had legs rather than limbs; and that all children were born with natural sexual appetites. He wondered if he would live long enough to see any change come over the minds of men. Darwin had wondered this too. Sigmund had read some of the abuse heaped on Darwin's head; it was as brutal as the maledictions he, Sigmund, suffered in his own press. The universality of man as a bigot was consoling to him . . . in a bleak fashion.

Working rapidly now, he finished Psychopathology of Everyday Life and sent it to Ziehen, who promised to publish it during the summer months. Martha asked quietly, while they were walking to his mother's for Sunday dinner, the highlight of Amalie's month:

"Sigi, you said you wrote this long article for the general public. Then why are you offering it to the *Monthly Magazine for Psychiatry and Neurology,* instead of a general newspaper? Is it because you took the Dora Giesl manuscript away from them?"

"Only partly. It simply isn't proper for a physician to publish medical materials in a popular paper. He is confined to the scientific journals."

"Then how does your material reach the general public?"

"By osmosis. It leaks. Like gas from the earth or water from a flat roof."

Then, for the first time in five years, since his ill-fated lecture on The Etiology of Hysteria before the Society for Psychiatry and Neurology, he was invited to lecture in Vienna before the Philosophical Society, which included in its membership authorities in every department of the university. In its early years the group had met informally in the Kaiserhof Coffeehouse, but in 1888 they had been adopted by the Philosophy Department of the university and given a lecture hall for their rapidly expanding membership. Over the years Sigmund had heard brilliant lectures and discussions offered by the Philosophical Society not only in medicine but in philosophy. Though the Society had only two women enrolled as members, there were many who attended the lectures with their husbands and parents. Socially and culturally it played an important part in the intellectual life of Vienna.

The officers of the Society, having no contact with Dr. Sigmund Freud, approached him through Josef Breuer. Breuer wrote Sigmund a note urging him to accept. Sigmund was filled with joy. Though he had lectured on dreams several times to the B'nai B'rith, and to the few who signed for his course, the lectures had been given at his own request, when his isolation had become unbearable. While he would not assume that this invitation was a gesture of sponsorship, it would provide him with one of the most respected platforms in Europe. He determined to write a strong, convincing and lucid paper.

When he reread what he had written he realized that it contained a great deal of sexual material which a mixed audience would find shocking and unacceptable. He sent word to the Society suggesting that the lecture be canceled. Two of the directors came to the Berggasse to urge him to reconsider.

"Very well, gentlemen, but on one condition: that you return to my house one evening next week and listen to the lecture. If you find nothing objectionable in it, I will be happy to give it before your Society."

The men returned, listened to Sigmund's hour-long presentation, and were absorbed. When they thanked him for giving of his time, one of them remarked:

"Our membership is well educated, Herr Doktor; they travel widely and are sophisticated. Your theses will cause some surprise, perhaps even some shock, but certainly no outbursts of moral indignation. We are a proper audience for such a point of departure in neurology."

The lecture was announced in the *Neue Freie Presse* and stirred considerable interest. On the morning of the meeting an express letter was delivered to the Berggasse. Apologetically, the spokesman for the Philosophical Society explained: word had leaked out about the content of Dr. Freud's lecture; some of the members, the men, not the women, had taken exception. Would Dr. Freud be so considerate as to commence with inoffensive, non-sexual cases and examples? Then, when he came to the material which some might consider offensive, would he, as delicately as possible, announce that he was about to detail certain objectionable matters; then wait for a few moments, in silence of course, "during which the ladies could leave the hall"?

He canceled the lecture with a note so indignant that the words almost seared the stationery. Martha asked:

"Couldn't you have lectured on the psychopathology of everyday life? You yourself have said that that was the easy road to the unconscious, and there is very little sexual reference in the book."

"Yes, I could have, if in the beginning they had asked me to give that lecture. But after I have presented the main body of my work, to declare ninety percent of it indecent or reprehensible would be an admission that I am doing something wrong. If these men think that their women's ears are too delicate to hear about the sexual life of *Homo sapiens*, then I think I had best withdraw from their bull-fight arena."

"Given a choice," twitted Minna, "which would you rather be, the matador or the bull?"

"At each fiesta I go out gloriously garbed as the matador but by the end of the contest I have somehow been transformed into the bull with the sword in the hump of my neck, down on my knees in the sawdust."

12.

Alexander, who was teaching freight scheduling and tariffs several nights a week at the Export Academy across the street, often dropped in for a cup of coffee when his lectures were over. He was now thirty-four, owned the major interest in his shipping business, was dressing nattily and going out more; particularly to his beloved light operas. As far as Sigmund or Martha could determine he still had no inclination to fall seriously in love or to marry.

"Plenty of time for settling down. In another five years Moritz Muenz will retire, and I will be sole owner of the business. That's when I'll look for a wife."

When Leopold Königstein finally got his associate professorship, Martha gave a Saturday night supper party to celebrate, inviting old friends Sigmund had not been seeing, after which Sigmund installed the *Tarock* game on the heavy dining table overlooking the Berggasse. Then Alexander was appointed associate professor of tariffs at the Export Academy. Martha invited the family to a festive Sunday dinner. The party was somewhat spoiled for Sigmund when his mother announced at table:

"I never expected my younger son to become a professor before my older one."

Sigmund refrained from replying, "Mother, the Export Academy is a trade school. It is not the University of Vienna." Instead he said:

"We produce only geniuses in the Freud family."

Nevertheless, as the days went by, his mother's unguarded remark nettled him. He thought, "I've got to renew my efforts with the Minister of Education. But how?"

Wilhelm Fliess wrote that he was attempting to persuade a Frau Doblhoff to come to Vienna and put herself in Sigmund's care, since the Berlin neurologists had failed to help her. Wilhelm had assured Frau and Herr Professor Doblhoff that Privatdozent Sigmund Freud could help her with his new therapeutic techniques. Sigmund was confounded by this piece of intelligence. He exclaimed:

"He's doing the precise thing Professor Nothnagel does: 'I don't believe in your methods, but here is a patient whom no one else can cure. Perhaps you can!'" Was he still a Court of Last Appeals?

At the beginning of June he went on a scouting expedition through Bavaria to find a place for the family for the summer, taking the train directly to Salzburg where he visited with Minna and Mrs. Bernays, who were vacationing in Reichenhall, and then on a carriage trip lost his heart to the neighboring Thumsee: a little green lake, Alpine roses descending the mountain to the roadway, magnificent woods all around, strawberries, flowers in profusion, mushrooms . . . There were no villas available for rent, but the doctor who had owned the small local inn had just died and Sigmund made a bid for his spacious rooms.

Thumsee proved to be a little paradise for the family. The children ate ravenously, fought for the few available boats on the lake and were gone for the day, carrying massive picnic luncheons. Martin, now eleven, Oliver, ten, and Ernst, nine, were dressed by their mother in identical outfits: short leather pants with patch pockets, boots, heavy socks ending just below the knee, soft jackets cut straight down from the collar, white shirts, polka-dot ties and round hats with a feather in the band. Sigmund sometimes went with them but he complained that life among the fish made him feel stupid. More often he took the three girls, Mathilde, now thirteen, Sophie, eight, and Anna, five, for walks in the woods to gather baskets of wild berries. Martha was enchanted with the surroundings and the little inn.

Yet Sigmund was restless. Since completing *The Psychopathology of Everyday Life* he had felt mentally tired. He was irked with himself because no new ideas occurred to him. He had enjoyed a satisfactory year with his clients; since there had been fewer of them, the strain had been less. He should have been in top spirits; yet he was hard put to fill his free time. He had been haunted by daydreams as well as nightdreams of spending Easter in Rome. Though he had been reading widely in Greek archaeology and "reveling in journeys which I shall never make and treasures which I shall never possess" he now turned his attention back to Rome, studying street maps so that he would know his way around if he could ever summon the courage to break the strong inhibitions against going. He asked himself, "I've learned from my own analysis why I have repressed this lifetime desire. Why should I not be free now to go? I must make the journey!"

"What I need is a couple of weeks in the land of wine and olive oil," he told Martha.

"Then why not go, my dear? New places refresh you for the coming year's work."

He could not get himself organized. He took Martha to Salzburg to hear the opera, then was trapped in the inn for several days by raw, driving rainstorms. He read the introduction to Dr. Ludwig Laistner's *The Riddle of the Sphinx*, which attempted to prove that myths could be traced back to dreams; then put the volume aside, lazily, when he saw that the author had no concept of what lay behind dreams. The only news in the papers that excited him was the report of Arthur Evans's excavation of the palace of Knossos, on Crete, birthplace of the earliest Greek culture, 1500 B.C., and reputed to be the site of the original labyrinth of Minos.

The excitement of these finds in Greek archaeology brought his thinking back sharply to his unrequited desire: to visit Rome. A thunderstorm caught him while tramping in the woods. From behind the swift-flying dark clouds came a bolt of lightning.

"But of course!" he cried aloud. He had been a fool not to see it! He had thought that because his self-analysis was complete he would now be free to go to Rome. It was the other way round: his arrival in Rome would officially signal the end of the analysis, the symptomatic act he needed to perform to establish his independence.

He rushed back to the inn in the splattering rain, found Martha in their sitting room reading to the young by the light of a kerosene lamp. She saw the look of snapping excitement in his eyes.

"Sigi, what has happened? You look as though something enormous has hit you."

"It has. That bolt of lightning. We're leaving for Rome on the first of September. For a two-week visit. What do you say to that, Marty?"

"I say, Hallelujah. I know how long and ardently you've wanted to go." She cherished a contemplative moment, then put her arms about Sigmund's waist and said gently, "I appreciate your being willing to share this great experience with me. But I can just see you trying to absorb two thousand years of Roman history in two weeks, and all in what you have always described as 'the beastly heat and malaria of the Roman summer.' Let me go with you next time, when you know more about the city and can take it philosophically."

In the end he decided to invite Alexander to join him.

They arrived at noon of the second day at the Central Station and took a carriage to the Hotel Milano in the Piazza Montecitorio. Sigmund was so tense as they drove through the streets, particularly when they passed places he had read about, the lovely Fountain of the Naiades in the Piazza dell' Esedra, the column of Marcus Aurelius in the Piazza Colonna; the obelisk brought from Heliopolis to Rome by Augustus and placed in the Field of Mars, that he was afraid he would stop breathing.

The Hotel Milano had reserved a spacious room equipped with electric lights rather than the gas lamps to which he was accustomed during his travels. He promptly had a hot bath, dressed in fresh clothes and, surveying himself in the mirror of the wardrobe, exclaimed:

"Now I feel like a proper Roman, though I would much rather have soaked in the hot waters of the Baths of Caracalla surrounded by a hundred senators and members of the nobility, playing games of chance on the patterned tile floors."

"You sound like the guidebook you have in your coat pocket," exclaimed Alex.

"Come, Alex, let's find a good restaurant; and then we'll wander footloose on our first afternoon. All the other days I have rigidly organized."

"I haven't the slightest doubt!" groused Alexander. "We'd better get to sleep early tonight. We'll doubtless watch the sun come up in the Colosseum."

"Not this time. This is a high spot of my life and I plan to savor every moment of it. You simply can't know how happy I am to be in Rome, or how much it means to me."

They started the next morning at seven-thirty with a visit to St. Peter's, having had an inspiring view of Michelangelo's Dome the afternoon before from the terrace of the Piazzale del Pincio. They entered the massive central door and walked quickly to the central nave where they stood in awe at the superbly balanced immensity of the Mother Church of Christendom. He observed the early worshipers kissing the already worn foot of St. Peter; went down the winding steps beneath the central altar to the tomb of St. Peter; then climbed the hundreds of steps to the top of the Dome to study the vastness of the cathedral beneath them. They walked out onto the open balconies with their gigantic sculptures for a majestic view of Rome, the Castle Sant'Angelo in front of them, the Tiber flowing through the city.

Leaving St. Peter's, they visited the Vatican. Nothing that Sigmund had read or seen had prepared him for the vault of the Sistine Chapel where Michelangelo had transcribed the Old Testament. He paced the chapel floor, his head craned back trying to absorb this miracle in paint, the Prophets, Sibyls, Creation of Man, the Flood . . . almost unable to grasp its immensity. It was a chastening and inspiring art experience. Almost the same emotion gripped him when he went to the end of the chapel to look at the *Last Judgment,* with its powerful male Christ hurling the evil ones into hell, an exquisitely beautiful Mary sitting beside him in diaphanous robes.

He returned to the Hotel Milano numb. He wrote to Martha:

"And to think that for years I was afraid to come to Rome!"

The next morning they spent two and a half hours in the Museo Nazionale Romano, with its collection of ancient Greek sculptures; then walked in the warm sunshine to the little Trevi piazza and threw a coin into the robust spray of the fountain to insure their return to Rome. They had midday dinner at a sidewalk restaurant shaded by an awning with a close view of the enormous stone Tritons bearing a winged chariot. After a delicious *fettuccine* and *ossi bucchi*, digging out the marrow from the bones with a long grooved knife, they continued across the city to the ancient Pantheon with its sixteen monolithic columns, so huge inside as to stagger the imagination; its circular opening at the top pinpointing the clear Italian sky. The afternoon they spent in the Colosseum.

Later they had a light supper at a sidewalk restaurant in the Piazza Navona, overlooking Bernini's splendid baroque fountains, then walked home in the warm evening air, Sigmund amused to see how the Romans lived in their streets, mothers breast-feeding their children on the doorsteps, families buying their supper from open stalls and eating as they continued onward, singing, arguing, gesticulating; young couples locked in each other's arms, even as they had been on the streets of Paris, leaning against the walls as they kissed.

"I like the modern Romans as well as I do the ancient ones," Sigmund observed to Alexander; "they live their lives *en plein air.* In Vienna we can do anything indoors but nothing outdoors except drink a coffee."

The days went by in a phantasmagoria of sights, sounds and revelations. He had never felt so well. They rented a carriage for four hours so that they could get a general impression of the city; visited the Palatine, which became Sigmund's favorite hill in Rome, even more dear than Michelangelo's brilliantly designed Capitoline with its Senatorial Palace and statue of Marcus Aurelius. He went to see the Moses in San Pietro in Vincoli, vowing that one day he would write a book about the marble carving. At an antique dealer's he found an old Roman head, a female marble torso from Asia Minor, two standing Egyptian figures, small but exquisite in detail, and finally a Greek-Roman intaglio with a head of Jupiter carved in the semiprecious stone. He had it set in a simple gold ring, which he adored and rarely took off.

On the ninth day the sirocco struck, the hot south wind coming up from Africa; it drained Sigmund's energy, but still he continued to enjoy the marvels of ancient Rome: the Forum with its Arch of Septimius Severus, Caesar's Basilica Julia, the House of the Vestal Virgins. They walked along the Via dei Fori Imperiali, past the noble Forums built in turn by Augustus, Caesar, Trajan. It was on his very last day that Sigmund stumbled into his single most meaningful experience: a small, dank underground pagan temple with its sacrificial altar preserved intact; above it, though still largely underground, an early Christian church of the first or second century, unadorned; and above that a third church: large, ornate, seventeenth century. For Sigmund this was the symbol for the derivation and structure of his own work: the unconscious, the preconscious and the conscious mind, all resting upon each other, in precisely that order.

On the twelfth day the brothers took the train back to Vienna. Sigmund sighed with contentment as they settled into their compartment for the two-day ride.

13.

When he returned to Vienna he had three interesting patients awaiting his care, two of whom were to have an important influence on his life. The first was the Baroness Maria von Ferstel, nee Thorsch, in her mid-thirties, regal in bearing, with a broad, strong, handsome face and magnificently large dark eyes. She had been born in Prague, of an international family of bankers and wholesalers, and was raised in the Palais Thorsch, so large that it covered almost a square block. Her own father, David, had eschewed business to become a civil engineer. Maria Thorsch had married Baron Erwin von Ferstel, a wealthy General Konsul in the Emperor's Foreign Ministry. The couple had been married in the Votivkirche, which the Baron's father, Heinrich von Ferstel, had designed and built. As one of the most prominent architects of Vienna, he had also built the University of Vienna. The *Baronin*, as she was called, had four daughters and conducted one of the more exciting salons in the Imperial City. She had wit and presence. The Thorsches were Jews, but Maria had converted to Catholicism before she married Baron von Ferstel, a gesture which was accepted as sincere.

"Herr Doktor, I was recommended to you by Frau Hofrat Gomperz; she said you cured her ailment in a month."

"It was little more than a sprain of the wrist. Would you like to tell me your problem?"

"I suffer from headaches. When I wake in the morning I feel fine, I am rested and approach the day's tasks with pleasure. But as the day wears on, as I open my mail, and couriers arrive with messages about meetings, charity affairs, I begin to feel as though I have a tight hat on my head."

"Would you please show me where the pain first begins."

"Yes, here where my neck joins my head." She patted the area with her left hand. "The pain seems to radiate to the top of my head and then spreads downward to my forehead. Sometimes my head feels so heavy that I think it is a separate body that moves in any direction it wants."

"Baronin, it sounds like a textbook example of the headache coming from tension."

He found tenderness over the occipital nerve but nothing else. He asked for a detailed account of her day, from the time she awoke until she retired for the night. What emerged was a portrait of one of the most active women in the Austro-Hungarian Empire. When it came to requests to serve the Emperor, the Parliament or Mayor, a religious, educational or art group, she lacked the capacity to say "No." As far as Sigmund could gather, there were no family problems; the Baron and Baroness although married for eleven years, still loved each other. The Baroness did not have a neurosis, nor did she suffer from hysteria.

At one session she asked, "Herr Doktor, how can all these activities possibly be wrong when the causes are all so worthwhile?"

"Perhaps you have overstretched your commitments."

"My days do seem to grow increasingly complex."

"Would it be fair to say that you have a compulsive need to be active?"

The Baroness sat with her head down for a moment, then raised her eyes to his in full candor.

"Yes. I feel a driving force within me. Call it *noblesse oblige*. But from your expression I can see that you feel it is more complicated than that. I don't want to be the one who is always called upon, and yet at the same time I do not want to be left out of anything. Does a contradiction of this sort make sense, Herr Doktor?"

"Indeed. Few human beings go through life without some kind of dichotomy."

Baroness von Ferstel turned her head sideways, the better to think, then said, "Since my husband is a diplomat we entertain interesting and important people. Both my husband's family and mine have been financially secure for generations. We have no quarrels with in-laws or children. There have been no deep shocks or disappointments in my life. Why then would I be in conflict with myself?"

"That's what we're going to find out. And I do not think it is going to take deep analysis to get at the cause."

During the first two months he was able to bring the woman little relief. However what began to emerge was her need to compete with her mother, a *grande dame* who had conducted a brilliant salon. The older Mrs. Thorsch had achieved high distinction in the Empire, had been a regular at the court of Emperor Franz Josef; and was known for her charities, not only to the Jewish hospital and Institute for the Blind and Orphanage, but to a good many Catholic causes as well. This mother figure, larger than life size, was the one Baroness von Ferstel was competing with, apparently beyond her nervous strength or real desire. The second element arose from her conversion to Catholicism. Conversion frequently carried with it a residue of guilt. What came out was the feeling that because she had not been born a Catholic the Baroness had to do more, accomplish more than anyone around her in order that no one could say she refused to do this, or failed to fulfill that, because she had been born a Jew.

She accepted Herr Doktor Freud's reasoning and began finding further proof of his deductions in her own mind. The headaches diminished. She grew less tense. The sense of having a tight hat on her head returned only occasionally. She began cutting down on tasks which she realized others could do equally well. She enjoyed her sessions with Sigmund, was impressed by his techniques for giving human beings weapons with which to rout an unseen enemy. At the end of three months she felt quite well.

His second new patient brought a sharp pang of pleasure. Dr. Wilhelm Stekel was the first practicing physician to come to his office seeking analytical help. Stekel was thirty-three, a graduate of the University of Vienna Medical School, though born and raised in Austrian Bucovina. He was a colorful character, a self-conceived actor with an upsweeping mustache, immaculately rounded goatee; eye sockets so large that the irises seemed adrift at sea. He dressed debonairly, with flowing ties, a rakish hat. He wrote articles for the Sunday newspapers, was an accomplished pianist who set his own poems to music, and an authority on the bicycle, having published a book called *Health and the Bicycle*. He had also published a monograph entitled *Coitus in Children*, from which Sigmund had quoted a passage in one of his own papers. He managed the miracle of spouting whole stretches of monologue without stopping to breathe.

"Max Kahane told me about you. Said your lectures at the university were original, packed with ideas. Kahane told me you had quoted from my *Coitus in Children*. I had never heard your name or seen any of your books. A couple of days after Kahane mentioned your name I read a review of your *Interpretation of Dreams*. The review was so bad, the reviewer called it abstruse and unscientific, that I knew it had to be good. I have frequently been frustrated by patients who have nervous disorders yet have nothing organically wrong with them. I did not know about that discovery of yours, the unconscious. Can you lend me a copy of *Interpretation of Dreams*? I want to learn how dreams reveal buried material. I'm sure I can help my patients once I have mastered your methods.

"But you'll want to know why I came to you. I have a very dangerous condition. My marriage is breaking up. I married the girl because she loved beautiful books and played duets with me. Now we can't stand each other, good as I have been to her. . . . I have had homosexual dreams, but Max Kahane told me of the concept of bisexuality, so that doesn't make me abnormal, does it? I have also had incestuous dreams about my mother; but Caesar and Alexander had similar dreams, didn't they?

"But before you can answer my questions, you'll want the story of my life, particularly my childhood. I shall leave nothing out, I assure you, including all youthful sexual experience; after all, who is the world authority on coitus in children but myself? Well then, let us start at the beginning . . ."

Stekel spoke for two solid hours without interrupting himself. Sigmund was amused; Stekel was a superb storyteller who did not feel constricted by the harsh boundaries of truth. Words and sentences flowed out of him like a mountain spring gushing forth to make a river. Out poured some of the freest association Sigmund had ever heard: dozens of fantasies about his schooldays, apprenticeship to a shoemaker, his work with the university Pacifist Club, his six years as an army surgeon, training under Krafft-Ebing in the psychiatric wards; all interspersed with current stories of the Viennese coffeehouses, where he spent his leisure time reading through half a dozen newspapers every day and writing his articles.

He returned several times a week, stayed as long as Sigmund was free, and entertained him as thoroughly as any comedy at the Volkstheater. Sigmund found that he talked too fast, thought too fast, judged too fast, remembered too fast, wrote too fast, moved in his imaginative flights too fast. Emotionally, Stekel had to reach a climax every few moments; in finishing a thought, a tale, a judgment.

He made it clear to Sigmund that "I don't want a total analysis. That might mean character change. I am delighted with myself the way I am. All I ask is that you clear up my one unfortunate condition. But you must discover my ailment by yourself. Only then can I be certain that you are on the right track and can cure me."

It took Sigmund some three weeks to deduce that Wilhelm Stekel suffered from ejaculation praecox. In a sense, Stekel's entire personality was one of ejaculation before penetration; yet in his sexual life this had not come into focus until he developed an intense dislike for his wife. It was Sigmund's assumption that, unconsciously, Stekel was revenging himself on her for having called him a miser, an incompetent and a windbag. On those occasions when he was moved to make love to her he ejaculated before she could have any satisfaction from him.

All this Sigmund had to surmise, for Stekel, although he was roundly abusive of his wife, refused to discuss marital intercourse. Nor did Sigmund think it would be good for Stekel's psyche to be told he had been caught out. Sigmund worked tangentially, managing within two months to slow down many of Stekel's precipitous processes: talking too fast, eating too fast; climaxing too fast. Stekel wanted to quit at the end of eight weeks, saying:

"I'm better now. The dangerous condition has passed. Besides, I'm leaving my wife. . . ."

Sigmund, who would accept no fee from a fellow physician, felt free to prevail on Stekel to continue the visits for a few more weeks. Stekel agreed:

"I feel that we have become friends. I am enraptured with the *Interpretation of Dreams*. My talks with you are like sunshine after rain. I am writing a long paper, in two parts, for the *Neues Wiener Tageblatt* in which I declare that your book inaugurates a whole new science. I want to learn everything about psychoanalysis. Perhaps someday you will deem me qualified to practice analysis on my patients!"

Frau Theresa Doblhoff was the attractive wife of a Berlin professor who had been referred to him by Wilhelm Fliess. The professor, a short, portly man, brought his wife to the *Parterre* office, studied Dr. Freud carefully and then after a few days returned to Berlin, leaving his wife to stay with friends. It was not until her husband had left Vienna that Frau Doblhoff was ready to cooperate in the analysis. Frau Theresa, as she urged Dr. Freud to call her, was in her early thirties, with a superb figure; an exhibitionist in the extreme styling of her gowns. She was seductive in manner, a vain woman though not a silly one, given to gales of sudden laughter which displayed her magnificent white teeth; and equally sudden drops into despondency. She described her symptoms to Sigmund as "ennui, leading to depression; I'm not happy with my life, my husband, my home . . . I'm childless, you know; or my social position. The idea of suicide flashes across my mind."

"And your physical disturbances, Frau Theresa?"

"Pains in the abdomen, headaches that feel as though there are splinters lodged beneath my scalp; and a skin rash between my breasts."

Sigmund did not consider that his month of training in dermatology rendered him capable of diagnosing Frau Theresa's skin rash. He sent her to his former instructor in dermatology at the Allgemeine Krankenhaus. Professor Maximilian von Zeissl reported that the rash was nervous in origin, confirming Sigmund's supposition.

Frau Theresa gave herself over to a free association of her thoughts and images, pouring forth a wealth of sexual material: molestation by a favorite uncle, which Sigmund established as fantasy; fantasies of a Prince Charming, of Sleeping Beauty, of royal blood, of being mistress to the Emperor and to famous stars of the theater; and finally achieved a complete transference to Dr. Freud.

"You're so like my uncle, the one I adored. I can feel myself slipping back into childhood in the same room with him. He was such a virile man, so handsome . . ." Suddenly she cried, "Uncle, why don't you love me? You know I adore you, I dream about you at night. Why do you prefer those hussies you bring home to dinner . . . ?"

Frau Theresa had all the symptoms of a classical hysteria. By the end of a month the rich flow of materials left no doubt that she suffered from frigidity. Nor did her intense involvement with her doctor, her admiration of him because he had six children whereas her husband had given her none, and the delight with which she overcame her childhood amnesia and related sexually meaningful material, blind him to the fact that he had before him an aggravated case of narcissism, self-love. Theresa had discovered masturbation at an early age, masturbation with climax; she declared how much pleasure she had taken from it. Now, as an adult, she was unwilling to give up the control of her pleasure.

"Why should I give my body to someone who is outside of me? Someone who would dictate when I could or could not have my satisfactions? Besides, I don't like my husband; I find him physically repugnant."

"Do you find him undesirable, or merely less desirable than the Prince Charmings you fantasy when you are masturbating?"

Theresa laughed without embarrassment.

"There is no way for my husband to make me feel Queen of the World, as I think the sexual act should. That's why I have not let him have intercourse with me for several years now. Of course he is insanely jealous, accuses me of getting my satisfactions elsewhere . . ."

"Which is true. In your imagination!"

"Yes. Sometimes he tries to take me by force. I become terrified . . . and all the more inhibited against him. I am not the kind of woman who can lie supinely on my back while my husband has an orgasm inside me, and I lie there with my eyes and fists clenched."

"Since you live in the same house, and I gather in the same bedroom, how have you managed?"

"At bedtime I develop stomach cramps, authentic ones, and real headaches. Of course I must keep this rash on my bosom covered with a medicinal cream. My husband screams, 'If you're so tired and ill all the time, why don't you go to see a doctor?' That's how I managed to get to you: Dr. Wilhelm Fliess felt you could help me."

Professor Doblhoff returned after five weeks. Sigmund had no idea what his wife told him about their analytical hours together, but the irate husband came to the office outraged, having transferred his jealousy from unknown seducers in Berlin to Dr. Sigmund Freud of Vienna, a city famous for its freedom of intercourse.

"I'm not accusing you of having seduced my wife, Herr Doktor, that would be stupid of me. But I do accuse you of encouraging improper subjects to be brought up in this office."

"Of what nature, Herr Professor?"

"Of a sexual nature."

"But that is the basis of your wife's illness; and of the malfunction of your marriage."

The professor went almost black in the face.

"My wife had no right to tell you about that!"

"But isn't that why you brought her to Vienna?"

The professor had little neck, and so he could not hang his head. Instead he leaned over from the waist, staring at the floor.

". . . yes. Do you think you can cure her . . . make her a . . . normal . . . wife?"

"I have reason to hope."

Professor Doblhoff returned to Berlin. Sigmund had another five weeks to work with Frau Theresa, one hour every day. He taught her the meaning of regression, after which she was able to recall infantile material from the anal and oral stages. Each day he brought her fresh sexual insights about herself and the basic sexual nature of man. He got to the base of her narcissistic problem, working the material out into the open, and felt that he was making important progress because of her breakthrough to her infantile sexual conflicts. Once he could help her move to a higher level of emotional maturity, from the psychosexual point of view, she would develop understanding and sympathy for her husband, take a more tolerant attitude toward married love and in all probability have children. She could rid herself of her hysteria and achieve a life of common human unhappiness.

Dr. Freud's concept appealed to Theresa. She counted on additional treatment to enable her to return home and build a married life based on her knowledge of herself. Sigmund was pleased with the further testimony that his therapy could cure.

Then Professor Doblhoff broke into a session unannounced, saw his wife lying on the couch with her eyes closed, Dr. Freud sitting behind her, their conversation flowing in intimate fashion, and yanked his wife to her feet. To Sigmund he screamed:

"I have no more money to waste on this kind of nonsense! Nor time to spare, running back and forth from Berlin to Vienna to make sure my wife is all right. You will see no more of her!"

14.

After his sojourn in Rome, Sigmund felt that his self-analysis was complete. A restraining set of chains was unlocked in his attitude toward his professorship. He had uttered not one word in his own behalf since Frankl-Hochwart had been awarded the title. The Minister of Education had apparently forgotten about Privatdozent Sigmund Freud.

"Enough of the puritan ethic," he announced to Martha. "I've earned the title, and if I have to become a careerist to get it, *tant pis*, as they say in Paris. I'm going to see my old friend Exner, who is now

Councilor to the Minister of Education in charge of reforming the educational system at the university, in particular the Medical Faculty. I'm going to provide him with one reform which he can put into effect immediately."

But as he walked up the Berggasse to the Physiology Institute he realized that he was seeking something quite different from what he had wanted four years before when Nothnagel and Krafft-Ebing wrote their enthusiastic endorsements of his work and the Medical Faculty had recommended his appointment. Then he had wanted a full academic career. Now all that was changed. He knew that, considering the equivocal nature of his work and its total repudiation, nay, bitter condemnation, there was not the slightest chance of his being accepted by the Medical Faculty as a full-time professor and administrator of the Medical School. In addition, he no longer thought this academic life imperative. His achievement in getting to Rome had given him the courage to stand alone and make his own way, not only for himself and his family, but for the twentieth-century philosophy of the unconscious. When he had first applied for the role of associate professor, the concept of an honorary title involving no obligation on the part of the recipient or the Medical School was almost unknown, only one such title had been granted, to Dr. Gustav Gärtner in 1890. Now, in 1901, a number of titles of *Extraordinarius* had been granted by the Minister: to Drs. Ehrmann, Pal, Redlich; there was no longer any excuse to deny him the title, which would cost the university nothing but would be so urgently important in gaining respectability for his unknown and unwanted psychoanalysis.

He crossed the Währinger Strasse and entered the Physiology Institute, his nostrils assailed by the familiar odors of the oxidation of electric batteries and the chemicals used for anatomical preparations, remembering his final conference with Professor Brücke of the agate-blue eyes. Professor Brücke had wisely pointed out that pure science was for rich men. Sigmund was glad that Brücke had turned him out; what he was learning about the human mind seemed infinitely more important than documenting the structure of the nerve fibers of the crayfish.

Sigmund Exner was now head of the Physiology Institute, as he had always planned to be. He had taken the job as Councilor to the Minister of Education because he was vitally concerned with reform of Austria's medical colleges. His colleagues wanted him in the Ministry so that they would have a strong voice in all medical decisions made at a governmental level. He had a desk at the Ministry in an old palace in the Minoritenplatz 7, spent some five hours there one day a week for meetings. He earned twenty-four hundred gulden a year for his labors; but he did not do this work for money, any more than the work he did for the Board of Health. Spread over what had formerly been Professor Brücke's work-table were his drawings for new electrical machines to measure the speed and strength of muscle movements; the manuscript for the staining of tissue; and mixed in, helter-skelter, reports from the Ministry. Sigmund von Exner was acknowledged to be one of Vienna's great men of science and government, a rare and valuable combination.

Herr Hofrat Exner was now fifty-five years old, almost completely bald. He tenderly combed his few scraggly tissue-thin hairs across the blank white space of his head. His beard was more gray than black; but the absorbed gray eyes, overhung with heavy brows and lids, had not aged: one glance and they understood everything. He looked up, took in Sigmund's face and posture, knew what he had come for. Sigmund had not seen Exner for several years; Exner found it impossible to conceive that a medical man would abandon physiology.

"Oh, it's you, Herr Doktor Freud."

"Now, Hofrat Exner, that's not the most friendly greeting. I can remember several years of very amused greetings between you and Fleischl and myself at eight o'clock every morning in the Physiology Laboratory."

"It is not eight o'clock in the morning. It is four o'clock in the afternoon and I have two experiments going in my laboratory."

"You always did have. And most of them came out extremely well. Fleischl said that once he was dead you would be the greatest physiologist in Europe."

"And so I would be," growled Exner, "if I didn't have to sit behind this desk and conduct interviews with people for whom I can do nothing."

Sigmund did not take Exner's crustiness seriously. He was beloved by the students at the Physiology Institute because, after each lecture, he remained to answer all of their questions, even the stupid ones.

"How can you be sure you can do nothing for me, Hofrat Exner, until you hear what I'm here for? Perhaps I only want to borrow ten kronen. Or ask to see your file on a young neurologist looking for an assistantship."

"You're looking for no such thing!"

"Granted. What I am seeking to know is why four and a half years have gone by since the Medical Faculty endorsed me for the title of associate professor. Yet each year I am passed by. There has to be an explanation."

Exner shrugged eloquently.

"Not necessarily. Certainly not in government. Cause and effect, yes, but a rational explanation, no."

A tinge of sarcasm entered Sigmund's voice.

"I really don't think, looking back on our years of friendly association, even though you were my superior and my teacher, that it is absolutely necessary for you to be disagreeable. I have a strong feeling that Professor Brücke would not approve of your attitude."

Exner wheeled about in his chair and stared blindly at the top of the Berggasse. In a moment he turned around and there was a different expression in his eyes, not one of anger, which Sigmund had thought he might as well invoke since he was getting nowhere, but somewhat unfocused, as though Exner for the first time were looking back through the maze of twenty years and was remembering the excitement of working with Brücke and Fleischl, and the two bright, eager young men helping them, Josef Paneth and Sigmund Freud.

"Yes . . . well . . . I'm sorry. I'm irritable when the official paper-work piles up."

"I understand, Exner; you really have no desire to play the high official. What I came to tell you is that I am no longer interested in the academic appointment, but only the honorary title of assistant professor."

"Yes . . . well . . ." Exner paused, then planted his elbow firmly on the desk in front of him and looked up at Sigmund. "Sig, these appointments are a matter of pressures; who can bring the most pressure to put a man into office . . . or to keep him out of office. At the Ministry we sit in the middle of a seesaw trying to make sure that the people at either end keep our educational system balanced."

"Just between us, are you saying that there are certain pressures being exerted upon the Minister to keep him from giving me an appointment?"

"I didn't say that. I was simply suggesting the general nature of politics as it spreads its dark cloak over education. My advice to you is to assume that there are personal influences exerted against you with His Excellency. You must seek a personal counterinfluence. What I am suggesting is that you get a lot more weight on your end of the plank; pretty soon it will thump down to the ground and you will have what you want."

Sigmund thought for a moment, then said, "I could approach an old friend and former patient, Frau Hofrat Gomperz. Would this be the right direction?"

"Unquestionably so. Frau Hofrat Gomperz and the Hofrat himself are very highly regarded in the Ministry. In addition, His Excellency was appointed professor of philology at the same time as Hofrat Gomperz; they were close associates for many years. You could not do better."

Sigmund wrote a note to Elise Gomperz asking if he might drop in for coffee at six o'clock one afternoon. He received an express letter asking him to come that very evening. Frau Gomperz received him in the drawing room; they chatted for a few moments, then Sigmund said:

"Frau Hofrat Gomperz, I want to confess that I have come to ask a favor. It's nothing customary that I will be asking, nor can I take it for granted that you may be willing to help. So I will understand if you cannot . . ."

"Herr Doktor, my good right hand is at your service."

"Thank you. The situation is this. Four and a half years ago I was highly recommended by Professors Nothnagel and Krafft-Ebing for the title of associate professor. When I first went to see Von Härtel's predecessor, Baillet-Latour, he said, 'Oh yes, I've heard excellent things of you.' That is the last good word, in fact any word, I've heard from the Minister. I feel that my long years of work in neurology and children's paralyses, as well as my newer researches and my books and articles, have earned me the title of associate professor, and I am asking now only for the honorary title."

Elise Gomperz looked puzzled, shook her head from side to side.

"Indeed it has. I did not realize that you didn't have it. What do you suppose is standing in your way? Please be quite honest with me; it is necessary if we are to be helpful."

He suggested briefly that anti-Semitism was gaining strength in Vienna; but that he did not believe this was the major problem. He then gave her an exposition of the nature of his work in psychoanalysis. Elise Gomperz listened carefully.

"Herr Doktor, you did not come to me for an evaluation. You came for help. May I ask whether your recommendation by Nothnagel and Krafft-Ebing, as well as by the Medical Faculty, has been renewed lately?"

"Once the recommendations are in the file at the Ministry of Education they are there permanently."

"Yes, permanently lost at the bottom of a drawer. You should write to Nothnagel and Krafft-Ebing requesting that they renew your application."

"I shall do so at once."

"Once this has been done, I shall go to the Minister of Education. He has dined at my board for some thirty years now; I should think that would entitle me to an appointment."

"Thank you, Frau Hofrat."

Nothnagel and Krafft-Ebing, who was about to retire from the Medical Faculty, wrote new letters urging the Minister and Emperor Franz Josef to bestow upon Privatdozent Sigmund Freud the honorary title of associate professor. Elise Gomperz secured an appointment with Minister von Härtel, who was gracious, listened to her in full, and then pretended never to have heard of Dr. Freud. Were his contributions really so important that he was entitled to an *Extraordinarius?* Elise Gomperz gave back in full everything Sigmund had told her a few days before. The Minister promised that he would give the matter his closest attention.

She got nowhere. Minister von Härtel begged for time, suggested that the matter of these appointments always took years, that he would certainly bring the papers out from the file. Yes, he had received the new application; yes, Exner had spoken of Dr. Freud. Everything was being done that could be done. However during the weeks that followed he dodged a meeting with Hofrat Theodor Gomperz. Hofrat Gomperz did not feel that he was being purposely evaded or shut out; however through the entire month of December he never was able to speak a word to Minister von Härtel.

The combined efforts of the Gomperz family were to no avail . . . except for an accidental happening. Elise Gomperz was having afternoon coffee with her long-time friend, Baroness Maria von Ferstel, on New Year's Day of 1902. She told the Baroness about her efforts and those of her husband to move the Minister to grant Dr. Freud his title. The Baroness stormed into Sigmund's *Parterre* late that afternoon looking like a goddess out of Greek mythology, angry and about to punish mortals.

"Herr Doktor, grateful patients frequently bring their doctor a 'thank you' gift."

"You are kind, Baronin, but I have been well compensated for my work."

"I am going to get you your long-overdue *Extraordinarius.*"

Sigmund frowned, then broke into a hearty laugh.

"Now, Baronin, you are disobeying my orders. You are taking on yourself still one more obligation for which you have no real need, and which can only complicate your life."

The Baroness's eyes flashed.

"My husband has been posted to Berlin and I shall not leave until I have the privilege of calling you 'Excellency.'"

There was a message every few days. On the first skirmish she met Minister von Härtel at a ball and made herself agreeable to him. A few days later she wangled an invitation to a dinner party where she had heard he was to be. A few days later she invited the Minister to her home for dinner, assembling a fashionable group of royalty and heads of government.

Her next move was the pivotal one: she invited the Minister to Saturday afternoon coffee, just the two of them. The Minister was by now apparently enchanted with her. She let him talk about the importance of his work and his close relationship with the Emperor Franz Josef and the Prime Ministers of the great countries of Europe. When she considered that he had expounded himself into a state of euphoria, she said:

"Speaking of the importance of your accomplishments, Excellency, there is a little thing you could do that I think would bring honor both upon you and upon our Empire."

"What might that be, my dear Baronin?"

"Granting a professorship to the doctor who has cured me."

"But you always appear in magnificent health."

"Thank you, my dear Minister, I am. But much of that I owe to my doctor. I was having miserable headaches, the feeling of steel bands around my head . . ."

". . . indeed!" the Minister broke in. "I have had periods when I suffered from precisely that. I have always had to suffer them for days, perhaps weeks, and simply pray for them to go away."

"I found a doctor in Vienna who has a new method. His name is Privatdozent Dr. Sigmund Freud. He has made some fascinating discoveries about the nature of the human mind and the relation of our emotional lives to our physical well-being . . ."

In the course of her compulsion to lead Vienna's social work, she had become an eloquent pleader for special causes. She held the Minister spellbound while she talked of Dr. Freud and his theories. When she had finished, he replied slowly:

"Baronin, you know that I have been in charge of the building of a modern art museum, which we are going to open in a month or two. I trust that you will be one of our guests of honor at the formal opening? The Emperor will be there of course, and the entire court."

"I shall be delighted."

"The building itself is superb. Our other museums have fine collections. However each museum has to make its own acquisitions. We have the strongest desire to have Böcklin represented. I know that your aunt has one of the greatest of the Böcklins, *Ruined Castle*, hanging in her home. Do you suppose she could be persuaded to give it to the new museum?"

"I know the picture very well. I grew up with it. It is indeed a glorious canvas. With your permission I shall attempt to persuade my aunt that she should give the canvas to the museum for its opening. If it were my own possession, Excellence, you may be assured that you could walk out the front door this very afternoon with the painting under your arm."

The Baroness showed up at the Freud apartment the following Sunday at coffee time. They were vastly entertained. However, Sigmund asked the key question:

"Is there any possibility of your aunt's parting with the Böcklin?"

"I really don't know. I feel certain I can persuade her to bequeath the painting to the museum, but she is a hearty old girl and is going to live a lot of years."

Baroness von Ferstel's aunt did not yield to the blandishments of her niece, but the Baronin was keeping the Minister at her side. She reported to the Freuds, "Every time he comes to the house I sit him in front of one of my own favorite paintings, a church in a Moravian village, by Emil Orlik. It is becoming a part of the Minister's landscape."

Weeks later, on an icy day in March, she dashed out of her family carriage and into the *Parterre* waving an express letter from the Minister.

"Herr *Professor* Freud. It is done! I want to be the first to congratulate you!"

A wave of mingled joy, relief and letdown surged through Sigmund. "Did your aunt give him the Böcklin?"

"No. My aunt will not part with it. I told the Minister so yesterday while we were standing in front of the Orlik. It really is a valuable painting and will make a fine addition to the opening exhibit. I simply said, 'Excellency, it is too early to get the Böcklin from my aunt. May I offer you my superb Emil Orlik?' Härtel gazed at me wide-eyed; he was obviously disappointed but took his defeat with good grace. He studied the painting for several moments, bowed and said, 'Baronin, I accept the Orlik for the museum.'"

Sigmund took the Baroness upstairs to tell the family the good news. Minna opened a bottle of wine and they all drank to Professor Sigmund Freud and Frau Professor Martha Freud. That evening Sigmund sat in his study and wrote to Fliess, sarcastically:

"The *Wiener Zeitung* has not yet published it, but the news spread quickly from the Ministry. The public enthusiasm is immense! Congratulations and bouquets keep pouring in, as if the role of sexuality had been suddenly recognized by His Majesty, the interpretation of dreams confirmed by the Council of Ministers, and the necessity of the psychoanalytic therapy of hysteria carried by a two-thirds majority in Parliament. I have obviously become reputable again, and my shiest admirers now greet me from a distance in the street."

One of the first to appear was the effervescent Wilhelm Stekel. His face was awash with pride. Sigmund was touched.

"Excellency! Now that you are Professor Sigmund Freud instead of a mere and lowly *Dozent*, hasn't the time arrived to carry out your plan to start your own group? I believe you called it a seminar, a circle of people interested in psychoanalysis . . ."

Sigmund rose from his desk, came around to thank Stekel for his well wishes, and then found himself moved by a sense of anticipation.

"I've wanted that little circle ever since the political demonstrations closed down the university and I had my class of eleven meet here in this *Parterre* for my Great Neuroses lectures. Thank you for remembering. I was waiting for something . . . doubtless the professorship . . . but now it's here. We will want only physicians, of course, so that we can keep our papers and discussions on a scientific level. Max Kahane and Rudolf Reitler took my lecture course last year, and drop in occasionally for coffee and discussion. I think they may want to participate. How about you, Wilhelm? Say every Wednesday evening during the medical season?"

"I wouldn't miss it for the world."

"That makes four of us. Can you think of anyone else?"

". . . well . . . let's see . . . yes, there is one, Dr. Alfred Adler. My *Stammtisch* was next to his at the Cafe Dom when we were fledgling intellectuals and beginning physicians. Now that we've both built our practices, we've moved to the Cafe Central where the political arguments are more exciting. Adler is reputed to have one of the fastest-moving and most intuitive minds in Vienna."

"What makes you think that he might be interested in participating in our discussions?"

"That's just the point: he knew about your work before I did. He read *Interpretation of Dreams* shortly after it came out. Adler didn't tell me the story himself, but his close friend Furtmüller did. It seems that after Adler finished your book he exclaimed with what Furtmüller described as 'great earnestness':

" 'This man has something to say to us!' "

"Good! Adler sounds interesting. I'll send out the four postcards, but not now, it's too close to Easter and the annual trek to the mountains. I'll send them out in the fall, when everyone has returned, and we can look forward to a full season of meetings."

After Stekel had left, Sigmund took a postcard from his desk and jotted down:

Dear Colleague:

It has been suggested that some of us might meet for a scientific discussion. May I ask you to come to me at Berggasse 19 on ——— at eight-thirty o'clock?

With best regards,

Very truly yours,

Dr. Sigm. Freud

BOOK TWELVE

THE MEN

The Men

HE TURNED the key in the double lock of his inner study of the
Parterre office, opened the door and stood aside to allow his young
companion, Otto Rank, to enter. Otto was twenty-two, small,
dark, clean-shaven, with jet-black hair brushed neatly back and melancholy
eyes magnified by thick glasses. Once inside the room an enchanted
smile lighted his homely face, and the melancholy fled, as indeed had
most of his sadness a year before when he had come, near terror-stricken,
to see Professor Freud. Dr. Alfred Adler had sent him after Otto attended one of Adler's lectures; he had brought with him a manuscript of
The Artist, written from his love of literature, the theater, painting,
sculpture.

"When I step into this room, Professor Freud, my confusions fall
away, and I know that the world and human life have meaning."

"At least it has continuity. Look at this long-necked Greek vase I
picked up at the antique dealer's down the street. Study the figures
carefully, the headdress and robe; they could go back almost to the time
of Knossos. Take it; that's the way we should hold history, clasped in our
hands."

This room held history for him. What a wealth of memories and
excitements it evoked. From a pariah he had become a man with a
small circle of friends and disciples. He remembered the first meeting
four years before in response to his postcard summons. Martha had
prepared coffee and cake. The men had sounded each other out, the
professor tentatively initiating them into his studies, though Rudolf Reitler
and Max Kahane had already taken his course on dreams at the university, Alfred Adler and Wilhelm Stekel had read his books. The five
physicians had had a sound basis for discussion.

These new friendships were particularly needed, for Wilhelm Fliess
had disappeared again. After Fliess sent Frau Doblhoff to him from
Berlin, Sigmund had imagined their relationship could be renewed; and
so it might have been if not for a row over "priorities." Sigmund had
described Wilhelm's bisexuality to a neurosis patient by the name of
Swoboda. Swoboda revealed the materials to a brilliant but disturbed
friend by the name of Weininger, who hastily put together a little book

on the subject and published it. Fliess was outraged. There was an exchange of letters; Sigmund had to confess that he had seen part of Weininger's manuscript but had thought it too poor to comment on. Fliess had then published his own book, in which he accused Swoboda and Weininger of plagiarism, with Sigmund damned by the implication of having helped them. Sigmund had never heard from Wilhelm Fliess again.

The growth of his little group, Sigmund realized, had been modest enough; but then, he had done no proselytizing. Each man who came was a volunteer who had heard about the discussions or had read Sigmund's publications. By the end of the first year two men had joined the original four to whom he had sent his summons: Max Graf, a Ph.D. in music who taught at the Konservatorium; and Hugo Heller, a booksellerpublisher. The year 1903 had brought two more members, Dr. Paul Federn, who was directed to the group by Professor Nothnagel, and Dr. Alfred Meisl, who practiced general medicine in a suburb of Vienna. No new applicant had joined the ranks in 1904; Dr. Eduard Hitschmann, of vast erudition and dry, coruscating wit, had become a regular in 1905, along with Otto Rank, Dr. Adolf Deutsch, a physiotherapist in the tradition of Max Kahane, brought in by Paul Federn; and Philipp Frey, a schoolteacher in a private academy who had published a book, *The Battle of the Sexes*. At this first fall meeting of 1906 there would be another new member, Dr. Isidor Sadger, a gifted man with an involuted personality who had shown Sigmund manuscripts on Perversion and Homosexuality which Sigmund considered penetrating.

In all, seventeen men now belonged to the Psychological Wednesday Society, which was without officers, by-laws or dues. More than half of the members attended each Wednesday meeting, for which the members, in turn, researched and wrote a paper on a psychoanalytical subject, to be read to the group and then discussed. Sigmund was proud that several of these papers had already been published, while others had grown into book-length manuscripts. It also brought him considerable pleasure to recall that not one member had withdrawn over the four years, though some of the response to the papers had been intensely critical. This was the best tribute.

He took heart too from the manner in which his own publications were spreading through the medical and educational worlds. Prior to the formation of these Wednesday Evenings, he had considered himself fortunate if he received two letters a week from people asking questions about his work. Now, although none of the books and only a couple of the articles had been translated into other languages, he received several letters a day, from Russia in the east to Italy and Spain in the south; from Australia, India, South America, asking for further information and instruction. Sigmund looked upon all the correspondents as potential students and made it a point to answer each letter the day it arrived. The growth of his Wednesday Evening group, and of his correspondence, were living proof to him that his ideas slowly were beginning to penetrate. It renewed his confidence and courage.

The men had become his loyal friends; he was grateful to every one of them for ending his eight years of isolation. A good deal else had changed, now that he was Professor Sigmund Freud. By virtue of having achieved the most awesome title in Central Europe, his practice had increased. It meant little to the public that his title was an honorary one. His patients assumed the same attitude that the Turks in Bosnia had toward their physicians:

"Herr, if I could be saved, I know you would help me."

The personal attacks against him at the Medical College had ceased, except for one obsessed Assistant to Wagner-Jauregg in the Psychiatric Clinic, Professor Raimann who was assiduously trailing Sigmund's failures with patients in order to publish them in book form, thus hoping to put an end to the evils of psychoanalysis. However the attitude of the Medical Faculty, which had invited him back to the Society of Medicine to lecture on neurology after a lapse of nine years, was simply put:

"We do not spit in the face of our family."

It was not yet eight-thirty; there were still a few moments before the Psychological Wednesday Society would arrive for their October meeting at the beginning of the new medical season. Otto Rank had had supper upstairs with the family as he often did; Martha had adopted him a year before as a kind of younger brother to Sigmund. Adoption had been precisely what Otto needed: son of an alcoholic father and a disinterested mother, he had been sent to a technical school, then been apprenticed in a factory as a machine maker, a task for which he had neither the strength nor aptitude. He had turned in his misery to books, then to the theater and, having an absorptive mind, had so thoroughly educated himself that when at twenty-one he had brought Sigmund his manuscript, Sigmund was stirred by its originality. He had made a friend of the youth, walked the streets of Vienna with him for late-night discussions of how to reorganize his manuscript so that it had now been accepted for book publication. In the meanwhile Sigmund had paid Otto Rank's way through a year of the *Gymnasium*, to earn the academic credits he needed; and Otto was entered in the University of Vienna. In order not to put the young man in his debt, Sigmund had made him the salaried secretary of the Psychological Wednesday Society, paying his wage out of his own pocket.

Otto Rank put the Greek vase on Sigmund's desk with the other Egyptian, Assyrian and Oriental figures standing there. In the midst of the antiquities was a medallion which had been presented to Sigmund the previous spring in honor of his fiftieth birthday by the Wednesday

Evening group. The medal was created by the sculptor Schwerdtner: Sigmund's portrait was on one side in bas-relief, and on the other was a carving of Oedipus replying to the Sphinx. Under it was cut the line from Sophocles:

Who divined the famed riddle and was a man most mighty.

Rank sorted some papers out of a shabby briefcase.

"Would you like me to take the task of recording secretary off your hands for tonight?" Sigmund asked.

"Why so, Herr Professor?"

"You have a full hour of reading on your paper. Might you not be too keyed up to take accurate notes on the discussion?"

"Ah no, it's a job for which I've trained myself."

"But remember that the other members will give you no quarter."

Sigmund let his eyes roam the room. Between the windows overlooking the garden he had a four-shelf cabinet filled with superb antiques, some of them dating from three thousand years before Christ. On the top of the cabinet sat an ancient Mediterranean boat, with the rowers in place, a Pegasus, mounted on a rod, an Indian Buddha, a Chinese camel, an Egyptian Sphinx and a pre-Columbian mask. On the opposite wall there was a textured Persian rug, while above it were shelves for his special books on dream interpretation, psychiatry and psychology, each specialized group separated by a fragment of marble sarcophagus or bas-relief. The archaeological pieces were an integral part of his life, refreshing him during the hours that he treated patients, and when he wrote the two volumes he had published the year before: *Jokes and Their Relation to the Unconscious* and *Three Essays on Sexuality.* Though he had surrounded himself with these antiquities for the joy they gave him in living amidst a dozen civilizations, he found that their effect on his patients was also a salutary one, helping them to grasp his concept of the unconscious mind, and suggesting to the distressed ones that neither they nor their troubles were fresh born, but rather had come, as Charles Darwin proved, from accumulated millennia stretching back beyond man to time inconceivable.

Sigmund heard voices outside, rose to welcome his colleagues. First came Drs. Max Kahane and Rudolf Reitler, who had rarely missed a meeting during the past four winters: Reitler, slim, blond, unblemished by the years except for a faintly receding hairline; and Kahane, whose deeply furrowed face had accepted middle age long before he reached it chronologically.

Sigmund exchanged warm greetings with his friends; they had not seen each other since the previous June. Reitler was now practicing psychoanalysis on those patients who he thought could benefit from the therapy, though he was of necessity maintaining his general practice. He had begun tentatively and with discretion, bringing the material of his more difficult cases to Sigmund for assistance. In a remote corner of his mind Sigmund was pleased that Reitler, the first man in Vienna to follow in his footsteps, was a Catholic with a Catholic practice.

Max Kahane still declined to try psychoanalysis on the patients in his growing and prosperous sanatorium.

"But I understand them so much better, Professor," he volunteered; "there are many subtle ways of redesigning burnt-out or useless apartments in people's unconscious. Those clues, straight out of your therapy, are getting good results."

Sigmund heard voices in his consultation room, around whose oval table the members met. He recognized that of Philipp Frey, teacher in a private school, who had written a favorable review of Sigmund's *Jokes and Their Relation to the Unconscious* for the *Austrian Review* the year before. He was now working on the first draft of an article, Toward Clearing Up the Sex Problem in the School, a subject no one had dared to touch. He was talking to the other non-medical member, Hugo Heller, who besides being a bookseller and publisher was booking agent for the concert and theatrical world. In his shop in the Bauernmarkt there gathered the young, unknown artists and writers of Vienna for coffee and conversation. He was a shaggy kind of man, wrapped in an enveloping coat which seemed too large for him, with a head of dark curls, a blond mustache, pince-nez glasses which he wore in a near horizontal position when he was not reading. He was a lively public speaker but with a nervous disposition which displayed itself in occasional fits of anger, and was what the Austrians called *konfessionslos*, a believer without religious affiliation, who was raising his sons as Lutherans.

There loomed in the doorway the most scintillating personality to have joined the group, Dr. Alfred Adler. An early protégé of Professor Nothnagel, Adler was said to practice medicine as though it were as simple as scrambling eggs. His patients reported that he combined swift and sure judgment with extreme cautiousness. Even before he had received Sigmund's postcard and agreed to participate in the discussions, he had already become a psychological physician, going into matters which had never been thought to be germane to medicine, asking his patients what they described as "far-away questions." He was a faithful member of the Wednesday Evenings.

"But," Sigmund ruminated, while he and Adler shook hands, murmuring *Grüss Gott*, "with a difference."

All of the other members, doctors and laymen alike, considered themselves disciples, followers, students of Professor Sigmund Freud. Not so Alfred Adler; he had made it clear from the outset that he was a colleague, a co-worker in the psychology of the neuroses, of equal standing even though fourteen years younger than Sigmund. He had joined a group of University of Vienna students in the early years to read and discuss Das Kapital. He had never become a Marxist, his anti-doctrinaire nature precluded him from swallowing systems whole, but the years of reading and study had turned his mind to social justice and political reform. Though he was raised in a prosperous family of corn merchants, he deliberately threw in his lot with what was becoming known as the "common man," by opening his office in the Praterstrasse, among poor people and the employees from the Prater. In the beginning of their relationship he had attempted to lend Sigmund Freud books by Marx, Engels, Sorel, but Sigmund had replied wryly:

"Dr. Adler, I can't take on the class war. It will take me a lifetime to win the sex war."

It was only when Adler sent Stekel to Freud for treatment that Sigmund had learned that Adler was an enthusiast who had tested Sigmund's methods on a few of his patients . . .

". . . with sometimes quite gratifying results," he confided to Sigmund, early on.

"That's as well as I do," Sigmund had confessed; "but then, we are not out to prove statistically how infallible psychoanalysis is. It's more important to take on increasingly difficult cases in order to broaden our field of knowledge. That's what I've been doing this last year, trying to treat schizophrenia and other withdrawn patients who seem beyond communication. I can't cure them, not even Professor Bleuler in the Burghölzli in Zurich can do that."

Dr. Alfred Adler had retreated behind his hooded eyes and pince-nez glasses. Though he acknowledged that Sigmund's findings had opened new vistas, he had at the same time strained psychoanalysis and the realm of the unconscious through his own mind and declined to accept the entire credo. This, Sigmund reasoned, was why Adler had refused to become an intimate, as had the others, who frequently dropped in for coffee, took long walks with him in the evenings and in the Wienerwald on Sundays while they discussed techniques. At the Wednesday Evenings Adler had made it clear that, although Dr. Freud was the host and pioneer, he, Dr. Alfred Adler, was going his own way. Sigmund, on his part, had assured him that everyone's views would be respected. The chapter Adler had read from his manuscript on Study of Organ Inferiority, scheduled for publication the following year, shifted the interpretation of human character from the mind to individual organs within the body. Sigmund admired the paper though it was based more on physiology than the psyche and seemed to revise parts of his own theories. However Adler had been helpful and generous to the younger men of the group, most of whom aspired to become psychoanalysts.

2.

The men dropped into their chairs about the oval table, Sigmund at the head, Otto Rank at his left, the others taking any seat available . . . except Alfred Adler, who always occupied the same position in the center, not because he demanded authority, he was not egocentric, but because the lucidity and daring of his published papers, his experience in the field of neuroses, made him a natural leader in the exhilarating discussions. Sigmund liked it that way; he remained in the background, reading no more papers than anyone else, taking only his proportionate share of the discussion time that followed.

The consultation room, where Sigmund held his interviews with patients before deciding whether psychoanalysis could help them, was sandwiched between his rear office-study and the outside waiting room; it was a tranquil, non-committed room, had an Oriental rug on the floor, paintings on the walls of the three stone-carved Pharaohs of the Luxor Valley; reproductions of his favorite Italian painters.

Sigmund gazed about the table. There were nine men present this evening, including himself. He leaned back in his chair. His vision unreeled the four years that had passed since the night in October 1902 when Adler, Stekel, Reitler, Kahane and he had had their first discussion around this table. Very quickly he had created a friendly atmosphere, in which a spark seemed to jump from one mind to the other. He had avoided pontificating, yet had confided all he had learned about the unconscious and the emerging structure of the human psyche, simply, as starting points for further research and exploration. In his role as host he was sometimes able, by a soft word or gesture, to keep the argument from running wild, or becoming personal in rebuttal instead of objective. Because he had eschewed the role of professor, preferring to use his age, experience and skills to maintain harmony, the little group had grown continually closer in friendship and respect. They considered themselves pioneers.

The first two years during which they met had been reflective ones for him, while he regrouped his thoughts and energies for the next drive. Though he kept the Dora manuscript locked up, he had written a chapter on *Psychoanalytic Procedure* for Löwenfeld's textbook on *Obsessional Neuroses*, in 1903. In 1904 he had written out his lecture *On Psychotherapy* for the *Doktorenkollegium*, and then published it; as well as a chapter on *Psychical (or Mental) Treatment* for a semi-popular volume on medicine, published in Germany.

The two years of lying dormant had led to a renewed creative explosion. He began writing avidly, with overwhelming force and joy, on two manuscripts which he kept on separate tables in his study, working on each in turn as new thoughts and ideas came to him: Jokes and Their Relation to the Unconscious, and Three Essays on the Theory of Sexuality. He had finished the two manuscripts almost at the same time, and sent them to press simultaneously. Then, prepared for the storm which must burst over his head because of the content of Three Essays on the Theory of Sexuality, he took the Dora manuscript out of his locked desk, read it ruminatively, and decided that this detailed case study could help substantiate his theories; that the time was ripe for another bout with the scientists of the world.

"Strange," he thought, "how similar the medical profession is to my patients. It's no use to coddle or mollify them; that method changes nothing in their minds or conduct. I must first get down to their repressions, allow them their emotional rage, then their transference to me of the agony, hatred, humiliation and guilt of childhood. Only from that kind of catharsis can they come to judge the truth or falsity of my work on the basis of the evidence."

Sigmund watched Otto Rank sort his papers while fussing his glasses over the bridge of his nose before starting to read The Incest Drama and Its Complications. Rank was slight and boyish amidst the older men. He began to speak in the simple, direct tone he had learned to use by auditing Sigmund's lectures at the university during the winter of 1905 and 1906 on Introduction to Psychotherapy. His presentation was to be spread over three weeks, a sizable assignment for a youth on his maiden voyage. Yet Sigmund felt a sense of security for his protégé; he had given unstintingly of his time to make sure that Otto matured each aspect of his theme. This room was the proper caldron in which to have it boiled in oil. Otto had read widely and documented his thesis about the presence of the incest theme throughout the ages.

Otto Rank finished his presentation on the dot of ten. The maid arrived from the upstairs kitchen with coffee and a tray of plain cake covered with nuts. She placed the tray in the center of the oval table. The men rose, put hot milk or whipped cream in their coffee, moved about the room chatting and chaffing each other amiably for a few moments before picking a number out of a bowl on the table and returning to their seats. Otto Rank now transformed himself from a budding scholar into a secretary who had a talent for reproducing an entire discussion as faithfully as though it had been recorded on one of the phonographs recently invented by an American named Thomas A. Edison.

Philipp Frey, the teacher, had pulled the number one card from the bowl. All eyes turned toward him. He was now working on a monograph called Suicide and Habit which Sigmund believed to be a point of departure in documenting the human death wish.

"Rank, I failed to perceive any structural base for your theme. You present fragmentary and isolated details, all interpreted through the Freudian method, and consequently you are reading too much into the material, where it would have been better simply to state the facts."

Otto Rank gulped but did not look up.

Rudolf Reitler flicked a card with the number two on it, began speaking in a high but unhurried tone.

"First, Otto, I can buttress your argument by calling your attention to incestuous illusions in student songs; you will find the examples plentiful as you move along at the university. I feel that you would profit from a closer study of the part played by penitence in the history of the saints. I could give you an example of paternal hate: when God the Father killed His Son Jesus, indirectly of course, His Son who, together with God the Father, is part of the Trinity."

Sigmund thought, bemused, "Only our Catholic member would have felt free to come up with that heretical concept!"

Dr. Eduard Hitschmann spoke next. He was thirty-five, a successful internist. He was clean-shaven, except for a briskly clipped mustache, and although he was prematurely bald, was an attractive man, with laughing sardonic eyes. He was the one who usually came up with a line which Sigmund would remember the first thing the following morning: "Intercourse is the supper of the poor." "One usually wants to have coitus when one is unhappy." Upon being introduced to the group he had said:

"Professor Freud, my major interest in your work applies to the past rather than the future. I think your methods of psychoanalysis can be used not only on the living but on the dead. I am referring to the great dead. It has occurred to me that these men leave magnificent records in letters, diaries, journals, speeches, which can reveal to the trained psychoanalyst almost as much about their unconscious motivations as free association reveals of the patient on the couch. I should like to write such psychoanalytic biographies once I am sufficiently versed in the technique."

To Otto Rank he now said, "You are wrong to assume that love between relatives is always incestuous at base. It could be a simple matter of parental love. Wouldn't you say that the reason poets write so much about incest is that they are drawn to pathological themes? I think you will severely limit yourself if you confine your thinking to Professor Freud's Oedipus complex."

Sigmund felt a mild annoyance that Hitschmann was still not convinced of the Oedipal situation as a focal point around which psychoanalysis revolved. He wondered:

"How do you maintain the second floor of a building if you obliterate the ground floor? But *pazienza*; the grain ripens in the field when the summer is done."

Dr. Paul Federn was one of the homeliest men Sigmund had ever seen, with a flat bald head twice as long from front to back as it was high, and a hooked beak that made him look like the most vicious anti-Semitic caricatures published in the *Deutsches Volksblatt*. Yet thirty-five-year-old Paul Federn had not allowed his physical ugliness to influence his life; he was a man of singular sweetness, a loyal friend who had stood as a bulwark for Sigmund Freud since he joined the group in 1903. He was one of the best internists in Vienna.

"Friend Hitschmann, I take exception to your criticism. Otto's paper contains important contributions. I am astonished to learn of the frequency of incestuous impulses. I do agree that the paper would be even more valuable if it traced the historical development of incest from primeval man to the individual family. Isn't it interesting that incest between father and daughter is not as strictly forbidden as between mother and son? I suppose that's why we find it less frequently in literature. Otto, I do think you could expand your castration theme to primeval times, when it was indicated for any despised man or mortal rival."

Sigmund listened intently as Alfred Adler began to speak, for his comments were always in season. He had so beautiful a voice that his friends had urged him to train for the opera; though his spoken German had been influenced by the modulation of the Viennese vernacular, it was of a scholarly, almost literary tone. He had grown up in the prosperous suburbs of Vienna, where his playmates and friends were all Christians, so that he had never witnessed any difference between Jew and Gentile. At an early age he had converted to Protestantism. His eyes sparkled as he spoke directly to Otto Rank. He wore only a small mustache, his hair was combed back neatly from a high brow, and his face, although a trifle pudgy, with a cleft chin, was a highly sensitive organ of expression.

"I consider your paper important because it confirms my own experience in treating psychoneuroses. Bearing out your sexual interpretation of Oedipus' removal of his father's belt, I have a hysteric woman patient who keeps untying her belt; through analysis we got down to her sexual meaning in this act. Concerning your point about Orestes biting off his finger, another of my female patients found that during a dream she had bitten her finger until it bled. The finger had taken the place of the penis in her dream; her act was a defense against oral perversion. As regards your theory of the sexual symbolism of the serpent, one of my patients informed me, 'There is a link between me and my father, which is shaped partly like a serpent and partly like a bird.' When I asked her to make me a drawing of this connecting link, what emerged from her pen was unmistakably a penis."

Sigmund knew that unlike the fast-talking Wilhelm Stekel, who invented cases on the spur of the moment in order to make the discussions more interesting, Adler reported only on cases he had actually treated. Sigmund reported that in medieval pictures devils were frequently depicted with genitals shaped like a serpent.

He then turned his attention to Otto Rank. It was his task as Rank's mentor, one who would have to see this manuscript on Incest through to publication, to slip unostentatiously into the role of Professor Freud, instructing a promising young student just as his own professors had taught him during his years at the University Medical School.

"First of all, Otto, work done is work accomplished."

Otto smiled his wistful, homely, little-boy smile.

"Professor Freud, my wounds are salved; my psyche is in good state of repair."

"Quite so! Then let us tick off a few points on the fingers of two hands. First, I think you must learn to outline your topic more clearly, then discipline yourself to stay within the limits of your subject. Second, you are not proving for the reader the disputed subjects which you feel you yourself already understand. I think you should quote the more important results of your researches. But take heed! It is a matter of personal taste and skill to stop at the right place, and not use remote evidence from poetry or mythology which will tend to obscure your central theme. . . ."

Otto Rank was writing his notes with a high flush on his dark cheeks. Sigmund knew the young man would not be hurt by such an overhauling. When he had finished his critique, the meeting was over; but the group liked to hear of each new case that came to him. For ten days he had been treating a female hysteric who had come forth with the material that in her fourth year she had undressed in front of her brother, who revolted against the act. However from the time she was eleven they used to undress together and show each other their sexual development. Between her eleventh and fourteenth years they had intimate bodily contact, lying on top of each other and simulating intercourse. With the onset of the menses the patient had made an end to all of this; and there had seemed to be no injurious effect . . . until she grew older and men started courting her. With the prospect of marriage a sense of guilt had taken possession of her, she knew not why. How best to lead her back to the why?

3.

By ten o'clock the next morning he had lost one of his most interesting patients, a tall, stout, self-assured bachelor of forty-five who suffered from such an obsession against germs and dirt that he washed and ironed the paper currency with which he insisted upon paying after each day's session. It had taken months before the patient revealed his sexual pattern: he did not care for "affairs" or the public women of Vienna; instead he preferred little girls. He had become the attentive "Uncle" to several families in town, each of which had a twelve- or thirteen-year-old daughter. When he had gained the confidence of the family he would take the girl into the country for an all-day picnic, and then manage to miss the last train home. A comfortable hotel room had been reserved in advance; here they would have supper and go to sleep in the same, because only, bed. And here "Uncle" would slowly move over, slip his fingers into the girl's vagina from behind, and slowly masturbate while he massaged her.

Sigmund asked, "Since you have this phobia about germs, aren't you afraid to put your dirty fingers into the vagina?"

The patient sprang up from the couch, his face a beet red with rage.

"How dare you say such a thing! You know better than to think I would put dirty fingers inside those pure, innocent little girls' private parts!"

With which he stormed out of the office, never to return, forgetting to hand over the washed and ironed bills so neatly stacked in his wallet; and leaving Sigmund to wonder what particular circumstances in "Uncle's" childhood had led him to this form of sexual intercourse; from the guilt of which he would need to be cleansed.

At eleven o'clock there arrived a married woman, thirty-two years of age, who, though she came from a wealthy, aristocratic family, had made up her mind very early that she must marry a poor man. At twenty-eight, although her parents did their best to dissuade her, she did marry a handsome well-educated man of thirty, one without means. The first five years of their married life were happy ones; the woman had borne three children. However in the middle of her last pregnancy certain character alterations began to appear. She convinced herself that her husband was being unfaithful to her and became intensely jealous, lighting upon the nursemaid in the home. She gave as proof of her suspicions the fact that her husband was so handsome he could attract anyone, and the nursemaid so attractive that she must be highly desirable to the husband.

At this point the family physician recommended that the husband and wife separate. In her husband's absence the patient began writing amatory letters to young men of her acquaintance inviting them to clandestine meetings. She also began talking to strange men in the streets. When her parents caught her at this she cried, "If my husband is unfaithful to me, I have the right to be unfaithful to him." She was reunited with her husband, and shortly after was recommended to Sigmund by the family physician.

After a few sessions Sigmund asked the husband to come for a consultation. The husband assured him, as had the parents, that there was no truth to the accusations. Her father now vouchsafed that as a child she had not behaved normally. The husband, for his part, conceded that during their engagement his wife had acted very peculiarly, often, as though by accident and involuntarily, pushing against men in the street. During the third month of her third pregnancy he had noticed a striking increase in her sexual desire. He confessed that it was no longer possible to satisfy her. Lately she had taken to what he described as perverse desires. She insisted that he masturbate her, that he look at her private parts from below, and that he have intercourse through the anus. She had dropped all inhibitions, even in front of the servants, speaking and acting shamelessly; she had masturbated in her husband's presence, sexually attacked him at any hour of the day and night, mocked him for being not enough man, and cried, "I need other men besides you."

Sigmund concluded that it was a case of nymphomania, one which had begun ideationally in childhood and come into flower in youth. The early years of marriage to a handsome virile man had satisfied her temporarily. Then there had been a regressive development of the libido, the energies associated with one's sex drive from object love, this case her husband, back to autoeroticism. The delusional system she had created, the jealousies, accusations of unfaithfulness, the hearing of voices accusing her husband, all these had been developed by her unconscious to overcome her psychic inhibitions and give her free reign in her nymphomania.

Sigmund described it as a case of exquisite paranoia, incurable by psychotherapy because the mania had a tendency to spread to more and more reaches of the mind, and to become permanent. The patient had been brought to him too late. Had the family physician brought her in at the beginning of the pathological jealousies, when she was in a state of neurosis, before the nymphomania had been given a chance to break through, there might have been an opportunity for transference, a chance for him to demonstrate that "pathological jealousy is usually based on the projection of one's own desires."

His noon patient too was perplexing; a young man with a consistent death wish, who had confided an episode which had happened in his sixth year.

". . . one occasion . . . I was sharing my mother's bed . . . I misused the opportunity . . . inserted my finger into her genitals . . . while she was asleep."

Sigmund had been unable to tie the young man's obsession with death to this isolated incident; the other manifestations of guilt were not strong enough to induce a suicide wish. Now the man related a dream:

"I was visiting a house that I had been in twice before. What meaning can that have, Professor? How can it be a fulfillment of a wish?"

"Let us think in terms of symbols. What house, symbolically, have you been in twice before which you still dream about wanting to return to, perhaps permanently?"

The young man stared at him, aghast.

"Yes, your mother's womb. Where you spent nine months before you were born. And to which you returned in your sixth year. Your obsession is not with death but with birth. The longing of your life is to return to your mother's womb . . . in various ways. Now that we grasp the nature of the problem, let's see if we cannot set you on the straight path: the desire is to return to a loved one's womb. With mature men, it is to a surrogate for the mother, to a sweetheart or a wife. With this, your obsession with death should vanish, you will begin to think of creating life."

Though he had the seminar for which he had longed, his connection with the University of Vienna, aside from his Saturday night extracurricular lectures to which he now attracted twenty-eight registrants, remained strictly an honorary one. Neither Wagner-Jauregg nor the Hofrat in charge of Neurology invited Professor Freud to give an authorized course to the medical students. Nor did any other Medical School, except the one conducted by the Burghölzli, the hospital and sanatorium attached to the University of Zurich. Here Sigmund Freud had found a supporter very early, Dr. Eugen Bleuler, who had written fourteen years before, in 1892, the only favorable review published about On Aphasia, praising Sigmund for being the first to introduce psychological factors into aphasia. Even Josef Breuer, to whom Sigmund had dedicated the book, had rejected it because of this point of departure. Sigmund sent Bleuler his books as they appeared, and Professor Bleuler had become an advocate of psychoanalysis, using it in a limited way with his dementia praecox patients; but more importantly, teaching it to his medical students. In Zurich, Freudian psychology was highly respected.

The favorable climate of Switzerland bore fruit in the form of a thirty-one-year-old psychiatrist by the name of Dr. Carl Jung, son of a Swiss pastor, now Chief Assistant to Bleuler. Dr. Jung had read The Interpretation of Dreams and become converted. Earlier in 1906 Jung had sent Sigmund a copy of his new book, Studies in Word-Association, a field being opened for psychological research in Zurich. Jung dedicated his essay, Psychoanalysis and Word-Association Experiments, to Dr. Sigmund Freud. This began a vital correspondence between the two men in which they exchanged ideas and knowledge. Carl Jung took upon himself the role of defender of Sigmund's work.

The previous May, at a Congress of Neurologists and Psychiatrists held in Baden-Baden, Professor Gustav Aschaffenburg had devoted his speech to an attack on Sigmund's recent publication, Fragment of an Analysis of a Case of Hysteria, the story of Dora. Professor Aschaffenburg had decreed to the Congress:

"Freud's method is wrong in most cases, objectionable in many and superfluous in all."

Carl Jung went to work on Aschaffenburg at once, writing a reply that was published in the same *Münchener medizinische Wochenschrift* as Aschaffenburg's attack, the first such spirited and public defense of Sigmund Freud to be seen by the medical profession. Jung pointed out that Aschaffenburg's criticism had been "confined exclusively to the role which sexuality, according to Freud, plays in the formation of the psychoneuroses. What he says, therefore, does not affect the wider range of Freud's psychology, that is, the psychology of dreams, jokes and disturbances of ordinary thinking caused by feeling-toned constellations." He had given Sigmund high credit for unique achievements which could be denied only by those who had not bothered to "check Freud's thought processes experimentally.

"I say 'achievements,'" Jung continued, "though this does not mean that I subscribe unconditionally to all Freud's theorems. But it is also an achievement, and often no small one, to propound ingenious problems."

However the first enthusiast to reach Sigmund Freud from Zurich was neither Eugen Bleuler nor Carl Jung, but a cultivated young man of twenty-five by the name of Max Eitingon, who had just completed his medical studies under Bleuler and Jung but had not yet been awarded his medical degree. Bleuler had asked him to bring to Dr. Freud a disturbed patient for whom they could do nothing at the Burghölzli. It took Dr. Freud only two hours of consultation to be convinced that his methods were powerless to reach the unfortunate person who saw the outside world as a faithful portrait of his inner, chaotic psyche.

But Max Eitingon proved to be a delight. Born into a wealthy Russian family, of independent means himself, he had gone to school in Leipzig, where his family had settled, but had dropped out at an early age because of severe stuttering which made it almost impossible for him to participate in classroom work. It was not until he discovered medicine, learned that one does not have to talk much when hovering over a microscope or Bunsen burner, that he found his role in life. He had transferred from the Medical School at Marburg to Zurich to work under Eugen Bleuler. During the past two years he had devoured all six of Sigmund's published books, as well as the twenty-four articles on psychoanalysis in the technical journals, having been led to them by Carl Jung.

In spite of his excruciating handicap, Max Eitingon had already made his commitment, as he now confided to Sigmund during a fast walk around the Votivkirche of a late, cold but miraculously clear January night. He wanted to become a psychoanalyst, to be trained by Sigmund Freud and follow in his footsteps. But he did not want to settle in Vienna.

"I ha . . . ha . . . have a fr . . . fr . . . friend in Zurich, de . . . devo . . . devoted to you, K . . . K . . . Karl Abra . . . Abra . . . ham, being tra . . . tra . . . trained by Ju . . . Jung, wa . . . wants to p . . . prac . . . practice in Ber . . . Berlin. M . . . m . . . me too."

Sigmund liked the young man. During the years that he was out of school he had read voraciously and knew the world's literature. Sigmund found him to be extraordinarily kind and gentle. He explained to Sigmund with an apologetic smile on the round plain face dominated by rimless spectacles that he needed kindness from others "wh . . . wh . . . when I g . . . g . . . get m . . . myself in . . . invol . . . involved in ta . . . ta . . . talking." Stutter or no, Sigmund soon found that Max Eitingon could, given a little time, drive to the heart of any psychoanalytic problem. He was touched by Max's obvious pride in at last being at the fountainhead. When Max showed him a list of questions sent along by Bleuler in the hope that Sigmund Freud could shed some light on troublesome problems in psychiatry, Sigmund said:

"You must attend our Psychological Wednesday Society meeting and put these questions before the group. I hope you are not in a hurry to leave Vienna . . . ?"

". . . no . . . no . . . I c . . . can . . . st . . . remain as l . . . long as I like."

"Good. These questions will take us at least two meetings to clarify; and then the rest of our lives to resolve. But I must tell you with what joy I will welcome you; up to now we have had only Viennese. You will be the first foreign guest to honor us with your presence. We can then say that we are an international body!"

Max Eitingon laughed; the beautiful deep sounds that came from his throat, since they did not have to form words, were uninhibited. His eyes behind the glasses were filled with joy at having been accepted.

Sigmund introduced Max Eitingon to the group on Wednesday evening, January 23, 1907. His pleasure at having this first foreign visitor was shared by the members. Eitingon had gone to the trouble of writing out ten copies of Bleuler's questions so that his stuttering would not slow down the discussion:

"What other factors have to be at work, in addition to the mechanisms known to us, for a neurosis to develop? Are social components perhaps of some account? What is the essence of therapy? Is it or is it not directed against the *symptom*? Does one substitute something for the symptom, or does one only 'take away,' as Freud expressed it in his simile of sculpture?"

A spirited discussion ensued. Everyone wanted to talk at once. Otto Rank had to write furiously to keep up. Sigmund sat back in his chair with a pleased smile on his lips, listening to the younger men, all of whom he had trained. Sadger said, "Hysteria is the neurosis of love par excellence" Federn commented, "The severe neurotic always comes from an unhappy marriage." Kahane observed, "The psyche lives by means of charges which it receives. . . . The complete assimilation of these charges is the condition for health." Rank put down his pen and decreed. "Between the illness and its cure, the symptom and its resolution, there is, one might say, the normal life of the patient; there his social, religious, artistic instincts come to the fore, and it is from there that one can start. . . ."

Alfred Adler tapped the palm of his left hand with the fingertips of his right, to indicate applause for Rank, the youngest man present, then spoke in his ringingly musical voice:

"Therapy consists primarily in strengthening certain psychic fields through a kind of psychic training. The hysteric shows a growth of his psychic qualities during treatment. The patient surprises us by his ideas and a discovery of connections which sometimes astonishes the physician. During and after the treatment, he masters material which was entirely strange to him before. As he progresses in understanding, the patient gains the peace of mind which he needs so badly. From an unwitting pawn of circumstance, he becomes a conscious antagonist or sufferer of his fate."

The maid entered with the tray of coffee and cakes. During the lull Max Eitingon told about word-association, of how Dr. Carl Jung used a stop-watch to measure and record the amount of reaction time taken by a patient to respond to a given word; and how the physician was able to judge the depth and severity of the repression by how long it took the patient to answer. Then, after a moment of silence, all eyes turned toward Sigmund, at the head of the table.

"Pro . . . Pro . . . Professor Fr . . . Freud, won't you pl . . . please t . . . t . . . tell us what you th . . . thin . . . think?"

Sigmund chuckled, said, "Ah, I had no intention of remaining silent! At this table every man gets his turn. I've just been thinking, in the manner of all aging professors, how to recapitulate, briefly, what has been proffered here tonight. Let me try it this way:

"The sexual component of psychic life has more bearing on the causation of the neuroses than all other factors. Through sexuality, the intimate relation of psyche to soma is established. The neurotic is ill only to the extent that he suffers. Where he does not suffer, therapy is ineffectual. Perhaps all of us are somewhat neurotic. Practical considerations really determine whether an individual is characterized as ill. The actual difference between mild and severe illness lies only in the localization, the topography of the symptom. As long as the pathological element obtains an outlet in insignificant performances, man is 'healthy.' But if it attacks functions essential for living, then he is considered ill. Thus illness develops through a quantitative increase. As to the problem of the choice of neurosis, this is what we know least about."

4.

Jokes and Their Relation to the Unconscious was paid considerable attention because the book revealed the non-sexual side of the unconscious. It was not an original field of research, such philosophers as Lipps, Fischer and Vischer had published volumes on the classification and nature of the comic; yet these books, as with the eighty volumes on dreams which had been published prior to *The Interpretation of Dreams*, served only as Sigmund's starting point. He had broken down jokes and the field of wit into their various components, under chapters on The Mechanism of Pleasure and the Psychogenesis of Jokes, The Motives of Jokes, Jokes as a Social Process, The Relation of Jokes to Dreams and to the Unconscious, and had come to the conclusion that jokes served a purpose beyond that of provoking an instant of laughter. They were most often fashioned by the unconscious with a specific motive: jealousy, spite, the desire to humiliate, repudiate or simply inflict pain. A "good" joke was one that came to everyone's assistance, at which all could laugh, and was rare.

The two major subdivisions, he decided, were hostile jokes, which served the purpose of aggression or self-defense; and obscene jokes which made it possible to satisfy a lustful instinct in the face of an obstacle: usually respectable woman's inability to accept undisguised sexuality, or anatomical references, so frequently centered around the processes of defecation. He made the observation, "A person who laughs at smut that he hears is laughing as though he were the spectator of an act of sexual aggression. . . . Smut is like an exposure of the sexually different person to whom it is directed."

Jokes involving excrement were particularly popular. In childhood, what is sexual and what is excremental can barely be distinguished; jokes involving excrement, therefore, were a return to the pleasures of childhood.

To illustrate the use of wit as fulfillments of wishes, he used Heine's story of the lottery agent who said, "As true as God shall grant me all good things, I sat beside Salomon Rothschild and he treated me quite as his equal, quite famillionairely."

From his own collection Sigmund brought forth examples that were used as social weapons or as means of revenge: in discussing a friend, one man said of another, "Vanity is one of his four Achilles' heels." Another commented, "I drove out with Charles *tête-a-bête* (He is a stupid ass)." An opponent said of a young political figure, "He has a great future behind him." Karl Kraus wrote of a yellow journalist, "He is traveling to one of the Balkan states by *Orienterpresszug*," a combination of Orient Express and *Erpressung*, blackmail. A young bachelor who had lived a gay life abroad returned to Vienna wearing a wedding ring. "What!" exclaimed a friend. "Are you married?" "Yes," the young man replied, "*Trauring* (a combination of wedding ring and sad) but true."

For Sigmund, jokes had certain elements in common with dreams: each had a manifest or open meaning, and behind that, a latent or buried purpose. He recalled a joke from Medical School: "When one asks a young patient whether he has ever masturbated, the answer will always be, '*O na, nie!* Oh, no, never'"; which emerged as *Onanie*, the basic word for masturbation. Then there were the jokes satirizing marriage. A doctor, called in to see a woman patient, said to her husband in an aside, "I don't like her looks." The husband replied, "I haven't liked her looks for a long time."

A marriage broker asks, "What do you require in a bride?" "She must be beautiful, she must be rich, and educated." "Very good," said the broker, "but that is three matches."

Humor was rarely unmotivated; it served means not readily available in serious relationships, such as the servitude of a citizen to his government. Here satire allowed the most pungent criticism to surface: the thorn embedded in the cream puff. It also served as social commentary.

"A man who was hard of hearing consulted the doctor, who correctly diagnosed that the patient probably drank too much brandy and was on that account deaf. He advised him against it and the deaf man promised to take his advice. After a while the doctor met him in the street and asked in a loud voice how the man was. 'You needn't shout so loud, Doctor. I've given up drinking and hear quite well again.' A little while later they met once more. The doctor asked him how he was in an ordinary voice, but noticed that his question had not been understood. 'It seems to me you're drinking brandy again,' shouted the doctor in his ear, 'and that's why you're deaf again.' 'You may be right,' replied the deaf man, 'I *have* begun drinking brandy again and I'll tell you why. So long as I didn't drink I was able to hear. But nothing I heard was as good as the brandy.'"

Heine was said to have made a blasphemous joke on his deathbed. When a friendly priest reminded him of God's mercy and gave hope that God would forgive him his sins, Heine was said to have replied: "*Bien sûr qu'il me pardonnera: c'est son métier.* Of course He'll forgive me: that's His job."

During his years of isolation Sigmund had derived relief by collecting Jewish ethnic jokes, jokes which had served the purpose over the centuries of keeping the race alive by poking fun at itself, and at the same time subtly suggesting its virtues. He used many of them for his chapter The Purposes of Jokes:

"There is really no advantage in being a rich man if one is a Jew. Other people's misery makes it impossible to enjoy one's own happiness."

Another portrayed the relationship between poor and rich Jews, since the Torah says that the poor should be cared for and treated as equals:

"A *Schnorrer*, beggar, who was allowed as a guest into the same house every Sunday appeared one day in the company of an unknown young man who gave signs of being about to sit down to table. 'Who is this?' asked the householder. 'He's been my son-in-law,' was the reply, 'since last week. I've promised him his board for the first year.'

"The *Schnorrer* begged the Baron for some money for a journey to Ostend; his doctor had recommended sea bathing for his troubles. The Baron thought Ostend was a particularly expensive resort; a cheaper one would do equally well. The *Schnorrer*, however, rejected the proposal with the words: 'Herr Baron, I consider nothing too expensive for my health.'"

He paid special attention to the façade behind which apparently nonsensical jokes concealed their meanings; the amount of brutal derision that could lie submerged in comic stories. A joke, a witty comment or riposte, could bring forth repressed sentiments which had been simmering on the back burner of the mind for weeks, perhaps months. They often came not only as a jolt to the listener but as a revelation and a relief to the one whose true state of mind had been prised out of him. Shakespeare had said in *Love's Labour's Lost*:

> A jest's prosperity lies in the ear
> Of him that hears it, never in the tongue
> Of him that makes it.

Ah, but the pleasure the teller received from the release of excessive stored-up psychic energy, enabling him to laugh uproariously at his transitory triumph!

Readers of *Jokes and Their Relation to the Unconscious* acknowledged the validity of Sigmund Freud's arguments; they had either been at the painful receiving end of someone else's bit of tendentious humor or had had something pop out of them which had been smoldering in their preconscious waiting for a chance to escape. If he was getting nowhere with his sexual etiology of the neuroses except among his followers, he was at least beginning to convince a small part of the world that there was an unconscious mind which dominated a portion of their characters and lives. A few of his colleagues, Sigmund had learned through correspondence, particularly with Carl Jung, felt that he should be content with this, that the exploration of the unconscious held out far more hope for the solving of both normal and abnormal psychology than did his psychotherapy for patients.

But he was not content; it was like asking him to be the engineer of the train that crossed the sixteen viaducts and went through the seventeen tunnels on the way up to Semmering, with wheels on only one side of the engine and carriages. Without both sets of wheels the train simply could not run, let alone make the steep grade up to Semmering. The sexual etiology of the neuroses was not only the second set of wheels, it was also the second engine which would carry man up to the Schneeberg of self-knowledge, where before he had had to grovel at its base in dark forests.

Three Essays on the Theory of Sexuality, which Deuticke published almost simultaneously, was born under no such favorable constellation; nor could Sigmund have expected it to be, since its three longish essays dealt with The Sexual Aberrations, Infantile Sexuality and The Transformations of Puberty, the last of which he opened with a scientific barrage which was certain to bring down the enemy's heaviest artillery shells upon his head.

"With the arrival of puberty, changes set in which are destined to give infantile sexual life its final, normal shape. The sexual instinct has hitherto been predominantly autoerotic; it now finds a sexual object. Its activity has hitherto been derived from a number of separate instincts and erotogenic zones which, independently of one another, have pursued a certain sort of pleasure as their sole sexual aim. Now, however, a new sexual aim appears, and all the component instincts combine to attain it, while the erotogenic zones become subordinated to the primacy of the genital zone."

It was getting increasingly difficult for his opponents to find new terms of opprobrium for his sexual heresies; but the neurologists and psychiatrists moving from congress to congress in Europe did not give up hope. He was accused of preaching Old Wives' Psychiatry, a form of mysticism and theatricality derived straight from his spiritual progenitor, Dr. Anton Mesmer. Sigmund Freud was one whom no alienist could read without a sense of horror.

"Little wonder!" exclaimed the ebullient Wilhelm Stekel, who had had supper with the Freuds and was now in Sigmund's upstairs study leafing through the copy he had bought that noon at Deuticke's bookstore. "In it you announce your intention of demolishing the established basis of thinking about our animal nature. Listen to what you write here, just in case it has slipped your mind:

"'Popular opinion has quite definite ideas about the nature and characteristics of this sexual instinct. It is generally understood to be absent in childhood, to set in at the time of puberty in connection with the process of coming to maturity and to be revealed in the manifestations of an irresistible attraction exercised by one sex upon the other; while its aim is presumed to be sexual union, or at all events actions leading in that direction. We have every reason to believe, however, that these views give a very false picture of the true situation. If we look into them more closely we shall find that they contain a number of errors, inaccuracies and hasty conclusions.' "

Stekel chuckled. Sigmund used the cigar cutter at the end of the knife he carried on his gold watch chain, to cut off the tip of a cigar.

"The closer you cut to the bone called *instinct*," Stekel exclaimed, "the louder the patient is going to scream; the patient in this case being your fellow neurologists and psychiatrists on whom you are operating without an anesthetic. It's indecent and unchivalrous of you to upset their secure, comfortable way of thinking. Never mind that there is a broad spectrum of neuroses which they can't relieve, let alone cure; that's the patients' bad luck. Here you come along with the nerve to tell them that you have opened a door to a new world of understanding, but one into which they'll have to walk barefooted over burning coals. They'll chain you to a mountain crag the way Zeus did Prometheus for giving fire to mankind."

Sigmund smiled wanly.

"Wilhelm, I already have a pain in the side!" Recovering his good humor, he added, "Still and all, it's better than being ignored. It's traditional to attack savagely what one fears most."

5.

At ten o'clock on a Sunday morning in early March, Dr. Carl Jung rang the doorbell at the Freud apartment. The maid brought him to Sigmund's study. The two men stood gazing at each other, big-eyed, for they had been looking forward to this meeting for months. It was a moment before they shook hands: warmly, admiringly, each glowing with pleasure; yet in this brief instant Sigmund was able to record one of the rare instants of Carl Jung caught in suspension, at rest.

He was a big man, well over six feet tall, broad across the shoulders and chest, with the powerful gnarled hands of a Renaissance stone carver. The head was big too, with short cropped brown hair and mustache, spectacles unconcealing of wise, dancing eyes; a personality that suffused a glow of strength and inner vitality that pushed back the book-lined walls of Sigmund's study, making the room seem infinitely larger because of the superb presence. Sigmund thought, as the two men clasped hands as though they had been intimate friends for years:

"He is the kind of mountain peak that raises the stature of everything around him."

Carl Jung, thirty-two years old, was the son of a parson; on his mother's side there were six parsons, on his father's, two uncles were also clergymen. He first dropped into the deep chair Sigmund offered him, then sprang up and paced the room, fitting long strides to the sentences tumbling happily out of him. His voice was high-pitched but in no way strident.

"Highly Revered Professor, I have looked forward to this moment for several years. Without your work I would never have had a key to my own work. We have been using Freudian psychoanalysis in Zurich with gratifying results. I bring you these cases, which seem to me gifts more valuable than rubies, for they prove that you have lighted up the scientific sky with the new sun of the unconscious. Before you began to explore the unconscious we lived in a dark cave as far as understanding human motivation or character was concerned. It's the difference between our ancestors who lived in the forests with clubs as their only means of procuring food, and those who came out into the bright sunlight to plant and till the fields. We can never return to that primitive stage. You have looked at the same materials that thousands of doctors since Hippocrates have faced, and only you have penetrated to the truth. You have proved to us that man is an event which cannot judge itself but, for better or worse, is left to the judgment of others. The pathological variants of so-called normality fascinated me, because they offered me the longed-for opportunity to obtain a deeper insight into the psyche in general. You have observed Charcot's instruction to the letter: you have become our greatest see-er into the psyche."

Sigmund was so unaccustomed to praise of this nature that he literally blanched.

"I've been using your therapeutic procedures for the treatment of neuroses," Jung continued, "sometimes with partial success, sometimes with failure; but medical psychotherapy is only part of your contribution, and perhaps not even the more important half; it's what your discoveries will do to the interpreting and evaluating of anthropology, of the arts, the humanities, that will leave an ineradicable mark on the face of the Western world. The blind have been made to see. Your work will enable man to understand himself in the light of inner happenings, not only his own, but those of his progenitors back through what you call 'time inconceivable,' to that shrouded period when man first became man."

Carl Jung thrust aside the curtains and stood staring out the window at the Export Academy across the street. Having calmed himself, he turned back to Sigmund with an eager smile.

"I am by nature a heretic. That was one reason I was immediately drawn to your heretical views."

Sigmund laughed, answered, "One generation's heresy is the next generation's orthodoxy."

"Let me tell you of the first case in which I used the psychoanalytic method," said Jung. "A woman was admitted to the hospital suffering from melancholia. The diagnosis was dementia praecox, the prognosis poor. It appeared to me that she was suffering from ordinary depression. I used my word-association method, then discussed her dreams with her. She had been deeply in love with the son of a wealthy industrialist; because she was pretty she thought she had a chance. But the young man paid little attention to her, and so she married a second choice, had two children by her husband, only to learn five years later that the first young man had indeed been interested in her. She became depressed, allowed her baby daughter to suck the sponge in a bath of impure water, with the result that the child died of typhoid fever. That was when she was admitted to the hospital and came under my care. Up to this point she had been given narcotics against insomnia, guarded against suicide. Using your methods, I perceived what she was suppressing: the desire to undo her marriage, banish the children. She was accusing herself of murdering the little girl, and was determined to die for it. Did I dare bring forth the suppressed materials? I could not ask my colleagues, for they would have warned me against it. Yet you had provided the technique; how could I let her die? She's back home now, not free from moral responsibility for her daughter's death, but making it up to the rest of her family. . . ."

Sigmund settled back in his chair with a deep sense of gratification, watching Jung circle the room with words, ideas, cases, dreams from his childhood, stories of the years of work that had led him over the pitted road of psychiatry to Sigmund Freud's psychoanalysis, his voice high, filled with passion for what he called "our new era," his effervescent mind pouring out the varied matters he had stored up for years to communicate to Sigmund Freud.

"I have an arcane nature which I inherited from my mother; in me it is linked with the gift, not always pleasant, of seeing people and things as they are. I can be deceived when I don't want to recognize something, and yet at bottom I know quite well how matters stand.

"You are looking at my hands. Yes, I like best to work with my hands. All my life I have carved wood. Now I mean to turn to stone. I want a harder, more worthy adversary. In the garden of my parents' home there was an old wall. In front of the wall, on a slope, was a stone that jutted out. I named it 'My Stone.' Often when I was alone I sat down on it but after a number of years I began to wonder, 'Am I sitting on the stone, or is the stone sitting on me?'

"Revered Professor, I must be honest with you at the outset, as I have tried to be in my letters. I cannot agree with you wholly on the sexual etiology of the neuroses. I know you understand that, because you wrote me last October that you have long suspected from my writings that I cannot wholly appreciate your psychology when it comes to sexuality. You will remember that I confessed at the end of last year that my education, my environment and my scientific premises are, in any event, very different from yours. I urged you not to believe that I am desperately eager to distinguish myself just by holding the most divergent views possible. You have suggested that in the course of time I will come closer to you than I now think possible. A consummation devoutly to be wished! But please recall what I wrote to you from Zurich last December when I was asking for this appointment with you:

"When we are writing, lecturing, and in other ways advocating the spread of psychoanalysis, do you not think it would be wiser to keep the subject of therapy out of the foreground of our exposition? Not that you have not achieved significant and meaningful results—even I, in my modest beginnings, have brought considerable help—but rather because you have given us a wholly new and revolutionary science of psychology, one which we will be able to apply to all activities of man. Why then risk the reputation and validity of psychoanalysis, whose ultimate meaning will be a thousand times broader than the therapy itself, to the hands of doctors who could well take unsuitable cases, who may even come into the field because they imagine psychoanalytic therapy to be easy, and who will hurt our movement by their lack of knowledge of our techniques. Wouldn't it be better, in our public statements, to play down our claims for the healing powers of our therapy until we ourselves can give expert training to a group of doctors who will then be qualified to practice Freudian analysis?"

Sigmund reached for a cigar, lighted it thoughtfully. Was he again being asked to be the engineer of a train with wheels on one side only? He had already written to Carl Jung during the last December, "I . . . have taken care not to maintain in my writings more than that 'the method effects more than any other.'" He thought back to what he already knew about Carl Jung. He was born in Kesswil, Switzerland, to the churchmouse-poor pastor of a small-town congregation, an embittered man who had never wanted to go into theology but had stumbled there when his father, an eminent physician, died young. The boy's only chance at an education was controlled by an aunt who proffered money for the theological training but nothing else. Carl Jung had gone to Basel to the *Gymnasium,* then on to Zurich, the intellectual capital of Switzerland, for his medical training at the University of Zurich in order to follow his grandfather's profession. He had come to psychiatry circuitously; before he could graduate he had had to read a textbook by Krafft-Ebing, *Psychiatry,* and thinking it was going to be dull stuff, he put it off until the last . . . only to find that Krafft-Ebing had opened a world more interesting than anything he had learned in internal medicine. After graduation he had attached himself to Professor Eugen Bleuler at the university sanatorium, done psychological experiments in the new concept of "association tests" which showed what was concealed from a patient's conscious mind. Already the author of two well-known books, he was still a poor young man when he fell in love with the delightful daughter of the wealthy industrialist family Rauschenbach. He had thought he had no chance, but Emma Rauschenbach and her parents sensed the superb mind, character and drive of this handsome and brainy young doctor, and welcomed him into the family. Jung and Emma had married in 1903, living in a bungalow on the Burghölzli hospital grounds. Emma Jung had had a considerable fortune left to her in trust by her grandfather, but the young couple lived off Carl Jung's tiny salary as an Assistant to Professor Bleuler, the position Sigmund Freud had sought twenty-five years before from Professor Brücke, as a first step toward marrying Martha Bernays.

Carl Jung was no arrant egoist, Sigmund observed, in spite of the fact that through his natural gifts he walked almost like a god among ordinary mortals. During the three-hour cornucopia Sigmund interrupted Jung not even once. Jung spoke of himself only to illuminate the long, frequently dark road that had led him to Sigmund Freud: dreams. He wanted Professor Freud to know about his dreams so that he could understand Carl Jung's unconscious.

He outlined one dream: that he was making slow headway against a heavy wind, and cupped a tiny light in his hands. He turned around to see a gigantic black figure following him, but he was conscious of the fact that he had to keep the light going. When he woke he realized that the figure was "my own shadow on the swirling mists, brought into being by the little light I was carrying. I knew, too, that this little light was my consciousness, the only light I have."

In science he was well trained in zoology, paleontology and geology, as well as the humanities including Greco-Roman, Egyptian and pre-historic archaeology, subjects which had long fascinated Sigmund. Yet there was implicit in his approach to work and discovery the permeating sense of destiny, as though his life had been assigned to him by fate and had to be fulfilled. It was clear to Sigmund that what Carl Jung wanted was a lifetime of deep-pitted, consecrated work; his manner showed not the tiniest effluvium of desire for the external rewards of fame or fortune. Jung had a robust sense of humor, loved to laugh and make other people laugh; most of his jokes and witticisms were turned against himself.

"I must tell you about my most brilliant cure! It was a middle-aged woman, with a patch quilt of neuroses. She heard voices coming from the nipple of each breast. I tried every therapeutic hint in your books, plus a few you haven't invented yet. Nothing! After several months I exclaimed to her: 'Whatever am I to do with you?' 'Oh, I know, Herr Professor,' she replied sweetly; 'let us read the Bible together.' We did . . . for a month; first one voice disappeared, then the other, after which the patient discharged herself as cured! I ask you, doesn't that make me a great therapist!"

The gratifying part of the morning was that Carl Jung appeared to be holding nothing back. With every gesture of those huge encircling arms, every relevant sentence that came forth in his unabashed delight was an avowal that he was a Freudian; that he intended to stand shoulder to shoulder with the older man; to teach the meaning and measure of the unconscious mind to a disinterested world. There was a strong difference between Jung and Alfred Adler, who came closest to Jung in brain power and personality among Sigmund's group. Jung did not feel it necessary or even proper to keep a distance between himself and Sigmund Freud, to maintain a formal relationship, to let the medical world know that he was neither student nor follower. Jung was exulting in the fact that Sigmund Freud was his teacher, guide, inspiration; he made it clear in every ringing sentence that:

"I am a disciple of Sigmund Freud!"

Sigmund took the gold watch out of his vest pocket and studied it for a moment.

"For the purposes of our discussion for the remainder of the day, I suggest that we organize our materials into manageable categories. So far this morning you have discussed . . ." and he broke down Jung's monologue into its different areas. Carl Jung gaped in astonishment, then cried:

"My God! You've collated my three-hour diatribe and marshaled it into an intelligible structure!"

6.

It was one o'clock when Sigmund and Jung walked up the Berggasse to the Hotel Regina to fetch Emma Jung for dinner. Emma was twenty-four, tall, willowy, with a lovely face, perceptive eyes, glossy black hair parted on the left side and then puffed up in a wave to the right. Martha and Emma liked each other immediately.

Sigmund seated Jung at the table in the midst of the six children, surrounded by Martha, Tante Minna, Sigmund's mother, Amalie, and sister Dolfi, Rosa and her husband Heinrich Graf from across the hall. Alexander brought his fiancée, Sophie Sabine Schreiber. Alexander, who was now forty and owned the freight company, had advertised for a secretary. Twenty-eight-year-old Sophie Schreiber had proved such an irresistible combination of capability and loveliness that Alexander had not only hired her but was planning to marry her. With all of the extra boards in the dining table, it extended the full length of the room.

Carl Jung was a physical creature, just as strongly as he was a mental being. He loved everything about the out of doors and was particularly fond of sailing, going to the far end of Lake Zurich to sail and then camp among the uninhabited islands. He fascinated the Freud children with his tales of adventure. He wrote his manuscripts in enormous double-ledger writing books in which he also painted and drew with colored block letters at the beginning of each page, somewhat in the manner of the monks of medieval times illuminating their manuscripts. The art work sprang from his own dreams and fantasies but was frequently expressed in the forms of Oriental art which he had studied, and examples of which he had in the books on his library shelves.

Archaeology had been his first love, and still was one of his most intense interests. However there had been no Chair of Archaeology in Switzerland, and the young man had had a living to make and a place to hollow out for himself. Now he was finding to his intense gratification that his two fields of interest had conjoined; everything that was unearthed about earlier civilizations revealed to psychoanalysis the thinking, the gods, the religion, the myths, the fears, the communal values.

"All of which," observed Jung, "affords us a deeper understanding of the psyche of modern man."

Jung never counted the value of one kind of work against another; he would spend hours painting a picture of a dream he had had, and think the time well spent. Puzzled, Sigmund asked:

"How does the painting enable you to interpret the dream?"

"Because I don't attempt to control either the content or the form of the painting. I let it flow spontaneously from my unconscious. When I finish the painting, and study it, I learn as much about the latent content of that dream as I could by writing in language the meaning of its content. There are many fantasy fragments which arise from the unconscious for which there is no suitable language. That is why we must use other means of communication, chief among them being drawing and painting."

"How do you refresh your own wellsprings, Dr. Jung?" Martha asked.

"I go far enough down Lake Zurich to find untouched sandbanks," Jung replied with a broad grin, "where I spend the whole day searching for hidden springs, releasing them and making channels for an inner network of waterways . . . while at the same time searching for the hidden springs in my own mind. The thoughts come forth, cool and clear, from hidden underground wells. When I return to my office I have new insights, new divinations, new theories to set down on paper. I adore that uninhabited end of the lake; all of my suppressed energies and creative juices flow when I am there, in the quiet and the beauty of the marshes and the little primitive islands surrounded by snow-capped mountains. I don't know how much longer I want to remain at the Burghölzli, perhaps only a year or two, long enough to learn everything that the asylum can give me. In a sense it is a blind alley for me; Professor Eugen Bleuler is the world's authority on dementia praecox, and is a talented administrator; certainly he will be the director for another thirty years. There is no place for me to go . . ."

". . . except to the other end of Lake Zurich?" Sigmund interrupted with smiling eyes.

"Precisely! My private practice is building. As you know, my wife has a substantial inheritance and she is as eager as I to find land and build a house toward the north end of the lake. There I could practice, write, paint, spend a wholly creative life."

"And your patients will follow you, those from Zurich who come to you now?"

"I would hope so. There is the boat, there is the train. I would be a poor doctor indeed if patients who needed help would not travel a short distance to reach me. I am the only psychoanalyst practicing in Zurich. I believe that life is long enough to accomplish everything. I feel longevity in my bones. That's why I feel calm, with a great sense of patience, why I can stay on a sandbank all day and search for hidden springs or paint my dream fantasies."

After dinner the two men walked up the Berggasse and along the Währinger Strasse so that Sigmund could point out the Physiology Institute and the main buildings of the Allgemeine Krankenhaus, including the Fools' Tower which had been converted into cell-like rooms for the resident nurses. Jung towered over Sigmund. As they walked through the hospital courts, he said tentatively:

"I have no method, as you do. I could define analysis as 'mutual influence.' Perhaps I am more of an artist and not so much a professional technician as you are. I read everything and I try to learn everything; but when I am faced with a patient I forget all this and think only what concerns this one person."

"But without psychoanalytic procedures" countered Sigmund mildly, "aren't we like children without a trail in a dense woods? —Is there something in Vienna you would particularly like to see?"

"What is your most ancient structure?"

"St. Ruprecht, but St. Stephan's Cathedral is more interesting. The first church on the site was built in the mid-twelfth century. It is very beautiful, with its colored slate roof."

As they walked down the Schottengasse Jung shook his head in mock despair.

"Since I was six I have not been able to enter a Catholic church without terrible fear and trepidation. Oh, I had reason enough; when my parents took me on a trip to Arlesheim one Easter my mother said, 'This is a Catholic church.' I was both frightened and curious—Swiss Protestants do not go into Catholic churches—broke away, ran to the open church, got one quick look at the flower-laden altar, then tripped on a step and hit my chin against a piece of iron. It was a big gash and bled profusely. I screamed, upset the congregation and felt a sense of guilt at being punished for some wrongdoing."

The last of the Sunday masses was long since over. St. Stephan's was warm and fragrant with the incense of the ceremonies. The two men walked about slowly, arm in arm. As they emerged into the cold March sunlight, the Platz filled with *Einspännern* and *Fiakern*, the horses eating from their bags of oats, Sigmund looked up at Carl Jung affectionately and asked:

"No fear and trepidation, no blood from the gash in your chin?"

Jung laughed in an easy way.

"No, you made me feel comfortable. The lovely things you said about the stained-glass windows and the stone carvings, the frescoes, the tombs, the comparisons with the cathedrals you've seen in Italy. It gave me a historical perspective. I began to see Catholic churches somewhat as you do: as repositories for some of the greatest art the world has produced." He glanced sideways at Sigmund, a mischievous glint in his eyes, said:

"Isn't it droll that you, as a broad-gauged Jew, should enable me, a provincial Calvinist Protestant, to confront *mater ecclesia* without a sense of guilt or oppression? If this is part of my analysis, I thank you, Revered Professor, for releasing me from the narrow fears and the repressions of my childhood."

"Isn't that the broadest road to freedom, the release from the fears and tyrannies imposed upon us before we were capable of judgment?"

"I would be obliged to agree," replied Carl Jung, suddenly gone very serious. "Again when I was six, my aunt took me to the Natural Museum in Basel to look at the animals. I was so fascinated that I could not tear myself away when the closing bell rang. As a consequence we were locked into the main building. We had to go out by a side wing; and there I saw beautiful displays of human figures who wore nothing but meager fig leaves. They were marvelous. I was enchanted by them. But my aunt shouted at me, 'Disgusting boy, shut your eyes!' She was as outraged as though she had been dragged through a pornographic exhibition. She did her best to persuade me that the human body, in particular the erogenous zone, was ugly, evil and dirty. It had never occurred to me that this might be true, and I fought it as best I could during my adolescence; but always shouting in my ear was my aunt's terrified voice, 'Disgusting boy, shut your eyes!' Well, Professor Freud, you opened my eyes and made me see that the erogenous zone was not diabolically inserted between the soft intestine and the thigh by Satan himself while God was napping. Either the entire human body, including the brain, the spirit, the soul and the reproductive organs are a masterful creation by God; or else it is a dirty and senseless structure and should be obliterated from an otherwise beautiful earth."

"Bravo! You have a felicity of phrase that I could envy. Now explain to me how you divine so many of your patients' ills."

"My therapy is active rather than receptive," Jung replied as they dug in their heels to slacken their pace down the Berggasse hill. "I am interested in the *action* that can take place in the patient, the action that will enable him to overthrow his problems. Even in the asylum it is not my practice to analyze the daytime fantasies of the dementia praecox patients so much as to create in those patients the opportunity to fight the fantasy back, to reply to it. A young man who was married and having serious troubles with his bride had a daytime fantasy: they were in a cold area and the lake had been frozen over and he could not skate, but his bride skated very well. He was standing on the bank watching her and suddenly the ice broke and she fell in. That was the end of the fantasy. I was very angry with this young man and said, 'Well, what did you do about it? Didn't you go out to save her? Did you just stand there and let her drown?' This is the concept, it seems to me, of how to meet these fantasies. You don't stop with the dream and dwell on it as such; you force your mind to make the next step. You force yourself to get into that lake and save her. *You finish the fantasy by doing something about it.* This is therapy!"

They settled into Sigmund's rear study in the *Parterre.* When the discussions got too hectic they moved first to the consultation room, then to the waiting room, needing some kind of physical movement to match the ferment of their minds. For Carl Jung had a bigness and openness of the psyche that corresponded to the bigness and openness of his physical stature. He said:

"Anything that men are willing to give their minds to, I am willing to give credence to, and put my mind to, to see if there is some element of truth. I know that you are not interested in spiritualism or parapsychology, but I want to have an affinity with the whole world instead of just a corner of it. In treating my patients I let them express their own peculiar content in the form of writing, painting, drawing. In this way they find their own symbolic expression and portray clearly their own pathology. After all, science is the art of creating suitable illusions. We help our patients wipe out destructive neuroses, and put in their place illusions with which they can live. Is it not life to paint the world with divine colors?"

Sigmund's mind went back to Wilhelm Fliess, to his almost hypnotic persuasiveness, yet he felt differently about Carl Jung. Fliess could not abide criticism. Jung was a man who called forth total honesty. Sigmund felt free to differ, dispute, set forth divergent views.

"Forgive me, Herr Doktor, if I do not get into a discussion of religion," Sigmund replied. "It is important, certainly, in what it has done to shape our beliefs and fantasies. The history of religion is that of shivering, frightened peoples who have attempted to put a roof over their heads against the night and the blackness and fears and terrors of the unknown. That is why man has invented God; how many gods since the beginning of time: hundreds? Perhaps thousands? All with different names, shapes, natures, powers. Admittedly, religion can tell us much about the present condition of the human psyche; but I haven't found any way to use religion as therapy, despite the old lady who simply wanted to read the Scriptures with you."

Carl Jung digested this intelligence soberly, but ended by shaking his head "No," then saying:

"Man is a dream in which he is repeatedly executed by hanging. After each death the voice calls out, 'The stillness increases.' What do we use for protection? For my own part, there is a mystical fool in me that has proved to be stronger than all of my science. I frequently have a dream which gives me great happiness: I am the last man on earth, around me there is a cosmic stillness and I laugh like a Homeric hero."

Sigmund smiled indulgently, then said: "I remember a line from one of your letters: 'No one can escape suffering. The best that we can do is to avoid blind suffering.' But there is no way to understand the abnormal, and treat it properly, until we have a thorough grasp of what is normal in human nature, and how all of our instincts got there, how deep they lie buried, which are constructive and which destructive; and what each human being needs to keep him on balance, functioning in a complex world in which greed, envy, jealousy, hatred, bitterness, disillusion, niggardliness of spirit and the will to destroy surrounds us all. How do we help man to achieve normal, human infelicity? By explaining scientifically how the human mind came to be what it is, what the forces were that shaped it, how we can control these forces within ourselves and within our society. In short, we have to know as much about the human mind as we do about the body: what makes the blood flow, what keeps the heart pumping, feeds oxygen to the brain, what antidotes can kill off viruses, infections, malignant growths."

At eight o'clock the maid brought them a light supper. They ate hungrily, for they had expended tremendous emotional and physical energy. When they had finished, they gathered up Mrs. Jung from the apartment upstairs and escorted her back to the hotel because she wanted to retire early. Then Sigmund took Carl Jung for his favorite walk around the Ring. The streets were quiet. Jung was fascinated by the multi-architecture, the Parliament, the museums, the Burgtheater, all the lines softened in the starlit night. Sigmund walked fast; although a slight figure alongside the powerful frame of Carl Jung, it was he who led the break-neck pace. The evening proved to be a nostalgic time for Jung, who wanted to share the confidence of his early youth with his new friend.

"I slept in my father's room for a number of years. My mother had had a breakdown and went to the hospital. When she came back she slept in her own room behind a locked door. From this door I sometimes heard frightening sounds. I knew of course that there were serious difficulties in my parents' relationship; and it would have been impossible for me not to know that my mother was disturbed emotionally and mentally. Do you suppose that is why, when I read Krafft-Ebing's book, *Psychiatry*, I was quite overwhelmed? I would not have been able to formulate it clearly then, but I felt I had touched a focus. That moment was the real origin of my career as a medical scientist. Would I have been equally receptive had I not experienced the devastating results of such psychiatric illness?"

"I think it must have influenced you. Judging by the men in the Wednesday Psychological circle who are beginning to practice psychoanalysis, I would say that we all grew up with neuroses with which we have had to come to terms."

Passing one of the churches which boomed ten o'clock, they returned to the Freud apartment where Martha was waiting to serve them hot chocolate.

At one in the morning Sigmund walked Jung to his hotel. When they shook hands good night, having been together and talking for thirteen solid hours, leaving out the time required to eat, Jung said softly:

"Revered Professor, you are the first man of real importance I have encountered. In my experience, up to this time, no one else can compare with you. There is nothing in the least trivial in your attitude. I have found you extremely intelligent, shrewd and altogether remarkable. And yet my first impressions of you remain somewhat tangled. I cannot yet make you out."

Sigmund reached up, put the fingertips of one hand gently on Carl Jung's shoulder and said, "My good Doctor, you will. Let us stay very close to each other in our minds and hearts. We need each other and we can fulfill each other."

As Sigmund entered their bedroom, Martha turned a shy smile to him and said:

"I've never seen you so engrossed. Is he as magnificent as he appears?"

Sigmund kissed her good night, holding his cheek against hers for a moment.

"Yes, I think perhaps the greatest I've ever met. But caution, caution, this is all too important to me. He could be the man for whom I've been searching for years to lead our movement."

7.

And still they came: The Men: as though impelled by some centripetal force: Alfred Adler's intimates from the Cafe Central, interested in learning whether they could use psychoanalysis for their social revolution; physicians working alone in outlying towns such as Guido Brecher

of Meran, who wrote, asking permission to attend; or simply knocked on
the door and introduced themselves. And of course the friends and relatives of the long-time members, such as Dr. Fritz Wittels, twenty-seven-
year-old nephew of Dr. Sadger, who was the author of several successful
novels, including *The Jeweler of Bagdad,* and was about to publish a
daring study called The Sexual Need. He had been trained in Wagner-
Jauregg's Psychiatric Clinic and wanted to read to the group his newly
completed paper, The Motives of Female Assassins, which indicated
that suppressed eroticism lay at the base of such murders.

Fritz Wittels was a natural for the group; yet Sigmund hesitated. His
uncle, Isidor Sadger, had the personality of an African thornbush; no
matter how slight the encounter, anyone who brushed against him came
away with an ugly scratch or welt. Nothing was known of his personal
life, which he kept a deep secret; he was a personality in distress who
struck back by causing distress to his intimates. Sigmund believed that
Sadger's problem was a rigidly suppressed homosexuality which seeped
out only in the penetrating papers Sadger wrote about deviates.

Could he take a chance on Fritz Wittels? The young man was arrogant,
thought himself superior to other doctors because he was a creative writer
as well, and had already earned the reputation of an *enfant terrible* in
other groups. Yet, like Wilhelm Stekel, he had charm and gusto, was
witty and a gifted physician. His provocative mind could be an asset to
the group; and again, as with Wilhelm Stekel, he was a prolific contributor
to Vienna's newspapers, with an audience not generally available to
Sigmund Freud. Sigmund decided that he could control the pyrotechnical young man.

Looking backwards is like walking backwards: you can get a good view
of what you have just passed but you are liable to bump into something behind you. Sigmund had spent a good many of his years looking
backward at *Homo sapiens'* childhood, deducing what went on at the
age of two, three, four and five from the conduct and free association of
the adults on his couch. He had never had an opportunity to study infants
or young children head on; assuredly not in his own nursery, where
Martha had made it explicit from the beginning that he was to be a
normal father to his brood of six, and was not to watch them or use their
play or chatter for research purposes. This had proven no hardship; for
Sigmund had not believed that young children could be analyzed. He
doubted in fact whether even a trained observer could get an accurate
portrait of what went on in their minds.

Now all of this was turned around for him in a dramatic fashion. One
of his friends in the Wednesday Evening group was thirty-three-year-old
Dr. Max Graf, an unlikely combination of graduate in jurisprudence who
also had his doctorate in music. The son of an editor and owner of a

printing house, he was the editor of the *Neues Wiener Journal*, wrote widely for Austrian newspapers on the subject of music, was professor of musicology at the Konservatorium, and had occasionally invited Sigmund and Martha to his home to hear quartets. He was an amiable man, sensitive without being an introvert.

Graf wore horned-rimmed spectacles with his sideburns chopped short, almost at the sidelines of the glasses; he had thinning hair at the brow, and a modest dimple in his chin. He liked to wear clothes with a very slight check in them so that he would be marked off from the businessmen of Vienna and be recognized as someone who lived, if not at the heart of the arts, at least on one of its more companionable fringes. He was fascinated by the group's discussions because of his training in philosophy.

Max Graf was married to a warmhearted wife who came with her husband to have late afternoon coffee with the Freuds. She had read several of Sigmund's books and eagerly awaited her husband's report on the Wednesday evening discussions. They had a son by the name of Hans, four and a half years old, a bright child who had grown anxious and depressed, developing a phobia about going out into the streets of Vienna for fear he would be bitten by a horse. His fear of horses became so great that he would no longer go with his nurse to the Stadtpark for his afternoon play or to Schönbrunn with his father on Sunday. Since Hans Graf had never been bitten by a horse, or hurt or frightened by one, with the exception of the time he was walking with his mother and saw a bus horse fall down and kick his legs about as though he were dying, there was evidently a neurotic cause for his disturbance.

Hans had also become obsessed with the idea that every living creature had a "widdler or a wee-wee-doer." When he was taken to the zoo he always looked first for the animals' organs. He continually questioned his mother about whether she had a penis or widdler. He described the cow's udder as a penis, and could not understand how milk came from it. When he had been three and a half and his sister Hannah was born, he watched her being bathed so that he could search for her widdler.

Sigmund told Max Graf that Hans "was faced with the great riddle of where babies come from," which is perhaps the first problem to engage a child's mental powers, and of which the riddle of the Theban Sphinx is probably no more than a distorted version. Hans had rejected the proffered solution of the stork having brought Hannah, for he had noticed that months before the baby's birth his mother's body had grown big, that then she had gone to bed, and when she got up she was thin again. He therefore inferred that Hannah had been inside his mother's body and had come out like a "lumf." He was able to imagine the act of giving birth as a pleasurable one by relating it to his own first feelings of pleasure in passing stool. He thus had a motive for wishing to have children of his own.

Hans would frequently cry when away from his mother because he wanted to be "coaxed," caressed by her; sometimes in the evening or early morning he would go into his mother's bedroom and tell her how much he was afraid he would lose her; and the mother would react sentimentally by taking the boy into bed and holding him close. It was a struggle on the part of both his mother and father to keep him from putting his hands on his penis. When his mother first found him playing with himself, just a little past the age of three, she made what, in Sigmund's estimate, was a serious mistake: she threatened that his penis would be cut off if he touched it. This had given rise to a strong castration fear and was at the base of a good deal of his anxiety, both waking and in dreams. However it was Max Graf rather than Sigmund Freud who came up with the starting point of the analysis. Max confided to Sigmund, when the boy's neurosis had reached its height:

"I think where his trouble lies is that he may have been frightened by a large penis, and the only place I can think of one large enough would be on the horses we see around the streets of Vienna. Does that give you something to go on, Professor?"

"Yes, Max, but first I think we ought to use a childlike method in dealing with a child. I suggest that you tell him that his fear about being bitten is a lot of nonsense; that he is using it as a substitute. What he really wants is to be taken into his mother's bed and be 'coaxed' by her; and I think you might begin to suggest very delicately that getting into his mother's bed is also tied up with his refusal to stop handling his penis."

Hans's father had given him some rudimentary explanation about the differences between male and female, and why females did not have a penis. For a time this seemed to dissolve Hans's anxiety, but now he fell into absolute terror if he were obliged to go out of the house. Graf begged Sigmund to undertake the case. They were afraid the phobia would seriously injure both the nervous and physical health of their son.

Sigmund took a daring step, the outcome of which he could not predict; not could he have made the attempt except with parents who were versed in psychoanalysis. He urged both Max Graf and his wife to tell Hans, slowly and gently, something about the nature of the Oedipal situation, and to explain that Hans's desire to be caressed by his mother was normal, as was his desire to replace his father. This came from Hans's story of how he had seen a horse fall down; in his mind the horse had become converted into his father, who was thrashing about and dying.

Hans listened carefully, seemed to absorb much of what was told to him. Though he was now only five, he quite resourcefully made the transition to where in his fantasy he could possess his mother and yet not destroy his father. The solution was revealed to Sigmund by Max Graf, who kept a record of the dialogue.

"April 30th. Seeing Hans playing with his imaginary children again, 'Hullo,' I said to him, 'are your children still alive? You know quite well a boy can't have any children.'

"Hans: 'I know. I was their Mummy before, now I'm their Daddy.'

"I: 'And who's the children's Mummy?'

"Hans: 'Why, Mummy, and you're their Granddaddy.'

"I: 'So then you'd like to be as big as me, and be married to Mummy, and then you'd like her to have children.'

"Hans: 'Yes, that's what I'd like. . . .'"

With this resolution Hans's fear of horses disappeared. He made no mention of horses biting him, and asked no more questions about "widdlers" or where babies came from. He was able to go out freely. His father reported to Sigmund that the boy was eating and sleeping well, that all manifestations of his phobia were gone. Sigmund replied with a grin that was halfway between bafflement and pride:

"Our little Oedipus has found a happier solution than that which is described by destiny. Instead of putting you, his father, out of the way, he has granted you the same happiness that he desires for himself. He has turned you into his grandfather, and he has been kind enough to let you marry your own mother. In his mind that is a perfect solution."

8.

When the heat of summer clamped down, Sigmund felt drained from the months of hard work, writing and publishing. He and Martha decided to make a change in their plans; instead of searching out a villa they decided to wander about Carinthia and the Dolomite Alps, staying at whatever pleasant hotels they happened upon. They found an agreeable spot at St. Christina, swimming in the lake, taking mountain trips and picking gentian. Sigmund came down with influenza, which proved to be a stubborn case. Early in September they moved on to Lake Ossiacher. Sigmund had thought he would make the journey to Sicily to see the Roman ruins there, but he decided not to risk his health to the sirocco which was reported blowing across Palermo and Syracuse. The only writing activity he enjoyed was his letters to Carl Jung, who was spending most of his time on the firing line, defending Sigmund Freud and his work. For his own peace of mind he told himself that Jung made a much more suitable propagandist because people found in Professor Freud's personality and his ideas something alien. He wrote Jung:

"To you all hearts are open. . . . People just don't want to be enlightened. That is why for the present they can't understand the simplest thing. Once they are ready for it, you will see they are capable of understanding the most complicated ideas. Until then there is nothing to be done but to go on working and to argue as little as possible. . . . Any young, fresh mind that turns up is bound to be on our side."

By the middle of September his energies began to revive. He decided that he wanted a week or two in Rome, by himself, to think slowly and quietly through some problems which had to be faced during the coming work year. Martha would take the children to Thalhof until the end of September. Tante Minna had also been ill, and had been for some time in Meran, under medical care. The family felt that a few days in Florence would revive her drooping spirits. By means of an exchange of telegrams Tante Minna met Sigmund on the train at Franzensfeste. In Florence, Sigmund took her to see the Benozzo Gozzoli frescoes in the Medici Chapel, and the next day for a carriage ride to Fiesole with its magnificent view of Florence. After lunch on an open terrace overlooking the valley of the Arno, they inspected the Etruscan sculptures and walls which the invading Roman armies had never been able to destroy; and then rode along the ridge of the hills to Settignano, where Michelangelo was raised.

Minna took the train back to Meran. Sigmund bought an inlaid cabinet and a small Tuscan mirror frame which he shipped to Martha, then caught the train to Orvieto, where he had an opportunity to renew his acquaintance with Signorelli's monumental frescoes in the Duomo, the painting he had remembered so vividly when he could not recall the artist's name, giving rise to his diagrammatic approach to the subject of symptomatic slips of the memory or tongue.

The Hotel Milano in Rome, at which he had first stayed with his brother Alexander, had reserved the same room for him. He spent a day in the Villa Borghese, visiting the castle and museum where he saw Titian's *Sacred and Profane Love*. The park reminded him of Schönbrunn with its wandering gazelles and pheasants. The next day he spent in the Baths of Diocletian which Michelangelo had converted into a church, Santa Maria degli Angeli, and the Monastery, to the rear of which was the National Museum which he loved for its Greek marbles. He prowled the antique shops, buying marble bowls, a Tuscan warrior and a Buddha. In the evenings he went into the Piazza Colonna near his hotel. There was a full moon in the clear sky, a military band played, lantern slides were projected, advertisements interspersed with scenes of nature, on the roof of a house at the other end of the square. He enjoyed walking alone among the crowds, observing that all Roman women were beautiful, even the ugly ones; watching the newsboys hurl themselves into the piazza every hour with another strident edition, even as the news vendors had in Paris; and then about eight o'clock, dropping into a wicker chair in front of a confectioner's shop to have a dessert and cool drink until it was time to retire to the hotel. He wrote to Martha:

"What a pity one can't live here always!"

He visited Christian and Jewish catacombs, got locked into one when the female guide suddenly realized that she had forgotten her keys. But this was his only misadventure. For the rest his mind began working alertly, making several decisions toward which he had been reaching for months. Now that Carl Jung was setting up a formal group in Zurich to be called the Freudian Association, it was time he redesigned his own Wednesday group and clarified its purpose. It was five years old and had served as a center for the dissemination of their growing knowledge. Nevertheless too few publications had come out of the group of twenty-odd who were now interested. The reason was clear: the scientific journals of mid-Europe were hostile to psychoanalysis. Even when they were neutral in their attitude, they simply did not have space for so young and disputed a science. The time had come, he decided while crossing the Piazza Venezia, to begin their own *Jahrbuch*, in which their people would have a medium for publishing their experimental papers. He got off a letter to Jung suggesting that this Yearbook should be designed and put into work as quickly as possible.

Then too, the Wednesday Evening group should graduate to a formal organization to be called the Vienna Psychoanalytic Society. They would elect officers, pay dues, finance the publication of the Yearbook and other books by their members. Before too long they could afford to build their own reference library, engage halls for public lectures and become an integral part of the German-speaking scientific world. Since the neurologists and psychologists were spending much of their time at their Congresses attacking Freudian theory, why would it not make good sense for the Freudians to have their own Congress, where a number of well-written papers could be read, based on specific cases which embodied their own documentary proof?

Why should they not make their presence felt?

BOOK THIRTEEN

A COMING TOGETHER

A Coming Together

FOR SIGMUND FREUD the new medical year opened on October first in the form of a bright advocate by the name of Lertzing, just short of thirty years old, who had by chance picked up a copy of *The Psychopathology of Everyday Life*. After six years of deep emotional disturbance, during which no physician had been able to help him, Lertzing thought he had at last found a doctor who understood how the human mind worked. He suffered from obsessional neuroses and, although he had become highly qualified in the handling of commercial law, had only recently been able to pass the final examination for criminal law because for years his obsessions had kept him from work.

Lertzing was a man of high intelligence and sound academic background. What was the power of a disciplined mind to overcome fantasy and delusion? Could the arduous training that had helped make him a lawyer conquer the obsessions that had bored into his unconscious and felled him?

Advocate Lertzing was a tall, lean, fair-complected young man with intense blue eyes and nervous gestures. In his first sentence he told Sigmund that the basis of his illness was recurrent fears of what would happen to the two most important people in his life, his father and the young woman with whom he had been in love for ten years. He constantly had to fight the impulse, when shaving, to cut his throat with the sharp razor. After volunteering these two bits of information, he then plunged into the history of his sexual life: there had been almost no masturbation except between his sixteenth and seventeenth years; he had not had intercourse until the age of twenty-six; he was frustrated by the lack of opportunity, since he felt a physical repugnance at lying with prostitutes. When Sigmund asked him why he laid so much stress on his sexual life during this first session, Lertzing replied:

"Professor Freud, I know about your theories. But I never made any connection between your sexual theory and my illness until I read your book."

Lertzing claimed his sexuality began between his fourth and fifth year, and took place with an attractive young governess whom he called by her family name, Fräulein Peter, rather than by the customary first name.

Sigmund noted with interest that the family name was also a man's name. On this particular afternoon Fräulein Peter was stretched out on a sofa wearing only a shift and reading. The boy had asked if he could creep under the skirt. She had agreed providing he would tell no one about it. Lertzing described how he had run his hands over the lower part of her body and her genitals, the structure of which had seemed strange to him. This created an overpowering desire to see the naked female form; he became a voyeur. For a considerable time he had been allowed to get into bed with Fräulein Peter, undress her and run his hands over her. He not unnaturally began having erections, the first of which he took to his mother to complain about how much it hurt.

He had no memory of what his mother had answered; but from that time he became obsessed with the idea that his parents knew everything he was thinking. The additional fear grew that he was speaking his thoughts out loud, and that he was the only one who could not hear them. His greatest anxiety at the moment was that his father might die. It was not until weeks later that Sigmund learned, through something Lertzing said, that his father had been dead for a good many years.

Lertzing's illness had been brought to a crisis during the military maneuvers in which he had participated as an officer the past summer. During a long day's march he had lost his glasses. Although he knew he could easily find them if he wanted to hold up the regiment, he decided against this. During a later halt he rested with two brother officers, one of them a captain whom Lertzing feared because he seemed to enjoy cruelty for its own sake. During this time the captain told Lertzing of a brutal punishment inflicted on prisoners. . . .

The patient sprang up from the sofa, pleaded not to be obliged to tell what the punishment was, nervously paced the room, his blue eyes darting about and becoming unfocused. Sigmund informed him that overcoming resistances was a major part of the treatment and that, since Lertzing had brought up this punishment himself without any urging or influence on the doctor's part, he would have to continue his story. Lertzing, pale and distraught, blurted out:

". . . a criminal was tied up . . . a pot was turned upside down on his buttocks . . . some rats were put into it . . . and they . . . bored their way into . . ."

He collapsed onto the sofa, unable to continue. Sigmund suggested: "Into his anus?"

Lertzing whispered, "Yes."

Sigmund noted that the expression on Lertzing's face was a combination of horror and pleasure. After a bit Lertzing added:

"At that moment the idea flashed through my mind that this was happening to persons who were very dear to me."

The individuals turned out to be his father, whom Lertzing still fantasied to be alive; and his long-time fiancée. The only way he could combat these now omnipresent images of the rats gnawing at the anuses of his father and his fiancée was by shaking his head violently and exclaiming to himself:

"Whatever are you thinking!"

Lertzing's obsession then became convoluted; the captain, whom he feared as a violent man, became a surrogate for his father. When the new glasses arrived at the post office near the military base, the captain delivered the package to Lertzing, telling him that their friend Lieutenant Nahl had paid 3.80 kronen at the post office for him. Lertzing told himself:

"You must pay back the money to Lieutenant Nahl."

But in Lertzing's mind this order became one that had been issued by his father; he was determined to pay the debt and yet at the same time even more determined not to pay back the money or his entire fantasy about the rats would come true with his father and the young woman he loved! The rats in the pot and the new eyeglasses became inseparably woven into his thought structure.

Among Lertzing's assorted guilts was the fact that he had fallen asleep somewhere around midnight in an adjoining room, and his father had died at one-thirty in the morning without the son being able to say farewell, in spite of the fact that the father had called out his name. He had become so obsessed with his guilt that he had had to abandon his legal studies. After a month of treatment, Sigmund decided that he could risk giving Lertzing his first clue. Toward the end of one of the hour sessions, he said to him:

"When there is a mésalliance between an affect and its ideational content (in this instance, between the intensity of the self-reproach and the occasion for it), a layman will say that the affect is too great for the occasion, that it is exaggerated, and that consequently the inference following from the self-reproach is false. . . . On the contrary, the physician says: 'No. The affect is justified. The sense of guilt is not in itself open to further criticism. But it belongs to some other content, which is unknown (unconscious), and which requires to be looked for. The known ideational content has only got into its actual position owing to a false connection. We are not used to feeling strong affects without their having any ideational content, and therefore if the content is missing, we seize as a substitute upon some other content which is in some way or other suitable."

The time had come for the distressed young man to start making discoveries of the unknown content of his mind. Sigmund added, "There are psychological differences between the conscious and the unconscious; everything conscious is subject to a process of wearing away, while what is unconscious is relatively unchangeable. It's this latter content that we must now try to get at." He explained also that, in psychoanalytical theory, "Every fear corresponds to a former wish which is now repressed." He suggested that a number of patients took genuine satisfaction from their sufferings and held back their own recovery. The suffering satisfies because it released unconscious guilt.

Advocate Lertzing began telling the story of how many times he had wished for his father's death, a good many of them in the latter years because he then would inherit enough money to marry the poor young girl he loved. He remembered the one time his father had given him a ferocious beating because he had bitten someone. After imparting this piece of intelligence, Lertzing said:

"Bite him. That's what rats do, isn't it? That's what I've been obsessed by, the image of rats biting their way up into the anus."

It was only after several months that a chance remark on the part of Lertzing enabled Sigmund to learn what had been the precipitating cause of the illness, six years before. His mother had announced that one of their wealthy cousins had agreed to have Lertzing marry one of his daughters, and was offering him a position in his firm which would make him an immediate success in the legal profession. Lertzing did not want to marry a girl whom he barely knew and did not love; yet the temptations of money and success were very strong. By falling ill with fantasies and obsessions he had been able to walk away from any need for a decision.

He now went through a complete transference: Dr. Sigmund Freud became the wealthy cousin who wanted to take him into the family; a young girl he had met on the lower steps at Berggasse 19 became Professor Freud's daughter. Dr. Freud was beleaguering him to marry this supposed daughter. He roundly abused Dr. Freud for tempting him to abandon his true love and to marry for money and position, something which in his mind was unthinkable. Then the doctor became his father, who was beating him on the buttocks. After that he became the father's surrogate, the sadistic captain. In all these transferences, including the one in which Dr. Freud became Fräulein Peter, Lertzing heaped reproaches, abuse, rage, vilifying names, tears, deep emotional outbursts, then protestations of love upon the doctor. The over-all effect was salutary; Lertzing heard these outpourings of his unconscious mind, and he was able to understand the character of his illness.

The problem now was to attempt to solve the obsession of the rats and the patient's anal eroticism. Lertzing had suffered almost continual irritation of the anus due to worms in his early years. When he was a little child, prior to his snuggling under Fräulein Peter's skirt, the family had called his tiny penis a worm. He had also come to associate rats with money, which was one of the preoccupations of the anal personality. When Dr. Freud had told him what his fee would be for an hour's treatment, Lertzing had said to himself, "So many florins, so many rats!"

During his father's service in the army, the older man had been known as a "playrat" for his gambling debts which he never managed to repay. The cruel captain's story coupled with the command to pay back the money debt for the eyeglasses had further tied rats and money together in his associations.

But more important was the inference of intercourse per anus. His revulsion against the army captain was in part a homosexual attraction. A good part of his illness had been devised to punish himself for this crime.

Lertzing required eleven months of daily sessions to thrash out every last piece of the childhood material that had lodged in his unconscious, and the fantasy-structure which had overtaken him with the rat obsession. The patient, who at first had shrunk from the pathological productions of his unconscious mind, opened his eyes wide and began taking a good long look at the fantasies, repressions and phobias which had taken possession of him. Now that the forgotten memories and conflicts had broken into the conscious, he understood that his father was irrevocably dead; that he had committed no crimes against him; that his obsessions resulted from experiences in his childhood years over which he could have had little control, and had long since forgotten.

Once Advocate Lertzing was rid of his rat phobia, Sigmund was able to pronounce him cured. The advocate resumed his practice of law, including criminal cases. Before Sigmund dismissed him he asked for consent to publish the case, assuring Lertzing that his identity would be totally concealed. Lertzing agreed.

Sigmund set a time for the following summer when he would have the freedom to write.

2.

Karl Abraham arrived from Berlin in mid-December of 1907 to spend a full Sunday with Sigmund Freud, even as had Carl Jung some nine months before. Sigmund welcomed Abraham heartily, for he had received several letters from the thirty-year-old doctor, assuring Sigmund that Abraham thought of him as his teacher. Although veneration shone from Karl Abraham's clear candid eyes, he was basically a reserved man and by nature a listener. Carl Jung had talked up a storm through the first three hours of his visit; Karl Abraham obviously wanted to listen for the three full hours, or perhaps the three full days he had in Vienna. He was a medium-sized man, built compactly, with a big open, honest face and gentle eyes that looked out with untroubled optimism on a complex world. He was clean-shaven, with a modest mustache, hair close-cropped except in the center, short sideburns; he was formally and handsomely dressed in a black suit and tie, with cuff links showing in the immaculate white cuffs. He wore a wedding ring on his right hand.

"You've made a permanent decision, then, to leave the world of the institutions?" Sigmund asked, after Martha had come in to be introduced and had had the maid serve them coffee.

"Yes, Professor Freud. I put in four years at the Berlin Municipal Mental Hospital at Dalldorf, even though I went there without any basic interest in psychiatry. My background has been very much the same as yours: I spent my early years being trained in histology, pathology and brain anatomy. But after working in mental institutions for a time I began to become interested in the patients themselves. We had absolutely no understanding of what was going on inside their brains or nervous systems. Nor was there any desire to learn. It was custodial work, really. That's why I wrote to Professor Eugen Bleuler at the Burghölzli; I had read some of their material and come to the conclusion that they were searching for causes. It seemed to me to be the most open-minded mental hospital in Europe. I became engaged on the basis of that appointment, and two years later, when Carl Jung recommended to Bleuler that I become his Assistant, I went back to Berlin to be married and brought my bride to live in an apartment about ten minutes from the Burghölzli."

Sigmund smiled as the picture of his and Martha's first apartment in the *Sühnhaus* flashed into his mind; and of how his sister Rosa had bought the heavy, carved mahogany furniture.

"I chose the right place," Karl Abraham continued in his serious well-modulated voice, "but for the wrong reasons. I did learn a great deal about dementia praecox from Bleuler and Jung, and from my three years of observation of patients. However my good fortune at the Burghölzli turned out to be something quite different: I met Professor Sigmund Freud and his studies of the unconscious mind. Both Bleuler and Jung encouraged me to read your books. For a period of almost two years we spent our late afternoon tea hour, when the doctors collected for relaxation, discussing your theories and relating them to our patients."

"Now you have opened an office in Berlin and are going to become the first psychoanalyst in Germany?"

"Yes. I know it will be difficult in the beginning, as we have no money except what I can earn. The usual fate of the young doctor, no? I am determined to become known as a Freudian psychoanalyst; though for a few years I may have to practice psychiatry as well. Dr. Hermann Oppenheim, who owns a private sanatorium, is a cousin by marriage; he is going to let me work one day a week in the outpatient clinic. Oh, not through psychoanalysis, he made that quite clear! But I have other friends in the medical world who I think will refer cases." He looked up at Sigmund with a shy smile. "Though not until every other form of treatment has proved hopeless! With your permission I shall form a Psycho-analytic Society and hold meetings in my home in Berlin, as you have held them here for the past five years."

Sigmund gave his hearty approval, then said, "If I describe you as my pupil and disciple, you don't strike me as a man who would be ashamed of this, then I can take actual steps on your behalf. Frequently patients need help in Germany, and I have had no one to whom I may refer them. Now I will have you."

Karl Abraham was a man of a sunny and tranquil disposition. As far as Sigmund could perceive there were no pockets of anxiety, confusion or withdrawal. He believed that if a man were patient he could persuade fate to behave in a rational manner. This came out when Sigmund tried to forewarn Abraham of the antagonisms and repudiations he would face. Abraham listened quietly while Sigmund recapitulated his own stormy years, then replied in a self-assured tone:

"In spite of the opposition and enemies and attacks—I have read much of the abuse heaped upon you in the Psychiatric Congresses and the press —I still believe that if I can sit down and reason quietly with the most violent of these attackers in Berlin we can probably reach some middle ground of agreement."

They spent the next hours, until Martha summoned them to dinner with the family, going through a number of Sigmund's case histories and the methods he had used. It was apparent to Sigmund that Karl Abraham, who had never been in private practice, would have benefited from several months of analytical training, but the subject never even came up. Abraham could remain only through the Wednesday Evening meeting and then had to return to Berlin. He was highly perceptive and absorbed insights from what, in effect, Sigmund turned into a seminar.

The basis for Abraham's sanguine attitude towards life, Sigmund discovered, as they bundled up in overcoats and big woolen scarves against the December cold, to walk for an hour along the Donau Kanal, with the winter-bare Vienna Woods etched sharply on the horizon, was that he was one of those rare young men who had lived an almost completely happy childhood. His father had been a teacher of Hebrew in the old Hanseatic League town of Bremen. After twelve years he had fallen in love with a cousin, whose parents did not favor the match because they knew that teachers earned modest wages. Abraham's father had then become a wholesale merchant, somewhat in the fashion of Jakob Freud. Karl's older brother had not been well and could not indulge in sports, so Karl had been mildly restrained, but managed to find his joy in swimming and mountain climbing with a young uncle for a companion. During his *Gymnasium* years he was fascinated by languages and philology, and at the age of fifteen had written a small book on comparative language study, with a chapter on the word "father" in three hundred and twenty languages. He had taken great pride in perfecting his Latin and Greek; by the time he reached the university he could also read and speak English, Spanish and Italian. Just as Carl Jung, who had wanted to become an archaeologist, had been forced to decide against it because there was no Chair of Archaeology in Zurich, so Karl Abraham, who wanted to become a teacher in the history of languages, had had to forgo that ambition because there was no university in Bremen and no chair in the other German universities to which he could sensibly aspire. His family wanted him to become a dentist. However after one semester at Würzburg University in southern Germany he returned home to inform his parents that he was going to become a medical doctor. He transferred to Freiburg University, where he came under the influence of a young professor who specialized in histology and embryology. He then moved on to Berlin where he would have an opportunity to do brain anatomy. That was the road which had led him to Berggasse 19.

Sigmund invited Abraham back for supper on Monday evening and again on Wednesday before the group was to meet. He found him a lovable man, as did Martha and the children; he inspired trust. Sigmund commented to Martha when she waited up for him on Monday evening:

"I think that Karl Abraham is a man of integrity. I don't mean only in his personal relationships, but in his scientific work as well. He has deep insights; although he has practiced no psychoanalysis, he has a strong grasp on the nature and working of the unconscious. I think he is going to be so scrupulous in his treatment of patients and in his presentation of materials that he will earn the respect of Berlin. I doubt if we could have found a better man to begin the psychoanalytical movement in Germany."

For Wednesday evening, because he would be presenting Karl Abraham to a dozen of the regulars, Sigmund had suggested that no paper be read but that they turn the discussion toward Abraham's lecture *On the Significance of Sexual Trauma in Childhood for the Symptomatology of Dementia Praecox* which he had given as a paper before the German Society for Psychiatry at Frankfurt the previous April, and which had recently been published in a medical journal. When they came to the subject of sexual enlightenment there was a spirited argument about what was the proper age, and what kind of sexual and anatomical knowledge to give to children, and in which stages of their development. Karl Abraham listened intently; he was much too reserved in front of such a large group of strangers to offer anything but brief comments.

Abraham had mentioned the interest in archaeology and Egyptology which he had shared with Carl Jung at the Burghölzli. Before he left on Wednesday evening, Sigmund took two small Egyptian statuettes which he had bought in Rome the summer before and put them into Abraham's battered briefcase without the younger man's knowing it. They parted as friends. There had been only one disquieting moment, and that had come when Sigmund spoke with high regard of Carl Jung. Abraham too praised Jung's skill as a psychiatrist and his uses of psychoanalysis for therapy at the Burghölzli, but then he said in a low tone:

"I am sure you must know by now that Jung cannot accept in toto your concept of the sexual etiology of the neuroses."

"Yes, he spoke of the many other possible causes of neurosis. But I feel confident that he will come around; in the meanwhile he is one of our greatest possible assets to the movement. Don't you agree?"

Abraham turned his face just a fraction of an inch from Sigmund's direct gaze; it was the first time that he had done this. Sigmund was puzzled. Seeing his expression, Karl Abraham said:

"Carl Jung and I were very close during the two years that I lived as a bachelor at the Burghölzli. We had dinner together nearly every day, and many wonderful discussions. Then, when I returned with my wife, the Jungs invited us to their home and were most friendly. I had to leave our apartment a little after six each morning, and I rarely finished a day before seven or eight at night. Frau Jung used to call on my wife quite frequently, knowing that she was alone in Zurich and had neither friends nor relatives there. It was a very happy relationship . . ."

Karl Abraham shook his head in perplexity. "Then something happened. We never found out what. She stopped calling on my wife. Nor were we again invited to their home for evenings. Frau Jung did call when my daughter Hilda was born, and was helpful. But then the relationship terminated. I never detected any difference in Jung's attitude while we worked together at the hospital. But the close friendship that had existed between us for more than two years was gone. Perhaps this was another factor in my determination to leave Zurich. My wife was lonely, and there was literally no place for me to go at the Burghölzli. Professor Bleuler would surely remain the head of the hospital for years to come. We decided to return to Berlin where my wife's family lives and to start private practice."

"How very strange! Carl Jung has nobility of heart and mind. Assuredly he is the man to lead our movement in Switzerland. As you know, since you participated in the first discussions of the Zurich Psychoanalytic Society, as many as twenty doctors have attended the meetings . . ."

Abraham's sensitive face was flushed.

"Please believe me, Professor Freud, I am extremely hesitant to speak about personal or family affairs. To the best of my knowledge I have no enemies in this world; and I think ill of no man. But you asked; and I thought it better that you be forewarned."

3.

And still the men came, with a greater frequency now, and from different parts of the earth. Some had been communicating with Sigmund for a year or two, telling of their enthusiasm, asking hard-bitten questions about psychoanalytical techniques. Sigmund answered them all, at considerable length, for he considered them pupils who happened to live too far away to attend his Wednesday Evenings or his Saturday night lectures at the University of Vienna.

Dr. Maximilian Steiner was a valuable addition to the group and quickly earned a warm spot in Sigmund's heart. Born in Hungary, he had taken his medical degree at the University of Vienna, becoming a specialist in venereal and other skin diseases. Since there was a plethora of these disturbances in Vienna, Dr. Steiner had a large practice. He had joined the group in 1907; by the beginning of the following year he had watched Sigmund with enough of the younger and poorer men to hatch a plan of his own. One Wednesday evening he asked Sigmund if he might speak to him privately after the meeting was over. Though only eight years younger than Sigmund, he treated him with the utmost deference.

"Professor Freud, I've learned that you are helping our younger doctors when they begin their practice of psychoanalysis. That is good of you; but I do not think the burden should rest solely on your shoulders. As you know, I earn a very substantial income. I've put a few hundred kronen in this envelope. May I please place it in your desk drawer, and add a similar amount each month? I'll never miss it, and it will be there whenever you see a member in distress. I think there are others who might like to help, in a modest way."

Sigmund reached for Steiner's hand, deeply touched at the generous gesture.

When Sandor Ferenczi first walked into the apartment Sigmund exclaimed to himself, "There is a well-rounded man!" He was short, just a little over five feet, with a round head, a round face, a round stomach and a round backside. Despite the fact that physically he was on the flabby side, he was agile, constantly in motion; the very act of talking seemed to be a total physical, nervous, emotional and mental commitment. He also managed the miracle of being ugly and attractive at alternate moments.

Sandor Ferenczi, thirty-four, was the fifth son in a family of eleven boys and girls. His father owned a prosperous bookstore and lending library in the town of Miskolc, ninety miles from Budapest. His father had also published a resistance newspaper for which the Austrians had put him in jail for a short time as being an excessively patriotic Hungarian. Connected with the bookstore was an artists' bureau through which musicians and other performers were engaged for the town, as a consequence of which the Ferenczi family had a wide circle among writers, musicians and painters. As one of the middle children, and something of an ugly duckling, Sandor very soon learned that he had to compete for attention. Instead of doing so aggressively he eagerly sought the love of those older than he, while at the same time serving as an ardent protector and champion of the younger ones. The children were raised as much in the bookstore as in the home. Sandor grew up absorbing the new volumes as they reached the family shop. Like Otto Rank, Alfred Adler and all of the other young men who had come into Sigmund's circle, he was an omnivorous reader. After passing his *Matura* in the *Gymnasium* in Miskolc he chose the Vienna Medical School as the best in Europe, received his medical degree in 1896 with the evaluation of *Genügend*, sufficiently good; for he had spent considerable time during the years writing sentimental poetry and attending the daily concerts which Vienna afforded. He did his year of military service and sometime before the turn of the century returned to Budapest to set up a practice in neurology.

In Budapest he served in the Municipal Hospital, where he was put to work in the female wards for emergencies, many of which were attempted suicides. Another of his duties was to examine the Budapest prostitutes for gonorrhea and syphilis. He took a room in the Hotel Royal where he lived for many years, spending his spare hours and evenings at the coffeehouse next door, part of a permanent round table reserved for the artists, writers and musicians. Ferenczi became friends with the editors of a medical journal, began writing reviews of medical books and then articles, and finally case reports on what he called borderline situations between medicine and psychiatry.

"At the outset I have to confess my single greatest idiocy, Herr Professor. The editor of the medical journal gave me your *Interpretation of Dreams* to review. I read perhaps twenty or thirty pages, decided it was dull stuff, and returned the copy, saying I didn't want to bother writing a review. It wasn't until several years later, when I read Carl Jung's praise of your book, that I bought a copy. That day proved to be the turning point in my life." He threw his arms out wide.

"*But*, Herr Professor, that opening chapter! Where for a hundred pages you quote what other psychologists have thought about dreams, only to prove them wrong because they had never heard of the unconscious mind! Were it not a criminal act, I would go around to every bookstore and tear out that chapter with my bare hands!"

Sigmund laughed, and made a mental note to tell Martha how right she had been.

"It's my fate in life, Ferenczi, to want to be an exact scientist. But we have finally sold out the first printing. I am revising the text now for a second edition. I have received literally hundreds of letters from physicians and laymen alike, recounting specimen dreams which bear out the theses of my book. I am incorporating a number of them in an expanded version."

Ferenczi enjoyed his bachelor life, going about to the small Budapest restaurants with his friends, eating, drinking vintage Tokay wine, listening to gypsy music. He became chief neurologist for the Elizabeth Poorhouse, and by 1905 had sufficiently distinguished himself to be appointed psychiatric expert to the Royal Court of Justice.

In his overwhelming desire to be loved, Ferenczi gave of his interest and devotion to the problems of everyone about him: the waiters, the clerks, male and female, in the shops where he traded, the government employees connected with the courts and the hospitals. By the time he reached Sigmund Freud he was already becoming known as "Budapest's doctor." All doctors were called Herr Doktor, but not Ferenczi; he was called plain Doktor, an impossible title. He had two outstanding talents: the ability to free people to talk about themselves; and the intuitive wisdom to pierce to the heart of their problem. He was a charming companion, full of laughter, with a childlike quality which apparently went back to his earliest need to be loved and to be recognized in the welter of brothers and sisters surrounding him.   ·

In 1906 Ferenczi had heard about Carl Jung's experiments in Zurich, the word-association tests and the work which indicated that emotional reaction could be measured with a stopwatch.

"During my stopwatch experiments," he laughed, "no one in Budapest was safe, not even the cloakroom people."

Ferenczi had written a couple of weeks earlier, asking if he might be received in Vienna:

"It is not only because I am very eager to meet you, Herr Professor, since I have been occupied uninterruptedly for about a year in studying your work, but also because I promise myself much useful and instructive help from this meeting. . . . I am going to represent the whole complex of your discoveries before a medical audience which is in part wholly ignorant and in part erroneously informed on the subject. . . ."

Sigmund found within the hour that Ferenczi had absorbed the books so thoroughly, and his fertile mind had reached out so far in the direction of their implications, that already he had moved down paths and tested theories on patients which further documented Sigmund's theses and in a significant way were an extension of the original ideas.

It was a case of love at first sight. Ferenczi was seventeen years the younger, just about the right age to enable Sigmund to think of him as the kind of adoring young son who comes into a father's profession and slowly takes the burdens off the older man's shoulders, a similar relation-ship to the one he had enjoyed for so many years with Josef Breuer. The two men launched into the structure of Ferenczi's coming lecture, which would introduce psychoanalysis to the medical world of Hungary. Sig-mund found that Ferenczi already had the entire lecture laid out in his mind, beginning with the premises in *Three Essays on the Theory of Sexuality.* Ferenczi asked Sigmund to take him through the therapeutic techniques on his last dozen patients to indicate the beautiful intellectual work behind free association; the widespread and ingenious resources of repression; the significance of the patient's flight from unconscious mate-rials such as the Oedipal situation; the value of transference, the point where the doctor becomes someone whom the patient had loved, or with whom he had had difficulties many years before, and is thus able to make the voyage backwards through the dark seas.

Sigmund found him to be remarkable in his powers of assimilation.

Sandor Ferenczi asked for help in his own procedures. He was now treating three cases of impotence. The first was a thirty-two-year-old who told the doctor, "All my life I have been unable to perform the sexual act satisfactorily. Inadequate erections and premature ejaculation have made cohabitation impossible for me. Now I have met a young girl whom I want to marry."

A physical examination had shown nothing wrong organically; nor did free association bring out anything more illuminating than the fact that he was unable to urinate in the presence of other men. Ferenczi then turned to the patient's dreams and, using Freudian methods, worked his way back to the cause of the disturbance. When the patient was three or four years old he was often cared for by a sister ten years older than him-self who was fat (this image had emerged from his dreams as a two-hundred-pound faceless figure which unnerved him and made him awaken filled with anxiety and dread) and who let her little brother "ride on her naked leg." As the sister grew older she refused the boy's request for this play, admonishing him; it was his sense of guilt about incestuous love that rendered him impotent.

The second case was a forty-year-old cardiac patient suffering nervous impotence, who was able to relate through free association the story of his sexual attraction to his now dead stepmother which had resulted because she had allowed him to sleep in her bed until he was ten years old, and in other playful ways had encouraged his erotic attachment to her. The third one was rather simpler, a twenty-eight-year-old suffering from impotence because of an Oedipal situation and recurring hostile fantasies, both waking and dreaming, against his father. Ferenczi had been able to help all three of the men, though in varying degrees. He said:

"Herr Professor, I have come to a conclusion based on these three cases. I wrote down the material. May I read it to you?"

Sigmund sat back in his big leather chair, lighted a cigar and puffed on it contentedly, pleased to find that he had a pupil, advocate, follower and practitioner already going full blast in Budapest. Ferenczi lisped a bit with his *s*'s, but his darkish blue eyes behind the pince-nez glasses were enormously alive, almost an erupting volcano in the series of speculative flights, hypotheses and challenging ideas which transformed him into a glowing personality.

"Male psychosexual impotence is always a single manifestation of a psychoneurosis, and accords with Freud's conception of the genesis of psychoneurotic symptoms. Thus it is always the symbolic expression of repressed memory-traces of infantile sexual experiences, of unconscious wishes striving for repetition of these, and of the mental conflicts provoked in this way. These memory-traces and wish-impulses in sexual impotence are always of such a kind . . . as to be incompatible with the conscious thought of adult civilized human beings. The sexual inhibition is thus an interdiction on the part of the unconscious, which becomes extended to sexual gratification altogether."

During dinner Ferenczi captured the hearts of the Freud children. He had the capacity to reach out and engulf them with affection, laced with a playful mélange of stories, anecdotes, fairy tales. The children were sorry when Sigmund took him away for a long walk. Though he was half a head shorter than Sigmund, and his only exercise had been walking to the coffeehouse in the evenings after his day's work in the hospital and the court, Ferenczi nevertheless managed to keep up by taking two quick steps to each of Sigmund's long driven strides. The younger man saw by now that he had been accepted.

"I wish I could settle here in Vienna and be near you. I need education, training, advice . . ."

"No, no, you must remain in Budapest. You will create a psychoanalytical movement there. It is invaluable for us to have you in Budapest."

"But I may consider myself a part of your Psychological Wednesday Society? Quite frankly I need to belong to something. You can see in my nature the need to belong."

Sigmund took a shrewd sideward glance at Sandor Ferenczi, said, "Yes, but it works to your advantage. You give more of yourself. You will have your own group. Watch the men you work with and to whom you lecture. Within a year or two you should be able to form a Budapest Psychoanalytic Society."

"I want to give up neurology, and also my position as psychiatrist in the courts. But I will need six or seven analytical patients before then, if I want to concentrate. Don't you think this is right?"

"I can't say, because you've told me little of your private affairs. Apparently you enjoy the bachelor life?"

Ferenczi flushed, slackened his pace so that Sigmund was obliged to slow down, and then said, lisping a little more than usual:

"I have a permanent love affair with Gisela Palos. She comes from my home town of Miskolc. She is a few years older than I am, has two daughters, and is separated from her husband, who refuses to give her a divorce. I admired her in Miskolc as a youth and now I love her. She is comfortably fixed and so there are no money problems. We have not talked about marriage; she can have no more children, and I dread growing old without young children around me. Our arrangement is satisfactory to both of us, and that leaves me the free years to study and wait for enough of the right cases to become a psychoanalyst.

"But there is another matter I wanted to suggest." He ran a step or two ahead of Sigmund so that he could turn at a sharp angle and see his entire face. "I myself need analysis. I am a fearful hypochondriac. If I can clear the time to come to you every two or three months, let's say for a week or two, will you analyze me so that I can achieve objectivity, and not be trapped anywhere along the line by my patients getting me involved in their own subterfuges?"

"Yes, come as often as you like. I will give you whatever spare hours I have. We will walk the streets of Vienna and we will talk about why you cannot analyze your own hypochondria. Do you not have other hypochondriacal patients in your office?"

"Yes, several, and sometimes I manage to get at the base of their disturbances. But I cannot do it with myself. You had to complete your self-analysis to continue your work; but you also had to do the job alone because there was no one ahead of you. For me there is Sigmund Freud."

Sigmund felt a warmth spread through him, a glowing gratification.

"I have an idea. We always rent a place in the mountains for the summer. Why not join us for a couple of weeks? Before we left the house, Frau Professor Freud said to me, 'Your young Dr. Ferenczi is an endearing soul, is he not?' I find that true. Come to us for a vacation, then we can wander the woods and swim in the lake and climb high mountains . . ."

4.

It was pleasant for Martha to have Rosa living just across the hall. While both families maintained their privacy, the friendship between the Grafs and the Freuds deepened. Martha had little time for making new friends with Sigmund bringing in the foreign doctors who showed up with increasing frequency, and his colleagues for dinner or supper nearly every day; some, like Otto Rank, becoming family. Martha did all her own shopping at a market on Nussdorfer Strasse, not even taking a maid to trail behind her in the hallowed Vienna tradition. She shopped cautiously, buying the finest meats, vegetables and dairy products at the best possible price; for although Tante Minna jokingly referred to the Freud board as the "Psychoanalytical Commissary," Sigmund's income was still irregular and modest. Martha managed shrewdly in order to make her week's *Haushaltsgeld* last through Sunday, when she frequently had to go through the back door of a grocery store, the law said they had to be closed on Sunday, to buy additional food for guests who showed up unannounced at ten o'clock on Sunday mornings to discuss a case and whom Sigmund would invite to stay for dinner. Hardly a day went by that she did not have from one to five of Sigmund's colleagues at her family board; it was a tribute to the basic goodness of her nature that all felt wanted.

"No woman ever better earned the title of Frau Professor," Rosa commented; "my Heinrich's clientele is growing by leaps and bounds, as you know. His office is filled all day with clients; yet he never brings any of them home. He says our few hours together are too precious to him."

"It's different, Rosa dear; Sigi's colleagues are his pupils and advocates, the men he is training to carry on his work."

Minna, who was fascinated by the colorful characters Sigmund brought to the family table, quipped, "He keeps up not only their moral courage but their physical stamina as well."

Since Heinrich Graf's only relatives in Vienna were a cousin and married niece he happily let himself be absorbed into the Freud circle, having the entire family for dinner one Sunday a month, going to Amalie's with the rest of the clan a second Sunday; and across the hall to Sigmund's and Martha's for a third. One Sunday morning in his long-time office on the Werdertorgasse where he had gone to complete a brief, Heinrich died suddenly of cerebral apoplexy. He was only fifty-six, an enormously vital, energetic man who had looked ten years younger than his age.

Sigmund, at the funeral, wondered if he should buy a plot here for Martha and himself, since Heinrich's totally unexpected death made it painfully clear that "all roads lead to the Central Cemetery."

Rosa was inconsolable and barely rational. Tremendous bouts of weeping overcame her, followed by agonized despair and demands for an explanation. "Why? Why my Heinrich? He was so well, so happy . . . we were all so happy together. Why did this have to happen to him? He never hurt anyone: he was a good man, a gentle loving man. Why does he have to be taken in the prime of his life? To leave me a widow, and his two children fatherless. It makes no sense! It's cruel. Now I'll be alone all the rest of my life . . ."

"That's not true, Rosa, you have your son and daughter, whom you love. You have to take this terrible blow bravely, for their sakes. They're frightened and unhappy."

Martha took ten-year-old Hermann and nine-year-old Caecilie to bunk with her older children. Tante Minna moved across the hall to be with Rosa during the night; for although Sigmund was giving her a tranquilizing drug she could not achieve sleep, and mourned through all the dark lonely hours. Minna soothed her, bathed her feverish face with cold washrags; tried to divert her. Nothing worked; Rosa seemed to grow more despondent each day. Sigmund worried about her health, her sanity, even her life. In one of her more rational moments she seized his hand and with tears streaming down her cheek, cried:

"Sigi, you'll be the children's guardian, won't you? I mean legally. You must promise to watch over them . . ."

"I will, Rosa, as though they were my own children."

"Another thing, Sigi, you must get me out of this apartment. It's too expensive. I must conserve Heinrich's resources for the children."

Sigmund put his arm protectively around her shoulder.

"Rosa, my dear, you have no money worries. Alex has seen the will; Heinrich died a rich man, according to our standards. Even when he signed it, back in 1904, there were a hundred thousand kronen in the estate."

". . . no . . . no . . . I must move. I can't bear to be here, where I see Heinrich's face in every corner. I must get away. Can you arrange with the landlord to terminate the lease? Minna said she would look for a smaller apartment for me."

"Rosa, you have just lost your husband. Why must you also inflict upon yourself the loss of your home? Please talk it over with Martha."

But Martha's efforts were also fruitless. Rosa insisted upon moving. A week after Heinrich's death, Sigmund told his wife:

"If Rosa is determined to move out, then we must help her. I have a solution for the lease problem; we'll simply take it over and I'll give up the *Parterre*. I've been wanting for a long time to avoid that up-and-down-the-staircase trip half a dozen times a day. We could use the two extra bedrooms on the street to give the children more space. We'll have a carpenter seal off the two front rooms, adding them to the family apartment. The three rooms at the rear would serve well for my offices. It will be far more convenient for everyone to have us all on the same floor."

His oldest daughter Mathilde, now twenty, came into his study one evening after supper, closed the door and locked it behind her. Sigmund was surprised; he could not remember one of his children having done this before. On her face was a worried look. Mathilde, as their first-born, had been a young mother to the little ones as they came along, not only caring for them in tender ways but serving as a confidante. By the time she was twelve, Sigmund had described her as a "complete little woman." In her childhood she had suffered three major illnesses. Oskar Rie had brought her through them all safely, but not without some depletion of strength and self-confidence. There had also been a badly performed appendicitis operation which had kept her down for months. She was now suffering from what Sigmund diagnosed as a floating kidney. He was not alarmed, but he had taken the precaution of making arrangements with a doctor friend in Meran for the girl to vacation there.

Mathilde was rather plain, with a broad flat facial structure more reminiscent of Tante Minna than of her mother. Perhaps because of the illnesses, her hair was lackluster. However she was a lovely human being; every thought and emotion was honest. She had done well at the girls' school, and during the four years since her graduation had continued her reading.

"Papa, I think I need a little help."

"That's a refreshing change, Mathilde, because for years I can remember coming to you for help, which you never denied me, by the way."

"I am anxious about this newest illness. Will it make things difficult for me . . . in marriage . . . ?"

"No, I don't think it's anything harmful. It will vanish within a month or two. But there is something else that is troubling you, isn't there?"

"Yes, Papa."

"I have sensed that you have been fretting yourself the past couple of years over the fact that you think you are not pretty enough to attract a husband. I have not taken this seriously, because you seem quite pretty to me."

Mathilde smiled wistfully, said in her low, pleasant voice:

"But you can't marry me, Papa, you're already married."

"Mathilde dear, let me make a suggestion: in families enjoying our social and material circumstances, girls don't marry young. Otherwise they grow old too soon. You know that your mother was twenty-five before we married. I have never told you this specifically, but it has always been my hope to keep you at home until you were at least twenty-four, till you had regained your full strength and would be prepared for the bearing of children and carrying on the frequently arduous duties of married life."

"It seems like such a long time, Papa, four years, and with nothing to do, not even any useful work around the house."

"I don't think it's the length of time that worries you. If you had confidence that you would find love and a husband, you would not worry so much."

"No, I wouldn't. That is the base of my uneasiness."

Sigmund rose, went to his oldest daughter and held her in his arms. "My dear girl, when you go back to your room, take a good look at yourself in the mirror. You are attractive. There is nothing common in your features. In reality, since I know men fairly well because of my profession, I can assure you that it is not sheer physical beauty which decides what will happen to a girl, but rather the impact of her entire personality. The young men I grew up with wanted their young women to be cheerful, gentle, with a talent for making their lives more beautiful. You have an emotional fluidity that does not always serve you well because it brings you too many ups and downs; however you come by it legitimately, for I suffered the same kind of neurosis when I was younger, and so did your Aunt Rosa. You must not let your Uncle Heinrich's death frighten you; no one is ever totally safe. That is why life has special flavor and meaning for us: we know it cannot go on forever.

"Someone whom you care for will love you as a human being, as all of us around you have. That you are Mathilde Freud shouldn't do you any harm either; men searching for a lifetime companion want a respected name, and look for a warm atmosphere in her home. You have always had confidence in my judgment. You have no reason to be downhearted. So go to Meran now, and stay there as long as Herr Dr. and Frau Raab remain, hopefully late into May."

Mathilde paled, said with a touch of hoarseness in her voice:

"I don't think I fantasy about this matter of spinsterhood; I have two models very close at hand that could give me cause to worry: Tante Minna and Tante Dolfi."

"Your Tante Minna is an intensely moral person. She gave her heart to Ignaz Schönberg when she was young. Most surely she could have married after Ignaz's death; but she believes that a woman is afforded only one love in her life, not more. It was a deliberate choice on her part."

"What about Tante Dolfi?"

Sigmund sighed, a privilege he rarely allowed himself within the bosom of his family.

"That is perhaps my fault and your Uncle Alex's. We did think about it, but with your Grandpa Jackob dead, and your other aunts married, someone was needed to take care of your grandmother. We assured Dolfi that she would always have everything she wanted. And so she has had . . . except a husband. But if at any time over the years Dolfi had brought home someone and said, 'This is the man I want to marry,' there would have been another family wedding. Every woman who genuinely wants a husband can find one. You genuinely want a husband, ergo . . . Does that syllogism make sense to you?"

"Yes, Papa, you always make sense. But you deal in universals, while lone individuals like myself have to deal in particulars, in this case a particular man."

"He will materialize: out of the air, the sea. It is a recurring miracle, my dear Mathilde, how the male and female of the species manage to make contact, sometimes under highly implausible circumstances."

Mathilde broke into a smile which transformed her plain face into a charming one.

"And I have your promise that I shall be married by the time I am twenty-four?"

"I promise. I am a prophet not only of people's pasts but of their futures as well."

Mathilde kissed him on both cheeks, her eyes bright with affection.

"Thank you, Papa. I must leave now before I overrun my hour."

5.

Martha and Minna found Rosa a small apartment close by and did all the work of settling her in. Then Sigmund arranged to move into her old one. The apartment was immaculate and did not need painting. First he had a carpenter install a door between the new apartment and the old flat so that he did not have to go into the public hallway any more; placed the hat and umbrella stand he and Martha had bought for their first apartment in the *Sühnhaus*, almost twenty-two years before, in the attractive foyer with its wood paneling and diffused light admitted from colored glass windows; then put up eighteen hooks for the Wednesday Evening group so that everyone would have a place to hang his coat. What had been Rosa's kitchen, just off the entrance hall, he converted into his waiting room with its oval table and leather chairs. The middle room became his medical office, the black couch now covered by a worn Persian rug, with a bolster and white pillow at its head, a blanket at the foot. Next to it, fitting just comfortably into the corner, under the bust of a Roman Emperor and framed mosaic fragments from Pompeii, was his own chair, at the same height as the bolster so that he could sit in back of the patient's head, where the patient could not see him. Between this consultation room and the waiting room he installed tightly fitted double doors, with heavy curtains on either side. Further to protect the patients' privacy he made another alteration so that the patient could leave his office without being seen by anyone in the waiting room.

The rear room he converted into his private study, covering the back wall completely with bookshelves, except for a space in the center where he had a five-shelf glass cabinet for his dozens of ancient figurines. The bookshelves were brought around the corner to the tall window overlooking the garden with its chestnut trees. He placed his writing desk at a right angle to the center of the window so that he could get all of the available light and warmth, so highly desirable in the Viennese winter. In the center of the room, the side wall of which contained several cases of antiques, he placed a chair for the patients with whom he wished to consult before agreeing to take their cases. In the event they might be embarrassed at the symptoms they would have to reveal, he placed a table between them and on it put a large seventh-century Chinese terra cotta figure, with a seated Egyptian on either side so that he could focus on these three sculptures and thus give the patient the freedom to talk.

In his office, in addition to his desk, he had a long wide table where he wrote his books and the articles for the scientific journals. He kept his manuscripts meticulously organized in leather folders which he closed at the end of each day's work. The back of the table was occupied by a tight-packed row of small figures not more than a foot high, some of them coming from early civilizations, the Hittite, Etruscan. On a smaller table, which formed a right angle to his desk and to which he could swing from the chair, he kept his correspondence, growing heavier day by day now that he was receiving letters from Jung, Abraham, Ferenczi and other young doctors who were becoming interested, describing their cases and asking for scientific guidance. The double doors between the middle office and his study were painted off-gray; the door from the waiting room to his office was upholstered in red, with brass buttons, conforming to the style of the Viennese doctors. The floors, a beautiful fishbone parquet, he covered with his Oriental rugs; but the ceilings, with their hanging gas lamps, were left in their original white to give the rooms the appearance of height. The waiting room was kept simple, as always, with a few very large framed pictures on the wall. However his other two rooms, from the moment he finished them, were crammed with the hundreds of antiques he had been buying over the years. There was very little space to walk around in either of the rooms, which now also housed his collection of ancient tools, miniature ox-drawn carts, clay and marble horses purchased at modest prices. A few feet beyond the couch was the tall, handsomely decorated ceramic stove which kept the room comfortable throughout the winter. One of the new telephones was installed in the outside hallway.

On the door of his new apartment he attached the plaque giving the hour during which he would consult with prospective patients.

Prof. Dr Freud

3-4

When Martha and Tante Minna came in to inspect the finished offices, Minna could not refrain from saying:

"Sigi, any time you want to give up the practice of medicine, you can operate an antique shop. You now have considerably more pieces than your dealer around the corner."

Sigmund smiled.

"I'm like a squirrel, hoarding nuts against the winter. But the more I am surrounded by these figures of the past, the better I am able to concentrate on the future."

The first meeting of his Wednesday Evening group in the new apartment was held on April 15, 1908. A round dozen members came, inspected the rooms, discussed how different the sculptures looked in the stronger light and set out more boldly on tables, desks and tops of cabinets. Each member had brought him a little gift to commemorate the opening of his new offices: a faun from Pompeii, a female Indian stone figure, a piece of Coptic vestment.

Sigmund proposed that in celebration of their new home they transform themselves into the Vienna Psychoanalytic Society, as he had planned the previous summer in Rome. There was hearty approval. Sigmund was elected president, Otto Rank secretary. Alfred Adler suggested they begin to collect a complete scientific library of all fields surrounding their subject. Modest dues were set, collected and recorded in a fresh notebook. Subscriptions were voted for several medical journals that hitherto had been available only at the university library. They agreed that their entire membership should attend the first Psychoanalytic Congress, in Salzburg, at the end of April, for which Carl Jung had already reserved rooms and made the necessary arrangements.

President Sigmund Freud introduced, as the subject for the evening's discussion, a lengthy questionnaire sent by Dr. Magnus Hirschfeld of Berlin on The Purpose of Exploring the Sex Instinct, the aim of which was to determine, from a medical point of view, what factors contributed to the sex life of both healthy and ill people. Each member agreed to answer the questions within his own frame of reference. If they were pleased with the final result they would collate the materials and perhaps publish it under the imprint of the Vienna Psychoanalytic Society, manifesting to the world that there was now an official body of psychoanalysts, just as there were psychiatrists, neurologists and psychologists.

At ten o'clock, when Martha and Minna brought in coffee and cake, Sigmund asked them to remain and help celebrate the birth of the Society.

Oskar Rie telephoned to Sigmund and refused to give the message when Sigmund, who hated the telephone and avoided it except in emergencies, would not respond. When Sigmund came on, Oskar said:

"The Ries and the Königsteins want you for supper on Sunday evening. That's Easter."

"In honor of what, Oskar? The Resurrection?"

The Ries had an old-fashioned, large apartment in the Stubenring. Oskar had taken the Freuds' advice to "get married, so you'll have a wife to give presents to," and married Melanie Bondy, and had their three children in quick succession. Now forty-four, he had just resigned from the Kassowitz Institute, where he had taken Sigmund's place as the head of the Department of Children's Paralyses, to give his full time to private practice, specializing in children's communicable diseases. Oskar had received *Genügend* marks all through Medical School; he was still "sufficiently good," the stable, conscientious, patient, plodding physician whom children trusted. He had never cared for research or to publish; his entire satisfaction came from the day-by-day effort to cure children of their illnesses.

Leopold Königstein, now fifty-eight, had received his honorary professorship a year before Sigmund, and had moved his *Dozentur* lectures from the Allgemeine Krankenhaus to the Polyclinic Hospital, where he continued to make significant advances in surgery on the eye. Leopold was the kind of man who grew handsome with age, even though his receding brow was a battlefield where a few straggling hairs were fighting to escape annihilation. His eyes, now that they had no mop of hair to compete with, had seemed to double in size and power.

"Come now," Sigmund cried. "I'm certain one of you has been made dean of the Medical Faculty."

After a gay, chattering meal, Oskar opened a bottle of champagne with a resounding pop.

"It was exactly ten years ago," said Königstein, "that we were walking home from the hospital together. I told you you were too much absorbed in your favorite hobby of the unconscious. In fact you mentioned this in your *Interpretation of Dreams*."

"How odd that you should remember, Leopold. I thought you didn't read my books."

"I didn't; but I do now. I've read them straight through, and with the utmost care. In the bosom of our three families, I should like to confess that you were right all along and I was wrong. As a sign of public contrition I should like your permission to join the Viennese delegation at the Salzburg meeting."

Sigmund flushed with pleasure. Oskar Rie puckered up his mouth in a repentant smile and said:

"Martha, remember that liqueur I brought you for your birthday when you were summering in Bellevue; that bottle that smelled like fusel oil? That incident is also in *The Interpretation of Dreams*. Sigmund, I still smell that fusel oil when I remember how I reacted to the manuscript you showed me on the sexual etiology of the neuroses. I read a page or two, handed the manuscript back to you and said, 'There's nothing in that.' That was at Kassowitz Institute thirteen years ago. Well, I was wrong. There's a great deal in that. I can't get away for the meeting in Salzburg, but I would like you to propose me for membership in the Vienna Psychoanalytic Society in the fall."

"Well, well," murmured Martha as she went to Leopold and Oskar and kissed each of them on the cheek, "there is more joy in heaven over one sinner that repenteth . . ."

6.

He arrived in Salzburg early of a Sunday morning, went directly to the Hotel Bristol in the wide, flower-ringed Makartplatz, bathed, changed his clothes and returned to the lobby. Two men were standing at the registration desk; they exchanged a comment, and smiled at him. Though he did not recognize either of the men, he assumed from the steadfastness of their gaze that they had come for the meeting. He walked to them, put out his hand.

"Freud, Vienna."

"Jones, London."

"Brill, New York."

"Gentlemen, have you had breakfast? Even so, would you join me for coffee?"

"We'd be delighted."

They went into a small dining room that was reserved for the few guests who did not choose to have breakfast in their rooms. All three started talking at once and all in English, Sigmund in a somewhat literary manner since he had learned the language mainly from reading; Jones with a faintly lingering Welsh accent, and Brill with a slight German accent. They were young, Jones only twenty-nine, Brill thirty-three; both had come down from Zurich, where they had been working with Eugen Bleuler and Carl Jung, a day ahead of the Swiss group which Sigmund was delighted to learn would include not only Bleuler and Jung but Max Eitingon, to whom Sigmund had given what amounted to the first training analysis; Franz Riklin, Hans Bertschinger, and Edouard Claparède of Geneva, the first doctor in that city to become interested in psychoanalysis.

After breakfast Sigmund asked Jones and Brill if they would like a walk.

"I'd like to get the kinks out of my legs after those hours in the train compartment."

"It will give us a chance to compare the neuroses of Vienna, London and New York," said Brill.

They crossed the Makart, filled with Salzburgian families dressed in their Sunday best and headed for the church; the city had been the see of the bishop-princes for well over a thousand years. Then they made their way in the clear, sunlit air to the Mirabell Gardens, from which they had a superb view over the spires and churches of the Old Town to the staggering stone fortress which crowned the mountain peak across the river.

Sigmund turned to Ernest Jones and thanked him for first suggesting this meeting to Carl Jung, who had then done the organizational work necessary to bring forty-two men from six countries together.

"It is an historic occasion," said Jones; "that is why I wanted to call it the International Psychoanalytic Congress."

"Next year, if this meeting is a success. Now please do tell me about the road that brought you to psychoanalysis."

They moved on to the Old Town, with its narrow curving streets and colorful shopwindows. Ernest Jones walked between Sigmund and Brill, a little man, only a couple of inches above five feet, with a heroic head built for a man much taller and heavier, yet somehow not out of proportion.

"I should like to have been taller," he said with a wry grin; "but I accept the inevitable. By way of compensation, I have become a Napoleon buff."

Like most small men, he dressed himself elegantly, and would allow no one to select any article of apparel for him, not even a necktie.

His hair was as fine as silk, a bright brown in color; his eyes large, dark brown, perceptive. Yet his outstanding characteristic was his pallor, the result of a minor blood disease he suffered from childhood. He also had dark, strongly arched eyebrows which enhanced the pallor. Into the strong face was built an imposing Roman nose, ears slotted low on the head, and a silky mustache. As for his mouth, whenever Ernest Jones had used his mordant wit on a member of the family, his mother would point to his tongue and exclaim:

"It's sharp as a needle!"

Like Sigmund Freud, he was the first-born son of an adoring mother, as well as of a permissive father; the main difference being that Ernest Jones's father was a prosperous man well able to afford his son's medical education. Jones also considered that he came from an abused minority: the Welsh. Born to Baptist parents, his mother socially advanced herself to the Anglican Church, whereupon her husband and son became atheists. He already had his medical degree at twenty-one and had picked up his first Gold Medals in the examinations all the way through the preparatory years and the University of London Medical School. During his obstetric service at the hospital, when he had to go out to the homes of women about to be delivered, he had by chance been assigned to one of the poorest Jewish districts in London. He liked the people, was intrigued with their warm, emotional way of life, and developed a sympathy which lasted him the days of his life.

Trained as a neurologist, he had spent three years as house physician at the Children's Hospital. In his eagerness to do a tremendous job as surgeon, neurologist, pathologist, he ran roughshod over the nurses and the matron, who did not know why they had to work so unrelentingly hard. His troubles did not begin until near the end of his third year when he diagnosed an abscess in the chest of a very sick girl. The visiting physician, an authority, countermanded Jones's suggestion by insisting that it was a solid condition in the lung. The following Saturday the child's abscess burst. Seeing the pus she was spitting up, Jones decided to operate at once to save her life. When the physician returned the next week, he was thoroughly angry. A short time later Jones's then fiancée was being operated on for appendicitis. Jones wanted to be with the girl during the operation. As house physician he was not permitted to leave the hospital, but he asked the surgeon in charge if it would be all right for him to take the Saturday night off. The surgeon said he thought it would be; however the matron reported him and he was immeditely discharged. This was the beginning of the process he described as "giving me a bad name."

At the moment the setback had not seemed serious. He spent the next month studying for his final examinations and came out at the top of the list with another Gold Medal. He was certain he would secure the post in neurology at the National Hospital. There was no one in England with any part of his qualifications. However, sitting as chairman of the Board at the National Hospital was the consulting physician whose judgment Jones had proven wrong. He declared young Dr. Ernest Jones to be "difficult to work with"; then secured the position for his own nephew.

"I was cut adrift in the London medical world as a marked man."

Any possible connection with the medical elite, or with his Alma Mater to which he wished to return, was now terminated as effectively as Sigmund Freud had managed to terminate his connection with the Vienna Medical School by publishing *The Etiology of Hysteria.* Jones had set up private offices in Harley Street with an older and better-known doctor, his own father taking out the lease and demanding no rent; then spent the better part of two years going down the list of hospitals in London, the teaching hospital at Charing Cross, the West End Hospital for Nervous Diseases, even second- and third-rate hospitals for children's or nervous diseases; in every case he was rejected because of his past history, until finally he managed to get an appointment at the obscure Faringdon Dispensary, and a little later the Dreadnought Seamen's Hospital where he lectured on neurology. He also managed to earn an extra guinea here and there by becoming a reporter for the medical press, taking the notes of extemporaneous lecturers.

A friend had introduced him to the Fabian Society, where he went to hear talks given by Bernard Shaw, H. G. Wells and Sidney Webb. Here he met a young Dutch girl named Loe, with whom he fell in love. She was a woman of indomitable courage, coupled with a psychoneurotic constitution. The couple spent seven years together, living in each other's flats and going abroad for trips. Loe called herself Mrs. Ernest Jones even though there had never been a marriage ceremony.

Then had come the harshest blow of all. He had been researching on aphasia, some of his tests being carried out at a school for mental defectives. Two young girls accused him of behaving indecently during a speech test. Dr. Ernest Jones was arrested, spent three days in a jail cell before he was bailed out, and then went through months of agonizing postponements until a magistrate dismissed the case as absurd. The medical press now acclaimed his innocence; medical men he had worked with in the hospitals got up the funds to help him pay his legal fees. He himself was convinced that the girls had been guilty of sexual acts between themselves and were transferring their sense of guilt to him.

By this time, in 1906, he was treating convulsion cases that had no somatic source, and had witnessed cases of anesthesia and paralysis of limbs and organs of the body that were impossible to account for. His experience in the Children's Hospital had also convinced him of the sexuality of children.

"The English are the worst hypocrites in the world when it comes to sex; yet we all knew the facts of life by the time we entered primary school. One of my friends, the nine-year-old son of a prominent minister, who was rolling on the floor with a bellyache, said to me, 'Oh, God, it hurts so much I don't think I could fuck a girl if she was under me at this minute.' No sexuality in children, indeed!"

He was practicing psychotherapy in a mild sort of way, though he had not yet read Sigmund Freud's books, when he got into a final bit of trouble. At the West End Hospital for Nervous Diseases there was a ten-year-old girl with a hysterical paralysis of the left arm. Dr. Savill, in charge of the girl, had published a book on neurasthenia; he diagnosed her trouble as "one of imperfect blood supply to one side of the brain." Jones examined the girl, found that she had made a practice of going to school early in order to play with a slightly older boy who finally had tried to seduce her. She had turned away and warded off the attack with her arm, which thereupon went numb and became paralyzed, though she had been struck no actual blow.

The young patient told the other girls in the ward that the doctor had talked to her about sexual matters. Since sex was not allowed to be mentioned in the hospital, this became a matter of scandal. The girl's parents heard about it, complained to the Hospital Committee, which promptly advised Jones to resign from the staff.

At that moment Dr. C. K. Clarke, professor of psychiatry at the University of Toronto, had come through Europe studying psychiatric clinics and looking for a director for an institute which he had been authorized to set up in Canada. Young Jones, desperate, welcomed the opportunity to start a new life. He asked for a six months' period of grace in which to secure training at the Burghölzli under Bleuler and Jung.

The first publication of Sigmund's he read was the Dora analysis; although his German was not good enough to follow the fine details, he was deeply impressed by Sigmund's method. He decided that he had to learn the German language thoroughly, and began studying *The Interpretation of Dreams*.

"I came away with a deep impression of there being a man in Vienna who actually listened with attention to every word his patients said to him. . . . It meant that he was that *rara avis*, a true psychologist. It meant that, whereas men had often taken a moral or political interest in mental processes, here for the first time was a man who took a scientific interest in them. Hitherto scientific interest had been confined to what Sherrington calls the world of energy, the 'material' world. Now at last it was being applied to the equally valid world of mind."

The three men had made a circle of the town. Sigmund turned to Brill.

"If you don't mind talking while walking uphill, I'd like to climb high enough on the Mönchsberg to get a good view of the town."

"Walking uphill? Bah! I could talk to you, Herr Professor Freud, if I were buried in a mine shaft!"

Abraham Arden Brill was a short-necked, stocky man of medium height with heavy eyelids and eyes that were on the sentimental side, though they had seen a good deal of hardship and cruelty. Life for him had so long been an obstacle course that he thought obstacles to be a normal part of the landscape. At rest he was homely in an appealing sort of way, but when animated his personality came on fire. He gazed fascinatedly at the world and people through steel-rimmed spectacles; a shock of black hair rather high on the brow stood straight up and then looped backward. He wore the enormously high American collars which seemed to be a foundation upon which his jawbones rested. He was so eager to know, to experience, to live, that a stranger might have gained the impression that he was a malleable man. Only one thing gave him away: his chin, which he would thrust out if it appeared he was about to be frustrated or defeated.

Brill, an Austrian by birth, had persuaded his parents, when he was only fifteen, to buy him a steamship ticket to the United States where, although he would have neither friend nor relative, he was determined to complete his education and fit himself into the New World. Some sharpers on shipboard had defrauded him of the few dollars his parents had been able to spare, and so he landed in New York without one word of English or one dollar. But he was strong, resourceful and filled to the brim with an optimistic view of life, much like Karl Abraham's. A saloonkeeper let him sleep on the floor in exchange for his keeping the place clean; later he met a doctor who again allowed him to sleep on the floor of his medical offices . . . during which time he was completing his high school course.

At the age of eighteen he made the decision which had brought him at this very moment to this Meeting for Freudian Psychology: though he still had not a cent in the world, he decided that he was going to become a physician. He graduated from New York City College, went to New York University on a scholarship to earn his Bachelor of Philosophy degree, after which he was admitted to the College of Physicians and Surgeons at Columbia University. Whenever his savings ran out he would stop his university work for a semester, find two or three jobs, live on a subsistence and save the money needed to go back for another year of study.

After he had secured his medical degree at the age of twenty-nine, Brill put in four years at the Central Islip Hospital, working with patients who were psychiatrically disturbed. Since the therapeutic methods available to him were achieving no useful results, he turned in discouragement to neurology; at the same time reading the psychiatric literature being published in German, translating some of what he considered the more valuable pieces into English, particularly Kraepelin's studies coming out of his Institute in Munich. In 1907 he had gone to Paris to work in the Hospice de Bicêtre under Dr. Pierre Marie, who had welcomed Sigmund to Charcot's group at the Salpêtrière. Disappointed with the results that Dr. Marie was getting with the psychiatrically disturbed, Brill, on the advice of a doctor friend, went to Zurich to work under Professor Eugen Bleuler and Dr. Carl Jung, there to be appointed as an Assistant by Bleuler, to take the place of Karl Abraham.

"This past year at the Burghölzli has been the turning point of my life," Brill exclaimed with a radiant smile, as they zigzagged up the steep mountain path, working their way toward the green forest above them. "I had never heard of your psychoanalysis. Within forty-eight hours I was plunged into my first session and heard cases being analyzed from the Freudian point of view. I thought the top of my head would come off! The first patient we discussed sometimes poured red ink or red wine onto the sheet of her bed. At the State Hospital in New York, at the Hospice de Bicêtre this simply would have been considered another piece of unreasonable conduct. But Bleuler and Jung agreed that this was an act out of the woman's unconscious which had a meaning. They were right, the woman had completed her menopause, and in her unconscious mind was rejecting the proof of growing old. She was attempting to revert to an earlier and better time of her life when she could menstruate. I left that staff meeting with a copy of *The Interpretation of Dreams* under my arm. During the next months I consumed everything you had written.

"My dear Professor Freud, there was I in 1903, starting my work at the State Hospital in New York after *Studies on Hysteria* had been published, *The Interpretation of Dreams*, *The Psychopathology of Everyday Life*, not to mention your monographs on *Obsessions and Phobias*, and *The Neuropsychoses of Defense*, and not having read a word you had written! There was I, thirty-two years old, and half of my life already gone before I got to you. Even then it was just damn fool luck; if one of my teachers in New York, Adolf Meyer, hadn't also been trained at the Burghölzli, I probably would have gone to Kraepelin in Munich, where I would have learned only to make still more classifications of psychoses."

They had reached the first line of trees. Above them, dominating the rocky crag, was the Fortress Hohensalzburg, on the very end of the Mönchsberg, seat of the archbishops and impregnable fortress for the Salzburgians since A.D. 100. Below them lay the city, sparkling in the sunshine as it sat on the banks of the Salzach River. The Celts had first settled the area in 500 B.C.; then the Romans had conquered it in A.D. 40. In the fourth century St. Maximus had introduced Christianity and built the first catacombs under the Mönchsberg; in the eighth century St. Rupert had built St. Peter's Monastery in front of the catacombs and Salzburg had been famous and beloved ever since.

Gazing down at the town, pointing out the landmarks to Brill and Jones, Sigmund felt a wave of happiness pass over him at the acquisition of two such bright, young, ardent friends of psychoanalysis. He linked his arm lightly through each of theirs, said:

"It's been a fine walk, but I think we had better return to the Bristol now. The rest of our delegates will be checking in."

"Herr Professor, we are coming to Vienna when the meeting is over," said Brill. "Will you have time to see us?"

"But of course. Every evening. And if you can remain until Sunday, we will have the entire day."

"Excellent!" exclaimed Ernest Jones. "And next time we promise to do all the listening. We are coming to be trained."

7.

When he got back to the hotel a group of men were standing together in the lobby. The first one Sigmund saw was Carl Jung, who had been waiting for him to return from his walk. The two men greeted each other affectionately. Sigmund had forgotten how big and robust a man Jung was, and for that matter how powerful the stone-cutter's hand that now crushed his. Once again, as had happened the year before, Sigmund felt himself engulfed in Jung's magnificent spirit.

"My dear colleague, I want to thank you most heartily for all the work you have done to bring about this meeting."

Jung waved aside the thanks.

"It was a labor of love, my esteemed Professor."

"I have decided to present the history of the Rat Man, with whom I have been working for eight months," said Sigmund. "It is an extraordinary obsessional case, showing how a man can feel both love and hate for a person; and the results of this unconscious conflict."

"This is what we have come to hear, a full case history which will reveal your methods. But let me introduce you to a lot of the doctors who are eager to meet you: Arend, Löwenfeld and Ludwig from Munich; Stegmann from Dresden; our friend Karl Abraham from Berlin; my relative Franz Riklin, along with your friend Max Eitingon from Zurich; and a pleasant surprise, Edouard Claparède from Geneva, where he too will spread the gospel. Your follower Sandor Ferenczi has arrived from Budapest. Bleuler is due at suppertime; the Viennese delegation, twenty-six strong! have come in from the station . . ."

"Have you asked Professor Bleuler to sit as chairman of our Congress?"

"He would refuse. Bleuler insists on retaining total freedom for himself and his beliefs. To chair this meeting would mean, at least to him, that he has not only joined the organization . . ."

"There is no organization!"

". . . but also that he approves and stands behind the papers that will be read. He comes here, as he goes to many Congresses, as an interested but independent spectator. Above all, my dear Professor, you are in error if you think of Bleuler as a follower, to quote the term you used in your letter to me. Interested, yes, but a follower, no."

Sigmund replied soberly, "Bleuler is of the utmost importance to our group. We'll proceed at his pace. But in that event I think we'll just do without a chairman, and without a secretary, treasurer or business meeting. We will keep it informal. We need only the order in which the papers are to be read."

It was one of the most gratifying days of Sigmund's life, for when Bleuler arrived there would be forty-two men on hand, who had come from all over Europe to attend this meeting, almost as large a group as attended the established Neurological and Psychiatric Congresses. He found the men to be highly compatible, not only tied together by a bond of interest but sharing a feeling of expectancy. Sigmund had dinner in the Goldener Hirsch with the five men from Germany, enjoying the restaurant's famous wild game and *Salzburger Nockerl*; strolled through the beautiful and historic Residenzplatz with Jung, Eitingon and the new men from Switzerland; spent the rest of the afternoon discussing individual cases with the doctors who were seeking guidance. At sundown he arranged for his Vienna cohorts to act as hosts at the Sternbräu, a huge brewery restaurant which had music and dancing groups in Tyrolese costumes, where the beer was served in one-liter mugs, and one inspected the restaurant's own butcher and sausage shops before sitting at the tables. It was a favorite spot for country people, inexpensive, noisy, filled with the gusto of life. Martha had always liked to come once during the summer, when the Freuds were vacationing in the nearby mountains.

When they returned from the party, Carl Jung took Sigmund up to Eugen Bleuler's room. He called a soft "Come in" to Jung's knock, met Sigmund in the center of the room, hand outstretched, a smile on his face. Jung murmured the introduction, then excused himself. Sigmund felt awkward, constrained. He thought how much he owed to Eugen Bleuler, the first to recognize his work, to introduce it into a university, to teach it to doctors at an asylum; who had started Carl Jung, Riklin, Abraham, Eitingon, Jones, Brill on the path to Sigmund Freud. How did one express gratitude to such a man, who had literally converted psychoanalysis from a parochial Viennese fad into a world movement!

Sigmund thought Eugen Bleuler a marvelous-looking man, perhaps the most favored since Ernst von Fleischl before his infected thumb had drained the beauty from his face. He had something of the look of an eagle, with his Renaissance sculptured head perched proudly on his neck; yet with no hint of arrogance. His eyes, light in color, wide open, all-seeing; a long craglike nose, a high sloping brow, soft gray hair, the faintest shadow of a luminous gray face beard, ears molded flat to the head, a sturdy mustache gave an over-all expression of perceptiveness, courage and tact; for Eugen Bleuler managed to keep himself aloof from the pettiness of the world, while at the same time being deeply involved in the plight of humanity.

While Bleuler spoke of his pleasure in meeting Herr Professor Freud after years of admiring his work, Sigmund bowed his head slightly, then raised it with a warm smile of greeting.

Eugen Bleuler was a few months younger than Sigmund, fifty-one; he had succeeded Forel as director of the Burghölzli, the same Forel whose book, *Hypnotism*, Sigmund had defended against Professor Meynert's irrelevant attacks. Bleuler, who was professor of psychiatry at the University of Zurich, had earned the reputation of being a courageous man. Since his wide experience with dementia praecox had led him to disagree with Kraepelin, the world's authority, he had published his findings slowly, tentatively, always documented by painstaking research, never offending Kraepelin or his zealous admirers. Kraepelin was interested in the form, the type and the category of the illness; Bleuler had turned his attention to the ideational content of the patient's mind.

Though Carl Jung had formed the Psychoanalytic Society in Zurich and was clearly its leader, that had been a matter of choice on the part of his superior. Even here in Salzburg, Bleuler would sit back quietly and let Jung manage not only the Swiss group but the details of the meeting.

They sat on a comfortable sofa, their discussion roving over the sciences of psychiatry and psychoanalysis, and how they could serve each other in a useful manner. Yet it did not take Sigmund long to perceive that Jung had been right; Eugen Bleuler would never have accepted the chairmanship, and would have thought it in bad taste for the position to be offered to him. Unlike any of the other men assembled for this meeting, Sigmund perceived that Bleuler had a fortress within; a guarded area where no human being might intrude. In spite of the fact that he appeared open and hearty in expressing his view, Bleuler seemed to a certain degree unapproachable. Yet before they bade each other good night Bleuler said:

"My wife and I hope to visit Vienna for a vacation within a few months. Could we have the great pleasure of calling on you and Frau Professor Freud?"

Sigmund rose early the next morning, took breakfast in his room, had the hotel barber cut his dark rich hair and trim the short sideburns, graying chin beard and handsome mustache. He then donned the new gray woven suit he had had made for the occasion and the white linen shirt, the collar coming down to a V with a black bow tie tucked under its wings, and the stiff white cuffs held together by the cuff links Martha had given him for his last birthday. He glanced at himself in the mirror of the wardrobe before he left the room, decided that he did not look old for fifty-two, and that although he sometimes thought of death, and imagined that it had a predetermined pattern, he was in a sense really just beginning life.

He reached the special meeting room set aside for them several minutes before eight, and found twenty men already seated on each side of a long table. The head of the table had been left open for him. He would read the first paper. He bade everyone a quiet good morning, and on the stroke of eight began his presentation, without notes, of the Rat Man case. He spoke in a low, comradely tone, as one would with honored colleagues; yet his voice had body, and his enunciation was so distinct that not a word was lost at the end of the table.

He told the group about Advocate Lertzing, his obsessions over suicide and the well-being of his fiancée which had kept him from passing his final bar examinations; his fear that his already dead father might die; the brutal captain on military maneuvers who had told him of the criminal who had had a pot turned upside down on his buttocks, the rats put into it, who bored their way into the anus; the loss of the eyeglasses; the identification of the captain with the father; the patient's anal eroticism and repressed homosexuality.

He spoke for three hours, uninterrupted. Everyone listened with rapt attention; for the Rat Man case was, as Sigmund had decided during the treatments, one in which an entire rostrum of psychoanalytical symptoms were tied together in one neat bundle. At eleven, he broke off.

"Gentlemen, I have spoken much too long!"

"No, no, please, Herr Professor. Continue!"

Sigmund looked about the table, ordered coffee for the group, and resumed his analysis of his conclusions and cure.

The men had midday dinner, took a walk about town and then returned to the meeting room. Ernest Jones led off brilliantly with a paper on Rationalization in Everyday Life, a psychological field in which he was pioneering. Alfred Adler followed with an equally well-documented paper on Sadism in Life and Neurosis, an area which he had marked out for special research; Ferenczi gave a pyrotechnical delivery of a paper on Psychoanalysis and Pedagogy, which earned him cheers; Isidor Sadger read a pugnacious account of The Etiology of Homosexuality; Carl Jung and Karl Abraham reported on two aspects of dementia praecox. This produced the only unpleasant moment of the meeting, for Abraham had written into his paper his acknowledgment to Jung for his discoveries in the field, and then failed to read Jung's name. Jung was properly irritated, and Abraham crestfallen.

"My unconscious betrayed me!" he groaned when he got a moment alone with Sigmund. "I had every intention of acknowledging my indebtedness to Jung. My eyes just skipped over his name."

"I should be most unwilling to see serious dissension arising between you two. There are still so few of us that disagreements, based perhaps on personal 'complexes,' ought to be excluded."

8.

When the papers and discussions were completed the men adjourned to a room set aside for them for a celebration banquet. Sigmund was in fine fettle, for the meeting had gone superbly, each of the papers had opened a rewarding field.

The day had demonstrated that psychoanalysis was not and never again would be a one-man movement. The Swiss contingent had shown a high enthusiasm, far more even than his own Viennese, who had somehow seemed inhibited.

Though Eugen Bleuler would permit no alcohol to be served, the banquet was hilarious. Sigmund seated himself with Jung on one side and Bleuler on the other. Guido Brecher of Meran, a newer Austrian member, wittily satirized the Congresses of the neurological and psychiatric groups, then mercilessly pulled the leg of that day's speakers, including Sigmund, by making a *reductio ad absurdum* of their theses. The laughter was annealing after the serious day's work; each man rose in turn to tell a funny story out of his practice or his fund of national wit.

It was coming on eleven o'clock and the one subject Sigmund most wanted to discuss, the establishment of a *Jahrbuch* or Yearbook, had not yet been mentioned. He did not want the meeting to break up without at least the beginning plans for the publication. However he wanted the Swiss to play the leading role. Just before the dinner ended, Jung leaned over to him and said in a low voice:

"We are ready to discuss the formation of the Yearbook now. Would you like to join us in Bleuler's room?"

Sigmund felt his heart palpitate.

"I should be delighted."

"Are there a few others you would like to include?"

"Yes, some of the members from countries where we are just beginning: Jones, Brill, Ferenczi, Abraham."

"Good. I'll ask them to drop in."

When Sigmund reached Bleuler's room he found it pervaded by a high sense of expectation. Each member of the Swiss group wrung his hand and congratulated him on the successful realization of the Meeting for Freudian Psychology. Brill, Jones, Abraham, and Ferenczi were pleased to be included. Though the meeting was being held in Director Professor Bleuler's room, Carl Jung was obviously in charge . . . and enjoying every moment of it. Sigmund sat quietly, mentally listing his objectives:

The establishment of a Yearbook would take psychoanalysis out of the realm of being a local idiom and convert it into an international movement. With Zurich sponsoring the publication, it would connect psychoanalysis with the major University of Zurich, highly regarded throughout Europe, and with the Burghölzli, whose fame extended as far as the United States. It would stop the accusation that the new science had emerged from the most lascivious and sexually depraved city in the world, and deserved to remain there. It would put an end to the venal whispering campaign that this was "a Jewish science." It would assure a continuing flow of material from the Swiss physicians, which could influence the German psychiatrists to contribute. Most important of all, it would make them independent of the journals which printed only a fraction of what the Freudian group was turning out.

Carl Jung took the center of the floor, suggesting that the time was ripe to create a Yearbook. Ernest Jones suggested they publish it in three languages; Edouard Claparède urged a French edition on the grounds that too few French doctors and medical students read German. Max Eitingon stuttered through an assurance that the publication costs could be met from the Society's modest dues, and that he knew where the help could be found (himself) if there was a deficit. Sandor Ferenczi insisted the editorial standards be set extremely high, so that critics would be hard put to find fault; Karl Abraham suggested that, in addition to the major articles, a department be set up to review new and relevant books. Jung, to indicate that he was no longer upset over Abraham's failure to acknowledge his indebtedness, cried:

"The department is yours, Dr. Abraham!"

To Sigmund Freud's astonishment, the heartiest support came from Eugen Bleuler, who rose, turned a chair about, leaned against its back and spoke in enthusiastic terms about the value of such a magazine, its power to find its way around the scientific world, as well as its urgency for all members, who could now be assured that their papers would be published. He welcomed the opportunity of a joint Swiss-Austrian publication.

All eyes now turned to Sigmund Freud. The endorsement by Bleuler made the Yearbook a certainty.

"This group is the culmination of our meeting and the realization of one of my fondest dreams. We will now be able to take our place on the world scene. In order to make certain that we have a superbly edited Yearbook, I think you will all agree with me that Herr Dr. Carl Jung should be that editor. I don't think I'm being presumptuous, for we have corresponded about this matter."

There was spontaneous applause for Carl Jung. His face lit up with a heartwarming, engulfing smile as he exclaimed:

"I accept. With pride and joy."

Franz Riklin, a quiet man who appeared content to walk in Jung's shadow, but who had given a telling paper that day on Problems of Myth Interpretation, said:

"Herr Professor Freud, now that we have an editor, surely you know that you must become the director."

"Thank you, Herr Dr. Riklin. I would be pleased of course. But I must be only one of the directors. We should have someone in Switzerland to share the responsibility and the policy decisions."

No one looked at Eugen Bleuler, not even Sigmund Freud. If Bleuler would refuse to chair a simple two-day meeting, how would it be possible for him to accept responsibility as director of an ongoing Yearbook? No, the idea was unthinkable . . .

. . . to everyone but Eugen Bleuler.

"I would be happy to become co-director with you, Herr Professor Freud, if I am acceptable to everyone in the room. I think that, working together, we can publish a highly creditable *Jahrbuch.*"

His announcement had an electrifying effect. Sigmund felt himself drenched in exultation. The Swiss heartily congratulated Bleuler, then Sigmund. Then the outlanders, Jones, Brill, Abraham, Ferenczi, added their congratulations to the new editor and directors. Sigmund whispered in an aside to Abraham:

"Do you think I might order a bottle of champagne? This is a memorable occasion and calls for a toast."

Abraham shuddered.

"Not in alcohol. Bleuler and Jung are teetotalers!"

His pleasure was short-lived. The moment he entered the compartment on the train and saw the expression on the faces of his fellow Viennese, he knew he was in for trouble. With a start he realized that he had paid little attention to his old friends during the past two days; but then, what was there special to talk about? He had helped all of them with the papers they had read. There had been so many new men to meet and become friends with. He saw his colleagues in Vienna every Wednesday. Surely it was wise and proper for him to spend these days developing bonds with the men from other countries?

His Viennese colleagues did not think so. There were anger and resentment on the faces of Alfred Adler, Wilhelm Stekel, Isidor Sadger, Rudolf Reitler, Paul Federn and Fritz Wittels as they ranged themselves on the six seats of the compartment, facing each other. As a mark of their displeasure, no one rose to offer Sigmund a seat. He stood in the center of the compartment with the train lurching beneath him as it sped through the outlying districts of Salzburg. Outside in the corridor was another group: Otto Rank, who had squeezed his arm as he passed; Eduard Hitschmann, who had tendered him a sardonic wink, as though to say, "What else can you expect from human nature?"; Leopold Königstein, who had given him a sympathetic nod of the head as he entered the compartment . . . Sigmund noted that the six seats were occupied by medical men; the non-professionals, such as Hugo Heller and Max Graf, were in the corridor, too far away to hear the discussion. From the flaming red of Wilhelm Stekel's face, it was obvious that he had elected himself to be the spokesman.

"Very well, Wilhelm, what is it?"

"We are grossly disappointed."

"In what?"

"In your conduct toward us at the Congress. You neglected us, your oldest friends, the ones who helped you start this movement . . ."

". . . and without whom there could have been no Congress," rasped Isidor Sadger.

Sigmund recalled for them that they had hosted the Congress together at the Sternbräu.

"But you treated us as poor relations," said Fritz Wittels hoarsely; "people you have known so long you have become bored with."

"I was meeting some dozen new men for the first time. I considered it important to give them every spare moment before they returned home."

Leopold Königstein poked his head into the compartment, said tentatively, "May I speak as an outsider? I believe that Professor Freud is right in thinking . . ."

"No, you may not speak as an outsider!" cried Rudolf Reitler. "We have all been members of this group from the earliest days, and we are the ones who have a right to speak."

"Granted, Rudolf," replied Sigmund, "but there is obviously more behind this rump meeting than my seeming neglect."

"Why did you surround yourself with the Zurichers, and the new men from England and America, while we Viennese were put at the other end of the room?" It was Stekel again.

"Same reason, Wilhelm. But we are still not getting down to your real complaint. Dr. Adler, you obviously share the compartment's sentiments. Won't you tell me quite honestly what is troubling the group?"

"Yes, Herr Professor, since you insist. There is dissatisfaction over your meeting about the *Jahrbuch*."

Alfred Adler fell silent; he had no intention of participating in a disagreement. Max Kahane moved into the compartment.

"Since I don't join in this sense of hostility and jealousy, perhaps I am the one to state the case objectively. Your Viennese colleagues feel they were purposely excluded from the meeting. That you wanted the Swiss to control the discussion so that they would come out with the Yearbook they want, and consequently will help publish."

"True. But not the way you tell it. I was asked by Carl Jung if I would like to come to Eugen Bleuler's room for a discussion about a possible Yearbook. I said I had been awaiting the moment eagerly. Jung asked if there were some people I would specially like to ask. I said, 'Yes, a man from each of the countries represented: Brill from America, Jones from England, Abraham from Germany, Ferenczi from Hungary . . ."

". . . and why no Viennese?" Reitler broke in.

"Because I felt myself capable of representing you."

"And who is to control the *Jahrbuch?*"

"Jung will be the editor . . ."

"We thought so!"

". . . Bleuler and I will be the directors."

"Why aren't there more Viennese in that special little group?" Fritz Wittels demanded, not at all politely. "Why are we outnumbered two to one by the Swiss?"

"Fritz, this is not a soccer game, and the Swiss are not our opponents. They are our friends and comrades in arms. Though they occupy two of the three executive posts—and admittedly I wanted it that way—we Viennese will fill two thirds of each issue with our articles, since we have more members than all the other societies put together. Isn't that what we really want?"

There was silence for a moment. The expression on Alfred Adler's face lightened. Since he above all the Viennese, by reason of his originality, research and brilliant writings, had the best reason to be on the Editorial Board, and since he was now apparently accepting Sigmund Freud's explanation, the tension in the compartment eased. There was a babble of relieved voices in the corridor. Sigmund heard Otto Rank say:

"Thank heavens that's over!"

But it was not. Wilhelm Stekel was as upset as he had been when Sigmund walked in. He cried:

"There's one thing more; and all of us in the group agree: you are making a fatal judgment."

"About what, Wilhelm?"

"Carl Jung. We've watched you court him. You think he can become the most important man, next to you, on the international scene. You imagine he can do great good to psychoanalysis. You think he is as loyal and dependable as all of us who have surrounded you for almost six years. But you're wrong, Freud. Carl Jung will never work for or with anyone for long. He will walk out, and be his own man. When he leaves he will do us irreparable harm."

"I see nothing of this in Carl Jung," Sigmund replied placatingly. "He is passionately devoted to psychoanalysis and the unconscious. He has years of work planned which will expand our field and earn us new supporters. If I feel this strongly and confidently about him, Wilhelm, what is the special power that enables you to perceive his coming desertion and apostasy?"

Stekel replied in a voice as cold as a piece of iron in a field at sunrise:

"Hate has a keen eye!"

BOOK FOURTEEN

PARADISE IS UNPAVED

Paradise Is Unpaved

MARTHA was in Hamburg caring for her mother, who was ill, when Ernest Jones and A. A. Brill came to dinner on Thursday at the end of April. The cook outdid herself with Frau Professor away: a *Tafelspitz* with a special horseradish sauce, new potatoes with parsley.

Sigmund welcomed his two new friends. Jones was nattily dressed, sporting a debonair necktie. Though his face was pale as always, his eyes mirrored his excitement like large dark brown reflecting pools. Brill wore his American choke collar; his usually heavy eyelids were raised as the three men started a marathon in English, all speaking and listening at the same time. After dinner they went across the hall to Sigmund's study and examined his collection of antiquities. Brill cleared his throat. He had something he wanted to say.

"Herr Professor, it is now twelve years since you began publishing your books on psychoanalysis, and not one of them has been translated into English."

"No, no one has ever volunteered, or asked for the rights."

Brill ran his index finger inside the rim of his high collar.

"Jones and I were talking about that during the train trip. We decided the time is long overdue. If you consider me worthy, I would like to undertake the translation. I would start with *The Psychopathology of Everyday Life* as being the simplest, then, when I have sharpened my techniques, move on to the *Interpretation of Dreams* and *Three Essays on the Theory of Sexuality*. If I am to start a psychoanalytic movement in the United States, I must make your books available to the American people." Then, with a mischievous grin, he added, "I asked Jones, 'How can I start a new religion in New York without a Bible? After all, the Jews had their Old Testament; the Christians their Gospel after Matthew, Luke and Mark; Islam its Koran . . .'"

Sigmund was pleased. Except for the early article in *Brain*, nothing of his work had appeared in English. It would open new worlds for him. He glanced over at Jones to make sure that he was not feeling left out.

"Do we need two translations, one for the United States and one for England?"

"By no means," Jones replied, fingering back the silky brown hair that had fallen over his brow. "One good translation will serve both countries equally."

"Then it's done!"

Both men stayed over for the Wednesday Evening meeting, since Brill intended to form a New York Psychoanalytic Society as soon as he could gather a nucleus about him. Jones had scant hopes of forming a Toronto Society but was planning to remain there only a few years.

"From what I can gather from the temper of my colleagues in England," he said tartly, "psychoanalysis will be precisely where it was when I left there. Mark my words as a prophet without honor, or assets, for that matter, in his own country, I will be the one who founds the London Psychoanalytic Society when I return."

This was the first meeting of the Vienna group since Salzburg. As Sigmund greeted thirteen of the members, renewed their introductions to Ernest Jones and A. A. Brill, and watched them take their favorite places around the long oval table, he saw with considerable relief that there was no residue of resentment against him; the confrontation on the train had exhausted their anger. Yet he realized that the Viennese would never become as enthusiastic about the Zurichers as he was. The mercurial Wilhelm Stekel, about to read a freshly hatched paper on The Genesis of Psychic Impotence, had forgotten the incident; only Alfred Adler, Sigmund observed, had pulled a centimeter deeper into the shell of his formal attitude toward Professor Freud.

In the first days after his return from Salzburg, Sigmund often sat at his desk reliving the meeting's wonderful exhilaration. He admitted to himself that he had made a mistake in not inviting Alfred Adler and Wilhelm Stekel, since Stekel was knowledgeable about publications, to the conference in Bleuler's room over the *Jahrbuch*. The omission was not an accident; he had not wanted any of the Viennese present. He had wanted to shape the Yearbook with the Swiss group, whom he was wooing, and with the eager new young converts, Jones, Brill, Sandor Ferenczi, Karl Abraham, in whom he sensed a future for psychoanalysis. Though he had not been aware of it consciously, he had been afraid that the Viennese would interfere, not allow him to put two thirds of the control in the hands of the Zurichers. It had been clear to his intimates how elated he was at the presence of these outsiders; it had not sat well. Had they been invited to the discussion they might have become hostile, opposing what the Zurichers suggested.

He believed this to be his first error in behavior in the six years of their coming together. He had been the paterfamilias, encouraging them to do original work, rewriting their manuscripts, helping them to get published, sending patients to the doctors in the group, welcoming them to his dinner table and his study for hours of training, lending them money when they were in debt. Whenever he could, he wrote introductions for their books, as he had for Wilhelm Stekel's *Nervous Anxiety States and Their Treatment*. In the Wednesday Evening meetings he had been incisive in his comments, but always in a comradely fashion; nor had he permitted his criticism to sound like *obiter dicta*. There had developed the normal differences between members of a professional group: personality clashes, hurt feelings, jealousy, cliquishness, jockeying for position. But none of this had been manifested toward himself; and he had always been able to salve the wounds. This had been the first break with him. He must exercise extreme caution not to let it happen again.

In the paper he read this evening, Stekel ticked off his points in rapid succession: impotence arising at a later age derived from the unconscious; if a man gets an idea that he is impotent that idea would prevent him from having an erection, except for the early morning, wake-up erections. As he fails to function sexually, anxiety sets in, strengthening the prohibiting idea; most of his impotent patients had erections when not with women; hence the presence of a homosexual tendency arising from the incestuous ideas of youth. Impotence also set in when the first, early sexual experience became "permanently associated with unpleasure."

In the discussion that followed, Stekel took his usual thrashing. Jones and Brill had been warned of the intense critical activity. Now they listened as Reitler accused Stekel of going too far in his theorizing from the available facts. Steiner agreed with the thesis but said the classifications of impotence would not last; in addition, morning erections were a result of prostate trouble. Sadger wanted to extend the concept of psychic impotence to include "the mother as prostitute," found in those impotent patients who had had considerable contact with prostitutes. Alfred Adler, to whom Stekel was closest, tore the paper apart. "If a man during intercourse needs to moan and express pain . . . then all of these factors indicate an accumulation of various impulses in the instinct of aggression." Was not impotence, then, caused by fear and the putting down of the aggression built into sex?

Sigmund in a mild tone chastised Stekel for indulging in "surface psychology." His etiology of psychic impotence was too narrowly conceived. Man did not become impotent a second time because he had been impotent before; the first, second and tenth times had a common cause. All men were born with differing quotients of the sexual instinct, from very weak to very strong. This had to be considered an element in potence. Impotence was a psychiatric disturbance. There was also the factor of "the choice of neurosis," the unconscious mind had a rather wide variety at hand, and could choose, even as the *Hausfrau* did at the open-air fish market on the bank of the Donau Kanal. However, Sigmund agreed, Stekel had a point about early sexual unpleasure: two of his patients had originally been seduced by ugly or elderly women. The same was true of several of his women patients who were sexually anesthetic, lacking all sensibility.

Jones and Brill spoke briefly, as behooved first-time guests, but they were fascinated by the give and take, and by Sigmund Freud's warning against rash dogmatic publishing. "Let us behave as exact scientists," he said, "waiting to make absolutely sure there are no organic factors involved, factors which can be measured by our colleagues in other branches of medicine, before we state categorically that the case is one of psychiatric impotence."

After the meeting Sigmund walked Jones and Brill up to the Hotel Regina. They were leaving for Budapest the next morning to spend several days working with Sandor Ferenczi, whom they admired. Brill was then returning to New York to rejoin his doctor-bride; Jones was spending the balance of the six months in Munich and Paris before leaving for Canada to open the Psychiatric Clinic.

Martha returned from Hamburg with the news that the doctors suspected her seventy-eight-year-old mother of having cancer. Tante Minna left at once to care for Mrs. Bernays.

Two guests arrived from Zurich: Max Eitingon, who had already had several training sessions the winter before, and Ludwig Binswanger, who had also visited Sigmund briefly the previous winter. Eitingon, clean-shaven except for a shy mustache, combed his hair on the extreme left side of his head, almost directly above his ear. His expression was still diffident, claiming nothing; his eyes saw but did not assert. Even as his face put up no front, his psyche was not a litigant in the court of his contemporaries. His attitudes were as inconspicuous as his modest dark suits: a man who had nothing to gain or prove, to Sigmund something of a relief from the rambunctious egos that surrounded him in his own group. Yet there was one issue about which Max Eitingon permitted no doubt: he was a committed Freudian psychoanalyst, and nothing would ever change him. His warmth overcame his stutter.

No one could have been farther from Eitingon's character than his companion, Dr. Ludwig Binswanger. He was a handsome young man with a high, vertical brow, dark hair as thickly virginal as the trees on the mountainside of the Black Forest; grave eyes, a high collar inside which the ends of his mustache took refuge; sideburns down to the lobes of his ears; a thick gold watch chain sprawled across his vest. His expression was one of "Tell me. I'm interested. But don't put me off with banalities. I shouldn't care for that. I'm seeking the Kingdom of Truth, though I'm in no desperate hurry to reach there. Each time I put one foot in front of the other I want to learn something. But it's no use to spout at me, make unverified claims based on dubious documentation. I'll go to any lengths to be convinced; but I'll not be swindled."

Sigmund did not consider it wise to give a dinner party for the Zurichers; feelings were a little too tender among the Vienna group. Besides, Martha did not care for formal entertaining. She acknowledged that their apartment was Sigi's University of Vienna, Allgemeine Krankenhaus and Society of Medicine.

"This dining table is as important to your work as your oval conference table."

"You're right, Martha; many a time I've seen your Thursday liver dumplings quiet ulcers that had flared during the discussion the night before."

Martha laughed good-naturedly. "I adore your colleagues, one and all. I also know your Zurichers think the Viennese are a little bohemian, even flamboyant, with their flowing cloaks and upswept hats."

Sigmund invited Otto Rank, who was using his library to research a paper, to remain for supper with Eitingon and Binswanger. The two men liked Otto: his dark, serious face, the scent of the scholar. After supper the four men retired to Sigmund's office, where they talked until one in the morning. Sigmund judged Binswanger to be correct and honest, yet he found himself squabbling with the young man. Binswanger was a truthteller; he did not know any other way.

"You've detected a trace of hesitancy in me. I'll explain why. I consider you the great model and master. Yet my primary allegiance must be to Carl Jung, who has trained me. I have a basic conflict in my loyalties to psychiatry as practiced by Jung and the Burghölzli, and Freudian psychoanalysis."

"The two branches are not in conflict," Sigmund declared. "Psychoanalysis cannot help the dementia praecox patient who has fled all reality and is a victim of autism, living in the fantasy world he has created. But we can help, far better than psychiatry, those people suffering neuroses who can still communicate and make their way back to reality."

"True. Since beginning work with Carl Jung I have believed that almost every patient must be analyzed. But I have had disappointments. I'm just beginning to distinguish between a full analysis and a 'psychotherapeutic treatment guided by psychoanalytic viewpoints.'"

Sigmund replied gently, "Follow me as far as you can, and for the rest let us remain good friends."

2.

They rented a summer house called Dietfeldhof, in an isolated spot above Berchtesgaden. Mathilde was still in Meran and refused to join the family for their summer vacation. Martin, now eighteen and a half, had passed his final examinations at the Humanistic Gymnasium at the top of his class, to everyone's amazement, since he had been at the bottom of the class for years. Sigmund credited Martha with this miracle; invited to the school along with the other parents, she alone went to see Martin's physical training teacher. Martin was his worst student, weak, undersized, clumsy at athletics, put upon by the bigger boys. Flattered by her visit, the teacher gave Martin special training and introduced him to a pamphlet on physical development. Martin asked his father for a bedroom of his own, and each night went through the exercises. As his strength grew he took on the schoolboys who had been bullying him, and thrashed them, one after the other. He tackled his subjects in the same fashion. His self-confidence soared as well as his grades. He was admitted to the University of Vienna for the October term, and as a reward, Sigmund gave his son a summer tour of Europe with a school chum.

"You should be practicing psychoanalysis," Sigmund told Martha; "one visit to a physical training teacher and you turn an incipient *Dummkopf* into a scholar!"

"He was just a late bloomer," replied Martha smugly. "Didn't I once hear you tell your mother that we produce only geniuses in the Freud family?"

Sigmund fulfilled his promise to Sandor Ferenczi, inviting him to spend two weeks near them, engaging a room at the closest hotel, the Bellevue.

"He is an ebullient character," Sigmund explained to Martha, "flavorsome, like those Tokay wines he's so fond of. Much of it comes from his soaring imagination. His mind makes creative leaps that sometimes astonish me."

Ferenczi promptly treated Oliver, now seventeen, and Ernst, sixteen, as brothers; Sophie, fifteen, and Anna, twelve and a half, as younger sisters. He was invited each day for noon dinner, walking the several miles with a gift in his arms, flowers, candy, a bottle of wine, or books for the young. After dinner they would all go mountain climbing or bathe in nearby Aschauer pond. There were wild strawberries and mushrooms to be picked, and clumps of asters. Ferenczi, who loathed all forms of physical exercise, even took Oliver and Ernst on a tour to the Hochkönig, while Sigmund remained at home to correct the beginning fourteen galley sheets of the first issue of the *Jahrbuch*, on which Jung was doing a splendid job of editing and organizing. It was almost impossible not to like outgoing Sandor.

"He's like a puppy," Tante Minna observed when she returned from Hamburg for a visit, "scampering around at your heels and begging for attention. I enjoy him. I'm glad I was able to get a companion for Mother and join you for a while."

Ferenczi was a spontaneous man, rarely at rest. He considered it sound medicine to talk to people. At the St. Rochus Hospital in Budapest he had been in charge of the female ward of attempted suicides. He explained to Sigmund:

"These women who had tried to kill themselves, though not very skillfully, which meant they were ambivalent about wanting to die, had no one to talk to about their anxieties and fears. What good is life if you can't communicate? Talking is the most valuable of all the arts; and certainly the most difficult in which to be truly creative. The day I left Budapest to come here, I went into a florist's to order some flowers for my friend Gisela. The woman who owned the shop was in trouble. I enabled her to talk out her complex situation. I was skillful at it, if you will permit me to say so, so that she told things she had been unable to utter before. It was a full hour of give and take, but the result was extraordinary: a catharsis. By the time I left the shop she had seen her way clear through her painful dilemma and said to me, 'Doktor, I know now what I must do, and you have given me the courage to act.' She even refused to accept money for my flowers, which made it the largest hour's fee I've yet received for a psychoanalytical session."

Sigmund was amused by Ferenczi, bouncing along at his side; at thirty-five he was still very much a child, seeking love and praise from the surrogates for the dozen sisters and brothers he had grown up with. Perhaps because of this unlost innocence he was able to penetrate deeper and with starker clarity. At the moment he was puzzled by a patient suffering from female frigidity, a young wife with vaginal anesthesia.

"She wants to be the male who inserts the penis rather than the female who merely is allowed to harbor it. She cannot achieve an orgasm, of course, because she is resentful, tense, full of aggression against her husband. The marriage was about to be dissolved when her parents persuaded her to come to me. Using your techniques, Herr Professor, I have managed to work her back to her early identification with her mother, whom she thought of as constantly 'filled up' by the father; her love for her father, she slept in the same bedroom with her parents until puberty, her fantasy desires for him, in which the normal penis envy of young girls, who feel cheated and bereft because they have no genital appendage, became subverted to envy of the father's penis which she wanted in her."

"Is she able to accept these findings, Sandor?"

"In part, yes. Now at least she knows what her unnamed guilts are about. As her rejection of her own femininity lessens, she is beginning to feel some sensation during intercourse. It will be a long road. . . ."

At the end of the first week of his stay, Sigmund said to Martha: "I wish Mathilde were here. Do you think she might like Sandor as much as the rest of us do?"

Martha cocked her head to one side, quizzically.

"Sigi, you wouldn't be matchmaking? Well, at least you have the honesty to blush! Isn't he quite a lot older than Mathilde?"

"Fifteen years. He has the most brilliant mind . . ."

". . . and you'd like to incorporate that brilliant mind into the family?"

"Just an errant thought, my dear; it grows out of a little conversation Mathilde and I had last spring, before she left for Meran."

Ferenczi continued his analytical training with Sigmund, attempting to conquer his own neuroses.

"How does it happen, Sandor, that you cannot come to grips with your hypochondria?"

"When I feel well, I am the master of it. When I don't feel well, it takes over . . . or does hypochondria take over first, and cause me to feel unwell, sending me to my medicine cabinet to swallow purgatives to eliminate my organic diseases?"

The fields around Berchtesgaden were as lush and brilliantly green as he had remembered them; the haystacks had not changed their structure by the tiniest variation; there was the amazing variety of trees, the mountains rolling back to infinity, six ranges piled behind each other, the vast icy peaks sticking like prongs into the sky. There were trails running in every direction through the woods, little rivulets with plank bridges.

One afternoon a week Sigmund hired a carriage to carry Martha and himself into Berchtesgaden for a few companionable hours of privacy. The air was fresh, the streets were up-and-down narrow, the women were charming in their dirndls: cotton dresses with short puffed sleeves and little aprons. Martha particularly enjoyed the Berchtesgaden shops, filled with a variety of foods, hundreds of items in each window, all in very small quantities and elaborately prepared. The bakeries were heaped with cakes covered with sugar, chocolate and whipped cream. The buildings were painted with murals of the countryside, particularly of harvesting. The men wore leather shorts, high socks, Tyrolean hats, carried canes and rucksacks on their backs. On Sunday the people walked through the streets with flowers in their hands, two roses or two blue cornflowers. Martha and Sigmund would end the day at the Kursaal, where they sat out in the open, drank a glass of beer, read the local newspaper; but mostly watched the parade of townspeople taking their leisurely, late afternoon walk. They appeared healthy and happy, with rosy cheeks and animated conversation. Martha commented:

"I'm afraid a psychoanalyst would have a hard time earning a living here. It's not only the cattle that look sleek and content; it's the people too. They look as though they take what comes along without questioning it. Sigi, could there be neuroses in this friendly and beautiful countryside?"

"There could be. When I worked as a *Sekundararzt* in Meynert's Psychiatric Clinic, at least half the patients I took care of came from farms and villages."

3.

The transition from summer to autumn brought Sigmund several shocks. The group of twenty physicians in and around Zurich, which had been meeting since the previous September in what they called their "Freudian Association," did not resume their discussions. No reasons were given; Sigmund could get no information by mail. He decided to go to Zurich and find out what had caused the unfortunate cessation.

Carl Jung met him at the railroad station, a hearty welcoming smile on his attractive blond face. He had a carriage waiting to take them through the central city, clustered around the sparkling blue lake, and then on the long uphill ride through the business and residential districts to the Burghölzli, located in the outskirts, even as the newly opened Steinhof Asylum was in Vienna. The Jungs had invited Sigmund to be their house guest.

Frau Emma Jung received him at the door of the living quarters they had occupied for the five years of their marriage, and in which their two daughters had been born. Though Emma was seven months' pregnant, she carried herself with almost regal grace. She had been entertained by Martha and Sigmund and, hospitable by nature, was pleased to be able to reciprocate. Despite the differences in their backgrounds, Emma was very like Martha, speaking a pure German, and thoroughly disliking travel. Carl Jung was adventuresome; he would try any strange country, food, way of life; Emma was conservative in her eating habits and living habits. Again, like Martha, she was precise in her ways, liked everything to be in its proper place, and believed in the rigorous exercise of etiquette. In a picture taken shortly after their marriage, which Sigmund saw in Carl's library, Emma looked the stronger of the two, which amused Sigmund, since no one he had ever known could conceivably be stronger than Dr. Carl Jung.

After Sigmund had unpacked his bag, Jung took him for a tour of the Burghölzli, where he had trained and worked for eight years, since 1900.

The Cantonal Asylum was enormous, containing hundreds of beds. Though it was connected with the University of Zurich and was used to train medical students, it in no way resembled Professor Meynert's Psychiatric Clinic at the Allgemeine Krankenhaus. The patients Sigmund had treated had been kept only long enough to study and record the nature of their disturbance, and had then been moved out, returned home if that were possible, or placed in an asylum. The Burghölzli was a custodial hospital; many of the patients Sigmund now saw in the wards had been there for years, hopeless cases of paranoia or dementia praecox. He was sorry to miss Eugen Bleuler, who was traveling at the moment. To Sigmund's trained eye the Burghölzli seemed magnificently run.

"Bleuler must be a fine administrator," Sigmund observed; "it's a rare gift, one I've admired but never possessed."

"Yes, he is," replied Jung a bit ruefully; "we don't like each other, but I have to give him his due. In fact this inspection tour I'm taking you on is almost like a farewell visit for me. As soon as the baby is born and Emma has fully recovered, we are moving out to Küsnacht, and the house we are just completing on the lake. I have to leave the Burghölzli and my assistantship with Bleuler. That means, perforce, the end of my teaching at the University of Zurich, as well. I'll do a little independent work in the laboratory here, but that's really only a gesture to the outside world that there is not a total rupture. Either you adhere, and travel the prescribed route, or you are a heretic. Heresy, in any form, is not popular in Switzerland. I will be pretty much in isolation for a while, even as you were in Vienna. But I will make my own way, with my studies and writings to sustain me. Sunday we will ride out to Küsnacht on Lake Zurich. I would like to show you the house."

There was rejoicing in Carl Jung's voice, but also a touch of bitterness. Sigmund had sensed from Jung's letters that Jung had come to dislike his superior. It might appear to be because Bleuler was the omnipresent authority figure, whose presence would block Jung's advance to the directorship. However, Sigmund suspected the real reasons for Jung's insistence upon breaking the relationship were repressed; short of analysis, they would not be brought to the surface. In any event it would be indiscreet to ask any questions. Although the Swiss might quarrel among themselves, even as his own Viennese did, they were intensely chauvinistic about not letting their differences escape the national borders.

That evening Ludwig Binswanger came in with Franz Riklin, Jung's relative, for supper. The four physicians discussed the usefulness of psychoanalysis in certain serious cases of mental disturbance. During the course of the evening Sigmund subtly inquired about the dissolving of the Zurich Freudian Association. No one of the men wished to explain.

Despite the fact that Jung was busy in the hospital, he and Sigmund managed to get in eight hours of hard-bitten talk each day: examining the materials of their recent cases, the expansion of psychoanalytic thinking into the broader fields of religion, anthropology, political economy, literature, the better to reveal the intricacies of man's instinctual nature, and what he had had to give up, modify, repress, in order to live peaceably in society. They also realistically discussed the beginning attacks from the Swiss pulpit and press against Freudian psychoanalysis, and the abandonment of the Swiss Freudian Association. Had it been a mistake, perhaps, for them to call their group a Freudian Association? It had given their opponents too sharp a target to shoot at. The membership had simply fallen off. Jung believed that the nucleus of the group would be re-formed in the not too distant future as the Zurich Psychoanalytic Society.

Sigmund decided that this was an appropriate time to press Jung for his stand on the sexual etiology of the neuroses; and how far he intended to deviate from Sigmund's fundamental tenets. Jung assured him that his days of vacillation were over . . .

Sigmund glanced up sharply.

". . . but Bleuler's are not!" Jung declared.

Yet Carl Jung did not want to be forced into a position where he would have to choose between Zurich psychiatry and Vienna psychoanalysis; he was already isolating himself sufficiently by moving out of the Burghölzli, the university and the city itself. Sigmund wondered if the reason Carl Jung had expressed his willingness to lend himself to the sexual etiology at this time, to move closer to Sigmund Freud, might be because he faced a possible void. Was Jung perhaps uncertain, even confused about his future? Would his few patients really follow him out to Küsnacht? Would he miss the activity of the Burghölzli?

As if reading Sigmund's thoughts, Jung said:

"I am going to be my own master, but in fact I do not have many patients. I am not sure, once I leave the city, whether I will function as a pure scientist, just read and spend time working on the new house, or whether I will get on with my practice." His light brown eyes were self-mocking. "You might say that I am in a bit of a fog."

On a Friday early in October, Eugen Bleuler and his wife Hedwig arrived in Vienna. They came to the Freuds' for dinner. Sigmund was struck, as he had been in Salzburg, by how attractive Bleuler was, his good looks and quiet charm enhanced by his slight aura of unapproachability. Sigmund was a little awed by him: his authority, his high, unassailable position at the pinnacle of academic science. It was the reverence he had felt for Professors Brücke and Meynert. When he intimated something of this to Bleuler, the director was astonished.

"I represent for you a person of authority? For God's sake, why? You are a discoverer; I did not accomplish anything like that."

Sigmund murmured a half-felt banality, but Bleuler was not to be put off; he apparently had some deeper purpose in mind than merely handing out praise.

"One compares your work with that of Darwin, Copernicus and Semmelweis. I believe too that for psychology your discoveries are equally fundamental, whether or not one evaluates advancements in psychology as highly as those in other sciences."

Sigmund was numbed by the encomium.

Martha had heard that Professor and Frau Professor Bleuler were somewhat formal by nature, and had banished the children to the kitchen for an earlier dinner. Tante Minna asked to be allowed to join the youngsters, suggesting that she did not feel up to meeting the Frau Professor, who was said to carry herself with a modicum of affectation.

When the roasted veal had been dispatched and the maid brought in the dessert, Bleuler cocked his handsome head to one side and said with a bright, purposeful gleam in his eye:

"Professor Freud, I must confess that I do have something serious on my mind for this meeting, pleasant as I knew it would be for our two families to become better acquainted. I am most hopeful that I can persuade you not to put so much emphasis on sex, and to find another name for whatever does not coincide with sexuality in the popular sense. I sincerely believe that if you would do this, all resistance and misunderstanding would cease."

Sigmund replied, with all the dignity he could summon:

"I do not believe in household remedies."

Frau Professor Bleuler was a serious-minded woman who understood the nature and worth of her husband's work. She gazed at Sigmund thoughtfully for a moment, then said:

"Please do not misunderstand us, Professor Freud; we are not suggesting that you change your beliefs or give up a single principle of psychoanalysis. It is purely a matter of semantics. I can tell you that in Switzerland the word 'sex' is utterly forbidden. In the Middle Ages people were burned at the stake because of one word: 'heretic.' Unless you find a more acceptable term than 'sexual,' your psychoanalysis is going to be burned at the stake!"

Martha had been watching the color rise in Sigmund's cheeks. She attempted to relieve the tension.

"Sigi, I've sometimes wondered whether there might be a more bland term. Why don't we try the association tests that come out of the Burghölzli?"

They spent the next hour conjuring and conjoining strange syllables, while the Bleulers tried to take the Freuds by storm: Pantheality, Nymph-

ism, Joinage, Corporeality, Juncturalis, Infibuation, Confluential . . .
Martha and Sigmund made some suggestions on the absurd side: Un-
ionality, Ingraft, Viritality, Accouplement . . . It was no use, as the
Bleulers at last agreed: sexuality was sexuality, it had been present ever
since the first egg was fertilized.

"To try to describe sexuality in other terms," Sigmund said hoarsely,
when they had exhausted themselves with the word game, "is to succumb
to a form of sickness which sexuality gone wrong brings on our patients.
It is not enough that our society must behave toward sex in a healthy,
honest, enjoyable fashion; people must be free to speak about it as they do
about other phases of life."

"Granted," said Bleuler, "we have failed to find a proper replacement
for the word 'sexuality.' For the moment we will have to leave it alone.
All the more reason, then, for you to shift your emphasis to a plurality instead of a single etiology of the neuroses."

"And so I shall, Professor Bleuler! Just as soon as these other causes of
neuroses turn up in my patients. I did not invent man; millions of years
of evolution have accomplished that. All I am trying to do is to describe
him, to find out what makes this most complex and confusing of all animals behave the way he does."

4.

It was a good thing he had not been serious about acquiring Ferenczi
as a son-in-law through Mathilde, for his older daughter announced that
she was engaged to Robert Hollitscher, thirty-three, a representative
of a silk firm, whom she had known for the six months she had been in
Meran, and whom she loved and intended to marry. Sigmund was furious
when Mathilde's letter arrived.

"She doesn't even bother to tell us in advance, to give us a chance to
get used to the idea. Presto! she's engaged. Wants to be married! At
twenty-one! Without our knowing the man, without the right to offer our
judgment . . ."

"Now, Sigi, it is not written in the Austrian Constitution that girls have
to be twenty-five, as I was, before they marry. If Mathilde has fallen in
love, let her marry. That was the subject of your private little conversation
before she left for Meran, wasn't it? Then you know that she will be
happier married than single. But I will invite the young man to visit."

Mollified, as he invariably was when Martha took over a situation, he
murmured, "You're right, of course. I promise not to examine Robert
Hollitscher as though he were an applicant for the Vienna Medical School.
At fifty-two, it is too late to become the outraged father."

He got not only a son-in-law but a sister-in-law as well. Mathilde and her Uncle Alexander decided they wanted a joint wedding. None of the Freuds belonged to a temple, which made things a trifle awkward, but Alexander found a sanctuary in a synagogue on the Müllnergasse and engaged it for a Sunday morning. Alexander insisted that his niece and Robert Hollitscher be married first.

Mathilde and Sophie Schreiber were beautiful in their long white wedding gowns. There was an over-all joyous air in the sanctuary, perhaps because the double ceremonies had generated a sense of excitement. The room had an awesome dignity, the candlelight softening the wood paneling and lending to both ceremonies an air of enchantment. Sigmund found himself enjoying his role of Father of the Bride, as well as that of Best Man.

"And why not?" Martha asked. "We all very much like Robert; and Sophie has already become a part of our family. Now that we've got you broken in to ceremonies, it will be easier for you to give away your five other children in matrimony."

Sigmund groaned, but pleasurably. After the two marriages everyone returned to the nearby Berggasse, where Martha had prepared a wedding dinner for some fifty guests, not only the Freud family, with Amalie recovered from a bout of illness and presiding in the seat of honor, but Rosa and her two children, Pauli, who had been widowed in New York, and had returned to Vienna with her daughter; the Hollitschers, who had come into the city for the marriage of their son; and Sophie Schreiber's small family. It was a happy day; even the new in-laws liked each other.

The Jungs arrived for one of their frequent visits on the day that publisher Deuticke delivered the first copy of the *Jahrbuch* to Sigmund. He held the journal in his hands with as much joy and affection as he had the first of his books; for now psychoanalysis would have an official voice and be available to medical circles. The magazine was sturdily printed and bound; he showed it to Martha with parental pride. His own contribution was a 109-page monograph on the Little Hans case, which he scanned with considerable pleasure. Jung, the editor, had read and corrected galleys on all the contributions, but this was the first time he had seen a bound copy. He too was pleased.

The Freuds and Jungs enjoyed each other thoroughly. When Karl Abraham, who still heard from the Burghölzli, warned Sigmund that Jung was "reverting to his former spiritualistic inclinations," Sigmund ascribed this to Abraham's mistrust of Jung.

After supper Sigmund left Martha and Emma to chat in the living room, while he and Jung went to Sigmund's office, drew comfortable chairs up before the bookcase and settled in for an evening of talk.

They discussed the second issue of the *Jahrbuch* and the second International Psychoanalytic Congress, which they were planning for the following spring. Sigmund emphasized his total confidence in Jung and made it clear that the younger man must assume the role of "successor and Crown Prince," leader of the international movement. But Jung was in one of his mystical moods; he wanted to talk about what he called the "factuality of occult events." First he told Sigmund about how he became interested.

"While I was still a student I was invited by the children of some relatives to join the game of table-turning with which they were amusing themselves. One of the group, a girl of fifteen, went into a trance, exhibited the bearing and conversation of an educated woman.

"I wanted to understand something so arresting, so different from anything I had seen before. That my parents and the others accepted as an explanation the fact that the girl was always high-strung amazed me. I set about the solution of this difficult question systematically, by keeping a detailed diary of the séances, and I drew up a careful account of the girl's personality and behavior in the waking state. This record provided a mass of psychological problems which at that stage in my career I could not understand. I explored in vain the extensive literature on spiritualism. My teachers at the university showed no interest in the girl's peculiarities and thought I was wasting my time. Then I read Krafft-Ebing. I had never heard of 'diseases of the personality.' This was a new world of thought, and naturally it stirred up memories of the girl who had gone into a trance."

Sigmund moved in his chair, uneasy. He crushed his half-smoked cigar in one of Martha's omnipresent ashtrays. He admired Carl Jung for the enormous range of his interests, and for his inexhaustible energies which brought him authoritative knowledge in fields so remote from each other as the calligraphy of Chinese art and the worship of the totem animals among the aboriginal Australians. But this approach to some kind of nether world was dangerous for anyone who was working in a new field of medicine and attempting to put it on an objective, scientific base.

"My dear Jung, we are going to have to buy you one of those new Ouija boards that were demonstrated in Vienna only last week. You put your fingertips lightly on a wooden triangle on the board, close your eyes, and occult forces lead the triangle from letter to letter to spell out names and whole sentences, most of them applying to events in the future."

Jung looked pained. He pressed on his diaphragm with both hands, murmuring to himself, ". . . made of iron . . . red hot . . . a glowing vault."

At that instant there was a pistol-like retort in the bookcase above them. Both men sprang up, expecting to see it topple. Nothing appeared disarranged.

"There," exclaimed Jung triumphantly, "is an example of a so-called catalytic exteriorization phenomenon."

"Oh, come, that is bosh!"

"It is not. You are mistaken, Herr Professor. Since you are so fond of quoting Shakespeare, may I suggest that 'There are more things in heaven and earth, Horatio, than are dreamt of in your philosophy.' And to prove my point I now predict that in a moment there will be another such retort."

Instantly there was another cracking sound from behind the bookshelves. Sigmund stared at Jung, aghast. What kind of happening was this? It was almost a year since he had moved his books into this back study and, aided by Otto Rank, fastidiously put each volume in its place; there had been no such shotlike noises.

Jung looked triumphant.

"As well he might!" thought Sigmund. "He believes he has just given a flawless demonstration of a poltergeist in action. And from the persuasive way he's trying to convince me of the power of unseen forces and how they can be studied through séances and mediums, I could almost believe . . . at least for the moment . . . !"

"Carl, there's one sequence I don't understand: was it the 'red hot' burning in your diaphragm that caused the noise to happen? Or was it the approaching bang which communicated itself to you and caused your diaphragm to become a 'glowing vault'?"

"Now you are pulling my leg. The unexplainable can only be observed, it cannot be rationalized. But for us, as researchers, to say that what cannot be explained does not exist is to dry up one of the main founts of man's inquiring mind. But I know you don't want to discuss this further. Let's go back to the subject we were talking about before dinner, what I termed the two divisions of the unconscious, the personal and the collective. The personal embraces all the acquisitions of the personal existence, hence the forgotten, the repressed, the subliminally perceived, thought and felt. But, in addition to these personal unconscious contents, there exist other contents which do not originate in personal acquisitions but in the inherited possibility of psychic functioning in general, that is, in the inherited brain structure. These are the mythological associations; those motives and images which can spring anew in every age and clime, without historical tradition or migration. I term these contents the collective unconscious."

Sigmund walked the Jungs up to their hotel at the top of the hill. The Regina had by now become the official hotel for all visiting doctors and patients who came to Vienna to see Herr Professor Sigmund Freud. They chatted lightly of personal matters; how the house in Küsnacht was progressing; when Sigmund and Martha could come for a week's visit and enjoy the quiet, far reaches of Lake Zurich in Carl's boat.

Back at home, Sigmund gently rocked his head between the fingertips of both hands. He felt uncomfortable about the precognition incident, mostly because, under the spell of Jung's overwhelming personality, he had for the moment been convinced that such occult happenings could occur.

But not for long; two nights later when sitting at his table quietly working on a paper, there was a sharp, cracking sound from the book-case. With a sigh of relief he realized that the noise had come from the drying out of the green planks he had used for the bookshelves.

He was grateful to be able to put the incident out of his mind.

At the end of April the Reverend Oskar Pfister, thirty-six, with a parish in Zurich, married, with several children, made the pilgrimage to the Berggasse after four months of correspondence.

Pfister was a lean, sinewy man of good height, dressed in the every-day clothes of the Swiss layman; he wore a butterfly collar with the points turned down to frame the tight knot of a dark necktie. He was clean-shaven except for as modest a mustache as would have been considered respectable in his profession; dark hair, immaculately groomed, a lean face tapering to a resolute chin; alert eyes, at once gentle and gray-granite strong. From his letters Sigmund imagined him to be a different breed of man from any he had met.

Martha had read several of Parson Pfister's letters, so that she could take the measure of the man. But the Freud children were taken completely by surprise. They had expected someone in a clergyman's outfit, dark and foreboding; as well as one of the deadly serious, grim pastors they had read about. Oskar Pfister had an effervescent quality which enveloped them, a man whose whole being was an emanation of love for the young. During dinner all the Freud children wanted to talk at once, with Oskar Pfister's engulfing voice above them, speaking to each of them quite personally . . . or so they thought. It was the first time, after dinner, that the young Freuds gathered about the visitor, besieging their father not to take the guest away.

"I'm sure he'd rather be with us than talk medicine in your office," said Oliver.

Sigmund smiled, said to Pfister:

"Please don't imagine that this happens every time I bring a friend to Frau Professor Freud's table. In fact, it has never happened, except with Sandor Ferenczi. You have made a conquest. Very well, children, take the parson into the living room for a while. Then you simply must release him to me."

The Reverend Oskar Pfister had bought Sigmund's books as they appeared in the Zurich bookstores and was convinced, based on his experience with his parishioners, but mostly with the children in his religious classes, that psychoanalysis was sound in the basic principles

and should be converted to the purpose of public education where its
therapy was needed.

"You may be interested in knowing, Professor Freud, why I first
intended to become a teacher. It began in kindergarten, when one of
my little friends fell asleep during class. He was severely beaten by the
woman teacher. I have been unable to forget the hurt expression of
the sick child as he vomited over the dress of the disciplinarian. He
died a few days later. We chanted our songs of grief and mourning
at the open grave. . . . When we moved to Zurich, I was put in public
school under a confirmed alcoholic. He pounded knowledge into our
behinds with a huge ruler. He particularly enjoyed his encounter with
two feeble-minded girls whom he declared he could teach to read by
beating them savagely. The poor girls never learned to read, of course,
but the teacher went through an emotional orgasm each day as he
pounded them with his rod. I cringed and felt pity for those girls."

"Did you know, Parson Pfister, when you turned to theology that
you could combine it with education?"

"Only vaguely. I attended more psychology lectures at the University
of Basel than I did theology. I very nearly did not receive my doctorate in philosophy. Though I never doubted the grace of God, I
did begin to question the Christian belief in miracles. It was my belief that a devoted Christian had to question. Orthodox beliefs frightened
me; there was little love and even less understanding of what you have
called 'common human unhappiness.'"

Sigmund thought, "He shares one quality with Adler, Jung, Ferenczi:
he radiates empathy."

There was an inner tranquillity about the man, a sense that he understood the human condition and did not condemn it. But as Pfister's
professors had learned, and later his superiors in the Church, no one
could trifle with his independence; it was the rock of his faith. He
was a formidable fighter for what he defined as the Christian ethic:
love for one's neighbor. He had already declined a prestigious chair
at the University of Zurich because he preferred to remain with his parish
and to continue his work with adolescents.

Sigmund said quietly:

"As I address you in my letters, 'Dear Man of God,' can you know
how much pleasure it brings me, as an unrepentant heretic, to have
this trusting friendship with a Protestant clergyman?"

"Herr Professor, in the Judaeo-Christian tradition, I must insist that
you too are a good Christian."

Sigmund chuckled. "One of my friends in Prague, Christian von
Ehrenfels, who has just published an illuminating volume on sexual
ethics, had described us as 'Sexual Protestants.' Tell me about teaching
religion to four hundred children from many different districts."

"My only method of discipline is teaching in a lively way; if a student falls asleep, it's my fault. Second, I describe religion as salvation, as a source of joy and support in times of danger."

Sigmund replied soberly, "In earlier times religious faith stifled the neuroses. . . . In itself psychoanalysis is neither religious nor non-religious, but an impartial tool which both priest and layman can use in the service of a sufferer."

Pfister looked troubled.

"With adults, yes. I must train myself so that I can help those who come to me as blind sufferers. But what about the children?"

"What about the children?"

"Few if any of our teachers understand what goes on in a child's mind, let alone his unconscious. We have to teach them Freudian principles. If we can lead the young to a loving God, and to an enlightened teacher, half of their problems will be solved. That is my life ambition. You will see, Herr Professor, that before I am through I will have made an impression on both the gloomy Church and morbid classroom in Switzerland."

5.

The Freuds became a more closely knit family with each passing year. It was a happy household, despite the fact that during the winter months Sigmund's workdays were rigidly scheduled. By seven in the morning he was in his shower, the barber came in to trim his hair and beard, then he sat down with Martha and the children for a roll, sweet butter and coffee while he glanced at the pages of the *Neue Freie Presse*. By eight o'clock he was in his office ready to receive the first patient, the children were on their way to various schools, Martha was dressed and out doing her day's marketing. Sigmund no longer indulged himself in the *Kleines Gulasch* at eleven o'clock, or the coffee at five; his only indulgence was his cigars, but here he was profligate. Each day after dinner he walked to the Tabak Trafik close by the Michaeler Church to buy the twenty excellent cigars which were his day's quota. Once when he offered a friend a cigar, and the man declined on the grounds that he had just finished one, Sigmund laughed and said, "That's the most irrelevant excuse I can think of."

His medical practice, after years of inexplicable ups and downs, was now constant, as was his weekly routine. He analyzed as many as ten and twelve patients a day, yet he was able to make frequent referrals of patients to the young doctors in his psychoanalytical group. Now that his income was stable, and he was receiving forty kronen for each hour, he was at last able to buy life insurance for Martha and to

invest part of his savings in government bonds to insure the education
and the travel of his offspring.

The children had grown up liking each other, sharing, rarely indulging in the arguments which sometimes plagued large households.
They went together to Saturday night dances; when the girls had tickets
for the theater, Sigmund timed his evening walk so that he would be
waiting for them when the performance was over and he would accompany them home. He provided them with an adequate allowance
and insisted that they be well dressed, since this was important for their
psyches. He did not want them to suffer the painful, straitened circumstances of his own youth. Now that they were older and needed
more spending money, he set aside the modest royalties from his books
to be divided equally among them.

He taught them how to play *Tarock* because it was such a companionable game, and managed to find a couple of hours a week
to play with them. Mathilde and her husband often joined them. Martha
never did learn, but she liked the sound and sight of her family sitting
around one table enjoying each other.

Early each Sunday morning he walked to his mother's apartment
for a brief visit with Amalie and Dolfi. Amalie was now seventy-three
and in robust health. Martha frequently invited the family for informal
Sunday night supper, Rosa and her children, Alexander and his wife,
Pauli and her daughter, Amalie and Dolfi. She put a light repast on
the sideboard and they helped themselves when they wanted.

Occasionally of a Tuesday evening, Sigmund gave a paper at the
B'nai B'rith; he never ceased to be grateful to the members for giving
him an audience when he had no other. After the Wednesday Evening
meetings of the Vienna Psychoanalytic Society, he went with his
colleagues and a few guests to one of the nearby cafes for non-scientific
talk and companionship. After his Saturday night lecture at the University of Vienna, he would go at once to Leopold Königstein's house,
where supper would be waiting for him, and then he, Oskar Rie, and
Dr. Ludwig Rosenstein would play *Tarock*. Martha often went late
on a Saturday afternoon to visit and wait for Sigmund's arrival.

She too had her routine and little *Kaffeeplausch*. Frau Professor
Königstein, Frau Dr. Melanie Rie, other women whom she had met,
wives of Sigmund's colleagues, dropped in at five for coffee and cake
and talk.

On Sunday afternoons, when Sigmund was not too cluttered with
manuscripts, he took the children to the two excellent art museums.
By now they knew each picture, particularly the Rembrandts, Breughels,
the Baroness von Ferstel's *Ruined Castle*; their interest was enhanced
by the fact that Sigmund would compare the works of art to those

he had seen in Italy, for the Hapsburgs had collected fine examples of Titian, Tintoretto, Rubens, Veronese.

He was an affectionate father who allowed his children to grow up along the lines of their own natures. In many of the sterner households of Vienna he was thought to be too permissive. As long as they did their chores and took care of their schoolwork, he let them make their own decisions. As soon as they were old enough to travel, he sent them off on trips through Germany, Holland and Italy. Sixteen-year-old Sophie, the middle daughter, was the affectionate, happy-go-lucky elf of the family, known as the "Sunday child." She was pretty and tender and had inherited her mother's nature. She took every opportunity to cuddle on her father's lap when he was sitting in a big chair.

He and Anna, who was thirteen, were attached by the most powerful cords of love and understanding. She was a natural and penetrating student. There were no outward displays between them, since Anna's nature was diametrically opposed to Sophie's, but they enjoyed a rapport which was a source of joy and strength to both of them. Seventeen-year-old Ernst, bright and attractive, was known in the family as the "lucky child"; everything he wanted and everything he did seemed to come out right. The apartment on the Berggasse was frequently filled with young people, though Martha gave no formal parties for them. Sigmund's manner was warm and simple; and although he did not always have spare time, they knew very well that each of them was in his mind; if they were late for a meal or did not show up at all, he would be unhappy and point with a spoon or fork at the empty chair, inquiring silently of Martha:

"Why are we missing a member of our family?"

They knew that their father was becoming an increasingly important man, but because of Sigmund's intense work schedule and his innate modesty in the home, they were never brushed by the pollen-laden wings of arrogance. They grew up with his dry wit, which they came to enjoy; and at the same time they were exposed to Tante Minna's outrageous jokes and repartee. Like Ernest Jones, she had a "tongue as sharp as a needle," but it was directed only against the foibles of the outside world.

Martha was as disciplined in her activities as Sigmund. She could not sit down during the day with a book, to rest or read for a half hour, because her mother had taught her that that was not proper conduct for a housewife. However she did enjoy going out occasionally, to the home of a friend, to meet with other women for coffee. Sigmund often asked her to join him for the walk after dinner or supper, but she would go along only if he had a specific destination: delivering proofs to Deuticke or Heller, going to the Tabak Trafik for his cigars.

If he simply wanted an hour's fast walk, up to the Schottentor and then around the Ringstrasse and home along the Kai, she would reply:

"Thank you, no, I get enough exercise."

The evenings were the nicest time of the day for her. When Sigmund worked with patients until nine, Tante Minna would have supper with the children, leaving Martha and Sigmund to have a quiet hour together. Occasionally he would bring correspondence or a manuscript into his study to work there while she sat beside him in a deep chair reading Thomas Mann or Romain Rolland. If she did not feel like being left alone, and Sigmund remained in his office, she would take a book and read with him there until midnight.

It had long been evident that Minna was a born Tante; she had a natural gift for the role. The six children were as much hers as Martha's. She never violated their confidence. She did not interfere in the running of the household; if one of the servants came to her and asked for an instruction, Tante Minna replied:

"Ask Frau Professor."

She embroidered beautifully, making gifts for birthdays, anniversaries, Christmas. The older she got, the taller she seemed to grow, a big rawboned woman with a wide flat face, hair parted in the middle, broad shoulders and almost entirely flat-chested. She wore her skirts so long, covering her shoes, that Martin remarked:

"I have never had any realization that she has legs."

It was a hard-working, growing and accomplishing household, lived in by a compatible brood. One of the qualities Sigmund had wanted in a wife was that of sweetness. The children had inherited a touch of Martha's quality.

In one of the last few days of 1908, Sigmund had received a letter from President G. Stanley Hall of Clark University in Worcester, Massachusetts, inviting him to come to America for a series of lectures to help celebrate the twentieth anniversary of the founding of the university. President Hall, a well-known and respected educator, who had been teaching Freudian psychoanalysis in his classes, wrote:

"Although I have not the honor of your personal acquaintance, I have for many years been profoundly interested in your work, which I have studied with diligence, and also in that of your followers."

Sigmund knew this to be a true statement, because only the year before Hall had published a book called *Adolescence* with five references to *Studies on Hysteria*. He had also predicted in *Adolescence* that Dr. Sigmund Freud's work would become important to the psychology of art and religion.

He wanted Dr. Freud to come to America during the first week of

July, for a fee of four hundred dollars; the United States was now ready for a strong statement by the originator of psychoanalysis and the discoverer of the unconscious. Freud's lectures would "perhaps in some sense mark an epoch in the history of these studies in this country."

At the break between patients, Sigmund took the letter across the hall to show to Martha, exclaiming, "This is the first time any university in the world has invited me to give a statement of my beliefs. It's most gratifying."

"Of course you'll go."

"Alas. The university is almost four thousand miles away, and it would be a week's sea voyage. The four-hundred-dollar fee would pay my expenses, but I would lose a month of my practice. That is always one of my busiest times, trying to bring the patients into a state of reasonable good health so that they can enjoy their summer."

"What a pity!" Martha declared. "It would not only give you a chance to see the United States but to give a helping hand to Brill and Jones. How foolish of us to think that the only reason to save money is against misfortune; perhaps we ought to start a separate fund in the bank labeled 'good fortune.'"

President Hall was not a man to be put down. He answered Sigmund's letter of regret with a counterproposal: the fee would be raised to seven hundred and fifty dollars; Dr. Freud could give his lectures in September; and Clark University would like to confer upon him the honorary degree of Doctor of Laws.

"Now you have to go," cried Martha exultantly. "President Hall has blocked your every line of retreat."

Sigmund smiled shyly.

"One does not retreat from a Doctor of Laws; that is the oldest and most prestigious honorary degree there is. It will probably be the only honorary degree I ever receive, and so I had better make the most of my opportunity. I can write the lectures going over on the ship. Why don't I ask Sandor Ferenczi if he would be free to come along?"

The members of the Vienna Psychoanalytic Society were excited when Sigmund showed them the letter. Alfred Adler spoke for them all when he said with pride, "It is one more step along the road to official recognition. We must invade the universities; they are the first and most important stronghold of ideas. This is a rare opportunity, Professor Freud, and I trust that you will arrange to publish the lectures as well."

Ferenczi accepted at once. Sigmund was delighted to learn sometime later that Carl Jung had also been invited by Clark University, to lecture on the association tests which had originated in Zurich. Jung was also to be given an honorary Doctor of Laws. When Sigmund told Martha and Minna the news at the dinner table, he said:

"That magnifies the importance of the whole affair. I must write to Jung this very day and invite him to travel with Ferenczi and me."

6.

The year 1908 had proved to be a fertile one; five of his articles had appeared in scientific journals: on *Creative Writers and Day-Dreaming, Hysterical Fantasies and Their Relation to Bisexuality, "Civilized" Sexual Morality and Modern Nervous Illness, On the Sexual Theories of Children.* It was not until news of his monograph *Character and Anal Eroticism* got around that another violent storm burst over his head. The more clever of his opponents were now calling him, behind the backs of their hands, a "shit" and "the asshole of creation."

He pointed out that every child has available for sexual excitation such parts of the body as the genitals, the mouth and the anus, which he labeled the erotogenic zones. Working with his adult patients had taught him that some infants had a strong emphasis on the excitations of the anal zone. Their first characteristic was an unwillingness to empty their bowels because this gave them an early chance for self-assertion by exerting control over their feces; they also derived pleasure from denying their mothers satisfaction. These individuals later became fascinated with their own feces, took pride in their production, spent considerable time studying them, equated feces with wealth, in a kind of worship. If the parents so ardently wanted the feces passed, must they not be the most valuable gift the baby could offer up?

The idiosyncrasies vanished once the child matured and the concentration on the anal zone gave way to the genital zone. But it left permanent marks on the character; almost without fail these people turned out to be orderly, punctual, parsimonious and obstinate: character traits which derived from the sublimation of anal eroticism. Sigmund had handled many cases of chronic constipation which the internists had been unable to cure; they turned out to be neuroses based on the age-old identification of feces with gold.

"I will not give away my wealth."

By bringing forward to consciousness the origin of this disturbance, Sigmund was able to bring the patients relief, though sometimes he had to take them, unbelieving, all the way from ancient Babylonia, "Gold is the feces of Hell," to the modern, vulgar phrase "shitter of ducats" used to describe spendthrifts. Not everyone made the transition;

a considerable percentage of the homosexuals who came to Sigmund for help had simply never outgrown their anal eroticism.

Sigmund thought back to the outburst of rage when he had first published his findings on sexuality in children. He commented to Otto Rank, who was cataloguing a newly arrived batch of medical journals, that even doctors repressed their memories of childhood sexuality.

"All they have to do is to remember backward," murmured Rank, his dark eyes enormous behind the thick glasses.

"Quite right. It takes considerable ingenuity on the part of older people to overlook such early sexual activities or to explain them away. But who ever said that the human race was not ingenious? It can turn an obvious truth into a falsehood and then sell the illusion to a repressed society as though it were Holy Writ."

Rank grinned his eager homely grin.

"They won't have it easy, Professor. You are teaching people to understand that no truth is ugly, and no lie is beautiful."

Sigmund patted young Rank on the shoulder.

"Push ahead at the university, Otto, and earn your degree. You will become the first layman to practice, and help us get our job done."

The reason Sigmund was being so productive was that the source material that winter and the following spring was particularly rich. For him, learning was a process of growth; it was never a process of arriving and leeching. One of his patients was a cultured and sophisticated man of twenty-five, a clothes fetishist who demanded elegance of dress in himself and any young woman he was to be seen with. A fixation on his mother had rendered him psychologically impotent; and little wonder, for the mother was passionately in love with him, making the son, even now, the petted observer of her dressing and undressing. During his childhood he had been fascinated by his rectal excreta; from eight to ten he had used a string to keep a hard sausage hanging from his rectum, bits of which he would break off during the day when the impulse seized him. He was also a shoe fetishist, with an overdeveloped sense of smell. Sigmund had learned from earlier patients that "shoe fetishism goes back to an original (olfactory) pleasure in the dirty and stinking foot," a vestigial remain from the days when man's ancestor walked on all fours, with his nose close to the ground, and his sense of smell afforded him both defense and pleasure. Now for the first time Dr. Freud was able to tie together his patient's "coprophilic olfactory pleasure" from childhood and his present foot and shoe fetishism.

Analysis returned the young man to potency, but he remained unable to experience pleasure.

A kindred case was that of an attractive young housewife who adored her own feet, massaged them with creams for hours each day, kept

her toenails in an exquisite state of pedicure; and then went into the
shops of Vienna to buy shoes: all colors, all styles, all shapes, sometimes a dozen pairs a day to join the hundreds of pairs already in
her closet at home. It was the husband who came to Dr. Sigmund
Freud for help; not only was his wife neglecting their home and children, and earning the reputation of being somewhat crazy, but she
was also bankrupting the family by the expenditures. Could Dr. Freud
help his wife return to sanity?

Sigmund learned, after a number of sessions, that the young woman
bought the shoes as decoration for her feet. Unlike the foot fetish of
the earlier patient, it was in no way connected with olfactory pleasures.
This confused him at first; but after a time he found his patient returning more and more in her thoughts to her earliest memories of
the days when she had thought that she, like her baby brother, had
a penis. It had taken her a considerable time to learn that her clitoris
was not going to grow into a penis; and she was never reconciled. During
these painful days of disillusionment she had made a displacement downward, and fallen in love with her feet. Sigmund led her slowly to
this discovery; and again, he got a partial cure: the young woman
stopped buying shoes, but she continued to massage and pedicure her
feet every day of her life.

He was also treating a bright but peculiar man who suffered from
erythrophobia, fear of the color red, commonly associated with blood.
This was the third case of this nature he had handled; the first had
gone on with interruptions for five years; in the second, the patient
had terminated the treatments after two weeks. In this third case, the
man suffered from outbursts of perspiration, as well as furious blushing
accompanied by senseless rage, a fear of shaving because he might cut
himself and see blood; and the feeling of comfort only when he was
in intense cold. Sigmund diagnosed an anxiety hysteria, yet it was
difficult to find a place for it among the sexual neuroses. Shame appeared to be at the base of the anxiety; but shame over what? The
patient, who was known in Vienna as a great rogue and "sex scoundrel," finally came forth with his childhood materials: too early sexual
knowledge, occasioned by the patient's parents discussing intercourse in
terms that the six-year-old boy could not understand. Sigmund wrote:
"Erythrophobia consists of being ashamed for unconscious reasons."

The first case Sigmund had failed to cure even after five years, though
he had enabled the man to cope with life. The second patient vanished.
But now, knowing more, he was not only able to send the third
patient back to his profession, but so completely dried out his Don
Juan complex ("I must conquer new women all the time to prove to
myself that I am a man!") that he actually married and settled down.

A young man came to him because he was being harassed by "insane dreams." He had heard that Professor Freud had evolved an intelligible method of interpreting dreams. What could he do for example with the ridiculous dream he had had the night before?

"I was being treated by two university professors of my acquaintance instead of by you. One of them was doing something to my penis. I was afraid of an operation. The other was pushing against my mouth with an iron rod, so that I lost one or two of my teeth. I was tied up with four silk cloths."

Analysis made clear that the young man had never performed the act of coitus. Although the silk cloths led him to a homosexual he knew, he had never desired intercourse with men. In fact his ideas about intercourse were so confused that he imagined men and women made love by masturbating together. Sigmund interpreted the dream: the fear of an operation on his penis was the fear of castration from his childhood; the iron rod pushing against his mouth was the act of fellatio, also present in his unconscious from early, repressed desire; and the loss of his teeth the guilt price he made himself pay for the act of perversion.

A baffling case was one which he saw in an institution because the boy's desperate parents concealed the fact that he was psychotic. Sigmund got to the sanatorium in time to observe one of his attacks, a simulated act of coitus, or rage against the act of coitus, with a constant spitting during the violent charade, in such a fashion as to indicate that what was being ejaculated was sperm. Subsequently there were severe auditory hallucinations: a combination of hysteria and obsessional neurosis which he could treat; and dementia praecox, which he could not. Sigmund stayed with the patient long enough to determine that the simulated coitus, rage and spitting resulted from his having observed his parents go through the act. Against these outbreaks, Sigmund could help the boy, for which the parents were grateful. Then it occurred to him to give the boy a physical examination; to his surprise he found that the boy's genitals were infantile.

"I'm deeply sorry," he told the parents, "but I cannot honestly hold out hope of a cure."

During this period he had an influx of male patients. One of the most interesting, a patient whom he described as a "mental masochist," aggressive and sadistic by nature in wanting to inflict pain and punishment on others, had reversed these elements into a desire to have pain and punishment inflicted on himself, not physical pain but humiliation and mental torture. Under these circumstances he was destroying not only his human relationships but himself as well. His difficulties had begun a number of years earlier when he had fallen into a pattern of tormenting his older brother, to whom he was drawn in a repressed homosexual manner. Since he would not free associate, Sigmund had to work through the dreams, which the man had no hesitancy in relating.

"The dream came in three pieces: first, my older brother was chaffing me. Secondly, two grown men were caressing each other homosexually. Third, my brother had sold the business to which I myself had been looking forward to being the director. I awoke feeling terribly distressed."

"It was a masochistic wishful dream," Sigmund explained, "and might be translated thus: 'It would serve me right if my brother were to confront me with this sale as a punishment for all the torments he had to put up with from me.'"

When the patient accepted this interpretation, Sigmund added, "There is a masochistic component in the sexual constitution of many people, which arises from the reversal of an aggressive, sadistic component into its opposite."

The analysis went well from there, allowing Sigmund to do a study of the elements of sadism and masochism which lodged in the unconscious as opposite sides of the same shield; and how these childhood components later affected adult character and action.

7.

It was time to leave for the United States. The family saw him off from a North Tyrol villa on the nineteenth of August, with a good many hugs and kisses. He was in a rested and happy state of mind. He went through Oberammergau to Munich. In Munich he ate something that disagreed with him and had a bad train trip from Munich to Bremen, sleeping hardly at all. He felt a little better after he had had a warm bath at his hotel, took a walk about the city and through the colorful docks, and wrote three separate letters to Martha describing everything he had seen.

Carl Jung arrived from Zurich and Sandor Ferenczi from Budapest in time for Sigmund to be host at luncheon. He ordered a bottle of wine to celebrate their coming together. When Jung refused to break his rule of total abstinence, inherited from Bleuler, and Forel before him, Sigmund and Ferenczi persuaded him that a tiny glass of wine could not possibly hurt him; and at last he gave in. But the wine had a strange effect upon him; he began talking animatedly about the so-called bog corpses which were to be found in northern Europe, prehistoric men who had either drowned in the marshes or were buried there, hundreds of thousands of years before. Since there was humic acid in the bog water, the chemical consumed the bones but it also tanned the skin, so that the skin and hair were perfectly preserved. It was a process of natural mummification, in the course of which the bodies were pressed flat by the weight of the peat. But the wine had befuddled Jung a little; instead of locating the peat corpses in Scandinavia, he said that the mummies were to be found in the lead cellars of Bremen. Sigmund asked:

"Why are you so concerned with these corpses?"

"Because they have always fascinated me; it's a way of seeing what men and women really looked like all those thousands of years ago. Being here in the city where there are the corpses brought it back to my mind. I'd like to see some of them."

"I don't really think that peat-bog corpses go very well with my *Schnitzel*," Sigmund said; "besides, those corpses don't exist in Bremen, they're turned up by the peat diggers farther north in Denmark and Sweden."

Jung put down his fork, straightened up, shook his head in a puzzled sort of way.

"You're absolutely right. Now why do you suppose I transported those corpses all the distance down to Bremen? You say that no one ever makes a mistake by accident. What could have been my motivation?"

Sigmund felt dizzy, and then faint. He tried to take a sip of the wine but could not raise the glass. He felt himself slipping away. The next thing he knew he was lying on a couch in the manager's office. Jung had picked him up from the floor where he had fallen, but had carried him out so unostentatiously that almost no one in the restaurant knew what had happened. Ferenczi was holding an icebag on his forehead. When he opened his eyes he saw Jung hovering above him. Jung said:

"A fine thing. I take my first taste of wine in fifteen years and you pass out! Seriously, what happened to you?"

Sigmund sat up, his head still spinning.

"I don't know. Perhaps it was the food that disagreed with me in Munich. Perhaps it was the fact that I was up all night on the train coming into Bremen. Perhaps it was overstimulation at the thought of boarding the ship tomorrow. But I have never fainted in my life before, and so there has to be a deeper-lying cause. All that chatter about corpses unnerved me. I was the one who was in Bremen, not the bog corpses. Could there be a connection? Could you have had a death wish toward me? That was the last, unwelcome thought I had just before I lost consciousness."

They sailed into New York Harbor late Friday afternoon, August 27, a brilliantly clear day. Sigmund stood well forward on the prow with Jung on one side of him and Ferenczi on the other, while the skyline of Manhattan came into view, first a blur on the horizon and then the buildings particularizing themselves: tall, majestic, seeming to rest squarely on the waters of the bay. Sigmund was fascinated by the contour of the island, its needle point at the Battery broadening as it moved north. He thought:

"I wonder if I am looking at the United States the way Eli Bernays did? He was seeking a new home and a new way of life; he was asking himself, 'Is this where I belong? Am I going to become an American?' Millions of Europeans have had that same hope and question when they first saw this thrilling sight. But I am only here for a few weeks. When the lectures are over, I shall go out into the courtyard of the inn, find my own pack, put it on my back and return to Vienna."

As they passed the Statue of Liberty, Sigmund exclaimed:

"Won't they get a surprise when they hear what we have to say to them!"

Jung turned, replied, not unkindly:

"How ambitious you are!"

A. A. Brill was on the dock to greet them. He looked as though he wanted to hug each one of the three men, so great was his sense of triumph in their being invited to bring psychoanalysis to the United States. The only ship's reporter who seemed interested in the little group of European doctors was so unimpressed that he misspelled Sigmund's name; the next morning word appeared in the paper that a "Professor Freund of Vienna" had arrived in the country. However he had found his cabin steward reading a copy of *The Psychopathology of Everyday Life*, and so his feelings were not hurt. The young man had said: "Dr. Freud, I know that what you have written in this book is true because I have committed every one of the acts myself."

It was dusk by the time they cleared customs, and Brill had the carriage driver take the party uptown to the Manhattan Hotel, just east of Fifth Avenue on Forty-second Street. There was a letter awaiting Sigmund from President Hall inviting him to be his guest in the President's House for his week's stay in Worcester. Sigmund tried to telephone his sister Anna and Eli Bernays but they were away on their summer vacation.

While Brill helped Jung and Ferenczi make themselves comfortable in the rooms he had booked for them, Sigmund went quickly into the city again, eager to possess New York in the tactile sense, even as he had Paris when he went to work at the Salpêtrière: by walking the streets, feeling the pavement beneath his legs, studying the store windows, looking at the faces of the people rushing by, in a hurry to return to their families and sit down to their suppers; no leisurely pace, but an onslaught against time, as though more than enough of the day had been given to work, and now one wanted to return to the security of home.

Brill had slipped a map of the city into his pocket. At Fifth Avenue he saw diggings where a great Public Library was to be built. He realized that Vienna had no such accumulation of books which the entire public was free to use. He then walked with his light, swift steps up Fifth Avenue past elegant homes, churches and expensive shops. At Fifty-ninth Street he saw a beautiful hotel, the Plaza, newly opened, and wandered through its garden court where an orchestra was playing and some unhurried New Yorkers were lingering over late afternoon tea.

He returned to the Manhattan tired but triumphant. New York City, though he had seen only a dozen and a half blocks of it, was no longer strange or alien. Had he not held some part of it under his feet, even as he had the Humpback World above Semmering? He could not liken New York to anything in Vienna, Berlin, Paris or Rome. It was, in its own busy, fast-paced teeming energy and jams of people, a new experience. The city with its tall buildings looked, sounded, almost tasted on his tongue, extraordinarily different from the cities he knew.

Brill treated them to a light supper and, because they had been up since five that morning, amidst the ship's excitement at approaching port, saw that they were bedded down; promising to reappear at breakfast to take them on a sightseeing tour.

He started their adventure at the Battery, where they had a superb early morning view of the bay. Then he walked them past the buildings of the great shipping firms, the few blocks to Wall Street, a narrow canyon filled with the aromatic scents of coffee and spices, some of the bales and boxes still standing in the streets in front of the import and export houses near the docks. Sigmund recognized several famous banks, with the company names attached in heavy gold lettering.

He wanted to know where the foreign settlements were, so Brill took them to the East Side to the pushcart neighborhood which Sigmund likened to the Naschmarkt, filled as it was with delicious fragrances and all manner of foods, the housewives shopping early to get the best pick. Next he moved them south to Chinatown where, for the first time, Sigmund saw Chinese men with their hair in long queues hanging down their backs, dressed in long black silk or satin robes, he could not tell which, long coats with wide sleeves, talking in high-pitched voices among themselves as they entered shops selling exotic Chinese foods and herbs. He remarked that there was not one Chinese woman to be seen on the streets; but there was the fragrance of burning incense.

Brill had no organized plan, quickly shuttling his indefatigable friends through the colorful Italian neighborhood around Houston Street, then for a brief spell into the Bowery where they watched artists tattooing sailors in New York on leave from their ships. When he decided their feet must be hurting, he hired a carriage and took them out to Coney Island, whose magnificent Luna Park amusement area was world famous. Sigmund described it as a somewhat larger Prater. Back in Manhattan, Brill pointed out the big department stores, John Wanamaker at Broadway and Eighth Street, the Flatiron Building, twenty-nine stories high, the world's tallest, the men's garment center starting at Twenty-seventh Street, the millinery section at Thirty-first, the sweatshops that functioned inside former red brick private homes. Despite the height of the buildings, the variety of the avenues and vehicles, the numbers and diversity of the people impressed the men the most.

Back at the hotel, Sigmund soaked his feet in hot water in the bathtub. He said to Brill:

"This is the first time in my life my feet ever came out of a day's joust as the loser. But now I know what Eli Bernays meant when he wrote about New York as a melting pot. Will all the ingredients melt? And what will America be when the fires die down under the pot?"

The following morning Sigmund asked Brill to take him to the Metropolitan Museum so that he could see the Greek antiquities. After an hour of exploring the marble sculptures he turned to Brill and said with eyes dancing:

"I know I am now in the country of the future, I can tell it by the speed with which people walk and talk and eat. Nevertheless, I am happier right here in the civilization of the past."

"That's a strange thing for you to say, Professor Freud," Brill answered, his heavy-lidded eyes serious; "your work is going to do more to change and shape the future than anything I showed you in New York. But come along to Columbia University. I hope to teach Freudian psychoanalysis there one day, and so you should see its beautiful setting."

That afternoon Ernest Jones arrived from Toronto. There was a hearty reunion, and that evening the five colleagues had dinner at Hammerstein's Roof Garden, one of the most fashionable of New York's restaurants. Sigmund was impressed by the noisy though elegant restaurant, the lavishly gowned women, many of them in décolleté, and the men who, according to Brill, were powerful businessmen converting America into a rich industrial nation.

"Their food is also rich," Sigmund groaned after he had finished his dinner. "I don't think American cooking agrees with me. I have a stomach ache. I shall fast all day tomorrow."

Carl Jung chuckled, said, "Herr Professor, that is not entirely fair to the American cuisine. You told us in Bremen that your dinner in Munich had not agreed with you and that it gave you a bad night."

Before retiring they went to see one of the first comedy-chase films; Sigmund was amused. The next morning they woke up to dreary weather, made more gloomy by the fact that the entire party was suffering from diarrhea. They left in midafternoon for Worcester, taking the elevated railroad downtown from Forty-second Street to the piers along the Hudson River, where they boarded a white-decked steamer. Each man had his own cabin. The ship circled the point of Manhattan, made its way up the East River, passing under the Brooklyn and Manhattan bridges, steering through the damp, chilly air among barges, tugs and ferryboats.

From Fall River they took a train to Boston. While Ernest Jones was showing them historical sites, the Old State House, Old North Church, and then the harbor where the Boston Tea Party had been held, Sigmund said to him in an aside, "Where is the nearest urinal?"

"There aren't any, Herr Professor."

"What! Then what is a man supposed to do?"

"We'd better make our way back to the business district and find an office or a government building."

When Jones finally piloted Sigmund into a large building, he had to go down to an underground floor and walk along an enormously long corridor before he came to the men's room. He barely made it. When they emerged, he demanded of Jones, "What kind of country is this that doesn't have public urinals? In creating their new civilization, they are leaving out one of the most important contributions of the Old World."

"You see, Professor Freud," laughed Jones, "this is a Puritan country, more inhibited than my Victorian England. The processes of elimination are kept hidden and never referred to. You will find this equally true about the other functions of the erogenous zone. By the by, you are going to have a fine reception here in New England, for your work is already known. Last year, when I was a house guest of Dr. Morton Prince in Boston, we had two or three evenings in which some sixteen doctors and university professors were present, including Dr. James Putnam, who is professor of neurology at Harvard University and several of the leading psychiatrists in this region. Last May, Professor Putnam and I gave papers on psychoanalysis and the unconscious at a meeting in New Haven. We aroused considerable interest; some opposition, naturally, but also a good deal of animated discussion. I also have heard that the famous philosopher, William James, is coming down from Harvard to hear your lectures. Do you think I might read one or two before you give them?"

Sigmund shook his head in bemused perplexity.

"I haven't written a line. The six days with Ferenczi and Jung on board ship became a total vacation. We interpreted each other's dreams, played some silly deck sports and told funny stories. By the way, Jung thinks I ought to confine my lectures to the interpretation of dreams, as the best open doorway with which to welcome an American audience. What do you think?"

"I heartily disagree. You would be constricting yourself. You must devote considerable time to interpretation of dreams, of course, but you must also give the picture of your discoveries from the beginning, so that the audience will understand where you came from scientifically and where you are going."

The country around Worcester was characterful: low-lying hills, forests, a rocky terrain with many small lakes and villages with the houses painted in attractive green or gray, and an occasional one in red. While the others were left at the Standish Hotel, Sigmund was taken to President Hall's home: a big, open, comfortable house with people coming and going all the time. The entire house was carpeted, and books lined half the walls. The Halls greeted him with affection. The president, approaching seventy, was distinguished-looking; his wife had been described as "plump, jolly, good-natured, extremely ugly, and a wonderful cook." Sigmund was given a spacious corner room overlooking a stand of majestic trees. Two solemn Negroes in white jackets served the meals, and there was a box of cigars in every room.

When he stepped out onto the stage of Jonas Clark Hall, a granite and brick building which was the focus of activities on the campus, he saw that the auditorium, which seated four hundred, was filled. He had been told that in the audience were some of the most distinguished faculty members of Harvard, including Franz Boas, the famous anthropologist, William James, the philosopher, and Dr. James Putnam. He still had not written the lecture, nor did he have any notes before him on the lectern. Earlier that morning he had taken a half-hour walk with Ferenczi, discussing both its structure and content. It was his only preparation. He spoke in German; quietly and in a conversational tone. A considerable portion of his audience understood the language.

"Ladies and gentlemen, it is with novel and bewildering feelings that I find myself in the New World, lecturing before an audience of expectant inquirers. No doubt I owe this honor only to the fact that my name is linked with the topic of psychoanalysis; and it is of psychoanalysis, therefore, that I intend to speak to you. I shall attempt to give you, as succinctly as possible, a survey of the history and subsequent development of this new method of examination and treatment.

"If it is a merit to have brought psychoanalysis into being, that merit is not mine. I had no share in its earliest beginnings. I was a student and working for my final examinations at the time when another Viennese physician, Dr. Josef Breuer, first in 1880–82 made use of this procedure on a girl who was suffering from hysteria. Let us turn our attention straightaway to the history of this case and its treatment, which you will find set out in detail in the *Studies on Hysteria*, which was published later by Breuer and myself. . . ."

As he gazed out at the audience for a moment in silence, he thought to himself:

"This is like recognition of some incredible daydream; psychoanalysis is no longer a product of delusion; it has become a valuable part of reality."

He spoke for almost an hour, and received an ovation. After many in the audience had congratulated him and shaken his hand, Jung said:

"I have been prepared for opposition. You appear to be in seventh heaven, and I am glad with all my heart to see you so."

Sigmund was indeed thrilled.

"Thank you, Carl. I feel despised in Europe, but here today some of the foremost men of America have treated me as an equal."

"As well they might! We are gaining ground here, and our following is growing."

Sigmund patted Jung paternally on the shoulder.

"I'm pleased to hear you use the word 'our.' It *is* our following, for you are going to be the man to take over when I can no longer lead."

The week of lectures went extraordinarily well. There was warm applause at the end of each hour. He described in detail the process whereby individuals saved themselves unpleasure by driving out of their consciousness, and hence out of their memories, ideas which had become intolerable and would have to be repressed, with the repressed wishful impulses continuing to exist in the unconscious. He went on to describe the process whereby disguised substitutes for the repressed ideas moved into consciousness and became attached to the unpleasure which had existed there originally, ending as phobias or obsessions.

He took his listeners very carefully through the field of male hysteria, free association, dream interpretation, concepts of repression, regression, infantile sexuality.

When he came to the sexual etiology of the neuroses, which he saved for his fourth lecture, he admitted frankly that as late as 1895, when he and Breuer published *Studies on Hysteria,* he had not yet come to this scientific conclusion. He related his difficulties with patients in getting them to speak of their sexual lives and admitted wryly, "People are in general not candid over sexual matters." Then he made his categorical statement: "Psychoanalytic research traces back the symptoms of patients' illnesses with really surprising regularity to impressions from their *erotic life.* It shows us that the pathogenic wishful impulses are in the nature of erotic instinctual components; and it forces us to suppose that, among the influences leading to the illness, the predominant significance must be assigned to erotic disturbances, and that this is the case in both sexes.

"I am aware that this assertion of mine will not be willingly believed. Even workers who are ready to follow my psychological studies are inclined to think that I overestimate the part played by sexual factors; they meet me with the question why *other* mental excitations should not lead to the phenomena I have described of repression and the formation of substitutes. I can only answer that I do not know why they should not, and that I should have no objection to their doing so; but experience shows that they do not carry this weight, that at most they *support* the operation of the sexual factors but cannot replace them. . . . There are among my present audience a few of my closest friends and followers, who have traveled with me here to Worcester. Inquire from them, and you will hear that they all began by completely disbelieving my assertion that sexual etiology was of decisive importance, until their own analytic experiences compelled them to accept it."

What surprised Sigmund was the friendliness of the press. The Worcester *Telegram*, though it refrained from any effort at a critical assessment, did its best to report the main thrust of Sigmund's thinking. The conservative Boston *Transcript* gave the lectures faithful coverage, and sent a reporter to interview Sigmund at President Hall's home. The reporter proved to be intelligent and eager to learn; as a result the interview published in the *Transcript* was an accurate, sympathetic presentation of Freudian psychoanalysis and its therapeutics. When Ernest Jones read the article, he commented to Sigmund:

"This is a fine bit of irony. It was in Boston that American Puritanism was born. Yet here in Boston we have a conservative newspaper giving Freudian psychoanalysis the most friendly reception I have yet seen. Perhaps this *is* the New World."

A. A. Brill, who, as a converted American, was a more ardent patriot than most of the native-born, added:

"There hasn't been one adverse criticism either of his ideas or of the fact that Clark University invited him here. I will make a prediction right now, at the beginning of our endeavors in America: this country will become the most fertile field for the practice and development of psychoanalysis."

The days passed in a phantasmagoria of faces, scenes, students and classrooms, lectures in history, the Far East, education; a series of luncheons and dinners at several of which Sigmund was the guest of honor. He could attend only one of Jung's three lectures on the psychological results of Zurich's word-association tests and the manner in which they corroborated Freudian psychoanalysis. Jung was well received.

When at the end of the week Sigmund donned his cap and gown in President Hall's home and joined the academic procession to the Clark gymnasium, with Carl Jung also in black cap and gown striding alongside him, he had a feeling of a job well done. He took his seat on the stage. President Hall placed the colorful hood around his neck and read the citation:

> "*Sigmund Freud of the University of Vienna, founder of a school of pedagogy already rich in new methods and achievements, leader today among students of the psychology of sex, and of psychotherapy and analysis,*
>
> > Doctor of Laws."

While the large and distinguished audience applauded, Sigmund thought:

"This is the first official recognition of my endeavors. It is also the end of infancy for psychoanalysis."

8.

His success and acceptance in the United States made no impression on Europe. Neither the lectures nor the outstanding Americans who attended them were reported in the press. As far as Vienna and the German-speaking world were concerned, Professor Sigmund Freud had never left home.

It was partly this sense of disappointment, joined to the importunings of President Hall, James Putnam, Ernest Jones and A. A. Brill in the new country, as well as Otto Rank, Abraham and Ferenczi in Europe, that he agreed to set down the five lectures, precisely as he had given them. The writing took him a month and a half; though he had total recall, he preferred to go back to the original thinking that had determined the architectural structure as well as the content of the forward-moving series. When they were translated and published in the *American Journal of Psychology*, edited by Stanley Hall, Brill and Jones were delighted; they now had a textbook in the English language.

The event he looked forward to now was the second Congress, set for Nuremberg at the end of March. He hoped to have almost a hundred delegates from a dozen countries; and to form the International Psychoanalytic Society, with working chapters in New York, London, Berlin, Zurich, Budapest. That would make psychoanalysis an official entity, put a solid structure under their body of knowledge, with officers, a constitution, dues collected for publications, and an annual Congress, such as the neurological and psychiatric societies had.

In the meanwhile he was working well on his new book on Leonardo da Vinci and a Memory of His Childhood, and his lecture for the Nuremberg Congress, The Future Prospects of Psychoanalytic Therapy. There was the good news that Deuticke was at long last going to release a second, expanded version of *The Interpretation of Dreams*; it had taken almost a decade to sell the original six hundred copies. Karger in Berlin was printing a third, enlarged edition of *The Psychopathology of Everyday Life*. His satisfaction grew as rich material poured in both from his own group and from doctors and patients around the world, verifying the truth of his conclusions. Both publishers were confident, now that Sigmund Freud could no longer be ignored, but had to be read if only to be attacked, that they could put out revised and enlarged editions every couple of years.

"So you were not given a basket, back in 1900!" Martha teased. "You just had to wait awhile for new suitors to come seeking your hand."

Despite the progress being made elsewhere, at home he faced difficulties with the Vienna group. They were not unlike any other family seeing each other too often, dependent upon each other, fighting for their place in the sun and for Sigmund's attention: to have more of his time for the evolving of an idea or the editing of a manuscript; one doctor wishing to receive more patients from him than the other. They competed for space in the pages of the *Jahrbuch*. A big bone of contention, as it was with other scientific bodies, was the element of priority: who first discovered a new idea or developed an old one into a broader and more meaningful stance. They were all working along similar lines; frequently two of them came up with the same idea, the same paper, at the same moment. Who was to have credit for it on the international scene? If one man achieved a startling concept, but another researched it and developed it to where it could be published, who had the priority? When Sigmund agreed to write the introductions for the books, or even for a chapter of one of the books, as he did for Otto Rank in *Myth of the Birth of the Hero*, and a follower carried the idea to its logical conclusion, either through a leap of imagination or a hard reading and testing of patients, who was to be given the credit?

Sigmund worried about holding down the troublesome question of priority, which had destroyed many a professional society. When one man felt neglected because another had been given an advantage, he worked with the man for weeks to help him develop an approach which would bring official credit. Yet it was an unending battle to keep the members of the group at peace. They had all started together, they were all involved in the limited number of postulates Sigmund had so far set up as being the science of psychoanalysis.

They had always been fiercely critical of each other's work. Each Wednesday evening everyone was obliged to comment whether he wished to or not. There might be a modest amount of praise, but for the most part each member had found something to minimize or to reject in the other man's paper, frequently indicating that he thought his own source material and conclusions were more valid, that his techniques were more thorough. Sigmund increasingly found himself having to intervene with his mild:

"Let us not be personal; let us confine our criticisms to the theories at stake."

When two of his people were rowing, he invited them to supper together and made it an exciting evening for them, going over case materials, bringing each of them into the conversation, listening carefully, admiring their grasp of the subject, building their confidence not only in themselves but in each other so they would leave Berggasse 19 arm in arm and walk each other home. If he were going to be paterfamilias there simply was no choice: these disparate children were all living inside his ideological household. He had to find ways to keep them happy. Nevertheless there were times when several of the older members saddened him by their internecine wars.

One of the bruising personalities was Dr. Isidor Sadger. After four years he remained a complete stranger. No one knew where he lived or whether he had a family, except for his thirty-year-old nephew, Dr. Fritz Wittels, whom he had brought into the group. Certainly he never showed up at any of the coffeehouses where Sigmund occasionally stopped for an hour's conversation. Though it had long been obvious to Sigmund from the nature of Sadger's monographs, which were superbly researched and written, that his problem was one of a repressed homosexuality, there was no opportunity to help him to relieve the obviously agonizing clashes of character within himself, which he took out on the other members of the group. Everyone respected him, everyone felt sorry for him; and no one knew what to do with him.

Another source of discomfort was Dr. Eduard Hitschmann's coruscating wit, with which he injured the pride of those who were neither as fast nor as smart as he was. Hitschmann had a very successful general practice and a growing group of psychoanalytical patients; he was a generous man, and there was no malice in him. It was simply that a funny retort would come to his mind, albeit one which would slash another man's throat or rip open the paradigm he was presenting, which Hitschmann simply could not prevent himself from uttering. Nearly everyone in the group had suffered from his barbs and had vowed revenge. Because there seemed no way to surpass Hitschmann's remarks, the members took out their hurt pride by slashing his papers, no matter how well prepared or true they might be.

It was an omnipresent difficulty, Sigmund found, that when one man read a paper, and the others criticized it, though the points may have been minor, the words of criticism burned deep into the mind, and the man waited until his adversaries had papers of their own to give, then took his revenge.

Here Wilhelm Stekel was the worst offender, doing his best to annihilate every newly conceived approach. When his turn came to read portions of his nearly completed book on Nervous People, his earlier victims tore the manuscript to shreds, mercilessly. Although he treated patients, and had a flair for therapy, his papers were often useless, based on the veriest conjecture. Sigmund was grateful for his newspaper articles, whose purpose was to popularize psychoanalysis; at the same time he was often vexed at the sloppy writing and oversimplified, frequently erroneous portraits which he dashed off at the Cafe Central for the Sunday edition. When Sigmund brought him to heel for inadequate preparation, Stekel replied:

"I have the original ideas. Let others do the research that will prove me right."

No matter what paper was read, on what subject, Stekel would exclaim with great excitement:

"That's exactly the case of the patient I had in my office this morning!"

He had long been a source of mockery in the group because of his "Wednesday morning patients."

Stekel was not only hurt but astonished.

Some of the young men who had been accepted for the group brought with them a lifetime portfolio of problems. Such a one was Viktor Tausk, a handsome, blue-eyed, tormented Croatian who said of himself, "I am incurably ill in my soul. My whole past appears to me to be nothing but a preparation for this terrible collapse of my personality."

Tausk's emotional life, composed of rags and tatters, went back directly to his parents. So bitterly did he loathe his father that he organized the other children in the household to ostracize the old man. His mother beat him in an effort to stop the machinations. He was a talented linguist who did well in school until he got into a row with his teacher over religion, and was expelled just before his *Matura* for leading a strike against the faculty. Penniless and suffering from lung trouble, he nonetheless had completed the course at the University of Vienna, taking his degree in law, which he hated, since he had always wanted to be a doctor.

At twenty-one he had married the daughter of a prosperous printer in Vienna, but took his wife to Croatia, largely because of the unbounded hatred between himself and his father-in-law. He found work as a lawyer, had two sons; then he and his wife separated. Tausk went to Berlin, where he made the faintest facsimile of a living as a poet, musician, artist, journalist. His good looks won him a whole series of women. When he was thirty he chanced upon a monograph by Sigmund Freud in a medical journal, wrote to Professor Freud and asked if he could visit him in Vienna. Sigmund somehow derived from the letter that Viktor Tausk was already a physician. He encouraged Tausk to come. The invitation saved Tausk's life, for he had been on the verge of suicide.

Sigmund had spent several hours with Viktor Tausk on an early Sunday in the spring of 1909, then took one hundred and fifty kronen from his desk and slipped the money into Tausk's pocket. The young man was a walking mass of psychiatric wounds, but there was no mistaking the intellectual qualities of his mind. Sigmund introduced him to the Wednesday Evening group. The men perceived the depth of Tausk's emotional crisis but believed that his determination to return to the University of Vienna and take his medical degree, so that he could become a psychoanalyst, might set him straight. Hitschmann, Federn and Steiner gave him four thousand kronen; Sigmund added enough to guarantee his first two years in Medical School. Tausk was so overcome by this generosity that he stumbled out of the room weeping; but not before he had sworn a lifetime of allegiance.

Occasionally Sigmund had to dissuade an enthusiast. Chief among them was Rudolf von Urbantschitsch, son of a renowned ear specialist, who had taken his medical degree from the University of Vienna six years earlier and was the owner and director of the fashionable Cottage Sanatorium. He had read Freud's monographs and several of his books as extracurricular work while working for his degree, and was one of the few who had praised Freudian psychoanalysis at the Medical School. He had several times been warned for his indiscretions. Rudolf, thirty, was a clean-shaven young man with a big-eyed, wistful face; a Catholic, with an all-Catholic practice. When he applied for admission to the Vienna group he was received with open arms. Then the news leaked out to the medical profession, and he was threatened with the closing down of his sanatorium. He came to see Sigmund.

"Professor Freud, I simply cannot give in to these threats. I feel that my manhood and my integrity are at stake, that I will remain a servant to the medical profession all of my life. I must stand up to them, even though I lose my sanatorium. I can always earn a living in Vienna . . ."

Sigmund put an arm about the young man's shoulders.

"You are only at the threshold of your career; you are too young to engage in an Arezzo jousting match. Give yourself a chance to get securely established in your profession, and give us a chance to earn a reputation for ourselves."

"Professor Freud, your Wednesday Evening meetings afford the only opportunity for me to be trained in psychoanalysis."

"It would do neither of us any good to have the world know that association with us can cost a man his practice," Sigmund persisted. "My fond advice to you is to withdraw, but let us remain friends."

Like other close-knit family groups, they battled in private but presented a solid front to the public. They also managed to be aware of each other, and sometimes, knowing they had caused suffering, went out of their way to send a patient or secure publication for the victim's paper. They were generous with financial help, reminding Sigmund of the fraternal days when he was a *Sekundararzt* at the Allgemeine Krankenhaus, and the forty young men working there shared their few gulden as the need arose. Sigmund kept close tabs on the members, making sure they were always in funds. He gave small sums of money when they were much needed; or if this seemed indelicate, gave a larger amount as a "loan" which he never intended to collect.

He held his followers together, too, by sending the younger doctors patients when their practice was barren or they had no material to develop, being careful never to send a case too complicated for their period of advancement or technique. He was also glad occasionally to pass along a patient with the kind of neurosis he had treated steadily these past twenty-odd years, and which had nothing more to teach him.

This was simple enough as long as he had eight or ten patients of his own and could earn the continually increasing expenses of running his house, entertaining outside guests nearly every day for dinner and supper, and educating his growing children. At the age of fifty-three his practice was reasonably steady but he was rarely able to put aside more than a few thousand kronen in a savings bank. Since he had no genuine understanding of the business world, he made no attempt to invest these savings so that they might earn a larger return. In any event the two and a half months of summer vacation, travel and book writing nearly always depleted the medical year's accumulation.

More serious than the personal differences was the cliquishness that had been growing stronger in the past year or two. Most of it centered between those who supported Sigmund Freud, and Alfred Adler's *Stammtisch*, which he had brought in one by one from the Cafe Central, some nine in number, D. J. Bach, Stefan Maday, Baron Franz von Hye, Carl Furtmüller, Franz and Gustav Grüner, Margarete Hilferding, a doctor and the first woman to be admitted, Paul Klemperer, David Oppenheim. Though few were doctors, Sigmund had approved these memberships thinking that psychoanalysis needed friends in Vienna more than it needed anything else; but now Alfred Adler's newly emerging psychology, his declared theories of organ inferiority as the major formation factor in character, and not the sexual etiology; of masculine protest as the dominant factor in neuroses, was splitting the group. No member loyal to Freud praised Adler's contributions, brilliant and informative though they were, though Sigmund himself had said that the theory of organ inferiority was an important one in the building of the human psyche.

By the same token, Adler's friends were also intensely loyal to him and were reluctant to praise a paper by anyone in the Freud group. As Adler's work progressed, it was becoming increasingly clear that he no longer wanted to be considered a Freudian psychoanalyst. Why should he be, when his Adlerian psychology was very different from Sigmund Freud's, and in effect owed Freud's original theories little or nothing!

He was also beginning to hint that the group should no longer meet in Sigmund's waiting room, because that made it a ward of Professor Sigmund Freud and exerted undue influence over the members. Would they not be better advised to find an attractive hall or lecture room so that they could sometimes invite the public to hear the more interesting papers, and in that way become a recognized institution rather than a family group meeting in the father's home?

Wilhelm Stekel, who had so vigorously helped form the original group in 1902, fell victim to Alfred Adler's charisma, which was considerable, and joined his *Stammtisch* at the Cafe Central. Sigmund was stung by the hints of defection. Martha, who knew his every mood, said:

"Sigi, these Wednesday Evenings used to bring you so much joy. They are now proving disagreeable. What has happened?"

He shook his head, murmured, "No use to go into the problems. I'll simply have to find ways of resolving them."

9.

Carl Jung was called to America for a series of lectures in Chicago. Sigmund feared this might endanger the Congress in Nuremberg, Bavaria, scheduled for the end of March, but the indefatigable Jung made all the necessary arrangements before he left, and gave Sigmund his word that he would return in time to preside. Abraham, Eitingon, Hirschfeld, Heinrich Körber and Löwenfeld would represent Germany; J. Honegger, Alphonse Maeder and an American, Trigant Burrow, a student of Jung's, were coming from Switzerland. Because of the time of the year no one from America could make the journey: Brill, Jones, Putnam of Harvard University, were involved with teaching and other responsibilities.

An untoward incident occurred during the preparations. Dr. Max Isserlin, a Munich psychiatrist, asked permission to read a paper. Sigmund agreed. It was the Vienna group which somehow got word that Isserlin's paper, rather than being an exposition of an interesting psychoanalytical case or theory, was in fact a violent attack on the concept of the unconscious. Several of them met together in a coffeehouse to discuss procedure, then went to Sigmund to demand that Isserlin's paper be canceled. Sigmund asked for proof of its content. Within a few days he was provided with sufficient quotes to prove the charges true. It was to be only a two-day meeting. The number of papers that could be read was limited. What sense to give Isserlin valuable platform time, and then have his attack published as emerging from an official psychoanalytical Congress? Since Jung was in America, Sigmund sent word under his own signature to Isserlin that his request was canceled. He thought he had avoided a disagreeable and destructive incident. The repercussions were to prove unfortunate.

The case of Dr. Hans W. Maier, of the Burghölzli and a member of the Psychoanalytic Society, had a different base but was to cause an equal amount of uproar. Maier was a perceptive physician and a good writer who contributed to the psychiatric journals. He was attempting to make a synthesis of psychiatry and psychoanalysis, with psychoanalysis coming out second best. Sigmund resented this but said nothing until Maier began emptying out the contents of the Freudian portfolio, disparaging or discrediting each of its theories. He was also demanding the right, as was his privilege as a member, to have his papers published in the *Jahrbuch*. When the articles got to the point of being ninety percent Kraepelin-Bleuler psychiatry and ten percent Freudian icing, which was supposed to sweeten the cake for his fellow members, Sigmund decided that action had to be taken. It was Otto Rank who actually put the question into words, when he finished reading the last of Maier's articles in a journal which had always been unfriendly.

"Why do we need a traitor in our midst? For that matter, why should Dr. Maier want to continue to remain a member? He obviously doesn't approve of us, let alone agree with us. What's more, it will encourage people to sneer, to say, 'Even the members of the Society don't believe in their mumbo-jumbo.' Is there some delicate way to suggest to Dr. Maier that he not pay his dues next time around?"

"Since he is a Swiss, perhaps the suggestion should come from one of his fellow Zurichers, rather than from us."

Rank was respectful but persistent.

"Now, Professor Freud, you know that no Swiss is going to ask another Swiss to resign from an organization. They would consider it an act of treason."

"Then we will have to take it up with the Vienna group on Wednesday evening."

The discussion the following Wednesday was entirely one-sided; they had all read Maier's articles attacking their basic elements of faith; they disliked the Zurichers anyway. The vote was unanimous for inviting Dr. Maier out. This Sigmund did; it caused hard feelings in Zurich.

Hard feelings abounded in Zurich. In the growing feud between Carl Jung and Eugen Bleuler, Jung had now completely divorced himself from the Burghölzli and was carrying on his practice in his house in Küsnacht. He was looking forward to teaching at the Free, or Trade, School, which had no connection with the University of Zurich. Sigmund still did not know what the quarrel was about, for both men were respected in half a dozen countries of Europe, each with a host of friends. Sigmund more and more felt that there had to be elements of revolt by Carl Jung against the father figure. He had heard Jung dress down Bleuler during their times together but he had never heard Bleuler say a single syllable against his young Assistant. It was not unlike the falling away which Abraham had faced with Jung.

The trouble became serious. Jung, like Sigmund, believed in the establishment of a broad base for psychoanalysis while at the same time keeping out the hostile voices with no helpful purpose in mind. Bleuler did not agree. He believed that every science, as well as the arts and the humanities, was strengthened by letting the most lucid and loquacious opponents make their best attacks. He believed this procedure sharpened the minds of the faithful and enabled them to put down, through hard effort, the charges of their opponents. The rumors coming out of Zurich were that Jung intended to force Bleuler out of the Swiss Psychoanalytic Society! To Sigmund this appeared a tragedy beyond measure.

He left for Nuremberg a day ahead of the twenty-man Vienna delegation in order to have some time with Karl Abraham, and to talk with Sandor Ferenczi about a proposal he wanted Ferenczi to present to the Congress. It was over two years since Abraham had first visited Vienna and become Sigmund's fast friend, avowed pupil and the first psychoanalyst to practice in Berlin. The going had been difficult, as it always was when there was but one analyst in a big city. Karl Abraham, not yet thirty-three, was not only steadfast by nature but incurably optimistic. He was good to look at: clean-shaven, except for a non-assertive mustache, wide-set honest eyes reflecting the goodness of his nature, soft curly black hair rolling across a finely sculptured head; light gray tie, a tailored coat of many buttons and a short collar. The better part of his modest living was still being earned by writing psychiatric reports to be used in court cases. Karl had kept his promise to "argue reasonably" with the other physicians of Berlin and, as a result, though he had as yet converted no one, he had not made any enemies. The attacks on Freud continued in the Berlin Congresses, but they were not directed against Karl Abraham.

"Which is something of a minor miracle," Sigmund told Abraham as they walked about the streets of Nuremberg. "Keep following my technique with opponents: treat them like patients under psychoanalysis, calmly ignoring their denials, and continuing your explanation without telling them anything that too much resistance makes inaccessible to them."

Abraham wanted help with some of his more difficult cases. His wife's cousin, Dr. Hermann Oppenheim, founder of a respected psychiatric clinic in Berlin, had been sending him patients on whom all other methods and physicians had failed. Abraham confided to Sigmund:

"What am I to do about my persistent paranoid querulent, who after two years of treatment with me still sues everyone with whom he comes in contact? How does one avoid getting stuck in cleaning up neurotics?"

"I must publish those technical rules of mine soon," said Sigmund.

"They would be a great help, Herr Professor." Shyly, "I have few spectacular cures to exhibit, but in almost every case I am able to alleviate the symptoms."

There was the usual array of homosexuals, seeking help but dreading the finding of it; the forty-two-year-old man who had been married for ten years but was impotent in the marriage; two stubborn cases of obsessional neurosis: the first, a severe form of compulsive brooding accompanied by compulsive praying. Free association uncovered the origin of the disturbance: at the age of seven the boy had accidentally seen a woman, during a quarrel with her neighbors, pull up her skirt and show

her bare buttocks in a gesture of contempt. When he told the family maid
about the incident, she threatened to have him arrested for being naughty;
whereupon the boy became frightened, began to pray, covered every scrap
of paper with words of prayer. Deeper analysis proved the scene to be a
screen memory covering earlier exposures: pulling his nurse's nightgown
up over her buttocks; doing the same when he slept with his mother. Everything he took in his hand he turned around, to look at from the backside.
The alternate brooding and praying, which had vanished during his early
manhood, returned in middle age; the symptoms became so acute they
threatened his sanity.

The second case Abraham described concerned a patient who in early
childhood had loved his mother possessively and was jealous of his father
and his brother. When he was sent to a boarding school the boy felt an
unbearable sense of sexual rejection, cut his mother cold, destroyed her
gifts, never mentioned her again; all of which resulted in fits of screaming.
Reproved by his father, he answered:

"It screams by itself, Daddy."

His compulsion now was to utter obscene words when with the family,
especially those referring to the female genitals.

"I am revealing the Oedipal situation to him slowly," Abraham explained. "And I have put an end to the screams of protest at being rejected, as well as of feeling guilty about his desire for his mother. But
where do I probe now?"

"Dear colleague, mental changes are never quick. A problem like 'Where
should I probe now?' should not exist. The patient shows the way by
saying everything that comes into his head. He displays his mental surface
from moment to moment. Obsession must be dealt with early, in persons
who are still young, and then the treatment is a triumph and a pleasure.
But do not allow yourself to become discouraged with the middle-aged
man; keep him as long as possible. Such patients are often satisfied when
the physician is not. You mentioned his switching from devout prayer to
atheism and back to prayer. This is characteristic of obsessional neurotics; they have to express both contradictory voices, generally in immediate
juxtaposition."

The two men circled the ancient walls and moats of the town. Abraham
related how he had spoken privately to the wife of his middle-aged
patient, to reassure her about her husband's impotence.

"Hardly had I said to her that potency could be restored when the lady,
who had hitherto held her handbag quietly by its chain, began opening
and shutting it!"

The noon chimes were ringing in the churches. They started back to the
hotel. Abraham continued:

"The two psychotic women patients I wrote you about share a symptom:
they both complain of a tense puckered feeling about the mouth, as if it

were constricted. Is this not a displacement upward? I know that both patients have an aversion, in one of them repressed, to their husbands. One hardly tolerates any sexual intercourse and even reacts at times with physical symptoms of revulsion and disgust. Could the constricting sensation around the mouth stand for displaced vaginismus? The latter is, after all, only an expression of revulsion."

They found Sandor Ferenczi waiting for them when they returned to the Grand Hotel. Abraham excused himself. Sigmund took Ferenczi to his room, where they could confer in private.

Ferenczi's position in Budapest was different from Abraham's in Berlin. He was known and well liked not only by the medical profession and the government but by a considerable portion of the population as one of the city's more colorful characters. He had a robust general practice and was able to sustain himself until he could teach Hungary what psychoanalysis was about. The antagonism to Sigmund's ideas was nowhere near as violent in Budapest. Ferenczi's first lecture to the Budapest Society of Psychiatry and Nervous Diseases did not act like a "red rag to a bull." He had been diplomatic when addressing his Hungarian medical audiences, discussing "only quite obvious, easily understandable facts which will consequently be convincing." He had written to Sigmund, "I should only do harm to the cause by a sudden tactless assault, and I mean to behave at any rate as a master of restraint."

So he had, teaching slowly, skillfully, without giving offense, until a group of physicians came to the conclusion that there was something in this Freudian psychology after all, and began sending Ferenczi patients.

Sigmund plunged into the discussion for which he had asked Ferenczi to come to Nuremberg a day early.

"Sandor, when the papers have been read, and we have completed the scientific discussions, we have to convert ourselves into a business meeting and create a permanent organization. I want you to present a memorandum to the meeting."

Ferenczi flushed with pride, took off his glasses and polished them energetically with his handkerchief as though better to see the honor that had just been conferred on him.

"I accept with pleasure, Herr Professor; but shouldn't you perhaps choose one of your older followers from the Vienna group?"

"No." Peremptorily. "The Viennese no longer give me any pleasure. I have a heavy cross to bear with the older generation, Stekel, Sadger, Adler. I have the feeling that they will soon find me something of an obstacle and treat me as such."

Ferenczi was genuinely shocked.

"I can't believe that, Herr Professor. But let us get back to the business at hand." He took a note pad from his inside coat pocket. "Now if you will tell me precisely what structure you want for the organization . . ."

"First, I would like to move that we set up an International Psycho-analytic Association, with societies in each country to be formed as soon as they are ready. I should like Carl Jung to be elected president of the International Association . . . for life."

Ferenczi whistled softly, but did not look up from his writing pad.

"For this reason I would like to have the focal center of psychoanalysis moved from Vienna, which is a totally inhospitable spot, to Zurich, which has been receptive from the beginning despite the fact that the group had to reorganize under a different name. Riklin has agreed to act as secretary, handle the dues as they come in, arrange for our publications, in short, serve as a business manager. Another important step we should take to protect ourselves against frauds and inept amateurs is to keep unacceptable material out of the *Yearbook*. We should give Carl Jung the right to ex-amine all papers submitted and decide which he wants to publish."

"Since you are also on the Board, that would be safe . . . as long as you and Jung remain friends. . . ."

It was Sigmund's turn to be astonished.

"But we will always be friends! I consider him my successor."

"Very well, Herr Professor. I believe I have everything. I will write it up early tomorrow morning, over coffee."

"Just one warning, Ferenczi, the Viennese will not be enthusiastic about some of these suggestions. But you will be clever enough to handle their objections."

The scientific part of the meeting went well. Abraham's paper on Fetishism and Adler's on Psychic Hermaphroditism were enthusiastically received; Jung, Maeder and Löwenfeld also presented valuable papers, though Sigmund's paper on the future of psychoanalytic techniques aroused considerably less excitement than had his history of the Rat Man case two years earlier in Salzburg. Ferenczi's opening suggestion that an International Psychoanalytic Association be formed was greeted with ap-plause; but when he proposed that Carl Jung be named president for life there began an uneasy movement among the Viennese, a murmur of dis-sent. Ferenczi held up his hand for silence, then continued in an authori-tarian tone:

"The headquarters for the International Psychoanalytic Association will be in Zurich. Dr. Riklin has agreed to serve as executive secretary; in this capacity he will officially recognize new chapters as they open in Berlin, Budapest, London, New York. He will collect the annual dues, supervise publications, start a bimonthly paper to bring to members news of the As-sociation's activities."

This further concentration of power in the hands of the Swiss was re-ceived by the Viennese in icy silence. It was not until Ferenczi made his final announcement that they exploded.

"All materials to be published in the *Yearbook* are first to be approved by the president, Carl Jung. Only in this way can we keep psychoanalysis a pure science."

A half dozen men were on their feet at once: Stekel, Adler, Federn, Sadger, Wittels, Hitschmann, all shouting. To Sigmund it seemed that pandemonium had broken loose. He could hear some of the cries over the body of protest:

"We'll have nothing to do with a dictator!" "That is censorship in its worst form!" "We insist on free elections!"

Then, in a sudden silence, in a crevice between the solid cliffs of outrage, came a cry of anguish:

"Why are we Viennese being put down in favor of Zurich?"

Sandor Ferenczi, the well-rounded man, showed a sharp cutting edge.

"Because their approach is more scientific in form and content. They are all university-trained psychiatrists, which you Viennese are not. They are respected in the medical profession. You are outcasts, without a university, a hospital or even a respected clinic to your name!"

The Viennese were on their feet again, waving their fists and shouting at Ferenczi. The chairman banged his gavel, three sharp raps, and cried over the tumult below him:

"This meeting is adjourned!"

Sigmund slipped out the back of the meeting room, heartsick. He spoke to no one, ran up the one flight of stairs to his room and locked the door behind him. He drank a glass of cold water to quiet himself, then sank despondently into a deep velours chair and tried to assess the damage that had been done. It was unfortunate that Ferenczi had been placed in a position where he had had to belittle the Viennese before a Congress of their peers. There would be a small civil war. . . .

He rose from the chair and paced the room. The fault was his! He had complained to Ferenczi about the Viennese, told him that they were quarrelsome, that Stekel was inventing some of his Wednesday morning clients; that by their cliquishness, backbiting and striving for priority they were causing him considerable discomfort. That was what had emerged when Ferenczi was attacked; he minimized the Viennese because of the seeds he, Sigmund, had planted in Sandor's mind. He had been indiscreet with Ferenczi.

"It is I who am putting the Viennese aside," he said aloud.

There was a knock on the door. He opened it to see Otto Rank standing there, his dark face bloodless.

"Herr Professor, I think you had better come to Stekel's room immediately. Most of our Viennese are there. They are hurt and angry, and are threatening to walk out of the Congress."

Rank had not exaggerated. There were a dozen men churning about in Stekel's room, even his own loyal followers, all of them outraged. They fell silent when Sigmund entered; but it was the hostile silence of a family whose father has betrayed them. Adler spoke first; it was obvious that the group had turned to him for leadership in the crisis.

"Herr Professor, we want to know first of all what prompted Ferenczi's attack on us."

"Dr. Adler, those critical remarks should not have been made. But since Ferenczi was my spokesman, I must take the blame for them. I apologize, and ask that you put that unfortunate incident out of your minds."

"Very well," cried Stekel, "but how do we put out of our minds the fact that we, your oldest supporters, are again being pushed aside in favor of the Zurichers? We have suffered with you through these seven and a half difficult years, shared in your hardships, sacrifices, abuse. We have been loyal to you, faithful to your teachings. Now what about the Zurichers? They held weekly meetings for Freudian psychoanalysis for a few months and then abandoned them. Bleuler refuses to join our organization. Jung, whom you want to install as permanent president, is only half a Freudian; he frequently attacks the sexual etiology of the neuroses . . ."

Sigmund held up a hand to stanch the flow.

"Gentlemen, I turn to the Swiss because we need them desperately. It is not possible for a new branch of medical science to be accepted unless it is attached to a university medical school and hospital. The Burghölzli is our only hope." He took a deep breath. "I could almost say that it was only by Jung's appearance on the scene that psychoanalysis escaped the danger of becoming a Jewish national affair. It is only by having Jung as president, with headquarters in Zurich, that we can escape the growing virulent anti-Semitism which our opponents are using as a lethal weapon against us."

His plea, quietly made, had been an impassioned one; he was still choked with emotion when he finished. But his words had had no effect on his stung and humiliated cohorts. Sensing that everything he had built over the years was on the point of being lost, he said hoarsely:

"My enemies would be willing to see us starve; they would tear my very coat off my back!"

The anger and repudiation drained out of the belligerent group when they saw how sorely distressed their professor was; and how old he looked. Paul Federn spoke up; he had been one of Sigmund's closest friends.

"Very well, Professor Freud, we will accept Zurich as administrative headquarters for the International Association. But we will agree to Jung being president for no more than two years. After that, we must have free and open elections."

"I agree, Federn. It will be done that way."

Eduard Hitschmann spoke next; he too had been consistently loyal.

"Nor will we accept a censor over our published writings. If Jung is to have sole control over what goes into the *Yearbook*, he can turn Freudian psychoanalysis around and lead it down the garden path of mysticism."

"I never wanted that, Eduard. I urged him to assure everyone of their scholarly freedom. I wanted only to protect us from poor work, from the 'Maier' kind of paper you also condemned. I will suggest that we have an editorial board, composed of people from both cities."

The tension in the room diminished. Most of the men were saddened at seeing Professor Freud chastised. But Sigmund had no intention of leaving the mood in this mixed-up state. He was in full possession of himself now, his voice was calm and a fragment of a smile raised one corner of his lips.

"Now that we have bandaged the wounds and redressed just grievances, let us move forward to more creative ideas. For a long time I have wanted to step down as president of the Vienna Psychoanalytic Society. I have always known that the natural one to succeed me is Dr. Alfred Adler. At our next meeting in Vienna, I shall resign and nominate Adler in my place."

There was applause. Alfred Adler seemed quite startled by the announcement.

"Second, I think we very much need a second publication, to be edited and published in Vienna, which will provide additional space for our own contributors. I've even thought of a title: *Zentralblatt für Psychoanalyse*. The two logical editors would be Stekel and Adler."

Again there was applause. Somebody cried, "Now, Herr Professor, the forces have been equalized. With Dr. Adler the president of our group, and a monthly magazine of our own, the capital of the kingdom of psychoanalysis will remain in Vienna."

Sigmund returned to his room, got into his nightclothes and, for one of the few times in his life, remained wide awake until dawn. As a man who had analyzed himself, he was free to acknowledge that he had suffered a minor breakdown, and had indulged in hysteria. He had thought himself cured of all neuroses; but apparently the strains, pressures, attacks, defeats, had bitten more deeply into his psyche than he had known. He had been unwise in not conferring with his own group in advance. It should have been Adler who presented the memorandum. Having chosen Ferenczi, he should never have allowed his exasperation with his home group to show. But all was mended now; in the morning the International Psychoanalytic Association would be born. Jung would be elected for a two-year term. Riklin would be elected to assist Jung. That was what he had come to Nuremberg to achieve. In spite of his errors in judgment everything was repaired, and the Congress would be a success.

He fell asleep as the first ray of sunshine painted his window sill a pale yellow.

BOOK FIFTEEN

ARMAGEDDON

BOOK THIRTEEN

ARMAGEDDON

Armageddon

THE International Psychoanalytic Congress of March 1910 had eventually ended on a pleasant note. This was confirmed by a letter from
Karl Abraham which said that he and the German group had talked
for nine hours on their way back to Berlin about the interesting papers
and theories that had been presented. Abraham announced that the
Berlin Psychoanalytic Society had joined the International Association,
with ten starting members.

Back in Vienna, it was refreshing for Sigmund to have a selfless man
join the group. Dr. Ludwig Jekels was originally from Lemberg, and
studied medicine at the University of Vienna. He had been a general
practitioner for seventeen years before joining the Vienna Psychoanalytic
Society, and had put away enough money to be able to give up his practice at the age of forty-two and devote full time to psychoanalysis. He was
a hollow-cheeked man with a sharp, pointed nose, bald except for one
thin strand of hair which he combed from his right ear straight across his
head, on an exact line with his eyebrows.

The members appreciated Jekels' rare qualities; he was self-effacing,
preferring to write rather than talk, and became known as "a gentleman
of the old school, for whom the terms 'dignity' and 'honor' had meaning." He had an insatiable thirst for knowledge and insisted upon thinking every psychological problem through to its ultimate conclusion. This
slowed down his writing for publication, but when a paper was finished,
Jekels had achieved truth. He also began a translation of Sigmund's books
into Polish, his mother tongue.

Sigmund provided him with his first psychoanalytic case. He handled it
well. When Sigmund congratulated him, Jekels replied shyly:

"I am glad that I could help."

Sigmund's problems with Wilhelm Stekel continued, but for once they
were not of Stekel's volition. When Sigmund talked to Hugo Heller
about publishing their new Journal for Psychoanalysis, Heller replied
firmly:

"Professor Freud, if you are to be the editor of the *Zentralblatt*, I will
certainly be happy to publish it. However I will not do so with Wilhelm

Stekel as its editor. I do not approve of his careless writing and his failure to face up to research."

Sigmund was silent for a moment, then murmured:

"Let us say nothing more about it."

He urged Stekel to inquire around and see if he could find a proper publishing house. Stekel encountered three or four further refusals but finally found a firm in Wiesbaden which took the assignment. Sigmund suggested to Alfred Adler that as co-editor of the Journal he should read and edit each piece according to his own high standards of excellence.

It took several Wednesday Evenings before the Vienna group accepted Alfred Adler as president, making Sigmund Freud scientific chairman. In late April, Adler got his wish: the Vienna Psychoanalytic Society, after seven and a half years of meeting in Sigmund Freud's medical offices, was moved to the *Doktorenkollegium*. Here the public was invited. However the old rule that every member of the Society must participate in the discussions had to be abandoned. Now there was a formal lecture, one or two comments, and the evening ended. A group gathered around Sigmund after each lecture. They walked to the Alte Elster or the Ronacher Cafe, where they sat about a table for several hours, talking not only of psychoanalysis and the lecture they had just heard, but of the new plays and books, political developments.

Adler was unable to conceal his dislike for Sandor Ferenczi, and spoke frequently about Ferenczi's "clumsy memorandum, against which one had to defend the Vienna school." More benignly he added, "As far as the scientific work itself is concerned, our pleasure in working together will unquestionably increase as soon as we can have confidence in each other. And this will enable us to enjoy in the future too the so far unchallenged reputation of the Vienna school as the leading scientific force."

Sigmund was pleased to hear this announcement. Fritz Wittels, who could sting to the very core of a situation with a sentence or two, observed:

"The Zurichers are trained clinically to become Freudians; they would probably champion any other doctrine with the same righteousness and the same tearful tone. The Vienna Society, on the other hand, has grown historically; each one of us has a neurosis, which is necessary for entry into Freud's teachings; whether the Swiss have is questionable."

This earned a laugh around the table; who ever heard of a Swiss developing a neurosis? Yet Sigmund knew that the Burghölzli was filled with neuroses; the Zurichers handled the same classical cases.

It was disquieting that the German neurologists meeting in Hamburg, and discussing a report of the papers that had been read by the psychoanalysts at Nuremberg, had passed a resolution "to boycott those sanatoria in which Freud's method of treatment is employed." This might be a hardship for Max Kahane, many of whose patients came from Germany. Max practiced little or no psychoanalysis in his sanatorium, yet he kept assuring Sigmund that he came away from each Wednesday Evening with new psychological insights which helped him to take care of his patients.

The by-laws of the Vienna Psychonanalytic Society read: "The Society aims to cultivate and further the psychoanalytic science founded in Vienna by Prof. Sigmund Freud." Yet a few weeks later Alfred Adler gave a paper which indicated that he had almost completely broken with Freud's sexual theory. Sexuality should be considered only in a symbolic sense. What in essence Adler was saying was:

"Women in our culture have a tendency to become neurotic not because they covet the penis, but because they envy the pre-eminence of man in contemporary culture. To women, then, the penis symbolizes the overexalted position of men in society. Should they wish to become men, renouncing their femininity, they suffer from such neurotic symptoms as painful menses, painful intercourse, or even homosexuality, all expressive of masculine protest reactions." Men "who try to become excessively masculine are not reacting to anxiety over fear of castration but are overcompensating for their feelings of inadequacy as men."

Sigmund complained to Martha that Wednesday now represented his weekly headache; but Adler frequently came up with illuminating phrases. One of these was the "confluence of drives" which clarified some of the complexity of the libido, the energy with which the instincts are endowed, and its content, which Adler believed was derived not from one source or stimulation but from many. Sigmund immediately acknowledged his indebtedness to Adler for the phrase and introduced it into his work. Another Adlerian concept was that of "the feeling of inferiority" which grew out of his original concept of organ inferiority as the background formation for most of character. Organ inferiority was defined as a somatic defect in which any organ, limb or portion of the body is weak, defective, diseased, a condition which must be remedied, compensated for or adapted to, or it will lead to emotional disturbances. Sigmund was unable to accept Adler's idea, though he knew that certain anxiety states did arise from inferiority in the face of a given situation. He explained to the members:

"I am not always able to accept new ideas the first time I hear them. I have to conjure with them for days, sometimes for weeks, before I can integrate them into my thinking."

He succeeded with this one; before long the term *inferiority complex* was being used as a tentpole for psychoanalysis.

Adler was too creative a thinker, too much a leader and contributor of original materials, to be content to play a subsidiary role to Carl Jung in Zurich. He had suffered all his life from his revolt against his older brother, who had been sickly and favored by his mother. Playing a secondary role was anathema to him. This had been part of his drive during the past two years to separate himself from Freudian analysis; from its basic Oedipal complex and sexual etiology of the neuroses, putting in their place organ inferiority and masculine protest. Sigmund knew that there was no dishonesty or pretense about any of this; Alfred Adler was a man of integrity. His relationships with his patients, his family and his wide circle of friends were beyond criticism. Yet every Wednesday evening, whether he read a paper or gave a lengthy critique of someone else's lecture, he brought distress to Sigmund, as he whittled away tiny shavings from the trunk of Freudian psychoanalysis.

2.

Sigmund submerged himself in work. The previous February, before he went to the Nuremberg Congress, he had accepted as a patient a wealthy young Russian who had been under the care of Kraepelin in Munich, as well as the best psychiatrists in Berlin, all of whom had abandoned him as being a manic depressive, incurable. Sergei Petrov suffered acute bouts of melancholia, as well as inability to take care of himself in any way, even to the feeding or dressing of himself. His constipation was so severe that he had to have his feces removed twice a week by means of an enema administered by male nurses.

He came to Sigmund six days a week after some early sessions at the Cottage Sanatorium, and appeared willing, even eager, to be on the analytical couch; yet for the entire hour he divulged nothing of his background or childhood, neither in free association nor controlled materials. After several months Sigmund grew discouraged; but there was no turning back. He had already devoted too much time to educating Sergei in the process of psychoanalysis and what is inscribed on the unconscious mind. He was convinced that the young man's illness was a result of an infantile neurosis, that it had nothing to do with the gonorrhea he had contracted in his eighteenth year, which the patient thought marked the beginning of his troubles.

Sigmund decided that he would set a firm date to terminate the analysis, if by that time he had been unable to do Sergei any good. Sergi did not believe him at first, but in a matter of weeks, as they approached the final session, became convinced that the doctor was in earnest. Since he had spent months listening to Professor Freud, and had decided that this was an honest and capable man, his fear that he would be ejected, together with his affection for the doctor, enabled him to open up.

Sergei had been born on a large estate in Russia to young parents very much in love with each other. What should have been a happy childhood was soon twisted out of shape by a series of mishaps. His mother became ill with an abdominal disorder and consequently had little time for her son. His father, who favored the boy during his earlier years, before turning his attention to an older daughter, began suffering bouts of melancholia and ended in a sanatorium. Sergei's sister, two years older, took pleasure in tormenting the boy with a picture of a wolf walking upright, from a popular picture book. Whenever Sergei saw the picture, or was forced to catch a sight of it, he began screaming that the wolf was coming to eat him up.

During his first few years he had been a quiet, amenable child who gave no trouble. One summer, when the boy was four and a half, the parents returned from a holiday to find his personality changed. He had been raised by an old peasant woman, Nanya, who had been good to him, but during their absence the parents had sent in an English governess who had quarreled violently with the children and with Nanya. For the next eight years Sergei was ill, bad-tempered and next to impossible to live with.

Sergei free-associated back to an incident that took place when he was a year and a half old. He was suffering from malaria, and his crib had been placed in his parents' bedroom. He awakened late on a summer afternoon in the room where his parents were taking a siesta, to see them indulging in coitus *a tergo*, from behind. The action was repeated three times. Because of the particular position, the child had seen his father's organ in erection as well as his mother's genitalia.

This was what Sigmund labeled the "primal scene"; it had no meaning for Sergei, or any effect upon his nervous health, until he had a dream at the age of four which brought back its content, albeit in symbolic terms. He dreamt that he was lying in his bed, which stood with its foot toward the window, in front of which there was a row of old walnut trees.

"I know it was winter when I had the dream, and nighttime. Suddenly the window opened of its own accord, and I was terrified to see that some white wolves were sitting on the big walnut tree in front of the window. There were six or seven of them. The wolves were quite white, and looked more like foxes or sheep dogs, for they had big tails like foxes and they had their ears pricked like dogs when they pay attention to something. In great terror, evidently of being eaten up by the wolves, I screamed and woke up."

Sergei added a drawing of the tree and the white wolves; an interesting detail was that the old wolf had his tail docked. After much meandering through stories such as *Little Red Riding Hood and the Wolf*, with which his sister had terrorized him, they finally came to the question of why the wolves were white. Sergei told the doctor that he was struck by two elements in the dream: the absolute stillness of the wolves, and the rigid tension with which they were all gazing at him. He also felt a strong sense of reality about the scene, which in Sigmund's experience meant that the content of the dream was bound to an incident which actually took place, and not fantasy.

Before Sergei was five his sister had introduced him to some childish sexual practices. When they went to the lavatory together, she would say, "Let's show our bottoms," and they would uncover for each other. When they were alone she would take his penis in her hand and play with it, giving him explanations of how his Nanya used to do the same thing with the gardener. To revenge himself on his beloved Nanya, he began to play with his penis in her presence. Nanya had exclaimed:

"That is not a good thing to do. Boys who do that lose their little members and they get a 'wound' instead."

Sergei's unconscious, by now fully shaped, motivated him into a rage against himself and the world around him. The passing months grudgingly revealed Sergei's resentment because he had been the passive member of the sexual relationship with his sister, and had permitted her to play the masculine or aggressive role. When he reached the age of five, at which time his psyche should have been controlled by normal concentration on the genital zone, he suffered a regression to the anal stage, out of which came acts of sadism, such as pulling the wings off flies, crushing beetles under his boots, and fantasies of beating horses. He also revealed fantasies of young boys being beaten on the penis, usually young heirs to the throne, evidently projections of himself. That fitted into the slowly emerging configuration as another motive for his rages and screamings; he wanted to be beaten, and actually did force his now sick father to whip him in order to stop the misconduct.

During the second year of treatment each timber built into the construction of Sergei's neurosis returned to the old wolf whose tail had been docked; which led Sergei back to the act of coitus *a tergo* he had witnessed. His father had always been his model; he identified with him and had wanted to grow up to be precisely like him. Because of the sight he had seen, his father rather than his mother became the object-choice of his sexuality. This again threw him into a passive role in his burgeoning sexual life, causing still another trauma to his psyche: that his male genitals would disappear and in their place would come a "wound," or the female genitalia.

Sergei worked his way through the manifest content of the dream about the wolf and finally to the latent element: in the dream he had opened his eyes suddenly and seen the wolves sitting motionless outside his window. Months of painful searching brought him the clues as to why the wolves were white: his parents had been wearing white shifts when he caught them in the act of making love. In his dream he had opened his eyes suddenly; this led him to the primal scene when he had awakened, opened his eyes suddenly, and had seen the contortions of his parents on their bed. But why were the white wolves absolutely still in the tree, when his parents had been the exact opposite on the bed? Sigmund explained that this had been a defense mechanism. Sergei in his dreams had converted violent motion, which was repugnant and unacceptable to him, into the stillness of his wolf-parents sitting in the tree. For years he had suffered from depression which accelerated during the late afternoon. Sergei was able to trace back the normal siesta time on their estate in Russia on hot summer afternoons; it would generally come to an end about five. The height of his depression came when his unconscious once again flushed the emotion that had been engendered in the year-and-a-half-old child in the bedroom.

For Sigmund this was a remarkable documentation of the evidence from patients that the illness had arisen because of an early witnessing of the sexual act.

Toward the end of the second year, light was thrown on another of Sergei's obsessions. Since he had achieved maturity he had been unable to fall in love with any woman unless he saw her down on her hands and knees. When he did come upon such a sight, a young servant girl scrubbing a floor, either on his parents' estate or in his own home later, there would be a rush of libido and sexual excitement which he could not contain. He had fallen in love with several such girls after seeing them in precisely that position, and he would have intercourse with them in no way except *a tergo*. Though he had tried the normal posture, it had given him little pleasure, and he had abandoned it. His case of gonorrhea had been acquired this way: copulation from behind with a servant girl whom he had come upon in that position. He had not known why he suffered this obsession; now it was he who perceived the motivation and offered it to his doctor as part of the ongoing analysis.

The primal scene which Sergei had witnessed had splintered his sexual life. The anxiety dream of the wolves which took place before he was five, and referred back to the primal scene, was simply a case of deferred action. It would be another three or more years before the emotional and nervous impact would traumatize the growing boy and cause the wound in his psyche; and it would be another twenty years before he could understand what was going on inside his mental apparatus, and what had caused his wolf phobia.

In his copious notes, written over several years of steady treatment of Sergei Petrov, Sigmund referred to him as the Wolf Man. It was his intention to write the case whole and publish it; not for the near cure he had achieved, but for the story of the childhood origins of the obsessional neurosis. This was the urgent point he had to prove to the medical world, to the psychologists who maintained that all neuroses developed out of conflicts in adult life, and could have no point of origin in childhood; and to the dissenters in his own midst. The value of the Wolf Man case was that after a year of intensive training Sergei had been able to reach many of his own conclusions, the key ones that freed him from his obsessions and sent him back into the world, almost healed.

After Sigmund had told Martha of his satisfactions in the case, she asked:

"What would happen if you could persuade Sergei Petrov to return to Munich and confront Kraepelin with the conquering of his melancholia and phobias, after Kraepelin had declared him incurable? Wouldn't he have to admit the validity of your science?"

Sigmund laughed, throwing his arms in playful affection around his wife.

"Fantasy! Let me be the one who is accused of inventing fantasies for my cases, and then subtly forcing them upon defenseless patients!"

3.

The rich ore of the unconscious presented itself again in a book called *Memoirs of a Nerve Patient*, by Daniel Paul Schreber, who had formerly been a judge of the Appeals Court in Germany. Schreber had had a nervous breakdown as far back as October 1884, when he had been presiding over an Inferior Court. The main symptom had been hypochondria, but the expert medical care given to him by a Dr. Flechsig of the Leipzig Psychiatric Clinic, where Schreber spent six months, had brought him what appeared to be a complete cure. The reverence of the Schreber family for Dr. Flechsig was so great that Frau Schreber kept a framed photograph of Dr. Flechsig in their bedroom.

The second attack came when Schreber was promoted to a higher court and Mrs. Schreber had to be away from her husband for four days. During this time Schreber went into an intensive period of fantasying, which resulted in several emissions each night. He was harassed by dreams that his nervous breakdown was going to recur; toward early morning, when he was still half awake and half asleep, it came to him that:

"After all, it really must be very nice to be a woman submitting to the act of copulation."

He returned to the Leipzig Psychiatric Clinic where the breakdown became so complete that he had to be transferred to the Sonnenstein Asylum. He was obsessed with the idea that he had the plague, that his body was being manhandled in revolting ways; that he was dead and his body was decomposing. He attempted to drown himself in his bath and begged the attendants for "the cyanide that was intended for him."

The death wish was superseded by a "delusional structure," in which he became the Redeemer, with God as his natural ally. His new religious order would create a state of bliss for all mankind in which the rays of God would enter each worthy one, enabling them to experience spiritual voluptuousness. However he could not redeem the world or restore it to its state of bliss until he was "first transformed from a man into a woman." He did not wish to be transformed into a woman, but it was an imperative part of what he called the Divine Order of Things; he had to suffer the transformation in order to save the world. His hypochondria had returned with a parallel set of delusions; he was living without lungs, intestines, a stomach or a bladder; each time he took a bite of food he swallowed part of his own larynx with it. However God sent divine miracles in the form of rays not only to cure him but to speed up the transition to his "femaleness." Because God had now endowed him with a set of female "nerves," from his body there was going to emerge a new and glorious race of men which would be directly impregnated by God. Everything Schreber learned came to him in voices from what he called "miracles of talking birds."

After more than eight and a half years in the asylum Judge Schreber petitioned the state to secure his release. When free, he published his book. Much of it was concerned with a bitter attack upon Dr. Flechsig, detailing the horrible things Flechsig had done while he was Flechsig's patient.

It was during Sigmund's vacation of August 1910, spent at the seaside in Holland with his family, that he picked up a copy of the book and read it twice with total fascination. When he returned to Vienna, Otto Rank found in their catalogue of psychiatric and neurological journals a number of reviews and discussions that had already taken place around the book. It had been reviewed as a classical case of paranoia based on religious obsessions, for Schreber had ultimately gone through the phase of being Jesus Christ's redeemer, before he went on to the role of being Mother to the World.

The psychiatrists of Europe had decided that the core of Schreber's paranoia was his religious delusions. The statement that in order to accomplish his mission he had to be transformed into a female was passed by as a minor element in the sickness, largely because the psychiatrists believed Schreber's statement that he wanted to remain a man and only unwillingly became a woman in order to be impregnated by God and bear a new breed of men.

When he had finished the first reading, Sigmund exclaimed:

"They've got the cart before the horse! The religious system that he has constructed emerges from his suppressed homosexuality. There is a connection between his desire to be transformed into a woman and his intimate relationship with God the Father. If we do not proceed from Schreber's suppressed homosexuality, we will be in the position of the man described by Kant in his *Critique of Pure Reason:*

"'Holding a sieve under a he-goat while someone else milks it.'"

Schreber, in his brilliantly insane way, had revealed in print almost the full content of his unconscious mind. Sigmund saw in this case an opportunity to reach a wide audience with the insights of psychoanalysis. He would publish an analysis of the Schreber case, first in the *Yearbook,* and later in book form.

According to Schreber, it was Dr. Flechsig who had been his original "soul murderer," the head of a ritualistic conspiracy to destroy him. Yet for eight years after his release from the Leipzig Psychiatric Clinic he had loved and honored Dr. Flechsig and had seen his picture every night when he went to bed! Schreber had not revealed in his book the fantasies which had caused his emissions during the four days of his wife's absence, but the dreams were connected with his former illness and the attentions of Dr. Flechsig. The unconscious homosexuality in Schreber had found its natural target in the man he loved and honored. Since those yearnings were buried deep, he had lived comfortably with his wife for the eight years between attacks. Then the emotion of love was turned into hate in order to give it expression. Now he could think about Dr. Flechsig and talk about him most of the day, hear voices not only of the birds but all sorts of people in Flechsig's image and bearing Flechsig's messages, even write a book in which Dr. Flechsig became the central soul-destroying villain. During the course of the book Schreber suggested his ever present fear of a sexual attack upon himself by Dr. Flechsig; even while being cured of his first illness in Leipzig he had sometimes been afraid that he "was to be thrown to the attendants for the purpose of sexual abuse." Schreber's unconscious homosexual fantasies were so strong they enabled him to create a religion with a new vocabulary.

There was no way for Sigmund to know why Schreber had survived eight good years and then fallen ill at the particular moment his wife was away: the tension caused by the promotion, the unusual absence of his wife from his bed. Schreber's age might have had a good deal to do with it, for he was then fifty-three, and subject to the male climacteric. There had been stored up at this point a very high quantity of libido, erotic energy, which had to be discharged. It came first in what Schreber described as nocturnal emissions; then in the form of a defense against his homosexuality; and ultimately in a vigorous act of suppression of the reality he could not face. All had caused his breakdown: his refusal to accept his wife when she returned after the four-day absence, the resumption of his hypochondria, the illusions and obsessions which very quickly landed him in the asylum. Endemic to this form of paranoia, the persecution mania had set in, accusing voices which evolved into talking birds; and, as Sigmund had found with his own patients, the persecutor, the one at the center of the destructive plot, was the one who was the best loved.

Sigmund did not ask the question that could have embarrassed the psychiatric profession: how could it happen that this book had been available for seven years and yet no psychiatrist had realized that the basis of Schreber's paranoia was his repressed homosexuality; that "the neuroses arise in the main from a conflict between the ego and the sexual instinct"? Psychiatry had refused to accept the basic sexual instincts of man; it had refused to accept the idea that there was an unconscious mind. What could it say now, faced with unmistakable documentation?

He took great pleasure in writing the sixty-page monograph.

Though he had promised Otto Rank that when he was graduated from the University of Vienna he could open an office as the first lay analyst, Sigmund was not sympathetic to the idea in general. He still hoped that psychoanalysis would be adjudged a medical science; the presence of laymen in the profession would injure this image.

Hanns Sachs helped change his mind. Sachs came from a family of successful and cultivated lawyers. He too had taken his law degree, and gone into practice with a brother. However he was more interested in literature than law, writing poetry and translating Kipling's *Barrack-Room Ballads* into German. In 1904 his life was changed by reading *The Interpretation of Dreams*. He studied Freud's books for two years, then went with a cousin to one of Sigmund's Saturday night lectures at the university. He was too shy to allow himself to be introduced to Professor Freud; in fact it took him another four years to work up the courage, as a layman, to seek membership in the Vienna Psychoanalytic Society.

Sigmund liked him at once, and he became popular with all the members, in particular forming close friendships with Otto Rank and Ernest Jones, who came often to Vienna. Sachs was the perfect portrait of the Viennese man of the world: exquisite manners, broad literary and artistic background, uncrushable sense of humor which included anecdotes from half a dozen languages. He was of medium height, a bit on the portly side, with full cheeks and a double chin. Women found him ugly, described him as "repelling, a face like an egg, with no chin." The men of the Wednesday Evening group enjoyed him thoroughly; his wit, his urbanity and his humility. When Sigmund asked him about his law practice, Sachs answered:

"What kind of lawyer was I? The kind you always have to push uphill."

Yet behind the fashionable clothes, addiction to passing love affairs, an early marriage which had lasted only a few years, the epicurean tastes, the life in the theater, opera, constant travel, his early writings were so perceptive that within a few months of joining he was invited to prepare a paper to be read at the next Congress, to be held in Weimar in September 1911.

4.

Carl Jung had not forced Eugen Bleuler out of the Swiss Society for Psychoanalysis. Bleuler had resigned on his own. This was a severe blow to Sigmund, who had been counting on Bleuler to take the presidency of the Swiss Society. One of the sharpest points of contention was the canceled paper of Dr. Max Isserlin. To Sigmund and the Vienna group, this had simply seemed an act of disarming the enemy; but Bleuler had taken the cancellation hard. Sigmund wrote long, expository letters. Bleuler's replies were friendly, but when Sigmund found that the interchange of letters was not going to keep Bleuler in the Swiss group, he asked for a face-to-face encounter in the hope of settling their differences. Bleuler agreed. They planned to meet in Munich, which had direct rail connections with both cities. The date was set for Christmas Day, when they would be free to take time off.

The two men gripped each other's hands with pleasure as they met at the Bayerischer Hof. There was a warm feeling between them. They had reserved a parlor suite on the top floor of the hotel so that they would have a quiet place to talk. After the usual amenities, inquiries about the health of wives and children, they plunged at once into the subject at hand.

"Professor Bleuler, please let me clarify something I have been trying to say through the mails: our Society does not stifle divergent opinion. It was formed for two important reasons, first, to present to the public authentic psychoanalysis; second, because of the abuse that is being heaped upon us. You were present when your colleague, Hoche, called me a crazy sectarian, and you know that Ziehen has declared to the world that I am writing nonsense. Since we must be ready to answer our opponents, it is no longer proper to leave the replies to the whim of one individual. It is in the interest of our cause to relegate polemics to a central office."

"Aren't you afraid, Professor Freud, of falling into orthodoxy?"

"Why do you suggest that? We are not rigid people. Our minds are open to all hypotheses."

"Because 'who is not with us is against us,' the principle 'all or nothing' is necessary for religious sects and for political parties. I can understand such a policy, but for science I consider it harmful. There is no ultimate truth. From a complex of notions one person will accept one detail, another person another detail. I recognize in science neither open nor closed doors, but no doors, no barriers at all."

"Assuredly, Professor Bleuler. But one cannot fault the International Psychoanalytic Association because it accepts only members who accept psychoanalysis. The Association, however, never goes so far as to declare all non-members as gangsters or idiots. The Association is not exclusive in the sense that it would forbid its members to belong to other humanitarian and social societies, even to the Association of German Nerve Specialists, which treats us so 'lovely' in Berlin! Jung and I belong to this latter society."

Bleuler rose, asked quietly:

"Shall we walk down the main street, past that marvelous City Hall? The people will just be returning from church on their way home for Christmas dinner."

The store windows were aglow with Christmas decorations. The Munichers, bundled up against the intense cold, were walking along with their arms draped around their young, chatting animatedly about the gifts that had been exchanged that morning.

Bleuler was able to disagree in a calm manner.

"The greater one evaluates the significance of the cause one supports, the more one can accept the disadvantages. I know from my own experience, as well as from experiences of others, that I would only do harm and would not help should I participate in a fashion which is against my feelings. There is a difference between us. For you, evidently, it became the aim and interest of your whole life to establish firmly your theory and to secure its acceptance. I decline to believe that psychoanalysis is the one true faith. I stand up for it because I consider it valid and because I feel that I am able to judge it since I am working in a related field. But for me it is not a major issue whether the validity of these views will be recognized a few years sooner or later. I am therefore less tempted than you to sacrifice my whole personality for the advancement of the cause."

Sigmund was silent for a long time. Then he said soberly:

"We appointed Adler president of the Vienna group even though, in the psychological area, he is so against my inner convictions that he makes me angry every single week. Yet I did not demand his exclusion. I feel entitled to stick to my own fifteen-years-older views. One should not confuse steadfastness with intolerance."

He paused for a moment, took a deep breath.

"You accuse us of isolationism; yet there is no group that less wants to be isolated. We want this to be a world movement in every sense of the term. We have been brutally rejected by psychiatrists and neurologists. That is why we must hold ourselves together as a homogeneous group, with our own inner force. It is the strongest of all my desires that you should be the link for us between theoretical psychoanalysis and academic psychiatry."

"I understand your desire for this connection," Bleuler said. "I also genuinely believe that you attribute too much influence to me, Professor Freud. But for the sake of argument, how can we move away from a certain sense of intolerance that I begin to perceive?"

"Professor Bleuler, I would like to make you a concrete proposition. Please tell me what changes you need in the Association to make it acceptable to you, and what modifications of our foreign policies toward our opponents you consider as correct. I personally will give the greatest possible consideration to your wishes and ideas and thus make it possible for you to implement them."

Bleuler smiled, linked his arm through Sigmund's for a moment as they crunched through the winter snows, their breath vaporizing before them.

"Psychoanalysis as a science will prove its value with me or without me, because it contains a great many truths and because it is led by persons like you and Jung. The introduction of the 'closed door' policy scared away a great many friends and made of some of them emotional opponents." He turned honest, concerned eyes on Sigmund. "No matter how great your scientific accomplishments are, psychologically you impress me as an artist. From this point of view it is understandable that you do not want your art product to be destroyed. In art we have a unit which cannot be torn apart. In science you made a great discovery which has to stay. How much of what is loosely connected with it will survive is not important. But I will make one prediction: you will find in the long run that I will remain closer to your beliefs than your second in command, Carl Jung."

There is something about the turning of a New Year which leads men who have long contemplated a change to make it. This was true of Dr. Alfred Adler as the calendar date changed to 1911. What had formerly been a slow, point-by-point withdrawal from Sigmund's sexual etiology of the neuroses now became an attitude of rejection, a sense that his own theories and Sigmund Freud's were mutually exclusive. Sigmund and the Wednesday group decided that Adler should have the opportunity to make a total statement of his beliefs so that they would all know precisely where he stood. They offered him three consecutive Wednesdays starting in mid-January for a course of lectures to carry through the entire evening, without any discussion or criticism until the conclusion of the third lecture. No visitors would be permitted in the hall.

Adler was pleased at the suggestion and shook Sigmund's hand with more warmth than at any time since the Nuremberg dispute. When he started reading his first lecture, in his beautifully melodic voice, he had the attention of the full Society. His major point of departure centered around Sigmund's definition of libido as the energy associated with the sexual issues. He preferred to consider the libido as plain psychic energy, not necessarily connected with the instincts.

"We ask if that which the neurotic shows as libido is to be taken at face value. We would say no. His sexual prematurity is forced. His compulsion to masturbate serves his defiance and as a safeguard against the demon woman . . . his perverted fantasies, even his active perversions, serve him only to keep him away from actual love. How, then, does sexuality come into the neurosis and what part does it play there? It is awakened early and stimulated when existing inferiority and a strong masculine protest are present. . . ."

Those were the key words, "inferiority" and "masculine protest," around which Adler was building his new psychology. His second lecture carried forward his beginning thesis:

"Organic repression appears, then, as nothing but an emergency exit, showing that changes in the modes of operation are possible. It has hardly any bearing on the theory of the neuroses. Repressed drives and drive components, repressed complexes, repressed fantasies, repressed events from life, and repressed wishes are considered under organic repression. . . . Freud says: 'Man cannot forgo any pleasure he has ever experienced.' Although this method created an important step forward, it tended to reify and freeze the psyche which, in reality, is constantly at work contemplating future events."

When Adler finished, Sigmund and his friends, who had been jotting down observations, closed their notebooks and left the hall one by one without saying good night to each other. When Adler appeared for his third lecture, he seemed flushed with pleasure. He mounted the platform with a jaunty step and a bright sparkle in his eye. He wanted to make it clear once again that he did not consider the energy of the libido as sexual in origin; any more than he would accept infantile sexuality, or that there was any such compartment as the unconscious in which repressions could be stored, not even the Oedipal complex.

"For our consideration, the constant factor is the culture, the society and its institutions. Our drives, the satisfaction of which has been considered the end, act merely as the direction-giving means to initiate the satisfactions in the distant future. Here increased tensions are as urgent as repressions. In these relations rests the necessity for an extensive system of safeguards, one small part of which we must recognize in the neurosis. Drive-satisfaction, and consequently the quality and strength of the drive, are at all times variable and therefore not measurable. In the talk on Sexuality and Neurosis, I likewise came to the conclusion that the apparently libidinous and sexual tendencies in the neurotic, as in the normal individual, in no way permit any conclusion regarding the strength or composition of his sex drive. Once one appreciates the masculine protest in the Oedipus complex, one is no longer justified in speaking of a complex of fantasies and wishes. One will then learn to understand that the apparent Oedipus complex is only a small part of the overpowering neurotic dynamic, a stage of the masculine protest, a stage which in itself is insignificant although instructive in its context."

Sigmund Freud went cold. When Adler finished, he sat down, certain that he had made an unanswerable case. From his expression, Sigmund could see that he expected to be congratulated and applauded. It was as though, eight years before, Sigmund Freud had presented Alfred Adler with a pocket knife with inlaid ivory handles. One by one Adler had lost the blades, replacing them, then the ivory insets, replacing them as well, then the springs and casings for the blades, until every last piece of the knife had been replaced. Now he was showing Sigmund Freud what great care he had taken of the gift, exclaiming:

"See, I have the very knife you gave me eight years ago! With the blades sharpened to a razor's edge."

"No," Sigmund said to himself grimly, "that is not my knife. It is a totally new and different knife. I never gave it to him; he gave it to himself, piece by piece. And it's his to keep!"

He had never spoken in anger at one of these meetings, no matter how objectionable, obtuse or irresponsible some of the members had become. But he decided that only hot, logical anger could sweep clean the Augean stable of Adler's surface psychology. He pre-empted the right to speak first. He rose to his feet and, after suggesting that Adler's paper suffered from the simple shortcoming of obscurity, continued:

"Personally I take it ill of the author that he speaks of the same things without designating them by the same names, which they already have, and without trying to bring his new terms into relation with the old. Thus one has the impression that repression exists in the masculine protest; either the latter coincides with the former or it is the same phenomenon under different viewpoints. Even our old idea of bisexuality is called psychic hermaphroditism, as if it were something else. He has swept away the unconscious, advocates asexual infantile history, and deprecates the value of the details of neuroses. This trend is methodically deplorable and condemns his whole work to sterility."

Adler cried out:

"The masculine protest in a male individual indicates that he has never fully recovered from an infantile doubt as to whether he really is male. He strives for an ideal masculinity invariably conceived as the possession by himself of freedom, love and power . . . the *conquest* of women or friends, and the surpassing or overthrowing of others."

Sigmund replied quickly:

"The whole doctrine has a reactionary and retrograde character. For the most part it deals with biology instead of psychology, and instead of the psychology of the unconscious it concerns surface phenomena."

One by one Freud's followers began consulting their notes. They took the floor to combat Adler's concept that there was no such thing as an unconscious, that infants were asexual, that the theory of repression was fallacious, that the sexual drive had no primary importance. The attacks were so thoroughgoing that Wilhelm Stekel jumped to his feet, crying:

"This group has organized its attack on Dr. Adler's psychology!"

Sigmund denied this. Adler had now turned ashen.

"Please accept my word for it, Dr. Adler, nothing was organized. I have not discussed your lectures with any of our colleagues. We have all taken our notes separately; that is why you see written pages before each of us. This is nothing more than proper procedure, so that we could quote you accurately if we wished to contradict your thesis."

Adler replied hoarsely, "The accusation was not mine. I could never impute any personal wrongdoing to you. But you mistake my motive. You believe that I have tried to replace Freudian psychoanalysis with Adlerian psychoanalysis. That was not my intent. I tried to achieve a synthesis, taking the best out of both of our sciences. Apparently I have failed."

"Dr. Adler, you are a biologist, half of your thinking is based on organ inferiority. You are a sociologist, the other half of your psychology is based upon the influence of society, the world in which a man grows up, on the formation of his individual character. While there are elements of truth in both areas, they do not offer a working hypothesis upon which to build a psychoanalytic science."

Adler rose, picked up his papers, said coolly:

"You will permit me to differ." Then, sweeping the room with his eyes, he said, "I am sure you will understand that there is no longer a place for me here. I resign my position as president of the Vienna Psychoanalytic Society. I shall also resign as co-editor of the *Journal for Psychoanalysis*. Good evening, gentlemen."

He started for the door. His own group of friends and colleagues, whom he had brought into the organization, rose to leave with him. Wilhelm Stekel also rose, a stern look of displeasure on his face as he joined the Adlerian group. Sigmund went quickly to Adler, asked if he could have a moment with him in private. Adler stood still, his warm personality frozen, his mobile face expressionless. The rest of the men left the room, both Adler's cohorts and Freud's. Sigmund said nostalgically, in spite of the year of discomfort Adler had caused him:

"This is a sad moment in my life. It is the first time in the nine years our group has met that I have lost a disciple."

Adler replied firmly, "I am not, and never was, a disciple."

"I accept the correction: a colleague. It is not a happy event when one loses a long-time colleague. But then in actuality you have been lost to us for some time."

Adler took off his pince-nez. His eyes were hooded. He said, without looking directly at Sigmund:

"The break was of your doing."

"How so, Doctor?"

"By committing the same scientific crime I have heard you ascribe to Charcot and Bernheim: *you have frozen your own revolution!*"

Sigmund was profoundly shocked. The accusation hurt him more deeply than anything attributed to him by his enemies. His voice was hoarse, as though his laryngitis had returned in full flower.

"On the contrary, Doctor, when I have made errors I have admitted them, and continued the search. I have proudly incorporated into the body of psychoanalysis ideas which you yourself have contributed. What is your real reason for resigning from the Vienna Psychoanalytic Society?"

Anguish flooded Adler's proud, sensitive face.

"Why should I always do my work under your shadow?"

5.

Martin Freud broke his thigh while skiing on the Schneeberg, and had to be nursed in a sanatorium. Psychoanalysis was also tobogganing up and down metaphorical mountains, enjoying the sport but splintering a bone here and there.

An Australian neurologist was dismissed from his post for practicing Freudian psychoanalysis; but Dr. Poul Bjerre, a Swedish psychiatrist, read a paper before the Association of Swedish Physicians on Freud's Psychoanalytic Method, then came to Vienna to tell Sigmund that things were going well in Sweden. Although there was a Berlin Psychoanalytic Society, Abraham was in difficulties; he could get no other physician to practice psychoanalysis in that city. Only Wilhelm Fliess had communicated with Abraham, asking if they could become friends. Sandor Ferenczi was taking some lumps in Budapest; where in the beginning the Hungarians had treated psychoanalysis lightly, now a formidable opposition had been formed inside the medical profession, which had come to understand its implications. A. A. Brill founded the New York Psychoanalytic Society, and shortly thereafter Ernest Jones, on leave from his hospital duties in Toronto, took the train to Baltimore and founded the American Psychoanalytic Association there. Sigmund had visits from Sutherland of India, who was translating *The Interpretation of Dreams*; two Hollanders arrived at the Berggasse, Jan van Emden, to study under Sigmund, and August Stärcke, who turned up with the astonishing information that he had been practicing psychoanalysis in Holland since 1905. A doctor by the name of M. D. Eder read for the first time an account of psychoanalysis to the Neurological Section of the British Medical Association. Ernest Jones decided that he would return to London to start not only his practice but a Psychoanalytic Society there.

The word was spreading through Russia. A Dr. L. Drosnés of Odessa came to tell him of the beginning of the Russian Psychoanalytic Society. Dr. M. E. Ossipow and a group of his colleagues were translating the books into Russian; the Moscow Academy offered a prize for the best essay on psychoanalysis; one doctor announced in St. Petersburg that his office was open for patients wanting psychotherapy. When Dr. M. Wulff was fired from his job in a Berlin institution because he believed in Freud's views, he promptly moved to Odessa and took further training by correspondence from Sigmund and Ferenczi.

Dr. G. Modena of Ancona translated Sigmund's *Three Essays on the Theory of Sexuality* into Italian. But little work was being done in France, perhaps because Dr. Pierre Janet, who had succeeded Charcot as France's greatest neurologist, first claimed that he had invented psychoanalysis because he had used the word "unconscious" before Freud had, albeit in different context; and then, having staked out his priority, announced to the medical world that he repudiated his discovery! However an independent neurologist named R. Morichau-Beauchant wrote from Poitiers, apologizing for France's neglect of his work and promising a more fertile field for the future.

There was a group of doctors in Sydney, Australia, making concerted studies of Freudian psychology under the direction of Dr. Donald Fraser, who was both a physician and a minister of the Presbyterian Church. Despite the fact that Sigmund was also invited by Dr. Andrew Davidson, secretary of the section of Psychological Medicine, to come to Sydney to address an Australasian Medical Congress, Dr. Fraser was forced to resign as minister of his church because he advocated study of the Freud books; a fate that was staring the Reverend Oskar Pfister in the face in Zurich, where his superiors were trying to have him recant or be defrocked. The most serious attack was launched against their friend Dr. Morton Prince; the police in Boston were threatening to prosecute him because he had published "obscenities" in his *Journal of Abnormal Psychology*. In Canada, because Ernest Jones had written articles for the *Asylum Bulletin*, the *Bulletin* was closed down on the grounds that it was advocating psychoanalysis. Sigmund felt as though his mind and heart were a battlefield where he increasingly won victories, but which nonetheless was strewn with corpses and carnage.

Tante Minna's health seemed to get worse each winter, though Sigmund was never able to determine precisely what the ailment was. He tried to take her for a vacation each year, sometimes with Martha and the children to Holland, when the weather was good, or on a short trip into Italy. Ernest Jones's common-law wife of seven years, Loe, became psychologically ill and addicted to morphia. Sigmund agreed to take her under his care. Jones brought her to Vienna where Sigmund, through analysis, slowly brought her use of morphia down to a half, then to a quarter.

Another generation was being born in the Freudian circle: Alexander had a son, Karl Abraham a daughter, the Binswangers also had a child, the Carl Jungs had taken their new son out to Küsnacht. One of the more promising of the Swiss psychoanalysts, Dr. J. Honegger, committed suicide, and no one in Zurich knew why. Martha's mother, Emmeline Bernays, died at the age of eighty, of cancer. Martha and Tante Minna attended her funeral.

Sigmund's own health was on and off: he went for a walk on a raw winter night and came down with influenza. After Martha had kept him in bed for several days, plying him with hot drinks that cured him, he began to suffer mental obfuscation, ending each day with a severe headache. He thought that there must be something seriously wrong with him, until he found that there was a gas leak in his lamp which had been slowly poisoning the air in his office.

"I'm lucky," he observed to Martha; "the old watchmaker down in the *Parterre* got blown out of his apartment because of a gas leak. I merely lost a month of writing. I thought for a while that my creative energies were at an end."

Sigmund had had an early fantasy that he was going to die at forty-one or forty-two. He frequently wrote to his followers that he was growing old and would soon need to be superseded. But when Dr. James Putnam wrote favorably about Sigmund's Clark University lectures in the *Journal of Abnormal Psychology*, and observed that Dr. Freud was no longer young, Sigmund lost most of his pleasure in the publication.

After imagining that he would die at forty-one, he substituted the hallucination that he would die at the age of fifty-one, the sum of Wilhelm Fliess's twenty-eight and twenty-three numerical cycles. When he passed that age in good health, he decided that the age of sixty-one was a more logical figure; and then was amused to find that he always gave himself a full decade leeway!

Sigmund and his committed group of twenty settled down. There were four laymen: Max Graf, Hugo Heller, Otto Rank and Hanns Sachs, but no one of them was yet practicing psychoanalysis or treating patients.

As Sigmund looked around at his loyal followers, he was once again surprised and pleased to see how young they were. Otto Rank was only twenty-eight, Fritz Wittels thirty-two, Viktor Tausk thirty-three, Guido Brecher thirty-five. Most of the rest were in their early forties: Eduard Hitschmann and Josef Friedjung forty-one, Paul Federn forty-two, Sadger and Jekels forty-four, Reitler and Steiner forty-seven. . . . If their fewer years made him feel old at fifty-five, it also gave him a feeling that there would be a younger generation to carry on.

Now that the disaffection in their ranks was removed, each man dug in on a research project and began writing a paper, many of them aimed at the International Congress to be held in Weimar in September. The productivity was high, only part of it technically about medicine. They decided to create a non-medical psychoanalytical journal to be called Imago, of which Otto Rank and his close friend Hanns Sachs became the editors. Here they could publish the articles growing out of their studies of anthropology, political economy, the arts, literature and the humanities. Sigmund had trouble finding a publisher because no one thought he could sell enough copies to earn back the printing costs. Finally Hugo Heller took it over, more out of a sense of loyalty to the Society than with any idea that he could make a profit. He told Sigmund:

"At least I have a bookstore, and I can give Imago a display, both in the window and on the inside tables. We should be able to sell some copies that way."

The family spent the summer in the Tyrol where Sigmund began the writing of four long papers which he intended to publish in succeeding issues of the projected magazine, and then put out as a book. By August he wrote Ferenczi that he was "wholly Totem and Taboo," so deeply immersed was he in the fascinating materials.

On September 14, 1911, Martha and Sigmund celebrated their silver anniversary. Since the day fell on a Thursday, at which time there was to be a celebration dinner, Sigmund asked his relatives and friends to come the weekend before. He scouted the countryside, renting rooms in the neighboring villas. The Oskar Ries arrived, and the Leopold Königsteins. Otto Rank checked the guests into their scattered rooms in the forest villas. There were hikes in the mountains, berry pickings and all-day picnics, swimming and fishing parties, evenings of storytelling and laughter around a roaring fire, while they roasted apples on long sticks. Mathilde was there with her husband, happily blooming in her marriage; Ernst, the youngest son, had managed to turn up an ulcer at examination time; and Sophie, the happy-go-lucky middle daughter, though only eighteen, announced that, like Mathilde, she had no intention of waiting until she was twenty-four to marry.

Sigmund looked down the length of the dining-room table to where Martha presided in her simple dignity. It was now twenty-nine years since that fateful Saturday when they had climbed to the top of the mountain behind Mödling with Martha's brother Eli Bernays, and then returned to the back garden of their friend's house where they sat under a lime tree eating the white blossoms of the elderberry bushes. Twenty-nine years since their lips had met for the first time; the first "intimation" to Sigmund that he might have Martha Bernays in marriage. The first four years had been the hardest because they were separated most of the time, and he was struggling at the Allgemeine Krankenhaus to find a proper discipline with which to support them, and in which he could make a modest contribution to medical science. But the twenty-five years of marriage, ah! that was a different story. The bearing of six children, the isolation and obloquy, the sometimes inadequate funds, had not dimmed the kindliness of Martha's nature.

She had just passed her fiftieth birthday. But she had not grown old; she had been too busy. She had maintained the structure of her domicile with so much tender precision that one of Sigmund's colleagues commented:

"Your home is like an island in the sea of Vienna."

The years had taken something of a physical toll: there was a gray mist in the hair that she puffed up and wore rolled high and backwards on her head; there were little pockets of darkness under her eyes, and the lines of her cheeks were deepening where they ran from the top of her nostrils down to her mouth. But these were the normal forfeits to time. They had happened so gradually that Sigmund took no more notice of them than he had of the whitening of his own hair at the temples. He had had his neuroses, and learned to live with them; but in the one most important relationship in his life, he was as normal as sun or rain water: marriage.

"Bless her," he thought, "for the goodness and joy she has brought me, and for enduring all that she has without acknowledging that the enemy was pounding at the gate."

The twenty-fifth anniversary dinner was a merry one. Martha had commandeered several of the young women of the neighborhood to help her cook and serve it. It was a noisy, jubilant dinner. By midafternoon, when all the toasts had been drunk, the gifts of books, antique figurines, jewelry, opened and declared over, the Tyrolean band began to play, and everyone danced.

When darkness fell, Sigmund asked if he might tell something about the pages he had been writing on Totem and Taboo. Martha was pleased at what the creative surge had done for Sigmund's health and spirits over the summer. She shepherded everyone out to the veranda; chairs were placed in a semicircle before Sigmund. Then, without lamp or candle, he began speaking in a soft, intimate voice, lighting up the night as did the gleaming stars overhead.

What he was attempting to do was to "bridge the gap between students of such subjects as social anthropology, philology and folklore on the one hand, and psychoanalysis on the other." All cultures had evolved out of a suppression of instincts. There were a great many taboos in contemporary society, but totemism had long since been abandoned and replaced by newer forms. The best way to get at the original meaning of totemism was to study the vestiges of it remaining in childhood.

What was there in prehistory, in the events and conditions prior to recorded history, which still survived in the mind of modern man? Making a study of the aborigines of Australia, who were described as "the most backward and miserable of savages," who worshiped no higher being, he had written, "Yet we find that they set before themselves with the most scrupulous care and the most painful severity the aim of avoiding incestuous sexual relations. Indeed, their whole social organization seems to serve that purpose, or to have been brought into relation with its attainment."

Every clan had its own totem and took the name of that totem, usually an animal. This totem, Sigmund suggested, became the common ancestor of each clan; it was also the guardian spirit and helper, peculiar to its own group, which no other could appropriate, and no one abandon. Every individual in the clan gave it total loyalty and adherence.

But why was the totem so all-powerful, so all-present that not a single clan among the Australian aborigines existed without it? And what was the relationship of the totemic system to psychoanalysis?

He called for a lamp and his manuscript, and then read from it.

"In almost every place where we find totems we also find a law against persons of the same totem having sexual relations with one another and consequently against their marrying. This, then, is 'exogamy.'" The aim and structure of the totemic clan was to regulate the marriage choice, even to the extent of preventing group incest and forbidding marriage between distant relatives within a clan.

"A neurotic invariably exhibits some degree of psychical infantilism. It is therefore of no small importance that we are able to show that these same incestuous wishes, which are later destined to become unconscious, are still regarded by savage peoples as immediate perils against which the most severe measures of defense must be enforced."

He had taken such enjoyment from the writing of the first essay that he moved very quickly to the second phase, Taboo and Emotional Ambivalence. Here he drew the distinction between taboo restrictions and religious and moral prohibitions, showing that often the origin of taboos could not be traced, were frequently unintelligible, yet were never disobeyed by primitive man because such defiance would bring immediate and drastic punishment. This conduct was very similar to that of his obsessional patients; they suffered from a "taboo sickness." With neurotics the taboos, as with primitives, appeared to be lacking in motive and indeterminate in origin. Once an obsession seized an individual it was maintained by fear of punishment.

It seemed apparent to him that the prohibitions growing out of taboos had to be concerned with "activities towards which there was a strong inclination." The Australian primitives "must therefore have an ambivalent attitude towards their taboos. In their unconscious there is nothing they would like more than to violate them, but they are afraid to do so; they are afraid precisely because they would like to, and the fear is stronger than the desire. The desire is unconscious, however, in every individual member of the tribe, as it is in neurotics. . . .

"Here, then, we have an exact counterpart of the obsessional act in the neurosis, in which the suppressed impulse and the impulse that suppresses it find simultaneous and common satisfaction. The obsessional act is *ostensibly* a protection against the prohibited act; but *actually*, in our view, it is a repetition of it."

His third essay, which he planned to call Animism, Magic and the Omnipotence of Thoughts, would trace the origins of formal religion, including its techniques of magic and sorcery. The relation between animistic thinking and that of the neurotic was that both believed in the "omnipotence of thought." Just as people practicing magic and sorcery lived in a world apart, so did neurotics, in a world where only "neurotic currency" could be considered legal tender.

"The primary obsessive acts of these neurotics are of an entirely magical character. If they are not charms, they are at all events counter-charms, designed to ward off the expectations of disaster with which the neurosis usually starts. Whenever I have succeeded in penetrating the mystery, I have found that the expected disaster was death."

There was a sharp intake of breath on the part of the friends sitting around him.

It was with a sense of exhilaration that he approached the materials of the fourth and last essay, to be called The Return of Totemism in Childhood. The primitive directed his fear toward the totem animal. In the contemporary life of all young males the totem animal was replaced by the father.

"If the totem animal is the father, then the two principal ordinances of totemism, the two taboo prohibitions which constitute its core, not to kill the totem and not to have sexual relations with a woman of the same totem, coincide in their content with the two crimes of Oedipus, who killed his father and married his mother, as well as the two primal wishes of children, the insufficient repression or the reawakening of which forms the nucleus of perhaps every psychoneurosis. If this equation is anything more than a misleading trick of chance, it must enable us to throw a light upon the origin of totemism in the inconceivably remote past. In other words, it would enable us to make it probable that the totem system, like little Hans's animal phobia, was a product of the conditions involved in the Oedipus complex. . . .

"Sexual desires do not unite men but divide them," divide son from father. Totemic religion arose from this filial sense of guilt, in "an attempt to allay that feeling and to appease the father by deferred obedience to him. All later religions are seen to be attempts at solving the same problem."

This led to one of the oldest totemic practices, the sacrifice at one time each year of the totem animal, whose flesh was eaten by each member of the clan. "Everywhere a sacrifice involved a feast and a feast cannot be celebrated without a sacrifice." The clan sacrifice of the clan animal was in effect a triumph over the father figure. This also applied to modern religion. "Totemic religion not only comprised expressions of remorse and attempts at atonement, it also served as a remembrance of the triumph over the father." Since the killing of the father was the wish in the unconscious of every male child, so with primitive man it became part of the system to commit parricide at a given time, sacrificing the totem and partaking of its flesh. As far as modern religion went, psychoanalysis revealed that each man's god is formed in the likeness of his father.

There were several moments of silence. No one moved. Then came a soft murmuring: of excitement? of shock? Sigmund could not be sure. He rose. Martha stood beside him. The others surrounded them, expressing their thanks for the marvelous day:

"Many more happy anniversaries! For the future, *Alles in Butter!*"

6.

Sigmund left for Zurich to visit with Carl Jung at Küsnacht for four days before they would go together to the Weimar Congress. Jung met him at the station in Zurich. They were too reserved to embrace in public; yet the radiant joy on both their faces reflected unmistakably the deep admiration and love they felt for each other.

They went by train to the little village of Küsnacht. The Jung house had been designed by a relative of Jung's. Unlike most of the other houses along the lake, its style was out of the eighteenth century, with a remarkable sense of spaciousness which impressed Sigmund deeply. There was a long path in from the road, lined by newly planted trees, a handsome front door with a carving in the stone lintel above it, which Carl Jung had put there for himself and his wife, and which read, *This laughing spot.* From the foyer a broad, handsome staircase led up to the second floor, guarded by a superbly carved wooden balustrade. The architect had worked to achieve everything Carl and Emma Jung wanted for gracious living for themselves and their children.

Off the foyer to one side was a French baroque music room with a piano in one corner, silk and brocaded walls of a turquoise color, very elaborate in its finery. Straight in from the foyer and fronting on the lake was the central room of the house, a drawing room of great size with a huge fireplace at one end and, clustered around it, a sofa, settee, lounge chairs, coffee tables. In the middle of the room, in the center of the big carpet, was an expandable dining table. Here the family ate its meals, and here the family entertained.

Sigmund was happily received by Emma Jung and then taken upstairs to a guest room overlooking the lake. Jung took him to see the wing of the house that he had helped design, the quarters for his consultation offices and workshop. At first there had not been very many patients. Carl Jung concentrated on research and writing; but soon people were coming out by train and by boat. The word spread that he had an absolute genius as a healer.

There was a modest-sized waiting room and a suite of two charming rooms, the larger one with several big windows overlooking the lake and the sloping lawn which reached down to the boathouse in which Jung kept the sailboat he had had built in Zurich. Jung saw his patients in this room with its colorful stained-glass windows. He wrote his books in the smaller of the two rooms, on a large ·desk on which he kept the enormous double ledger in which he painted and drew. Sigmund noticed that there was no couch in the consultation room as there was in his own office, merely a big comfortable chair in which the patient would sit facing Jung across his desk. There was a fireplace against the winter chill, though the rest of the family complained that, since Father was never cold, the house was usually freezing. Despite the fact that Jung had wanted to be an archaeologist and had already traveled extensively, he brought back few archaeological specimens, an occasional spear and shield. What he collected bountifully were ideas and images which he later carved into wood, and sometimes into stone. He was not at all attracted to the antique figures Sigmund loved so dearly. Sigmund thought with affection:

"In the best sense, he is the complete man, the artist contained within himself."

Sigmund rose at six-thirty to help Carl Jung work in his garden and vegetable patch. They would eat a light breakfast and go for a row on the lake, or the family would join them and go out to the far end of the lake to sail among the islands, one of which Carl Jung wanted to buy, and build there a summer retreat. When the two men were alone they discussed psychoanalysis. They had only minor differences, in the matter of technique, on how one approached the patient to get the greatest flow of material. Jung had accepted with grace the fact that he was the successor to Sigmund's empire, and was working hard to make the *Yearbook* an important and exciting one.

As Sigmund watched Carl Jung carve away at a block of wood, or gather stones for a new piece of wall, he was moved by the sharp contrast between the way Jung lived here at Küsnacht and the way he, Sigmund, lived in Vienna. He and Martha owned nothing but the furniture and household goods of their apartment, most of which had been bought at the time of their marriage. The apartment, for which they paid rent, carried no sense of ownership, except in the Viennese concept that one's domicile was a lifetime residence. The Jungs owned their own lovely home, encompassing acres of land, with vegetable and flower gardens, and with trails through their own woods along the beach. He thought:

"They own a piece of the world. It's theirs forever. What a good feeling that must be. They are living in a house they have designed, which sits on the lakeside in the precise direction they want to face, with tall windows off their bedroom taking in the beauty of the mountains opposite, and the sunrise and sunset on the waters. It must breed a particular kind of life philosophy: not exactly a relaxation, though there would be an element of that too; but mostly of longevity, of continuity. Obviously Küsnacht had been built to stand a century on these spacious grounds; its owner too could have the freedom to live perhaps as much as a full century.

"Well," he thought, "I am happy for Carl and Emma and their children. They did indeed pick a happy place. Carl will do great work here, slowly, carefully, and become famous."

He did not feel the slightest twinge of envy, since he could not have it at all, and it was not in the Viennese tradition anyway. But the contrast in the life style was amazing.

After two days Dr. James Putnam arrived from Boston. He was an urbane, gracious man, well trained in both psychology and philosophy. The three men spoke English together, although Putnam's German was quite good. Putnam was encouraging about the growth of psychoanalysis in America. On his many visits from Canada, Ernest Jones had rounded up a loyal nucleus in New England; A. A. Brill had already collected some twenty members into the New York Psychoanalytic Society. Jung twitted Sigmund:

"How can you even suspect that a country which is so hospitable to psychoanalysis could have given you a case of colitis?"

Sigmund, Carl Jung, James Putnam, Franz Riklin and Ludwig Binswanger made the train journey to Weimar together. It was a ninth-century city, still medieval in character because of its narrow winding streets in the older part of town and the busy, colorful market place, closed in by private homes with high-pitched gables. Before they settled into the hotel, the five men dropped off their suitcases and walked to the former palace, the building of which had been supervised by Goethe himself.

In contrast to the Nuremberg one the year before, the Weimar Congress turned out to be relaxed and friendly. Some fifty-five adherents were present, including several women doctors who were beginning to specialize in the field of psychoanalysis. This time four Americans attended. Dr. James Putnam opened the Congress with a paper on The Importance of Philosophy for the Further Development of Psychoanalysis. His modest manner and high moral purpose were received with enthusiasm. All knew of the brilliant fight he was waging in America for Freudian psychoanalysis. Carl Jung was in excellent form. He presided with wit and an easy hand, took his turn to read a paper on Symbolism in the Psychoses and Neuroses. Sigmund had been happy to see Eugen Bleuler arrive with a group from Zurich. He was cordial to everyone, and read an incisive paper on Autism. The Reverend Oskar Pfister brought a fellow Swiss clergyman, the Reverend Adolf Keller. Dr. Jan van Emden came in from Leiden, Dr. A. W. van Renterghem from Amsterdam; and from Germany, Magnus Hirschfeld, an authority on homosexuality. Karl Abraham earned the respect of the Congress with his study of Manic-Depressive Insanity; Hanns Sachs read a paper on the Interrelation Between Psychoanalysis and the Mental Sciences; Ferenczi's contribution to the understanding of homosexuality was approved by Dr. Hirschfeld. Otto Rank's paper was of the highest order, The Motif of Nudity in Poetry and Legends. The Congress had a laugh at breakfast; the local newspaper reported that "interesting papers were read on nudity and other current topics."

Though it had been known that Alfred Adler and his cohorts had resigned from the Vienna Psychoanalytic Society, and that Adler had founded his own Society for Free Psychoanalysis, no one brought up his name or seemed concerned that he had moved in directions of his own.

One of the more interesting visitors to the Congress was a woman whom Sigmund had long known about, Lou Andreas-Salomé, who had been given an intensive course in psychoanalysis by her then lover, the Swedish psychotherapist, Dr. Poul Bjerre, who had brought her to the Congress as a guest. Lou Andreas-Salomé was Russian-born, from a prosperous and cultivated family. She had married Andreas because he threatened to commit suicide if she did not. Her one condition was that she would never be obliged to have intercourse with him, a condition which Andreas accepted. A young serving girl had been brought in to take care of his needs, and had by now given him two sons. This freed Lou Andreas-Salomé to wander the world. She was a published novelist, poet, essayist, friend of the literati of a good many countries. She had been Rainer Maria Rilke's mistress during the years in which he produced his most creative poetry; and had been Friedrich Nietzsche's last and most desperate love. Nietzsche had said about her:

"She was prepared like none other for that part of my philosophy that has hardly yet been uttered."

Dr. Bjerre told Sigmund:

"Lou's grasp of psychoanalysis is instantaneous and profound."

Lou Andreas-Salomé was now fifty. She had never been a beautiful woman, but she remained enormously attractive, with an intelligence and spontaneity, an outgoing charm which attracted all men and most women, except Nietzsche's sister, who had jealously called her "an arch fiend," even though Lou Andreas-Salomé had refused Nietzsche's importunings to marry him. She rejected contemptuously the idea that she was a *femme fatale;* she simply claimed to be a free spirit, with money of her own and the liberty to travel; an "independent human being." She never fell in love except with men of talent, and usually great talent, and never gave herself completely to her love affairs. When the bloom wore off, and she met another interesting man, she terminated one affair and commenced another. No one knew how many of these affairs she had had in the past thirty years, but neither did anyone think of her as promiscuous. She reserved her inner core for herself, moving on to the next man and to a higher stage of her own intellectual and artistic development. Sigmund was struck by the grasp and clarity of her mind. There was nothing coy or flirtatious in her manner. She asked if she might write to him in Vienna and come to see him. He agreed.

The two-day Congress adjourned with a feeling of accomplishment and high hope for the future. Sigmund remained behind for several days of conferences with Abraham, Brill and Jones about their cases in progress, their problems and projected therapeutic techniques. He returned to Vienna in the best health and spirits he could remember for years.

7.

It is in the nature of a pendulum to swing.

The attacks in the Swiss press intensified, articles denouncing not so much the validity of psychoanalysis as its morality. It was declared to be a black science, evil in nature, an emanation of Satan to corrupt the world. Nor were they isolated attacks; they were organized and integrated. It appeared evident to Sigmund, as the blistering stories reached his desk, that they did not originate in newspaper or magazine offices. There was always a deeply theological involvement which indicated that the Church was inspiring much of the material. Another phase seemed to come from high government levels; the practice of psychoanalysis in Switzerland was declared to be against the national interests of the Swiss. It was demanded of the psychiatrists that they cease working in this muckish field; the Swiss public was warned not to go to a physician who believed in Freudian psychoanalysis.

Sigmund's friends in Zurich, particularly the members of the Swiss Society for Psychoanalysis which had been founded the year before, felt the effects immediately. Many of their patients stopped coming; few new patients appeared on the scene. Riklin wrote to Sigmund asking if he could not send them patients from Austria or Germany, not merely to help them make a living, but to allow them to remain in psychoanalysis, and not have to revert to general practice or their earlier forms of neurology.

At about the same time there appeared in the New York *Times* the report of an indictment made by Dr. Allen Starr before the Neurological Section of the New York Academy of Medicine, in which Dr. Starr claimed that he had worked with Sigmund Freud in Meynert's laboratory in Vienna, that Freud was a Viennese libertine, "not a man who lived on a particularly high plane."

The only American Sigmund had met in Meynert's laboratory was Bernard Sachs. If the New York *Times* report had not been so damaging to the infant movement A. A. Brill had just headed, it could have been considered funny: during his undergraduate years with Professor Meynert, Sigmund had been a penniless bookworm, without a girl or a glass of beer to his name. During his graduate years in Meynert's Clinic and laboratory, he had been engaged to Martha and was living the life of an anchorite. Sigmund checked out the records at Meynert's Clinic, also at the Allgemeine Krankenhaus; the name of Allen Starr did not appear. He might have been at the Medical School briefly as a guest physician. The brunt of the *Times* story, which was simply reporting Dr. Starr's comments, was that Sigmund Freud's theories were based on his immoral life. The family refused to take the article seriously. Minna teased:

"Just think, we have had a Viennese libertine living in our midst all these years, and we never suspected."

In April Sigmund received a letter from Ludwig Binswanger from Switzerland, telling him that an operation for appendicitis had revealed a malignant tumor. His life expectancy was one to three years. The news was painful; Binswanger had remained a loyal and courageous friend under fire.

On the heels of this, Amalie became ill. His mother was still a vital woman at the age of seventy-six. Sigmund called in an internist, who examined her thoroughly, though not without considerable protest on her part that she did not need a doctor. The internist prescribed bed rest and heavy doses of medication, which Dolfi promised she would somehow get

down her mother's throat. When Amalie was feeling well again, Sigmund
wrote to Carl Jung that he was going to Kreuzlingen, which was on Lake
Constance, to visit Ludwig Binswanger. Although he would have only
two days, surely they could meet and have a talk?

He found Binswanger in a good state of recovery after removal of the
tumor. They went for short walks along the lake, discussing how best to
outlive the concerted Swiss attack. On Sunday Binswanger took Sigmund
to his family's estate where a group of friends and relatives had been invited to meet Ludwig's teacher. It was a pleasant day; but by midafternoon Sigmund found himself growing uneasy. Why had Carl Jung not
come? It was only a distance of thirty or forty miles from Küsnacht to
Lake Constance. There was a good train connection. Sigmund would
have to return to Vienna that night to be on hand for his early Monday
morning patients. Surely Carl and Emma Jung would have wanted to
spend a day with Ludwig Binswanger, who was an old friend, and with
Sigmund himself.

Carl Jung never did appear, nor did he send word. Sigmund was disappointed. What could have happened?

The answer arrived a few days later in a letter from Jung, an extremely
hurt and angry letter. Why had Sigmund come to Switzerland and not
seen him? Why had he written so late that Carl Jung could not have
received the news in time to come to Lake Constance? What had happened to their friendship that Sigmund would make the long trip from
Vienna and not be sufficiently interested to spend a few hours with the
Jungs at Küsnacht, where he had been so welcome only the year before?

Sigmund answered at once, telling about the letter he had written
a sufficient number of days in advance for Jung to have received it, and to
have known that Sigmund was going to be passing the weekend with
Binswanger to cheer him up and speed him on his recovery. It was a quiet
note, simply giving the facts of his journey.

Shortly thereafter Jung wrote that he had been invited to give a series
of lectures that September at Fordham University in New York, and was
now accepting. This meant, he explained, that he could not be at the
next Congress, nor would he be able to make the arrangements for it. He
would simply have to be left out this year. There seemed to Sigmund to be
the suggestion between the lines that as long as President Carl Jung
could not be in Europe in September, no Congress should be held.

It was a dilemma. Sigmund did not feel it proper that he himself preside.
If he called the Congress without Jung, it might seem that Carl Jung had
taken the lecture series in order to avoid the Congress. By the same token,
if he put someone else in the chair, he could easily offend Jung and loosen
his bond to the movement. He agonized for a number of days, then
decided to postpone the Congress until the following year, though he
regretted the loss deeply.

Hugo Heller had already published two issues of *Imago* with the first two parts of Sigmund's *Totem and Taboo*. The magazine had been sold and read with interest by a small circle. Now Heller came thundering into his office. He was prone to fits of anger, and was in the midst of a real one.

"Hugo, you look as though the heavens were about to fall in on you."

"They have! In the form of a dozen of my customers. Ones who have been with me since the store opened. They declare that if I don't take all the copies of *Imago* out of my window and out of the shop itself, they will discontinue their trade. It's blackmail! But what am I to do? These are some of my best accounts. I would have a difficult time surviving without them."

Sigmund asked quietly, "How are the subscriptions going, and the sale in other cities?"

"The subscription list is surprisingly good, nearly two hundred by now. I am not worrying about losing money on the magazine. I just don't like being told how to run my own bookstore. It demeans me."

No more copies of *Imago* were displayed or sold in Vienna.

Carl Jung's next letter deepened Sigmund's sense of unease. Over the past years he had addressed these letters "Dear Friend." Now Sigmund received one which began "Dear Doctor." The tone of the letter was perceptibly cooler than any he had had from Jung, contained ideological differences and disputes, and pointed out elements of Sigmund's thinking with which Jung could no longer agree. It would have been impossible for Sigmund not to suspect that Jung's outburst of rage over Sigmund's trip to Lake Constance, his failure either to read the Viennese postmark or to ask his wife when the letter had arrived, along with the sudden trip to New York in September, were not a series of accidents, but were representative of other materials in Carl Jung's mind, repressed, but beginning to emerge.

By now Sigmund was considerably distressed. He pondered the problem in his every free moment. He had an enormous affection and regard for Carl Jung. He also believed the future of the psychoanalytical movement revolved about him. Jung's dedication, his strength, loyalty and enthusiasm, his administration of the details of the Congresses, chairing of the meetings, his obvious delight in all of the people who came, the papers that were read, the publications that followed, these were at the core of the movement.

He wrote to Jung suggesting that any differences they might have in ideology would certainly be honest differences and should never cause a breach in their relationship.

Their middle daughter, Sophie, on vacation in Hamburg, announced her engagement. The man was a photographer by the name of Max Halberstadt.

"She's only nineteen!" cried Sigmund. "What is her hurry? And why does she write us a letter making this announcement? Why couldn't she come home and tell us? Who is Max Halberstadt?"

Martha shrugged. "I don't know, dear. Mathilde announced her engagement from Meran, and we didn't know Robert Hollitscher. Yet you are very fond of Robert, and you're as pleased as I am that she is pregnant, and that we will soon become grandparents. As you said about Mathilde, it is time for us to have sons-in-law; it is also time for us to have grandchildren."

Misfortune struck Mathilde. She developed a high fever, and the pregnancy, as Sigmund wrote to Ernest Jones, "had to be interrupted." The obstetrician was not sure whether Mathilde could, or ever should, try to have another child. It was a bitter blow for the family.

The departure of Alfred Adler and his friends had not left any ugly scars, and no harsh words had been exchanged in the months that had passed. In 1911, Adler published three articles in the *Zentralblatt* on the subjects of resistance and female neurotics, and was working on a book to be called The Neurotic Constitution, to be published in Wiesbaden the following year, which would attempt to rend the cloth of Freudian psychoanalysis. His followers, less mindful of the amenities than Adler himself, took the occasion to make personal attacks, accusing Sigmund of building a "captured" psychology in contrast to the Adlerian "free" psychology, of being a tyrant who would brook no opposition and would allow no one to rise high enough to supersede him.

Otto Rank, who had recorded more than a hundred and fifty sets of notes on the meetings over a period of six years, came up with some interesting figures.

"Look, Professor Freud, at what the Minutes reveal. Adler gave as many papers as you did, and for long stretches occupied more of the discussion time than you. Nor can I find anything that could be called stern criticism of Adler, except for his final three lectures. I would like your permission to circulate this material."

Sigmund sighed.

"No, Otto. It would do no good. Rumors die as fast as the Florentine moths that live only long enough to fly to the first light."

8.

Storm signals appear well in advance; they can be missed by people concentrating on other problems, or ignored under the illusion that "it will blow over."

Sigmund Freud counted the warnings on his fingers: two years before, Carl Jung had sent him the first half of a manuscript tentatively entitled, Changes and Symbols of the Libido. Sigmund had found numerous points of departure from his own premises, yet he wrote Jung several pages suggesting how he might strengthen his main thrust. When he had visited Carl and Emma Jung that summer, Jung had wanted to dissect the manuscript, but Sigmund changed the subject. Emma observed this scene and said to Sigmund later:

"You seem reserved on the subject of Carl's new book."

"Emma, I have already given Carl the benefit of any criticism I might offer. There would be no point in my haranguing him. Carl would reject it; in any event, he must follow the dictates of his own mind."

Emma put her hand lightly on Sigmund's where he had rested it on a coffee table.

"That is very understanding, Professor. You are the most important man in Carl's life, and I would never want differences to arise between you."

In May of the following year, Carl Jung informed him that the work was going forward with the manuscript, but that he was widening Sigmund's concept of the libido, which he regarded merely as an extension of general tension, and not necessarily or exclusively related to sexuality.

Sigmund had thought it the better part of wisdom not to reply to the letter. However in November he received a personal note from Emma Jung, affectionate, but sounding an alarm.

"I have the fear, dear Professor Freud, that you will neither like nor approve of what my husband is setting forth in the second half of Symbols of the Libido. My point in writing is to make sure you are forewarned; and to urge you to remember our little talk at Küsnacht: Carl must go his own way, but it must not cost him your friendship."

Sigmund showed Emma's letter to Martha.

"It was good of Emma to write me, but I already know the general direction in which Carl is moving. Next, he is going to maintain that the Oedipal situation and the incest wishes are not an active, personal part of the unconscious but symbols representing higher ideals."

"By 'higher,' does he mean religious?"

"Not in the conventional sense. Carl's mystical ideas spring from other sources."

Martha studied his face. There were perplexity wrinkles between his eyebrows.

"Sigi, can you live with these differences?"

"Yes, though not comfortably. He has been defending me publicly for years, when it was dangerous and unprofitable for him to do so. No one has more fully earned my love and gratitude."

This particular storm did not veer from its course. Carl Jung was a good administrator when he had his wind up; but he began neglecting his duties as president of the Society. He no longer wanted to give his time to organizational work but was guarding it for his research and writing.

"I can't blame him for that," Sigmund confessed to Martha as they walked in the pleasant summer evening; "that's one of the reasons I myself did not want the presidency. Yet Carl has the energy, the dash, the skill of managing people."

"Do you think the honor of being president is wearing a trifle thin?" she asked.

"Perhaps. But he is also laboring under a strong repression: he wants to remain by my side, but at the same time he wants to move as far away as possible. That too is understandable: there are tremendous pressures being brought upon him by every segment of Swiss officialdom to abandon my thinking. In his last several lectures he has avoided mentioning my name."

Franz Riklin took his cue from Carl Jung and began to neglect his duties as secretary-treasurer of the Society. Correspondence was not answered, dues remained uncollected, publishing bills unpaid. Sigmund was determined to replace him at the next Congress, called for Munich the following year; but by whom? Would Jung permit his relative to be put down?

The reports from New York where Jung was giving his lecture series were even less heartening. Dr. James Putnam made the trip down from Boston to visit with Jung and to hear some of the addresses. He sent a report to Vienna via his friend Ernest Jones: Jung had suggested to his audience at Fordham University that, although he still believed in the value of psychoanalytic technique, he no longer believed in infantile fixations in the etiology of a neurosis; in fact they seemed negligible to him. A psychiatrist had to come to grips with the problems and environmental conditions which arose just before the neurosis began.

"Shades of Alfred Adler!" Sigmund exclaimed to Otto Rank, who was watching him owl-eyed. "The next thing we know, Jung will be calling himself a social psychologist."

When Jung returned from America he wrote to Sigmund:

"I have been able to make psychoanalysis much more palatable to the Americans by the simple stratagem of avoiding sexual themes."

Sigmund replied tartly:

"I fail to find anything clever in that. All one has to do is avoid the sexual nature of man entirely, and psychoanalysis will become even more acceptable."

The peripatetic Ernest Jones, who moved about the world more than Sigmund Freud and all of his Viennese combined, arrived in Vienna for one of his frequent visits with the Freuds. Sigmund had just received a neurological journal in which Carl Jung had disavowed the validity of penis envy, and expressed his disbelief in any form of childhood sexuality. When Jones read the article he cried in astonishment:

"How is that possible? Not long ago he published an analytical study of his own child, depicting as discerningly as possible the stages in the development of her infantile sexual life."

Sigmund smiled wanly.

"Our patients are not the only ones who have fluctuations of insight. As analysts our knowledge should render us immune to retrogression."

"Analysts can be as fallible as other mortals."

"Yes, Ernest, and we shall see a lot of it before we have finished playing our roles."

The difficulties with Jung had, for Sigmund, profound emotional, intellectual and professional implications. Youth was the time for close companionship, particularly among students and colleagues. Sigmund had loved Ignaz Schönberg, Ernst Fleischl and Josef Paneth, all of whom died young. He had enjoyed the close friendship of Josef Breuer and Wilhelm Fliess over a period of fruitful years, during which these men had helped make the earth an inhabitable planet. He did not honestly see, searching his own psyche with a powerful light, where the fault for the loss of either of these marvelous companions had been his. Alfred Adler had never been a close friend. Adler had not wanted intimacy; but Adler's departure was at least half his own fault. If he had been wise enough to move Adler into the heart of the Zurich group, and allowed him to play a key part in the formation and control of the International Psychoanalytic Society, that would have helped for a time. But in the end Alfred Adler would have had to go his own way, to be independent, to form a group of which he would be the head.

The widening breach between himself and the nineteen-years-younger Carl Jung was quite another matter. Sigmund had loved Jung with the wholehearted warmth and loyalty he gave to Breuer and Fliess. There was no way to compare human minds when they worked in sharply demarcated fields; it had been Sigmund's good fortune to work with some of the most creative brains of the age: Brentano in philosophy, Brücke in physiology, Meynert in psychiatry, Nothnagel in internal medicine, Billroth in surgery, Charcot in neurology, Bernheim in hypnotism; talented friends such as Breuer, Exner, Fleischl; Weiss, dead by his own hand; Wilhelm Fliess, who had given him a scientific audience and encouragement during the years that he had been banished. Carl Jung was as brilliant as the best of them.

Sigmund was monogamous by nature; he had married Martha for life, and he had adopted Carl Jung as his successor for life. It was inconceivable to him that a relationship of six years which had been so close, so beautiful, so mutually sustaining, could disappear in a fog bank of dispute, particularly since they had recognized their differences at the outset, and accepted them. Or had they? It was heartbreaking to contemplate the possible loss of Carl Jung; yet he had to admit that something in the relationship had already been undermined.

His colleagues sensed his unhappiness and, each in his own way, Oskar Pfister, Ludwig Binswanger, Ferenczi, Abraham, Jones, made overtures to Carl Jung to heal the breach. Sigmund Freud did not discourage them; rather he assured everyone that once their personal feelings could be re-established there would be no danger of a break.

A new development came from a highly unlikely source, for there was nothing conspiratorial in Ernest Jones's open nature. Earlier that summer Sigmund had gone with Martha to Karlsbad to take the waters in an effort to cure up his "American colitis." Minna exclaimed:

"Sigi, the nationality is wrong. You haven't got American colitis, you've got Swiss colitis. Get Carl Jung to stop tearing the bark off your tree of knowledge and your colon will behave itself."

Ernest Jones was working with Sandor Ferenczi in Budapest when a letter reached him from Sigmund Freud, in which Sigmund suggested that psychoanalysis was no longer solely his own affair, that it concerned Jones and many others. Jones showed the letter to Ferenczi, who commented:

"If we continue to have defectors such as Adler and Stekel, and now possibly Carl Jung, we're going to have to assume that we will suffer more and more splits as our Society grows. The most workable plan for us, to protect ourselves against schisms and the resultant splinter psychologies, would be to organize a small group of doctors who have been thoroughly analyzed by Professor Freud, one in each country. They would rebut the fallacies being attributed to Freudian psychoanalysis."

"That is not possible, Ferenczi, since you and Max Eitingon are the only ones who can really claim to have been analyzed by Professor Freud. However, I have another suggestion. Why couldn't we form a small, secret group of trustworthy analysts as a sort of 'old guard'? It would give Professor Freud the assurance of a stable body of firm friends. It would be a comfort to him in the event of further dissension; and, as you suggest, it should be possible for us to be of practical assistance by replying to criticism."

"Excellent! Why don't you write to the professor?"

Ernest Jones wrote to Sigmund that very evening, laying out such a provisional plan. Sigmund read the letter while he was breakfasting at the Goldener Schlüssel in Karlsbad with Martha, Minna, Sophie and Anna. When Sigmund finished, he broke into a radiant smile. Martha said:

"Share the good news with us, Sigi. You've been dour these past days."

He passed the letter around. Everyone was highly pleased with the idea. Minna proved to be quite right, for his diarrhea stopped as suddenly as though he had taken paregoric. That afternoon, sitting in the warm sunshine in the bay of his room, he replied to Jones:

"What took hold of my imagination immediately is your idea of a secret council composed of the best and most trustworthy among our men to take care of the further development of psychoanalysis and defend the cause against personalities and accidents when I am no more. . . . I know there is a boyish and perhaps romantic element too in this conception, but perhaps it could be adapted to meet the necessities of reality. . . .

"I daresay it would make living and dying easier for me if I knew of such an association existing to watch over my creation."

When Sigmund returned to Vienna, he did not mention the formation of the new group to Otto Rank, who was with him several hours each day. The Vienna Psychoanalytic Society was planning to buy Otto a typewriter so that he could answer the routine mail that was not directly sent to Professor Freud, as well as send out notices of lectures and publications. It was Sigmund's feeling that he should not ask anyone to join the special group; then he would not know if someone were to refuse.

It was several months after the original exchange of letters before Ernest Jones spoke to Otto Rank. Otto was enthralled. Though he had now taken his degree from the university, and Sigmund had given him as a graduation present a trip to Greece, which fulfilled the dream of his lifetime, he still had no way of earning a living. Sigmund had said two years before that Otto Rank was to be the first lay analyst; he still intended this. But he felt that Rank needed more training in analysis, and consequently did not feel secure in turning patients over to him. Neither was Hanns Sachs taking patients; he was practicing law. The Vienna Psychoanalytic Society was still paying Rank a modest wage as secretary, one he earned tenfold over, and Sigmund made up the rest of Otto's modest living expenses out of his own pocket.

Ernest Jones, who was something of a *bon vivant* himself, dressing in expensive clothes and enjoying the best restaurants, hotels and wines, had become fast friends with Hanns Sachs, the Viennese "gentleman of the world." After Jones had brought Otto Rank into the fold, he then went to Hanns Sachs and outlined the plan. Sachs joined the Committee at once. The only other one whom Jones and Ferenczi thought should be tapped, but to whom they had not spoken, was Karl Abraham. Over a period of months nobody got to Berlin, and they were unwilling to confide the invitation to the mail. It was a full six months after Jones suggested his plan to Ferenczi and Professor Freud that Karl Abraham came to Vienna for a week to work with Sigmund. The task of approaching him was assigned to Otto Rank. Otto let the first three days go by while Abraham discussed his most urgent cases with Sigmund, seeking understanding and counsel. It was only when these matters were off Abraham's mind that Rank took him for a walk one day and told him what had been going on. He received Abraham's hearty assent.

9.

Wilhelm Stekel had taken the *Zentralblatt* with him when he left, since he was the one who had found the publisher for it after Hugo Heller had refused to accept him as editor. Sigmund had resigned from the staff, as had his followers; but now they faced the problem of creating a journal in its place. Sigmund considered it urgent that the new journal become an official one of the International Psychoanalytic Society. Heller agreed to publish it. A meeting was called for Munich in November 1912, to be attended by Sigmund Freud, Carl Jung, Ernest Jones, Sandor Ferenczi, Karl Abraham, Franz Riklin and Alphonse Maeder of Zurich. Carl Jung would continue as editor of the *Yearbook*. Sigmund had strong hope that when they met in Munich there would be a genuine reconciliation. In all the days he had spent with Jung, there had never been a time when he and Jung had not achieved a rapport, stimulating and enjoying each other. Surely when he and Jung met, their personal love for each other would enable them to resolve their problems.

Sigmund took the night train to Munich. Installed in his room at the Park Hotel, he bathed and changed clothes just in time to receive Ernest Jones, who had come to have breakfast with him. Jones had been in Florence for a month's vacation. There was a bemused twinkle in his eye.

"Professor, Carl Jung has just made another contribution to your *Psychopathology of Everyday Life.* Instead of sending the invitation to this conference to my regular address in England, Jung somehow managed to send it to my father up in Wales. In addition, he put down the date of our conference for tomorrow, November twenty-fifth instead of November twenty-fourth, so that I would have reached here just in time to find you all gone. It was only by the chance arrival of a letter from one of our colleagues in Vienna that I learned the meeting was today, and made a fast dash up from Florence. It was no doubt an unconscious slip."

Sigmund laughed, then replied dryly:

"A gentleman wouldn't have that sort of unconscious."

The meeting began at nine o'clock in the morning in a corner of the deserted Park Hotel lounge. Everyone seemed to be in excellent spirits. Carl Jung greeted Sigmund, and then Jones, Abraham and Ferenczi, with all the cordiality and naturalness they had known in the previous years. Dr. Johan van Ophuijsen, a Dutch psychoanalyst, had replaced

Alphonse Maeder. When Sigmund suggested that he would like to retrace his difficulties with Wilhelm Stekel over the *Zentralblatt*, Jung said amiably:

"My dear Professor, we all know what you have been through. We accept your judgment in the matter, and I for one agree that we should move forward to the establishing of our new journal to replace it. I like your title very much, Internationale Zeitschrift für Psychoanalyse."

"Thank you, that's generous of you, but I feel a need to go on record. Please do let me sketch for everyone the many complications we have been through."

The meeting lasted two hours. There was complete accord down the line. The three Zurichers felt that the new Zeitschrift should be published in Vienna. The format and nature of its contents were sketched out rapidly, as well as the decision to publish it as a quarterly, with Ferenczi and Hanns Sachs as editors. By eleven o'clock the official business was concluded.

Sigmund rose, went to Carl Jung and said with a smile:

"Shall we take a walk? Let's go down the Maximilianstrasse to the Isar and see those wonderful outdoor sculptures. Then we can go across the Max Joseph-Platz for a look at the royal palace and the Byzantine court church."

They set forth at a brisk pace. Walking was the one activity in which Sigmund could outstrip the younger man. Jung said at once:

"I owe you an apology, Professor. I understand now what happened at Whitsun. I was away that entire weekend but I forgot about it when I heard you had been visiting Binswanger at Kreuzlingen. I assumed that the letter had reached my desk early Monday morning, just before my return, and consequently that it had been posted from Vienna too late for me to know that you would be just a few miles away. I was so upset I did not ask Emma when the letter was received, nor did I trouble to look at the Vienna date mark."

"I assumed something like that had happened."

"As you see, Professor, I still have my neuroses. I sometimes find them hard to forgive in myself, but I must beg you to forgive them. They arise out of my childhood, the sense of being alone, different in many ways . . ."

"Dear friend, I really must lecture you like a Dutch uncle. You simply must not lose confidence in me and fly off the handle. It could mean that there are other things, deeper in your mind, that you are really crying out about."

"No, Professor, that's not true. I fluctuate, and sometimes I think you are wrong. For example, on the subject of incest. To me incest signified a personal complication only in the rarest cases. Usually incest has a highly religious aspect, for which reason the incest theme plays a decisive part in almost all cosmogonies and in numerous myths. I believe that you are clinging to the literal interpretation of it, and that you do not grasp the spiritual significance of incest as a symbol. But as you have written me from the very beginning of our correspondence, and as you have made plain a dozen times while we were together, any forking of the main road of our ideas, which either of us feels impelled to take, should never lessen our personal affection for each other."

"Thank you, I am glad you said that. It was worth coming to Munich, even without our settling on the Zeitschrift, to be sure that our relationship is whole again."

They returned to the hotel in time to join their companions for a one o'clock dinner in the hotel dining room. Sigmund was in high spirits. He felt that his troubles were over. Jung had been explicit in his promise to give sufficient time to his tasks as president of the International Psychoanalytic Society and was optimistic about the content and growth of the *Yearbook*. Riklin too had assured him that he would resume his secretarial duties as soon as he got back to Zurich.

But by the time Sigmund had finished his main course, a sense of unease began to steal over him. When the dessert was served, a question popped out of the back of his mind which he had no intention of asking, and which was really superfluous now that he had settled his differences with Jung. He fixed his attention on Jung and asked soberly:

"My dear colleague, how does it happen that in your recent lectures and publications you no longer mention my name?"

There was an uncomfortable moment of silence, after which Carl Jung smiled and said offhandedly:

"My dear Professor, everyone knows that Sigmund Freud is the founder of psychoanalysis. There is no longer any need to mention your name when we make historical recapitulations."

A sharp stab of pain went through Sigmund's bosom. He had been deceiving himself! Jung's cavalier answer revealed the truth. Deep in Carl Jung's unconscious there was a powerful force which was slowly gathering strength to blow their relationship wide open. In his conscious mind, Jung very much wanted to reconcile, he still loved and revered Sigmund Freud, and he had not been pretending on their two-hour walk when he assured Sigmund that everything good in their relationship was restored and that they would work together in the years ahead. But in that one wisp of a smile on Jung's face, and in the offhand reply, Sigmund sensed the repression that could not very much longer be denied; it was Carl Jung's need to be free, and be independent, to break through and become his own man.

He began to feel faint. The dining room swung elliptically around his head. He made an effort to grasp the edge of the table with both hands, but failed. He blinked his eyes hard, tried to speak, to focus on one of his friends sitting next to him. Then he slumped in his chair, felt consciousness recede, and fell to the floor.

As he had three years before, Carl Jung picked Sigmund up in his arms as though he were a boy and carried him to a sofa in the lounge. Ernest Jones massaged Sigmund's wrists and forehead to bring him around. After a moment or two, Sigmund opened his eyes, looked up at Jones hovering above him and whispered:

"How sweet dying must be."

10.

All of the older physicians now had substantial practices. Sigmund confined himself to eleven patients, for eleven hours a day, six days a week, because he wanted several hours in the evening to continue writing on Totem and Taboo, his monographs on The Occurrence in Dreams of Material from Fairy Tales and Two Lies Told by Children, both revealed by women patients, and arising out of excessive love for their fathers. In the first a "wild, happy, self-confident child" had been turned into a shy and timid one because, wanting a few pennies to buy paints to color Easter eggs for her father, and being refused the money, she had kept it out of a larger sum he had given her for a different purpose, then lied about buying the paints. This "turning point in my life," as she described it to Dr. Freud, had come after a severe punishment, which she interpreted as a rejection by her father. The second patient, wanting to please her father by being the best in the class, had lied about using a compass to draw a circle, and been caught and exposed by her teacher.

Karl Abraham had been able to give up his medical reports for the psychiatric courts because he was averaging ten patients a day, and was pleading with Sigmund to send him a trained analyst to help share the load.

One of the newest and most talented young men was Theodor Reik, who was just about to take his Doctor of Philosophy degree at the University of Vienna. Reik was a native Viennese, more than thirty years younger than Sigmund, the son of a civil servant. He was first attracted to Professor Freud's work by an attack upon him. He read The Interpretation of Dreams and became an enthusiast. At the university, though his major subject was psychology, he did a great deal of work in French and German literature and, at the age of twenty-two, just before he worked up the courage to introduce himself to Professor Freud, published a book on Beer-Hofmann, the Austrian poet and dramatist, which included a reference to Sigmund Freud. Reik was a lean young man with an agreeable nature, attractive, clean-shaven, with a bony ridged nose, full mouth and dancing eyes behind his glasses, but short of neck.

Reik had joined the Vienna Psychoanalytic Society in 1910, and had taken the daring path of arguing with his professors at the university about the validity of psychoanalysis, insisting upon writing a thesis on the subject, the first one ever submitted for a doctorate. Reik, when he first came to see Sigmund, had been willing to go through Medical School to become a psychoanalyst, but Sigmund had discouraged him because Reik had no inclination toward medicine. The clinching argument was the one which Reik confided to him when he dropped in to supper one night, sharing Sigmund's light meal of Quaegel, which smelled worse than Limburger cheese, and bread, served with salami and coffee:

"Since my late teens I have been looking for sources which can satisfy my passionate curiosity about the mysterious underground of the human soul. I think I have a gift for finding hidden traces of a forgotten past in the phenomenon of the present, of the ancient which is covered up in the new."

Theodor Reik knew about Sigmund's walk around the Ring at nine o'clock every evening. He waited for the professor at the Opera at half past the hour, knowing that Sigmund had gone first to the Freyung, and would be coming along the Kärntner Strasse. Now that Otto Rank was treating some few patients and beginning to earn a modest living, Sigmund had Theodor Reik elected secretary of the Society, so that he in turn could earn the wage. Reik linked his arm lightly through Sigmund's, accompanying him around the Rathausstrasse and home. He asked for advice on whether he should marry his childhood sweetheart, and how he should proceed toward his life work. Sigmund replied:

"For minor decisions, search your conscious mind. For the major decisions of your life, let your unconscious mind be the master. That way, you will make no mistakes."

Reik was about to finish a paper called The Puberty Ritual of Primitive Tribes. Sigmund persuaded him to go to Berlin with his bride, where Reik could be analyzed by Karl Abraham and make himself useful to Abraham with his editorial and publishing chores. Sigmund footed the bill.

It took Wilhelm Stekel only two years after he broke with Sigmund to exhaust his interest in Alfred Adler's group and to abandon the Zentralblatt, since it was no longer receiving serious contributions and had lost most of its subscribers. Sigmund learned that Stekel was attempting to set up an association for sexual science. He tried to get Karl Abraham, in Berlin, to join. Also in Berlin, Dr. Wilhelm Fliess proved to be the figure behind a group which had established a Society for Sexology. Both Wilhelm Stekel's and Wilhelm Fliess's attempts to carve a corner of psychoanalysis for themselves proved abortive.

The Freud family liked Sophie's Max Halberstadt. Martha gave her daughter a charming wedding in the middle of January. Hugo Heller, despite the threats of his customers over the magazine *Imago*, prepared the four essays on *Totem and Taboo* for book form. A number of the younger members of the Wednesday Evening group completed manuscripts and Sigmund wrote introductions to help get them published: the Reverend Oskar Pfister's *The Psychoanalytic Method*, Max Steiner's *The Psychical Disorders of Male Potency*. In the United States A. A. Brill had completed his tremendous labors in translating *The Psychopathology of Everyday Life* and *The Interpretation of Dreams*. These two of Sigmund's earliest books had already had several printings in Europe. The American editions received less opposition than they had in Austria and Germany.

Carl Jung's reconversion was short-lived. Once back in Switzerland, he renounced more of the Freudian concepts in which he no longer believed: the sexual symbols in dreaming, resistance, repression. Jung did not seem happy about this, his letters were churned and sometimes unintelligible. Sigmund said to Martha, to whom he had reported the wonderful meeting in Munich only a few months before:

"I consider there is no hope of rectifying the errors of the Zurich people. I am resolved to give up private relations with Jung. It's too difficult for us to maintain our friendship in the face of his divergences."

His own young people were coming along splendidly. Otto Rank's new book, *The Incest Motif in Poetry and Saga*, was earning a good audience. Sandor Ferenczi was publishing unique papers on Transference in the *Yearbook*. Ernest Jones had published seven articles in the *Zentralblatt*, was becoming the authority on sublimation, and now gave his writings to Sigmund's new *Zeitschrift* and the *Journal of Abnormal Psychology*. Karl Abraham's articles were appearing regularly in *Imago*, *Zeitschrift* and the Berlin *Psychoanalytische Verlag*. He was now writing a thesis which would earn him his professorship at the university. Oskar Pfister was writing on pedagogy for the *Berner Seminarblätter*.

One of the more gratifying experiences was that the young Italian student Edoardo Weiss from Trieste, who had come to him when he was only nineteen years old asking how best to be trained to become a psychoanalyst, took his medical degree from the University of Vienna, joined the Society and very quickly gave a paper on Rhyme and Refrain. Sigmund had recommended four years before that Weiss be analyzed by Paul Federn, with whom Edoardo had now become firm friends.

Lou Andreas-Salomé also came to Vienna to be trained by Professor Freud. She was an attractive, serious-minded woman, rather tall, favoring Russian blouses with a row of buttons up one side, and high collars. She had a handsome face, deep-set eyes, a full expressive mouth and glossy hair parted in the center. Sigmund liked her personality, enjoyed her spontaneity.

He fell into the habit of addressing his Saturday evening university lectures to her. When she missed one he wrote her a note telling her of his disappointment. She was admitted to the Wednesday Evening discussions as a guest, where she showed an intuitive grasp of psychoanalysis. When she pleaded for some hours alone with Sigmund to talk about personal and non-medical matters, he let her come to his office of a Sunday evening at ten, when he would be finished with his writing. They would chat until one in the morning, when he would walk her back to her hotel. Martha also enjoyed Lou Andreas-Salomé and invited her for supper once a week. She did not hold it against Frau Andreas-Salomé that she had promptly taken Viktor Tausk as her lover. Sigmund explained to his womenfolk that the liaison was good for Tausk, despite the fact that he was eighteen years younger than Lou Andreas-Salomé; that it was making him more stable emotionally. The Russian woman told wonderful stories at the Freud supper table, though Minna asked:

"Have you noticed that Lou Andreas-Salomé always ends up at the center of these tales?"

Sigmund was having difficulties with Tausk. Tausk, sometimes accused of being a slavish follower of Sigmund Freud, periodically felt the need to rise up in public and proclaim his manhood by attempting to refute one of Professor Freud's theories. He had such a daring, improvisational mind that he occasionally came close to succeeding. He was also aggressive and argumentative with the Vienna group, when his psychic wounds surfaced. At such times Sigmund sought help from Lou Andreas-Salomé in an effort to understand his most difficult disciple, who was nevertheless writing incisive papers on masochism and the theory of knowledge.

Alfred Adler had moved the Wednesday Evening meetings out of Sigmund's offices and into the public lecture halls, which Sigmund had not appreciated at first. Now he was grateful for the change because after each meeting he went with his close associates, Rank, Federn, Sachs, Tausk and, for the months that she was in Vienna, Lou Andreas-Salomé, to the Alte Elster Restaurant, or more frequently the Cafe Landtmann, a symphony in quiet browns, where they gathered around a central table and talked of many things that Sigmund preferred not to discuss in public: thought transference, parapsychology. It was interesting to see how his students were branching out on their own, approaching fields he had not thought germane, or which he had not seen with total clarity and had neither time nor desire to illuminate.

Carl Jung left to give a five-week lecture course in America.

"More to advance Carl Jung than the field of psychoanalysis," observed Sigmund.

At Easter he took his youngest daughter, Anna, to Venice for a sightseeing trip. They paused first in Verona, one of the most delightful of medieval cities in northern Italy, home of Romeo Montague and Juliet

Capulet, then took the train from there to Venice, and a gondola to their hotel. Anna was now seventeen, slender, almost as tall as her father, resembling him slightly, with a wholesome face, crowned by a wealth of light fine-textured hair which she parted in the middle and combed softly above the ear on either side.

With Mathilde and Sophie married and gone from the home, Anna was now *the* daughter, and over the past couple of years had grown close to her father. She was the brightest of the girls, a natural student whom Martha and Sigmund had favored with her own bedroom overlooking the Berggasse when they took Rosa's apartment, in order that she might have privacy and quiet for her studies, even as Sigmund had had his *Kabinett* in the Freud home on the Kaiser Josefs-Strasse. She was also the child who was devotedly interested in her father's work. The two older girls had passed it by as being something which was not truly for young ladies. Anna, on the contrary, had no such sense of embarrassment; she read the books as soon as she was able to understand them, and most of her father's monographs. When the material was too techincal for her comprehension, at the age of sixteen and then seventeen, she took it to Sigmund and asked if he would please explain it to her in simpler terms. She was by now, as far as her youth and inexperience allowed, well trained in the Oedipal situation, the incest drives, repression and the subtle workings of the unconscious mind. Though she did not attend the Wednesday Evening meetings, she sometimes asked permission to sit in during the informal discussions when Jones, Ferenczi or Abraham was visiting. Or in fact when any of the Viennese dropped in for supper; for she had slowly and carefully made friends with Otto Rank, Hanns Sachs, and particularly Max Eitingon, whom she favored. It was a tribute to the high quality of her mind and her already professional attitude, adopted directly from her father, that Sigmund's colleagues were neither abashed nor restrained by her presence, but spoke of their patients and their writings as though Anna were a young colleague. Unlike Mathilde and Sophie, she was not obsessed by the desire for an early marriage; she was content to continue her studies at home and to share as much of her father's time as his responsibilities allowed.

Sigmund found her to be a marvelous traveling companion. Her mind was so like his own that there was no need for them to talk a great deal; they seemed to know what each other was thinking by the recognition of a glance, an expression, a passing mood. Sigmund thought how curious it was that this youngest of his six children, and a girl to boot, should be closer to him in temperament than his three sons, with whom he had spent so many wonderful summers in the mountains, climbing, boating, fishing, hunting mushrooms, enjoying the cool fragrant mountain woods. Had Anna been a boy, Sigmund reflected, she would be enrolling in the Vienna Medical School the following autumn. Ernst, his youngest son, now twenty-one, was at the University of Vienna studying architecture, for which he had shown a genuine talent. Oliver, twenty-two, was about to complete his course in mathematical engineering; while Martin, who was twenty-three, was still studying at the commercial college across the street from the Berggasse, the Export Academy, where Alexander had beaten Sigmund to the title of professor. Sigmund had not been enthusiastic about Martin's going to the Export Academy, but he had not opposed his oldest son. There had not seemed any possibility of the boys following in his footsteps as a physician, partly because Sigmund had seen neither interest nor aptitude on the part of his sons, but also because he had lost his taste for his own profession, which had ostracized him so early and for so long. The three boys seemed quite happy with their choices.

An occasional woman was now graduating from the Medical School. He had had one in his own group, Dr. Margarete Hilferding. Yet Anna seemed content and happy to go to school to her father, who gave unstintingly of himself to his interested and interesting youngest daughter.

For the pictures and pleasures of the eye, Sigmund said, there was almost no sight in the world to equal Venice, particularly the first time one visited the city built on alluvial islands in a vast lagoon. Anna loved the Piazza San Marco, the Duomo, the figures striking the clock opposite the Campanile, Sansovino's Loggetta, the boat ride down the Grand Canal and the Ponte dell' Accademia; the visits to the colorful fish markets on the opposite side of the Ponte di Rialto, juxtaposed to visits to the Galleria dell' Accademia with its superb collection of paintings by Veneziano, Mantegna, the Titians and Tintorettos; and then trips by steamer to Murano and to Torcello, the first village to be created in the lagoon.

Two pieces of good news were waiting for him when he returned to Vienna. Sandor Ferenczi had at last been successful in founding a Budapest Psychoanalytical Society, with half a dozen doctors. There was also word that all five members of the Committee would assemble at the Berggasse toward the end of May to make their organization a formal one, and to plan their strategy for the months ahead, including the coming Congress in Munich in September 1913.

Sigmund glanced down at the gold ring he was wearing, in which he had had mounted his favorite Greek-Roman intaglio, with a head of Jupiter. He had bought a dozen of these intaglios, small carved gems and seals, in the antique shops of Italy. Now he selected five from his collection, those containing the finest carving, took them to Martha and laid them out on the palm of his hand.

"Martha, I thought it would be nice to give each member of the Committee one of these stones. They could carry them in their vest pockets as a sort of charm if they liked . . ."

". . . or have them mounted as a ring the way you did, Sigi. I think it

is a fine idea." She mocked him a little with her eyes. "It will be like a
blood brotherhood."

Sigmund smiled.

"Sentimental, I grant, and romantic."

The five members arrived together for dinner, each presenting Martha
with a little bouquet of flowers. It was truly a family gathering, on this
evening late in May, for all three of the boys were at home; they dispersed during the summer vacation to go their own adventuresome ways.
Martha surrounded each member of the Committee by two Freuds.
While the maid brought in the heavy soup tureen, Sigmund glanced
affectionately around the table. Next to Anna sat Otto Rank, dark of complexion and hair, barely hiding an expression of beatitude behind his dark
glasses. Next to Tante Minna was Ernest Jones of the heavy black eyebrows, pale skin and magnificent head. Next to Martha was Hanns Sachs
of the sagging jowls and lively tongue. Sandor Ferenczi was happily ensconced between Ernst and Oliver, sounding for all the world like a
Hungarian actor. Next to Sigmund was Karl Abraham, of the short cropped
hair and self-disciplined eyes. In the glass door of the china closet opposite
him, Sigmund caught a reflected image of himself.

"For a man who has recently passed his fifty-seventh birthday," he
mused, "I do not look too bad."

His hair was still black, showing signs of gray only at the slightly
balding part on the right side of his head. Yet his mustache and small
chin beard had turned almost totally white. He knew that when he was
concentrating there were furrows in his forehead and lines in his cheeks;
but now, surrounded by his family, friends and disciples, he was happy
and relaxed. Only his dark eyes were grave.

After dinner they went into Sigmund's office, where the men puffed
away on their cigars in contented comradeship. Sigmund shook the five
intaglios from an envelope into the palm of his hand:

"Gentlemen, I have for you the official seal of the Order. Would you
please take one of the gems from my hand, but with your eyes closed as
you make the choice. Then each will get the stone meant for him by fate."

One by one the men took a gem from Sigmund's hand. They waited
until all five had theirs so that they could study their new possessions
together. There were exclamations of joy and gratification. Ernest Jones,
who had been elected chairman because he was the founder, said:

"My dear Professor, we are deeply touched. There's no gift you could
have given us which would have brought more satisfaction or feeling of
closeness. May we have your permission to mount these stones in a gold
ring similar to yours? No one else will know what they signify, but for us
they will be on hand night and day."

After laughing at Jones's pun, Sigmund declared:

"I consent, most heartily."

They got down to the business of the meeting: precisely what were the duties and requisites of such a group? They would write to each other frequently, reporting in detail what was going on in each man's city, the new publications in the field of psychoanalysis, those which attacked and those which approved, interesting cases they were treating; new thoughts on therapy. They planned to meet at least twice a year, not only in Vienna but in Budapest, Berlin and London. Since they all took their vacations at the same time, in August or September, they agreed to spend several weeks together each year, perhaps in the high mountains or by the sea, during which time they could enjoy their freedom, their contact with nature, the heartwarming sense of being together.

11.

In spite of the efforts of Sigmund's colleagues to lessen the growing gap between Zurich and Vienna, the silences grew longer and were in fact preferable to the occasional communications between Sigmund Freud and Carl Jung, which were increasingly disputatious. Every time Sigmund received an antagonistic letter from Küsnacht, he developed laryngitis. The climax came in June when Dr. Alphonse Maeder, who for several years had been one of the more important psychoanalysts practicing in Switzerland, wrote Sandor Ferenczi saying, in effect, that it was quite natural and normal for there to be a scientific divergence between the two groups, since the Zurichers were Aryan and the Viennese Jews. When Ferenczi came to Vienna a couple of weeks later, accompanied by Ernest Jones, who had been spending two months with Ferenczi for analysis, Ferenczi showed the letter to Sigmund. Sigmund read it, then replied:

"There should not be such a thing as Aryan or Jewish science. Results in science must be identical, though the presentation of them may vary."

Ernest Jones, sharp-tongued, exclaimed:

"It's obvious that I am going to have to move my practice to Vienna. Otherwise how are we going to put a stop to Maeder's scintillating observations? In one of your two Obstetrical Clinics at the Allgemeine Krankenhaus, women died by the thousands from puerperal fever . . . until Semmelweis taught the doctors to wash their hands with soap and hot water. Is asepsis a Jewish science?"

Carl Jung indulged in none of this nonsense. He kept his promise to Sigmund to become an active president again and made the arrangements for the September 1913 Munich Congress. When he learned that Sigmund was not planning to read a paper, he wrote a strong letter contending that the Congress could not achieve its full stature or significance unless Professor Freud read a paper there. Abraham, Ferenczi and

Jones had also been adamant on this point. Finally Sigmund agreed. He was vacationing with Martha and Anna in Marienbad, where he began a monograph on the Predisposition to Obsessional Neurosis. The weather was cold and wet and he developed such a severe neuralgia that he could hardly move his writing arm across the page. He wrote to Ernest Jones:

"I scarcely can recall a time so full of petty mischiefs and annoyances as this. It is like a shower of bad weather, you have to wait to see who will hold out better, you or the evil genius of this time."

They left Marienbad and went to San Martino di Castrozza, five thousand feet high in the Dolomites, where there was warm sun. Here the family was joined by Abraham and Ferenczi, the neuralgia was cured, the depression vanished and they had some pleasant weeks of vacation before starting out for the Bayerischer Hof in Munich. Sigmund expressed his hope that it would be a peaceful Congress, like the one in Weimar; that their differences would be submerged in the interests of their embattled science. He edited and softened Ernest Jones's manuscript, in which Jones made some critical comments about Jung's approach to therapy.

Sigmund asked Martha if she would like to join them and go to the Congress, where there would be a number of wives and women doctors, and then visit with him in Rome for two weeks. Martha thanked him for the invitation but preferred to spend the weeks in the cooler mountains. Tante Minna had been in poor health all year, rarely getting out of the house. Minna was the one who loved to travel and was particularly fond of Rome. Martha thought the trip would do her sister good, and Sigmund assented.

Sigmund and Ferenczi took the night train to Munich. They went directly to the Bayerischer Hof. Sigmund had insisted that they stay at the same hotel as the Zurichers, as had been done from the beginning. The Committee came in to breakfast with him: Abraham, Sachs, Rank, Ferenczi and Jones. Over coffee, rolls, butter and jam they decided which members would make replies to criticisms that might arise in the discussions.

Professor Freud was not to participate in these imbroglios!

In Munich the prior November, the group had agreed that only the main paper should be followed by a discussion. Now Carl Jung insisted that the time for the papers be cut short, so that a discussion could follow each of them. The danger in this was that time would be used up, papers would have to be canceled; the Congress could degenerate into a wrangling contest, be terminated with each side bruised and resentful.

The first morning of the Congress was a success. Eighty-seven members and guests were present, though Sigmund was sad to see that Eugen Bleuler did not attend. Ernest Jones read a paper on sublimation, a field which he had pioneered. Dr. Jan van Emden, the Dutch psychoanalyst, gave an analysis of pseudoepilepsy. Viktor Tausk read a solid article on narcissism. One of the Swiss wound up with a strong paper on the causes of homosexuality. Tausk was the only one cut short in his paper; the criticism had to do largely with methodology.

A serious breach occurred at the midday dinner. Somehow Carl Jung and his group sat at one table, Sigmund Freud and his friends at another. Sigmund did not understand how this happened. Gone was the fellowship and socializing of their meeting. Sigmund said unhappily to Hanns Sachs:

"I had hoped that by staying at the same hotel we would mingle at the dinner hour."

The fireworks started when Ferenczi and then Abraham rose to give their papers. They had been written to occupy a full hour; the hour was needed to carry out the thematic progression. However Carl Jung kept an eye on the gold watch he kept pulling out of his vest pocket; if he gave these men a full hour there could be no discussion. He decreed they would have to stop short. Both men protested, as did the Viennese group from the floor, but it was to no avail; Jung was chairman, his word was law. Jung himself opened the critical attack, denying aspects of the Oedipal situation, infantile sexuality, the incest wish and the force of the sexual etiology. Other members of the Swiss group took up the argument. The Viennese were on their feet, trying to make a counter-statement. Jung banged his gavel and cried:

"The hour is over. We must proceed to the next paper."

When the afternoon session ended, the Viennese were upset and angry. They thought Carl Jung had been heavy-handed and arbitrary, that he had structured the afternoon so that criticisms of the Freudian papers could be made public. Elections were to be held the following day. Private meetings were going on in half a dozen rooms of the hotel. Sandor Ferenczi said sardonically:

"The Jung no longer believe in Freud."

Karl Abraham added soberly:

"I don't think any of us should vote to renew his presidency! Why don't we simply leave our ballots blank?"

Sigmund's face flushed.

"I urge you not to make this futile and, for Carl Jung, humiliating gesture. He will be re-elected anyway; he has a majority. So in spite of our disappointments . . ."

". . . aggrievements," cried Ferenczi.

"Very well, aggrievements, let us not open the chasm any wider. This breach is painful to Jung too. Part of his arbitrary conduct on the platform was due to a conflict being waged in his own mind. This breakup is tearing him apart! You must take my word for this. His hand is being forced: by his own nature and background, by the Swiss and German

medical societies, by the Swiss clergy, government and press. He fought
for us when no one else had the courage to do so. We cannot let such a
man down publicly. At the next election we can be prepared, put up one
of our own men as candidate."

It was an eloquent plea, albeit delivered with a touch of laryngitis. No
one of his twenty-two followers doubted his sincerity. Neither did any one
of them yield to his request. When the ballots were counted the following
day, Jung had his name on fifty-two of them; the other twenty-two were
blank. Jung was infuriated by the slap in the face. He said nothing to
Sigmund but did corner Ernest Jones on the way out of the hall.

"Jones, you left your ballot blank, didn't you?"

"I'm afraid I had to, Jung."

"I thought you were a Christian!"

Welshman Jones had an overly sensitive nose for national or religious
prejudice. He went directly to Sigmund's room.

"Herr Professor, do I detect the slightest stench of anti-Semitism in
that remark?"

Sigmund thought about this frightening possibility.

"I honestly don't think so, Ernest. Jung is a universal man. He respects
all religions and cultures."

"Then what the devil did he mean?"

"Perhaps that he expected you to exercise true Christian charity and
vote for him in spite of the pressures from your Viennese friends to
abstain."

Rome was warm, but not oppressively so. The first morning he met
Minna in the lobby after they had breakfasted in their rooms, and they
walked through the streets, already teeming with life, down the Via dei
Fori Imperiali past the ruins of the ancient forums. Just before they got
to the Colosseum, they swung around to the left and walked up the hill
to San Pietro in Vincoli to see Michelangelo's *Moses*. His wounds from
the Munich Congress had cut deep; both he and the psychoanalytical
movement were in for troubled times. But as he stood in front of the
sculpture, studying the fingers twined in the beard, the hand leaning on
the stone tablets of the Ten Commandments; the look on Moses' face
which had been described as "a mixture of wrath, pain and contempt,"
his mind was washed clean. He felt a sense of sheer ecstasy in the presence
of the magnificent work of art. He had brought a notebook with him
and jotted down his reactions to The Law Giver.

Each morning he and Minna set out for the specific sight they wanted
to see: the Palatine, the Piazza del Campidoglio, with its statue of Marcus
Aurelius, the Theater of Marcellus, begun by Julius Caesar, the Raphael
Rooms in the Vatican, or went by train to the excavations of Ostia
Antica. In the afternoons and evenings he wrote an introduction to

Totem and Taboo and a monograph on narcisissm. He enlarged his Munich paper on Obsessional Neurosis and, for a change of pace, wrote a rough draft of an article on the *Moses*.

12.

He returned to the opening of his medical year to find his waiting room full of patients. The first case was that of a young boy who had shot himself in the head and could not explain why. His parents brought him to Professor Freud to seek an explanation, since the boy had been in good health and spirits right up to the moment of the shooting. It did not take long for Sigmund to get to the primary cause. The boy's older sister had married the year before and had moved to another city with her husband. She had returned for a visit to the family in her seventh month of pregnancy. The boy had taken one look at his pregnant sister, gone into his room and shot himself. Fortunately his aim was as bad as his will to die was weak. However his parents were frightened that he might try it again.

Since the boy was too young to grasp the meaning of *Totem and Taboo*, Sigmund slowly taught him the materials involved in incest, and why from the time of the aborigines a marriage within a family was forbidden. Proceeding cautiously, he led the boy to understand that the incest motive was not unnatural, but that it had to be recognized and controlled; that within a few years, when he became a young man, he would find another love object outside his own clan. The boy grasped the implications. At the end of two months he was able to assure his parents that they need have no further fear about his well-being.

For the next patient he could do nothing at all, a case of obsessional neurosis on the part of a young man who each night fantasied or dreamed that he heard people coming over the roof to castrate him.

The mail brought the news that Jones was having difficulty in London with his newly formed Psychoanalytic Society. He had no sooner got started than the reverberations of the Jungian revolt spread to England. The *British Medical Journal* commented:

"The Swiss are returning to normal good sense."

Some of Jones's members were abdicating to Carl Jung and his collective unconscious. There was also a report from America that Dr. Stanley Hall, who had invited Sigmund to Clark University and expounded Freudian theories, was now becoming converted to Adler's individual psychology.

Sigmund and Carl Jung exchanged an occasional formal letter having to do with the *Yearbook* and the International Psychoanalytic Society; nothing more. Sigmund Freud had fathered his own dilemma: both the International Society and the *Yearbook* had been created to present

Freudian psychoanalysis. Carl Jung wanted no more of Freudian psycho-analysis. The pages of the *Yearbook* could be closed to the Viennese, as well as to all supporters of Sigmund Freud. The annual Congresses were in Jung's hands, to call them when he wished, to indicate who would read papers and what the official stand of the Society would be on psychiatric theory.

"I've done myself in," he groaned, "but I can't say that I wasn't forewarned. Karl Abraham . . . Eugen Bleuler . . . my Viennese . . ."

Letters between the members of the Committee went back and forth in rapid succession. Ferenczi wanted all of the Freudians to resign from the Society. Karl Abraham and Ernest Jones deplored this thinking. They said:

"If we resign, we leave the Society in Jung's hands entirely. We render ourselves powerless. We must remain in, and wait for developments. Jung is not likely to stay very long. When he is ready, he will retreat into Küsnacht and build a personal following."

Sigmund agreed with the cooler reasoning. Abraham and Jones proved to be right. The next month, in October 1913, Carl Jung resigned as editor of the *Yearbook*. Could his resignation as president of the International Psychoanalytic Society be far behind?

Sigmund received the news of the resignation with mixed feelings. He was relieved; at the same time saddened over the loss of his friend. He had truly loved Carl Jung. In some deep recess of his mind he would always be grateful to him and love him. He had explored the love-hate emotion as he found it in his patients. Hate was the other side of the shield. He would not permit himself to hate Carl Jung, or to downgrade him. If, as he had said these many years, there were no accidents in the mind, it was equally true that neither could there be concealment. He grimaced as he recalled a line from Jung, in which Jung was replying to an accusation that he was beginning to sound like Alfred Adler. Jung had written Sigmund in hot indignation:

"No one could ever accuse me of being an Adlerian, or of having joined *your* group." He had meant to write *their* group. Jung's unconscious had broken through and spoken the truth.

Carl Jung was not an Alfred Adler. He would never exclaim, "Why should I always do my work under your shadow?" He would be incapable of such a thought. He would believe only that he had valuable contributions to make which would make him an equal. Nor would he start a rival, antagonistic group in Küsnacht, in the way Adler had in his own apartment on the Dominikanerbastei. His intent would never be to harm Sigmund Freud or the psychoanalysis he had evolved.

Sigmund reviewed the last year of correspondence; the dozens of letters indicating the severity of the strain Jung was undergoing. For Carl Jung, as for himself, the break would be a traumatic shock. Jung had been teaching and extolling Freudian psychoanalysis since 1900, thirteen years, and he had done a tremendous job. It was six and a half years since he had come to Vienna and he and Sigmund had responded so strongly to each other. Carl Jung had to know that, once he left Sigmund Freud, he was separating himself from his dearest friend, the master to whom he was indebted more than he was to his former chief, Eugen Bleuler. He would know that he was giving up two prestigious positions, editor of the *Yearbook* and president of the International Psychoanalytic Society. Sigmund also granted that there would be no way for a man of Carl Jung's strength and stature to walk away from his own convictions, to pretend that he followed the Freudian dictum once he felt that he had superseded it by a broader, more universal belief.

In the final analysis this did not make the loss of Carl Jung any the less sad or bitter. He, above all the others, grasped the power of Jung's mind and personality. As Jung continued to work and enunciate his psychology, the world would be split into separate and frequently warring camps. There was no way to minimize the severity of the blow.

When he had permitted himself the proper period of mourning, he knew there was only one way to fight back, to lessen the impact of Jung's defaulting. He must write a book on the history of psychoanalysis and its techniques, showing precisely where its truths lay. When he attacked Carl Jung, it must be on the basis of Jung's mysticism, his wanderings into the realms of saga and myth.

It was during his opening lecture at the university, on October 26, 1913, in which he had twelve students and was discussing his relationship with Josef Breuer, that he was suddenly struck by a realization. He exclaimed to himself with silent intensity:

"The complete analogy can be drawn between the first running away from the discovery of sexuality behind the neurosis by Breuer, and the latest one by Jung! That makes it the more certain that this is the core of psychoanalysis."

Very well then, he was engaged in a battle for men's minds. The truth would emerge. He did not underestimate his opponent: much of what Carl Jung wrote would be true because he was a profound scholar of archaeology, anthropology, the world's art and literature. But much of it would be mystical, would not lend itself to the tests of reason or logic. Its heavy spiritual overlay created a mystique which would in some way reconcile man to his fate.

That was not Sigmund's desire or intent. His major purpose was to enable man to understand his unconscious mind, his instinctive drives, the forces that were at play within him. In short, a knowledge of man himself, and of other men, which was the last great hope on earth.

13.

At Christmas he took the train to Hamburg to visit his daughter Sophie, who was six months pregnant. He and Max Halberstadt got along well because Sigmund declined the role of interfering father-in-law. Sophie was well and strong, stirred by the carrying of a child. Sigmund was eagerly looking forward to becoming a grandfather. He remembered Martha's comment when she returned from a visit with Sophie.

"For a mother there is something very special when one's daughter is pregnant. It's a woman's only chance of carving her name on a rock. Womb of my womb . . ."

He stopped in Berlin on the way home for consultations with Karl Abraham, whom he wanted to see become acting president of the International Psychoanalytic Society once Carl Jung's formal resignation was at hand. Abraham was entirely willing. Sigmund also had an opportunity to visit with his sister Marie and her husband Moritz Freud and their four children.

There had been times during the past year when he had spent as much as thirteen hours a day with patients. Now, as he returned to Vienna to celebrate New Year's Day of 1914 with his family, he found that for some inexplicable reason his practice had been cut in half. Sometimes there were only four or five patients.

A woman patient who could not face reality, and who made up incredible stories about the gifts and largess her husband showered upon her, was led back in her mind to the early years when, as the daughter of an impecunious merchant, she had bragged in school about having ice cream for dinner every day, which her prosperous father brought home, when in fact she had never tasted ice cream. She was now extending these fantasies to protect the husband who had replaced the father.

Then there was the young woman who was having troubles in the marriage bed. She could not be trusted with money because she promptly threw it into the street as something "bad, dirty." It took considerable time before she brought forth the memories of having watched, on several occasions, her nurse having sexual intercourse with a doctor in his office. Each time the nurse and doctor had given her "hush money," pennies with which to buy candy. Now, in marriage, money and sexual pleasure had become synonymous. She threw the "bad" money into the street with the same gesture of repudiation with which she threw her husband out of her bed. Professor Freud was able to alleviate the symptoms: she no longer felt obliged to throw money away; and she was able to suffer her husband's conjugal rights. But Sigmund doubted that she would enjoy a robust sexual life.

Still a third case involved a woman who liked to think of herself as high-spirited, and who demanded masochistic satisfaction from her husband as a guarantee that she would remain faithful to him. The husband had to hit her, call her degrading names, forcibly spread her legs, examine her genitals before rudely making his entry. While engaged in intercourse she fantasied that a number of spectators were present, enjoying the spectacle. In between such sessions she suffered attacks of vertigo. It was not until Dr. Freud put together two pieces of evidence: that her father also suffered from attacks of dizziness, and that he was frequently present as a spectator in her fantasies while in the middle of coitus, that the analysis began moving down the track. As a child she had identified with her father, whom she had heard abuse and then roughly force her mother in the bedroom, where the child also slept. Dr. Freud cleared up the vertigo, then led the woman to self-discovery of her compulsive need for masochism in the sexual act. The patient thanked him, albeit tentatively:

"Herr Professor, now that you have made me normal, how will I be able to remain faithful to my husband?"

The lightness of his practice was a blessing in disguise, for it was his strongest wish to write the entire manuscript On the History of the Psychoanalytic Movement in the early months of the year, so that it could be published in the Yearbook by the time the news of Carl Jung's resignation spread throughout Europe, England and America. It had been his policy never to go on the defensive, yet this manuscript would be defensive. There was a need to set forth the truth about the birth and growth of psychoanalysis, what he had discovered, developed, set in motion; and what subsequent contributions had been made by Alfred Adler or Carl Jung. He would try to write the history in full candor and honesty.

"No one need be surprised at the subjective character of the contribution I propose to make here to the history of the psychoanalytic movement, nor need anyone wonder at the part I play in it. For psychoanalysis is my creation; for ten years I was the only person who concerned himself with it, and all the dissatisfaction which the new phenomenon aroused in my contemporaries has been poured out in the form of criticisms on my head. Although it is a long time now since I was the only psychoanalyst, I consider myself justified in maintaining that even today no one can know better than I do what psychoanalysis is, how it differs from other ways of investigating the life of the mind, and precisely what should be called psychoanalysis and what would better be described by some other name."

He told the story of how he discovered psychoanalysis, starting with Josef Breuer's Bertha Pappenheim case, coming down through Charcot's male hysteria, his rejection at the hands of Professor Meynert and the

Medical Faculty; his work in Nancy with Bernheim and Liébeault, the first use of suggestion through hypnotism, the putting of pressure on the patient's forehead, and the evolving of the technique of free association; the coming to light of the unconscious mind, the Oedipal situation, infantile sexuality, repression, transference. . . .

He told a good deal of his personal story, including the departure of Alfred Adler and Carl Jung; as well as the effects upon him of being guilty, in Hebbel's words, of having "disturbed the sleep of the world."

"*Whatever personal sensitiveness I possessed became blunted during those years, to my advantage. I was saved from becoming embittered, however, by a circumstance which is not always present to help lonely discoverers. Such people are as a rule tormented by the need to account for the lack of sympathy or the aversion of their contemporaries, and feel this attitude as a distressing contradiction of the security of their own sense of conviction. There was no need for me to feel so; for psychoanalytic theory enabled me to understand this attitude in my contemporaries and to see it as a necessary consequence of fundamental analytic premises. If it was true that the set of facts I had discovered were kept from the knowledge of patients themselves by internal resistances of an affective kind, then these resistances would be bound to appear in healthy people too, as soon as some external source confronted them with what was repressed. It was not surprising that they should be able to justify this rejection of my ideas on intellectual grounds though it was actually affective in origin. The same thing happened equally often with patients; the arguments they advanced were the same and were not precisely brilliant. In Falstaff's words, reasons are 'as plenty as blackberries.' The only difference was that with patients one was in a position to bring pressure to bear on them so as to induce them to get insight into their resistances and overcome them, whereas one had to do without this advantage in dealing with people who were ostensibly healthy.*"

How to compel these healthy people to examine the matter in a cool and scientifically objective spirit was an unsolved problem which was best left to time to clear up.

"*In the history of science one can clearly see that often the very proposition which has at first called out nothing but contradiction has later come to be accepted, although no new proofs in support of it have been brought forward.*"

He completed the manuscript by the end of February 1914 and sent it to press. Karl Abraham, who had replaced Jung as editor of the *Yearbook*, thought he could publish it in the first issue under his control, hopefully in June. Sigmund was enormously relieved that the historical review would soon be available. A few days later his daughter Sophie contributed to his well-being by giving birth to a husky boy.

By the beginning of May, Sigmund began to feel ill. He told Martha: "Aside from Ernest Jones's illness in London, things are going well. We have received Jung's official resignation as president. Karl Abraham will act in his place, and arrange the next Congress for Dresden. I plan to write up the Wolf Man case. For sheer weight of documentary evidence, it could be the most convincing statement I have yet been able to make. I have been invited to lecture at the University of Leiden in the fall, the first such recognition in Europe. Dr. A. W. van Renterghem, the leading Dutch psychiatrist, has publicly proclaimed the validity of our dream interpretation and neurosis theories . . ."

Martha was genuinely worried, for the first time since his supposed heart trouble a full twenty years before. Her concern had been caused by Dr. Walter Zweig, a gastro-intestinal specialist, who planned to carry out a rectoscopy to make certain that Sigmund did not have a cancer of the bowel. Sigmund had been reluctant to admit that many of his passing disturbances had been caused by pressure, anxiety, exhaustion.

"You've had more than your share of setbacks, Sigi. The Jung affair has bled you; and now Dr. Stanley Hall has announced that he is backing Alfred Adler in his series of lectures in America."

The examination was painful but Dr. Zweig found no trace of malignancy. Sigmund announced this to Martha as:

"A reprieve from the gods. Though as a matter of fact Dr. Zweig couldn't find anything wrong at all, in spite of what I so fondly refer to as my American colitis. Let's just assume that I've been feeling with the wrong end of my carcass. The *Yearbook* will be out soon with my history, and that should set things in proper perspective for me. In the meanwhile, let's start planning the summer."

"Yes. Anna wants to visit Sophie and the baby."

"Good. She can stop off there on the way to England. I've promised her a summer with Emanuel's family, the kind I had at her age, when my father gave me the trip as a reward for passing my *Matura.*"

"Does Dr. Zweig think we ought to go back to Karlsbad?"

"He recommends it. Why don't we spend most of July in the Villa Fasolt, then August in Seis in the southern Dolomites? Then in September you can accompany me to Dresden for the Congress. It is an exquisite town, perhaps the most colorful in Germany."

He had only a layman's interest in politics. He read a newspaper each day, but the international news had no special meaning for him, as it had for Alfred Adler and his *Stammtisch,* who read several foreign papers each day. The one political crisis that had threatened Sigmund, his family and friends had been the investiture of Karl Lueger as Mayor of Vienna, after he had been elected to the post but kept out of office by Emperor

Franz Josef because of the anti-Semitic platform on which he had run. However once Lueger was re-elected and sworn into office, he had declared:

"I am the one to determine who is a Jew and who isn't!"

Whereupon he declared a number of his friends to be unofficial Aryans, and appointed a few to posts in his administration. Lueger proved to be a progressive Mayor. Anti-Semitism was muted during his reign until his death in 1910. It was reassuring.

War clouds had been darkening Vienna's newspapers for several years. Sigmund read the dispatches but had no way of knowing which were bluff and which thunder. Karl Abraham reassured him from Berlin that there would be no war. Sandor Ferenczi did the same from Budapest. Ernest Jones, in London, did not seem concerned. Neither did Pfister in Zurich. Though Sigmund knew that the Serbians were attempting to take the Croats out of the Austro-Hungarian Empire, to form their own union; that the Archduke Franz Ferdinand had promised the Croats their autonomy as soon as he succeeded aged Franz Josef to the throne, and that this act might mean a war with Russia, which usually had troops poised at the Austrian border; these alarums and proclamations had been going on for too long for anyone to take seriously, least of all a man who had his own war on his hands.

He said, "I will leave the war discussions to the coffeehouses."

He was taken totally by surprise when Archduke Franz Ferdinand was assassinated on the bridge at Serajevo, killed by a Serbian national, working in conspiracy with the Serbs, who wanted to absorb the Croatians, and not have them become independent at the hand of the Archduke. After reading the news, he wrote to Ferenczi:

"I am writing while still under the impact of the astonishing murder at Serajevo, the consequences of which cannot be foreseen."

When the Archduke's coffin was spirited through Vienna in the dark hours of the morning and the deserted streets, even as Crown Prince Rudolf's was after his death at Mayerling twenty-five years before, he exclaimed to Martha:

"There is something dirty going on behind this. But how can one know what it means?"

"I'm frightened, Sigi." There were tears in her eyes. "If there is a war, we have three grown sons . . ."

He took her in his arms.

"Don't you remember, Martha, back in December of 1912, we were on the verge of war with Russia over Serbia? That was a stormy political situation, but nothing happened."

The expected furor did not arise, at least not in the Viennese newspapers. The only excited talk was in the coffeehouses, about frantic notes and negotiations going on among the Foreign Offices of Europe. When, after a week, there was no sign of war, Sigmund sent Anna to Hamburg to visit Sophie, and then to England for the rest of the summer.

He made plans to take Martha with him to the Congress in Dresden. This one would be pure psychoanalysis, with the papers read in an aura of agreement and sympathy, without Alfred Adler and dissident Viennese, without Carl Jung and dissident Zurichers. His closest associates would meet him a few days early to discuss their cases in progress, and a new structure for the Society. The Committee would spend pleasurable hours together. Brill was coming from New York, James Putnam from Boston, Theodor Reik and Abraham from Berlin, Pfister from Zurich, Ossipow from Moscow, Edoardo Weiss from Trieste. . . .

BOOK SIXTEEN

DANGEROUS VOYAGE

Dangerous Voyage

B UT there was war.
Emperor Wilhelm II of Germany assured Emperor Franz Josef that if Austria were brought into conflict with Russia, because of Austria's punitive action against Serbia, Germany would "stand behind her as an ally."

Austria declared war on Serbia. Russia mobilized. Germany declared war on Russia. France mobilized. Germany declared war on France and invaded Belgium the same day. England, honoring her treaty with Belgium, declared war on Germany.

Martin Freud volunteered as a gunner. Ernst Freud joined the army. Oliver dug a tunnel in the Carpathians.

Both the Committee and the Vienna Psychoanalytic Society went to war. Viktor Tausk, Hanns Sachs, Otto Rank were called up for military service. Paul Federn became an army doctor. Sandor Ferenczi was inducted in Budapest. Karl Abraham was put on hospital service in Germany.

Professor Sigmund Freud, too old at fifty-eight to be inducted into the army, became filled with patriotic fervor. For the first time in years he was conscious of being an Austrian and was proud that Austria had demonstrated its virility to the world. Its army would quickly conquer the Serbs, capture Belgrade, put an end to the unrest in the Balkans. The Austro-Hungarian Empire, which had been shrinking, would regain its lost territories and once again become a major world power. He had no doubt about the justification of the war. Nor its outcome. Austria had been right in beginning the war. Germany had done the proper thing in honoring its promise to Austria. He said to Alexander:

"All my libido is given to Austro-Hungary."

He was also giving considerable of his energy to worrying about Anna, who was in England. The Austrian Ambassador brought her back safely to Vienna.

He admired the speed with which the German army pulverized its opponents. He feared that the German successes, which would end the war by Christmas, might also cause the nation to become haughty.

Most of the neuroses of Europe were absorbed by the war fervor. Sigmund's patients vanished. Since only the genuinely ill were given medical papers which would allow them to escape the draft, he was called on by strangers for certification that they were nervously unfit to fight. Two Hungarian patients made their way to him, but one quickly left. Sigmund used his time to write the story of the Wolf Man.

Letters smuggled through neutral countries surprised him. Ernest Jones wrote from London that the English and French would win the war. Sigmund wondered whether Jones had taken leave of his senses. Dr. Trigant Burrow, who had attended meetings of the Zurich Psychoanalytic Society, wrote from Baltimore to offer him refuge because of the plight of Austria. Sigmund understood this myopia: was not Dr. Burrow four thousand miles away from the scene?

His euphoria lasted a short time. It began to crumble when Emperor Franz Josef's imperial army suffered its first defeats at the hands of the Serbs. It received another blow when the Germans failed to capture Paris. He was disturbed by a joke in the coffeehouses:

"Our retreats in Galicia were ordered purposely to tire the enemy."

He still expected to win the war, but he began to perceive that victory was in the distance; perhaps by the second Christmas?

He did not come to his senses until the first sons of his friends and colleagues were killed in action. Martin wrote home that bullets had passed through his cap and sleeve. Sigmund went into the hospitals and saw young men with an arm or leg shot off, parts of their heads blown away.

Then it was that he realized what a fool he had been, what a blind, dangerous fool. To exalt war! To feel a youthful thrill, a surge of patriotism, because his country was going to conquer the world! Nobody was going to conquer anybody. The sole victor would be death. How many would die, ten thousand? A hundred thousand? And how many more would be maimed for life?

He found it humiliating that he, Professor Sigmund Freud, who had spent the better part of his life clarifying man's thinking about his instinctual and unconscious motivations, had permitted himself to become a dupe, unquestioning, falling victim to man's most primitive urge: to fight, to kill, to conquer! There was no way he could have prevented the war; but he could have used his training to see through the lies with which they all had been deceived. He was as much to blame as the most ignorant peasant who had gloried in the adventure of this senseless war, until he died in the mud of another peasant's farm, or ended in the observation ward which Karl Abraham was organizing for psychopathic soldiers.

Deep in the back of his mind was the feeling that he should suffer for his personal folly. As the months wore on he felt that a state of exhaustion had already overtaken Vienna. He saw the coming years filled with bitterness and ruthlessness.

At his busiest he had too few patients to pay even half of his expenditures. Martha economized. His savings were drained away. The government made no bid for his services as a neurologist.

He suffered bouts of depression after still another bloody battle, and the full horror of the brutality of war was borne in upon him. He thought:

"It is a long polar night. . . . One must wait for the sun to rise again."

Food became scarce, even for those who had the money to buy it. Many staples disappeared from the stores. Soon there was no meat to be bought. Even the butcher shop on the ground floor of the Berggasse house was emptied. This was a deprivation to Sigmund, who considered meat his main sustenance. He lost weight, as did Martha, Minna, Anna.

Next it was wood and coal that were in short supply. Prices, as had happened to food and clothing, rose to two and three times their prewar level. Then there was no coal at all, and their green and yellow tile stoves stood empty. In the evenings he sat in his office with Hanns Sachs, who had been discharged from the army for poor eyesight, wrapped in his heaviest overcoat, wool scarf tied around his neck, hat on his head, trying to write with half-frozen fingers.

Oliver finished his engineering work on the tunnel and enlisted in the army. Max Halberstadt was wounded in action. They commiserated with Sophie.

The *Jahrbuch* ceased publication. The *Zeitschrift* appeared sporadically.

The International Psychoanalytic Society existed only on a sheet of paper in Sigmund's office. No Congress could be held.

As 1916 limped wearily into 1917, as the Russian Revolution overthrew the Czar, and the United States entered the war on the side of England and France, the family's hardships increased. Inflation was undermining the value of their remaining kronen. Their nephew Hermann Graf, Rosa's son, was killed on the Italian front.

Their three sons were frequently under fire. Martha dreaded to get out of bed in the morning for fear there might be a message that one of the boys had been wounded or killed. Sometimes, when the news seeped into Vienna of Austrian casualties, she was unnerved.

Eli Bernays, suspecting the Freuds' financial plight, had transferred a substantial sum to Vienna before the United States declared war. Friends in Holland sent Sigmund boxes of cigars, knowing that his Tabak Trafik had few available. Ferenczi used his position as an officer to ship in forbidden boxes of food from Hungary. Dr. Robert Baranyi of Uppsala nominated Sigmund for the Nobel Prize. A patient, whom Sigmund had cured earlier, died and left him $2026 in his will, which he shared with his children and his two widowed sisters.

He resumed his *Dozent* lectures at the university, where he had nine students. He decided to write the lectures beforehand so that they could be published under the title of Introductory Lectures on Psychoanalysis. *The Psychopathology of Everyday Life* went into its fifth edition, though paper was becoming scarce. Brill was still translating and publishing volumes in America. Ernest Jones smuggled letters in through Switzerland or Holland, complaining that Brill's translations were so poor and misleading that they were injuring the cause of psychoanalysis.

Early in the war Sigmund and Martha had gone to Berchtesgaden for a few weeks because Amalie was at nearby Ischl, and they wanted to celebrate her eightieth birthday with her. The following summer they managed to gather in Salzburg, Sophie and her baby, Mathilde and Robert Hollitscher, Alexander and his wife, Anna, and best of all, their two sons Martin and Ernst, who were on leave, for a two-week family reunion. After returning to the service Ernst developed tuberculosis.

Toward the end of 1917 Sigmund's practice revived. He knew why. Though there was still some lingering optimism in Germany, the Austrians were becoming reconciled to the fact that they had to lose and the war would soon be over. Sigmund's patients, as many as nine each day, decided that as long as they had to live with defeat they might try to cure their neuroses; war excitement could no longer make the disturbances sufferable. They came to Professor Freud seeking help that was long overdue.

The last summer of the war, 1918, Ferenczi arranged for the Freuds to vacation at a resort in the Tatra Mountains. Ernst was in a sanatorium close by. Ferenczi also set up an International Psychoanalytic Congress to be held in Budapest, in September. Martha and Ernst attended with Sigmund, as did forty-two analysts and enthusiasts, a few from Holland and Germany, the rest from Austria and Hungary. They were put up at the newly opened Hotel Gellért-fürdö, with its hot springs baths and magnificent gardens. The mayor formally welcomed the delegates, a boat was made available to them for trips on the Danube, there were official receptions and dinners given in their honor.

Government officials from Germany, Austria and Hungary were present, seeking help for their soldiers with war neuroses. Budapest arranged to open a center for treating shellshock psychoses, with a psychoanalyst in charge. Ferenczi was promised a professorship at the university, and a full course of lectures on psychoanalysis for the students. He had achieved good results with war neurosis patients in Budapest, as had Eitingon in Berlin and Abraham in the army hospital in Allenstein.

"We're really wanted!" Sigmund commented to the Committee, Ferenczi, Abraham, Sachs and Otto Rank. "It's the first time we've been received as an established scientific body . . ."

". . . with something valuable to contribute," broke in Ferenczi exultantly. "Professor Freud, we're not merely *wanted*, we're *needed*. Ah! to be indispensable! I've fantasied about that for years."

The war ended on November 11, 1918. Franz Josef's successor, Emperor Karl, was deposed in a brief revolution. The Hapsburgs were gone. Hungary declared its independence. The Empire was gone. Martin had disappeared, lost in the final weeks of confusion. Sigmund and Martha were racked by anxiety: was the boy dead? Wounded beyond recovery? How were they to find him? Weeks passed before they received a postcard from him saying that he was in an Italian hospital. He had been captured, suffered with fever.

Vienna was in a state of collapse. "Meatless weeks" were replaced by "meatless months." The Austrian currency depreciated so rapidly it took a suitcase full of kronen to buy a loaf of bread. The Freuds lost everything, including the savings Sigmund had put into Austrian bonds, and a life insurance policy for Martha.

His patients stayed away for want of funds.

Ernest Jones urged him to come to London, where he could guarantee Sigmund a practice. Jones had nine patients, analysands, with sixteen more on the waiting list. Martha asked:

"Would you want to go, Sigi? The future seems so dark here."

After all this time, the question was the same as it had been shortly after they married.

He permitted himself a sigh.

"No, Vienna is my battlefield. I must remain at my post."

He turned his full energies to writing, not only to set down on paper the ideas that had been germinating during the past years, but as a form of retribution for his chauvinistic follies. During the war Deuticke had published *Remembering, Repeating and Working Through*, which investigated the neurotic's compulsion to repeat. Sigmund followed this with a new study on *Repression*, then a monograph on *Instincts and Their Vicissitudes*, and *Observations on Transference Love*, detailing the process whereby some women patients fall in love with their doctors as a surrogate for the father they loved in childhood. *Mourning and Melancholia* had followed in 1917, and now in 1918 Heller published the Wolf Man case under the title of *From the History of an Infantile Neurosis*. The story ran to a hundred pages, emerging as the clearest and most persuasive exposition he had yet written about the childhood origin of neuroses and the psychoanalytical techniques which can resolve them. He then started a series of twelve essays on metapsychology, an attempt at theory formation about the function of the mind: its origin, structure, physiology. Heller published the *Introductory Lectures on Psychoanalysis* in three volumes.

The polar night was over. But it was a gray dawn, overcast and cheerless.

2

The newly born Republic of Austria had little to go on. The war had left everyone exhausted. Vienna was desolate, her currency worthless, her stores empty, her hospitals full. There was little food, coal, work. Large portions of the population were starving. None of the three Freud sons could find a job. With scarcely any money coming in Sigmund was the sole support of his mother and Dolfi, his widowed sisters Rosa and Pauli and their children; Martin, Oliver and Ernst; Martha, Minna, Anna and himself. At a loose count he had some sixteen mouths to feed, with no practice whatever. He also tried to help Alexander and his family, since the railroads were no longer running in Central Europe.

It was an inconceivable situation.

Martha doggedly went her way. She left the house early each morning with her shopping basket, making the rounds of the markets, finding a few limp greens here, a soupbone there, perhaps a small fish for the soup, and on fortunate days a few lentils, split peas, beans or barley at the grocer's. The soup tureen was as big as ever, but its content was thin. Everyone felt a numb kind of hunger most of the time, but no one commented on it.

Sigmund wrote to Ernest Jones:

"We are living through a bad time, but science is a mighty power to stiffen one's neck."

During the last summer of the war, when he had taken Martha and Anna to the Tatra Mountains in Hungary, Sigmund had become the physician and friend of a wealthy, thirty-seven-year-old brewer, Anton von Freund, several of whose relatives had been helped through analysis by Ferenczi. Toni, as he asked Sigmund to call him, was a Doctor of Philosophy, and a man of extraordinary intellectual gifts.

Anton von Freund had a serious problem: he had developed carcinoma of the testicles. During an operation a few months earlier, the surgeon had had to remove one of the testicles. Although the doctor had assured Anton that he had removed every trace of the cancer, and that there was no physiological reason why he could not resume a normal sex life, the usually high-spirited Von Freund had become depressed and psychologically impotent, unable to make love to his attractive young wife, Rozsi.

Von Freund and Sandor Ferenczi had been close friends for too long. Ferenczi could not help Anton. "Besides, Professor Freud is coming to Hungary shortly," Ferenczi said, "you will do better with the master."

Toni von Freund asked Professor Freud if he would accept him as a patient. Sigmund readily consented. They agreed to spend their afternoons hiking in the Tatra Mountains, using the walks for therapy.

"Toni, we have neither the time nor the need for what we psychoanalysts call working through, which is a lengthy process leading to character transformation. You've had some psychoanalytic training from Ferenczi, and so we're going to work together to achieve symptom relief. We will go directly to catharsis, hoping to achieve a sudden, almost explosive discovery of the origin of the anxiety."

"How do you accomplish this, Professor Freud?"

"I don't accomplish it, Toni, you do. Through a teaching force which will enable you to break down a fear into its discreet and understandable elements. You think that your temporary impotence was caused by the operation. But that was only the immediate stimulus. It would have to tie back to childhood fears and anxieties to have worked up this much psychical power."

"I understand, Professor."

"Then we can proceed with a rapid production of ideas, with emphasis on the sexual aspects of your childhood, almost to the exclusion of all other facets."

Toni remembered that somewhere between his fourth and sixth years he had seen the cook cutting poultry and slicing sausage, and had feared that the sharp knife would cut something off him. He had been both fascinated and frightened by the knife sharpeners who carried their emery wheels through the streets. He also recalled hearing a joke at that time: that the difference between boys and girls was that the girls had had their "little widdler" cut off; he became terrorized at being anywhere near a sharp knife or scissors.

As the days passed, Anton von Freund recounted quickly and honestly his first masturbatory manipulations, at which his father had caught him and, half jocularly, warned the boy that if he did not stop playing with himself he would lose his private parts. Toni could not stop handling his penis; but each time he did so, his sense of guilt and the fear of castration deepened. In his fantasies his penis was no longer there; *or it had gone dead.* The removal of his testicle through surgery had brought forth from his unconscious these childhood fears of genital loss.

With this material uncovered, Sigmund moved to put Anton into a position of strength by taking an affirmative attitude toward everything he said.

"All men fear castration. I feared it too. All men fear the discovery of the feminine side of their bisexual nature. I feared it too. All men have threats and problems in their daily lives which interfere with the genital function. I have had them too."

Still another light turned on behind Toni's blue eyes. He smiled for the first time in days.

"I grasp what you are saying: genital dysfunction does not imply anything wrong with the genital! It is an expression of difficulty in another area."

"Quite so! Now we should be able to transmit your former libidinal concern about the genitals to other aspects of your life."

As Anton steadily built the potency of his whole personality, he gained the confidence in himself needed to banish the impotence of the one area where he had been most vulnerable.

He achieved symptom relief.

The two men were spending a day together on Lake Csorba, four thousand feet high in the midst of beautiful forests. There had been rain, storms and intense cold, but this day was clear and they basked in the warm sunhsine.

"Professor Freud, I've been hatching a plan. I've talked it over with my family, in particular with my mother and my sister Katá. We are agreed: I am going to create a fund for you of one million crowns (a quarter of a million dollars) to be used for the development of psychoanalysis."

Sigmund gasped. They were standing in a woodcutter's clearing above the lake. He leaned against a neatly stacked pile of logs, needing support.

"A million crowns! I cannot believe it! Our movement has always been poverty-stricken. Almost none of our publications earned back their cost. We will be able to resume publication of the *Jahrbuch* and put the *Zeitschrift* back on its quarterly basis. This is a godsend."

Anton sat on a shorter pile of logs, a look of satisfaction and fulfillment on his attractive face.

"There are no strings attached, Professor Freud. I'll put the crowns into the account when I return to Budapest. As you move along in your work and have a need for money, simply let me know and the necessary funds will be forwarded to you."

Sigmund was deeply moved.

"Toni, you are the sort of person one would have to invent if you did not already exist."

That evening Sigmund spun his dreams to Martha. A fierce rainstorm was beating on the roof over their bedroom. Sigmund's voice rang out, fading the noise above them into distant thunder.

"Our greatest need, of course, is for a publishing house of our own. Not only for the revived *Jahrbuch*, the *Zeitschrift* and *Imago*, but for our books as well. We'd never again have to go begging for a firm to put out our work. We could establish new scientific journals as they were needed, establish regular publishing schedules. We could commission books to be written, books that might not otherwise be created, or if written, would lie in desk drawers because no commercial publisher can see a profit in them."

Martha was sitting propped up by the pillows Sigmund had stood against the headboard. The war years had taken their toll, there were semicircular lines at the corners of her mouth, and her hair had thinned, but her eyes had regained their philosophic calm. She listened, engrossed, to Sigmund's plans.

"Yes, Sigi, I can see the advantages. There would not be another Wilhelm Stekel to take away a *Zentralblatt* because he had originally found the house to issue it. But won't it require trained men?"

"Assuredly. But they will come along once we have the money to open a plant, buy printing presses . . ."

He brought back fifty thousand crowns of the Anton von Freund fund to Vienna and rented quarters for the press which was to be called *Internationaler Psychoanalytischer Verlag*, or *Verlag*, publishing house, for short. Otto Rank, who had suffered severe bouts of depression in Cracow, where he had been stationed during the war, because he had been separated from Professor Freud and psychoanalysis, but had managed to marry beautiful Beata Tola Mincer, took over the *Verlag* immediately upon his return to Vienna with a vitality and enthusiasm that had been repressed for four years. He announced that he was going to put out The Collected Works of Sigmund Freud in a handsomely bound leather edition so that the reading public would know how worthy were its contents.

The fifty thousand crowns (ten thousand dollars), were quickly spent on furnishing an office and storeroom, buying paper stock which was rapidly disappearing from Vienna, securing equipment and setting up printing contracts. Sigmund was not concerned, for there were another nine hundred and fifty thousand crowns in the Budapest fund.

Slowly the members of the Vienna Psychoanalytic Society returned home, took up their practices. Communications between the Committee members were resumed. Sandor Ferenczi, in Budapest, started his postwar career brilliantly. A thousand students at the university signed a petition for his lecture course. When Béla Kun's Communist regime took over, after Hungary became independent from Austria, it gave Ferenczi full backing as a professor at the university, and made plans for starting a psychoanalytical institute to train physicians. Since psychoanalysis was officially recognized in Budapest, and the Von Freund funds were there, Sigmund considered sending Otto Rank to Budapest to create the *Verlag*. Had it not become the center of European psychoanalysis?

The Wednesday Evening sessions reconvened at the beginning of 1919. Each of the men had been affected by the war; now the group suffered a new setback.

Viktor Tausk had been thwarted in his attempt to practice psycho-analysis by being drafted immediately upon his graduation from Medical

School. The war years, which he had been obliged to spend in Lublin and Belgrade, had done little to dissipate his lifetime neuroses. Lou Andreas-Salomé had returned to her house in Göttingen, Germany, to practice lay psychoanalysis. Tausk needed Sigmund more than ever as a father surrogate; he wanted to be admired, absorbed. He also yearned to be independent of Professor Freud, and so he contested Sigmund's thinking and theorizing at the Wednesday Evening meetings. Sigmund respected the nimbleness of Tausk's mind but was frequently made uncomfortable by his schizophrenia.

At long last, at the age of forty, Viktor Tausk was able to open an office to practice psychoanalysis. When he fell in love with a young musician, Hilde Loewi, whom he described as "the dearest woman who ever entered into my life . . . noble, pure and kind," Sigmund believed that Tausk would achieve an emotionally stable love life and the professional practice he had sought for these eleven years.

It was not to be. When Viktor Tausk was to go for his wedding license, he wrote farewell letters to his fiancée and to Professor Sigmund Freud, inventoried his possessions, tied a curtain cord around his neck, put his army pistol to his right temple, blew off part of his head and strangled himself as he fell.

The farewell letter was brought to Freud. Sigmund was stunned, experiencing shock, pity, anger. Why had Viktor done this witless thing just as he was on the verge of fulfilling his personal and professional life . . . after the endless energy, affection, money the group had poured into his development and medical degree? The farewell note revealed little:

> Dear Professor . . . I thank you for all the good which you have done me. It was much and has given meaning to the last ten years of my life. Your work is genuine and great, I shall take leave of this life knowing that I was one of those who witnessed the triumph of one of the greatest ideas of mankind . . .
> I greet you warmly.
>
> Yours,
Tausk

The funeral in the Central Cemetery was ghastly. Though there were members of his family present, as well as his first wife's family, no one had made any arrangement for a religious service. Sigmund and the Vienna group were there in force, but no one had planned an oration. Tausk's coffin was lowered into the grave in dead silence: only the earth resounded as it was shoveled downward by the gravediggers.

Sigmund went home sick at heart. He blamed himself that he could feel no love for Viktor at this moment, only pity . . . and a sense of hopeless frustration. Tausk had been needed!

He recalled the insight which Wilhelm Stekel had first enunciated:

"No one kills himself who did not want to kill another, or at least wish death to another."

Was suicide an act of aggression? Of revenge? Of escape from a worse fate, murder or madness? There was so much that psychoanalysis had to learn about suicide.

Sigmund wrote Viktor Tausk's obituary for the *Zeitschrift*. Later he wrote in a separate context:

"Probably no one finds the mental energy required to kill himself unless, in the first place, in doing so he is at the same time killing an object with whom he has identified himself and, in the second place, is turning against himself a death wish which had been directed against someone else."

In November 1919, Béla Kun's Hungarian government was ousted by counterrevolutionary forces and the Rumanian army. Admiral Horthy, who had led the counterrevolution, was put in charge of the government and early in 1920 became Regent. He was a rightist dictator, bitterly anti-Semitic. One of his early acts was to fire Sandor Ferenczi from the university, close the war neuroses clinic, and force Ferenczi to resign from the Hungarian Medical Society. Admiral Horthy then dictated that all bank accounts were to be frozen; that no money could be sent out of the country without the government's approval.

That was the end of Budapest as the center of psychoanalysis; and the end of the Anton von Freund fund. Commitments Sigmund had made for the *Verlag* would now have to be fulfilled out of his own empty pockets.

There was additional tragic news. Anton von Freund's carcinoma had returned and spread to his chest and liver. He came to Vienna hoping for better medical treatment. Sigmund arranged a room for him at the Sanatorium Fürth. The cancer was too widespread to be operable. There was nothing Sigmund could do except sit by Anton's bedside and comfort him. Later he wrote to Anton's wife, Rozsi:

"Toni was well aware of his fate, which he endured like a hero; but like a true human, Homeric hero he was able from time to time to give free vent to his grief about his lot."

Sigmund was holding Anton's hand the afternoon that he died. He gently closed the eyelids and put the blanket over the man's face. Walking home in the brittle coldness of the late January afternoon, shivering inside his overcoat, he thought of Anton's desire to become a friend to the psychoanalytic movement, which he had described to Sigmund as the greatest promise and adventure of his life. Remembering his own joy in finding Anton, and then his hopes for the future of the *Verlag*, Sigmund recalled the adage:

"Who drinks wine for supper wants water for breakfast."

3.

A virulent postwar influenza had been sweeping across Europe. Martha became ill. Sigmund and Minna nursed her at home for several months until she was strong enough to be moved to a sanatorium in Salzburg, where she made a good recovery. That had been during the spring and summer before. Now, on the very day that Sigmund and the Vienna Society buried Anton von Freund, Sigmund received a telegram from Max Halberstadt in Hamburg that their daughter Sophie had been stricken.

Sigmund went to Alexander for help.

"Sig, I'm bitterly sorry. There are no trains running to Berlin, and you have to go through there to get to Hamburg."

"What about tomorrow, Alex?"

Alex's face was gray.

"Not tomorrow. Perhaps an Entente train in a few days. Are Oliver and Ernst still looking for jobs in Berlin? Then telegraph them. They can reach Hamburg from there."

Oliver and Ernst went by train to Hamburg. Max Eitingon accompanied them to make sure everything was cared for. Martha said:

"Sophie is young and healthy. If I pulled through, being thirty-two years older than she, she will have no trouble."

That evening they reminisced about their visits to Sophie and her older son Ernst, now three months short of six years, and one-year-old Heinz, whom the grandparents had not yet seen. Sophie, as a mother, was more than ever their Sunday child: cheerful by nature, full of affection for her parents, proud and happy to share her bright, attractive children with the family.

Sophie died from influenzal pneumonia. Oliver, Ernst and Max Eitingon reached Hamburg only in time for the cremation. Sigmund sent Mathilde and her husband Robert on the Entente train to console the bereaved Max Halberstadt, and care for the two little boys. Martha, dry-eyed and inconsolable, took to her bed. Sigmund knew that he could not succumb to grief; Martha needed him. For four years of war they had worried about the possible death of their three sons; and now it was their daughter who had been taken.

Eli Bernays had helped the Freuds considerably during the war by returning tenfold the money Sigmund had loaned Eli to get to the United States. Now it was Eli's twenty-eight-year-old son Edward, robustious and dynamic, with a wholehearted devotion to his Uncle Sigmund and his work, who took over. His first move when he arrived in Paris in 1919 had been to send to Vienna a box of good cigars. Next, when Edward received the German copy of Sigmund's *Introductory Lectures on Psychoanalysis*, he asked for the translation rights, promising good royalties. Sigmund consented. Edward, who moved like lightning, secured a generous contract from Boni & Liveright, avant-garde publishers in New York, farmed out the chapters to several Columbia University graduates to speed up the process of translation and then, as a genuine coup, convinced the publishers that they should offer Professor Freud ten thousand dollars to come to New York and promote the book by a series of lectures. Sigmund declined the offer, though he needed the money, saying to Martha:

"Edward is apparently one of the great promoters of all time. Alas! I am not."

Edward fulfilled his promise about the royalties; unfortunately the translation, done hastily, by several hands, was uneven and shot through with errors.

Only a few months before, Sigmund had had to borrow two thousand marks from Max Eitingon because he needed foreign, or sound, money in order to travel to Berlin and Hamburg. Now the wheel of fortune spun round once again. He was appointed a full professor at the university. Though the title was still honorary, and he was not invited to teach regular classes at the Medical School, nevertheless the "promotion" was accepted as an important one throughout Austria, and stimulated a resurgence of his local practice. Dr. David Forsyth, a British physician came for seven weeks of training. Ernest Jones sent him an American dentist working in England. A patient arrived from the United States because he had heard about "an alienist in Vienna who was getting good results." Difficult cases were referred to him by his colleagues everywhere. He charged them all the same fee, five dollars for the hour, considerably below his prewar rates, but cash was hard to come by, and he was grateful to be paid in foreign currency, which enabled him to support his family. Sergei Petrov, the "Wolf Man," who had lost his fortune in the Russian Revolution, came to Vienna seeking renewed analytical help. He had paid well over the several years of his analysis, and now Sigmund reciprocated by treating him without charge.

By March 1920, Sigmund had saved enough money to repay his debt to Eitingon. Oliver and Ernst had found jobs in Berlin. Martin was working for a newly organized bank in Vienna. Alexander was back in business; the railroad lines had been repaired, the rolling stock replenished. Conditions were returning to normal.

"If by normal," Sigmund commented wryly to Martha, "we mean that our roadbed has been mended!"

A new Swiss Psychoanalytic Society was established by the ever loyal Pastor Pfister, Ludwig Binswanger and Hermann Rorschach, who was devising psychological tests to measure the content of the unconscious by a patient's reaction to what he saw in inkblots. Hanns Sachs, who had fallen ill during the war and gone to Switzerland presumably to die, recovered and opened an office in Zurich to engage in psychoanalysis. Ernest Jones and Sandor Ferenczi made their way to Vienna, not without difficulties from their own governments, and settled into the Hotel Regina at the top of the Berggasse.

Sandor Ferenczi had finally married his Gisela, after her long separated husband had killed himself in 1919; but not until a rumor had reached Vienna that Ferenczi had been carrying on a love affair with one of Gisela's young daughters, and had had a difficult time deciding which to marry: mother or child. Despite the loss of his professorship, Ferenczi had a good private practice.

Ernest Jones brought his new wife, shortly after their marriage, to meet the Freuds. Young Katherine Jokl was a Viennese who had moved to Zurich in order to study at the School of Economics there. She was working as secretary to the proprietor of the Hotel Baur-au-Lac to support herself and her mother, when she met Hanns Sachs, who had previously had a love affair with Katherine's older sister. Sachs invited Katherine and her mother for tea the following afternoon at the Cafe Terrace. When they arrived, there was no Hanns Sachs, but an attractive man in a white suit jumped up, introduced himself as Dr. Ernest Jones, a friend of Sachs, and asked if he might give the two ladies tea.

The next day, Saturday, Jones sent Katherine a large basket of sweet peas; and on Sunday invited her for a walk. They had been out for about an hour when he said:

"What would you say if I asked you to go to Italy with me . . . as my wife?"

Sigmund, who had been observing Katherine, said in an undertone to Jones:

"You have chosen well. And in only three days!"

Ferenczi and Sachs teased Ernest Jones, suggesting that he had married Katherine in order to become a member of the Chosen People.

The Committee now had its first meeting since the beginning of the war. Max Eitingon had been invited to join and had accepted. Sigmund gave him a gold ring with an intaglio mounted in it. It was decided that Ernest Jones should open a branch of the *Verlag* in London for the translation of psychoanalytical works and the publication of their scientific journals for the English-speaking world. Jones had brought with him an advance copy of the American edition of *Introductory Lectures on Psychoanalysis*. He cried:

"Professor Freud, you simply cannot give away these English translation rights so cavalierly. Now we will have difficulty getting publication in England." He pulled on his ears, which sat so low on the majestic head that the tips of the lobes were on a level with his mouth. "My dear Professor, we are going to have to abandon all the Brill translations as inadequate."

"No," replied Sigmund firmly. "I would rather have a good friend than a good translator."

"We cannot afford that luxury," Jones insisted.

Those who suffered most in the war's aftermath were the Austrian children who had been orphaned in great numbers and had no one to care for them. Their plight was so desperate that a group of American physicians created a fund of three million crowns ($608,000) to found a convalescent home for them. They asked Professor Freud to join the dean of the Medical Faculty and the Mayor of Vienna in administering the fund. A few weeks later Eli Bernays added a million crowns ($202,333), in his wife Anna's name, to the same fund. The orphans were now housed, fed and clothed. The Medical Faculty was astonished that the American physicians had singled out Dr. Freud for this post. Why Sigmund Freud, of all people?

Max Eitingon, whose fortune came from the United States, decided that Berlin should have the first psychoanalytic training school. He commissioned young Ernst Freud to design the building. Ernst did a splendid job, providing for a lecture hall, library, classrooms and private offices for the training analysts. Eitingon paid for the entire structure and its furnishings, handing over ownership to the Berlin Psychoanalytic Society. Karl Abraham took charge. Hanns Sachs agreed to go to Berlin from Zurich to help train young doctors. With the opening of the Berlin center the Vienna group became eager for their own clinical center. Sigmund was opposed to the idea on the grounds that Vienna had always been antagonistic to psychoanalysis, and "a raven should not don a white shirt." He was overruled by the Society and plans were begun to open an Ambulatorium.

The venture was postponed when Dr. Sigmund Freud again fell into disfavor with the Viennese medical profession, the incident arising from his testimony in the hearing against Ordinarius Wagner-Jauregg for the electrical treatment of war neuroses.

Professor Freud had not been asked to practice psychoanalysis on the Austrian soldiers returned to Viennese hospitals suffering from war neuroses. Instead, Wagner-Jauregg had administered electrical shock. He was now accused by former army patients of brutality, of using or permitting his psychiatric clinic to use excessive, and hence cruelly painful, amounts of shock. Sigmund was asked by the court to submit a report, and later to testify on the value of shock treatment; whether excessive amounts were purposely used on what Wagner-Jauregg called "malingerers from battle." Sigmund agreed that there might be malingering, but that it would be unconscious; that it was poor therapy to make the electric shock more horrendous than anything faced in battle so that the soldier would return to the front lines. He testified that he knew of cases where excessive shock had been used for this purpose, but that he was "personally convinced that it was never intensified to a cruel pitch by the initiative of Professor Wagner-Jauregg. I cannot vouch for other physicians whom I did not know. The psychological education of medical men is in general decidedly deficient. . . ."

Though Sigmund thought he had exonerated his former colleague, Wagner-Jauregg was hurt because Professor Freud had not defended him more vigorously, and Wagner-Jauregg's displeasure was as nothing compared to the psychiatrists who had had charge of the nervously afflicted soldiers. They openly attacked Freudian psychoanalysis as a fraud. Sigmund responded by distributing copies of Dr. Ernst Simmel's pamphlet, published in 1918, in which Dr. Simmel, a psychoanalyst from Berlin who had been head of a hospital for war neuroses patients in Posen, gave the "extraordinarily favorable results achieved in severe cases of war neurosis by the psychotherapeutic method introduced by me."

He had sufficient patients now to save enough money to permit the family a summer vacation. When Martha went to Ischl to visit with Mathilde, who was in poor health again, Minna kept Sigmund company at Gastein, where they took the waters together. Sigmund and Anna visited Hamburg to be with Max Halberstadt and Sigmund's two grandchildren; and then went on to The Hague for the September 1920 Congress, the first International Congress since the war.

Their Dutch colleagues, knowing that the members from Central Europe had lost their savings and would have trouble raising travel money, gathered together the sum of fifty thousand crowns to pay their expenses. They also offered the hospitality of their homes for the four-day meeting. As Sigmund let his eyes wander over the group of one hundred and nineteen members and guests assembled for the first session he saw with deep satisfaction that the International Psychoanalytic Association had been reformed, that no friendships had been broken, and no ugly scars resulted from the war. He thought:

"It is a true test of brotherhood that we have come together again; for many of us as nationals were at war with each other less than two years ago. It is good to be a physician: we heal the victims of war."

Ernest Jones and the British group gave a luncheon honoring Professor Sigmund Freud and his daughter. Anna gave the "thank you" speech in excellent English, which pleased the British Psychoanalytic Society and delighted her father.

4.

He approached his sixty-fifth birthday, May 6, 1921, with the realization that he had achieved the early ambition of his years in Professor Brücke's physiology laboratory: to become a researcher and teacher, rather than a medical practitioner. He now had more pupils whom he was training than he did patients. There were more applications for training analysis than there were hours in the workday. He had already accepted ten analysands for the fall, a heavy schedule since he was continuing to write in the evenings and on Sundays.

One of his delights was the growth and talent of the young second-generation analysts, the majority of them medical doctors, the others Ph.D.s: Helene Deutsch, Felix Deutsch, Georg Groddeck, Heinrich Meng, Hans Zulliger, August Aichhorn, Siegfried Bernfeld, Heinz Hartmann, Ernst Kris, Géza Róheim. Two trainees gave him particular pleasure: a tall, lean, bright English couple, James and Alix Strachey, each of whom had quite independently arrived at the conclusion that psychology was the most fascinating subject of the future. James Strachey had discovered *The Interpretation of Dreams*, taught himself German so that he could read it in the original, then gone to Ernest Jones to ask how he could become a psychoanalyst. Jones had replied:

"Study to become a doctor."

Strachey worked at a hospital for six weeks, decided that medicine was not for him, secured Sigmund Freud's permission to come to Vienna for analytical training. Sigmund found him to be one of the most perceptive of students. Before long Alix Strachey, fascinated by what she heard from her husband about Professor Freud's methods, asked if she too could undergo analysis. Sigmund agreed, commenting:

"I have never psychoanalyzed a husband and wife at the same time. It should be fascinating."

When the Stracheys first arrived, in October of 1920, Sigmund had written Jones, "I have taken Mr. Strachey at one guinea the hour, do not regret it but for his speech being so indistinct and strange to my ear, that he is a torture to my attention." In a matter of weeks he was describing James Strachey as "a good acquisition." What most impressed Sigmund about thirty-three-year-old Strachey was the excellence of his translations; for Strachey spent most of his spare hours studying German, translating Sigmund's shorter pieces into English, and then showing Professor Freud how muddled and unreadable the earlier translations were. Sigmund was also impressed by the quality of Strachey's fervor, for he was even more adamant than Ernest Jones that the earlier translations were inadequate or misleading and had to be taken over by a capable group of psychoanalysts and redone under the guidance of the British Psycho-analytic Society.

"Strachey, I have a proposal to make. How would you like to undertake the translation of a group of five clinical cases: Dora, The Rat Man, Little Hans, Schreber and The Wolf Man? They would give us a nice volume for our library, if Jones is agreeable."

"I'd like that very much, Professor Freud."

"Good. That would make a valuable teaching tool. The volume will take you a considerable time. In the meanwhile, I'd like you to consider two shorter monographs, *Beyond the Pleasure Principle*, which was published last autumn, and Group Psychology, which I am just finishing and which will appear this summer. It deals with the study of the changes and differences in the group mind when people meet together either accidentally or for specific purposes, from the individual mind when it is functioning out of its own instincts and character directives. Why not come on Sunday for early supper, with your wife, and we can discuss it."

Strachey's light blue eyes showed their pleasure.

"We'd be delighted, Professor. Alix is also going to be an excellent translator."

The Sunday evening supper was most pleasant. Martha developed the same kind of maternal fondness for the Stracheys that she had for young Katherine Jones. Sigmund took James and Alix into his study where they sat among the room-filling collection of antique figures and got involved at once in an intense discussion of *Beyond the Pleasure Principle* which the Stracheys had studied together, and which Sigmund considered the most important point of departure he had made in the past few years. He read aloud from the monograph:

"In the theory of psychoanalysis we have no hesitation in assuming that the course taken by mental events is automatically regulated by the pleasure principle. We believe, that is to say, that the course of those events is invariably set in motion by an unpleasurable tension, and that it takes a direction such that its final outcome coincides with a lowering of that tension—that is, with an avoidance of unpleasure or a production of pleasure. . . ."

Sigmund set forth what he felt was a new and important turn for psychoanalysis: pleasure and unpleasure were related to the quantity of excitation present in the mind. Unpleasure corresponded to an increase in the quantity of excitation and pleasure to a diminution. The mental apparatus endeavored to keep the quantity of excitation as low as possible, or at least to keep it constant. This was the best way to state the pleasure principle, "for if the work of the mental apparatus is directed towards keeping the quantity of excitation low, then anything that is calculated to increase that quantity is bound to be felt as adverse to the functioning of the apparatus, that is as unpleasure." He made the point to the Stracheys that "the pleasure principle follows from the principle of constancy."

His mind went back to the days when he had tried to convince Josef Breuer that psychoanalysis could be an exact science, and attempted to hitch his concept to Helmholtz's theory of constancy which he had studied in Brücke's laboratory. He had even drawn diagrams for Josef to prove his point.

Because of the influence of the ego's instincts towards self-preservation, the pleasure principle had to be replaced by the *reality* principle, which demanded and carried into effect the "postponement of satisfaction, the abandonment of a number of possibilities of gaining satisfaction and the temporary toleration of unpleasure as a step on the long indirect road to pleasure." It was his opinion that all neurotic unpleasure was pleasure that could not be felt as such.

He drew a sharp distinction between the instincts which, because they strive for inertia, exercise pressure towards death, and the sexual instincts which work towards a prolongation of life. Eros and Thanatos. Love and Death. The two polarized forces of human nature.

In order to bring a patient beyond the pleasure principle into the reality principle, what had been unconscious had to be made conscious. The patient who could not remember the whole of what had been repressed in his mind, and often could not remember the essential part of it, was obliged to repeat the repressed material as a contemporary experience. The physician had to help him to remember it as belonging to something in the past.

"It seems, then, that an instinct is an urge inherent in organic life to restore an earlier state of things which the living entity has been obliged to abandon under the pressure of external disturbing forces." It was a truth which knew no exception "that everything living dies for internal reasons, becomes inorganic once again." Therefore he felt compelled to say that the aim of all life was death. "If we firmly maintain the exclusively conservative nature of instincts, we cannot arrive at any other notions as to the origin and aim of life. . . . The hypothesis of self-preservative instincts, such as we attribute to all living beings, stands in marked opposition to the idea that instinctual life as a whole serves to bring about death." Yet the instincts of self-preservation served only "to assure that the organism shall follow its own path to death."

The sexual instincts were the true life instincts. They "operate against the purpose of the other instincts, which lead, by reason of their function, to death; and this fact indicates that there is an opposition between them and the other instincts, an opposition whose importance was long ago recognized by the theory of the neuroses." Apart from the sexual instincts, there were no instincts that did not seek to restore an earlier state of things . . . of non-existence.

One of the most fascinating analysands to reach him was a tall, beautiful Englishwoman by the name of Mrs. Joan Riviere. She had already had three years of analysis and training with Ernest Jones and had completed an excellent translation of *Introductory Lectures*. James Strachey had known Joan Verrall Riviere ever since he had been at Cambridge. When Sigmund asked him something about her, Strachey replied:

"We came out of the same middle-class professional, cultured, later Victorian box. She frightened me somewhat, but she possesses three invaluable gifts: a thorough knowledge of the German language, a highly accomplished literary style, and a penetrating intellect."

Sigmund observed about her that she was "concentrated acid, not to be used until duly diluted." She could not tolerate praise, triumph or success, any more than she could failure, blame or repudiation. Sigmund diagnosed it as a narcissistic problem. It did not take long for him to develop a kind feeling towards her, based partly on her practical efficiency, particularly when she brought him an over-all plan for the Collected Works which was better than anything that had yet been proposed. What Joan Riviere seemed to be fighting for at this early stage was not a clearing up of her neurosis but the title of "Translating Editor" on the inside of the cover of the English translations of all Freudian publications.

5.

In the beginning of his book *On the History of the Psychoanalytic Movement*, published in 1914, Sigmund had used the legend from the coat of arms of the City of Paris, which showed a ship, and under it the words *Fluctuat nec mergitus: It is tossed by the waves but does not sink.* As he moved through the rest of 1921 and 1922, he decided that this comforting adage fitted him as well as it did Paris.

Through the indefatigable efforts of Paul Federn and Eduard Hitschmann the Ambulatorium was finally opened in Vienna; but after six months the city government, harassed by Viennese psychiatrists, ordered the clinic closed without giving any reason.

The Vienna *Verlag*, which had started out so auspiciously, was an unending source of vexation and anxiety. Sigmund poured his royalties into the publishing house, and whatever he could spare from his earnings, but the press was forever in debt. Otto Rank kept it alive by heroic efforts. When there was no paper available for the journals he scrounged until he had accumulated it sheet by sheet. When they lacked type, ink, printers, he begged, borrowed, connived until he could get the printed material off the presses. When they found it to be cheaper to print in Czechoslovakia they contracted to have the books and maga-zines printed there; but the printers knew no German and made incredible errors.

The press in London was in an equally desperate situation. Ernest Jones had no money with which to finance the newly founded *International Journal of Psychoanalysis*, which had contributions in English as well as translations from the German journals. If the errors in German were bad, the errors in English were ludicrous. Jones sent a young Englishman to live in Vienna and supervise the galleys; Anna Freud also pitched in. Yet it sometimes took a year and more for Jones to get back, in printed form, a manuscript he had sent to Vienna.

Otto Rank, overworked, overwrought, found the need for a scapegoat, and not unnaturally selected Ernest Jones, who sent back poorly printed galleys insisting that Germanisms, such as *Frau* instead of *Mrs.*, be eliminated. Rank poured out his complaints to Sigmund, who was at first distressed that two key members of the Committee should be quarreling, and then so worn down by Rank's unending complaints against the character and performance of Ernest Jones that Sigmund wrote Jones a critical, even harsh letter. Jones answered calmly, replying to Sigmund's criticisms one by one, showing that the delays and frustra-tions did not as a matter of fact take place at his end. Sigmund decided, belatedly, that he had better investigate. Then, shamefacedly, he apolo-gized to Jones, thanked him for not taking offense, and started to worry about Otto Rank, particularly since he observed him carrying an army pistol around with him. There was no question but that Rank's nervous system was shattered. Sigmund did everything he could to lighten the work load and free Otto for the revitalizing practice of psychoanalysis. Rank did not seem eager for patients; he wanted his free time for two manuscripts he was writing.

Sigmund's niece, twenty-three-year-old Caecilie, became pregnant and killed herself. His sister Marie, widowed in Berlin, had returned to Vienna. Hermann Rorschach died suddenly in Switzerland of peritonitis.

Yet the ship stayed afloat. The Ambulatorium was revived. Anna Freud served as secretary and was elected to the Vienna Psychoanalytic Society after reading a paper "Beating Fantasies and Day Deams." The world-wide translations and voluminous printing of his works brought new and famous friends to Berggasse 19: H. G. Wells, the English novelist; William C. Bullitt, who had been with the American Peace Commission in 1919; Arthur Schnitzler, one of the few writers who knew and reported the truth about the sexual nature of man; the German philosopher, Count Hermann Keyserling.

The University of London announced a course of lectures on five great Jewish philosophers: Philo, Maimonides, Spinoza, Freud and Einstein.

Sigmund, Martha and Minna had a spirited discussion about it over supper. Minna cried:

"Albert Einstein a philosopher! I thought he got the Nobel Prize last year for physics?"

"Putting my name next to Maimonides and Spinoza!" Sigmund said with a grin. "That is exalted company. A lesser person might have his head turned by such a compliment. But I am a modest man . . ."

". . . who hides his light under a bushel," retorted Martha. "By the way, Sigi, what does that saying mean? A bushel of corn? Of fish? Or of rocks on which you have disdained to carve your name?"

The high point of the postwar years was the Berlin Congress of 1922. He refreshed himself with six weeks of rest in the cool beauty of Obersalzberg where he spent the crisp mornings writing a draft of The Ego and the Id, and the afternoons walking the winding trails through the woods with Martha and Anna. Since the Armistice, the International Psychoanalytic Society had grown tremendously; it now had two hundred and thirty-nine members, of whom one hundred and twelve attended the Congress, with the addition of almost another hundred and fifty interested guests. Eleven members had made the journey from America, thirty-one from England, ninety-one from Berlin, a testimonial to the work that had been done by Karl Abraham, Max Eitingon, and then Hanns Sachs and Theodor Reik at the training center. In spite of the continuing opposition and adversity, twenty members came from Switzerland. Looking over the large hall and remembering the unfortunate disruptions at the Munich Congress a decade before, Sigmund mused:

"We have the numbers and the strength to sustain ourselves. We have arrived! We may lose individuals over the years, for reasons relevant or irrelevant; but we are as steady on our feet as any psychiatric or neurological society."

Psychoanalysis was here to stay.

Abraham's paper on melancholia and Ferenczi's on genital theory fascinated the Congress. But for Sigmund Freud the great joy was hearing the papers of the new young people: Franz Alexander, Karen Horney on problems of feminine psychology, Géza Róheim who was introducing psychoanalysis into anthropological thinking. Sigmund gave his own paper the title Some Remarks on the Unconscious, based on his The Ego and the Id manuscript. In it he made plain to the assemblage that he had been but partially right in the past in stressing only the conscious and unconscious mind. He had oversimplified. Growing knowledge led him to a fresh concept. For in science, yesterday's knowledge is today's half-truth.

In terms of architecture, the unconscious was held at bay by something called the ego, the mediator between the individual and reality. As he had written three years before in Beyond the Pleasure Principle, "It may be that much of the ego is itself unconscious." Under his new terminology he broke up man's mental structure into the Id, the Ego and the Superego. The Id had first surfaced in the writings of the physician-novelist Georg Groddeck, whose concept the *It* went back to Nietzsche. Sigmund changed it to the *Id* and writing at a later period, clarified its meaning:

"It is the dark, inaccessible part of our personality; what little we know of it we have learnt from our study of the dream-work and of the construction of neurotic symptoms, and most of that is of a negative character and can be described only as a contrast to the ego. We approach the id with analogies: we call it a chaos, a caldron full of seething excitations. We picture it as being open at its end to somatic influences, and as there taking up into itself instinctual needs which find their psychical expression in it, but we cannot say in what substratum. It is filled with energy reaching it from the instincts, but it has no organization, produces no collective will, but only a striving to bring about the satisfaction of the instinctual needs subject to the observance of the pleasure principle."

The Ego he used as a term which described the most rational part of a person's self as a whole.

"The ego seeks to bring the influence of the external world to bear upon the id and its tendencies, and endeavors to substitute the reality principle for the pleasure principle which reigns unrestrictedly in the id. For the ego, perception plays the part which in the id falls to instinct. The ego represents what may be called reason and common sense, in contrast to the id, which contains the passions."

He made the observation that "The id . . . has no means of showing the ego either love or hate. It cannot say what it wants; it has achieved no unified will. Eros and the death instinct struggle within it. . . . It would be possible to picture the id as under the domination of the mute but powerful death instincts, which desire to be at peace and (prompted by the pleasure principle) to put Eros, the mischief-maker, to rest."

The new identity was the Superego, which was derived from a child's earliest object-relations, what he had formerly thought of as the "ego ideal," the representative of society within the psyche, including conscience, morality, aspirations. The Superego served as the watchdog over the ego, differentiated between right and wrong, and attempted to keep the ego away from wrongdoing which brought guilt in its train, and the consequent anxiety.

Then he set down what he thought was the crux of the paper:

"Psychoanalysis is an instrument to enable the ego to achieve a progressive conquest of the id."

It was also a way of looking at things, an attitude, a frame of reference, a point of view, an approach to understanding the human mind in terms of its repressions, its ongoing conflict between Eros and Thanatos, love and death.

6.

It started when he noticed a little blood on a piece of bread he had been eating. By stretching out his right cheek with one finger and lifting his upper lip with another, he was able to see in the mirror the spot from which the blood was coming. He paid it no further attention; it would dry. And so it did, for a couple of days; but then the bleeding returned. He examined the area with his tongue, but when he put a finger on the edge of the tongue he saw a spot of blood. He remembered a working phrase from medical school, "Beware of painless bleeding." However the blood was coming from an area just beyond the last tooth, and he put it down to a swollen gum or an impacted tooth. As the weeks passed and he kept exploring a growth, it felt increasingly rough to his tongue. Then, when he saw that the growth was extending toward his palate, he decided he had better consult a doctor.

The obvious choice seemed to be Dr. Markus Hajek, whom he had known slightly over the years, a professor and head of the university clinic of laryngology and rhinology at the Allgemeine Krankenhaus. Hajek had published authoritatively on the diseases of the mouth. Much as Sigmund disliked using the telephone, he called Dr. Hajek when no member of his family could hear him, and made an appointment for Hajek's office-apartment on the Beethovengasse.

Markus Hajek at sixty-one was five years younger than Sigmund Freud. He had been born in the Balkans, studied medicine at the University of Vienna and taken his medical degree in 1879, two years before the lagging Sigmund Freud. He was a tousled looking man with a salt and pepper beard, bald except for a thin patch which stood straight up in the middle of his head and then curled over in a whimsical puff. It was a good head, sympathetic, a face dominated by a marvelous pair of eyes: wide, sad, sentimental.

Dr. Hajek did not take long for his examination. He straightened up and said casually:

"Nothing serious. Just a growth of leucoplakia. It's on the mucosa of the hard palate."

"Will it go away if we give it sufficient time?"

"I think not. It would be wiser to have it out. It's a minor operation. Just come into my ambulatorium at the Allgemeine Krankenhaus early one morning. I can excise it for you and have you home by noon."

A few days later the young internist Felix Deutsch came to the Freud apartment. He had been one of Martin Freud's tutors at the university, had become a friend of Sigmund's years before, and subsequently the family doctor. He was an advocate of psychoanalysis and had published a paper called *The Meaning of Psychoanalytical Knowledge for Internal Medicine.* His wife, Helene Deutsch, was also a graduate of the University of Vienna Medical School, and had been trained for a number of years by Wagner-Jauregg in psychiatry, as well as by Kraepelin in Munich. In the middle of the war she had come across a Sigmund Freud book, had read straight through his published works and began attending his lectures. She had asked Sigmund if he would analyze her. He had done so for one year and then informed her, "You do not need any more analysis, you are not neurotic." She entered into analytical work with cases which Sigmund sent her, and now both Helene and Felix Deutsch were stalwarts of the Psychoanalytic Society.

Sigmund asked Felix Deutsch to look at the sore spot and showed him where it was, on the roof of his mouth, at the extreme right, just beyond where the upper row of teeth ended. Dr. Deutsch's expression was noncommittal when he finished his examination.

"Dr. Hajek's diagnosis looks to me to be correct; it's a simple leucoplakia. It would be wise to remove it before it grows any larger."

For the first time Sigmund was disturbed, not from anything Felix Deutsch had said but from the slightly strained expression on his face.

"Deutsch, deceiving the patient for his own peace of mind in cases like this really doesn't afford a longtime assurance. I'm concerned about two things: one is my mother, who is now eighty-seven, and who would find my death quite unbearable . . ."

He rose from his chair and walked about his office blindly for a moment, then returned to Dr. Deutsch.

". . . and I should like to die in dignity. That is why it is important for me to know the truth."

Felix Deutsch shrugged his shoulders and smiled affectionately.

"My dear Professor, why do you distress yourself with such ideas? From my superficial examination I would say that Dr. Hajek is right. Once it has been removed you will be able to forget about it."

During the two months that passed Sigmund had mentioned nothing to the family about the growth in his mouth. What was there to talk about? Neither did he tell them, this particular morning when he left the house at eight, that he was going to Dr. Hajek's clinic at the Allgemeine Krankenhaus to have it removed. Since he would be home for the noon dinner, with his mouth just a little sore, why worry them?

He strode vigorously up the Berggasse, turned right along the Währinger Strasse to the Allgemeine Krankenhaus, then crossed to what was known as the "New Clinic." Since this was an outpatient clinic, where patients could come without appointment for examinations and minor surgery of the mouth, Sigmund passed a dozen people sitting on a wooden bench in the long corridor, then a number more in the waiting room, sitting back to back on a double bench. A young nurse in an immaculate white uniform, her hair covered by a white veil which flowed down her back, took him immediately to Dr. Hajek. It was a high-ceilinged room, flooded with April sunlight from the tall corner windows. There were two straight-backed chairs with tables alongside, a revolving stool for the doctor and a bowl standing high on a rod into which the patient could expectorate during the operation.

Dr. Markus Hajek seated him in the chair under the corner window, asked Sigmund to unloosen his collar and tie and then to wash out his mouth with a strong antiseptic. He examined the growth once again with a magnifying glass, tied a bib around Sigmund's neck. After spraying the area with cocaine to deaden the pain as much as possible, he injected a local anesthetic around the portion of the mouth that he was to excise. A wooden wedge was placed at the opposite end of the mouth to give Hajek open space in which to cut around the margins of the tumor and core out the center of the growth. His nurse took a scalpel out of the boiling water of the instrument tray and handed it to the doctor.

There was the usual bleeding when he made his first incision. Dr. Hajek expected that he would have fifteen or twenty minutes in which to remove the surface blemish. Sigmund began coughing and spitting blood into the receptacle at his side. The deeper Hajek cut into the tumor, the more persistent and uncontrollable the bleeding became. Sigmund, attempting to clear his mouth of the blood, spat out the wedge, which closed Hajek's operating space. This interfered with Hajek's custom of rapidly removing the growth so that he could quickly stem the anticipated flow of blood. He cried to Sigmund:

"Professor Freud, please keep your mouth open! Try not to gag! Nurse, keep the professor's mouth open."

Because of the great speed with which he was now obliged to work, Hajek's delineation with the scalpel became less certain. He had the growth almost entirely out, and was about to make the final plunge to cut the restraining tissue, when suddenly he hit a large blood vessel. The blood gushed forth, some of it straight into Hajek's face. Hajek, who had not yet extracted the growth and needed another moment, cried:

"Keep your mouth open, Professor, keep it open!"

The blood was now pouring down Sigmund's shirt and pants, had bespattered Hajek and the nurse who was helping him. Sigmund was not only gagging and coughing, but because of the flow of blood lurched forward in his chair in a series of contortive movements, with the nurse trying to hold him back. Now that Hajek needed the most possible exposure, he could see almost nothing. However he was a skilled and experienced craftsman; he made one final incision with the scalpel and removed the growth, a bluish-red color, berrylike in composition, about the size of a quarter.

While Sigmund coughed and spat out the blood so that he would not inhale it and die in the chair, Hajek quickly got a gauze packing and stuffed it up into the wound. It was necessary to ram the packing in deep and hold it firmly. Hajek did, with his thumb clamped into the right side of Sigmund's jaw. Both patient and doctor had become panicky when the blood gushed out. Sigmund still did not trust himself to speak, but his eyes asked a very large question of Hajek, who was unnerved. Hajek answered:

"As I told you, Professor, it looked to me like a surface lesion; but the deeper I went the more tumor there seemed to be. I was almost forced to quit before I could get to the bottom, once I hit that large blood vessel. No surgeon could proceed in the face of marked bleeding. However, I think with my last completed cut I got it all out. We'll just keep you in this chair for an hour or so, and the nurse and I will take turns pressing a pack in your wound. As soon as the bleeding stops we'll move you to a more comfortable place."

Sigmund was in a state of partial shock. He knew that Hajek had not been careless. If the doctor had been forced to cut deeper than the quarter inch he thought he would have to go to take out the growth, then this was certainly more than a simple lesion. Had Hajek really gotten the whole of it with that final slash of his scalpel? Or had the gush of blood from the artery concealed everything and left Hajek in the dark about the nature of the growth?

He heard the doctor say, "I will telephone your family."

The bleeding having been arrested, Sigmund was helped out of the operating room by an assistant. They sat him down on a hard chair in the waiting room. A nurse held the pack in place for a considerable time, then asked Sigmund to clamp it with his thumb. A number of questions went cascading across the foreground of his mind.

In less time than he would have imagined possible, Martha and Anna were standing before him, with a valise containing some nightclothes. There was an unasked question in their eyes:

"Why didn't you tell us? Why did you come here for an operation and not let us know?"

No one offered any explanation of what had gone wrong; it was clear that no one knew. Martha and Anna were making a heroic effort to conceal their distress over the fact that Sigmund's clothing was covered with blood. They were an owl-like trio gazing at each other, unable to say anything, least of all a word of reproach. The silence was broken by the arrival of Dr. Hajek's assistant, who said, shaking his head in frustration:

"This is a stupid state of affairs! There is not a single bed to be had in the clinic. Every last one of them is filled with a patient. Let me try again; perhaps we can find a cot."

Again they were left to sit in silence, Sigmund, Martha, Anna, three people who loved each other more than anyone in the world, but could find no words to express their tumultuous feelings. The assistant returned, a look of mock despair on his face.

"Professor Freud, please forgive me, I have found a bed, but the only place we can set it up is in a small room where we are treating a cretinous dwarf. Would you mind terribly?"

Sigmund murmured:

"That will make two of us."

The assistant, Martha and Anna led Sigmund through the corridor and into a side room, one seldom used, undressed him and got him into bed without any resumption of the bleeding. The cretinous dwarf observed all this up on one elbow from the adjoining bed. Sigmund knew there was an explanation due his wife and daughter, but any attempt to talk would put a strain on the packing inside the wound and might cause the bleeding to start again. Martha and Anna understood this.

Shortly before noon Dr. Hajek came in to examine the packing. He now appeared calm and unworried. He reassured them that everything was in order, that the bleeding had stopped and that Sigmund would be able to return home the following day. Promptly at noon one of the older nurses came in and announced:

"I am sorry, Frau Professor Freud and Fräulein Freud, but it is the dinner hour and we must feed our patients. No visitors are allowed in the hospital during that time."

Anna seemed about to remonstrate but Sigmund raised his hand, palm outward, and she refrained. Martha went to the head of the bed and spoke for the first time, patting Sigmund's hair down gently on either side of the part.

"Try to get some sleep, dear. We will be back at two o'clock when the visiting hours start."

Sigmund felt weak and tried to sleep but he could not in spite of the sedative Dr. Hajek had given him; there was a throbbing pain in his mouth.

Then he started to bleed again. At first just a trickle down his throat. He sat up abruptly, and leaned over to spit it into the basin on the nightstand beside him. This loosened the packing, and now the bleeding grew in intensity, once again pouring out of his mouth, over his nightclothes and the bedclothes. He reached his right arm backwards and rang the bell which hung over the bed, but no response came out of it. He rang it several times more before he realized that it was not working. The blood was coming too fast now for him to cry out for help; and who was there to cry out to?

The dwarf, who had been watching all of this with wide eyes, jumped out of bed in his nightshirt, ran out into the hall and summoned help. Hajek's assistant and a nurse came running. It took a considerable time, but at last a new packing was inserted and the flow of blood was stopped. The nurse changed the bedclothes.

When Martha and Anna returned at two o'clock they were shocked and frightened. If Sigmund's roommate had not summoned help, what would have happened? Might he not have bled to death? Anna announced her intention of remaining in the room until Sigmund could be taken home the following day. No relative was allowed to stay overnight with a patient, it was against the rules. But this did not faze her. She secured permission from Dr. Hajek to remain the night. Martha left, reluctantly, when the nurses insisted that she had already overstayed the visiting hours.

For Sigmund it was a long night, filled with half-conscious suffering. Dr. Hajek had given him the strongest possible sedative, but Sigmund's mouth throbbed so bruisingly that he could not fall asleep.

During the dark hours before dawn Anna became frightened that her father was growing weaker and the pain was too much for him to endure. She found the night nurse, who had been looking in frequently and seemed concerned about Professor Freud's condition. Together they tried to rouse the house surgeon, but he refused to leave his bed. Anna returned to her father's room to make him as comfortable as she could until morning.

Dr. Hajek arrived early. He made no comment about the loss of blood. The bleeding had stopped now. Hajek repacked the wound, declared that there would be no more bleeding and that he could return home that afternoon.

"But I should like to demonstrate your case to a group of students who are coming in this morning. Would that be all right, Professor Freud?"

Anna was about to protest, but Sigmund replied:

"This is a teaching institution. The students have a right to learn, and Dr. Hajek is obliged to demonstrate all interesting cases that pass through this clinic."

The demonstration went off without incident, Dr. Hajek being careful not to disturb the dressing. When the students had trooped out and Hajek was alone in the room with him, Sigmund asked quietly:

"One question, Dr. Hajek. Do you have a report on the biopsy?"

"Yes."

"What does the laboratory say?"

"Exactly what I diagnosed: benign."

"Then there is no cancerous growth?"

"None. It is perfectly safe for you to go home this afternoon. Just take it easy for a couple of days and regain your strength."

7.

Sophie's youngest son, Heinz, who was now four and a half years old, had been plagued by a series of infections and colds in Hamburg. The doctor recommended having his tonsils out but the operation had not helped. He was a frail child, little more than skin and bones. While his father, Max Halberstadt, was doing his best, Sigmund reasoned that he could provide the boy with better care in Vienna. Mathilde, the oldest Freud daughter, was childless and eager to have Heinz live with her. At the end of May, when the weather turned warm, the boy was brought from Hamburg.

He had his mother's bright face and laughing eyes, an alert child with an ever present fund of good nature. At each meeting Sigmund realized with a sense of shock that he was gazing at Sophie as she had looked at her son's age. After midday dinner Sigmund and Martha walked over to Mathilde's apartment to visit with him. Sigmund called him by the pet name of Heinele, and for the first time in his life sat on the floor to help a child with a set of building toys. It became a standing joke in the family that Heinele could build a bridge or an apartment house faster than Grandfather could bolt four wheels onto a flat-bed truck.

Heinz reached Vienna a month after Sigmund's operation. Although Sigmund had been back at work, he had been low in spirits, with the suspicion that Hajek's operation might not have excised the entire growth, and that Hajek had been deceiving him. The attractive grandson, with his quick intelligence, brought a glow of joy into Sigmund's life. When the weather was warm, Mathilde and Robert Hollitscher would bring the boy to the Berggasse apartment for a glass of milk and soft cookies, while Sigmund joined him with a cup of coffee. Because of the tonsillectomy Heinz still had trouble in swallowing.

"Grandfather, I can eat crusts already. Can you?"

Sigmund laughed, held the child to him.

"No, not yet, Heinele, you've beat me again, just as you always do with the Meccano set."

Heinz went down with fever. Sigmund summoned Dr. Oskar Rie, who brought with him the best young pediatrician in Vienna. There could be no mistake about it: Heinz was suffering from miliary tuberculosis. Sigmund cast about frantically for a way to save the boy. Mathilde and Robert would take him at once to the hot dry climate of Egypt. . . . But little Heinz was lost. His eager spirit and bright mind were not enough to restore his lungs. He died on June nineteenth, after only a few months of having brightened his grandparents' lives with the radiant glow of love. Sigmund felt as though something had died within him, that he would never be able to give himself to love so wholeheartedly again. He wept openly at the funeral. It was the first time the family had seen him shed tears in public.

At the end of June Sigmund and Tante Minna went to Bad Gastein to take the waters, their usual cure. Martha twitted them:

"You two remind me of the Italian women who go to a spa every summer for a cure of their *fegato*. It's a conversation piece; they look forward to that excursion during the long cold winters. There is nothing more wrong with their livers than there is with your stomachs; but I'm sure it helps you psychologically."

On August first he joined Martha and Anna at the Hotel du Lac in Lavarone, where the family had been many times before, and were cared for solicitously by the owners. The Committee was meeting at San Cristoforo, down the mountain. Sigmund knew that they were having troubled times; the quarrels between Otto Rank and Ernest Jones over the way Jones was running their publishing house in London had increased. Rank had Ferenczi on his side, though not Abraham or Sachs. Sigmund had heard that Rank was going to ask for Jones's resignation from the Committee, but he was confident that the other members would not allow this to happen. The Committee had to be kept intact! Yet Sigmund did not feel that it would be proper for him to interfere. The men had to settle their own internal problems if they were going to continue to work together as the cohesive force they had been over the eleven years of the intimate group's existence.

The Committee settled its difficulties as best it could, then came up to Lavarone to spend a day with the Freuds. Sigmund was going through a period of torture because the wound in his palate was not healing properly. He had known that it would take two or three months to coat over, but now it was four months, and a new growth seemed to be spreading from the original excision toward his lower jaw. He asked Dr. Felix Deutsch to come to Lavarone. Deutsch made a careful examination but once again declined to speak about the growth. Sigmund had long been planning to take Anna to Rome for the month of September to show her the city he loved best.

"That's an excellent idea," Deutsch exclaimed. "Show Anna everything you love in Rome, but be sure to come back home at the end of the month. Then we'll see what has to be done."

The day after Sigmund and Anna returned to the Berggasse, Felix Deutsch came to the house. He listened to their stories about Rome, then the two men went across the hall into Sigmund's study. Deutsch did not ask to examine Sigmund's mouth again, but said with a serious expression:

"Professor Freud, I have arranged an appointment for you later in the week with Professor Hans Pichler. He is the most famous oral surgeon in Europe."

"I have not heard of him."

Deutsch grimaced.

"Nor has he heard of you. That is what has happened to our medical profession in this day of specialization."

"Tell me about him."

"Hans Pichler is forty-six years old, is Viennese, took his medical degree in 1900 at the university and began his training in ear, nose and throat surgery from Dr. Anton von Eiselsberg, who is the pioneer in the field. However his career was halted very early by an extreme case of eczema. He had to give up surgery. He went to Chicago, to the North-western Dental School where he passed his examinations, got rid of his eczema and returned to Vienna to open a dental practice. This was successful but the pull of oral surgery was undiminished, so he returned to the Eiselsberg Clinic to continue his work on surgery of the mouth. The war provided him with more than ample opportunity to work on soldiers whose mouths, jaws or faces had been shot away. It is said of him that he gave back to wounded soldiers faces that one could look upon again. He is a man in whom you may have total confidence. I will make an appointment for you at the Sanatorium Auersperg. You know where it is, close to the Josefstädter Theater."

This time Sigmund told Martha and Anna, in an uninflected voice, that he was going to see Dr. Pichler for an examination. He assured them that no operation would take place. The two women received the information in silence.

The Sanatorium Auersperg was charming architecturally, with the first two floors constructed of tan stone; between it and the three higher stories was a line of windowboxes sporting pink, yellow and red flowers.

When Sigmund entered Dr. Hans Pichler's consulting office he found to his surprise that Pichler looked more like an American than an Austrian. He was a little man, filled with a quiet vitality, clean-shaven; he chopped his sideburns almost level with the tops of his ears and wore his hair cropped close to his head. The low soft collar and gray flannel suit were similar to those Sigmund remembered from his stay in New York and Boston. Apparently Chicago had not only cured his eczema and returned him to his profession, but also given him an American appearance which he had been unwilling to relinquish.

Dr. Markus Hajek was also present, a professional courtesy. Sigmund recognized Hajek's record of his case on Pichler's desk.

While Dr. Pichler examined Sigmund's mouth, Sigmund kept his eyes open, staring up into the handsome, stern, bony-nose, aesthetic face of the doctor, his resolute mouth and chin, deep solitary eyes. Pichler was thoroughgoing; he took his time, yet the examination required no more

than ten minutes. He motioned for Sigmund to button the collar of
his shirt, then went to the sink at the side of the room, washed his hands
in hot water, dried them on a white towel. To Sigmund his eyes seemed
more inscrutable than before. However there was nothing inscrutable in
his tone of voice.

"Professor Freud, you are a physician and a man of science. You will
want to know the full truth."

"Certainly, Dr. Pichler."

"You have a very serious cancer in your mouth. The only way we
can control it is to operate. This will leave you with a disabling feature,
a hole in the roof of your mouth, which fortunately we will be able to
correct with a prosthetic appliance. I will have to perform the operation
in two stages, in order to control the bleeding which accompanies this
kind of operation."

Sigmund had a sinking feeling through his innards. He had suspected
all along; but there had been room for a less serious diagnosis and a less
serious operation. Cancer was a death warrant, a distasteful disease, news
of which had to be concealed somewhat in a manner that syphilis had to
be concealed, though for different reasons. Any person with cancer had
to face the fact that this most invasive disease could take a sharp turn for
the worse in a very short period. He heard Dr. Pichler speaking.

"First I will have to remove a number of your teeth on the right side.
A few days later I will have to perform surgery on your right upper
neck. Through this incision the external carotid artery will be ligated;
then I will remove the upper cervical lymph nodes to prevent the spread
of the cancer to more vital organs."

Sigmund knew why Dr. Pichler would have to open his upper neck
to ligate the external carotid artery, which sent blood only to the outer
part of the head and to the site of the cancer. Although he would have no
further use of this artery during his lifetime, there would be no severe
loss, for other arteries would eventually take over the task of supplying
blood to the scalp and mouth.

"And the second part, Dr. Pichler?"

"That will be the serious aspect, in which we'll have to get rid of all
traces of the cancer. From my examination I would say that the growth
had originally been confined to the region of the hard palate, but now
has extended downward to the tissue covering the mandible (jawbone),
and the adjacent parts of the tongue and inner surface of the right cheek.
I will have to remove part of your right soft palate, the adjacent parts
of the tongue and the inner surface of the right cheek, and part of your
mandible just beyond where your teeth end."

Sigmund thought for a moment, then asked:

"That is a critical operation, is it not?"

"Yes, but I am only taking out what you are destined to lose. It is better for me to take it out than for the cancer to destroy this tissue and have the cancer remain. However I will not remove any more than is necessary. Before I extract the teeth I will make a mold for your prosthesis and it will be ready for your use as soon as you mend. The mold will cover the hole in your palate, giving you a partition between your mouth and nasal passage."

Dr. Pichler took Sigmund to the door. Sigmund stopped abruptly, turned and said:

"Dr. Pichler, I would like it to be understood that I am paying the regular fee for the operation, and all postoperative care. I should not want to become a burden."

Pichler smiled for the first time, a tiny twitching of his lips.

"Ah yes, I have been learning about your work in the unconscious mind. You feel that if you make considerable demands on me, without my even knowing it I might give you short shrift in favor of my paying clients!"

8.

He would have to take the news home with him now; it would be just as difficult as receiving the sentence from Dr. Pichler. He did not wish to alarm the family, nor would it be sensible to deceive them. Best to tell them the truth, matter-of-factly, even as he had described the symptoms and the necessary treatment of some of his early patients to Martha. He felt that he could rely on Martha, Minna and Anna not to make a scene; the two older women knew enough about life to accept its irreversible judgments. Anna was young, yet her sense of attachment and loyalty to him was so absolute that she would accept, without being instructed, his version of how they were all going to see this through.

The three pairs of feminine eyes that gazed at him from different parts of the living room somehow achieved the stoic attitude they knew he wanted. But no one ate supper that night, and no one slept.

The extracting of his teeth was a preliminary move. Then, on the late afternoon of October 3, 1923, he moved into the sanatorium. His room was furnished with a comfortable homelike bed, night table with reading lamp and two handsomely carved wood chiffoniers, a small desk at which to write, cheerful wallpaper, a bath and toilet draped off at the far end. The room, which overlooked a pleasant enclosed garden, had been made to appear as much as possible like quarters in a private club rather than a hospital.

He was rolled into the operating room early in the morning on a stretcher. He had had no breakfast. A mild sedative had quieted his apprehensions.

The operating room was a marvel of modern design, with extremely high ceilings, an enormous "surgical" window facing north, and immediately in front of it the operating chair which could recline backward if Dr. Pichler needed a better angle.

When Sigmund was helped into the operating chair by two assistants, Dr. Pichler entered and said, "Good morning," then asked:

"How do you feel, Professor Freud?"

"As a physician, all I am hoping for is that you get it out. What remains of me I know I can adjust myself to, as long as I don't have to live with this malignancy with its daily threat to my mental and physical existence."

He had already been shaved.

His face was coated with an iodine solution, then his eyes and forehead were covered with drapes, leaving exposed only his cheeks, nose, mouth and chin. Dr. Pichler was on his right side draped in a gown, gloved and masked; one of his assistants was on the other side. To the right of the surgeon was the instrument nurse; two other nurses moved about securing materials.

The first operation was the simpler of the two. Dr. Pichler used a combination of Pantopon and Scopolamine as a local anesthetic along the line where he would cut. He made a curved incision on the right hand side of Sigmund's neck, starting at the back over the mastoid process, passing about two fingers below the angle of the jaw and terminating at the front of the neck at the upper level of the voice box. Pichler quickly found his way inside the incision to the external carotid artery. Sigmund sensed a pulling and stretching inside his neck. Pichler warned him:

"There will be a sharp pain for an instant, while we tie off the artery, but it will pass quickly."

Pichler then went to work, inside the same incision, on the lymph nodes which he found hard and rough, and into which cancerous cells could drain. He gave Sigmund a fresh injection in the area of the lymph nodes, then dexterously extracted them. Sigmund gritted his teeth for the pain which never arrived. There was little bleeding, and so Pichler was able to work slowly and meticulously. He then sutured the incision. The operation took an hour and three quarters.

He was taken to his room on a stretcher, feeling a trifle weak and dazed, but not at all bad. He sat up and ate a fairly good supper, for the sanatorium prided itself on its kitchen. By the next day he was able to walk to the bathroom himself, though his legs were a little unsteady. He quickly regained his strength and by the third day felt like his old self except for the soreness in his neck. He was able to go down to the social room and sink into a comfortable chair to read. He invited Martha, Minna and Anna to have midday dinner with him in the charming private dining room with its elegant appointments. Martha brought him a number of the novels he had been wanting to read, and several which he had read once and was always determined to go back to: Merezhkovsky's *The Romance of Leonardo da Vinci*, Zola's *Fécondité*, Mark Twain's *Sketches, New and Old*, Kipling's *Jungle Books*, C. F. Meyer's *Huttens letzte Tage*.

Friends were allowed to visit at any time except late at night. Sigmund had an opportunity to see some of his colleagues.

The second operation took place a week later. The surgeon, who had just been handed a syringe with a local anesthetic, said, "Professor Freud, I'm going to put a needle in; it will be only a momentary hurt." He thereupon plunged the needle along the line of the new incision. Each syringe was good for four or five injections; the nurse had to hand him a sufficient number of syringes to make a full twenty injections around the tumor. Pichler waited for about five minutes for the novocain to take effect, quietly reassuring Sigmund that everything was coming along nicely.

"If you need anything, Professor Freud, please let me know."

Sigmund could think of no answer to this invitation. With his eyes veiled he could not see, but as a trained physician who had spent months in Billroth's operating room, he could follow Pichler's movements. Pichler split his upper lip through and through with a scalpel. He then carried his incision swiftly around the right margin of the nose to the level of the eye. Sigmund felt no considerable pain, but visualized his whole cheek being lifted over the bone. Pichler's assistants controlled the mild bleeding. Some blood got into his mouth from his split lip, and he started to cough, but Pichler called sharply: "Nurse, suction!" The nurse put a suction tube into his mouth to take out the blood and saliva.

Using his scalpel with precision, Dr. Pichler cut out the cancerous growth at the back of Sigmund's mouth, including the involved areas of the tongue and cheek. The nurse took the scalpel, handing Pichler a chisel and mallet.

"You are going to feel me pounding, Professor Freud."

The doctor now cut into the condemned portion of Sigmund's palate bone, which came out as one piece with the cancer of the soft palate. The pounding inside his mouth made Sigmund feel as though he were a granite quarry, and workmen were removing slabs of stone. Next Dr. Pichler was handed a bone-cutting instrument. He proceeded to remove the upper end of Sigmund's right lower jawbone, which had also been invaded by the cancer.

Sigmund kept saying to himself:

"I must not gag! Yet all those hands and instruments in my mouth! Now I know how my claustrophobia patients must suffer."

For the moment he was not concerned about what Dr. Pichler was taking out of his mouth; he was more frightened about how he would withstand the ordeal.

He was gagging and bleeding now. He thought how difficult it was for patients to have to undergo this kind of operation under local anesthetic; at the same time he knew that a general anesthetic could not be used because the patient might inhale his own blood.

Pichler had been operating for two hours. He had removed the cancer and the bony parts that had been involved. The hole in Sigmund's palate was packed to control the bleeding. This brought on a momentary crisis, when Sigmund tried to cry out:

"There is too much stuff in my throat. I can't breathe!"

He motioned to the operating team. They readjusted the pack to make it more comfortable. Pichler waited for five or ten minutes to make sure he had the bleeding under control. He then inspected the entire area of the wound. Satisfied that he had removed all of the malignancy, he made a Thiersch-graft of skin from Sigmund's left upper arm. He then sutured Sigmund's cheek back into position. The nurse took the cloths off Sigmund's eyes and forehead. Sigmund saw a glint of approval in Pichler's eyes, though he was not sure whether this was Pichler congratulating himself on his own artistry, or congratulating Professor Freud on his restraint under hammer and chisel, bone cruncher and scalpel.

The two assistants put him back onto the stretcher and took him into his room. There he was given another sedative. The nurse remained with him constantly, gauze in hand to keep his mouth dry.

Sigmund lay back on the pillow. His first feeling was one of relief that the operation was over and that he had come through it satisfactorily. He felt like a person who had been partially intoxicated. He was not apprehensive, now that it was over. Dr. Pichler came into the room in his street clothes to congratulate Sigmund on the success of the operation, and to give him an analgesic against the pain that would commence fairly soon.

The recovery period was slow and awkward. For the first few days Sigmund had to undergo nasal feeding, since no food could be put into his mouth. This was bad for the first twenty-four hours, until his tissues accommodated the tube. Since he was getting nothing but liquids, he lost weight and strength, looked tired to Martha and Anna as they came twice a day to visit with him; and went through considerable anguish during the frequent changes of the packing in the hole in his palate. At night he was given an injection of morphine to put him to sleep; the night nurse renewed it around midnight. After a week, when he could use his mouth again, he was still permitted only liquids. Pichler took the stitches out in ten days. Sigmund's right cheek was paralyzed. He had little strength to read, and only a touch more with which to concentrate; but he did know one thing for sure: Pichler had said that he could be released from the hospital at the end of October, and he was determined to start seeing patients again on November first. The way to regain one's strength was to work. His mouth was tender, he could handle no solid food of any kind; but Dr. Pichler, who stopped in once or twice a day, assured him that this was normal and that the healing process would accelerate. He would never be able to chew again in the same vigorous fashion as before the operation, but adequately to enjoy the softer foods. Pichler made no attempt to insert the prosthesis to see if it would fit or to accustom Sigmund to its use; this was the mold which would take the place of his upper palate and give him freedom to eat and speak. Dr. Pichler felt that the tissue of his mouth was still too sensitive.

When he told the surgeon that he was going to commence treating patients on November first, and that in fact he had had appointments made for him at that time, Pichler patted his shoulder reassuringly, but his expression said:

"My dear Professor, you just don't know what you're up against!"

The determination to return to work on November first, just a few days after his release from the hospital, had been a sustaining force, but it was an illusory one. He simply was not strong enough physically to lend himself to other people's problems; besides, his mouth was still too sore to try the prosthesis. The plug in the hole in his palate was still painful and became fetid after he had eaten once or twice. He went back to Dr. Pichler each day for examination. In November Pichler noticed a recurrence on the soft palate. He took a small cut for a biopsy. The tissue was cancerous. The shock was a great one to Sigmund. The sentence formed in his mind, though he did not utter it:

"Will I ever be through?"

Pichler had said, "We'll get it all," yet he had not. Pichler read this in Sigmund's eyes. He replied firmly, "I did not cut wide enough, trying to keep the wound as small as possible. It was a calculated risk. I will now have to remove most of your right soft palate."

9.

He did go back to work the day after New Year's, 1924. Outwardly there was little change. He wore his mustache and chin beard a little fuller to cover the operating scars. He had to make a number of adaptive changes: since the operation had cost him his hearing in his right ear, the one he had turned toward the patients all these years, he had to reverse the position of the patients on the couch and sit at the opposite end. It was at this point that Tante Minna created the joke which would reverberate through the decades:

"Sigi, don't tell me you actually listen to all that nonsense!"

His strength returned. He began with six patients a day, a goodly chore even for a healthy man. Most of his patients were referrals now, coming in from Edoardo Weiss in Trieste, Oskar Pfister in Zurich, from Ernest Jones, the Stracheys and Joan Riviere in London, A. A. Brill and his group in New York, as well as his followers in Boston. He continued his writing at night, though he did not work as late as he used to. For a book, *These Eventful Years*, he wrote a chapter called Psychoanalysis: Exploring the Hidden Recesses of the Mind; as well as a letter to the French periodical *Le Disque Vert* which was devoting an issue to Sigmund Freud and psychoanalysis. Determined not to let his illness interfere with his creativity, he wrote exploratory papers on Neurosis and Psychosis, The Loss of Reality in Neurosis and Psychosis, and The Economic Problem of Masochism.

The prosthesis was his big problem. On one occasion when he was attempting to eat at the family table the food came out of his nose. He found this not only distressing but embarrassing. Although no one of his three women seemed to notice, he was self-conscious about the difficulty. After dinner he took Martha aside and said:

"I think I should take my meals alone until I manage to eat properly."

Martha's eyelids flared with indignation.

"I shall eat alone when I am a widow!"

The problem with the prosthesis, which plugged the large hole left by the removal of half of the roof of his mouth, was that it was required to fit securely in a corklike fashion. However the tighter the clasps fit the more it irritated the adjacent healthy tissue. He was taking X-ray treatments on a prescribed course set out by Dr. Pichler, who felt that the X ray would prevent the return of the cancer; however the radiated tissues of his mouth were sensitive to the hard, intrusive prosthesis and the pain became so unbearable that at times Sigmund simply had to thumb the whole contraption out. This gave him relief, but he dared not leave it out very long, for then his mouth tissue would contract, and he would be unable to fit it back in.

He went to Pichler's office every afternoon, where the doctor examined the healing tissues and made minor adjustments on the prosthesis so that Sigmund's mouth could abide it. The addition of a set of hinges to the clasps helped; but sometimes the construction was so tightly shut that, when he wanted to put a cigar between his lips he had to use a clothespin to pry open the two halves.

During the day, while he was treating patients, he dared not take the prosthesis out no matter how excruciating the pain. His patients were already suffering from several of his handicaps; the split lip could never be normal again, and his voice was now hoarse and nasal, almost as though he had been born with a harelip. No one commented on this, certainly not the patients; but Sigmund himself missed the sound of his former professorial voice as he guided his patients toward an amelioration of their symptoms.

It soon became evident that he was going to need help with the prosthesis, which was now called "The Monster." The nurses at the hospital had been good, yet he did not want a stranger in the house, or hovering about him as he went about his chores. The need was quickly filled by Anna; she had spent her days at the hospital watching the nurses taking care of her father's mouth, and now slipped into the position in her cool, unannounced way.

When Sigmund struggled for a half hour to get the prosthesis back into his mouth, with no success, and was in a state of exhaustion, Anna took over and accomplished the task with a minimum of discomfort. Sigmund took a long hard look at his youngest daughter. He whispered: "I will forgo self-pity in return for your not expressing sympathy."

Anna nodded. It was a pact they never broke.

Leopold Königstein died, one of Sigmund's oldest friends. He felt the loss, yet at the same time Ernst and Lucie, his wife of four years, had a son. Martin and Esti, his wife of five years, had a daughter: the generations were succeeding each other.

The City of Vienna gave him an honorary citizenship for his sixty-eighth birthday, instead of waiting for the customary seventieth.

"Because they do not think I will last until seventy," Sigmund commented to Martha, who did not enjoy the sardonic humor.

The earth rotated on its axis. Sigmund frequently found that axis to have an ironic base. Romain Rolland, one of the best loved and most talented of the French writers, came to visit, announcing that he had known Professor Freud's work and had admired him for a solid twenty years, but had never told him! Some twenty-five years before, Sigmund had, at Martha's insistence, taken a copy of *The Interpretation of Dreams* to the hotel room of Georg Brandes, the famous Danish critic, whom he and Martha had just heard lecture. Brandes had never acknowledged receipt of the book. Now, when he came to Vienna, he sent a note to Sigmund urging him to come and spend an evening in his hotel room for a good discussion.

Aside from manipulating The Monster, his only serious problem was the internal difficulties of the Committee. Dissension was deepening because of two books which were written and published almost secretly. The first of the two, *The Development of Psychoanalysis*, by Rank and Ferenczi, Sigmund had known something about, for both men had discussed parts of it with him. When there was strong objection from other members of the Committee, and Sigmund pointed out certain areas of error, Ferenczi agreed and made peace with the group.

However this was not true of Otto Rank, who seemed to be growing unhappier and more disturbed as the years passed. It had been a shock when he was informed that his master and father figure had cancer of the mouth, with a dubious future. When the news was told to the Committee, Otto Rank had burst out in hysterical laughter. When Sigmund heard about this, he quoted the French maxim:

"It is necessary to laugh in order not to cry."

Rank had been doing a heroic job on the publishing end in Vienna, as had Jones in London, both men working out of love and dedication, without compensation. The new problem arose over the second book, which Otto Rank had published without letting anyone see the manuscript. He called it *The Trauma of Birth*. It set forth the effect of the violent act of birth on the individual, coming out of the warm, well-fed security of the womb into an alien and hostile world, getting little more for his pains than a sharp slap on the buttocks which made him gasp for air, and hunger which made him cry for food. Rank attributed man's nervous and mental ills, his complexities, his anxieties, fears, confusions, phobias and failures to cope, with this original birth trauma.

As far as the Freudian group was concerned, it undercut the Oedipal situation as the basis for man's neuroses. Sigmund found some good things in the book; at the same time he felt that much of *The Trauma of Birth* was based on false premises. He decided the best thing to do would be to ignore it and let it disappear quietly.

When Hanns Sachs wrote to Berlin to tell of Freud's doubts about the book, it increased the bitterness already felt there about Rank's theory. In an attempt to quiet the dispute, Sigmund wrote a circular letter asking for harmony, even though "complete agreement in all scientific details on all fresh themes is quite impossible among half a dozen men with different temperaments, and is not even desirable."

Karl Abraham, one of the most peaceful of men, had also been a prophet of apostasy and had shown, as Sigmund later acknowledged, better judgment of human character than Professor Freud himself. It was Abraham who had watched Alfred Adler and Carl Jung, and predicted that they would split off and become a world unto themselves. Strict constructionist that he was when it came to psychoanalytical theory, he did not abide what he felt to be falsification or error. When he could not persuade Sigmund to do an analysis of Rank's book, he wrote to Professor Freud warning him of the dangers involved in this "scientific regression."

Otto Rank took this hard. He knew that he was going through a trauma of his own, the need to break away from Professor Sigmund Freud, upon whom his entire adult life had depended. Like Alfred Adler and Carl Jung and Wilhelm Stekel before him, he felt that the time had come for him to be his own man, to strike out along independent paths, no longer to work under the wing or the shadow of Professor Freud. This revolution going on inside his psyche brought him little pleasure; in fact it felled him, and he took to his bed. When he was able to get up he received an invitation to go to New York to lecture for a series of months; this seemed a sensible solution to his impasse of not being able to cut the umbilical cord which bound him to Sigmund Freud, yet being as unable to stand its restraints as Sigmund the prosthesis in his mouth. Rank accepted the invitation.

Dr. Pichler made a new prosthesis which seemed worse than the old. His health improved with the passing of the months, though he was undergoing a constant series of X-ray treatments, and some of the dosages proved to be so excessive that they brought on a toxic illness.

He did an analytical piece called *The Resistances to Psychoanalysis;* and wrote *An Autobiographical Study* which was published as a short book. It turned out to be an autobiography of psychoanalysis rather than of Sigmund Freud, which amused Tante Minna.

"Sigi, when you look into the mirror, do you see a reflection of yourself, or of Jung's Collective Unconscious?"

Minna was one of the few left who could still get a laugh out of Sigmund. He rejoined:

"Not Jung's Collective Unconscious, Minna; if he heard you say that he would accuse me of being a Peeping Tom. What I see is the collected unconscious of all the patients I have treated. It makes a much more interesting portrait than these sad features of mine."

Karl Abraham went to Holland in May 1925 to give a series of three lectures, and returned to take to his bed with a feverous bronchitis. Shortly after, in June, Josef Breuer died. A strong wash of memories flooded Sigmund's hours, recollections of his student days, his first meeting with Breuer in Brücke's physiology laboratory, all the years when he was free to come and go in the Breuer home as a younger brother surrounded with affection and encouragement. Sigmund wrote a tender letter to Mathilde Breuer. He also wrote an obituary for the *Zeitschrift* in which he set forth frankly that Josef Breuer was the "creator of the cathartic method, whose name is for that reason indissolubly linked with the beginnings of psychoanalysis."

Josef could resist the honor no longer!

Breuer's death reminded him that he and Martha had frequently seen Bertha Pappenheim's name in the German newspapers and magazines, for she had become one of the leading figures in the women's rights movement, successfully achieving safety legislation for factories, raises in wage scales, and legal protection for women in marriage. Bertha Pappenheim had never married, but Josef Breuer's treatment had saved her life and made her a valuable member of society.

The Freud family spent the summer of 1925 at Semmering. Sigmund took only one patient with him, an American boy who thought he had demons lurking at the base of his skull. It was a trying case, but Sigmund helped to make the demons disappear. There was to be a Congress in Homburg in Prussia, in September. Sigmund decided he would not go. He sent Anna instead to read his paper: Some Pyschological Consequences of the Anatomical Distinction between the Sexes.

All sorts of what he considered ludicrous affairs happened to him. There were several offers to make a motion picture about psychoanalysis. He was offered one hundred thousand dollars by Samuel Goldwyn to come to Hollywood to help film the great love stories of history. William Randolph Hearst offered to send a ship to bring Sigmund and his family to New York to report the Loeb-Leopold case, the trial of two young Chicago boys who had killed a fourteen-year-old acquaintance in an attempt to commit the perfect crime. Within a matter of days Colonel McCormick of the Chicago *Tribune* cabled him an offer of twenty-five thousand dollars if he would come to Chicago to psychoanalyze Loeb and Leopold.

Tante Minna cried:

"Sigi, why couldn't all of this have happened to you while you were a beautiful youth of thirty? Just think, you would have been a film star, and the highest-paid newspaper reporter in the world."

The bad news of that autumn was that Karl Abraham's condition worsened. He had apparently gotten a fishbone stuck in his lung during the Holland visit, and a serious infection had resulted. Dr. Felix Deutsch went to Berlin to see if there was anything he could do to help. But Karl Abraham died on Christmas Day of 1925, at the age of forty-eight. Sigmund, who had thought that after the loss of his grandchild Heinz he could never be heartbroken at a death again, was desolated by this death. Karl Abraham had been the genius of the German movement; he had gone into Berlin when no one believed one syllable of psychoanalysis; he had created faith and respect for that branch of medical science, had built a training center and had gathered around him a superb group of young doctors. His contributions had always been meticulously reasoned, and written with the utmost care. If he did not engage in the speculative flights of a Sandor Ferenczi, that simply was not in his temperament. He was the steadiest and most self-disciplined of the Committee, a man who brooked neither idleness nor foolishness on the part of his contemporaries. Sigmund had never suffered the illusion that man's fate was logical; but with the death of Karl Abraham he cried:

"Karl Abraham was forty-eight. He had thirty years of creative work ahead of him. Here am I sixty-nine, with half of my mouth carved away, yet I remain on earth while Karl is lost to us."

10.

For a very long time we worry about how to stay alive; then we concern ourselves about how not to die; there is a subtle distinction.

After a time he stopped keeping count of the number of operations, electro-desiccations and X-ray treatments. Dr. Pichler had to excise a small papillary area of leucoplakia; then he had to insert another Thiersch skin graft, then remove still another growth by diathermy. In the months that followed there were more excisions and more skin grafts.

The harder he tried to stop the birthday celebrations the larger the parties grew. Max Eitingon was still the inspirer of the celebrations; there was no way to cut him off. For Sigmund's seventieth birthday the house was filled with flowers, there were hundreds of letters, telegrams and cablegrams from all over the world, gifts of Egyptian and Greek figurines. He did not attempt to conceal his pleasure at the letters of congratulations from people he admired. He had no word from Carl Jung, but Eugen Bleuler wrote from the Burghölzli. Bleuler had told him many years before that he would still be loyal long after Carl Jung had taken his departure. Bleuler congratulated him on such papers as *Beyond the Pleasure Principle, The Ego and the Id.* He was still teaching his students Freudian psychoanalysis, though there was no such course at the University of Vienna Medical School.

There was never an hour of the day that was free of pain. The prosthesis was remodeled and reshaped day after day, but still kept irritating the tissues of his mouth, causing agonizing painful ulcers. He had an entirely new one made by a doctor from Berlin, hoping for a miracle that never materialized; and still another by an expert from Boston who charged him six thousand dollars for the trip and the work. It was no better than the others. In one particularly galling year there were six more surgical operations by excision and electro-coagulation, so that it seemed as though Dr. Pichler forever had his scalpel inside Sigmund's mouth, cutting something away. His only comfort was that none of the growths was cancerous. The constant use of X ray kept the fatal beast at bay.

The operations continued, cauterization with caustic potash, excisions of small papillomata, contact radium, destruction of dry scaling ulcers by diathermy. It was his dearly beloved friend Ernst von Fleischl's infected thumb all over again; Dr. Billroth's operations several times a year trying to get rid of the recurring "proud flesh," agonizing operations that afforded Von Fleischl only temporary relief.

"We learn to live in dignity," Sigmund declared. "To justify what I'm going through, I should be doing some of my very best work."

He refused to take so much as aspirin to dull the pain, for fear that his mind might be clouded when he needed the exact right thought or the precise sentence for the paper he was writing. He rarely had his friends in for dinner because of the embarrassment over his awkward process of chewing. But he did not feel lonely; he took joy in the quality of the work being published by the younger men and women he had helped to mature. In a true sense he had become a paterfamilias; each day there were a dozen letters lying on his desk from as many different countries, from young people who were studying and writing and publishing, nearly all of them expanding the sphere of psychoanalysis beyond anything its founder had dreamed. He wrote introductions and prefaces to works by Max Eitingon, Edoardo Weiss, Hermann Nunberg, August Aichhorn.

He particularly admired Dr. Georg Groddeck, a poet and novelist who owned a private sanatorium in Baden-Baden. Groddeck had turned to psychoanalysis in an effort to cure physical illnesses which appeared to have no organic base. He had been warmly received by Sigmund at The Hague Congress of 1920, but had alienated all those present except Professor Freud by announcing from the platform:

"I am a wild (untrained) analyst."

Groddeck had coined the phrase *pyschosomatic medicine* to describe the Freudian methods of treating physical disorders whose etiology was related to or largely caused by emotional factors. This phrase helped the public to understand the uses and purposes of psychoanalysis. Another of Groddeck's ideas in which Sigmund had found merit was that "what we call our ego behaves essentially passively in life: we are lived by unknown and uncontrollable forces."

It had been Sigmund's task to make these forces known and controllable.

Sometimes when he took his hour of rest in the afternoon, with a hot water bottle pressed against his aching jawbone, he wondered how long it would take after his death before a professor at the Medical School would be teaching the science of psychoanalysis; and how long it would take before the patients in the psychiatric wards, who had formerly been under the care of Professors Meynert, Krafft-Ebing and Wagner-Jauregg, no one of whom had attempted to get at the base of their disturbances through the Freudian methods, would be allowed to benefit from his therapy? How long did it take to dissipate prejudice? Forever? But then, what right had he to complain when Galileo Galilei had still not officially been forgiven for his apostasy of suggesting that the earth revolved around the sun?

The most extraordinary woman to enter his life, after Lou Andreas-Salomé returned to Göttingen, was Princess Marie Bonaparte, forty-three years old, down in a straight line from the brother of Napoleon I, and married to Prince George of Greece. She had inherited a fortune from her mother, who died of an embolism a month after Marie's birth. While keeping vigil at her father's deathbed in 1924 at the family mansion in St. Cloud outside of Paris, she had started reading *Introduction to Psycho-analysis*. The book proved to be a touchstone for her own emotional and sexual problems, and for those among the female mental patients with whom she worked at Ste. Anne Hospital in Paris. Marie Bonaparte wrote several times asking Professor Freud if he would take her as a patient. Suspecting that she was a dilettante from the world of high society, he refused.

She was not a woman to be put off. She arrived in Vienna and made a strongly favorable impact on Sigmund, who found in her a woman of courage, character and penetrating mental powers. Her background was a tortured one: raised by a stern grandmother, in a sad and lonely house in the woods, she was allowed no playmates except an occasional cousin. She suffered from melancholia, carried the burden of guilt over her mother's death, and in particular suffered from what she termed "hole anxiety," since the hole had come to be for her the symbol of womanhood. She had always felt that being a woman carried intellectual shame; consequently she longed to be a man. For years she maintained a protective neurotic illness which she felt would save her from the ignominy of marriage and the pregnancy which would take her life. She had wanted to become a doctor, which her father had refused to allow on the grounds that it would hurt her chances for a fashionable marriage. But Marie Bonaparte got the better of her father by studying medicine by herself, and putting in long days at Ste. Anne's where the women found her sympathetic and poured out the sexual problems which had turned them into mental patients. Marie had been astonished to learn how many of them suffered from frigidity.

While sorting the papers in her father's estate, she came across five little black notebooks which she had filled with stories from her seventh year until her tenth. She had no memory of having written these notebooks; yet their strange, symbolic content, which she could no longer understand, frightened her. She came to the conclusion that their implications could be freed from her unconscious mind only by Freudian analysis. The year before she had published anonymously *Notes on the Anatomical Causes of Frigidity in Women*, which stressed the clitoridean nature of many of the patients at Ste. Anne's who relied on their own clitorises for sexual gratification.

Sigmund found her to be tall, broad-shouldered, with a regal bearing, handsome, with something of a masculine stance in her manner and carriage. She came to Professor Freud with love and loyalty, believing him to be the prophet who could lead the mental patients out of Ste. Anne's Hospital, as well as the untold number of individuals who were imprisoned in psychiatric wards inside their own heads. She had enjoyed a reasonably happy marriage with Prince George, who was considerably older than she; and had borne a daughter in robust physical and mental health. Now that she had found Professor Freud, she was determined to fulfill her youthful ambition and become a medical researcher.

Since Marie Bonaparte intended to study female sexuality and frigidity with the hope of writing on these still obscure subjects, her treatment with Sigmund was a combination of therapy and training in psychoanalysis. After months of working over the little black notebooks, Sigmund was able to lead her back to her childhood memories, fears, anxieties, guilts, her early conflict of "the hole" as fearful punishment visited upon females. He brought the meaning of the early notebooks into her conscious mind, where she had the strength and vision to face them. Yet Sigmund found something in her analysis which puzzled him. Through the interpreting of Marie Bonaparte's dreams, he came to a conclusion:

"There is no longer any doubt in my mind that as a baby you were present at an act of coitus."

There was no truth, no matter how disturbing, which Marie Bonaparte could not face. But this concept shocked her.

"It simply cannot be true, Professor Freud. There were no acts of coitus going on in my home. Aside from my nurse, there was no one there except my father and grandmother."

"All your unconscious memories point in the same direction."

"I regret deeply that I must disagree with you. I have got to reject this reconstruction. To me it seems not only implausible but impossible."

"Then let us not pursue it further."

After Marie Bonaparte had returned to Paris, she found one of her father's grooms, who was a bastard son of her grandfather. Through skillful questioning the groom at length admitted that he had had sexual relations with her wet nurse while she was in the same room, not yet a year old. She wrote Professor Freud a full statement of her interview with the groom and his corroboration of Sigmund's conclusion from the dream materials. Sigmund wrote back:

"Now you understand how contradiction and recognition can be completely indifferent when one knows oneself to possess a real certainty. That was my case, and it was why I have held out against scorn and disbelief without even getting bitter."

It was an attitude at which he was well practiced. When visiting with Ernst in Berlin a meeting was arranged between himself and Albert Einstein, who had already published his theory of relativity and was recognized as the world's greatest mathematician and physicist. The two men were wary of each other, sat on opposite sides of the room, each speaking his own dialectic, Einstein in terms of mathematics and Sigmund in terms of psychoanalysis. Neither one understood a word the other was saying. The main difference was that Professor Freud accepted Einstein's scientific discoveries as incontrovertible truths, while Einstein was frankly skeptical about the unconscious mind, and whether it could be plumbed for the purpose of improving human health or knowledge.

Though Sigmund had been nominated several times for the Nobel Prize, the award, when it came to Austria, went to Wagner-Jauregg for his work in using malaria to cure paresis. Few begrudged Wagner-Jauregg his award, and certainly not Sigmund Freud; for Wagner-Jauregg had made a daring leap of the imagination.

11.

It was only natural that the constant cutting away of his mouth, the heavy dosages of X ray and diathermy, the demands of the prosthesis, should cause disturbances elsewhere in his body. The heart trouble of his early years returned; the upsets of his digestive system became organic rather than psychosomatic; he had frequent colds, influenza, fever. He was in need of a personal physician. One day in March 1929 when Marie Bonaparte reached the house and found him ill and miserable, she said:

"Professor Freud, would I be permitted to make a suggestion? There is a thirty-two-year-old internist in Vienna who has also been trained in analysis. I met him some months ago when Dr. Edelman sent him to me to take some blood tests. He has a kind of bone-deep honesty that shines out of his too closely shaven face. When I fell ill recently, and Dr. Edelman was out of town, Max Schur took care of me in exemplary fashion. Dr. Edelman, who has been a teacher and friend to Max Schur since he graduated from the Vienna Medical School, suggested that I become Dr. Schur's patient since we were both 'psychoanalysis addicts.' May I bring Dr. Schur to see you? His apartment is only ten minutes away, in the Mölker Gasse."

"Please do. What you say about Dr. Schur interests me."

Dr. Schur was there within the hour. He was over medium height, most of his brown hair had taken itself elsewhere, and he was the kind of man who lived his clothes rather than wore them. Marie Bonaparte had already warned Sigmund:

"The first day Max Schur wears a new suit, none of his friends recognize him. The second day, none of us recognize the suit!"

But Sigmund liked what he saw in the well-scrubbed face, the poised air of self-confidence. Sigmund judged that here was a psyche that was at peace with itself. Dr. Schur took Sigmund's case record, then examined him, yet Sigmund noted that he was very like the young Dr. Josef Breuer who had won his reputation by "divining" people's illnesses.

The word "divining" had been wrongly used, Sigmund now realized; both Josef Breuer and Max Schur were inspired psychoanalysts who knew the intricate relationships between the psyche and the soma.

After Dr. Schur had made Sigmund more comfortable and written out a prescription, Sigmund said:

"I think that you and I can establish a patient-doctor relationship based on mutual respect and confidence. However I have had some unfortunate experiences with your predecessors, and so I must extract a promise from you."

"What would that be, Professor Freud?"

"That you will always tell me the truth."

Max Schur replied:

"I make that promise. I mean to keep that promise."

"I am reassured. Thank you."

Dr. Max Schur made a great difference to the Freud family. He accompanied Sigmund each day to Dr. Pichler's office, to observe the results of the work done on the prosthesis. Schur shared with Anna the intuitive faculty of knowing how Professor Freud felt without any word being spoken. Martha felt more secure, for they no longer needed to fear that they were being deceived. The relationship between patient and doctor became a deep and trusting one. Although Sigmund was forty-one years older than Schur, a friendship sprang up. Professor Freud became foremost in Max Schur's life. Sigmund sent Dr. Schur patients for evaluation and treatment, when he himself was not certain precisely how much of the illness was organic and how much psychological. Max Schur began bringing his fiancée, Helen, to the Berggasse on a Sunday. She was studying medicine at the University of Vienna, a lovely, bright and at the same time gentle girl whom the Freuds accepted with the same affection that they did Schur himself.

In 1930, shortly after publishing one of his most profound monographs, *Civilization and Its Discontents*, Sigmund was awarded the Goethe Prize for Literature. He sent Anna to Frankfurt to acknowledge the honor, but he was not unaware of the twist of fate which had denied him the Nobel Prize in medical science, and given it to him in an art form. Many of his critics had said that there was more art than science in psychoanalysis. The Goethe Prize seemed to confirm at least part of this puzzling question. He opened his acceptance speech by writing:

"My life's work has been directed to a single aim. I have observed the more subtle disturbances of mental function in healthy and sick people and have sought to infer—or, if you prefer it, to guess—from signs of this kind how the apparatus which serves these functions is constructed and what concurrent and mutually opposing forces are at work in it. What we, I, my friends and collaborators, have managed to learn in following this path has seemed to us of importance for the construction of a mental science which makes it possible to understand both normal and pathological processes as parts of the same natural course of events."

The early years of life are slow-moving and as laden as a string of tightly packed boxcars. The latter years flash by like falling stars. There was so much that Sigmund still wanted to think through, to write and publish, so that he would leave behind fruitful clues in areas where he had done only the beginning work. Time sped by so fast that he sometimes felt he was being encapsulated. He wrote every night and on Sundays after he had visited with Amalie, now in her nineties and quite feeble, yet waiting at the head of the stairs, even with all of her children, grandchildren and great-grandchildren behind her in the living room, listening for Sigmund's step on the staircase. She died quietly in her sleep that September, at the age of ninety-five.

The following year his home town of Freiberg honored him by putting a plaque on the locksmith's house in which he had been born, and where Monica Zajic had been his nurse. Sigmund commented caustically: "I am beginning to feel like a monument."

12.

The longer one lived the fewer months there seemed to be in a year; and then the fewer days there were in a month. Time had lost its substance. What started out in the morning to be a new day quickly contracted into a fatigued night. Boundaries were lost; borders grew dim as a year ended before anyone had noticed it had begun. He no sooner lost a skirmish not to have a birthday celebrated than still another birthday was upon him. There would have been no necessity to kill time: what formerly had been a solid became a liquid, and then a gas and then steam and then evaporated. Time was a train, he thought, and people were merely unticketed passengers . . . who would get to Karlsbad if their constitutions could stand it! Good old Papa Jakob with his Peter Simpleton stories! Their combination of childlike humor and wisdom had sustained Sigmund all his life.

His Committee was being decimated.

It was clear that he had lost Otto Rank, who had fled to Paris, made a precipitous return to secure forgiveness and reconciliation, but had been unable to sustain the healing of the breach. In New York he had preached short-term analysis based on *The Trauma of Birth*, at last achieving his independence. A. A. Brill was outraged, writing to Professor Freud that Rank had repudiated the sexual etiology of the neuroses, was dispensing with the analysis of dreams, and was confining analysis to the interpretation of the birth trauma.

Sigmund was sad to lose Otto Rank. He wrote Rank a couple of conciliatory letters but without attempting to hide the fact that he believed him in error about the trauma of birth. Otto Rank could not return to Vienna, physically or symbolically. He divided his time between Paris and New York. Difficult as it was to lose a talented man who had served as a good right arm for fifteen years, there was compensation in the fact that others who had drifted away, such as Wilhelm Stekel and Fritz Wittels, wrote to ask if they might come back into the family.

But there was no possible compensation for the loss of Sandor Ferenczi, to whom Sigmund had the deepest emotional attachment of any man in the movement, and whom he had on several occasions addressed as "Son." The first strain on their long friendship had occurred with the book Ferenczi wrote and published secretly with Otto Rank. He had then backed Rank's book *The Trauma of Birth*. But these differences were quickly dispelled. No problem arose again until 1931, when Ferenczi stopped communicating for long stretches; and then came forth with a new therapeutic method. When a patient had regressed to an infantile stage during his analysis, and was once again caught in the trauma which had been caused by the cruelty, indifference or neglect of a parent, Dr. Ferenczi believed that he had to play the part of a loving parent, in particular the mother, and give to the patient the love he had been denied as an infant, thus erasing the early trauma and its effects. He was allowing his patients to embrace and kiss him; giving them physical love when they thought they needed it.

Sigmund Freud learned of this through a patient whom both he and Ferenczi were treating. He was profoundly shocked, for he and the analysts he had trained had been adamant on this crucial point: no physical contact with the patient! It was a monstrous perversion of treatment which destroyed the scientific detachment between physician and patient, and which would scandalize the medical world if word leaked out. There was no question but that it would be lethal to psychoanalysis. He wrote to Ferenczi:

"You have not made a secret of the fact that you kiss your patients and let them kiss you. . . . Soon we shall have accepted . . . petting parties. . . ."

Ferenczi simply stopped writing. By April of 1932 Sigmund wrote to Eitingon that he found Ferenczi a tribulation.

"He is offended because one is not delighted to hear how he plays mother and child with his *female* patients." Nevertheless he announced that he would back Ferenczi for the presidency of the International Psychoanalytic Society; he thought it would settle Ferenczi down. Ferenczi declined. A few harsh words were exchanged by mail, but there was never an open break. Then Ferenczi's letters became warm and friendly again. A year later he was dead from pernicious anemia. Sigmund wrote sadly to Oskar Pfister:

"The loss is very distressing."

‹ The Verlag was in such a hopeless situation that Martin quit his secure job at the bank to take over its management. The press was in debt, its future obscure; but Martin, the early poet, knew how important the continuing publications were to his father's cause. It was an act of loyalty and faith which Sigmund deeply appreciated in his son.

The press seemed to lose more money with each new publication it put out, and had frequently to be rescued from bankruptcy by its friends. Sigmund decided that the only way to save the firm was to write a new book which he hoped would be popular. He called it New Introductory Lectures on Psychoanalysis. The New Introductory Lectures accomplished their purpose; although there was nothing startlingly new in them, Sigmund had presented the material in such a reasonable fashion that the book gained new students and adherents, and was translated into a number of languages, bringing in sufficient funds for Martin Freud to keep the firm solvent.

Germany's postwar Weimar Republic had fallen. A militant dictator and party were in power. An exchange of letters between Sigmund Freud and Albert Einstein called Why War? was published in Paris in German, French and English simultaneously, the League of Nations participating with translations. However the Nazis forbade the work's circulation in Germany. Einstein left Germany for the safety of Belgium. Arnold Zweig, the writer, sent his wife and children to Palestine where he intended to follow them. Alfred Adler packed his possessions and left for America. The German psychoanalysts fled, almost in a body. Oliver and Ernst Freud and Max Halberstadt wrote that they too were looking to leave Germany.

"Our horizon has been darkly clouded by the events in Germany."

Ernst Freud moved his wife and children to England.

In Vienna one knew about Adolf Hitler, for he had been born in Upper Austria, had taken a few art courses in Munich and then returned to Vienna in hopes of being admitted to the art academy. Rejected, poverty-stricken, he had found a focus for his hatred of society in the early anti-Semitic speeches of Mayor Karl Lueger. The Vienna press had reported Hitler's beer-hall putsch in Munich in 1923, his trial and imprisonment, and had dismissed him as little more than an amusing conversation piece for the coffeehouses.

Now the hollow joke was over. Adolf Hitler had developed a political acumen and personality that were to prove mesmeric to the middle-class Germans who had been impoverished by the depression following 1929; to the working-class unemployed, on a hopeless dole; and to the industrialists who feared the rise of Communism. Hitler, whose National Socialist Party had grown into a smartly uniformed body of terrorists and propagandists, won a majority of seats in the Reichstag. Hitler was appointed Chancellor by Hindenburg, and then blamed the mysterious burning of the Reichstag on the Communists, uniting a considerable portion of the German people under two slogans:

"The Third Reich will endure for a thousand years!"

"Death to all Jews!"

The Germans who opposed Hitler's terrorism were either in exile, dead, in concentration camps or silent and powerless. With the last of the opposition crushed, Hitler began his relentless war on the Jews: loss of their homes, businesses, jobs, possessions; then physical violence, including attacks on women and children; then the detention camps, work camps and ultimately the extermination camps. Those Jews of Germany who perceived the danger early, fled the country, often empty-handed but alive, to whatever countries would accept them. The others remained, unbelieving, hoping for the best.

The Austrian Jews were not overly alarmed. Though an ally of Germany, Austria was an independent republic. The sort of thing that was happening in Germany could never happen in Austria. The German army would never invade; the rights of minorities in Austria were guaranteed by the Treaty of Versailles. . . .

Though he described himself as a pessimist in evaluating man's instinctive nature, Sigmund was no more prepared for Nazism than he had been for the war of 1914. There were signs aplenty: his books were burned in the giant bonfire in Berlin; the Berlin Psychoanalytic Society was wiped out, the analysts fleeing for their lives. Many of the Gentile analysts left with their colleagues, unwilling to live or work under the Nazis. He did not perceive his own danger in Austria, or that of his remaining family. He, Martha, Tante Minna, his sisters, were all in their mid- or late seventies; how much time could any of them have left? The only ones in Vienna he had to worry about were Martin and his family, and Anna. They did not discuss the matter.

He continued to see patients and to write at his big desk. If sitting in the coffeehouses with his students after the Saturday night lectures and tearing around the Ring were lost to him, he was surrounded with the art he loved, the endless civilizations that enthralled him. There were times when he grew depressed, imagining that his writing since *Totem and Taboo* had lost its importance. Yet in the postscript to his autobiographical study he wrote:

"My interest, after making a lifelong détour through the natural sciences, medicine and psychotherapy, returned to the cultural problems which had fascinated me long before when I was a youth scarcely old enough for thinking."

His world reputation continued to grow and to spread. But the compensation for his increasing old age, the terror of the recurrent operations in his mouth, was Annerl, the pet name by which he called his youngest daughter. She had made her lifetime decision and had come down on the side of her father and psychoanalysis. Anna was forty now. Her grasp of the field had impressed the members of the Committee as well as the psychoanalysts from other countries whom she met at the Congresses where she read her father's papers. She continued in the role of Sigmund's nurse: quiet, casual, tireless, helping him to adjust the flesh-searing prosthesis, and to adjust to it. They never mentioned The Monster, except when it was necessary to take it back to Dr. Pichler or one of his successors to be supplied with gutta-percha, vulcanized, fitted with new steel-spring holders in unending attempts to make it bearable, to bring the hope of some relief. Anna was good company; she knew what Sigmund was going through and felt every pang of it inside herself, yet she betrayed no emotion and kept the pact of "no self-pity, no sympathy." Yet she was considerably more than a nurse; he was delighted with the way her mind matured and how she began exploring the field of education and children's psychology. He wrote to Pfister:

"Of all the applications of psychoanalysis the only one that is really flourishing is that initiated by you in the field of education. It gives me great pleasure that my daughter is beginning to do good work in that field."

Many young people had come into Vienna to take training analysis, and here Anna had an opportunity for friendship and social activity. She had attended the theater with James and Alix Strachey; they took her as far as the Regina Hotel, then let her walk down the Berggasse alone. The next day Sigmund had berated them soundly for letting Anna come home alone at night. Strachey commented:

"That analytical hour was a fright!"

Occasionally she became friends with one of Sigmund's patients, though not until the analysis had been concluded. One of these was an American woman by the name of Dorothy Burlingham, married and with several children, who had crossed the Atlantic seeking help from Professor Freud. She became so attached to Vienna and to the Freuds that she rented an apartment upstairs at Berggasse 19. She helped Anna in opening a school for children, where Anna could test her burgeoning theories on the very young. They took a weekend farm cottage together in the country at Hochroterd, about forty-five minutes by car from Vienna. Sigmund sometimes went to visit them during the summer months.

There was a book he had been wanting to write under the title The Man Moses, a Historical Novel, a book which would give him leeway to speculate. Years before he had written a short piece about

Michelangelo's Moses. Moses had long fascinated him, the man whose legendary origin coincided with that of so many mythical leaders of religions and dynasties, as Otto Rank had pointed out in *The Myth of the Birth of the Hero*. He had no desire to deprive his people of a man in whom they took pride as the greatest of their sons. He agreed with the historians that Moses was a real person who led an exodus out of Egypt in the thirteenth or fourteenth century before Christ. But was Moses truly a Hebrew, or was he an Egyptian? The name was Egyptian, not Hebrew.

If there were even the faintest possibility of Moses being an Egyptian, why would he have deserted his own people and led a foreign people out of a crumbling Egyptian dynasty? Could it have been that he was a follower of the Aten religion, which had been formed in an earlier dynasty by Akhenaten, who preached strict monotheism, truth and justice as the highest aim in life, which banished ceremony and magic? The Aten religion had been destroyed by later Pharaohs; if Moses wished to preserve it somewhere in the world, where could he turn better than to a minority group, lead them out of their bondage and re-create for them the religion of Aten with which, Sigmund reflected, "the later Jewish religion agrees in some remarkable respects"?

Sigmund knew that he was on tenuous ground. He put the manuscript away for long periods, yet the question continued to intrigue him.

He had always enjoyed his extensive correspondence. In the days of his pariahdom it had been his chief encouragement. Now that he entertained few guests and was handling only three training analysands a day, he had ample time and energy for the writing of his letters. He wrote to Arnold Zweig, whose novel, *The Case of Sergeant Grischa*, he admired:

"I still have so much capacity for enjoyment that I am dissatisfied with the resignation that is forced upon me. It is a bitter winter here in Vienna and I have not been out for months. I also find it hard to adapt myself to the role of the hero suffering for mankind, which you kindly assign me. My mood is bad, little pleases me, my self-criticism has grown much more acute. I would diagnose it as senile depression in anyone else. I see a cloud of disaster passing over the world, even over my own little world. I must remind myself of the one bright spot, and that is that my daughter Anna is making such excellent analytic discoveries just now and, they all tell me, is delivering masterly lectures on them. An admonition therefore not to believe that the world will end with my death."

Equally enjoyable was the kind of letter that came from Albert Einstein, now safely ensconced at Princeton University:

Verehrter Herr Freud:
I am happy that this generation has the good fortune to have the opportunity of expressing their respect and gratitude to you as

one of its greatest teachers. You have undoubtedly not made it easy for the skeptical laity to come to an independent judgment. Until recently I could only apprehend the speculative power of your train of thought, together with its enormous influence on the *Weltanschaung* of the present era, without being in a position to form a definite opinion about the amount of truth it contains. Not long ago, however, I had the opportunity of hearing about a few instances, not very important in themselves, which in my judgment exclude any other interpretation than that provided by the theory of repression. I was delighted to come across them; since it is always delightful when a great and beautiful conception proves to be consonant with reality.

As he plowed painfully toward eighty, missing so many friends now dead, he came to the point in his life where he was able to forgive his detractors, past and present. Only one infection remained. Edouard Pichon, Pierre Janet's son-in-law, friendly to Sigmund, wrote to ask if Janet might visit him. From the beginning Janet had been a consistent and severe critic of psychoanalysis. Freud wrote to Marie Bonaparte:

"No, I will not see Janet. I could not refrain from reproaching him with having behaved unfairly to psychoanalysis and also to me personally and having never corrected it. He was stupid enough to say that the idea of a sexual etiology for the neuroses could only arise in the atmosphere of a town like Vienna. Then when the libel was spread by French writers that I had listened to his lectures and stolen his ideas he could with a word have put an end to such talk, since actually I never saw him or heard his name in the Charcot time: he has never spoken this word."

He had reached the age of recapitulation, when a man tends to look backward over his eighty years on earth to make a summation of his failures and accomplishments. The cancer of his mouth had returned; there would have to be more drastic operations. But had he not survived almost thirty operations and thirteen years of life and work since that dread announcement in Dr. Pichler's office? There had been times when he had not believed that he could endure another hour of the agonizing pain; yet to this very day he was treating patients, training more young analysts, writing the third section of his book Moses and Monotheism. His indestructible love of life had enabled him to stave off death. He would have scoffed at the word, but there were those among his friends and followers who declared it a "heroic" accomplishment. He had also managed to preserve his sense of humor. When a woman caller inquired about his health, he replied:

"How a man of eighty feels is not a topic for conversation."

Psychoanalysis was still not included in the curricula of the Austrian

medical schools, yet every university used his books and a whole generation was being raised on them. The *Introductory Lectures on Psychoanalysis*, in a Russian translation, was selling thousands of copies in
Moscow. It had long been charged that psychoanalysis, if true at all,
could apply only to Western man, yet not too long before he had
held in his hands a considerable number of his books translated into
Japanese. The Freudian psychology of the unconscious was spreading
through Asia. It was a gratifying thought.

A whole decade of novels in the 1920s had been based on the
stream-of-consciousness which had evolved from his own therapeutic
method of free association. Dramatist Eugene O'Neill's play *Strange
Interlude* was world-famous; it was completely Freudian. As was the
actor John Barrymore's new interpretation of *Hamlet*.

His name had entered the language. How small would a city have
to be in which, during the course of a day, someone did not exclaim:
"That's a Freudian slip!"

He had changed man's way of thinking about himself. One was
no longer obliged to be ignorant about the forces at play in human
nature. Yet there were certain kinds of mentalities which he had failed
to reach, those who still felt that investigation into the sexual nature of
man was immoral and degrading. He wondered if these people could
ever be reached.

He had not completed his work in many areas where he had started
it. He consoled himself with the saying from the Old Testament: "It
is not for you to complete the work, but neither are you free to
refrain from it." There were people coming behind him whose researches
were creating substantive knowledge in these fields.

He had made his errors, acknowledged them and gone forward. There
were still misconceptions, half-truths, false leads in what would come
to twenty-three sizable volumes of his writings when they were all
retranslated and published in England; but ah! the young people he
had trained, physician and layman alike: how many of them were there,
at this last count? They would go beyond his mistakes and shortcomings,
modify and change psychology in ways inconceivable to him, sitting in his
study at Berggasse 19 in the year 1936. It was not necessary for everything he had written to stand as gospel. Had he not said in many of his
volumes, on sociology, anthropology, history, that he was speculating on
the available evidence? His methods of psychotherapy would change too;
already schools were springing up which advocated short analysis, group
analysis, personal, adjust-to-society-and-you-will-be-well analysis.

Yet he was convinced that the body of his findings about the
unconscious mind and psychoanalytical theory was sound, and would
remain intact. After all of the mutations which would be sure to spring
up in the decades to come, at least eighty percent of his work would

stand as inescapable, viable, even for those burgeoning analysts in revolt against the father figure, who were determined to start their own, different, independent branches of therapy. What scientist would not be pleased to achieve positive results of eighty percent in his laboratory researches? The other twenty percent would be made right by younger minds, starting where he had left off.

Looking back from the vantage point of the years, he realized that his life had come full circle. The early criticism that his conclusions applied only to middle-class Viennese Jews in a particular period of history could no longer be made with any pretext of seriousness, for his discoveries of the unconscious mind were being documented in nearly every country of the world, among all races, religions, classes, cultures, creeds, educational levels.

Most rewarding was the address Thomas Mann had written and delivered before the Academic Society for Psychological Medicine on his eightieth birthday. Mann had come to their summer villa in Grinzing to see Professor Freud, and read to him a second similar address which had been signed by two hundred of the foremost artists and writers of the world: H. G. Wells, Romain Rolland, Jules Romains, Virginia Woolf, Stefan Zweig . . .

"The eightieth birthday of Sigmund Freud gives us a welcome opportunity to convey to the pioneer of a new and deeper knowledge of man our congratulation and our veneration. In every important sphere of his activity, as physician and psychologist, as philosopher and artist, this courageous seer and healer has for two generations been a guide to hitherto undreamed-of regions of the human soul. An independent spirit, 'a man and knight, grim and stern of visage' as Nietzsche said of Schopenhauer, a thinker and investigator who knew how to stand alone and then drew many to him and with him, he went his way and penetrated to truths which seemed dangerous because they revealed what had been anxiously hidden, and illumined dark places. Far and wide he disclosed new problems and changed the old standards; in his seeking and perceiving he extended many times the field of mental research, and made even his opponents indebted to him through the creative stimulus they derived from him. Even should the future remold and modify one result or another of his researches, never again will the questions be stilled which Sigmund Freud put to mankind; his gains for knowledge cannot permanently be denied or obscured. The conceptions he built, the words he chose for them, have already entered the living language and are taken for granted. In all spheres of humane science, in the study of literature and art, in the evolution of religion and prehistory, mythology, folklore and pedagogics, and last not least in poetry itself his achievement has left a deep mark; and, we feel sure, if any deed of our race remains unforgotten it will be his deed of penetrating into the depths of the human mind."

The summation Sigmund liked best was the one written by the ever faithful Eugen Bleuler from Zurich. He rummaged in his files, found the letter and read the closing lines:

"Anyone who would try to understand neurology or psychiatry without possessing a knowledge of psychoanalysis would seem to me like a dinosaur. I say 'would seem' not 'seems,' for there no longer are such people, even among those who enjoy depreciating psychoanalysis!"

Smiling was difficult. Sigmund laughed inwardly.

He had begun by telling Martha, during their courtship, that he had no need to carve his name on a rock. That had been what Ernest Jones would later call a "rationalization." At just about the age at which his father Jakob had died, he was willing to admit with a whimsical smile that that need had been one of the dominating elements in his nature. He had carved the name of Freud on a rock, one which might become slightly worn about the edges by nature's hailstorms and the pickaxes of assailants; but which in its basic structure would weather the ages.

13.

As late as March 1938, Sigmund still felt secure in Vienna, for Chancellor Schuschnigg was a strong leader and a dedicated Austrian who had held out against both the threats and blandishments of Adolf Hitler. He had decreed that a plebiscite be held to determine whether the Republic of Austria should join the Third Reich. While Sigmund knew that a good portion of the Austrian youth had become infatuated with the uniforms, parades, slogans of the Nazis, it was his opinion, shared by middle-class Vienna, that in the plebiscite the Austrians would reject *Anschluss* and maintain their independence.

The plebiscite was never allowed to take place.

On March 11, 1938, the German army invaded and took possession of Austria. German planes seized the airports. Vienna crawled with Nazi tanks. Long concealed Austrian Nazis swarmed through the streets in brown shirts with swastika armbands.

The Board of the Vienna Psychoanalytic Society was dissolved. It was agreed that everyone who could should flee. Sigmund had been urged for several years to leave Vienna and take refuge with long-time friends in France, Holland, Sweden, England, the United States. He had refused. He wrote to a friend that he considered it inconceivable that the Nazis would not honor the Versailles Treaty rules on the rights of minorities. Were not the Jews a minority, even though not the kind of political minority specified by the treaty?

The following Sunday he learned differently. The doorbell rang insistently. There stood a uniformed and armed squad of the Storm Troopers, the S.A. They rushed into the apartment, leaving a guard standing just inside the open door so that no one could escape. Martha watched the S.A. man nervously lifting and then dropping the butt of his rifle against the parquet floor of her foyer. She said firmly:

"Please be so kind as to rest your gun in the umbrella stand!"

The Nazi was so startled that he did as he was directed.

The other S.A. men had made their way into the dining room. Martha followed, unruffled.

"Won't the gentlemen be seated?"

They were embarrassed but only shifted from one foot to another.

Martha asked, "For what purpose have you come to our home?"

After a moment one of them muttered, "We are ordered to confiscate all alien funds."

Martha went into the kitchen, got her week's household money and placed the bills in the center of the dining-room table, then said in the same High German with which she had greeted her husband's guests for half a century:

"Won't the gentlemen help themselves?"

The S.A. men scowled; it was not a large enough sum to be divided decently. Anna sensed their anger. She asked the men to accompany her to a safe in another room. She opened it. The S.A. men went through hurriedly, emerging with six thousand schillings ($840). Sigmund, who heard their loud voices counting the money, came out of his study, a frail man whom any gust of wind could blow away. The young Nazis blanched under the fire of his gaze. They quickly left.

"What did they want?" he asked Martha.

"Money."

"How much did they get?"

"Six thousand Austrian schillings."

"That's more than I ever got for a single visit."

Martin Freud arrived, accompanied by Ernest Jones. The Freuds had not known he was in Vienna. Martin looked as though he had been put through a wringer. He had been working on the accounts at the Verlag when a gang of young Austrians, armed and calling themselves Nazis, had taken over his offices, put him under arrest, taken the contents of the cashbox and threatened to burn all the books he had in stock. At this moment Ernest Jones stumbled in, having been urged over the long-distance telephone by Dorothy Burlingham in Vienna and Marie Bonaparte in Paris to rescue Freud and his family before it was too late. Jones too had been placed under arrest, until a Nazi officer in uniform had arrived and dismissed the young bravoes.

The family made no further comment on the invasion of their household. Martin and Jones were given something to eat, then Jones asked Sigmund in an undertone if he could speak to him alone. They went through Anna's corner room overlooking the Berggasse, and then through Sigmund's medical suite to his study at the rear where the two men had been holding private conversations for the past thirty years.

"Professor Freud, there were moments on that wild dash from London to Prague, and then in a small monoplane, when I thought I would never reach Vienna to make my plea. You must see, after what happened today, that you must leave Vienna with your family as quickly as possible. Thousands of Viennese are on the sidewalks shouting, 'Heil Hitler!'"

"I hear them. How can you not?"

"Then you know that you must get out."

"No, my place is here."

"But, my dear Professor, you are not alone in the world," Ernest Jones cried in anguish. "Your life is dear to many people."

"Alone! Ah, if I were only alone. I am too weak to travel. I couldn't even climb up to a compartment on a continental train."

"No need. We'll carry you."

"But no country will allow me to enter; and certainly not to work."

"Marie Bonaparte can get you a visa for France; though you will not be allowed to practice there. England is the logical place; we have wanted you for years. I have confidence that my government will welcome you, and permit you to practice."

"I cannot leave my native land. It would be the equivalent of a soldier deserting his post."

"Professor, have you heard the story about the officer of the *Titanic* who was blown to the surface when a boiler exploded? He was asked, 'At which moment did you leave the ship?' He replied proudly, 'I never left the ship, sir; she left me.'"

A glint of a smile came into Sigmund's somber eyes.

"I'll think about it. Thank you, dear friend."

Marie Bonaparte arrived from Paris, just as determined as Ernest Jones to get the Freud family out of Austria. Jones returned to London to plead for the necessary permits.

A week later a group of S.S. arrived, older men and more determined. They searched every nook and cranny of the house, declaring that they were looking for "subversive literature." Sigmund and Martha sat silent and motionless, side by side on the velours sofa, while the Nazis continued their systematic search. They found nothing they wanted to take away with them . . . except Anna Freud.

"What is the meaning of this?" Sigmund cried. "Why are you taking my daughter? And where to?"

"Hotel Metropol. We wish to ask her some questions."

"Hotel Metropol," Martha whispered, "that's Gestapo headquarters!"

"My daughter knows nothing that can be of interest to you," Sigmund cried. "If you are seeking information, I am the only one who can provide it. I volunteer to come with you."

The Nazi officer bowed stiffly, replied:

"We have orders to arrest your daughter."

Anna tried to comfort them with her calm gaze as she left the apartment, an S.S. man on either side of her.

Martha was pale but she did not weep, despite the fact that it was known that Viennese Jews who had been arrested and taken to Gestapo headquarters had been physically abused, many of them shipped out, nameless, to labor camps. This could happen to Anna; they could torture her, send her that night to a concentration camp from which she would never return.

"Is it possible that I have murdered my own daughter?" Sigmund demanded, puffing furiously at his cigar while attempting to disguise his agitation from Martha. "I've been stupid, willful . . .

"Everyone else has fled, with their families, all who had any chance of getting out. But not me! I would not desert my post. But why was I not thinking of Anna and Martin! We are old, Martha. Minna is old. My sisters are old. It doesn't matter what happens to us. But Anna and Martin have their lives before them.

"What was there left for me to desert? Why did I not oblige Anna and Martin to join Oliver and Ernst, where they would have been safe? My God, what have I done to my daughter? What will they do to her at the Gestapo?"

All of his operations put together had not caused him this much anguish. He went through the agonies of the damned, minute by minute as the hours ate themselves up in excruciating slowness. When the phone rang he ran to it, held the receiver in trembling hands. It was the American Chargé d'Affaires, a Mr. Wiley, who had come to offer his services the Sunday before when he learned that the Nazis had invaded the Freud home.

"Professor Freud, I learned of your daughter's arrest, and immediately made an official call of protest. I managed to reach an officer of rank. I believe he took my protest seriously. You may be sure that I will continue until your daughter is released."

The hours crawled by on their hands and knees. Sigmund roamed from room to room, trying to deaden his dread by smoking a chain of cigars. The house was as silent as a morgue at midnight. No one tried to comfort anyone else. What was there to say? All they could do was pray, and listen for the moment when they would hear Anna's footstep on the outside stairs.

Midafternoon came, four o'clock, five . . . still no word, no sign. Sigmund told himself:

"If I lose Anna, if she is harmed, or deported, it will be the end of the world for me. And I alone will have brought this dreadful ending upon our family."

Darkness brought terror. No one lighted a lamp. Coffee was brought in. No one touched it. Sigmund's remaining strength was spent. Martha stood up best under the strain, but this was one time she could not help her husband. Martin arrived, charged from room to room like a caged tiger.

Then at last there was Anna, letting herself in with her house key. All eyes turned to her. She walked into the room, said:

"I am all right."

The American Chargé d'Affaires had helped; but in the last analysis it was Anna's acute observation and good sense that had saved her. She knew that all those arrested who were not questioned during the day were swept out as so much human offal at night, to be placed in trucks, and then freight cars, and taken away to an unknown destination. She had not allowed this to happen to her. She had made her presence felt. She had insisted upon being interrogated. They had finally questioned her for an hour or more, then released her.

Sigmund cried, "Thank God, you are safe. Tomorrow we start our preparations to leave Vienna!"

Ernest Jones worked indefatigably in London to secure British visas and work permits. Refugees were not welcome in England during this unfortunate period; their support had to be guaranteed by British citizens, and work permits were almost unknown. Jones went directly to the Royal Society, which had honored Sigmund Freud two years before; the Royal Society rarely interfered in political matters. Sir William Bragg, world-famous physicist and president of the Society, pledged his support and gave Jones a letter of introduction to the Home Secretary, Sir Samuel Hoare. Jones pleaded the Freud case brilliantly; in the middle of his presentation he realized that the Home Secretary was sympathetic to his every word. He gave Jones carte blanche to fill in permits for Professor Freud, his family, doctor, all those necessary for his well-being.

Now came the critical time. Three months spun themselves out, three months of frustration and anxiety because the Nazis would not release their most famous hostage. Sigmund spent his days answering correspondence, writing the third section of Moses and Monotheism, translating, with Anna's help, Marie Bonaparte's book about her chow Topsy.

Professor Freud had become a *cause célèbre*. The Nazis seized his bank accounts, confiscated all the books at the *Verlag*, obliged Martin to bring back publications and money he had deposited safely in Switzerland. The American Ambassador in Paris, William C. Bullitt, asked President Franklin D. Roosevelt to intercede on Sigmund Freud's behalf. President Roosevelt complied. Ambassador Bullitt urged the German Ambassador in Paris to secure the necessary papers. Benito Mussolini, to whom Sigmund had once sent an autographed copy of one of his books at the request of an Italian patient's father, made a direct request of Hitler to let the Freuds depart from Vienna.

Tante Minna was in a sanatorium, having been operated on for cataracts of the eyes. Dorothy Burlingham, who had an American passport, managed to take her to London.

Martin escaped to join his wife and children in Paris.

Mathilde and Robert Hollitscher fled to England ten days later.

Harry Freud, Alexander's son, had seen the swastika on the wall a lot earlier than the older generation. After failing to convince his parents, he had managed what appeared to be a routine business trip to Switzerland. His cousin in New York, Edward Bernays, was generously making it possible for Harry to come to America. The Gestapo came to Alexander's apartment to arrest Harry. Alexander saw the light. He appointed a prominent Nazi lawyer who was also a member of the S.S. as his trustee, turning over to him their considerable savings on the condition that he secure for them the necessary passports and visas. The exit permits came through in May. They came to the Berggasse to bid good-by to Sigmund and the family. The farewells were quiet, everyone saying that they would meet soon in London.

"Next year in Jerusalem," Sigmund murmured to Martha as he stood at the front window, watching Alexander and Sophie get into a taxi that would take them to the railroad station, carrying only a small bag and the clothes on their backs.

Though Sigmund had been unwilling to help himself, he was able to rescue a number of friends and colleagues. The widow of Josef Breuer's oldest son came to report that she and her daughter were about to be arrested. Sigmund got A. A. Brill in New York to secure American visas. He helped Theodor Reik and his family secure visas for the United States, where Helene and Felix Deutsch had already gone, as well as Max Graf, Franz Alexander, Karen Horney. When Theodor Rik came to say good-by, Sigmund put his arm about Reik's shoulder.

"I've always liked you," he said. Reik bowed his head, unable to speak. Sigmund continued in a low voice, "People do not need to be glued together when they belong together."

A story originated in Boston and spread over the United States, that Sigmund was being held for ransom. Funds began to be collected. Sigmund sent out word through a reporter that the story was not true.

In essence it was true: the Nazis were demanding a sum of $4824 in taxes, the nature of which no one was able to explain. Princess Marie Bonaparte, who had been working through her connections with the French and Greek governments to secure the Freuds' release, promptly paid the sum in cash.

That appeared to be the last obstacle. An officer arrived at the Berggasse apartment with a formal document in his dispatch case.

"Professor Freud, you have only to sign this release paper, and exit visas will be granted for your family and associates. It merely states that since the *Anschluss* of Austria to the German Reich you have been treated by the German authorities, and particularly by the Gestapo, with all of the respect and consideration due to your scientific reputation."

Sigmund scanned the sheet, said with a smile more twisted than his paralyzed right cheek made necessary:

"I will gladly sign it, providing I may add a sentence."

"If that is your wish, Herr Professor."

Under his signature, Sigmund wrote:

"I can heartily recommend the Gestapo to anyone."

On June 4, 1938, they took the Orient Express westward through Austria and Germany, crossing the Rhine at three in the morning at Kehl, just below Strassburg. They had a compartment to themselves, Sigmund, Martha, Anna and two domestics who had been with them for years. Ernest Jones had also secured entry permits for Dr. Max Schur and his wife Helen. Dr. Schur went down with appendicitis, and Helen Schur remained behind to care for him. At the last moment they were able to secure an exit visa for a friend of Anna's, Dr. Josephine Stross, to care for Sigmund on the journey.

No one in the Freud compartment attempted to sleep. The German border guards were wide awake and coolly efficient at three in the morning. Every last paper was triple checked. As the train crossed the Rhine, Sigmund sighed, exchanged relieved glances with his wife and daughter. The French officials on the other side were much less ceremonious; the Freud party had only transit visas across France, which the officers stamped, and then bade the Freuds a courteous good night. Now, safe but exhausted physically and emotionally from the strain, Sigmund fell asleep.

They reached Paris in the morning. Ernst was waiting for them, having crossed from England to escort them on the last leg of the journey. Marie Bonaparte was there, with a car and driver. Ambassador William C. Bullitt was in the welcoming group, a smile on his face at the happy outcome of his efforts. Harry Freud had come to Paris to welcome them, and to assure them that his parents would soon join the family in

London, where Mathilde and Robert Hollitscher had set up a home for them.

Marie Bonaparte took everyone home with her. They bathed away the night's grime from the long train ride, then sat down to a cheering breakfast in the dining room of the Bonaparte palace. They sat on the roof garden in the warm and friendly French sun. Marie Bonaparte came to them, hiding something behind her back.

"See what I purloined from your study the last time I left the Berggasse. This exquisite Athene. I've always known it was one of your favorites. Now you can take her to England and entrench her on your work desk."

Sigmund took the Athene in his hands, gently caressing it as he had so many times before.

"Thank you, dear friend. Now we shall live under her protection. She will have to represent my lifetime collection, lost now, lost forever."

"Don't imagine it!" cried Marie Bonaparte. "My people in Vienna have rescued a part of it. And a portion of your library as well, not to mention your manuscripts. They may have to be shipped to the Greek Embassy in London; but when you start work again in London, you will be surrounded by the memorabilia of your life."

Sigmund and his family spent a golden day in the Bonaparte home. "Surrounded," Sigmund said, "by love for twelve hours." That night they took the ferry across the English Channel. A sense of peace and calm engulfed him; the day in Paris had restored his sense of dignity.

In the morning they disembarked at Dover. Sigmund let the rest of his party go ahead. He gazed at the white cliffs, his mind flashing a long way backwards as he remembered his visit to England when he had been a boy of nineteen. He thought:

"Here I shall die in freedom."

He turned, walked as close as he could to the water's edge, stood gazing across the Channel. In his mind's eye he made the journey eastward across France, Germany, Austria, until he came home. Vienna.

ACKNOWLEDGMENTS

This book involved six years of uninterrupted research and writing, yet the road was lighted at every turn by the kindness and generosity of almost everyone who had known Sigmund Freud or worked with him.

Mrs. Katherine Jones gave a number of days to the recounting of Ernest Jones's life story; and permitted me to use the unpublished letters of Sigmund Freud to Jones. Dr. Hilda Abraham, with Mrs. Karl Abraham helping, sketched Dr. Karl Abraham's background, and afforded me unpublished materials about Karl Abraham's life. Harry Freud, Sigmund Freud's nephew, wrote a thirty-page biography about his father, Alexander. Dr. Max Schur, Freud's personal physician for the last eleven years of his life, helped me to insights that would not otherwise have been possible. Dr. Helen Schur kindly made available to me portions of Max Schur's unpublished manuscript *Freud: Living and Dying*.

James and Alix Strachey were a mine of information about Freud's personal and professional life. Edward L. Bernays was magnificently helpful about his parents, Anna Bernays, Freud's sister, and Eli Bernays, Martha Freud's brother. Mr. and Mrs. Heinrich Schnitzler allowed me access to Arthur Schnitzler's then unpublished autobiography. Dr. Michael Balint made available character materials from his still unpublished *Life and Letters of Sandor Ferenczi*, and Mrs. Carl Furtmüller from her husband's unpublished biography of Alfred Adler. Dr. Richard Friedenthal supplied me with a set of unpublished letters between Freud and Stefan Zweig.

It is impossible to speak too highly of the Jung family in Zurich. Franz Jung, Carl Jung's son, and his wife welcomed me at Küsnacht and at Bollingen as well. Franz Jung gave me background personality portraits of his father that had not been made public before. Jung's disciples, in Zurich, Mrs. Aniela Jaffé, Dr. Jolande Jacobi and Dr. Marie-Louise von Franz, afforded me invaluable material on Jung's professional life and talents. I was also permitted to read a considerable portion of the Freud-Jung letters, now being prepared for publication.

It was my good fortune to be able to work with men whom Sigmund Freud liked and admired: Heinz Hartmann, Theodor Reik, Edward Glover, Franz Alexander, Edoardo Weiss. Anna Freud permitted me to visit the Freud home in Maresfield Gardens in London, so that I was able to see part of Sigmund Freud's library and collection of antique figures. Ernst

Freud kindly mapped my journey through Bavaria and Austria, so that I could locate the villas and hotels where the Freud family spent its summer vacations.

At the Allgemeine Krankenhaus in Vienna I am deeply indebted to the director, Dr. Franz Ritschl, Oberamtsrat Hans Denk and to Oberamtsrat Bernhard Grois. The Institute für Geschichte der Medizin an der Universität Wien was indispensable, particularly the director, Frau Prof. Erna Lesky; also Dr. Karl Sablik and Dr. Hilde Dönt; at the Neurologische Abteilung der Allgemeinen Poliklinik der Stadt Wien, Prof. Dr. Viktor E. Frankl; at the Psychiatrische-neurologische Klinik Prof. Hans Hoff, Prof. Dr. Josef Quatember, Dr. O. H. Arnold, Doz. H. Tschabitscher, Dr. E. Ringel, Doz. Dr. W. Spiel; at the Austro-American Institute of Education, Franz Dolezal, Gloria Grimus von Grimburg, Siegfried F. Richter, director.

In Vienna I am also indebted to Dr. Franz Patzer at the Kultor Büro; Amtsrat Johann Raitmar at the Police Archives; Dr. Josef Vass and Dr. Karl Gladt at the Stadtbibliothek; Prof. Dr. Leopold Mazakarini at the University of Vienna. At Berggasse 19 I am indebted to Hans Pfeifer for permitting me to make detailed sketches of the Freud apartment; as well as to Alois Henkel for the apartment which was Freud's medical suite; to Dr. Hans Kultur and Elsebeth Bisanz at the Historisches Museum der Stadt Wien; and to Frau Dr. August Aichhorn, for permitting me to copy the set of photographs of Sigmund Freud and his work quarters; to Frau Renée Gicklhorn, who provided me with documents on some disputed points in the Freud story. Others who helped are Prof. Franz Brücke, who provided me with material about Freud's beloved teacher, Prof. Ernst Brücke; Mr. Bacher; Ernst Beer; Joseph A. Gasser; Dr. Hofer; Rudolf Karin; Dr. Arthur Kline; Reg.-Rat Wilhelm Krell; Mrs. Inge Zimmer-Lehmann; Ann Tizia Leitich; Anastasyin Lohr; Dr. Jonny Moser; Mrs. Karl Nagel; Frau Prof. Annie Politzer; Prim. Dr. Wilhelm Podhajsky; Brian and Ruth Sadelson; Gertrude Sandner; Mr. and Mrs. Karl Seitz; Brigitte Silberbauer-Haffner; Nada Skerly; Doz. Dr. Wilhelm Solms-Roedelheim; Mrs. Rosetta Spalt; Hilde Spiel; Prof. Otto Stradal; Frau A. Urell; Hofrat Arnold Večer; Hans Wickenburg.

In England I am particularly indebted to Masud Khan, as well as Gerhard Adler; Dr. J. Bowlby; Dr. W. H. Gillespie; Dr. Willi Hoffer; Miss H. Shiehan-Dare; Prof. E. Stengel; Dr. H. A. Thorner; Kathleen Wacher; Dr. D. W. Winnicott. The Hogarth Press and the Institute of Psychoanalysis kindly gave me permission to quote from their twenty-three-volume Standard Edition of the *Complete Psychological Works* of Sigmund Freud.

In Paris I was enabled to work at the Hôpital de la Salpêtrière by Prof. Dr. P. Castaigne. Madame François Mauriac, whose family bought the Charcot home, made available her memories and photographs of the house and garden. Princess Eugénie of Greece made me welcome in the family home in St. Cloud, where Marie Bonaparte was born and raised.

In Nancy, Dr. Dominique Barrucand enabled me to work at the hospital where Dr. Hippolyte Bernheim had performed his experiments, and took me to the home of Dr. Ambroise-Auguste Liébeault. Mademoiselle G. Koest at the Bibliothèque de l'Université, Section "Médecine," in Nancy helped me secure copies of unpublished materials on Drs. Bernheim and Liébeault.

In Zurich, Prof. Manfred Bleuler acquainted me with the Cantonale Heilanstalt Burghölzli, as well as providing biographical and professional materials about his father. I was also helped there by Dr. Ambrosius Uchterhagen, Dr. Alfonse Maeder, Thilde Dinkelkamp and Martha Sennhauser. At the Medizinhistorisches Institut der Universität Zürich I was assisted by Prof. Dr. Erwin Ackerknecht. Also in Zurich there was help from Wolfgang Binswanger, Barbara Hannah, Mr. and Mrs. James Hillman, Dr. C. A. Meier, Hilda Procter, Dr. Schwöbel and Leon Steinig.

I have been particularly fortunate with the medical profession in Southern California. Dr. Milton Heifetz was my consultant on neurology and brain anatomy, and also read manuscript. Dr. Marcus Rabwin taught me what I needed to know about general surgery; Dr. Samuel L. Perzik, jaw and mouth surgery; Dr. Theodore Massell, medical history. Dr. Hilda Rollman-Branch was my psychoanalytical consultant from the beginning; she also read manuscript. Dr. Martin Grotjahn and Dr. Malvin Braverman rescued me when I needed assistance on technical aspects of psychoanalysis. Help in Southern California came from Dr. Peter Amacher, medical historian, of the U.C.L.A. Bio-Medical Library; Dr. Judd Marmor; Dr. Sheldon Selesnick; Dr. Emil Krahulik; Dr. and Mrs. Paul Koretz; Mrs. Alfred Zinner; Austrian Consul-General and Mrs. Thomas Klestil; Henry Seldis, Los Angeles *Times* art editor; Mrs. Olga Shnearer.

For assistance in New York I want to express my appreciation to F. Thomas Heller; Edmund Engelman; William McQuire of the Bollingen Foundation; James W. Montgomery and Dr. Lothar Gidro-Frank of the New York State Psychiatric Institute; Dr. Phillip Polatin of the Columbia-Presbyterian Medical Center; Prof. Ernst Simon; Dr. and Mrs. Emery Wells. In Chicago to Dr. George H. Pollock of The Institute of Psychoanalysis; Dr. Bina Rosenberg; the University of Chicago Press for the right to use the translation of *Oedipus Rex*; Dr. Lewis F. Wheelock, director of the Museum and Archives of the Menninger Foundation. In Detroit, to Dr. Alexander Grinstein for the manuscript of his book *On Sigmund Freud's Dreams*. Also to Dr. Lawrence S. Kubie in Maryland; Mrs. Marie K. Chaffee in Massachusetts; Hans W. Hannau in Florida.

My wife, Jean Stone, was the editor on the entire project. Her efforts in Vienna, Zurich and London to secure unpublished and usually unavailable research materials was little short of heroic. Without her superb editing and polishing of the manuscript, which occupied the best part of her time for four years, this book would have been twice as long and half as readable.

GLOSSARY OF PSYCHOANALYTIC TERMS

All definitions are from *Psychiatric Dictionary* (Leland E. Hinsie, M.D., and Robert J. Campbell, M.D., Oxford University Press, 1960), except when otherwise noted, or without quote marks.

ABREACTION: The bringing to consciousness and expression of material which had been repressed in the unconscious.

AFFECT: "The feeling-tone accompaniment of an idea or mental representation."

AMBIVALENCE: "Bipolarity; the co-existence of antithetic emotions, attitudes, ideas, or wishes toward a given object or situation. The term was coined by Bleuler, who differentiated between affective or emotional ambivalence, intellectual ambivalence, and ambivalence of the will. In current usage, the term ambivalence without further qualification ordinarily refers to affective ambivalence."

AMENTIA: "Subnormal development of the mind, with particular reference to intellectual capacities. . . . Its synonyms are: feeblemindedness, mental deficiency, intellectual inadequacy. . . . Amentia implies intellectual incapacity prevalent from birth or from the early months of life."

ANAL EROTICISM: "According to psychoanalytic formulations, during the infancy period, libido spreads diffusely over the body, but certain areas, known as erotogenic zones, take up a large quantity of libido. Three such zones merit special consideration: the oral, anal, and genital. The earliest concentration of libido is in the oral zone; with further development most of the oral libido shifts to the anal region, which in turn gives up a fair portion of its libido to the third or genital area. The localization of libido in the anal zone is known as anal eroticism."

ANESTHESIA: "Absence of sensation. Any organ of the body, including the skin, may suffer loss of sensibility; anesthesia may be occasioned by organic or by psychic causes."

ANOREXIA: Loathing for food. "Loss of appetite."

ANXIETY: "An affect which differs from other affects in its specific unpleasurable character. Anxiety consists of a somatic, physiological side (disturbed breathing, increased heart activity, vasomotor changes, musculoskeletal disturbances such as trembling or paralysis, increased sweating, etc.) and of a psychological side (perceptions of specific unpleasurable feelings and sensations, apprehension, etc.). Anxiety is to be differentiated from fear; the latter is a reaction to a real or threatened danger, while anxiety is more typically a reaction to an unreal or imagined danger. Freud's earlier view was that anxiety arises by transformation of libido which cannot otherwise be discharged. He later abandoned this view and came to believe that anxiety arises automatically whenever the psyche is overwhelmed by an influx of stimuli too great to be mastered or discharged."

ANXIETY NEUROSIS: "In 1894, Freud detached the particular syndrome of anxiety-neurosis from neurasthenia and described the clinical characteristics of anxiety-neurosis as: general irritability, anxious expectation and pangs of conscience, the anxiety-attack, and phobias."

"Neurotic anxiety is anxiety in regard to a danger which we do not know." (Freud: Dictionary of Psychoanalysis, Nandor Fodor and Frank Gaynor, eds., Philosophical Library, 1950.)

APHASIA: "A general term for all disturbances of language due to brain lesions but not a result of faulty innervation of the speech muscles, involvement of the organs of articulation, or general mental or intellectual deficiency. The word, language, as used in this definition, refers not only to the expression or communication of thought by word, writing, and gesture, but also to the retention, recall, and visualization of the symbols involved."

BILATERALISM: "The condition of having the right and left sides, as of the body, counterparts one of the other." (Webster's.)

BISEXUALITY: "The presence of the qualities of both sexes in the same individual."

CASTRATION: "In its original and broadest biological sense, this term simply means the surgical operation of removing the sex organs (gonads) which are essential to reproduction as well as to the development of the secondary sex characters, that is, the ovaries in the female or the testes in the male. . . . In psychological medicine castration implies the penis alone."

CASTRATION ANXIETY: "A male child commonly suffers from anxiety lest his father rob him of his male member; and so castration anxiety is one of the strongest influences on the development of his character, and decisive for his sexual tendencies later." (Freud: Dictionary of Psychoanalysis.)

CATHARSIS: Psychotherapy which brings repressed traumatic material into the conscious.

COITUS INTERRUPTUS: "Cessation of sexual intercourse before emission."

COMPULSION: "Action due to irresistible impulse. As a morbid phenomenon it is an act contrary to the conscious will of the subject at the time the act is performed."

CONVERSION: Transforming of an excitation into a somatic seizure.

"The term, taken from psychoanalysis, means in psychiatry the symbolic representation of a psychical conflict in terms of motor or sensory manifestations. The symbolization is the means by which repressed instinctual tendencies gain external expression; usually, as for instance in hysteria, the symbolization also contains the defense set up against the instinctual impulses."

DEFENSE: "The mental attribute or mechanism or dynamism, which serves to protect the individual against danger arising from his impulses or affects."

DEFENSE MECHANISM: "From the very outset the ego has to try to fulfill its task of acting as an intermediary between the id and the external world in the service of the pleasure principle, to protect the id from the dangers of the external world. . . . In this battle on two fronts . . . the ego makes use of various methods of fulfilling its task, i.e. to put it in general terms of avoiding danger, anxiety and unpleasure. We call these devices *defensive mechanisms*." (*Freud: Dictionary of Psychoanalysis.*)

DEMENTIA PRAECOX: "A term coined by Morel in 1857 to describe those psychoses ('vesania') with a poor prognosis, i.e. those ending in deterioration (dementia) and incurability. Praecox was meant to refer to the fact that the onset of the disorders was early in life—typically, in adolescence."

DISSOCIATION: The splitting of the content of consciousness.

EGO: In psychoanalytic psychology, the ego is that part of the psychic apparatus which is the mediator between the individual and reality. Its prime function is the perception of reality and adaptation to it."

"We recognize in man a psychical organization which is interpolated between his sensory stimuli and perception of his bodily needs on the one hand, and his motor activity on the other; and which mediates between them with a certain purpose. We call this organization his 'I' [Ego]." (*Freud: Dictionary of Psychoanalysis.*)

EJACULATIO PRAECOX: "The ejaculation of semen and seminal fluid during the act of preparation for sexual intercourse, i.e. before there is penetration."

ETIOLOGY: "The division of medical science relating to the cause of disease."

FANTASY: "From the psychiatric point of view this is the equivalent of *day-dream*, and in psychoanalysis, at times, also the equivalent of *night-dream*." The unreal, conjured up by a human mind, as opposed to reality.

FREE ASSOCIATION: "The trends of thought or chains of ideas which spontaneously arise when restraint and censorship upon logical thinking are removed and the individual orally reports everything that passes through his mind. This fundamental technique of modern psychoanalysis assumes that when relieved of the necessity of logical thinking and reporting verbally everything going through his mind, the individual will bring forward basic psychic material and thus make it available to analytical interpretation."

HYPNOTISM: "The theory and practice of inducing hypnosis or a state resembling sleep induced by psychical means."

ID: "The id, as a psychoanalytic formulation, is part of the energy system of the psyche. It is regarded as the reservoir of psychic energy or libido; it contains all phylogenetic acquisitions and is the source of instinctive energy. The pleasure-principle reigns supreme in it and has control over the erotic and thanatotic (death) instincts. The id resides in the unconscious, far removed from reality, to which the id pays no attention. The id recognizes only its own needs and does not itself undertake to modify its needs in any way. Modifications of id impulses are brought about through other agencies, the superego and ego."

INFANTILE SEXUALITY: "The expression *infantile sexuality* is common in psychoanalysis. It is maintained by psychoanalysts that 'this period of life, during which a certain degree of directly sexual pleasure is produced by the stimulation of various cutaneous areas (erotogenic zones), by the activity of certain biological impulses and as an accompanying excitation during many affective states, is designated by an expression introduced by Havelock Ellis as the period of auto-erotism.'"

INFERIORITY COMPLEX: "Inferiority, feeling of. By this term Adler indicates that through the whole period of development, the child possesses a feeling of inadequacy in its relation both to parents and the world at large."

LIBIDO: The energy with which instincts are endowed.

LOCALIZATION: "The doctrine of the localization of functional centers, as sight, smell, speech, etc. in the cerebrum." (Webster's.)

MANIA: "The principal characteristics of mania are expressed in three fields; of ideas, feelings, and motility. Each of the three shows pronounced exaggeration, in the sense that ideas are voluminous, feelings are intensely elevated, and there is marked psychomotor overactivity."

NARCISSISM: "The term first used by Näcke to indicate the form of auto-erotism characterized by self-love, often without genitality as an object. . . . In psychoanalytic psychology, narcissism is a stage in the development of object relationships in which the child's estimation of his capacities is heightened to the degree of omnipotence."

NEUROPSYCHOSIS OF DEFENSE: "In 1896 Freud wrote that 'in a short paper published in 1894 I included hysteria, obsessions, and certain cases of acute hallucinatory confusion under one heading as "Defense Neuro-Psychoses." I did this because one point of view showed itself as applying in common to all these affections: their symptoms arise through the psychical mechanism of (unconscious) defense, that is, through an attempt to repress an intolerable idea which was in painful opposition to the patient's ego.'"

NEUROSIS: "As used today, this term is interchangeable with the term psychoneurosis. At one time it was used to refer to any somatic disorder of the nerves (the present-day term for this meaning is neuropathy) or to any disorder of nerve function. In psychoanalytic terminology, neurosis often is used more broadly to include all psychical disorders; thus Freud spoke of actual neuroses (neurasthenia, including hypochondriasis, and anxiety-neurosis); transference or psychoneuroses (anxiety-hysteria, conversion-hysteria, obsessional and compulsive neurosis . . .); narcissistic neuroses (the schizophrenias and manic-depressive psychoses); and traumatic neuroses."

NOXA or SEXUAL NOXAE: "Any injurious agent, mental or physical."

OBSESSION: "An idea or an emotion (an impulse) that persists in the mind of an individual and cannot be gotten rid of by any conscious processes."

OEDIPAL SITUATION: "Freud states that, in all instances of neuroses, it is desirable to assume the existence of what he calls the *complete Oedipus*. The expression refers to the simultaneous presence of both a positive and a negative (or inverted) Oedipus situation; the child displays mother object-love and father identification, and father object-love and mother identification."

ONANISM: "Strictly speaking *onanism* is sexual intercourse interrupted before ejaculation. . . . Some writers use the term *onanism* interchangeably with masturbation."

PARANOIA: "'The general concept of paranoia which has been prevalent for many years is that of a psychosis presenting delusions of persecution of a clearly defined type, well supported and defended by the patient, in other words, systematized. These delusions generally involve a more or less circumscribed portion of the mentality, although they tend to spread out slowly and involve more and more. With this state of mind there is no marked tendency toward deterioration, the disease having essentially a chronic course. Associated with the delusions and harmonized with them in content are frequently auditory hallucinations—voices.'"

PHOBIA: "A phobia is a morbid fear associated with morbid anxiety."

PRECONSCIOUS: "Foreconscious; in psychoanalysis, one of the three topographical divisions of the psyche. The preconscious division includes those thoughts, memories, and similar mental elements which, although not conscious at the moment, can readily be brought into consciousness by an effort of attention. This is in contrast to the unconscious division, whose elements are barred from access to consciousness by some intrapsychic force such as repression."

PREHISTORY: The period before a child knows what is happening to him.

"The study of prehistoric man; a history of the antecedents of an event or situation." (Webster's.)

PSYCHE: "The most comprehensive schematization of the psyche is that drawn by Freud, consisting in general of the conscious and unconscious divisions, each of which is made up of a great number of components. The mind, like all other organs of the body, has its own local functions and those functions that are intimately associated with adjacent and distant organs. It is like the cardiovascular system in that it reaches all parts of the body; it also serves to adjust the total organism to the needs or demands of the environment."

PSYCHIATRY: "The science of curing or healing disorders of the psyche."

PSYCHOANALYSIS: "The separation or resolution of the psyche into its constituent elements. The term has three separate meanings: (1) a procedure, devised by Sigmund Freud, for investigating mental processes by means of free-association, dream-interpretation, and interpretation of resistance and transference manifestations; (2) a theory of psychology developed by Freud out of his clinical experience with hysterical patients; and (3) a form of psychiatric treatment developed by Freud which utilizes the psychoanalytic procedure (definition 1 above) and which is based on psychoanalytic psychology (definition 2 above). Freud considered the cornerstones of psychoanalytic theory to be: the assumption of unconscious mental processes, recognition of resistance and repression, appreciation of the importance of sexuality (and aggressivity), and the Oedipus complex."

PSYCHOSIS: "A psychosis is usually a severer type of mental disorder in the sense that all the forms of adaptation (e.g. social, intellectual, professional, religious, etc.) are disrupted. In other words, the disorganization of the personality is extensive. The principal psychotic syndromes are schizophrenia and manic-depressive psychosis. When the psychic disorder is associated with an organic disease, such as general paresis, brain tumor, etc., the term *organic psychosis* is used for the sake of convenience."

REGRESSION: "From the psychiatric point of view *regression* refers to the act of returning to some earlier level of adaptation. The mentally healthy individual progresses through many so-called levels. . . . From the psychoanalytic standpoint, regression and *fixation* are commonly associated with each other. When fixation is intense, frustrations on the part of reality may easily lead to regression."

REPRESSION: "The concept is used extensively in psychiatry. The most exhaustive description of it was made by Freud. It may be briefly defined as the active process of keeping out and ejecting, banishing from consciousness, the ideas or impulses that are unacceptable to it."

RESISTANCE: "From the psychoanalytic point of view resistance is 'the instinctive opposition displayed towards any attempt to lay bare the unconscious; a manifestation of the repressing forces.'"

"We call all the forces which oppose the work of cure the patient's "resistances.'" (*Freud: Dictionary of Psychoanalysis.*)

SCREEN MEMORY: "When a memory, a real thought, not a fantasied one, is used as a shield to conceal an allied memory, it is called a screen-memory. Thus, when a patient recalls playing in the basement, but does not remember the nature of the play, he is said to be providing a screen-memory."

"The period of infantile amnesia is often interrupted by isolated fragmentary memories, the so-called 'screen-memories.'" (*Freud: Dictionary of Psychoanalysis.*)

SOMA: "The organic tissues of the body. Thus, the brain, heart, musculature, bone, constitute parts of the soma."

SUBLIMATION: "In psychoanalytic psychology the process of modifying an instinctual impulse in such a way as to conform to the demands of society. Sublimation is a substitute activity which gives some measure of gratification to the infantile impulse which has been repudiated in its original form. Sublimation is an unconscious process and is a function of the normal ego. . . . Unlike the usual defenses, in sublimation the ego is not acting in opposition to the id; on the contrary, it is helping the id to gain external expression. Sublimation, in other words, does not involve repression. It is to be noted that the original impulse is never conscious in sublimation."

SUPEREGO: "In psychoanalytic psychology, there are three functional divisions of the psyche: the id, the ego, and the superego. The superego is the last of these to be differentiated. It is the representative of society within the psyche (i.e. conscience or morality) and also includes the ideal aspirations (ego-ideal). The superego is mainly unconscious; its functions include: (1) approval or disapproval of the ego's actions, i.e. judgment that an act is 'right' or 'wrong'; (2) critical self-observation; (3) self-punishment; (4) demands that the ego repent or make reparation for wrongdoing; (5) self-love or self-esteem as the ego reward for having done right. In general, the superego may be regarded as a split-off portion of the ego which arises on the basis of identification with certain aspects of the introjected parents."

"The Superego is the successor and representative of the parents (and educators) who superintend the actions of the individual in his first years of life; it perpetuates their functions almost without a change." (*Freud: Dictionary of Psychoanalysis.*)

SYMBOLISM: "The act or process of representing an object or idea by a substitute object, sign, or signal. In psychiatry, symbolism is of particular importance since it can serve as a defense mechanism of the ego, as where unconscious (and forbidden) aggressive or sexual impulses come to expression through symbolic representation and thus are able to avoid censorship. The symbolic expression of the unconscious impulse may then appear as the patient's symptom."

TRANSFERENCE: "In psychoanalytic therapy, the phenomenon of projection of feelings, thoughts, and wishes onto the analyst, who has come to represent an object from the patient's past."

"The patient sees in his analyst the return—the reincarnation—of some important figure out of his childhood or past, and consequently transfers on to him feelings and reactions that undoubtedly applied to this model." (*Freud: Dictionary of Psychoanalysis.*)

TRAUMA: "The term *trauma* means the same in psychiatry as it means in general medicine, namely, an injury, something hurtful. In psychoanalysis, any stimulation of such intensity that it cannot be mastered or adequately discharged is traumatic."

UNCONSCIOUS: "The expression *unconscious* may be used as a noun or an adjective. In psychiatry it is used with two different and separate meanings. The first meaning has to do with the absence of participation of the conscious ego or the so-called perceptive-self. When the conscious part of the mind is not functioning, the individual is said to be unconscious. Unconsciousness is usually associated with absence of orientation and perception, particularly in its extreme expression.

"The second meaning of *unconscious* (used as a noun) refers to a division of the psyche. One then speaks of *the unconscious* or of *unconsciousness*. In general it may be stated that all psychic material not in the immediate field of awareness is in the unconscious. When it is near enough to the former to be more or less easily accessible to it, it is said to be in the foreconscious or preconscious."

THIS IS VIENNA

Probably the words *Gemütlich* and *Gemütlichkeit* are the best known of the Viennese descriptive terms. This homey, gentle properness pervades Viennese social life. It is embodied in the soft-spoken hellos and good-bys, the *Guten Morgen* of good morning and the *Guten Abend* of good evening, the *Auf Wiedersehen* of until we meet again, as well as the *Grüss Gott* and *Küss' die Hand* of greeting and the *Servus*, at your service, parting. Politeness is required. One addresses a married woman as my gracious lady, *Gnädige Frau*, the young woman as *Fräulein*, and the aunt as *Frau Tante*.

Titles abound: over all was the embossed K.K., *Kaiserlich Königlich*, the Imperial Royalty of Franz Josef and the Austro-Hungarian Empire. There was: *Baron* and *Baronin*, *Herr Professor*, *Herr Hofrat*, *Herr Doktor*, *Extraordinarius*, Assistant Professor, *Ordinarius*, Full Professor, *Primarius*, *Dozent*, and *Privatdozent*, *Sekundararzt*, for intern, *Regimentsarzt* for Regimental Medical Officer, and *Abteilungsleiter* for the Department Head, the *Doktorenkollegium* or *Professorenkollegium*, and *Ärztegesellschaft*, the faculties. One wishes *Alles Gute*, may all be good, and *Alles in Butter*, a colloquialism implying the prosperity of always using the good rich Austrian butter in cooking; and is eternally grateful with *Gott sei Dank*, thanks to God, when things go well.

The custom of the coffeehouse is supremely Vienna's, and a vital part of the life and social structure. Hours are spent in these informal "clubs." *Stamm* is family, a man's *Stammlokal*, the cafe he favors, his *Stammtisch*, the table reserved for himself and his friends, and the *Marqueur*, waiter, who knows each *Stammgast*, or guest. At the coffeehouse one drinks a *kaffetscherl*, a little coffee, or a *Kleinen Braunen*, a small coffee with milk, or a *Grosser Braunen*, a large cup, talks animatedly or reads the wide variety of newspapers, or plays *Tarock* with large colorful illustrated cards and loud cries of *Stich oder Schmier*, a kind of put up or shut up, and *Ultimo!*, that does it!

In the *Weinstube* the Viennese will drink all vintages of wine, but in the *Heurigen Stüberln* with the *Büschel*, or clump of fresh leaves over its front door, he will drink only the fresh wine of the neighborhood, and listen to special *Heurigenmusik*, informal country music. In the *Bierstube* he will drink endless quantities of *Gösser Bier*, an excellent beer, toasting with *Prosit!* or *Giesshübler*, mineral water. On the trail in the Wienerwald, he will drink soda pop, literally thumbing down the *Kracherl*, round marble placed in the neck of the bottle to close it.

The women for the most part will consume their coffee at the *Kaffeeklatsch*, or *Kaffeeplausch* held at home for their lady friends. They will talk *bassena* gossip, from the gathering of the women at the central basin, or water supply, in many of the buildings, of their *Kinder*, children, *Kirche*, church, *Küche*, kitchen . . . recipes.

Stadt is the City, and the word is affixed to theaters, parks, government buildings; the *Stadtbahn* is the railway, to indicate its ownership; the *Volk* are the people, with their *Volkstheater* and *Volksküchenverein*, kitchen. The *Hof* indicates a square or open triangle, *Strasse* is street.

Haus is house, and the apartment building, generally with a mezzanine apartment or *Parterre*, is run by the *Hausmeister*, or *Hausbesorger*. The *Hausfrau* runs her home and is given a weekly *Haushaltsgeld*, allowance, with which to do it. She will have a *Zimmermädchen*, a cleaning maid, or *Dienstmädchen*, day help, and a *Wäschermädel* to do the laundry. In her apartment of many *Zimmer*, rooms, there will be the formal *Wohnzimmer*, living room, with its *Kredenz* of chinaware, and Oriental *Tapis*, rug, a *Kabinett*, small oddment of space too small to be a *Zimmer*, and doubtless a *Tröpferlbad*, trickle bath or shower. *Füllöfen*, large ceramic stoves fed with *Kohle*, charcoal, heat the rooms.

The *Allgemeine Krankenhaus*, General Hospital, had its *Hausordnung*, resident, its *Journal*, Admittance Room, and *Journaldienst*, attendant; the Departments had their *Beobachtungszimmer*, B.Z. Observation or Examining Rooms.

A *Dienstmann*, stationed on the street corners, the uniformed owner of a cart, carries everything from letters and messages to the trunks and *Handkoffer*, valises, of the Viennese in their summer exodus to the *Sommerwohnung*, vacation refresher in the mountains. Furniture, *Möbel*, was moved in a *Hofwagen*, or *Möbelwagen*. One got about the streets on foot, in horse-drawn cars, in an *Einspänner*, a sturdy one-horse carriage or in a *Fiaker*, a more elegant two-horse cab, equivalent of the German *Droschke*, used by the professional and required of the *Mittelstand*, the middle class.

Trades were practiced in shops, by the *Börsenmakler*, on the Stock Exchange, and in the streets; the women in colorful *Dirndlkleid*, wide skirt, apron, and scarf, the countrymen in *Lederhosen*, short leather pants, and *Hosenträger*, suspenders. Women cried out selling *Lavendl*, prettily tied bunches of dried lavender; the *Schokoladenmacher* had chocolate, hot or cold; the *Wurstelmann*, sausages; the *Limonehandler*, lemonade, the *Sieder*, coffee. One paid with *Kreutzer*, *Gulden*, *Kronen*. The *Laternenanzünder* was the official lamplighter, with his *Zundstongen*, long pole.

Children filled the streets returning from the *Gymnasium*, where .they worked toward their *Matura* and prayed for grades at least *Genügend*, good enough, satisfactory. For the girls attending the *Töchterschule*, daughterschool, girls' school, it was not as important.

Young men walked arm in arm with their *Süsse Mädel*, their sweet girls, in Vienna, young mistresses. But not the "Yeshivabucher," he had his nose in a book, and his eye on the university, and a lectureship, *Dozentur*.

The Viennese ate well and often. There were five set meals a day; the coffee and rolls, or *Kipfeln*, of the early *Frühstück*, breakfast; the *Kleines Gulasch*, small pieces of veal and potatoes in a paprika sauce, of the *Gabelfrühstück*, or fork breakfast. The dinner, or main meal, came at midday, and a favorite was *Tafelspitz*, or boiled beef. There was always a soup: a *Bouillon mit Ei*, a clear soup with an egg in it, and the ubiquitous *Knödel*, dumpling. At five o'clock everyone stopped for the *Jause*, frequently a pair of sausages, and always cake, a *Guglhupf* or *Nusstrudel*. There might also be little *Schinkensemmel*, buns with ham, or *Selzstangerl*, long salt sticks with *Kümmel* seeds. A thick whipped cream, *Schlagobers* in its deep round bowl, smothered all pastries including the rich Sacher or *Wiener Torte*. The *Nachtmahl*, or supper, consisted of leftovers from the day's dinner, a slice of *Hausbrot* from the large round loaf, simple bread and butter, or *Mohnkipfel*, poppy seed rolls, cheese or cold meats, or perhaps a *Kraut mit Rahm*, finely shredded cabbage cooked with sour cream and sprinkled with caraway seeds.

Next to the beloved, omnipresent music, be it symphonic or opera, and the proud possession of an *Abonnement*, season ticket to the concerts, *Naschen*, to nibble, was endemic. A colorful fairground was the *Naschmarkt* where one could buy everything from *Kuttelkraut*, an Austrian thyme, to *Gemischter Salat*, a mixture of pickled *Kohl*, cabbage, cauliflower, peppers; to *Lungenbraten*, a loin of beef, to *Fogosch*, a lake fish, to veal for the *Gulasch* and the *Wienerschnitzel*, and *Rindfleisch* for the *Tafelspitz*; to *Kleine Vögel*, small birds, and *Geflügel*, wild fowl, to *Schwammerl*, wild mushrooms. There were sausages of all kinds and in the *Konditorei* a variety of cakes: *Kuchen* and *Strudel*: *Hönigkuchen*, honey cake, *Königskuchen*, *Kaffeekuchen*, coffeecakes, *Linzertorte* and *Palatschinken*, pancakes.

Noodles were made at home, with a *Nudelwalze*, a noodlewalker.

But every now and then everything went *Kraut und Rüben, topsy-turvy*. One was *Erschüttert*, shocked; perhaps cried, *Verdammt*, Damn!

And over all was a lovely looseness, a denial of *Verboten*, forbidden, what was gaily pronounced *Schlamperei*.

Fertig! Done.

BIBLIOGRAPHY

WORKS BY SIGMUND FREUD

"A New Histological Method for the Study of Nerve-Tracts in the Brain and Spinal Cord," *Brain*, Vol. VII, 1885; *The Cocaine Papers*, 1963; *On Aphasia: A Critical Study*, 1953; *Sigmund Freud: Collected Papers*, translation under supervision of Joan Riviere, Alix and James Strachey, 5 vols., 1959; *The Standard Edition of the Complete Psychological Works of Sigmund Freud*, translated from the German under the general editorship of James Strachey in collaboration with Anna Freud, 23 vols., 1953–66; Sigmund Freud and William C. Bullitt, *Thomas Woodrow Wilson: A Psychological Study*, 1967.

WORKS CONTAINING LETTERS BY SIGMUND FREUD

Franz Alexander and Sheldon T. Selesnick, "Freud-Bleuler Correspondence," *Archives of General Psychiatry*, Vol. 12, No. 1, January 1965; Ludwig Binswanger, *Sigmund Freud: Reminiscences of a Friendship*, trans. Norbert Guterman, 1957; *Letters of Sigmund Freud*, ed. Ernst L. Freud, trans. Tania and James Stern, 1960; *The Letters of Sigmund Freud and Arnold Zweig*, ed. Ernst L. Freud, trans. Elaine and William Robson-Scott, 1970; *The Origins of Psychoanalysis: Letters to Wilhelm Fliess, Drafts and Notes: 1887–1902*, ed. Marie Bonaparte, Anna Freud, Ernst Kris, trans. Eric Mosbacher and James Strachey, 1954; *Psychoanalysis and Faith: The Letters of Sigmund Freud and Oskar Pfister*, ed. Heinrich Meng and Ernst L. Freud, trans. Eric Mosbacher, 1963; *A Psychoanalytic Dialogue: The Letters of Sigmund Freud and Karl Abraham, 1907–1926*, ed. Hilda C. Abraham and Ernst L. Freud, trans. Bernard Marsh and Hilda C. Abraham, 1965; "Sigmund Freud as a Consultant and Therapist: From Sigmund Freud's Letters to Edoardo Weiss," ed. Martin Grotjahn, *Psychoanalytic Forum*, Vol. I, No. 2, 1966; "Freud as a Psychoanalytic Consultant: From Some Unknown Letters to Edoardo Weiss," ed. Martin Grotjahn, *Psychoanalytic Forum*, Vol. I, No. 1, 1966; Ernest Jones, *The Life and Work of Sigmund Freud*, 3 vols., 1953–57; C. G. Jung, *Memories, Dreams, Reflections*, ed. Aniela Jaffé, trans. Richard and Clara Winston, 1963; A. A. Roback, *Freudiana*, 1957; Milton Rosenbaum, "Freud-Eitingon-Magnes Correspondence: Psychoanalysis at the Hebrew University," *Journal of the American Psychoanalytic Association*, Vol. II, No. 2, April 1954; Edoardo Weiss, *Sigmund Freud as a Consultant*, 1970.

WRITINGS ABOUT SIGMUND FREUD

ARTICLES. Leslie Adams, "Sigmund Freud's Correct Birthday: Misunder-
standing and Solution," *Psychoanalytic Review*, Vol. 41, No. 4, October 1954;
Franz Alexander, "Recollections of Berggasse 19," *Psychoanalytic Quarterly*,
Vol. 9, 1940; Peter Amacher, "Freud's Neurological Education and Its In-
fluence on Psychoanalytic Theory," *Psychological Issues*, Vol. IV, No. 4,
Monograph 16, 1965; Franz Baumeyer, "The Schreber Case," *International
Journal of Psychoanalysis*, Vol. XXXVII, Pt. 1, January–February 1956; Otto
Beer, article on Sigmund Freud, *Neus Österreich*, September 23, 1954;
Anna Freud Bernays, "My Brother, Sigmund Freud," *American Mercury*,
Vol. LI, No. 203, November 1940; Siegfried Bernfeld, "Freud's Earliest
Theories and the School of Helmholtz," *Psychoanalytic Quarterly*, Vol. XIII,
No. 3, 1944; Siegfried Bernfeld, "Freud's Scientific Beginnings," *American
Imago*, Vol. 6, No. 3, September 1949; Siegfried Bernfeld, "Freud's Studies
on Cocaine, 1884–1887," *Yearbook of Psychoanalysis*, Vol. 10, 1954; Siegfried
Bernfeld, "Sigmund Freud, M.D., 1882–1885," *International Journal of
Psychoanalysis*, Vol. XXXII, 1951; Siegfried Bernfeld and Suzanne Cassirer
Bernfeld, "Freud's Early Childhood," *Bulletin of the Menninger Clinic*,
Vol. 8, No. 4, July 1944; Siegfried Bernfeld and Suzanne Cassirer Bernfeld,
"Freud's First Year in Practice, 1886–1887," *Bulletin of the Menninger
Clinic*, Vol. 16, No. 2, March 1952; A. A. Brill, "Reminiscences of Freud,"
Psychoanalytic Quarterly, Vol. 9, 1940; Benjamin Brody, "Freud's Case-
Load," *Psychotherapy: Theory, Research and Practice*, Vol. 7, No. 1,
Spring 1970; Edith Buxbaum, "Freud's Dream Interpretation in the Light of
His Letters to Fliess," *Bulletin of the Menninger Clinic*, Vol. 15, No. 6,
November 1951; Helene Deutsch, "Freud and His Pupils," *Psychoanalytic
Quarterly*, Vol. 9, 1940; Richard Dyck, interview with Harry Freud, *Neues
Österreich*, September 19, 1964; Max Eastman, "A Significant Memory of
Freud," *New Republic*, Vol. 104, No. 20, May 19, 1941; K. R. Eissler,
"Freud and the Psychoanalysis of History," *Journal of the American Psycho-
analytic Association*, Vol. XI, No. 4, October 1963; K. R. Eissler, "Zwei
bisher übersehene Dokumente zur akademischen Laufbahn Sigmund Freuds,"
Wiener klinische Wochenschrift, Nr. 1, S. 16–19, 1966; Nandor Fodor,
"Freud and the Poltergeist," *Journal of Psychoanalytic Psychology*, Vol. 4,
No. 2, Winter 1955–56; Louis Fraiberg, "Freud's Writings on Art," *Inter-
national Journal of Psychoanalysis*, Vol. XXXVII, Pt. 1, January–February
1956; Renée Gicklhorn, "Eine Episode aus S. Freuds Mittelschulzeit,"
Unsere Heimat, Jahrgang 36, NR. 1/3, 1965; Renée Gicklhorn, "The Frei-
berg Period of the Freud Family," *Journal of the History of Medicine and
Allied Sciences*, Vol. XXIV, No. 1, January 1969; Max Graf, "Freud and
Vienna," *Weltpresse*, February 10, 1955; Max Graf, "Reminiscences of Pro-
fessor Sigmund Freud," *Psychoanalytic Quarterly*, Vol. 11, 1942; Martin
Grotjahn, "A Letter by Sigmund Freud with Recollections of His Adoles-
cence," *Journal of the American Psychoanalytic Association*, Vol. IV, No. 4,
October 1956; Judith Bernays Heller, "Freud's Mother and Father: A
Memoir," *Commentary*, Vol. 21, No. 5, May 1956; Smith Ely Jelliffe,

"Sigmund Freud as a Neurologist," *Journal of Nervous and Mental Disease,* Vol. 85, No. 6, June 1937; Ernest Jones, "The Inception of 'Totem and Taboo,'" *International Journal of Psychoanalysis,* Vol. XXXVII, Pt. 1, January–February 1956; Donald M. Kaplan, "Freud and His Own Patients," *Harper's* magazine, Vol. 235, No. 1411, December 1967; William A. Koelsch, "Freud Discovers America," *Virginia Quarterly Review,* Vol. 46, No. 1, Winter 1970; Emil Lorenz, "When Freud Still Gave Out 'Einlass-cheine,'" *Forum,* May 1956; Peter Madison, "Freud's Repression Concept," *International Journal of Psychoanalysis,* Vol. XXXVII, Pt. 1, January–February 1956; Thomas Mann, "Freud and the Future," *International Journal of Psychoanalysis,* Vol. XXXVII, Pt. 1, January–February 1956; Philip Merlan, "Brentano and Freud," *Journal of the History of Ideas,* Vol. VI, No. 3, June 1945; Philip Merlan, "Brentano and Freud—A Sequel," *Journal of the History of Ideas,* Vol. X, No. 3, June 1949; Odette Pannetier, "Appointment in Vienna," *Living Age,* Vol. 351, October 1936; Martin W. Peck, "A Brief Visit with Freud," *The Psychoanalytic Quarterly,* Vol. 9, 1940; Karl Sablik, "Sigmund Freud und die Gesellschaft der Ärzte in Wien," *Wiener klinische Wochenschrift,* Nr. 6, S. 107, 1968; Josef Sajner, "Sigmund Freud's Beziehungen zu seinem Geburtsort Freiberg (Příbor) und zu Mären"; Manfred Scheuch, "On Freud's Relationship to Vienna," *Arbeiter-Zeitung,* September 20, 1964; Max Schur, "Some Additional 'Day Residues' of 'The Specimen Dream of Psychoanalysis,'" reprinted from *Psychoanalysis—A General Psychology,* 1966; Ernst Simmel, "Sigmund Freud: The Man and His Work," *Psychoanalytic Quarterly,* Vol. 9, 1940; Robert I. Simon, "Great Paths Cross: Freud and James at Clark University, 1909," *American Journal of Psychiatry,* 124:6, December 1967; Fritz Wittels, "Revision of a Biography," *Psychoanalytic Review,* Vol. XX, No. 4, October 1933.

BOOKS. Jacob A. Arlow, *The Legacy of Sigmund Freud,* 1956; Percival Bailey, *Sigmund the Unserene: A Tragedy in Three Acts,* 1965; David Bakan, *Sigmund Freud and the Jewish Mystical Tradition,* 1958; A. A. Brill, *Freud's Contribution to Psychiatry,* 1944; Vincent Brome, *Freud and His Early Circle,* 1968; J. A. C. Brown, *Freud and the Post-Freudians,* 1961; Ruth Mack Brunswick, "A Supplement to Freud's 'History of an Infantile Neurosis,' (1928)," *The Psychoanalytic Reader,* Vol. I, 1948; H.D., *Tribute to Freud,* 1956; K. R. Eissler, *Sigmund Freud und die Wiener Universität,* 1966; Nandor Fodor and Frank Gaynor, eds., *Freud: Dictionary of Psychoanalysis,* 1950; *The Freud Centenary Exhibit* of the American Psychoanalytic Association, 1956; Martin Freud, *Glory Reflected: Sigmund Freud—Man and Father,* 1957; Erich Fromm, *Sigmund Freud's Mission: An Analysis of His Personality and Influence,* 1959; Iago Galdston, *Freud and Contemporary Culture,* 1957; Josef Gicklhorn and Renée Gicklhorn, *Sigmund Freud's akademische Laufbahn: im Lichte der Dokumente,* 1960; Alexander Grinstein, *On Sigmund Freud's Dreams,* 1968; Walter Hollitscher, *Sigmund Freud: An Introduction,* 1947; Stanley Edgar Hyman, *The Tangled Bank: Darwin, Marx, Frazer and Freud as Imaginative Writers,* 1962; Ernest Jones, *The Life and Work of Sigmund Freud,* 3 vols., 1953–57; Ernest Jones, *The*

Life and Work of Sigmund Freud, edited and abridged by Lionel Trilling and Steven Marcus, Introduction by Lionel Trilling, 1961; Ernest Jones, *Sigmund Freud: Four Centenary Addresses*, 1956; Milton V. Kline, *Freud and Hypnosis: The Interaction of Psychodynamics and Hypnosis*, 1958; Rudolph M. Loewenstein, *Freud: Man and Scientist*, 1951; Emil Ludwig, *Doctor Freud: An Analysis and a Warning*, 1947; Herbert Marcuse, *Eros and Civilization*, 1966; Maurice Natenberg, *The Case History of Sigmund Freud: A Psycho-Biography*, 1955; Benjamin Nelson, ed., *Freud and the 20th Century*, 1957; Helen Walker Puner, *Freud: His Life and His Mind*, 1947; Wilhelm Reich, *Reich Speaks of Freud*, ed. Mary Higgins and Chester M. Raphael, trans. Therese Pol, 1967; Theodor Reik, *From Thirty Years with Freud*, 2nd ed., trans. Richard Winston, 1949; Philip Rieff, *Freud: The Mind of the Moralist*, 1959; Paul Roazen, *Freud: Political and Social Thought*, 1968; Marthe Robert, *The Psychoanalytic Revolution: Sigmund Freud's Life and Achievement*, trans. Kenneth Morgan, 1966; Hendrik M. Ruitenbeek, *Freud and America*, 1966; Hanns Sachs, *Freud: Master and Friend*, 1945; Richard L. Schoenwald, *Freud: The Man and His Mind, 1856–1956*, 1956; Ernst Simon, *Sigmund, the Jew*, 1957; Rainer Spehlmann, *Sigmund Freud's Neurologische Schriften*, 1953; David Stafford-Clark, *What Freud Really Said*, 1966; Bartlett H. Stoodley, *The Concepts of Sigmund Freud*, 1959; Lionel Trilling, *Freud and the Crisis of Our Culture*, 1955; Robert Waelder, *The Living Thoughts of Freud*, 1942; Harry K. Wells, *Sigmund Freud: A Pavlovian Critique*, 1960; Fritz Wittels, *Freud and His Time*, 1931; Fritz Wittels, *Sigmund Freud: His Personality, His Teaching and His School*, trans. Eden and Cedar Paul, 1924; Joseph Wortis, *Fragments of an Analysis with Freud*, 1954; Gregory Zilboorg, *Sigmund Freud: His Exploration of the Mind of Man*, 1951.

WRITINGS BY AND ABOUT SIGMUND FREUD'S CONTEMPORARIES

GENERAL. Franz Alexander, Samuel Eisenstein and Martin Grotjahn, eds., *Psychoanalytic Pioneers*, 1966; *The Jewish Encyclopedia*, 1902; Erna Lesky, *Die Wiener Medizinische Schule im 19. Jahrhundert*, 1965; Herman Nunberg and Ernst Federn, eds., *Minutes of the Vienna Psychoanalytic Society*, Vol. I: 1906–8, trans. M. Nunberg, 1962; Herman Nunberg and Ernst Federn, eds., *Minutes of the Vienna Psychoanalytic Society*, Vol. II: 1908–10, trans. M. Nunberg, 1967; Paul A. Robinson, *The Freudian Left: Wilhelm Reich, Geza Roheim, Herbert Marcuse*, 1969; Olga Székely-Kovács and Robert Berény, *Caricatures of 88 Pioneers in Psychoanalysis: Drawn from Life at the Eighth International Psychoanalytic Congress*, 1954.

KARL ABRAHAM. Karl Abraham, *Clinical Papers and Essays on Psychoanalysis*, ed. Hilda Abraham, trans. Hilda Abraham and D. R. Ellison, 1955; Karl Abraham, *Selected Papers of Karl Abraham, M.D.*, trans. Douglas Bryan and Alix Strachey, 1953; *A Psychoanalytic Dialogue: The Letters of Sigmund Freud and Karl Abraham, 1907–1926*, ed. Hilda C. Abraham and Ernst L. Freud, trans. Bernard Marsh and Hilda C. Abraham, 1965.

ALFRED ADLER. Alfred Adler, *The Individual Psychology of Alfred Adler: A Systematic Presentation in Selections from His Writings,* ed. Heinz L. Ansbacher and Rowena R. Ansbacher, 1956; Alfred Adler, *What Life Should Mean to You,* ed. Alan Porter, 1958; Phyllis Bottome, *Alfred Adler: A Portrait from Life,* 1957; Kenneth Mark Colby, "On the Disagreement Between Freud and Adler," *American Imago,* Vol. 8, No. 3, September 1951; Madelaine Ganz, *The Psychology of Alfred Adler,* 1953; Hertha Orgler, *Alfred Adler: The Man and His Work: Triumph over the Inferiority Complex,* 1963.

AUGUST AICHHORN. August Aichhorn, *Wayward Youth,* 1955.

FRANZ ALEXANDER. Franz Alexander, *Fundamentals of Psychoanalysis,* 1948; Franz Alexander, *Psychosomatic Medicine: Its Principles and Applications,* 1950; Franz Alexander, *Psychoanalysis and Psychotherapy: Developments in Theory, Technique and Training,* 1956.

LOU ANDREAS-SALOMÉ. Lou Andreas-Salomé, *The Freud Journal of Lou Andreas-Salomé,* trans. Stanley A. Leavy, 1964; Rudolph Binion, *Frau Lou: Nietzsche's Wayward Disciple,* 1968; H. F. Peters, *My Sister, My Spouse: A Biography of Lou Andreas-Salomé,* 1962.

BERNAYS FAMILY. Edward L. Bernays, *Biography of an Idea: Memoirs of Public Relations Counsel Edward L. Bernays,* 1965.

HIPPOLYTE BERNHEIM. H. Bernheim, *Hypnosis and Suggestion in Psychotherapy,* trans. Christian A. Herter, 1964.

THEODOR BILLROTH. Hans Barkan, ed. and trans., *Johannes Brahms and Theodor Billroth: Letters from a Musical Friendship,* 1957; Theodor Billroth, *The Medical Sciences in the German Universities: A Study in the History of Civilization,* trans. William H. Welch, 1924.

LUDWIG BINSWANGER. Ludwig Binswanger, *Sigmund Freud: Reminiscences of a Friendship,* trans. Norbert Guterman, 1957.

EUGEN BLEULER. Franz Alexander and Sheldon T. Selesnick, "Freud-Bleuler Correspondence," *Archives of General Psychiatry,* Vol. 12, No. 1, January 1965; Eugen Bleuler, *Dementia Praecox or the Group of Schizophrenias,* trans. Joseph Zinkin, 1950; Eugen P. Bleuler, "The Physiogenic and Psychogenic in Schizophrenia," *American Journal of Psychiatry,* Vol. X, No. 2, September 1930; M. Bleuler, *Geschichte des Burghölzlis und der Psychiatrischen Universitätsklinik,* 1951; Manfred Bleuler, "Schizophrenia: Review of the Work of Prof. Eugen Bleuler," *Archives of Neurology and Psychiatry,* Vol. 26, 1931.

MARIE BONAPARTE. Marie Bonaparte, *Female Sexuality,* 1953; Max Schur, ed., *Drives, Affects, Behavior: Essays in Memory of Marie Bonaparte,* Vol. 2, 1965.

JOSEF BREUER. Josef Breuer, "Autobiography of Josef Breuer (1842–1925)," ed. and trans. C. P. Oberndorf, *International Journal of Psychoanalysis,* Vol. XXXIV, Pt. 1, 1953; Josef Breuer and Sigmund Freud, "On the Psychical Mechanism of Hysterical Phenomena," *International Journal of Psychoanalysis*, Vol. XXXVII, Pt. 1, January–February 1956; Paul F. Cranefield, "Josef Breuer's Evaluation of His Contribution to Psychoanalysis," *International Journal of Psychoanalysis*, Vol. XXXIX, Pt. V, September–October 1958; George H. Pollock, *The Possible Significance of Childhood Object Loss in the Josef Breuer-Bertha Pappenheim (Anna O.) Sigmund Freud Relationship:* I. Josef Breuer, unpublished.

A. A. BRILL. A. A. Brill, *Basic Principles of Psychoanalysis*, 1949; A. A. Brill, *Freud's Contribution to Psychiatry*, 1944; A. A. Brill, *Lectures on Psychoanalytic Psychiatry*, 1946; A. A. Brill, "Reminiscences of Freud," *Psychoanalytic Quarterly*, Vol. 9, 1940.

ERNST BRÜCKE. E. T. H. Brücke, *Ernst Brücke*, 1928.

J. M. CHARCOT. J. M. Charcot, *Clinical Lectures on Diseases of the Nervous System*, trans. Thomas Savill, 1889; J. M. Charcot, *Lectures on the Diseases of the Nervous System*, 2nd Series, trans. George Sigerson, 1962; Georges Guillain, *J.-M. Charcot, 1825–1893, His Life—His Work*, ed. and trans. Pearce Bailey, 1959.

CHARLES DARWIN. Charles Darwin, *The Origin of Species* and *The Descent of Man*; Benjamin Farrington, *What Darwin Really Said*, 1966.

FELIX DEUTSCH. Felix Deutsch, ed., *On the Mysterious Leap from the Mind to the Body: A Workshop Study on the Theory of Conversion*, 1959; Felix Deutsch, ed., *The Psychosomatic Concept in Psychoanalysis*, 1953.

HELENE DEUTSCH. Helene Deutsch, *Psychoanalysis of the Neuroses*, trans. W. D. Robson-Scott, 1951; Helene Deutsch, *The Psychology of Women*, 2 vols., 1944–45.

DAVID EDER. J. B. Hobman, *David Eder: Memoirs of a Modern Pioneer*, 1945.

MAX EITINGON. Milton Rosenbaum, "Freud-Eitingon-Magnes Correspondence: Psychoanalysis at the Hebrew University," *Journal of the American Psychoanalytic Association*, Vol. II, No. 2, April 1954.

HAVELOCK ELLIS. Havelock Ellis, *My Life*, 1939; H. Havelock Ellis, *The Psychology of Sex*, 1933; H. Havelock Ellis, *Sex in Relation to Society*, 1937; Havelock Ellis, *Studies in the Psychology of Sex*, 2 vols., 1942; Joseph Ishill, ed., *Havelock Ellis: In Appreciation*, 1929; Houston Peterson, *Philosopher of Love: Havelock Ellis*, 1928.

ERIK H. ERIKSON. Erik H. Erikson, *Childhood and Society*, 1950; Erik H. Erikson, *Identity and the Life Cycle*, 1959; Erik H. Erikson, *Insight and Responsibility: Lectures on the Ethical Implications of Psychoanalytic Insight*, 1964; Erik H. Erikson, *Young Man Luther: A Study in Psychoanalysis and History*, 1958.

PAUL FEDERN. Paul Federn, *Ego Psychology and the Psychoses*, ed. Edoardo Weiss, 1952.

OTTO FENICHEL. Otto Fenichel, *The Psychoanalytic Theory of Neurosis*, 1945; Otto Fenichel, *The Collected Papers of Otto Fenichel*, ed. Dr. Hanna Fenichel and Dr. David Rapaport, 1953.

SANDOR FERENCZI. Sandor Ferenczi, *Final Contributions to the Problems and Methods of Psychoanalysis*, ed. Michael Balint, trans. Eric Mosbacher and others, 1955; Sandor Ferenczi, *Further Contributions to the Theory and Technique of Psychoanalysis*, comp. John Rickman, trans. Jane Isabel Suttie, 1952; Sandor Ferenczi, *Sex in Psychoanalysis (Contributions to Psychoanalysis)*, trans. Ernest Jones, Sandor Ferenczi and Otto Rank, *The Development of Psychoanalysis*, trans. Caroline Newton, 1956; Sandor Ferenczi, "Ten Letters to Freud," *International Journal of Psychoanalysis*, Vol. XXX, 1949; Nandor Fodor, "Sandor Ferenczi's Psychic Adventures," *International Journal of Parapsychology*, Vol. 3, No. 3, 1961.

ERNST FLEISCHL VON MARXOW. Ernst Fleischl von Marxow, *Gesammelte Abhandlungen*, ed. Dr. Otto Fleischl von Marxow, 1893.

WILHELM FLIESS. Wilhelm Fliess, *Zur Periodenlehre: Gesammelte Aufsätze*, 1925; Sigmund Freud, *The Origins of Psychoanalysis: Letters to Wilheim Fleiss, Drafts and Notes: 1887–1902*, ed. Marie Bonaparte, Anna Freud, Ernst Kris, trans. Eric Mosbacher and James Strachey, 1954; Georg Riebold, *Einblicke in den periodischen Ablauf des Lebens*, 1942.

FREUD FAMILY. Anna Freud Bernays, "My Brother, Sigmund Freud," *American Mercury*, Vol. LI, No. 203, November 1940; Judith Bernays Heller, "Freud's Mother and Father: A Memoir," *Commentary*, Vol. 21, No. 5, May 1956.

ANNA FREUD. Anna Freud, *The Ego and the Mechanisms of Defence*, trans. Cecil Baines, 1961; Anna Freud, *Normality and Pathology in Childhood: Assessments of Development*, 1965; Anna Freud, *The Psychoanalytical Treatment of Children*, trans. Nancy Procter-Gregg, 1946.

EDWARD GLOVER. Edward Glover, *The Technique of Psychoanalysis*, 1955.

GEORG GRODDECK. Georg Groddeck, *The Book of the It*, 1961; Carl M. Grossman and Sylva Grossman, *The Wild Analyst: The Life and Work of Georg Groddeck*, 1965.

HEINZ HARTMANN. Heinz Hartmann, *Ego Psychology and the Problem of Adaptation*, trans. David Rapaport, 1958; Heinz Hartmann, *Psychoanalysis and Moral Values*, 1960.

HUGO HELLER. *Literarischer Festalmanach auf das Jahr 1930.*

EDWARD HITSCHMANN. Edward Hitschmann, *Great Men: Psychoanalytic Studies*, ed. Sydney G. Margolin, 1956.

KAREN HORNEY. Karen Horney, *Neurosis and Human Growth: The Struggle Toward Self-Realization*, 1950; Karen Horney, *The Neurotic Per-*

sonality of Our Time, 1937; Karen Horney, *New Ways in Psychoanalysis*, 1939; Karen Horney, *Self-Analysis*, 1942.

WILLIAM JAMES. Gay Wilson Allen, *William James: A Biography*, 1967.

PIERRE JANET. Ernest Jones, "Professor Janet on Psychoanalysis: A Rejoinder," *Journal of Abnormal Psychology*, Vol. IX, No. 5, December 1914–January 1915.

ERNEST JONES. Ernest Jones, *Essays in Applied Psychoanalysis*, 2 vols., 1951; Ernest Jones, *Free Associations: Memories of a Psychoanalyst*, 1959; Ernest Jones, *Hamlet and Oedipus*, 1949; Elizabeth R. Zetzel, "Ernest Jones: His Contribution to Psychoanalytic Theory," *International Journal of Psychoanalysis*, Vol. XXXIX, Pt. V, September–October 1958.

CARL JUNG. E. A. Bennet, *C. G. Jung*, 1961; E. A. Bennet, *What Jung Really Said*, 1967; Richard Evans, *Conversations with Carl Jung and Reactions from Ernest Jones*, 1964; Frieda Fordham, *An Introduction to Jung's Psychology*, 1959; Edward Glover, *Freud or Jung*, 1950; Jolande Jacobi, "Freud and Jung—Meeting and Parting," *Swiss Review of World Affairs*, August 1956; Jolande Jacobi, "Jung, Carl Gustav," *International Encyclopedia of the Social Sciences*, 1968; Jolande Jacobi, *The Psychology of C. G. Jung*, 1962; Jolande Jacobi, *Two Essays on Freud and Jung*, 1958; Aniela Jaffé, "C. G. Jung and Parapsychology," *Science and ESP*, ed. J. R. Smythies, 1967; C. G. Jung, *The Basic Writings of C. G. Jung*, ed. Violet S. DeLaszlo, 1959; C. G. Jung, *Freud and Psychoanalysis*, trans. R. F. C. Hull, 1961; Carl G. Jung, M.-L. von Franz, Joseph L. Henderson, Jolande Jacobi, Aniela Jaffé, *Man and His Symbols*, 1964; C. G. Jung, *Memories, Dreams, Reflections*, ed. Aniela Jaffé, trans. Richard and Clara Winston, 1963; C. G. Jung, *Psychological Types*, trans. H. G. Baynes, 1959; C. G. Jung, *Symbols of Transformation: An Analysis of the Prelude to a Case of Schizophrenia*, trans. R. F. C. Hull, 1956; C. G. Jung, *Two Essays on Analytical Psychology*, trans. R. F. C. Hull, 1953.

MELANIE KLEIN. Melanie Klein, *The Psychoanalysis of Children*, 6th ed., trans. Alix Strachey, 1959.

KARL KOLLER. Hortense Koller Becker, "Carl Koller and Cocaine," *Psychoanalytic Quarterly*, Vol. XXXII, No. 3, 1963.

RICHARD VON KRAFFT-EBING. Richard von Krafft-Ebing, *Psychopathia Sexualis: With Especial Reference to the Antipathic Sexual Instinct: A Medico-Forensic Study*, trans. Franklin S. Klaf, 1965; Richard von Krafft-Ebing, *Text-Book of Insanity Based on Clinical Observations*, trans. Charles Gilbert Chaddock, 1905.

AMBROISE-AUGUSTE LIÉBEAULT. A. W. van Renterghem, "Liébeault et son école," *Zeitschrift für Hypnotismus*, Vol. 5, 1897.

THEODOR MEYNERT. H. Hartmann, review of Dorer, M.: "Historische Grundlagen der Psychoanalyse," *Imago*, XIX, 1933; Theodor Meynert, *Psychiatry*, trans. B. Sachs, 1885.

AXEL MUNTHE. Axel Munthe, *The Story of San Michele*, 1953.

OSKAR PFISTER. *Psychoanalysis and Faith: The Letters of Sigmund Freud and Oskar Pfister*, ed. Heinrich Meng and Ernst L. Freud, trans. Eric Mosbacher, 1963; Oskar Pfister, *Love in Children and Its Aberrations: A Book for Parents and Teachers*, 1924; Oskar Pfister, *The Psychoanalytic Method*, trans. Charles Rockwell Payne, 1917; Oskar Pfister, *Some Applications of Psychoanalysis*, 1923.

J. J. PUTNAM. J. J. Putnam, *Addresses on Psychoanalysis*, 1951.

OTTO RANK. Otto Rank, *Beyond Psychology*, 1941; Otto Rank, *The Myth of the Birth of the Hero and Other Writings*, ed. Philip Freund, 1959; Otto Rank, *The Trauma of Birth*, 1952; Jessie Taft, *Otto Rank*, 1958.

WILHELM REICH. Wilhelm Reich, *Character Analysis*, trans. Theodore P. Wolfe, 1958; Wilhelm Reich, *The Function of the Orgasm: Sex-Economic Problems of Biological Energy*, trans. Theodore P. Wolfe, 1961; Wilhelm Reich, *Reich Speaks of Freud*, ed. Mary Higgins and Chester M. Raphael, trans. Therese Pol, 1967.

THEODOR REIK. Theodor Reik, *Fragment of a Great Confession: A Psychoanalytic Autobiography*, 1949; Theodor Reik, *From Thirty Years with Freud*, 2nd ed., trans. Richard Winston, 1949; Theodor Reik, *Listening with the Third Ear: The Inner Experience of a Psychoanalyst*, 1954; Theodor Reik, *The Search Within: The Inner Experiences of a Psychoanalyst*, 1958.

JOAN RIVIERE. Obituary of Joan Riviere by James Strachey, Paula Heimann, Lois Munro, *International Journal of Psychoanalysis*, Vol. 44, Pt. 2, 1963.

HANNS SACHS. Hanns Sachs, *Freud: Master and Friend*, 1945; Hanns Sachs, *Masks of Love and Life: The Philosophical Basis of Psychoanalysis*, ed. A. A. Roback, 1948.

WILHELM STEKEL. Wilhelm Stekel, *The Autobiography of Wilhelm Stekel: The Life Story of a Pioneer Psychoanalyst*, ed. Emil A. Gutheil, 1950; Wilhelm Stekel, *Conditions of Nervous Anxiety and Their Treatment*, 1950; Wilhelm Stekel, *The Interpretation of Dreams: New Developments and Technique*, trans. Eden and Cedar Paul, 2 vols., 1943.

VIKTOR TAUSK. Paul Roazen, *Brother Animal: The Story of Freud and Tausk*, 1969.

BRUNO WALTER. Bruno Walter, *Theme and Variations: An Autobiography*, trans. James A. Galston, 1946.

EDOARDO WEISS. Martin Grotjahn, ed., "Freud as a Psychoanalytic Consultant: From Some Unknown Letters to Edoardo Weiss," *Psychoanalytic Forum*, Vol. I, No. 1, 1966; Martin Grotjahn, ed., "Sigmund Freud as a Consultant and Therapist: From Sigmund Freud's Letters to Edoardo Weiss," *Psychoanalytic Forum*, Vol. I, No. 2, 1966; Edoardo Weiss, *Sigmund Freud as a Consultant*, 1970.

FRITZ WITTELS. Fritz Wittels, *Freud and His Time*, 1931; Fritz Wittels, "Revision of a Biography," *Psychoanalytic Review*, Vol. XX, No. 4, October 1933; Fritz Wittels, *Sigmund Freud: His Personality, His Teaching, and His School*, trans. Eden and Cedar Paul, 1924.

STEFAN ZWEIG. Stefan Zweig, *The World of Yesterday*, 1953.

PSYCHOLOGY AND PSYCHIATRY

Erwin H. Ackerknecht, *A Short History of Psychiatry*, trans. Sulammith Wolff, 1959; Franz G. Alexander and Sheldon T. Selesnick, *The History of Psychiatry: An Evaluation of Psychiatric Thought and Practice from Pre-historic Times to the Present*, 1966; Clifford Allen, *Modern Discoveries in Medical Psychology*, 1952; John Balt, *By Reason of Insanity*, 1966; Dominique Barrucand, *Histoire de l'hypnose en France*, 1967; James Braid, *Braid on Hypnotism: The Beginnings of Modern Hypnosis*, rev. ed. by Arthur Edward Waite, 1960; Robert Edward Brennan, *History of Psychology: From the Standpoint of a Thomist*, 1945; Brigid Brophy, *Black Ship to Hell*, 1962; John Chynoweth Burnham, "Psychoanalysis and American Medicine: 1894–1918: Medicine, Science, and Culture," *Psychological Issues*, Vol. V, No. 4, Monograph 20, 1967; Norman Dain, *Concepts of Insanity in the United States, 1789–1865*, 1964; Albert Deutsch, *The Mentally Ill in America: A History of Their Care and Treatment from Colonial Times*, 2nd ed., 1949; John Dewey, *Human Nature and Conduct*; Henri F. Ellenberger, *The Discovery of the Unconscious*, 1970; O. Spurgeon English and Stuart M. Finch, *Introduction to Psychiatry*, 2nd ed., 1957; J. C. Flugel, *A Hundred Years of Psychology: 1833–1933*, with an additional Part: *1933–1963* by Donald J. West, 1964; James George Frazer, *The New Golden Bough*, ed. Theodor H. Gaster, 1959; Lucy Freeman and Marvin Small, *The Story of Psychoanalysis*, 1960; Erich Fromm, *Escape from Freedom*, 1941; Erving Goffman, *Asylums: Essays on the Social Situation of Mental Patients and Other Inmates*, 1961; Alexander Grinstein, *The Index of Psychoanalytic Writings*, 5 vols., 1956–60; G. Stanley Hall, *Founders of Modern Psychology*, 1912; Leland E. Hinsie and Robert Jean Campbell, *Psychiatric Dictionary*, 3rd ed., 1960; Joint Commission on Mental Illness and Health, *Action for Mental Health*, 1961; Walter Kaufmann, *The Faith of a Heretic*, 1963; Richard Lewinsohn, *A History of Sexual Customs*, 1961; Steven Marcus, *The Other Victorians: A Study of Sexuality and Pornography in Mid-Nineteenth-Century England*, 1966; Robin McKown, *Pioneers in Mental Health*, 1961; Carl Murchison, ed., *A History of Psychology in Autobiography*, Vol. I, 1930; I. P. Pavlov, *Conditioned Reflexes: An Investigation of the Physiological Activity of the Cerebral Cortex*, trans. G. V. Anrep, 1960; A. A. Roback, *History of Psychology and Psychiatry*, 1961; Charles Rolo, ed., *Psychiatry in American Life*, 1963; Karl Stern, *The Third Revolution: A Study of Psychiatry and Religion*, 1961; Walter A. Stewart, *Psychoanalysis: The First Ten Years, 1888–1898*, 1967; Harry Stack Sullivan, *Conceptions of Modern Psychiatry*, 2nd ed., 1953; Cornelius Tabori, *My Occult Diary*, trans. Paul Tabori, 1951; Heinz Werner, *Comparative Psy-*

chology of Mental Development, 1961; Allen Wheelis, *The Quest for Identity*, 1958; Victor White, *God and the Unconscious*, 1961; Gregory Zilboorg in collaboration with George W. Henry, *A History of Medical Psychology*, 1941; Stefan Zweig, *Mental Healers*, trans. Eden and Cedar Paul, 1933.

PSYCHOANALYTIC TECHNIQUE AND THEORY

ARTICLES. Gerhard Adler, "Methods of Treatment in Analytical Psychology," *Psychoanalytic Techniques*, ed. Benjamin B. Wolman, 1967; K. R. Eissler, "Mankind at Its Best," *Journal of the American Psychoanalytic Association*, Vol. XII, No. 1, January 1964; Gerda Frank, "The Enigma of Michelangelo's Pietà Rondanini: A Study of Mother-loss in Childhood," *American Imago*, Vol. 23, No. 4, Winter 1966; Martin Grotjahn, "Jewish Jokes and Their Relation to Masochism," *Journal of the Hillside Hospital*, Vol. X, Nos. 3–4, July–October 1961; Masud R. Khan, "Dream Psychology and the Evolution of the Psychoanalytic Situation," *International Journal of Psychoanalysis*, Vol. XLIII, Pt. 1, 1962; Marianne Pollack, "The Anna, the Marie, the Wetti, and the Poldi," *Arbeiter-Zeitung*, July 31, 1949; George H. Pollock, "Mourning and Adaptation," *International Journal of Psychoanalysis*, Vol. XLII, Pts. IV–V, 1961; Albert Reissner, "Religion and Classical Psychotherapy," *Christian Century*, Vol. LXXVIII, No. 15, April 12, 1961; Hilda S. Rollman-Branch, "The First Born Child, Male: Vicissitudes of Preoedipal Problems," *International Journal of Psychoanalysis*, Vol. 47, Pts. 2–3, 1966.

BOOKS. Franz Alexander, Thomas Morton French and others, *Psychoanalytic Therapy: Principles and Application*, 1946; Camilla M. Anderson, *Beyond Freud: A Creative Approach to Mental Health*, 1957; Michael Balint, *The Doctor, His Patient and the Illness*, 1957; Michael Balint, *Primary Love and Psychoanalytic Technique*, 1965; Michael Balint, *Problems of Human Pleasure and Behaviour*, 1957; Michael and Enid Balint, *Psychotherapeutic Techniques in Medicine*, 1961; Michael Balint, *Thrills and Regressions*, with a chapter on "Distance in Space and Time" by Enid Balint, 1959; Roy P. Basler, *Sex, Symbolism, and Psychology in Literature*, 1948; Ivy Bennett, *Delinquent and Neurotic Children: A Comparative Study*, 1960; Edmund Bergler, *The Superego: Unconscious Conscience—The Key to the Theory and Therapy of Neurosis*, 1952; Bruno Bettelheim, *The Informed Heart: Autonomy in a Mass Age*, 1960; Irving Bieber and others, *Homosexuality: A Psychoanalytic Study*, 1962; Gerald S. Blum, *Psychoanalytic Theories of Personality*, 1953; Trygve Braatøy, *Fundamentals of Psychoanalytic Technique*, 1954; Marjorie Brierley, *Trends in Psychoanalysis*, 1951; Norman O. Brown, *Life Against Death: The Psychoanalytical Meaning of History*, 1959; Kenneth Mark Colby, *Energy and Structure in Psychoanalysis*, 1955; James C. Coleman, *Abnormal Psychology and Modern Life*, 2nd ed., 1956; Robert S. DeRopp, *Drugs and the Mind*, 1957; Edwin Diamond, *The Science of Dreams*, 1962; K. R. Eissler, *Goethe: A Psychoanalytic*

Study, 1775–1786, 2 vols., 1963; K. R. Eissler, *Leonardo da Vinci: Psycho-analytic Notes on the Enigma*, 1961; K. R. Eissler, *Medical Orthodoxy and the Future of Psychoanalysis*, 1965; O. Spurgeon English and Gerald H. J. Pearson, *Emotional Problems of Living: Avoiding the Neurotic Pattern*, rev. and enlarged ed., 1955; E. Pickworth Farrow, *Psychoanalyze Yourself*, 1953; Herman Feifel, ed., *The Meaning of Death*, 1959; David Harold Fink, *Release from Nervous Tension*, 1943; Robert Fliess, *Erogeneity and Libido: Addenda to the Theory of the Psychosexual Development of the Human*, 1956; Robert Fliess, *The Revival of Interest in the Dream*, 1953; Nandor Fodor, *On the Trail of the Poltergeist*, 1958; Paul Friedman, ed., *On Suicide*, 1967; Erich Fromm, *The Sane Society*, 1955; Frieda Fromm-Reichmann, *Principles of Intensive Psychotherapy*, 1950; Phyllis Greenacre, *Trauma, Growth, and Personality*, 1953; Ralph R. Greenson, *The Technique and Practice of Psychoanalysis*, Vol. I, 1967; Harold Greenwald, ed., *Great Cases in Psychoanalysis*, 1959; Martin Grotjahn, *Beyond Laughter*, 1957; D. O. Hebb, *The Organization of Behavior: A Neuropsychological Theory*, 1961; Ives Hendrick, *Facts and Theories of Psychoanalysis*, 3rd ed., 1958; Frederick J. Hoffman, *Freudianism and the Literary Mind*, 2nd ed., 1957; Melanie Klein, Paula Heimann and R. E. Money-Kyrle, eds., *New Direc-tions in Psychoanalysis: The Significance of Infant Conflict in the Pattern of Adult Behaviour*, 1955; Lawrence S. Kubie, *Neurotic Distortion of the Creative Process*, 1961; Lawrence S. Kubie, *Practical and Theoretical As-pects of Psychoanalysis*, 1950; R. D. Laing and A. Esterson, *Sanity, Mad-ness, and the Family*, 1964; Konradi Leitner, *How to Hypnotize: A Master Key to Hypnotism*, 1950; Robert Lindner, *The Fifty-Minute Hour: A Col-lection of True Psychoanalytic Tales*, 1954; Perry London, *The Modes and Morals of Psychotherapy*, 1964; Sandor Lorand, *Technique of Psychoanalytic Therapy*, 1946; Konrad Lorenz, *On Aggression*, trans. Marjorie Kerr Wilson, 1963; Helen Merrell Lynd, *On Shame and the Search for Identity*, 1961; Norman R. F. Maier, *Frustration: The Study of Behavior without a Goal*, 1961; William H. Masters and Virginia E. Johnson, *Human Sexual Re-sponse*, 1966; Karl Menninger, *Theory of Psychoanalytic Technique*, 1961; Albert Mordell, *The Erotic Motive in Literature*, rev. ed., 1962; O. Hobart Mowrer, *The Crisis in Psychiatry and Religion*, 1961; Warner Muensterberger and Sidney Axelrad, eds., *The Psychoanalytic Study of Society*, Vol. I, 1960; Ruth L. Munroe, *Schools of Psychoanalytic Thought: An Exposition, Critique, and Attempt at Integration*, 1955; Erich Neumann, *The Origins and History of Consciousness*, trans. R. F. C. Hull, 2 vols., 1962; William Phillips, ed., *Art and Psychoanalysis*, 1957; Phillip Polatin, *A Guide to Treat-ment in Psychiatry*, 1966; Phillip Polatin and Ellen G. Philtine, *How Psychia-try Helps*, 1965; Phillip Polatin and Ellen C. Philtine, *Marriage in the Modern World*, 1964; David Rapaport, *Emotions and Memory*, 1961; Fredrick C. Redlich and Daniel X. Freedman, *The Theory and Practice of Psychiatry*, 1966; Philip Rieff, *The Triumph of the Therapeutic: Uses of Faith after Freud*, 1966; David Shapiro, *Neurotic Styles*, 1965; Thomas S. Szasz, *The Ethics of Psychoanalysis: The Theory and Method of Autonomous Psycho-therapy*, 1965; Helmut Thomä, *Anorexia Nervosa*, trans. Gillian Brydone,

1967; Clara M. Thompson, *Interpersonal Psychoanalysis: The Selected Papers of Clara M. Thompson*, ed. Maurice R. Green, 1964; Edward Burnett Tylor, *Religion in Primitive Culture*, 1958; Robert Waelder, *Basic Theory of Psychoanalysis*, 1960; Charles William Wahl, ed., *New Dimensions in Psychosomatic Medicine*, 1964; Nigel Walker, *A Short History of Psychotherapy: In Theory and Practice*, 1959; George J. Wayne and Ronald R. Koegler, eds., *Energy Psychiatry and Brief Therapy*, 1966; Benjamin Wolstein, *Counter-Transference*, 1959; Benjamin Wolstein, *Transference: Its Meaning and Function in Psychoanalytic Therapy*, 1954; Gregory Zilboorg, *Psychoanalysis and Religion*, ed. Margaret Stone Zilboorg, 1962.

MEDICAL HISTORY

Theodor Billroth, *The Medical Sciences in the German Universities: A Study in the History of Civilization*, trans. William H. Welch, 1924; Samuel M. Bluefarb, *Kaposi's Sarcoma*, 1957; Benjamin D. Brodie, *Lectures Illustrative of Certain Local Nervous Affections*, 1837; A. Ross Defendorf, *Clinical Psychiatry*, abstracted and adapted from the 6th German ed. of Kraepelin's *Lehrbuch der Psychiatrie*, 1902; A. Denker and O. Kahler, eds., *Handbuch der Hals- Nasen- Ohren- Heilkunde*, 1926; Dujardin-Beaumetz, *Clinical Therapeutics*, trans. E. P. Hurd, 1885; Wilhelm Erb, *Handbook of Electro-Therapeutics*, trans. L. Putzel, 1883; Austin Flint, *Clinical Medicine: A Systematic Treatise on the Diagnosis and Treatment of Diseases*, 1879; Frank R. Ford, *Diseases of the Nervous System in Infancy, Childhood and Adolescence*, 3rd ed., 1952; J. Milner Fothergill, *The Physiological Factor in Diagnosis*, 1883; Wilhelm Griesinger, *Mental Pathology and Therapeutics*, trans. C. Lockhart Robertson and James Rutherford, 1867; Bernhard Grois, *Das Allgemeine Krankenhaus in Wien und seine Geschichte*, 1965; Richard D. Hoblyn, *A Dictionary of Terms Used in Medicine and the Collateral Sciences*, rev. by John A. P. Price, 1900; Erna Lesky, *Die Wiener Medizinische Schule im 19. Jahrhundert*, 1965; William P. Letchworth, *The Insane in Foreign Countries*, 1889; Alfred L. Loomis, *Lessons in Physical Diagnosis*, 3rd ed., 1887; Ralph H. Major, *A History of Medicine*, Vol. II, 1954; Henry E. Sigerist, *The Great Doctors: A Biographical History of Medicine*, trans. Eden and Cedar Paul, 1958; Norman Burke Taylor, ed., *Stedman's Practical Medical Dictionary*, 16th rev. ed., 1946; Morton Thompson, *The Cry and the Covenant*, 1949; D. Hack Tuke, ed., *A Dictionary of Psychological Medicine*, 2 vols., 1892; Lancelot Law Whyte, *The Unconscious Before Freud*, 1962; Hans Zinsser, *Rats, Lice and History*, 1963.

HISTORY

H. Benedikt, ed., *Geschichte der Republik Öesterreich*, 1954; Julius Braunthal, *The Tragedy of Austria*, 1948; Alan Bullock, *Hitler: A Study in Tyranny*, 1953; Egon Caesar Conte Corti, *Der alte Kaiser*, 1955; Egon Caesar Conte Corti, *Mensch und Kaiser*, 1955; Egon Caesar Conte Corti,

Vom Kind zum Kaiser, 1955; Edward Crankshaw, *The Fall of the House of Habsburg*, 1963; Oswald Dutch, *Thus Died Austria*, 1938; M. W. Fodor, "The Austrian Roots of Hitlerism," *Foreign Affairs*, Vol. XIV, 1935–36; A. Fuchs, *Geistige Strömungen in Österreich, 1867–1918*, 1949; M. Fuchs, *A Pact with Hitler*, 1939; Jürgen Gehl, *Austria, Germany, and the Anschluss: 1931–1938*, 1963; C. A. Gullick, *Austria from Habsburg to Hitler*, 2 vols., 1948; Harry Hanak, *Great Britain and Austria-Hungary During the First World War: A Study in the Formation of Public Opinion*, 1962; Bertita Harding, *Imperial Twilight: The Story of Karl and Zita of Austria-Hungary*, 1941; Adolf Hitler, *The Speeches of Adolf Hitler, 1922–1939*, ed. Norman H. Baynes, 2 vols., 1942; Admiral Nicholas Horthy, *Memoirs of Admiral Nicholas Horthy, Regent of Hungary*, 1956; Carl Lonyay, *Rudolph: The Tragedy of Mayerling*, 1949; DeWitt C. Poole, "Light on Nazi Foreign Policy," *Foreign Affairs*, Vol. XXV, 1956; Stoyan Pribichevich, *World without End: The Saga of Southeastern Europe*, 1939; Wolf von Schierbrand, *Austria-Hungary: The Polyglot Empire*, 1917; Kurt von Schuschnigg, *Austrian Requiem*, 1947; Kurt von Schuschnigg, *Farewell Austria*, 1938; Ernst Rüdiger Prince von Starhemberg, *Between Hitler and Mussolini*, 1942; A. J. P. Taylor, *The Course of German History: A Survey of the Development of Germany Since 1815*, 1962; A. J. P. Taylor, *The Habsburg Monarchy: 1809–1918*, 1948; A. J. P. Taylor, *The Struggle for Mastery in Europe, 1848–1918*, 1954; Barbara W. Tuchman, *The Guns of August*, 1962; Barbara W. Tuchman, *The Proud Tower: A Portrait of the World Before the War, 1890–1914*, 1966; Z. A. B. Zeman, *The Break-Up of the Habsburg Empire, 1914–1918: A Study in National and Social Revolution*, 1961; Guido Zernatto, *Die Wahrheit über Oesterreich*, 1938.

THE ARTS AND LITERATURE

Heimito von Doderer, *The Waterfalls of Slunj*, trans. Eithne Wilkins and Ernst Kaiser, 1966; Ernst Jos. Gorlich, comp., *Einführung in die Geschichte der Österreichischen Literatur*, 1946; Heinrich Heine, *Heinrich Heine: Lyric Poems and Ballads*, trans. Ernst Feise, 1961; Arthur Jacobs and Stanley Sadie, *The Pan Book of Opera*, 1964; Robert A. Kann, *A Study in Austrian Intellectual History: From Late Baroque to Romanticism*, 1960; Heinz Kindermann, ed., *Wegweiser durch die moderne Literatur in Österreich*, 1954; Hans Kohn, *The Mind of Germany: The Education of a Nation*, 1960; Josef Nadler, *Literaturgeschichte Österreichs*, 1951; Johann Willibald Nagl and Jakob Ziedler, *Deutsch-Österreichische Literaturgeschichte*, 1937; Nagler-Zeidle, *Deutsch-Österreichische Literaturgeschichte*, Vol. IV; Friedrich Nietzsche, *The Portable Nietzsche*, ed. and trans. Walter Kaufmann, 1954; J. G. Robertson, *A History of German Literature*, 3rd ed. rev. by Edna Purdie, 1959; Arthur Schnitzler, *La Ronde*, trans. Frank and Jacqueline Marcus, 1964; William Shakespeare, *The Comedies and Tragedies of Shakespeare*, 4 vols., 1944; Sophocles, *The Complete Greek Tragedies*, Vol. II, ed. David Grene and Richard Lattimore, 1959.

LIFE IN AUSTRIA AND VIENNA

Austria: Facts and Figures, 1955; *Austria: Facts and Figures*, trans. Richard Rickett, 1963; James Baker, *Austria: Her People and Their Homelands*, 1913; Ilsa Barea, *Vienna*, 1966; Friedrich Bauer, Franz Jelinek and Franz Streinz, *Deutsches Lesebuch für Österreichische Mittel-Schüler*, 1907; Rudolf Bienenfeld, *Die Religion der religionslosen Juden*, 1938; Felix Braun, *Das musische Land: Versuche über Österreichs Landschaft und Dichtung*, 1952; E. H. Buschbeck, *Austria*, 1949; *Collection des Guides-Joanne: Etats du Danube et des Balkans*, 1888; *Drei Jahrunderte Strassenverkehr in Wien*, 1962; Eugene Fodor, ed., *Austria*, 1967; L. C. Friedlaender, *Wien*, 1961; Victor Wallace Germains, *Austria of To-Day*, 1932; Alfred Grund, *Landeskunde von Österreich*, 1905; Felix Halmer, *Castles in Austria*; Helen Hilsenrad, *Brown Was the Danube: A Memoir of Hitler's Vienna*, 1966; Count Hans Huyn, *Tragedy of Errors: The Chronicle of a European*, trans. Countess Nora Wydenbruck, 1939; *The Intellectual Vienna*, 1892; Julius Jakob, *Wörtenbuch des Wiener Dialektes*; L. Kellner, Madame Paula Arnold and Arthur L. Delisle, *Austria of the Austrians and Hungary of the Hungarians*, 1914; Ann Knox, *Austria Cooking*; Ann Knox, *Cooking the Austrian Way*, 1960; Moritz Ledeli, *Wien bie Nacht*, 1891; Ann Tizia Leitich, *Die Wienerin*, 1953; Ann Tizia Leitich, *Genie und Leidenschaft: Die Frauen um Grillparzer*, 1965; Ernst Lothar, extract of *Das Wunder des Überlebens*, *Presse*, October 16, 1960; Jul Löwy, *Geschichten aus der Wienerstadt*, 1889; C. A. Macartney, *The Social Revolution in Austria*, 1926; J. Alexander Mahan, *Vienna Yesterday and Today*, 1928; Ernst Marboe, comp., *The Book of Austria*, 1958; Alfred May, *Wien in alten Ansichten*, II, 1965; Michelin's *Austria and the Bavarian Alps*, 1965; Jonny Moser, *Von der Emanzipation zur antisemitischen Bewegung*; Francis H. E. Palmer, *Austro-Hungarian Life in Town and Country*, 1903; *Plan von Wien*; Eduard Poetzl, *Klein-Wiener. Skizzen in Wiener Art und Mundart*, 1890; Karl Renner, *An der Wende zweier zeiten: Lebenserinnerungen*, 1946; James Reynolds, *Panorama of Austria*, 1956; Hans Schikola, *Sprachlehre der Wiener Mundart*, 1956; Henry Schnitzler, "'Gay Vienna'—Myth and Reality," *Journal of the History of Ideas*, Vol. XV, No. 1, January 1954; Henry Swight Sedgwick, *Vienna: The Biography of a Bygone City*, 1939; Adalbert Seligmann, *Ein Bilderbuch aus dem alten Wien*, 1913; Herta Singer, *Im Wiener Kaffeehaus*, 1959; Otto Stradal, *Manch gastlich Haus in Österreich*, 1961; Fritz Stüber-Gunther, ed., *Vienna Humor*, Vol. V; Hans Tietze, *Die Juden Wiens*, 1953; *Vienna: A Faithful Sketch of the Austrian Metropolis*, 1869; *Vienna: A Faithful Sketch of the Austrian Metropolis*, 1873; *Vienna and Environs*, 7th ed., 1951; Robert Waissenberger, *Introducing Vienna*, 2nd ed., trans. David Hermges, 1964; *Wien und die Wiener*, 1844; *Wien und die Wiener-Grossstädtische Charakterbilder*, 1892; *Wienerstadt, Lebensbilder aus der Gegenwart: Geschildert von Wiener Schriftstellern*, 1895; *Zweites Programm des K.K. Akademischen Straats-Gymnasium zu Innsbruck, veröffentlicht am Schlusse des Schuljahres 1851*, 1851.

NEWSPAPERS

Arbeiter-Zeitung; Deutsche Zeitung; Deutsches Volksblatt; Die Presse; Figaro; Freie Presse; Fremdenblatt; Illustrierte Beilage des Wiener Extrablattes; Das Interessante Blatt; Konstitutionelle Vorstadt-Zeitung; Neue Freie Presse; Neues Wiener Tagblatt; Welt-Blatt; Wiener Allgemeine Zeitung; Wiener Zeitung.

COUNTRIES

FRANCE. Findlay Muirhead and Marcel Monmarché, eds., *North-Eastern France*, 1922; Doré Ogrizek, ed., *France: Paris and the Provinces*, 1948; Doré Ogrizek, ed., *The Provinces of France*, 1951; *Sites et Monuments: La Lorraine*, 1906.

ITALY. Hachette World Guides, *Italy*, 1956.

GERMANY. Karl Baedeker, *Berlin and Its Environs*, 2nd ed., 1905; Otto Beneke, *Von unehrlichen Leuten*, 1863; Albert Borcherdt, *Das lustige alte Hamburg*, 1910; Theodor Böttiger, *Kulinarische Streifzüge Durch Hamburg*, 1966; *Hamburg: Ein Stadtführer*, 1963; *Hamburg: Her Political, Economic and Cultural Aspects*, trans. Wilhelm J. Eggers, 1922; Irmgard Heilmann, *Hamburger Bilderbuch*, 1963; Wilson King, *Chronicles of Three Free Cities: Hamburg, Bremen, Lübeck*, 1914; Felix Lampe, *Berlin und die Mark Brandenburg*, 1909; Hans O. Modrow, *Berlin 1900*, 1936; Minerva Brace Norton, *In and Around Berlin*, 1890; Friedrich Schwieter, *Hamburg: Eine landschaftskundliche Stadtuntersuchung*, 1925; Albert Shaw, "Hamburg's New Sanitary Impulse," *Atlantic Monthly*, Vol. LXXIII, June 1894; Henry Vizetelly, *Berlin Under the New Empire*, 2 vols., 1879.

UNITED STATES. *Fifty Years on Fifth: 1907–1957*, 1957; John A. Kouwenhoven, *The Columbia Historical Portrait of New York*, 1953; Grace M. Mayer, *Once Upon a City*, 1958; Allon Schoener, ed., *Portalto America: The Lower East Side 1870–1925*, 1967.